The Short Story in English

The Short Story in English

Edited by
Neil Besner and David Staines

Toronto
Oxford University Press

Oxford University Press, 70 Wynford Drive, Don Mills, Ontario M3C 1J9

Oxford New York
Athens Auckland Bangkok Bombay Calcutta Cape Town
Dar es Salaam Delhi Florence Hong Kong Istanbul Karachi
Kuala Lumpur Madras Madrid Melbourne Mexico City
Nairobi Paris Singapore Taipei Tokyo Toronto

and associated companies in
Berlin Ibadan

Canadian Cataloguing in Publication Data

Main entry under title:

The Short story in English

Includes index.
ISBN 0-19-540683-4

1. Short stories, English. 2. Short stories, Canadian (English).* 3. Short stories, American. I. Besner, Neil Kalman, 1949- II. Staines, David, 1946-

PN6120.2.S48 1991 823'.0108 C91-093124-0

4 5 6 7 8 - 02 01 00 99 98

Printed in Canada by Webcom Limited

Contents

Acknowledgements

MARGARET ATWOOD. Used by permission of the Canadian Publishers, McClelland and Stewart, Toronto: 'Bluebeard's Egg' and 'Significant Moments in the Life of My Mother' from *Bluebeard's Egg* by Margaret Atwood.

MORLEY CALLAGHAN. 'Ancient Lineage' and 'Two Fishermen' from *Morley Callaghan Stories* by Morley Callaghan © 1959. Reprinted by permission of Macmillan of Canada, A Division of Canada Publishing Corporation.

RAYMOND CARVER. 'Cathedral' from *Cathedral by Raymond Carver*. Copyright © 1981, 1982, 1983 by Raymond Carver. Reprinted by permission of Alfred A. Knopf Inc. 'Why Don't You Dance?' from *What We Talk About When We Talk About Love* by Raymond Carver. Copyright © 1981 by Raymond Carver. Reprinted by permission of Alfred A. Knopf Inc.

WILLIAM FAULKNER. Reprinted from *Collected Stories of William Faulkner*, by permission of Random House Inc.: 'Dry September' copyright 1930 and renewed 1958 by William Faulkner; 'A Rose for Emily' copyright 1930 and renewed 1958 by William Faulkner.

MAVIS GALLANT. 'In Youth is Pleasure' from *Home Truths* by Mavis Gallant © 1956 and 'The Moslem Wife' from *From the Fifteenth District* by Mavis Gallant © 1973. Reprinted by permission of Macmillan of Canada, a Division of Canada Publishing Corporation.

NADINE GORDIMER. From *Selected Stories* by Nadine Gordimer. 'No Place Like' copyright © 1971 by Nadine Gordimer. 'The Train from Rhodesia' copyright 1950, 1952, 1952 by Nadine Gordimer. Reprinted by permission of the publisher, Viking Penguin, a division of Penguin Books USA Inc.

ERNEST HEMINGWAY. 'A Clean, Well-Lighted Place'. Reprinted with permission of Charles Scribner's Sons, an imprint of Macmillan Publishing Company, from *Winner Take Nothing* by Ernest Hemingway. Copyright 1933 by Charles Scribner's Sons, renewed 1961 by Mary Hemingway.

MARGARET LAURENCE. Used by permission of the Canadian Publishers, McClelland and Stewart, Toronto: 'The Tomorrow-Tamer' from *The Tomorrow-Tamer* by Margaret Laurence and 'To Set Our House in Order' from *A Bird in the House* by Margaret Laurence.

STEPHEN LEACOCK. 'My Financial Career' from *Literary Lapses* by Stephen Leacock and 'The Marine Excursion of the Knights of Pythias' from *Sunshine Sketches of a Little Town* by Stephen Leacock. Used by permission of the Canadian Publishers, McClelland and Stewart, Toronto.

DORIS LESSING. Reprinted by permission of Jonathan Clowes Ltd, London, on behalf of Doris Lessing: 'Our Friend Judith' from *A Man and Two Women* by Doris Lessing, ©

Preface

What is the short story? It is a comparatively modern literary genre, dating back only to the mid-nineteenth century. By that time the novel – with its wide scope, its capacity for panoramic social depiction, and its seemingly stronger commitment to realism – had already been developed. Because of its brevity, the short story does not aspire to the larger dimensions of the novel, nor does it usually concern itself with the social implications of the novel's universe. And it does not cleave so closely to the kind of realism evident, for example, in the British novel of the nineteenth century.

The short story had its first flowering in the writings of Edgar Allan Poe, who also gave it one of its most enduring descriptions. In the May 1842 issue of *Graham's Magazine*, Poe reviewed Nathaniel Hawthorne's *Twice-Told Tales* and set out the earliest definition of the short story: 'the short prose narrative, requiring from a half-hour to one or two hours in its perusal'. His emphasis on the reader's participation is strikingly modern, and his focus on the shortness of the form leads directly to his understanding of the story's major advantage over the novel:

> The ordinary novel is objectionable, from its length. . . . As it cannot be read at one sitting, it deprives itself, of course, of the immense force derivable from *totality*. Worldly interests intervening during the pauses of perusal, modify, annul, or counteract, in a greater or less degree, the impressions of the book. But simple cessation in reading would, of itself, be sufficient to destroy the true unity. In the brief tale, however, the author is enabled to carry out the fulness of his intention, be it what it may. During the hour of perusal the soul of the reader is at the writer's control. There are no external or extrinsic influences – resulting from weariness or interruption.

Such uninterrupted communion between writer and reader allows for the 'unique or single *effect*' of the story's concentrated focus:

> A skilful literary artist has constructed a tale. If wise, he has not fashioned his thoughts to accommodate his incidents; but having conceived, with deliberate care, a certain unique or single *effect* to be wrought out, he then invents such incidents – he then combines such events as may best aid him in establishing this preconceived effect.

The short-story writer, according to Poe, has in the limited space and focus of the form the ability 'to carry out the fulness of his intention, be it what it may'.

As a creator of both the horror story and the detective story, Poe found the form the perfect vehicle for his relentless exploration of the terrors hidden within the human soul.

Poe's theories about the short story originate in his close and intelligent reading of the tales of Hawthorne, who allowed for a movement away from strict realism in his own fiction in order to discover the 'truth of the human heart'. Herman Melville, Hawthorne's contemporary and close friend, identified the power of 'blackness, ten times black' in Hawthorne's work and sought in fiction not strict realism, which he defined as 'severe fidelity to real life', but heightened reality, another world that is a part of and yet apart from everyday life, where the reader finds 'nature unfettered, exhilarated, in effect transformed'.

This American strain of romance, as Hawthorne named it, as opposed to the realism of nineteenth-century British fiction, finds its completion in many of Henry James's novels and novellas. Romance, James maintained in the preface to the New York edition of *The American*, offers a welcome disentanglement from the experience the realist writer wishes to render in fiction, and presents

> experience liberated, so to speak; experience disengaged, disembroiled, disencumbered, exempt from the conditions that we usually know to attach to it and, if we wish so to put the matter, drag upon it, and operating in a medium which relieves it, in a particular interest, of the inconvenience of a *related*, a measurable state, a state subject to all our vulgar communities.

An accomplished realist himself, James recognized in romance an opportunity to present a reality that only seems to be 'fidelity to real life':

> The balloon of experience is in fact of course tied to the earth, and under that necessity we swing, thanks to a rope of remarkable length, in the more or less commodious car of the imagination; but it is by the rope we know where we are, and from the moment that cable is cut we are at large and unrelated: we only swing apart from the globe – though remaining as exhilarated, naturally, as we like, especially when all goes well. The art of the romancer is, 'for the fun of it', insidiously to cut the cable, to cut it without our detecting him.

In his own short stories – and he wrote more than one hundred – he often leaves the 'cable' intact when his purpose shifts and he leaves the realm of romance in order to become a chronicler of manners and social behaviour, especially of people in foreign environments. In this pursuit James is followed by such writers as Sara Jeannette Duncan, whose perspective on manners and codes of conduct abroad is both British and Canadian, and whose stories are infused with a sentimentality less noticeable in James's own fiction. And Stephen Leacock's stories, indebted to the comic sketches of Dickens and Thackeray, ground their humorous and hyperbolic flights more firmly on

Canadian soil, at once cutting James's 'cable' and deftly skewering individual and social pretensions.

The stories of James Joyce return to and advance from Poe's 'unique or single effect' to reach the most enduring modern incarnation of Poe's definition. For many readers, the major reward of the short story is its culmination in a moment of insight – a seemingly spiritual moment in which reality reveals itself, in which a perception, often as fleeting as it is powerful, illuminates a relationship, a state of mind, a setting. Joyce's term for such a moment, borrowed from a religious frame of reference, is 'epiphany', and he first defined this moment in his novel, *Stephen Hero*, to be the one in which 'we recognize that it is *that* thing which it is. Its soul, its whatness, leaps to us from the vestment of its appearance.' Like Gabriel Conroy in 'The Dead', Joyce's characters often reach such a moment in isolation, in reflection, or in reverie. And the depiction of human loneliness and isolation, along with the often tenuous connections between individuals and their societies, has been central in the twentieth-century short story.

Virginia Woolf's fiction turned away from the nineteenth-century realism that governed the British novel. Her stories show how her imagination appropriates the form to explore consciousness in a new way. In her 1919 essay 'Modern Novels', Woolf instructs the writer to examine the inner life:

> The mind, exposed to the ordinary course of life, receives upon its surface a myriad impressions – trivial, fantastic, evanescent, or engraved with the sharpness of steel. From all sides they come, an incessant shower of innumerable atoms, composing in their sum what we might venture to call life itself; and to figure further as the semi-transparent envelope, or luminous halo, surrounding us from the beginning of consciousness to the end. Is it not perhaps the chief task of the novelist to convey this incessantly varying spirit with whatever stress or sudden deviation it may display, and as little admixture of the alien and external as possible? We are not pleading merely for courage and sincerity; but suggesting that the proper stuff for fiction is a little other than custom would have us believe it.

With D.H. Lawrence's stories, realism is refashioned again, this time to serve his purpose of revealing moral obtuseness and the encroachments of materialism. For Lawrence, the short story offered itself as an ideal form for the depiction of childhood and adult fantasies and obsessions that reveal the social realities suppressing love and sexuality.

Katherine Mansfield's New Zealand stories also widen the bounds of the form, both in their depictions of the decline of the Empire and in their 'slice of life' realism. In her fiction, detailed renderings of consciousness coalesce with a heightened apprehension of natural settings. The exploration of class, which informs a story such as 'The Garden-Party', is a reminder that the short story can offer sharp insights into social reality.

The short stories of William Faulkner, F. Scott Fitzgerald, and Ernest Hemingway offer three related American incarnations of the genre. Faulkner shows how powerfully short fiction can serve the purposes of a regional vision, imbued, as in Lawrence's stories, with the resonances of a local setting and society. In 'Babylon Revisited', Fitzgerald's vision of the American experience in Europe reshapes James's earlier renditions of the theme, and 'Winter Dreams' reveals how the short story, as distinct from the novel, renders the rhythms of a North American initiation. Hemingway's fiction explores isolation not only as a modern condition, but as the spur for a way of seeing and being, an apprehension of a circumscribed reality that Hemingway evokes through his use of a spare and terse style.

Hemingway has been traditionally recognized as the originator of the laconic style often associated with his concept of a male code of honour. Morley Callaghan, his friend and contemporary, used an even sparer style to record the dramas in ordinary lives and their moral consequences; his characters struggle to act with dignity in a world of often hostile social forces and institutions. In Raymond Carver's stories, an equally spare style takes the reader into the lives of American working-class people frustrated by glimpses of the narrow possibilities for love, insight, and self-transformation. Joyce Carol Oates's explorations of American middle-class alienation focus on young women trapped in a violent, urban, male-dominated world.

In Canada as in the United States, the regional vision has found powerful expression in the short story. The prominence of regionalism is no accident; it may well be related to the propensity of the form for depictions of isolated characters, groups, and settings. In Sinclair Ross's stories, the prairie and small-town milieu of Western Canada finds one of its more evocative renditions. For Ross and other regionalists, setting becomes the imaginative ground for their stories' explorations of character. And just as Ross's fiction opened the way for Margaret Laurence's Canadian stories, Faulkner's renditions of the American South are refashioned in Eudora Welty's stories and, in a form shaped more explicitly by the religious dimensions of her characters' actions, in Flannery O'Connor's stories too. And the short fiction of Bernard Malamud and Bharati Mukherjee provides an ethnic counterpart to such regionalism.

The aims of realism and regionalism are, of course, never mutually exclusive, and Alice Munro and Alistair MacLeod, with stories set in different Canadian regions, rely on a precise rendering of detail to capture what Munro describes as the 'emotional core' of the short story. Realism is shaped to another end in Mavis Gallant's stories, where her characters' memories come into conflict with the forces of history. Doris Lessing, who believes that the 'realist story' is the 'highest form of prose writing', reveals her characters in all their troubled complexity without explaining away their isolation in psychological terms.

And in the fiction of Ethel Wilson, Edna O'Brien, and Margaret Atwood, the short story often accommodates itself to an ironic stripping away of illusion as women's perceptions of their relationships undergo painful revision when their self-deception is suddenly revealed to them.

What, then, is the short story? It is a comparatively modern literary genre that defies any simple or singular definition.

When Nadine Gordimer published her *Selected Stories* in 1975, she cautioned her readers in the Introduction:

> Nobody has ever succeeded in defining a short story in a manner to satisfy all who write or read them, and I shall not, here. I sometimes wonder if one shouldn't simply state flatly: a short story is a piece of fiction short enough to be read at one sitting? No, that will satisfy no one, least myself. But for me certainly there is a clue, there, to the choice of the short story by writers, as a form: whether or not it has a narrative in the external or internal sense, whether it sprawls or neatly bites its own tail, a short story is a concept that the writer can 'hold', fully realized, in his imagination, at one time. A novel is, by comparison, staked out, and must be taken possession of stage by stage; it is impossible to contain, all at once, the proliferation of concepts it ultimately may use. For this reason I cannot understand how people can suppose one makes a conscious choice, *after* knowing what one wants to write about, between writing a novel or a short story. A short story *occurs*, in the imaginative sense. To write one is to express from a situation in the exterior or interior world the life-giving drop—sweat, tear, semen, saliva—that will spread an intensity on the page; burn a hole in it.

For Gordimer, the short-story writer can hold the concept of the story, 'fully realized, in his imagination, at one time'. For Poe, the short story must be a fiction that can be read—'perused'—at a single sitting. The emphasis, both contemporary and traditional, falls on both writers' and readers' perspectives on the short story's singleness of focus amid the seemingly infinite variety of its forms.

Nathaniel Hawthorne

1804-64

In his preface to *The House of the Seven Gables* (1851), Nathaniel Hawthorne distinguished between the novel and the romance. The novel 'is presumed to aim at a very minute fidelity, not merely to the possible, but to the probable and ordinary course of man's experience.' The romance, Hawthorne's preferred genre, allows 'a certain latitude, both as to its fashion and material,' but 'sins unpardonably so far as it may swerve aside from the truth of the human heart.' As long as the writer remains true to the human heart, 'he has a right to present that truth under circumstances' that are of his 'own choosing or creation.' Hawthorne's world, then, is the realm of the human heart with all its hidden recesses and shadows.

Born in Salem, Massachusetts, Hawthorne attended Bowdoin College in Maine, where he began his writing. He published his first novel, *Fanshawe*, in 1828, then continued to write while holding a variety of jobs, including customhouse officer in Boston and later in Salem. Summarily dismissed from the Salem position in 1849, he turned his full-time attention to fiction and produced *The Scarlet Letter* (1850), which won immediate acclaim. In 1853 President Franklin Pierce, another Bowdoin graduate, appointed Hawthorne to the consulship in Liverpool, England, where he lived for five years before moving to Italy. He returned to the United States in 1860 and died in Plymouth, New Hampshire.

Throughout Hawthorne's fiction broods the Puritan obsession with evil and doom. Often Hawthorne turned to the past in American history, not as history, but as a setting to examine the deepest secrets of the human heart. 'This great power of blackness in Hawthorne derives its force from its appeals to that Calvinistic sense of Innate Depravity and Original Sin, from whose visitations, in some shape or other, no deeply thinking mind is always and wholly free,' concluded Herman Melville.

Beneath this 'power of blackness' in Hawthorne's fiction is an ultimately life-affirming vision. For Hawthorne, the heart is a cavern with depths that are bright and peaceful: 'the gloom and terror may lie deep; but deeper still is the eternal beauty.' The artist must present both good and evil as they appear in this life. 'Purify that inward sphere,' Hawthorne commented, 'and the many shapes of evil that haunt the outward, and which now seem almost our only realities, will turn to shadowy phantoms and vanish of their own accord.'

'My Kinsman, Major Molineux' presents Robin's journey of initiation into an unfamiliar world of evil. From its dreamlike atmosphere at the beginning, 'It was near nine o'clock of a moonlight evening,' to the similar atmosphere at the end, the tale centres on the night of a planned riot in Boston when the inexperienced protagonist embarks on his search for his kinsman, Major Molineux, who, Robin expects, will help to advance him in the city. But the city turns out to be a waste land, and Robin loses his innocence through the night's experience.

Melville regarded 'Young Goodman Brown' as the strongest of all of Hawthorne's tales and as 'deep as Dante' in its exploration of the mystery of evil. Like Robin, Young Goodman Brown also sets out on a journey of initiation, though he does so willingly and proudly, bent 'on his present evil purpose.'

'My Kinsman, Major Molineux' was first published in the fiction anthology *The Token: A Christmas and New Year's Present* (1831) and then collected in *The Snow-Image, and Other Twice-Told Tales* (1851). 'Young Goodman Brown' was first published in the April 1835 issue of *New-England Magazine* and then collected in *Mosses from an Old Manse* (1846).

My Kinsman, Major Molineux

After the kings of Great Britain had assumed the right of appointing the colonial governors, the measures of the latter seldom met with the ready and general approbation, which had been paid to those of their predecessors, under the original charters. The people looked with most jealous scrutiny to the exercise of power, which did not emanate from themselves, and they usually rewarded the rulers with slender gratitude, for the compliances, by which, in softening their instructions from beyond the sea, they had incurred the reprehension of those who gave them. The annals of Massachusetts Bay will inform us, that of six governors, in the space of about forty years from the surrender of the old charter, under James II, two were imprisoned by a popular insurrection; a third, as Hutchinson inclines to believe, was driven from the province by the whizzing of a musket ball; a fourth, in the opinion of the same historian, was hastened to his grave by continual bickerings with the House of Representatives; and the remaining two, as well as their successors, till the Revolution, were favoured with few and brief intervals of peaceful sway. The inferior members of the court party, in times of high political excitement, led scarcely a more desirable life. These remarks may serve as preface to the following adventures, which chanced upon a summer night, not far from a hundred years ago. The reader, in order to avoid a long and dry detail of colonial affairs, is requested to dispense with an account of the train of circumstances, that had caused much temporary inflammation of the popular mind.

It was near nine o'clock of a moonlight evening, when a boat crossed the ferry with a single passenger, who had obtained his conveyance, at that unusual hour, by the promise of an extra fare. While he stood on the landing-place, searching in either pocket for the means of fulfilling his agreement, the ferryman lifted a lantern, by the aid of which, and the newly risen moon, he took a very accurate survey of the stranger's face. He was a youth of barely eighteen years, evidently country-bred, and now, as it should seem, upon his first visit to town. He was clad in a coarse grey coat, well worn, but in excellent repair; his under garments were durably constructed of leather, and sat tight to a pair of serviceable and well-shaped limbs; his stockings of blue yarn, were the incontrovertible handiwork of a mother or a sister; and on his head was a three-cornered hat, which in its better days had perhaps sheltered the graver brow of the lad's father. Under his left arm was a heavy cudgel, formed of an oak sapling, and retaining a part of the hardened root; and his equipment was completed by a wallet, not so abundantly stocked as to incommode the vigorous shoulders on which it hung. Brown, curly hair, well-shaped features, and bright, cheerful eyes, were nature's gifts, and worth all that art could have done for his adornment.

The youth, one of whose names was Robin, finally drew from his pocket the half of a little province-bill of five shillings, which, in the depreciation of that sort of currency, did but satisfy the ferryman's demand, with the surplus of a sexangular piece of parchment valued at three pence. He then walked forward into the town, with as light a step, as if his day's journey had not already exceeded thirty miles, and with as eager an eye, as if he were entering London city, instead of the little metropolis of a New England colony. Before Robin had proceeded far, however, it occurred to him, that he knew not whither to direct his steps; so he paused, and looked up and down the narrow street, scrutinizing the small and mean wooden buildings, that were scattered on either side.

'This low hovel cannot be my kinsman's dwelling,' thought he, 'nor yonder old house, where the moonlight enters at the broken casement; and truly I see none hereabouts that might be worthy of him. It would have been wise to inquire my way of the ferryman, and doubtless he would have gone with me, and earned a shilling from the Major for his pains. But the next man I meet will do as well.'

He resumed his walk, and was glad to perceive that the street now became wider, and the houses more respectable in their appearance. He soon discerned a figure moving on moderately in advance, and hastened his steps to overtake it. As Robin drew nigh, he saw that the passenger was a man in years, with a full periwig of grey hair, a wide-skirted coat of dark cloth, and silk stockings rolled about his knees. He carried a long and polished cane, which he struck down perpendicularly before him, at every step; and at regular intervals he uttered two successive hems, of a peculiarly solemn and sepulchral intonation. Having made these observations, Robin laid hold of the skirt of the old man's coat, just when the light from the open door and windows of a barber's shop, fell upon both their figures.

'Good evening to you, honoured Sir,' said he, making a low bow, and still retaining his hold of the skirt. 'I pray you to tell me whereabouts is the dwelling of my kinsman, Major Molineux?'

The youth's question was uttered very loudly; and one of the barbers, whose razor was descending on a well-soaped chin, and another who was dressing a Ramillies wig, left their occupations, and came to the door. The citizen, in the meantime, turned a long favoured countenance upon Robin, and answered him in a tone of excessive anger and annoyance. His two sepulchral hems, however, broke into the very centre of his rebuke, with most singular effect, like a thought of the cold grave obtruding among wrathful passions.

'Let go my garment, fellow! I tell you, I know not the man you speak of. What! I have authority, I have—hem, hem—authority; and if this be the respect you show your betters, your feet shall be brought acquainted with the stocks, by daylight, tomorrow morning!'

Robin released the old man's skirt, and hastened away, pursued by an ill-mannered roar of laughter from the barber's shop. He was at first considerably surprised by the result of his question, but, being a shrewd youth, soon thought himself able to account for the mystery.

'This is some country representative,' was his conclusion, 'who has never seen the inside of my kinsman's door, and lacks the breeding to answer a stranger civilly. The man is old, or verily—I might be tempted to turn back and smite him on the nose. Ah, Robin, Robin! even the barber's boys laugh at you, for choosing such a guide! You will be wiser in time, friend Robin.'

He now became entangled in a succession of crooked and narrow streets, which crossed each other, and meandered at no great distance from the water-side. The smell of tar was obvious to his nostrils, the masts of vessels pierced the moonlight above the tops of the buildings, and the numerous signs, which Robin paused to read, informed him that he was near the centre of business. But the streets were empty, the shops were closed, and lights were visible only in the second storeys of a few dwelling-houses. At length, on the corner of a narrow lane, through which he was passing, he beheld the broad countenance of a British hero swinging before the door of an inn, whence proceeded the voices of many guests. The casement of one of the lower windows was thrown back, and a very thin curtain permitted Robin to distinguish a party at supper, round a well-furnished table. The fragrance of the good cheer steamed forth into the outer air, and the youth could not fail to recollect, that the last remnant of his travelling stock of provision had yielded to his morning appetite, and that noon had found, and left him, dinnerless.

'Oh, that a parchment three-penny might give me a right to sit down at yonder table,' said Robin, with a sigh. 'But the Major will make me welcome to the best of his victuals; so I will even step boldly in, and inquire my way to his dwelling.'

He entered the tavern, and was guided by the murmur of voices, and fumes of tobacco, to the public room. It was a long and low apartment, with oaken walls, grown dark in the continual smoke, and a floor, which was thickly sanded, but of no immaculate purity. A number of persons, the larger part of whom appeared to be mariners, or in some way connected with the sea, occupied the wooden benches, or leather-bottomed chairs, conversing on various matters, and occasionally lending their attention to some topic of general interest. Three or four little groups were draining as many bowls of punch, which the great West India trade had long since made a familiar drink in the colony. Others, who had the aspect of men who lived by regular and laborious handicraft, preferred the insulated bliss of an unshared potation, and became more taciturn under its influence. Nearly all, in short, evinced a predilection for the Good Creature in some of its various shapes, for this is a vice, to which, as the Fast-day sermons of a hundred years ago will testify, we have a long hereditary claim. The only guests to whom Robin's sympathies inclined him, were two or three sheepish countrymen, who were using the inn somewhat after the fashion of a Turkish Caravansary; they had gotten themselves into the darkest corner of the room, and, heedless of the Nicotian atmosphere, were supping on the bread of their own ovens, and the bacon cured in their own chimney-smoke. But though Robin felt a sort of brotherhood with these strangers, his eyes were attracted from them, to a person who stood near the door, holding whispered conversation with a group of ill-dressed associates. His features were separately striking almost to grotesqueness, and the whole face left a deep impression in the memory. The forehead bulged out into a double prominence, with a vale between; the nose came boldly forth in an irregular curve, and its bridge was of more than a finger's breadth; the eyebrows were deep and shaggy, and the eyes glowed beneath them like fire in a cave.

While Robin deliberated of whom to inquire respecting his kinsman's dwelling, he was accosted by the innkeeper, a little man in a stained white apron, who had come to pay his professional welcome to the stranger. Being in the second generation from a French Protestant, he seemed to have inherited the courtesy of his parent nation; but no variety of circumstance was ever known to change his voice from the one shrill note in which he now addressed Robin.

'From the country, I presume, Sir?' said he, with a profound bow. 'Beg to congratulate you on your arrival, and trust you intend a long stay with us. Fine town here, Sir, beautiful buildings, and much that may interest a stranger. May I hope for the honour of your commands in respect to supper?'

'The man sees a family likeness! the rogue has guessed that I am related to the Major!' thought Robin, who had hitherto experienced little superfluous civility.

All eyes were now turned on the country lad, standing at the door, in his worn three-cornered hat, grey coat, leather breeches, and blue yarn stockings, leaning on an oaken cudgel, and bearing a wallet on his back.

Robin replied to the courteous innkeeper, with such an assumption of consequence, as befitted the Major's relative.

'My honest friend,' he said, 'I shall make it a point to patronize your house on some occasion, when—' here he could not help lowering his voice—'I may have more than a parchment three-pence in my pocket. My present business,' continued he, speaking with lofty confidence, 'is merely to inquire the way to the dwelling of my kinsman, Major Molineux.'

There was a sudden and general movement in the room, which Robin interpreted as expressing the eagerness of each individual to become his guide. But the innkeeper turned his eyes to a written paper on the wall, which he read, or seemed to read, with occasional recurrences to the young man's figure.

'What have we here?' said he, breaking his speech into little dry fragments. ' "Left the house of the subscriber, bounden servant, Hezekiah Mudge—had on, when he went away, grey coat, leather breeches, master's third best hat. One pound currency reward to whoever shall lodge him in any jail in the province." Better trudge, boy, better trudge!'

Robin had begun to draw his hand towards the lighter end of the oak cudgel, but a strange hostility in every countenance, induced him to relinquish his purpose of breaking the courteous innkeeper's head. As he turned to leave the room, he encountered a sneering glance from the bold-featured personage whom he had before noticed; and no sooner was he beyond the door, than he heard a general laugh, in which the innkeeper's voice might be distinguished, like the dropping of small stones into a kettle.

'Now is it not strange,' thought Robin, with his usual shrewdness, 'is it not strange, that the confession of an empty pocket, should outweigh the name of my kinsman, Major Molineux? Oh, if I had one of these grinning rascals in the woods, where I and my oak sapling grew up together, I would teach him that my arm is heavy, though my purse be light!'

On turning the corner of the narrow lane, Robin found himself in a spacious street, with an unbroken line of lofty houses on each side, and a steepled building at the upper end, whence the ringing of a bell announced the hour of nine. The light of the moon, and the lamps from numerous shop windows, discovered people promenading on the pavement, and amongst them, Robin hoped to recognize his hitherto inscrutable relative. The result of his former inquiries made him unwilling to hazard another, in a scene of such publicity, and he determined to walk slowly and silently up the street, thrusting his face close to that of every elderly gentleman, in search of the Major's lineaments. In his progress, Robin encountered many gay and gallant figures. Embroidered garments, of showy colours, enormous periwigs, gold-laced hats, and silver hilted swords, glided past him and dazzled his optics. Travelled youths, imitators of the European fine gentlemen of the period, trod jauntily along, half-dancing to the fashionable tunes which they hummed, and making poor Robin ashamed of his quiet and natural gait. At length, after many pauses to examine the gorgeous display of goods in the shop windows, and after suffering some rebukes for the impertinence of his scrutiny into people's faces, the Major's kinsman found himself near the steepled building, still unsuccessful in his search. As yet, however, he had seen only one side of the thronged street; so Robin crossed, and continued the same sort of inquisition down the opposite pavement, with stronger hopes than the philosopher seeking an honest man, but with no better fortune. He had arrived about mid-way towards the lower end, from which his course began, when he overheard the approach of some one, who struck down a cane on the flag-stones at every step, uttering, at regular intervals, two sepulchral hems.

'Mercy on us!' quoth Robin, recognizing the sound.

Turning a corner, which chanced to be close at his right hand, he hastened to pursue his researches, in some other part of the town. His patience was now wearing low, and he seemed to feel more fatigue from his rambles since he crossed the ferry, than from his journey of several days on the other side. Hunger also pleaded loudly within him, and Robin began to balance the propriety of demanding, violently and with lifted cudgel, the necessary guidance from the first solitary passenger, whom he should meet. While a resolution to this effect was gaining strength, he entered a street of mean appearance, on either side of which, a row of ill-built houses was straggling towards the harbour. The moonlight fell upon no passenger along the whole extent, but in the third domicile which Robin passed, there was a half-opened door, and his keen glance detected a woman's garment within.

'My luck may be better here,' said he to himself.

Accordingly, he approached the door, and beheld it shut closer as he did so; yet an open space remained, sufficing for the fair occupant to observe the stranger, without a corresponding display on her part. All that Robin could discern was a strip of scarlet petticoat, and the occasional sparkle of an eye, as if the moonbeams were trembling on some bright thing.

'Pretty mistress'—for I may call her so with a good conscience, thought the shrewd youth, since I know nothing to the contrary—'my sweet pretty mistress, will you be kind enough to tell me whereabouts I must seek the dwelling of my kinsman, Major Molineux?'

Robin's voice was plaintive and winning, and the female, seeing nothing to be shunned in the handsome country youth, thrust open the door, and came forth into the moonlight. She was a dainty little figure, with a white neck, round arms, and a slender waist, at the extremity of which her scarlet petticoat jutted out over a hoop, as if she were standing in a balloon. Moreover, her face was oval and pretty, her hair dark beneath the little cap, and her bright eyes possessed a sly freedom, which triumphed over those of Robin.

'Major Molineux dwells here,' said this fair woman.

Now her voice was the sweetest Robin had heard that night, the airy counterpart of a stream of melted silver; yet he could not help doubting whether that sweet voice spoke Gospel truth. He looked up and down the mean street, and then surveyed the house before which they stood. It was a small, dark edifice of two storeys, the second of which projected over the lower floor; and the front apartment had the aspect of a shop for petty commodities.

'Now truly I am in luck,' replied Robin, cunningly, 'and so indeed is my kinsman, the Major, in having so pretty a housekeeper. But I prithee trouble him to step to the door; I will deliver him a message from his friends in the country, and then go back to my lodgings at the inn.'

'Nay, the Major has been a-bed this hour or more,' said the lady of the scarlet petticoat; 'and it would be to little purpose to disturb him to-night, seeing his evening draught was of the strongest. But he is a kind-hearted man, and it would be as much as my life's worth, to let a kinsman of his turn away from the door. You are the good old gentleman's very picture, and I could swear that was his rainy-weather hat. Also, he has garments very much resembling those leather—But come in, I pray, for I bid you hearty welcome in his name.'

So saying, the fair and hospitable dame took our hero by the hand; and though the touch was light, and the force was gentleness, and though Robin read in her eyes what he did not hear in her words, yet the slender waisted woman, in the scarlet petticoat, proved stronger than the athletic country youth. She had drawn his half-willing footsteps nearly to the threshold, when the opening of a door in the neighbourhood, startled the Major's housekeeper, and, leaving the Major's kinsman, she vanished speedily into her own domicile. A heavy yawn preceded the appearance of a man, who, like the Moonshine of Pyramus and Thisbe, carried a lantern, needlessly aiding his sister luminary in the heavens. As he walked sleepily up the street, he turned his broad, dull face on Robin, and displayed a long staff, spiked at the end.

'Home, vagabond, home!' said the watchman, in accents that seemed to fall asleep as soon as they were uttered. 'Home, or we'll set you in the stocks by peep of day!'

'This is the second hint of the kind,' thought Robin. 'I wish they would end my difficulties, by setting me there tonight.'

Nevertheless, the youth felt an instinctive antipathy towards the guardian of midnight order, which at first prevented him from asking his usual question. But just when the man was about to vanish behind the corner, Robin resolved not to lose the opportunity, and shouted lustily after him—

'I say, friend! will you guide me to the house of my kinsman, Major Molineux?'

The watchman made no reply, but turned the corner and was gone; yet Robin seemed to hear the sound of drowsy laughter stealing along the solitary street. At that moment, also, a pleasant titter saluted him from the open window above his head; he looked up, and caught the sparkle of a saucy eye; a round arm beckoned to him, and next he heard light footsteps descending the staircase within. But Robin, being of the household of a New England clergyman, was a good youth, as well as a shrewd one; so he resisted temptation, and fled away.

He now roamed desperately, and at random, through the town, almost ready to believe that a spell was on him, like that, by which a wizard of his country, had once kept three pursuers wandering, a whole winter night, within twenty paces of the cottage which they sought. The streets lay before him, strange and desolate, and the lights were extinguished in almost every house. Twice, however, little parties of men, among whom Robin distinguished individuals in outlandish attire, came hurrying along, but though on both occasions they paused to address him, such intercourse did not at all enlighten his perplexity. They did but utter a few words in some language of which Robin knew nothing, and perceiving his inability to answer, bestowed a curse upon him in plain English, and hastened away. Finally, the lad determined to knock at the door of every mansion that might appear worthy to be occupied by his kinsman, trusting that perseverance would overcome the fatality which had hitherto thwarted him. Firm in this resolve, he was passing beneath the walls of a church, which formed the corner of two streets, when, as he turned into the shade of its steeple, he encountered a bulky stranger, muffled in a cloak. The man was proceeding with the speed of earnest business, but Robin planted himself full before him, holding the oak cudgel with both hands across his body, as a bar to further passage.

'Halt, honest man, and answer me a question,' said he, very resolutely. 'Tell me, this instant, whereabouts is the dwelling of my kinsman, Major Molineux?'

'Keep your tongue between your teeth, fool, and let me pass,' said a deep, gruff voice, which Robin partly remembered. 'Let me pass, I say, or I'll strike you to the earth!'

'No, no, neighbour!' cried Robin, flourishing his cudgel, and then thrusting its larger end close to the man's muffled face. 'No, no, I'm not the fool you take me for, nor do you pass, till I have an answer to my question. Whereabouts is the dwelling of my kinsman, Major Molineux?'

The stranger, instead of attempting to force his passage, stept back into the moonlight, unmuffled his own face and stared full into that of Robin.

'Watch here an hour, and Major Molineux will pass by,' said he.

Robin gazed with dismay and astonishment, on the unprecedented physiognomy of the speaker. The forehead with its double prominence, the broad-hooked nose, the shaggy eyebrows, and fiery eyes, were those which he had noticed at the inn, but the man's complexion had undergone a singular, or, more properly, a two-fold change. One side of the face blazed of an intense red, while the other was black as midnight, the division line being in the broad bridge of the nose; and a mouth, which seemed to extend from ear to ear, was black or red, in contrast to the colour of the cheek. The effect was as if two individual devils, a fiend of fire and a fiend of darkness, had united themselves to form this infernal visage. The stranger grinned in Robin's face, muffled his parti-coloured features, and was out of sight in a moment.

'Strange things we travellers see!' ejaculated Robin.

He seated himself, however, upon the steps of the church-door, resolving to wait the appointed time for his kinsman's appearance. A few moments were consumed in philosophical speculations, upon the species of the *genus homo*, who had just left him, but having settled this point shrewdly, rationally, and satisfactorily, he was compelled to look elsewhere for amusement. And first he threw his eyes along the street; it was of more respectable appearance than most of those into which he had wandered, and the moon, 'creating, like the imaginative power, a beautiful strangeness in familiar objects,' gave something of romance to a scene, that might not have possessed it in the light of day. The irregular, and often quaint architecture of the houses, some of whose roofs were broken into numerous little peaks; while others ascended, steep and narrow, into a single point; and others again were square; the pure milk-white of some of their complexions, the aged darkness of others, and the thousand sparklings, reflected from bright substances in the plastered walls of many; these matters engaged Robin's attention for awhile, and then began to grow wearisome. Next he endeavoured to define the forms of distant objects, starting away with almost ghostly indistinctness, just as his eye appeared to grasp them; and finally he took a minute survey of an edifice, which stood on the opposite side of the street, directly in front of the church-door, where he was stationed. It was a large square mansion, distinguished from its neighbours by a balcony, which rested on tall pillars, and by an elaborate Gothic window, communicating therewith.

'Perhaps this is the very house I have been seeking,' thought Robin.

Then he strove to speed away the time, by listening to a murmur, which swept continually along the street, yet was scarcely audible, except to an unaccustomed ear like his; it was a low, dull, dreamy sound, compounded of many noises, each of which was at too great a distance to be separately heard. Robin marvelled at this snore of a sleeping town, and marvelled more, whenever its continuity was broken, by now and then a distant shout, apparently loud where it originated. But altogether it was a sleep-inspiring sound, and to shake off its drowsy influence, Robin arose, and climbed a window-frame, that he might view the interior of the church. There the moonbeams came trembling in, and fell down upon the deserted pews, and extended along the quiet aisles. A fainter, yet more awful radiance, was hovering round the pulpit, and one solitary ray had dared to rest upon the opened page of the great Bible. Had Nature, in that deep hour, become a worshipper in the house, which man had builded? Or was that heavenly light the visible sanctity of the place, visible because no earthly and impure feet were within the walls? The scene made Robin's heart shiver with a sensation of loneliness, stronger than he had ever felt in the remotest depths of his native woods; so he turned away, and sat down again before the door. There were graves around the church, and now an uneasy thought obtruded into Robin's breast. What if the object of his search, which had been so often and so strangely thwarted, were all the time mouldering in his shroud? What if his kinsman should glide through yonder gate, and nod and smile to him in passing dimly by?

'Oh, that any breathing thing were here with me!' said Robin.

Recalling his thoughts from this uncomfortable track, he sent them over forest, hill, and stream, and attempted to imagine how that evening of ambiguity and weariness, had been spent by his father's household. He pictured them assembled at the door, beneath the tree, the great old tree, which had been spared for its huge twisted trunk, and venerable shade, when a thousand leafy brethren fell. There, at the going down of the summer sun, it was his father's custom to perform domestic worship, that the neighbours might come and join with him like brothers of the family, and that the wayfaring man might pause to drink at that fountain, and keep his heart pure by freshening the memory of home. Robin distinguished the seat of every individual of the little audience; he saw the good man in the midst, holding the Scriptures in the golden light that shone from the western clouds; he beheld him close the book, and all rise up to pray. He heard the old thanksgivings for daily mercies, the old supplications for their continuance, to which he had so often listened in weariness, but which were now among his dear remembrances. He perceived the slight inequality of his father's voice when he came to speak of the Absent One; he noted how his mother turned her face to the broad and knotted trunk; how his elder brother scorned, because the beard was rough upon his upper lip, to permit his features to be moved; how his younger sister drew down a low hanging branch before her eyes; and how the little one of all, whose sports had hitherto broken the decorum of the scene, understood the prayer for her playmate, and burst into clamorous grief. Then he saw them go in at the door; and when Robin would have entered also, the latch tinkled into its place, and he was excluded from his home.

'Am I here, or there?' cried Robin, starting; for all at once, when his thoughts had become visible and audible in a dream, the long, wide, solitary street shone out before him.

He aroused himself, and endeavoured to fix his attention steadily upon the large edifice which he had surveyed before. But still his mind kept vibrating between fancy and reality; by turns, the pillars of the balcony lengthened into the tall, bare stems of pines, dwindled down to human figures, settled again in their true shape and size, and then commenced a new succession of changes. For a single moment, when he deemed himself awake, he could have sworn that a visage, one which he seemed to remember, yet could not absolutely name as his kinsman's, was looking towards him from the Gothic window. A deeper sleep wrestled with, and nearly overcame him, but fled at the sound of footsteps along the opposite pavement. Robin rubbed his eyes, discerned a man passing at the foot of the balcony, and addressed him in a loud, peevish, and lamentable cry.

'Halloo, friend! must I wait here all night for my kinsman, Major Molineux?'

The sleeping echoes awoke, and answered the voice; and the passenger, barely able to discern a figure sitting in the oblique shade of the steeple, traversed the street to obtain a nearer view. He was himself a gentleman in his prime, of open, intelligent, cheerful, and altogether prepossessing countenance. Perceiving a country youth, apparently homeless and without friends, he accosted him in a tone of real kindness, which had become strange to Robin's ears.

'Well, my good lad, why are you sitting here?' inquired he. 'Can I be of service to you in any way?'

'I am afraid not, Sir,' replied Robin, despondingly; 'yet I shall take it kindly, if you'll answer me a single question. I've been searching half the night for one Major Molineux; now, Sir, is there really such a person in these parts, or am I dreaming?'

'Major Molineux! The name is not altogether strange to me,' said the gentleman, smiling. 'Have you any objection to telling me the nature of your business with him?'

Then Robin briefly related that his father was a clergyman, settled on a small salary, at a long distance back in the country, and that he and Major Molineux were brothers' children. The Major, having inherited riches, and acquired civil and military rank, had visited his cousin in great pomp a year or two before; had manifested much interest in Robin and an elder brother, and, being childless himself, had thrown out hints respecting the future establishment of one of them in life. The elder brother was destined to succeed to the farm, which his father cultivated, in the interval of sacred duties; it was therefore determined that Robin should profit by his kinsman's generous intentions, especially as he had seemed to be rather the favourite, and was thought to possess other necessary endowments.

'For I have the name of being a shrewd youth,' observed Robin, in this part of his story.

'I doubt not you deserve it,' replied his new friend, good naturedly; 'but pray proceed.'

'Well, Sir, being nearly eighteen years old, and well-grown, as you see,' continued Robin, raising himself to his full height, 'I thought it high time to begin the world. So my mother and sister put me in handsome trim, and my father gave me half the remnant of his last year's salary, and five days ago I started for this place, to pay the Major a visit. But would you believe it, Sir? I crossed the ferry a little after dusk, and have yet found nobody that would show me the way to his dwelling; only an hour or two since, I was told to wait here, and Major Molineux would pass by.'

'Can you describe the man who told you this?' inquired the gentleman.

'Oh, he was a very ill-favoured fellow, Sir,' replied Robin, 'with two great bumps on his forehead, a hook nose, fiery eyes, and, what struck me as the strangest, his face was of two different colours. Do you happen to know such a man, Sir?'

'Not intimately,' answered the stranger, 'but I chanced to meet him a little time previous to your stopping me. I believe you may trust his word, and that the Major will very shortly pass through this street. In the mean time, as I have a singular curiosity to witness your meeting, I will sit down here upon the steps, and bear you company.'

He seated himself accordingly, and soon engaged his companion in animated discourse. It was but of brief continuance, however, for a noise of shouting, which had long been remotely audible, drew so much nearer, that Robin inquired its cause.

'What may be the meaning of this uproar?' asked he. 'Truly, if your town be always as noisy, I shall find little sleep, while I am an inhabitant.'

'Why, indeed, friend Robin, there do appear to be three or four riotous fellows abroad to-night,' replied the gentleman. 'You must not expect all the stillness of your native woods, here in our streets. But the watch will shortly be at the heels of these lads, and—'

'Aye, and set them in the stocks by peep of day,' interrupted Robin, recollecting his own encounter with the drowsy lantern-bearer. 'But, dear Sir, if I may trust my ears, an army of watchmen would never make head against such a multitude of rioters. There were at least a thousand voices went to make up that one shout.'

'May not one man have several voices, Robin, as well as two complexions?' said his friend.

'Perhaps a man may; but Heaven forbid that a woman should!' responded the shrewd youth, thinking of the seductive tones of the Major's housekeeper.

The sounds of a trumpet in some neighbouring street now became so evident and continual, that Robin's curiosity was strongly excited. In addition to the shouts, he heard frequent bursts from many instruments of discord, and a wild and confused laughter filled up the intervals. Robin rose from the steps, and looked wistfully towards a point, whither several people seemed to be hastening.

'Surely some prodigious merrymaking is going on,' exclaimed he. 'I have laughed very little since I left home, Sir, and should be sorry to lose an opportunity. Shall we just step round the corner by that darkish house, and take our share of the fun?'

'Sit down again, sit down, good Robin,' replied the gentleman, laying his hand on the skirt of the grey coat. 'You forget that we must wait here for your kinsman; and there is reason to believe that he will pass by, in the course of a very few moments.'

The near approach of the uproar had now disturbed the neighbourhood; windows flew open on all sides; and many heads, in the attire of the pillow, and confused by sleep suddenly broken, were protruded to the gaze of whoever had leisure to observe them. Eager voices hailed each other from house to house, all demanding the explanation, which not a soul could give. Half-dressed men hurried towards the unknown commotion, stumbling as they went over the stone steps, that thrust themselves into the narrow foot-walk. The shouts, the laughter, and the tuneless bray, the antipodes of music, came onward with increasing din, till scattered individuals, and then denser bodies, began to appear round a corner, at the distance of a hundred yards.

'Will you recognize your kinsman, Robin, if he passes in this crowd?' inquired the gentleman.

'Indeed, I can't warrant it, Sir; but I'll take my stand here, and keep a bright look out,' answered Robin, descending to the outer edge of the pavement.

A mighty stream of people now emptied into the street, and came rolling slowly towards the church. A single horseman wheeled the corner in the midst of them, and close behind him came a band of fearful wind-instruments, sending forth a fresher discord, now that no intervening buildings kept it from the ear. Then a redder light disturbed the moonbeams, and a dense multitude of torches shone along the street, concealing by their glare whatever object they illuminated. The single horseman, clad in a military dress, and bearing a drawn sword, rode onward as the leader, and, by his fierce and variegated countenance, appeared like war personified; the red of one cheek was an emblem of fire and sword; the blackness of the other betokened the mourning which attends them. In his train, were wild figures in the Indian dress, and many fantastic shapes without a model, giving the whole march a visionary air, as if a dream had broken forth from some feverish brain, and were sweeping visibly through the midnight streets. A mass of people, inactive, except as applauding spectators, hemmed the procession in, and several women ran along the sidewalks, piercing the confusion of heavier sounds, with their shrill voices of mirth or terror.

'The double-faced fellow has his eye upon me,' muttered Robin, with an indefinite but uncomfortable idea, that he was himself to bear a part in the pageantry.

The leader turned himself in the saddle, and fixed his glance full upon the country youth, as the steed went slowly by. When Robin had freed his eyes from those fiery ones, the musicians were passing before him, and the torches were close at hand; but the unsteady brightness of the latter formed a veil which he could not penetrate. The rattling of wheels over the stones sometimes found its way to his ear, and confused traces of a human form appeared at intervals, and then melted into the vivid light. A moment more, and the leader thundered a command to halt; the trumpets vomited a horrid breath, and held their peace; the shouts and laughter of the people died away, and there remained only a universal hum, nearly allied to silence. Right before Robin's eyes was an uncovered cart. There the torches blazed the brightest, there the moon shone out like day, and there, in tar-and-feathery dignity, sate his kinsman, Major Molineux!

He was an elderly man, of large and majestic person, and strong, square features, betokening a steady soul; but steady as it was, his enemies had found the means to shake it. His face was pale as death, and far more ghastly; the broad forehead was contracted in his agony, so that his eyebrows formed one grizzled line; his eyes were red and wild, and the foam hung white upon his quivering lip. His whole frame was agitated by a quick, and continual tremor, which his pride strove to quell, even in those circumstances of overwhelming humiliation. But perhaps the bitterest pang of all was when his eyes met those of Robin; for he evidently knew him on the instant, as the youth stood witnessing the foul disgrace of a head that had grown grey in honour. They stared at each other in silence, and Robin's knees shook, and his hair bristled, with a mixture of pity and terror. Soon, however, a bewildering excitement began to seize upon his mind; the preceding adventures of the night, the unexpected appearance of the crowd, the torches, the confused din, and the hush that followed, the spectre of his kinsman reviled by that great multitude, all this, and more than all, a perception of tremendous ridicule in the whole scene, affected him with a sort of mental inebriety. At that moment a voice of sluggish merriment saluted Robin's ears; he turned instinctively, and just behind the corner of the church stood the lantern-bearer, rubbing his eyes, and drowsily enjoying the lad's amazement. Then he heard a peal of laughter like the ringing of silvery bells; a woman twitched his arm, a saucy eye met his, and he saw the lady of the scarlet petticoat. A sharp, dry cachinnation appealed to his memory, and, standing on tiptoe in the crowd, with his white apron over his head, he beheld the courteous little innkeeper. And lastly, there sailed over the heads of the multitude a great, broad laugh, broken in the midst by two sepulchral hems; thus—

'Haw, haw, haw—hem, hem—haw, haw, haw, haw!'

The sound proceeded from the balcony of the opposite edifice, and thither Robin turned his eyes. In front of the Gothic window stood the old citizen, wrapped in a wide gown, his grey periwig exchanged for a nightcap, which was thrust back from his forehead, and his silk stockings hanging down about his legs. He supported himself on his polished cane in a fit of convulsive merriment, which manifested itself on his solemn old features, like a funny inscription on a tombstone. Then Robin seemed to hear the voices of the barbers; of the guests of the inn; and of all who had made sport of him that night. The contagion was spreading among the multitude, when, all at once, it seized upon Robin, and he sent forth a shout of laughter that echoed through the street; every man shook his sides, every man emptied his lungs, but Robin's shout was the loudest there. The cloud-spirits peeped from their silvery islands, as the congregated mirth went roaring up the sky! The Man in the Moon heard the far bellow; 'Oho,' quoth he, 'the old Earth is frolicsome to-night!'

When there was a momentary calm in that tempestuous sea of sound, the leader gave the sign, the procession resumed its march. On they went, like fiends that throng in mockery round some dead potentate, mighty no more, but majestic still in his agony. On they went, in counterfeited pomp, in senseless uproar, in frenzied merriment, trampling all on an old man's heart. On swept the tumult, and left a silent street behind.

'Well, Robin, are you dreaming?' inquired the gentleman, laying his hand on the youth's shoulder.

Robin started, and withdrew his arm from the stone post, to which he had instinctively clung, while the living stream rolled by him. His cheek was somewhat pale, and his eye not quite so lively as in the earlier part of the evening.

'Will you be kind enough to show me the way to the ferry?' said he, after a moment's pause.

'You have then adopted a new subject of inquiry?' observed his companion, with a smile.

'Why, yes, Sir,' replied Robin, rather drily. 'Thanks to you, and to my other friends, I have at last met my kinsman, and he will scarce desire to see my face again. I begin to grow weary of a town life, Sir. Will you show me the way to the ferry?'

'No, my good friend Robin, not to-night, at least,' said the gentleman. 'Some few days hence, if you continue to wish it, I will speed you on your journey. Or, if you prefer to remain with us, perhaps, as you are a shrewd youth, you may rise in the world, without the help of your kinsman, Major Molineux.'

1831

Young Goodman Brown

Young Goodman Brown came forth, at sunset, into the street of Salem village, but put his head back, after crossing the threshold, to exchange a parting kiss with his young wife. And Faith, as the wife was aptly named, thrust her own pretty head into the street, letting the wind play with the pink ribbons of her cap, while she called to Goodman Brown.

'Dearest heart,' whispered she, softly and rather sadly, when her lips were close to his ear, 'pr'y thee, put off your journey until sunrise, and sleep in your own bed to-night. A lone woman is troubled with such dreams and such thoughts, that she's afeard of herself, sometimes. Pray, tarry with me this night, dear husband, of all nights in the year!'

'My love and my Faith,' replied young Goodman Brown, 'of all nights in the year, this one night must I tarry away from thee. My journey, as thou callest it, forth and back again, must needs be done 'twixt now and sunrise. What, my sweet, pretty wife, dost thou doubt me already, and we but three months married!'

'Then, God bless you!' said Faith, with the pink ribbons, 'and may you find all well, when you come back.'

'Amen!' cried Goodman Brown. 'Say thy prayers, dear Faith, and go to bed at dusk, and no harm will come to thee.'

So they parted; and the young man pursued his way, until, being about to turn the corner by the meeting-house, he looked back, and saw the head of Faith still peeping after him, with a melancholy air, in spite of her pink ribbons.

'Poor little Faith!' thought he, for his heart smote him. 'What a wretch am I, to leave her on such an errand! She talks of dreams, too. Methought, as she spoke, there was trouble in her face, as if a dream had warned her what work is to be done to-night. But, no, no! 'twould kill her to think it. Well; she's a blessed angel on earth; and after this one night, I'll cling to her skirts and follow her to Heaven.'

With this excellent resolve for the future, Goodman Brown felt himself justified in making more haste on his present evil purpose. He had taken a dreary road, darkened by all the gloomiest trees of the forest, which barely stood aside to let the narrow path creep through, and closed immediately behind. It was all as lonely as could be; and there is this peculiarity in such a solitude, that the traveller knows not who may be concealed by the innumerable trunks and the thick boughs overhead; so that, with lonely footsteps, he may yet be passing through an unseen multitude.

'There may be a devilish Indian behind every tree,' said Goodman Brown, to himself; and he glanced fearfully behind him, as he added, 'What if the devil himself should be at my very elbow!'

His head being turned back, he passed a crook of the road, and looking forward again, beheld the figure of a man, in grave and decent attire, seated at the foot of an old tree. He arose, at Goodman Brown's approach, and walked onward, side by side with him.

'You are late, Goodman Brown,' said he. 'The clock of the Old South was striking as I came through Boston; and that is full fifteen minutes agone.'

'Faith kept me back awhile,' replied the young man, with a tremor in his voice, caused by the sudden appearance of his companion, though not wholly unexpected.

It was now deep dusk in the forest, and deepest in that part of it where these two were journeying. As nearly as could be discerned, the second traveller was about fifty years old, apparently in the same rank of life as Goodman Brown, and bearing a considerable resemblance to him, though perhaps more in expression than features. Still, they might have been taken for father and son. And yet, though the elder person was as simply clad as the younger, and as simple in manner too, he had an indescribable air of one who knew the world, and would not have felt abashed at the governor's dinner-table, or in King William's court, were it possible that his affairs should call him thither. But the only thing about him, that could be fixed upon as remarkable, was his staff, which bore the likeness of a great black snake, so curiously wrought, that it might almost be seen to twist and wriggle itself, like a living serpent. This, of course, must have been an ocular deception, assisted by the uncertain light.

'Come, Goodman Brown!' cried his fellow-traveller, 'this is a dull pace for the beginning of a journey. Take my staff, if you are so soon weary.'

'Friend,' said the other, exchanging his slow pace for a full stop, 'having kept covenant by meeting thee here, it is my purpose now to return whence I came. I have scruples, touching the matter thou wot'st of.'

'Sayest thou so?' replied he of the serpent, smiling apart. 'Let us walk on, nevertheless, reasoning as we go, and if I convince thee not, thou shalt turn back. We are but a little way in the forest, yet.'

'Too far, too far!' exclaimed the goodman, unconsciously resuming his walk. 'My father never went into the woods on such an errand, nor his father before him. We have been a race of honest men and good Christians, since the days of the martyrs. And shall I be the first of the name of Brown, that ever took this path, and kept—'

'Such company, thou wouldst say,' observed the elder person, interpreting his pause. 'Well said, Goodman Brown! I have been as well acquainted with your family as with ever a one among the Puritans; and that's no trifle to say. I helped your grandfather, the constable, when he lashed the Quaker woman so smartly through the streets of Salem. And it was I that brought your father a pitch-pine knot, kindled at my own hearth, to set fire to an Indian village, in King Philip's war. They were my good friends, both; and many a pleasant walk have we had along this path, and returned merrily after midnight. I would fain be friends with you, for their sake.'

'If it be as thou sayest,' replied Goodman Brown, 'I marvel they never spoke of these matters. Or, verily, I marvel not, seeing that the least rumour of the sort would have driven them from New-England. We are a people of prayer, and good works, to boot, and abide no such wickedness.'

'Wickedness or not,' said the traveller with the twisted staff, 'I have a very general acquaintance here in New-England. The deacons of many a church have drunk the communion wine with me; the selectmen, of divers towns, make me their chairman; and a majority of the Great and General Court are firm supporters of my interest. The governor and I, too—but these are state-secrets.'

'Can this be so!' cried Goodman Brown, with a stare of amazement at his undisturbed companion. 'Howbeit, I have nothing to do with the governor and council; they have their own ways, and are no rule for a simple husbandman, like me. But, were I to go on with thee, how should I meet the eye of that good old man, our minister, at Salem village? Oh, his voice would make me tremble, both Sabbath-day and lecture-day!'

Thus far, the elder traveller had listened with due gravity, but now burst into a fit of irrepressible mirth, shaking himself so violently, that his snake-like staff actually seemed to wriggle in sympathy.

'Ha! ha! ha!' shouted he, again and again; then composing himself, 'Well, go on, Goodman Brown, go on; but pr'y thee, don't kill me with laughing!'

'Well, then, to end the matter at once,' said Goodman Brown, considerably nettled, 'there is my wife, Faith. It would break her dear little heart, and I'd rather break my own!'

'Nay, if that be the case,' answered the other, 'e'en go thy ways, Goodman Brown. I would not, for twenty old women like the one hobbling before us, that Faith should come to any harm.'

As he spoke, he pointed his staff at a female figure on the path, in whom Goodman Brown recognized a very pious and exemplary dame, who had taught him his catechism, in youth, and was still his moral and spiritual adviser, jointly with the minister and Deacon Gookin.

'A marvel, truly, that Goody Cloyse should be so far in the wilderness, at night-fall!' said he. 'But, with your leave, friend, I shall take a cut through the woods, until we have left this Christian woman behind. Being a stranger to you, she might ask whom I was consorting with, and whither I was going.'

'Be it so,' said his fellow-traveller. 'Betake you to the woods, and let me keep the path.'

Accordingly, the young man turned aside, but took care to watch his companion, who advanced softly along the road, until he had come within a staff's length of the old dame. She, meanwhile, was making the best of her way, with singular speed for so aged a woman, and mumbling some indistinct words, a prayer, doubtless, as she went. The traveller put forth his staff, and touched her withered neck with what seemed the serpent's tail.

'The devil!' screamed the pious old lady.

'Then Goody Cloyse knows her old friend?' observed the traveller, confronting her, and leaning on his writhing stick.

'Ah, forsooth, and is it your worship, indeed?' cried the good dame. 'Yea, truly is it, and in the very image of my old gossip, Goodman Brown, the grandfather of the silly fellow that now is. But—would your worship believe it?—my broomstick hath strangely disappeared, stolen, as I suspect, by that unhanged witch, Goody Cory, and that, too, when I was all anointed with the juice of smallage and cinque-foil and wolf's-bane—'

'Mingled with fine wheat and the fat of a new-born babe,' said the shape of old Goodman Brown.

'Ah, your worship knows the receipt,' cried the old lady, cackling aloud. 'So, as I was saying, being all ready for the meeting, and no horse to ride on, I made up my mind to foot it; for they tell me, there is a nice young man to be taken into communion to-night. But now your good worship will lend me your arm, and we shall be there in a twinkling.'

'That can hardly be,' answered her friend. 'I may not spare you my arm, Goody Cloyse, but here is my staff, if you will.'

So saying, he threw it down at her feet, where, perhaps, it assumed life, being one of the rods which its owner had formerly lent to the Egyptian Magi. Of this fact, however, Goodman Brown could not take cognizance. He had cast up his eyes in astonishment, and looking down again, beheld neither Goody Cloyse nor the serpentine staff, but his fellow-traveller alone, who waited for him as calmly as if nothing had happened.

'That old woman taught me my catechism!' said the young man; and there was a world of meaning in this simple comment.

They continued to walk onward, while the elder traveller exhorted his companion to make good speed and persevere in the path, discoursing so aptly, that his arguments seemed rather to spring up in the bosom of his auditor, than to be suggested by himself. As they went, he plucked a branch of maple, to serve for a walking-stick, and began to strip it of the twigs and little boughs, which were wet with evening dew. The moment his fingers touched them, they became strangely withered and dried up, as with a week's sunshine. Thus the pair proceeded, at a good free pace, until suddenly, in a gloomy hollow of the road, Goodman Brown sat himself down on the stump of a tree, and refused to go any farther.

'Friend,' said he, stubbornly, 'my mind is made up. Not another step will I budge on this errand. What if a wretched old woman do choose to go to the devil, when I thought she was going to Heaven! Is that any reason why I should quit my dear Faith, and go after her?'

'You will think better of this, by-and-by,' said his acquaintance, composedly. 'Sit here and rest yourself awhile; and when you feel like moving again, there is my staff to help you along.'

Without more words, he threw his companion the maple stick, and was as speedily out of sight, as if he had vanished into the deepening gloom. The young man sat a few moments, by the road-side, applauding himself greatly, and thinking with how clear a conscience he should meet the minister, in his morning-walk, nor shrink from the eye of good old Deacon Gookin. And what calm sleep would be his, that very night, which was to have been spent so wickedly, but purely and sweetly now, in the arms of Faith! Amidst these pleasant and praiseworthy meditations, Goodman Brown heard the tramp of horses along the road, and deemed it advisable to conceal himself within the verge of the forest, conscious of the guilty purpose that had brought him thither, though now so happily turned from it.

On came the hoof-tramps and the voices of the riders, two grave old voices, conversing soberly as they drew near. These mingled sounds appeared to pass along the road, within a few yards of the young man's hiding-place; but owing, doubtless, to the depth of the gloom, at that particular spot, neither the travellers nor their steeds were visible. Though their figures brushed the small boughs by the way-side, it could not be seen that they intercepted, even for a moment, the faint gleam from the strip of bright sky, athwart which they must have passed. Goodman Brown alternately crouched and stood on tip-toe, pulling aside the branches, and thrusting forth his head as far as he durst, without discerning so much as a shadow. It vexed him the more, because he could have sworn, were such a thing possible, that he recognized the voices of the minister and Deacon Gookin, jogging along quietly, as they were wont to do, when bound to some ordination or ecclesiastical council. While yet within hearing, one of the riders stopped to pluck a switch.

'Of the two, reverend Sir,' said the voice like the deacon's, 'I had rather miss an ordination-dinner than to-night's meeting. They tell me that some of our community are to be here from Falmouth and beyond, and others from Connecticut and Rhode-Island; besides several of the Indian pow-wows, who, after their fashion, know almost as much deviltry as the best of us. Moreover, there is a goodly young woman to be taken into communion.'

'Mighty well, Deacon Gookin!' replied the solemn old tones of the minister. 'Spur up, or we shall be late. Nothing can be done, you know, until I get on the ground.'

The hoofs clattered again, and the voices, talking so strangely in the empty air, passed on through the forest, where no church had ever been gathered, nor solitary Christian prayed. Whither, then, could these holy men be journeying, so deep into the heathen wilderness? Young Goodman Brown caught hold of a tree, for support, being ready to sink down on the ground, faint and overburthened with the heavy sickness of his heart. He looked up to the sky, doubting whether there really was a Heaven above him. Yet, there was the blue arch, and the stars brightening in it.

'With Heaven above, and Faith below, I will yet stand firm against the devil!' cried Goodman Brown.

While he still gazed upward, into the deep arch of the firmament, and had lifted his hands to pray, a cloud, though no wind was stirring, hurried across the zenith, and hid the brightening stars. The blue sky was still visible, except directly overhead, where this black mass of cloud was sweeping swiftly northward. Aloft in the air, as if from the depths of the cloud, came a confused and doubtful sound of voices. Once, the listener fancied that he could distinguish the accents of town's-people of his own, men and women, both pious and ungodly, many of whom he had met at the communion-table, and had seen others rioting at the tavern. The next moment, so indistinct were the sounds, he doubted whether he had heard aught but the murmur of the old forest, whispering without a wind. Then came a stronger swell of those familiar tones, heard daily in the sunshine, at Salem village, but never, until now, from a cloud of night. There was one voice, of a young woman, uttering lamentations, yet with an uncertain sorrow, and entreating for some favour, which, perhaps, it would grieve her to obtain. And all the unseen multitude, both saints and sinners, seemed to encourage her onward.

'Faith!' shouted Goodman Brown, in a voice of agony and desperation; and the echoes of the forest mocked him, crying—'Faith! Faith!' as if bewildered wretches were seeking her, all through the wilderness.

The cry of grief, rage, and terror, was yet piercing the night, when the unhappy husband held his breath for a response. There was a scream, drowned immediately in a louder murmur of voices, fading into far-off laughter, as the dark cloud swept away, leaving the clear and silent sky above Goodman Brown. But something fluttered lightly down through the air, and caught on the branch of a tree. The young man seized it, and beheld a pink ribbon.

'My Faith is gone!' cried he, after one stupefied moment. 'There is no good on earth; and sin is but a name. Come, devil! for to thee is this world given.'

And maddened with despair, so that he laughed loud and long, did Goodman Brown grasp his staff and set forth again, at such a rate, that he seemed to fly along the forest-path, rather than to walk or run. The road grew wilder and drearier, and more faintly traced, and vanished at length, leaving him in the heart of the dark wilderness, still rushing onward, with the instinct that guides mortal man to evil. The whole forest was peopled with frightful sounds; the creaking of the trees, the howling of wild beasts, and the yell of Indians; while, sometimes, the wind tolled like a distant church-bell, and sometimes gave a broad roar around the traveller, as if all Nature were laughing him to scorn. But he was himself the chief horror of the scene, and shrank not from its other horrors.

'Ha! ha! ha!' roared Goodman Brown, when the wind laughed at him. 'Let us hear which will laugh loudest! Think not to frighten me with your deviltry! Come witch, come wizard, come Indian powwow, come devil himself! and here comes Goodman Brown. You may as well fear him as he fear you!'

In truth, all through the haunted forest, there could be nothing more frightful than the figure of Goodman Brown. On he flew, among the black pines, brandishing his staff with frenzied gestures, now giving vent to an inspiration of horrid blasphemy, and now shouting forth such laughter, as set all the echoes of the forest laughing like demons around him. The fiend in his own shape is less hideous, than when he rages in the breast of man. Thus sped the demoniac on his course, until, quivering among the trees, he saw a red light before him, as when the felled trunks and branches of a clearing have been set on fire, and throw up their lurid blaze against the sky, at the hour of midnight. He paused, in a lull of the tempest that had driven him onward, and heard the swell of what seemed a hymn, rolling solemnly from a distance, with the weight of many voices. He knew the tune; it was a familiar one in the choir of the village meeting-house. The verse died heavily away, and was lengthened by a chorus, not of human voices, but of all the sounds of the benighted wilderness, pealing in awful harmony together. Goodman Brown cried out; and his cry was lost to his own ear, by its unison with the cry of the desert.

In the interval of silence, he stole forward, until the light glared full upon his eyes. At one extremity of an open space, hemmed in by the dark wall of the forest, arose a rock, bearing some rude, natural resemblance either to an altar or a pulpit, and surrounded by four blazing pines, their tops aflame, their stems untouched, like candles at an evening meeting. The mass of foliage, that had overgrown the summit of the rock, was all on fire, blazing high into the night, and fitfully illuminating the whole field.

Each pendent twig and leafy festoon was in a blaze. As the red light arose and fell, a numerous congregation alternately shone forth, then disappeared in shadow, and again grew, as it were, out of the darkness, peopling the heart of the solitary woods at once.

'A grave and dark-clad company!' quoth Goodman Brown.

In truth, they were such. Among them, quivering to-and-fro, between gloom and splendour, appeared faces that would be seen, next day, at the council-board of the province, and others which, Sabbath after Sabbath, looked devoutly heavenward, and benignantly over the crowded pews, from the holiest pulpits in the land. Some affirm, that the lady of the governor was there. At least, there were high dames well known to her, and wives of honoured husbands, and widows, a great multitude, and ancient maidens, all of excellent repute, and fair young girls, who trembled, lest their mothers should espy them. Either the sudden gleams of light, flashing over the obscure field, bedazzled Goodman Brown, or he recognized a score of church-members of Salem village, famous for their especial sanctity. Good old Deacon Gookin had arrived, and waited at the skirts of that venerable saint, his revered pastor. But, irreverently consorting with these grave, reputable, and pious people, these elders of the church, these chaste dames and dewy virgins, there were men of dissolute lives and women of spotted fame, wretches given over to all mean and filthy vice, and suspected even of horrid crimes. It was strange to see, that the good shrank not from the wicked, nor were the sinners abashed by the saints. Scattered, also, among their pale-faced enemies, were the Indian priests, or powwows, who had often scared their native forest with more hideous incantations than any known to English witchcraft.

'But, where is Faith?' thought Goodman Brown; and, as hope came into his heart, he trembled.

Another verse of the hymn arose, a slow and mournful strain, such as the pious love, but joined to words which expressed all that our nature can conceive of sin, and darkly hinted at far more. Unfathomable to mere mortals is the love of fiends. Verse after verse was sung, and still the chorus of the desert swelled between, like the deepest tone of a mighty organ. And, with the final peal of that dreadful anthem, the howling beasts, and every other voice of the unconverted wilderness, were mingling and according with the voice of guilty man, in homage to the prince of all. The four blazing pines threw up a loftier flame, and obscurely discovered shapes and visages of horror on the smoke-wreaths, above the impious assembly. At the same moment, the fire on the rock shot redly forth, and formed a glowing arch above its base, where now appeared a figure. With reverence be it spoken, the figure bore no slight similitude, both in garb and manner, to some grave divine of the New-England churches.

'Bring forth the converts!' cried a voice, that echoed through the field and rolled into the forest.

At the word, Goodman Brown stept forth from the shadow of the trees, and approached the congregation, with whom he felt a loathful brotherhood, by the sympathy of all that was wicked in his heart. He could have well nigh sworn, that the shape of his own dead father beckoned him to advance, looking downward from a smoke-wreath, while a woman, with dim features of despair, threw out her hand to warn him back. Was it his mother? But he had no power to retreat one step, nor to resist, even in thought, when the minister and good old Deacon Gookin seized his arms, and led him to the blazing rock. Thither came also the slender form of a veiled female, led between Goody Cloyse, that pious teacher of the catechism, and Martha Carrier, who had received the devil's promise to be queen of hell. A rampant hag was she! And there stood the proselytes, beneath the canopy of fire.

'Welcome, my children,' said the dark figure, 'to the communion of your race! Ye have found, thus young, your nature and your destiny. My children, look behind you!'

They turned; and flashing forth, as it were, in a sheet of flame, the fiend-worshippers were seen; the smile of welcome gleamed darkly on every visage.

'There,' resumed the sable form, 'are all whom ye have reverenced from youth. Ye deemed them holier than yourselves, and shrank from your own sin, contrasting it with their lives of righteousness, and prayerful aspirations heavenward. Yet, here are they all, in my worshipping assembly! This night it shall be granted you to know their secret deeds; how hoary-bearded elders of the church have whispered wanton words to the young maids of their households; how many a woman, eager for widow's weeds, has given her husband a drink at bed-time, and let him sleep his last sleep in her bosom; how beardless youths have made haste to inherit their fathers' wealth; and how fair damsels—blush not, sweet ones!—have dug little graves in the garden, and bidden me, the sole guest, to an infant's funeral. By the sympathy of your human hearts for sin, ye shall scent out all the places—whether in church, bed-chamber, street, field, or forest—where crime has been committed, and shall exult to behold the whole earth one stain of guilt, one mighty blood-spot. Far more than this! It shall be yours to penetrate, in every bosom, the deep mystery of sin, the fountain of all wicked arts, and which inexhaustibly supplies more evil impulses than human power—than my power, at its utmost!—can make manifest in deeds. And now, my children, look upon each other.'

They did so; and, by the blaze of the hell-kindled torches, the wretched man beheld his Faith, and the wife her husband, trembling before that unhallowed altar.

'Lo! there ye stand, my children,' said the figure, in a deep and solemn tone, almost sad, with its despairing awfulness, as if his once angelic nature could yet mourn for our miserable race. 'Depending upon one another's hearts, ye had still hoped, that virtue were not all a dream. Now are ye undeceived! Evil is the nature of mankind. Evil must be your only happiness. Welcome, again, my children, to the communion of your race!'

'Welcome!' repeated the fiend-worshippers, in one cry of despair and triumph.

And there they stood, the only pair, as it seemed, who were yet hesitating on the verge of wickedness, in this dark world. A basin was hollowed, naturally, in the rock. Did it contain water, reddened by the lurid light? or was it blood? or, perchance, a liquid flame? Herein did the Shape of Evil dip his hand, and prepare to lay the mark of baptism upon their foreheads, that they might be partakers of the mystery of sin, more conscious of the secret guilt of others, both in deed and thought, than they could now be of their own. The husband cast one look at his pale wife, and Faith at him. What polluted wretches would the next glance shew them to each other, shuddering alike at what they disclosed and what they saw!

'Faith! Faith!' cried the husband. 'Look up to Heaven, and resist the Wicked One!'

Whether Faith obeyed, he knew not. Hardly had he spoken, when he found himself amid calm night and solitude, listening to a roar of the wind, which died heavily away through the forest. He staggered against the rock and felt it chill and damp, while a hanging twig, that had been all on fire, besprinkled his cheek with the coldest dew.

The next morning, young Goodman Brown came slowly into the street of Salem village, staring around him like a bewildered man. The good old minister was taking a walk along the grave-yard, to get an appetite for breakfast and meditate his sermon, and bestowed a blessing, as he passed, on Goodman Brown. He shrank from the venerable saint, as if to avoid an anathema. Old Deacon Gookin was at domestic worship, and the holy words of his prayer were heard through the open window. 'What God doth the wizard pray to?' quoth Goodman Brown. Goody Cloyse, that excellent old Christian, stood in the early sunshine, at her own lattice, catechising a little girl, who had brought her a pint of morning's milk. Goodman Brown snatched away the child, as from the grasp of the fiend himself. Turning the corner by the meeting-house, he spied the head of Faith, with the pink ribbons, gazing anxiously forth, and bursting into such joy at sight of him, that she skipt along the street, and almost kissed her husband before the whole village. But, Goodman Brown looked sternly and sadly into her face, and passed on without a greeting.

Had Goodman Brown fallen asleep in the forest, and only dreamed a wild dream of a witch-meeting?

Be it so, if you will. But, alas! it was a dream of evil omen for young Goodman Brown. A stern, a sad, a darkly meditative, a distrustful, if not a desperate man, did he become, from the night of that fearful dream. On the Sabbath-day, when the congregation were singing a holy psalm, he could not listen, because an anthem of sin rushed loudly upon his ear, and drowned all the blessed strain. When the minister spoke from the pulpit, with power and fervid eloquence, and, with his hand on the open Bible, of the sacred truths of our religion, and of saint-like lives and triumphant deaths, and of future bliss or misery unutterable, then did Goodman Brown turn pale, dreading, lest the roof should thunder down upon the grey blasphemer and his hearers. Often, awakening suddenly at midnight, he shrank from the bosom of Faith, and at morning or eventide, when the family knelt down at prayer, he scowled, and muttered to himself, and gazed sternly at his wife, and turned away. And when he had lived long, and was borne to his grave, a hoary corpse, followed by Faith, an aged woman, and children and grand-children, a goodly procession, besides neighbours, not a few, they carved no hopeful verse upon his tomb-stone; for his dying hour was gloom.

1835

Edgar Allan Poe

1809-49

Both in theory and in practice Edgar Allan Poe's contributions to the development of the short story are of major importance. He was one of the originators of two kinds of story that now have a venerable history—the psychological horror story and the detective story.

In a short story, Poe maintains, the writer should aim for a single 'effect': 'A skilful literary artist has constructed a tale. If wise, he has not fashioned his thoughts to accommodate his incidents; but having conceived, with deliberate care, a certain unique or single *effect* to be wrought out, he then invents such incidents—he then combines such effects as may best aid him in establishing this preconceived effect. If his very initial sentence tend not to the outbringing of this effect, then he has failed in his first step. In the whole composition there should be no word written, of which the tendency, direct or indirect, is not to the one pre-established design. And by such means, with such care and skill, a picture is at length painted which leaves in the mind of him who contemplates it with a kindred art, a sense of the fullest satisfaction. The idea of the tale has been presented unblemished, because undisturbed; and this is an end unattainable by the novel.'

Born in Boston, Poe was taken in by John and Frances Allan after his mother died when he was three. Educated in private academies, he travelled with the Allans to Scotland and England in 1815, returning to Richmond, Virginia, in 1820. After attending the University of Virginia for a year in 1826, he enlisted in the army; his first book, *Tamerlane and Other Poems*, appeared in 1827. He left the army in 1829, attending West Point Academy briefly in 1830; the following year, he began to concentrate on writing short stories. He married in 1836, moved to New York the next year, and then to Philadelphia a year and a half later. *Tales of the Grotesque and Arabesque* (1840), Poe's first collection of fiction, includes the twenty-five stories he had already published. He died in Baltimore.

'The Fall of the House of Usher' presents the narrator's account of the psychic disintegration of Roderick Usher, which is inextricably bound up with the disintegration of the family house. This horror story's projection of a psychological state onto a physical setting—of a mind onto a house, and *vice-versa*—is so carefully wrought that Poe's single 'effect' appears to work both ways in the narrator's perspective, and character and setting become inseparable.

Poe commented that the detective story 'The Purloined Letter' was 'perhaps the best of [his] tales of ratiocination.' 'Ratiocination' is what readers find rewarding in Poe's detective stories. It is not the surface plot—that Dupin is able to find the letter that has eluded Paris's police for so long—that most engages readers; rather, it is the artful presentation of Dupin's processes of inference, hypotheses, and deduction, intertwined with his many asides.

'The Fall of the House of Usher' was first published in the September 1839 issue of *Burton's Magazine* then collected in *Tales of the Grotesque and Arabesque*. 'The Purloined Letter' was first published in the 1845 issue of *Gift* and then collected in *Tales by Edgar A. Poe* (1845).

The Fall of the House of Usher

Son coeur est un luth suspendu;
Sitôt qu'on le touche il résonne.
[His heart is a hanging lute;
As soon as touched, it reverberates.]
—*De Béranger*

During the whole of a dull, dark, and soundless day in the autumn of the year, when the clouds hung oppressively low in the heavens, I had been passing alone, on horseback, through a singularly dreary tract of country; and at length found myself, as the shades of the evening drew on, within view of the melancholy House of Usher. I know not how it was—but, with the first glimpse of the building, a sense of insufferable gloom pervaded my spirit. I say insufferable; for the feeling was unrelieved by any of that half-pleasurable, because poetic, sentiment, with which the mind usually receives even the sternest natural images of the desolate or terrible. I looked upon the scene before me—upon the mere house, and the simple landscape features of the domain—upon the bleak walls—upon the vacant eye-like windows—upon a few rank sedges—and upon a few white trunks of decayed trees—with an utter depression of soul which I can compare to no earthly sensation more properly than to the after-dream of the reveller upon opium—the bitter lapse into common life—the hideous dropping off of the veil. There was an iciness, a sinking, a sickening of the heart—an unredeemed dreariness of thought which no goading of the imagination could torture into aught of the sublime. What was it—I paused to think—what was it that so unnerved me in the contemplation of the House of Usher? It was a mystery all insoluble; nor could I grapple with the shadowy fancies that crowded upon me as I pondered. I was forced to fall back upon the unsatisfactory conclusion, that while, beyond a doubt, there *are* combinations of very simple natural objects which have the power of thus affecting us, still the reason, and the analysis of this power lies among considerations beyond our depth. It was possible, I reflected, that a mere different arrangement of the particulars of the scene, of the details of the picture, would be sufficient to modify, or perhaps to annihilate its capacity for sorrowful impression; and, acting upon this idea, I reined my horse to the precipitous brink of a black and lurid tarn that lay in unruffled lustre by the dwelling, and gazed down—but with a shudder even more thrilling than before—upon the remodelled and inverted images of the grey sedge, and the ghastly tree-stems, and the vacant and eye-like windows.

Nevertheless, in this mansion of gloom I now proposed to myself a sojourn of some weeks. Its proprietor, Roderick Usher, had been one of my boon companions in boyhood; but many years had elapsed since our last meeting. A letter, however, had lately reached me in a distant part of the country—a letter from him—which, in its wildly importunate nature, had admitted of no other than a personal reply. The MS gave evidence of nervous agitation. The writer spoke of acute bodily illness—of a pitiable mental idiosyncrasy which oppressed him—and of an earnest desire to see me, as his best, and indeed his only personal friend, with a view of attempting, by the cheerfulness of my society, some alleviation of his malady. It was the manner in which all this, and much more, was said—it was the apparent *heart* that went with his request—which allowed me no room for hesitation; and I accordingly obeyed what I still considered a very singular summons, forthwith.

Although, as boys, we had been even intimate associates, yet I really knew little of my friend. His reserve had been always excessive and habitual. I was aware, however, that his very ancient family had been noted, time out of mind, for a peculiar sensibility of temperament, displaying itself, through long ages, in many works of exalted art, and manifested, of late, in repeated deeds of munificent yet unobtrusive charity, as well as in a passionate devotion to the intricacies, perhaps even more than to the orthodox and easily recognizable beauties, of musical science. I had learned, too, the very remarkable fact, that the stem of the Usher race, all time-honoured as it was, had put forth, at no period, any enduring branch; in other words, that the entire family lay in the direct line of descent, and had always, with very trifling and very temporary variation, so lain. It was this deficiency, I considered, while running over in thought the perfect keeping of the character of the premises with the accredited character of the people, and while speculating upon the possible influence which the one, in the long lapse of centuries, might have exercised upon the other—it was this deficiency, perhaps, of collateral issue, and the consequent undeviating transmission, from sire to son, of the patrimony with the name, which had, at length, so identified the two as to merge the original title of the estate in the quaint and equivocal appellation of the 'House of Usher'—an appellation which seemed to include, in the minds of the peasantry who used it, both the family and the family mansion.

I have said that the sole effect of my somewhat childish experiment—of looking down within the tarn—had been to deepen the first singular impression. There can be no doubt that the consciousness of the rapid increase of my superstition—for why should I not so term it?—served mainly to accelerate the increase itself. Such, I have long known, is the paradoxical law of all sentiments having terror as a basis. And it might have been for this reason only, that, when I again uplifted my eyes to the house itself, from its image in the pool, there grew in my mind a strange fancy—a fancy so ridiculous, indeed, that I but mention it to show the vivid force of the sensations which oppressed me. I had so worked upon my imagination as really to believe that around about the whole mansion and domain there hung an atmosphere peculiar to themselves and their immediate vicinity—an atmosphere which had no affinity with the air of heaven, but which had reeked up from the decayed trees, and the grey walls, and in the silent tarn, in the form of an inelastic vapour or gas—dull, sluggish, faintly discernible, and leaden-hued.

Shaking off from my spirit what *must* have been a dream, I scanned more narrowly the real aspect of the building. Its principal feature seemed to be that of an excessive antiquity. The discoloration of ages had been great. Minute fungi overspread the whole exterior, hanging in a fine tangled web-work from the eaves. Yet all the masonry had fallen; and there appeared to be a wild inconsistency between its still perfect adaptation of parts, and the utterly porous, and evidently decayed condition of the individual stones. In this there was much that reminded me of the specious totality of old wood-work which has rotted for long years in some neglected vault, with no disturbance from the breath of the external air. Beyond this indication of extensive decay, however, the fabric gave little token of instability. Perhaps the eye of a scrutinizing observer might have discovered a barely perceptible fissure, which, extending from the roof of the building in front, made its way down the wall in a zigzag direction, until it became lost in the sullen waters of the tarn.

Noticing these things, I rode over a short causeway to the house. A servant in waiting took my horse, and I entered the Gothic archway to the hall. A valet, of stealthy step, thence conducted me, in silence, through many dark and intricate passages in my progress to the studio of his master. Much that I encountered on the way contributed, I know not how, to heighten the vague sentiments of which I have already spoken. While the objects around me—while the carvings of the ceilings, the sombre tapestries of the walls, the ebon blackness of the floors, and the phantasmagoric armorial trophies which rattled as I strode, were but matters to which, or to such as which, I had been accustomed from my infancy—I still wondered to find how unfamiliar were the fancies which ordinary images were stirring up. On one of the staircases, I met the physician of the family. His countenance, I thought, wore a mingled expression of low cunning and perplexity. He accosted me with trepidation and passed on. The valet now threw open a door and ushered me into the presence of his master.

The room in which I found myself was very large and excessively lofty. The windows were long, narrow, and pointed, and at so vast a distance from the black oaken floor as to be altogether inaccessible from within. Feeble gleams of encrimsoned light made their way through the trellised panes, and served to render sufficiently distinct the more prominent objects around; the eye, however, struggled in vain to reach the remoter angles of the chamber, or the recesses of the vaulted and fretted ceiling. Dark draperies hung upon the walls. The general furniture was profuse, comfortless, antique, and tattered. Many books and musical instruments lay scattered about, but failed to give any vitality to the scene. I felt that I breathed an atmosphere of sorrow. An air of stern, deep, and irredeemable gloom hung over and pervaded all.

Upon my entrance, Usher arose from a sofa upon which he had been lying at full length, and greeted me with a vivacious warmth which had much in it, I at first thought, of an overdone cordiality—of the constrained effort of the *ennuyé* man of the world. A glance, however, at his countenance, convinced me of his perfect sincerity. We sat down; and for some moments, while he spoke not, I gazed upon him with a feeling half of pity, half of awe. Surely, man had never before so terribly altered, in so brief a period, as had Roderick Usher! It was with difficulty that I could bring myself to admit the identity of the wan being before me with the companion of my early boyhood. Yet the character of his face had been at all times remarkable. A cadaverousness of complexion; an eye large, liquid, and luminous beyond comparison; lips somewhat thin and very pallid, but of a surpassingly beautiful curve; a nose of a delicate Hebrew model, but with a breadth of nostril unusual in similar formations; a finely moulded chin, speaking, in its want of prominence, of a want of moral energy; hair of a more than web-like softness and tenuity; these features, with an inordinate expansion above the regions of the temple, made up altogether a countenance not easily to be forgotten. And now in the mere exaggeration of the prevailing character of these features, and of the expression they were wont to convey, lay so much of change that I doubted to whom I spoke. The now ghastly pallor of the skin, and the now miraculous lustre of the eye, above all things startled and even awed me. The silken hair, too, had been suffered to grow all unheeded, and as, in its wild gossamer texture, it floated rather than fell about the face, I could not, even with effort, connect its Arabesque expression with any idea of simple humanity.

In the manner of my friend I was at once struck with an incoherence—an inconsistency; and I soon found this to arise from a series of feeble and futile struggles to overcome an habitual trepidancy—an excessive nervous agitation. For something of this nature I had indeed been prepared, no less by his letter, than by reminiscences of certain boyish traits, and by conclusions deduced from his peculiar physical conformation and temperament. His action was alternately vivacious and sullen. His voice varied rapidly from a tremulous indecision (when the animal spirits seemed utterly in abeyance) to that species of energetic concision—that abrupt, weighty, unhurried, and hollow-sounding enunciation—that leaden, self-balanced, and perfectly modulated guttural utterance, which may be observed in the moments of the intensest excitement of the lost drunkard, or the irreclaimable eater of opium.

It was thus that he spoke of the object of my visit, of his earnest desire to see me, and of the solace he expected me to afford him. He entered, at some length, into what he conceived to be the nature of his malady. It was, he said, a constitutional and a family evil, and one for which he despaired to find a remedy—a mere nervous affection, he added in a breath, which would undoubtedly soon pass. It displayed itself in a host of unnatural sensations. Some of these, as he detailed them, interested and bewildered me; although, perhaps, the terms, and the general manner of the narration had their weight. He suffered much from a morbid acuteness of the senses; the most insipid food was alone endurable; he could wear only garments of certain texture; the odours of all flowers were oppressive; his eyes were tortured by even a faint light; and there were but peculiar sounds, and these from stringed instruments, which did not inspire him with horror.

To an anomalous species of terror I found him a bounden slave. 'I shall perish,' said he, 'I *must* perish in this deplorable folly. Thus, thus, and not otherwise, shall I be lost. I dread the events of the future, not in themselves, but in their results. I shudder at the thought of any, even the most trivial, incident, which may operate upon this intolerable agitation of soul. I have, indeed, no abhorrence of danger, except in its absolute effect—in terror. In this unnerved—in this pitiable condition—I feel that I must inevitably abandon life and reason together, in my struggles with some fatal demon of fear.'

I learned, moreover, at intervals, and through broken and equivocal hints, another singular feature of his mental condition. He was enchained by certain superstitious impressions in regard to the dwelling which he tenanted, and from which, for many years, he had never ventured forth—in regard to an influence whose supposititious force was conveyed in terms too shadowy here to be restated—an influence which some peculiarities in the mere form and substance of his family mansion, had, by dint of long sufferance, he said, obtained over his spirit—an effect which the *physique* of the grey walls and turrets, and of the dim tarn into which they all looked down, had, at length, brought about upon the *morale* of his existence.

He admitted, however, although with hesitation, that much of the peculiar gloom which thus afflicted him could be traced to a more natural and far more palpable origin—to the severe and long-continued illness—indeed to the evidently approaching dissolution—of a tenderly beloved sister—his sole companion for long years—his last and only relative on earth. 'Her decease,' he said, with a bitterness which I can never forget, 'would leave him (him the hopeless and the frail) the last of the ancient race of the Ushers.' As he spoke, the lady Madeline (for so was she called) passed slowly through a remote portion of the apartment, and without having noticed my presence, disappeared. I regarded her with an utter astonishment not unmingled with dread. Her figure, her air, her features—all, in their very minutest development were those—were identically (I can use no other sufficient term) were identically those of the Roderick Usher who sat beside me. A feeling of stupor oppressed me, as my eyes followed her retreating steps. As a door, at length, closed upon her exit, my glance sought instinctively and eagerly the countenance of the brother—but he had buried his face in his hands, and I could only perceive that a far more than ordinary wanness had overspread the emaciated fingers through which trickled many passionate tears.

The disease of the lady Madeline had long baffled the skill of her physicians. A settled apathy, a gradual wasting away of the person, and frequent although transient affections of a partially cataleptical character, were the unusual diagnosis. Hitherto she had steadily borne up against the pressure of her malady, and had not betaken herself finally to bed; but, on the closing in of the evening of my arrival at the house, she succumbed (as her brother told me at night with inexpressible agitation) to the prostrating power of the destroyer; and I learned that the glimpse I had obtained of her person would thus probably be the last I should obtain—that the lady, at least while living, would be seen by me no more.

For several days ensuing, her name was unmentioned by either Usher or myself: and during this period I was busied in earnest endeavours to alleviate the melancholy of my friend. We painted and read together; or I listened, as if in a dream, to the wild improvisations of his speaking guitar. And thus, as a closer and still closer intimacy admitted me more unreservedly into the recesses of his spirit, the more bitterly did I perceive the futility of all attempt at cheering a mind from which darkness, as if an inherent positive quality, poured forth upon all objects of the moral and physical universe, in one unceasing radiation of gloom.

I shall ever bear about me, as Moslemin their shrouds at Mecca, a memory of the many solemn hours I thus spent alone with the master of the House of Usher. Yet I should fail in any attempt to convey an idea of the exact character of the studies, or of the occupations, in which he involved me, or led me the way. An excited and highly distempered ideality threw a sulphurous lustre over all. His long improvised dirges will ring forever in my ears. Among other things, I bear painfully in mind a certain singular perversion and amplification of the wild air of the last waltz of Von Weber. From the paintings over which his elaborate fancy brooded, and which grew, touch by touch, into vagueness at which I shuddered the more thrillingly, because I shuddered knowing not why;—from these paintings (vivid as their images now are before me) I would in vain endeavour to educe more than a small portion which should lie within the compass of merely written words. By the utter simplicity, by the nakedness of his designs, he arrested and overawed attention. If ever mortal painted an idea, that mortal was Roderick Usher. For me at least—in the circumstances then surrounding me—there arose out of the pure abstractions which the hypochondriac contrived to throw upon his canvas an intensity of intolerable awe, no shadow of which felt I ever yet in the contemplation of the certainly glowing yet too concrete reveries of Fuseli.

One of the phantasmagoric conceptions of my friend, partaking not so rigidly of the spirit of abstraction, may be shadowed forth, although feebly, in words. A small picture presented the interior of an immensely long and rectangular vault or tunnel, with low walls, smooth, white, and without interruption or device. Certain accessory points of the design served well to convey the idea that this excavation lay at an exceeding depth below the surface of the earth. No outlet was observed in any portion of its vast extent, and no torch, or other artificial source of light was discernible; yet a flood of intense rays rolled throughout, and bathed the whole in a ghastly and inappropriate splendour.

I have just spoken of that morbid condition of the auditory nerve which rendered all music intolerable to the sufferer with the exception of certain effects of stringed instruments. It was, perhaps, the narrow limits to which he thus confined himself upon the guitar, which gave birth, in great measure, to the fantastic character of his performances. But the fervid *facility* of his impromptus could not be so accounted for. They must have been, and were, in the notes, as well as in the words of his wild fantasias (for he not unfrequently accompanied himself with rhymed verbal improvisations), the result of that intense mental collectedness and concentration to which I have previously alluded as observable only in particular moments of the highest artificial excitement. The words of one of these rhapsodies I have easily borne away in memory. I was, perhaps, the more forcibly impressed with it, as he gave it, because, in the under or mystic current of its meaning, I fancied that I perceived, and for the first time, a full consciousness on the part of Usher, of the tottering of his lofty reason upon her throne. The verses, which were entitled 'The Haunted Palace', ran very nearly, if not accurately, thus:

[THE HAUNTED PALACE]

I

In the greenest of our valleys
    By good angels tenanted,
Once a fair and stately palace—
    Snow-White palace—reared its head.
In the monarch Thought's dominion—
    It stood there!
Never seraph spread his pinion
    Over fabric half so fair!

II

Banners yellow, glorious, golden,
    On its roof did float and flow—
(This—all this—was in the olden
    Time long ago)
And every gentle air that dallied,
    In that sweet day,
Along the rampart plumed and pallid,
    A winged odour went away.

III
All wanderers in that happy valley,
    Through two luminous windows, saw
Spirits moving musically,
    To a lute's well-tuned law,
Round about a throne where, sitting,
    Porphyrogene,
In state his glory well befitting
    The sovereign of the realm was seen.

IV
And with all pearl and ruby glowing
    Was the fair palace door,
Through which came flowing, flowing, flowing,
    And sparkling evermore,
A troop of Echoes whose sweet duty
    Was but to sing,
In voices of surpassing beauty,
    The wit and wisdom of their king.

V
But evil things, in robes of sorrow,
    Assailed the monarch's high estate.
(Ah, let us mourn!—for never morrow
    Shall dawn upon him, desolate!)
And round about his home the glory
    That blushed and bloomed,
Is but a dim-remembered story
    Of the old-time entombed.

VI
And travellers, now, within that valley,
    Through the encrimsoned windows see
Vast forms that move fantastically
    To a discordant melody,
While, like a rapid ghastly river,
    Through the pale door
A hideous throng rush out forever
    And laugh—but smile no more.

I well remember that suggestions arising from this ballad led us into a train of thought wherein there became manifest an opinion of Usher's which I mention not so much on account of its novelty (for other men have thought thus), as on account of the pertinacity with which he maintained it. This opinion, in its general form, was that of the sentience of all vegeta-ble things. But, in his disordered fancy, the idea had assumed a more daring character, and trespassed under certain conditions, upon the kingdom of inorganization. I lack words to express the full extent, or the earnest *abandon* of his persuasion. The belief, however, was connected (as I have previously hinted) with the grey stones of the home of his forefathers. The condition of the sentience had been here, he imagined, fulfilled in the method of collocation of these stones—in the order of their arrangement, as well as in that of the many fungi which overspread them, and of the decayed trees which stood around—above all, in the long undisturbed endurance of this arrangement, and in its reduplication in the still waters of the tarn. Its evidence—the evidence of the sentience—was to be seen, he said, (and I here started as he spoke), in *the gradual yet certain condensation of an atmosphere of their own about the waters and the walls.* The result was discoverable, he added, in that silent, yet importunate and terrible influence which for centuries had moulded the destinies of his family, and which made *him* what I now saw him—what he was. Such opinions need no comment and I will make none.

Our books—the books which, for years, had formed no small portion of the mental existence of the invalid—were, as might be supposed, in strict keeping with this character of phantasm. We pored together over such works as the *Ververt et Chartreuse* of Gresset; the *Belphegor of Machiavelli*; the *Selenography* of Brewster; the *Heaven and Hell* of Swedenborg; the *Subterranean Voyage* of Nicholas Klimm de Holberg; the *Chiromancy* of Robert Flud, of Jean D'Indaginé, and of De la Chambre; the *Journey into the Blue Distance* of Tieck; and the *City of the Sun* of Campanella. One favourite volume was a small octavo edition of the *Directorium Inquisitorum* [Office of the Chief Inquisitor] by the Dominican Eymeric de Gironne, and there were passages in Pomponius Mela, about the old African Satyrs and Œgipans, over which Usher would sit dreaming for hours. His chief delight, however, was found in the earnest and repeated perusal of an exceedingly rare and curious book in quarto Gothic—the manual of a forgotten church—the *Vigilae Mortuorum secundum Chorum Ecclesiae Maguntinae* [Vigils of the Dead According to the Chorus of the Church of Mainz].

I could not help thinking of the wild ritual of this work, and of its probable influence upon the hypochondriac, when, one evening, having informed me abruptly that the lady Madeline was no more, he stated his intention of preserving her corpse for a fortnight (previously to its final interment), in one of the numerous vaults within the main walls of the building. The worldly reason, however, assigned for this singular proceeding, was one which I did not feel at liberty to dispute. The brother had been led to his resolution (so he told me) by considerations of the unusual character of the malady of the deceased, of certain obtrusive and eager inquiries on the part of her medical men, and of the remote and exposed situation of the burial-ground of the family. I will not deny that when I called to mind the sinister countenance of the person whom I met upon the staircase, on the day of my arrival at the house, I had no desire to oppose what I regarded as at best but a harmless, and not by any means an unnatural, precaution.

At the request of Usher, I personally aided him in the arrangements for the temporary entombment. The body having been encoffined, we two alone bore it to its rest. The vault in which we placed it (and which had been so long unopened that our torches, half smothered in its oppressive atmosphere, gave us little opportunity for investigation) was small, damp, and utterly without means of admission for light; lying, at great depth, immediately beneath that portion of the building in which was my own sleeping apartment. It had been used, apparently, in remote feudal times, for the worst purposes of a donjon-keep, and, in later days, as a place of deposit for powder, or other highly combustible substance, as a portion of its floor, and the whole interior of a long archway through which we reached it, were carefully sheathed with copper. The door, of massive iron, had been, also, similarly protected. Its immense weight caused an unusually sharp grating sound, as it moved upon its hinges.

Having deposited our mournful burden upon tressels within this region of horror, we partially turned aside the yet unscrewed lid of the coffin, and looked upon the face of the tenant. The exact similitude between the brother and sister even here again startled and confounded me. Usher, divining, perhaps, my thought, murmured out some few words from which I learned that the deceased and himself had been twins, and that sympathies of a scarcely intelligible nature had always existed between them. Our glances, however, rested not long upon the dead—for we could not regard her unawed. The disease which had thus entombed the lady in the maturity of youth, had left, as usual in all maladies of a strictly cataleptical character, the mockery of a faint blush upon the bosom and the face, and that suspiciously lingering smile upon the lip which is so terrible in death. We replaced and screwed down the lid, and having secured the door of iron, made our way, with toil, into the scarcely less gloomy apartments of the upper portion of the house.

And now, some days of bitter grief having elapsed, an observable change came over the features of the mental disorder of my friend. His ordinary manner had vanished. His ordinary occupations were neglected or forgotten. He roamed from chamber to chamber with hurried, unequal, and objectless step. The pallor of his countenance had assumed, if possible, a more ghastly hue—but the luminousness of his eye had utterly gone out. The once occasional huskiness of his tone was heard no more; and a tremulous quaver, as if of extreme terror, habitually characterized his utterance. There were times, indeed, when I thought his mind was labouring with an oppressive secret, to divulge which he struggled for the necessary courage. At times, again, I was obliged to resolve all into the mere inexplicable vagaries of madness, as I beheld him gazing upon vacancy for long hours, in an attitude of the profoundest attention, as if listening to some imaginary sound. It was no wonder that his condition terrified—that it infected me. I felt creeping upon me, by slow yet certain degrees, the wild influences of his own fantastic yet impressive superstitions.

It was, most especially, upon retiring to bed late in the night of the seventh or eighth day after the entombment of the lady Madeline, that I experienced the full power of such feelings. Sleep came not near my couch—while the hours waned and waned away. I struggled to reason off the nervousness which had dominion over me. I endeavoured to believe that much, if not all of what I felt, was due to the phantasmagoric influence of the gloomy furniture of the room—of the dark and tattered draperies, which, tortured into motion by the breath of a rising tempest, swayed fitfully to and fro upon the walls, and rustled uneasily about the decorations of the bed. But my efforts were fruitless. An irrepressible tremor gradually pervaded my frame; and, at length, there sat upon my very heart an incubus of utterly causeless alarm. Shaking this off with a gasp and a struggle, I uplifted myself upon the pillows, and peering earnestly within the intense darkness of the chamber, harkened—I know not why, except that an instinctive spirit prompted me—to certain low and indefinite sounds which came, through the pauses of the storm, at long intervals, I knew not whence. Overpowered by an intense sentiment of horror, unaccountable yet unendurable, I threw on my clothes with haste (for I felt that I should sleep no more during the night), and endeavoured to arouse myself from the pitiable condition into which I had fallen, by pacing rapidly to and fro through the apartment.

I had taken but few turns in this manner, when a light step on an adjoining staircase arrested my attention. I presently recognized it as that of Usher. In an instant afterwards he rapped, with a gentle touch, at my door, and entered, bearing a lamp. His countenance was, as usual, cadaverously wan—but there was a species of mad hilarity in his eyes—an evidently restrained hysteria in his whole demeanour. His air appalled me—but anything was preferable to the solitude which I had so long endured, and I even welcomed his presence as a relief.

'And you have not seen it?' he said abruptly, after having stared about him for some moments in silence—'you have not then seen it?—but, stay! you shall.' Thus speaking, and having carefully shaded his lamp, he hurried to one of the gigantic casements, and threw it freely open to the storm.

The impetuous fury of the entering gust nearly lifted us from our feet. It was, indeed, a tempestuous yet sternly beautiful night, and one wildly singular in its terror and its beauty. A whirlwind had apparently collected its force in our vicinity; for there were frequent and violent alterations in the direction of the wind; and the exceeding density of the clouds (which hung so low as to press upon the turrets of the house) did not prevent our perceiving the life-like velocity with which they flew careering from all points against each other, without passing away into the distance. I say that even their exceeding density did not prevent our perceiving this—yet we had no glimpse of the moon or stars—nor was there any flashing forth of the lightning. But the under surfaces of the huge masses of agitated vapour, as well as all terrestrial objects immediately around us, were glowing in the unnatural light of a faintly luminous and distinctly visible gaseous exhalation which hung about and enshrouded the mansion.

'You must not—you shall not behold this!' said I, shudderingly, to Usher, as I led him, with a gentle violence, from the window to a seat. 'These appearances, which bewilder you, are merely electrical phenomena not uncommon—or it may be that they have their ghastly origin in the rank miasma of the tarn. Let us close this casement;—the air is chilling and dangerous to your frame. Here is one of your favourite romances. I will read, and you shall listen;—and so we will pass away this terrible night together.'

The antique volume which I had taken up was the *Mad Trist* of Sir Launcelot Canning; but I had called it a favourite of Usher's more in sad jest than in earnest; for, in truth, there is little in its uncouth and unimaginative prolixity which could have had interest for the lofty and spiritual ideality of my friend. It was, however, the only book immediately at hand; and I indulged a vague hope that the excitement which now agitated the hypochondriac, might find relief (for the history of mental disorder is full of similar anomalies) even in the utterness of the folly which I should read. Could I have judged, indeed, by the wild overstrained air of vivacity with which he harkened, or apparently harkened, to the words of the tale, I might have well congratulated myself upon the success of my design.

I had arrived at that well-known portion of the story where Ethelred, the hero of the *Trist*, having sought in vain for peaceable admission into the dwelling of the hermit, proceeds to make good an entrance by force. Here, it will be remembered, the words of the narrative run thus:

'And Ethelred, who was by nature of a doughty heart, and who was now mighty withal, on account of the powerfulness of the wine which he had drunken, waited no longer to hold parley with the hermit, who, in sooth, was of an obstinate and maliceful turn, but, feeling the rain upon his shoulders, and fearing the rising of the tempest, uplifted his mace outright, and, with blows, made quickly room in the plankings of the door for his gauntleted hand; and now pulling therewith sturdily, he so cracked, and ripped, and tore all asunder, that the noise of the dry and hollow-sounding wood alarummed and reverberated throughout the forest.'

At the termination of this sentence I started, and for a moment, paused; for it appeared to me (although I at once concluded that my excited fancy had deceived me)—it appeared to me that, from some very remote portion of the mansion or of its vicinity, there came, indistinctly, to my ears, what might have been, in its exact similarity of character, the echo (but a stifled and dull one certainly) of the very cracking and ripping sound which Sir Launcelot had so particularly described. It was, beyond doubt, the coincidence alone which had arrested my attention; for, amid the rattling of the sashes of the casements, and the ordinary commingled noises of the still increasing storm, the sound, in itself, had nothing, surely, which should have interested or disturbed me. I continued the story:

'But the good champion Ethelred, now entering within the door, was sore enraged and amazed to perceive no signal of the maliceful hermit; but, in the stead thereof, a dragon of a scaly and prodigious demeanour, and of a fiery tongue, which sate in guard before a palace of gold, with a floor of silver; and upon the wall there hung a shield of shining brass with this legend enwritten—

Who entereth herein, a conqueror hath bin;
Who slayeth the dragon, the shield he shall win;

And Ethelred uplifted his mace, and struck upon the head of the dragon, which fell before him, and gave up his pesty breath, with a shriek so horrid and harsh, and withal so piercing, that Ethelred had fain to close his ears with his hands against the dreadful noise of it, the like whereof was never before heard.'

Here again I paused abruptly, and now with a feeling of utter amazement—for there could be no doubt whatever that, in this instance, I did actually hear (although from what direction it proceeded I found it impossible to say) a low and apparently distant, but harsh, protracted, and most unusual screaming or grating sound—the exact counterpart of what my fancy had already conjured up as the sound of the dragon's unnatural shriek as described by the romancer.

Oppressed, as I certainly was, upon the occurrence of this second and most extraordinary coincidence, by a thousand conflicting sensations, in which wonder and extreme terror were predominant, I still retained sufficient presence of mind to avoid exciting by any observation, the sensitive nervousness of my companion. I was by no means certain that he had noticed the sounds in question; although, assuredly, a strange alteration had, during the last few minutes, taken place in his demeanour. From a position fronting my own, he had gradually brought round his chair, so as to sit with his face to the door of the chamber; and thus I could but partially perceive his features, although I saw that his lips trembled as if he were murmuring inaudibly. His head had dropped upon his breast—yet I knew that he was not asleep, from the wide and rigid opening of the eye as I caught a glance of it in profile. The motion of his body, too, was at variance with this idea—for he rocked from side to side with a gentle yet constant and uniform sway. Having rapidly taken notice of all this, I resumed the narrative of Sir Launcelot, which thus proceeded:

'And now, the champion, having escaped from the terrible fury of the dragon, bethinking himself of the brazen shield, and of the breaking up of the enchantment which was upon it, removed the carcass from out of the way before him, and approached valorously over the silver pavement of the castle to where the shield was upon the wall; which in sooth tarried not for his full coming, but fell down at his feet upon the silver floor, with a mighty great and terrible ringing sound.'

No sooner had these syllables passed my lips, than—as if a shield of brass had indeed, at the moment, fallen heavily upon a floor of silver—I became aware of a distinct, hollow, metallic, and clangorous, yet apparently muffled reverberation. Utterly unnerved, I started convulsively to my feet; but the measured rocking movement of Usher was undisturbed. I rushed to the chair in which he sat. His eyes were bent fixedly before him, and throughout his whole countenance there reigned a more than stony rigidity. But, as I laid my hand upon his shoulder, there came a strong shudder over his frame; a sickly smile quivered about his lips; and I saw that he spoke in a low, hurried, and gibbering murmur, as if unconscious of my presence. Bending closely over his person, I at length drank in the hideous import of his words.

'Not hear it?—yes, I hear it, and *have* heard it. Long—long—long—many minutes, many hours, many days, have I heard it—yet I dared not—oh, pity me, miserable wretch that I am!—I dared not—I *dared* not speak! We *have put her living in the tomb!* Said I not that my senses were acute? I *now* tell you that I heard her first feeble movements in the hollow coffin. I heard them—many, many days ago—yet I dared not—I *dared not speak!* And now—to-night—Ethelred—ha! ha!—the breaking of the hermit's door, and the death-cry of the dragon, and the clangour of the shield!—say, rather, the rending of the coffin, and the grating of the iron hinges, and her struggles within the coppered arch-way of the vault! Oh whither shall I fly? Will she not be here anon? Is she not hurrying to upbraid me for my haste? Have I not heard her footsteps on the stair? Do I not distinguish that heavy and horrible beating of her heart? Madman!'—here he sprung violently to his feet, and shrieked out his syllables, as if in the effort he were giving up his soul—'Madman! *I tell you that she now stands without the door!*'

As if in the superhuman energy of his utterance there had been found the potency of a spell—the huge antique panels to which the speaker pointed, threw slowly back, upon the instant, their ponderous and ebony jaws. It was the work of the rushing gust—but then without those doors there *did* stand the lofty and enshrouded figure of the lady Madeline of Usher. There was blood upon her white robes, and the evidence of some bitter struggle upon every portion of her emaciated frame. For a moment she remained, trembling and reeling to and fro upon the threshold—then, with a low moaning cry, fell heavily inward upon the person of her brother, and in her horrible and now final death-agonies bore him to the floor a corpse, and a victim to the terrors he had dreaded.

From that chamber, and from that mansion, I fled aghast. The storm was still abroad in all its wrath as I found myself crossing the old causeway. Suddenly there shot along the path a wild light, and I turned to see whence a gleam so unusual could have issued; for the vast house and its shadows were alone behind me. The radiance was that of the full, setting, and blood-red moon, which now shone vividly through that once barely-discernible fissure, of which I have before spoken as extending from the roof of the building, in a zigzag direction, to the base. While I gazed, this fissure rapidly widened—there came a fierce breath of the whirlwind—the entire orb of the satellite burst at once upon my sight—my brain reeled as I saw the mighty walls rushing asunder—there was a long tumultuous shouting sound like the voice of a thousand waters—and the deep and dank tarn at my feet closed sullenly and silently over the fragments of the '*House of Usher*'.

1839

The Purloined Letter

Nil sapientia odiosius acumine nimio [Nothing is more hateful to wisdom than too much cleverness]. —*Seneca*

At Paris, just after dark one gusty evening in the autumn of 18—, I was enjoying the twofold luxury of meditation and a meerschaum, in company with my friend C. Auguste Dupin, in his little back library, or book-closet, *au troisième, No. 33, Rue Dunôt, Faubourg St Germain*. For one hour at least we had maintained a profound silence; while each, to any casual observer, might have seemed intently and exclusively occupied with the curling eddies of smoke that oppressed the atmosphere of the chamber. For myself, however, I was mentally discussing certain topics which had formed matter for conversation between us at an earlier period of the evening; I mean the affair of the Rue Morgue, and the mystery attending the murder of Marie Rogêt. I looked upon it, therefore, as something of a coincidence, when the door of our apartment was thrown open and admitted our old acquaintance, Monsieur G---, the Prefect of the Parisian police.

We gave him a hearty welcome; for there was nearly half as much of the entertaining as of the contemptible about the man, and we had not seen him for several years. We had been sitting in the dark, and Dupin now arose for the purpose of lighting a lamp, but sat down again, without doing so, upon G---'s saying that he had called to consult us, or rather to ask the opinion of my friend, about some official business which had occasioned a great deal of trouble.

'If it is any point requiring reflection,' observed Dupin, as he forbore to enkindle the wick, 'we shall examine it to better purpose in the dark.'

'That is another of your odd notions,' said the Prefect, who had a fashion of calling every thing 'odd' that was beyond his comprehension, and thus lived amid an absolute legion of 'oddities'.

'Very true,' said Dupin, as he supplied his visitor with a pipe, and rolled towards him a very comfortable chair.

'And what is the difficulty now?' I asked. 'Nothing more in the assassination way, I hope?'

'Oh no; nothing of that nature. The fact is, the business is *very* simple indeed, and I make no doubt that we can manage it sufficiently well ourselves; but then I thought Dupin would like to hear the details of it, because it is so excessively *odd*.'

'Simple and odd,' said Dupin.

'Why, yes; and not exactly that, either. The fact is, we have all been a good deal puzzled because the affair *is* so simple, and yet baffles us altogether.'

'Perhaps it is the very simplicity of the thing which puts you at fault,' said my friend.

'What nonsense you *do* talk!' replied the Prefect, laughing heartily.

'Perhaps the mystery is a little *too* plain,' said Dupin.

'Oh, good heavens! who ever heard of such an idea?'

'A little *too* self-evident.'

'Ha! ha! ha!—ha! ha! ha!—ho! ho! ho!' roared out our visitor, profoundly amused, 'oh, Dupin, you will be the death of me yet!'

'And what, after all, *is* the matter on hand?' I asked.

'Why, I will tell you,' replied the Prefect, as he gave a long, steady, and contemplative puff, and settled himself in his chair. 'I will tell you in a few words; but, before I begin, let me caution you that this is an affair demanding the greatest secrecy, and that I should most probably lose the position I now hold, were it known that I confided it to any one.'

'Proceed,' said I.

'Or not,' said Dupin.

'Well, then; I have received personal information, from a very high quarter, that a certain document of the last importance, has been purloined from the royal apartments. The individual who purloined it is known; this beyond a doubt; he was seen to take it. It is known also that it still remains in his possession.'

'How is this known?' asked Dupin.

'It is clearly inferred,' replied the Prefect, 'from the nature of the document, and from the non-appearance of certain results which would at once arise from its passing *out* of the robber's possession;—that is to say, from his employing it as he must design in the end to employ it.'

'Be a little more explicit,' I said.

'Well, I may venture so far as to say that the paper gives its holder a certain power in a certain quarter where such power is immensely valuable.' The Prefect was fond of the cant of diplomacy.

'Still I do not quite understand,' said Dupin.

'No? Well; the disclosure of the document to a third person, who shall be nameless, would bring in question the honour of a personage of most exalted station; and this fact gives the holder of the document an ascendancy over the illustrious personage whose honour and peace are so jeopardized.'

'But this ascendancy,' I interposed, 'would depend upon the robber's knowledge of the loser's knowledge of the robber. Who would dare—'

'The thief,' said G---, 'is the Minister D---, who dares all things, those unbecoming as well as those becoming a man. The method of the theft was not less ingenious than bold. The document in question—a letter, to be frank—had been received by the personage robbed while alone in the royal *boudoir*. During its perusal she was suddenly interrupted by the entrance of the other exalted personage from whom especially it was her wish to conceal it. After a hurried and vain endeavour to thrust it in a drawer, she was forced to place it, open as it was, upon a table. The address, however, was uppermost, and, the contents thus unexposed, the letter escaped notice. At this juncture enters the Minister D---. His lynx eye immediately perceives the paper, recognizes the handwriting of the address, observes the confusion of the personage addressed, and fathoms her secret. After some business transactions, hurried through in his ordinary manner, he produces a letter somewhat similar to the one in question, opens it, pretends to read it, and then places it in close juxtaposition to the other. Again he converses, for some fifteen minutes, upon the public affairs. At length, in taking leave, he takes also from the table the letter to which he had no claim. Its rightful owner saw, but, of course, dared not call attention to the act, in the presence of the third personage who stood at her elbow. The minister decamped; leaving his own letter—one of no importance—upon the table.'

'Here, then,' said Dupin to me, 'you have precisely what you demand to make the ascendancy complete—the robber's knowledge of the loser's knowledge of the robber.'

'Yes,' replied the Prefect; 'and the power thus attained has, for some months past, been wielded, for political purposes, to a very dangerous extent. The personage robbed is more thoroughly convinced, every day, of the necessity of reclaiming her letter. But this, of course, cannot be done openly. In fine, driven to despair, she has committed the matter to me.'

'Than whom,' said Dupin, amid a perfect whirlwind of smoke, 'no more sagacious agent could, I suppose, be desired, or even imagined.'

'You flatter me,' replied the Prefect; 'but it is possible that some such opinion may have been entertained.'

'It is clear,' said I, 'as you observe, that the letter is still in possession of the minister; since it is this possession, and not any employment of the letter, which bestows the power. With the employment the power departs.'

'True,' said G---; 'and upon this conviction I proceeded. My first care was to make thorough search of the minister's hotel; and here my chief embarrassment lay in the necessity of searching without his knowledge. Beyond all things, I have been warned of the danger which would result from giving him reason to suspect our design.'

'But,' said I, 'you are quite *au fait* in these investigations. The Parisian police have done this thing often before.'

'O yes; and for this reason I did not despair. The habits of the minister gave me, too, a great advantage. He is frequently absent from home all night. His servants are by no means numerous. They sleep at a distance from their master's apartments, and, being chiefly Neapolitans, are readily made drunk. I have keys, as you know, with which I can open any chamber or cabinet in Paris. For three months a night has not passed, during the greater part of which I have not been engaged, personally, in ransacking the D--- Hotel. My honour is interested, and, to mention a great secret, the reward is enormous. So I did not abandon the search until I had become fully satisfied that the thief is a more astute man than myself. I fancy that I have investigated every nook and corner of the premises in which it is possible that the paper can be concealed.'

'But is it not possible,' I suggested, 'that although the letter may be in possession of the minister, as it unquestionably is, he may have concealed it elsewhere than upon his own premises?'

'This is barely possible,' said Dupin. 'The present peculiar condition of affairs at court, and especially of those intrigues in which D--- is known to be involved, would render the instant availability of the document—its susceptibility of being produced at a moment's notice—a point of nearly equal importance with its possession.'

'Its susceptibility of being produced?' said I.

'That is to say, of being *destroyed*,' said Dupin.

'True,' I observed; 'the paper is clearly then upon the premises. As for its being upon the person of the minister, we may consider that as out of the question.'

'Entirely,' said the Prefect. 'He has been twice waylaid, as if by footpads, and his person rigorously searched under my own inspection.'

'You might have spared yourself this trouble,' said Dupin. 'D---, I presume, is not altogether a fool, and, if not, must have anticipated these waylayings, as a matter of course.'

'Not *altogether* a fool,' said G---, 'but then he's a poet, which I take to be only one remove from a fool.'

'True,' said Dupin, after a long and thoughtful whiff from his meerschaum, 'although I have been guilty of certain doggerel myself.'

'Suppose you detail,' said I, 'the particulars of your search.'

'Why the fact is, we took our time, and we searched *everywhere*. I have had long experience in these affairs. I took the entire building, room by room; devoting the nights of a whole week to each. We examined, first, the furniture of each apartment. We opened every possible drawer; and I presume you know that, to a properly trained police agent, such a thing as a *secret* drawer is impossible. Any man is a dolt who permits a "secret" drawer to escape him in a search of this kind. The thing is so plain. There is a certain amount of bulk—of space—to be accounted for in every cabinet. Then we have accurate rules. The fiftieth part of a line could not escape us. After the cabinets we took the chairs. The cushions we probed with the fine long needles you have seen me employ. From the tables we removed the tops.'

'Why so?'

'Sometimes the top of a table, or other similarly arranged piece of furniture, is removed by the person wishing to conceal an article; then the leg is excavated, the article deposited within the cavity, and the top replaced. The bottoms and tops of bedposts are employed in the same way.'

'But could not the cavity be detected by sounding?' I asked.

'By no means, if, when the article is deposited, a sufficient wadding of cotton be placed around it. Besides, in our case, we were obliged to proceed without noise.'

'But you could not have removed—you could not have taken to pieces *all* articles of furniture in which it would have been possible to make a deposit in the manner you mention. A letter may be compressed into a thin spiral roll, not differing much in shape or bulk from a large knitting-needle, and in this form it might be inserted into the rung of a chair, for example. You did not take to pieces all the chairs?'

'Certainly not; but we did better—we examined the rungs of every chair in the hotel, and, indeed, the jointings of every description of furniture, by the aid of a most powerful microscope. Had there been any traces of recent disturbance we should not have failed to detect it *instanter*. A single grain of gimlet-dust, or saw-dust, for example, would have been as obvious as an apple. Any disorder in the gluing—any unusual gaping in the joints—would have sufficed to insure detection.'

'Of course you looked to the mirrors, between the boards and the plates, and you probed the beds and the bed-clothes, as well as the curtains and carpets.'

'That of course; and when we had absolutely completed every particle of the furniture in this way, then we examined the house itself. We divided its entire surface into compartments, which we numbered, so that none might be missed; then we scrutinized each individual square inch throughout the premises, including the two houses immediately adjoining, with the microscope, as before.'

'The two houses adjoining!' I exclaimed; 'you must have had a great deal of trouble.'

'We had; but the reward offered is prodigious.'

'You include the *grounds* about the houses?'

'All the grounds are paved with brick. They gave us comparatively little trouble. We examined the moss between the bricks, and found it undisturbed.'

'And the roofs?'

'We surveyed every inch of the external surface, and probed carefully beneath every tile.'

'You looked among D---'s papers, of course, and into the books of the library?'

'Certainly; we opened every package and parcel; we not only opened every book, but we turned over every leaf in each volume, not contenting ourselves with a mere shake, according to the fashion of some of our police officers. We also measured the thickness of every book-*cover*, with the most jealous scrutiny of the microscope. Had any of the bindings been recently meddled with, it would have been utterly impossible that the fact should have escaped observation. Some five or six volumes, just from the hands of the binder, we carefully probed, longitudinally, with the needles.'

'You explored the floors beneath the carpets?'

'Beyond doubt. We removed every carpet, and examined the boards with the microscope.'

'And the paper on the walls?'

'Yes.'

'You looked into the cellars?'

'We did; and, as time and labour were no objects, we dug up every one of them to the depth of four feet.'

'Then,' I said, 'you have been making a miscalculation, and the letter is *not* upon the premises, as you suppose.'

'I fear you are right there,' said the Prefect. 'And now, Dupin, what would you advise me to do?'

'To make a thorough re-search of the premises.'

'That is absolutely needless,' replied G---. 'I am not more sure that I breathe than I am that the letter is not at the Hotel.'

'I have no better advice to give you,' said Dupin. 'You have, of course, an accurate description of the letter?'

'Oh yes!'—And here the Prefect, producing a memorandum-book, proceeded to read aloud a minute account of the internal, and especially of the external appearance of the missing document. Soon after finishing the perusal of this description, he took his departure, more entirely depressed in spirits than I had ever known the good gentleman before.

In about a month afterwards he paid us another visit, and found us occupied very nearly as before. He took a pipe and a chair and entered into some ordinary conversation. At length I said,—

'Well, but G---, what of the purloined letter? I presume you have at last made up your mind that there is no such thing as overreaching the Minister?'

'Confound him, say I—yes; I made the re-examination, however, as Dupin suggested—but it was all labour lost, as I knew it would be.'

'How much was the reward offered, did you say?' asked Dupin.

'Why, a very great deal—a *very* liberal reward—I don't like to say how much, precisely; but one thing I *will* say, that I wouldn't mind giving my individual cheque for fifty thousand francs to any one who could obtain me that letter. The fact is, it is becoming of more and more importance every day; and the reward has been lately doubled. If it were trebled, however, I could do no more than I have done.'

'Why, yes,' said Dupin, drawlingly, between the whiffs of his meerschaum, 'I really—think, G---, you have not exerted yourself—to the utmost in this matter. You might—do a little more, I think, eh?'

'How?—in what way?'

'Why—puff, puff—you might—puff, puff—employ counsel in the matter, eh?—puff, puff, puff. Do you remember the story they tell of Abernethy?'

'No; hang Abernethy!'

'To be sure! hang him and welcome. But, once upon a time, a certain rich miser conceived the design of sponging upon this Abernethy for a medical opinion. Getting up, for this purpose, an ordinary conversation in a private company, he insinuated his case to the physician, as that of an imaginary individual.

' "We will suppose," said the miser, "that his symptoms are such and such; now, doctor, what would *you* have directed him to take?"

' "Take!" said Abernethy, "why, take *advice*, to be sure." '

'But,' said the Prefect, a little discomposed, 'I am *perfectly* willing to take advice, and to pay for it. I would *really* give fifty thousand francs, every *centime* of it, to any one who would aid me in the matter.'

'In that case,' replied Dupin, opening a drawer, and producing a cheque-book, 'you may as well fill me up a cheque for the amount mentioned. When you have signed it, I will hand you the letter.'

I was astonished. The Prefect appeared absolutely thunder-stricken. For some minutes he remained speechless and motionless, looking incredulously at my friend with open mouth, and eyes that seemed starting from their sockets; then, apparently recovering himself in some measure, he seized a pen, and after several pauses and vacant stares, finally filled up and signed a cheque for fifty thousand francs, and handed it across the table to Dupin. The latter examined it carefully and deposited it in his pocket-book; then, unlocking an *escritoire*, took thence a letter and gave it to the Prefect. This functionary grasped it in a perfect agony of joy, opened it with a trembling hand, cast a rapid glance at its contents, and then, scrambling and struggling to the door, rushed at length unceremoniously from the room and from the house, without having uttered a solitary syllable since Dupin had requested him to fill up the cheque.

When he had gone, my friend entered into some explanations.

'The Parisian police,' he said, 'are exceedingly able in their way. They are persevering, ingenious, cunning, and thoroughly versed in the knowledge which their duties seem chiefly to demand. Thus, when G--- detailed to us his mode of searching the premises at the Hotel D---, I felt entire confidence in his having made a satisfactory investigation—so far as his labours extended.'

'So far as his labours extended?' said I.

'Yes,' said Dupin. 'The measures adopted were not only the best of their kind, but carried out to absolute perfection. Had the letter been deposited within the range of their search, these fellows would, beyond a question, have found it.'

I merely laughed—but he seemed quite serious in all that he said.

'The measures, then,' he continued, 'were good in their kind, and well executed; their defect lay in their being inapplicable to the case, and to the man. A certain set of highly ingenious resources are, with the Prefect, a sort of Procrustean bed, to which he forcibly adapts his designs. But he perpetually errs by being too deep or too shallow, for the matter in hand; and many a schoolboy is a better reasoner than he. I knew one about eight years of age, whose success at guessing in the game of "even and odd" attracted universal admiration. This game is simple, and is played with marbles. One player holds in his hand a number of these toys, and demands of another whether that number is even or odd. If the guess is right, the guesser wins one; if wrong, he loses one. The boy to whom I allude won all the marbles of the school. Of course he had some principle of guessing; and this lay in mere observation and admeasurement of the astuteness of his opponents. For example, an arrant simpleton is his opponent, and, holding up his closed hand, asks, "are they even or odd?" Our schoolboy replies, "odd," and loses; but upon the second trial he wins, for he then says to himself, "the simpleton had them even upon the first trial, and his amount of cunning is just sufficient to make him have them odd upon the second, I will therefore guess odd;" —he guesses odd, and wins. Now, with a simpleton a degree above the first, he would have reasoned thus: "This fellow finds that in the first instance I guessed odd, and, in the second, he will propose to himself, upon the first impulse, a simple variation from even to odd, as did the first simpleton; but then a second thought will suggest that this is too simple a variation, and finally he will decide upon putting it even as before. I will therefore guess even;" —he guesses even, and wins. Now this mode of reasoning in the schoolboy, whom his fellows termed "lucky",—what, in its last analysis, is it?'

'It is merely,' I said, 'an identification of the reasoner's intellect with that of his opponent.'

'It is,' said Dupin; 'and, upon inquiring of the boy by what means he effected the *thorough* identification in which his success consisted, I received answer as follows: "When I wish to find out how wise, or how stupid, or how good, or how wicked is any one, or what are his thoughts at the moment, I fashion the expression of my face, as accurately as possible, in accordance with the expression of his, and then wait to see what thoughts or sentiments arise in my mind or heart, as if to match or correspond with the expression." This response of the schoolboy lies at the bottom of all the spurious profundity which has been attributed to Rochefoucault, to La Bruyère, to Machiavelli, and to Campanella.'

'And the identification,' I said, 'of the reasoner's intellect with that of his opponent, depends, if I understand you aright, upon the accuracy with which the opponent's intellect is admeasured.'

'For its practical value it depends upon this,' replied Dupin; 'and the Prefect and his cohort fail so frequently, first, by default of this identification, and, secondly, by ill-admeasurement, or rather through non-admeasurement, of the intellect with which they are engaged. They consider only their *own* ideas of ingenuity; and, in searching for anything hidden, advert only to the modes in which *they* would have hidden it. They are right in this much—that their own ingenuity is a faithful representative of that of *the mass*; but when the cunning of the individual felon is diverse in character from their own, the felon foils them, of course. This always happens when it is above their own, and very usually when it is below. They have no variation of principle in their investigations; at best, when urged by some unusual emergency—by some extraordinary reward—they extend or exaggerate their old modes of *practice*, without touching their principles. What, for example, in this case of D---, has been done to vary the principle of action? What is all this boring, and probing, and sounding, and scrutinizing with the microscope, and dividing the surface of the building into registered square inches—what is it all but an exaggeration of *the application* of the one principle or set of principles of search, which are based upon the one set of notions regarding human ingenuity, to which the Prefect, in the long routine of his duty, has been accustomed? Do you not see he has taken it for granted that *all* men proceed to conceal a letter,—not exactly in a gimlet-hole bored in a chair-leg—but, at least, in *some* out-of-the-way hole or corner suggested by the same tenor of thought which would urge a man to secrete a letter in a gimlet-hole bored in a chair-leg? And do you not see also, that such *recherchés* nooks for concealment are adapted only for ordinary occasions, and would be adopted only by ordinary intellects; for, in all cases of concealment, a disposal of the article concealed—a disposal of it in this *recherché* manner,—is, in the very first instance, presumed and presumable; and thus its discovery depends, not at all upon the acumen, but altogether upon the mere care, patience, and determination of the seekers; and where the case is of importance—or, what amounts to the same thing in the policial eyes, when the reward is of magnitude,—the qualities in question have *never* been know to fail. You will now understand what I meant in suggesting that, had the purloined letter been hidden anywhere within the limits of the Prefect's examination—in other words, had the principle of its concealment been comprehended within the principles of the Prefect—its discovery would have been a matter altogether beyond question. This functionary, however, has been thoroughly mystified; and the remote source of his defeat lies in the supposition that the Minister is a fool, because he has acquired renown as a poet. All fools are poets; this the Prefect *feels*; and he is merely guilty of a *non distributio medii* [fallacy of the undistributed middle] in thence inferring that all poets are fools.'

'But is this really the poet?' I asked. 'There are two brothers, I know; and both have attained reputation in letters. The Minister I believe has written learnedly of the Differential Calculus. He is a mathematician, and no poet.'

'You are mistaken; I know him well; he is both. As poet *and* mathematician, he would reason well; as poet, profoundly; as mere mathematician, he could not have reasoned at all, and thus would have been at the mercy of the Prefect.'

'You surprise me,' I said, 'by these opinions, which have been contradicted by the voice of the world. You do not mean to set at naught the well-digested idea of centuries. The mathematical reason has been long regarded as *the* reason *par excellence*.'

'"*Il y a à parier*,"' replied Dupin, quoting from Chamfort, '"*que toute idée publique, toute convention reçue, est une sottise, car elle a convenu au plus grand nombre* [It's a good bet that every public idea, every received convention, is foolish; since it appeals to the majority]." The mathematicians, I grant you, have done their best to promulgate the popular error to which you allude, and which is none the less an error for its promulgation as truth. With an art worthy a better cause, for example, they have insinuated the term "analysis" into application to algebra. The French are the originators of this particular deception; but if a term is of any importance—if words derive any value from applicability—then "analysis" conveys "algebra" about as much as, in Latin, "*ambitus*" implies "ambition", "*religio*" "religion", or "*homines honesti*", a set of *honourable* men.'

'You have a quarrel on hand, I see,' said I, 'with some of the algebraists of Paris; but proceed.'

'I dispute the availability, and thus the value, of that reason which is cultivated in any especial form other than the abstractly logical. I dispute, in particular, the reason educed by mathematical study. The mathematics are the science of form and quantity; mathematical reasoning is merely logic applied to observation upon form and quantity. The great error lies in supposing that even the truths of what is called *pure* algebra, are abstract or general truths. And this error is so egregious that I am confounded at the universality with which it has been received. Mathematical axioms are *not* axioms of general truth. What is true of *relation*—of form and quantity—is often grossly false in regard to morals, for example. In this latter science it is very usually *un*true that the aggregated parts are equal to the whole. In chemistry also the axiom fails. In the consideration of motive it fails; for two motives, each of a given value, have not, necessarily, a value when united, equal to the sum of their values apart. There are numerous other mathematical truths which are only truths within the limits of *relation*. But the mathematician argues, from his *finite truths*, through habit, as if they were of an absolutely general applicability—as the world indeed imagines them to be. Bryant, in his very learned "Mythology", mentions an analogous source of error, when he says that "although the Pagan fables are not believed, yet we forget ourselves continually, and make inferences from them as existing realities." With the algebraists, however, who are Pagans themselves, the "Pagan fables" *are* believed, and the inferences are made, not so much through lapse of memory, as through an unaccountable addling of the brains. In short, I never yet encountered the mere mathematician who could be trusted out of equal roots, or one who did not clandestinely hold it as a point of his faith that $x^2 + px$ was absolutely and unconditionally equal to q. Say to one of these gentlemen, by way of experiment, if you please, that you believe occasions may occur where $x^2 + px$ is *not* altogether equal to q, and, having made him understand what you mean, get out of his reach as speedily as convenient, for, beyond doubt, he will endeavour to knock you down.

'I mean to say,' continued Dupin, while I merely laughed at his last observations, 'that if the Minister had been no more than a mathematician, the Prefect would have been under no necessity of giving me this cheque. Had he been no more than a poet, I think it probable that he would have foiled us all. I knew him, however, as both mathematician and poet, and my measures were adapted to his capacity, with reference to the circumstances by which he was surrounded. I knew him as a courtier, too, and as a bold *intriguant*. Such a man, I considered, could not fail to be aware of the ordinary policial modes of action. He could not have failed to anticipate—and events have proved that he did not fail to anticipate—the waylayings to which he was subjected. He must have foreseen, I reflected, the secret investigations of his premises. His frequent absences from home at night, which were hailed by the Prefect as certain aids to his success, I regarded only as *ruses*, to afford opportunity for thorough search to the police, and thus the sooner to impress them with the conviction to which G---, in fact, did finally arrive—the conviction that the letter was not upon the premises. I felt, also, that the whole train of thought, which I was at some pains in detailing to you just now, concerning the invariable principle of policial action in searches for articles concealed—I felt that this whole train of thought would necessarily pass through the mind of the Minister. It would imperatively lead him to despise all the ordinary *nooks* of concealment. *He* could not, I reflected, be so weak as not to see that the most intricate and remote recess of his hotel would be as open as his commonest closets to the eyes, to the probes, to the gimlets, and to the microscopes of the Prefect. I saw, in fine, that he would be driven, as a matter of course, to *simplicity*, if not deliberately induced to it as a matter of choice. You will remember, please, how desperately the Prefect laughed when I suggested, upon our first interview, that it was just possible this mystery troubled him so much on account of its being so *very* self-evident.'

'Yes,' said I, 'I remember his merriment well. I really thought he would have fallen into convulsions.'

'The material world,' continued Dupin, 'abounds with very strict analogies to the immaterial; and thus some colour of truth has been given to the rhetorical dogma, that metaphor, or simile, may be made to strengthen an argument, as well as to embellish a description. The principle of the *vis inertiæ* [force of inertia], for example, with the amount of *momentum* proportionate with it and consequent upon it, seems to be identical in physics and metaphysics. It is not more true in the former, that a large body is with more difficulty set in motion than a smaller one, and that its subsequent impetus is commensurate with this difficulty, than it is, in the latter, that intellects of the vaster capacity, while more forcible, more constant, and more eventful in their movements than those of inferior grade, are yet the less readily moved, and more embarrassed and full of hesitation in the first few steps of their progress. Again: have you ever noticed which of the street signs, over the shop-doors, are the most attractive of attention?'

'I have never given the matter a thought,' I said.

'There is a game of puzzles,' he resumed, 'which is played upon a map. One party playing requires another to find a given word—the name of town, river, state, or empire—any word, in short, upon the motley and perplexed surface of the chart. A novice in the game generally seeks to embarrass his opponents by giving them the most minutely lettered names; but the adept selects such words as stretch, in large characters, from one end of the chart to the other. These, like the over-largely lettered signs and placards of the street, escape observation by dint of being excessively obvious; and here the physical oversight is precisely analogous with the moral inapprehension by which the intellect suffers to pass unnoticed those considerations which are too obtrusively and too palpably self-evident. But this is a point, it appears, somewhat above or beneath the understanding of the Prefect. He never once thought it probable, or possible, that the Minister had deposited the letter immediately beneath the nose of the whole world, by way of best preventing any portion of that world from perceiving it.

'But the more I reflected upon the daring, dashing, and discriminating ingenuity of D---; upon the fact that the document must always have been *at hand*, if he intended to use it to good purpose; and upon the decisive evidence, obtained by the Prefect, that it was not hidden within the limits of that dignitary's ordinary search—the more satisfied I became that, to conceal this letter, the Minister had resorted to the comprehensive and sagacious expedient of not attempting to conceal it at all.

'Full of these ideas, I prepared myself with a pair of green spectacles, and called one fine morning, quite by accident, at the Ministerial hotel. I found D--- at home, yawning, lounging, and dawdling, as usual, and pretending to be in the last extremity of *ennui*. He is, perhaps, the most really energetic human being now alive—but that is only when nobody sees him.

'To be even with him, I complained of my weak eyes, and lamented the necessity of the spectacles, under cover of which I cautiously and thoroughly surveyed the whole apartment, while seemingly intent only upon the conversation of my host.

'I paid especial attention to a large writing-table near which he sat, and upon which lay confusedly, some miscellaneous letters and other papers, with one or two musical instruments and a few books. Here, however, after a long and very deliberate scrutiny, I saw nothing to excite particular suspicion.

'At length my eyes, in going the circuit of the room, fell upon a trumpery filigree card-rack of pasteboard, that hung dangling by a dirty blue riband, from a little brass knob just beneath the middle of the mantelpiece. In this rack, which had three or four compartments, were five or six visiting cards and a solitary letter. This last was much soiled and crumpled. It was torn nearly in two, across the middle—as if a design, in the first instance, to tear it entirely up as worthless, had been altered, or stayed, in the second. It had a large black seal, bearing the D--- cipher *very* conspicuously, and was addressed, in a diminutive female hand, to D---, the minister, himself. It was thrust carelessly, and even, as it seemed, contemptuously, into one of the uppermost divisions of the rack.

'No sooner had I glanced at this letter, than I concluded it to be that of which I was in search. To be sure, it was, to all appearance, radically different from the one of which the Prefect had read us so minute a description. Here the seal was large and black, with the D--- cipher; there it was small and red, with the ducal arms of the S--- family. Here, the address, to the Minister, was diminutive and feminine; there the superscription, to a certain royal personage, was markedly bold and decided; the size alone formed a point of correspondence. But, then, the *radicalness* of these differences, which was excessive; the dirt; the soiled and torn condition of the paper, so inconsistent with the *true* methodical habits of D---, and so suggestive of a design to delude the beholder into an idea of the worthlessness of the document; these things, together with the hyperobtrusive situation of this document, full in view of every visitor, and thus exactly in accordance with the conclusions to which I had previously arrived; these things, I say, were strongly corroborative of suspicion, in one who came with the intention to suspect.

'I protracted my visit as long as possible, and, while I maintained a most animated discussion with the Minister, upon a topic which I knew well had never failed to interest and excite him, I kept my attention really riveted upon the letter. In this examination, I committed to memory its external appearance and arrangement in the rack; and also fell, at length, upon a discovery which set at rest whatever trivial doubt I might have entertained.

In scrutinizing the edges of the paper, I observed them to be more *chafed* than seemed necessary. They presented the *broken* appearance which is manifested when a stiff paper, having been once folded and pressed with a folder, is refolded in a reversed direction, in the same creases or edges which had formed the original fold. This discovery was sufficient. It was clear to me that the letter had been turned, as a glove, inside out, re-directed, and re-sealed. I bade the Minister good morning, and took my departure at once, leaving a gold snuff-box upon the table.

'The next morning I called for the snuff-box, when we resumed, quite eagerly, the conversation of the preceding day. While thus engaged, however, a loud report, as if of a pistol, was heard immediately beneath the windows of the hotel, and was succeeded by a series of fearful screams, and the shoutings of a terrified mob. D--- rushed to a casement, threw it open, and looked out. In the meantime, I stepped to the card-rack, took the letter, put it in my pocket, and replaced it by a *fac-simile*, so far as regards externals, which I had carefully prepared at my lodgings—imitating the D--- cipher, very readily, by means of a seal formed of bread.

'The disturbance in the street had been occasioned by the frantic behaviour of a man with a musket. He had fired it among a crowd of women and children. It proved, however, to have been without ball, and the fellow was suffered to go his way as a lunatic or a drunkard. When he had gone, D--- came from the window, whither I had followed him immediately upon securing the object in view. Soon afterwards I bade him farewell. The pretended lunatic was a man in my own pay.'

'But what purpose had you,' I asked, 'in replacing the letter by a *fac-simile*? Would it not have been better, at the first visit, to have seized it openly, and departed?'

'D---,' replied Dupin, 'is a desperate man, and a man of nerve. His hotel, too, is not without attendants devoted to his interests. Had I made the wild attempt you suggest, I should never have left the Ministerial presence alive. The good people of Paris would have heard of me no more. But I had an object apart from these considerations. You know my political prepossessions. In this matter, I act as a partisan of the lady concerned. For eighteen months the Minister has had her in his power. She has now him in hers—since, being unaware that the letter is not in his possession, he will proceed with his exactions as if it was. Thus will he inevitably commit himself, at once, to his political destruction. His downfall, too, will not be more precipitate than awkward. It is all very well to talk about the *facilis descensus Averni* [the path down to Hell is an easy one], but in all kinds of climbing, as Catalani said of singing, it is far more easy to get up than to come down. In the present instance I have no sympathy—at least no pity—for him who descends. He is that *monstrum horrendum* [frightful monstrosity], an unprincipled man of genius. I confess, however, that I should like very well to know the precise character of his thoughts, when, being defied by her whom the Prefect terms "a certain personage", he is reduced to opening the letter which I left for him in the card-rack.'

'How? did you put any thing particular in it?'

'Why—it did not seem altogether right to leave the interior blank—that would have been insulting. To be sure, D---, at Vienna once, did me an evil turn, which I told him, quite good-humouredly, that I should remember. So, as I knew he would feel some curiosity in regard to the identity of the person who had outwitted him, I thought it a pity not to give him a clue. He is well acquainted with my MS, and I just copied into the middle of the blank sheet the words—

—Un dessein si funeste,
S'il n'est digne d'Atrée, est digne de Thyeste.
[—A plan so sinister,
If unworthy of Atreus, is worthy of Thyestes.]

They are to be found in Crébillon's *Atrée*.'

1845

Herman Melville

1819-91

Like his friend Nathaniel Hawthorne, to whom he dedicated *Moby-Dick* (1851), Herman Melville sought in his fiction to heighten everyday reality. He did not believe that fiction should maintain 'severe fidelity to real life'. Readers, he observed, 'look not only for more entertainment, but, at bottom, even for more reality, than real life itself can show. Thus, though they want novelty, they want nature, too; but nature unfettered, exhilarated, in effect transformed. In this way of thinking, the people in a fiction, like the people in a play, must dress as nobody exactly dresses, talk as nobody exactly talks, act as nobody exactly acts. It is with fiction as with religion; it should present another world, and yet one to which we feel the tie.'

Born in New York City, Melville attended the Albany Academy and the Albany Classical School, then worked as a bank clerk, a farm helper, and as a schoolteacher before deciding to seek his fortune at sea. He signed on a trading ship bound for Liverpool in 1839; the experience, however, proved disillusioning, and he returned to teaching. Two years later he set sail again, signing on a whaler bound for the South Seas; he jumped ship in the Marquesas Islands and spent a month among the natives of the Typee Valley, escaping to Tahiti on another whaling ship. He returned home in 1844 as a sailor in the United States Navy. Turning to fiction writing, he sought to record and recreate his sea experiences. Despite initial success with *Typee* (1846) and *Omoo* (1847)—two novels of the South Seas—he never made enough money from his writing to support himself and his family. He returned to farming, and eventually, in 1866, found a job as a district inspector of customs in New York City, where he worked in relative obscurity for the next two decades until his death.

In his short fiction, Melville usually employs a first-person narrator, often an older man who reminisces about or recounts some episode or event of long ago. The story's centre is the self-delineation of the narrator and his reflections on the intruding figure who creates the tale's confrontation.

The narrator of 'Bartleby the Scrivener', a mild-mannered and unassuming lawyer who leads an ordinary life, admires and even envies in others their sense of adventure and challenge. Into his life comes Bartleby, the unexpected rebel, consciously cutting himself off from his past and living his own life. The tale contrasts the lawyer's isolated world of insecurity and fear with Bartleby's independence and 'humanity'.

The narrator of 'The Lightning-Rod Man' dwells in a cottage in the mountains, where he receives a visit from a pedlar trying to sell lightning rods. Insistent upon calling the salesman Jupiter Tonans [Jupiter the Thunderer], the solitary narrator seems contemptuous of his visitor's belief in reason and order.

'Bartleby the Scrivener' was first published in the November and December 1853 issues of *Putnam's Monthly Magazine*. 'The Lightning-Rod Man' was first published in the August 1854 issue of *Putnam's Monthly Magazine*. Both were then collected in *The Piazza Tales* (1856).

Bartleby the Scrivener: A Story of Wall Street

I am a rather elderly man. The nature of my avocations for the last thirty years has brought me into more than ordinary contact with what would seem an interesting and somewhat singular set of men, of whom as yet nothing that I know of has ever been written:—I mean the law-copyists or scriveners. I have known very many of them, professionally and privately, and if I pleased, could relate divers histories, at which good-natured gentlemen might smile, and sentimental souls might weep. But I waive the biographies of all other scriveners for a few passages in the life of Bartleby, who was a scrivener the strangest I ever saw or heard of. While of other law-copyists I might write the complete life, of Bartleby nothing of that sort can be done. I believe that no materials exist for a full and satisfactory biography of this man. It is an irreparable loss to literature. Bartleby was one of those beings of whom nothing is ascertainable, except from the original sources, and in his case those are very small. What my own astonished eyes saw of Bartleby, *that* is all I know of him, except, indeed, one vague report which will appear in the sequel.

Ere introducing the scrivener, as he first appeared to me, it is fit I make some mention of myself, my *employés*, my business, my chambers, and general surroundings; because some such description is indispensable to an adequate understanding of the chief character about to be presented.

Imprimis: I am a man who, from his youth upward, has been filled with a profound conviction that the easiest way of life is the best. Hence, though I belong to a profession proverbially energetic and nervous, even to turbulence, at times, yet nothing of that sort have I ever suffered to invade my peace. I am one of those unambitious lawyers who never addresses a jury, or in any way draws upon public applause; but in the cool tranquillity of a snug retreat, do a snug business among rich men's bonds and mortgages and title-deeds. All who know me, consider me an eminently *safe* man. The late John Jacob Astor, a personage little given to poetic enthusiasm, had no hesitation in pronouncing my first grand point to be prudence; my next, method. I do not speak it in vanity, but simply record the fact, that I was not unemployed in my profession by the late John Jacob Astor; a name which, I admit, I love to repeat, for it hath a rounded and orbicular sound to it, and rings like unto bullion. I will freely add, that I was not insensible to the late John Jacob Astor's good opinion.

Some time prior to the period at which this little history begins, my avocations had been largely increased. The good old office, now extinct in the State of New York, of a Master in Chancery, had been conferred upon me. It was not a very arduous office, but very pleasantly remunerative. I seldom lose my temper; much more seldom indulge in dangerous indignation at wrongs and outrages; but I must be permitted to be rash here and declare, that I consider the sudden and violent abrogation of the office of

Master in Chancery, by the new Constitution, as a -------- premature act; inasmuch as I had counted upon a life-lease of the profits, whereas I only received those of a few short years. But this is by the way.

My chambers were upstairs at No. --- Wall Street. At one end they looked upon the white wall of the interior of a spacious sky-light shaft, penetrating the building from top to bottom. This view might have been considered rather tame than otherwise, deficient in what landscape painters call 'life'. But if so, the view from the other end of my chambers offered, at least, a contrast, if nothing more. In that direction my windows commanded an unobstructed view of a lofty brick wall, black by age and everlasting shade; which wall required no spy-glass to bring out its lurking beauties, but for the benefit of all near-sighted spectators, was pushed up to within ten feet of my window panes. Owing to the great height of the surrounding buildings, and my chambers being on the second floor, the interval between this wall and mine not a little resembled a huge square cistern.

At the period just preceding the advent of Bartleby, I had two persons as copyists in my employment, and a promising lad as an office-boy. First, Turkey; second, Nippers; third, Ginger Nut. These may seem names, the like of which are not usually found in the Directory. In truth they were nicknames, mutually conferred upon each other by my three clerks, and were deemed expressive of their respective persons or characters. Turkey was a short, pursy Englishman of about my own age, that is, somewhere not far from sixty. In the morning, one might say, his face was of a fine florid hue, but after twelve o'clock, meridian—his dinner hour—it blazed like a grate full of Christmas coals; and continued blazing—but, as it were, with a gradual wane—till 6 o'clock p.m. or thereabouts, after which I saw no more of the proprietor of the face, which, gaining its meridian with the sun, seemed to set with it, to rise, culminate, and decline the following day, with the like regularity and undiminished glory. There are many singular coincidences I have known in the course of my life, not the least among which was the fact, that exactly when Turkey displayed his fullest beams from his red and radiant countenance, just then, too, at that critical moment, began the daily period when I considered his business capacities as seriously disturbed for the remainder of the twenty-four hours. Not that he was absolutely idle, or averse to business then; far from it. The difficulty was, he was apt to be altogether too energetic. There was a strange, inflamed, flurried, flighty recklessness of activity about him. He would be incautious in dipping his pen into his inkstand. All his blots upon my documents, were dropped there after twelve o'clock, meridian. Indeed, not only would he be reckless and sadly given to making blots in the afternoon, but some days he went further, and was rather noisy. At such times, too, his face flamed with augmented blazonry, as if cannel coal had been heaped on anthracite. He made an unpleasant racket with his chair; spilled his sand-box; in mending his pens, impatiently split them all to pieces, and threw them on the floor in a sudden passion; stood up and leaned over his table, boxing his papers about in a most indecorous manner, very sad to behold in an elderly man like him. Nevertheless, as he was in many ways a most valuable person to me, and all the time before twelve o'clock, meridian, was the quickest, steadiest creature, too, accomplishing a great deal of work in a style not easy to be matched—for these reasons, I was willing to overlook his eccentricities, though indeed, occasionally, I remonstrated with him. I did this very gently, however, because, though the civilest, nay, the blandest and most reverential of men in the morning, yet in the afternoon he was disposed, upon provocation, to be slightly rash with his tongue, in fact, insolent. Now, valuing his morning services as I did, and resolving not to lose them—yet, at the same time, made uncomfortable by his inflamed ways after twelve o'clock; and being a man of peace, unwilling by my admonitions to call forth unseemly retorts from him—I took upon me, one Saturday noon (he was always worse on Saturdays), to hint to him, very kindly, that perhaps now that he was growing old, it might be well to abridge his labours; in short, he need not come to my chambers after twelve o'clock, but, dinner over, had best go home to his lodgings and rest himself till tea-time. But no; he insisted upon his afternoon devotions. His countenance became intolerably fervid, as he oratorically assured me—gesticulating, with a long ruler, at the other side of the room—that if his services in the morning were useful, how indispensable, then, in the afternoon?

'With submission, sir,' said Turkey on this occasion, 'I consider myself your right-hand man. In the morning I but marshal and deploy my columns; but in the afternoon I put myself at their head, and gallantly charge the foe, thus!'—and he made a violent thrust with the ruler.

'But the blots, Turkey,' intimated I.

'True,—but, with submission, sir, behold these hairs! I am getting old. Surely, sir, a blot or two of a warm afternoon is not to be severely urged against grey hairs. Old age—even if it blot the page—is honourable. With submission, sir, we *both* are getting old.'

This appeal to my fellow-feeling was hardly to be resisted. At all events, I saw that go he would not. So I made up my mind to let him stay, resolving, nevertheless, to see to it, that during the afternoon he had to do with my less important papers.

Nippers, the second on my list, was a whiskered, sallow, and, upon the whole, rather piratical-looking young man of about five and twenty. I always deemed him the victim of two evil powers—ambition and indigestion. The ambition was evinced by a certain impatience of the duties of a mere copyist—an unwarrantable usurpation of strictly professional affairs, such as the original drawing up of legal documents. The indigestion seemed betokened in an occasional nervous testiness and grinning irritability, causing the teeth to audibly grind together over mistakes committed in copying; unnecessary maledictions, hissed, rather than spoken, in the heat of business; and especially by a continual discontent with the height of the table where he worked. Though of a very ingenious mechanical turn, Nippers could never get this table to suit him. He put chips under it, blocks of various sorts, bits of pasteboard, and at last went so far as to attempt an exquisite adjustment by final pieces of folded blotting-paper. But no invention would answer. If, for the sake of easing his back, he brought the table lid at a sharp angle well up toward his chin, and wrote there like a man using the steep roof of a Dutch house for his desk—then he declared that it stopped the circulation in his arms. If now he lowered the table to his waistbands, and stooped over it in writing, then there was a sore aching in his back. In short, the truth of the matter was, Nippers knew not what he wanted. Or, if he wanted anything, it was to be rid of a scrivener's table altogether. Among the manifestations of his diseased ambition was a fondness he had for receiving visits from certain ambiguous-looking fellows in seedy coats, whom he called his clients. Indeed I was aware that not only was he, at times, considerable of a ward-politician, but he occasionally did a little business at the Justices' courts, and was not unknown on the steps of the Tombs. I have good reason to believe, however, that one individual who called upon him at my chambers, and who, with a grand air, he insisted was his client, was no other than a dun, and the alleged title-deed, a bill. But with all his failings, and the annoyances he caused me, Nippers, like his compatriot Turkey, was a very useful man to me; wrote a neat, swift hand; and, when he chose, was not deficient in a gentlemanly sort of deportment. Added to this, he always dressed in a gentlemanly sort of way; and so, incidentally, reflected credit upon my chambers. Whereas with respect to Turkey, I had much ado to keep him from being a reproach to me. His clothes were apt to look oily and smell of eating-houses. He wore his pantaloons very loose and baggy in summer. His coats were execrable; his hat not to be handled. But while the hat was a thing of indifference to me, inasmuch as his natural civility and deference, as a dependent Englishman, always led him to doff it the moment he entered the room, yet his coat was another matter. Concerning his coats, I reasoned with him; but with no effect. The truth was, I suppose, that a man with so small an income, could not afford to sport such a lustrous face and a lustrous coat at one and the same time. As Nippers once observed, Turkey's money went chiefly for red ink. One winter day I presented Turkey with a highly respectable-looking coat of my own, a padded grey coat, of a most comfortable warmth, and which buttoned straight up from the knee to the neck. I thought Turkey would appreciate the favour, and abate his rashness and obstreperousness of afternoons. But no. I verily believe that buttoning himself up in so downy and blanket-like a coat had a pernicious effect upon him; upon the same principle that too much oats are bad for horses. In fact, precisely as a rash, restive horse is said to feel his oats, so Turkey felt his coat. It made him insolent. He was a man whom prosperity harmed.

Though concerning the self-indulgent habits of Turkey I had my own private surmises, yet touching Nippers I was well persuaded that whatever might be his faults in other respects, he was, at least, a temperate young man. But, indeed, nature herself seemed to have been his vintner, and at his birth charged him so thoroughly with an irritable, brandy-like disposition, that all subsequent potations were needless. When I consider how, amid the stillness of my chambers, Nippers would sometimes impatiently rise from his seat, and stooping over his table, spread his arms wide apart, seize the whole desk, and move it, and jerk it, with a grim, grinding motion on the floor, as if the table were a perverse voluntary agent, intent on thwarting and vexing him; I plainly perceive that for Nippers, brandy and water were altogether superfluous.

It was fortunate for me that, owing to its peculiar cause—indigestion—the irritability and consequent nervousness of Nippers, were mainly observable in the morning, while in the afternoon he was comparatively mild. So that Turkey's paroxysms only coming on about twelve o'clock, I never had to do with their eccentricities at one time. Their fits relieved each other like guards. When Nipper's was on, Turkey's was off; and *vice versa*. This was a good natural arrangement under the circumstances.

Ginger Nut, the third on my list, was a lad some twelve years old. His father was a carman, ambitious of seeing his son on the bench instead of a cart, before he died. So he sent him to my office as student at law, errand boy, and cleaner and sweeper, at the rate of one dollar a week. He had a little desk to himself, but he did not use it much. Upon inspection, the drawer exhibited a great array of the shells of various sorts of nuts. Indeed, to this quick-witted youth the whole noble science of the law was contained in a nut-shell. Not the least among the employments of Ginger Nut, as well as one which he discharged with the most alacrity, was his duty as cake and apple purveyor for Turkey and Nippers. Copying law papers being proverbially a dry, husky sort of business, my two scriveners were fain to moisten their mouths very often with Spitzenbergs to be had at the numerous stalls nigh the Custom House and Post Office. Also, they sent Ginger Nut very frequently for that peculiar cake—small, flat, round, and very spicy—after which he had been named by them. Of a cold morning, when business was but dull, Turkey would gobble up scores of these cakes, as if they were mere wafers—indeed they sell them at the rate of six or eight for a penny—the scrape of his pen blending with the crunching of the crisp particles in his mouth. Of all the fiery afternoon blunders and flurried rashnesses of Turkey, was his once moistening a ginger-cake between his lips, and clapping it on to a mortgage for a seal. I came within an ace of dismissing him then. But he mollified me by making an oriental bow and saying—'With submission, sir, it was generous of me to find you in stationery on my own account.'

Now my original business—that of a conveyancer and title hunter, and drawer-up of recondite documents of all sorts—was considerably increased by receiving the master's office. There was now great work for scriveners. Not only must I push the clerks already with me, but I must have additional help. In answer to my advertisement, a motionless young man one morning stood upon my office threshold, the door being open, for it was summer. I can see that figure now—pallidly neat, pitiably respectable, incurably forlorn! It was Bartleby.

After a few words touching his qualifications, I engaged him, glad to have among my corps of copyists a man of so singularly sedate an aspect, which I thought might operate beneficially upon the flighty temper of Turkey, and the fiery one of Nippers.

I should have stated before that ground glass folding-doors divided my premises into two parts, one of which was occupied by my scriveners, the other by myself. According to my humour I threw open these doors, or closed them. I resolved to assign Bartleby a corner by the folding-doors, but on my side of them, so as to have this quiet man within easy call, in case any trifling thing was to be done. I placed his desk close up to a small side-window in that part of the room, a window which originally had afforded a lateral view of certain grimy back-yards and bricks, but which, owing to subsequent erections, commanded at present no view at all, though it gave some light. Within three feet of the panes was a wall, and the light came down from far above, between two lofty buildings, as from a very small opening in a dome. Still further to a satisfactory arrangement, I procured a high green folding screen, which might entirely isolate Bartleby from my sight, though not remove him from my voice. And thus, in a manner, privacy and society were conjoined.

At first Bartleby did an extraordinary quantity of writing. As if long famishing for something to copy, he seemed to gorge himself on my documents. There was no pause for digestion. He ran a day and night line, copying by sun-light and by candle-light. I should have been quite delighted with his application, had he been cheerfully industrious. But he wrote on silently, palely, mechanically.

It is, of course, an indispensable part of a scrivener's business to verify the accuracy of his copy, word by word. Where there are two or more scriveners in an office, they assist each other in this examination, one reading from the copy, the other holding the original. It is a very dull, wearisome, and lethargic affair. I can readily imagine that to some sanguine temperaments it would be altogether intolerable. For example, I cannot credit that the mettlesome poet Byron would have contentedly sat down with Bartleby to examine a law document of, say five hundred pages, closely written in a crimpy hand.

Now and then, in the haste of business, it had been my habit to assist in comparing some brief document myself, calling Turkey or Nippers for this purpose. One object I had in placing Bartleby so handy to me behind the screen, was to avail myself of his services on such trivial occasions. It was on the third day, I think, of his being with me, and before any necessity had arisen for having his own writing examined, that, being much hurried to complete a small affair I had in hand, I abruptly called to Bartleby. In my haste and natural expectancy of instant compliance, I sat with my head bent over the original on my desk, and my right hand sideways, and somewhat nervously extended with the copy, so that immediately upon emerging from his retreat, Bartleby might snatch it and proceed to business without the least delay.

In this very attitude did I sit when I called to him, rapidly stating what it was I wanted him to do—namely, to examine a small paper with me. Imagine my surprise, nay, my consternation, when without moving from his privacy, Bartleby in a singularly mild, firm voice, replied, 'I would prefer not to.'

I sat awhile in perfect silence, rallying my stunned faculties. Immediately it occurred to me that my ears had deceived me, or Bartleby had entirely misunderstood my meaning. I repeated my request in the clearest tone I could assume. But in quite as clear a one came the previous reply, 'I would prefer not to.'

'Prefer not to,' echoed I, rising in high excitement, and crossing the room with a stride. 'What do you mean? Are you moon-struck? I want you to help me compare this sheet here—take it,' and I thrust it toward him.

'I would prefer not to,' said he.

I looked at him steadfastly. His face was leanly composed; his grey eye dimly calm. Not a wrinkle of agitation rippled him. Had there been the least uneasiness, anger, impatience or impertinence in his manner; in other words, had there been anything ordinarily human about him; doubtless I should have violently dismissed him from the premises. But as it was, I should have as soon thought of turning my pale plaster-of-paris bust of Cicero out of doors. I stood gazing at him awhile, as he went on with his own writing, and then reseated myself at my desk. This is very strange, thought I. What had one best do? But my business hurried me. I concluded to forget the matter for the present, reserving it for my future leisure. So calling Nippers from the other room, the paper was speedily examined.

A few days after this, Bartleby concluded four lengthy documents, being quadruplicates of a week's testimony taken before me in my High Court of Chancery. It became necessary to examine them. It was an important suit, and great accuracy was imperative. Having all things arranged, I called Turkey, Nippers and Ginger Nut from the next room, meaning to place the four copies in the hands of my four clerks, while I should read from the original. Accordingly Turkey, Nippers and Ginger Nut had taken their seats in a row, each with his document in hand, when I called to Bartleby to join this interesting group.

'Bartleby! quick, I am waiting.'

I heard a slow scrape of his chair legs on the uncarpeted floor, and soon he appeared standing at the entrance of his hermitage.

'What is wanted?' said he mildly.

'The copies, the copies,' said I hurriedly. 'We are going to examine them. There'—and I held toward him the fourth quadruplicate.

'I would prefer not to,' he said, and gently disappeared behind the screen.

For a few moments I was turned into a pillar of salt, standing at the head of my seated column of clerks. Recovering myself, I advanced toward the screen, and demanded the reason for such extraordinary conduct.

'*Why* do you refuse?'

'I would prefer not to.'

With any other man I should have flown outright into a dreadful passion, scorned all further words, and thrust him ignominiously from my presence. But there was something about Bartleby that not only strangely disarmed me, but in a wonderful manner touched and disconcerted me. I began to reason with him.

'These are your own copies we are about to examine. It is labour saving to you, because one examination will answer for your four papers. It is common usage. Every copyist is bound to help examine his copy. Is it not so? Will you not speak? Answer!'

'I prefer not to,' he replied in a flute-like tone. It seemed to me that while I had been addressing him, he carefully revolved every statement that I made; fully comprehended the meaning; could not gainsay the irresistible conclusion; but, at the same time, some paramount consideration prevailed with him to reply as he did.

'You are decided, then, not to comply with my request—a request made according to common usage and common sense?'

He briefly gave me to understand that on that point my judgement was sound. Yes: his decision was irreversible.

It is not seldom the case that when a man is browbeaten in some unprecedented and violently unreasonable way, he begins to stagger in his own plainest faith. He begins, as it were, vaguely to surmise that, wonderful as it may be, all the justice and all the reason are on the other side. Accordingly, if any disinterested persons are present, he turns to them for some reinforcement for his own faltering mind.

'Turkey,' said I, 'what do you think of this? Am I not right?'

'With submission, sir,' said Turkey, with his blandest tone, 'I think that you are.'

'Nippers,' said I, 'what do *you* think of it?'

'I think I should kick him out of the office.'

(The reader of nice perceptions will here perceive that, it being morning, Turkey's answer is couched in polite and tranquil terms but Nippers's reply in ill-tempered ones. Or, to repeat a previous sentence, Nippers's ugly mood was on duty, and Turkey's off.)

'Ginger Nut,' said I, willing to enlist the smallest suffrage in my behalf, 'what do *you* think of it?'

'I think, sir, he's a little *luny*,' replied Ginger Nut, with a grin.

'You hear what they say,' said I, turning towards the screen, 'come forth and do your duty.'

But he vouchsafed no reply. I pondered a moment in sore perplexity. But once more business hurried me. I determined again to postpone the consideration of this dilemma to my future leisure. With a little trouble we made out to examine the papers without Bartleby, though at every page or two, Turkey deferentially dropped his opinion that this proceeding was quite out of the common; while Nippers, twitching in his chair with a dyspeptic nervousness, ground out between his set teeth occasional hissing maledictions against the stubborn oaf behind the screen. And for his (Nippers's) part, this was the first and the last time he would do another man's business without pay.

Meanwhile Bartleby sat in his hermitage, oblivious to everything but his own peculiar business there.

Some days passed, the scrivener being employed upon another lengthy work. His late remarkable conduct led me to regard his ways narrowly. I observed that he never went to dinner; indeed that he never went any where. As yet I had never of my personal knowledge known him to be outside of my office. He was a perpetual sentry in the corner. At about eleven o'clock, though, in the morning, I noticed that Ginger Nut would advance towards the opening in Bartleby's screen, as if silently beckoned thither by a gesture invisible to me where I sat. The boy would then leave the office jingling a few pence, and reappear with a handful of ginger-nuts which he delivered in the hermitage, receiving two of the cakes for his trouble.

He lives, then, on ginger-nuts, thought I; never eats a dinner, properly speaking; he must be a vegetarian then; but no; he never eats even vegetables, he eats nothing but ginger-nuts. My mind then ran on in reveries concerning the probable effects upon the human constitution of living entirely on ginger-nuts. Ginger-nuts are so called because they contain ginger as one of their peculiar constituents, and the final flavouring one. Now what was ginger? A hot, spicy thing. Was Bartleby hot and spicy? Not at all. Ginger, then, had no effect upon Bartleby. Probably he preferred it should have none.

Nothing so aggravates an earnest person as a passive resistance. If the individual so resisted be of a not inhumane temper, and the resisting one perfectly harmless in his passivity; then, in the better moods of the former, he will endeavour charitably to construe to his imagination what proves impossible to be solved by his judgement. Even so, for the most part, I regarded Bartleby and his ways. Poor fellow! thought I, he means no mischief; it is plain he intends no insolence; his aspect sufficiently evinces that his eccentricities are involuntary. He is useful to me. I can get along with him. If I turn him away, the chances are he will fall in with some less indulgent employer, and then he will be rudely treated, and perhaps driven forth miserably to starve. Yes. Here I can cheaply purchase a delicious self-approval. To befriend Bartleby; to humour him in his strange wilfulness, will cost me little or nothing, while I lay up in my soul what will eventually prove a sweet morsel for my conscience. But this mood was not invariable with me. The passiveness of Bartleby sometimes irritated me. I felt strangely goaded on to encounter him in new opposition, to elicit some angry spark from him answerable to my own. But indeed I might as well have essayed to strike fire with my knuckles against a bit of Windsor soap. But one afternoon the evil impulse in me mastered me, and the following little scene ensued:

'Bartleby,' said I, 'when those papers are all copied, I will compare them with you.'

'I would prefer not to.'

'How? Surely you do not mean to persist in that mulish vagary?'

No answer.

I threw open the folding-doors near by, and turning upon Turkey and Nippers, exclaimed in an excited manner:

'He says, a second time, he won't examine his papers. What do you think of it, Turkey?'

It was afternoon, be it remembered. Turkey sat glowing like a brass boiler, has bald head steaming, his hands reeling among his blotted papers.

'Think of it?' roared Turkey; 'I think I'll just step behind his screen, and black his eyes for him!'

So saying, Turkey rose to his feet and threw his arms into a pugilistic position. He was hurrying away to make good his promise, when I detained him, alarmed at the effect of incautiously rousing Turkey's combativeness after dinner.

'Sit down, Turkey,' said I, 'and hear what Nippers has to say. What do you think of it, Nippers? Would I not be justified in immediately dismissing Bartleby?'

'Excuse me, that is for you to decide, sir. I think his conduct quite unusual, and indeed unjust, as regards Turkey and myself. But it may only be a passing whim.'

'Ah,' exclaimed I, 'you have strangely changed your mind then—you speak very gently of him now.'

'All beer,' cried Turkey; 'gentleness is effects of beer—Nippers and I dined together to-day. You see how gentle *I* am, sir. Shall I go and black his eyes?'

'You refer to Bartleby, I suppose. No, not to-day, Turkey,' I replied; 'pray, put up your fists.'

I closed the doors, and again advanced towards Bartleby. I felt additional incentives tempting me to my fate. I burned to be rebelled against again. I remembered that Bartleby never left the office.

'Bartleby,' said I, 'Ginger Nut is away; just step round to the Post Office, won't you? (it was but a three minutes' walk), and see if there is anything for me.'

'I would prefer not to.'

'You *will* not?'

'I *prefer* not.'

I staggered to my desk, and sat there in a deep study. My blind inveteracy returned. Was there any other thing in which I could procure myself to be ignominiously repulsed by this lean, penniless wight?—my hired clerk? What added thing is there, perfectly reasonable, that he will be sure to refuse to do?

'Bartleby!'

No answer.

'Bartleby,' in a louder tone.

No answer.

'Bartleby,' I roared.

Like a very ghost, agreeably to the laws of magical invocation, at the third summons, he appeared at the entrance of his hermitage.

'Go to the next room, and tell Nippers to come to me.'

'I prefer not to,' he respectfully and slowly said, and mildly disappeared.

'Very good, Bartleby,' said I, in a quiet sort of serenely severe self-possessed tone, intimating the unalterable purpose of some terrible retribution very close at hand. At the moment I half intended something of the kind. But upon the whole, as it was drawing towards my dinner-hour, I thought it best to put on my hat and walk home for the day, suffering much from perplexity and distress of mind.

Shall I acknowledge it? The conclusion of this whole business was, that it soon became a fixed fact of my chambers, that a pale young scrivener, by the name of Bartleby, had a desk there; that he copied for me at the usual rate of four cents a folio (one hundred words); but he was permanently exempt from examining the work done by him, that duty being transferred to Turkey and Nippers, out of compliment doubtless to their superior acuteness; moreover, said Bartleby was never on any account to be despatched on the most trivial errand of any sort; and that even if entreated to take upon him such a matter, it was generally understood that he would prefer not to—in other words, that he would refuse point-blank.

As days passed on, I became considerably reconciled to Bartleby. His steadiness, his freedom from all dissipation, his incessant industry (except when he chose to throw himself into a standing reverie behind his screen), his great stillness, his unalterableness of demeanour under all circumstances, made him a valuable acquisition. One prime thing was this,—*he was always there*;—first in the morning, continually through the day, and the last at night. I had a singular confidence in his honesty. I felt my most precious papers perfectly safe in his hands. Sometimes to be sure I could not, for the very soul of me, avoid falling into sudden spasmodic passions with him. For it was exceeding difficult to bear in mind all the time those strange peculiarities, privileges, and unheard of exemptions, forming the tacit stipulations of Bartleby's part under which he remained in my office. Now and then, in the eagerness of despatching pressing business, I would inadvertently summon Bartleby, in a short, rapid tone, to put his finger, say, on the incipient tie of a bit of red tape with which I was about compressing some papers. Of course, from behind the screen the usual answer, 'I prefer not to,' was sure to come; and then, how could a human creature with the common infirmities of our nature, refrain from bitterly exclaiming upon such perverseness—such unreasonableness. However, every added repulse of this sort which I received only tended to lessen the probability of my repeating the inadvertence.

Here it must be said, that according to the custom of most legal gentlemen occupying chambers in densely-populated law buildings, there were several keys to my door. One was kept by a woman residing in the attic, which person weekly scrubbed and daily swept and dusted my apartments. Another was kept by Turkey for convenience sake. The third I sometimes carried in my own pocket. The fourth I knew not who had.

Now, one Sunday morning I happened to go to Trinity Church, to hear a celebrated preacher, and finding myself rather early on the ground, I thought I would walk round to my chambers for awhile. Luckily I had my key with me; but upon applying it to the lock, I found it resisted by something inserted from the inside. Quite surprised, I called out; when to my consternation a key was turned from within; and thrusting his lean visage at me, and holding the door ajar, the apparition of Bartleby appeared, in his shirt sleeves, and otherwise in a strangely tattered dishabille, saying quietly that he was sorry, but he was deeply engaged just then, and—preferred not admitting me at present. In a brief word or two, he moreover added, that perhaps I had better walk round the block two or three times, and by that time he would probably have concluded his affairs.

Now, the utterly unsurmised appearance of Bartleby, tenanting my law-chambers of a Sunday morning, with his cadaverously gentlemanly *nonchalance*, yet withal firm and self-possessed, had such a strange effect upon me, that incontinently I slunk away from my own door, and did as desired. But not without sundry twinges of impotent rebellion against the mild effrontery of this unaccountable scrivener. Indeed, it was his wonderful mildness chiefly, which not only disarmed me, but unmanned me, as it were. For I consider that one, for the time, is in a way unmanned when he tranquilly permits his hired clerk to dictate to him, and order him away from his own premises. Furthermore, I was full of uneasiness as to what Bartleby could possibly be doing in my office in his shirt sleeves, and in an otherwise dismantled condition of a Sunday morning. Was anything amiss going on? Nay, that was out of the question. It was not to be thought of for a moment that Bartleby was an immoral person. But what could he be doing there—copying? Nay again, whatever might be his eccentricities,

Bartleby was an eminently decorous person. He would be the last man to sit down to his desk in any state approaching to nudity. Besides, it was Sunday; and there was something about Bartleby that forbade the supposition that he would by any secular occupation violate the proprieties of the day.

Nevertheless, my mind was not pacified; and full of a restless curiosity, at last I returned to the door. Without hindrance I inserted my key, opened it, and entered. Bartleby was not to be seen. I looked round anxiously, peeped behind his screen; but it was very plain that he was gone. Upon more closely examining the place, I surmised that for an indefinite period Bartleby must have ate, dressed, and slept in my office, and that too without plate, mirror, or bed. The cushioned seat of a rickety old sofa in one corner bore the faint impress of a lean, reclining form. Rolled away under his desk, I found a blanket; under the empty grate, a blacking box and brush; on a chair, a tin basin, with soap and a ragged towel; in a newspaper a few crumbs of ginger-nuts and a morsel of cheese. Yes, thought I, it is evident enough that Bartleby has been making his home here, keeping bachelor's hall all by himself. Immediately then the thought came sweeping across me, What miserable friendlessness and loneliness are here revealed! His poverty is great; but his solitude, how horrible! Think of it. Of a Sunday, Wall Street is deserted as Petra; and every night of every day it is an emptiness. This building too, which of week-days hums with industry and life, at nightfall echoes with sheer vacancy, and all through Sunday is forlorn. And here Bartleby makes his home; sole spectator of a solitude which he has seen all populous—a sort of innocent and transformed Marius brooding among the ruins of Carthage!

For the first time in my life a feeling of overpowering stinging melancholy seized me. Before, I had never experienced aught but a not-unpleasing sadness. The bond of a common humanity now drew me irresistibly to gloom. A fraternal melancholy! For both I and Bartleby were sons of Adam. I remembered the bright silks and sparkling faces I had seen that day, in gala trim, swan-like sailing down the Mississippi of Broadway; and I contrasted them with the pallid copyist, and thought to myself, Ah, happiness courts the light, so we deem the world is gay; but misery hides aloof, so we deem that misery there is none. These sad fancyings—chimeras, doubtless, of a sick and silly brain—led on to other and more special thoughts, concerning the eccentricities of Bartleby. Presentiments of strange discoveries hovered round me. The scrivener's pale form appeared to me laid out, among uncaring strangers, in its shivering winding sheet.

Suddenly I was attracted by Bartleby's closed desk, the key in open sight left in the lock.

I mean no mischief, seek the gratification of no heartless curiosity, thought I; besides, the desk is mine, and its contents, too, so I will make bold to look within. Everything was methodically arranged, the papers smoothly placed. The pigeon holes were deep, and, removing the files of documents, I groped into their recesses. Presently I felt something there, and dragged it out. It was an old bandanna handkerchief, heavy and knotted. I opened it, and saw it was a savings' bank.

I now recalled all the quiet mysteries which I had noted in the man. I remembered that he never spoke but to answer; that though at intervals he had considerable time to himself, yet I had never seen him reading—no, not even a newspaper; that for long periods he would stand looking out, at his pale window behind the screen, upon the dead brick wall; I was quite sure he never visited any refectory or eating-house; while his pale face clearly indicated that he never drank beer like Turkey, or tea and coffee even, like other men; that he never went anywhere in particular that I could learn; never went out for a walk, unless indeed that was the case at present; that he had declined telling who he was, or whence he came, or whether he had any relatives in the world; that though so thin and pale, he never complained of ill health. And more than all, I remembered a certain unconscious air of pallid—how shall I call it?—of pallid haughtiness, say, or rather an austere reserve about him, which had positively awed me into my tame compliance with his eccentricities, when I had feared to ask him to do the slightest incidental thing for me, even though I might know, from his long-continued motionlessness, that behind his screen he must be standing in one of those dead-wall reveries of his.

Revolving all these things, and coupling them with the recently discovered fact that he made my office his constant abiding place and home, and not forgetful of his morbid moodiness; revolving all these things, a prudential feeling began to steal over me. My first emotions had been those of pure melancholy and sincerest pity; but just in proportion as the forlornness of Bartleby grew and grew to my imagination, did that same melancholy merge into fear, that pity into repulsion. So true it is, and so terrible, too, that up to a certain point the thought or sight of misery enlists our best affections; but, in certain special cases, beyond that point it does not. They err who would assert that invariably this is owing to the inherent selfishness of the human heart. It rather proceeds from a certain hopelessness of remedying excessive and organic ill. To a sensitive being, pity is not seldom pain. And when at last it is perceived that such pity cannot lead to effectual succour, common sense bids the soul be rid of it. What I saw that morning persuaded me that the scrivener was the victim of innate and incurable disorder. I might give alms to his body; but his body did not pain him; it was his soul that suffered, and his soul I could not reach.

I did not accomplish the purpose of going to Trinity Church that morning. Somehow, the things I had seen disqualified me for the time from church-going. I walked homeward, thinking what I would do with Bartleby. Finally, I resolved upon this:—I would put certain calm questions to him the next morning, touching his history, &c., and if he declined to answer them openly and unreservedly (and I supposed he would prefer not), then to give him a twenty dollar bill over and above whatever I might owe him, and tell him his services were no longer required; but that if in any other way I could assist him, I would be happy to do so, especially if he desired to return to his native place, wherever that might be, I would willingly help to defray the expenses. Moreover, if, after reaching home, he found himself at any time in want of aid, a letter from him would be sure of a reply.

The next morning came.

'Bartleby,' said I, gently calling to him behind his screen.

No reply.

'Bartleby,' said I, in a still gentler tone, 'come here; I am not going to ask you to do anything you would prefer not to do—I simply wish to speak to you.'

Upon this he noiselessly slid into view.

'Will you tell me, Bartleby, where you were born?'

'I would prefer not to.'

'Will you tell me *anything* about yourself?'

'I would prefer not to.'

'But what reasonable objection can you have to speak to me? I feel friendly towards you.'

He did not look at me while I spoke, but kept his glance fixed upon my bust of Cicero, which, as I then sat, was directly behind me, some six inches above my head.

'What is your answer, Bartleby?' said I, after waiting a considerable time for a reply, during which his countenance remained immovable, only there was the faintest conceivable tremor of the white attenuated mouth.

'At present I prefer to give no answer,' he said, and retired into his hermitage.

It was rather weak in me I confess, but his manner on this occasion nettled me. Not only did there seem to lurk in it a certain calm disdain, but his perverseness seemed ungrateful, considering the undeniable good usage and indulgence he had received from me.

Again I sat ruminating what I should do. Mortified as I was at his behaviour, and resolved as I had been to dismiss him when I entered my office, nevertheless I strangely felt something superstitious knocking at my heart, and forbidding me to carry out my purpose, and denouncing me for a villain if I dared to breathe one bitter word against this forlornest of mankind. At last, familiarly drawing my chair behind his screen, I sat down and said: 'Bartleby, never mind then about revealing your history; but let me entreat you, as a friend, to comply as far as may be with the usages of this office. Say now you will help to examine papers to-morrow or next day: in short, say now that in a day or two you will begin to be a little reasonable:—say so, Bartleby.'

'At present I would prefer not to be a little reasonable,' was his mildly cadaverous reply.

Just then the folding-doors opened, and Nippers approached. He seemed suffering from an unusually bad night's rest, induced by severer indigestion than common. He overheard those final words of Bartleby.

'*Prefer not*, eh?' gritted Nippers—'I'd *prefer* him, if I were you, sir,' addressing me—'I'd *prefer* him; I'd give him preferences, the stubborn mule! What is it, sir, pray, that he *prefers* not to do now?'

Bartleby moved not a limb.

'Mr Nippers,' said I, 'I'd prefer that you would withdraw for the present.'

Somehow, of late I had got into the way of involuntarily using this word 'prefer' upon all sorts of not exactly suitable occasions. And I trembled to think that my contact with the scrivener had already and seriously affected me in a mental way. And what further and deeper aberration might it not yet produce? This apprehension had not been without efficacy in determining me to summary means.

As Nippers, looking very sour and sulky, was departing, Turkey blandly and deferentially approached.

'With submission, sir,' said he, 'yesterday I was thinking about Bartleby here, and I think that if he would but prefer to take a quart of good ale every day, it would do much towards mending him, and enabling him to assist in examining his papers.'

'So you have got the word, too,' said I, slightly excited.

'With submission, what word, sir?' asked Turkey, respectfully crowding himself into the contracted space behind the screen, and by so doing, making me jostle the scrivener. 'What word, sir?'

'I would prefer to be left alone here,' said Bartleby, as if offended at being mobbed in his privacy.

'*That's* the word, Turkey,' said I—'*that's* it.'

'Oh, *prefer*? oh, yes—queer word. I never use it myself. But, sir, as I was saying, if he would but prefer—'

'Turkey,' interrupted I, 'you will please withdraw.'

'Oh certainly, sir, if you prefer that I should.'

As he opened the folding-door to retire, Nippers at his desk caught a glimpse of me, and asked whether I would prefer to have a certain paper copied on blue paper or white. He did not in the least roguishly accent the word prefer. It was plain that it involuntarily rolled from his tongue. I thought to myself, surely I must get rid of a demented man, who already has in some degree turned the tongues, if not the heads, of myself and clerks. But I thought it prudent not to break the dismission at once.

The next day I noticed that Bartleby did nothing but stand at his window in his dead-wall reverie. Upon asking him why he did not write, he said that he had decided upon doing no more writing.

'Why, how now? what next?' exclaimed I, 'do no more writing?'

'No more.'

'And what is the reason?'

'Do you not see the reason for yourself?' he indifferently replied.

I looked steadfastly at him, and perceived that his eyes looked dull and glazed. Instantly it occurred to me, that his unexampled diligence in copying by his dim window for the first few weeks of his stay with me might have temporarily impaired his vision.

I was touched. I said something in condolence with him. I hinted that, of course, he did wisely in abstaining from writing for a while, and urged him to embrace that opportunity of taking wholesome exercise in the open air. This, however, he did not do. A few days after this, my other clerks being absent, and being in a great hurry to despatch certain letters by the mail, I thought that, having nothing else earthly to do, Bartleby would surely be less inflexible than usual, and carry these letters to the Post Office. But he blankly declined. So, much to my inconvenience, I went myself.

Still added days went by. Whether Bartleby's eyes improved or not, I could not say. To all appearance, I thought they did. But when I asked him if they did, he vouchsafed no answer. At all events, he would do no copying. At last, in reply to my urgings, he informed me that he had permanently given up copying.

'What!' exclaimed I; 'suppose your eyes should get entirely well—better than ever before—would you not copy then?'

'I have given up copying,' he answered and slid aside.

He remained, as ever, a fixture in my chamber. Nay—if that were possible—he became still more of a fixture than before. What was to be done? He would do nothing in the office: why should he stay there? In plain fact, he had now become a millstone to me, not only useless as a necklace, but afflictive to bear. Yet I was sorry for him. I speak less than truth when I say that, on his own account, he occasioned me uneasiness. If he would but have named a single relative or friend, I would instantly have written, and urged their taking the poor fellow away to some convenient retreat. But he seemed alone, absolutely alone in the universe. A bit of wreckage in the mid-Atlantic. At length, necessities connected with my business tyrannized over all other considerations. Decently as I could, I told Bartleby that in six days' time he must unconditionally leave the office. I warned him to take measures, in the interval, for procuring some other abode. I offered to assist him in this endeavour, if he himself would but take the first step towards a removal. 'And when you finally quit me, Bartleby,' added I. 'I shall see that you go away not entirely unprovided. Six days from this hour, remember.'

At the expiration of that period, I peeped behind the screen, and lo! Bartleby was there.

I buttoned up my coat, balanced myself; advanced slowly towards him, touched his shoulder, and said, 'The time has come; you must quit this place; I am sorry for you; here is money; but you must go.'

'I would prefer not,' he replied, with his back still towards me.

'You *must*.'

He remained silent.

Now I had an unbounded confidence in this man's common honesty. He had frequently restored to me sixpences and shillings carelessly dropped upon the floor, for I am apt to be very reckless in such shirt-button affairs. The proceeding then which followed will not be deemed extraordinary.

'Bartleby,' said I, 'I owe you twelve dollars on account; here are thirty-two; the odd twenty are yours.—Will you take it?' and I handed the bills towards him.

But he made no motion.

'I will leave them here then,' putting them under a weight on the table. Then taking my hat and cane and going to the door, I tranquilly turned and added—'After you have removed your things from these offices, Bartleby, you will of course lock the door—since every one is now gone for the day but you—and if you please, slip your key underneath the mat, so that I may have it in the morning. I shall not see you again; so good-bye to you. If hereafter in your new place of abode I can be of any service to you, do not fail to advise me by letter. Good-bye, Bartleby, and fare you well.'

But he answered not a word; like the last column of some ruined temple, he remained standing mute and solitary in the middle of the otherwise deserted room.

As I walked home in a pensive mood, my vanity got the better of my pity. I could not but highly plume myself on my masterly management in getting rid of Bartleby. Masterly I call it, and such it must appear to any dispassionate thinker. The beauty of my procedure seemed to consist in its perfect quietness. There was no vulgar bullying, no bravado of any sort, no choleric hectoring, no striding to and fro across the apartment, jerking out vehement commands for Bartleby to bundle himself off with his beggarly traps. Nothing of the kind. Without loudly bidding Bartleby depart—as an inferior genius might have done—I *assumed* the ground that depart he must; and upon that assumption built all I had to say. The more I thought over my procedure, the more I was charmed with it. Nevertheless, next morning, upon awakening, I had my doubts,—I had somehow slept off the fumes of vanity. One of the coolest and wisest hours a man has, is just after he awakes in the morning. My procedure seemed as sagacious as ever,—but only in theory. How it would prove in practice—there was the rub. It was truly a beautiful thought to have assumed Bartleby's departure; but, after all, that assumption was simply my own, and none of Bartleby's. The great point was, not whether I had assumed that he would quit me, but whether he would prefer so to do. He was more a man of preferences than assumptions.

After breakfast, I walked down town, arguing the probabilities *pro* and *con*. One moment I thought it would prove a miserable failure, and Bartleby would be found all alive at my office as usual; the next moment it seemed certain that I should see his chair empty. And so I kept veering about. At the corner of Broadway and Canal Street, I saw quite an excited group of people standing in earnest conversation.

'I'll take odds he doesn't,' said a voice as I passed.

'Doesn't go?—done!' said I, 'put up your money.'

I was instinctively putting my hand in my pocket to produce my own, when I remembered that this was an election day. The words I had overheard bore no reference to Bartleby, but to the success or non-success of some candidate for the mayoralty. In my intent frame of mind, I had, as it were, imagined that all Broadway shared in my excitement, and were debating the same question with me. I passed on, very thankful that the uproar of the street screened my momentary absent-mindedness.

As I had intended, I was earlier than usual at my office door. I stood listening for a moment. All was still. He must be gone. I tried the knob. The door was locked. Yes, my procedure had worked to a charm; he indeed must be vanished. Yet a certain melancholy mixed with this: I was almost sorry for my brilliant success. I was fumbling under the door mat for the key, which Bartleby was to have left there for me, when accidentally my knee knocked against a panel, producing a summoning sound, and in response a voice came to me from within—'Not yet; I am occupied.'

It was Bartleby.

I was thunderstruck. For an instant I stood like the man who, pipe in mouth, was killed one cloudless afternoon long ago in Virginia, by summer lightning; at his own warm open window he was killed, and remained leaning out there upon the dreamy afternoon, till some one touched him, and he fell.

'Not gone!' I murmured at last. But again obeying that wondrous ascendency which the inscrutable scrivener had over me—and from which ascendency, for all my chafing, I could not completely escape—I slowly went down stairs and out into the street, and while walking round the block, considered what I should next do in this unheard-of perplexity. Turn the man out by an actual thrusting I could not; to drive him away by calling him hard names would not do; calling in the police was an unpleasant idea; and yet, permit him to enjoy his cadaverous triumph over me,—this too I could not think of. What was to be done? or, if nothing could be done, was there anything further that I could *assume* in the matter? Yes, as before I had prospectively assumed that Bartleby would depart, so now I might retrospectively assume that departed he was. In the legitimate carrying out of this assumption, I might enter my office in a great hurry, and pretending not to see Bartleby at all, walk straight against him as if he were air. Such a proceeding would in a singular degree have the appearance of a home-thrust. It was hardly possible that Bartleby could withstand such an application of the doctrine of assumptions. But, upon second thought, the success of the plan seemed rather dubious. I resolved to argue the matter over with him again.

'Bartleby,' said I, entering the office, with a quietly severe expression, 'I am seriously displeased. I am pained, Bartleby. I had thought better of you. I had imagined you of such a gentlemanly organization, that in any delicate dilemma a slight hint would suffice—in short, an assumption; but it appears I am deceived. Why,' I added, unaffectedly starting, 'you have not even touched that money yet,' pointing to it, just where I had left it the evening previous.

He answered nothing.

'Will you or will you not, quit me?' I now demanded in a sudden passion, advancing close to him.

'I would prefer *not* to quit you,' he replied, gently emphasizing the *not*.

'What earthly right have you to stay here? Do you pay any rent? Do you pay my taxes? Or is this property yours?'

He answered nothing.

'Are you ready to go on and write now? Are your eyes recovered? Could you copy a small paper for me this morning? or help examine a few lines? or step round to the Post Office? In a word, will you do any thing at all, to give a colouring to your refusal to depart the premises?'

He silently retired into his hermitage.

I was now in such a state of nervous resentment that I thought it but prudent to check myself, at present, from further demonstrations. Bartleby and I were alone. I remembered the tragedy of the unfortunate Adams and the still more unfortunate Colt in the solitary office of the latter; and how poor Colt, being dreadfully incensed by Adams, and imprudently permitting himself to get wildly excited, was at unawares hurried into his fatal act—an act which certainly no man could possibly deplore more than the actor himself. Often it had occurred to me in my ponderings upon the subject, that had that altercation taken place in the public street, or at a private residence, it would not have terminated as it did. It was the circumstance of being alone in a solitary office, upstairs, of a building entirely unhallowed by humanizing domestic associations—an uncarpeted office, doubtless, of a dusty, haggard sort of appearance;—this it must have been, which greatly helped to enhance the irritable desperation of the hapless Colt.

But when this old Adam of resentment rose in me and tempted me concerning Bartleby, I grappled him and threw him. How? Why, simply by recalling the divine injunction: 'A new commandment give I unto you, that ye love one another.' Yes, this it was that saved me. Aside from higher considerations, charity often operates as a vastly wise and prudent principle—a great safeguard to its possessor. Men have committed murder for jealousy's sake, and anger's sake, and hatred's sake, and selfishness' sake, and spiritual pride's sake; but no man that ever I heard of, ever committed a diabolical murder for sweet charity's sake. Mere self-interest, then, if no better motive can be enlisted, should, especially with high-tempered men, prompt all beings to charity and philanthropy. At any rate, upon the occasion in question, I strove to drown my exasperated feelings toward the scrivener by benevolently construing his conduct. Poor fellow, poor fellow! thought I, he doesn't mean any thing; and besides, he has seen hard times, and ought to be indulged.

I endeavoured also immediately to occupy myself, and at the same time to comfort my despondency. I tried to fancy that in the course of the morning, at such time as might prove agreeable to him, Bartleby, of his own free accord, would emerge from his hermitage, and take up some decided line of march in the direction of the door. But no. Half-past twelve o'clock came; Turkey began to glow in the face, overturn his ink-stand, and become generally obstreperous; Nippers abated down into quietude and courtesy; Ginger Nut munched his noon apple; and Bartleby remained standing at his window in one of his profoundest dead-wall reveries. Will it be credited? Ought I to acknowledge it? That afternoon I left the office without saying one further word to him.

Some days now passed, during which at leisure intervals I looked a little into 'Edwards on the Will', and 'Priestley on Necessity'. Under the circumstances, those books induced a salutary feeling. Gradually I slid into the persuasion that these troubles of mine, touching the scrivener, had been all predestinated from eternity, and Bartleby was billeted upon me for some mysterious purpose of an all-wise Providence, which it was not for a mere mortal like me to fathom. Yes, Bartleby, stay there behind your screen, thought I; I shall persecute you no more; you are harmless and noiseless as any of these old chairs; in short, I never feel so private as when I know you are here. At least I see it, I feel it; I penetrate to the predestinated purpose of my life. I am content. Others may have loftier parts to enact; but my mission in this world, Bartleby, is to furnish you with office room for such period as you may see fit to remain.

I believe that this wise and blessed frame of mind would have continued with me had it not been for the unsolicited and uncharitable remarks obtruded upon me by my professional friends who visited the rooms. But thus it often is, that the constant friction of illiberal minds wears out at last the best resolves of the most generous. Though to be sure, when I reflected upon it, it was not strange that people entering my office should be struck by the peculiar aspect of the unaccountable Bartleby, and so be tempted to throw out some sinister observations concerning him. Sometimes an attorney having business with me, and calling at my office, and finding no one but the scrivener there, would undertake to obtain some sort of precise information from him touching my whereabouts; but without heeding his idle talk, Bartleby would remain standing immovable in the middle of the room. So, after contemplating him in that position for a time, the attorney would depart, no wiser than he came.

Also, when a Reference was going on, and the room full of lawyers and witnesses and business was driving fast, some deeply occupied legal gentleman present, seeing Bartleby wholly unemployed, would request him to run round to his (the legal gentleman's) office and fetch some papers for him. Thereupon, Bartleby would tranquilly decline, and yet remain idle as before. Then the lawyer would give a great stare, and turn to me. And what could I say? At last I was made aware that all through the circle of my professional acquaintance, a whisper of wonder was running round, having reference to the strange creature I kept at my office. This worried me very much. And as the idea came upon me of his possibly turning out a long-lived man, and keep occupying my chambers, and denying my authority; and perplexing my visitors; and scandalizing my professional reputation; and casting a general gloom over the premises; keeping soul and body together to the last upon his savings (for doubtless he spent but half a dime a day), and in the end perhaps outlive me, and claim possession of my office by right of his perpetual occupancy: as all these dark anticipations crowded upon me more and more, and my friends continually intruded their relentless remarks upon the apparition in my room, a great change was wrought in me. I resolved to gather all my faculties together, and for ever rid me of this intolerable incubus.

Ere revolving any complicated project, however, adapted to this end, I first simply suggested to Bartleby the propriety of his permanent departure. In a calm and serious tone, I commended the idea to his careful and mature consideration. But having taken three days to meditate upon it, he apprised me that his original determination remained the same; in short, that he still preferred to abide with me.

What shall I do? I now said to myself, buttoning up my coat to the last button. What shall I do? what ought I to do? what does conscience say I *should* do with this man, or rather ghost? Rid myself of him, I must; go he shall. But how? You will not thrust him, the poor, pale, passive mortal,—you will not thrust such a helpless creature out of your door? you will not dishonour yourself by such cruelty? No, I will not, I cannot do that. Rather would I let him live and die here, and then mason up his remains in the wall. What then will you do? For all your coaxing, he will not budge. Bribes he leaves under your own paper-weight on your table; in short, it is quite plain that he prefers to cling to you.

Then something severe, something unusual must be done. What! surely you will not have him collared by a constable, and commit his innocent pallor to the common jail? And upon what ground could you procure such a thing to be done?—a vagrant, is he? What! he a vagrant, a wanderer, who refuses to budge? It is because he will *not* be a vagrant, then, that you seek to count him *as* a vagrant. That is too absurd. No visible means of support: there I have him. Wrong again: for indubitably he *does* support himself, and that is the only unanswerable proof that any man can show of his possessing the means so to do. No more then. Since he will not quit me, I must quit him. I will change my offices; I will move elsewhere; and give him fair notice, that if I find him on my new premises I will then proceed against him as a common trespasser.

Acting accordingly, next day I thus addressed him: 'I find these chambers too far from the City Hall; the air is unwholesome. In a word, I propose to remove my offices next week, and shall no longer require your services. I tell you this now, in order that you may seek another place.'

He made no reply, and nothing more was said.

On the appointed day I engaged carts and men, proceeded to my chambers, and having but little furniture, everything was removed in a few hours. Throughout all, the scrivener remained standing behind the screen, which I directed to be removed the last thing. It was withdrawn; and being folded up like a huge folio, left him the motionless occupant of a naked room. I stood in the entry watching him a moment, while something from within me upbraided me.

I re-entered, with my hand in my pocket—and—and my heart in my mouth.

'Good-bye, Bartleby; I am going—good-bye, and God some way bless you; and take that,' slipping something in his hand. But it dropped upon the floor and then—strange to say—I tore myself from him whom I had so longed to be rid of.

Established in my new quarters, for a day or two I kept the door locked, and started at every footfall in the passages. When I returned to my rooms after any little absence, I would pause at the threshold for an instant, and attentively listen, ere applying my key. But these fears were needless. Bartleby never came nigh me.

I thought all was going well, when a perturbed looking stranger visited me, inquiring whether I was the person who had recently occupied rooms at No. --- Wall Street.

Full of forebodings, I replied that I was.

'Then sir,' said the stranger, who proved a lawyer, 'you are responsible for the man you left there. He refuses to do any copying, he refuses to do anything; and he says he prefers not to; and he refuses to quit the premises.'

'I am very sorry, sir,' said I, with assumed tranquillity, but an inward tremor, 'but, really, the man you allude to is nothing to me—he is no relation or apprentice of mine, that you should hold me responsible for him.'

'In mercy's name, who is he?'

'I certainly cannot inform you. I know nothing about him. Formerly I employed him as a copyist; but he has done nothing for me now for some time past.'

'I shall settle him then,—good morning, sir.'

Several days passed, and I heard nothing more; and though I often felt a charitable prompting to call at the place and see poor Bartleby, yet a certain squeamishness of I know not what withheld me.

All is over with him, by this time, thought I at last, when through another week no further intelligence reached me. But coming to my room the day after, I found several persons waiting at my door in a high state of nervous excitement.

'That's the man—here he comes,' cried the foremost one, whom I recognized as the lawyer who had previously called upon me alone.

'You must take him away, sir, at once,' cried a portly person among them, advancing upon me, and whom I knew to be the landlord of No. — Wall Street. 'These gentlemen, my tenants, cannot stand it any longer; Mr B—,' pointing to the lawyer, 'has turned him out of his room, and he now persists in haunting the building generally, sitting upon the banisters of the stairs by day, and sleeping in the entry by night. Everybody here is concerned; clients are leaving the offices; some fears are entertained of a mob; something you must do, and that without delay.'

Aghast at this torrent, I fell back before it, and would fain have locked myself in my new quarters. In vain I persisted that Bartleby was nothing to me—no more than to any one else there. In vain:—I was the last person known to have anything to do with him, and they held me to the terrible account. Fearful then of being exposed in the papers (as one person present obscurely threatened) I considered the matter, and at length said, that if the lawyer would give me a confidential interview with the scrivener, in his (the lawyer's) own room, I would that afternoon strive my best to rid them of the nuisance they complained of.

Going up stairs to my old haunt, there was Bartleby silently sitting upon the banister at the landing.

'What are you doing here, Bartleby?' said I.

'Sitting upon the banister,' he mildly replied.

I motioned him into the lawyer's room, who then left us.

'Bartleby,' said I, 'are you aware that you are the cause of great tribulation to me, by persisting in occupying the entry after being dismissed from the office?'

No answer.

'Now one of two things must take place. Either you must do something, or something must be done to you. Now what sort of business would you like to engage in? Would you like to re-engage in copying for some one?'

'No; I would prefer not to make any change.'

'Would you like a clerkship in a dry-goods store?'

'There is too much confinement about that. No, I would not like a clerkship; but I am not particular.'

'Too much confinement,' I cried, 'why you keep yourself confined all the time!'

'I would prefer not to take a clerkship,' he rejoined, as if to settle that little item at once.

'How would a bartender's business suit you? There is no trying of the eyesight in that.'

'I would not like it at all; though, as I said before, I am not particular.'

His unwonted wordiness inspirited me. I returned to the charge.

'Well then, would you like to travel through the country collecting bills for the merchants? That would improve your health.'

'No, I would prefer to be doing something else.'

'How then would going as a companion to Europe to entertain some young gentleman with your conversation,—how would that suit you?'

'Not at all. It does not strike me that there is anything definite about that. I like to be stationary. But I am not particular.'

'Stationary you shall be then,' I cried, now losing all patience, and for the first time in all my exasperating connection with him fairly flying into a passion. 'If you do not go away from these premises before night, I shall feel bound—indeed I *am* bound—to—to—to quit the premises myself!' I rather absurdly concluded, knowing not with what possible threat to try to frighten his immobility into compliance. Despairing of all further efforts, I was precipitately leaving him, when a final thought occurred to me—one which had not been wholly unindulged before.

'Bartleby,' said I, in the kindest tone I could assume under such exciting circumstances, 'will you go home with me now—not to my office, but my dwelling—and remain there till we can conclude upon some convenient arrangement for you at our leisure? Come, let us start now, right away.'

'No: at present I would prefer not to make any change at all.'

I answered nothing, but effectually dodging every one by the suddenness and rapidity of my flight, rushed from the building, ran up Wall Street toward Broadway, and then jumping into the first omnibus was soon removed from pursuit. As soon as tranquillity returned I distinctly perceived that I had now done all that I possibly could, both in respect to the demands of the landlord and his tenants, and with regard to my own desire and sense of duty, to benefit Bartleby, and shield him from rude persecution. I now strove to be entirely care-free and quiescent; and my conscience justified me in the attempt; though indeed it was not so successful as I could have wished. So fearful was I of being again hunted out by the incensed landlord and his exasperated tenants, that, surrendering my business to Nippers, for a few days I drove about the upper part of the town and through the suburbs, in my rockaway; crossed over to Jersey City and Hoboken, and paid fugitive visits to Manhattanville and Astoria. In fact I almost lived in my rockaway for the time.

When again I entered my office, lo, a note from the landlord lay upon the desk. I opened it with trembling hands. It informed me that the writer had sent to the police, and had Bartleby removed to the Tombs as a vagrant. Moreover, since I knew more about him than any one else, he wished me to appear at that place, and make a suitable statement of the facts. These tidings had a conflicting effect upon me. At first I was indignant; but at last almost approved. The landlord's energetic, summary disposition had led him to adopt a procedure which I do not think I would have decided upon myself; and yet as a last resort, under such peculiar circumstances, it seemed the only plan.

As I afterwards learned, the poor scrivener, when told that he must be conducted to the Tombs, offered not the slightest obstacle, but in his own pale, unmoving way silently acquiesced.

Some of the compassionate and curious bystanders joined the party; and headed by one of the constables, arm-in-arm with Bartleby the silent procession filed its way through all the noise, and heat, and joy of the roaring thoroughfares at noon.

The same day I received the note I went to the Tombs, or, to speak more properly, the Halls of Justice. Seeking the right officer, I stated the purpose of my call, and was informed that the individual I described was indeed within. I then assured the functionary that Bartleby was a perfectly honest man, and greatly to be a compassionated (however unaccountable) eccentric. I narrated all I knew, and closed by suggesting the idea of letting him remain in as indulgent confinement as possible till something less harsh might be done—though indeed I hardly knew what. At all events, if nothing else could be decided upon, the alms-house must receive him. I then begged to have an interview.

Being under no disgraceful charge, and quite serene and harmless in all his ways, they had permitted him freely to wander about the prison, and especially in the enclosed grass-platted yards thereof. And so I found him there, standing all alone in the quietest of the yards, his face toward a high wall—while all around, from the narrow slits of the jail windows, I thought I saw peering out upon him the eyes of murderers and thieves.

'Bartleby!'

'I know you,' he said, without looking round—'and I want nothing to say to you.'

'It was not I that brought you here, Bartleby,' said I, keenly pained at his implied suspicion. 'And to you, this should not be so vile a place. Nothing reproachful attaches to you by being here. And see, it is not so sad a place as one might think. Look, there is the sky and here is the grass.'

'I know where I am,' he replied, but would say nothing more, and so I left him.

As I entered the corridor again a broad, meat-like man in an apron accosted me, and jerking his thumb over his shoulder said—'Is that your friend?'

'Yes.'

'Does he want to starve? If he does, let him live on the prison fare, that's all.'

'Who are you?' asked I, not knowing what to make of such an unofficially speaking person in such a place.

'I am the grub-man. Such gentlemen as have friends here, hire me to provide them with something good to eat.'

'Is this so?' said I, turning to the turnkey.

He said it was.

'Well then,' said I, slipping some silver into the grub-man's hands (for so they called him), 'I want you to give particular attention to my friend there; let him have the best dinner you can get. And you must be as polite to him as possible.'

'Introduce me, will you?' said the grub-man, looking at me with an expression which seemed to say he was all impatience for an opportunity to give a specimen of his breeding.

Thinking it would prove of benefit to the scrivener, I acquiesced; and asking the grub-man his name, went up with him to Bartleby.

'Bartleby, this is Mr Cutlets; you will find him very useful to you.'

'Your sarvant, sir, your sarvant,' said the grub-man, making a low salutation behind his apron. 'Hope you find it pleasant here, sir;—spacious grounds—cool apartments, sir—hope you'll stay with us some time—try to make it agreeable. May Mrs Cutlets and I have the pleasure of your company to dinner, sir, in Mrs Cutlets' private room?'

'I prefer not to dine to-day,' said Bartleby, turning away. 'It would disagree with me; I am unused to dinners.' So saying, he slowly moved to the other side of the enclosure and took up a position fronting the dead-wall.

'How's this?' said the grub-man, addressing me with a stare of astonishment. 'He's odd, ain't he?'

'I think he is a little deranged,' said I, sadly.

'Deranged? deranged is it? Well now, upon my word, I thought that friend of yourn was a gentleman forger; they are always pale and genteel-like, them forgers. I can't help pity 'em—can't help it, sir. Did you know Monroe Edwards?' he added touchingly, and paused. Then, laying his hand pityingly on my shoulder, sighed, 'he died of the consumption at Sing-Sing. So you weren't acquainted with Monroe?'

'No, I was never socially acquainted with any forgers. But I cannot stop longer. Look to my friend yonder. You will not lose by it. I will see you again.'

Some few days after this, I again obtained admission to the Tombs, and went through the corridors in quest of Bartleby; but without finding him.

'I saw him coming from his cell not long ago,' said a turnkey, 'maybe he's gone to loiter in the yards.'

So I went in that direction.

'Are you looking for the silent man?' said another turnkey passing me. 'Yonder he lies—sleeping in the yard there. 'Tis not twenty minutes since I saw him lie down.'

The yard was entirely quiet. It was not accessible to the common prisoners. The surrounding walls, of amazing thickness, kept off all sounds behind them. The Egyptian character of the masonry weighed upon me with its gloom. But a soft imprisoned turf grew under foot. The heart of the eternal pyramids, it seemed, wherein by some strange magic, through the clefts grass-seed, dropped by birds, had sprung.

Strangely huddled at the base of the wall—his knees drawn up, and lying on his side, his head touching the cold stones—I saw the wasted Bartleby. But nothing stirred. I paused; then went close up to him; stooped over, and saw that his dim eyes were open; otherwise he seemed profoundly sleeping. Something prompted me to touch him. I felt his hand, when a tingling shiver ran up my arm and down my spine to my feet.

The round face of the grub-man peered upon me now. 'His dinner is ready. Won't he dine to-day, either? Or does he live without dining?'

'Lives without dining,' said I, and closed the eyes.

'Eh!—he's asleep, ain't he?'

'With kings and counsellors,' murmured I.

There would seem little need for proceeding further in this history. Imagination will readily supply the meagre recital of poor Bartleby's interment. But ere parting with the reader, let me say, that if this little narrative has sufficiently interested him, to awaken curiosity as to who Bartleby was, and what manner of life he led prior to the present narrator's making his acquaintance, I can only reply, that in such curiosity I fully share—but am wholly unable to gratify it. Yet here I hardly know whether I should divulge one little item of rumour, which came to my ear a few months after the scrivener's decease. Upon what basis it rested, I could never ascertain; and hence, how true it is I cannot now tell. But inasmuch as this vague report has not been without a certain strange suggestive interest to me, however sad, it may prove the same with some others; and so I will briefly mention it. The report was this: that Bartleby had been a subordinate clerk in the Dead Letter Office at Washington, from which he had been suddenly removed by a change in the administration. When I think over this rumour I cannot adequately express the emotions which seize me. Dead letters! does it not sound like dead men? Conceive a man by nature and misfortune prone to a pallid hopelessness: can any business seem more fitted to heighten it than that of continually handling these dead letters, and assorting them for the flames? For by the cartload they are annually burned. Sometimes from out the folded paper the pale clerk takes a ring:—the finger it was meant for, perhaps, moulders in the grave; a bank-note sent in swiftest charity:—he whom it would relieve, nor eats nor hungers any more; pardon for those who died despairing; hope for those who died unhoping; good tidings for those who died stifled by unrelieved calamities. On errands of life, these letters speed to death.

Ah Bartleby! Ah humanity!

1853

The Lightning-Rod Man

What grand irregular thunder, thought I, standing on my hearth-stone among the Acroceraunian hills, as the scattered bolts boomed overhead, and crashed down among the valleys, every bolt followed by zigzag irradiations, and swift slants of sharp rain, which audibly rang, like a charge of spear-points, on my low shingled roof. I suppose, though, that the mountains hereabouts break and churn up the thunder, so that it is far more glorious here than on the plain. Hark!—some one at the door. Who is this that chooses a time of thunder for making calls? And why don't he, man-fashion, use the knocker, instead of making that doleful undertaker's clatter with his fist against the hollow panel? But let him in. Ah, here he comes. 'Good day, sir': an entire stranger. 'Pray be seated.' What is that strange-looking walking-stick he carries: 'A fine thunder-storm, sir.'

'Fine?—Awful.'

'You are wet. Stand here on the hearth before the fire.'

'Not for worlds!'

The stranger still stood in the exact middle of the cottage, where he had first planted himself. His singularity impelled a closer scrutiny. A lean, gloomy figure. Hair dark and lank, mattedly streaked over his brow. His sunken pitfalls of eyes were ringed by indigo halos, and played with an innocuous sort of lightning: the gleam without the bolt. The whole man was dripping. He stood in a puddle on the bare oak floor: his strange walking-stick vertically resting at his side.

It was a polished copper rod, four feet long, lengthwise attached to a neat wooden staff, by insertion into two balls of greenish glass, ringed with copper bands. The metal rod terminated at the top tripodwise, in three keen tines, brightly gilt. He held the thing by the wooden part alone.

'Sir,' said I, bowing politely, 'have I the honour of a visit from the illustrious god, Jupiter Tonans? So stood he in the Greek statue of old, grasping the lightning-bolt. If you be he, or his viceroy, I have to thank you for this noble storm you have brewed among our mountains. Listen: that was a glorious peal. Ah, to a lover of the majestic, it is a good thing to have the Thunderer himself in one's cottage. The thunder grows finer for that. But pray be seated. This old rush-bottomed arm-chair, I grant, is a poor substitute for your evergreen throne on Olympus; but, condescend to be seated.'

While I thus pleasantly spoke, the stranger eyed me, half in wonder, and half in a strange sort of horror; but did not move a foot.

'Do, sir, be seated; you need to be dried ere going forth again.'

I planted the chair invitingly on the broad hearth, where a little fire had been kindled that afternoon to dissipate the dampness, not the cold; for it was early in the month of September.

But without heeding my solicitation, and still standing in the middle of the floor, the stranger gazed at me portentously and spoke.

'Sir,' said he, 'excuse me; but instead of my accepting your invitation to be seated on the hearth there, I solemnly warn *you*, that you had best accept *mine*, and stand with me in the middle of the room. Good Heavens!' he cried, starting—'there is another of those awful crashes. I warn you, sir, quit the hearth.'

'Mr Jupiter Tonans,' said I, quietly rolling my body on the stone, 'I stand very well here.'

'Are you so horridly ignorant then,' he cried, 'as not to know, that by far the most dangerous part of a house, during such a terrific tempest as this, is the fire-place?'

'Nay, I did not know that,' involuntarily stepping upon the first board next to the stone.

The stranger now assumed such an unpleasant air of successful admonition, that—quite involuntarily again—I stepped back upon the hearth, and threw myself into the erectest, proudest posture I could command. But I said nothing.

'For Heaven's sake,' he cried, with a strange mixture of alarm and intimidation—'for Heaven's sake, get off the hearth! Know you not, that the heated air and soot are conductors;—to say nothing of those immense iron fire-dogs? Quit the spot—I conjure—I command you.'

'Mr Jupiter Tonans, I am not accustomed to be commanded in my own house.'

'Call me not by that pagan name. You are profane in this time of terror.'

'Sir, will you be so good as to tell me your business? If you seek shelter from the storm, you are welcome, so long as you be civil; but if you come on business, open it forthwith. Who are you?'

'I am a dealer in lightning-rods,' said the stranger, softening his tone; 'my special business—Merciful Heaven! what a crash!—Have you ever been struck—your premises, I mean? No? It's best to be provided,'—significantly rattling his metallic staff on the floor,—'by nature, there are no castles in thunder-storms; yet, say but the word, and of this cottage I can make a Gibraltar by a few waves of this wand. Hark, what Himalayas of concussions!'

'You interrupted yourself; your special business you were about to speak of.'

'My special business is to travel the country for orders for lightning-rods. This is my specimen rod;' tapping his staff; 'I have the best of references'—fumbling in his pockets. 'In Criggan last month, I put up three-and-twenty rods on only five buildings.'

'Let me see. Was it not at Criggan last week, about midnight on Saturday, that the steeple, the big elm, and the assembly-room cupola were struck? Any of your rods there?'

'Not on the tree and cupola, but the steeple.'

'Of what use is your rod, then?'

'Of life-and-death use. But my workman was heedless. In fitting the rod at top to the steeple, he allowed a part of the metal to graze the tin sheeting. Hence the accident. Not my fault, but his. Hark!'

'Never mind. That clap burst quite loud enough to be heard without finger-pointing. Did you hear of the event at Montreal last year? A servant girl struck at her bed-side with a rosary in her hand; the beads being metal.

Does your beat extend into the Canadas?'

'No. And I hear that there, iron rods only are in use. They should have *mine*, which are copper. Iron is easily fused. Then they draw out the rod so slender, that it has not body enough to conduct the full electric current. The metal melts; the building is destroyed. My copper rods never act so. Those Canadians are fools. Some of them knob the rod at the top, which risks a deadly explosion, instead of imperceptibly carrying down the current into the earth, as this sort of rod does. *Mine* is the only true rod. Look at it. Only one dollar a foot.'

'This abuse of your own calling in another might make one distrustful with respect to yourself.'

'Hark! The thunder becomes less muttering. It is nearing us, and nearing the earth, too. Hark! One crammed crash! All the vibrations made one by nearness. Another flash. Hold.'

'What do you?' I said, seeing him now instantaneously relinquishing his staff, lean intently forward towards the window, with his right fore and middle fingers on his left wrist.

But ere the words had well escaped me, another exclamation escaped him.

'Crash! only three pulses—less than a third of a mile off—yonder, somewhere in that wood. I passed three stricken oaks there, ripped out new and glittering. The oak draws lightning more than other timber, having iron in solution in its sap. Your floor here seems oak.'

'Heart-of-oak. From the peculiar time of your call upon me, I suppose you purposely select stormy weather for your journeys. When the thunder is roaring, you deem it an hour peculiarly favourable for producing impressions favourable to your trade.

'Hark!—Awful!'

'For one who would arm others with fearlessness, you seem unbeseemingly timorous yourself. Common men choose fair weather for their travels: you choose thunder-storms; and yet—'

'That I travel in thunder-storms, I grant; but not without particular precautions, such as only a lightning-rod man may know. Hark! Quick—look at my specimen rod. Only one dollar a foot.'

'A very fine rod, I dare say. But what are these particular precautions of yours? Yet first let me close yonder shutters; the slanting rain is beating through the sash. I will bar up.'

'Are you mad? Know you not that yon iron bar is a swift conductor? Desist.'

'I will simply close the shutters, then, and call my boy to bring me a wooden bar. Pray, touch the bell-pull there.'

'Are you frantic? That bell-wire might blast you. Never touch bell-wire in a thunder-storm, nor ring a bell of any sort.'

'Nor those in belfries? Pray, will you tell me where and how one may be safe in a time like this? Is there any part of my house I may touch with hopes of my life?'

'There is; but not where you now stand. Come away from the wall. The current will sometimes run down a wall, and—a man being a better conductor than a wall—it would leave the wall and run into him. Swoop! *That* must have fallen very nigh. That must have been globular lightning.'

'Very probably. Tell me at once, which is, in your opinion, the safest part of this house?'

'This room, and this one spot in it where I stand. Come hither.'

'The reasons first.'

'Hark!—after the flash the gust—the sashes shiver—the house, the house!—Come hither to me!'

'The reasons, if you please.'

'Come hither to me!'

'Thank you again, I think I will try my old stand—the hearth. And now, Mr Lightning-rod-man, in the pauses of the thunder, be so good as to tell me your reasons for esteeming this one room of the house the safest, and your own one stand-point there the safest spot in it.'

There was now a little cessation of the storm for a while. The Lightning-rod man seemed relieved, and replied:—

'Your house is a one-storeyed house, with an attic and a cellar; this room is between. Hence its comparative safety. Because lightning sometimes passes from the clouds to the earth, and sometimes from the earth to the clouds. Do you comprehend?—and I choose the middle of the room, because, if the lightning should strike the house at all, it would come down the chimney or walls; so, obviously, the further you are from them, the better. Come hither to me, now.'

'Presently. Something you just said, instead of alarming me, has strangely inspired confidence.'

'What have I said?'

'You said that sometimes lightning flashes from the earth to the clouds.'

'Aye, the returning-stroke, as it is called; when the earth, being overcharged with the fluid, flashes its surplus upward.'

'The returning-stroke; that is, from earth to sky. Better and better. But come here on the hearth and dry yourself.'

'I am better here, and better wet.'

'How?'

'It is the safest thing you can do—Hark, again!—to get yourself thoroughly drenched in a thunder-storm. Wet clothes are better conductors than the body; and so, if the lightning strike, it might pass down the wet clothes without touching the body. The storm deepens again. Have you a rug in the house? Rugs are non-conductors. Get one, that I may stand on it here, and you, too. The skies blacken—it is dusk at noon. Hark!—the rug, the rug!'

I gave him one; while the hooded mountains seemed closing and tumbling into the cottage.

'And now, since our being dumb will not help us,' said I, resuming my place, 'let me hear your precautions in travelling during thunder-storms.'

'Wait till this one is passed.'

'Nay, proceed with the precautions. You stand in the safest possible place according to your own account. Go on.'

'Briefly, then. I avoid pine-trees, high houses, lonely barns, upland pastures, running water, flocks of cattle and sheep, a crowd of men. If I travel on foot—as to-day—I do not walk fast; if in my buggy, I touch not its back or sides; if on horseback, I dismount and lead the horse. But of all things, I avoid tall men.'

'Do I dream? Man avoid man? and in danger-time, too.'

'Tall men in a thunder-storm I avoid. Are you so grossly ignorant as not to know, that the height of a six-footer is sufficient to discharge an electric cloud upon him? Are not lonely Kentuckians, ploughing, smit in the unfinished furrow? Nay, if the six-footer stand by running water, the cloud will sometimes *select* him as its conductor to that running water. Hark! Sure, yon black pinnacle is split. Yes, a man is a good conductor. The lightning goes through and through a man, but only peels a tree. But sir, you have kept me so long answering your questions, that I have not yet come to business. Will you order one of my rods? Copper's the best conductor. Your house is low; but being upon the mountains, that lowness does not one whit depress it. You mountaineers are most exposed. In mountainous countries the lightning-rod man should have most business. Look at the specimen, sir. One rod will answer for a house so small as this. Look over these recommendations. Only one rod, sir; cost, only twenty dollars. Hark! There go all the granite Taconics and Hoosics dashed together like pebbles. By the sound, that must have struck something. An elevation of five feet above the house, will protect twenty feet radius all about the rod. Only twenty dollars, sir—a dollar a foot. Hark!—Dreadful!—Will you order? Will you buy? Shall I put down your name? Think of being a heap of charred offal, like a haltered horse burnt in his stall; and all in one flash!'

'You pretended envoy extraordinary and minister plenipotentiary to and from Jupiter Tonans,' laughed I; 'you mere man who come here to put you and your pipestem between clay and sky, do you think that because you can strike a bit of green light from the Leyden jar, that you can thoroughly avert the supernal bolt? Your rod rusts, or breaks, and where are you? Who has empowered you, you Tetzel, to peddle round your indulgences from divine ordinations? The hairs of our heads are numbered, and the days of our lives. In thunder as in sunshine, I stand at ease in the hands of my God. False negotiator, away! See, the scroll of the storm is rolled back; the house is unharmed; and in the blue heavens I read in the rainbow, that the Deity will not, of purpose, make war on man's earth.'

'Impious wretch!' foamed the stranger, blackening in the face as the rainbow beamed, 'I will publish your infidel notions.'

'Begone! move quickly! if quickly you can, you that shine forth into sight in moist times like the worm.'

The scowl grew blacker on his face; the indigo-circles enlarged round his eyes as the storm-rings round the midnight moon. He sprang upon me, his tri-forked thing at my heart.

I seized it; I snapped it; I dashed it; I trod it; and dragging the dark lightning-king out of my door, flung his elbowed, copper sceptre after him.

But spite of my treatment, and spite of my dissuasive talk of him to my neighbours, the Lightning-rod man still dwells in the land; still travels in storm-time, and drives a brave trade with the fears of man.

1854

Henry James

1843-1916

For Henry James, the measure of good fiction is 'the success with which the author has produced the illusion of life. The cultivation of this success, the study of this exquisite process, form, to my taste, the beginning and the end of the art of the novelist. They are his inspiration, his despair, his reward, his torment, his delight. It is here in very truth that he competes with life.' In this formulation, James is articulating the realist's credo that governed his art—that fiction should 'produce the illusion of life.'

James, the second eldest of four boys and a girl, was born in New York City. His father, Henry James Sr, was a wealthy philosopher; his older brother, William, became a famous philosopher himself. The family travelled frequently to Europe for extended periods when James was a child, returning to Newport, Rhode Island when he was eighteen. From 1862-63 he attended Harvard Law School, but spent most of his time reading and attending lectures on literature and began writing stories and reviews. In 1869 he took his first trip on his own to Europe; the cycle of European travel and returns to the United States became a lifelong pattern for him, although from 1875 on he spent more time in Europe, and in 1896 settled in Lamb House, a mansion in Rye, England, for the rest of his life. His first major novel, *The Portrait of a Lady*, appeared in 1881. Throughout his career, James wrote prolifically, alternating fictional forms with criticism and drama.

In his many stories, novellas, and novels, James strove to render, both through his style and his choice of subjects, the developments of his characters' consciousnesses, the psychological intricacies of their interior lives, and the ways in which their experience modified their perceptions. His fiction uses plot to reveal character, and setting—often, the European settings that James lived his adult life in—to dramatize the subtle unfolding of motivation, self-deception, delusion, and insight, that mark his finest portraits. In his Preface to the New York edition of 'The Pupil', James recalled the story's genesis: a doctor in Italy had told him about 'a wonderful American family, an odd adventurous, extravagant band, of high but rather unauthenticated pretensions, the most stimulating member of which was a small boy, acute and precocious, afflicted with a heart of weak action, but beautifully intelligent, who saw their prowling precarious life exactly as it was, and measured and judged it, and measured and judged *them*, all round ever so quaintly; presenting himself in short as an extraordinary little person.' The style of James' description is a good example of his fictional signature; in 'The Pupil' he recreates this 'extraordinary little person' through the character of Morgan, exploring the boy's relationship with his tutor to reveal both the family's composite character and the causes of the unnaturally intense connection between Pemberton and the child.

James described 'The Beast in the Jungle'—an example of the form he called a 'nouvelle'—as 'an elaborated fantasy—which, I must add, I hold a successful thing only as its motive may seem to the reader to stand out sharp.' Through his character study of John Marcher, James shows how Marcher's obsession with the 'beast' that is, in part, his own nature and feelings, prevents him from ever living his life—particularly, from allowing him to love May Bartram. The consequences of the unlived life, James shows, are fatal, both to Marcher and, perhaps, to May Bartram.

'The Pupil' was first published in the March-April 1891 issue of *Longman's Magazine* and then collected in *The Lesson of the Master, The Marriages, The Pupil, Brooksmith, The Solution, Sir Edmund Orme* (1892). 'The Beast in the Jungle' was first published in *The Better Sort* (1903).

The Pupil

I

The poor young man hesitated and procrastinated: it cost him such an effort to broach the subject of terms, to speak of money to a person who spoke only of feelings and, as it were, of the aristocracy. Yet he was unwilling to take leave, treating his engagement as settled, without some more conventional glance in that direction than he could find an opening for in the manner of the large affable lady who sat there drawing a pair of soiled *gants de Suède* through a fat jewelled hand and, at once pressing and gliding, repeated over and over everything but the thing he would have liked to hear. He would have liked to hear the figure of his salary; but just as he was nervously about to sound that note the little boy came back—the little boy Mrs Moreen had sent out of the room to fetch her fan. He came back without the fan, only with the casual observation that he couldn't find it. As he dropped this cynical confession he looked straight and hard at the candidate for the honour of taking his education in hand. This personage reflected somewhat grimly that the first thing he should have to teach his little charge would be to appear to address himself to his mother when he spoke to her—especially not to make her such an improper answer as that.

When Mrs Moreen bethought herself of this pretext for getting rid of their companion Pemberton supposed it was precisely to approach the delicate subject of his remuneration. But it had been only to say some things about her son that it was better a boy of eleven shouldn't catch. They were extravagantly to his advantage save when she lowered her voice to sigh, tapping her left side familiarly, 'And all over-clouded by *this*, you know; all at the mercy of a weakness—!' Pemberton gathered that the weakness was in the region of the heart. He had known the poor child was not robust: this was the basis on which he had been invited to treat, through an English lady, an Oxford acquaintance, then at Nice, who happened to know both his needs and those of the amiable American family looking out for something really superior in the way of a resident tutor.

The young man's impression of his prospective pupil, who had come into the room as if to see for himself the moment Pemberton was admitted, was not quite the soft solicitation the visitor had taken for granted. Morgan Moreen was somehow sickly without being 'delicate', and that he looked intelligent—it is true Pemberton wouldn't have enjoyed his being stupid—only added to the suggestion that, as with his big mouth and big ears he really couldn't be called pretty, he might too utterly fail to please. Pemberton was modest, was even timid; and the chance that his small scholar would prove cleverer than himself had quite figured, to his anxiety, among the dangers of an untried experiment. He reflected, however, that these were risks one had to run when one accepted a position, as it was called, in a private family; when as yet one's university honours had, pecuniarily speaking, remained barren. At any rate when Mrs Moreen got up as to intimate that, since it was understood he would enter upon his duties within the week she would let him off now, he succeeded, in spite of the presence of the child, in squeezing out a phrase about the rate of payment. It was not the fault of the conscious smile which seemed a reference to the lady's expensive identity, it was not the fault of this demonstration, which had, in a sort, both vagueness and point, if the allusion didn't sound rather vulgar. This was exactly because she became still more gracious to reply: 'Oh I can assure you that all that will be quite regular.'

Pemberton only wondered, while he took up his hat, what 'all that' was to amount to—people had such different ideas. Mrs Moreen's words, however, seemed to commit the family to a pledge definite enough to elicit from the child a strange little comment in the shape of the mocking foreign ejaculation 'Oh la-la!'

Pemberton, in some confusion, glanced at him as he walked slowly to the window with his back turned, his hands in his pockets and the air in his elderly shoulders of a boy who didn't play. The young man wondered if he should be able to teach him to play, though his mother had said it would never do and that this was why school was impossible. Mrs Moreen exhibited no discomfiture; she only continued blandly: 'Mr Moreen will be delighted to meet your wishes. As I told you, he has been called to London for a week. As soon as he comes back you shall have it out with him.'

This was so frank and friendly that the young man could only reply, laughing as his hostess laughed: 'Oh I don't imagine we shall have much of a battle.'

'They'll give you anything you like,' the boy remarked unexpectedly, returning from the window. 'We don't mind what anything costs—we live awfully well.'

'My darling, you're too quaint!' his mother exclaimed, putting out to caress him a practised but ineffectual hand. He slipped out of it, but looked with intelligent innocent eyes at Pemberton, who had already had time to notice that from one moment to the other his small satiric face seemed to change its time of life. At this moment it was infantine, yet it appeared also to be under the influence of curious intuitions and knowledges. Pemberton rather disliked precocity and was disappointed to find gleams of it in a disciple not yet in his teens. Nevertheless he divined on the spot that Morgan wouldn't prove a bore. He would prove on the contrary a source of agitation. This idea held the young man, in spite of a certain repulsion.

'You pompous little person! We're not extravagant!' Mrs Moreen gaily protested, making another unsuccessful attempt to draw the boy to her side. 'You must know what to expect,' she went on to Pemberton.

'The less you expect the better!' her companion interposed. 'But we *are* people of fashion.'

'Only so far as *you* make us so!' Mrs Moreen tenderly mocked. 'Well then, on Friday—don't tell me you're superstitious—and mind you don't fail us. Then you'll see us all. I'm so sorry the girls are out. I guess you'll like the girls. And, you know, I've another son, quite different from this one.'

'He tries to imitate me,' Morgan said to their friend.

'He tries? Why he's twenty years old!' cried Mrs Moreen.

'You're very witty,' Pemberton remarked to the child—a proposition his mother echoed with enthusiasm, declaring Morgan's sallies to be the delight of the house.

The boy paid no heed to this; he only enquired abruptly of the visitor, who was surprised afterwards that he hadn't struck him as offensively forward: 'Do you *want* very much to come?'

'Can you doubt it after such a description of what I shall hear?' Pemberton replied. Yet he didn't want to come at all; he was coming because he had to go somewhere, thanks to the collapse of his fortune at the end of a year abroad spent on the system of putting his scant patrimony into a single full wave of experience. He had had his full wave but couldn't pay the score at his inn. Moreover he had caught in the boy's eyes the glimpse of a far-off appeal.

'Well, I'll do the best I can for you,' said Morgan; with which he turned away again. He passed out of one of the long windows; Pemberton saw him go and lean on the parapet of the terrace. He remained there while the young man took leave of his mother, who, on Pemberton's looking as if he expected a farewell from him, interposed with: 'Leave him, leave him; he's so strange!' Pemberton supposed her to fear something he might say. 'He's a genius—you'll love him,' she added. 'He's much the most interesting person in the family.' And before he could invent some civility to oppose to this she wound up with: 'But we're all good, you know!'

'He's a genius—you'll love him!' were words that recurred to our aspirant before the Friday, suggesting among many things that geniuses were not invariably lovable. However, it was all the better if there was an element that would make tutorship absorbing: he had perhaps taken too much for granted it would only disgust him. As he left the villa after his interview he looked up at the balcony and saw the child leaning over it. 'We shall have great larks!' he called up.

Morgan hung fire a moment and then gaily returned: 'By the time you come back I shall have thought of something witty!'

This made Pemberton say to himself 'After all he's rather nice.'

II

On the Friday he saw them all, as Mrs Moreen had promised, for her husband had come back and the girls and the other son were at home. Mr Moreen had a white moustache, a confiding manner and, in his buttonhole, the ribbon of a foreign order—bestowed, as Pemberton eventually learned, for services. For what services he never clearly ascertained: this was a point—one of a large number—that Mr Moreen's manner never confided. What it emphatically did confide was that he was even more a man of the world than you might first make out. Ulick, the firstborn, was in visible training for the same profession—under the disadvantage as yet, however, of a buttonhole but feebly floral and a moustache with no pretensions to type. The girls had hair and figures and manners and small fat feet, but had never been out alone. As for Mrs Moreen Pemberton saw on a nearer view that her elegance was intermittent and her parts didn't always match. Her husband, as she had promised, met with enthusiasm Pemberton's ideas in regard to a salary. The young man had endeavoured to keep these stammerings modest, and Mr Moreen made it no secret that *he* found them wanting in 'style'. He further mentioned that he aspired to be intimate with his children, to be their best friend, and that he was always looking out for them. That was what he went off for, to London and other places—to look out; and this vigilance was the theory of life, as well as the real occupation, of the whole family. They all looked out, for they were very frank on the subject of its being necessary. They desired it to be understood that they were earnest people, and also that their fortune, though quite adequate for earnest people, required the most careful administration. Mr Moreen, as the parent bird, sought sustenance for the nest. Ulick invoked support mainly at the club, where Pemberton guessed that it was usually served on green cloth. The girls used to do up their hair and their frocks themselves, and our young man felt appealed to to be glad, in regard to Morgan's education, that, though it must naturally be of the best, it didn't cost too much. After a little he *was* glad, forgetting at times his own needs in the interest inspired by the child's character and culture and the pleasure of making easy terms for him.

During the first weeks of their acquaintance Morgan had been as puzzling as a page in an unknown language—altogether different from the obvious little Anglo-Saxons who had misrepresented childhood to Pemberton. Indeed the whole mystic volume in which the boy had been amateurishly bound demanded some practice in translation. To-day, after a considerable interval, there is something phantasmagoric, like a prismatic reflexion or a serial novel, in Pemberton's memory of the queerness of the Moreens. If it were not for a few tangible tokens—a lock of Morgan's hair cut by his own hand, and the half-dozen letters received from him when they were disjoined—the whole episode and the figures peopling it would seem too inconsequent for anything but dreamland. Their supreme quaintness was their success—as it appeared to him for a while at the time; since he had never seen a family so brilliantly equipped for failure. Wasn't it success to have kept him so hatefully long? Wasn't it success to have drawn him in that first morning at déjeuner, the Friday he came—it was enough to *make* one superstitious—so that he utterly committed himself, and this not by calculation or on a signal, but from a happy instinct which made them, like a band of gypsies, work so neatly together? They amused him as much as if they had really been a band of gypsies. He was still young and had not seen much of the world—his English years had been properly arid; therefore the reversed conventions of the Moreens—for they had *their* desperate proprieties—struck him as topsy-turvy. He had encountered nothing like them at Oxford; still less had any such note been struck to his younger American ear during the four years at Yale in which he had richly supposed himself to be reacting against a Puritan strain. The reaction of the Moreens, at any rate, went ever so much further. He had thought himself very sharp that first day in hitting them all off in his mind with the 'cosmopolite' label. Later it seemed feeble and colourless—confessedly helplessly provisional.

He yet when he first applied it felt a glow of joy—for an instructor he was still empirical—rise from the apprehension that living with them would really be to see life. Their sociable strangeness was an intimation of that—their chatter of tongues, their gaiety and good humour, their infinite dawdling (they were always getting themselves up, but it took for ever, and Pemberton had once found Mr Moreen shaving in the drawing-room), their French, their Italian and, cropping up in the foreign fluencies, their cold tough slices of American. They lived on macaroni and coffee—they had these articles prepared in perfection—but they knew recipes for a hundred other dishes. They overflowed with music and song, were always humming and catching each other up, and had a sort of professional acquaintance with Continental cities. They talked of 'good places' as if they had been pickpockets or strolling players. They had at Nice a villa, a carriage, a piano, and a banjo, and they went to official parties. They were a perfect calendar of the 'days' of their friends, which Pemberton knew them, when they were indisposed, to get out of bed to go to, and which made the week larger than life when Mrs Moreen talked of them with Paula and Amy. Their initiations gave their new inmate at first an almost dazzling sense of culture. Mrs Moreen had translated something at some former period—an author whom it made Pemberton feel *borné* never to have heard of. They could imitate Venetian and sing Neapolitan, and when they wanted to say something very particular communicated with each other in an ingenious dialect of their own, an elastic spoken cipher which Pemberton at first took for some *patois* of one of their countries, but which he 'caught on to' as he would not have grasped provincial development of Spanish or German.

'It's the family language—Ultramoreen,' Morgan explained to him drolly enough; but the boy rarely condescended to use it himself, though he dealt in colloquial Latin as if he had been a little prelate.

Among all the 'days' with which Mrs Moreen's memory was taxed she managed to squeeze in one of her own, which her friends sometimes forgot. But the house drew a frequented air from the number of fine people who were freely named there and from several mysterious men with foreign titles and English clothes whom Morgan called the Princes and who, on sofas with the girls, talked French very loud—though sometimes with some oddity of accent—as if to show they were saying nothing improper. Pemberton wondered how the Princes could ever propose in that tone and so publicly: he took for granted cynically that this was what was desired of them. Then he recognized that even for the chance of such an advantage Mrs Moreen would never allow Paula and Amy to receive alone. These young ladies were not at all timid, but it was just the safeguards that made them so candidly free. It was a houseful of Bohemians who wanted tremendously to be Philistines.

In one respect, however, certainly, they achieved no rigour—they were wonderfully amiable and ecstatic about Morgan. It was a genuine tenderness, an artless admiration, equally strong in each. They even praised his beauty, which was small, and were as afraid of him as if they felt him of finer clay. They spoke of him as a little angel and a prodigy—they touched on his want of health with long, vague faces. Pemberton feared at first an extravagance that might make him hate the boy, but before this happened he had become extravagant himself. Later, when he had grown rather to hate the others, it was a bribe to patience for him that they were at any rate nice about Morgan, going on tiptoe if they fancied he was showing symptoms, and even giving up somebody's 'day' to procure him a pleasure. Mixed with this too was the oddest wish to make him independent, as if they had felt themselves not good enough for him. They passed him over to the new members of their circle very much as if wishing to force some charity of adoption on so free an agent and get rid of their own charge. They were delighted when they saw Morgan take so to his kind playfellow, and could think of no higher praise for the young man. It was strange how they contrived to reconcile the appearance, and indeed the essential fact, of adoring the child with their eagerness to wash their hands of him. Did they want to get rid of him before he should find them out? Pemberton was finding them out month by month. The boy's fond family, however this might be, turned their backs with exaggerated delicacy, as if to avoid the reproach of interfering. Seeing in time how little he had in common with them—it was by *them* he first observed it; they proclaimed it with complete humility—his companion was moved to speculate on the mysteries of transmission, the far jumps of heredity. Where his detachment from most of the things they represented had come from was more than an observer could say—it certainly had burrowed under two or three generations.

As for Pemberton's own estimate of his pupil, it was a good while before he got the point of view, so little had he been prepared for it by the smug young barbarians to whom the tradition of tutorship, as hitherto revealed to him, had been adjusted. Morgan was scrappy and surprising, deficient in many properties supposed common to the *genus* and abounding in others that were the portion only of the supernaturally clever. One day his friend made a great stride: it cleared up the question to perceive that Morgan *was* supernaturally clever and that, though the formula was temporarily meagre, this would be the only assumption on which one could successfully deal with him. He had the general quality of a child for whom life had not been simplified by school, a kind of homebred sensibility which might have been bad for himself but was charming for others, and a whole range of refinement and perception—little musical vibrations as taking as picked-up airs—begotten by wandering about Europe at the tail of his migratory tribe. This might not have been an education to recommend in advance, but its results with so special a subject were as appreciable as the marks on a piece of fine porcelain. There was at the same time in him a small strain of stoicism, doubtless the fruit of having had to begin early to bear pain, which counted for pluck and made it of less consequence that he might have been thought at school rather a polyglot little beast. Pemberton indeed quickly found himself rejoicing that school was out of the question: in any million of boys it was probably good for all but one, and Morgan was that millionth. It would have made him comparative and superior—it might have made him really require kicking. Pemberton would try to be school himself—a bigger seminary than five hundred grazing donkeys, so that, winning no prizes, the boy would remain unconscious and irresponsible and amusing—amusing, because, though life was already intense in his childish nature, freshness still made there a strong draught for jokes. It turned out that even in the still air of Morgan's various disabilities jokes flourished greatly. He was a pale lean acute undeveloped little cosmopolite, who liked intellectual gymnastics and who also, as regards the behaviour of mankind, had noticed more things than you might suppose, but who nevertheless had his proper playroom of superstitions, where he smashed a dozen toys a day.

III

At Nice once, towards evening, as the pair rested in the open air after a walk, and looked over the sea at the pink western lights, he said suddenly to his comrade: 'Do you like it, you know—being with us all in this intimate way?'

'My dear fellow, why should I stay if I didn't?'

'How do I know you'll stay? I'm almost sure you won't, very long.'

'I hope you don't mean to dismiss me,' said Pemberton.

Morgan debated, looking at the sunset. 'I think if I did right I ought to.'

'Well, I know I'm supposed to instruct you in virtue; but in that case don't do right.'

'You're very young—fortunately,' Morgan went on, turning to him again.

'Oh yes, compared with you!'

'Therefore it won't matter so much if you do lose a lot of time.'

'That's the way to look at it,' said Pemberton accommodatingly.

They were silent a minute; after which the boy asked: 'Do you like my father and my mother very much?'

'Dear me, yes. Charming people.'

Morgan received this with another silence; then unexpectedly, familiarly, but at the same time affectionately, he remarked: 'You're a jolly old humbug!'

For a particular reason the words made our young man change colour. The boy noticed in an instant that he had turned red, whereupon he turned red himself and pupil and master exchanged a longish glance in which there was a consciousness of many more things than are usually touched upon, even tacitly, in such a relation. It produced for Pemberton an embarrassment; it raised in a shadowy form a question—this was the first glimpse of it—destined to play a singular and, as he imagined, owing to the altogether peculiar conditions, an unprecedented part in his intercourse with his little companion. Later, when he found himself talking with the youngster in a way in which few youngsters could ever have been talked with, he thought of that clumsy moment on the beach at Nice as the dawn of an understanding that had broadened. What had added to the clumsiness then was that he thought it his duty to declare to Morgan that he might abuse him, Pemberton, as much as he liked, but must never abuse his parents. To this Morgan had the easy retort that he hadn't dreamed of abusing them; which appeared to be true: it put Pemberton in the wrong.

'Then why am I a humbug for saying *I* think them charming?' the young man asked, conscious of a certain rashness.

'Well—they're not your parents.'

'They love you better than anything in the world—never forget that,' said Pemberton.

'Is that why you like them so much?'

'They're very kind to me,' Pemberton replied evasively.

'You *are* a humbug!' laughed Morgan, passing an arm into his tutor's. He leaned against him looking off at the sea again and swinging his long thin legs.

'Don't kick my shins,' said Pemberton while he reflected 'Hang it, I can't complain of them to the child!'

'There's another reason too,' Morgan went on, keeping his legs still.

'Another reason for what?'

'Besides their not being your parents.'

'I don't understand you,' said Pemberton.

'Well, you will before long. All right!'

He did understand fully before long, but he made a fight even with himself before he confessed it. He thought it the oddest thing to have a struggle with the child about. He wondered he didn't hate the hope of the Moreens for bringing the struggle on. But by the time it began any such sentiment for that scion was closed to him. Morgan was a special case, and to know him was to accept him on his own odd terms. Pemberton had spent his aversion to special cases before arriving at knowledge. When at last he did arrive his quandary was great. Against every interest he had attached himself. They would have to meet things together. Before they went home that evening at Nice the boy had said, clinging to his arm:

'Well, at any rate you'll hang on to the last.'

'To the last?'

'Till you're fairly beaten.'

'*You* ought to be fairly beaten!' cried the young man, drawing him closer.

IV

A year after he had come to live with them Mr and Mrs Moreen suddenly gave up the villa at Nice. Pemberton had got used to suddenness, having seen it practised on a considerable scale during two jerky little tours—one in Switzerland the first summer, and the other late in the winter, when they all ran down to Florence and then, at the end of ten days, liking it much less than they had intended, straggled back in mysterious depression. They had returned to Nice 'for ever,' as they said; but this didn't prevent their squeezing, one rainy muggy May night, into a second-class railway-carriage—you could never tell by which class they would travel—where Pemberton helped them to stow away a wonderful collection of bundles and bags. The explanation of this manoeuvre was that they had determined to spend the summer 'in some bracing place'; but in Paris they dropped into a small furnished apartment—a fourth floor in a third-rate avenue, where there was a smell on the staircase and the *portier* was hateful—and passed the next four months in blank indigence.

The better part of this baffled sojourn was for the preceptor and his pupil, who, visiting the Invalides and Notre Dame, the Conciergerie and all the museums, took a hundred remunerative rambles. They learned to know their Paris, which was useful, for they came back another year for a longer stay, the general character of which in Pemberton's memory to-day mixes pitiably and confusedly with that of the first. He sees Morgan's shabby knickerbockers—the everlasting pair that didn't match his blouse and that as he grew longer could only grow faded. He remembers the particular holes in his three or four pair of coloured stockings.

Morgan was dear to his mother, but he never was better dressed than was absolutely necessary—partly, no doubt, by his own fault, for he was as indifferent to his appearance as a German philosopher. 'My dear fellow, you *are* coming to pieces,' Pemberton would say to him in sceptical remonstrance; to which the child would reply, looking at him serenely up and down: 'My dear fellow, so are you! I don't want to cast you in the shade.' Pemberton could have no rejoinder for this—the assertion so closely represented the fact. If however the deficiencies of his own wardrobe were a chapter by themselves he didn't like his little charge to look too poor.

Later he used to say 'Well, if we're poor, why, after all, shouldn't we look it?' and he consoled himself with thinking there was something rather elderly and gentlemanly in Morgan's disrepair—it differed from the untidiness of the urchin who plays and spoils his things. He could trace perfectly the degrees by which, in proportion as her little son confined himself to his tutor for society, Mrs Moreen shrewdly forbore to renew his garments. She did nothing that didn't show, neglected him because he escaped notice, and then, as he illustrated this clever policy, discouraged at home his public appearances. Her position was logical enough—those members of her family who did show had to be showy.

During this period and several others Pemberton was quite aware of how he and his comrade might strike people; wandering languidly through the Jardin des Plantes as if they had nowhere to go, sitting on the winter days in the galleries of the Louvre, so splendidly ironical to the homeless, as if for the advantage of the *calorifère*. They joked about it sometimes: it was the sort of joke that was perfectly within the boy's compass. They figured themselves as part of the vast vague hand-to-mouth multitude of the enormous city and pretended they were proud of their position in it—it showed them 'such a lot of life' and made them conscious of a democratic brotherhood. If Pemberton couldn't feel a sympathy in destitution with his small companion—for after all Morgan's fond parents would never have let him really suffer—the boy would at least feel it with him, so it came to the same thing. He used sometimes to wonder what people would think they were—to fancy they were looked askance at, as if it might be a suspected case of kidnapping. Morgan wouldn't be taken for a young patrician with a preceptor—he wasn't smart enough; though he might pass for his companion's sickly little brother. Now and then he had a five-franc piece, and except once, when they bought a couple of lovely neckties, one of which he made Pemberton accept, they laid it out scientifically in old books. This was sure to be a great day, always spent on the quays, in a rummage of the dusty boxes that garnish the parapets. Such occasions helped them to live, for their books ran low very soon after the beginning of their acquaintance. Pemberton had a good many in England, but he was obliged to write to a friend and ask him kindly to get some fellow to give him something for them.

If they had to relinquish that summer the advantage of the bracing climate the young man couldn't but suspect this failure of the cup when at their very lips to have been the effect of a rude jostle of his own. This had represented his first blow-out, as he called it, with his patrons; his first successful attempt—though there was little other success about it—to bring them to a consideration of his impossible position. As the ostensible eve of a costly journey the moment had struck him as favourable to an earnest protest, the presentation of an ultimatum. Ridiculous as it sounded, he had never yet been able to compass an uninterrupted private interview with the elder pair or with either of them singly. They were always flanked by their elder children, and poor Pemberton usually had his own little charge at his side. He was conscious of its being a house in which the surface of one's delicacy got rather smudged; nevertheless he had preserved the bloom of his scruple against announcing to Mr and Mrs Moreen with publicity that he shouldn't be able to go on longer without a little money. He was still simple enough to suppose Ulick and Paula and Amy might not know that since his arrival he had only had a hundred and forty francs; and he was magnanimous enough to wish not to compromise their parents in their eyes. Mr Moreen now listened to him, as he listened to every one and to every thing, like a man of the world, and seemed to appeal to him—though not of course too grossly—to try and be a little more of one himself. Pemberton recognized in fact the importance of the character—from the advantage it gave Mr Moreen. He was not even confused or embarrassed, whereas the young man in his service was more so than there was any reason for. Neither was he surprised—at least any more than a gentleman had to be who freely confessed himself a little shocked—though not perhaps strictly at Pemberton.

'We must go into this, mustn't we, dear?' he said to his wife. He assured his young friend that the matter should have his very best attention; and he melted into space as elusively as if, at the door, he were taking an inevitable but deprecatory precedence. When, the next morning, Pemberton found himself alone with Mrs Moreen it was to hear her say 'I see, I see'—stroking the roundness of her chin and looking as if she were only hesitating between a dozen easy remedies. If they didn't make their push Mr Moreen could at least disappear for several days. During his absence his wife took up the subject again spontaneously, but her contribution to it was merely that she had thought all the while they were getting on so beautifully. Pemberton's reply to this revelation was that unless they immediately put down something on account he would leave them on the spot and for ever. He knew she would wonder how he would get away, and for a moment expected her to enquire. She didn't, for which he was almost grateful to her, so little was he in a position to tell.

'You won't, you *know* you won't—you're too interested,' she said. 'You *are* interested, you know you are, you dear kind man!' She laughed with almost condemnatory archness, as if it were a reproach—though she wouldn't insist; and flirted a soiled pocket-handkerchief at him.

Pemberton's mind was fully made up to take his step the following week. This would give him time to get an answer to a letter he had dispatched to England. If he did in the event nothing of the sort—that is if he stayed another year and then went away only for three months—it was not merely because before the answer to his letter came (most unsatisfactory when it did arrive) Mr Moreen generously counted out to him, and again with the sacrifice to 'form' of a marked man of the world, three hundred francs in elegant ringing gold. He was irritated to find that Mrs Moreen was right, that he couldn't at the pinch bear to leave the child. This stood out clearer for the very reason that, the night of his desperate appeal to his patrons, he had seen fully for the first time where he was. Wasn't it another proof of the success with which those patrons practised their arts that they had managed to avert for so long the illuminating flash? It descended on our friend with a breadth of effect which perhaps would have struck a spectator as comical, after he had returned to his little servile room, which looked into a close court where a bare dirty opposite wall took, with the sound of shrill clatter, the reflexion of lighted back windows. He had simply given himself away to a band of adventurers. The idea, the word itself, wore a romantic horror for him—he had always lived on such safe lines. Later it assumed a more interesting, almost a soothing, sense: it pointed a moral, and Pemberton could enjoy a moral. The Moreens were adventurers not merely because they didn't pay their debts, because they lived on society, but because their whole view of life, dim and confused and instinctive, like that of clever colour-blind animals, was speculative and rapacious and mean. Oh they were 'respectable', and that only made them more *immondes*! The young man's analysis, while he brooded, put it at last very simply—they were adventurers because they were toadies and snobs. That was the completest account of them—it was the law of their being. Even when this truth became vivid to their ingenious inmate he remained unconscious of how much his mind had been prepared for it by the extraordinary little boy who had now become such a complication in his life. Much less could he then calculate on the information he was still to owe the extraordinary little boy.

V

But it was during the ensuing time that the real problem came up—the problem of how far it was excusable to discuss the turpitude of parents with a child of twelve, of thirteen, of fourteen. Absolutely inexcusable and quite impossible it of course at first appeared; and indeed the question didn't press for some time after Pemberton had received his three hundred francs. They produced a temporary lull, a relief from the sharpest pressure. The young man frugally amended his wardrobe and even had a few francs in his pocket. He thought the Moreens looked at him as if he were almost too smart, as if they ought to take care not to spoil him. If Mr Moreen hadn't been such a man of the world he would perhaps have spoken of the freedom of such neckties on the part of a subordinate. But Mr Moreen was always enough a man of the world to let things pass—he had certainly shown that. It was singular how Pemberton guessed that Morgan, though saying nothing about it, knew something had happened. But three hundred francs, especially when one owed money, couldn't last for ever; and when the treasure was gone—the boy knew when it had failed—Morgan did break ground. The party had returned to Nice at the beginning of the winter, but not to the charming villa. They went to an hotel, where they stayed three months, and then moved to another establishment, explaining that they had left the first because, after waiting and waiting, they couldn't get the rooms they wanted. These apartments, the rooms they wanted, were generally very splendid; but fortunately they never *could* get them—fortunately, I mean, for Pemberton, who reflected always that if they had got them there would have been a still scanter educational fund. What Morgan said at last was said suddenly, irrelevantly, when the moment came, in the middle of a lesson, and consisted of the apparently unfeeling words: 'You ought to *filer*, you know—you really ought.'

Pemberton stared. He had learnt enough French slang from Morgan to know that to *filer* meant to cut sticks. 'Ah my dear fellow, don't turn me off!'

Morgan pulled a Greek lexicon toward him—he used a Greek-German—to look out a word, instead of asking it of Pemberton. 'You can't go on like this, you know.'

'Like what, my boy?'

'You know they don't pay you up,' said Morgan, blushing and turning his leaves.

'Don't pay me?' Pemberton stared again and feigned amazement. 'What on earth put that into your head?'

'It has been there a long time,' the boy replied rummaging his book.

Pemberton was silent, then he went on: 'I say, what are you hunting for? They pay me beautifully.'

'I'm hunting for the Greek for awful whopper,' Morgan dropped.

'Find that rather for gross impertinence and disabuse your mind. What do I want of money?'

'Oh that's another question!'

Pemberton wavered—he was drawn in different ways. The severely correct thing would have been to tell the boy that such a matter was none of his business and bid him go on with his lines. But they were really too intimate for that; it was not the way he was in the habit of treating him; there had been no reason it should be. On the other hand Morgan had quite lighted on the truth—he really shouldn't be able to keep it up much longer; therefore why not let him know one's real motive for forsaking him? At the same time it wasn't decent to abuse to one's pupil the family of one's pupil; it was better to misrepresent than to do that. So in reply to his comrade's last exclamation he just declared, to dismiss the subject, that he had received several payments.

'I say—I say!' the boy ejaculated, laughing.

'That's all right,' Pemberton insisted. 'Give me your written rendering.'

Morgan pushed a copybook across the table, and he began to read the page, but with something running in his head that made it no sense. Looking up after a minute or two he found the child's eyes fixed on him and felt in them something strange. Then Morgan said: 'I'm not afraid of the stern reality.'

'I haven't yet seen the thing you *are* afraid of—I'll do you that justice!'

This came out with a jump—it was perfectly true—and evidently gave Morgan pleasure. 'I've thought of it a long time,' he presently resumed.

'Well, don't think of it any more.'

The boy appeared to comply, and they had a comfortable and even an amusing hour. They had a theory that they were very thorough, and yet they seemed always to be in the amusing part of lessons, the intervals between the dull dark tunnels, where there were waysides and jolly views. Yet the morning was brought to a violent end by Morgan's suddenly leaning his arms on the table, burying his head in them and bursting into tears: at which Pemberton was the more startled that, as it then came over him, it was the first time he had ever seen the boy cry and that the impression was consequently quite awful.

The next day, after much thought, he took a decision and, believing it to be just, immediately acted on it. He cornered Mr and Mrs Moreen again and let them know that if on the spot they didn't pay him all they owed him he wouldn't only leave their house but would tell Morgan exactly what had brought him to it.

'Oh you *haven't* told him?' cried Mrs Moreen with a pacifying hand on her well-dressed bosom.

'Without warning you? For what do you take me?' the young man returned.

Mr and Mrs Moreen looked at each other; he could see that they appreciated, as tending to their security, his superstition of delicacy, and yet that there was a certain alarm in their relief. 'My dear fellow,' Mr Moreen demanded, 'what use *can* you have, leading the quiet life we all do, for such a lot of money?'—a question to which Pemberton made no answer, occupied as he was in noting that what passed in the mind of his patrons was something like: 'Oh then, if we've felt that the child, dear little angel, has judged us and how he regards us, and we haven't been betrayed, he must have guessed—and in short it's *general*!' an inference that rather stirred up Mr and Mrs Moreen, as Pemberton had desired it should. At the same time, if he had supposed his threat would do something towards bringing them round, he was disappointed to find them taking for granted—how vulgar their perception *had* been!—that he had already given them away. There was a mystic uneasiness in their parental breasts, and that had been the inferior sense of it. None the less, however, his threat did touch them; for if they had escaped it was only to meet a new danger. Mr Moreen appealed to him, on every precedent, as a man of the world; but his wife had recourse, for the first time since his domestication with them, to a fine *hauteur*, reminding him that a devoted mother, with her child, had arts that protected her against gross misrepresentation.

'I should misrepresent you grossly if I accused you of common honesty!' our friend replied; but as he closed the door behind him sharply, thinking he had not done himself much good, while Mr Moreen lighted another cigarette, he heard his hostess shout after him more touchingly:

'Oh you do, you *do*, put the knife to one's throat!'

The next morning, very early, she came to his room. He recognized her knock, but had no hope she brought him money; as to which he was wrong, for she had fifty francs in her hand. She squeezed forward in her dressing-gown, and he received her in his own, between his bath-tub and his bed. He had been tolerably schooled by this time to the 'foreign ways' of his hosts. Mrs Moreen was ardent, and when she was ardent she didn't care what she did; so she now sat down on his bed, his clothes being on the chairs, and, in her preoccupation, forgot, as she glanced round, to be ashamed of giving him such a horrid room. What Mrs Moreen's ardour now bore upon was the design of persuading him that in the first place she was very good-natured to bring him fifty francs, and that in the second, if he would only see it, he was really too absurd to expect to be *paid*. Wasn't he paid enough without perpetual money—wasn't he paid by the comfortable luxurious home he enjoyed with them all, without a care, an anxiety, a solitary want? Wasn't he sure of his position, and wasn't that everything to a young man like him, quite unknown, with singularly little to show, the ground of whose exorbitant pretensions it had never been easy to discover? Wasn't he paid above all by the sweet relation he had established with Morgan—quite ideal as from master to pupil—and by the simple privilege of knowing and living with so amazingly gifted a child; than whom really (and she meant literally what she said) there was no better company in Europe? Mrs Moreen herself took to appealing to him as a man of the world; she said 'Voyons, mon cher,' and 'My dear man, look here now'; and urged him to be reasonable, putting it before him that it was truly a chance for him. She spoke as if, according as he *should* be reasonable, he would prove himself worthy to be her son's tutor and of the extraordinary confidence they had placed in him.

After all, Pemberton reflected, it was only a difference of theory and the theory didn't matter much. They had hitherto gone on that of remunerated, as now they would go on that of gratuitous, service; but why should they have so many words about it? Mrs Moreen at all events continued to be convincing; sitting there with her fifty francs she talked and reiterated, as women reiterate, and bored and irritated him, while he leaned against the wall with his hands in the pockets of his wrapper, drawing it together round his legs and looking over the head of his visitor at the grey negations of his window. She wound up with saying: 'You see I bring you a definite proposal.'

'A definite proposal?'

'To make our relations regular, as it were—to put them on a comfortable footing.'

'I see—it's a system,' said Pemberton. 'A kind of organized blackmail.'

Mrs Moreen bounded up, which was exactly what he wanted. 'What do you mean by that?'

'You practise on one's fears—one's fears about the child if one should go away.'

'And pray what would happen to him in that event?' she demanded with majesty.

'Why he'd be alone with *you*.'

'And pray with whom *should* a child be but with those whom he loves most?'

'If you think that, why don't you dismiss me?'

'Do you pretend he loves you more than he loves *us*?' cried Mrs Moreen.

'I think he ought to. I make sacrifices for him. Though I've heard of those *you* make I don't see them.'

Mrs Moreen stared a moment; then with emotion she grasped her inmate's hand. '*Will* you make it—the sacrifice?'

He burst out laughing. 'I'll see. I'll do what I can. I'll stay a little longer. Your calculation's just—I *do* hate intensely to give him up; I'm fond of him and he thoroughly interests me, in spite of the inconvenience I suffer. You know my situation perfectly. I haven't a penny in the world and, occupied as you see me with Morgan, am unable to earn money.'

Mrs Moreen tapped her undressed arm with her folded bank-note. 'Can't you write articles? Can't you translate as *I* do?'

'I don't know about translating; it's wretchedly paid.'

'I'm glad to earn what I can,' said Mrs Moreen with prodigious virtue.

'You ought to tell me who you do it for.' Pemberton paused a moment, and she said nothing; so he added: 'I've tried to turn off some little sketches, but the magazines won't have them—they're declined with thanks.'

'You see then you're not such a phoenix,' his visitor pointedly smiled—'to pretend to abilities you're sacrificing for our sake.'

'I haven't time to do things properly,' he ruefully went on. Then as it came over him that he was almost abjectly good-natured to give these explanations he added: 'If I stay on longer it must be on one condition—that Morgan shall know distinctly on what footing I am.'

Mrs Moreen demurred. 'Surely you don't want to show off to a child?'

'To show *you* off, do you mean?'

Again she cast about, but this time it was to produce a still finer flower. 'And *you* talk of blackmail!'

'You can easily prevent it,' said Pemberton.

'And *you* talk of practising on fears!' she bravely pushed on.

'Yes, there's no doubt I'm a great scoundrel.'

His patroness met his eyes—it was clear she was in straits. Then she thrust out her money at him. 'Mr Moreen desired me to give you this on account.'

'I'm much obliged to Mr Moreen, but we *have* no account.'

'You won't take it?'

'That leaves me more free,' said Pemberton.

'To poison my darling's mind?' groaned Mrs Moreen.

'Oh your darling's mind—!' the young man laughed.

She fixed him a moment, and he thought she was going to break out tormentedly, pleadingly: 'For God's sake, tell me what *is* in it!' But she checked this impulse—another was stronger. She pocketed the money—the crudity of the alternative was comical—and swept out of the room with the desperate concession: 'You may tell him any horror you like!'

VI

A couple of days after this, during which he had failed to profit by so free a permission, he had been for a quarter of an hour walking with his charge in silence when the boy became sociable again with the remark: 'I'll tell you how I know it; I know it through Zénobie.'

'Zénobie? Who in the world is *she*?'

'A nurse I used to have—ever so many years ago. A charming woman. I liked her awfully, and she liked me.'

'There's no accounting for tastes. What is it you know through her?'

'Why what their idea is. She went away because they didn't fork out. She did like me awfully, and she stayed two years. She told me all about it—that at last she could never get her wages. As soon as they saw how much she liked me they stopped giving her anything. They thought she'd stay for nothing—just *because*, don't you know?' And Morgan had a queer little conscious lucid look. 'She did stay ever so long—as long as she could. She was only a poor girl. She used to send money to her mother. At last she couldn't afford it any longer, and went away in a fearful rage one night—I mean of course in a rage against *them*. She cried over me tremendously, she hugged me nearly to death. She told me all about it,' the boy repeated. 'She told me it was their idea. So I guessed, ever so long ago, that they have had the same idea with you.'

'Zénobie was very sharp,' said Pemberton. 'And she made you so.'

'Oh that wasn't Zénobie; that was nature. And experience!' Morgan laughed.

'Well, Zénobie was a part of your experience.'

'Certainly I was a part of hers, poor dear!' the boy wisely sighed. 'And I'm part of yours.'

'A very important part. But I don't see how you know I've been treated like Zénobie.'

'Do you take me for the biggest dunce you've known?' Morgan asked. 'Haven't I been conscious of what we've been through together?'

'What we've been through?'

'Our privations—our dark days.'

'Oh our days have been bright enough.'

Morgan went on in silence for a moment. Then he said: 'My dear chap, you're a hero!'

'Well, you're another!' Pemberton retorted.

'No I'm not, but I ain't a baby. I won't stand it any longer. You must get some occupation that pays. I'm ashamed, I'm ashamed!' quavered the boy with a ring of passion, like some high silver note from a small cathedral chorister, that deeply touched his friend.

'We ought to go off and live somewhere together,' the young man said.

'I'll go like a shot if you'll take me.'

'I'd get some work that would keep us both afloat,' Pemberton continued.

'So would I. Why shouldn't *I* work? I ain't such a beastly little muff as *that* comes to.'

'The difficulty is that your parents wouldn't hear of it. They'd never part with you; they worship the ground you tread on. Don't you see the proof of it?' Pemberton developed. 'They don't dislike me; they wish me no harm; they're very amiable people; but they're perfectly ready to expose me to any awkwardness in life for your sake.'

The silence in which Morgan received his fond sophistry struck Pemberton somehow as expressive. After a moment the child repeated: 'You *are* a hero!' Then he added: 'They leave me with you altogether. You've all the responsibility. They put me off on you from morning till night. Why then should they object to my taking up with you completely? I'd help you.'

'They're not particularly keen about my being helped, and they delight in thinking of you as *theirs*. They're tremendously proud of you.'

'I'm not proud of *them*. But you know that,' Morgan returned.

'Except for the little matter we speak of they're charming people,' said Pemberton, not taking up the point made for his intelligence, but wondering greatly at the boy's own, and especially at this fresh reminder of something he had been conscious of from the first—the strangest thing in his friend's large little composition, a temper, a sensibility, even a private ideal, which made him as privately disown the stuff his people were made of. Morgan had in secret a small loftiness which made him acute about betrayed meanness; as well as a critical sense for the manners immediately surrounding him that was quite without precedent in a juvenile nature, especially when one noted that it had not made this nature 'old-fashioned', as the word is of children—quaint or wizened or offensive. It was as if he had been a little gentleman and had paid the penalty by discovering that he was the only such person in his family. This comparison didn't make him vain, but it could make him melancholy and a trifle austere. While Pemberton guessed at these dim young things, shadows of shadows, he was partly drawn on and partly checked, as for a scruple, by the charm of attempting to sound the little cool shallows that were so quickly growing deeper. When he tried to figure to himself the morning twilight of childhood, so as to deal with it safely, he saw it was never fixed, never arrested, that ignorance, at the instant he touched it, was already flushing faintly into knowledge, that there was nothing that at a given moment you could say an intelligent child didn't know. It seemed to him that he himself knew too much to imagine Morgan's simplicity and too little to disembroil his tangle.

The boy paid no heed to his last remark; he only went on: 'I'd have spoken to them about their idea, as I call it, long ago, if I hadn't been sure what they'd say.'

'And what would they say?'

'Just what they said about what poor Zénobie told me—that it was a horrid dreadful story, that they had paid her every penny they owed her.'

'Well, perhaps they had,' said Pemberton.

'Perhaps they've paid you!'

'Let us pretend they have, and *n'en parlons plus*.'

'They accused her of lying and cheating'—Morgan stuck to historic truth. 'That's why I don't want to speak to them.'

'Lest they should accuse me too?' To this Morgan made no answer, and his companion, looking down at him—the boy turned away his eyes, which had filled—saw that he couldn't have trusted himself to utter. 'You're right. Don't worry them,' Pemberton pursued. 'Except for that, they *are* charming people.'

'Except for *their* lying and *their* cheating?'

'I say—I say!' cried Pemberton, imitating a little tone of the lad's which was itself an imitation.

'We must be frank, at the last; we *must* come to an understanding,' said Morgan with the importance of the small boy who lets himself think he is arranging great affairs—almost playing at shipwreck or at Indians. 'I know all about everything.'

'I dare say your father has his reasons,' Pemberton replied, but too vaguely, as he was aware.

'For lying and cheating?'

'For saving and managing and turning his means to the best account. He has plenty to do with his money. You're an expensive family.'

'Yes, I'm very expensive,' Morgan concurred in a manner that made his preceptor burst out laughing.

'He's saving for *you*,' said Pemberton. 'They think of you in everything they do.'

'He might, while he's about it, save a little—' The boy paused, and his friend waited to hear what. Then Morgan brought out oddly: 'A little reputation.'

'Oh there's plenty of that. That's all right!'

'Enough of it for the people they know, no doubt. The people they know are awful.'

'Do you mean the princes? We mustn't abuse the princes.'

'Why not? They haven't married Paula—they haven't married Amy. They only clean out Ulick.'

'You *do* know everything!' Pemberton declared.

'No I don't after all. I don't know what they live on, or how they live, or *why* they live! What have they got and how did they get it? Are they rich, are they poor, or have they a *modeste aisance*? Why are they always chivvying me about—living one year like ambassadors and the next like paupers? Who are they, anyway, and what are they? I've thought of all that—I've thought of a lot of things. They're so beastly worldly. That's what I hate most—oh I've *seen* it! All they care about is to make an appearance and to pass for something or other. What the dickens do they want to pass for? What *do* they, Mr Pemberton?'

'You pause for a reply,' said Pemberton, treating the question as a joke, yet wondering too and greatly struck with his mate's intense if imperfect vision. 'I haven't the least idea.'

'And what good does it do? Haven't I seen the way people treat them—the "nice" people, the ones they want to know? They'll take anything from them—they'll lie down and be trampled on. The nice ones hate that—they just sicken them. You're the only really nice person we know.'

'Are you sure? They don't lie down for me!'

'Well, you shan't lie down for them. You've got to go—that's what you've got to do,' said Morgan.

'And what will become of you?'

'Oh I'm growing up. I shall get off before long. I'll see you later.'

'You had better let me finish you,' Pemberton urged, lending himself to the child's strange superiority.

Morgan stopped in their walk, looking up at him. He had to look up much less than a couple of years before—he had grown, in his loose leanness, so long and high. 'Finish me?' he echoed.

'There are such a lot of jolly things we can do together yet. I want to turn you out—I want you to do me credit.'

Morgan continued to look at him. 'To give you credit—do you mean?'

'My dear fellow, you're too clever to live.'

'That's just what I'm afraid you think. No, no; it isn't fair—I can't endure it. We'll separate next week. The sooner it's over the sooner to sleep.'

'If I hear of anything—any other chance—I promise to go,' Pemberton said.

Morgan consented to consider this. 'But you'll be honest,' he demanded; 'you won't pretend you haven't heard?'

'I'm much more likely to pretend I have.'

'But what can you hear of, this way, stuck in a hole with us? You ought to be on the spot, to go to England—you ought to go to America.'

'One would think you were *my* tutor,' said Pemberton.

Morgan walked on and after a little had begun again: 'Well, now that you know I know and that we look at the facts and keep nothing back—it's much more comfortable, isn't it?'

'My dear boy, it's so amusing, so interesting, that it will surely be quite impossible for me to forego such hours as these.'

This made Morgan stop once more. 'You *do* keep something back. Oh you're not straight—*I* am!'

'How am I not straight?'

'Oh you've got your idea!'

'My idea?'

'Why that I probably shan't make old—make older—bones, and that you can stick it out till I'm removed.'

'You *are* too clever to live!' Pemberton repeated.

'I call it a mean idea,' Morgan pursued. 'But I shall punish you by the way I hang on.'

'Look out or I'll poison you!' Pemberton laughed.

'I'm stronger and better every year. Haven't you noticed that there hasn't been a doctor near me since you came?'

'*I'm* your doctor,' said the young man, taking his arm and drawing him tenderly on again.

Morgan proceeded and after a few steps gave a sigh of mingled weariness and relief. 'Ah now that we look at the facts it's all right!'

VII

They looked at the facts a good deal after this; and one of the first consequences of their doing so was that Pemberton stuck it out, in his friend's parlance, for the purpose. Morgan made the facts so vivid and so droll, and at the same time so bald and so ugly, that there was fascination in talking them over with him, just as there would have been heartlessness in leaving him alone with them. Now that the pair had such perceptions in common it was useless for them to pretend they didn't judge such people; but the very judgement and the exchange of perceptions created another tie. Morgan had never been so interesting as now that he himself was made plainer by the sidelight of these confidences. What came out in it most was the small fine passion of his pride. He had plenty of that, Pemberton felt—so much that one might perhaps wisely wish for it some early bruises. He would have liked his people to have a spirit and had waked up to the sense of their perpetually eating humble-pie. His mother would consume any amount, and his father would consume even more than his mother. He had a theory that Ulick had wriggled out of an 'affair' at Nice: there had once been a flurry at home, a regular panic, after which they all went to bed and took medicine, not to be accounted for on any other supposition. Morgan had a romantic imagination, fed by poetry and history, and he would have liked those who 'bore his name'—as he used to say to Pemberton with the humour that made his queer delicacies manly—to carry themselves with an air. But their one idea was to get in with people who didn't want them and to take snubs as if they were honourable scars. Why people didn't want them more he didn't know—that was people's own affair; after all they weren't superficially repulsive, they were a hundred times cleverer than most of the dreary grandees, the 'poor swells' they rushed about Europe to catch up with. 'After all they *are* amusing—they are!' he used to pronounce with the wisdom of the ages. To which Pemberton always replied: 'Amusing—the great Moreen troupe? Why they're altogether delightful; and if it weren't for the hitch that you and I (feeble performers!) make in the *ensemble* they'd carry everything before them.'

What the boy couldn't get over was the fact that this particular blight seemed, in a tradition of self-respect, so undeserved and so arbitrary. No doubt people had a right to take the line they liked; but why should *his* people have liked the line of pushing and toadying and lying and cheating? What had their forefathers—all decent folk, so far as he knew—done to them, or what had *he* done to them? Who had poisoned their blood with the fifth-rate social ideal, the fixed idea of making smart acquaintances and getting into the *monde chic*, especially when it was foredoomed to failure and exposure? They showed so what they were after; that was what made the people they wanted not want *them*. And never a wince for dignity, never a throb of shame at looking each other in the face, never any independence or resentment or disgust. If his father or his brother would only knock some one down once or twice a year! Clever as they were they never guessed the impression they made. They were good-natured, yes—as good-natured as Jews at the doors of clothing-shops! But was that the model one wanted one's family to follow? Morgan had dim memories of an old grandfather, the maternal, in New York, whom he had been taken across the ocean at the age of five to see: a gentleman with a high neck-cloth and a good deal of pronunciation, who wore a dress-coat in the morning, which made one wonder what he wore in the evening, and had, or was supposed to have, 'property' and something to do with the Bible Society. It couldn't have been but that *he* was a good type. Pemberton himself remembered Mrs Clancy, a widowed sister of Mr Moreen's, who was as irritating as a moral tale and had paid a fortnight's visit to the family at Nice shortly after he came to live with them. She was 'pure and refined', as Amy said over the banjo, and had the air of not knowing what they meant when they talked, and of keeping something rather important back. Pemberton judged that what she kept back was an approval of many of their ways; therefore it was to be supposed that she too was of a good type, and that Mr and Mrs Moreen and Ulick and Paula and Amy might easily have been of a better one if they would.

But that they wouldn't was more and more perceptible from day to day. They continued to 'chivvy', as Morgan called it, and in due time became aware of a variety of reasons for proceeding to Venice. They mentioned a great many of them—they were always strikingly frank and had the brightest friendly chatter, at the late foreign breakfast in especial, before the ladies had made up their faces, when they leaned their arms on the table, had something to follow the *demi-tasse*, and, in the heat of familiar discussion as to what they 'really ought' to do, fell inevitably into the languages in which they could *tutoyer*. Even Pemberton liked them then; he could endure even Ulick when he heard him give his little flat voice for the 'sweet sea-city'. That was what made him have a sneaking kindness for them—that they were so out of the workaday world and kept him so out of it. The summer had waned when, with cries of ecstasy, they all passed out on the balcony that overhung the Grand Canal. The sunsets then were splendid and the Dorringtons had arrived. The Dorringtons were the only reason they hadn't talked of at breakfast; but the reasons they didn't talk of at breakfast always came out in the end. The Dorringtons on the other hand came out very little; or else when they did they stayed—as was natural—for hours, during which periods Mrs Moreen and the girls sometimes called at their hotel (to see if they had returned) as many as three times running. The gondola was for the ladies, as in Venice too there were 'days', which Mrs Moreen knew in their order an hour after she arrived. She immediately took one herself, to which the Dorringtons never came, though on a certain occasion when Pemberton and his pupil were together at Saint Mark's—where, taking the best walks they had ever had and haunting a hundred churches, they spent a great deal of time—they saw the old lord turn up with Mr Moreen and Ulick, who showed him the dim basilica as if it belonged to them. Pemberton noted how much less, among its curiosities, Lord Dorrington carried himself as a man of the world; wondering too whether, for such services, his companions took a fee from him. The autumn at any rate waned, the Dorringtons departed, and Lord Verschoyle, the eldest son, had proposed neither for Amy nor for Paula.

One sad November day, while the wind roared round the old palace and the rain lashed the lagoon, Pemberton, for exercise and even somewhat for warmth—the Moreens were horribly frugal about fires; it was a cause of suffering to their inmate—walked up and down the big bare sala with his pupil. The scagliola floor was cold, the high battered casements shook in the storm, and the stately decay of the place was unrelieved by a particle of furniture. Pemberton's spirits were low, and it came over him that the fortune of the Moreens was now even lower. A blast of desolation, a portent of disgrace and disaster, seemed to draw through the comfortless hall. Mr Moreen and Ulick were in the Piazza, looking out for something, strolling drearily, in mackintoshes, under the arcades; but still, in spite of mackintoshes, unmistakable men of the world. Paula and Amy were in bed—it might have been thought they were staying there to keep warm. Pemberton looked askance at the boy at his side, to see to what extent he was conscious of these dark omens. But Morgan, luckily for him, was now mainly conscious of growing taller and stronger and indeed of being in his fifteenth year. This fact was intensely interesting to him and the basis of a private theory—which, however, he had imparted to his tutor—that in a little while he should stand on his own feet. He considered that the situation would change—that in short he should be 'finished', grown up, producible in the world of affairs and ready to prove himself of sterling ability. Sharply as he was capable at times of analysing, as he called it, his life, there were happy hours when he remained, as he also called it—'jolly' superficial; the proof of which was his fundamental assumption that he should presently go to Oxford, to Pemberton's college, and aided and abetted by Pemberton, do the most wonderful things. It depressed the young man to see how little in such a project he took account of ways and means: in other connexions he mostly kept to the measure. Pemberton tried to imagine the Moreens at Oxford and fortunately failed; yet unless they were to adopt it as a residence there would be no *modus vivendi* for Morgan. How could he live without an allowance, and where was the allowance to come from? He, Pemberton, might live on Morgan; but how could Morgan live on *him*? What was to become of him anyhow? Somehow the fact that he was a big boy now, with better prospects of health, made the question of his future more difficult. So long as he was markedly frail the great consideration he inspired seemed enough of an answer to it. But at the bottom of Pemberton's heart was the recognition of his probably being strong enough to live and not yet strong enough to struggle or to thrive. Morgan himself at any rate was in the first flush of the rosiest consciousness of adolescence, so that the beating of the tempest seemed to him after all but the voice of life and the challenge of fate. He had on his shabby little overcoat, with the collar up, but was enjoying his walk.

It was interrupted at last by the appearance of his mother at the end of the sala. She beckoned him to come to her, and while Pemberton saw him, complaisant, pass down the long vista and over the damp false marble, he wondered what was in the air. Mrs Moreen said a word to the boy and made him go into the room she had quitted. Then, having closed the door after him, she directed her steps swiftly to Pemberton. There *was* something in the air, but his wildest flight of fancy wouldn't have suggested what it proved to be. She signified that she had made a pretext to get Morgan out of the way, and then she enquired—without hesitation—if the young man could favour her with the loan of three louis. While, before bursting into a laugh, he stared at her with surprise, she declared that she was awfully pressed for the money; she was desperate for it—it would save her life.

'Dear lady, *c'est trop fort*!' Pemberton laughed in the manner and with the borrowed grace of idiom that marked the best colloquial, the best anecdotic, moments of his friends themselves. 'Where in the world do you suppose I should get three louis, *du train dont vous allez*?'

'I thought you worked—wrote things. Don't they pay you?'

'Not a penny.'

'Are you such a fool as to work for nothing?'

'You ought surely to know that.'

Mrs Moreen stared, then she coloured a little. Pemberton saw she had quite forgotten the terms—if 'terms' they could be called—that he had ended by accepting from herself; they had burdened her memory as little as her conscience. 'Oh yes, I see what you mean—you've been very nice about that; but why drag it in so often?' She had been perfectly urbane with him ever since the rough scene of explanation in his room the morning he made her accept *his* 'terms'—the necessity of his making his case known to Morgan. She had felt no resentment after seeing there was no danger Morgan would take the matter up with her. Indeed, attributing this immunity to the good taste of his influence with the boy, she had once said to Pemberton 'My dear fellow, it's an immense comfort you're a gentleman.' She repeated this in substance now. 'Of course you're a gentleman—that's a bother the less!' Pemberton reminded her that he had not 'dragged in' anything that wasn't already in as much as his foot was in his shoe; and she also repeated her prayer that, somewhere and somehow, he would find her sixty francs. He took the liberty of hinting that if he could find them it wouldn't be to lend them to *her*—as to which he consciously did himself injustice, knowing that if he had them he would certainly put them at her disposal. He accused himself, at bottom and not unveraciously, of a fantastic, a demoralized sympathy with her. If misery made strange bedfellows it also made strange sympathies. It was moreover a part of the abasement of living with such people that one had to make vulgar retorts, quite out of one's own tradition of good manners. 'Morgan, Morgan, to what pass have I come for you?' he groaned while Mrs Moreen floated voluminously down the *sala* again to liberate the boy, wailing as she went that everything was too odious.

Before their young friend was liberated there came a thump at the door communicating with the staircase, followed by the apparition of a dripping youth who poked in his head. Pemberton recognised him as the bearer of a telegram and recognized the telegram as addressed to himself. Morgan came back as, after glancing at the signature—that of a relative in London—he was reading the words: 'Found jolly job for you, engagement to coach opulent youth on own terms. Come at once.' The answer happily was paid and the messenger waited. Morgan, who had drawn near, waited too and looked hard at Pemberton; and Pemberton, after a moment, having met his look, handed him the telegram. It was really by wise looks—they knew each other so well now—that, while the telegraph-boy, in his waterproof cape, made a great puddle on the floor, the thing was settled between them. Pemberton wrote the answer with a pencil against the frescoed wall, and the messenger departed. When he was gone the young man explained himself.

'I'll make a tremendous charge; I'll earn a lot of money in a short time, and we'll live on it.'

'Well, I hope the opulent youth will be a dismal dunce—he probably will,' Morgan parenthesized—'and keep you a long time a-hammering of it in.'

'Of course the longer he keeps me the more we shall have for our old age.'

'But suppose *they* don't pay you!' Morgan awfully suggested.

'Oh there are not two such—!' But Pemberton pulled up; he had been on the point of using too invidious a term. Instead of this he said 'Two such fatalities.'

Morgan flushed—the tears came to his eyes. '*Dites toujours* two such rascally crews!' Then in a different tone he added: 'Happy opulent youth!'

'Not if he's a dismal dunce.'

'Oh they're happier then. But you can't have everything, can you?' the boy smiled.

Pemberton held him fast, hands on his shoulders—he had never loved him so. 'What will become of *you*, what will you do?' He thought of Mrs Moreen, desperate for sixty francs.

'I shall become an *homme fait*.' And then as if he recognized all the bearings of Pemberton's allusion: 'I shall get on with them better when you're not here.'

'Ah don't say that—it sounds as if I set you against them!'

'You do—the sight of you. It's all right; you know what I mean. I shall be beautiful. I'll take their affairs in hand; I'll marry my sisters.'

'You'll marry yourself!' joked Pemberton; as high, rather tense pleasantry would evidently be the right, or the safest, tone for their separation.

It was, however, not purely in this strain that Morgan suddenly asked: 'But I say—how will you get to your jolly job? You'll have to telegraph to the opulent youth for money to come on.'

Pemberton bethought himself. 'They won't like that, will they?'

'Oh look out for them!'

Then Pemberton brought out his remedy. 'I'll go to the American Consul; I'll borrow some money of him—just for the few days, on the strength of the telegram.'

Morgan was hilarious. 'Show him the telegram—then collar the money and stay!'

Pemberton entered into the joke sufficiently to reply that for Morgan he was really capable of that; but the boy, growing more serious, and to prove he hadn't meant what he said, not only hurried him off to the Consulate—since he was to start that evening, as he had wired to his friend—but made sure of their affair by going with him. They splashed through the tortuous perforations and over the humpbacked bridges, and they passed through the Piazza, where they saw Mr Moreen and Ulick go into a jeweller's shop. The Consul proved accommodating—Pemberton said it wasn't the letter, but Morgan's grand air—and on their way back they went into Saint Mark's for a hushed ten minutes. Later they took up and kept up the fun of it to the very end; and it seemed to Pemberton a part of that fun that Mrs Moreen, who was very angry when he had announced her his intention, should charge him, grotesquely and vulgarly and in reference to the loan she had vainly endeavoured to effect, with bolting lest they should 'get something out' of him. On the other hand he had to do Mr Moreen and Ulick the justice to recognize that when on coming in *they* heard the cruel news they took it like perfect men of the world.

VIII

When he got at work with the opulent youth, who was to be taken in hand for Balliol, he found himself unable to say if his aspirant had really such poor parts or if the appearance were only begotten of his own long association with an intensely living little mind. From Morgan he heard half a dozen times: the boy wrote charming young letters, a patchwork of tongues, with indulgent postscripts in the family Volapuk and, in little squares and rounds and crannies of the text, the drollest illustrations—letters that he was divided between the impulse to show his present charge as a vain, a wasted incentive, and the sense of something in them that publicity would profane. The opulent youth went up in due course and failed to pass; but it seemed to add to the presumption that brilliancy was not expected of him all at once that his parents, condoning the lapse, which they good-naturedly treated as little as possible as if it were Pemberton's, should have sounded the rally again, begged the young coach to renew the siege.

The young coach was now in a position to lend Mrs Moreen three louis, and he sent her a post-office order even for a larger amount. In return for this favour he received a frantic scribbled line from her: 'Implore you to come back instantly—Morgan dreadfully ill.' They were on the rebound, once more in Paris—often as Pemberton had seen them depressed he had never seen them crushed—and communication was therefore rapid. He wrote to the boy to ascertain the state of his health, but awaited the answer in vain. He accordingly, after three days, took an abrupt leave of the opulent youth and, crossing the Channel, alighted at the small hotel, in the quarter of the Champs Elysées, of which Mrs Moreen had given him the address. A deep if dumb dissatisfaction with this lady and her companions bore him company: they couldn't be vulgarly honest, but they could live at hotels, in velvety *entresols*, amid a smell of burnt pastilles, surrounded by the most expensive city in Europe. When he had left them in Venice it was with an irrepressible suspicion that something was going to happen; but the only thing that could have taken place was again their masterly retreat. 'How is he? where is he?' he asked of Mrs Moreen; but before she could speak these questions were answered by the pressure round his neck of a pair of arms, in shrunken sleeves, which still were perfectly capable of an effusive young foreign squeeze.

'Dreadfully ill—I don't see it!' the young man cried. And then to Morgan: 'Why on earth didn't you relieve me? Why didn't you answer my letter?'

Mrs Moreen declared that when she wrote he was very bad, and Pemberton learned at the same time from the boy that he had answered every letter he had received. This led to the clear inference that

Pemberton's note had been kept from him so that the game to be practised should not be interfered with. Mrs Moreen was prepared to see the fact exposed, as Pemberton saw the moment he faced her that she was prepared for a good many other things. She was prepared above all to maintain that she had acted from a sense of duty, that she was enchanted she had got him over, whatever they might say, and that it was useless of him to pretend he didn't know in all his bones that his place at such a time was with Morgan. He had taken the boy away from them and now had no right to abandon him. He had created for himself the gravest responsibilities and must at least abide by what he had done.

'Taken him away from you?' Pemberton exclaimed indignantly.

'Do it—do it for pity's sake; that's just what I want. I can't stand *this*—and such scenes. They're awful frauds—poor dears!' These words broke from Morgan, who had intermitted his embrace, in a key which made Pemberton turn quickly to him and see that he had suddenly seated himself, was breathing in great pain and was very pale.

'*Now* do you say he's not in a state, my precious pet?' shouted his mother, dropping on her knees before him with clasped hands, but touching him no more than if he had been a gilded idol. 'It will pass—it's only for an instant; but don't say such dreadful things!'

'I'm all right—all right,' Morgan panted to Pemberton, whom he sat looking up at with a strange smile, his hands resting on either side of the sofa.

'Now do you pretend I've been dishonest, that I've deceived?' Mrs Moreen flashed at Pemberton as she got up.

'It isn't *he* says it, it's I!' the boy returned, apparently easier but sinking back against the wall; while his restored friend, who had sat down beside him, took his hand and bent over him.

'Darling child, one does what one can; there are so many things to consider,' urged Mrs Moreen. 'It's his *place*—his only place. You see *you* think it is now.'

'Take me away—take me away,' Morgan went on, smiling to Pemberton with his white face.

'Where shall I take you, and how—oh *how*, my boy?' the young man stammered, thinking of the rude way in which his friends in London held that, for his convenience, with no assurance of prompt return, he had thrown them over; of the just resentment with which they would already have called in a successor, and of the scant help in finding fresh employment that resided for him in the grossness of his having failed to pass his pupil.

'Oh we'll settle that. You used to talk about it,' said Morgan. 'If we can only go all the rest's a detail.'

'Talk about it as much as you like, but don't think you can attempt it. Mr Moreen would never consent—it would be so *very* hand-to-mouth,' Pemberton's hostess beautifully explained to him. Then to Morgan she made it clearer: 'It would destroy our peace, it would break our hearts. Now that he's back it will be all the same again. You'll have your life, your work and your freedom, and we'll all be happy as we used to be. You'll bloom and grow perfectly well, and we won't have any more silly experiments, will we? They're too absurd. It's Mr Pemberton's place—every one in his place. You in yours, your papa in his, me in mine—*n'est-ce pas, chéri*? We'll all forget how foolish we've been and have lovely times.'

She continued to talk and to surge vaguely about the little draped stuffy salon while Pemberton sat with the boy, whose colour gradually came back; and she mixed up her reasons, hinting that there were going to be changes, that the other children might scatter (who knew?—Paula had her ideas) and that then it might be fancied how much the poor old parent-birds would want the little nestling. Morgan looked at Pemberton, who wouldn't let him move; and Pemberton knew exactly how he felt at hearing himself called a little nestling. He admitted that he had had one or two bad days, but he protested afresh against the wrong of his mother's having made them the ground of an appeal to poor Pemberton. Poor Pemberton could laugh now, apart from the comicality of Mrs Moreen's mustering so much philosophy for her defence—she seemed to shake it out of her agitated petticoats, which knocked over the light gilt chairs—so little did their young companion, *marked*, unmistakably marked at the best, strike him as qualified to repudiate any advantage.

He himself was in for it at any rate. He should have Morgan on his hands again indefinitely; though indeed he saw the lad had a private theory to produce which would be intended to smooth this down. He was obliged to him for it in advance; but the suggested amendment didn't keep his heart rather from sinking, any more than it prevented him from accepting the prospect on the spot, with some confidence moreover that he should do so even better if he could have a little supper. Mrs Moreen threw out more hints about the changes that were to be looked for, but she was such a mixture of smiles and shudders—she confessed she was very nervous—that he couldn't tell if she were in high feather or only in hysterics. If the family was really at last going to pieces why shouldn't she recognize the necessity of pitching Morgan into some sort of lifeboat? This presumption was fostered by the fact that they were established in luxurious quarters in the capital of pleasure; that was exactly where they naturally *would* be established in view of going to pieces. Moreover didn't she mention that Mr Moreen and the others were enjoying themselves at the opera with Mr Granger, and wasn't *that* also precisely where one would look for them on the eve of a smash? Pemberton gathered that Mr Granger was a rich vacant American—a big bill with a flourishy heading and no items; so that one of Paula's 'ideas' was probably that this time she hadn't missed fire—by which straight shot indeed she would have shattered the general cohesion. And if the cohesion was to crumble what would become of poor Pemberton? He felt quite enough bound up with them to figure to his alarm as a dislodged block in the edifice.

It was Morgan who eventually asked if no supper had been ordered for him; sitting with him below, later, at the dim delayed meal, in the presence of a great deal of corded green plush, a plate of ornamental biscuit and an aloofness marked on the part of the waiter. Mrs Moreen had explained that they had been obliged to secure a room for the visitor out of the house; and Morgan's consolation—he offered it while Pemberton reflected on the nastiness of luke-warm sauces—proved to be, largely, that this circumstance would facilitate their escape. He talked of their escape—recurring to it often afterwards—as if they were making up a 'boy's book' together. But he likewise expressed his sense that there was something in the air, that the Moreens couldn't keep it up much longer. In point of fact, as Pemberton was to see, they kept it up for five or six months. All the while, however, Morgan's contention was designed to cheer him. Mr Moreen and Ulick, whom he had met the day after his return, accepted that return like perfect men of the world. If Paula and Amy treated it even with less formality an allowance was to be made for them, inasmuch as Mr Granger hadn't come to the opera after all. He had only placed his box at their service, with a bouquet for each of the party; there was even one apiece, embittering the thought of his profusion, for Mr Moreen and Ulick. 'They're all like that,' was Morgan's comment; 'at the very last, just when we think we've landed them they're back in the deep sea!'

Morgan's comments in these days were more and more free; they even included a large recognition of the extraordinary tenderness with which he had been treated while Pemberton was away. Oh yes, they couldn't do enough to be nice to him, to show him they had him on their mind and make up for his loss. That was just what made the whole thing so sad and caused him to rejoice after all in Pemberton's return—he had to keep thinking of their affection less, had less sense of obligation. Pemberton laughed out at this last reason, and Morgan blushed and said 'Well, dash it, you know what I mean.' Pemberton knew perfectly what he meant; but there were a good many things that—dash it too!—it didn't make any clearer. This episode of his second sojourn in Paris stretched itself out wearily, with their resumed readings and wanderings and maunderings, their potterings on the quays, their hauntings of the museums, their occasional lingerings in the Palais Royal when the first sharp weather came on and there was a comfort in warm emanations, before Chevet's wonderful succulent window. Morgan wanted to hear all about the opulent youth—he took an immense interest in him. Some of the details of his opulence—Pemberton could spare him none of them—evidently fed the boy's appreciation of all his friend had given up to come back to him; but in addition to the greater reciprocity established by that heroism he had always his little brooding theory, in which there was a frivolous gaiety too, that their long probation was drawing to a close. Morgan's conviction that the Moreens couldn't go on much longer kept pace with the unexpended impetus with which, from month to month, they did go on. Three weeks after Pemberton had rejoined them they went on to another hotel, a dingier one than the first; but Morgan rejoiced that his tutor had at least still not sacrificed the advantage of a room outside. He clung to the romantic utility of this when the day, or rather the night, should arrive for their escape.

For the first time, in this complicated connexion, our friend felt his collar gall him. It was, as he had said to Mrs Moreen in Venice, *trop fort*—everything was *trop fort*. He could neither really throw off his blighting burden nor find in it the benefit of a pacific conscience or of a rewarded affection. He had spent all the money accruing to him in England, and he saw his youth going and that he was getting nothing back for it. It was all very well of Morgan to count it for reparation that he should now settle on him permanently—there was an irritating flaw in such a view. He saw what the boy had in his mind; the conception that as his friend had had the generosity to come back he must show his gratitude by giving him his life. But the poor friend didn't desire the gift—what could he do with Morgan's dreadful little life? Of course at the same time that Pemberton was irritated he remembered the reason, which was very honourable to Morgan and which dwelt simply in his making one so forget that he was no more than a patched urchin. If one dealt with him on a different basis one's misadventures were one's own fault. So Pemberton waited in a queer confusion of yearning and alarm for the catastrophe which was held to hang over the house of Moreen, of which he certainly at moments felt the symptoms brush his cheek and as to which he wondered much in what form it would find its liveliest effect.

Perhaps it would take the form of sudden dispersal—a frightened *sauve qui peut*, a scuttling into selfish corners. Certainly they were less elastic than of yore; they were evidently looking for something they didn't find. The Dorringtons hadn't re-appeared, the princes had scattered; wasn't that the beginning of the end? Mrs Moreen had lost her reckoning of the famous 'days'; her social calendar was blurred—it had turned its face to the wall. Pemberton suspected that the great, the cruel discomfiture had been the unspeakable behaviour of Mr Granger, who seemed not to know what he wanted, or, what was much worse, what *they* wanted. He kept sending flowers, as if to bestrew the path of his retreat, which was never the path of a return. Flowers were all very well, but—Pemberton could complete the proposition. It was now positively conspicuous that in the long run the Moreens were a social failure; so that the young man was almost grateful the fun had not been short. Mr Moreen indeed was still occasionally able to get away on business and, what was more surprising, was likewise able to get back. Ulick had no club, but you couldn't have discovered it from his appearance, which was as much as ever that of a person looking at life from the window of such an institution; therefore Pemberton was doubly surprised at an answer he once heard him make his mother in the desperate tone of a man familiar with the worst privations.

Her question Pemberton had not quite caught; it appeared to be an appeal for a suggestion as to whom they might get to take Amy. 'Let the Devil take her!' Ulick snapped; so that Pemberton could see that they had not only lost their amiability but had ceased to believe in themselves. He could also see that if Mrs Moreen was trying to get people to take her children she might be regarded as closing the hatches for the storm. But Morgan would be the last she would part with.

One winter afternoon—it was a Sunday—he and the boy walked far together in the Bois de Boulogne. The evening was so splendid, the cold lemon-coloured sunset so clear, the stream of carriages and pedestrians so amusing and the fascination of Paris so great, that they stayed out later than usual and became aware that they should have to hurry home to arrive in time for dinner. They hurried accordingly, arm-in-arm, good-humoured and hungry, agreeing that there was nothing like Paris after all and that after everything too that had come and gone they were not yet sated with innocent pleasures. When they reached the hotel they found that, though scandalously late, they were in time for all the dinner they were likely to sit down to. Confusion reigned in the apartments of the Moreens—very shabby ones this time, but the best in the house—and before the interrupted service of the table, with objects displaced almost as if there had been a scuffle and a great wine-stain from an overturned bottle, Pemberton couldn't blink the fact that there had been a scene of the last proprietary firmness. The storm had come—they were all seeking refuge. The hatches were down, Paula and Amy were invisible—they had never tried the most casual art upon Pemberton, but he felt they had enough of an eye to him not to wish to meet him as young ladies whose frocks had been confiscated—and Ulick appeared to have jumped overboard. The host and his staff, in a word, had ceased to 'go on' at the pace of their guests, and the air of embarrassed detention, thanks to a pile of gaping trunks in the passage, was strangely commingled with the air of indignant withdrawal.

When Morgan took all this in—and he took it in very quickly—he coloured to the roots of his hair. He had walked from his infancy among difficulties and dangers, but he had never seen a public exposure. Pemberton noticed in a second glance at him that the tears had rushed into his eyes and that they were tears of a new and untasted bitterness. He wondered an instant, for the boy's sake, whether he might successfully pretend not to understand. Not successfully, he felt, as Mr and Mrs Moreen, dinnerless by their extinguished hearth, rose before him in their little dishonoured salon, casting about with glassy eyes for the nearest port in such a storm. They were not prostrate but were horribly white, and Mrs Moreen had evidently been crying. Pemberton quickly learned however that her grief was not for the loss of her dinner, much as she usually enjoyed it, but the fruit of a blow that struck even deeper, as she made all haste to explain. He would see for himself, so far as that went, how the great change had come, the dreadful bolt had fallen, and how they would now all have to turn themselves about. Therefore cruel as it was to them to part with their darling she must look to him to carry a little further the influence he had so fortunately acquired with the boy—to induce his young charge to follow him into some modest retreat. They depended on him—that was the fact—to take their delightful child temporarily under his protection: it would leave Mr Moreen and herself so much more free to give the proper attention (too little, alas! had been given) to the readjustment of their affairs.

'We trust you—we feel we *can*,' said Mrs Moreen, slowly rubbing her plump white hands and looking with compunction hard at Morgan, whose chin, not to take liberties, her husband stroked with a tentative paternal forefinger.

'Oh yes—we feel that we *can*. We trust Mr Pemberton fully, Morgan,' Mr Moreen pursued.

Pemberton wondered again if he might pretend not to understand; but everything good gave way to the intensity of Morgan's understanding. 'Do you mean he may take me to live with him for ever and ever?' cried the boy. 'May take me away, away, anywhere he likes?'

'For ever and ever? *Comme vous-y-allez*!' Mr Moreen laughed indulgently. 'For as long as Mr Pemberton may be so good.'

'We've struggled, we've suffered,' his wife went on; 'but you've made him so your own that we've already been through the worst of the sacrifice.'

Morgan had turned away from his father—he stood looking at Pemberton with a light in his face. His sense of shame for their common humiliated state had dropped; the case had another side—the thing was to clutch at *that*. He had a moment of boyish joy, scarcely mitigated by the reflexion that with this unexpected consecration of his hope—too sudden and too violent; the turn taken was away from a *good* boy's book—the 'escape' was left on their hands. The boyish joy was there an instant, and Pemberton was almost scared at the rush of gratitude and affection that broke through his first abasement. When he stammered 'My dear fellow, what do you say to *that*?' how could one not say something enthusiastic? But there was more need for courage at something else that immediately followed and that made the lad sit down quickly on the nearest chair. He had turned quite livid and had raised his hand to his left side. They were all three looking at him, but Mrs Moreen suddenly bounded forward. 'Ah his darling little heart!' she broke out; and this time, on her knees before him and without respect for the idol, she caught him ardently in her arms. 'You walked him too far, you hurried him too fast!' she hurled over her shoulder at Pemberton. Her son made no protest, and the next instant, still holding him, she sprang up with her face convulsed and with the terrified cry 'Help, help! he's going, he's gone!' Pemberton saw with equal horror, by Morgan's own stricken face, that he was beyond their wildest recall. He pulled him half out of his mother's hands, and for a moment, while they held him together, they looked all their dismay into each other's eyes. 'He couldn't stand it with his weak organ,' said Pemberton—'the shock, the whole scene, the violent emotion.'

'But I thought he *wanted* to go to you!' wailed Mrs Moreen.

'I *told* you he didn't, my dear,' her husband made answer. Mr Moreen was trembling all over and was in his way as deeply affected as his wife. But after the very first he took his bereavement as a man of the world.

1891

The Beast in the Jungle

I

What determined the speech that startled him in the course of their encounter scarcely matters, being probably but some words spoken by himself quite without intention—spoken as they lingered and slowly moved together after their renewal of acquaintance. He had been conveyed by friends an hour or two before to the house at which she was staying; the party of visitors at the other house, of whom he was one, and thanks to whom it was his theory, as always, that he was lost in the crowd, had been invited over to luncheon. There had been after luncheon much dispersal, all in the interest of the original motive, a view of Weatherend itself and the fine things, intrinsic features, pictures, heirlooms, treasures of all the arts, that made the place almost famous; and the great rooms were so numerous that guests could wander at their will, hang back from the principal group and in cases where they took such matters with the last seriousness give themselves up to mysterious appreciations and measurements. There were persons to be observed, singly or in couples, bending toward objects in out-of-the-way corners with their hands on their knees and their heads nodding quite as with the emphasis of an excited sense of smell. When they were two they either mingled their sounds of ecstasy or melted into silences of even deeper import, so that there were aspects of the occasion that gave it for Marcher much the air of the 'look round', previous to a sale highly advertised, that excites or quenches, as may be, the dream of acquisition. The dream of acquisition at Weatherend would have had to be wild indeed, and John Marcher found himself, among such suggestions, disconcerted almost equally by the presence of those who knew too much and by that of those who knew nothing. The great rooms caused so much poetry and history to press upon him that he needed some straying apart to feel in a proper relation with them, though this impulse was not, as happened, like the gloating of some of his companions, to be compared to the movements of a dog sniffing a cupboard. It had an issue promptly enough in a direction that was not to have been calculated.

It led, briefly, in the course of the October afternoon, to his closer meeting with May Bartram, whose face, a reminder, yet not quite a remembrance, as they sat much separated at a very long table, had begun merely by troubling him rather pleasantly. It affected him as the sequel of something of which he had lost the beginning. He knew it, and for the time quite welcomed it, as a continuation, but didn't know what it continued, which was an interest or an amusement the greater as he was also somehow aware—yet without a direct sign from her—that the young woman herself hadn't lost the thread. She hadn't lost it, but she wouldn't give it back to him, he saw, without some putting forth of his hand for it; and he not only saw that, but saw several things more, things odd enough in the light of the fact that at the moment some accident of grouping brought them face to face he was still merely fumbling with the idea that any contact between them in the past would have had no importance. If it had had no importance he scarcely knew why his actual impression of her should so seem to have so much; the answer to which, however, was that in such a life as they all appeared to be leading for the moment one could but take things as they came. He was satisfied, without in the least being able to say why, that this young lady might roughly have ranked in the house as a poor relation; satisfied also that she was not there on a brief visit, but was more or less a part of the establishment—almost a working, a remunerated part. Didn't she enjoy at periods a protection that she paid for by helping, among other services, to show the place and explain it, deal with the tiresome people, answer questions about the dates of the building, the styles of the furniture, the authorship of the pictures, the favourite haunts of the ghost? It wasn't that she looked as if you could have given her shillings—it was impossible to look less so. Yet when she finally drifted toward him, distinctly handsome, though ever so much older—older than when he had seen her before—it might have been as an effect of her guessing that he had, within the couple of hours, devoted more imagination to her than to all the others put together, and had thereby penetrated to a kind of truth that the others were too stupid for. She *was* there on harder terms than any one; she was there as a consequence of things suffered, one way and another, in the interval of years; and she remembered him very much as she was remembered—only a good deal better.

By the time they at last thus came to speech they were alone in one of the rooms—remarkable for a fine portrait over the chimney-place—out of which their friends had passed, and the charm of it was that even before they had spoken they had practically arranged with each other to stay behind for talk. The charm, happily, was in other things too—partly in there being scarce a spot at Weatherend without something to stay behind for. It was in the way the autumn day looked into the high windows as it waned; the way the red light, breaking at the close from under a low sombre sky, reached out in a long shaft and played over old wainscots, old tapestry, old gold, old colour. It was most of all perhaps in the way she came to him as if, since she had been turned on to deal with the simpler sort, he might, should he choose to keep the whole thing down, just take her mild attention for a part of her general business. As soon as he heard her voice, however, the gap was filled up and the missing link supplied; the slight irony he divined in her attitude lost its advantage. He almost jumped at it to get there before her. 'I met you years and years ago in Rome. I remember all about it.' She confessed to disappointment—she had been so sure he didn't; and to prove how well he did he began to pour forth the particular recollections that popped up as he called for them. Her face and her voice, all at his service now, worked the miracle—the impression operating like the torch of a lamplighter who touches into flame, one by one, a long row of gas-jets. Marcher flattered himself the illumination was brilliant, yet he was really still more pleased on her showing him, with amusement, that in his haste to make everything right he had got most things rather wrong. It hadn't been at Rome—it had been at Naples; and it hadn't been eight years before—it had been more nearly ten. She hadn't been, either, with her uncle and aunt, but with her mother and her brother; in addition to which it was not with the Pembles *he* had been, but with the Boyers, coming down in their company from Rome—a point on which she insisted, a little to his confusion, and as to which she had her evidence in hand. The Boyers she had known, but didn't know the Pembles, though she had heard of them, and it was the people he was with who had made them acquainted. The incident of the thunderstorm that had raged round them with such violence as to drive them for refuge into an excavation—this incident had not occurred at the Palace of the Cæsars, but at Pompeii, on an occasion when they had been present there at an important find.

He accepted her amendments, he enjoyed her corrections, though the moral of them was, she pointed out, that he *really* didn't remember the least thing about her; and he only felt it as a drawback that when all was made strictly historic there didn't appear much of anything left. They lingered together still, she neglecting her office—for from the moment he was so clever she had no proper right to him—and both neglecting the house, just waiting as to see if a memory or two more wouldn't again breathe on them. It hadn't taken them many minutes, after all, to put down on the table, like the cards of a pack, those that constituted their respective hands; only what came out was that the pack was unfortunately not perfect—that the past, invoked, invited, encouraged, could give them, naturally, no more than it had. It had made them anciently meet—her at twenty, him at twenty-five; but nothing was so strange, they seemed to say to each other, as that, while so occupied, it hadn't done a little more for them. They looked at each other as with the feeling of an occasion missed; the present would have been so much better if the other, in the far distance, in the foreign land, hadn't been so stupidly meagre. There weren't apparently, all counted, more than a dozen little old things that had succeeded in coming to pass between them; trivialities of youth, simplicities of freshness, stupidities of ignorance, small possible germs, but too deeply buried—too deeply (didn't it seem?) to sprout after so many years. Marcher could only feel he ought to have rendered her some service—saved her from a capsized boat in the Bay or at least recovered her dressing-bag, filched from her cab in the streets of Naples by a lazzarone with a stiletto. Or it would have been nice if he could have been taken with fever all alone at his hotel, and she could have come to look after him, to write to his people, to drive him out in convalescence. *Then* they would be in possession of the something or other that their actual show seemed to lack. It yet somehow presented itself, this show, as too good to be spoiled; so that they were reduced for a few minutes more to wondering a little helplessly why—since they seemed to know a certain number of the same people—their reunion had been so long averted. They didn't use that name for it, but their delay from minute to minute to join the others was a kind of confession that they didn't quite want it to be a failure. Their attempted supposition of reasons for their not having met but showed how little they knew of each other. There came in fact a moment when Marcher felt a positive pang. It was vain to pretend she was an old friend, for all the communities were wanting, in spite of which it was as an old friend that he saw she would have suited him. He had new ones enough—was surrounded with them for instance on the stage of the other house; as a new one he probably wouldn't have so much as noticed her. He would have liked to invent something, get her to make-believe with him that some passage of a romantic or critical kind *had* originally occurred. He was really almost reaching out in imagination—as against time—for something that would do, and saying to himself that if it didn't come this sketch of a fresh start would show for quite awkwardly bungled. They would separate, and now for no second or no third chance. They would have tried and not succeeded. Then it was, just at the turn, as he afterwards made it out to himself, that, everything else failing, she herself decided to take up the case and, as it were, save the situation. He felt as soon as she spoke that she had been consciously keeping back what she said and hoping to get on without it; a scruple in her that immensely touched him when, by the end of three or four minutes more, he was able to measure it. What she brought out, at any rate, quite cleared the air and supplied the link—the link it was so odd he should frivolously have managed to lose.

'You know you told me something I've never forgotten and that again and again has made me think of you since; it was that tremendously hot day when we went to Sorrento, across the bay, for the breeze. What I allude to was what you said to me, on the way back, as we sat under the awning of the boat enjoying the cool. Have you forgotten?'

He had forgotten and was even more surprised than ashamed. But the great thing was that he saw in this no vulgar reminder of any 'sweet' speech. The vanity of women had long memories, but she was making no claim on him of a compliment or a mistake. With another woman, a totally different one, he might have feared the recall possibly even of some imbecile 'offer'. So, in having to say that he had indeed forgotten, he was conscious rather of a loss than a gain; he already saw an interest in the matter of her mention. 'I try to think—but I give it up. Yet I remember the Sorrento day.'

'I'm not very sure you do,' May Bartram after a moment said; 'and I'm not very sure I ought to want you to. It's dreadful to bring a person back at any time to what he was ten years before. If you've lived away from it,' she smiled, 'so much the better.'

'Ah if *you* haven't why should I?' he asked.

'Lived away, you mean, from what I myself was?'

'From what *I* was. I was of course an ass,' Marcher went on; 'but I would rather know from you just the sort of ass I was than—from the moment you have something in your mind—not know anything.'

Still, however, she hesitated. 'But if you've completely ceased to be that sort—?'

'Why I can then all the more bear to know. Besides, perhaps I haven't.'

'Perhaps. Yet if you haven't,' she added, 'I should suppose you'd remember. Not indeed that *I* in the least connect with my impression the invidious name you use. If I had only thought you foolish,' she explained, 'the thing I speak of wouldn't so have remained with me. It was about yourself.' She waited as if it might come to him; but as, only meeting her eyes in wonder, he gave no sign, she burnt her ships. 'Has it ever happened?'

Then it was that, while he continued to stare, a light broke for him and the blood slowly came to his face, which began to burn with recognition. 'Do you mean I told you—?' But he faltered, lest what came to him shouldn't be right, lest he should only give himself away.

'It was something about yourself that it was natural one shouldn't forget—that is if one remembered you at all. That's why I ask you,' she smiled, 'if the thing you then spoke of has ever come to pass?'

Oh then he saw, but he was lost in wonder and found himself embarrassed. This, he also saw, made her sorry for him, as if her allusion had been a mistake. It took him but a moment, however, to feel it hadn't been, much as it had been a surprise. After the first little shock of it her knowledge on the contrary began, even if rather strangely, to taste sweet to him. She was the only other person in the world then who would have it, and she had had it all these years, while the fact of his having so breathed his secret had unaccountably faded from him. No wonder they couldn't have met as if nothing had happened. 'I judge,' he finally said, 'that I know what you mean. Only I had strangely enough lost any sense of having taken you so far into my confidence.'

'Is it because you've taken so many others as well?'

'I've taken nobody. Not a creature since then.'

'So that I'm the only person who knows?'

'The only person in the world.'

'Well,' she quickly replied, 'I myself have never spoken. I've never, never repeated of you what you told me.' She looked at him so that he perfectly believed her. Their eyes met over it in such a way that he was without a doubt. 'And I never will.'

She spoke with an earnestness that, as if almost excessive, put him at ease about her possible derision. Somehow the whole question was a new luxury to him—that is from the moment she was in possession. If she didn't take the sarcastic view she clearly took the sympathetic, and that was what he had had, in all the long time, from no one whomsoever. What he felt was that he couldn't at present have begun to tell her, and yet could profit perhaps exquisitely by the accident of having done so of old. 'Please don't then. We're just right as it is.'

'Oh I am,' she laughed, 'if you are!' To which she added: 'Then you do still feel in the same way?'

It was impossible he shouldn't take to himself that she was really interested, though it all kept coming as perfect surprise. He had thought of himself so long as abominably alone, and lo he wasn't alone a bit. He hadn't been, it appeared, for an hour—since those moments on the Sorrento boat. It was *she* who had been, he seemed to see as he looked at her—she who had been made so by the graceless fact of his lapse of fidelity. To tell her what he had told her—what had it been but to ask something of her? something that she had given, in her charity, without his having, by a remembrance, by a return of the spirit, failing another encounter, so much as thanked her. What he had asked of her had been simply at first not to laugh at him. She had beautifully not done so for ten years, and she was not doing so now. So he had endless gratitude to make up. Only for that he must see just how he had figured to her. 'What, exactly, was the account I gave—?'

'Of the way you did feel? Well, it was very simple. You said you had had from your earliest time, as the deepest thing within you, the sense of being kept for something rare and strange, possibly prodigious and terrible, that was sooner or later to happen to you, that you had in your bones the foreboding and the conviction of, and that would perhaps overwhelm you.'

'Do you call that very simple?' John Marcher asked.

She thought a moment. 'It was perhaps because I seemed, as you spoke, to understand it.'

'You do understand it?' he eagerly asked.

Again she kept her kind eyes on him. 'You still have the belief?'

'Oh!' he exclaimed helplessly. There was too much to say.

'Whatever it's to be,' she clearly made out, 'it hasn't yet come.'

He shook his head in complete surrender now. 'It hasn't yet come. Only, you know, it isn't anything I'm to *do*, to achieve in the world, to be distinguished or admired for. I'm not such an ass as *that*. It would be much better, no doubt, if I were.'

'It's to be something you're merely to suffer?'

'Well, say to wait for—to have to meet, to face, to see suddenly break out in my life; possibly destroying all further consciousness, possibly annihilating me; possibly, on the other hand, only altering everything, striking at the root of all my world and leaving me to the consequences, however they shape themselves.'

She took this in, but the light in her eyes continued for him not to be that of mockery. 'Isn't what you describe perhaps but the expectation—or at any rate the sense of danger, familiar to so many people—of falling in love?'

John Marcher wondered. 'Did you ask me that before?'

'No—I wasn't so free-and-easy then. But it's what strikes me now.'

'Of course,' he said after a moment, 'it strikes you. Of course it strikes *me*. Of course what's in store for me may be no more than that. The only thing is,' he went on, 'that I think if it had been that I should by this time know.'

'Do you mean because you've *been* in love?' And then as he but looked at her in silence: 'You've been in love, and it hasn't meant such a cataclysm, hasn't proved the great affair?'

'Here I am, you see. It hasn't been overwhelming.'

'Then it hasn't been love,' said May Bartram.

'Well, I at least thought it was. I took it for that—I've taken it till now. It was agreeable, it was delightful, it was miserable,' he explained. 'But it wasn't strange. It wasn't what *my* affair's to be.'

'You want something all to yourself—something that nobody else knows or *has* known?'

'It isn't a question of what I "want"—God knows I don't want anything. It's only a question of the apprehension that haunts me—that I live with day by day.'

He said this so lucidly and consistently that he could see it further impose itself. If she hadn't been interested before she'd have been interested now. 'Is it a sense of coming violence?'

Evidently now too again he liked to talk of it. 'I don't think of it as—when it does come—necessarily violent. I only think of it as natural and as of course above all unmistakable. I think of it simply as *the* thing. *The* thing will of itself appear natural.'

'Then how will it appear strange?'

Marcher bethought himself. 'It won't—to *me*.'

'To whom then?'

'Well,' he replied, smiling at last, 'say to you.'

'Oh then I'm to be present?'

'Why you *are* present—since you know.'

'I see.' She turned it over. 'But I mean at the catastrophe.'

At this, for a minute, their lightness gave way to their gravity; it was as if the long look they exchanged held them together. 'It will only depend on yourself—if you'll watch with me.'

'Are you afraid?' she asked.

'Don't leave me *now*,' he went on.

'Are you afraid?' she repeated.

'Do you think me simply out of my mind?' he pursued instead of answering. 'Do I merely strike you as a harmless lunatic?'

'No,' said May Bartram. 'I understand you. I believe you.'

'You mean you feel how my obsession—poor old thing!—may correspond to some possible reality?'

'To some possible reality.'

'Then you *will* watch with me?'

She hesitated, then for the third time put her question. 'Are you afraid?'

'Did I tell you I was—at Naples?'

'No, you said nothing about it.'

'Then I don't know. And I should *like* to know,' said John Marcher. 'You'll tell me yourself whether you think so. If you'll watch with me you'll see.'

'Very good then.' They had been moving by this time across the room, and at the door, before passing out, they paused as for the full wind-up of their understanding. 'I'll watch with you,' said May Bartram.

II

The fact that she 'knew'—knew and yet neither chaffed him nor betrayed him—had in a short time begun to constitute between them a goodly bond, which became more marked when, within the year that followed their afternoon at Weatherend, the opportunities for meeting multiplied. The event that thus promoted these occasions was the death of the ancient lady her great-aunt, under whose wing, since losing her mother, she had to such an extent found shelter, and who, though but the widowed mother of the new successor to the property, had succeeded—thanks to a high tone and a high temper—in not forfeiting the supreme position at the great house. The deposition of this personage arrived but with her death, which, followed by many changes, made in particular a difference for the young woman in whom Marcher's expert attention had recognized from the first a dependent with a pride that might ache though it didn't bristle. Nothing for a long time had made him easier than the thought that the aching must have been much soothed by Miss Bartram's now finding herself able to set up a small house in London. She had acquired property, to an amount that made that luxury just possible, under her aunt's extremely complicated will, and when the whole matter began to be straightened out, which indeed took time, she let him know that the happy issue was at last in view. He had seen her again before that day, both because she had more than once accompanied the ancient lady to town and because he had paid another visit to the friends who so conveniently made of Weatherend one of the charms of their own hospitality. These friends had taken him back there; he had achieved there again with Miss Bartram some quiet detachment; and he had in London succeeded in persuading her to more than one brief absence from her aunt. They went together, on these latter occasions, to the National Gallery and the South Kensington Museum, where, among vivid reminders, they talked of Italy at large—not now attempting to recover, as at first, the taste of their youth and their ignorance. That recovery, the first day at Weatherend, had served its purpose well, had given them quite enough; so that they were, to Marcher's sense, no longer hovering about the head-waters of their stream, but had felt their boat pushed sharply off and down the current.

They were literally afloat together; for our gentleman this was marked, quite as marked as that the fortunate cause of it was just the buried treasure of her knowledge. He had with his own hands dug up this little hoard, brought to light—that is to within reach of the dim day constituted by their discretions and privacies—the object of value the hiding-place of which he had, after putting it into the ground himself, so strangely, so long forgotten. The rare luck of his having again just stumbled on the spot made him indifferent to any other question; he would doubtless have devoted more time to the odd accident of his lapse of memory if he hadn't been moved to devote so much to the sweetness, the comfort, as he felt, for the future, that this accident itself had helped to keep fresh. It had never entered into his plan that any one should 'know', and mainly for the reason that it wasn't in him to tell any one. That would have been impossible, for nothing but the amusement of a cold world would have waited on it. Since, however, a mysterious fate had opened his mouth betimes, in spite of him, he would count that a compensation and profit by it to the utmost. That the right person *should* know tempered the asperity of his secret more even than his shyness had permitted him to imagine; and May Bartram was clearly right, because—well, because there she was. Her knowledge simply settled it; he would have been sure enough by this time had she been wrong. There was that in his situation, no doubt, that disposed him too much to see her as a mere confidant, taking all her light for him from the fact—the fact only—of her interest in his predicament; from her mercy, sympathy, seriousness, her consent not to regard him as the funniest of the funny. Aware, in fine, that her price for him was just in her giving him this constant sense of his being admirably spared, he was careful to remember that she had also a life of her own, with things that might happen to *her*, things that in friendship one should likewise take account of. Something fairly remarkable came to pass with him, for that matter, in this connexion—something represented by a certain passage of his consciousness, in the suddenest way, from one extreme to the other.

He had thought himself, so long as nobody knew, the most disinterested person in the world, carrying his concentrated burden, his perpetual suspense, ever so quietly, holding his tongue about it, giving others no glimpse of it nor of its effect upon his life, asking of them no allowance and only making on his side all those that were asked. He hadn't disturbed people with the queerness of their having to know a haunted man, though he had had moments of rather special temptation on hearing them say they were forsooth 'unsettled'. If they were as unsettled as he was—he who had never been settled for an hour in his life—they would know what it meant. Yet it wasn't, all the same, for him to make them, and he listened to them civilly enough. This was why he had such good—though possibly such rather colourless—manners; this was why, above all, he could regard himself, in a greedy world, as decently—as in fact perhaps even a little sublimely—unselfish. Our point is accordingly that he valued this character quite sufficiently to measure his present danger of letting it lapse, against which he promised himself to be much on his guard. He was quite ready, none the less, to be selfish just a little, since surely no more charming occasion for it had come to him. 'Just a little', in a word, was just as much as Miss Bartram, taking one day with another, would let him. He never would be in the least coercive, and would keep well before him the lines on which consideration for her—the very highest—ought to proceed. He would thoroughly establish the heads under which her affairs, her requirements, her peculiarities—he went so far as to give them the latitude of that name—would come into their intercourse. All this naturally was a sign of how much he took the intercourse itself for granted. There was nothing more to be done about *that*. It simply existed; had sprung into being with her first penetrating question to him in the autumn light there at Weatherend. The real form it should have taken on the basis that stood out large was the form of their marrying. But the devil in this was that the very basis itself put marrying out of the question. His conviction, his apprehension, his obsession, in short, wasn't a privilege he could invite a woman to share; and that consequence of it was precisely what was the matter with him. Something or other lay in wait for him, amid the twists and the turns of the months and the years, like a crouching beast in the jungle. It signified little whether the crouching beast were destined to slay him or to be slain. The definite point was the inevitable spring of the creature; and the definite lesson from that was that a man of feeling didn't cause himself to be accompanied by a lady on a tiger-hunt. Such was the image under which he had ended by figuring his life.

They had at first, none the less, in the scattered hours spent together, made no allusion to that view of it; which was a sign he was handsomely alert to give that he didn't expect, that he in fact didn't care, always to be talking about it. Such a feature in one's outlook was really like a hump on one's back. The difference it made every minute of the day existed quite independently of discussion. One discussed of course *like* a hunchback, for there was always, if nothing else, the hunchback face. That remained, and she was watching him; but people watched best, as a general thing, in silence, so that such would be predominantly the manner of their vigil. Yet he didn't want, at the same time, to be tense and solemn; tense and solemn was what he imagined he too much showed for with other people. The thing to be, with the one person who knew, was easy and natural—to make the reference rather than be seeming to avoid it, to avoid it rather than be seeming to make it, and to keep it, in any case, familiar, facetious even, rather than pedantic and portentous. Some such consideration as the latter was doubtless in his mind for instance when he wrote pleasantly to Miss Bartram that perhaps the great thing he had so long felt as in the lap of the gods was no more than this circumstance, which touched him so nearly, of her acquiring a house in London. It was the first allusion they had yet again made, needing any other hitherto so little; but when she replied, after having given him the news, that she was by no means satisfied with such a trifle as the climax to so special a suspense, she almost set him wondering if she hadn't even a larger conception of singularity for him than he had for himself. He was at all events destined to become aware little by little, as time went by, that she was all the while looking at his life, judging it, measuring it, in the light of the thing she knew, which grew to be at last, with the consecration of the years, never mentioned between them save as 'the real truth' about him. That had always been his own form of reference to it, but she adopted the form so quietly that, looking back at the end of a period, he knew there was no moment at which it was traceable that she had, as he might say, got inside his idea, or exchanged the attitude of beautifully indulging for that of still more beautifully believing him.

It was always open to him to accuse her of seeing him but as the most harmless of maniacs, and this, in the long run—since it covered so much ground—was his easiest description of their friendship. He had a screw loose for her, but she liked him in spite of it and was practically, against the rest of the world, his kind wise keeper, unremunerated but fairly amused and, in the absence of other near ties, not disreputably occupied. The rest of the world of course thought him queer, but she, she only, knew how, and above all why, queer; which was precisely what enabled her to dispose the concealing veil in the right folds. She took his gaiety from him—since it had to pass with them for gaiety—as she took everything else; but she certainly so far justified by her unerring touch his finer sense of the degree to which he had ended by convincing her. *She* at least never spoke of the secret of his life as 'the real truth about you,' and she had in fact a wonderful way of making it seem, as such, the secret of her own life too. That was in fine how he so constantly felt her as allowing for him; he couldn't on the whole call it anything else. He allowed for himself, but she, exactly, allowed still more; partly because, better placed for a sight of the matter, she traced his unhappy perversion through reaches of its course into which he could scarce follow it. He knew how he felt, but, besides knowing that, she knew how he *looked* as well; he knew each of the things of importance he was insidiously kept from doing, but she could add up the amount they made, understand how much, with a lighter weight on his spirit, he might have done, and thereby establish how, clever as he was, he fell short. Above all she was in the secret of the difference between the forms he went through—those of his little office under Government, those of caring for his modest patrimony, for his library, for his garden in the country, for the people in London whose invitations he accepted and repaid—and the detachment that reigned beneath them and that made of all behaviour, all that could in the least be called behaviour, a long act of dissimulation. What it had come to was that he wore a mask painted with the social simper, out of the eye-holes of which there looked eyes of an expression not in the least matching the other features. This the stupid world, even after years, had never more than half-discovered. It was only May Bartram who had, and she achieved, by an art indescribable, the feat of at once—or perhaps it was only alternately—meeting the eyes from in front and mingling her own vision, as from over his shoulder, with their peep through the apertures.

So while they grew older together she did watch with him, and so she let this association give shape and colour to her own existence. Beneath *her* forms as well detachment had learned to sit, and behaviour had become for her, in the social sense, a false account of herself. There was but one account of her that would have been true all the while and that she could give straight to nobody, least of all to John Marcher. Her whole attitude was a virtual statement, but the perception of that only seemed called to take its place for him as one of the many things necessarily crowded out of his consciousness. If she had moreover, like himself, to make sacrifices to their real truth, it was to be granted that her compensation might have affected her as more prompt and more natural. They had long periods, in this London time, during which, when they were together, a stranger might have listened to them without in the least pricking up his ears; on the other hand the real truth was equally liable at any moment to rise to the surface, and the auditor would then have wondered indeed what they were talking about. They had from an early hour made up their mind that society was, luckily, unintelligent, and the margin allowed them by this had fairly become one of their commonplaces. Yet there were still moments when the situation turned almost fresh—usually under the effect of some expression drawn from herself. Her expressions doubtless repeated themselves, but her intervals were generous. 'What saves us, you know, is that we answer so completely to so usual an appearance: that of the man and the woman whose friendship has become such a daily habit—or almost—as to be at last indispensable.' That for instance was a remark she had frequently enough had occasion to make, though she had given it at different times different developments. What we are especially concerned with is the turn it happened to take from her one afternoon when he had come to see her in honour of her birthday. This anniversary had fallen on a Sunday, at a season of thick fog and general outward gloom; but he had brought her his customary offering, having known her now long enough to have established a hundred small traditions. It was one of his proofs to himself, the present he made her on her birthday, that he hadn't sunk into real selfishness. It was mostly nothing more than a small trinket, but it was always fine of its kind, and he was regularly careful to pay for it more than he thought he could afford. 'Our habit saves you at least, don't you see? because it makes you, after all, for the vulgar, indistinguishable from other men. What's the most inveterate mark of men in general? Why the capacity to spend endless time with dull women—to spend it I won't say without being bored, but without minding that they are, without being driven off at a tangent by it; which comes to the same thing. I'm your dull woman, a part of the daily bread for which you pray at church. That covers your tracks more than anything.'

'And what covers yours?' asked Marcher, whom his dull woman could mostly to this extent amuse. 'I see of course what you mean by your saving me, in this way and that, so far as other people are concerned—I've seen it all along. Only what is it that saves *you*? I often think, you know, of that.'

She looked as if she sometimes thought of that too, but rather in a different way. 'Where other people, you mean, are concerned?'

'Well, you're really so in with me, you know—as a sort of result of my being so in with yourself. I mean of my having such an immense regard for you, being so tremendously mindful of all you've done for me. I sometimes ask myself if it's quite fair. Fair I mean to have so involved and—since one may say it—interested you. I almost feel as if you hadn't really had time to do anything else.'

'Anything else but be interested?' she asked. 'Ah what else does one ever want to be? If I've been "watching" with you, as we long ago agreed I was to do, watching's always in itself an absorption.'

'Oh certainly,' John Marcher said, 'if you hadn't had your curiosity—! Only doesn't it sometimes come to you as time goes on that your curiosity isn't being particularly repaid?'

May Bartram had a pause. 'Do you ask that, by any chance, because you feel at all that yours isn't? I mean because you have to wait so long.'

Oh he understood what she meant! 'For the thing to happen that never does happen? For the beast to jump out? No, I'm just where I was about it. It isn't a matter as to which I can *choose*, I can decide for a change. It's in the lap of the gods. One's in the hands of one's law—there one is. As to the form the law will take, the way it will operate, that's its own affair.'

'Yes,' Miss Bartram replied; 'of course one's fate's coming, of course it *has* come in its own form and its own way, all the while. Only, you know, the form and the way in your case were to have been—well, something so exceptional and, as one may say, so particularly *your* own.'

Something in this made him look at her with suspicion. 'You say "were to *have* been", as if in your heart you had begun to doubt.'

'Oh!' she vaguely protested.

'As if you believed,' he went on, 'that nothing will now take place.'

She shook her head slowly but rather inscrutably. 'You're far from my thought.'

He continued to look at her. 'What then is the matter with you?'

'Well,' she said after another wait, 'the matter with me is simply that I'm more sure than ever my curiosity, as you call it, will be but too well repaid.'

They were frankly grave now; he had got up from his seat, had turned once more about the little drawing-room to which, year after year, he brought his inevitable topic; in which he had, as he might have said, tasted their intimate community with every sauce, where every object was as familiar to him as the things of his own house and the very carpets were worn with his fitful walk very much as the desks in old counting-houses are worn by the elbows of generations of clerks. The generations of his nervous moods had been at work there, and the place was the written history of his whole middle life. Under the impression of what his friend had just said he knew himself, for some reason, more aware of these things; which made him, after a moment, stop again before her. 'Is it possibly that you've grown afraid?'

'Afraid?' He thought, as she repeated the word, that his question had made her, a little, change colour; so that, lest he should have touched on a truth, he explained very kindly: 'You remember that that was what you asked *me* long ago—that first day at Weatherend.'

'Oh yes, and you told me you didn't know—that I was to see for myself. We've said little about it since, even in so long a time.'

'Precisely,' Marcher interposed—'quite as if it were too delicate a matter for us to make free with. Quite as if we might find, on pressure, that I *am* afraid. For then,' he said, 'we shouldn't, should we? quite know what to do.'

She had for the time no answer to this question.

'There have been days when I thought you were. Only, of course,' she added, 'there have been days when we have thought almost anything.'

'Everything. Oh!' Marcher softly groaned as with a gasp, half-spent, at the face, more uncovered just then than it had been for a long while, of the imagination always with them. It had always had its incalculable moments of glaring out, quite as with the very eyes of the very Beast, and, used as he was to them, they could still draw from him the tribute of a sigh that rose from the depths of his being. All they had thought, first and last, rolled over him; the past seemed to have been reduced to mere barren speculation. This in fact was what the place had just struck him as so full of—the simplification of everything but the state of suspense. That remained only by seeming to hang in the void surrounding it. Even his original fear, if fear it had been, had lost itself in the desert. 'I judge, however,' he continued, 'that you see I'm not afraid now.'

'What I see, as I make it out, is that you've achieved something almost unprecedented in the way of getting used to danger. Living with it so long and so closely you've lost your sense of it; you know it's there, but you're indifferent, and you cease even, as of old, to have to whistle in the dark. Considering what the danger is,' May Bartram wound up, 'I'm bound to say I don't think your attitude could well be surpassed.'

John Marcher faintly smiled. 'It's heroic?'

'Certainly—call it that.'

It was what he would have liked indeed to call it. 'I *am* then a man of courage?'

'That's what you were to show me.'

He still, however, wondered. 'But doesn't the man of courage know what he's afraid of—or *not* afraid of? I don't know *that*, you see. I don't focus it. I can't name it. I only know I'm exposed.'

'Yes, but exposed—how shall I say?—so directly. So intimately. That's surely enough.'

'Enough to make you feel then—as what we may call the end and the upshot of our watch—that I'm not afraid?'

'You're not afraid. But it isn't,' she said, 'the end of our watch. That is, it isn't the end of yours. You've everything still to see.'

'Then why haven't *you*?' he asked. He had had, all along, to-day, the sense of her keeping something back, and he still had it. As this was his first impression of that it quite made a date. The case was the more marked as she didn't at first answer; which in turn made him go on. 'You know something I don't.' Then his voice, for that of a man of courage, trembled a little. 'You know what's to happen.' Her silence, with the face she showed, was almost a confession—it made him sure. 'You know, and you're afraid to tell me. It's so bad that you're afraid I'll find out.'

All this might be true, for she did look as if, unexpectedly to her, he had crossed some mystic line that she had secretly drawn round her. Yet she might, after all, not have worried; and the real climax was that he himself, at all events, needn't. 'You'll never find out.'

III

It was all to have made, none the less, as I have said, a date; which came out in the fact that again and again, even after long intervals, other things that passed between them wore in relation to this hour but the character of recalls and results. Its immediate effect had been indeed rather to lighten insistence—almost to provoke a reaction; as if their topic had dropped by its own weight and as if moreover, for that matter, Marcher had been visited by one of his occasional warnings against egotism. He had kept up, he felt, and very decently on the whole, his consciousness of the importance of not being selfish, and it was true that he had never sinned in that direction without promptly enough trying to press the scales the other way. He often repaired his fault, the season permitting, by inviting his friend to accompany him to the opera; and it not infrequently thus happened that, to show he didn't wish her to have but one sort of food for her mind, he was the cause of her appearing there with him a dozen nights in the month. It even happened that, seeing her home at such times, he occasionally went in with her to finish, as he called it, the evening, and, the better to make this point, sat down to the frugal but always careful little supper that awaited his pleasure. His point was made, he thought, by his not eternally insisting with her on himself; made for instance, at such hours, when it befell that, her piano at hand and each of them familiar with it, they went over passages of the opera together. It chanced to be on one of these occasions, however, that he reminded her of her not having answered a certain question he had put to her during the talk that had taken place between them on her last birthday. 'What is it that saves *you*?'—saved her, he meant, from that appearance of variation from the usual human type. If he had practically escaped remark, as she pretended, by doing, in the most important particular, what most men do—find the answer to life in patching up an alliance of a sort with a woman no better than himself—how had she escaped it, and how could the alliance, such as it was, since they must suppose it had been more or less noticed, have failed to make her rather positively talked about?

'I never said,' May Bartram replied, 'that it hadn't made me a good deal talked about.'

'Ah well then you're not "saved".'

'It hasn't been a question for me. If you've had your woman I've had,' she said, 'my man.'

'And you mean that makes you all right?'

Oh it was always as if there were so much to say!

'I don't know why it shouldn't make me—humanly, which is what we're speaking of—as right as it makes you.'

'I see,' Marcher returned. '"Humanly", no doubt, as showing that you're living for something. Not, that is, just for me and my secret.'

May Bartram smiled. 'I don't pretend it exactly shows that I'm not living for you. It's my intimacy with you that's in question.'

He laughed as he saw what she meant. 'Yes, but since, as you say, I'm only, so far as people make out, ordinary, you're—aren't you?—no more than ordinary either. You help me to pass for a man like another. So if I *am*, as I understand you, you're not compromised. Is that it?'

She had another of her waits, but she spoke clearly enough. 'That's it. It's all that concerns me—to help you to pass for a man like another.'

He was careful to acknowledge the remark handsomely. 'How kind, how beautiful, you are to me! How shall I ever repay you?'

She had her last grave pause, as if there might be a choice of ways. But she chose. 'By going on as you are.'

It was into this going on as he was that they relapsed, and really for so long a time that the day inevitably came for a further sounding of their depths. These depths, constantly bridged over by a structure firm enough in spite of its lightness and of its occasional oscillation in the somewhat vertiginous air, invited on occasion, in the interest of their nerves, a dropping of the plummet and a measurement of the abyss. A difference had been made moreover, once for all, by the fact that she had all the while not appeared to feel the need of rebutting his charge of an idea within her that she didn't dare to express—a charge uttered just before one of the fullest of their later discussions ended. It had come up for him then that she 'knew' something and that what she knew was bad—too bad to tell him. When he had spoken of it as visibly so bad that she was afraid he might find it out, her reply had left the matter too equivocal to be let alone and yet, for Marcher's special sensibility, almost too formidable again to touch. He circled about it at a distance that alternately narrowed and widened and that still wasn't much affected by the consciousness in him that there was nothing she could 'know', after all, any better than he did. She had no source of knowledge he hadn't equally—except of course that she might have finer nerves. That was what women had where they were interested; they made out things, where people were concerned, that the people often couldn't have made out for themselves. Their nerves, their sensibility, their imagination, were conductors and revealers, and the beauty of May Bartram was in particular that she had given herself so to his case. He felt in these days what, oddly enough, he had never felt before, the growth of a dread of losing her by some catastrophe—some catastrophe that yet wouldn't at all be *the* catastrophe: partly because she had almost of a sudden begun to strike him as more useful to him than ever yet, and partly by reason of an appearance of uncertainty in her health, coincident and equally new. It was characteristic of the inner detachment he had hitherto so successfully cultivated and to which our whole account of him is a reference, it was characteristic that his complications, such as they were, had never yet seemed so as at this crisis to thicken about him, even to the point of making him ask himself if he were, by any chance, of a truth, within sight or sound, within touch or reach, within the immediate jurisdiction, of the thing that waited.

When the day came, as come it had to, that his friend confessed to him her fear of a deep disorder in her blood, he felt somehow the shadow of a change and the chill of a shock. He immediately began to imagine aggravations and disasters, and above all to think of her peril as the direct menace for himself of personal privation. This indeed gave him one of those partial recoveries of equanimity that were agreeable to him—it showed him that what was still first in his mind was the loss she herself might suffer. 'What if she should have to die before knowing, before seeing—?' It would have been brutal, in the early stages of her trouble, to put that question to her; but it had immediately sounded for him to his own concern, and the possibility was what most made him sorry for her. If she did 'know', moreover, in the sense of her having had some—what should he think?—mystical irresistible light, this would make the matter not better, but worse, inasmuch as her original adoption of his own curiosity had quite become the basis of her life. She had been living to see what would *be* to be seen, and it would quite lacerate her to have to give up before the accomplishment of the vision. These reflexions, as I say, quickened his generosity; yet, make them as he might, he saw himself, with the lapse of the period, more and more disconcerted. It lapsed for him with a strange steady sweep, and the oddest oddity was that it gave him, independently of the threat of much inconvenience, almost the only positive surprise his career, if career it could be called, had yet offered him. She kept the house as she had never done; he had to go to her to see her—she could meet him nowhere now, though there was scarce a corner of their loved old London in which she hadn't in the past, at one time or another, done so; and he found her always seated by her fire in the deep old-fashioned chair she was less and less able to leave. He had been struck one day, after an absence exceeding his usual measure, with her suddenly looking much older to him than he had ever thought of her being; then he recognized that the suddenness was all on his side—he had just simply and suddenly noticed. She looked older because inevitably, after so many years, she *was* old, or almost; which was of course true in still greater measure of her companion. If she was old, or almost, John Marcher assuredly was, and yet it was her showing of the lesson, not his own, that brought the truth home to him. His surprises began here; when once they had begun they multiplied; they came rather with a rush: it was as if, in the oddest way in the world, they had all been kept back, sown in a thick cluster, for the late afternoon of life, the time at which for people in general the unexpected has died out.

One of them was that he should have caught himself—for he *had* so done—*really* wondering if the great accident would take form now as nothing more than his being condemned to see this charming woman, this admirable friend, pass away from him. He had never so unreservedly qualified her as while confronted in thought with such a possibility; in spite of which there was small doubt for him that as an answer to his long riddle the mere effacement of even so fine a feature of his situation would be an abject anticlimax. It would represent, as connected with his past attitude, a drop of dignity under the shadow of which his existence could only become the most grotesque of failures. He had been far from holding it a failure—long as he had waited for the appearance that was to make it a success. He had waited for quite another thing, not for such a thing as that. The breath of his good faith came short, however, as he recognized how long he had waited, or how long at least his companion had. That she, at all events, might be recorded as having waited in vain—this affected him sharply, and all the more because of his at first having done little more than amuse himself with the idea. It grew more grave as the gravity of her condition grew, and the state of mind it produced in him, which he himself ended by watching as if it had been some definite disfigurement of his outer person, may pass for another of his surprises. This conjoined itself still with another, the really stupefying consciousness of a question that he would have allowed to shape itself had he dared. What did everything mean—what, that is, did *she* mean, she and her vain waiting and her probable death and the soundless admonition of it all—unless that, at this time of day, it was simply, it was overwhelmingly too late? He had never at any stage of his queer consciousness admitted the whisper of such a correction; he had never till within these last few months been so false to his conviction as not to hold that what was to come to him had time, whether *he* struck himself as having it or not. That at last, at last, he certainly hadn't it, to speak of, or had it but in the scantiest measure—such, soon enough, as things went with him, became the inference with which his old obsession had to reckon: and this it was not helped to do by the more and more confirmed appearance that the great vagueness casting the long shadow in which he had lived had, to attest itself, almost no margin left. Since it was in Time that he was to have met his fate, so it was in Time that his fate was to have acted; and as he waked up to the sense of no longer being young, which was exactly the sense of being stale, just as that, in turn, was the sense of being weak, he waked up to another matter beside. It all hung together; they were subject, he and the great vagueness, to an equal and indivisible law. When the possibilities themselves had accordingly turned stale, when the secret of the gods had grown faint, had perhaps even quite evaporated, that, and that only, was failure. It wouldn't have been failure to be bankrupt, dishonoured, pilloried, hanged; it was failure not to be anything. And so, in the dark valley into which his path had taken its unlooked-for twist, he wondered not a little as he groped. He didn't care what awful crash might overtake him, with what ignominy or what monstrosity he might yet be associated—since he wasn't after all too utterly old to suffer—if it would only be decently proportionate to the posture he had kept, all his life, in the threatened presence of it. He had but one desire left—that he shouldn't have been 'sold'.

IV

Then it was that, one afternoon, while the spring of the year was young and new she met all in her own way his frankest betrayal of these alarms. He had gone in late to see her, but evening hadn't settled and she was presented to him in that long fresh light of waning April days which affects us often with a sadness sharper than the greyest hours of autumn. The week had been warm, the spring was supposed to have begun early, and May Bartram sat, for the first time in the year, without a fire; a fact that, to Marcher's sense, gave the scene of which she formed part a smooth and ultimate look, an air of knowing, in its immaculate order and cold meaningless cheer, that it would never see a fire again. Her own aspect—he could scarce have said why—intensified this note. Almost as white as wax, with the marks and signs in her face as numerous and as fine as if they had been etched by a needle, with soft white draperies relieved by a faded green scarf on the delicate tone of which the years had further refined, she was the picture of a serene and exquisite but impenetrable sphinx, whose head, or indeed all whose person, might have been powdered with silver. She was a sphinx, yet with her white petals and green fronds she might have been a lily too—only an artificial lily, wonderfully imitated and constantly kept, without dust or stain, though not exempt from a slight droop and a complexity of faint creases, under some clear glass bell. The perfection of household care, of high polish and finish, always reigned in her rooms, but they now looked most as if everything had been wound up, tucked in, put away, so that she might sit with folded hands and with nothing more to do. She was 'out of it', to Marcher's vision; her work was over; she communicated with him across some gulf or from some island of rest that she had already reached, and it made him feel strangely abandoned. Was it—or rather wasn't it—that if for so long she had been watching with him the answer to their question must have swum into her ken and taken on its name, so that her occupation was verily gone? He had as much as charged her with this in saying to her, many months before, that she even then knew something she was keeping from him. It was a point he had never since ventured to press, vaguely fearing as he did that it might become a difference, perhaps a disagreement, between them. He had in this later time turned nervous, which was what he in all the other years had never been; and the oddity was that his nervousness should have waited till he had begun to doubt, should have held off so long as he was sure. There was something, it seemed to him, that the wrong word would bring down on his head, something that would so at least ease off his tension. But he wanted not to speak the wrong word; that would make everything ugly. He wanted the knowledge he lacked to drop on him, if drop it could, by its own august weight. If she was to forsake him it was surely for her to take leave. This was why he didn't directly ask her again what she knew; but it was also why, approaching the matter from another side, he said to her in the course of his visit: 'What do you regard as the very worst that at this time of day *can* happen to me?'

He had asked her that in the past often enough; they had, with the odd irregular rhythm of their intensities and avoidances, exchanged ideas about it and then had seen the ideas washed away by cool intervals, washed like figures traced in sea-sand. It had ever been the mark of their talk that the oldest allusions in it required but a little dismissal and reaction to come out again, sounding for the hour as new. She could thus at present meet his enquiry quite freshly and patiently. 'Oh yes, I've repeatedly thought, only it always seemed to me of old that I couldn't quite make up my mind. I thought of dreadful things, between which it was difficult to choose; and so must you have done.'

'Rather! I feel now as if I had scarce done anything else. I appear to myself to have spent my life in thinking of nothing *but* dreadful things. A great many of them I've at different times named to you, but there were others I couldn't name.'

'They were too, too dreadful?'

'Too, too dreadful—some of them.'

She looked at him a minute, and there came to him as he met it an inconsequent sense that her eyes, when one got their full clearness, were still as beautiful as they had been in youth, only beautiful with a strange cold light—a light that somehow was a part of the effect, if it wasn't rather a part of the cause, of the pale hard sweetness of the season and the hour. 'And yet,' she said at last, 'there are horrors we've mentioned.'

It deepened the strangeness to see her, as such a figure in such a picture, talk of 'horrors', but she was to do in a few minutes something stranger yet—though even of this he was to take the full measure but afterwards—and the note of it already trembled. It was, for the matter of that, one of the signs that her eyes were having again the high flicker of their prime. He had to admit, however, what she said. 'Oh yes, there were times when we did go far.' He caught himself in the act of speaking as if it all were over. Well, he wished it were; and the consummation depended for him clearly more and more on his friend.

But she had now a soft smile. 'Oh far—!'

It was oddly ironic. 'Do you mean you're prepared to go further?'

She was frail and ancient and charming as she continued to look at him, yet it was rather as if she had lost the thread. 'Do you consider that we went far?'

'Why I thought it the point you were just making—that we *had* looked most things in the face.'

'Including each other?' She still smiled. 'But you're quite right. We've had together great imaginations, often great fears; but some of them have been unspoken.'

'Then the worst—we haven't faced that. I *could* face it, I believe, if I knew what you think it. I feel,' he explained, 'as if I had lost my power to conceive such things.' And he wondered if he looked as blank as he sounded. 'It's spent.'

'Then why do you assume,' she asked, 'that mine isn't?'

'Because you've given me signs to the contrary. It isn't a question for you of conceiving, imagining, comparing. It isn't a question now of choosing.' At last he came out with it. 'You know something I don't. You've shown me that before.'

These last words had affected her, he made out in a moment, exceedingly, and she spoke with firmness. 'I've shown you, my dear, nothing.'

He shook his head. 'You can't hide it.'

'Oh, oh!' May Bartram sounded over what she couldn't hide. It was almost a smothered groan.

'You admitted it months ago, when I spoke of it to you as of something you were afraid I should find out. Your answer was that I couldn't, that I wouldn't, and I don't pretend I have. But you had something therefore in mind, and I now see how it must have been, how it still is, the possibility that, of all possibilities, has settled itself for you as the worst. This,' he went on, 'is why I appeal to you. I'm only afraid of ignorance to-day—I'm not afraid of knowledge.' And then as for a while she said nothing: 'What makes me sure is that I see in your face and feel here, in this air and amid these appearances, that you're out of it. You've done. You've had your experience. You leave me to my fate.'

Well, she listened, motionless and white in her chair, as on a decision to be made, so that her manner was fairly an avowal, though still, with a small fine inner stiffness, an imperfect surrender. 'It *would* be the worst,' she finally let herself say. 'I mean the thing I've never said.'

It hushed him for a moment. 'More monstrous than all the monstrosities we've named?'

'More monstrous. Isn't that what you sufficiently express,' she asked, 'in calling it the worst?'

Marcher thought. 'Assuredly—if you mean, as I do, something that includes all the loss and all the shame that are thinkable.'

'It would if it *should* happen,' said May Bartram. 'What we're speaking of, remember, is only my idea.'

'It's your belief,' Marcher returned. 'That's enough for me. I feel your beliefs are right. Therefore if, having this one, you give me no more light on it, you abandon me.'

'No, no!' she repeated. 'I'm with you—don't you see?—still.' And as to make it more vivid to him she rose from her chair—a movement she seldom risked in these days—and showed herself, all draped and all soft, in her fairness and slimness. 'I haven't forsaken you.'

It was really, in its effort against weakness, a generous assurance, and had the success of the impulse not, happily, been great, it would have touched him to pain more than to pleasure. But the cold charm in her eyes had spread, as she hovered before him, to all the rest of her person, so that it was for the minute almost a recovery of youth. He couldn't pity her for that; he could only take her as she showed—as capable even yet of helping him. It was as if, at the same time, her light might at any instant go out; wherefore he must make the most of it. There passed before him with intensity the three or four things he wanted most to know; but the question that came of itself to his lips really covered the others. 'Then tell me if I shall consciously suffer.'

She promptly shook her head. 'Never!'

It confirmed the authority he imputed to her, and it produced on him an extraordinary effect. 'Well, what's better than that? Do you call that the worst?'

'You think nothing is better?' she asked.

She seemed to mean something so special that he again sharply wondered, though still with the dawn of a prospect of relief. 'Why not, if one doesn't *know*?' After which, as their eyes, over his question, met in a silence, the dawn deepened and something to his purpose came prodigiously out of her very face. His own, as he took it in, suddenly flushed to the forehead, and he gasped with the force of a perception to which, on the instant, everything fitted. The sound of his gasp filled the air; then he became articulate. 'I see—if I don't suffer!'

In her own look, however, was doubt. 'You see what?'

'Why what you mean—what you've always meant.'

She again shook her head. 'What I mean isn't what I've always meant. It's different.'

'It's something new?'

She hung back from it a little. 'Something new. It's not what you think. I see what you think.'

His divination drew breath then; only her correction might be wrong. 'It isn't that I *am* a blockhead?' he asked between faintness and grimness. 'It isn't that it's all a mistake?'

'A mistake?' she pityingly echoed. *That* possibility, for her, he saw, would be monstrous; and if she guaranteed him the immunity from pain it would accordingly not be what she had in mind. 'Oh no,' she declared; 'it's nothing of that sort. You've been right.'

Yet he couldn't help asking himself if she weren't, thus pressed, speaking but to save him. It seemed to him he should be most in a hole if his history should prove all a platitude. 'Are you telling me the truth, so that I shan't have been a bigger idiot than I can bear to know? I *haven't* lived with a vain imagination, in the most besotted illusion? I haven't waited but to see the door shut in my face?'

She shook her head again. 'However the case stands *that* isn't the truth. Whatever the reality, it *is* a reality. The door isn't shut. The door's open,' said May Bartram.

'Then something's to come?'

She waited once again, always with her cold sweet eyes on him. 'It's never too late.' She had, with her gliding step, diminished the distance between them, and she stood nearer to him, close to him, a minute, as if still charged with the unspoken. Her movement might have been for some finer emphasis of what she was at once hesitating and deciding to say. He had been standing by the chimney-piece, fireless and sparely adorned, a small perfect old French clock and two morsels of rosy Dresden constituting all its furniture; and her hand grasped the shelf while she kept him waiting, grasped it a little as for support and encouragement. She only kept him waiting, however; that is he only waited. It had become suddenly, from her movement and attitude, beautiful and vivid to him that she had something more to give him; her wasted face delicately shone with it—it glittered almost as with the white lustre of silver in her expression. She was right, incontestably, for what he saw in her face was the truth, and strangely, without consequence, while their talk of it as dreadful was still in the air, she appeared to present it as inordinately soft. This, prompting bewilderment, made him but gape the more gratefully for her revelation, so that they continued for some minutes silent, her face shining at him, her contact imponderably pressing, and his stare all kind but all expectant. The end, none the less, was that what he had expected failed to come to him. Something else took place instead, which seemed to consist at first in the mere closing of her eyes. She gave way at the same instant to a slow fine shudder, and though he remained staring—though he stared in fact but the harder—turned off and regained her chair. It was the end of what she had been intending, but it left him thinking only of that.

'Well, you don't say—?'

She had touched in her passage a bell near the chimney and had sunk back strangely pale. 'I'm afraid I'm too ill.'

'Too ill to tell me?' It sprang up sharp to him, and almost to his lips, the fear she might die without giving him light. He checked himself in time from so expressing his question, but she answered as if she had heard the words.

'Don't you know—now?'

'"Now"—?' She had spoken as if some difference had been made within the moment. But her maid, quickly obedient to her bell, was already with them. 'I know nothing.' And he was afterwards to say to himself that he must have spoken with odious impatience, such an impatience as to show that, supremely disconcerted, he washed his hands of the whole question.

'Oh!' said May Bartram.

'Are you in pain?' he asked as the woman went to her.

'No,' said May Bartram.

Her maid, who had put an arm round her as if to take her to her room, fixed on him eyes that appealingly contradicted her; in spite of which, however, he showed once more his mystification. 'What then has happened?'

She was once more, with her companion's help, on her feet, and, feeling withdrawal imposed on him, he had blankly found his hat and gloves and had reached the door. Yet he waited for her answer. 'What *was* to,' she said.

V

He came back the next day, but she was then unable to see him, and as it was literally the first time this had occurred in the long stretch of their acquaintance he turned away, defeated and sore, almost angry—or feeling at least that such a break in their custom was really the beginning of the end—and wandered alone with his thoughts, especially with the one he was least able to keep down. She was dying and he would lose her; she was dying and his life would end. He stopped in the Park, into which he had passed, and stared before him at his recurrent doubt. Away from her the doubt pressed again; in her presence he had believed her, but as he felt his forlornness he threw himself into the explanation that, nearest at hand, had most of a miserable warmth for him and least of a cold torment. She had deceived him to save him—to put him off with something in which he should be able to rest. What could the thing that was to happen to him be, after all, but just this thing that had begun to happen? Her dying, her death, his consequent solitude—*that* was what he had figured as the Beast in the Jungle, that was what had been in the lap of the gods. He had had her word for it as he left her—what else on earth could she have meant? It wasn't a thing of a monstrous order; not a fate rare and distinguished; not a stroke of fortune that overwhelmed and immortalized; it had only the stamp of the common doom. But poor Marcher at this hour judged the common doom sufficient. It would serve his turn, and even as the consummation of infinite waiting he would bend his pride to accept it. He sat down on a bench in the twilight. He hadn't been a fool. Something had *been*, as she had said, to come. Before he rose indeed it had quite struck him that the final fact really matched with the long avenue through which he had had to reach it. As sharing his suspense and as giving herself all, giving her life, to bring it to an end, she had come with him every step of the way. He had lived by her aid, and to leave her behind would be cruelly, damnably to miss her. What could be more overwhelming than that?

Well, he was to know within the week, for though she kept him a while at bay, left him restless and wretched during a series of days on each of which he asked about her only again to have to turn away, she ended his trial by receiving him where she had always received him. Yet she had been brought out at some hazard into the presence of so many of the things that were, consciously, vainly, half their past, and there was scant service left in the gentleness of her mere desire, all too visible, to check his obsession and wind up his long trouble. That was clearly what she wanted, the one thing more for her own peace while she could still put out her hand. He was so affected by her state that, once seated by her chair, he was moved to let everything go; it was she herself therefore who brought him back, took up again, before she dismissed him, her last word of the other time. She showed how she wished to leave their business in order. 'I'm not sure you understood. You've nothing to wait for more. It *has* come.'

Oh how he looked at her! 'Really?'

'Really.'

'The thing that, as you said, *was* to?'

'The thing that we began in our youth to watch for.'

Face to face with her once more he believed her; it was a claim to which he had so abjectly little to oppose. 'You mean that it has come as a positive definite occurrence, with a name and a date?'

'Positive. Definite. I don't know about the "name", but oh with a date!'

He found himself again too helplessly at sea. 'But come in the night—come and passed me by?'

May Bartram had her strange faint smile. 'Oh no, it hasn't passed you by!'

'But if I haven't been aware of it and it hasn't touched me—?'

'Ah your not being aware of it'—and she seemed to hesitate an instant to deal with this—'your not being aware of it is the strangeness *in* the strangeness. It's the wonder *of* the wonder.' She spoke as with the softness almost of a sick child, yet now at last, at the end of all, with the perfect straightness of a sibyl. She visibly knew that she knew, and the effect on him was of something co-ordinate, in its high character, with the law that had ruled him. It was the true voice of the law; so on her lips would the law itself have sounded. 'It *has* touched you,' she went on. 'It has done its office. It has made you all its own.'

'So utterly without my knowing it?'

'So utterly without your knowing it.' His hand, as he leaned to her, was on the arm of her chair, and, dimly smiling always now, she placed her own on it. 'It's enough if *I* know it.'

'Oh!' he confusedly breathed, as she herself of late so often had done.

'What I long ago said is true. You'll never know now, and I think you ought to be content. You've *had* it,' said May Bartram.

'But had what?'

'Why what was to have marked you out. The proof of your law. It has acted. I'm too glad,' she then bravely added, 'to have been able to see what it's *not*.'

He continued to attach his eyes to her, and with the sense that it was all beyond him, and that *she* was too, he would still have sharply challenged her hadn't he so felt it an abuse of her weakness to do more than take devoutly what she gave him, take it hushed as to a revelation. If he did speak, it was out of the foreknowledge of his loneliness to come. 'If you're glad of what it's "not" it might then have been worse?'

She turned her eyes away, she looked straight before her; with which after a moment: 'Well, you know our fears.'

He wondered. 'It's something then we never feared?'

On this slowly she turned to him. 'Did we ever dream, with all our dreams, that we should sit and talk of it thus?'

He tried for a little to make out that they had; but it was as if their dreams, numberless enough, were in solution in some thick cold mist through which thought lost itself. 'It might have been that we couldn't talk?'

'Well'—she did her best for him—'not from this side. This, you see,' she said, 'is the *other* side.'

'I think,' poor Marcher returned, 'that all sides are the same to me.' Then, however, as she gently shook her head in correction: 'We mightn't, as it were, have got across—?'

'To where we are—no. We're *here*'—she made her weak emphasis.

'And much good does it do us!' was her friend's frank comment.

'It does us the good it can. It does us the good that *it* isn't here. It's past. It's behind,' said May Bartram. 'Before—' but her voice dropped.

He had got up, not to tire her, but it was hard to combat his yearning. She after all told him nothing but that his light had failed—which he knew well enough without her. 'Before—?' he blankly echoed.

'Before, you see, it was always to *come*. That kept it present.'

'Oh I don't care what comes now! Besides,' Marcher added, 'it seems to me I liked it better present, as you say, than I can like it absent with *your* absence.'

'Oh mine!'—and her pale hands made light of it.

'With the absence of everything.' He had a dreadful sense of standing there before her for—so far as anything but this proved, this bottomless drop was concerned—the last time of their life. It rested on him with a weight he felt he could scarce bear, and this weight it apparently was that still pressed out what remained in him of speakable protest. 'I believe you; but I can't begin to pretend I understand. *Nothing*, for me, is past; nothing *will* pass till I pass myself, which I pray my stars may be as soon as possible. Say, however,' he added, 'that I've eaten my cake, as you contend, to the last crumb—how can the thing I've never felt at all be the thing I was marked out to feel?'

She met him perhaps less directly, but she met him unperturbed. 'You take your "feelings" for granted. You were to suffer your fate. That was not necessarily to know it.'

'How in the world—when what is such knowledge but suffering?'

She looked up at him a while in silence. 'No—you don't understand.'

'I suffer,' said John Marcher.

'Don't, don't!'

'How can I help at least *that*?'

'*Don't*!' May Bartram repeated.

She spoke it in a tone so special, in spite of her weakness, that he stared an instant—stared as if some light, hitherto hidden, had shimmered across his vision. Darkness again closed over it, but the gleam had already become for him an idea. 'Because I haven't the right—?'

'Don't *know*—when you needn't,' she mercifully urged. 'You needn't—for we shouldn't.'

'Shouldn't?' If he could but know what she meant!

'No—it's too much.'

'Too much?' he still asked but, with a mystification that was the next moment of a sudden to give way. Her words, if they meant something, affected him in this light—the light also of her wasted face—as meaning *all*, and the sense of what knowledge had been for herself came over him with a rush which broke through into a question. 'Is it of that then you're dying?'

She but watched him, gravely at first, as to see, with this, where he was, and she might have seen something or feared something that moved her sympathy. 'I would live for you still—if I could.' Her eyes closed for a little, as if, withdrawn into herself, she were for a last time trying. 'But I can't!' she said as she raised them again to take leave of him.

She couldn't indeed, as but too promptly and sharply appeared, and he had no vision of her after this that was anything but darkness and doom. They had parted for ever in that strange talk; access to her chamber of pain, rigidly guarded, was almost wholly forbidden him; he was feeling now moreover, in the face of doctors, nurses, the two or three relatives attracted doubtless by the presumption of what she had to 'leave', how few were the rights, as they were called in such cases, that he had to put forward, and how odd it might even seem that their intimacy shouldn't have given him more of them. The stupidest fourth cousin had more, even though she had been nothing in such a person's life. She had been a feature of features in *his*, for what else was it to have been so indispensable? Strange beyond saying were the ways of existence, baffling for him the anomaly of his lack, as he felt it to be, of producible claim. A woman might have been, as it were, everything to him, and it might yet present him in no connexion that any one seemed held to recognize. If this was the case in these closing weeks it was the case more sharply on the occasion of the last offices rendered, in the great grey London cemetery, to what had been mortal, to what had been precious, in his friend. The concourse at her grave was not numerous, but he saw himself treated as scarce more nearly concerned with it than if there had been a thousand others. He was in short from this moment face to face with the fact that he was to profit extraordinarily little by the interest May Bartram had taken in him. He couldn't quite have said what he expected, but he hadn't surely expected this approach to a double privation. Not only had her interest failed him, but he seemed to feel himself unattended—and for a reason he couldn't seize—by the distinction, the dignity, the propriety, if nothing else, of the man markedly bereaved. It was as if in the view of society he had not *been* markedly bereaved, as if there still failed some sign or proof of it, and as if none the less his character could never be affirmed nor the deficiency ever made up. There were moments as the weeks went by when he would have liked, by some almost aggressive act, to take his stand on the intimacy of his loss, in order that it *might* be questioned and his retort, to the relief of his spirit, so recorded; but the moments of an irritation more helpless followed fast on these, the moments during which, turning things over with a good conscience but with a bare horizon, he found himself wondering if he oughtn't to have begun, so to speak, further back.

He found himself wondering indeed at many things, and this last speculation had others to keep it company. What could he have done, after all, in her lifetime, without giving them both, as it were, away? He couldn't have made known she was watching him, for that would have published the superstition of the Beast. This was what closed his mouth now—now that the Jungle had been threshed to vacancy and that the

Beast had stolen away. It sounded too foolish and too flat; the difference for him in this particular, the extinction in his life of the element of suspense, was such as in fact to surprise him. He could scarce have said what the effect resembled; the abrupt cessation, the positive prohibition, of music perhaps, more than anything else, in some place all adjusted and all accustomed to sonority and to attention. If he could at any rate have conceived lifting the veil from his image at some moment of the past (what had he done, after all if not lift it to *her*?) so to do this to-day, to talk to people at large of the Jungle cleared and confide to them that he now felt it as safe, would have been not only to see them listen as to a goodwife's tale, but really to hear himself tell one. What it presently came to in truth was that poor Marcher waded through his beaten grass, where no life stirred, where no breath sounded, where no evil eye seemed to gleam from a possible lair, very much as if vaguely looking for the Beast, and still more as if acutely missing it. He walked about in an existence that had grown strangely more spacious, and, stopping fitfully in places where the undergrowth of life struck him as closer, asked himself yearningly, wondered secretly and sorely, if it would have lurked here or there. It would have at all events *sprung*; what was at least complete was his belief in the truth itself of the assurance given him. The change from his old sense to his new was absolute and final: what was to happen *had* so absolutely and finally happened that he was as little able to know a fear for his future as to know a hope; so absent in short was any question of anything still to come. He was to live entirely with the other question, that of his unidentified past, that of his having to see his fortune impenetrably muffled and masked.

The torment of this vision became then his occupation; he couldn't perhaps have consented to live but for the possibility of guessing. She had told him, his friend, not to guess; she had forbidden him, so far as he might, to know, and she had even in a sort denied the power in him to learn: which were so many things, precisely, to deprive him of rest. It wasn't that he wanted, he argued for fairness, that anything past and done should repeat itself; it was only that he shouldn't, as an anticlimax, have been taken sleeping so sound as not to be able to win back by an effort of thought the lost stuff of consciousness. He declared to himself at moments that he would either win it back or have done with consciousness for ever; he made this idea his one motive in fine, made it so much his passion that none other, to compare with it, seemed ever to have touched him. The lost stuff of consciousness became thus for him as a strayed or stolen child to an unappeasable father; he hunted it up and down very much as if he were knocking at doors and enquiring of the police. This was the spirit in which, inevitably, he set himself to travel; he started on a journey that was to be as long as he could make it; it danced before him that, as the other side of the globe couldn't possibly have less to say to him, it might, by a possibility of suggestion, have more. Before he quitted London, however, he made a pilgrimage to May Bartram's grave, took his way to it through the endless avenues of the grim suburban metropolis, sought it out in the wilderness of tombs, and, though he had come but for the renewal of the act of farewell, found himself, when he had at last stood by it, beguiled into long intensities. He stood for an hour, powerless to turn away and yet powerless to penetrate the darkness of death; fixing with his eyes her inscribed name and date, beating his forehead against the fact of the secret they kept, drawing his breath, while he waited, as if some sense would in pity of him rise from the stones. He kneeled on the stones, however, in vain; they kept what they concealed; and if the face of the tomb did become a face for him it was because her two names became a pair of eyes that didn't know him. He gave them a last long look, but no palest light broke.

VI

He stayed away, after this, for a year; he visited the depths of Asia, spending himself on scenes of romantic interest, of superlative sanctity; but what was present to him everywhere was that for a man who had known what *he* had known the world was vulgar and vain. The state of mind in which he had lived for so many years shone out to him, in reflexion, as a light that coloured and refined, a light beside which the glow of the East was garish cheap and thin. The terrible truth was that he had lost—with everything else—a distinction as well; the things he saw couldn't help being common when he had become common to look at them. He was simply now one of them himself—he was in the dust, without a peg for the sense of difference; and there were hours when, before the temples of gods and the sepulchres of kings, his spirit turned for nobleness of association to the barely discriminated slab in the London suburb. That had become for him, and more intensely with time and distance, his one witness of a past glory. It was all that was left to him for proof or pride, yet the past glories of Pharaohs were nothing to him as he thought of it. Small wonder then that he came back to it on the morrow of his return. He was drawn there this time as irresistibly as the other, yet with a confidence, almost, that was doubtless the effect of the many months that had elapsed. He had lived, in spite of himself, into his change of feeling, and in wandering over the earth had wandered, as might be said, from the circumference to the centre of his desert. He had settled to his safety and accepted perforce his extinction; figuring to himself, with some colour, in the likeness of certain little old men he remembered to have seen, of whom, all meagre and wizened as they might look, it was related that they had in their time fought twenty duels or been loved by ten princesses. They indeed had been wondrous for others while he was but wondrous for himself; which, however, was exactly the cause of his haste to renew the wonder by getting back, as he might put it, into his own presence. That had quickened his steps and checked his delay. If his visit was prompt it was because he had been separated so long from the part of himself that alone he now valued.

It's accordingly not false to say that he reached his goal with a certain elation and stood there again with a certain assurance. The creature beneath the sod *knew* of his rare experience, so that, strangely now, the place had lost for him its mere blankness of expression. It met him in mildness—not, as before, in mockery; it wore for him the air of conscious greeting that we find, after absence, in things that have closely belonged to us and which seem to confess of themselves to the connexion. The plot of ground, the graven tablet, the tended flowers affected him so as belonging to him that he resembled for the hour a contented landlord reviewing a piece of property. Whatever had happened—well, had happened. He had not come back this time with the vanity of that question, his former worrying 'What, *what*?' now practically so spent. Yet he would none the less never again so cut himself off from the spot; he would come back to it every month, for if he did nothing else by its aid he at least held up his head. It thus grew for him, in the oddest way, a positive resource; he carried out his idea of periodical returns, which took their place at last among the most inveterate of his habits. What it all amounted to, oddly enough, was that in his finally so simplified world this garden of death gave him the few square feet of earth on which he could still most live. It was as if, being nothing anywhere else for any one, nothing even for himself, he were just everything here, and if not for a crowd of witnesses or indeed for any witness but John Marcher, then by clear right of the register that he could scan like an open page. The open page was the tomb of his friend, and *there* were the facts of the past, there the truth of his life, there the backward reaches in which he could lose himself. He did this from time to time with such effect that he seemed to wander through the old years with his hand in the arm of a companion who was, in the most extraordinary manner, his other, his younger self; and to wander, which was more extraordinary yet, round and round a third presence—not wandering she, but stationary, still, whose eyes, turning with his revolution, never ceased to follow him, and whose seat was his point, so to speak, of orientation. Thus in short he settled to live—feeding all on the sense that he once *had* lived, and dependent on it not alone for a support but for an identity.

It sufficed him in its way for months and the year elapsed; it would doubtless even have carried him further but for an accident, superficially slight, which moved him, quite in another direction, with a force beyond any of his impressions of Egypt or of India. It was a thing of the merest chance—the turn, as he afterwards felt, of a hair, though he was indeed to live to believe that if light hadn't come to him in this particular fashion it would still have come in another. He was to live to believe this, I say, though he was not to live, I may not less definitely mention, to do much else. We allow him at any rate the benefit of the conviction, struggling up for him at the end, that, whatever might have happened or not happened, he would have come round of himself to the light. The incident of an autumn day had put the match to the train laid from of old by his misery.

With the light before him he knew that even of late his ache had only been smothered. It was strangely drugged, but it throbbed; at the touch it began to bleed. And the touch, in the event, was the face of a fellow mortal. This face, one grey afternoon when the leaves were thick in the alleys, looked into Marcher's own, at the cemetery, with an expression like the cut of a blade. He felt it, that is, so deep down that he winced at the steady thrust. The person who so mutely assaulted him was a figure he had noticed, on reaching his own goal, absorbed by a grave a short distance away, a grave apparently fresh, so that the emotion of the visitor would probably match it for frankness. This fact alone forbade further attention, though during the time he stayed he remained vaguely conscious of his neighbour, a middle-aged man apparently, in mourning, whose bowed back, among the clustered monuments and mortuary yews, was constantly presented. Marcher's theory that these were elements in contact with which he himself revived, had suffered, on this occasion, it may be granted, a marked, an excessive check. The autumn day was dire for him as none had recently been, and he rested with a heaviness he had not yet known on the low stone table that bore May Bartram's name. He rested without power to move, as if some spring in him, some spell vouchsafed, had suddenly been broken for ever. If he could have done that moment as he wanted he would simply have stretched himself on the slab that was ready to take him, treating it as a place prepared to receive his last sleep. What in all the wide world had he now to keep awake for? He stared before him with the question, and it was then that, as one of the cemetery walks passed near him, he caught the shock of the face.

His neighbour at the other grave had withdrawn, as he himself, with force enough in him, would have done by now, and was advancing along the path on his way to one of the gates. This brought him close, and his pace was slow, so that—and all the more as there was a kind of hunger in his look—the two men were for a minute directly confronted. Marcher knew him at once for one of the deeply stricken—a perception so sharp that nothing else in the picture comparatively lived, neither his dress, his age, nor his presumable character and class; nothing lived but the deep ravage of the features he showed. He *showed* them—that was the point; he was moved, as he passed, by some impulse that was either a signal for sympathy or, more possibly, a challenge to an opposed sorrow. He might already have been aware of our friend, might at some previous hour have noticed in him the smooth habit of the scene, with which the state of his own senses so scantly consorted, and might thereby have been stirred as by an overt discord. What Marcher was at all events conscious of was in the first place that the image of scarred passion presented to him was conscious too—of something that profaned the air; and in the second that, roused, startled, shocked, he was yet the next moment looking after it, as it went, with envy. The most extraordinary thing that had happened to him—though he had given that name to other matters as well—took place, after his immediate vague stare, as a consequence of this impression. The stranger passed, but the raw glare of his grief remained, making our friend wonder in pity what wrong, what wound it expressed, what injury not to be healed. What had the man *had*, to make him by the loss of it so bleed and yet live?

Something—and this reached him with a pang—that *he*, John Marcher, hadn't; the proof of which was precisely John Marcher's arid end. No passion had ever touched him, for this was what passion meant; he had survived and maundered and pined, but where had been *his* deep ravage? The extraordinary thing we speak of was the sudden rush of the result of this question. The sight that had just met his eyes named to him, as in letters of quick flame, something he had utterly, insanely missed, and what he had missed made these things a train of fire, made them mark themselves in an anguish of inward throbs. He had seen *outside* of his life, not learned it within, the way a woman was mourned when she had been loved for herself: such was the force of his conviction of the meaning of the stranger's face, which still flared for him as a smoky torch. It hadn't come to him, the knowledge, on the wings of experience; it had brushed him, jostled him, upset him, with the disrespect of chance, the insolence of accident. Now that the illumination had begun, however, it blazed to the zenith, and what he presently stood there gazing at was the sounded void of his life. He gazed, he drew breath, in pain; he turned in his dismay, and, turning, he had before him in sharper incision than ever the open page of his story. The name on the table smote him as the passage of his neighbour had done, and what it said to him, full in the face, was that *she* was what he had missed. This was the awful thought, the answer to all the past, the vision at the dread clearness of which he grew as cold as the stone beneath him. Everything fell together, confessed, explained, overwhelmed; leaving him most of all stupefied at the blindness he had cherished. The fate he had been marked for he had met with a vengeance—he had emptied the cup to the lees; he had been the man of his time, *the* man, to whom nothing on earth was to have happened. That was the rare stroke—that was his visitation. So he saw it, as we say, in pale horror, while the pieces fitted and fitted. So *she* had seen it while he didn't, and so she served at this hour to drive the truth home. It was the truth, vivid and monstrous, that all the while he had waited the wait was itself his portion. This the companion of his vigil had at a given moment made out, and she had then offered him the chance to baffle his doom. One's doom, however, was never baffled, and on the day she told him his own had come down she had seen him but stupidly stare at the escape she offered him.

The escape would have been to love her; then, *then* he would have lived. *She* had lived—who could say now with what passion?—since she had loved him for himself; whereas he had never thought of her (ah how it hugely glared at him!) but in the chill of his egotism and the light of her use. Her spoken words came back to him—the chain stretched and stretched. The Beast had lurked indeed, and the Beast, at its hour, had sprung; it had sprung in that twilight of the cold April when, pale, ill, wasted, but all beautiful, and perhaps even then recoverable, she had risen from her chair to stand before him and let him imaginably guess. It had sprung as he didn't guess; it had sprung as she hopelessly turned from him, and the mark, by the time he left her, had fallen where it *was* to fall. He had justified his fear and achieved his fate; he had failed, with the last exactitude, of all he was to fail of; and a moan now rose to his lips as he remembered she had prayed he mightn't know. This horror of waking—*this* was knowledge, knowledge under the breath of which the very tears in his eyes seemed to freeze. Through them, none the less, he tried to fix it and hold it; he kept it there before him so that he might feel the pain. That at least, belated and bitter, had something of the taste of life. But the bitterness suddenly sickened him, and it was as if, horribly, he saw, in the truth, in the cruelty of his image, what had been appointed and done. He saw the Jungle of his life and saw the lurking Beast; then, while he looked, perceived it, as by a stir of the air, rise, huge and hideous, for the leap that was to settle him. His eyes darkened—it was close; and, instinctively turning, in his hallucination, to avoid it, he flung himself, face down, on the tomb.

1903

Sara Jeannette Duncan

1862-1922

'Literature should at its best be true not only to the objects upon and about which it constructs itself, but faithful also to all the delicate attractions and repulsions which enter so intimately into the highest art,' wrote Sara Jeannette Duncan in seeming support of realism in fiction. At the same time, however, such support was always qualified and even ambivalent: 'The modern school of fiction, if it is fairly subject to any reproach, may bear the blame of dealing too exclusively in the corporealities of human life, to the utter and scornful neglect of its idealities.' And so Duncan, the seeming advocate of realism, still understood the appeal of romance with its idealities and often wavered in her own fiction between romance and realism.

Born in Brantford, Ontario, Duncan attended the Toronto Normal School, then left teaching for a career in journalism. She worked as editorial writer and book reviewer for the Washington *Post*, then as columnist for the Toronto *Globe* and the Montreal *Star*, where she also served as parliamentary correspondent. In 1888 she set off on a round-the-world trip as correspondent for the *Star* and the New York *World*. In Calcutta she met Everard Cotes, an Englishman serving there as curator of the Indian Museum; they married in 1890 and lived in Calcutta and in Simla, at that time the Himalayan summer capital of India, for the next three decades. A prolific and popular writer, Duncan wrote more than twenty volumes of fiction, many of them set in India. *The Imperialist* (1904), generally considered her finest novel, is the only one with a Canadian setting. During her later years Duncan devoted much of her time to playwrighting. She and her husband retired to England in 1922.

In her fiction and in her journalism, Duncan is a careful and telling observer of social roles and manners, often following the responses to foreign cultures and customs of her English and American characters. Her portraits of women reflect her own muted feminism: while Duncan advocated advanced education and opportunities for women, she often expressed sympathy for traditional female roles. 'There is one thing which the women of today, with all their new accomplishments, high aims, and wide opportunities, are utterly and irretrievably losing. That is the repose of manner that our grandmothers possessed in so marked and pleasing a degree . . .' she wrote. 'There are worse places in the world than woman's domestic sphere, contracted though it seems to be; and while necessity and the laws of progress have driven us out of it to some extent, we can still look and sometimes go back to it with love and gratitude for so safe a haven.'

In 'The Pool in the Desert' the narrator examines two British ladies 'against the rather empty landscape of life in a frontier station.' The Anglo-Indian world of martial heroism is the background for romantic flirtation and unfulfilled love as the narrator studies a friend's romance with her best friend's son.

'A Mother in India' is an account of Cecily Farnham's childhood away from her parents and then her brief relationship with Dacres Tottenham. As Cecily's mother finds Tottenham's amorous attentions transferred from herself to her daughter, the story moves to an ironic ending for both mother and daughter.

'The Pool in the Desert' was first published in the May 1903 issue of *Century Magazine*. 'A Mother in India' was first published in the June/July 1903 issues of *Scribner's Magazine*. Both stories were then collected in *The Pool in the Desert* (1903).

The Pool in the Desert

I knew Anna Chichele and Judy Harbottle so well, and they figured so vividly at one time against the rather empty landscape of life in a frontier station, that my affection for one of them used to seem little more, or less, than a variant upon my affection for the other. That recollection, however, bears examination badly; Judy was much the better sort, and it is Judy's part in it that draws me into telling the story. Conveying Judy is what I tremble at: her part was simple. Looking back—and not so very far—her part has the relief of high comedy with the proximity of tears; but looking closely, I find that it is mostly Judy, and what she did is entirely second, in my untarnished picture, to what she was. Still I do not think I can dissuade myself from putting it down.

They would, of course, inevitably have found each other sooner or later, Mrs Harbottle and Mrs Chichele, but it was I who actually introduced them; my palmy veranda in Rawul Pindi, where the tea-cups used to assemble, was the scene of it. I presided behind my samovar over the early formalities that were almost at once to drop from their friendship, like the sheath of some bursting flower. I deliberately brought them together, so the birth was not accidental, and my interest in it quite legitimately maternal. We always had tea in the veranda in Rawul Pindi, the drawing-room was painted blue, blue for thirty feet up to the whitewashed cotton ceiling; nothing of any value in the way of a human relation, I am sure, could have originated there. The veranda was spacious and open, their mutual observation had room and freedom; I watched it to and fro. I had not long to wait for my reward; the beautiful candour I expected between them was not ten minutes in coming. For the sake of it I had taken some trouble, but when I perceived it revealing I went and sat down beside Judy's husband, Robert Harbottle, and talked about Pharaoh's split hoof. It was only fair; and when next day I got their impressions of one another, I felt single-minded and deserving.

I knew it would be a satisfactory sort of thing to do, but perhaps it was rather more for Judy's sake than for Anna's that I did it. Mrs Harbottle was only twenty-seven then and Robert a major, but he had brought her to India out of an episode too colour-flushed to tone with English hedges; their marriage had come, in short, of his divorce, and as too natural a consequence. In India it is well known that the eye becomes accustomed to primitive pigments and high lights; the aesthetic consideration, if nothing else, demanded Robert's exchange. He was lucky to get a Piffer* regiment, and the Twelfth were lucky to get him; we were all lucky, I thought,

*Punjabi Frontier Force

to get Judy. It was an opinion, of course, a good deal challenged, even in Rawul Pindi, where it was thought, especially in the beginning, that acquiescence was the most the Harbottles could hope for. That is not enough in India; cordiality is the common right. I could not have Judy preserving her atmosphere at our tea-parties and gymkhanas. Not that there were two minds among us about 'the case'; it was a preposterous case, sentimentally undignified, from some points of view deplorable. I chose to reserve my point of view, from which I saw it, on Judy's behalf, merely quixotic, preferring on Robert's just to close my eyes. There is no doubt that his first wife was odious to a degree which it is simply pleasanter not to recount, but her malignity must almost have amounted to a sense of humour. Her detestation of her cousin Judy Thynne dated much further back than Robert's attachment. That began in Paris, where Judy, a young widow, was developing a real vein at Julian's. I am entirely convinced that there was nothing, as people say, 'in it', Judy had not a thought at that time that was not based on Chinese white and permeated with good-fellowship; but there was a good deal of it, and no doubt the turgid imagination of the first Mrs Harbottle dealt with it honestly enough. At all events, she saw her opportunity, and the depths of her indifference to Robert bubbled up venomously into the suit. That it was undefended was the senseless mystery; decency ordained that he and Judy should have made a fight, even in the hope that it would be a losing one. The reason it had to be a losing one—the reason so immensely criticized—was that the petitioning lady obstinately refused to bring her action against any other set of circumstances than those to which, I have no doubt, Judy contributed every indiscretion. It is hard to imagine Robert Harbottle refusing her any sort of justification that the law demands short of beating her, but her malice would accept nothing of which the account did not go for final settlement to Judy Thynne. If her husband wanted his liberty, he should have it, she declared, at that price and no other. Major Harbottle did indeed deeply long for his liberty, and his interesting friend, Mrs Thynne, had, one can only say, the most vivid commiseration for his bondage. Whatever chance they had of winning, to win would be, for the end they had at heart, to lose, so they simply abstained, as it were, from comment upon the detestable procedure which terminated in the rule absolute. I have often wondered whether the whole business would not have been more defensible if there had been on Judy's part any emotional spring for the leap they made. I offer my conviction that there was none, that she was only extravagantly affected by the ideals of the Quarter—it is a transporting atmosphere—and held a view of comradeship which permitted the reversal of the modern situation filled by a blameless correspondent. Robert, of course, was tremendously in love with her; but my theory is that she married him as the logical outcome of her sacrifice and by no means the smallest part of it.

It was all quite unimaginable, as so many things are, but the upshot of it brought Judy to Rawul Pindi, as I have said, where I for one thought her mistake insignificant compared with her value. It would have been great, her value, anywhere; in the middle of the Punjab it was incalculable. To explain why would be to explain British India, but I hope it will appear; and I am quite willing, remember, to take the responsibility if it does not.

Somers Chichele, Anna's son, it is absurd to think, must have been about fifteen then, reflecting at Winchester with the other 'men' upon the comparative merits of tinned sardines and jam roll, and whether a packet of real Egyptians was not worth the sacrifice of either. His father was colonel of the Twelfth; his mother was still charming. It was the year before Dick Forsyth came down from the neighbourhood of Sheikhbudin with a brevet and a good deal of personal damage. I mention him because he proved Anna's charm in the only conclusive way before the eyes of us all; and the station, I remember, was edified to observe that if Mrs Chichele came out of the matter 'straight'—one relapses so easily into the simple definitions of those parts—which she undoubtedly did, she owed it in no small degree to Judy Harbottle. This one feels to be hardly a legitimate reference, but it is something tangible to lay hold upon in trying to describe the web of volitions which began to weave itself between the two that afternoon on my veranda and which afterward became so strong a bond. I was delighted with the thing; its simplicity and sincerity stood out among our conventional little compromises at friendship like an ideal. She and Judy had the assurance of one another; they made upon one another the finest and often the most unconscionable demands. One met them walking at odd hours in queer places, of which I imagine they were not much aware. They would turn deliberately off the Maidan and away from the band-stand to be rid of our irrelevant bows; they did their duty by the rest of us, but the most egregious among us, the Deputy-Commissioner for selection, could see that he hardly counted. I thought I understood, but that may have been my fatuity; certainly when their husbands inquired what on earth they had been talking of, it usually transpired that they had found an infinite amount to say about nothing. It was a little worrying to hear Colonel Chichele and Major Harbottle describe their wives as 'pals', but the fact could not be denied, and after all we were in the Punjab. They were pals too, but the terms were different.

People discussed it according to their lights, and girls said in pretty wonderment that Mrs Harbottle and Mrs Chichele were like men, they never kissed each other. I think Judy prescribed these conditions. Anna was far more a person who did as the world told her. But it was a poor negation to describe all that they never did; there was no common little convention of attachment that did not seem to be tacitly omitted between them. I hope one did not too cynically observe that they offered these to their husbands instead; the redeeming observation was their husbands' complete satisfaction. This they maintained to the end. In the natural order of things Robert Harbottle should have paid heavily for interfering as he did in Paris between a woman and what she was entitled to live for. As a matter of fact he never paid anything at all; I doubt whether he ever knew himself a debtor. Judy kept her temperament under like a current and swam with the tides of the surface, taking refreshing dips only now and then which one traced in her eyes and her hair when she and Robert came back from leave. That sort of thing is lost in the sands of India, but it makes an oasis as it travels, and it sometimes seemed to me a curious pity that she and Anna should sit in the shade of it together, while Robert and Peter Chichele, their titular companions, blundered on in the desert. But after all, if you are born blind—and the men were both immensely liked, and the shooting was good.

Ten years later Somers joined. The Twelfth were at Peshawur. Robert Harbottle was Lieutenant-Colonel by that time and had the regiment. Distinction had incrusted, in the Indian way, upon Peter Chichele, its former colonel; he was General Commanding the District and KCB. So we were all still together in Peshawur. It was great luck for the Chicheles, Sir Peter's having the district, though his father's old regiment would have made it pleasant enough for the boy in any case. He came to us, I mean, of course, to two or three of us, with the interest that hangs about a victim of circumstances; we understood that he wasn't a 'born soldier'. Anna had told me on the contrary that he was a sacrifice to family tradition made inevitable by the General's unfortunate investments. Bellona's bridegroom was not a role he fancied, though he would make a kind of compromise as best man; he would agree, she said, to be a war correspondent and write picturesque specials for the London halfpenny press. There was the humour of the poor boy's despair in it, but she conveyed it, I remember, in exactly the same tone with which she had said to me years before that he wanted to drive a milk-cart. She carried quite her half of the family tradition, though she could talk of sacrifice and make her eyes wistful, contemplating for Somers the limitations of the drill-book and the camp of exercise, proclaiming and insisting upon what she would have done if she could only have chosen for him. Anna Chichele saw things that way. With more than a passable sense of all that was involved, if she could have made her son an artist in life or a commander-in-chief, if she could have given him the seeing eye or the Order of the Star of India, she would not have hesitated for an instant. Judy, with her single mind, cried out, almost at sight of him, upon them both, I mean both Anna and Sir Peter. Not that the boy carried his condemnation badly, or even obviously; I venture that no one noticed it in the mess; but it was naturally plain to those of us who were under the same. He had put in his two years with a British regiment at Meerut—they nurse subalterns that way for the Indian army—and his eyes no longer played with the tinsel vision of India; they looked instead into the arid stretch beyond. This preoccupation conveyed to the Surgeon-Major's wife the suggestion that Mr Chichele was the victim of a hopeless attachment. Mrs Harbottle made no such mistake; she saw simply, I imagine, the beginnings of her own hunger and thirst in him, looking back as she told us across a decade of dusty sunsets to remember them. The decade was there, close to the memory of all of us; we put, from Judy herself downward, an absurd amount of confidence in it.

She looked so well the night she met him. It was English mail day; she depended a great deal upon her letters, and I suppose somebody had written her a word that brought her that happy, still excitement that is the inner mystery of words. He went straight to her with some speech about his mother having given him leave, and for twenty minutes she patronized him on a sofa as his mother would not have dreamed of doing.

Anna Chichele, from the other side of the room, smiled on the pair.

'I depend on you and Judy to be good to him while we are away,' she said. She and Sir Peter were going on leave at the end of the week to Scotland, as usual, for the shooting.

Following her glance I felt incapable of the proportion she assigned me. 'I will see after his socks with pleasure,' I said. 'I think, don't you, we may leave the rest to Judy?'

Her eyes remained upon the boy, and I saw the passion rise in them, at which I turned mine elsewhere. Who can look unperturbed upon such a privacy of nature as that?

'Poor old Judy!' she went on. 'She never would be bothered with him in all his dear hobble-dehoy time; she resented his claims, the unreasonable creature, used to limit me to three anecdotes a week; and now she has him on her hands, if you like. See the pretty air of deference in the way he listens to her! He has nice manners, the villain, if he is a Chichele!'

'Oh, you have improved Sir Peter's,' I said kindly.

'I do hope Judy will think him worth while. I can't quite expect that he will be up to her, bless him, she is so much cleverer, isn't she, than any of us? But if she will just be herself with him it will make such a difference.'

The other two crossed the room to us at that, and Judy gaily made Somers over to his mother, trailing off to find Robert in the billiard-room.

'Well, what has Mrs Harbottle been telling you?' Anna asked him.

The young man's eye followed Judy, his hand went musingly to his moustache.

'She was telling me,' he said, 'that people in India were sepulchres of themselves, but that now and then one came who could roll away another's stone.'

'It sounds promising,' said Lady Chichele to me.

'It sounds cryptic,' I laughed to Somers, but I saw that he had the key.

I can not say that I attended diligently to Mr Chichele's socks, but the part corresponding was freely assigned me. After his people went I saw him often. He pretended to find qualities in my tea, implied that he found them in my talk. As a matter of fact it was my inquiring attitude that he loved, the knowledge that there was no detail that he could give me about himself, his impressions and experiences, that was unlikely to interest me. I would not for the world imply that he was egotistical or complacent, absolutely the reverse, but he possessed an articulate soul which found its happiness in expression, and I liked to listen. I feel that these are complicated words to explain a very simple relation, and I pause to wonder what is left to me if I wished to describe his commerce with Mrs Harbottle. Luckily there is an alternative; one needn't do it. I wish I had somewhere on paper Judy's own account of it at this period, however. It is a thing she would have enjoyed writing and more enjoyed communicating, at this period.

There was a grave reticence in his talk about her which amused me in the beginning. Mrs Harbottle had been for ten years important enough to us all, but her serious significance, the light and the beauty in her, had plainly been reserved for the discovery of this sensitive and intelligent person not very long from Sandhurst and exactly twenty-six. I was barely allowed a familiar reference, and anything approaching a flippancy was met with penetrating silence. I was almost rebuked for lightly suggesting that she must occasionally find herself bored in Peshawur.

'I think not anywhere,' said Mr Chichele; 'Mrs Harbottle is one of the few people who sound the privilege of living.'

This to me, who had counted Mrs Harbottle's yawns on so many occasions! It became presently necessary to be careful, tactful, in one's implications about Mrs Harbottle, and to recognize a certain distinction in the fact that one was the only person with whom Mr Chichele discussed her at all.

The day came when we talked to Robert; it was bound to come in the progress of any understanding and affectionate colloquy which had his wife for inspiration. I was familiar, of course, with Somers's opinion that the Colonel was an awfully good sort; that had been among the preliminaries and become understood as the base of all references. And I liked Robert Harbottle very well myself. When his adjutant called him a born leader of men, however, I felt compelled to look at the statement consideringly.

'In a tight place,' I said—dear me, what expressions had the freedom of our little frontier drawing-rooms!—'I would as soon depend on him as on anybody. But as for leadership—'

'He is such a good fellow that nobody here does justice to his soldierly qualities,' said Mr Chichele, 'except Mrs Harbottle.'

'Has she been telling you about them?' I inquired.

'Well,' he hesitated, 'she told me about the Mulla Nulla affair. She is rather proud of that. Any woman would be.'

'Poor dear Judy!' I mused.

Somers said nothing, but looked at me, removing his cigarette, as if my words would be the better of explanation.

'She has taken refuge in them—in Bob Harbottle's soldierly qualities—ever since she married him,' I continued.

'Taken refuge,' he repeated, coldly, but at my uncompromising glance his eyes fell.

'Well?' I said.

'You mean—'

'Oh, I mean what I say,' I laughed. 'Your cigarette has gone out—have another.'

'I think her devotion to him splendid.'

'Quite splendid. Have you seen the things he brought her from the Simla Art Exhibition? He said they were nice bits of colour, and she has hung them in the drawing-room, where she will have to look at them every day. Let us admire her—dear Judy.'

'Oh,' he said, with a fine air of detachment, 'do you think they are so necessary, those agreements?'

'Well,' I replied, 'we see that they are not indispensable. More sugar? I have only given you one lump. And we know, at all events,' I added, unguardedly, 'that she could never have had an illusion about him.'

The young man looked up quickly. 'Is that story true?' he asked.

'There was a story, but most of us have forgotten it. Who told you?'

'The doctor.'

'The Surgeon-Major,' I said, 'has an accurate memory and a sense of proportion. As I suppose you were bound to get it from somebody, I am glad you got it from him.'

I was not prepared to go on, and saw with some relief that Somers was not either. His silence, as he smoked, seemed to me deliberate; and I had oddly enough at this moment for the first time the impression that he was a man and not a boy. Then the Harbottles themselves joined us, very cheery after a gallop from Wazir-Bagh. We talked of old times, old friendships, good swords that were broken, names that had carried far, and Somers effaced himself in the perfect manner of the British subaltern. It was a long, pleasant gossip, and I thought Judy seemed rather glad to let her husband dictate its level, which, of course, he did. I noticed when the three rode away together that the Colonel was beginning to sit down rather solidly on his big New Zealander; and I watched the dusk come over from the foot-hills for a long time thinking more kindly than I had spoken of Robert Harbottle.

I have often wondered how far happiness is contributed to a temperament like Judy Harbottle's, and how far it creates its own; but I doubt whether, on either count, she found as much in any other winter of her life except perhaps the remote ones by the Seine. Those ardent hours of hers, when everything she said was touched with the flame of her individuality, came oftener; she suddenly cleaned up her palate and began to translate in one study after another the language of the frontier country, that spoke only in stones and in shadows under the stones and in sunlight over them. There is nothing in the Academy of this year, at all events, that I would exchange for the one she gave me. She lived her physical life at a pace which carried us all along with her; she hunted and drove and danced and dined with such sincere intention as convinced us all that in hunting and driving and dancing and dining there were satisfactions that had been somehow overlooked. The Surgeon-Major's wife said it was delightful to meet Mrs Harbottle, she seemed to enjoy everything so thoroughly; the Surgeon-Major looked at her critically and asked her if she were quite sure she hadn't a night temperature. He was a Scotchman. One night Colonel Harbottle, hearing her give away the last extra, charged her with renewing her youth.

'No, Bob,' she said, 'only imitating it.'

Ah, that question of her youth. It was so near her—still, she told me once, she heard the beat of its flying, and the pulse in her veins answered the false signal. That was afterward, when she told the truth. She was not so happy when she indulged herself otherwise. As when she asked one to remember that she was a middle-aged woman, with middle-aged thoughts and satisfactions.

'I am now really happiest,' she declared, 'when the Commissioner takes me in to dinner, when the General Commanding leads me to the dance.'

She did her best to make it an honest conviction. I offered her a recent success not crowned by the Academy, and she put it down on the table. 'By and by,' she said. 'At present I am reading Pascal and Bossuet.' Well, she was reading Pascal and Bossuet. She grieved aloud that most of our activities in India were so indomitably youthful, owing to the accident that most of us were always so young. 'There is no dignified distraction in this country,' she complained, 'for respectable ladies nearing forty.' She seemed to like to make these declarations in the presence of Somers Chichele, who would look at her with a little queer smile—a bad translation, I imagine, of what he felt.

She gave herself so generously to her seniors that somebody said Mrs Harbottle's girdle was hung with brass hats. It seems flippant to add that her complexion was as honest as the day, but the fact is that the year before Judy had felt compelled, like the rest of us, to repair just a little the ravages of the climate. If she had never done it one would not have looked twice at the absurdity when she said of the powder-puff in the dressing-room, 'I have raised that thing to the level of an immorality,' and sailed in to dance with an uncompromising expression and a face uncompromised. I have not spoken of her beauty; for one thing it was not always there, and there were people who would deny it altogether, or whose considered comment was, 'I wouldn't call her plain.' They, of course, were people in who she declined to be interested, but even for those of us who could evoke some demonstration of her vivid self her face would not always light in correspondence. When it did there was none that I liked better to look at; and I envied Somers Chichele his way to make it the pale, shining thing that would hold him lifted, in return, for hours together, with I know not what mystic power of a moon upon the tide. And he? Oh, he was dark and delicate, by nature simple, sincere, delightfully intelligent. His common title to charm was the rather sweet seriousness that rested on his upper lip, and a certain winning gratification in his attention; but he had a subtler one in his eyes, which must be always seeking and smiling over what they found; those eyes of perpetual inquiry for the exquisite which ask so little help to create it. A personality to button up in a uniform, good heavens!

As I begin to think of them together I remember how the maternal note appeared in her talk about him.

'His youth is pathetic,' she told me, 'but there is nothing that he does not understand.'

'Don't apologize, Judy,' I said. We were so brusque on the frontier. Besides, the matter still suffered a jocular presentment. Mrs Harbottle and Mr Chichele were still 'great friends'; we could still put them next each other at our dinner-parties without the feeling that it would be 'marked'. There was still nothing unusual in the fact that when Mrs Harbottle was there Mr Chichele might be taken for granted. We were so broad-minded also, on the frontier.

It grew more obvious, the maternal note. I began positively to dread it, almost as much, I imagine, as Somers did. She took her privileges all in Anna's name, she exercised her authority quite as Lady Chichele's proxy. She went to the very limit. 'Anna Chichele,' she said actually in his presence, 'is a fortunate woman. She has all kinds of cleverness, and she has her tall son. I have only one little talent, and I have no tall son.' Now it was not in nature that she could have had a son as tall as Somers, nor was that desire in her eyes. All civilization implies a good deal of farce, but this was a poor refuge, a cheap device; I was glad when it fell away from her sincerity, when the day came on which she looked into my fire and said simply, 'An attachment like ours has no terms.'

'I wonder,' I said.

'For what comes and goes,' she went on dreamily, 'how could there be a formula?'

'Look here, Judy,' I said, 'you know me very well. What if the flesh leaps with the spirit?'

She looked at me, very white. 'Oh no,' she said, 'no.'

I waited, but there seemed nothing more that she could say; and in the silence the futile negative seemed to wander round the room repeating itself like an echo, 'Oh no, no.' I poked the fire presently to drown the sound of it. Judy sat still, with her feet crossed and her hands thrust into the pockets of her coat, staring into the coals.

'Can you live independently, satisfied with your interests and occupations?' she demanded at last. 'Yes, I know you can. I can't. I must exist more than half in other people. It is what they think and feel that matters to me, just as much as what I think and feel. The best of life is in that communication.'

'It has always been a passion with you, Judy,' I replied. 'I can imagine how much you must miss—'

'Whom?'

'Anna Chichele,' I said softly.

She got up and walked about the room, fixing here and there an intent regard upon things which she did not see. 'Oh, I do,' she said at one point, with the effect of pulling herself together. She took another turn or two, and then finding herself near the door she went out. I felt as profoundly humiliated for her as if she had staggered.

The next night was one of those that stand out so vividly, for no reason that one can identify, in one's memory. We were dining with the Harbottles, a small party, for a tourist they had with them. Judy and I and Somers and the traveller had drifted out into the veranda, where the scent of Japanese lilies came and went on the spring wind to trouble the souls of any taken unawares. There was a brightness beyond the foot-hills where the moon was coming, and I remember how one tall clump swayed out against it, and seemed in passionate perfume to lay a burden on the breast. Judy moved away from it and sat clasping her knees on the edge of the veranda. Somers, when his eyes were not upon her, looked always at the lily.

Even the spirit of the globe-trotter was stirred, and he said, 'I think you Anglo-Indians live in a kind of little paradise.'

There was an instant's silence, and then Judy turned her face into the lamplight from the drawing-room. 'With everything but the essentials,' she said.

We stayed late; Mr Chichele and ourselves were the last to go. Judy walked with us along the moonlit drive to the gate, which is so unnecessary a luxury in India that the servants always leave it open. She swung the stiff halves together.

'Now,' she said, 'it is shut.'

'And I,' said Somers Chichele, softly and quickly, 'am on the other side.'

Even over that depth she could flash him a smile. 'It is the business of my life,' she gave him in return, 'to keep this gate shut.' I felt as if they had forgotten us. Somers mounted and rode off without a word; we were walking in a different direction. Looking back, I saw Judy leaning immovable on the gate, while Somers turned in his saddle, apparently to repeat the form of lifting his hat. And all about them stretched the stones of Kabul valley, vague and formless in the tide of the moonlight . . .

Next day a note from Mrs Harbottle informed me that she had gone to Bombay for a fortnight. In a postscript she wrote, 'I shall wait for the Chicheles there, and come back with them.' I remember reflecting that if she could not induce herself to take a passage to England in the ship that brought them, it seemed the right thing to do.

She did come back with them. I met the party at the station. I knew Somers would meet them, and it seemed to me, so imminent did disaster loom, that some one else should be there, some one to offer a covering movement or a flank support wherever it might be most needed. And among all our smiling faces disaster did come, or the cold premonition of it. We were all perfect, but Somers's lip trembled. Deprived for a fortnight he was eager for the draft, and he was only twenty-six. His lip trembled, and there, under the flickering station-lamps, suddenly stood that of which there never could be again any denial, for those of us who saw.

Did we make, I wonder, even a pretense of disguising the consternation that sprang up among us, like an armed thing, ready to kill any further suggestion of the truth? I don't know. Anna Chichele's unfinished sentence dropped as if someone had given her a blow upon the mouth. Coolies were piling the luggage into a hired carriage at the edge of the platform. She walked mechanically after them, and would have stepped in with it but for the sight of her own gleaming landau drawn up within a yard or two, and the General waiting. We all got home somehow, taking it with us, and I gave Lady Chichele twenty-four hours to come to me with her face all one question and her heart all one fear. She came in twelve.

'Have you seen it—long?' Prepared as I was her directness was demoralizing.

'It isn't a mortal disease.'

'Oh, for Heaven's sake—'

'Well, not with certainty, for more than a month.'

She made a little spasmodic movement with her hands, then dropped them pitifully. 'Couldn't you do *any*thing?'

I looked at her, and she said at once, 'No, of course you couldn't.'

For a moment or two I took my share of the heavy sense of it, my trivial share, which yet was an experience sufficiently exciting. 'I am afraid it will have to be faced,' I said.

'What will happen?' Anna cried. 'Oh, what will happen?'

'Why not the usual thing?' Lady Chichele looked up quickly as if at a reminder. 'The ambiguous attachment of the country,' I went on, limping but courageous, 'half declared, half admitted, that leads vaguely nowhere, and finally perishes as the man's life enriches itself—the thing we have seen so often.'

'Whatever Judy is capable of it won't be the usual thing. You know that.'

I had to confess in silence that I did.

'It flashed at me—the difference in her—in Bombay.' She pressed her lips together and then went on unsteadily. 'In her eyes, her voice. She was mannered, extravagant, elaborate. With me! All the way up I wondered and worried. But I never thought—' She stopped; her voice simply shook itself into silence. I called a servant.

'I am going to give you a good stiff peg,' I said. I apologize for the 'peg', but not for the whisky and soda. It is a beverage on the frontier, of which the vulgarity is lost in the value. While it was coming I tried to talk of other things, but she would only nod absently in the pauses.

'Last night we dined with him, it was guest night at the mess, and she was there. I watched her, and she knew it. I don't know whether she tried, but anyway, she failed. The covenant between them was written on her forehead whenever she looked at him, though that was seldom. She dared not look at him. And the little conversation that they had—you would have laughed—it was a comedy of stutters. The facile Mrs Harbottle!'

'You do well to be angry, naturally,' I said; 'but it would be fatal to let yourself go, Anna.'

'Angry? Oh, I am *sick*. The misery of it! The terror of it! If it were anybody but Judy! Can't you imagine the passion of a temperament like that in a woman who has all these years been feeding on herself? I tell you she will take him from my very arms. And he will go—to I dare not imagine what catastrophe! Who can prevent it? Who can prevent it?'

'There is you,' I said.

Lady Chichele laughed hysterically. 'I think you ought to say, "There are you." I—what can I do? Do you realize that it's *Judy!* My friend—my other self? Do you think we can drag all that out of it? Do you think a tie like that can be broken by an accident—by a misfortune? With it all I *adore* Judy Harbottle. I love her, as I have always loved her, and—it's damnable, but I don't know whether, whatever happened, I wouldn't go on loving her.'

'Finish your peg,' I said. She was sobbing.

'Where I blame myself most,' she went on, 'is for not seeing in him all that makes him mature to her—that makes her forget the absurd difference between them, and take him simply and sincerely as I know she does, as the contemporary of her soul if not of her body. I saw none of that. Could I, as his mother? Would he show it to me? I thought him just a charming boy, clever, too, of course, with nice instincts and well plucked; we were always proud of that, with his delicate physique. Just a boy! I haven't yet stopped thinking how different he looks without his curls. And I thought she would be just kind and gracious and delightful to him because he was my son.'

'There, of course,' I said, 'is the only chance.'

'Where—what?'

'He is your son.'

'Would you have me appeal to her? Do you know I don't think I could?'

'Dear me, no. Your case must present itself. It must spring upon her and grow before her out of your silence, and if you can manage it, your confidence. There is a great deal after all, remember, to hold her in that. I can't somehow imagine her failing you. Otherwise—'

Lady Chichele and I exchanged a glance of candid admission.

'Otherwise she would be capable of sacrificing everything—everything. Of gathering her life into an hour. I know. And do you know if the thing were less impossible, less grotesque, I should not be so much afraid? I mean that the *absolute* indefensibility of it might bring her a recklessness and a momentum which might—'

'Send her over the verge,' I said. 'Well, go home and ask her to dinner.'

There was a good deal more to say, of course, than I have thought proper to put down here, but before Anna went I saw that she was keyed up to the heroic part. This was none the less to her credit because it was the only part, the dictation of a sense of expediency that despaired while it dictated. The noble thing was her capacity to take it, and, amid all that warred in her, to carry it out on the brave high lines of her inspiration. It seemed a literal inspiration, so perfectly calculated that it was hard not to think sometimes, when one saw them together, that Anna had been lulled into a simple resumption of the old relation. Then from the least thing possible—the lift of an eyelid—it flashed upon one that between these two every moment was dramatic, and one took up the word with a curious sense of detachment and futility, but with one's heart beating like a trip-hammer with the mad excitement of it. The acute thing was the splendid sincerity of Judy Harbottle's response. For days she was profoundly on her guard, then suddenly she seemed to become practically, vividly aware of what I must go on calling the great chance, and passionately to fling herself upon it. It was the strangest co-operation without a word or a sign to show it conscious—a playing together for stakes that could not be admitted, a thing to hang upon breathless. It was there between them—the tenable ground of what they were to each other: they occupied it with almost an equal eye upon the tide that threatened, while I from my mainland tower also made an anguished calculation of the chances. I think in spite of the menace, they found real beatitudes; so keenly did they set about the business that it brought them moments finer than any they could count in the years that were behind them, the flat and colourless years that were gone. Once or twice the wild idea even visited me that it was, after all, the projection of his mother in Somers that had so seized Judy Harbottle, and that the original was all that was needed to help the happy process of detachment. Somers himself at the time was a good deal away on escort duty: they had a clear field.

I can not tell exactly when—between Mrs Harbottle and myself—it became a matter for reference more or less overt, I mean her defined problem, the thing that went about between her and the sun. It will be imagined that it did not come up like the weather; indeed, it was hardly ever to be envisaged and never to be held; but it was always there, and out of our joint consciousness it would sometimes leap and pass, without shape or face. It might slip between two sentences, or it might remain, a dogging shadow, for an hour. Or a week would go by while, with a strong hand, she held it out of sight altogether and talked of Anna—always of Anna. Her eyes shone with the things she told me then: she seemed to keep herself under the influence of them as if they had the power of narcotics. At the end of a time like this she turned to me in the door as she was going and stood silent, as if she could neither go nor stay. I had been able to make nothing of her that afternoon: she had seemed preoccupied with the pattern of the carpet which she traced continually with her riding crop, and finally I, too, had relapsed. She sat haggard, with the fight forever in her eyes, and the day seemed to sombre about her in her corner. When she turned in the door, I looked up with sudden prescience of a crisis.

'Don't jump,' she said, 'it was only to tell you that I have persuaded Robert to apply for furlough. Eighteen months. From the first of April. Don't touch me.' I suppose I made a movement towards her. Certainly I wanted to throw my arms about her; with the instinct, I suppose, to steady her in her great resolution.

'At the end of that time, as you know, he will be retired. I had some trouble, he is so keen on the regiment, but I think—I have succeeded. You might mention it to Anna.'

'Haven't you?' sprang past my lips.

'I can't. It would be like taking an oath to tell her, and—I can't take an oath to go. But I mean to.'

'There is nothing to be said,' I brought out, feeling indeed that there was not. 'But I congratulate you, Judy.'

'No, there is nothing to be said. And you congratulate me, no doubt!'

She stood for a moment quivering in the isolation she made for herself; and I felt a primitive angry revolt against the delicate trafficking of souls that could end in such ravage and disaster. The price was too heavy; I would have denuded her, at the moment, of all that had led her into this, and turned her out a clod with fine shoulders like fifty other women in Peshawur. Then, perhaps, because I held myself silent and remote and she had no emotion of fear from me, she did not immediately go.

'It will beat itself away, I suppose, like the rest of the unreasonable pain of the world,' she said at last; and that, of course, brought me to her side. 'Things will go back to their proportions. This,' she touched an open rose, 'will claim its beauty again. And life will become—perhaps what it was before.' Still I found nothing to say, I could only put my arm in hers and walk with her to the edge of the veranda where the syce was holding her horse. She stroked the animal's neck. 'Everything in me answered him,' she informed me, with the grave intelligence of a patient who relates a symptom past. As she took the reins she turned to me again. 'His spirit came to mine like a homing bird,' she said, and in her smile even the pale reflection of happiness was sweet and stirring. It left me hanging in imagination over the source and the stream, a little blessed in the mere understanding.

Too much blessed for confidence, or any safe feeling that the source was bound. Rather I saw it leaping over every obstacle, flashing to its destiny. As I drove to the Club next day I decided that I would not tell Anna Chichele of Colonel Harbottle's projected furlough. If to Judy telling her would be like taking an oath that they would go, to me it would at least be like assuming sponsorship for their intention. That would be heavy indeed. From the first of April—we were then in March. Anna would hear it soon enough from the General, would see it soon enough, almost, in the *Gazette,* when it would have passed into irrecoverable fact. So I went by her with locked lips, kept out of the way of those eyes of the mother that asked and asked, and would have seen clear to any depth, any hiding-place of knowledge like that. As I pulled up at the Club I saw Colonel Harbottle talking concernedly to the wife of our Second-in-Command, and was reminded that I had not heard for some days how Major Watkins was going on. So I, too, approached Mrs Watkins in her victoria to ask. Robert Harbottle kindly forestalled her reply. 'Hard luck, isn't it? Watkins has been ordered home at once. Just settled in their new house, too—last of the kit came up from Calcutta yesterday, didn't it, Mrs Watkins? But it's sound to go—Peshawur is the worst hole in Asia to shake off dysentery in.'

We agreed upon this and discussed the sale-list of her new furniture that Mrs Watkins would have to send round the station, and considered the chances of a trooper—to the Watkinses with two children and not a penny but his pay it did make it easier not to have to go by a liner—and Colonel Harbottle and I were half-way to the reading-room before the significance of Major Watkin's sick-leave flashed upon me.

'But this,' I cried, 'will make a difference to your plans. You won't—'

'Be able to ask for that furlough Judy wants. Rather not. I'm afraid she's disappointed—she was tremendously set on going—but it doesn't matter tuppence to me.'

I sought out Mrs Harbottle, at the end of the room. She looked radiant; she sat on the edge of the table and swung a light-hearted heel. She was talking to people who in themselves were a witness to high spirits, Captain the Hon. Freddy Gisborne, Mrs Flamboys.

At sight of me her face clouded, fell suddenly into the old weary lines. It made me feel somehow a little sick; I went back to my cart and drove home.

For more than a week I did not see her except when I met her riding with Somers Chichele along the peach-bordered road that leads to the Wazir-Bagh. The trees were all in blossom and made a picture that might well catch dreaming hearts into a beatitude that would correspond. The air was full of spring and the scent of violets, those wonderful Peshawur violets that grow in great clumps, tall and double. Gracious clouds came and trailed across the frontier barrier; blue as an idyll it rose about us; the city smiled in her gardens.

She had it all in her face, poor Judy, all the spring softness and more, the morning she came, intensely controlled, to announce her defeat. I was in the drawing-room doing the flowers; I put them down to look at her. The wonderful telegram from Simla arrived—that was the wonderful part—at the same time; I remembered how the red, white, and blue turban of the telegraph peon bobbed up behind her shoulder in the veranda. I signed and laid it on the table; I suppose it seemed hardly likely that anything could be important enough to interfere at the moment with my impression of what love, unbound and victorious, could do with a face I thought I knew. Love sat there careless of the issue, full of delight. Love proclaimed that between him and Judith Harbottle it was all over—she had met him, alas, in too narrow a place—and I marvelled at the paradox with which he softened every curve and underlined every vivid note of personality in token that it had just begun. He sat there in great serenity, and though I knew that somewhere behind lurked a vanquished woman, I saw her through such a radiance that I could not be sure of seeing her at all . . .

She went back to the very first of it; she seemed herself intensely interested in the facts; and there is no use in pretending that, while she talked, the moral consideration was at all present with me either; it wasn't. Her extremity was the thing that absorbed us; she even, in tender thoughtfulness, diagnosed it from its definite beautiful beginning.

'It was there, in my heart, when I woke one morning, exquisite and strange, the assurance of a gift. How had it come there, while I slept? I assure you when I closed my eyes it did not exist for me. . . . Yes, of course, I had seen him, but only somewhere at dinner . . . As the day went on it changed—it turned into a clear pool, into a flower. And I—think of my not understanding! I was pleased with it! For a long time, for days, I never dreamed that it could be anything but a little secret joy. Then, suddenly—oh, I had not been perceiving enough!—it was in all my veins, a tide, an efflorescence, a thing of my very life.

'Then—it was a little late—I understood, and since—

'I began by hating it—being furious, furious—and afraid, too. Sometimes it was like a low cloud, hovering and travelling always with me, sometimes like a beast of prey that went a little way off and sat looking at me . . .

'I have—done my best. But there is nothing to do, to kill, to abolish. How can I say, "I will not let you in," when it is already there? How can I assume indifference when this thing is imposed upon every moment of my day? And it has grown so sweet—the longing—that—isn't it strange?—I could more willingly give him up than the desire of him. That seems as impossible to part with as life itself.'

She sat reflective for a moment, and I saw her eyes slowly fill.

'Don't—don't *cry,* Judy,' I faltered, wanting to horribly, myself.

She smiled them dry.

'Not now. But I am giving myself, I suppose, to many tears.'

'God help you,' I said. What else was there to say?

'There is no such person,' she replied, gaily. 'There is only a blessed devil.'

'Then you go all the way—to the logical conclusion?'

She hardly hesitated. 'To the logical conclusion. What poor words!'

'May I ask—when?'

'I should like to tell you that quite definitely, and I think I can. The English mail leaves tonight.'

'And you have arranged to take it?'

'We have arranged nothing. Do you know'—she smiled as if at the fresh colours of an idyll—'we have not even come to the admission? There has been between us no word, no vision. Ah, we have gone in bonds, and dumb! Hours we have had, exquisite hours of the spirit, but never a moment of the heart, a moment confessed. It was mine to give—that moment, and he has waited—I know—wondering whether perhaps it would ever come. And today—we are going for a ride today, and I do not think we shall come back.'

'O Judy,' I cried, catching at her sleeve, 'he is only a boy!'

'There were times when I thought that conclusive. Now the misery of it has gone to sleep; don't waken it. It pleases me to believe that the years are a convention. I never had any dignity, you know, and I seem to have missed the moral deliverance. I only want—oh, you know what I want. Why don't you open your telegram?'

I had been folding and fingering the brown envelope as if it had been a scrap of waste-paper.

'It is probably from Mrs Watkins about the victoria,' I said, feeling its profound irrelevance. 'I wired an offer to her in Bombay. However'—and I read the telegram, the little solving telegram from Army Headquarters. I turned my back on her to read it again, and then I replaced it very carefully and put it in my pocket. It was a moment to take hold of with both hands, crying on all one's gods for steadiness.

'How white you look!' said Mrs Harbottle, with concern. 'Not bad news?'

'On the contrary, excellent news. Judy, will you stay to lunch?'

She looked at me, hesitating. 'Won't it seem rather a compromise on your part? When you ought to be rousing the city—'

'I don't intend to rouse the city,' I said.

'I have given you the chance.'

'Thank you,' I said, grimly, 'but the only real favour you can do me is to stay and lunch.' It was then just on one.

'I'll stay,' she said, 'if you will promise not to make any sort of effort. I shouldn't mind, but it would distress you.'

'I promise absolutely,' I said, and ironical joy rose up in me, and the telegram burned in my pocket.

She would talk of it, though I found it hard to let her go on, knowing and knowing and knowing as I did that for that day at least it could not be. There was very little about herself that she wanted to tell me; she was there confessed a woman whom joy had overcome; it was understood that we both accepted that situation. But in the details which she asked me to take charge of it was plain that she also kept a watchful eye upon fate—matters of business.

We were in the drawing-room. The little round clock in its Amritsar case marked half-past three. Judy put down her coffee-cup and rose to go.

As she glanced at the clock the light deepened in her eyes, and I, with her hand in mine, felt like an agent of the Destroyer—for it was half-past three—consumed myself with fear lest the blow had miscarried. Then as we stood, suddenly, the sound of hoofs at a gallop on the drive, and my husband threw himself off at the door and tore through the hall to his room; and in the certainty that overwhelmed me even Judy, for an instant, stood dim and remote.

'Major Jim seems to be in a hurry,' said Mrs Harbottle, lightly. 'I have always liked your husband. I wonder whether he will say tomorrow that he always liked me.'

'Dear Judy, I don't think he will be occupied with you tomorrow.'

'Oh, surely, just a little, if I go tonight.'

'You won't go tonight.'

She looked at me helplessly. I felt as if I were insisting upon her abasement instead of her salvation. 'I wish—'

'You're not going—you're not! You can't! Look!'

I pulled it out of my pocket and thrust it at her—the telegram. It came, against every regulation, from my good friend the Deputy Adjutant-General, in Simla, and it read, '*Row Khurram 12th probably ordered front three hours' time*.'

Her face changed—how my heart leaped to see it change!—and that took command there which will command trampling, even in the women of the camp, at news like this.

'What luck that Bob couldn't take his furlough!' she exclaimed, single-thoughted. 'But you have known this for hours'—there was even something of the Colonel's wife, authority, incisiveness. 'Why didn't you tell me? Ah—I see.'

I stood before her abashed, and that was ridiculous, while she measured me as if I presented in myself the woman I took her to be. 'It wasn't like that,' she said. I had to defend myself. 'Judy,' I said, 'if you weren't in honour bound to Anna, how could I know that you would be in honour bound to the regiment? There was a train at three.'

'I beg to assure you that you have overcalculated,' said Mrs Harbottle. Her eyes were hard and proud. 'And I am not sure'—a deep red swept over her face, a man's blush—'in the light of this I am not sure that I am not in honour bound to Anna.'

We had reached the veranda, and at her signal her coachman drove quickly up. 'You have kept me here three hours when there was the whole of Bob's kit to see to,' she said, as she flung herself in; 'you might have thought of that.'

It was a more than usually tedious campaign, and Colonel Robert Harbottle was ambushed and shot in a place where one must believe pure boredom induced him to take his men. The incident was relieved, the newspapers said—and they are seldom so clever in finding relief for such incidents—by the dash and courage shown by Lieutenant Chichele, who, in one of those feats which it has lately been the fashion to criticize, carried the mortally wounded body of his Colonel out of range at conspicuous risk of depriving the Queen of another officer. I helped Judy with her silent packing; she had forgiven me long before that; and she settled almost at once into the flat in Chelsea which has since been credited with so delightful an atmosphere, went back straight into her own world. I have always kept her first letters about it, always shall. For months after, while the expedition still raged after snipers and rifle-thieves, I discussed with Lady Chichele the probable outcome of it all. I have sometimes felt ashamed of leaping as straight as I did with Anna to what we thought the inevitable. I based no calculation on all Mrs Harbottle had gone back to, just as I had based no calculation on her ten years' companionship in arms when I kept her from the three o'clock train. This last was a retrospection in which Anna naturally could not join me; she never knew, poor dear, how fortunate as to its moment was the campaign she deplored, and nothing to this day can have disturbed her conviction that the bond she was at such magnificent pains to strengthen, held against the strain, as long, happily, as the supreme need existed. 'How right you were!' she often said. 'She did, after all, love me best, dear, wonderful Judy!' Her distress about poor Robert Harbottle was genuine enough, but one could not be surprised at a certain ambiguity; one tear for Robert, so to speak, and two for her boy. It could hardly be, for him, a marriage after his mother's heart. And she laid down with some emphasis that Somers was brilliantly entitled to all he was likely to get—which was natural, too . . .

I had been from the beginning so much 'in it' that Anna showed me, a year later, though I don't believe she liked doing it, the letter in part of which Mrs Harbottle shall finally excuse herself.

'Somers will give you this,' I read, 'and with it take back your son. You will not find, I know, anything grotesque in the charming enthusiasm with which he has offered his life to me; you understand too well, you are too kind. And if you wonder that I can so render up a dear thing which I might keep and would once have taken, think how sweet in the desert is the pool and how barren was the prospect from Balclutha.'

It was like her to abandon in pride a happiness that asked so much less humiliation; I don't know why, but it was like her. And of course, when one thought of it, she had consulted all sorts of high expediencies. But I sat silent with remembrance, quieting a pang in my heart, trying not to calculate how much it had cost Judy Harbottle to take her second chance.

1903

A Mother in India

I

There were times when we had to go without puddings to pay John's uniform bills, and always I did the facings myself with a cloth-ball to save getting new ones. I would have polished his sword, too, if I had been allowed; I adored his sword. And once, I remember, we painted and varnished our own dog-cart, and very smart it looked, to save fifty rupees. We had nothing but our pay—John had his company when we were married, but what is that?—and life was made up of small knowing economies, much more amusing in recollection than in practice. We were sodden poor, and that is a fact, poor and conscientious, which was worse. A big fat spider of a money-lender came one day into the veranda and tempted us—we lived in a hut, but it had a veranda—and John threatened to report him to the police. Poor when everybody else had enough to live in the open-handed Indian fashion, that was what made it so hard; we were alone in our sordid little ways. When the expectation of Cecily came to us we made out to be delighted, knowing that the whole station pitied us, and when Cecily came herself, with a swamping burst of expense, we kept up the pretence splendidly. She was peevish, poor little thing, and she threatened convulsions from the beginning, but we both knew that it was abnormal not to love her a great deal, more than life, immediately and increasingly; and we applied ourselves honestly to do it, with the thermometer at a hundred and two, and the nurse leaving at the end of a fortnight because she discovered that I had only six of everything for the table. To find out a husband's virtues, you must marry a poor man. The regiment was under-officered as usual, and John had to take parade at daylight quite three times a week; but he walked up and down the veranda with Cecily constantly till two in the morning, when a little coolness came. I usually lay awake the rest of the night in fear that a scorpion would drop from the ceiling on her. Nevertheless, we were of excellent mind towards Cecily; we were in such terror, not so much of failing in our duty towards her as towards the ideal standard of mankind. We were very anxious indeed not to come short. To be found too small for one's place in nature would have been odious. We would talk about her for an hour at a time, even when John's charger was threatening glanders and I could see his mind perpetually wandering to the stable. I would say to John that she had brought a new element into our lives—she had indeed!—and John would reply, 'I know what you mean,' and to go on to prophesy that she would 'bind us together'. We didn't need binding together; we were more to each other, there in the desolation of that arid frontier outpost, than most husbands and wives; but it seemed a proper and hopeful thing to believe, so we believed it. Of course, the real experience would have come, we weren't monsters; but fate curtailed the opportunity. She was just five weeks old when the doctor told us that we must either pack her home immediately or lose her, and the very next day John went down with enteric. So Cecily was sent to England with a sergeant's wife who had lost her twins, and I settled down under the direction of a native doctor, to fight for my husband's life, without ice or proper food, or sickroom comforts of any sort. Ah! Fort Samila, with the sun glaring up from the sand!—however, it is a long time ago now. I trusted the baby willingly to Mrs Berry and to Providence, and did not fret; my capacity for worry, I suppose, was completely absorbed. Mrs Berry's letters, describing the child's improvement on the voyage and safe arrival came, I remember, the day on which John was allowed his first solid mouthful; it had been a long siege. 'Poor little wretch!' he said when I read it aloud; and after that Cecily became an episode.

She had gone to my husband's people; it was the best arrangement. We were lucky that it was possible; so many children had to be sent to strangers and hirelings. Since an unfortunate infant must be brought into the world and set adrift, the haven of its grandmother and its Aunt Emma and its Aunt Alice certainly seemed providential. I had absolutely no cause for anxiety, as I often told people, wondering that I did not feel a little all the same. Nothing, I knew, could exceed the conscientious devotion of all three Farnham ladies to the child. She would appear upon their somewhat barren horizon as a new and interesting duty, and the small additional income she also represented would be almost nominal compensation for the care she would receive. They were excellent persons of the kind that talk about matins and vespers, and attend both. They helped little charities and gave little teas, and wrote little notes, and made deprecating allowance for the eccentricities of their titled or moneyed acquaintances. They were the subdued, smiling, unimaginatively dressed women on a small definite income that you meet at every rectory garden-party in the country, a little snobbish, a little priggish, wholly conventional, but apart from these weaknesses, sound and simple and dignified, managing their two small servants with a display of the most exact traditions, and keeping a somewhat vague and belated but constant eye upon the doings of their country as chronicled in a bi-weekly paper. They were all immensely interested in royalty, and would read paragraphs aloud to each other about how the Princess Beatrice or the Princess Maud had opened a fancy bazaar, looking remarkably well in plain grey poplin trimmed with Irish lace—an industry which, as is well known, the Royal Family has set its heart on rehabilitating. Upon which Mrs Farnham's comment invariably would be, 'How thoughtful of them, dear!' and Alice would usually say, 'Well, if I were a princess, I should like something nicer than plain grey poplin.' Alice, being the youngest, was not always expected to think before she spoke. Alice painted in water-colours, but Emma was supposed to have the most common sense.

They took turns in writing to us with the greatest regularity about Cecily; only once, I think, did they miss the weekly mail, and that was when she threatened diphtheria and they thought we had better be kept in ignorance. The kind and affectionate terms of these letters never altered except with the facts they described—teething, creeping, measles, cheeks growing round and rosy, all were conveyed in the same smooth, pat, and proper phrases, so absolutely empty of any glimpse of the child's personality that after the first few months it was like reading about a somewhat uninteresting infant in a book. I was sure Cecily was not uninteresting, but her chroniclers were. We used to wade through the long, thin sheets and saw how much more satisfactory it would be when Cecily could write to us herself. Meanwhile we noted her weekly progress with much the feeling one would have about a far-away little bit of property that was giving no trouble and coming on exceedingly well. We would take possession of Cecily at our convenience; till then, it was gratifying to hear of our unearned increment in dear little dimples and sweet little curls.

She was nearly four when I saw her again. We were home on three months' leave; John had just got his first brevet for doing something which he does not allow me to talk about in the Black Mountain country; and we were fearfully pleased with ourselves. I remember that excitement lasted well up to Port Said. As far as the Canal, Cecily was only one of the pleasures and interests we were going home to: John's majority was the thing that really gave savour to life. But the first faint line of Europe brought my child to my horizon; and all the rest of the way she kept her place, holding out her little arms to me, beckoning me on. Her four motherless years brought compunction to my heart and tears to my eyes; she should have all the compensation that could be. I suddenly realized how ready I was—how ready—to have her back. I rebelled fiercely against John's decision that we must not take her with us on our return to the frontier; privately, I resolved to dispute it, and, if necessary, I saw myself abducting the child—my own child. My days and nights as the ship crept on were full of a long ache to possess her; the defrauded tenderness of the last four years rose up in me and sometimes caught at my throat. I could think and talk and dream of nothing else. John indulged me as much as was reasonable, and only once betrayed by a yawn that the subject was not for him endlessly absorbing. Then I cried and he apologized. 'You know,' he said, 'it isn't exactly the same thing. I'm not her mother.' At which I dried my tears and expanded, proud and pacified. I was her mother!

Then the rainy station and Alice, all-embracing in a damp waterproof, and the drive in the fly, and John's mother at the gate and a necessary pause while I kissed John's mother. Dear thing, she wanted to hold our hands and look into our faces and tell us how little we had changed for all our hardships; and on the way to the house she actually stopped to point out some alterations in the flower-borders. At last the drawing-room door and the smiling housemaid turning the handle and the unforgettable picture of a little girl, a little girl unlike anything we had imagined, starting bravely to trot across the room with the little speech that had been taught her. Half-way she came; I suppose our regards were too fixed, too absorbed, for there she stopped with a wail of terror at the strange faces, and ran straight back to the outstretched arms of her Aunt Emma. The most natural thing in the world, no doubt. I walked over to a chair opposite with my hand-bag and umbrella and sat down—a spectator, aloof and silent. Aunt Emma fondled and quieted the child, apologizing for her to me, coaxing her to look up, but the little figure still shook with sobs, hiding its face in the bosom that it knew. I smiled politely, like any other stranger, at Emma's deprecations, and sat impassive, looking at my alleged baby breaking her heart at the sight of her mother. It is not amusing even now to remember the anger that I felt. I did not touch her or speak to her; I simply sat observing my alien possession, in the frock I had not made and the sash I had not chosen, being coaxed and kissed and protected and petted by its Aunt Emma. Presently I asked to be taken to my room, and there I locked myself in for two atrocious hours. Just once my heart beat high, when a tiny knock came and a timid, docile little voice said that tea was ready. But I heard the rustle of a skirt, and guessed the directing angel in Aunt Emma, and responded, 'Thank you, dear, run away and say that I am coming,' with a pleasant visitor's inflection which I was able to sustain for the rest of the afternoon.

'She goes to bed at seven,' said Emma.

'Oh, does she?' said I. 'A very good hour, I should think.'

'She sleeps in my room,' said Mrs Farnham.

'We give her mutton broth very often, but seldom stock soup,' said Aunt Emma. 'Mamma thinks it is too stimulating.'

'Indeed?' said I, to all of it.

They took me up to see her in her crib, and pointed out, as she lay asleep, that though she had 'a general look' of me, her features were distinctively Farnham.

'Won't you kiss her?' asked Alice. 'You haven't kissed her yet, and she is used to so much affection.'

'I don't think I could take such an advantage of her,' I said.

They looked at each other, and Mrs Farnham said that I was plainly worn out. I mustn't sit up to prayers.

If I had been given anything like reasonable time I might have made a fight for it, but four weeks—it took a month each way in those days—was too absurdly little; I could do nothing. But I would not stay at mamma's. It was more than I would ask of myself, that daily disappointment under the mask of gratified discovery, for long.

I spent an approving, unnatural week, in my farcical character, bridling my resentment and hiding my mortification with pretty phrases; and then I went up to town and drowned my sorrows in the summer sales. I took John with me. I may have been Cecily's mother in theory, but I was John's wife in fact.

We went back to the frontier, and the regiment saw a lot of service.

That meant medals and fun for my husband, but economy and anxiety for me, though I managed to be allowed as close to the firing line as any woman.

Once the Colonel's wife and I, sitting in Fort Samila, actually heard the rifles of a punitive expedition cracking on the other side of the river—that was a bad moment. My man came in after fifteen hours' fighting, and went sound asleep, sitting before his food with his knife and fork in his hands. But service makes heavy demands besides those on your wife's nerves. We had saved two thousand rupees, I remember, against another run home, and it all went like powder, in the Mirzai expedition; and the run home diminished to a month in a boarding-house in the hills.

Meanwhile, however, we had begun to correspond with our daughter, in large round words of one syllable, behind which, of course, was plain the patient guiding hand of Aunt Emma. One could hear Aunt Emma suggesting what would be nice to say, trying to instil a little pale affection for the far-off papa and mamma. There was so little Cecily and so much Emma—of course, it could not be otherwise—that I used to take, I fear, but a perfunctory joy in these letters. When we went home again I stipulated absolutely that she was to write to us without any sort of supervision—the child was ten.

'But the spelling!' cried Aunt Emma, with lifted eyebrows.

'Her letters aren't exercises,' I was obliged to retort; 'she will do the best she can.'

We found her a docile little girl, with nice manners, a thoroughly unobjectionable child. I saw quite clearly that I could not have brought her up so well; indeed, there were moments when I fancied that Cecily, contrasting me with her aunts, wondered a little what my bringing up could have been like. With this reserve of criticism on Cecily's part, however, we got on very tolerably, largely because I found it impossible to assume any responsibility towards her, and in moments of doubt or discipline referred her to her aunts. We spent a pleasant summer with a little girl in the house whose interest in us was amusing, and whose outings it was gratifying to arrange; but when we went back, I had no desire to take her with us. I thought her very much better where she was.

Then came the period which is filled, in a subordinate degree, with Cecily's letters. I do not wish to claim more than I ought; they were not my only or even my principal interest in life. It was a long period; it lasted till she was twenty-one. John had had promotion in the meantime, and there was rather more money, but he had earned his second brevet with a bullet through one lung, and the doctors ordered our leave to be spent in South Africa. We had photographs, we knew she had grown tall and athletic and comely, and the letters were always very creditable. I had the unusual and qualified privilege of watching my daughter's development from ten to twenty-one, at a distance of four thousand miles, by means of the written word. I wrote myself as provocatively as possible; I sought for every string, but the vibration that came back across the seas to me was always other than the one I looked for, and sometimes there was none. Nevertheless, Mrs Farnham wrote me that Cecily very much valued my communications. Once when I had described an unusual excursion in a native state, I learned that she had read my letter aloud to the sewing circle. After that I abandoned description, and confined myself to such intimate personal details as no sewing circle could find amusing. The child's own letters were simply a mirror of the ideas of the Farnham ladies; that must have been so, it was not altogether my jaundiced eye. Alice and Emma and grandmamma paraded the pages in turn. I very early gave up hope of discoveries in my daughter, though as much of the original as I could detect was satisfactorily simple and sturdy. I found little things to criticize, of course, tendencies to correct; and by return post I criticized and corrected, but the distance and the deliberation seemed to touch my maxims with a kind of arid frivolity, and sometimes I tore them up. One quick, warm-blooded scolding would have been worth a sheaf of them. My studied little phrases could only inoculate her with a dislike for me without protecting her from anything under the sun.

However, I found she didn't dislike me, when John and I went home at last to bring her out. She received me with just a hint of kindness, perhaps, but on the whole very well.

II

John was recalled, of course, before the end of our furlough, which knocked various things on the head; but that is the sort of thing one learned to take with philosophy in any lengthened term of Her Majesty's service. Besides, there is usually sugar for the pill; and in this case it was a Staff command bigger than anything we expected for at least five years to come. The excitement of it when it was explained to her gave Cecily a charming colour. She took a good deal of interest in the General, her papa; I think she had an idea that his distinction would alleviate the situation in India, however it might present itself. She accepted that prospective situation calmly; it had been placed before her all her life. There would always be a time when she should go and live with papa and mamma in India, and so long as she was of age to receive the idea with rebel tears she was assured that pappa and mamma would give her a pony. The pony was no longer added to the prospect; it was absorbed no doubt in the general list of attractions calculated to reconcile a young lady to a parental roof with which she had no practical acquaintance. At all events, when I feared the embarrassment and dismay of a pathetic parting with darling grandmamma and the aunties, and the sweet cat and the dear vicar and all the other objects of affection, I found an agreeable unexpected philosophy.

I may add that while I anticipated such broken-hearted farewells I was quite prepared to take them easily. Time, I imagined, had brought philosophy to me also, equally agreeable and equally unexpected.

It was a Bombay ship, full of returning Anglo-Indians. I looked up and down the long saloon tables with a sense of relief and of solace; I was again among my own people. They belonged to Bengal and to Burma, to Madras and to Punjab, but they were all my people. I could pick out a score that I knew in fact, and there were none that in imagination I didn't know. The look of wider seas and skies, the casual experienced glance, the touch of irony and of tolerance, how well I knew it and how well I liked it! Dear old England, sitting in our wake, seemed to hold by comparison a great many soft, unsophisticated people, immensely occupied about very particular trifles. How difficult it had been, all the summer, to be interested! These of my long acquaintance belonged to my country's Executive, acute, alert, with the marks of travail on them. Gladly I went in and out of the women's cabins and listened to the argot of the men; my own ruling, administering, soldiering little lot.

Cecily looked at them askance. To her the atmosphere was alien, and I perceived that gently and privately she registered objections. She cast a disapproving eye upon the wife of a Conservator of Forests, who scanned with interest a distant funnel and laid a small wager that it belonged to the Messageries Maritimes. She looked with a straightened lip at the crisply stepping women who walked the deck in short and rather shabby skirts with their hands in their jacket-pockets talking transfers and promotions; and having got up at six to make a water-colour sketch of the sunrise, she came to me in profound indignation to say that she had met a man in his pyjamas; no doubt, poor wretch, on his way to be shaved. I was unable to convince her that he was not expected to visit the barber in all his clothes.

At the end of the third day she told me that she wished these people wouldn't talk to her; she didn't like them. I had turned in the hour we left the Channel and had not left my berth since, so possibly I was not in the most amiable mood to receive a douche of cold water. 'I must try to remember, dear,' I said, 'that you have been brought up altogether in the society of pussies and vicars and elderly ladies, and of course you miss them. But you must have a little patience. I shall be up tomorrow, if this beastly sea continues to go down; and then we will try to find somebody suitable to introduce to you.'

'Thank you, mamma,' said my daughter, without a ray of suspicion. Then she added consideringly, 'Aunt Emma and Aunt Alice do seem quite elderly ladies beside you, and yet you are older than either of them, aren't you? I wonder how that is.'

It was so innocent, so admirable, that I laughed at my own expense; while Cecily, doing her hair, considered me gravely. 'I wish you would tell me why you laugh, mamma,' quoth she; 'you laugh so often.'

We had not to wait after all for my good offices of the next morning. Cecily came down at ten o'clock that night quite happy and excited; she had been talking to a bishop, such a dear bishop. The bishop had been showing her his collection of photographs, and she had promised to play the harmonium for him at the eleven-o'clock service in the morning. 'Bless me!' said I, 'is it Sunday?' It seemed she had got on very well indeed with the bishop, who knew the married sister, at Tunbridge, of her very greatest friend. Cecily herself did not know the married sister, but that didn't matter—it was a link. The bishop was charming. 'Well, my love,' said I—I was teaching myself to use these forms of address for fear she would feel an unkind lack of them, but it was difficult—'I am glad that somebody from my part of the world has impressed you favourably at last. I wish we had more bishops.'

'Oh, but my bishop doesn't belong to your part of the world,' responded my daughter sleepily. 'He is travelling for his health.'

It was the most unexpected and delightful thing to be packed into one's chair next morning by Dacres Tottenham. As I emerged from the music saloon after breakfast—Cecily had stayed below to look over her hymns and consider with her bishop the possibility of an anthem—Dacres's face was the first I saw; it simply illuminated, for me, that portion of the deck. I noticed with pleasure the quick toss of the cigar overboard as he recognized and bore down upon me. We were immense friends; John liked him too. He was one of those people who make a tremendous difference; in all our three hundred passengers there could be no one like him, certainly no one whom I could be more glad to see. We plunged at once into immediate personal affairs, we would get at the heart of them later. He gave his vivid word to everything he had seen and done; we laughed and exclaimed and were silent in a concert of admirable understanding. We were still unravelling, still demanding and explaining when the ship's bell began to ring for church, and almost simultaneously Cecily advanced towards us. She had a proper Sunday hat on, with flowers under the brim, and a church-going frock; she wore gloves and clasped a prayer-book. Most of the women who filed past to the summons of the bell were going down as they were, in cotton blouses and serge skirts, in tweed caps or anything, as to a kind of family prayers. I knew exactly how they would lean against the pillars of the saloon during the psalms. This young lady would be little less than a rebuke to them. I surveyed her approach; she positively walked as if it were Sunday.

'My dear,' I said, 'how *endimanchée* you look! The bishop will be very pleased with you. This gentleman is Mr Tottenham, who administers Her Majesty's pleasure in parts of India about Allahabad. My daughter, Dacres.' She was certainly looking very fresh, and her calm grey eyes had the repose in them that has never known itself to be disturbed about anything. I wondered whether she bowed so distantly also because it was Sunday, and then I remembered that Dacres was a young man, and that the Farnham ladies had probably taught her that it was right to be very distant with young men.

'It is almost eleven, mamma.'

'Yes, dear. I see you are going to church.'

'Are you not coming, mamma?'

I was well wrapped up in an extremely comfortable corner. I had *La Duchesse Bleue* uncut in my lap, and an agreeable person to talk to. I fear that in any case I should not have been inclined to attend the service, but there was something in my daughter's intonation that made me distinctly hostile to the idea. I am putting things down as they were, extenuating nothing.

'I think not, dear.'

'I've turned up two such nice seats.'

'Stay, Miss Farnham, and keep us in countenance,' said Dacres, with his charming smile. The smile displaced a look of discreet and amused observation. Dacres had an eye always for a situation, and this one was even newer to him than to me.

'No, no. She must run away and not bully her mamma,' I said. 'When she comes back we will see how much she remembers of the sermon,' and as the flat tinkle from the companion began to show signs of diminishing, Cecily, with one grieved glance, hastened down.

'You amazing lady!' said Dacres. 'A daughter—and such a tall daughter! I somehow never—'

'You knew we had one?'

'There was theory of that kind, I remember, about ten years ago. Since then—excuse me—I don't think you've mentioned her.'

'You talk as if she were a skeleton in the closet!'

'You *didn't* talk—as if she were.'

'I think she was, in a way, poor child. But the resurrection day hasn't confounded me as I deserved. She's a very good girl.'

'If you had asked me to pick out your daughter—'

'She would have been the last you would indicate! Quite so,' I said. 'She is like her father's people. I can't help that.'

'I shouldn't think you would if you could,' Dacres remarked absently; but the sea air, perhaps, enabled me to digest his thoughtlessness with a smile.

'No,' I said, 'I am just as well pleased. I think a resemblance to me would confuse me, often.'

There was a trace of scrutiny in Dacres's glance. 'Don't you find yourself in sympathy with her?' he asked.

'My dear boy, I have seen her just twice in twenty-one years! You see, I've always stuck to John.'

'But between mother and daughter—I may be old-fashioned, but I had an idea that there was an instinct that might be depended on.'

'I am depending on it,' I said, and let my eyes follow the little blue waves that chased past the hand-rail. 'We are making very good speed, aren't we? Thirty-five knots since last night at ten. Are you in the sweep?'

'I never bet on the way out—can't afford it. Am I old-fashioned?' he insisted.

'Probably. Men are very slow in changing their philosophy about women. I fancy their idea of the maternal relation is firmest fixed of all.'

'We see it a beatitude!' he cried.

'I know,' I said wearily, 'and you never modify the view.'

Dacres contemplated the portion of the deck that lay between us. His eyes were discreetly lowered, but I saw embarrassment and speculation and a hint of criticism in them.

'Tell me more about it,' said he.

'Oh, for heaven's sake don't be sympathetic!' I exclaimed. 'Lend me a little philosophy instead. There is nothing to tell. There she is and there I am, in the most intimate relation in the world, constituted when she is twenty-one and I am forty.' Dacres started slightly at the ominous word; so little do men realize that the women they like can ever pass out of the constated years of attraction. 'I find the young lady very tolerable, very creditable, very nice. I find the relation atrocious. There you have it. I would like to break the relation into pieces,' I went on recklessly, 'and throw it into the sea. Such things should be tempered to one. I should feel it much less if she occupied another cabin, and would consent to call me Elizabeth or Jane. It is not as if I had been her mother always. One grows fastidious at forty—new intimacies are only possible then on a basis of temperament—'

I paused; it seemed to me that I was making excuses, and I had not the least desire in the world to do that.

'How awfully rough on the girl!' said Dacres Tottenham.

'That consideration has also occurred to me,' I said candidly, 'though I have perhaps been even more struck by its converse.'

'You had no earthly business to be her mother,' said my friend, with irritation.

I shrugged my shoulders—what would you have done?—and opened *La Duchesse Bleue*.

III

Mrs Morgan, wife of a judge of the High Court of Bombay, and I sat amidships on the cool side in the Suez Canal. She was outlining 'Soiled Linen' in chain-stitch on a green canvas bag; I was admiring the Egyptian sands. 'How charming,' said I, 'is this solitary desert in the endless oasis we are compelled to cross!'

'Oasis in the desert, you mean,' said Mrs Morgan; 'I haven't noticed any, but I happened to look up this morning as I was putting on my stockings, and I saw through my port-hole the most lovely mirage.'

I had been at school with Mrs Morgan more than twenty years agone, but she had come to the special enjoyment of the dignities of life while I still liked doing things. Mrs Morgan was the kind of person to make one realize how distressing a medium is middle age. Contemplating her precipitous lap, to which conventional attitudes were certainly more becoming, I crossed my own knees with energy, and once more resolved to be young until I was old.

'How perfectly delightful for you to be taking Cecily out!' said Mrs Morgan placidly.

'Isn't it?' I responded, watching the gliding sands.

'But she was born in sixty-nine—that makes her twenty-one. Quite time, I should say.'

'Oh, we couldn't put it off any longer. I mean—her father has such a horror of early débuts. He simply would not hear of her coming before.'

'Doesn't want her to marry in India, I dare say—the only one,' purred Mrs Morgan.

'Oh, I don't know. It isn't such a bad place. I was brought out there to marry, and I married. I've found it very satisfactory.'

'You always did say exactly what you thought, Helena,' said Mrs Morgan excusingly.

'I haven't much patience with people who bring their daughters out to give them the chance they never would have in England, and then go about devoutly hoping they won't marry in India,' I said. 'I shall be very pleased if Cecily does as well as your girls have done.'

'Mary in the Indian Civil and Jessie in the Imperial Service Troops,' sighed Mrs Morgan complacently. 'And both, my dear, within a year. It *was* a blow.'

'Oh, it must have been!' I said civilly.

There was no use in bandying words with Emily Morgan.

'There is nothing in the world like the satisfaction and pleasure one takes in one's daughters,' Mrs Morgan went on limpidly. 'And one can be in such *close* sympathy with one's girls. I have never regretted having no sons.'

'Dear me, yes. To watch oneself growing up again—call back the lovely April of one's prime, etcetera—to read every thought and anticipate every wish—there is no more golden privilege in life, dear Emily. Such a direct and natural avenue for affection, such a wide field for interest!'

I paused, lost in the volume of my admirable sentiments.

'How beautifully you talk, Helena! I wish I had the gift.'

'It doesn't mean very much,' I said truthfully.

'Oh, I think it's everything! And how companionable a girl is! I quite envy you, this season, having Cecily constantly with you and taking her about everywhere. Something quite new for you, isn't it?'

'Absolutely,' said I; 'I am looking forward to it immensely. But it is likely she will make her own friends, don't you think?' I added anxiously.

'Hardly the first season. My girls didn't. I was practically their only intimate for months. Don't be afraid; you won't be obliged to go shares in Cecily with anybody for a long long while,' added Mrs Morgan kindly. 'I know just how you feel about *that*.'

The muddy water of the Ditch chafed up from under us against its banks with a smell that enabled me to hide the emotions Mrs Morgan evoked behind my handkerchief. The pale desert was pictorial with the drifting, deepening purple shadows of clouds, and in the midst a blue glimmer of the Bitter Lakes, with a white sail on them. A little frantic Arab boy ran alongside keeping pace with the ship. Except for the smell, it was like a dream, we moved so quietly; on, gently on and on between the ridgy clay banks and the rows of piles. Peace was on the ship; you could hear what the Fourth in his white ducks said to the quartermaster in his blue denims; you could count the strokes of the electric bell in the wheel-house; peace was on the ship as she pushed on, an ever-venturing, double-funnelled impertinence, through the sands of the ages. My eyes wandered along a plankline in the deck till they were arrested by a petticoat I knew, when they returned of their own accord. I seemed to be always seeing that petticoat.

'I think,' resumed Mrs Morgan, whose glance had wandered in the same direction, 'that Cecily is a very fine type of our English girls. With those dark grey eyes, a *little* prominent possibly, and that good colour—it's rather high now perhaps, but she will lose quite enough of it in India—and those regular features, she would make a splendid Britannia. Do you know, I fancy she must have a great deal of character. Has she?'

'Any amount. And all of it good,' I responded, with private dejection.

'No faults at all?' chaffed Mrs Morgan.

I shook my head. 'Nothing,' I said sadly, 'that I can put my finger on. But I hope to discover a few later. The sun may bring them out.'

'Like freckles. Well, you are a lucky woman. Mine had plenty, I assure you. Untidiness was no name for Jessie, and Mary—I'm *sorry* to say that Mary sometimes fibbed.'

'How lovable of her! Cecily's neatness is a painful example to me, and I don't believe she would tell a fib to save my life.'

'Tell me,' said Mrs Morgan, as the lunch-bell rang and she gathered her occupation into her work-basket, 'who is that talking to her?'

'Oh, an old friend,' I replied easily; 'Dacres Tottenham, a dear fellow, and most benevolent. He is trying on my behalf to reconcile her to the life she'll have to lead in India.'

'She won't need much reconciling, if she's like most girls,' observed Mrs Morgan, 'but he seems to be trying very hard.'

That was quite the way I took it—on my behalf—for several days. When people have understood you very adequately for ten years you do not expect them to boggle at any problem you may present at the end of the decade. I thought Dacres was moved by a fine sense of compassion. I thought that with his admirable perception he had put a finger on the little comedy of fruitfulness in my life that laughed so bitterly at the tragedy of the barren woman, and was attempting, by delicate manipulation, to make it easier. I really thought so. Then I observed that myself had preposterously deceived me, that it wasn't like that at all. When Mr Tottenham joined us, Cecily and me, I saw that he listened more than he talked, with an ear specially cocked to register any small irony which might appear in my remarks to my daughter. Naturally he registered more than there were to make up perhaps for dear Cecily's obviously not registering any. I could see, too, that he was suspicious of any flavour of kindness; finally, to avoid the strictures of his upper lip, which really, dear fellow, began to bore me, I talked exclusively about the distant sails and the Red Sea littoral. When he no longer joined us as we sat or walked together, I perceived that his hostility was fixed and his *parti pris.* He was brimful of compassion, but it was all for Cecily, none for the situation or for me. (She would have marvelled, placidly, why he pitied her. I am glad I can say that.) The primitive man in him rose up as Pope of nature and excommunicated me as a creature recusant to her functions. Then deliberately Dacres undertook an office of consolation; and I fell to wondering, while Mrs Morgan spoke her convictions plainly out, how far an impulse of reparation for a misfortune with which he had nothing to do might carry a man.

I began to watch the affair with an interest which even to me seemed queer. It was not detached, but it was semi-detached, and, of course, on the side for which I seem, in this history, to be perpetually apologizing. With certain limitations it didn't matter an atom whom Cecily married. So that he was sound and decent, with reasonable prospects, her simple requirements and ours for her would be quite met. There was the ghost of a consolation in that; one needn't be anxious or exacting.

I could predict with a certain amount of confidence that in her first season she would probably receive three or four proposals, any one of which she might accept with as much propriety and satisfaction as any other one. For Cecily it was so simple; prearranged by nature like her digestion, one could not see any logical basis for difficulties. A nice upstanding sapper, a dashing Bengal Lancer—oh, I could think of half a dozen types that would answer excellently. She was the kind of young person, and that was the summing up of it, to marry a type and be typically happy. I hoped and expected that she would. But Dacres!

Dacres should exercise the greatest possible discretion. He was not a person who could throw the dice indifferently with fate. He could respond to so much, and he would inevitably, sooner or later, demand so much response! He was governed by a preposterously exacting temperament, and he wore his nerves outside. And what vision he had! How he explored the world he lived in and drew out of it all there was, all there was! I could see him in the years to come ranging alone the fields that were sweet and the horizons that lifted for him, and ever returning to pace the common dusty mortal road by the side of a purblind wife. On general principles, as a case to point at, it would be a conspicuous pity. Nor would it lack the aspect of a particular, a personal misfortune. Dacres was occupied in quite the natural normal degree with his charming self; he would pass his misery on, and who would deserve to escape it less than his mother-in-law?

I listened to Emily Morgan, who gleaned in the ship more information about Dacres Tottenham's people, pay, and prospects than I had ever acquired, and I kept an eye upon the pair which was, I flattered myself, quite maternal. I watched them without acute anxiety, deploring the threatening destiny, but hardly nearer to it than one is in the stalls to the stage. My moments of real concern for Dacres were mingled more with anger than with sorrow—it seemed inexcusable that he, with his infallible divining-rod for temperament, should be on the point of making such an ass of himself. Though I talk of the stage there was nothing at all dramatic to reward my attention, mine and Emily Morgan's. To my imagination, excited by its idea of what Dacres Tottenham's courtship ought to be, the attentions he paid to Cecily were most humdrum. He threw rings into buckets with her—she was good at that—and quoits upon the 'bull' board; he found her chair after the decks were swabbed in the morning and established her in it; he paced the deck with her at convenient times and seasons. They were humdrum, but they were constant and cumulative. Cecily took them with an even breath that perfectly matched. There was hardly anything, on her part, to note—a little discreet observation of his comings and goings, eyes scarcely lifted from her book, and later just a hint of proprietorship, as the evening she came up to me on deck, our first night in the Indian Ocean. I was lying in my long chair looking at the thick, low stars and thinking it was a long time since I had seen John.

'Dearest mamma, out here and nothing over your shoulders! You *are* imprudent. Where is your wrap? Mr Tottenham, will you please fetch mamma's wrap for her?

'If mamma so instructs me,' he said audaciously.

'Do as Cecily tells you,' I laughed, and he went and did it, while I by the light of a quartermaster's lantern distinctly saw my daughter blush.

Another time, when Cecily came down to undress, she bent over me as I lay in the lower berth with unusual solicitude. I had been dozing, and I jumped.

'What is it, child?' I said. 'Is the ship on fire?'

'No, mamma, the ship is not on fire. There is nothing wrong. I'm so sorry I startled you. But Mr Tottenham has been telling me all about what you did for the soldiers the time plague broke out in the lines at Mian-Mir. I think it was splendid, mamma, and so does he.'

'Oh, *Lord!*' I groaned. 'Good night.'

IV

It remained in my mind, that little thing that Dacres had taken the trouble to tell my daughter; I thought about it a good deal. It seemed to me the most serious and convincing circumstances that had yet offered itself to my consideration. Dacres was no longer content to bring solace and support to the more appealing figure of the situation; he must set to work, bless him!

to improve the situation itself. He must try to induce Miss Farnham, by telling her everything he could remember to my credit, to think as well of her mother as possible, in spite of the strange and secret blows which that mother might be supposed to sit up at night to deliver to her. Cecily thought very well of me already; indeed, with private reservations as to my manners and—no, *not* my morals, I believe I exceeded her expectations of what a perfectly new and untrained mother would be likely to prove. It was my theory that she found me all she could understand me to be. The maternal virtues of the outside were certainly mine; I put them on with care every morning and wore them with patience all day. Dacres, I assured myself, must have allowed his preconception to lead him absurdly by the nose not to see that the girl was satisfied, that my impatience, my impotence, did not at all make her miserable. Evidently, however, he had created our relations differently; evidently he had set himself to their amelioration. There was portent in it; things seemed to be closing in. I bit off a quarter of an inch of wooden pen-handle in considering whether or not I should mention it in my letter to John, and decided that it would be better just perhaps to drop a hint. Though I could not expect John to receive it with any sort of perturbation. Men are different; he would probably think Tottenham well enough able to look after himself.

I had embarked on my letter, there at the end of a corner-table of the saloon, when I saw Dacres saunter through. He wore a very conscious and elaborately purposeless air; and it jumped with my mood that he had nothing less than the crisis of his life in his pocket, and was looking for me. As he advanced towards me between the long tables doubt left me and alarm assailed me. 'I'm glad to find you in a quiet corner,' said he, seating himself, and confirmed my worst anticipations.

'I'm writing to John,' I said, and again applied myself to my pen-handle. It is a trick Cecily has since done her best in vain to cure me of.

'I am going to interrupt you,' he said. 'I have not had an opportunity of talking to you for some time.'

'I like that!' I exclaimed derisively.

'And I want to tell you that I am very much charmed with Cecily.'

'Well,' I said, 'I am not going to gratify you by saying anything against her.'

'You don't deserve her, you know.'

'I won't dispute that. But, if you don't mind—I'm not sure that I'll stand being abused, dear boy.'

'I quite see it isn't any use. Though one spoke with the tongues of men and of angels—'

'And had not charity,' I continued for him. 'Precisely. I won't go on, but your quotation is very apt.'

'I so bow down before her simplicity. It makes a wide and beautiful margin for the rest of her character. She is a girl Ruskin would have loved.'

'I wonder,' said I. 'He did seem fond of the simple type, didn't he?'

'Her mind is so clear, so transparent. The motive spring of everything she says and does is so direct. Don't you find you can most completely depend upon her?'

'Oh yes,' I said; 'certainly. I nearly always know what she is going to say before she says it, and under given circumstances I can tell precisely what she will do.'

'I fancy her sense of duty is very beautifully developed.'

'It is,' I said. 'There is hardly a day when I do not come in contact with it.'

'Well, that is surely a good thing. And I find that calm poise of hers very restful.'

'I would not have believed that so many virtues could reside in one young lady,' I said, taking refuge in flippancy, 'and to think that she should be my own daughter!'

'As I believe you know, that seems to me rather a cruel stroke of destiny, Mrs Farnham.'

'Oh yes, I know! You have a constructive imagination, Dacres. You don't seem to see that the girl is protected by her limitations, like a tortoise. She lives within them quite secure and happy and content. How determined you are to be sorry for her!'

Mr Tottenham looked at the end of this lively exchange as though he sought for a polite way of conveying to me that I rather was the limited person. He looked as if he wished he could say things. The first of them would be, I saw, that he had quite a different conception of Cecily, that it was illuminated by many trifles, nuances of feeling and expression, which he had noticed in his talks with her whenever they had skirted the subject of her adoption by her mother. He knew her, he was longing to say, better than I did; when it would have been natural to reply that one could not hope to compete in such a direction with an intelligent young man, and we should at once have been upon delicate and difficult ground. So it was as well perhaps that he kept silence until he said, as he had come prepared to say, 'Well, I want to put that beyond a doubt—her happiness—if I'm good enough. I want her, please, and I only hope that she will be half as willing to come as you are likely to be to let her go.'

It was a shock when it came, plump, like that; and I was horrified to feel how completely every other consideration was lost for the instant in the immense relief that it prefigured. To be my whole complete self again, without the feeling that a fraction of me was masquerading about in Cecily! To be freed at once, or almost, from an exacting condition and an impossible ideal! 'Oh!' I exclaimed, and my eyes positively filled. 'You *are* good, Dacres, but I couldn't let you do that.'

His undisguised stare brought me back to a sense of the proportion of things. I saw that in the combination of influences that had brought Mr Tottenham to the point of proposing to marry my daughter consideration for me, if it had a place, would be fantastic. Inwardly I laughed at the egotism of raw nerves that had conjured it up, even for an instant, as a reason for gratitude. The situation was not so peculiar, not so interesting, as that. But I answered his stare with a smile; what I had said might very well stand.

'Do you imagine,' he said, seeing that I did not mean to amplify it, 'that I want to marry her out of any sort of *good*ness?'

'Benevolence is your weakness, Dacres.'

'I see. You think one's motive is to withdraw her from a relation which ought to be the most natural in the world, but which is, in her particular and painful case, the most equivocal.'

'Well, come,' I remonstrated. 'You have dropped one or two things, you know, in the heat of your indignation, not badly calculated to give one that idea. The eloquent statement you have just made, for instance—it carries all the patness of old conviction. How often have you rehearsed it?'

I am a fairly long-suffering person, but I began to feel a little annoyed with my would-be son-in-law. If the relation were achieved it would give him no prescriptive right to bully me; and we were still in very early anticipation of that.

'Ah!' he said disarmingly. 'Don't let us quarrel. I'm sorry you think that; because it isn't likely to bring your favour to my project, and I want you friendly and helpful. Oh, confound it!' he exclaimed, with sudden temper. 'You ought to be. I don't understand this aloofness. I half suspect it's pose. You undervalue Cecily—well, you have no business to undervalue me. You know me better than anybody in the world. Now are you going to help me to marry your daughter?'

'I don't think so,' I said slowly, after a moment's silence, which he sat through like a mutinous schoolboy. 'I might tell you that I don't care a button whom you marry, but that would not be true. I do care more or less. As you say, I know you pretty well. I'd a little rather you didn't make a mess of it; and if you must I should distinctly prefer not to have the spectacle under my nose for the rest of my life. I can't hinder you, but I won't help you.'

'And what possesses you to imagine that in marrying Cecily I should make a mess of it? Shouldn't your first consideration be whether *she* would?'

'Perhaps it should, but, you see, it isn't. Cecily would be happy with anybody who made her comfortable. You would ask a good deal more than that, you know.'

Dacres, at this, took me up promptly. Life, he said, the heart of life, had particularly little to say to temperament. By the heart of life I suppose he meant married love. He explained that its roots asked other sustenance, and that it throve best of all on simple elemental goodness. So long as a man sought in women mere casual companionship, perhaps the most exquisite thing to be experienced was the stimulus of some spiritual feminine counterpart; but when he desired of one woman that she should be always and intimately with him, the background of his life, the mother of his children, he was better advised to avoid nerves and sensibilities, and try for the repose of the common—the uncommon—domestic virtues. Ah, he said, they were sweet, like lavender. (Already, I told him, he smelled the housekeeper's linen-chest.) But I did not interrupt him much; I couldn't, he was too absorbed. To temperamental pairing, he declared, the century owed its breed of decadents. I asked him if he had ever really recognized one; and he retorted that if he hadn't he didn't wish to make a beginning in his own family. In a quarter of an hour he repudiated the theories of a lifetime, a gratifying triumph for simple elemental goodness. Having denied the value of the subtler pretensions to charm in woman as you marry her, he went artlessly on to endow Cecily with as many of them as could possibly be desirable. He actually persuaded himself to say that it was lovely to see the reflections of life in her tranquil spirit; and when I looked at him incredulously he grew angry, and hinted that Cecily's sensitiveness to reflections and other things might be a trifle beyond her mother's ken. 'She responds instantly, intimately, to the beautiful everywhere,' he declared.

'Aren't the opportunities of life on board ship rather limited to demonstrate that?' I inquired. 'I know—you mean sunsets. Cecily is very fond of sunsets. She is always asking me to come and look at them.'

'I was thinking of last night's sunset,' he confessed. 'We looked at it together.'

'What did she say?' I asked idly.

'Nothing very much. That's just the point. Another girl would have raved and gushed.'

'Oh, well, Cecily never does that,' I responded. 'Nevertheless she is a very ordinary human instrument. I hope I shall have no temptation ten years hence to remind you that I warned you of her quality.'

'I wish, not in the least for my own profit, for I am well convinced already, but simply to win your cordiality and your approval—never did an unexceptional wooer receive such niggard encouragement!—I wish there were some sort of test for her quality. I would be proud to stand by it, and you would be convinced. I can't find words to describe my objection to your state of mind.'

The thing seemed to me to be a foregone conclusion. I saw it accomplished, with all its possibilities of disastrous commonplace. I saw all that I have here taken the trouble to foreshadow. So far as I was concerned, Dacres's burden would add itself to my philosophies, *voilà tout.* I should always be a little uncomfortable about it, because it had been taken from my back; but it would not be a matter for the wringing of hands. And yet—the hatefulness of the mistake! Dacres's bold talk of a test made no suggestion. Should my invention be more fertile? I thought of something.

'You have said nothing to her yet?' I asked.

'Nothing. I don't think she suspects for a moment. She treats me as if no such fell design were possible. I'm none too confident, you know,' he added, with longer face.

'We go straight to Agra. Could you come to Agra?'

'Ideal!' he cried. 'The memory of Mumtaz! the Garden of the Taj! I've always wanted to love under the same moon as Shah Jehan. How thoughtful of you!'

'You must spend a few days with us in Agra,' I continued. 'And as you say, it is the very place to shrine your happiness, if it comes to pass there.'

'Well, I am glad to have extracted a word of kindness from you at last,' said Dacres, as the stewards came to lay the table. 'But I wish,' he added regretfully, 'you could have thought of a test.'

V

Four days later we were in Agra. A time there was when the name would have been the key of dreams to me; now it stood for John's headquarters. I was rejoiced to think I would look again upon the Taj; and the prospect of living with it was a real enchantment; but I pondered most the kind of house that would be provided for the General Commanding the District, how many the dining-room would seat, and whether it would have a roof of thatch or of corrugated iron—I prayed against corrugated iron. I confess these my preoccupations. I was forty, and at forty the practical considerations of life hold their own even against domes of marble, world-renowned, and set about with gardens where the bulbul sings to the rose. I smiled across the years at the raptures of my first vision of the place at twenty-one, just Cecily's age. Would I now sit under Arjamand's cypresses till two o'clock in the morning to see the wonder of her tomb at a particular angle of the moon? Would I climb one of her tall white ministering minarets to see anything whatever? I very greatly feared that I would not. Alas for the aging of sentiment, of interest! Keep your touch with life and your seat in the saddle as long as you will, the world is no new toy at forty. But Cecily was twenty-one, Cecily who sat stolidly finishing her lunch while Dacres Tottenham talked about Akbar and his philosophy. 'The sort of man,' he said, 'that Carlyle might have smoked a pipe with.'

'But surely,' said Cecily reflectively, 'tobacco was not discovered in England then. Akbar came to the throne in 1526.'

'Nor Carlyle either for that matter,' I hastened to observe. 'Nevertheless, I think Mr Tottenham's proposition must stand.'

'Thanks, Mrs Farnham,' said Dacres. 'But imagine Miss Farnham's remembering Akbar's date! I'm sure you didn't!'

'Let us hope she doesn't know too much about him,' I cried gaily, 'or there will be nothing to tell!'

'Oh, really and truly very little!' said Cecily, 'but as soon as we heard papa would be stationed here Aunt Emma made me read up about those old Moguls and people. I think I remember the dynasty. Baber, wasn't he the first? and then Humayon, and after him Akbar, and then Jehangir, and then Shah Jehan. But I've forgotten every date but Akbar's.'

She smiled her smile of brilliant health and even spirits as she made the damaging admission, and she was so good to look at, sitting there simple and wholesome and fresh, peeling her banana with her well-shaped fingers, that we swallowed the dynasty as it were whole, and smiled back upon her. John, I may say, was extremely pleased with Cecily; he said she was a very satisfactory human accomplishment. One would have thought, positively, the way he plumed himself over his handsome daughter, that he alone was responsible for her. But John, having received his family, straightway set off with his Staff on a tour of inspection, and thereby takes himself out of this history. I sometimes think that if he had stayed—but there has never been the lightest recrimination between us about it, and I am not going to hint one now.

'Did you read,' asked Dacres, 'what he and the Court poet wrote over the entrance gate to the big mosque at Fattehpur-Sikri? It's rather nice. "The world is a looking-glass, wherein the image has come and is gone—take as thine own nothing more than what you lookest upon." '

My daughter's thoughtful gaze was, of course, fixed upon the speaker, and in his own glance I saw a sudden ray of consciousness; but Cecily transferred her eyes to the opposite wall, deeply considering, and while Dacres and I smiled across the table, I saw that she had perceived no reason for blushing. It was a singularly narrow escape.

'No,' said she, 'I didn't; what a curious proverb for an emperor to make! He couldn't possibly have been able to see all his possessions at once.'

'If you have finished,' Dacres addressed her, 'do let me show you what your plain and immediate duty is to the garden. The garden waits for you—all the roses expectant—'

'Why, there isn't one!' cried Cecily, pinning on her hat. It was pleasing, and just a trifle pathetic, the way he hurried her out of the scope of any little dart; he would not have her even within range of amused observation. Would he continue, I wondered vaguely, as, with my elbows on the table, I tore into strips the lemon-leaf that floated in my finger-bowl—would he continue, through life, to shelter her from his other clever friends as now he attempted to shelter her from her mother? In that case he would have to domicile her, poor dear, behind the curtain, like the native ladies—a good price to pay for a protection of which, bless her heart! she would be all unaware. I had quite stopped bemoaning the affair; perhaps the comments of my husband, who treated it with broad approval and satisfaction, did something to soothe my sensibilities. At all events, I had gradually come to occupy a high fatalistic ground towards the pair. If it was written upon their foreheads that they should marry, the inscription was none of mine; and, of course, it was true, as John had indignantly stated, that Dacres might do very much worse. One's interest in Dacres Tottenham's problematical future had in no way diminished; but the young man was so positive, so full of intention, so disinclined to discussion—he had not reopened the subject since that morning in the saloon of the Caledonia—that one's feeling about it rather took the attenuated form of a shrug. I am afraid, too, that the pleasurable excitement of such an impending event had a little supervened; even at forty there is no disallowing the natural interests of one's sex. As I sat there pulling my lemon-leaf to pieces, I should not have been surprised or in the least put about if the two had returned radiant from the lawn to demand my blessing. As to the test of quality that I had obligingly invented for Dacres on the spur of the moment without his knowledge or connivance, it had some time ago faded into what he apprehended it to be—a mere idyllic opportunity, a charming background, a frame for his project, of prettier sentiment than the funnels and the handrails of a ship.

Mr Tottenham had ten days to spend with us. He knew the place well; it belonged to the province to whose service he was dedicated, and he claimed with impressive authority the privilege of showing it to Cecily by degrees—the Hall of Audience to-day, the Jessamine Tower to-morrow, the tomb of Akbar another, and the Deserted City yet another day. We arranged the expeditions in conference, Dacres insisting only upon the order of them, which I saw was to be cumulative, with the Taj at the very end, on the night precisely of the full of the moon, with a better chance of roses. I had no special views, but Cecily contributed some; that we should do the Hall of Audience in the morning, so as not to interfere with the club tennis in the afternoon, that we should bicycle to Akbar's tomb and take a cold luncheon—if we were sure there would be no snakes—to the Deserted City, to all of which Dacres gave loyal assent. I endorsed everything; I was the encouraging chorus, only stipulating that my number should be swelled from day to day by the addition of such persons as I should approve. Cecily, for instance, wanted to invite the Bakewells because we had come out in the same ship with them; but I could not endure the Bakewells, and it seemed to me that our having made the voyage with them was the best possible reason for declining to lay eyes on them for the rest of our natural lives. 'Mamma has such strong prejudices,' Cecily remarked, as she reluctantly gave up the idea; and I waited to see whether the graceless Tottenham would unmurmuringly take down the Bakewells. How strong must be the sentiment that turns a man into a boa-constrictor without a pang of transmigration! But no, this time he was faithful to the principles of his pre-Cecilian existence. 'They are rather Boojums,' he declared. 'You would think so, too, if you knew them better. It is that kind of excellent person that makes the real burden of India.' I could have patted him on the back.

Thanks to the rest of the chorus, which proved abundantly available, I was no immediate witness to Cecily's introduction to the glorious fragments which sustain in Agra the memory of the Moguls. I may as well say that I arranged with care that if anybody must be standing by when Dacres disclosed them, it should not be I. If Cecily had squinted, I should have been sorry, but I would have found in it no personal humiliation. There were other imperfections of vision, however, for which I felt responsible and ashamed; and with Dacres, though the situation, Heaven knows, was none of my seeking, I had a little the feeling of a dealer who offers a defective *bibelot* to a connoisseur. My charming daughter—I was fifty times congratulated upon her appearance and her manners—had many excellent qualities and capacities which she never inherited from me; but she could see no more than the bulk, no further than the perspective; she could register exactly as much as a camera.

This was a curious thing, perhaps, to displease my maternal vanity, but it did; I had really rather she squinted; and when there was anything to look at I kept out of the way. I can not tell precisely, therefore, what the incidents were that contributed to make Mr Tottenham, on our return from these expeditions, so thoughtful, with a thoughtfulness which increased, towards the end of them, to a positive gravity. This would disappear during dinner under the influence of food and drink. He would talk nightly with new enthusiasm and fresh hope—or did I imagine it!—of the loveliness he had arranged to reveal on the following day. If again my imagination did not lead me astray, I fancied this occurred later and later in the course of the meal as the week went on; as if his state required more stimulus as time progressed. One evening, when I expected it to flag altogether, I had a whim to order champagne and observe the effect; but I am glad to say that I reproved myself, and refrained.

Cecily, meanwhile, was conducting herself in a manner which left nothing to be desired. If, as I sometimes thought, she took Dacres very much for granted, she took him calmly for granted; she seemed a prey to none of those fluttering uncertainties, those suspended judgements and elaborate indifferences which translate themselves so plainly in a young lady receiving addresses. She turned herself out very freshly and very well; she was always ready for everything, and I am sure that no glance of Dacres Tottenham's found aught but direct and decorous response. His society on these occasions gave her solid pleasure; so did the drive and the lunch; the satisfactions were apparently upon the same plane. She was aware of the plum, if I may be permitted a brusque but irresistible simile; and with her mouth open, her eyes modestly closed, and her head in a convenient position, she waited, placidly, until it should fall in. The Farnham ladies would have been delighted with the result of their labours in the sweet reason and eminent propriety of this attitude. Thinking of my idiotic sufferings when John began to fix himself upon my horizon, I pondered profoundly the power of nature in differentiation.

One evening, the last, I think, but one, I had occasion to go to my daughter's room, and found her writing in her commonplace-book. She had a commonplace-book, as well as a Where Is It? an engagement-book, an account-book, a diary, a Daily Sunshine, and others with purposes too various to remember. 'Dearest mamma,' she said, as I was departing, 'there is only one "p" in "opulence," isn't there?'

'Yes,' I replied, with my hand on the door-handle, and added curiously, for it was an odd word in Cecily's mouth, 'Why?'

She hardly hesitated. 'Oh,' she said, 'I am just writing down one or two things Mr Tottenham said about Agra before I forget them. They seemed so true.'

'He has a descriptive touch,' I remarked.

'I think he describes beautifully. Would you like to hear what he said to-day?'

'I would,' I replied, sincerely.

' "Agra," ' read this astonishing young lady, ' "is India's one pure idyll. Elsewhere she offers other things, foolish opulence, tawdry pageant, treachery of eunuchs and jealousies of harems, thefts of kings' jewels and barbaric retributions; but they are all actual, visualized, or part of a past that shows to the backward glance hardly more relief and vitality than a Persian painting"—I should like to see a Persian painting—"but here the immortal tombs and pleasure-houses rise out of colour delicate and subtle; the vision holds across three hundred years; the print of the court is still in the dust of the city." '

'Did you really let him go on like that?' I exclaimed. 'It has the license of a lecture!'

'I encouraged him to. Of course he didn't say it straight off. He said it naturally; he stopped now and then to cough. I didn't understand it all; but I think I have remembered every word.'

'You have a remarkable memory. I'm glad he stopped to cough. Is there any more?'

'One little bit. "Here the Moguls wrought their passions into marble, and held them up with great refrains from their religion, and set them about with gardens; and here they stand in the twilight of the glory of those kings and the noonday splendour of their own." '

'How clever of you!' I exclaimed. 'How wonderfully clever of you to remember!'

'I had to ask him to repeat one or two sentences. He didn't like that. But this is nothing. I used to learn pages letter-perfect for Aunt Emma. She was very particular. I think it is worth preserving, don't you?'

'Dear Cecily,' I responded, 'you have a frugal mind.'

There was nothing else to respond. I could not tell her just how practical I thought her, or how pathetic her little book.

VI

We drove together, after dinner, to the Taj. The moonlight lay in an empty splendour over the broad sandy road, with the acacias pricking up on each side of it and the gardens of the station bungalows stretching back into clusters of crisp shadows. It was an exquisite February night, very still. Nothing seemed abroad but two or three pariah dogs, upon vague and errant business, and the Executive Engineer going swiftly home from the club on his bicycle. Even the little shops of the bazaar were dark and empty; only here and there a light showed barred behind the carved balconies of the upper rooms, and there was hardly any tom-tomming. The last long slope of the road showed us the river curving to the left, through a silent white waste that stretched indefinitely into the moonlight on one side, and was crowned by Akbar's fort on the other. His long high line of turrets and battlements still guarded a hint of their evening rose, and dim and exquisite above them hovered the three dome-bubbles of the Pearl Mosque. It was a night of perfect illusion, and the illusion was mysterious, delicate, and faint. I sat silent as we rolled along, twenty years nearer to the original joy of things when John and I drove through the same old dream.

Dacres, too, seemed preoccupied; only Cecily was, as they say, herself. Cecily was really more than herself, she exhibited an unusual flow of spirits. She talked continually, she pointed out this and that, she asked who lived here and who lived there. At regular intervals of about four minutes she demanded if it wasn't simply too lovely. She sat straight up with her vigorous profile and her smart hat; and the silhouette of her personality sharply refused to mingle with the dust of any dynasty. She was a contrast, a protest; positively she was an indignity. 'Do lean back, dear child,' I exclaimed at last. 'You interfere with the landscape.'

She leaned back, but she went on interfering with it in terms of sincerest enthusiasm.

When we stopped at the great archway of entrance I begged to be left in the carriage. What else could one do, when the golden moment had come, but sit in the carriage and measure it? They climbed the broad stone steps together and passed under the lofty gravures into the garden, and I waited. I waited and remembered. I am not, as perhaps by this time is evident, a person of overwhelming sentiment, but I think the smile upon my lips was gentle. So plainly I could see, beyond the massive archway and across a score of years, all that they saw at that moment—Arjamand's garden, and the long straight tank of marble cleaving it full of sleeping water and the shadows of the marshalling cypresses; her wide dark garden of roses and of pomegranates, and at the end the Vision, marvellous, aerial, the soul of something—is it beauty? is it sorrow?—that great white pride of love in mourning such as only here in all the round of our little world lifts itself to the stars, the unpaintable, indescribable Taj Mahal. A gentle breath stole out with a scent of jessamine and such a memory! I closed my eyes and felt the warm luxury of a tear.

Thinking of the two in the garden, my mood was very kind, very conniving. How foolish after all were my cherry-stone theories of taste and temperament before that uncalculating thing which sways a world and builds a Taj Mahal! Was it probable that Arjamand and her Emperor had loved fastidiously, and yet how they had loved! I wandered away into consideration of the blind forces which move the world, in which comely young persons like my daughter Cecily had such a place; I speculated vaguely upon the value of the subtler gifts of sympathy and insight which seemed indeed, at that enveloping moment, to be mere flowers strewn upon the tide of deeper emotions. The garden sent me a fragrance of roses; the moon sailed higher and picked out the little kiosks set along the wall. It was a charming, charming thing to wait, there at the portal of the silvered, scented garden, for an idyll to come forth.

When they reappeared, Dacres and my daughter, they came with casual steps and cheerful voices. They might have been a couple of tourists. The moonlight fell full upon them on the platform under the arch. It showed Dacres measuring with his stick the length of the Sanskrit letters which declared the stately texts, and Cecily's expression of polite, perfunctory interest. They looked up at the height above them; they looked back at the vision behind. Then they sauntered towards the carriage, he offering a formal hand to help her down the uncertain steps, she gracefully accepting it.

'You—you have not been long,' said I. 'I hope you didn't hurry on my account.'

'Miss Farnham found the marble a little cold under foot,' replied Dacres, putting Miss Farnham in.

'You see,' explained Cecily, 'I stupidly forgot to change into thicker soles. I have only my slippers. But, mamma, how lovely it is! Do let us come again in the daytime. I am dying to make a sketch of it.'

Mr Tottenham was to leave us on the following day. In the morning, after 'little breakfast', as we say in India, he sought me in the room I had set aside to be particularly my own.

Again I was writing to John, but this time I waited for precisely his interruption. I had got no further than 'My dearest husband,' and my pen-handle was a fringe.

'Another fine day,' I said, as if the old, old Indian joke could give him ease, poor man!

'Yes,' said he, 'we are having lovely weather.'

He had forgotten that it was a joke. Then he lapsed into silence while I renewed my attentions to my pen.

'I say,' he said at last, with so strained a look about his mouth that it was almost a contortion, 'I haven't done it, you know.'

'No,' I responded, cheerfully, 'and you're not going to. Is that it? Well!'

'Frankly—' said he.

'Dear me, yes! Anything else between you and me would be grotesque,' I interrupted, 'after all these years.'

'I don't think it would be a success,' he said, looking at me resolutely with his clear blue eyes, in which still lay, alas! the possibility of many delusions.

'No,' I said, 'I never did, you know. But the prospect had begun to impose upon me.'

'To say how right you were would seem, under the circumstances, the most hateful form of flattery.'

'Yes,' I said, 'I think I can dispense with your verbal endorsement.' I felt a little bitter. It was, of course, better that the connoisseur should have discovered the flaw before concluding the transaction; but although I had pointed it out myself I was not entirely pleased to have the article returned.

'I am infinitely ashamed that it should have taken me all these days—day after day and each contributory—to discover what you saw so easily and so completely.'

'You forget that I am her mother,' I could not resist the temptation of saying.

'Oh, for God's sake don't jeer! Please be absolutely direct, and tell me if you have reason to believe that to the extent of a thought, of a breath—to any extent at all—she cares.'

He was, I could see, very deeply moved; he had not arrived at this point without trouble and disorder not lightly to be put on or off. Yet I did not hurry to his relief, I was still possessed by a vague feeling of offence. I reflected that any mother would be, and I quite plumed myself upon my annoyance. It was so satisfactory, when one had a daughter, to know the sensations of even any mother. Nor was it soothing to remember that the young man's whole attitude towards Cecily had been based upon criticism of me, even though he sat before me whipped with his own lash. His temerity had been stupid and obstinate; I could not regret his punishment.

I kept him waiting long enough to think all this, and then I replied, 'I have not the least means of knowing.'

I can not say what he expected, but he squared his shoulders as if he had received a blow and might receive another. Then he looked at me with a flash of the old indignation. 'You are not near enough to her for that!' he exclaimed.

'I am not near enough to her for that.'

Silence fell between us. A crow perched upon an opened venetian and cawed lustily. For years afterward I never heard a crow caw without a sense of vain, distressing experiment. Dacres got up and began to walk about the room. I very soon put a stop to that. 'I can't talk to a pendulum,' I said, but I could not persuade him to sit down again.

'Candidly,' he said at length, 'do you think she would have me?'

'I regret to say that I think she would. But you would not dream of asking her.'

'Why not? She is a dear girl,' he responded inconsequently.

'You could not possibly stand it.'

Then Mr Tottenham delivered himself of this remarkable phrase: 'I could stand it,' he said, 'as well as you can.'

There was far from being any joy in the irony with which I regarded him and under which I saw him gather up his resolution to go; nevertheless I did nothing to make it easy for him. I refrained from imparting my private conviction that Cecily would accept the first presentable substitute that appeared, although it was strong. I made no reference to my daughter's large fund of philosophy and small balance of sentiment. I did not even—though this was reprehensible—confess the test, the test of quality in these ten days with the marble archives of the Moguls, which I had almost wantonly suggested, which he had so unconsciously accepted, so disastrously applied. I gave him quite fifteen minutes of his bad quarter of an hour, and when it was over I wrote truthfully but furiously to John. . . .

That was ten years ago. We have since attained the shades of retirement, and our daughter is still with us when she is not with Aunt Emma and Aunt Alice—grandmamma has passed away. Mr Tottenham's dumb departure that day in February—it was the year John got his CB—was followed, I am thankful to say, by none of the symptoms of unrequited affection on Cecily's part. Not for ten minutes, so far as I was aware, was she the maid forlorn. I think her self-respect was of too robust a character, thanks to the Misses Farnham. Still less, of course, had she any reproaches to serve upon her mother, although for a long time I thought I detected—or was it my guilty conscience?—a spark of shrewdness in the glance she bent upon me when the talk was on Mr Tottenham and the probabilities of his return to Agra. So well did she sustain her experience, or so little did she feel it, that I believe the impression went abroad that Dacres had been sent disconsolate away. One astonishing conversation I had with her some six months later, which turned upon the point of a particularly desirable offer. She told me something then, without any sort of embarrassment, but quite lucidly and directly, that edified me much to hear. She said that while she was quite sure that Mr Tottenham thought of her only as a friend—she had never had the least reason for any other impression—he had done her a service for which she could not thank him enough—in showing her what a husband might be. He had given her a standard; it might be high, but it was unalterable. She didn't know whether she could describe it, but Mr Tottenham was different from the kind of man you seemed to meet in India. He had his own ways of looking at things, and he talked so well. He had given her an ideal, and she intended to profit by it. To know that men like Mr Tottenham existed, and to marry any other kind would be an act of folly which she did not intend to commit. No, Major the Hon. Hugh Taverel did not come near it—very far short, indeed! He had talked to her during the whole of dinner the night before about jackal-hunting with a bobbery pack—not at all an elevated mind. Yes, he might be a very good fellow, but as a companion for life she was surc hc would not bc at all suitablc. Shc would wait.

And she has waited. I never thought she would, but she has. From time to time men have wished to take her from us, but the standard has been inexorable, and none of them have reached it. When Dacres married the charming American whom he caught like a butterfly upon her Eastern tour, Cecily sent them as a wedding present an alabaster model of the Taj, and I let her do it—the gift was so exquisitely appropriate. I suppose he never looks at it without being reminded that he didn't marry Miss Farnham, and I hope that he remembers that he owes it to Miss Farnham's mother. So much I think I might claim; it is really very little considering what it stands for. Cecily is permanently with us—I believe she considers herself an intimate. I am very reasonable about lending her to her aunts, but she takes no sort of advantage of my liberality; she says she knows her duty is at home. She is growing into a firm and solid English maiden lady, with a good colour and great decision of character. That she always had.

I point out to John, when she takes our crumpets away from us, that she gets it from him. I could never take away anybody's crumpets, merely because they were indigestible, least of all my own parents'. She has acquired a distinct affection for us, by some means best known to herself; but I should have no objection to that if she would not rearrange my bonnetstrings. That is a fond liberty to which I take exception; but it is one thing to take exception and another to express it.

Our daughter is with us, permanently with us. She declares that she intends to be the prop of our declining years; she makes the statement often, and always as if it were humorous. Nevertheless I sometimes notice a spirit of inquiry, a note of investigation in her encounters with the opposite sex that suggests an expectation not yet extinct that another and perhaps a more appreciative Dacres Tottenham may flash across her field of vision—alas, how improbable! Myself I can not imagine why she should wish it; I have grown in my old age into a perfect horror of cultivated young men; but if such a person should by a miracle at any time appear, I think it is extremely improbable that I will interfere on his behalf.

1903

Stephen Leacock

1869-1944

Distinguished economist and political scientist by vocation, Stephen Leacock was humorist and humanist by avocation, delighting readers throughout the world with his comic writings. 'Personally,' he admitted, 'I would sooner have written *Alice in Wonderland* than the whole *Encyclopaedia Britannica*.' His political and scholarly treatises were instructive, his humorous books entertaining, though instructive too through their 'kindly contemplation of the incongruities of life.' The essence of Leacock's comic stories is 'the contrast between the fretting cares and the petty sorrows of the day and the long mystery of tomorrow. Here laughter and tears become one,' Leacock observed, 'and humour becomes the contemplation and interpretation of our life.'

Leacock was born in Swanmore, Hampshire, England. His family emigrated to Canada in 1876 and settled on a farm north of Toronto near Lake Simcoe. Leacock took his B.A. (1891) from the University of Toronto and his Ph.D. (1903) from the University of Chicago, where he studied under Thorstein Veblen, author of *The Theory of the Leisure Class*. In 1903 he went to teach economics at McGill University, where he chaired the Department of Political Science and Economics from 1908 until his retirement in 1936.

The author of nineteen books and countless articles on economics, history, and political science, Leacock published his first collection of humorous stories, *Literary Lapses*, in 1910, and from that time until his death he completed a volume of humour almost every year. The finest two are the complementary volumes, *Sunshine Sketches of a Little Town* (1912) and the urban satire *Arcadian Adventures of the Idle Rich* (1914). Humour, Leacock observed, 'cannot exist alongside of eager ambition, brisk success, and absorption in the game of life. Humour comes best to those who are down and out, or who have at least discovered their limitations and their failures. Humour is essentially a comforter, reconciling us to things as they are in contrast to things as they might be.'

'My Financial Career' illustrates Leacock's humour at its best. An innocent man becomes 'an irresponsible idiot' when he confronts the impersonal and forbidding world of a bank and its employees. Through the spare dialogue, Leacock captures the man's plight and discomfort.

Situated on Lake Wissanotti in Missinaba County, Mariposa is the archetypal Canadian small town, and 'The Marine Excursion of the Knights of Pythias' reveals the foibles and follies of the town's citizens. The narrator, once a town resident, looks back with nostalgia and affection on Mariposa in the late Victorian era. The incongruity between the townspeople's aspirations and their achievements, between the grandeur of their self-esteem and their less grand reality, is the focus of Leacock's kindly humour.

'My Financial Career' was first published in the 11 April 1895 issue of *Life* and then collected in *Literary Lapses*. 'The Marine Excursion of the Knights of Pythias' was first published in the 16 March 1912 issue of the *Montreal Star* and then became the third chapter of *Sunshine Sketches of a Little Town*.

My Financial Career

When I go into a bank I get rattled. The clerks rattle me; the wickets rattle me; the sight of the money rattles me; everything rattles me.

The moment I cross the threshold of a bank and attempt to transact business there, I become an irresponsible idiot.

I knew this beforehand, but my salary had been raised to fifty dollars a month and I felt that the bank was the only place for it.

So I shambled in and looked timidly round at the clerks. I had an idea that a person about to open an account must needs consult the manager.

I went up to a wicket marked 'Accountant'. The accountant was a tall, cool devil. The very sight of him rattled me. My voice was sepulchral.

'Can I see the manager?' I said, and added solemnly, 'alone.' I don't know why I said 'alone'.

'Certainly,' said the accountant, and fetched him.

The manager was a grave, calm man. I held my fifty-six dollars clutched in a crumpled ball in my pocket.

'Are you the manager?' I said. God knows I didn't doubt it.

'Yes,' he said.

'Can I see you,' I asked, 'alone?' I didn't want to say 'alone' again, but without it the thing seemed self-evident.

The manager looked at me in some alarm. He felt that I had an awful secret to reveal.

'Come in here,' he said, and led the way to a private room. He turned the key in the lock.

'We are safe from interruption here,' he said. 'Sit down.'

We both sat down and looked at each other. I found no voice to speak.

'You are one of Pinkerton's men, I presume,' he said.

He had gathered from my mysterious manner that I was a detective. I knew what he was thinking, and it made me worse.

'No, not from Pinkerton's,' I said, seeming to imply that I came from a rival agency.

'To tell the truth,' I went on, as if I had been prompted to lie about it, 'I am not a detective at all. I have come to open an account. I intend to keep all my money in this bank.'

The manager looked relieved but still serious; he concluded now that I was a son of Baron Rothschild or a young Gould.

'A large account, I suppose,' he said.

'Fairly large,' I whispered. 'I propose to deposit fifty-six dollars now and fifty dollars a month regularly.'

The manager got up and opened the door. He called to the accountant.

'Mr Montgomery,' he said unkindly loud, 'this gentleman is opening an account, he will deposit fifty-six dollars. Good morning.'

I rose.

A big iron door stood open at the side of the room.

'Good morning,' I said, and stepped into the safe.

'Come out,' said the manager coldly, and showed me the other way.

I went up to the accountant's wicket and poked the ball of money at him with a quick convulsive movement as if I were doing a conjuring trick.

My face was ghastly pale.

'Here,' I said, 'deposit it.' The tone of the words seemed to mean, 'Let us do this painful thing while the fit is on us.'

He took the money and gave it to another clerk.

He made me write the sum on a slip and sign my name in a book. I no longer knew what I was doing. The bank swam before my eyes.

'Is it deposited?' I asked in a hollow, vibrating voice.

'It is,' said the accountant.

'Then I want to draw a cheque.'

My idea was to draw out six dollars of it for present use. Someone gave me a cheque-book through a wicket and someone else began telling me how to write it out. The people in the bank had the impression that I was an invalid millionaire. I wrote something on the cheque and thrust it in at the clerk. He looked at it.

'What! are you drawing it all out again?' he asked in surprise. Then I realized that I had written fifty-six instead of six. I was too far gone to reason now. I had a feeling that it was impossible to explain the thing. All the clerks had stopped writing to look at me.

Reckless with misery, I made a plunge.

'Yes, the whole thing.'

'You withdraw your money from the bank?'

'Every cent of it.'

'Are you not going to deposit any more?' said the clerk, astonished.

'Never.'

An idiot hope struck me that they might think something had insulted me while I was writing the cheque and that I had changed my mind. I made a wretched attempt to look like a man with a fearfully quick temper.

The clerk prepared to pay the money.

'How will you have it?' he said.

'What?'

'How will you have it?'

'Oh'—I caught his meaning and answered without even trying to think—'in fifties.'

He gave me a fifty-dollar bill.

'And the six?' he asked dryly.

'In sixes,' I said.

He gave it to me and I rushed out.

As the big door swung behind me I caught the echo of a roar of laughter that went up to the ceiling of the bank. Since then I bank no more. I keep my money in cash in my trousers pocket and my savings in silver dollars in a sock.

1895

The Marine Excursion of the Knights of Pythias

Half-past six on a July morning! The Mariposa Belle is at the wharf, decked in flags, with steam up ready to start.

Excursion day!

Half-past six on a July morning, and Lake Wissanotti lying in the sun as calm as glass. The opal colours of the morning light are shot from the surface of the water.

Out on the lake the last thin threads of the mist are clearing away like flecks of cotton wool.

The long call of the loon echoes over the lake. The air is cool and fresh. There is in it all the new life of the land of the silent pine and the moving waters. Lake Wissanotti in the morning sunlight! Don't talk to me of the Italian lakes, or the Tyrol, or the Swiss Alps. Take them away. Move them somewhere else. I don't want them.

Excursion Day, at half-past six of a summer morning! With the boat all decked in flags and all the people in Mariposa on the wharf, and the band in peaked caps with big cornets tied to their bodies ready to play at any minute! I say! Don't tell me about the Carnival of Venice and the Delhi Durbar. Don't! I wouldn't look at them. I'd shut my eyes! For light and colour give me every time an excursion out of Mariposa down the lake to the Indian's Island out of sight in the morning mist. Talk of your Papal Zouaves and your Buckingham Palace Guard! I want to see the Mariposa band in uniform and the Mariposa Knights of Pythias with their aprons and their insignia and their picnic baskets and their five-cent cigars!

Half-past six in the morning, and all the crowd on the wharf and the boat due to leave in half an hour. Notice it!—in half an hour. Already she's whistled twice (at six, and six fifteen), and at any minute now, Christie Johnson will step into the pilot house and pull the string for the warning whistle that the boat will leave in half an hour. So keep ready. Don't think of running back to Smith's Hotel for the sandwiches. Don't be fool enough to try to go up to the Greek Store, next to Netley's, and buy fruit. You'll be left behind for sure if you do. Never mind the sandwiches and the fruit! Anyway, here comes Mr Smith himself with a huge basket of provender that would feed a factory. There must be sandwiches in that. I think I can hear them clinking. And behind Mr Smith is the German waiter from the caff with another basket—indubitably lager beer; and behind him, the bar-tender of the hotel, carrying nothing, as far as one can see. But of course if you know Mariposa you will understand that why he looks so nonchalant and empty-handed is because he has two bottles of rye whiskey under his linen duster. You know, I think, the peculiar walk of a man with two bottles of whisky in the inside pockets of a linen coat. In Mariposa, you see, to bring beer to an excursion is quite in keeping with public opinion. But, whisky,—well, one has to be a little careful.

Do I say that Mr Smith is here? Why, everybody's here. There's Hussell the editor of the Newspacket, wearing a blue ribbon on his coat, for the Mariposa Knights of Pythias are, by their constitution, dedicated to temperance; and there's Henry Mullins, the manager of the Exchange Bank, also a Knight of Pythias, with a small flask of Pogram's Special in his hip pocket as a sort of amendment to the constitution. And there's Dean Drone, the Chaplain of the Order, with a fishing-rod (you never saw such green bass as lie among the rocks at Indian's Island), and with a trolling line in case of maskinonge, and a landing net in case of pickerel, and with his eldest daughter, Lilian Drone, in case of young men. There never was such a fisherman as the Rev. Rupert Drone.

Perhaps I ought to explain that when I speak of the excursion as being of the Knights of Pythias, the thing must not be understood in any narrow sense. In Mariposa practically everybody belongs to the Knights of Pythias just as they do to everything else. That's the great thing about the town and that's what makes it so different from the city. Everybody is in everything.

You should see them on the seventeenth of March, for example, when everybody wears a green ribbon and they're all laughing and glad,—you know what the Celtic nature is,—and talking about Home Rule.

On St Andrew's Day every man in town wears a thistle and shakes hands with everybody else, and you see the fine old Scotch honesty beaming out of their eyes.

And on St George's Day!—well, there's no heartiness like the good old English spirit, after all; why shouldn't a man feel glad that he's an Englishman?

Then on the Fourth of July there are stars and stripes flying over half the stores in town, and suddenly all the men are seen to smoke cigars, and to know all about Roosevelt and Bryan and the Philippine Islands. Then you learn for the first time that Jeff Thorpe's people came from Massachusetts and that his uncle fought at Bunker Hill (it must have been Bunker Hill,—anyway Jefferson will swear it was in Dakota all right enough); and you find that George Duff has a married sister in Rochester and that her husband is all right; in fact, George was down there as recently as eight years ago. Oh, it's the most American town imaginable is Mariposa,—on the fourth of July.

But wait, just wait, if you feel anxious about the solidity of the British connection, till the twelfth of the month, when everybody is wearing an orange streamer in his coat and the Orangemen (every man in town) walk in the big procession. Allegiance! Well, perhaps you remember the address they gave to the Prince of Wales on the platform of the Mariposa station as he went through on his tour to the west. I think that pretty well settled that question.

So you will easily understand that of course everybody belongs to the Knights of Pythias and the Masons and Oddfellows, just as they all belong to the Snow Shoe Club and the Girls' Friendly Society.

And meanwhile the whistle of the steamer has blown again for a quarter to seven:—loud and long this time, for any one not here now is late for certain, unless he should happen to come down in the last fifteen minutes.

What a crowd upon the wharf and how they pile on to the steamer! It's a wonder that the boat can hold them all. But that's just the marvellous thing about the Mariposa Belle.

I don't know,—I have never known,—where the steamers like the Mariposa Belle come from. Whether they are built by Harland and Wolff of Belfast, or whether, on the other hand, they are not built by Harland and Wolff of Belfast, is more than one would like to say offhand.

The Mariposa Belle always seems to me to have some of those strange properties that distinguish Mariposa itself. I mean, her size seems to vary so. If you see her there in the winter, frozen in the ice beside the wharf with a snowdrift against the windows of the pilot house, she looks a pathetic little thing the size of a butternut. But in the summer time, especially after you've been in Mariposa for a month or two, and have paddled alongside of her in a canoe, she gets larger and taller, and with a great sweep of black sides, till you see no difference between the Mariposa Belle and the Lusitania. Each one is a big steamer and that's all you can say.

Nor do her measurements help you much. She draws about eighteen inches forward, and more than that,—at least half an inch more, astern, and when she's loaded down with an excursion crowd she draws a good two inches more. And above the water,—why, look at all the decks on her! There's the deck you walk on to, from the wharf, all shut in, with windows along it, and the after cabin with the long table, and above that the deck with all the chairs piled upon it, and the deck in front where the band stand round in a circle, and the pilot house is higher than that, and above the pilot house is the board with the gold name and the flag pole and the steel ropes and the flags; and fixed in somewhere on the different levels is the lunch counter where they sell the sandwiches, and the engine room, and down below the deck level, beneath the water line, is the place where the crew sleep. What with steps and stairs and passages and piles of cordwood for the engine,—oh no, I guess Harland and Wolff didn't build her. They couldn't have.

Yet even with a huge boat like the Mariposa Belle, it would be impossible for her to carry all of the crowd that you see in the boat and on the wharf. In reality, the crowd is made up of two classes,—all of the people in Mariposa who are going on the excursion and all those who are not. Some come for the one reason and some for the other.

The two tellers of the Exchange Bank are both there standing side by side. But one of them,—the one with the cameo pin and the long face like a horse,—is going, and the other,—with the other cameo pin and the face like another horse,—is not. In the same way, Hussell of the Newspacket is going, but his brother, beside him, isn't. Lilian Drone is going, but her sister can't; and so on all through the crowd.

And to think that things should look like that on the morning of a steamboat accident.

How strange life is!

To think of all these people so eager and anxious to catch the steamer, and some of them running to catch it, and so fearful that they might miss it,—the morning of a steamboat accident. And the captain blowing his whistle, and warning them so severely that he would leave them behind,—leave them out of the accident! And everybody crowding so eagerly to be in the accident.

Perhaps life is like that all through.

Strangest of all to think, in a case like this, of the people who were left behind, or in some way or other prevented from going, and always afterwards told of how they had escaped being on board the Mariposa Belle that day!

Some of the instances were certainly extraordinary.

Nivens, the lawyer, escaped from being there merely by the fact that he was away in the city.

Towers, the tailor, only escaped owing to the fact that, not intending to go on the excursion he had stayed in bed till eight o'clock and so had not gone. He narrated afterwards that waking up that morning at half-past five, he had thought of the excursion and for some unaccountable reason had felt glad that he was not going.

The case of Yodel, the auctioneer, was even more inscrutable. He had been to the Oddfellows' excursion on the train the week before and to the Conservative picnic the week before that, and had decided not to go on this trip. In fact, he had not the least intention of going. He narrated afterwards how the night before someone had stopped him on the corner of Nippewa and Tecumseh Streets (he indicated the very spot) and asked: 'Are you going to take in the excursion to-morrow?' and he had said, just as simply as he was talking when narrating it: 'No.' And ten minutes after that, at the corner of Dalhousie and Brock Streets (he offered to lead a party of verification to the precise place) somebody else had stopped him and asked: 'Well, are you going on the steamer trip to-morrow?' Again he had answered: 'No,' apparently almost in the same tone as before.

He said afterwards that when he heard the rumour of the accident it seemed like the finger of Providence, and he fell on his knees in thankfulness.

There was the similar case of Morison (I mean the one in Glover's hardware store that married one of the Thompsons). He said afterwards that he had read so much in the papers about accidents lately,—mining accidents, and aeroplanes, and gasoline,—that he had grown nervous. The night before his wife had asked him at supper: 'Are you going on the excursion?' He had answered: 'No, I don't think I feel like it,' and had added: 'Perhaps your mother might like to go.' And the next evening just at dusk, when the news ran through the town, he said the first thought that flashed through his head was: 'Mrs Thompson's on that boat.'

He told this right as I say it—without the least doubt or confusion. He never for a moment imagined she was on the Lusitania or the Olympic or any other boat. He knew she was on this one. He said you could have knocked him down where he stood. But no one had. Not even when he got half-way down,—on his knees, and it would have been easier still to knock him down or kick him. People do miss a lot of chances.

Still, as I say, neither Yodel nor Morison nor anyone thought about there being an accident until just after sundown when they—

Well, have you ever heard the long booming whistle of a steamboat two miles out on the lake in the dusk, and while you listen and count and wonder, seen the crimson rockets going up against the sky and then heard the fire bell ringing right there beside you in the town, and seen the people running to the town wharf?

That's what the people of Mariposa saw and felt that summer evening as they watched the Mackinaw life-boat go plunging out into the lake with seven sweeps to a side and the foam clear to the gunwale with the lifting stroke of fourteen men!

But, dear me, I am afraid that this is no way to tell a story. I suppose the true art would have been to have said nothing about the accident till it happened. But when you write about Mariposa, or hear of it, if you know the place, it's all so vivid and real that a thing like the contrast between the excursion crowd in the morning and the scene at night leaps into your mind and you must think of it.

But never mind about the accident,—let us turn back again to the morning.

The boat was due to leave at seven. There was no doubt about the hour,—not only seven, but seven sharp. The notice in the Newspacket said: 'The boat will leave sharp at seven'; and the advertising posters on the telegraph poles on Missinaba Street that began 'Ho, for Indian's Island!' ended up with the words: 'Boat leaves at seven sharp.' There was a big notice on the wharf that said: 'Boat leaves sharp on time.'

So at seven, right on the hour, the whistle blew loud and long, and then at seven fifteen three short peremptory blasts, and at seven thirty one quick angry call,—just one,—and very soon after that they cast off the last of the ropes and the Mariposa Belle sailed off in her cloud of flags, and the band of the Knights of Pythias, timing it to a nicety, broke into the 'Maple Leaf for Ever!'

I suppose that all excursions when they start are much the same. Anyway, on the Mariposa Belle everybody went running up and down all over the boat with deck chairs and camp stools and baskets, and found places, splendid places to sit, and then got scared that there might be better ones and chased off again. People hunted for places out of the sun and when they got them swore that they weren't going to freeze to please anybody; and the people in the sun said that they hadn't paid fifty cents to be roasted. Others said that they hadn't paid fifty cents to get covered with cinders, and there were still others who hadn't paid fifty cents to get shaken to death with the propeller.

Still, it was all right presently. The people seemed to get sorted out into the places on the boat where they belonged. The women, the older ones, all gravitated into the cabin on the lower deck and by getting round the table with needlework, and with all the windows shut, they soon had it, as they said themselves, just like being at home.

All the young boys and the toughs and the men in the band got down on the lower deck forward, where the boat was dirtiest and where the anchor was and the coils of rope.

And upstairs on the after deck there were Lilian Drone and Miss Lawson, the high school teacher, with a book of German poetry,—Gothey I think it was,—and the bank teller and the younger men.

In the centre, standing beside the rail, were Dean Drone and Dr Gallagher, looking through binocular glasses at the shore.

Up in front on the little deck forward of the pilot house was a group of the older men, Mullins and Duff and Mr Smith in a deck chair, and beside him Mr Golgotha Gingham, the undertaker of Mariposa, on a stool. It was part of Mr Gingham's principles to take in an outing of this sort, a business matter, more or less,—for you never know what may happen at these water parties. At any rate, he was there in a neat suit of black, not, of course, his heavier or professional suit, but a soft clinging effect as of burnt paper that combined gaiety and decorum to a nicety.

'Yes,' said Mr Gingham, waving his black glove in a general way towards the shore, 'I know the lake well, very well. I've been pretty well much all over it in my time.'

'Canoeing?' asked somebody.

'No,' said Mr Gingham, 'not in a canoe.' There seemed a peculiar and quiet meaning in his tone.

'Sailing, I suppose,' said somebody else.

'No,' said Mr Gingham. 'I don't understand it.'

'I never knowed that you went on to the water at all, Gol,' said Mr Smith, breaking in.

'Ah, not now,' explained Mr Gingham; 'it was years ago, the first summer I came to Mariposa. I was on the water practically all day. Nothing like it to give a man an appetite and keep him in shape.'

'Was you camping?' asked Mr Smith.

'We camped at night,' assented the undertaker, 'but we put in practically the whole day on the water. You see we were after a party that had come up here from the city on his vacation and gone out in a sailing canoe. We were dragging. We were up every morning at sunrise, lit a fire on the beach and cooked breakfast, and then we'd light our pipes and be off with the net for a whole day. It's a great life,' concluded Mr Gingham wistfully.

'Did you get him?' asked two or three together.

There was a pause before Mr Gingham answered.

'We did,' he said,—'down in the reeds past Horseshoe Point. But it was no use. He turned blue on me right away.'

After which Mr Gingham fell into such a deep reverie that the boat had steamed another half-mile down the lake before anybody broke the silence again.

Talk of this sort,—and after all what more suitable for a day on the water?—beguiled the way.

Down the lake, mile by mile over the calm water, steamed the Mariposa Belle. They passed Poplar Point where the high sand-banks are with all the swallows' nests in them, and Dean Drone and Dr Gallagher looked at them alternately through the binocular glasses, and it was wonderful how plainly one could see the swallows and the banks and the shrubs,—just as plainly as with the naked eye.

And a little further down they passed the Shingle Beach, and Dr Gallagher, who knew Canadian history, said to Dean Drone that it was strange to think that Champlain had landed there with his French explorers three hundred years ago; and Dean Drone, who didn't know Canadian history, said it was stranger still to think that the hand of the Almighty had piled up the hills and rocks long before that; and Dr Gallagher said it was wonderful how the French had found their way through such a pathless wilderness; and Dean Drone said that it was wonderful also to think that the Almighty had placed even the smallest shrub in its appointed place. Dr Gallagher said it filled him with admiration. Dean Drone said it filled him with awe. Dr Gallagher said he'd been full of it ever since he was a boy; and Dean Drone said so had he.

Then a little further, as the Mariposa Belle steamed on down the lake, they passed the Old Indian Portage where the great grey rocks are; and Dr Gallagher drew Dean Drone's attention to the place where the narrow canoe track wound up from the shore to the woods, and Dean Drone said he could see it perfectly well without the glasses.

Dr Gallagher said that it was just here that a party of five hundred French had made their way with all their baggage and accoutrements across the rocks of the divide and down to the Great Bay. And Dean Drone said that it reminded him of Xenophon leading his ten thousand Greeks over the hill passes of Armenia down to the sea. Dr Gallagher said that he had often wished he could have seen and spoken to Champlain, and Dean Drone said how much he regretted to have never known Xenophon.

And then after that they fell to talking of relics and traces of the past, and Dr Gallagher said that if Dean Drone would come round to his house some night he would show him some Indian arrow heads that he had dug up in his garden. And Dean Drone said that if Dr Gallagher would come round to the rectory any afternoon he would show him a map of Xerxes' invasion of Greece. Only he must come some time between the Infant Class and the Mothers' Auxiliary.

So presently they both knew that they were blocked out of one another's houses for some time to come, and Dr Gallagher walked forward and told Mr Smith, who had never studied Greek, about Champlain crossing the rock divide.

Mr Smith turned his head and looked at the divide for half a second and then said he had crossed a worse one up north back of the Wahnipitae and that the flies were Hades,—and then went on playing freezeout poker with the two juniors in Duff's bank.

So Dr Gallagher realized that that's always the way when you try to tell people things, and that as far as gratitude and appreciation goes one might as well never read books or travel anywhere or do anything.

In fact, it was at this very moment that he made up his mind to give the arrows to the Mariposa Mechanics' Institute,—they afterwards became, as you know, the Gallagher Collection. But, for the time being, the doctor was sick of them and wandered off round the boat and watched Henry Mullins showing George Duff how to make a John Collins without lemons, and finally went and sat down among the Mariposa band and wished that he hadn't come.

So the boat steamed on and the sun rose higher and higher, and the freshness of the morning changed into the full glare of noon, and they went on to where the lake began to narrow in at its foot, just where the Indian's Island is,—all grass and trees and with a log wharf running into the water. Below it the Lower Ossawippi runs out of the lake, and quite near are the rapids, and you can see down among the trees the red brick of the power house and hear the roar of the leaping water.

The Indian's Island itself is all covered with trees and tangled vines, and the water about it is so still that it's all reflected double and looks the same either way up. Then when the steamer's whistle blows as it comes into the wharf, you hear it echo among the trees of the island, and reverberate back from the shores of the lake.

The scene is all so quiet and still and unbroken, that Miss Cleghorn,—the sallow girl in the telephone exchange, that I spoke of—said she'd like to be buried there. But all the people were so busy getting their baskets and gathering up their things that no one had time to attend to it.

I mustn't even try to describe the landing and the boat crunching against the wooden wharf and all the people running to the same side of the deck and Christie Johnson calling out to the crowd to keep to the starboard and nobody being able to find it. Everyone who has been on a Mariposa excursion knows all about that.

Nor can I describe the day itself and the picnic under the trees. There were speeches afterwards, and Judge Pepperleigh gave such offence by bringing in Conservative politics that a man called Patriotus Canadiensis wrote and asked for some of the invaluable space of the Mariposa Times-Herald and exposed it.

I should say that there were races too, on the grass on the open side of the island, graded mostly according to ages,—races for boys under thirteen and girls over nineteen and all that sort of thing. Sports are generally conducted on that plan in Mariposa. It is realized that a woman of sixty has an unfair advantage over a mere child.

Dean Drone managed the races and decided the ages and gave out the prizes; the Wesleyan minister helped, and he and the young student, who was relieving in the Presbyterian Church, held the string at the winning point.

They had to get mostly clergymen for the races because all the men had wandered off, somehow, to where they were drinking lager beer out of two kegs stuck on pine logs among the trees.

But if you've ever been on a Mariposa excursion you know all about these details anyway.

So the day wore on and presently the sun came through the trees on a slant and the steamer whistle blew with a great puff of white steam and all the people came straggling down to the wharf and pretty soon the Mariposa Belle had floated out on to the lake again and headed for the town, twenty miles away.

I suppose you have often noticed the contrast there is between an excursion on its way out in the morning and what it looks like on the way home.

In the morning everybody is so restless and animated and moves to and fro all over the boat and asks questions. But coming home, as the afternoon gets later and later and the sun sinks beyond the hills, all the people seem to get so still and quiet and drowsy.

So it was with the people on the Mariposa Belle. They sat there on the benches and the deck chairs in little clusters, and listened to the regular beat of the propeller and almost dozed off asleep as they sat. Then when the sun set and the dusk drew on, it grew almost dark on the deck and so still that you could hardly tell there was anyone on board.

And if you had looked at the steamer from the shore or from one of the islands, you'd have seen the row of lights from the cabin windows shining on the water and the red glare of the burning hemlock from the funnel, and you'd have heard the soft thud of the propeller miles away over the lake.

Now and then, too, you could have heard them singing on the steamer,—the voices of the girls and the men blended into unison by the distance, rising and falling in long-drawn melody: '*O—Can-a-da—O—Can-a-da.*'

You may talk as you will about the intoning choirs of your European cathedrals, but the sound of 'O Can-a-da', borne across the waters of a silent lake at evening is good enough for those of us who know Mariposa.

I think that it was just as they were singing like this: '*O—Can-a-da*', that word went round that the boat was sinking.

If you have ever been in any sudden emergency on the water, you will understand the strange psychology of it,—the way in which what is happening seems to become known all in a moment without a word being said. The news is transmitted from one to the other by some mysterious process.

At any rate, on the Mariposa Belle first one and then the other heard that the steamer was sinking. As far as I could ever learn the first of it was that George Duff, the bank manager, came very quietly to Dr Gallagher and asked him if he thought that the boat was sinking. The doctor said no, that he had thought so earlier in the day but that he didn't now think that she was.

After that Duff, according to his own account, had said to Macartney, the lawyer, that the boat was sinking, and Macartney said that he doubted it very much.

Then somebody came to Judge Pepperleigh and woke him up and said that there was six inches of water in the steamer and that she was sinking. And Pepperleigh said it was a perfect scandal and passed the news on to his wife and she said that they had no business to allow it and that if the steamer sank that was the last excursion she'd go on.

So the news went all round the boat and everywhere the people gathered in groups and talked about it in the angry and excited way that people have when a steamer is sinking on one of the lakes like Lake Wissanotti.

Dean Drone, of course, and some others were quieter about it, and said that one must make allowances and that naturally there were two sides to everything. But most of them wouldn't listen to reason at all. I think, perhaps, that some of them were frightened. You see the last time but one that the steamer had sunk, there had been a man drowned and it made them nervous.

What? Hadn't I explained about the depth of Lake Wissanotti? I had taken it for granted that you knew; and in any case parts of it are deep enough, though I don't suppose in this stretch of it from the big reed beds up to within a mile of the town wharf, you could find six feet of water in it if you tried. Oh, pshaw! I was not talking about a steamer sinking in the ocean and carrying down its screaming crowds of people into the hideous depths of green water. Oh, dear me, no! That kind of thing never happens on Lake Wissanotti.

But what does happen is that the Mariposa Belle sinks every now and then, and sticks there on the bottom till they get things straightened up.

On the lakes round Mariposa, if a person arrives late anywhere and explains that the steamer sank, everybody understands the situation.

You see when Harland and Wolff built the Mariposa Belle, they left some cracks in between the timbers that you fill up with cotton waste every Sunday. If this is not attended to, the boat sinks. In fact, it is part of the law of the province that all the steamers like the Mariposa Belle must be properly corked,—I think that is the word,—every season. There are inspectors who visit all the hotels in the province to see that it is done.

So you can imagine now that I've explained it a little straighter, the indignation of the people when they knew that the boat had come uncorked and that they might be stuck out there on a shoal or a mud-bank half the night.

I don't say either that there wasn't any danger; anyway, it doesn't feel very safe when you realize that the boat is settling down with every hundred yards that she goes, and you look over the side and see only the black water in the gathering night.

Safe! I'm not sure now that I come to think of it that it isn't worse than sinking in the Atlantic. After all, in the Atlantic there is wireless telegraphy, and a lot of trained sailors and stewards. But out on Lake Wissanotti,—far out, so that you can only just see the lights of the town away off to the south,—when the propeller comes to a stop,—and you can hear the hiss of steam as they start to rake out the engine fires to prevent an explosion,—and when you turn from the red glare that comes from the furnace doors as they open them, to the black dark that is gathering over the lake,—and there's a night wind beginning to run among the rushes,—and you see the men going forward to the roof of the pilot house to send up the rockets to rouse the town,—safe? Safe yourself, if you like; as for me, let me once get back into Mariposa again, under the night shadow of the maple trees, and this shall be the last, last time I'll go on Lake Wissanotti.

Safe! Oh yes! Isn't it strange how safe other people's adventures seem after they happen? But you'd have been scared, too, if you'd been there just before the steamer sank, and seen them bringing up all the women on to the top deck.

I don't see how some of the people took it so calmly; how Mr Smith, for instance, could have gone on smoking and telling how he'd had a steamer 'sink on him' on Lake Nipissing and a still bigger one, a side-wheeler, sink on him in Lake Abbitibbi.

Then, quite suddenly, with a quiver, down she went. You could feel the boat sink, sink,—down, down,—would it never get to the bottom? The water came flush up to the lower deck, and then—thank heaven,—the sinking stopped and there was the Mariposa Belle safe and tight on a reed bank.

Really, it made one positively laugh! It seemed so queer and, anyway, if a man has a sort of natural courage, danger makes him laugh. Danger? pshaw! fiddlesticks! everybody scouted the idea. Why, it is just the little things like this that give zest to a day on the water.

Within half a minute they were all running round looking for sandwiches and cracking jokes and talking of making coffee over the remains of the engine fires.

I don't need to tell at length how it all happened after that.

I suppose the people on the Mariposa Belle would have had to settle down there all night or till help came from the town, but some of the men who had gone forward and were peering out into the dark said that it couldn't be more than a mile across the water to Miller's Point. You could almost see it over there to the left,—some of them, I think, said 'off on the port bow', because you know when you get mixed up in these marine disasters, you soon catch the atmosphere of the thing.

So pretty soon they had the davits swung out over the side and were lowering the old lifeboat from the top deck into the water.

There were men leaning out over the rail of the Mariposa Belle with lanterns that threw the light as they let her down, and the glare fell on the water and the reeds. But when they got the boat lowered, it looked such a frail, clumsy thing as one saw it from the rail above, that the cry was raised: 'Women and children first!' For what was the sense, if it should turn out that the boat wouldn't even hold women and children, of trying to jam a lot of heavy men into it?

So they put in mostly women and children and the boat pushed out into the darkness so freighted down it would hardly float.

In the bow of it was the Presbyterian student who was relieving the minister, and he called out that they were in the hands of Providence. But he was crouched and ready to spring out of them at the first moment.

So the boat went and was lost in the darkness except for the lantern in the bow that you could see bobbing on the water. Then presently it came back and they sent another load, till pretty soon the decks began to thin out and everybody got impatient to be gone.

It was about the time that the third boat-load put off that Mr Smith took a bet with Mullins for twenty-five dollars, that he'd be home in Mariposa before the people in the boats had walked round the shore.

No one knew just what he meant, but pretty soon they saw Mr Smith disappear down below into the lowest part of the steamer with a mallet in one hand and a big bundle of marline in the other.

They might have wondered more about it, but it was just at this time that they heard the shouts from the rescue boat—the big Mackinaw lifeboat—that had put out from the town with fourteen men at the sweeps when they saw the first rockets go up.

I suppose there is always something inspiring about a rescue at sea, or on the water.

After all, the bravery of the lifeboat man is the true bravery,—expended to save life, not to destroy it.

Certainly they told for months after of how the rescue boat came out to the Mariposa Belle.

I suppose that when they put her in the water the lifeboat touched it for the first time since the old Macdonald Government placed her on Lake Wissanotti.

Anyway, the water poured in at every seam. But not for a moment,—even with two miles of water between them and the steamer,—did the rowers pause for that.

By the time they were half-way there the water was almost up to the thwarts, but they drove her on. Panting and exhausted (for mind you, if you haven't been in a fool boat like that for years, rowing takes it out of you), the rowers stuck to their task. They threw the ballast over and chucked into the water the heavy cork jackets and lifebelts that encumbered their movements. There was no thought of turning back. They were nearer to the steamer than the shore.

'Hang to it, boys,' called the crowd from the steamer's deck, and hang they did.

They were almost exhausted when they got them; men leaning from the steamer threw them ropes and one by one every man was hauled aboard just as the lifeboat sank under their feet.

Saved! by Heaven, saved, by one of the smartest pieces of rescue work ever seen on the lake.

There's no use describing it; you need to see rescue work of this kind by lifeboats to understand it.

Nor were the lifeboat crew the only ones that distinguished themselves.

Boat after boat and canoe after canoe had put out from Mariposa to the help of the steamer. They got them all.

Pupkin, the other bank teller, with a face like a horse, who hadn't gone on the excursion,—as soon as he knew that the boat was signalling for help and that Miss Lawson was sending up rockets,—rushed for a row boat, grabbed an oar (two would have hampered him), and paddled madly out into the lake. He struck right out into the dark with the crazy skiff almost sinking beneath his feet. But they got him. They rescued him. They watched him, almost dead with exhaustion, make his way to the steamer, where he was hauled up with ropes. Saved! Saved!!

They might have gone on that way half the night, picking up the rescuers, only, at the very moment when the tenth load of people left for the shore,—just as suddenly and saucily as you please, up came the Mariposa Belle from the mud bottom and floated.

FLOATED?

Why, of course she did. If you take a hundred and fifty people off a steamer that has sunk, and if you get a man as shrewd as Mr Smith to plug the timber seams with mallet and marline, and if you turn ten bandsmen of the Mariposa band on to your hand pump on the bow of the lower decks—float? why, what else can she do?

Then, if you stuff in hemlock into the embers of the fire that you were raking out, till it hums and crackles under the boiler, it won't be long before you hear the propeller thud—thudding at the stern again, and before the long roar of the steam whistle echoes over to the town.

And so the Mariposa Belle, with all steam up again and with the long train of sparks careering from the funnel, is heading for the town.

But no Christie Johnson at the wheel in the pilot house this time.

'Smith! Get Smith!' is the cry.

Can he take her in? Well, now! Ask a man who has had steamers sink on him in half the lakes from Temiscaming to the Bay, if he can take her in? Ask a man who has run a York boat down the rapids of the Moose when the ice is moving, if he can grip the steering wheel of the Mariposa Belle? So there she steams safe and sound to the town wharf!

Look at the lights and the crowd! If only the federal census taker could count us now! Hear them calling and shouting back and forward from the deck to the shore! Listen! There is the rattle of the shore ropes as they get them ready, and there's the Mariposa band,—actually forming in a circle on the upper deck just as she docks, and the leader with his baton,—one—two—ready now,—

'O CAN-A-DA!'

1912

James Joyce

1882-1941

Explaining the title he chose for the book of stories published in 1914, James Joyce wrote: 'I call the series *Dubliners* to betray the soul of that hemiphelia or paralysis which many consider a city.' In much of his fiction, Joyce's vision is richly imbued with his celebrated recreations of Dublin, which figures as a realistic, symbolic, and mythological setting in his novels.

Born into a large Dublin family, Joyce went to school at Clongowes Wood College and then took his B.A. (1902) at University College before leaving for the continent. Although he returned to Ireland briefly on several occasions, he was to live the rest of his life in a self-imposed exile from his native country. He saw the writing of *Dubliners* as a way of freeing Ireland from its spiritual bondage: 'In composing my chapter of moral history in exactly the way I have composed it I have taken the first step towards the spiritual liberation of my country.' He moved from Trieste to Zurich in 1915, then to Paris in 1922, returning to Zurich two weeks before his death.

Although three of the stories in *Dubliners* first appeared in the *Irish Homestead* in 1904, Joyce only began to conceive of the collection of fifteen stories as a book in 1906. He saw the stories as showing the Irish who they were as a people and a culture—including the harsh realities of their experience: 'It is not my fault that the odour of ashpits and old weeds and offal hangs around my stories. I seriously believe that you will retard the course of civilisation in Ireland by preventing the Irish people from having a good look at themselves in my nicely-polished looking glass.'

In 'Araby,' Joyce traces the progress of a boy's infatuation with a girl who is his neighbour. The boy's inarticulate but powerfully felt longing builds to an epiphany, a moment of insight and initiation in the deserted bazaar, inviting reflections on the nature of the boy's feelings and also suggesting that he has not arrived at a final apprehension of his experience. In this story as in much of his fiction, Joyce saw the epiphany as a moment in which the true nature of a character is revealed, or a moment when perception is so sharpened that 'we recognize that it is *that* thing which it is. Its soul, its whatness leaps to us from the vestment of its appearance.'

'The Dead,' the longest and final story in *Dubliners*, opens with a richly nuanced depiction of a Christmas dance and dinner providing insight into the web of social relations that define Gabriel Conroy's character and vision. Gretta's response to the singing she hears at the party becomes the bridge to the story's exploration of the couple's relationship; the transformation of Gabriel's feelings for Gretta after he hears her memories of Michael Furey lead to his closing meditations on mortality, which meld beautifully with his apprehension of the snow descending at the window and all over Ireland. It is the pervasive presence of 'the dead,' as the story's title implies, that Gretta recalls, that Gabriel apprehends through her memories, and that is settling like winter weather over Ireland, modifying Gabriel's perception of love.

Joyce finished 'Araby' in October 1905. He wrote 'The Dead' in Trieste in the spring of 1907. Both stories were first published in *Dubliners*.

Araby

North Richmond Street, being blind, was a quiet street except at the hour when the Christian Brothers' School set the boys free. An uninhabited house of two storeys stood at the blind end, detached from its neighbours in a square ground. The other houses of the street, conscious of decent lives within them, gazed at one another with brown imperturbable faces.

The former tenant of our house, a priest, had died in the back drawing-room. Air, musty from having been long enclosed, hung in all rooms, and the waste room behind the kitchen was littered with old useless papers. Among these I found a few paper-covered books, the pages of which were curled and damp: *The Abbot*, by Walter Scott, *The Devout Communicant*, and *The Memoirs of Vidocq*. I liked the last best because its leaves were yellow. The wild garden behind the house contained a central apple-tree and a few straggling bushes under one of which I found the late tenant's rusty bicycle-pump. He had been a very charitable priest; in his will he had left all his money to institutions and the furniture of his house to his sister.

When the short days of winter came dusk fell before we had well eaten our dinners. When we met in the street the house had grown sombre. The space of sky above us was the colour of ever-changing violet and towards it the lamps of the street lifted their feeble lanterns. The cold air stung us and we played till our bodies glowed. Our shouts echoed in the silent street. The career of our play brought us through the dark muddy lanes behind the houses where we ran the gantlet of the rough tribes from the cottages, to the back doors of the dark dripping gardens where odours arose from the ashpits, to the dark odorous stables where a coachman smoothed and combed the horse or shook music from the buckled harness. When we returned to the street light from the kitchen windows had filled the areas. If my uncle was seen turning the corner we hid in the shadow until we had seen him safely housed. Or if Mangan's sister came out on the doorstep to call her brother in to his tea we watched her from our shadow peer up and down the street. We waited to see whether she would remain or go in and, if she remained, we left our shadow and walked up to Mangan's steps resignedly. She was waiting for us, her figure defined by the light from the half-opened door. Her brother always teased her before he obeyed and I stood by the railings looking at her. Her dress swung as she moved her body and the soft rope of her hair tossed from side to side.

Every morning I lay on the floor in the front parlour watching her door. The blind was pulled down to within an inch of the sash so that I could not be seen. When she came out on the doorstep my heart leaped. I ran to the hall, seized my books, and followed her. I kept her brown figure always in my eye and, when we came near the point at which our ways diverged, I quickened my pace and passed her. This happened morning after morning. I had never spoken to her, except for a few casual words, and yet her name was like a summons to all my foolish blood.

Her image accompanied me even in places the most hostile to romance. On Saturday evenings when my aunt went marketing I had to go to carry some of the parcels. We walked through the flaring streets, jostled by drunken men and bargaining women, amid the curses of labourers, the shrill litanies of shop-boys who stood on guard by the barrels of pigs' cheeks, the nasal chanting of street-singers, who sang a *come-all-you* about O'Donovan Rossa, or a ballad about the troubles in our native land. These noises converged in a single sensation of life for me: I imagined that I bore my chalice safely through a throng of foes. Her name sprang to my lips at moments in strange prayers and praises which I myself did not understand. My eyes were often full of tears (I could not tell why) and at times a flood from my heart seemed to pour itself out into my bosom. I thought little of the future. I did not know whether I would ever speak to her or not or, if I spoke to her, how I could tell her of my confused adoration. But my body was like a harp and her words and gestures were like fingers running upon the wires.

One evening I went into the back drawing-room in which the priest had died. It was a dark rainy evening and there was no sound in the house. Through one of the broken panes I heard the rain impinge upon the earth, the fine incessant needles of water playing in the sodden beds. Some distant lamp or lighted window gleamed below me. I was thankful that I could see so little. All my senses seemed to desire to veil themselves and, feeling that I was about to slip from them, I pressed the palms of my hands together until they trembled, murmuring: *O love! O love!* many times.

At last she spoke to me. When she addressed the first words to me I was so confused that I did not know what to answer. She asked me was I going to *Araby*. I forget whether I answered yes or no. It would be a splendid bazaar, she said; she would love to go.

—And why can't you? I asked.

While she spoke she turned a silver bracelet round and round her wrist. She could not go, she said, because there would be a retreat that week in her convent. Her brother and two other boys were fighting for their caps and I was alone at the railings. She held one of the spikes, bowing her head towards me. The light from the lamp opposite our door caught the white curve of her neck, lit up her hair that rested there and, falling, lit up the hand upon the railing. It fell over one side of her dress and caught the white border of a petticoat, just visible as she stood at ease.

—It's well for you, she said.

—If I go, I said, I will bring you something.

What innumerable follies laid waste my waking and sleeping thoughts after that evening! I wished to annihilate the tedious intervening days. I chafed against the work of school. At night in my bedroom and by day in the classroom her image came between me and the page I strove to read. The syllables of the word *Araby* were called to me through the silence in which my soul luxuriated and cast an Eastern enchantment over me. I asked for leave to go to the bazaar Saturday night. My aunt was surprised and hoped it was not some Freemason affair. I answered few questions in class. I watched my master's face pass from amiability to sternness; he hoped I was not beginning to idle. I could not call my wandering thoughts together. I had hardly any patience with the serious work of life which, now that it stood between me and my desire, seemed to me child's play, ugly monotonous child's play.

On Saturday morning I reminded my uncle that I wished to go to the bazaar in the evening. He was fussing at the hallstand, looking for the hat-brush, and answered me curtly:

—Yes, boy, I know.

As he was in the hall I could not go into the front parlour and lie at the window. I left the house in bad humour and walked slowly towards the school. The air was pitilessly raw and already my heart misgave me.

When I came home to dinner my uncle had not yet been home. Still it was early. I sat staring at the clock for some time and, when its ticking began to irritate me, I left the room. I mounted the staircase and gained the upper part of the house. The high cold empty gloomy rooms liberated me and I went from room to room singing. From the front window I saw my companions playing below in the street. Their cries reached me weakened and indistinct and, leaning my forehead against the cool glass, I looked over at the dark house where she lived. I may have stood there for an hour, seeing nothing but the brown-clad figure cast by my imagination, touched discreetly by the lamplight at the curved neck, at the hand upon the railings, and at the border below the dress.

When I came downstairs again I found Mrs Mercer sitting at the fire. She was an old garrulous woman, a pawnbroker's widow, who collected used stamps for some pious purpose. I had to endure the gossip of the tea-table. The meal was prolonged beyond an hour and still my uncle did not come. Mrs Mercer stood up to go: she was sorry she couldn't wait any longer, but it was after eight o'clock and she did not like to be out late, as the night air was bad for her. When she had gone I began to walk up and down the room, clenching my fists. My aunt said:

—I'm afraid you may put off your bazaar for this night of Our Lord.

At nine o'clock I heard my uncle's latchkey in the hall-door. I heard him talking to himself and heard the hallstand rocking when it had received the weight of his overcoat. I could interpret these signs. When he was midway through his dinner I asked him to give me the money to go to the bazaar. He had forgotten.

—The people are in bed and after their first sleep now, he said.

I did not smile. My aunt said to him energetically:

—Can't you give him the money and let him go? You've kept him late enough as it is.

My uncle said he was very sorry he had forgotten. He said he believed in the old saying: *All work and no play makes Jack a dull boy*. He asked me where I was going and, when I had told him a second time he asked me did I know *The Arab's Farewell to his Steed*. When I left the kitchen he was about to recite the opening lines of the piece to my aunt.

I held a florin tightly in my hand as I strode down Buckingham Street towards the station. The sight of the streets thronged with buyers and glaring with gas recalled to me the purpose of my journey. I took my seat in a third-class carriage of a deserted train. After an intolerable delay the train moved out of the station slowly. It crept onward among ruinous houses and over the twinkling river. At Westland Row Station a crowd of people pressed to the carriage doors; but the porters moved them back, saying that it was a special train for the bazaar. I remained alone in the bare carriage. In a few minutes the train drew up beside an improvised wooden platform. I passed out on to the road and saw by the lighted dial of a clock that it was ten minutes to ten. In front of me was a large building which displayed the magical name.

I could not find any sixpenny entrance and, fearing that the bazaar would be closed, I passed in quickly through a turnstile, handing a shilling to a weary-looking man. I found myself in a big hall girdled at half its height by a gallery. Nearly all the stalls were closed and the greater part of the hall was in darkness. I recognized a silence like that which pervades a church after a service. I walked into the centre of the bazaar timidly. A few people were gathered about the stalls which were still open. Before a curtain, over which the words *Café Chantant* were written in coloured lamps, two men were counting money on a salver. I listened to the fall of the coins.

Remembering with difficulty why I had come I went over to one of the stalls and examined porcelain vases and flowered tea-sets. At the door of the stall a young lady was talking and laughing with two young gentlemen. I remarked their English accents and listened vaguely to their conversation.

—O, I never said such a thing!

—O, but you did!

—O, but I didn't!

—Didn't she say that?

—Yes. I heard her.

—O, there's a . . . fib!

Observing me the young lady came over and asked me did I wish to buy anything. The tone of her voice was not encouraging; she seemed to have spoken to me out of a sense of duty. I looked humbly at the great jars that stood like eastern guards at either side of the dark entrance to the stall and murmured:

—No, thank you.

The young lady changed the position of one of the vases and went back to the two young men. They began to talk of the same subject. Once or twice the young lady glanced at me over her shoulder.

I lingered before her stall, though I knew my stay was useless, to make my interest in her wares seem the more real. Then I turned away slowly and walked down the middle of the bazaar. I allowed the two pennies to fall against the sixpence in my pocket. I heard a voice call from one end of the gallery that the light was out. The upper part of the hall was now completely dark.

Gazing up into the darkness I saw myself as a creature driven and derided by vanity; and my eyes burned with anguish and anger.

1914

The Dead

Lily, the caretaker's daughter, was literally run off her feet. Hardly had she brought one gentleman into the little pantry behind the office on the ground floor and helped him off with his overcoat than the wheezy hall-door bell clanged again and she had to scamper along the bare hallway to let in another guest. It was well for her she had not to attend to the ladies also. But Miss Kate and Miss Julia had thought of that and had converted the bathroom upstairs into a ladies' dressing-room. Miss Kate and Miss Julia were there, gossiping and laughing and fussing, walking after each other to the head of the stairs, peering down over the banisters and calling down to Lily to ask her who had come.

It was always a great affair, the Misses Morkan's annual dance. Everybody who knew them came to it, members of the family, old friends of the family, the members of Julia's choir, any of Kate's pupils that were grown up enough and even some of Mary Jane's pupils too. Never once had it fallen flat. For years and years it had gone off in splendid style as long as anyone could remember; ever since Kate and Julia, after the death of their brother Pat, had left the house in Stoney Batter and taken Mary Jane, their only niece, to live with them in the dark gaunt house on Usher's Island, the upper part of which they had rented from Mr Fulham, the cornfactor on the ground floor. That was a good thirty years ago if it was a day. Mary Jane, who was then a little girl in short clothes, was now the main prop of the household for she had the organ in Haddington Road. She had been through the Academy and gave a pupils' concert every year in the upper room of the Antient Concert Rooms. Many of her pupils belonged to better-class families on the Kingstown and Dalkey line. Old as they were, her aunts also did their share. Julia, though she was quite grey, was still the leading soprano in Adam and Eve's, and Kate, being too feeble to go about much, gave music lessons to beginners on the old square piano in the back room. Lily, the caretaker's daughter, did housemaid's work for them. Though their life was modest they believed in eating well; the best of everything; diamond-bone sirloins, three-shilling tea and the best bottled stout. But Lily seldom made a mistake in the orders so that she got on well with her three mistresses. They were fussy, that was all. But the only thing they would not stand was back answers.

Of course they had good reason to be fussy on such a night. And then it was long after ten o'clock and yet there was no sign of Gabriel and his wife. Besides they were dreadfully afraid that Freddy Malins might turn up screwed. They would not wish for worlds that any of Mary Jane's pupils should see him under the influence; and when he was like that it was sometimes very hard to manage him. Freddy Malins always came late but they wondered what could be keeping Gabriel: and that was what brought them every two minutes to the banisters to ask Lily had Gabriel or Freddy come.

—O, Mr Conroy, said Lily to Gabriel when she opened the door for him, Miss Kate and Miss Julia thought you were never coming. Goodnight, Mrs Conroy.

—I'll engage they did, said Gabriel, but they forget that my wife here takes three mortal hours to dress herself.

He stood on the mat, scraping the snow from his goloshes, while Lily led his wife to the foot of the stairs and called out:

—Miss Kate, here's Mrs Conroy.

Kate and Julia came toddling down the dark stairs at once. Both of them kissed Gabriel's wife, said she must be perished alive and asked was Gabriel with her.

—Here I am as right as the mail, Aunt Kate! Go on up. I'll follow, called out Gabriel from the dark.

He continued scraping his feet vigorously while the three women went upstairs, laughing, to the ladies' dressing-room. A light fringe of snow lay like a cape on the shoulders of his overcoat and like toecaps on the toes of his goloshes; and, as the buttons of his overcoat slipped with a squeaking noise through the snow-stiffened frieze, a cold fragrant air from out-of-doors escaped from crevices and folds.

—Is it snowing again, Mr Conroy? asked Lily.

She had preceded him into the pantry to help him off with his overcoat. Gabriel smiled at the three syllables she had given his surname and glanced at her. She was a slim, growing girl, pale in complexion and with hay-coloured hair. The gas in the pantry made her look still paler. Gabriel had known her when she was a child and used to sit on the lowest step nursing a rag doll.

—Yes, Lily, he answered, and I think we're in for a night of it.

He looked up at the pantry ceiling, which was shaking with the stamping and shuffling of feet on the floor above, listened for a moment to the piano and then glanced at the girl, who was folding his overcoat carefully at the end of a shelf.

—Tell me, Lily, he said in a friendly tone, do you still go to school?

—O no, sir, she answered. I'm done schooling this year and more.

—O, then, said Gabriel gaily, I suppose we'll be going to your wedding one of these fine days with your young man, eh?

The girl glanced back at him over her shoulder and said with great bitterness:

—The men that is now is only all palaver and what they can get out of you.

Gabriel coloured as if he felt he had made a mistake and, without looking at her, kicked off his goloshes and flicked actively with his muffler at his patent-leather shoes.

He was a stout tallish young man. The high colour of his cheeks pushed upwards even to his forehead where it scattered itself in a few formless patches of pale red; and on his hairless face there scintillated restlessly the polished lenses and the bright gilt rims of the glasses which screened his delicate and restless eyes. His glossy black hair was parted in the middle and brushed in a long curve behind his ears where it curled slightly beneath the groove left by his hat.

When he had flicked lustre into his shoes he stood up and pulled his waistcoat down more tightly on his plump body. Then he took a coin rapidly from his pocket.

—O Lily, he said, thrusting it into her hands, it's Christmas-time, isn't it? Just . . . here's a little. . . .

He walked rapidly towards the door.

—O no, sir! cried the girl, following him. Really, sir, I wouldn't take it.

—Christmas-time! Christmas-time! said Gabriel, almost trotting to the stairs and waving his hand to her in deprecation.

The girl, seeing that he had gained the stairs, called out after him:

—Well, thank you, sir.

He waited outside the drawing-room door until the waltz should finish, listening to the skirts that swept against it and to the shuffling of feet. He was still discomposed by the girl's bitter and sudden retort. It had cast a gloom over him which he tried to dispel by arranging his cuffs and the bows of his tie. Then he took from his waistcoat pocket a little paper and glanced at the headings he had made for his speech. He was undecided about the lines from Robert Browning for he feared they would be above the heads of his hearers. Some quotation that they could recognize from Shakespeare or from the Melodies would be better. The indelicate clacking of the men's heels and the shuffling of their soles reminded him that their grade of culture differed from his. He would only make himself ridiculous by quoting poetry to them which they could not understand. They would think that he was airing his superior education. He would fail with them just as he had failed with the girl in the pantry. He had taken up a wrong tone. His whole speech was a mistake from first to last, an utter failure.

Just then his aunts and his wife came out of the ladies' dressing-room. His aunts were two small plainly dressed old women. Aunt Julia was an inch or so taller. Her hair, drawn low over the tops of her ears, was grey; and grey also, with darker shadows, was her large flaccid face. Though she was stout in build and stood erect her slow eyes and parted lips gave her the appearance of a woman who did not know where she was or where she was going. Aunt Kate was more vivacious. Her face, healthier than her sister's, was all puckers and creases, like a shrivelled red apple, and her hair, braided in the same old-fashioned way, had not lost its ripe nut colour.

They both kissed Gabriel frankly. He was their favourite nephew, the son of their dead elder sister, Ellen, who had married T.J. Conroy of the Port and Docks.

—Gretta tells me you're not going to take a cab back to Monkstown tonight, Gabriel, said Aunt Kate.

—No, said Gabriel, turning to his wife, we had quite enough of that last year, hadn't we. Don't you remember, Aunt Kate, what a cold Gretta got out of it? Cab windows rattling all the way, and the east wind blowing in after we passed Merrion. Very jolly it was. Gretta caught a dreadful cold.

Aunt Kate frowned severely and nodded her head at every word.

—Quite right, Gabriel, quite right, she said. You can't be too careful.

—But as for Gretta there, said Gabriel, she'd walk home in the snow if she were let.

Mrs Conroy laughed.

—Don't mind him, Aunt Kate, she said. He's really an awful bother, what with green shades for Tom's eyes at night and making him do the dumb-bells, and forcing Eva to eat the stirabout. The poor child! And she simply hates the sight of it! . . . O, but you'll never guess what he makes me wear now!

She broke out into a peal of laughter and glanced at her husband, whose admiring and happy eyes had been wandering from her dress to her face and hair. The two aunts laughed heartily too, for Gabriel's solicitude was a standing joke with them.

—Goloshes! said Mrs Conroy. That's the latest. Whenever it's wet underfoot I must put on my goloshes. To-night even he wanted me to put them on, but I wouldn't. The next thing he'll buy me will be a diving suit.

Gabriel laughed nervously and patted his tie reassuringly while Aunt Kate nearly doubled herself, so heartily did she enjoy the joke. The smile soon faded from Aunt Julia's face and her mirthless eyes were directed towards her nephew's face. After a pause she asked:

—And what are goloshes, Gabriel?

—Goloshes, Julia! exclaimed her sister. Goodness me, don't you know what goloshes are? You wear them over your . . . over your boots, Gretta, isn't it?

—Yes, said Mrs Conroy. Guttapercha things. We both have a pair now. Gabriel says everyone wears them on the continent.

—O, on the continent, murmured Aunt Julia, nodding her head slowly.

Gabriel knitted his brows and said, as if he were slightly angered:

—It's nothing very wonderful but Gretta thinks it very funny because she says the word reminds her of Christy Minstrels.

—But tell me, Gabriel, said Aunt Kate, with brisk tact. Of course, you've seen about the room. Gretta was saying . . .

—O, the room is all right, replied Gabriel. I've taken one in the Gresham.

—To be sure, said Aunt Kate, by far the best thing to do. And the children, Gretta, you're not anxious about them?

—O, for one night, said Mrs Conroy. Besides, Bessie will look after them.

—To be sure, said Aunt Kate again. What a comfort it is to have a girl like that, one you can depend on! There's that Lily, I'm sure I don't know what has come over her lately. She's not the girl she was at all.

Gabriel was about to ask her aunt some questions on this point but she broke off suddenly to gaze after her sister who had wandered down the stairs and was craning her neck over the banisters.

—Now, I ask you, she said, almost testily, where is Julia going? Julia! Julia! Where are you going?

Julia, who had gone halfway down one flight, came back and announced blandly:

—Here's Freddy.

At the same moment a clapping of hands and a final flourish of the pianist told that the waltz had ended. The drawing-room door was opened from within and some couples came out. Aunt Kate drew Gabriel aside hurriedly and whispered into his ear:

—Slip down, Gabriel, like a good fellow and see if he's all right, and don't let him up if he's screwed. I'm sure he's screwed. I'm sure he is.

Gabriel went to the stairs and listened over the banisters. He could hear two persons talking in the pantry. Then he recognized Freddy Malins' laugh. He went down the stairs noisily.

—It's such a relief, said Aunt Kate to Mrs Conroy, that Gabriel is here. I always feel easier in my mind when he's here. . . . Julia, there's Miss Daly and Miss Power will take some refreshment. Thanks for your beautiful waltz, Miss Daly. It made lovely time.

A tall wizen-faced man, with a stiff grizzled moustache and swarthy skin, who was passing out with his partner said:

—And may we have some refreshment, too, Miss Morkan?

—Julia, said Aunt Kate summarily, and here's Mr Browne and Miss Furlong. Take them in, Julia, with Miss Daly and Miss Power.

—I'm the man for the ladies, said Mr Browne, pursing his lips until his moustache bristled and smiling in all his wrinkles. You know, Miss

Morkan, the reason they are so fond of me is—

He did not finish his sentence, but, seeing that Aunt Kate was out of earshot, at once led the three young ladies into the back room. The middle of the room was occupied by two square tables placed end to end, and on these Aunt Julia and the caretaker were straightening and smoothing a large cloth. On the sideboard were arrayed dishes and plates, and glasses and bundles of knives and forks and spoons. The top of the closed square piano served also as a sideboard for viands and sweets. At a smaller sideboard in one corner two young men were standing, drinking hop-bitters.

Mr Browne led his charges thither and invited them all, in jest, to some ladies' punch, hot, strong, and sweet. As they said they never took anything strong he opened three bottles of lemonade for them. Then he asked one of the young men to move aside, and, taking hold of the decanter, filled out for himself a goodly measure of whisky. The young men eyed him respectfully while he took a trial sip.

—God help me, he said, smiling, it's the doctor's orders.

His wizened face broke into a broader smile, and the three young ladies laughed in musical echo to his pleasantry, swaying their bodies to and fro, with nervous jerks of their shoulders. The boldest said:

—O, now, Mr Browne, I'm sure the doctor never ordered anything of the kind.

Mr Browne took another sip of his whisky and said, with sidling mimicry:

—Well, you see, I'm like the famous Mrs Cassidy, who is reported to have said: *Now, Mary Grimes, if I don't take it, make me take it, for I feel I want it*.

His hot face had leaned forward a little too confidentially and he had assumed a very low Dublin accent so that the young ladies, with an instinct, received his speech in silence. Miss Furlong, who was one of Mary Jane's pupils, asked Miss Daly what was the name of the pretty waltz she had played; and Mr Browne, seeing that he was ignored, turned promptly to the two young men who were more appreciative.

A red-faced young woman, dressed in pansy, came into the room, excitedly clapping her hands and crying:

—Quadrilles! Quadrilles!

Close on her heels came Aunt Kate, crying:

—Two gentlemen and three ladies, Mary Jane!

—O, here's Mr Bergin and Mr Kerrigan, said Mary Jane. Mr Kerrigan, will you take Miss Power? Miss Furlong, may I get you a partner, Mr Bergin. O, that'll just do now.

—Three ladies, Mary Jane, said Aunt Kate.

The two young gentlemen asked the ladies if they might have the pleasure, and Mary Jane turned to Miss Daly.

—O, Miss Daly, you're really awfully good, after playing for the last two dances, but really we're so short of ladies to-night.

—I don't mind in the least, Miss Morkan.

—But I've a nice partner for you, Mr Bartell D'Arcy, the tenor. I'll get him to sing later on. All Dublin is raving about him.

—Lovely voice, lovely voice! said Aunt Kate.

As the piano had twice begun the prelude to the first figure Mary Jane led her recruits quickly from the room. They had hardly gone when Aunt Julia wandered slowly into the room, looking behind her at something.

—What is the matter, Julia? asked Aunt Kate anxiously. Who is it?

Julia, who was carrying in a column of table-napkins, turned to her sister and said, simply, as if the question had surprised her:

—It's only Freddy, Kate, and Gabriel with him.

In fact right behind her Gabriel could be seen piloting Freddy Malins across the landing. The latter, a young man of about forty, was of Gabriel's size and build, with very round shoulders. His face was fleshy and pallid, touched with colour only at the thick hanging lobes of his ears and at the wide wings of his nose. He had coarse features, a blunt nose, a convex and receding brow, tumid and protruded lips. His heavy-lidded eyes and the disorder of his scanty hair made him look sleepy. He was laughing heartily in a high key at a story which he had been telling Gabriel on the stairs and at the same time rubbing the knuckles of his left fist backwards and forwards into his left eye.

—Good-evening, Freddy, said Aunt Julia.

Freddy Malins bade the Misses Morkan good-evening in what seemed an offhand fashion by reason of the habitual catch in his voice and then, seeing that Mr Browne was grinning at him from the sideboard, crossed the room on rather shaky legs and began to repeat in an undertone the story he had just told to Gabriel.

—He's not so bad, is he? said Aunt Kate to Gabriel.

Gabriel's brows were dark but he raised them quickly and answered:

—O no, hardly noticeable.

—Now, isn't he a terrible fellow! she said. And his poor mother made him take the pledge on New Year's Eve. But come on, Gabriel, into the drawing-room.

Before leaving the room with Gabriel she signalled to Mr Browne by frowning and shaking her forefinger in warning to and fro. Mr Browne nodded in answer and, when she had gone, said to Freddy Malins:

—Now, then, Teddy, I'm going to fill you out a good glass of lemonade just to buck you up.

Freddy Malins, who was nearing the climax of his story, waved the offer aside impatiently but Mr Browne, having first called Freddy Malins' attention to a disarray in his dress, filled out and handed him a full glass of lemonade. Freddy Malins' left hand accepted the glass mechanically, his right hand being engaged in the mechanical readjustment of his dress. Mr Browne, whose face was once more wrinkling with mirth, poured out for himself a glass of whisky while Freddy Malins exploded, before he had well reached the climax of his story, in a kink of high-pitched bronchitic laughter and, setting down his untasted and overflowing glass, began to rub the knuckles of his left fist backwards and forwards into his left eye, repeating words of his last phrase as well as his fit of laughter would allow him.

Gabriel could not listen while Mary Jane was playing her Academy piece, full of runs and difficult passages, to the hushed drawing-room. He liked music but the piece she was playing had no melody for him and he doubted whether it had any melody for the other listeners, though they had begged Mary Jane to play something. Four young men, who had come from the refreshment-room to stand in the door-way at the sound of the piano, had gone away quietly in couples after a few minutes. The only persons who seemed to follow the music were Mary Jane herself, her hands racing along the key-board or lifted from it at the pauses like those of a priestess in momentary imprecation, and Aunt Kate standing at her elbow to turn the page.

Gabriel's eyes, irritated by the floor, which glittered with beeswax under the heavy chandelier, wandered to the wall above the piano. A picture of the balcony scene in *Romeo and Juliet* hung there and beside it was a picture of the two murdered princes in the Tower which Aunt Julia had worked in red, blue, and brown wools when she was a girl. Probably in the school they had gone to as girls that kind of work had been taught, for one year his mother had worked for him as a birthday present a waistcoat of purple tabinet, with little foxes' heads upon it, lined with brown satin and having round mulberry buttons. It was strange that his mother had had no musical talent though Aunt Kate used to call her the brains carrier of the Morkan family. Both she and Julia had always seemed a little proud of their serious and matronly sister. Her photograph stood before the pier-glass. She held an open book on her knees and was pointing out something in it to Constantine who, dressed in a man-o'-war suit, lay at her feet. It was she who had chosen the names for her sons for she was very sensible of the dignity of family life. Thanks to her, Constantine was now senior curate in Balbriggan and, thanks to her, Gabriel himself had taken his degree in the Royal University. A shadow passed over his face as he remembered her sullen opposition to his marriage. Some slighting phrases she had used still rankled in his memory; she had once spoken of Gretta as being country cute and that was not true of Gretta at all. It was Gretta who had nursed her during all her last long illness in their house at Monkstown.

He knew that Mary Jane must be near the end of her piece for she was playing again the opening melody with runs of scales after every bar and while he waited for the end the resentment died down in his heart. The piece ended with a trill of octaves in the treble and a final deep octave in the bass. Great applause greeted Mary Jane as, blushing and rolling up her music nervously, she escaped from the room. The most vigorous clapping came from the four young men in the doorway who had gone away to the refreshment-room at the beginning of the piece but had come back when the piano had stopped.

Lancers were arranged. Gabriel found himself partnered with Miss Ivors. She was a frank-mannered talkative young lady, with a freckled face and prominent brown eyes. She did not wear a low-cut bodice and the large brooch which was fixed in the front of her collar bore on it an Irish device.

When they had taken their places she said abruptly:

—I have a crow to pluck with you.

—With me? said Gabriel.

She nodded her head gravely.

—What is it? asked Gabriel, smiling at her solemn manner.

—Who is G.C.? answered Miss Ivors, turning her eyes upon him.

Gabriel coloured and was about to knit his brows, as if he did not understand, when she said bluntly:

—O, innocent Amy! I have found out that you write for *The Daily Express*. Now, aren't you ashamed of yourself?

—Why should I be ashamed of myself? asked Gabriel, blinking his eyes and trying to smile.

—Well, I'm ashamed of you, said Miss Ivors frankly. To say you'd write for a rag like that. I didn't think you were a West Briton.

A look of perplexity appeared on Gabriel's face. It was true that he wrote a literary column every Wednesday in *The Daily Express*, for which he was paid fifteen shillings. But that did not make him a West Briton surely. The books he received for review were almost more welcome than the paltry cheque. He loved to feel the covers and turn over the pages of newly printed books. Nearly every day when his teaching in the college was ended he used to wander down the quays to the second-hand booksellers, to Hickey's on Bachelor's Walk, to Webb's or Massey's on Aston's Quay, or to O'Clohissey's in the by-street. He did not know how to meet her charge. He wanted to say that literature was above politics. But they were friends of many years' standing and their careers had been parallel, first at the University and then as teachers: he could not risk a grandiose phrase with her. He continued blinking his eyes and trying to smile and murmured lamely that he saw nothing political in writing reviews of books.

When their turn to cross had come he was still perplexed and inattentive. Miss Ivors promptly took his hand in a warm grasp and said in a soft friendly tone:

—Of course, I was only joking. Come, we cross now.

When they were together again she spoke of the University question and Gabriel felt more at ease. A friend of hers had shown her his review of Browning's poems. That was how she had found out the secret: but she liked the review immensely. Then she said suddenly:

—O, Mr Conroy, will you come for an excursion to the Aran Isles this summer? We're going to stay there a whole month. It will be splendid out in the Atlantic. You ought to come. Mr Clancy is coming, and Mr Kilkelly and Kathleen Kearney. It would be splendid for Gretta too if she'd come. She's from Connacht, isn't she?

—Her people are, said Gabriel shortly.

—But you will come, won't you? said Miss Ivors, laying her warm hand eagerly on his arm.

—The fact is, said Gabriel, I have already arranged to go—

—Go where? asked Miss Ivors.

—Well, you know, every year I go for a cycling tour with some fellows and so—

—But where? asked Miss Ivors.

—Well, we usually go to France or Belgium or perhaps Germany, said Gabriel awkwardly.

—And why do you go to France and Belgium, said Miss Ivors, instead of visiting your own land?

—Well, said Gabriel, it's partly to keep in touch with the languages and partly for a change.

—And haven't you your own language to keep in touch with—Irish? asked Miss Ivors.

—Well, said Gabriel, if it comes to that, you know, Irish is not my language.

Their neighbours had turned to listen to the cross-examination. Gabriel glanced right and left nervously and tried to keep his good humour under the ordeal which was making a blush invade his forehead.

—And haven't you your own land to visit, continued Miss Ivors, that you know nothing of, your own people, and your own country?

—O, to tell you the truth, retorted Gabriel suddenly, I'm sick of my own country, sick of it!

—Why? asked Miss Ivors.

Gabriel did not answer for his retort had heated him.

—Why? repeated Miss Ivors.

They had to go visiting together and, as he had not answered her, Miss Ivors said warmly:

—Of course, you've no answer.

Gabriel tried to cover his agitation by taking part in the dance with great energy. He avoided her eyes for he had seen a sour expression on her face. But when they met in the long chain he was surprised to feel his hand firmly pressed. She looked at him from under her brows for a moment quizzically until he smiled. Then, just as the chain was about to start again, she stood on tiptoe and whispered into his ear:

—West Briton!

When the lancers were over Gabriel went away to a remote corner of the room where Freddy Malins' mother was sitting. She was a stout feeble old woman with white hair. Her voice had a catch in it like her son's and she stuttered slightly. She had been told that Freddy had come and that he was nearly all right. Gabriel asked her whether she had had a good crossing. She lived with her married daughter in Glasgow and came to Dublin on a visit once a year. She answered placidly that she had had a beautiful crossing and that the captain had been most attentive to her. She spoke also of the beautiful house her daughter kept in Glasgow, and of all the nice friends they had there. While her tongue rambled on Gabriel tried to banish from his mind all memory of the unpleasant incident with Miss Ivors. Of course the girl or woman, or whatever she was, was an enthusiast but there was a time for all things. Perhaps he ought not to have answered her like that. But she had no right to call him a West Briton before people, even in joke. She had tried to make him ridiculous before people, heckling him and staring at him with her rabbit's eyes.

He saw his wife making her way towards him through the waltzing couples. When she reached him she said into his ear:

—Gabriel, Aunt Kate wants to know won't you carve the goose as usual. Miss Daly will carve the ham and I'll do the pudding.

—All right, said Gabriel.

—She's sending in the younger ones first as soon as this waltz is over so that we'll have the table to ourselves.

—Were you dancing? asked Gabriel.

—Of course I was. Didn't you see me? What words had you with Molly Ivors?

—No words. Why? Did she say so?

—Something like that. I'm trying to get that Mr D'Arcy to sing. He's full of conceit, I think.

—There were no words, said Gabriel moodily, only she wanted me to go for a trip to the west of Ireland and I said I wouldn't.

His wife clasped her hands excitedly and gave a little jump.

—O, do go, Gabriel, she cried. I'd love to see Galway again.

—You can go if you like, said Gabriel coldly.

She looked at him for a moment, then turned to Mrs Malins and said:

—There's a nice husband for you, Mrs Malins.

While she was threading her way back across the room Mrs Malins, without adverting to the interruption, went on to tell Gabriel what beautiful places there were in Scotland and beautiful scenery. Her son-in-law brought them every year to the lakes and they used to go fishing. Her son-in-law was a splendid fisher. One day he caught a fish, a beautiful big big fish, and the man in the hotel boiled it for their dinner.

Gabriel hardly heard what she said. Now that supper was coming near he began to think again about his speech and about the quotation. When he saw Freddy Malins coming across the room to visit his mother Gabriel left the chair free for him and retired into the embrasure of the window. The room had already cleared and from the back room came the clatter of plates and knives. Those who still remained in the drawing-room seemed tired of dancing and were conversing quietly in little groups. Gabriel's warm trembling fingers tapped the cold pane of the window. How cool it must be outside! How pleasant it would be to walk out alone, first along by the river and then through the park! The snow would be lying on the branches of the trees and forming a bright cap on the top of the Wellington Monument. How much more pleasant it would be there than at the supper-table!

He ran over the headings of his speech: Irish hospitality, sad memories, the Three Graces, Paris, the quotation from Browning. He repeated to himself a phrase he had written in his review: *One feels that one is listening to a thought-tormented music*. Miss Ivors had praised the review. Was she sincere? Had she really any life of her own behind all her propagandism? There had never been any ill-feeling between them until that night. It unnerved him to think that she would be at the supper-table, looking up at him while he spoke with her critical quizzing eyes. Perhaps she would not be sorry to see him fail in his speech. An idea came into his mind and gave him courage. He would say, alluding to Aunt Kate and Aunt Julia: *Ladies and Gentlemen, the generation which is now on the wane among us may have had its faults but for my part I think it had certain qualities of hospitality, of humour, of humanity, which the new and very serious and hypereducated generation that is growing up around us seems to me to lack*. Very good: that was one for Miss Ivors. What did he care that his aunts were only two ignorant old women?

A murmur in the room attracted his attention. Mr Browne was advancing from the door, gallantly escorting Aunt Julia, who leaned upon his arm, smiling and hanging her head. An irregular musketry of applause escorted her also as far as the piano and then, as Mary Jane seated herself on the stool, and Aunt Julia, no longer smiling, half turned so as to pitch her voice fairly into the room, gradually ceased. Gabriel recognized the prelude. It was that of an old song of Aunt Julia's—*Arrayed for the Bridal*. Her voice, strong and clear in tone, attacked with great spirit the runs which embellish the air and though she sang very rapidly she did not miss even the smallest of the grace notes. To follow the voice, without looking at the singer's face, was to feel and share the excitement of swift and secure flight. Gabriel applauded loudly with all the others at the close of the song and loud applause was borne in from the invisible supper-table. It sounded so genuine that a little colour struggled into Aunt Julia's face as she bent to replace in the music-stand the old leather-bound song-book that had her initials on the cover. Freddy Malins, who had listened with his head perched sideways to hear her better, was still applauding when everyone else had ceased and talking animatedly to his mother who nodded her head gravely and slowly in acquiescence. At last, when he could clap no more, he stood up suddenly and hurried across the room to Aunt Julia whose hand he seized and held in both his hands, shaking it when words failed him or the catch in his voice proved too much for him.

—I was just telling my mother, he said, I never heard you sing so well, never. No, I never heard your voice so good as it is to-night. Now! Would you believe that now? That's the truth. Upon my word and honour that's the truth. I never heard your voice sound so fresh and so . . . so clear and fresh, never.

Aunt Julia smiled broadly and murmured something about compliments as she released her hand from his grasp. Mr Browne extended his open hand towards her and said to those who were near him in the manner of a showman introducing a prodigy to an audience:

—Miss Julia Morkan, my latest discovery!

He was laughing very heartily at this himself when Freddy Malins turned to him and said:

—Well, Browne, if you're serious you might make a worse discovery. All I can say is I never heard her sing half so well as long as I am coming here. And that's the honest truth.

—Neither did I, said Mr Browne. I think her voice has greatly improved.

Aunt Julia shrugged her shoulders and said with meek pride:

—Thirty years ago I hadn't a bad voice as voices go.

—I often told Julia, said Aunt Kate emphatically, that she was simply thrown away in that choir. But she never would be said by me.

She turned as if to appeal to the good sense of the others against a refractory child while Aunt Julia gazed in front of her, a vague smile of reminiscence playing on her face.

—No, continued Aunt Kate, she wouldn't be said or led by anyone, slaving there in that choir night and day, night and day. Six o'clock on Christmas morning! And all for what?

—Well, isn't it for the honour of God, Aunt Kate? asked Mary Jane, twisting round on the piano-stool and smiling.

Aunt Kate turned fiercely on her niece and said:

—I know all about the honour of God, Mary Jane, but I think it's not at all honourable for the pope to turn out the women out of the choirs that have slaved there all their lives and put little whipper-snappers of boys over their heads. I suppose it is for the good of the Church if the pope does it. But it's not just, Mary Jane, and it's not right.

She had worked herself into a passion and would have continued in defence of her sister for it was a sore subject with her but Mary Jane, seeing that all the dancers had come back, intervened pacifically:

—Now, Aunt Kate, you're giving scandal to Mr Browne who is of the other persuasion.

Aunt Kate turned to Mr Browne, who was grinning at this allusion to his religion, and said hastily:

—O, I don't question the pope's being right. I'm only a stupid old woman and I wouldn't presume to do such a thing. But there's such a thing as common everyday politeness and gratitude. And if I were in Julia's place I'd tell that Father Healy straight up to his face . . .

—And besides, Aunt Kate, said Mary Jane, we really are all hungry and when we are hungry we are all very quarrelsome.

—And when we are thirsty we are also quarrelsome, added Mr Browne.

—So that we had better go to supper, said Mary Jane, and finish the discussion afterwards.

On the landing outside the drawing-room Gabriel found his wife and Mary Jane trying to persuade Miss Ivors to stay for supper. But Miss Ivors, who had put on her hat and was buttoning her cloak, would not stay. She did not feel in the least hungry and she had already overstayed her time.

—But only for ten minutes, Molly, said Mrs Conroy. That won't delay you.

—To take a pick itself, said Mary Jane, after all your dancing.

—I really couldn't, said Miss Ivors.

—I am afraid you didn't enjoy yourself at all, said Mary Jane hopelessly.

—Ever so much, I assure you, said Miss Ivors, but you really must let me run off now.

—But how can you get home? asked Mrs Conroy.

—O, it's only two steps up the quay.

Gabriel hesitated a moment and said:

—If you will allow me, Miss Ivors, I'll see you home if you really are obliged to go.

But Miss Ivors broke away from them.

—I won't hear of it, she cried. For goodness sake go in to your suppers and don't mind me. I'm quite well able to take care of myself.

—Well, you're the comical girl, Molly, said Mrs Conroy frankly.

—*Beannacht libh*, cried Miss Ivors, with a laugh, as she ran down the staircase.

Mary Jane gazed after her, a moody puzzled expression on her face, while Mrs Conroy leaned over the banisters to listen for the hall-door. Gabriel asked himself was he the cause of her abrupt departure. But she did not seem to be in ill humour: she had gone away laughing. He stared blankly down the staircase.

At that moment Aunt Kate came toddling out of the supper-room almost wringing her hands in despair.

—Where is Gabriel? she cried. Where on earth is Gabriel? There's everyone waiting in there, stage to let, and nobody to carve the goose!

—Here I am, Aunt Kate! cried Gabriel, with sudden animation, ready to carve a flock of geese, if necessary.

A fat brown goose lay at one end of the table and at the other end, on a bed of creased paper strewn with sprigs of parsley, lay a great ham, stripped of its outer skin and peppered over with crust crumbs, a neat paper frill round its shin and beside this was a round of spiced beef. Between these rival ends ran parallel lines of side-dishes: two little minsters of jelly, red and yellow; a shallow dish full of blocks of blancmange and red jam, a large green leaf-shaped dish with a stalk-shaped handle, on which lay bunches of purple raisins and peeled almonds, a companion dish on which lay a solid rectangle of Smyrna figs, a dish of custard topped with grated nutmeg, a small bowl full of chocolates and sweets wrapped in gold and silver papers, and a glass vase in which stood some tall celery stalks. In the centre of the table there stood, as sentries to a fruit-stand which upheld a pyramid of oranges and American apples, two squat old-fashioned decanters of cut glass, one containing port and the other dark sherry. On the closed square piano a pudding in a huge yellow dish lay in waiting and behind it were three squads of bottles of stout and ale and minerals, drawn up according to the colours of their uniforms, the first two black, with brown and red labels, the third and smallest squad white, with transverse green sashes.

Gabriel took his seat boldly at the head of the table and, having looked to the edge of the carver, plunged his fork firmly into the goose. He felt quite at ease now for he was an expert carver and liked nothing better than to find himself at the head of a well-laden table.

—Miss Furlong, what shall I send you? he asked. A wing or a slice of the breast?

—Just a small slice of the breast.

—Miss Higgins, what for you?

—O, anything at all, Mr Conroy.

While Gabriel and Miss Daly exchanged plates of goose and plates of ham and spiced beef Lily went from guest to guest with a dish of hot floury potatoes wrapped in a white napkin. This was Mary Jane's idea and she had also suggested apple sauce for the goose but Aunt Kate had said that plain roast goose without apple sauce had always been good enough for her and she hoped she might never eat worse. Mary Jane waited on her pupils and saw that they got the best slices and Aunt Kate and Aunt Julia opened and carried across from the piano bottles of stout and ale for the gentlemen and bottles of minerals for the ladies. There was a great deal of confusion and laughter and noise, the noise of orders and counter-orders, of knives and forks, of corks and glass-stoppers. Gabriel began to carve second helpings as soon as he had finished the first round without serving himself. Everyone protested loudly so that he compromised by taking a long draught of stout for he had found the carving hot work. Mary Jane settled down quietly to her supper but Aunt Kate and Aunt Julia were still toddling round the table, walking on each other's heels, getting in each other's way and giving each other unheeded orders. Mr Browne begged of them to sit down and eat their suppers and so did Gabriel but they said there was time enough so that, at last, Freddy Malins stood up and, capturing Aunt Kate, plumped her down on her chair amid general laughter.

When everyone had been well served Gabriel said, smiling:

—Now, if anyone wants a little more of what vulgar people call stuffing let him or her speak.

A chorus of voices invited him to begin his own supper and Lily came forward with three potatoes which she had reserved for him.

—Very well, said Gabriel amiably, as he took another preparatory draught, kindly forget my existence, ladies and gentlemen, for a few minutes.

He set to his supper and took no part in the conversation with which the table covered Lily's removal of the plates. The subject of talk was the opera company which was then at the Theatre Royal. Mr Bartell D'Arcy, the tenor, a dark-complexioned young man with a smart moustache, praised very highly the leading contralto of the company but Miss Furlong thought she had a rather vulgar style of production. Freddy Malins said there was a negro chieftain singing in the second part of the Gaiety pantomime who had one of the finest tenor voices he had ever heard.

—Have you heard him? he asked Mr Bartell D'Arcy across the table.

—No, answered Mr Bartell D'Arcy carelessly.

—Because, Freddy Malins explained, now I'd be curious to hear your opinion of him. I think he has a grand voice.

—It takes Teddy to find out the really good things, said Mr Browne familiarly to the table.

—And why couldn't he have a voice too? asked Freddy Malins sharply. Is it because he's only a black?

Nobody answered this question and Mary Jane led the table back to the legitimate opera. One of her pupils had given her a pass for *Mignon*. Of course it was very fine, she said, but it made her think of poor Georgina Burns. Mr Browne could go back farther still, to the old Italian companies that used to come to Dublin—Tietjens, Ilma de Murzka, Campanini, the great Trebelli, Giuglini, Ravelli, Aramburo. Those were the days, he said, when there was something like singing to be heard in Dublin. He told too of how the top gallery of the old Royal used to be packed night after night, of how one Italian tenor had sung five encores to *Let Me Like a Soldier Fall*, introducing a high C every time, and of how the gallery boys would sometimes in their enthusiasm unyoke the horses from the carriage of some great *prima donna* and pull her themselves through the streets to her hotel. Why did they never play the grand old operas now, he asked, *Dinorah*, *Lucrezia Borgia*? Because they could not get the voices to sing them: that was why.

—O, well, said Mr Bartell D'Arcy, I presume there are as good singers to-day as there were then.

—Where are they? asked Mr Browne defiantly.

—In London, Paris, Milan, said Mr Bartell D'Arcy warmly. I suppose Caruso, for example, is quite as good, if not better than any of the men you have mentioned.

—Maybe so, said Mr Browne. But I may tell you I doubt it strongly.

—O, I'd give anything to hear Caruso sing, said Mary Jane.

—For me, said Aunt Kate, who had been picking a bone, there was only one tenor. To please me, I mean. But I suppose none of you ever heard of him.

—Who was he, Miss Morkan? asked Mr Bartell D'Arcy politely.

—His name, said Aunt Kate, was Parkinson. I heard him when he was in his prime and I think he had then the purest tenor voice that was ever put into a man's throat.

—Strange, said Mr Bartell D'Arcy. I never even heard of him.

—Yes, yes, Miss Morkan is right, said Mr Browne. I remember hearing of old Parkinson but he's too far back for me.

—A beautiful pure sweet mellow English tenor, said Aunt Kate with enthusiasm.

Gabriel having finished, the huge pudding was transferred to the table. The clatter of forks and spoons began again. Gabriel's wife served out spoonfuls of the pudding and passed the plates down the table. Midway down they were held up by Mary Jane, who replenished them with raspberry or orange jelly or with blancmange and jam. The pudding was of Aunt Julia's making and she received praises for it from all quarters. She herself said that it was not quite brown enough.

—Well, I hope, Miss Morkan, said Mr Browne, that I'm brown enough for you because, you know, I'm all brown.

All the gentlemen, except Gabriel, ate some of the pudding out of compliment to Aunt Julia. As Gabriel never ate sweets the celery had been left for him. Freddy Malins also took a stalk of celery and ate it with his pudding. He had been told that celery was a capital thing for the blood and he was just then under doctor's care. Mrs Malins, who had been silent through the supper, said that her son was going down to Mount Melleray in a week or so. The table then spoke of Mount Melleray, how bracing the air was down there, how hospitable the monks were and how they never asked for a penny-piece from their guests.

—And do you mean to say, asked Mr Browne incredulously, that a chap can go down there and put up there as if it were a hotel and live on the fat of the land and then come away without paying a farthing?

—O, most people give some donation to the monastery when they leave, said Mary Jane.

—I wish we had an institution like that in our Church, said Mr Browne candidly.

He was astonished to hear that the monks never spoke, got up at two in the morning and slept in their coffins. He asked what they did it for.

—That's the rule of the order, said Aunt Kate firmly.

—Yes, but why? asked Mr Browne.

Aunt Kate repeated that it was the rule, that was all. Mr Browne still seemed not to understand. Freddy Malins explained to him, as best he could, that the monks were trying to make up for the sins committed by all the sinners in the outside world. The explanation was not very clear for Mr

Browne grinned and said:

—I like that idea very much but wouldn't a comfortable spring bed do them as well as a coffin?

—The coffin, said Mary Jane, is to remind them of their last end.

As the subject had grown lugubrious it was buried in a silence of the table during which Mrs Malins could be heard saying to her neighbour in an indistinct undertone:

—They are very good men, the monks, very pious men.

The raisins and almonds and figs and apples and oranges and chocolates and sweets were now passed about the table and Aunt Julia invited all the guests to have either port or sherry. At first Mr Bartell D'Arcy refused to take either but one of his neighbours nudged him and whispered something to him upon which he allowed his glass to be filled. Gradually as the last glasses were being filled the conversation ceased. A pause followed, broken only by the noise of the wine and by unsettlings of chairs. The Misses Morkan, all three, looked down at the tablecloth. Someone coughed once or twice and then a few gentlemen patted the table gently as a signal for silence. The silence came and Gabriel pushed back his chair and stood up.

The patting at once grew louder in encouragement and then ceased altogether. Gabriel leaned his ten trembling fingers on the tablecloth and smiled nervously at the company. Meeting a row of upturned faces he raised his eyes to the chandelier. The piano was playing a waltz tune and he could hear the skirts sweeping against the drawing-room door. People, perhaps, were standing in the snow on the quay outside, gazing up at the lighted windows and listening to the waltz music. The air was pure there. In the distance lay the park where the trees were weighted with snow. The Wellington Monument wore a gleaming cap of snow that flashed westward over the white field of Fifteen Acres.

He began:

—Ladies and Gentlemen.

—It has fallen to my lot this evening, as in years past, to perform a very pleasing task but a task for which I am afraid my poor powers as a speaker are all too inadequate.

—No, no! said Mr Browne.

—But, however that may be, I can only ask you to-night to take the will for the deed and to lend me your attention for a few moments while I endeavour to express to you in words what my feelings are on this occasion.

—Ladies and Gentlemen. It is not the first time that we have gathered together under this hospitable roof, around this hospitable board. It is not the first time that we have been the recipients—or perhaps, I had better say, the victims—of the hospitality of certain good ladies.

He made a circle in the air with his arm and paused. Everyone laughed or smiled at Aunt Kate and Aunt Julia and Mary Jane who all turned crimson with pleasure. Gabriel went on more boldly:

—I feel more strongly with every recurring year that our country has no tradition which does it so much honour and which it should guard so jealously as that of its hospitality. It is a tradition that is unique as far as my experience goes (and I have visited not a few places abroad) among the modern nations. Some would say, perhaps, that with us it is rather a failing than anything to be boasted of. But granted even that, it is, to my mind, a princely failing, and one that I trust will long be cultivated among us. Of one thing, at least, I am sure. As long as this one roof shelters the good ladies aforesaid—and I wish from my heart it may do so for many and many a long year to come—the tradition of genuine warm-hearted courteous Irish hospitality which our forefathers have handed down to us and which we in turn must hand down to our descendants, is still alive among us.

A hearty murmur of assent ran round the table. It shot through Gabriel's mind that Miss Ivors was not there and that she had gone away discourteously: and he said with confidence in himself:

—Ladies and Gentlemen.

—A new generation is growing up in our midst, a generation actuated by new ideas and new principles. It is serious and enthusiastic for these new ideas and its enthusiasm, even when it is misdirected, is, I believe, in the main sincere. But we are living in a sceptical and, if I may use the phrase, a thought-tormented age: and sometimes I fear that this new generation, educated or hypereducated as it is, will lack those qualities of humanity, of hospitality, of kindly humour which belonged to an older day. Listening to-night to the names of all those great singers of the past it seemed to me, I must confess, that we were living in a less spacious age. Those days might, without exaggeration, be called spacious days: and if they are gone beyond recall let us hope, at least, that in gatherings such as this we shall still speak of them with pride and affection, still cherish in our hearts the memory of those dead and gone great ones whose fame the world will not willingly let die.

—Hear, hear! said Mr Browne loudly.

—But yet, continued Gabriel, his voice falling into a softer inflection, there are always in gatherings such as this sadder thoughts that will recur to our minds: thoughts of the past, of youth, of changes, of absent faces that we miss here to-night. Our path through life is strewn with many such sad memories: and were we to brood upon them always we could not find the heart to go on bravely with our work among the living. We have all of us living duties and living affections which claim, and rightly claim, our strenuous endeavours.

—Therefore, I will not linger on the past. I will not let any gloomy moralizing intrude upon us here to-night. Here we are gathered together for a brief moment from the bustle and rush of our everyday routine. We are met here as friends, in the spirit of good-fellowship, as colleagues, also to a certain extent, in the true spirit of *camaraderie*, and as the guests of—what shall I call them?—the Three Graces of the Dublin musical world.

The table burst into applause and laughter at this sally. Aunt Julia vainly asked each of her neighbours in turn to tell her what Gabriel had said.

—He says we are the Three Graces, Aunt Julia, said Mary Jane.

Aunt Julia did not understand but she looked up, smiling, at Gabriel, who continued in the same vein:

—Ladies and Gentlemen.

—I will not attempt to play to-night the part that Paris played on another occasion. I will not attempt to choose between them. The task would be an invidious one and one beyond my poor powers. For when I view them in turn, whether it be our chief hostess herself, whose good heart, whose too good heart, has become a byword with all who know her, or her sister, who seems to be gifted with perennial youth and whose singing must have been a surprise and a revelation to us all to-night, or, last but not least, when I consider our youngest hostess, talented, cheerful, hard-working, and the best of nieces, I confess, Ladies and Gentlemen, that I do not know to which of them I should award the prize.

Gabriel glanced down at his aunts and, seeing the large smile on Aunt Julia's face and the tears which had risen to Aunt Kate's eyes, hastened to his close. He raised his glass of port gallantly, while every member of the company fingered a glass expectantly, and said loudly:

—Let us toast them all three together. Let us drink to their health, wealth, long life, happiness, and prosperity and may they long continue to hold the proud and self-won position which they hold in their profession and the position of honour and affection which they hold in our hearts.

All the guests stood up, glass in hand, and, turning towards the three seated ladies, sang in unison, with Mr Browne as leader:

For they are jolly gay fellows,
For they are jolly gay fellows,
For they are jolly gay fellows,
Which nobody can deny.

Aunt Kate was making frank use of her handkerchief and even Aunt Julia seemed moved. Freddy Malins beat time with his pudding-fork and the singers turned towards one another, as if in melodious conference, while they sang, with emphasis:

Unless he tells a lie,
Unless he tells a lie.

Then, turning once more towards their hostesses, they sang:

For they are jolly gay fellows,
For they are jolly gay fellows,

For they are jolly gay fellows,
Which nobody can deny.

The acclamation which followed was taken up beyond the door of the supper-room by many of the other guests and renewed time after time, Freddy Malins acting as officer with his fork on high.

The piercing morning air came into the hall where they were standing so that Aunt Kate said:

—Close the door, somebody. Mrs Malins will get her death of cold.

—Browne is out there, Aunt Kate, said Mary Jane.

—Browne is everywhere, said Aunt Kate, lowering her voice.

Mary Jane laughed at her tone.

—Really, she said archly, he is very attentive.

—He has been laid on here like the gas, said Aunt Kate in the same tone, all during the Christmas.

She laughed herself this time good-humouredly and then added quickly:

—But tell him to come in, Mary Jane, and close the door. I hope to goodness he didn't hear me.

At that moment the hall-door was opened and Mr Browne came in from the doorstep, laughing as if his heart would break. He was dressed in a long green overcoat with mock astrakhan cuffs and collar and wore on his head an oval fur cap. He pointed down the snow-covered quay from where the sound of shrill prolonged whistling was borne in.

—Teddy will have all the cabs in Dublin out, he said.

Gabriel advanced from the little pantry behind the office, struggling into his overcoat and, looking round the hall, said:

—Gretta not down yet?

—She's getting on her things, Gabriel, said Aunt Kate.

—Who's playing up there? asked Gabriel.

—Nobody. They're all gone.

—O no, Aunt Kate, said Mary Jane. Bartell D'Arcy and Miss O'Callaghan aren't gone yet.

—Someone is strumming at the piano, anyhow, said Gabriel.

Mary Jane glanced at Gabriel and Mr Browne and said with a shiver:

—It makes me feel cold to look at you two gentlemen muffled up like that. I wouldn't like to face your journey home at this hour.

—I'd like nothing better this minute, said Mr Browne stoutly, than a rattling fine walk in the country or a fast drive with a good spanking goer between the shafts.

—We used to have a very good horse and trap at home, said Aunt Julia sadly.

—The never-to-be-forgotten Johnny, said Mary Jane, laughing.

Aunt Kate and Gabriel laughed too.

—Why, what was wonderful about Johnny? asked Mr Browne.

—The late lamented Patrick Morkan, our grandfather, that is, explained Gabriel, commonly known in his later years as the old gentleman, was a glue-boiler.

—O, now, Gabriel, said Aunt Kate, laughing, he had a starch mill.

—Well, glue or starch, said Gabriel, the old gentleman had a horse by the name of Johnny. And Johnny used to work in the old gentleman's mill, walking round and round in order to drive the mill. That was all very well; but now comes the tragic part about Johnny. One fine day the old gentleman thought he'd like to drive out with the quality to a military review in the park.

—The Lord have mercy on his soul, said Aunt Kate compassionately.

—Amen, said Gabriel. So the old gentleman, as I said, harnessed Johnny and put on his very best tall hat and his very best stock collar and drove out in grand style from his ancestral mansion somewhere near Back Lane, I think.

Everyone laughed, even Mrs Malins, at Gabriel's manner and Aunt Kate said:

—O now, Gabriel, he didn't live in Back Lane, really. Only the mill was there.

—Out from the mansion of his forefathers, continued Gabriel, he drove with Johnny. And everything went on beautifully until Johnny came in sight of King Billy's statue: and whether he fell in love with the horse King Billy sits on or whether he thought he was back again in the mill, anyhow he began to walk round the statue.

Gabriel paced in a circle round the hall in his goloshes amid the laughter of the others.

—Round and round he went, said Gabriel, and the old gentleman, who was a very pompous old gentleman, was highly indignant. *Go on, sir! What do you mean, sir? Johnny! Johnny! Most extraordinary conduct! Can't understand the horse!*

The peals of laughter which followed Gabriel's imitation of the incident were interrupted by a resounding knock at the hall-door. Mary Jane ran to open it and let in Freddy Malins. Freddy Malins, with his hat well back on his head and his shoulders humped with cold, was puffing and steaming after his exertions.

—I could only get one cab, he said.

—O, we'll find another along the quay, said Gabriel.

—Yes, said Aunt Kate. Better not keep Mrs Malins standing in the draught.

Mrs Malins was helped down the front steps by her son and Mr Browne and, after many manoeuvres, hoisted into the cab. Freddy Malins clambered in after her and spent a long time settling her on the seat, Mr Browne helping him with advice. At last she was settled comfortably and Freddy Malins invited Mr Browne into the cab. There was a good deal of confused talk, and then Mr Browne got into the cab. The cabman settled his rug over his knees, and bent down for the address. The confusion grew greater and the cabman was directed differently by Freddy Malins and Mr Browne, each of whom had his head out through a window of the cab. The difficulty was to know where to drop Mr Browne along the route and Aunt Kate, Aunt Julia and Mary Jane helped the discussion from the doorstep with cross-directions and contradictions and abundance of laughter. As for Freddy Malins he was speechless with laughter. He popped his head in and out of the window every moment, to the great danger of his hat, and told his mother how the discussion was progressing till at last Mr Browne shouted to the bewildered cabman above the din of everybody's laughter:

—Do you know Trinity College?

—Yes, sir, said the cabman.

—Well, drive bang up against Trinity College gates, said Mr Browne, and then we'll tell you where to go. You understand now?

—Yes, sir, said the cabman.

—Make like a bird for Trinity College.

—Right, sir, cried the cabman.

The horse was whipped up and the cab rattled off along the quay amid a chorus of laughter and adieus.

Gabriel had not gone to the door with the others. He was in a dark part of the hall gazing up the staircase. A woman was standing near the top of the first flight, in the shadow also. He could not see her face but he could see the terracotta and salmon-pink panels of her skirt which the shadow made appear black and white. It was his wife. She was leaning on the banisters, listening to something. Gabriel was surprised at her stillness and strained his ear to listen also. But he could hear little save the noise of laughter and dispute on the front steps, a few chords struck on the piano and a few notes of a man's voice singing.

He stood still in the gloom of the hall, trying to catch the air that the voice was singing and gazing up at his wife. There was grace and mystery in her attitude as if she were a symbol of something. He asked himself what is a woman standing on the stairs in the shadow, listening to distant music, a symbol of. If he were a painter he would paint her in that attitude. Her blue felt hat would show off the bronze of her hair against the darkness and the dark panels of her skirt would show off the light ones. *Distant Music* he would call the picture if he were a painter.

The hall-door was closed; and Aunt Kate, Aunt Julia, and Mary Jane came down the hall, still laughing.

—Well, isn't Freddy terrible? said Mary Jane. He's really terrible.

Gabriel said nothing but pointed up the stairs towards where his wife was standing. Now that the hall-door was closed the voice and piano could be heard more clearly. Gabriel held up his hand for them to be silent. The song seemed to be in the old Irish tonality and the singer seemed uncertain both of his words and of his voice. The voice, made plaintive by distance and by the singer's hoarseness, faintly illuminated the cadence of the air with words expressing grief:

O, the rain falls on my heavy locks
And the dew wets my skin,
My babe lies cold . . .

—O, exclaimed Mary Jane. It's Bartell D'Arcy singing and he wouldn't sing all the night. O, I'll get him to sing a song before he goes.

—O do, Mary Jane, said Aunt Kate.

Mary Jane brushed past the others and ran to the staircase but before she reached it the singing stopped and the piano was closed abruptly.

—O, what a pity! she cried. Is he coming down, Gretta?

Gabriel heard his wife answer yes and saw her come down towards them. A few steps behind her were Mr Bartell D'Arcy and Miss O'Callaghan.

—O, Mr D'Arcy, cried Mary Jane, it's downright mean of you to break off like that when we were all in raptures listening to you.

—I have been at him all the evening, said Miss O'Callaghan, and Mrs Conroy too and he told us he had a dreadful cold and couldn't sing.

—O, Mr D'Arcy, said Aunt Kate, now that was a great fib to tell.

—Can't you see that I'm as hoarse as a crow? said Mr D'Arcy roughly.

He went into the pantry hastily and put on his overcoat. The others, taken aback by his rude speech, could find nothing to say. Aunt Kate wrinkled her brows and made signs to the others to drop the subject. Mr D'Arcy stood swathing his neck carefully and frowning.

—It's the weather, said Aunt Julia, after a pause.

—Yes, everybody has colds, said Aunt Kate readily, everybody.

—They say, said Mary Jane, we haven't had snow like it for thirty years; and I read this morning in the newspapers that the snow is general all over Ireland.

—I love the look of snow, said Aunt Julia sadly.

—So do I, said Miss O'Callaghan. I think Christmas is never really Christmas unless we have the snow on the ground.

—But poor Mr D'Arcy doesn't like the snow, said Aunt Kate, smiling.

Mr D'Arcy came from the pantry, fully swathed and buttoned, and in a repentant tone told them the history of his cold. Everyone gave him advice and said it was a great pity and urged him to be very careful of his throat in the night air. Gabriel watched his wife who did not join in the conversation. She was standing right under the dusty fanlight and the flame of the gas lit up the rich bronze of her hair which he had seen her drying at the fire a few days before. She was in the same attitude and seemed unaware of the talk about her. At last she turned towards them and Gabriel saw that there was colour on her cheeks and that her eyes were shining. A sudden tide of joy went leaping out of his heart.

—Mr D'Arcy, she said, what is the name of that song you were singing?

—It's called *The Lass of Aughrim*, said Mr D'Arcy, but I couldn't remember it properly. Why? Do you know it?

—*The Lass of Aughrim*, she repeated. I couldn't think of the name.

—It's a very nice air, said Mary Jane. I'm sorry you were not in voice to-night.

—Now, Mary Jane, said Aunt Kate, don't annoy Mr D'Arcy. I won't have him annoyed.

Seeing that all were ready to start she shepherded them to the door where good-night was said:

—Well, good-night, Aunt Kate, and thanks for the pleasant evening.

—Good-night, Gabriel. Good-night, Gretta!

—Good-night, Aunt Kate, and thanks ever so much. Good-night, Aunt Julia.

—O, good-night, Gretta, I didn't see you.

—Good-night, Mr D'Arcy. Good-night, Miss O'Callaghan.

—Good-night, Miss Morkan.

—Good-night, again.

—Good-night, all. Safe home.

—Good-night. Good-night.

The morning was still dark. A dull yellow light brooded over the houses and the river; and the sky seemed to be descending. It was slushy underfoot; and only streaks and patches of snow lay on the roofs, on the parapets of the quay, and on the area railings. The lamps were still burning redly in the murky air and, across the river, the palace of the Four Courts stood out menacingly against the heavy sky.

She was walking on before him with Mr Bartell D'Arcy, her shoes in a brown parcel tucked under one arm and her hands holding her skirt up from the slush. She had no longer any grace of attitude but Gabriel's eyes were still bright with happiness. The blood went bounding along his veins; and the thoughts went rioting through his brain, proud, joyful, tender, valorous.

She was walking on before him so lightly and so erect that he longed to run after her noiselessly, catch her by the shoulders, and say something foolish and affectionate into her ear. She seemed to him so frail that he longed to defend her against something and then to be alone with her. Moments of their secret life together burst like stars upon his memory. A heliotrope envelope was lying beside his breakfast-cup and he was caressing it with his hand. Birds were twittering in the ivy and the sunny web of the curtain was shimmering along the floor: he could not eat for happiness. They were standing on the crowded platform and he was placing a ticket inside the warm palm of her glove. He was standing with her in the cold, looking in through a grated window at a man making bottles in a roaring furnace. It was very cold. Her face, fragrant in the cold air, was quite close to his; and suddenly she called out to the man at the furnace:

—Is the fire hot, sir?

But the man could not hear her with the noise of the furnace. It was just as well. He might have answered rudely.

A wave of yet more tender joy escaped from his heart and went coursing in warm flood along his arteries. Like the tender fires of stars moments of their life together, that no one knew of or would ever know of, broke upon and illumined his memory. He longed to recall to her those moments, to make her forget the years of their dull existence together and remember only their moments of ecstasy. For the years, he felt, had not quenched his soul or hers. Their children, his writing, her household cares had not quenched all their souls' tender fire. In one letter that he had written to her then he had said: *Why is it that words like these seem to me so dull and cold? Is it because there is no word tender enough to be your name?*

Like distant music these words that he had written years before were borne towards him from the past. He longed to be alone with her. When the others had gone away, when he and she were in their room in the hotel, then they would be alone together. He would call her softly:

—Gretta!

Perhaps she would not hear at once: she would be undressing. Then something in his voice would strike her. She would turn and look at him. . . .

At the corner of Winetavern Street they met a cab. He was glad of its rattling noise as it saved him from conversation. She was looking out of the window and seemed tired. The others spoke only a few words, pointing out some building or street. The horse galloped along wearily under the murky morning sky, dragging his old rattling box after his heels, and Gabriel was again in a cab with her, galloping to catch the boat, galloping to their honeymoon.

As the cab drove across O'Connell Bridge Miss O'Callaghan said:

—They say you never cross O'Connell Bridge without seeing a white horse.

—I see a white man this time, said Gabriel.

—Where? asked Mr Bartell D'Arcy.

Gabriel pointed to the statue, on which lay patches of snow. Then he nodded familiarly to it and waved his hand.

—Good-night, Dan, he said gaily.

When the cab drew up before the hotel Gabriel jumped out and, in spite of Mr Bartell D'Arcy's protest, paid the driver. He gave the man a shilling over his fare. The man saluted and said:

—A prosperous New Year to you, sir.

—The same to you, said Gabriel cordially.

She leaned for a moment on his arm in getting out of the cab and while standing at the curbstone, bidding the others good-night. She leaned lightly on his arm, as lightly as when she had danced with him a few hours before. He had felt proud and happy then, happy that she was his, proud of her grace and wifely carriage. But now, after the kindling again of so many memories, the first touch of her body, musical and strange and perfumed, sent through him a keen pang of lust. Under cover of her silence he pressed her arm closely to his side; and, as they stood at the hotel door, he felt that they had escaped from their lives and duties, escaped from home and friends and run away together with wild and radiant hearts to a new adventure.

An old man was dozing in a great hooded chair in the hall. He lit a candle in the office and went before them to the stairs. They followed him in silence, their feet falling in soft thuds on the thickly carpeted stairs. She mounted the stairs behind the porter, her head bowed in the ascent, her frail shoulders curved as with a burden, her skirt girt tightly about her. He could have flung his arms about her hips and held her still for his arms were trembling with desire to seize her and only the stress of his nails against the palms of his hands held the wild impulse of his body in check. The porter halted on the stairs to settle his guttering candle. They halted too on the steps below him. In the silence Gabriel could hear the falling of the molten wax into the tray and the thumping of his own heart against his ribs.

The porter led them along the corridor and opened a door. Then he set his unstable candle down on a toilet-table and asked at what hour they were to be called in the morning.

—Eight, said Gabriel.

The porter pointed to the tap of the electric-light and began a muttered apology but Gabriel cut him short.

—We don't want any light. We have light enough from the street. And I say, he added, pointing to the candle, you might remove that handsome article, like a good man.

The porter took up his candle again, but slowly for he was surprised by such a novel idea. Then he mumbled good-night and went out. Gabriel shot the lock to.

A ghostly light from the street lamp lay in a long shaft from one window to the door. Gabriel threw his overcoat and hat on a couch and crossed the room towards the window. He looked down into the street in order that his emotion might calm a little. Then he turned and leaned against a chest of drawers with his back to the light. She had taken off her hat and cloak and was standing before a large swinging mirror, unhooking her waist. Gabriel paused for a few moments, watching her, and then said:

—Gretta!

She turned away from the mirror slowly and walked along the shaft of light towards him. Her face looked so serious and weary that the words would not pass Gabriel's lips. No, it was not the moment yet.

—You looked tired, he said.

—I am a little, she answered.

—You don't feel ill or weak?

—No, tired: that's all.

She went on to the window and stood there, looking out. Gabriel waited again and then, fearing that diffidence was about to conquer him, he said abruptly:

—By the way, Gretta!

—What is it?

—You know that poor fellow Malins? he said quickly.

—Yes. What about him?

—Well, poor fellow, he's a decent sort of chap after all, continued Gabriel in a false voice. He gave me back that sovereign I lent him and I didn't expect it really. It's a pity he wouldn't keep away from that Browne, because he's not a bad fellow at heart.

He was trembling now with annoyance. Why did she seem so abstracted? He did not know how he could begin. Was she annoyed, too, about something? If she would only turn to him or come to him of her own accord! To take her as she was would be brutal. No, he must see some ardour in her eyes first. He longed to be master of her strange mood.

—When did you lend him the pound? she asked, after a pause.

Gabriel strove to restrain himself from breaking out into brutal language about the sottish Malins and his pound. He longed to cry to her from his soul, to crush her body against his, to overmaster her. But he said:

—O, at Christmas, when he opened that little Christmas-card shop in Henry Street.

He was in such a fever of rage and desire that he did not hear her come from the window. She stood before him for an instant, looking at him strangely. Then, suddenly raising herself on tiptoe and resting her hands lightly on his shoulders, she kissed him.

—You are a very generous person, Gabriel, she said.

Gabriel, trembling with delight at her sudden kiss and at the quaintness of her phrase, put his hands on her hair and began smoothing it back, scarcely touching it with his fingers. The washing had made it fine and brilliant. His heart was brimming over with happiness. Just when he was wishing for it she had come to him of her own accord. Perhaps her thoughts had been running with his. Perhaps she had felt the impetuous desire that was in him and then the yielding mood had come upon her. Now that she had fallen to him so easily he wondered why he had been so diffident.

He stood, holding her head between his hands. Then, slipping one arm swiftly about her body and drawing her towards him, he said softly:

—Gretta dear, what are you thinking about?

She did not answer nor yield wholly to his arm. He said again, softly:

—Tell me what it is, Gretta. I think I know what is the matter. Do I know?

She did not answer at once. Then she said in an outburst of tears:

—O, I am thinking about that song, *The Lass of Aughrim*.

She broke loose from him and ran to the bed and, throwing her arms across the bed-rail, hid her face. Gabriel stood stock-still for a moment in astonishment and then followed her. As he passed in the way of the cheval-glass he caught sight of himself in full length, his broad, well-fitted shirt-front, the face whose expression always puzzled him when he saw it in a mirror, and his glimmering gilt-rimmed eyeglasses. He halted a few paces from her and said:

—What about the song? Why does that make you cry?

She raised her head from her arms and dried her eyes with the back of her hand like a child. A kinder note than he had intended went into his voice.

—Why, Gretta? he asked.

—I am thinking about a person long ago who used to sing that song.

—And who was the person long ago? asked Gabriel, smiling.

—It was a person I used to know in Galway when I was living with my grandmother, she said.

The smile passed away from Gabriel's face. A dull anger began to gather again at the back of his mind and the dull fires of his lust began to flow angrily in his veins.

—Someone you were in love with? he asked ironically.

—It was a young boy I used to know, she answered, named Michael Furey. He used to sing that song, *The Lass of Aughrim*. He was very delicate.

Gabriel was silent. He did not wish her to think that he was interested in this delicate boy.

—I can see him so plainly, she said after a moment. Such eyes as he had: big dark eyes! And such an expression in them—an expression!

—O then, you were in love with him? said Gabriel.

—I used to go out walking with him, she said, when I was in Galway.

A thought flew across Gabriel's mind.

—Perhaps that was why you wanted to go to Galway with that Ivors girl? he said coldly.

She looked at him and asked in surprise:

—What for?

Her eyes made Gabriel feel awkward. He shrugged his shoulders and said:

—How do I know? To see him perhaps.

She looked away from him along the shaft of light towards the window in silence.

—He is dead, she said at length. He died when he was only seventeen. Isn't it a terrible thing to die so young as that?

—What was he? asked Gabriel, still ironically.

—He was in the gasworks, she said.

Gabriel felt humiliated by the failure of his irony and by the evocation of this figure from the dead, a boy in the gasworks. While he had been full of memories of their secret life together, full of tenderness and joy and desire, she had been comparing him in her mind with another. A shameful consciousness of his own person assailed him. He saw himself as a ludicrous figure, acting as a pennyboy for his aunts, a nervous well-meaning sentimentalist, orating to vulgarians and idealizing his own clownish lusts, the pitiable fatuous fellow he had caught a glimpse of in the mirror. Instinctively he turned his back more to the light lest she might see the shame that burned upon his forehead.

He tried to keep up his tone of cold interrogation but his voice when he spoke was humble and indifferent.

—I suppose you were in love with this Michael Furey, Gretta, he said.

—I was great with him at that time, she said.

Her voice was veiled and sad. Gabriel, feeling now how vain it would be to try to lead her whither he had purposed, caressed one of her hands and said, also sadly:

—And what did he die of so young, Gretta? Consumption, was it?

—I think he died for me, she answered.

A vague terror seized Gabriel at this answer as if, at that hour when he had hoped to triumph, some impalpable and vindictive being was coming against him, gathering forces against him in its vague world. But he shook himself free of it with an effort of reason and continued to caress her hand. He did not question her again for he felt that she would tell him of herself. Her hand was warm and moist: it did not respond to his touch but he continued to caress it just as he had caressed her first letter to him that spring morning.

—It was in the winter, she said, about the beginning of the winter when I was going to leave my grandmother's and come up here to the convent. And he was ill at the time in his lodgings in Galway and wouldn't be let out and his people in Oughterard were written to. He was in decline, they said, or something like that. I never knew rightly.

She paused for a moment and sighed.

—Poor fellow, she said. He was very fond of me and he was such a gentle boy. We used to go out together, walking, you know, Gabriel, like the way they do in the country. He was going to study singing only for his health. He had a very good voice, poor Michael Furey.

—Well; and then? asked Gabriel.

—And then when it came to the time for me to leave Galway and come up to the convent he was much worse and I wouldn't be let see him so I wrote a letter saying I was going up to Dublin and would be back in the summer and hoping he would be better then.

She paused for a moment to get her voice under control and then went on:

—Then the night before I left I was in my grandmother's house in Nuns' Island, packing up, and I heard gravel thrown up against the window. The window was so wet I couldn't see so I ran downstairs as I was and slipped out the back into the garden and there was the poor fellow at the end of the garden, shivering.

—And did you not tell him to go back? asked Gabriel.

—I implored him to go home at once and told him he would get his death in the rain. But he said he did not want to live. I can see his eyes as well as well! He was standing at the end of the wall where there was a tree.

—And did he go home? asked Gabriel.

—Yes, he went home. And when I was only a week in the convent he died and he was buried in Oughterard where his people came from. O, the day I heard that, that he was dead!

She stopped, choking with sobs, and, overcome by emotion, flung herself face downward on the bed, sobbing in the quilt. Gabriel held her hand for a moment longer, irresolutely, and then, shy of intruding on her grief, let it fall gently and walked quietly to the window.

She was fast asleep.

Gabriel, leaning on his elbow, looked for a few moments unresentfully on her tangled hair and half-open mouth, listening to her deep-drawn breath. So she had had that romance in her life: a man had died for her sake. It hardly pained him now to think how poor a part he, her husband, had played in her life. He watched her while she slept as though he and she had never lived together as man and wife. His curious eyes rested long upon her face and on her hair: and, as he thought of what she must have been then, in that time of her first girlish beauty, a strange friendly pity for her entered his soul. He did not like to say even to himself that her face was no longer beautiful but he knew that it was no longer the face for which Michael Furey had braved death.

Perhaps she had not told him all the story. His eyes moved to the chair over which she had thrown some of her clothes. A petticoat string dangled to the floor. One boot stood upright, its limp upper fallen down: the fellow of it lay upon its side. He wondered at his riot of emotions of an hour before. From what had it proceeded? From his aunt's supper, from his own foolish speech, from the wine and dancing, the merry-making when saying good-night in the hall, the pleasure of the walk along the river in the snow. Poor Aunt Julia! She, too, would soon be a shade with the shade of Patrick Morkan and his horse. He had caught that haggard look upon her face for a moment when she was singing *Arrayed for the Bridal*. Soon, perhaps, he would be sitting in that same drawing-room, dressed in black, his silk hat on his knees. The blinds would be drawn down and Aunt Kate would be sitting beside him, crying and blowing her nose and telling him how Julia had died. He would cast about in his mind for some words that might console her, and would find only lame and useless ones. Yes, yes; that would happen very soon.

The air of the room chilled his shoulders. He stretched himself cautiously along under the sheets and lay down beside his wife. One by one they were all becoming shades. Better pass boldly into that other world, in the full glory of some passion, than fade and wither dismally with age. He thought of how she who lay beside him had locked in her heart for so many years that image of her lover's eyes when he had told her that he did not wish to live.

Generous tears filled Gabriel's eyes. He had never felt like that himself towards any woman but he knew that such a feeling must be love. The tears gathered more thickly in his eyes and in the partial darkness he imagined he saw the form of a young man standing under a dripping tree. Other forms were near. His soul had approached that region where dwell the vast hosts of the dead. He was conscious of, but could not apprehend, their wayward and flickering existence. His own identity was fading out into a grey impalpable world: the solid world itself which these dead had one time reared and lived in was dissolving and dwindling.

A few light taps upon the pane made him turn to the window. It had begun to snow again. He watched sleepily the flakes, silver and dark, falling obliquely against the lamplight. The time had come for him to set out on his journey westward. Yes, the newspapers were right: snow was general all over Ireland. It was falling on every part of the dark central plain, on the treeless hills, falling softly upon the Bog of Allen and, farther westward, softly falling into the dark mutinous Shannon waves. It was falling, too, upon every part of the lonely churchyard on the hill where Michael Furey lay buried. It lay thickly drifted on the crooked crosses and headstones, on the spears of the little gate, on the barren thorns. His soul swooned slowly as he heard the snow falling faintly through the universe and faintly falling, like the descent of their last end, upon all the living and the dead.

1914

Virginia Woolf

1882-1941

The most striking quality of Virginia Woolf's fiction is its evocation of consciousness from within. Woolf wanted her writing to break from what she called the 'materialism' of realist novelists, and, as she explained in a 1919 essay, she wanted fiction to portray the variegated workings of the mind, which 'receives upon its surface a myriad impressions—trivial, fantastic, evanescent, or engraved with the sharpness of steel. From all sides they come, an incessant shower of innumerable atoms, composing in their sum what we might venture to call life itself; and to figure further as the semi-transparent envelope, or luminous halo, surrounding us from the beginning of consciousness to the end.'

Woolf was born in London into a prominent literary family; her father, Sir Leslie Stephen, was a celebrated man of letters, and she was educated at home, reading at will in his library. After her father's death in 1904, she moved with her sister and two brothers to Bloomsbury, where she began her long association with the famous 'Bloomsbury Group' of artists and intellectuals. She married Leonard Woolf in 1912 and together with him established the Hogarth Press, which was to publish the works of new writers such as T.S. Eliot, Katherine Mansfield, and E.M. Forster; more importantly, the press gave her the freedom to experiment with her own fiction, knowing that Hogarth would publish it. Woolf suffered the first of a series of breakdowns at the death of her mother in 1895, and another more serious one in 1916; in 1941, fearing the onset of another crisis, she drowned herself near Rodmell, Sussex.

Woolf saw her stories in part as experiments in style and technique that would stand by themselves and lead to her experiments with the novel. 'A Haunted House', for example, leads to the 'Time Passes' section of *To the Lighthouse* (1927) and then to the interludes in *The Waves* (1931), and in 'Kew Gardens' she was developing her uses of point of view and interior monologue. 'Kew Gardens', with its couples strolling past the flower beds on a hot summer day, brings a finely focused attention both to the internal workings animating each couple's dialogue and to the flowers and the sunlight as it is refracted and reflected into various shades and colours. Finally, the focus on the several couples and their idiosyncrasies merges with a panoramic depiction of the larger scene, and the close attention to psychological detail and to the most minute elements in the natural setting informs the story's closing evocation of the languorous heat in the garden.

'A Haunted House' invokes the ghostly presences moving through the rooms of a house and through the consciousness of the present inhabitants. The effect of this mingling of past and present, dead and living consciousness is to imbue the house itself with a consciousness enduring over time and resonant with memory and love. Thus the house becomes a mind sensitive to its own workings, and responsive to its human ancestry and present inhabitants.

'Kew Gardens' first appeared as a separate publication of the Hogarth Press in May 1919 and was then collected in *Monday or Tuesday* (1921). 'A Haunted House' first appeared in *Monday or Tuesday*.

Kew Gardens

From the oval-shaped flower-bed there rose perhaps a hundred stalks spreading into heart-shaped or tongue-shaped leaves half way up and unfurling at the tip red or blue or yellow petals marked with spots of colour raised upon the surface; and from the red, blue or yellow gloom of the throat emerged a straight bar, rough with gold dust and slightly clubbed at the end. The petals were voluminous enough to be stirred by the summer breeze, and when they moved, the red, blue and yellow lights passed one over the other, staining an inch of the brown earth beneath with a spot of the most intricate colour. The light fell either upon the smooth grey black of a pebble, or the shell of a snail with its brown circular veins, or, falling into a raindrop, it expanded with such intensity of red, blue and yellow the thin walls of water that one expected them to burst and disappear. Instead, the drop was left in a second silver grey once more, and the light now settled upon the flesh of a leaf, revealing the branching thread of fibre beneath the surface, and again it moved on and spread its illumination in the vast green spaces beneath the dome of the heart-shaped and tongue-shaped leaves. Then the breeze stirred rather more briskly overhead and the colour was flashed into the air above, into the eyes of the men and women who walk in Kew Gardens in July.

The figures of these men and women straggled past the flower-bed with a curiously irregular movement not unlike that of the white and blue butterflies who crossed the turf in zig-zag flights from bed to bed. The man was about six inches in front of the woman, strolling carelessly, while she bore on with greater purpose, only turning her head now and then to see that the children were not too far behind. The man kept this distance in front of the woman purposely, though perhaps unconsciously, for he wanted to go on with his thoughts.

'Fifteen years ago I came here with Lily,' he thought. 'We sat somewhere over there by a lake, and I begged her to marry me all through the hot afternoon. How the dragon-fly kept circling around us: how clearly I see the dragon-fly and her shoe with the square silver buckle at the toe. All the time I spoke I saw her shoe and when it moved impatiently I knew without looking up what she was going to say: the whole of her seemed to be in her shoe. And my love, my desire, were in the dragon-fly; for some reason I thought that if it settled there, on that leaf, the broad one with the red flower in the middle of it, if the dragon-fly settled on the leaf she would say "Yes" at once. But the dragon-fly went round and round: it never settled anywhere—of course not, happily not, or I shouldn't be walking here with Eleanor and the children—Tell me, Eleanor, d'you ever think of the past?'

'Why do you ask, Simon?'

'Because I've been thinking of the past. I've been thinking of Lily, the woman I might have married . . . Well, why are you silent? Do you mind my thinking of the past?'

'Why should I mind, Simon? Doesn't one always think of the past, in a garden with men and women lying under the trees? Aren't they one's past, all that remains of it, those men and women, those ghosts lying under the trees, . . . one's happiness, one's reality?'

'For me, a square silver shoe-buckle and a dragon-fly—'

'For me, a kiss. Imagine six little girls sitting before their easels twenty years ago, down by the side of a lake, painting the water-lilies, the first red water-lilies I'd ever seen. And suddenly a kiss, there on the back of my neck. And my hand shook all the afternoon so that I couldn't paint. I took out my watch and marked the hour when I would allow myself to think of the kiss for five minutes only—it was so precious—the kiss of an old gray-haired woman with a wart on her nose, the mother of all my kisses all my life. Come Caroline, come Hubert.'

They walked on past the flower-bed, now walking four abreast, and soon diminished in size among the trees and looked half transparent as the sunlight and shade swam over their backs in large trembling irregular patches.

In the oval flower-bed the snail, whose shell had been stained red, blue and yellow for the space of two minutes or so, now appeared to be moving very slightly in its shell, and next began to labour over the crumbs of loose earth which broke away and rolled down as it passed over them. It appeared to have a definite goal in front of it, differing in this respect from the singular high-stepping angular green insect who attempted to cross in front of it, and waited for a second with its antennae trembling as if in deliberation, and then stepped off as rapidly and strangely in the opposite direction. Brown cliffs with deep green lakes in the hollows, flat blade-like trees that waved from root to tip, round boulders of grey stone, vast crumpled surfaces of a thin crackling texture—all these objects lay across the snail's progress between one stalk and another to his goal. Before he had decided whether to circumvent the arched tent of a dead leaf or to breast it there came past the bed the feet of the other human beings.

This time they were both men. The younger of the two wore an expression of perhaps unnatural calm; he raised his eyes and fixed them very steadily in front of him while his companion spoke, and directly his companion had done speaking he looked on the ground again and sometimes opened his lips only after a long pause and sometimes did not open them at all. The elder man had a curiously uneven and shaky method of walking, jerking his hand forward and throwing up his head abruptly, rather in the manner of an impatient carriage horse tired of waiting outside a house; but in the man these gestures were irresolute and pointless. He talked almost incessantly; he smiled to himself and again began to talk, as if the smile had been an answer. He was talking about spirits—the spirits of the dead, who, according to him, were even now telling him all sorts of odd things about their experiences in Heaven.

'Heaven was known to the ancients as Thessaly, William, and now, with this war, the spirit matter is rolling between the hills like thunder.' He paused, seemed to listen, smiled, jerked his head and continued:

'You have a small electric battery and a piece of rubber to insulate the wire—isolate?—insulate?—well, we'll skip the details, no good going into details that wouldn't be understood—and in short the little machine stands in any convenient position by the head of the bed, we will say, on a neat mahogany stand. All arrangements being properly fixed by workmen under my direction, the widow applies her ear and summons the spirit by sign as agreed. Women! Widows! Women in black—'

Here he seemed to have caught sight of a woman's dress in the distance, which in the shade looked a purple black. He took off his hat, placed his hand upon his heart, and hurried towards her muttering and gesticulating feverishly. But William caught him by the sleeve and touched a flower with the tip of his walking-stick in order to divert the old man's attention. After looking at it for a moment in some confusion the old man bent his ear to it and seemed to answer a voice speaking from it, for he began talking about the forests of Uruguay which he had visited hundreds of years ago in company with the most beautiful young woman in Europe. He could be heard murmuring about forests of Uruguay blanketed with the wax petals of tropical roses, nightingales, sea beaches, mermaids and women drowned at sea, as he suffered himself to be moved on by William, upon whose face the look of stoical patience grew slowly deeper and deeper.

Following his steps so closely as to be slightly puzzled by his gestures came two elderly women of the lower middle class, one stout and ponderous, the other rosy-cheeked and nimble. Like most people of their station they were frankly fascinated by any signs of eccentricity betokening a disordered brain, especially in the well-to-do; but they were too far off to be certain whether the gestures were merely eccentric or genuinely mad. After they had scrutinised the old man's back in silence for a moment and given each other a queer, sly look, they went on energetically piecing together their very complicated dialogue:

'Nell, Bert, Lot, Cess, Phil, Pa, he says, I says, she says, I says, I says, I says—'

'My Bert, Sis, Bill, Grandad, the old man, sugar,
Sugar, flour, kippers, greens
Sugar, sugar, sugar.'

The ponderous woman looked through the pattern of falling words at the flowers standing cool, firm and upright in the earth, with a curious expression. She saw them as a sleeper waking from a heavy sleep sees a brass candlestick reflecting the light in an unfamiliar way, and closes his eyes and opens them, and seeing the brass candlestick again, finally starts broad awake and stares at the candlestick with all his powers. So the heavy woman came to a standstill opposite the oval-shaped flower-bed, and ceased even to pretend to listen to what the other woman was saying. She stood there letting the words fall over her, swaying the top part of her body slowly backwards and forwards, looking at the flowers. Then she suggested that they should find a seat and have their tea.

The snail had now considered every possible method of reaching his goal without going round the dead leaf or climbing over it. Let alone the effort needed for climbing a leaf, he was doubtful whether the thin texture which vibrated with such an alarming crackle when touched even by the tip of his horns would bear his weight; and this determined him finally to creep beneath it, for there was a point where the leaf curved high enough from the ground to admit him. He had just inserted his head in the opening and was taking stock of the high brown roof and was getting used to the cool brown light when two other people came past outside on the turf. This time they were both young, a young man and a young woman. They were both in the prime of youth, or even in that season which precedes the prime of youth, the season before the smooth pink folds of the flower have burst their gummy case, when the wings of the butterfly, though fully grown, are motionless in the sun.

'Lucky it isn't Friday,' he observed.

'Why? D'you believe in luck?'

'They make you pay sixpence on Friday.'

'What's sixpence anyway? Isn't it worth sixpence?'

'What's "it"—what do you mean by "it"?'

'O anything—I mean—you know what I mean.'

Long pauses came between each of these remarks: they were uttered in toneless and monotonous voices. The couple stood still on the edge of the flower-bed, and together pressed the end of her parasol deep down into the soft earth. The action and the fact that his hand rested on the top of hers expressed their feelings in a strange way, as these short insignificant words also expressed something, words with short wings for their heavy body of meaning, inadequate to carry them far and thus alighting awkwardly upon the very common objects that surrounded them and were to their inexperienced touch so massive: but who knows (so they thought as they pressed the parasol into the earth) what precipices aren't concealed in them, or what slopes of ice don't shine in the sun on the other side? Who knows? Who has ever seen this before? Even when she wondered what sort of tea they gave you at Kew, he felt that something loomed up behind her words, and stood vast and solid behind them; and the mist very slowly rose and uncovered—O Heavens,—what were those shapes?—little white tables, and waitresses who looked first at her and then at him; and there was a bill that he would pay with a real two shilling piece, and it was real, all real, he assured himself, fingering the coin in his pocket, real to everyone except to him and to her; even to him it began to seem real; and then—but it was too exciting to stand and think any longer, and he pulled the parasol out of the earth with a jerk and was impatient to find the place where one had tea with other people, like other people.

'Come along, Trissie; it's time we had our tea.'

'Wherever *does* one have one's tea?' she asked with the oddest thrill of excitement in her voice, looking vaguely round and letting herself be drawn on down the grass path, trailing her parasol, turning her head this way and that way, forgetting her tea, wishing to go down there and then down there, remembering orchids and cranes among wild flowers, a Chinese pagoda and a crimson-crested bird; but he bore her on.

Thus one couple after another with much the same irregular and aimless movement passed the flower-bed and were enveloped in layer after layer of green-blue vapour, in which at first their bodies had substance and a dash of colour, but later both substance and colour dissolved in the green-blue atmosphere. How hot it was! So hot that even the thrush chose to hop, like a mechanical bird, in the shadow of the flowers, with long pauses between one movement and the next; instead of rambling vaguely the white butterflies danced one above another, making with their white shifting flakes the outline of a shattered marble column above the tallest flowers; the glass roofs of the palm house shone as if a whole market full of shiny green umbrellas had opened in the sun; and in the drone of the aeroplane the voice of the summer sky murmured its fierce soul. Yellow and black, pink and snow white, shapes of all these colours, men and women and children, were spotted for a second upon the horizon, and then, seeing the breadth of yellow that lay upon the grass, they wavered and sought shade beneath the trees, dissolving like drops of water in the yellow and green atmosphere, staining it faintly with red and blue. It seemed as if all gross and heavy bodies had sunk down in the heat motionless and lay huddled upon the ground, but their voices went wavering from them as if they were flames lolling from the thick waxen bodies of candles. Voices, yes, voices, wordless voices, breaking the silence suddenly with such depth of contentment, such passion of desire, or, in the voices of children, such freshness of surprise; breaking the silence? But there was no silence; all the time the motor omnibuses were turning their wheels and changing their gear; like a vast nest of Chinese boxes all of wrought steel turning ceaselessly one within another the city murmured; on the top of which the voices cried aloud and the petals of myriads of flowers flashed their colours into the air.

1919

A Haunted House

Whatever hour you woke there was a door shutting. From room to room they went, hand in hand, lifting here, opening there, making sure—a ghostly couple.

'Here we left it,' she said. And he added, 'Oh, but here too!' 'It's upstairs,' she murmured, 'And in the garden,' he whispered. 'Quietly,' they said, 'or we shall wake them.'

But it wasn't that you woke us. Oh, no. 'They're looking for it; they're drawing the curtain,' one might say, and so read on a page or two. 'Now they've found it,' one would be certain, stopping the pencil on the margin. And then, tired of reading, one might rise and see for oneself, the house all empty, the doors standing open, only the wood pigeons bubbling with content and the hum of the threshing machine sounding from the farm. 'What did I come in here for? What did I want to find?' My hands were empty. 'Perhaps it's upstairs then?' The apples were in the loft. And so down again, the garden still as ever, only the book had slipped into the grass.

But they had found it in the drawing-room. Not that one could ever see them. The window-panes reflected apples, reflected roses; all the leaves were green in the glass. If they moved in the drawing-room, the apple only turned its yellow side. Yet, the moment after, if the door was opened, spread about the floor, hung upon the walls, pendant from ceiling—what? My hands were empty. The shadow of a thrush crossed the carpet; from the deepest wells of silence the wood pigeon drew its bubble of sound. 'Safe, safe, safe,' the pulse of the house beat softly. 'The treasure buried; the room . . .' the pulse stopped short. Oh, was that the buried treasure?

A moment later the light had faded. Out in the garden then? But the trees spun darkness for a wandering beam of sun. So fine, so rare, coolly sunk beneath the surface the beam I sought always burnt behind the glass. Death was the glass; death was between us; coming to the woman first, hundreds of years ago, leaving the house, stealing all the windows; the rooms were darkened. He left it, left her, went North, went East, saw the stars turned in the southern sky; sought the house, found it dropped beneath the Downs. 'Safe, safe, safe,' the pulse of the house beat gladly, 'The treasure yours.'

The wind roars up the avenue. Trees stoop and bend this way and that. Moonbeams splash and spill wildly in the rain. But the beam of the lamp falls straight from the window. The candle burns stiff and still. Wandering through the house, opening the windows, whispering not to wake us, the ghostly couple seek their joy.

'Here we slept,' she says. And he adds, 'Kisses without number.' 'Waking in the morning—' 'Silver between the trees—' 'Upstairs—' 'In the garden—' 'When summer came—' 'In winter snowtime—' The doors go shutting far in the distance, gently knocking like the pulse of a heart.

Nearer they come; cease at the doorway. The wind falls, the rain slides silver down the glass. Our eyes darken; we hear no steps beside us; we see no lady spread her ghostly cloak. His hands shield the lantern. 'Look,' he breathes. 'Sound asleep. Love upon their lips.'

Stooping, holding their silver lamp above us, long they look and deeply. Long they pause. The wind drives straightly; the flame stoops slightly. Wild beams of moonlight cross both floor and wall, and, meeting, stain the faces bent; the faces pondering; the faces that search the sleepers and seek their hidden joy.

'Safe, safe, safe,' the heart of the house beats proudly. 'Long years—' he sighs. 'Again you found me.' 'Here,' she murmurs, 'sleeping; in the garden reading; laughing, rolling apples in the loft. Here we left our treasure—' Stooping, their light lifts the lids upon my eyes. 'Safe! safe! safe!' the pulse of the house beats wildly. Waking, I cry 'Oh, is this *your*—buried treasure? The light in the heart.'

1921

D.H. Lawrence

1885-1930

'The business of art is to reveal the relation between man and his circumambient universe, at the living moment. As mankind is always struggling in the toils of old relationships, art is always ahead of the "times", which themselves are always in the rear of the living moment,' wrote David Herbert Lawrence in 1925. For him, life '*consists in* this achieving of a pure relationship between ourselves and the living universe about us.' Fiction attempts, he maintained, to capture and explore that relatedness: 'The novel is the highest example of subtle interrelatedness that man has discovered. Everything is true in its own time, place, circumstance, and untrue outside of its own place, time, circumstance. . . . If a novel reveals true and vivid relationships, it is a moral work, no matter what the relationships may consist in.'

Born in Eastwood, Nottinghamshire, England, the fourth of five children of a miner and his middle-class wife, Lawrence attended Nottingham University College to obtain his teacher's certificate. In 1911 an illness, which was later identified as tuberculosis, brought his teaching career to an end; the same year he published his first novel, *The White Peacock*. While he was working on his autobiographical novel, *Sons and Lovers* (1913), he met Frieda von Richthofen, the wife of a former professor. They travelled to the continent, returning on the eve of the First World War to England, where they were then married. After the war they lived in self-appointed exile in Italy, New Mexico, and Mexico. They returned to Europe in 1929, and Lawrence died of tuberculosis the following year.

'The great relationship, for humanity, will always be the relation between man and woman,' Lawrence proclaimed. 'And the relation between man and woman will change for ever, and will for ever be the new central clue to human life. It is the *relation itself* which is the quick and the central clue to life.' And his fiction often contrasts the instinctive and life-affirming nature of love with the sterile death-in-life which is too often the human condition.

The poverty and spiritual deadness that pervade the Pervin household in 'The Horse Dealer's Daughter' are put in proper perspective by the intense love between the doctor and the woman he rescues from suicide. The story embodies Lawrence's own understanding of human love: 'A new relation, a new relatedness hurts somewhat in the attaining; and will always hurt. So life will always hurt. . . . Each [of the couple] must be true to himself, herself, his own manhood, her own womanhood, and let the relationship work out of itself. This means courage above all things: and then discipline. Courage to accept the life-thrust from within oneself, and from the other person. Discipline, not to exceed oneself any more than one can help. Courage, when one has exceeded oneself, to accept the fact and not whine about it.'

In 'The Rocking-horse Winner', the mother 'knew that at the centre of her heart was a hard little place that could not feel love, no, not for anybody.' As a consequence, her sterile home becomes the setting for an ultimately destructive commitment to materialism.

'The Horse Dealer's Daughter' was first published in the April 1922 issue of the *English Review* and then collected in *England, My England and Other Stories* (1922). 'The Rocking-horse Winner' was first published in the July 1926 issue of *Harper's Bazaar* and then collected in *The Lovely Lady* (1933).

The Horse Dealer's Daughter

'Well, Mabel, and what are you going to do with yourself?' asked Joe, with foolish flippancy. He felt quite safe himself. Without listening for an answer, he turned aside, worked a grain of tobacco to the tip of his tongue, and spat it out. He did not care about anything, since he felt safe himself.

The three brothers and the sister sat round the desolate breakfast-table, attempting some sort of desultory consultation. The morning's post had given the final tap to the family fortunes, and all was over. The dreary dining-room itself, with its heavy mahogany furniture, looked as if it were waiting to be done away with.

But the consultation amounted to nothing. There was a strange air of ineffectuality about the three men, as they sprawled at table, smoking and reflecting vaguely on their own condition. The girl was alone, a rather short, sullen-looking young woman of twenty-seven. She did not share the same life as her brothers. She would have been good-looking, save for the impressive fixity of her face, 'bull-dog', as her brothers called it.

There was a confused tramping of horses' feet outside. The three men all sprawled round in their chairs to watch. Beyond the dark holly bushes that separated the strip of lawn from the high-road, they could see a cavalcade of shire horses swinging out of their own yard, being taken for exercise. This was the last time. These were the last horses that would go through their hands. The young men watched with critical, callous look. They were all frightened at the collapse of their lives, and the sense of disaster in which they were involved left them no inner freedom.

Yet they were three fine, well-set fellows enough. Joe, the eldest, was a man of thirty-three, broad and handsome in a hot, flushed way. His face was red, he twisted his black moustache over a thick finger, his eyes were shallow and restless. He had a sensual way of uncovering his teeth when he laughed, and his bearing was stupid. Now he watched the horses with a glazed look of helplessness in his eyes, a certain stupor of downfall.

The great draught-horses swung past. They were tied head to tail, four of them, and they heaved along to where a lane branched off from the high-road, planting their great hoofs floutingly in the fine black mud, swinging their great rounded haunches sumptuously, and trotting a few sudden steps as they were led into the lane, round the corner. Every movement showed a massive, slumbrous strength, and a stupidity which held them in subjection. The groom at the head looked back, jerking the leading rope. And the cavalcade moved out of sight up the lane, the tail of the last horse, bobbed up tight and stiff, held out taut from the swinging great haunches as they rocked behind the hedges in a motion-like sleep.

Joe watched with glazed hopeless eyes. The horses were almost like his own body to him. He felt he was done for now. Luckily he was engaged to a woman as old as himself, and therefore her father, who was steward of a neighbouring estate, would provide him with a job. He would marry and go into harness. His life was over, he would be a subject animal now.

He turned uneasily aside, the retreating steps of the horses echoing in his ears. Then, with foolish restlessness, he reached for the scraps of bacon-rind from the plates, and making a faint whistling sound, flung them to the terrier that lay against the fender. He watched the dog swallow them, and waited till the creature looked into his eyes. Then a faint grin came on his face, and in a high, foolish voice he said:

'You won't get much more bacon, shall you, you little b—?'

The dog faintly and dismally wagged its tail, then lowered its haunches, circled round, and lay down again.

There was another helpless silence at the table. Joe sprawled uneasily in his seat, not willing to go till the family conclave was dissolved. Fred Henry, the second brother, was erect, clean-limbed, alert. He had watched the passing of the horses with more *sang-froid*. If he was an animal, like Joe, he was an animal which controls, not one which is controlled. He was master of any horse, and he carried himself with a well-tempered air of mastery. But he was not master of the situations of life. He pushed his coarse brown moustache upwards, off his lip, and glanced irritably at his sister, who sat impassive and inscrutable.

'You'll go and stop with Lucy for a bit, shan't you?' he asked. The girl did not answer.

'I don't see what else you can do,' persisted Fred Henry.

'Go as a skivvy,' Joe interpolated laconically.

The girl did not move a muscle.

'If I was her, I should go in for training for a nurse,' said Malcolm, the youngest of them all. He was the baby of the family, a young man of twenty-two, with a fresh, jaunty *museau*.

But Mabel did not take any notice of him. They had talked at her and round her for so many years, that she hardly heard them at all.

The marble clock on the mantelpiece softly chimed the half-hour, the dog rose uneasily from the hearth-rug and looked at the party at the breakfast-table. But still they sat on in ineffectual conclave.

'Oh, all right,' said Joe suddenly, apropos of nothing. 'I'll get a move on.'

He pushed back his chair, straddled his knees with a downward jerk, to get them free, in horsey fashion, and went to the fire. Still he did not go out of the room; he was curious to know what the others would do or say. He began to charge his pipe, looking down at the dog and saying in a high, affected voice:

'Going wi' me? Going wi' me are ter? Tha'rt goin' further than tha counts on just now, dost hear?'

The dog faintly wagged its tail, the man stuck out his jaw and covered his pipe with his hands, and puffed intently, losing himself in the tobacco, looking down all the while at the dog with an absent brown eye. The dog looked up at him in mournful distrust. Joe stood with his knees stuck out, in real horsey fashion.

'Have you had a letter from Lucy?' Fred Henry asked of his sister.

'Last week,' came the neutral reply.

'And what does she say?'

There was no answer.

'Does she *ask* you to go and stop there?' persisted Fred Henry.

'She says I can if I like.'

'Well, then, you'd better. Tell her you'll come on Monday.'

This was received in silence.

'That's what you'll do then, is it?' said Fred Henry, in some exasperation.

But she made no answer. There was a silence of futility and irritation in the room. Malcolm grinned fatuously.

'You'll have to make up your mind between now and next Wednesday,' said Joe loudly, 'or else find yourself lodgings on the kerbstone.'

The face of the young woman darkened, but she sat on immutable.

'Here's Jack Fergusson!' exclaimed Malcolm, who was looking aimlessly out of the window.

'Where?' exclaimed Joe loudly.

'Just gone past.'

'Coming in?'

Malcolm craned his neck to see the gate.

'Yes,' he said.

There was a silence. Mabel sat on like one condemned, at the head of the table. Then a whistle was heard from the kitchen. The dog got up and barked sharply. Joe opened the door and shouted:

'Come on.'

After a moment a young man entered. He was muffled up in overcoat and a purple woollen scarf, and his tweed cap, which he did not remove, was pulled down on his head. He was of medium height, his face was rather long and pale, his eyes looked tired.

'Hello, Jack! Well, Jack!' exclaimed Malcolm and Joe. Fred Henry merely said: 'Jack.'

'What's doing?' asked the newcomer, evidently addressing Fred Henry.

'Same. We've got to be out by Wednesday. Got a cold?'

'I have—got it bad, too.'

'Why don't you stop in?'

'*Me* stop in? When I can't stand on my legs, perhaps I shall have a chance.' The young man spoke huskily. He had a slight Scotch accent.

'It's a knock-out, isn't it,' said Joe, boisterously, 'if a doctor goes round croaking with a cold. Looks bad for the patients, doesn't it?'

The young doctor looked at him slowly.

'Anything the matter with *you*, then?' he asked sarcastically.

'Not as I know of. Damn your eyes, I hope not. Why?'

'I thought you were very concerned about the patients, wondered if you might be one yourself.'

'Damn it, no, I've never been patient to no flaming doctor, and hope I never shall be,' returned Joe.

At this point Mabel rose from the table, and they all seemed to become aware of her existence. She began putting the dishes together. The young doctor looked at her, but did not address her. He had not greeted her. She went out of the room with the tray, her face impassive and unchanged.

'When are you off then, all of you?' asked the doctor.

'I'm catching the eleven-forty,' replied Malcolm. 'Are you goin' down wi' th' trap, Joe?'

'Yes, I've told you I'm going down wi' th' trap, haven't I?'

'We'd better be getting her in then. So long, Jack, if I don't see you before I go,' said Malcolm, shaking hands.

He went out, followed by Joe, who seemed to have his tail between his legs.

'Well, this is the devil's own,' exclaimed the doctor, when he was left alone with Fred Henry. 'Going before Wednesday, are you?'

'That's the orders,' replied the other.

'Where, to Northampton?'

'That's it.'

'The devil!' exclaimed Fergusson, with quiet chagrin.

And there was silence between the two.

'All settled up, are you?' asked Fergusson.

'About.'

There was another pause.

'Well, I shall miss yer, Freddy, boy,' said the young doctor.

'And I shall miss thee, Jack,' returned the other.

'Miss you like hell,' mused the doctor.

Fred Henry turned aside. There was nothing to say. Mabel came in again, to finish clearing the table.

'What are *you* going to do, then, Miss Pervin?' asked Fergusson. 'Going to your sister's, are you?'

Mabel looked at him with her steady, dangerous eyes, that always made him uncomfortable, unsettling his superficial ease.

'No,' she said.

'Well, what in the name of fortune *are* you going to do? Say what you mean to do,' cried Fred Henry, with futile intensity.

But she only averted her head, and continued her work. She folded the white table-cloth, and put on the chenille cloth.

'The sulkiest bitch that ever trod!' muttered her brother.

But she finished her task with perfectly impassive face, the young doctor watching her interestedly all the while. Then she went out.

Fred Henry stared after her, clenching his lips, his blue eyes fixing in sharp antagonism, as he made a grimace of sour exasperation.

'You could bray her into bits, and that's all you'd get out of her,' he said, in a small, narrowed tone.

The doctor smiled faintly.

'What's she *going* to do, then?' he asked.

'Strike me if *I* know!' returned the other.

There was a pause. Then the doctor stirred.

'I'll be seeing you to-night, shall I?' he said to his friend.

'Ay—where's it to be? Are we going over to Jessdale?'

'I don't know. I've got such a cold on me. I'll come round to the "Moon and Stars", anyway.'

'Let Lizzie and May miss their night for once, eh?'

'That's it—if I feel as I do now.'

'All's one—'

The two young men went through the passage and down to the back door together. The house was large, but it was servantless now, and desolate. At the back was a small bricked house-yard and beyond that a big square, gravelled fine and red, and having stables on two sides. Sloping, dank, winter-dark fields stretched away on the open sides.

But the stables were empty. Joseph Pervin, the father of the family, had been a man of no education, who had become a fairly large horse dealer. The stables had been full of horses, there was a great turmoil and come-and-go of horses and of dealers and grooms. Then the kitchen was full of servants. But of late things had declined. The old man had married a second time, to retrieve his fortunes. Now he was dead and everything was gone to the dogs, there was nothing but debt and threatening.

For months, Mabel had been servantless in the big house, keeping the home together in penury for her ineffectual brothers. She had kept house for ten years. But previously it was with unstinted means. Then, however brutal and coarse everything was, the sense of money had kept her proud, confident. The men might be foul-mouthed, the women in the kitchen might have bad reputations, her brothers might have illegitimate children. But so long as there was money, the girl felt herself established, and brutally proud, reserved.

No company came to the house, save dealers and coarse men. Mabel had no associates of her own sex, after her sister went away. But she did not mind. She went regularly to church, she attended to her father. And she lived in the memory of her mother, who had died when she was fourteen, and whom she had loved. She had loved her father, too, in a different way, depending upon him, and feeling secure in him, until at the age of fifty-four he married again. And then she had set hard against him. Now he had died and left them all hopelessly in debt.

She had suffered badly during the period of poverty. Nothing, however, could shake the curious, sullen, animal pride that dominated each member of the family. Now, for Mabel, the end had come. Still she would not cast about her. She would follow her own way just the same. She would always hold the keys of her own situation. Mindless and persistent, she endured from day to day. Why should she think? Why should she answer anybody? It was enough that this was the end, and there was no way out. She need not pass any more darkly along the main street of the small town, avoiding every eye. She need not demean herself any more, going into the shops and buying the cheapest food. This was at an end. She thought of nobody, not even of herself. Mindless and persistent, she seemed in a sort of ecstasy to be coming nearer to her fulfilment, her own glorification, approaching her dead mother, who was glorified.

In the afternoon she took a little bag, with shears and sponge and a small scrubbing-brush, and went out. It was a grey, wintry day, with saddened, dark green fields and an atmosphere blackened by the smoke of foundries not far off. She went quickly, darkly along the causeway, heeding nobody, through the town to the churchyard.

There she always felt secure, as if no one could see her, although as a matter of fact she was exposed to the stare of everyone who passed along under the churchyard wall. Nevertheless, once under the shadow of the great looming church, among the graves, she felt immune from the world, reserved within the thick churchyard wall as in another country.

Carefully she clipped the grass from the grave, and arranged the pinky white, small chrysanthemums in the tin cross. When this was done, she took an empty jar from a neighbouring grave, brought water, and carefully, most scrupulously sponged the marble headstone and the coping-stone.

It gave her sincere satisfaction to do this. She felt in immediate contact with the world of her mother. She took minute pains, went through the park in a state bordering on pure happiness, as if in performing this task she came into a subtle, intimate connection with her mother. For the life she followed here in the world was far less real than the world of death she inherited from her mother.

The doctor's house was just by the church. Fergusson, being a mere hired assistant, was slave to the country-side. As he hurried now to attend to the out-patients in the surgery, glancing across the graveyard with his quick eye, he saw the girl at her task at the grave. She seemed so intent and remote, it was like looking into another world. Some mystical element was touched in him. He slowed down as he walked, watching her as if spellbound.

She lifted her eyes, feeling him looking. Their eyes met. And each looked again at once, each feeling, in some way, found out by the other. He lifted his cap and passed on down the road. There remained distinct in his consciousness, like a vision, the memory of her face, lifted from the tombstone in the churchyard, and looking at him with slow, large, portentous eyes. It *was* portentous, her face. It seemed to mesmerize him. There was a heavy power in her eyes which laid hold of his whole being, as if he had drunk some powerful drug. He had been feeling weak and done before. Now the life came back into him, he felt delivered from his own fretted, daily self.

He finished his duties at the surgery as quickly as might be, hastily filling up the bottles of the waiting people with cheap drugs. Then, in perpetual haste, he set off again to visit several cases in another part of his round, before tea-time. At all times he preferred to walk if he could, but particularly when he was not well. He fancied the motion restored him.

The afternoon was falling. It was grey, deadened, and wintry, with a slow, moist, heavy coldness sinking in and deadening all the faculties. But why should he think or notice? He hastily climbed the hill and turned across the dark green fields, following the black cinder-track. In the distance, across a shallow dip in the country, the small town was clustered like smouldering ash, a tower, a spire, a heap of low, raw, extinct houses. And on the nearest fringe of the town, sloping into the dip, was Oldmeadow, the Pervins' house. He could see the stables and the outbuildings distinctly, as they lay towards him on the slope. Well, he would not go there many more times! Another resource would be lost to him, another place gone: the only company he cared for in the alien, ugly little town he was losing. Nothing but work, drudgery, constant hastening from dwelling to dwelling among the colliers and the iron-workers. It wore him out, but at the same time he had a craving for it. It was a stimulant to him to be in the homes of the working people, moving, as it were, through the innermost body of their life. His nerves were excited and gratified. He could come so near, into the very lives of the rough, inarticulate, powerfully emotional men and women. He grumbled, he said he hated the hellish hole. But as a matter of fact it excited him, the contact with the rough, strongly-feeling people was a stimulant applied direct to his nerves.

Below Oldmeadow, in the green, shallow, soddened hollow of fields, lay a square, deep pond. Roving across the landscape, the doctor's quick eye detected a figure in black passing through the gate of the field, down towards the pond. He looked again. It would be Mabel Pervin. His mind suddenly became alive and attentive.

Why was she going down there? He pulled up on the path on the slope above, and stood staring. He could just make sure of the small black figure moving in the hollow of the failing day. He seemed to see her in the midst of such obscurity, that he was like a clairvoyant, seeing rather with the mind's eye than with ordinary sight. Yet he could see her positively enough, whilst he kept his eye attentive. He felt, if he looked away from her, in the thick, ugly falling dusk, he would lose her altogether.

He followed her minutely as she moved, direct and intent, like something transmitted rather than stirring in voluntary activity, straight down the field towards the pond. There she stood on the bank for a moment. She never raised her head. Then she waded slowly into the water.

He stood motionless as the small black figure walked slowly and deliberately towards the centre of the pond, very slowly, gradually moving deeper into the motionless water, and still moving forward as the water got up to her breast. Then he could see her no more in the dusk of the dead afternoon.

'There!' he exclaimed. 'Would you believe it?'

And he hastened straight down, running over the wet, soddened fields, pushing through the hedges, down into the depression of callous wintry obscurity. It took him several minutes to come to the pond. He stood on the bank, breathing heavily. He could see nothing. His eyes seemed to penetrate the dead water. Yes, perhaps that was the dark shadow of her black clothing beneath the surface of the water.

He slowly ventured into the pond. The bottom was deep, soft clay, he sank in, and the water clasped dead cold round his legs. As he stirred he could smell the cold, rotten clay that fouled up into the water. It was objectionable in his lungs. Still, repelled and yet not heeding, he moved deeper into the pond. The cold water rose over his thighs, over his loins, upon his abdomen. The lower part of his body was all sunk in the hideous cold element. And the bottom was so deeply soft and uncertain, he was afraid of pitching with his mouth underneath. He could not swim, and was afraid.

He crouched a little, spreading his hands under the water and moving them round, trying to feel for her. The dead cold pond swayed upon his chest. He moved again, a little deeper, and again, with his hands underneath, he felt all around under the water. And he touched her clothing. But it evaded his fingers. He made a desperate effort to grasp it.

And so doing he lost his balance and went under, horribly, suffocating in the foul earthy water, struggling madly for a few moments. At last, after what seemed an eternity, he got his footing, rose again into the air and looked around. He gasped, and knew he was in the world. Then he looked at the water. She had risen near him. He grasped her clothing, and drawing her nearer, turned to take his way to land again.

He went very slowly, carefully, absorbed in the slow progress. He rose higher, climbing out of the pond. The water was now only about his legs; he was thankful, full of relief to be out of the clutches of the pond. He lifted her and staggered on to the bank, out of the horror of wet, grey clay.

He laid her down on the bank. She was quite unconscious and running with water. He made the water come from her mouth, he worked to restore her. He did not have to work very long before he could feel the breathing begin again in her; she was breathing naturally. He worked a little longer. He could feel her live beneath his hands; she was coming back. He wiped her face, wrapped her in his overcoat, looked round into the dim, dark grey world, then lifted her and staggered down the bank and across the fields.

It seemed an unthinkably long way, and his burden so heavy he felt he would never get to the house. But at last he was in the stable-yard, and then in the house-yard. He opened the door and went into the house. In the kitchen he laid her down on the hearth-rug and called. The house was empty. But the fire was burning in the grate.

Then again he kneeled to attend to her. She was breathing regularly, her eyes were wide open and as if conscious, but there seemed something missing in her look. She was conscious in herself, but unconscious of her surroundings.

He ran upstairs, took blankets from a bed, and put them before the fire to warm. Then he removed her saturated, earthy-smelling clothing, rubbed her dry with a towel, and wrapped her naked in the blankets. Then he went into the dining-room, to look for spirits. There was a little whisky. He drank a gulp himself, and put some into her mouth.

The effect was instantaneous. She looked full into his face, as if she had been seeing him for some time, and yet had only just become conscious of him.

'Dr Fergusson?' she said.

'What?' he answered.

He was divesting himself of his coat, intending to find some dry clothing upstairs. He could not bear the smell of the dead, clayey water, and he was mortally afraid for his own health.

'What did I do?' she asked.

'Walked into the pond,' he replied. He had begun to shudder like one sick, and could hardly attend to her. Her eyes remained full on him, he seemed to be going dark in his mind, looking back at her helplessly. The shuddering became quieter in him, his life came back to him, dark and unknowing, but strong again.

'Was I out of my mind?' she asked, while her eyes were fixed on him all the time.

'Maybe, for the moment,' he replied. He felt quiet, because his strength had come back. The strange fretful strain had left him.

'Am I out of my mind now?' she asked.

'Are you?' he reflected a moment. 'No,' he answered truthfully, 'I don't see that you are.' He turned his face aside. He was afraid now, because he felt dazed, and felt dimly that her power was stronger than his, in this issue. And she continued to look at him fixedly all the time. 'Can you tell me where I shall find some dry things to put on?' he asked.

'Did you dive into the pond for me?' she asked.

'No,' he answered. 'I walked in. But I went in overhead as well.'

There was silence for a moment. He hesitated. He very much wanted to go upstairs to get into dry clothing. But there was another desire in him. And she seemed to hold him. His will seemed to have gone to sleep, and left him, standing there slack before her. But he felt warm inside himself. He did not shudder at all, though his clothes were sodden on him.

'Why did you?' she asked.

'Because I didn't want you to do such a foolish thing,' he said.

'It wasn't foolish,' she said, still gazing at him as she lay on the floor, with a sofa cushion under her head. 'It was the right thing to do. *I* knew best, then.'

'I'll go and shift these wet things,' he said. But still he had not the power to move out of her presence, until she sent him. It was as if she had the life of his body in her hands, and he could not extricate himself. Or perhaps he did not want to.

Suddenly she sat up. Then she became aware of her own immediate condition. She felt the blankets about her, she knew her own limbs. For a moment it seemed as if her reason were going. She looked round, with wild eye, as if seeking something. He stood still with fear. She saw her clothing lying scattered.

'Who undressed me?' she asked, her eyes resting full and inevitable on his face.

'I did,' he replied, 'to bring you round.'

For some moments she sat and gazed at him awfully, her lips parted.

'Do you love me, then?' she asked.

He only stood and stared at her, fascinated. His soul seemed to melt.

She shuffled forward on her knees, and put her arms round him, round his legs, as he stood there, pressing her breasts against his knees and thighs, clutching him with strange, convulsive certainty, pressing his thighs against her, drawing him to her face, her throat, as she looked up at him with flaring, humble eyes of transfiguration, triumphant in first possession.

'You love me,' she murmured, in strange transport, yearning and triumphant and confident. 'You love me. I know you love me, I know.'

And she was passionately kissing his knees, through the wet clothing, passionately and indiscriminately kissing his knees, his legs, as if unaware of everything.

He looked down at the tangled wet hair, the wild, bare, animal shoulders. He was amazed, bewildered, and afraid. He had never thought of loving her. He had never wanted to love her. When he rescued her and restored her, he was a doctor, and she was a patient. He had had no single personal thought of her. Nay, this introduction of the personal element was very distasteful to him, a violation of his professional honour. It was horrible to have her there embracing his knees. It was horrible. He revolted from it, violently. And yet—and yet—he had not the power to break away.

She looked at him again, with the same supplication of powerful love, and that same transcendent, frightening light of triumph. In view of the delicate flame which seemed to come from her face like a light, he was powerless. And yet he had never intended to love her. He had never intended. And something stubborn in him could not give way.

'You love me,' she repeated, in a murmur of deep, rhapsodic assurance. 'You love me.'

Her hands were drawing him, drawing him down to her. He was afraid, even a little horrified. For he had, really, no intention of loving her. Yet her hands were drawing him towards her. He put out his hand quickly to steady himself, and grasped her bare shoulder. A flame seemed to burn the hand that grasped her soft shoulder. He had no intention of loving her: his whole will was against his yielding. It was horrible. And yet wonderful was the touch of her shoulders, beautiful the shining of her face. Was she perhaps mad? He had a horror of yielding to her. Yet something in him ached also.

He had been staring away at the door, away from her. But his hand remained on her shoulder. She had gone suddenly very still. He looked down at her. Her eyes were now wide with fear, with doubt, the light was dying from her face, a shadow of terrible greyness was returning. He could not bear the touch of her eyes' question upon him, and the look of death behind the question.

With an inward groan he gave way, and let his heart yield towards her. A sudden gentle smile came on his face. And her eyes, which never left his face, slowly, slowly filled with tears. He watched the strange water rise in her eyes, like some slow fountain coming up. And his heart seemed to burn and melt away in his breast.

He could not bear to look at her any more. He dropped on his knees and caught her head with his arms and pressed her face against his throat. She was very still. His heart, which seemed to have broken, was burning with a kind of agony in his breast. And he felt her slow, hot tears wetting his throat. But he could not move.

He felt the hot tears wet his neck and the hollows of his neck, and he remained motionless, suspended through one of man's eternities. Only now it had become indispensable to him to have her face pressed close to him; he could never let her go again. He could never let her head go away from the close clutch of his arm. He wanted to remain like that for ever, with his heart hurting him in a pain that was also life to him. Without knowing, he was looking down on her damp, soft brown hair.

Then, as it were suddenly, he smelt the horrid stagnant smell of that water. And at the same moment she drew away from him and looked at him. Her eyes were wistful and unfathomable. He was afraid of them, and he fell to kissing her, not knowing what he was doing. He wanted her eyes not to have that terrible, wistful, unfathomable look.

When she turned her face to him again, a faint delicate flush was glowing, and there was again dawning that terrible shining of joy in her eyes, which really terrified him, and yet which he now wanted to see, because he feared the look of doubt still more.

'You love me?' she said, rather faltering.

'Yes.' The word cost him a painful effort. Not because it wasn't true. But because it was too newly true, the *saying* seemed to tear open again his newly-torn heart. And he hardly wanted it to be true, even now.

She lifted her face to him, and he bent forward and kissed her on the mouth, gently, with the one kiss that is an eternal pledge. And as he kissed her his heart strained again in his breast. He never intended to love her. But now it was over. He had crossed over the gulf to her, and all that he had left behind had shrivelled and become void.

After the kiss, her eyes again slowly filled with tears. She sat still, away from him, with her face drooped aside, and her hands folded in her lap. The tears fell very slowly. There was complete silence. He too sat there motionless and silent on the hearth-rug. The strange pain of his heart that was broken seemed to consume him. That he should love her? That this was love! That he should be ripped open in this way! Him, a doctor! How they would all jeer if they knew! It was agony to him to think they might know.

In the curious naked pain of the thought he looked again to her. She was sitting there drooped into a muse. He saw a tear fall, and his heart flared hot. He saw for the first time that one of her shoulders was quite uncovered, one arm bare, he could see one of her small breasts; dimly, because it had become almost dark in the room.

'Why are you crying?' he asked, in an altered voice.

She looked up at him, and behind her tears the consciousness of her situation for the first time brought a dark look of shame to her eyes.

'I'm not crying, really,' she said, watching him, half frightened.

He reached his hand, and softly closed it on her bare arm.

'I love you! I love you!' he said in a soft, low vibrating voice, unlike himself.

She shrank, and dropped her head. The soft, penetrating grip of his hand on her arm distressed her. She looked up at him.

'I want to go,' she said. 'I want to go and get you some dry things.'

'Why?' he said. 'I'm all right.'

'But I want to go,' she said. 'And I want you to change your things.'

He released her arm, and she wrapped herself in the blanket, looking at him rather frightened. And still she did not rise.

'Kiss me,' she said wistfully.

He kissed her, but briefly, half in anger.

Then, after a second, she rose nervously, all mixed up in the blanket. He watched her in her confusion as she tried to extricate herself and wrap herself up so that she could walk. He watched her relentlessly, as she knew. And as she went, the blanket trailing, and as he saw a glimpse of her feet and her white leg, he tried to remember her as she was when he had wrapped her in the blanket. But then he didn't want to remember, because she had been nothing to him then, and his nature revolted from remembering her as she was when she was nothing to him.

A tumbling, muffled noise from within the dark house startled him. Then he heard her voice: 'There are clothes.' He rose and went to the foot of the stairs, and gathered up the garments she had thrown down. Then he came back to the fire, to rub himself down and dress. He grinned at his own appearance when he had finished.

The fire was sinking, so he put on coal. The house was now quite dark, save for the light of a street-lamp that shone in faintly from beyond the holly trees. He lit the gas with matches he found on the mantelpiece. Then he emptied the pockets of his own clothes, and threw all his wet things in a heap into the scullery. After which he gathered up her sodden clothes, gently, and put them in a separate heap on the copper-top in the scullery.

It was six o'clock on the clock. His own watch had stopped. He ought to go back to the surgery. He waited, and still she did not come down. So he went to the foot of the stairs and called:

'I shall have to go.'

Almost immediately he heard her coming down. She had on her best dress of black voile, and her hair was tidy, but still damp. She looked at him—and in spite of herself, smiled.

'I don't like you in those clothes,' she said.

'Do I look a sight?' he answered.

They were shy of one another.

'I'll make you some tea,' she said.

'No, I must go.'

'Must you?' And she looked at him again with the wide, strained, doubtful eyes. And again, from the pain of his breast, he knew how he loved her. He went and bent to kiss her, gently, passionately, with his heart's painful kiss.

'And my hair smells so horrible,' she murmured in distraction. 'And I'm so awful, I'm so awful! Oh no, I'm too awful.' And she broke into bitter, heart-broken sobbing. 'You can't want to love me, I'm horrible.'

'Don't be silly, don't be silly,' he said, trying to comfort her, kissing her, holding her in his arms. 'I want you, I want to marry you, we're going to be married, quickly, quickly—to-morrow if I can.'

But she only sobbed terribly, and cried:

'I feel awful. I feel awful. I feel I'm horrible to you.'

'No, I want you, I want you,' was all he answered, blindly, with that terrible intonation which frightened her almost more than her horror lest he should *not* want her.

1922

The Rocking-horse Winner

THERE was a woman who was beautiful, who started with all the advantages, yet she had no luck. She married for love, and the love turned to dust. She had bonny children, yet she felt they had been thrust upon her, and she could not love them. They looked at her coldly, as if they were finding fault with her. And hurriedly she felt she must cover up some fault in herself. Yet what it was that she must cover up she never knew. Nevertheless, when her children were present, she always felt the centre of her heart go hard. This troubled her, and in her manner she was all the more gentle and anxious for her children, as if she loved them very much. Only she herself knew that at the centre of her heart was a hard little place that could not feel love, no, not for anybody. Everybody else said of her: 'She is such a good mother. She adores her children.' Only she herself, and her children themselves, knew it was not so. They read it in each other's eyes.

There were a boy and two little girls. They lived in a pleasant house, with a garden, and they had discreet servants, and felt themselves superior to anyone in the neighbourhood.

Although they lived in style, they felt always an anxiety in the house. There was never enough money. The mother had a small income, and the father had a small income, but not nearly enough for the social position which they had to keep up. The father went into town to some office. But though he had good prospects, these prospects never materialized. There was always the grinding sense of the shortage of money, though the style was always kept up.

At last the mother said: 'I will see if *I* can't make something.' But she did not know where to begin. She racked her brains, and tried this thing and the other, but could not find anything successful. The failure made deep lines comes into her face. Her children were growing up, they would have to go to school. There must be more money, there must be more money. The father, who was always very handsome and expensive in his tastes, seemed as if he never *would* be able to do anything worth doing. And the mother, who had a great belief in herself, did not succeed any better, and her tastes were just as expensive.

And so the house came to be haunted by the unspoken phrase: *There must be more money! There must be more money!* The children could hear it all the time, though nobody said it aloud. They heard it at Christmas, when the expensive and splendid toys filled the nursery. Behind the shining modern rocking-horse, behind the smart doll's house, a voice would start whispering: 'There *must* be more money! There *must* be more money!' And the children would stop playing, to listen for a moment. They would look into each other's eyes, to see if they had all heard. And each one saw in the eyes of the other two that they too had heard. 'There *must* be more money! There *must* be more money!'

It came whispering from the springs of the still-swaying rocking-horse, and even the horse, bending his wooden, champing head, heard it. The big doll, sitting so pink and smirking in her new pram, could hear it quite plainly, and seemed to be smirking all the more self-consciously because of it. The foolish puppy, too, that took the place of the teddy-bear, he was looking so extraordinarily foolish for no other reason but that he heard the secret whisper all over the house: 'There *must* be more money!'

Yet nobody ever said it aloud. The whisper was everywhere, and therefore no one spoke it. Just as no one ever says: 'We are breathing!' in spite of the fact that breath is coming and going all the time.

'Mother,' said the boy Paul one day, 'why don't we keep a car of our own? Why do we always use uncle's, or else a taxi?'

'Because we're the poor members of the family,' said the mother.

'But why *are* we, mother?'

'Well—I suppose,' she said slowly and bitterly, 'it's because your father has no luck.'

The boy was silent for some time.

'Is luck money, mother?' he asked, rather timidly.

'No, Paul. Not quite. It's what causes you to have money.'

'Oh!' said Paul vaguely. 'I thought when Uncle Oscar said *filthy lucker,* it meant money.'

'*Filthy lucre* does mean money,' said the mother. 'But it's lucre, not luck.'

'Oh!' said the boy. 'Then what *is* luck, mother?'

'It's what causes you to have money. If you're lucky you have money. That's why it's better to be born lucky than rich. If you're rich, you may lose your money. But if you're lucky, you will always get more money.'

'Oh! Will you? And is father not lucky?'

'Very unlucky, I should say,' she said bitterly.

The boy watched her with unsure eyes.

'Why?' he asked.

'I don't know. Nobody ever knows why one person is lucky and another unlucky.'

'Don't they? Nobody at all? Does *nobody* know?'

'Perhaps God. But He never tells.'

'He ought to, then. And aren't you lucky either, mother?'

'I can't be, if I married an unlucky husband.'

'But by yourself, aren't you?'

'I used to think I was, before I married. Now I think I am very unlucky indeed.'

'Why?'

'Well—never mind! Perhaps I'm not really,' she said.

The child looked at her to see if she meant it. But he saw, by the lines of her mouth, that she was only trying to hide something from him.

'Well, anyhow,' he said stoutly, 'I'm a lucky person.'

'Why?' said his mother, with a sudden laugh.

He stared at her. He didn't even know why he had said it.

'God told me,' he asserted, brazening it out.

'I hope He did, dear!' she said, again with a laugh, but rather bitter.

'He did, mother!'

'Excellent!' said the mother, using one of her husband's exclamations.

The boy saw she did not believe him; or rather, that she paid no attention to his assertion. This angered him somewhere, and made him want to compel her attention.

He went off by himself, vaguely, in a childish way, seeking for the clue to 'luck'. Absorbed, taking no heed of other people, he went about with a sort of stealth, seeking inwardly for luck. He wanted luck, he wanted it, he wanted it. When the two girls were playing dolls in the nursery, he would sit on his big rocking-horse, charging madly into space, with a frenzy that made the little girls peer at him uneasily. Wildly the horse careered, the waving dark hair of the boy tossed, his eyes had a strange glare in them. The little girls dared not speak to him.

When he had ridden to the end of his mad little journey, he climbed down and stood in front of his rocking-horse, staring fixedly into its lowered face. Its red mouth was slightly open, its big eye was wide and glassy-bright.

'Now!' he would silently command the snorting steed. 'Now, take me to where there is luck! Now take me!'

And he would slash the horse on the neck with the little whip he had asked Uncle Oscar for. He *knew* the horse could take him to where there was luck, if only he forced it. So he would mount again and start on his furious ride, hoping at last to get there. He knew he could get there.

'You'll break your horse, Paul!' said the nurse.

'He's always riding like that! I wish he'd leave off!' said his elder sister Joan.

But he only glared down on them in silence. Nurse gave him up. She could make nothing of him. Anyhow, he was growing beyond her.

One day his mother and his Uncle Oscar came in when he was on one of his furious rides. He did not speak to them.

'Hallo, you young jockey! Riding a winner?' said his uncle.

'Aren't you growing too big for a rocking-horse? You're not a very little boy any longer, you know,'' said his mother.

But Paul only gave a blue glare from his big, rather close-set eyes. He would speak to nobody when he was in full tilt. His mother watched him with an anxious expression on her face.

At last he suddenly stopped forcing his horse into the mechanical gallop and slid down.

'Well, I got there!' he announced fiercely, his blue eyes still flaring, and his sturdy long legs straddling apart.

'Where did you get to?' asked his mother.

'Where I wanted to go,' he flared back at her.

'That's right, son!' said Uncle Oscar. 'Don't you stop till you get there. What's the horse's name?'

'He doesn't have a name,' said the boy.

'Gets on without all right?' asked the uncle.

'Well, he has different names. He was called Sansovino last week.'

'Sansovino, eh? Won the Ascot. How did you know this name?'

'He always talks about horse-races with Bassett,' said Joan.

The uncle was delighted to find that his small nephew was posted with all the racing news. Bassett, the young gardener, who had been wounded in the left foot in the war and had got his present job through Oscar Cresswell, whose batman he had been, was a perfect blade of the 'turf'. He lived in the racing events, and the small boy lived with him.

Oscar Cresswell got it all from Bassett.

'Master Paul comes and asks me, so I can't do more than tell him, sir,'' said Bassett, his face terribly serious, as if he were speaking of religious matters.

'And does he ever put anything on a horse he fancies?'

'Well—I don't want to give him away—he's a young sport, a fine sport, sir. Would you mind asking him himself? He sort of takes a pleasure in it, and perhaps he'd feel I was giving him away, sir, if you don't mind.'

Bassett was serious as church.

The uncle went back to his nephew and took him off for a ride in the car.

'Say, Paul, old man, do you ever put anything on a horse?'' the uncle asked.

The boy watched the handsome man closely.

'Why, do you think I oughtn't to?' he parried.

'Not a bit of it! I thought perhaps you might give me a tip for the Lincoln.'

The car sped on into the country, going down to Uncle Oscar's place in Hampshire.

'Honour bright?' said the nephew.

'Honour bright, son!' said the uncle.

'Well, then, Daffodil.'

'Daffodil! I doubt it, sonny. What about Mirza?'

'I only know the winner,' said the boy. 'That's Daffodil.'

'Daffodil, eh?'

There was a pause. Daffodil was an obscure horse comparatively.

'Uncle!'

'Yes, son?'

'You won't let it go any further, will you? I promised Bassett.'

'Bassett be damned, old man! What's he got to do with it?'

'We're partners. We've been partners from the first. Uncle, he lent me my first five shillings, which I lost. I promised him, honour bright, it was only between me and him; only you gave me that ten-shilling note I started winning with, so I thought you were lucky. You won't let it go any further, will you?

The boy gazed at his uncle from those big, hot, blue eyes, set rather close together. The uncle stirred and laughed uneasily.

'Right you are, son! I'll keep your tip private. Daffodil, eh? How much are you putting on him?'

'All except twenty pounds,' said the boy. 'I keep that in reserve.'

The uncle thought it a good joke.

'You keep twenty pounds in reserve, do you, you young romancer? What are you betting, then?'

'I'm betting three hundred,' said the boy gravely. 'But it's between you and me, Uncle Oscar! Honour bright?'

The uncle burst into a roar of laughter.

'It's between you and me all right, you young Nat Gould,' he said, laughing. 'But where's your three hundred?'

'Bassett keeps it for me. We're partners.'

'You are, are you! And what is Bassett putting on Daffodil?'

'He won't go quite as high as I do, I expect. Perhaps he'll go a hundred and fifty.'

'What, pennies?' laughed the uncle.

'Pounds,' said the child, with a surprised look at his uncle. 'Bassett keeps a bigger reserve than I do.'

Between wonder and amusement Uncle Oscar was silent. He pursued the matter no further, but he determined to take his nephew with him to the Lincoln races.

'Now, son,' he said, 'I'm putting twenty on Mirza, and I'll put five on for you on any horse you fancy. What's your pick?'

'Daffodil, uncle.'

'No, not the fiver on Daffodil!'

'I should if it was my own fiver,' said the child.

'Good! Good! Right you are! A fiver for me and a fiver for you on Daffodil.'

The child had never been to a race-meeting before, and his eyes were blue fire. He pursed his mouth tight and watched. A Frenchman just in front had put his money on Lancelot. Wild with excitement, he flayed his arms up and down, yelling '*Lancelot! Lancelot!*' in his French accent.

Daffodil came in first, Lancelot second, Mirza third. The child, flushed and with eyes blazing, was curiously serene. His uncle brought him four five-pound notes, four to one.

'What am I to do with these?' he cried, waving them before the boy's eyes.

'I suppose we'll talk to Bassett,' said the boy. 'I expect I have fifteen hundred now; and twenty in reserve; and this twenty.'

His uncle studied him for some moments.

'Look here, son!' he said. 'You're not serious about Bassett and that fifteen hundred, are you?'

'Yes, I am. But it's between you and me, uncle. Honour bright?'

'Honour bright all right, son! But I must talk to Bassett.'

'If you'd like to be a partner, uncle, with Bassett and me, we could all be partners. Only, you'd have to promise, honour bright, uncle, not to let it go beyond us three. Bassett and I are lucky, and you must be lucky, because it was your ten shillings I started winning with. . . .'

Uncle Oscar took both Bassett and Paul into Richmond Park for an afternoon, and there they talked.

'It's like this, you see, sir,' Bassett said. 'Master Paul would get me talking about racing events, spinning yarns, you know, sir. And he was always keen on knowing if I'd made or if I'd lost. It's about a year since, now, that I put five shillings on Blush of Dawn for him: and we lost. Then the luck turned, with that ten shillings he had from you: that we put on Singhalese. And since that time, it's been pretty steady, all things considering. What do you say, Master Paul?'

'We're all right when we're sure,' said Paul. 'It's when we're not quite sure that we go down.'

'Oh, but we're careful then,' said Bassett.

'But when are you *sure?*' smiled Uncle Oscar.

'It's Master Paul, sir,' said Bassett in a secret, religious voice. 'It's as if he had it from heaven. Like Daffodil, now, for the Lincoln. That was as sure as eggs.'

'Did you put anything on Daffodil?' asked Oscar Cresswell.

'Yes, sir. I made my bit.'

'And my nephew?'

Bassett was obstinately silent, looking at Paul.

'I made twelve hundred, didn't I, Bassett? I told uncle I was putting three hundred on Daffodil.'

'That's right,' said Bassett, nodding.

'But where's the money?' asked the uncle.

'I keep it safe locked up, sir. Master Paul he can have it any minute he likes to ask for it.'

'What, fifteen hundred pounds?'

'And twenty! And forty, that is, with the twenty he made on the course.'

'It's amazing!' said the uncle.

'If Master Paul offers you to be partners, sir, I would, if I were you: if you'll excuse me,' said Bassett.

Oscar Cresswell thought about it.

'I'll see the money,' he said.

They drove home again, and sure enough, Bassett came round to the garden-house with fifteen hundred pounds in notes. The twenty pounds reserve was left with Joe Glee, in the Turf Commission deposit.

'You see, it's all right, uncle, when I'm *sure!* Then we go strong, for all we're worth. Don't we, Bassett?'

'We do that, Master Paul.'

'And when are you sure?' said uncle, laughing.

'Oh, well, sometimes I'm *absolutely* sure, like about Daffodil,' said the boy; 'and sometimes I have an idea; and sometimes I haven't even an idea, have I, Bassett? Then we're careful, because we mostly go down.'

'You do, do you! And when you're sure, like about Daffodil, what makes you sure, sonny?'

'Oh, well, I don't know,' said the boy uneasily. 'I'm sure, you know, uncle; that's all.'

'It's as if he had it from heaven, sir,' Bassett reiterated.

'I should say so!' said the uncle.

But he became a partner. And when the Leger was coming on Paul was 'sure' about Lively Spark, which was a quite inconsiderable horse. The boy insisted on putting a thousand on the horse, Bassett went for five hundred, and Oscar Cresswell two hundred. Lively Spark came in first, and the betting had been ten to one against him. Paul had made ten thousand.

'You see,' he said, 'I was absolutely sure of him.'

Even Oscar Cresswell had cleared two thousand.

'Look here, son,' he said, 'this sort of thing makes me nervous.'

'It needn't, uncle! Perhaps I shan't be sure again for a long time.'

'But what are you going to do with your money?' asked the uncle.

'Of course,' said the boy, 'I started it for mother. She said she had no luck, because father is unlucky, so I thought if *I* was lucky, it might stop whispering.'

'What might stop whispering?'

'Our house. I *hate* our house for whispering.'

'What does it whisper?'

'Why—why'—the boy fidgeted—'why, I don't know. But it's always short of money, you know, uncle.'

'I know it, son, I know it.'

'You know people send mother writs, don't you, uncle?'

'I'm afraid I do,' said the uncle.

'And then the house whispers, like people laughing at you behind your back. It's awful, that is! I thought if I was lucky—'

'You might stop it,' added the uncle.

The boy watched him with big blue eyes, that had an uncanny cold fire in them, and he said never a word.

'Well, then!' said the uncle. 'What are we doing?'

'I shouldn't like mother to know I was lucky,' said the boy.

'Why not, son?'

'She'd stop me.'

'I don't think she would.'

Oh!'—and the boy writhed in an odd way—'I *don't* want her to know, uncle.'

'All right, son! We'll manage it without her knowing.'

They managed it very easily. Paul, at the other's suggestion, handed over five thousand pounds to his uncle, who deposited it with the family lawyer, who was then to inform Paul's mother that a relative had put five thousand pounds into his hands, which sum was to be paid out a thousand pounds at a time, on the mother's birthday, for the next five years.

'So she'll have a birthday present of a thousand pounds for five successive years," said Uncle Oscar. 'I hope it won't make it all the harder for her later.'

Paul's mother had her birthday in November. The house had been 'whispering' worse than ever lately, and even in spite of his luck, Paul could not bear up against it. He was very anxious to see the effect of the birthday letter, telling his mother about the thousand pounds.

When there were no visitors, Paul now took his meals with his parents, as he was beyond the nursery control. His mother went into town nearly every day. She had discovered that she had an odd knack of sketching furs and dress materials, so she worked secretly in the studio of a friend who was the chief 'artist' for the leading drapers. She drew the figures of ladies in furs and ladies in silk and sequins for the newspaper advertisements. This young woman artist earned several thousand pounds a year, but Paul's mother only made several hundreds, and she was again dissatisfied. She so wanted to be first in something, and she did not succeed, even in making sketches for drapery advertisements.

She was down to breakfast on the morning of her birthday. Paul watched her face as she read her letters. He knew the lawyer's letter. As his mother read it, her face hardened and became more expressionless. Then a cold, determined look came on her mouth. She hid the letter under the pile of others, and said not a word about it.

'Didn't you have anything nice in the post for your birthday, mother?' said Paul.

'Quite moderately nice,' she said, her voice cold and absent.

She went away to town without saying more.

But in the afternoon Uncle Oscar appeared. He said Paul's mother had had a long interview with the lawyer, asking if the whole five thousand could not be advanced at once, as she was in debt.

'What do you think, uncle?' said the boy.

'I leave it to you, son.'

'Oh, let her have it, then! We can get some more with the other,' said the boy.

'A bird in the hand is worth two in the bush, laddie!' said Uncle Oscar.

'But I'm sure to *know* for the Grand National; or the Lincolnshire; or else the Derby. I'm sure to know for one of them,' said Paul.

So Uncle Oscar signed the agreement, and Paul's mother touched the whole five thousand. Then something very curious happened. The voices in the house suddenly went mad, like a chorus of frogs on a spring evening. There were certain new furnishings, and Paul had a tutor. He was *really* going to Eton, his father's school, in the following autumn. There were flowers in the winter, and a blossoming of the luxury Paul's mother had been used to. And yet the voices in the house, behind the sprays of mimosa and almond-blossom, and from under the piles of iridescent cushions, simply trilled and screamed in a sort of ecstasy: 'There *must* be more money? Oh-h-h; there *must* be more money. Oh, now, now-w! Now-w-w—there *must* be more money!—more than ever! More than ever!'

It frightened Paul terribly. He studied away at his Latin and Greek with his tutor. But his intense hours were spent with Bassett. The Grand National had gone by: he had not 'known', and had lost a hundred pounds. Summer was at hand. He was in agony for the Lincoln. But even for the Lincoln he didn't 'know', and he lost fifty pounds. He became wild-eyed and strange, as if something were going to explode in him.

'Let it alone, son! Don't you bother about it!' urged Uncle Oscar. But it was as if the boy couldn't really hear what his uncle was saying.

'I've got to know for the Derby! I've got to know for the Derby!' the child reiterated, his big blue eyes blazing with a sort of madness.

His mother noticed how overwrought he was.

'You'd better go to the seaside. Wouldn't you like to go now to the seaside, instead of waiting? I think you'd better,' she said, looking down at him anxiously, her heart curiously heavy because of him.

But the child lifted his uncanny blue eyes.

'I couldn't possibly go before the Derby, mother!' he said. 'I couldn't possibly!'

'Why not?' she said, her voice becoming heavy when she was opposed. 'Why not? You can still go from the seaside to see the Derby with your Uncle Oscar, if that's what you wish. No need for you to wait here. Besides, I think you care too much about these races. It's a bad sign. My family has been a gambling family, and you won't know till you grow up how much damage it has done. But it has done damage. I shall have to send Bassett away, and ask Uncle Oscar not to talk racing to you, unless you promise to be reasonable about it: go away to the seaside and forget it. You're all nerves!'

'I'll do what you like, mother, so long as you don't send me away till after the Derby,' the boy said.

'Send you away from where? Just from this house?'

'Yes,' he said, gazing at her.

'Why, you curious child, what makes you care about this house so much, suddenly? I never knew you loved it.'

He gazed at her without speaking. He had a secret within a secret, something he had not divulged, even to Bassett or to his Uncle Oscar.

But his mother, after standing undecided and a little bit sullen for some moments, said:

'Very well, then! Don't go to the seaside till after the Derby, if you don't wish it. But promise me you won't let your nerves go to pieces. Promise you won't think so much about horse-racing and *events,* as you call them!'

'Oh no,' said the boy casually. 'I won't think much about them, mother. You needn't worry. I wouldn't worry, mother, if I were you.'

'If you were me and I were you,' said his mother, 'I wonder what we *should* do!'

'But you know you needn't worry, mother, don't you?' the boy repeated.

'I should be awfully glad to know it,' she said wearily.

'Oh, well, you *can,* you know. I mean, you *ought* to know you needn't worry,' he insisted.

'Ought I? Then I'll see about it,' she said.

Paul's secret of secrets was his wooden horse, that which had no name. Since he was emancipated from a nurse and a nursery-governess, he had had his rocking-horse removed to his own bedroom at the top of the house.

'Surely you're too big for a rocking-horse!' his mother had remonstrated.

'Well, you see, mother, till I can have a *real* horse, I like to have *some* sort of animal about,' had been his quaint answer.

'Do you feel he keeps you company?' she laughed.

'Oh yes! He's very good, he always keeps me company, when I'm there,' said Paul.

So the horse, rather shabby, stood in an arrested prance in the boy's bedroom.

The Derby was drawing near, and the boy grew more and more tense. He hardly heard what was spoken to him, he was very frail, and his eyes were really uncanny. His mother had sudden strange seizures of uneasiness about him. Sometimes, for half an hour, she would feel a sudden anxiety about him that was almost anguish. She wanted to rush to him at once, and know he was safe.

Two nights before the Derby, she was at a big party in town, when one of her rushes of anxiety about her boy, her first-born, gripped her heart till she could hardly speak. She fought with the feeling, might and main, for she believed in common sense. But it was too strong. She had to leave the dance and go downstairs to telephone to the country. The children's nursery-governess was terribly surprised and startled at being rung up in the night.

'Are the children all right, Miss Wilmot?'

'Oh yes, they are quite all right.'

'Master Paul? Is he all right?'

'He went to bed as right as a trivet. Shall I run up and look at him?'

'No,' said Paul's mother reluctantly. 'No! Don't trouble. It's all right. Don't sit up. We shall be home fairly soon.' She did not want her son's privacy intruded upon.

'Very good,' said the governess.

It was about one o'clock when Paul's mother and father drove up to their house. All was still. Paul's mother went to her room and slipped off her white fur cloak. She had told her maid not to wait up for her. She heard her husband downstairs, mixing a whisky and soda.

And then, because of the strange anxiety at her heart, she stole upstairs to her son's room. Noiselessly she went along the upper corridor. Was there a faint noise? What was it?

She stood, with arrested muscles, outside his door, listening. There was a strange, heavy, and yet not loud noise. Her heart stood still. It was a soundless noise, yet rushing and powerful. Something huge, in violent, hushed motion. What was it? What in God's name was it? She ought to know. She felt that she knew the noise. She knew what it was.

Yet she could not place it. She couldn't say what it was. And on and on it went, like a madness.

Softly, frozen with anxiety and fear, she turned the door-handle.

The room was dark. Yet in the space near the window, she heard and saw something plunging to and fro. She gazed in fear and amazement.

Then suddenly she switched on the light, and saw her son, in his green pyjamas, madly surging on the rocking-horse. The blaze of light suddenly lit him up, as he urged the wooden horse, and lit her up, as she stood, blonde, in her dress of pale green and crystal, in the doorway.

'Paul!' she cried. 'Whatever are you doing?'

'It's Malabar!' he screamed in a powerful, strange voice. 'It's Malabar!'

His eyes blazed at her for one strange and senseless second, as he ceased urging his wooden horse. Then he fell with a crash to the ground, and she, all her tormented motherhood flooding upon her, rushed to gather him up.

But he was unconscious, and unconscious he remained, with some brain-fever. He talked and tossed, and his mother sat stonily by his side.

'Malabar! It's Malabar! Bassett, Bassett, I *know!* It's Malabar!'

So the child cried, trying to get up and urge the rocking-horse that gave him his inspiration.

'What does he mean by Malabar?' asked the heart-frozen mother.

'I don't know,' said the father stonily.

'What does he mean by Malabar?' she asked her brother Oscar.

'It's one of the horses running for the Derby,' was the answer.

And, in spite of himself, Oscar Cresswell spoke to Bassett, and himself put a thousand on Malabar: at fourteen to one.

The third day of the illness was critical: they were waiting for a change. The boy, with his rather long, curly hair, was tossing ceaselessly on the pillow. He neither slept nor regained consciousness, and his eyes were like blue stones. His mother sat, feeling her heart gone, turned actually into a stone.

In the evening, Oscar Cresswell did not come, but Bassett sent a message, saying could he come up for one moment, just one moment? Paul's mother was very angry at the intrusion, but on second thoughts she agreed. The boy was the same. Perhaps Bassett might bring him to consciousness.

The gardener, a shortish fellow with a little brown moustache and sharp little brown eyes, tiptoed into the room, touched his imaginary cap to Paul's mother, and stole to the bedside, staring with glittering, smallish eyes at the tossing, dying child.

'Master Paul!' he whispered. 'Master Paul! Malabar came in first all right, a clean win. I did as you told me. You've made over seventy thousand pounds, you have; you've got over eighty thousand. Malabar came in all right, Master Paul.'

'Malabar! Malabar! Did I say Malabar, mother? Did I say Malabar? Do you think I'm lucky, mother? I knew Malabar, didn't I? Over eighty thousand pounds! I call that lucky, don't you, mother? Over eighty thousand pounds! I knew, didn't I know I knew? Malabar came in all right. If I ride my horse till I'm sure, then I tell you, Bassett, you can go as high as you like. Did you go for all you were worth, Bassett?'

'I went a thousand on it, Master Paul.'

'I never told you, mother, that if I can ride my horse, and *get there,* then I'm absolutely sure—oh, absolutely! Mother, did I ever tell you? I *am* lucky!'

'No, you never did,' said his mother.

But the boy died in the night.

And even as he lay dead, his mother heard her brother's voice saying to her: 'My God, Hester, you're eighty-odd thousand to the good, and a poor devil of a son to the bad. But, poor devil, poor devil, he's best gone out of a life where he rides his rocking-horse to find a winner.'

1926

Katherine Mansfield

1888-1923

In one of her letters, Katherine Mansfield wrote: 'The artist takes a *long look* at life. He says softly, "So this is what life is, is it?" And he proceeds to express that. All the rest he leaves.' This formulation captures the essence of Mansfield's art: her sharply focused gaze, rendering details as precisely as possible, and the slice of life that each of her stories traces into a carefully shaped pattern. Although she made attempts at writing a novel, it was the short story that proved to be Mansfield's chosen form, accommodating her terse irony, her dissections of class, family, and relationship, and her evocations of natural setting, particularly of her beloved New Zealand.

Mansfield was born in Wellington, New Zealand, and spent her early years in the nearby village of Karoi. In 1903 she went to Queen's College in London and studied to become a cellist. When she returned to New Zealand in 1906 she found it oppressive and stifling and convinced her parents in 1908 to allow her to go back to London. She spent the rest of her life in Europe, always restlessly in search of a cure for the consumption that first afflicted her a few years after her return to London. Her first book of stories, *In A German Pension*, appeared in 1911; it was followed by four more books of stories during her lifetime. She died at thirty-four at the Gurdjieff Institute in France, where she had gone to seek a spiritual and physical cure for her ailments.

Describing 'At the Bay', Mansfield wrote that 'it's full of sand and seaweed, bathing dresses hanging over verandas, and sandshoes on window sills, and little pink "sea" convolvulus, and rather gritty sandwiches and the tide coming in. And it smells (oh, I *do* hope it smells) a little bit fishy.' Clearly much of the story's power derives from its evocation of the natural setting Mansfield took so many pains with, and she records how strongly the story took hold of her: 'It took me nearly a month to "recover" from *At the Bay*. I made at least three false starts. But I could not get away from the sound of the sea, and Beryl fanning her hair at the window. These things would not *die down*.' Her depiction of three generations of the Burnell family comprises a series of vignettes that offer sharp glimpses into children's, a mother's, and women's experience in the absence of men, culminating in Beryl's moment of longing and loneliness. The most intriguing element in the story may well be its recreation of an atmosphere in which desire, which seems as natural as the elements of the story's setting, is thwarted, distorted, or concealed.

In 'The Garden-Party', the rituals of the upper-class family as they prepare for the afternoon's festivities seem to provide the context for the ironic presentation of Laura's responses to the workmen setting up the marquee. The reactions of Laura and the family to the report of the fatal accident suggest the story's more complex perspective in Laura's inarticulate comments to her brother following her visit to the bereaved family.

'At the Bay' was first published in the January 1922 issue of *London Mercury*. 'The Garden-Party' was first published in three parts in the issues of 4, 11, and 22 February 1922 of the *Weekly Westminster Gazette*. Both stories were then collected in *The Garden-Party and Other Stories* (1922).

At the Bay

I

Very early morning. The sun was not yet risen, and the whole of Crescent Bay was hidden under a white sea-mist. The big bush-covered hills at the back were smothered. You could not see where they ended and the paddocks and bungalows began. The sandy road was gone and the paddocks and bungalows the other side of it; there were no white dunes covered with reddish grass beyond them; there was nothing to mark which was beach and where was the sea. A heavy dew had fallen. The grass was blue. Big drops hung on the bushes and did not fall; the silvery, fluffy toi-toi was limp on its long stalks, and all the marigolds and the pinks in the bungalow gardens were bowed to the earth with wetness. Drenched were the cold fuchsias, round pearls of dew lay on the flat nasturtium leaves. It looked as though the sea had beaten up softly in the darkness, as though one immense wave had come rippling, rippling—how far? Perhaps if you had waked up in the middle of the night you might have seen a big fish flicking in at the window and gone again. . . .

Ah-Aah! sounded the sleepy sea. And from the bush there came the sound of little streams flowing, quickly, lightly, slipping between the smooth stones, gushing into ferny basins and out again; and there was the splashing of big drops on large leaves, and something else—what was it?—a faint stirring and shaking, the snapping of a twig and then such silence that it seemed someone was listening.

Round the corner of Crescent Bay, between the piled-up masses of broken rock, a flock of sheep came pattering. They were huddled together, a small, tossing, woolly mass, and their thin, stick-like legs trotted along quickly as if the cold and the quiet had frightened them. Behind them an old sheep-dog, his soaking paws covered with sand, ran along with his nose to the ground, but carelessly, as if thinking of something else. And then in the rocky gateway the shepherd himself appeared. He was a lean, upright old man, in a frieze coat that was covered with a web of tiny drops, velvet trousers tied under the knee, and a wideawake with a folded blue handkerchief round the brim. One hand was crammed into his belt, the other grasped a beautifully smooth yellow stick. And as he walked, taking his time, he kept up a very soft light whistling, an airy, far-away fluting that sounded mournful and tender. The old dog cut an ancient caper or two and then drew up sharp, ashamed of his levity, and walked a few dignified paces by his master's side. The sheep ran forward in little pattering rushes; they began to bleat, and ghostly flocks and herds answered them from under the sea. 'Baa! Baaa!' For a time they seemed to be always on the same piece of ground. There ahead was stretched the sandy road with shallow puddles; the same soaking bushes showed on either side the same shadowy palings. Then something immense came into view; an enormous shock-haired giant with his arms stretched out. It was the big gum tree outside Mrs Stubbs's shop, and as they passed by there was a strong whiff of eucalyptus. And now big spots of light gleamed in the mist. The shepherd stopped whistling; he rubbed his red nose and wet beard on his wet sleeve and, screwing up his eyes, glanced in the direction of the sea. The sun was rising. It was marvellous how quickly the mist thinned, sped away, dissolved from the shallow plain, rolled up from the bush and was gone as if in a hurry to escape; big twists and curls jostled and shouldered each other as the silvery beams broadened. The far-away sky—a bright, pure blue—was reflected in the puddles, and the drops, swimming along the telegraph poles, flashed into points of light. Now the leaping, glittering sea was so bright it made one's eyes ache to look at it. The shepherd drew a pipe, the bowl as small as an acorn, out of his breast-pocket, fumbled for a chunk of speckled tobacco, pared off a few shavings and stuffed the bowl. He was a grave, fine-looking old man. As he lit up and the blue smoke wreathed his head, the dog, watching, looked proud of him.

'Baa! Baaa!' The sheep spread out into a fan. They were just clear of the summer colony before the first sleeper turned over and lifted a drowsy head; their cry sounded in the dreams of little children . . . who lifted their arms to drag down, to cuddle the darling little woolly lambs of sleep. Then the first inhabitant appeared; it was the Burnells' cat Florrie, sitting on the gatepost, far too early as usual, looking for their milk-girl. When she saw the old sheep-dog she sprang up quickly, arched her back, drew in her tabby head, and seemed to give a little fastidious shiver. 'Ugh! What a coarse, revolting creature!' said Florrie. But the old sheep-dog, not looking up, waggled past, flinging out his legs from side to side. Only one of his ears twitched to prove that he saw, and thought her a silly young female.

The breeze of morning lifted in the bush and the smell of leaves and wet black earth mingled with the sharp smell of the sea. Myriads of birds were singing. A goldfinch flew over the shepherd's head and, perching on the tiptop of a spray, it turned to the sun, ruffling its small breast feathers. And now they had passed the fisherman's hut, passed the charred-looking little *whare* where Leila the milk-girl lived with her old Gran. The sheep strayed over a yellow swamp and Wag, the sheep-dog, padded after, rounded them up and headed them for the steeper, narrower rocky pass that led out of Crescent Bay and towards Daylight Cove. 'Baa! Baaa!' Faint the cry came as they rocked along the fast-drying road. The shepherd put away his pipe, dropping it into his breast-pocket so that the little bowl hung over. And straightway the soft airy whistling began again. Wag ran out along a ledge of rock after something that smelled, and ran back again disgusted. Then pushing, nudging, hurrying, the sheep rounded the bend and the shepherd followed after out of sight.

II

A few moments later the back door of one of the bungalows opened, and a figure in a broad-striped bathing-suit flung down the paddock, cleared the stile, rushed through the tussock grass into the hollow, staggered up the sandy hillock, and raced for dear life over the big porous stones, over the cold, wet pebbles, on to the hard sand that gleamed like oil. Splish-Splosh! Splish-Splosh! The water bubbled round his legs as Stanley Burnell waded out exulting. First man in as usual! He'd beaten them all again. And he swooped down to souse his head and neck.

'Hail, brother! All hail, Thou Mighty One!' A velvety bass voice came booming over the water.

Great Scott! Damnation take it! Stanley lifted up to see a dark head bobbing far out and an arm lifted. It was Jonathan Trout—there before him! 'Glorious morning!' sang the voice.

'Yes, very fine!' said Stanley briefly. Why the dickens didn't the fellow stick to his part of the sea? Why should he come barging over to this exact spot? Stanley gave a kick, a lunge and struck out, swimming overarm. But Jonathan was a match for him. Up he came, his black hair sleek on his forehead, his short beard sleek.

'I had an extraordinary dream last night!' he shouted.

What was the matter with the man? This mania for conversation irritated Stanley beyond words. And it was always the same—always some piffle about a dream he'd had, or some cranky idea he'd got hold of, or some rot he'd been reading. Stanley turned over on his back and kicked with his legs till he was a living water-spout. But even then . . . 'I dreamed I was hanging over a terrifically high cliff, shouting to someone below.' You would be! thought Stanley. He could stick no more of it. He stopped splashing. 'Look here, Trout,' he said, 'I'm in rather a hurry this morning.'

'You're WHAT?' Jonathan was so surprised—or pretended to be—that he sank under the water, then reappeared again blowing.

'All I mean is,' said Stanley, 'I've no time to—to—to fool about. I want to get this over. I'm in a hurry. I've work to do this morning—see?'

Jonathan was gone before Stanley had finished. 'Pass, friend!' said the bass voice gently, and he slid away through the water with scarcely a ripple. . . . But curse the fellow! He'd ruined Stanley's bathe. What an unpractical idiot the man was! Stanley struck out to sea again, and then as quickly swam in again, and away he rushed up the beach. He felt cheated.

Jonathan stayed a little longer in the water. He floated, gently moving his hands like fins, and letting the sea rock his long, skinny body. It was curious, but in spite of everything he was fond of Stanley Burnell. True, he had a fiendish desire to tease him sometimes, to poke fun at him, but at bottom he was sorry for the fellow. There was something pathetic in his determination to make a job of everything. You couldn't help feeling he'd be caught out one day, and then what an almighty cropper he'd come! At that moment an immense wave lifted Jonathan, rode past him, and broke along the beach with a joyful sound. What a beauty! And now there came another. That was the way to live—carelessly, recklessly, spending oneself. He got on to his feet and began to wade towards the shore, pressing his toes into the firm, wrinkled sand. To take things easy, not to fight against the ebb and flow of life, but to give way to it—that was what was needed. It was this tension that was all wrong. To live—to live! And the perfect morning, so fresh and fair, basking in the light, as though laughing at its own beauty, seemed to whisper, 'Why not?'

But now he was out of the water Jonathan turned blue with cold. He ached all over; it was as though someone was wringing the blood out of him. And stalking up the beach, shivering, all his muscles tight, he too felt his bathe was spoilt. He'd stayed in too long.

III

Beryl was alone in the living-room when Stanley appeared, wearing a blue serge suit, a stiff collar, and a spotted tie. He looked almost uncannily clean and brushed; he was going to town for the day. Dropping into his chair, he pulled out his watch and put it beside his plate.

'I've just got twenty-five minutes,' he said. 'You might go and see if the porridge is ready, Beryl?'

'Mother's just gone for it,' said Beryl. She sat down at the table and poured out his tea.

'Thanks!' Stanley took a sip. 'Hallo!' he said in an astonished voice, 'you've forgotten the sugar.'

'Oh, sorry!' But even then Beryl didn't help him; she pushed the basin across. What did this mean? As Stanley helped himself his blue eyes widened; they seemed to quiver. He shot a quick glance at his sister-in-law and leaned back.

'Nothing wrong, is there?' he asked carelessly, fingering his collar.

Beryl's head was bent; she turned her plate in her fingers.

'Nothing,' said her light voice. Then she too looked up, and smiled at Stanley. 'Why should there be?'

'O-oh! No reason at all as far as I know. I thought you seemed rather—'

At that moment the door opened and the three little girls appeared, each carrying a porridge plate. They were dressed alike in blue jerseys and knickers; their brown legs were bare, and each had her hair plaited and pinned up in what was called a horse's tail. Behind them came Mrs Fairfield with the tray.

'Carefully, children,' she warned. But they were taking the very greatest care. They loved being allowed to carry things. 'Have you said good-morning to your father?'

'Yes, grandma.' They settled themselves on the bench opposite Stanley and Beryl.

'Good morning, Stanley!' Old Mrs Fairfield gave him his plate.

'Morning, mother! How's the boy?'

'Splendid! He only woke up once last night. What a perfect morning!' The old woman paused, her hand on the loaf of bread, to gaze out of the open door into the garden. The sea sounded. Through the wide-open window streamed the sun on to the yellow varnished walls and bare floor. Everything on the table flashed and glittered. In the middle there was an old salad bowl filled with yellow and red nasturtiums. She smiled, and a look of deep content shone in her eyes.

'You might *cut* me a slice of that bread, mother,' said Stanley. 'I've only twelve and a half minutes before the coach passes. Has anyone given my shoes to the servant girl?'

'Yes, they're ready for you.' Mrs Fairfield was quite unruffled.

'Oh, Kezia! Why are you such a messy child!' cried Beryl despairingly.

'Me, Aunt Beryl?' Kezia stared at her. What had she done now? She had only dug a river down the middle of her porridge, filled it, and was eating the banks away. But she did that every single morning, and no one had said a word up till now.

'Why can't you eat your food properly like Isabel and Lottie?' How unfair grown-ups are!

'But Lottie always makes a floating island, don't you, Lottie?'

'I don't,' said Isabel smartly. 'I just sprinkle mine with sugar and put on the milk and finish it. Only babies play with their food.'

Stanley pushed back his chair and got up.

'Would you get me those shoes, mother? And, Beryl, if you've finished, I wish you'd cut down to the gate and stop the coach. Run in to your mother, Isabel, and ask her where my bowler hat's been put. Wait a minute—have you children been playing with my stick?'

'No, father!'

'But I put it here,' Stanley began to bluster. 'I remember distinctly putting it in this corner. Now, who's had it? There's no time to lose. Look sharp! The stick's got to be found.'

Even Alice, the servant girl, was drawn into the chase. 'You haven't been using it to poke the kitchen fire with by any chance?'

Stanley dashed into the bedroom where Linda was lying. 'Most extraordinary thing. I can't keep a single possession to myself. They've made away with my stick, now!'

'Stick, dear? What stick?' Linda's vagueness on these occasions could not be real, Stanley decided. Would nobody sympathize with him?

'Coach! Coach, Stanley!' Beryl's voice cried from the gate.

Stanley waved his arm to Linda. 'No time to say good-bye!' he cried. And he meant that as a punishment to her.

He snatched his bowler hat, dashed out of the house, and swung down the garden path. Yes, the coach was there waiting, and Beryl, leaning over the open gate, was laughing up at somebody or other just as if nothing had happened. The heartlessness of women! The way they took it for granted it was your job to slave away for them while they didn't even take the trouble to see that your walking-stick wasn't lost. Kelly trailed his whip across the horses.

'Good-bye, Stanley,' called Beryl, sweetly and gaily. It was easy enough to say good-bye! And there she stood, idle, shading her eyes with her hand. The worst of it was Stanley had to shout good-bye too, for the sake of appearances. Then he saw her turn, give a little skip and run back to the house. She was glad to be rid of him!

Yes, she was thankful. Into the living-room she ran and called 'He's gone!' Linda cried from her room: 'Beryl! Has Stanley gone?' Old Mrs Fairfield appeared, carrying the boy in his little flannel coatee.

'Gone?'

'Gone!'

Oh, the relief, the difference it made to have the man out of the house. Their very voices were changed as they called to one another; they sounded warm and loving and as if they shared a secret. Beryl went over to the table. 'Have another cup of tea, mother. It's still hot.' She wanted, somehow, to celebrate the fact that they could do what they liked now. There was no man to disturb them; the whole perfect day was theirs.

'No, thank you, child,' said old Mrs Fairfield, but the way at that moment she tossed the boy up and said 'a-goos-a-goos-a-ga!' to him meant that she felt the same. The little girls ran into the paddock like chickens let out of a coop.

Even Alice, the servant girl, washing up the dishes in the kitchen, caught the infection and used the precious tank water in a perfectly reckless fashion.

'Oh, these men!' said she, and she plunged the teapot into the bowl and held it under the water even after it had stopped bubbling, as if it too was a man and drowning was too good for them.

IV

'Wait for me, Isa-bel! Kezia, wait for me!'

There was poor little Lottie, left behind again, because she found it so fearfully hard to get over the stile by herself. When she stood on the first step her knees began to wobble; she grasped the post. Then you had to put one leg over. But which leg? She never could decide. And when she did finally put one leg over with a sort of stamp of despair—then the feeling was awful. She was half in the paddock still and half in the tussock grass. She clutched the post desperately and lifted up her voice. 'Wait for me!'

'No, don't you wait for her, Kezia!' said Isabel. 'She's such a little silly. She's always making a fuss. Come on!' And she tugged Kezia's jersey. 'You can use my bucket if you come with me,' she said kindly. 'It's bigger than yours.' But Kezia couldn't leave Lottie all by herself. She ran back to her. By this time Lottie was very red in the face and breathing heavily.

'Here, put your other foot over,' said Kezia.

'Where?'

Lottie looked down at Kezia as if from a mountain height.

'Here where my hand is.' Kezia patted the place.

'Oh, *there* do you mean?' Lottie gave a deep sigh and put the second foot over.

'Now—sort of turn round and sit down and slide,' said Kezia.

'But there's nothing to sit down *on*, Kezia,' said Lottie.

She managed it at last, and once it was over she shook herself and began to beam.

'I'm getting better at climbing over stiles, aren't I, Kezia?'

Lottie's was a very hopeful nature.

The pink and the blue sunbonnet followed Isabel's bright red sunbonnet up that sliding, slipping hill. At the top they paused to decide where to go and to have a good stare at who was there already. Seen from behind, standing against the skyline, gesticulating largely with their spades, they looked like minute puzzled explorers.

The whole family of Samuel Josephs was there already with their lady-help, who sat on a camp-stool and kept order with a whistle that she wore tied round her neck, and a small cane with which she directed operations. The Samuel Josephs never played by themselves or managed their own game. If they did, it ended in the boys pouring water down the girls' necks or the girls trying to put little black crabs into the boys' pockets. So Mrs S. J. and the poor lady-help drew up what she called a 'brogramme' every morning to keep them 'abused and out of bischief.' It was all competitions or races or round games. Everything began with a piercing blast of the lady-help's whistle and ended with another. There were even prizes—large, rather dirty paper parcels which the lady-help with a sour little smile drew out of a bulging string kit. The Samuel Josephs fought fearfully for the prizes and cheated and pinched one another's arms—they were all expert pinchers. The only time the Burnell children ever played with them Kezia had got a prize, and when she undid three bits of paper she found a very small rusty button-hook. She couldn't understand why they made such a fuss. . . .

But they never played with the Samuel Josephs now or even went to their parties. The Samuel Josephs were always giving children's parties at the Bay and there was always the same food. A big washhand basin of very brown fruit salad, buns cut into four and a washhand jug full of something the lady-help called 'Limmonadear'. And you went away in the evening with half the frill torn off your frock or something spilled all down the front of your openwork pinafore, leaving the Samuel Josephs leaping like savages on their lawn. No! They were too awful.

On the other side of the beach, close down to the water, two little boys, their knickers rolled up, twinkled like spiders. One was digging, the other pattered in and out of the water, filling a small bucket. They were the Trout boys, Pip and Rags. But Pip was so busy digging and Rags was so busy helping that they didn't see their little cousins until they were quite close.

'Look!' said Pip. 'Look what I've discovered.' And he showed them an old, wet, squashed-looking boot. The three little girls stared.

'Whatever are you going to do with it?' asked Kezia.

'Keep it, of course!' Pip was very scornful. 'It's a find—see?'

Yes, Kezia saw that. All the same . . .

'There's lots of things buried in the sand,' explained Pip. 'They get chucked up from wrecks. Treasure. Why—you might find—'

'But why does Rags have to keep on pouring water in?' asked Lottie.

'Oh, that's to moisten it,' said Pip, 'to make the work a bit easier. Keep it up, Rags.'

And good little Rags ran up and down, pouring in the water that turned brown like cocoa.

'Here, shall I show you what I found yesterday?' said Pip mysteriously, and he stuck his spade into the sand. 'Promise not to tell.'

They promised.

'Say, cross my heart straight dinkum.'

The little girls said it.

Pip took something out of his pocket, rubbed it a long time on the front of his jersey, then breathed on it and rubbed it again.

'Now turn round!' he ordered.

They turned round.

'All look the same way! Keep still! Now!'

And his hand opened; he held up to the light something that flashed, that winked, that was a most lovely green.

'It's a nemeral,' said Pip solemnly.

'Is it really, Pip?' Even Isabel was impressed.

The lovely green thing seemed to dance in Pip's fingers. Aunt Beryl had a nemeral in a ring, but it was a very small one. This one was as big as a star and far more beautiful.

V

As the morning lengthened whole parties appeared over the sand-hills and came down on the beach to bathe. It was understood that at eleven o'clock the women and children of the summer colony had the sea to themselves. First the women undressed, pulled on their bathing dresses and covered their heads in hideous caps like sponge-bags; then the children were unbuttoned. The beach was strewn with little heaps of clothes and shoes; the big summer hats, with stones on them to keep them from blowing away, looked like immense shells. It was strange that even the sea seemed to sound differently when all those leaping, laughing figures ran into the waves. Old Mrs Fairfield, in a lilac cotton dress and a black hat tied under the chin, gathered her little brood and got them ready. The little Trout boys whipped their shirts over their heads, and away the five sped, while their grandma sat with one hand in her knitting-bag ready to draw out the ball of wool when she was satisfied they were safely in.

The firm compact little girls were not half so brave as the tender, delicate-looking little boys. Pips and Rags, shivering, crouching down, slapping the water, never hesitated. But Isabel, who could swim twelve strokes, and Kezia, who could nearly swim eight, only followed on the strict understanding they were not to be splashed. As for Lottie, she didn't follow at all. She liked to be left to go in her own way, please. And that way was to sit down at the edge of the water, her legs straight, her knees pressed together, and to make vague motions with her arms as if she expected to be wafted out to sea. But when a bigger wave than usual, an old whiskery one, came lolloping along in her direction, she scrambled to her feet with a face of horror and flew up the beach again.

'Here, mother, keep these for me, will you?'

Two rings and a thin gold chain were dropped into Mrs Fairfield's lap.

'Yes, dear. But aren't you going to bathe here?'

'No-o,' Beryl drawled. She sounded vague. 'I'm undressing further along. I'm going to bathe with Mrs Harry Kember.'

'Very well.' But Mrs Fairfield's lips set. She disapproved of Mrs Harry Kember. Beryl knew it.

Poor old mother, she smiled, as she skimmed over the stones. Poor old mother! Old! Oh, what joy, what bliss it was to be young. . . .

'You looked very pleased,' said Mrs Harry Kember. She sat hunched up on the stones, her arms round her knees, smoking.

'It's such a lovely day,' said Beryl, smiling down at her.

'Oh, my *dear*!' Mrs Harry Kember's voice sounded as though she knew better than that. But then her voice always sounded as though she knew something more about you than you did yourself. She was a long, strange-looking woman with narrow hands and feet. Her face, too, was long and narrow and exhausted-looking; even her fair curled fringe looked burnt out and withered. She was the only woman at the Bay who smoked, and she smoked incessantly, keeping the cigarette between her lips while she talked, and only taking it out when the ash was so long you could not understand why it did not fall. When she was not playing bridge—she played bridge every day of her life—she spent her time lying in the full glare of the sun. She could stand any amount of it; she never had enough. All the same, it did not seem to warm her. Parched, withered, cold, she lay stretched on the stones like a piece of toss-up driftwood. The women at the Bay thought she was very, very fast. Her lack of vanity, her slang, the way she treated men as though she was one of them, and the fact that she didn't care twopence about her house and called the servant Gladys 'Glad-eyes' was disgraceful. Standing on the veranda steps Mrs. Kember would call in her indifferent, tired voice, 'I say, Glad-eyes, you might heave me a handkerchief if I've got one, will you?' And Glad-eyes, a red bow in her hair instead of a cap, and white shoes, came running with an impudent smile. It was an absolute scandal! True, she had no children, and her husband . . . Here the voices were always raised; they became fervent. How can he have married her? How can he, how can he? It must have been money, of course, but even then!

Mrs Kember's husband was at least ten years younger than she was, and so incredibly handsome that he looked like a mask or a most perfect illustration in an American novel rather than a man. Black hair, dark blue eyes, red lips, a slow sleepy smile, a fine tennis player, a perfect dancer, and with it all a mystery. Harry Kember was like a man walking in his sleep. Men couldn't stand him, they couldn't get a word out of the chap; he ignored his wife just as she ignored him. How did he live? Of course there were stories, but such stories! They simply couldn't be told. The women he'd been seen with, the places he'd been seen in . . . but nothing was ever certain, nothing definite. Some of the women at the Bay privately thought he'd commit a murder one day. Yes, even while they talked to Mrs Kember and took in the awful concoction she was wearing, they saw her, stretched as she lay on the beach; but cold, bloody, and still with a cigarette stuck in the corner of her mouth.

Mrs Kember rose, yawned, unsnapped her belt buckle, and tugged at the tape of her blouse. And Beryl stepped out of her skirt and shed her jersey, and stood up in her short white petticoat, and her camisole with ribbon bows on the shoulders.

'Mercy on us,' said Mrs Harry Kember, 'what a little beauty you are!'

'Don't!' said Beryl softly; but, drawing off one stocking and then the other, she felt a little beauty.

'My dear—why not?' said Mrs Harry Kember, stamping on her own petticoat. Really—her underclothes! A pair of blue cotton knickers and a linen bodice that reminded one somehow of a pillow-case.. . . 'And you don't wear stays, do you?' She touched Beryl's waist, and Beryl sprang away with a small affected cry. Then 'Never!' she said firmly.

'Lucky little creature,' sighed Mrs Kember, unfastening her own.

Beryl turned her back and began the complicated movements of someone who is trying to take off her clothes and to pull on her bathing-dress all at one and the same time.

'Oh, my dear—don't mind me,' said Mrs Harry Kember. 'Why be shy? I shan't eat you. I shan't be shocked like those other ninnies.' And she gave her strange neighing laugh and grimaced at the other women.

But Beryl was shy. She never undressed in front of anybody. Was that silly? Mrs Harry Kember made her feel it was silly, even something to be ashamed of. Why be shy indeed! She glanced quickly at her friend standing so boldly in her torn chemise and lighting a fresh cigarette; and a quick, bold, evil feeling started up in her breast. Laughing recklessly, she drew on the limp, sandy-feeling bathing-dress that was not quite dry and fastened the twisted buttons.

'That's better,' said Mrs Harry Kember. They began to go down the beach together. 'Really, it's a sin for you to wear clothes, my dear. Somebody's got to tell you some day.'

The water was quite warm. It was that marvellous transparent blue, flecked with silver, but the sand at the bottom looked gold; when you kicked with your toes there rose a little puff of gold-dust. Now the waves just reached her breast. Beryl stood, her arms outstretched, gazing out, and as each wave came she gave the slightest little jump, so that it seemed it was the wave which lifted her so gently.

'I believe in pretty girls having a good time,' said Mrs Harry Kember. 'Why not? Don't you make a mistake, my dear. Enjoy yourself.' And suddenly she turned turtle, disappeared, and swam away quickly, quickly, like a rat. Then she flicked round and began swimming back. She was going to say something else. Beryl felt that she was being poisoned by this cold woman, but she longed to hear. But oh, how strange, how horrible! As Mrs Harry Kember came up close she looked, in her black waterproof bathing-cap, with her sleepy face lifted above the water, just her chin touching, like a horrible caricature of her husband.

VI

In a steamer chair, under a manuka tree that grew in the middle of the front grass patch, Linda Burnell dreamed the morning away. She did nothing. She looked up at the dark, close, dry leaves of the manuka, at the chinks of blue between, and now and again a tiny yellowish flower dropped on her. Pretty—yes, if you held one of those flowers on the palm of your hand and looked at it closely, it was an exquisite small thing. Each pale yellow petal shone as if each was the careful work of a loving hand. The tiny tongue in the centre gave it the shape of a bell. And when you turned it over the outside was a deep bronze colour. But as soon as they flowered, they fell and were scattered. You brushed them off your frock as you talked; the horrid little things got caught in one's hair. Why, then, flower at all? Who takes the trouble—or the joy—to make all these things that are wasted, wasted. . . . It was uncanny.

On the grass beside her, lying between two pillows, was the boy. Sound asleep he lay, his head turned away from his mother. His fine dark hair looked more like a shadow than like real hair, but his ear was a bright, deep coral. Linda clasped her hands above her head and crossed her feet. It was very pleasant to know that all these bungalows were empty, that everybody was down on the beach, out of sight, out of hearing. She had the garden to herself; she was alone.

Dazzling white the picotees shone; the golden-eyed marigolds glittered; the nasturtiums wreathed the veranda poles in green and gold flame. If only one had time to look at these flowers long enough, time to get over the sense of novelty and strangeness, time to know them! But as soon as one paused to part the petals, to discover the under-side of the leaf, along came Life and one was swept away. And, lying in her cane chair, Linda felt so light; she felt like a leaf. Along came Life like a wind and she was seized and shaken; she had to go. Oh dear, would it always be so? Was there no escape?

. . . Now she sat on the veranda of their Tasmanian home, leaning against her father's knee. And he promised, 'As soon as you and I are old enough, Linny, we'll cut off somewhere, we'll escape. Two boys together. I have a fancy I'd like to sail up a river in China.' Linda saw that river, very wide, covered with little rafts and boats. She saw the yellow hats of the boatmen and she heard their high, thin voices as they called . . .

'Yes, papa.'

But just then a very broad young man with bright ginger hair walked slowly past their house, and slowly, solemnly even, uncovered. Linda's father pulled her ear teasingly, in the way he had.

'Linny's beau,' he whispered.

'Oh, papa, fancy being married to Stanley Burnell!'

Well, she was married to him. And what was more she loved him. Not the Stanley whom every one saw, not the everyday one; but a timid, sensitive, innocent Stanley who knelt down every night to say his prayers, and who longed to be good. Stanley was simple. If he believed in people—as he believed in her, for instance—it was with his whole heart. He could not be disloyal; he could not tell a lie. And how terribly he suffered if he thought anyone—she—was not being dead straight, dead sincere with him! 'This is too subtle for me!' He flung out the words, but his open, quivering, distraught look was like the look of a trapped beast.

But the trouble was—here Linda felt almost inclined to laugh, though heaven knows it was no laughing matter—she saw *her* Stanley so seldom. There were glimpses, moments, breathing spaces of calm, but all the rest of the time it was like living in a house that couldn't be cured of the habit of catching fire, or a ship that got wrecked every day. And it was always Stanley who was in the thick of the danger. Her whole time was spent in rescuing him, and restoring him, and calming him down, and listening to his story. And what was left of her time was spent in the dread of having children.

Linda frowned; she sat up quickly in her steamer chair and clasped her ankles. Yes, that was her real grudge against life; that was what she could not understand. That was the question she asked and asked, and listened in vain for the answer. It was all very well to say it was the common lot of women to bear children. It wasn't true. She, for one, could prove that wrong. She was broken, made weak, her courage was gone, through childbearing. And what made it doubly hard to bear was, she did not love her children. It was useless pretending. Even if she had had the strength she never would have nursed and played with the little girls. No, it was as though a cold breath had chilled her through and through on each of those awful journeys; she had no warmth left to give them. As to the boy—well, thank heaven, mother had taken him; he was mother's, or Beryl's, or anybody's who wanted him. She had hardly held him in her arms. She was so indifferent about him, that as he lay there . . . Linda glanced down.

The boy had turned over. He lay facing her, and he was no longer asleep. His dark-blue, baby eyes were open; he looked as though he was peeping at his mother. And suddenly his face dimpled; it broke into a wide, toothless smile, a perfect beam, no less.

'I'm here!' that happy smile seemed to say. 'Why don't you like me?'

There was something so quaint, so unexpected about that smile that Linda smiled herself. But she checked herself and said to the boy coldly, 'I don't like babies.'

'Don't like babies?' The boy couldn't believe her. 'Don't like *me*?' He waved his arms foolishly at his mother.

Linda dropped off her chair on to the grass.

'Why do you keep on smiling?' she said severely. 'If you knew what I was thinking about, you wouldn't.'

But he only squeezed up his eyes, slyly, and rolled his head on the pillow. He didn't believe a word she said.

'We know all about that!' smiled the boy.

Linda was so astonished at the confidence of this little creature. . . . Ah no, be sincere. That was not what she felt; it was something far different, it was something so new, so . . . The tears danced in her eyes; she breathed in a small whisper to the boy, 'Hallo, my funny!'

But by now the boy had forgotten his mother. He was serious again. Something pink, something soft waved in front of him. He made a grab at it and it immediately disappeared. But when he lay back, another, like the first, appeared. This time he determined to catch it. He made a tremendous effort and rolled right over.

VII

The tide was out; the beach was deserted; lazily flopped the warm sea. The sun beat down, beat down hot and fiery on the fine sand, baking the grey and blue and black and white-veined pebbles. It sucked up the little drop of water that lay in the hollow of the curved shells; it bleached the pink convolvulus that threaded through and through the sand-hills. Nothing seemed to move but the small sand-hoppers. Pit-pit-pit! They were never still.

Over there on the weed-hung rocks that looked at low tide like shaggy beasts come down to the water to drink, the sunlight seemed to spin like a silver coin dropped into each of the small rock pools. They danced, they quivered, and minute ripples laved the porous shores. Looking down, bending over, each pool was like a lake with pink and blue houses clustered on the shores; and oh! the vast mountainous country behind those houses—the ravines, the passes, the dangerous creeks and fearful tracks that led to the water's edge. Underneath waved the sea-forest—pink thread-like trees, velvet anemones, and orange berry-spotted weeds. Now a stone on the bottom moved, rocked, and there was a glimpse of a black feeler; now a thread-like creature wavered by and was lost. Something was happening to the pink, waving trees; they were changing to a cold moonlight blue. And now there sounded the faintest 'plop'. Who made that sound? What was going on down there? And how strong, how damp the seaweed smelt in the hot sun. . . .

The green blinds were drawn in the bungalows of the summer colony. Over the verandas, prone on the paddock, flung over the fences, there were exhausted-looking bathing-dresses and rough striped towels. Each back window seemed to have a pair of sand-shoes on the sill and some lumps of rock or a bucket or a collection of pawa shells. The bush quivered in a haze of heat; the sandy road was empty except for the Trouts' dog Snooker, who lay stretched in the very middle of it. His blue eye was turned up, his legs stuck out stiffly, and he gave an occasional desperate sounding puff, as much as to say he had decided to make an end of it and was only waiting for some kind cart to come along.

'What are you looking at, my grandma? Why do you keep stopping and sort of staring at the wall?'

Kezia and her grandmother were taking their siesta together. The little girl, wearing only her short drawers and her under-bodice, her arms and legs bare, lay on one of the puffed-up pillows of her grandma's bed, and the old woman, in a white ruffled dressing-gown, sat in a rocker at the window, with a long piece of pink knitting in her lap. This room that they shared, like the other rooms of the bungalow, was of light varnished wood and the floor was bare. The furniture was of the shabbiest, the simplest. The dressing-table, for instance, was a packing-case in a sprigged muslin petticoat, and the mirror above was very strange; it was as though a little piece of forked lightning was imprisoned in it. On the table there stood a jar of sea-pinks, pressed so tightly together they looked more like a velvet pin-cushion, and a special shell which Kezia had given her grandma for a pin-tray, and another even more special which she had thought would make a very nice place for a watch to curl up in.

'Tell me, grandma,' said Kezia.

The old woman sighed, whipped the wool twice round her thumb, and drew the bone needle through. She was casting on.

'I was thinking of your Uncle William, darling,' she said quietly.

'My Australian Uncle William?' said Kezia. She had another.

'Yes, of course.'

'The one I never saw?'

'That was the one.'

'Well, what happened to him?' Kezia knew perfectly well, but she wanted to be told again.

'He went to the mines, and he got a sunstroke there and died,' said old Mrs Fairfield.

Kezia blinked and considered the picture again. . . . A little man fallen over like a tin soldier by the side of a big black hole.

'Does it make you sad to think about him, grandma?' She hated her grandma to be sad.

It was the old woman's turn to consider. Did it make her sad? To look back, back. To stare down the years, as Kezia had seen her doing. To look after *them* as a woman does, long after *they* were out of sight. Did it make her sad? No, life was like that.

'No, Kezia.'

'But why?' asked Kezia. She lifted one bare arm and began to draw things in the air. 'Why did Uncle William have to die? He wasn't old.'

Mrs Fairfield began counting the stitches in threes. 'It just happened,' she said in an absorbed voice.

'Does everybody have to die?' asked Kezia.

'Everybody!'

'*Me?*' Kezia sounded fearfully incredulous.

'Some day, my darling.'

'But, grandma.' Kezia waved her left leg and waggled the toes. They felt sandy. 'What if I just won't?'

The old woman sighed again and drew a long thread from the ball.

'We're not asked, Kezia,' she said sadly. 'It happens to all of us sooner or later.'

Kezia lay still thinking this over. She didn't want to die. It meant she would have to leave here, leave everywhere, for ever, leave—leave her grandma. She rolled over quickly.

'Grandma,' she said in a startled voice.

'What, my pet!'

'*You're* not to die.' Kezia was very decided.

'Ah, Kezia'—her grandma looked up and smiled and shook her head—'don't let's talk about it.'

'But you're not to. You couldn't leave me. You couldn't not be there.' This was awful. 'Promise me you won't ever do it, grandma,' pleaded Kezia.

The old woman went on knitting.

'Promise me! Say never!'

But still her grandma was silent.

Kezia rolled off the bed; she couldn't bear it any longer, and lightly she leapt on to her grandma's knees, clasped her hands round the old woman's throat, and began kissing her, under the chin, behind the ear, and blowing down her neck.

'Say never . . . say never . . . say never—' She gasped between the kisses. And then she began, very softly and lightly, to tickle her grandma.

'Kezia!' The old woman dropped her knitting. She swung back in the rocker. She began to tickle Kezia. 'Say never, say never, say never,' gurgled Kezia, while they lay there laughing in each other's arms. 'Come, that's enough, my squirrel! That's enough, my wild pony!' said old Mrs Fairfield, setting her cap straight. 'Pick up my knitting.'

Both of them had forgotten what the 'never' was about.

VIII

The sun was still full on the garden when the back door of the Burnells' shut with a bang and a very gay figure walked down the path to the gate. It was Alice, the servant girl, dressed for her afternoon out. She wore a white cotton dress with such large red spots on it, and so many that they made you shudder, white shoes, and a leghorn turned up under the brim with poppies. Of course she wore gloves, white ones, stained at the fastenings with iron-mould, and in one hand she carried a very dashed-looking sunshade which she referred to as her *perishall*.

Beryl, sitting in the window, fanning her freshly washed hair, thought she had never seen such a guy. If Alice had only blacked her face with a piece of cork before she started out the picture would have been complete. And where did a girl like that go to in a place like this? The heart-shaped Fijian fan beat scornfully at that lovely bright mane. She supposed Alice had picked up some horrible common larrikin and they'd go off into the bush together. Pity to make herself so conspicuous; they'd have hard work to hide with Alice in that rig-out.

But no, Beryl was unfair. Alice was going to tea with Mrs Stubbs, who'd sent her an 'invite' by the little boy who called for orders. She had taken ever such a liking to Mrs Stubbs ever since the first time she went to the shop to get something for her mosquitoes.

'Dear heart!' Mrs Stubbs had clapped her hand to her side. 'I never seen anyone so eaten. You might have been attacked by canningbals.'

Alice did wish there'd been a bit of life on the road though. Made her feel so queer, having nobody behind her. Made her feel all weak in the spine. She couldn't believe that someone wasn't watching her. And yet it was silly to turn round; it gave you away. She pulled up her gloves, hummed to herself and said to the distant gum tree, 'Shan't be long now.' But that was hardly company.

Mrs Stubbs's shop was perched on a little hillock just off the road. It had two big windows for eyes, a broad veranda for a hat, and the sign on the roof, scrawled MRS STUBBS'S, was like a little card stuck rakishly in the hat crown.

On the veranda there hung a long string of bathing-dresses, clinging together as though they'd just been rescued from the sea rather than waiting to go in, and beside them there hung a cluster of sand-shoes so extraordinarily mixed that to get at one pair you had to tear apart and forcibly separate at least fifty. Even then it was the rarest thing to find the left that belonged to the right. So many people had lost patience and gone off with one shoe that fitted and one that was a little too big. . . . Mrs Stubbs prided herself on keeping something of everything. The two windows, arranged in the form of precarious pyramids, were crammed so tight, piled so high, that it seemed only a conjuror could prevent them from toppling over. In the left-hand corner of one window, glued to the pane by four gelatine lozenges, there was—and there had been from time immemorial—a notice:

LOST! HANSOME GOLE BROOCH
SOLID GOLD
ON OR NEAR BEACH
REWARD OFFERED

Alice pressed open the door. The bell jangled, the red serge curtains parted, and Mrs Stubbs appeared. With her broad smile and the long bacon knife in her hand she looked like a friendly brigand. Alice was welcomed so warmly that she found it quite difficult to keep up her 'manners'. They consisted of persistent little coughs and hems, pulls at her gloves, tweaks at her skirt, and a curious difficulty in seeing what was set before her or understanding what was said.

Tea was laid on the parlour table—ham, sardines, a whole pound of butter, and such a large johnny cake that it looked like an advertisement for somebody's baking powder. But the Primus stove roared so loudly that it was useless to try to talk above it. Alice sat down on the edge of a basket-chair while Mrs Stubbs pumped the stove still higher. Suddenly Mrs Stubbs whipped the cushion off a chair and disclosed a large brown paper parcel.

'I've just had some new photers taken, my dear,' she shouted cheerfully to Alice. 'Tell me what you think of them.'

In a very dainty, refined way Alice wet her finger and put the tissue back from the first one. Life! How many there were! There were three dozzing at least. And she held hers up to the light.

Mrs Stubbs sat in an arm-chair, leaning very much to one side. There was a look of mild astonishment on her large face, and well there might be. For though the arm-chair stood on a carpet, to the left of it, miraculously skirting the carpet border, there was a dashing waterfall. On her right stood a Grecian pillar with a giant fern tree on either side of it, and in the background towered a gaunt mountain, pale with snow.

'It is a nice style, isn't it?' shouted Mrs Stubbs; and Alice had just screamed 'Sweetly' when the roaring of the Primus stove died down, fizzled out, ceased, and she said 'Pretty' in a silence that was frightening.

'Draw up your chair, my dear,' said Mrs Stubbs, beginning to pour out. 'Yes,' she said thoughtfully, as she handed the tea, 'but I don't care about the size. I'm having an enlargement. All very well for Christmas cards, but I never was the one for small photers myself. You get no comfort out of them. To say the truth, I find them dis'eartening.'

Alice quite saw what she meant.

'Size,' said Mrs Stubbs. 'Give me size. That was what my poor dear husband was always saying. He couldn't stand anything small. Gave him the creeps. And, strange as it may seem, my dear'—here Mrs Stubbs creaked and seemed to expand herself at the memory—'it was dropsy that carried him off at the larst. Many's the time they drawn one and a half pints from 'im at the 'ospital. . . . It seemed like a judgmint.'

Alice burned to know exactly what it was that was drawn from him. She ventured, 'I suppose it was water.'

But Mrs Stubbs fixed Alice with her eyes and replied meaningly, 'It was *liquid*, my dear.'

Liquid! Alice jumped away from the word like a cat and came back to it, nosing and wary.

'That's 'im!' said Mrs Stubbs, and she pointed dramatically to the life-size head and shoulders of a burly man with a dead white rose in the button-hole of his coat that made you think of a curl of cold mutton fat. Just below, in silver letters on a red cardboard ground, were the words, 'Be not afraid, it is I.'

'It's ever such a fine face,' said Alice faintly.

The pale-blue bow on the top of Mrs Stubbs's fair frizzy hair quivered. She arched her plump neck. What a neck she had! It was bright pink where it began and then it changed to warm apricot, and that faded to the colour of a brown egg and then to a deep creamy.

'All the same, my dear,' she said surprisingly, 'freedom's best!' Her soft, fat chuckle sounded like a purr. 'Freedom's best,' said Mrs Stubbs again.

Freedom! Alice gave a loud, silly little titter. She felt awkward. Her mind flew back to her own kitching. Ever so queer! She wanted to be back in it again.

IX

A strange company assembled in the Burnells' washhouse after tea. Round the table there sat a bull, a rooster, a donkey that kept forgetting it was a donkey, a sheep, and a bee. The washhouse was the perfect place for such a meeting because they could make as much noise as they liked and nobody ever interrupted. It was a small tin shed standing apart from the bungalow. Against the wall there was a deep trough and in the corner a copper with a basket of clothes-pegs on top of it. The little window, spun over with cobwebs, had a piece of candle and a mouse-trap on the dusty sill. There were clotheslines criss-crossed overhead and, hanging from a peg on the wall, a very big, a huge, rusty horseshoe. The table was in the middle with a form at either side.

'You can't be a bee, Kezia. A bee's not an animal. It's a ninseck.'

'Oh, but I do want to be a bee frightfully,' wailed Kezia. . . . A tiny bee, all yellow-furry, with striped legs. She drew her legs up under her and leaned over the table. She felt she was a bee.

'A ninseck must be an animal,' she said stoutly. 'It makes a noise. It's not like a fish.'

'I'm a bull, I'm a bull!' cried Pip. And he gave such a tremendous bellow—how did he make that noise?—that Lottie looked quite alarmed.

'I'll be a sheep,' said little Rags. 'A whole lot of sheep went past this morning.'

'How do you know?'

'Dad heard them. Baa!' He sounded like the little lamb that trots behind and seems to wait to be carried.

'Cock-a-doodle-do!' shrilled Isabel. With her red cheeks and bright eyes she looked like a rooster.

'What'll I be?' Lottie asked everybody, and she sat there smiling, waiting for them to decide for her. It had to be an easy one.

'Be a donkey, Lottie.' It was Kezia's suggestion. 'Hee-haw! You can't forget that.'

'Hee-haw!' said Lottie solemnly. 'When do I have to say it?'

'I'll explain, I'll explain,' said the bull. It was he who had the cards. He waved them round his head. 'All be quiet! All listen!' And he waited for them. 'Look here, Lottie.' He turned up a card. 'It's got two spots on it—see? Now, if you put that card in the middle and somebody else has one with two spots as well, you say "Hee-haw", and the card's yours.'

'Mine?' Lottie was round-eyed. 'To keep?'

'No, silly. Just for the game, see? Just while we're playing.' The bull was very cross with her.

'Oh, Lottie, you *are* a little silly,' said the proud rooster.

Lottie looked at both of them. Then she hung her head; her lip quivered. 'I don't not want to play,' she whispered. The others glanced at one another like conspirators. All of them knew what that meant. She would go away and be discovered somewhere standing with her pinny thrown over her head, in a corner, or against a wall, or even behind a chair.

'Yes, you *do*, Lottie. It's quite easy,' said Kezia.

And Isabel, repentant, said exactly like a grown-up, 'Watch *me*, Lottie, and you'll soon learn.'

'Cheer up, Lot,' said Pip. 'There, I know what I'll do. I'll give you the first one. It's mine, really, but I'll give it to you. Here you are.' And he slammed the card down in front of Lottie.

Lottie revived at that. But now she was in another difficulty. 'I haven't got a hanky,' she said; 'I want one badly, too.'

'Here, Lottie, you can use mine.' Rags dipped into his sailor blouse and brought up a very wet-looking one, knotted together. 'Be very careful,' he warned her. 'Only use that corner. Don't undo it. I've got a little star-fish inside I'm going to try and tame.'

'Oh, come on, you girls,' said the bull. 'And mind—you're not to look at your cards. You've got to keep your hands under the table till I say "Go." '

Smack went the cards round the table. They tried with all their might to see, but Pip was too quick for them. It was very exciting, sitting there in the washhouse; it was all they could do not to burst into a little chorus of animals before Pip had finished dealing.

'Now, Lottie, you begin.'

Timidly Lottie stretched out a hand, took the top card off her pack, had a good look at it—it was plain she was counting the spots—and put it down.

'No, Lottie, you can't do that. You mustn't look first. You must turn it the other way over.'

'But then everybody will see it the same time as me,' said Lottie.

The game proceeded. Mooe-ooo-er! The bull was terrible. He charged over the table and seemed to eat the cards up.

Bss-ss! said the bee.

Cock-a-doodle-do! Isabel stood up in her excitement and moved her elbows like wings.

Baa! Little Rags put down the King of Diamonds and Lottie put down the one they called the King of Spain. She had hardly any cards left.

'Why don't you call out, Lottie?'

'I've forgotten what I am,' said the donkey woefully.

'Well, change! Be a dog instead! Bow-wow!'

'Oh yes. That's *much* easier.' Lottie smiled again. But when she and Kezia both had one Kezia waited on purpose. The others made signs to Lottie and pointed. Lottie turned very red; she looked bewildered, and at last she said, 'Hee-haw! Ke-zia.'

'Ss! Wait a minute!' They were in the very thick of it when the bull stopped them, holding up his hand. 'What's that? What's that noise?'

'What noise? What do you mean?' asked the rooster.

'Ss! Shut up! Listen!' They were mouse-still. 'I thought I heard a—a sort of knocking,' said the bull.

'What was it like?' asked the sheep faintly.

No answer.

The bee gave a shudder. 'Whatever did we shut the door for?' she said softly. Oh, why, why had they shut the door?

While they were playing, the day had faded; the gorgeous sunset had blazed and died. And now the quick dark came racing over the sea, over the sand-hills, up the paddock. You were frightened to look in the corners of the washhouse, and yet you had to look with all your might. And somewhere, far away, grandma was lighting a lamp. The blinds were being pulled down; the kitchen fire leapt in the tins on the mantelpiece.

'It would be awful now,' said the bull, 'if a spider was to fall from the ceiling on to the table, wouldn't it?'

'Spiders don't fall from ceilings.'

'Yes, they do. Our Min told us she'd seen a spider as big as a saucer, with long hairs on it like a gooseberry.'

Quickly all the little heads were jerked up; all the little bodies drew together, pressed together.

'Why doesn't somebody come and call us?' cried the rooster.

Oh, those grown-ups, laughing and snug, sitting in the lamp-light, drinking out of cups! They'd forgotten about them. No, not really forgotten.

That was what their smile meant. They had decided to leave them there all by themselves.

Suddenly Lottie gave such a piercing scream that all of them jumped off the forms, all of them screamed too. 'A face—a face looking!' shrieked Lottie.

It was true, it was real. Pressed against the window was a pale face, black eyes, a black beard.

'Grandma! Mother! Somebody!'

But they had not got to the door, tumbling over one another, before it opened for Uncle Jonathan. He had come to take the little boys home.

X

He had meant to be there before, but in the front garden he had come upon Linda walking up and down the grass, stopping to pick off a dead pink or give a top-heavy carnation something to lean against, or to take a deep breath of something, and then walking on again, with her little air of remoteness. Over her white frock she wore a yellow, pink-fringed shawl from the Chinaman's shop.

'Hallo, Jonathan!' called Linda. And Jonathan whipped off his shabby panama, pressed it against his breast, dropped on one knee, and kissed Linda's hand.

'Greeting, my Fair One! Greeting, my Celestial Peach Blossom!' boomed the bass voice gently. 'Where are the other noble dames?'

'Beryl's out playing bridge and mother's giving the boy his bath. . . . Have you come to borrow something?'

The Trouts were for ever running out of things and sending across to the Burnells' at the last moment.

But Jonathan only answered, 'A little love, a little kindness'; and he walked by his sister-in-law's side.

Linda dropped into Beryl's hammock under the manuka tree and Jonathan stretched himself on the grass beside her, pulled a long stalk, and began chewing it. They knew each other well. The voices of children cried from the other gardens. A fisherman's light cart shook along the sandy road, and from far away they heard a dog barking; it was muffled as though the dog had its head in a sack. If you listened you could just hear the soft swish of the sea at full tide sweeping the pebbles. The sun was sinking.

'And so you go back to the office on Monday, do you, Jonathan?' asked Linda.

'On Monday the cage door opens and clangs to upon the victim for another eleven months and a week,' answered Jonathan.

Linda swung a little. 'It must be awful,' she said slowly.

'Would ye have me laugh, my fair sister? Would ye have me weep?'

Linda was so accustomed to Jonathan's way of talking that she paid no attention to it.

'I suppose,' she said vaguely, 'one gets used to it. One gets used to anything.'

'Does one? Hum!' The 'Hum' was so deep it seemed to boom from underneath the ground. 'I wonder how it's done,' brooded Jonathan; 'I've never managed it.'

Looking at him as he lay there, Linda thought again how attractive he was. It was strange to think that he was only an ordinary clerk, that Stanley earned twice as much money as he. What was the matter with Jonathan? He had no ambition; she supposed that was it. And yet one felt he was gifted, exceptional. He was passionately fond of music; every spare penny he had went on books. He was always full of new ideas, schemes, plans. But nothing came of it all. The new fire blazed in Jonathan; you almost heard it roaring softly as he explained, described, and dilated on the new thing; but a moment later it had fallen in and there was nothing but ashes, and Jonathan went about with a look like hunger in his black eyes. At these times he exaggerated his absurd manner of speaking, and he sang in church—he was the leader of the choir—with such fearful dramatic intensity that the meanest hymn put on an unholy splendour.

'It seems to me just as imbecile, just as infernal, to have to go to the office on Monday,' said Jonathan, 'as it always has done and always will do. To spend all the best years of one's life sitting on a stool from nine to five, scratching in somebody's ledger! It's a queer use to make of one's . . . one and only life, isn't it? Or do I fondly dream?' He rolled over on the grass and looked up at Linda. 'Tell me, what is the difference between my life and that of an ordinary prisoner. The only difference I can see is that I put myself in jail and nobody's ever going to let me out. That's a more intolerable situation than the other. For if I'd been—pushed in, against my will—kicking, even—once the door was locked, or at any rate in five years or so, I might have accepted the fact and begun to take an interest in the flight of flies or counting the warder's steps along the passage with particular attention to variations of tread and so on. But as it is, I'm like an insect that's flown into a room of its own accord. I dash against the walls, dash against the windows, flop against the ceiling, do everything on God's earth, in fact, except fly out again. And all the while I'm thinking, like that moth, or that butterfly, or whatever it is, "The shortness of life!' The shortness of life!" I've only one night or one day, and there's this vast dangerous garden, waiting out there, undiscovered, unexplored.'

'But, if you feel like that, why—' began Linda quickly.

'*Ah!*' cried Jonathan. And that 'Ah!' was somehow almost exultant. 'There you have me. Why? Why indeed? There's the maddening, mysterious question. Why don't I fly out again? There's the window or the door or whatever it was I came in by. It's not hopelessly shut—is it? Why don't I find it and be off? Answer me that, little sister.' But he gave her no time to answer.

'I'm exactly like that insect again. For some reason'—Jonathan paused between words—'it's not allowed, it's forbidden, it's against the insect law, to stop banging and flopping and crawling up the pane even for an instant. Why don't I leave the office? Why don't I seriously consider, this moment, for instance, what it is that prevents me leaving? It's not as though I'm tremendously tied. I've two boys to provide for, but, after all, they're boys. I could cut off to sea, or get a job up-country, or—' Suddenly he smiled at Linda and said in a changed voice, as if he were confiding a secret, 'Weak . . . weak. No stamina. No anchor. No guiding principle, let us call it.' But then the dark velvety voice rolled out:

Would ye hear the story
How it unfolds itself . . .

and they were silent.

The sun had set. In the western sky there were great masses of crushed-up rose-coloured clouds. Broad beams of light shone through the clouds and beyond them as if they would cover the whole sky. Overhead the blue faded; it turned a pale gold, and the bush outlined against it gleamed dark and brilliant like metal. Sometimes when those beams of light show in the sky they are very awful. They remind you that up there sits Jehovah, the jealous God, the Almighty, Whose eye is upon you, ever watchful, never weary. You remember that at His coming the whole earth will shake into one ruined graveyard; the cold, bright angels will drive you this way and that, and there will be no time to explain what could be explained so simply. . . . But to-night it seemed to Linda there was something infinitely joyful and loving in those silver beams. And now no sound came from the sea. It breathed softly as if it would draw that tender, joyful beauty into its own bosom.

'It's all wrong, it's all wrong,' came the shadowy voice of Jonathan. 'It's not the scene, it's not the setting for . . . three stools, three desks, three inkpots, and a wire blind.'

Linda knew that he would never change, but she said, 'Is it too late, even now?'

'I'm old—I'm old,' intoned Jonathan. He bent towards her, he passed his hand over his head. 'Look!' His black hair was speckled all over with silver, like the breast plumage of a black fowl.

Linda was surprised. She had no idea that he was grey. And yet, as he stood up beside her and sighed and stretched, she saw him, for the first time, not resolute, not gallant, not careless, but touched already with age. He looked very tall on the darkening grass, and the thought crossed her mind, 'He is like a weed.'

Jonathan stooped again and kissed her fingers.

'Heaven reward thy sweet patience, lady mine,' he murmured. 'I must go seek those heirs to my fame and fortune. . . .' He was gone.

XI

Light shone in the windows of the bungalow. Two square patches of gold fell upon the pinks and the peaked marigolds. Florrie, the cat, came out on to the veranda and sat on the top step, her white paws close together, her tail curled round. She looked content, as though she had been waiting for this moment all day.

'Thank goodness, it's getting late,' said Florrie. 'Thank goodness, the long day is over.' Her greengage eyes opened.

Presently there sounded the rumble of the coach, the crack of Kelly's whip. It came near enough for one to hear the voices of the men from town, talking loudly together. It stopped at the Burnells' gate.

Stanley was half-way up the path before he saw Linda. 'Is that you, darling?'

'Yes, Stanley.'

He leapt across the flower-bed and seized her in his arms. She was enfolded in that familiar, eager, strong embrace.

'Forgive me, darling, forgive me,' stammered Stanley, and he put his hand under her chin and lifted her face to him.

'Forgive you?' smiled Linda. 'But whatever for?'

'Good God! You can't have forgotten,' cried Stanley Burnell. 'I've thought of nothing else all day. I've had the hell of a day. I made up my mind to dash out and telegraph, and then I thought the wire mightn't reach you before I did. I've been in tortures, Linda.'

'But, Stanley,' said Linda, 'what must I forgive you for?'

'Linda!'—Stanley was very hurt—'didn't you realize—you must have realized—I went away without saying good-bye to you this morning? I can't imagine how I can have done such a thing. My confounded temper, of course. But—well'—and he sighed and took her in his arms again—'I've suffered for it enough to-day.'

'What's that you've got in your hand?' asked Linda. 'New gloves? Let me see.'

'Oh, just a cheap pair of wash-leather ones,' said Stanley humbly. 'I noticed Bell was wearing some in the coach this morning, so, as I was passing the shop, I dashed in and got myself a pair. What are you smiling at? You don't think it was wrong of me, do you?'

'On the *con*-trary, darling,' said Linda, 'I think it was most sensible.'

She pulled one of the large, pale gloves on her own fingers and looked at her hand, turning it this way and that. She was still smiling.

Stanley wanted to say, 'I was thinking of you the whole time I bought them.' It was true, but for some reason he couldn't say it. 'Let's go in,' said he.

XII

Why does one feel so different at night? Why is it so exciting to be awake when everybody else is asleep? Late—it is very late! And yet every moment you feel more and more wakeful, as though you were slowly, almost with every breath, waking up into a new, wonderful, far more thrilling and exciting world than the daylight one. And what is this queer sensation that you're a conspirator? Lightly, stealthily you move about your room. You take something off the dressing-table and put it down again without a sound. And everything, even the bedpost, knows you, responds, shares your secret. . . .

You're not very fond of your room by day. You never think about it. You're in and out, the door opens and slams, the cupboard creaks. You sit down on the side of your bed, change your shoes and dash out again. A dive down to the glass, two pins in your hair, powder your nose and off again. But now—it's suddenly dear to you. It's a darling little funny room. It's yours. Oh, what a joy it is to own things! Mine—my own!

'My very own for ever?'

'Yes.' Their lips met.

No, of course, that had nothing to do with it. That was all nonsense and rubbish. But, in spite of herself, Beryl saw so plainly two people standing in the middle of her room. Her arms were round his neck; he held her. And now he whispered, 'My beauty, my little beauty!' She jumped off her bed, ran over to the window and kneeled on the window-seat, with her elbows on the sill. But the beautiful night, the garden, every bush, every leaf, even the white palings, even the stars, were conspirators too. So bright was the moon that the flowers were bright as by day; the shadow of the nasturtiums, exquisite lilylike leaves and wide-open flowers, lay across the silvery veranda. The manuka tree, bent by the southerly winds, was like a bird on one leg stretching out a wing.

But when Beryl looked at the bush, it seemed to her the bush was sad.

'We are dumb trees, reaching up in the night, imploring we know not what,' said the sorrowful bush.

It is true when you are by yourself and you think about life, it is always sad. All that excitement and so on has a way of suddenly leaving you, and it's as though, in the silence, somebody called your name, and you heard your name for the first time. 'Beryl!'

'Yes, I'm here. I'm Beryl. Who wants me?'

'Beryl!'

'Let me come.'

It is lonely living by oneself. Of course, there are relations, friends, heaps of them; but that's not what she means. She wants someone who will find the Beryl they none of them know, who will expect her to be that Beryl always. She wants a lover.

'Take me away from all these people, my love. Let us go far away. Let us live our life, all new, all ours, from the very beginning. Let us make our fire. Let us sit down to eat together. Let us have long talks at night.'

And the thought was almost, 'Save me, my love. Save me!'

. . . 'Oh, go on! Don't be a prude, my dear. You enjoy yourself while you're young. That's my advice.' And a high rush of silly laughter joined Mrs Harry Kember's loud, indifferent neigh.

You see, it's so frightfully difficult when you've nobody. You're so at the mercy of things. You can't just be rude. And you've always this horror of seeming inexperienced and stuffy like the other ninnies at the Bay. And—and it's fascinating to know you've power over people. Yes, that is fascinating. . . .

Oh why, oh why doesn't 'he' come soon?

If I go on living here, thought Beryl, anything may happen to me.

'But how do you know he is coming at all?' mocked a small voice within her.

But Beryl dismissed it. She couldn't be left. Other people, perhaps, but not she. It wasn't possible to think that Beryl Fairfield never married, that lovely, fascinating girl.

'Do you remember Beryl Fairfield?'

'Remember her! As if I could forget her! It was one summer at the Bay that I saw her. She was standing on the beach in a blue'—no, pink—'muslin frock, holding on a big cream'—no, black—'straw hat. But it's years ago now.'

'She's as lovely as ever, more so if anything.'

Beryl smiled, bit her lip, and gazed over the garden. As she gazed, she saw somebody, a man, leave the road, step along the paddock beside their palings as if he was coming straight towards her. Her heart beat. Who was it? Who could it be? It couldn't be a burglar, certainly not a burglar, for he was smoking and he strolled lightly. Beryl's heart leapt; it seemed to turn right over and then to stop. She recognized him.

'Good evening, Miss Beryl,' said the voice softly.

'Good evening.'

'Won't you come for a little walk?' it drawled.

Come for a walk—at that time of night! 'I couldn't. Everybody's in bed. Everybody's asleep.'

'Oh,' said the voice lightly, and a whiff of sweet smoke reached her. 'What does everybody matter? Do come! It's such a fine night. There's not a soul about.'

Beryl shook her head. But already something stirred in her, something reared its head.

The voice said, 'Frightened?' It mocked, 'Poor little girl!'

'Not in the least,' said she. As she spoke that weak thing within her seemed to uncoil, to grow suddenly tremendously strong; she longed to go!

And just as if this was quite understood by the other, the voice said, gently and softly, but finally, 'Come along!'

Beryl stepped over her low window, crossed the veranda, ran down the grass to the gate. He was there before her.

'That's right,' breathed the voice, and it teased, 'You're not frightened, are you? You're not frightened?'

She was; now she was here she was terrified and it seemed to her everything was different. The moonlight stared and glittered; the shadows were like bars of iron. Her hand was taken.

'Not in the least,' she said lightly. 'Why should I be?'

Her hand was pulled gently, tugged. She held back.

'No, I'm not coming any further,' said Beryl.

'Oh, rot!' Harry Kember didn't believe her. 'Come along! We'll just go as far as that fuchsia bush. Come along!'

The fuchsia bush was tall. It fell over the fence in a shower. There was a little pit of darkness beneath.

'No, really, I don't want to,' said Beryl.

For a moment Harry Kember didn't answer. Then he came close to her, turned to her, smiled, and said quickly, 'Don't be silly! Don't be silly!'

His smile was something she'd never seen before. Was he drunk? That bright, blind, terrifying smile froze her with horror. What was she doing? How had she got here? The stern garden asked her as the gate pushed open, and quick as a cat Harry Kember came through and snatched her to him.

'Cold little devil! Cold little devil!' said the hateful voice.

But Beryl was strong. She slipped, ducked, wrenched free.

'You are vile, vile,' said she.

'Then why in God's name did you come?' stammered Harry Kember.

Nobody answered him.

A cloud, small, serene, floated across the moon. In that moment of darkness the sea sounded deep, troubled. Then the cloud sailed away, and the sound of the sea was a vague murmur, as though it waked out of a dark dream. All was still.

1922

The Garden-Party

And after all the weather was ideal. They could not have had a more perfect day for a garden-party if they had ordered it. Windless, warm, the sky without a cloud. Only the blue was veiled with a haze of light gold, as it is sometimes in early summer. The gardener had been up since dawn, mowing the lawns and sweeping them, until the grass and the dark flat rosettes where the daisy plants had been seemed to shine. As for the roses, you could not help feeling they understood that roses are the only flowers that impress people at garden-parties; the only flowers that everybody is certain of knowing. Hundreds, yes, literally hundreds, had come out in a single night; the green bushes bowed down as though they had been visited by archangels.

Breakfast was not yet over before the men came to put up the marquee.

'Where do you want the marquee put, mother?'

'My dear child, it's no use asking me. I'm determined to leave everything to you children this year. Forget I am your mother. Treat me as an honoured guest.'

But Meg could not possibly go and supervise the men. She had washed her hair before breakfast, and she sat drinking her coffee in a green turban, with a dark wet curl stamped on each cheek. Jose, the butterfly, always came down in a silk petticoat and a kimono jacket.

'You'll have to go, Laura; you're the artistic one.'

Away Laura flew, still holding her piece of bread-and-butter. It's so delicious to have an excuse for eating out of doors and, besides, she loved having to arrange things; she always felt she could do it so much better than anybody else.

Four men in their shirt-sleeves stood grouped together on the garden path. They carried staves covered with rolls of canvas and they had big tool-bags slung on their backs. They looked impressive. Laura wished now that she was not holding that piece of bread-and-butter, but there was nowhere to put it and she couldn't possibly throw it away. She blushed and tried to look severe and even a little bit short-sighted as she came up to them.

'Good morning,' she said, copying her mother's voice. But that sounded so fearfully affected that she was ashamed, and stammered like a little girl, 'Oh—er—have you come—is it about the marquee?'

'That's right, miss,' said the tallest of the men, a lanky, freckled fellow, and he shifted his tool-bag, knocked back his straw hat and smiled down at her. 'That's about it.'

His smile was so easy, so friendly, that Laura recovered. What nice eyes he had, small, but such a dark blue! And now she looked at the others, they were smiling too. 'Cheer up, we won't bite,' their smile seemed to say. How very nice workmen were! And what a beautiful morning! She mustn't mention the morning; she must be business-like. The marquee.

'Well, what about the lily-lawn? Would that do?'

And she pointed to the lily-lawn with the hand that didn't hold the bread-and-butter. They turned, they stared in the direction. A little fat chap thrust out his underlip and the tall fellow frowned.

'I don't fancy it,' said he. 'Not conspicuous enough. You see, with a thing like a marquee'—and he turned to Laura in his easy way—'you want to put it somewhere where it'll give you a bang slap in the eye, if you follow me.'

Laura's upbringing made her wonder for a moment whether it was quite respectful of a workman to talk to her of bangs slap in the eye. But she did quite follow him.

'A corner of the tennis-court,' she suggested. 'But the band's going to be in one corner.'

'H'm, going to have a band, are you?' said another of the workmen. He was pale. He had a haggard look as his dark eyes scanned the tennis-court. What was he thinking?

'Only a very small band,' said Laura gently. Perhaps he wouldn't mind so much if the band was quite small. But the tall fellow interrupted.

'Look here, miss, that's the place. Against those trees. Over there. That'll do fine.'

Against the karakas. Then the karaka trees would be hidden. And they were so lovely, with their broad, gleaming leaves, and their clusters of yellow fruit. They were like trees you imagined growing on a desert island, proud, solitary, lifting their leaves and fruits to the sun in a kind of silent splendour. Must they be hidden by a marquee?

They must. Already the men had shouldered their staves and were making for the place. Only the tall fellow was left. He bent down, pinched a sprig of lavender, put his thumb and forefinger to his nose and snuffed up the smell. When Laura saw that gesture she forgot all about the karakas in her wonder at him caring for things like that—caring for the smell of lavender. How many men that she knew would have done such a thing. *Oh, how extraordinarily nice workmen were*, she thought. Why couldn't she have workmen for friends rather than the silly boys she danced with and who came to Sunday night supper? She would get on much better with men like these.

It's all the fault, she decided, as the tall fellow drew something on the back of an envelope, something that was to be looped up or left to hang, of these absurd class distinctions. Well, for her part, she didn't feel them. Not a bit, not an atom. . . . And now there came the chock-chock of wooden hammers. Someone whistled, someone sang out, 'Are you right there, matey?' 'Matey!' The friendliness of it, the—the— Just to prove how happy she was, just to show the tall fellow how at home she felt, and how she despised stupid conventions, Laura took a big bite of her bread-and-butter as she stared at the little drawing. She felt just like a work-girl.

'Laura, Laura, where are you? Telephone, Laura!' a voice cried from the house.

'Coming!' Away she skimmed, over the lawn, up the path, up the steps, across the veranda, and into the porch. In the hall her father and Laurie were brushing their hats ready to go to the office.

'I say, Laura,' said Laurie very fast, 'you might just give a squiz at my coat before this afternoon. See if it wants pressing.'

'I will,' said she. Suddenly she couldn't stop herself. She ran at Laurie and gave him a small, quick squeeze. 'Oh, I do love parties, don't you?' gasped Laura.

'Ra-ther,' said Laurie's warm, boyish voice, and he squeezed his sister too and gave her a gentle push. 'Dash off to the telephone, old girl.'

The telephone. 'Yes, yes; oh yes. Kitty? Good morning, dear. Come to lunch? Do, dear. Delighted, of course. It will only be a very scratch meal—just the sandwich crusts and broken meringue-shells and what's left over. Yes, isn't it a perfect morning? Your white? Oh, I certainly should. One moment—hold the line. Mother's calling.' And Laura sat back. 'What, mother? Can't hear.'

Mrs Sheridan's voice floated down the stairs. 'Tell her to wear that sweet hat she had on last Sunday.'

'Mother says you're to wear that *sweet* hat you had on last Sunday. Good. One o'clock. Bye-bye.'

Laura put back the receiver, flung her arms over her head, took a deep breath, stretched and let them fall. 'Huh,' she sighed, and the moment after the sigh she sat up quickly. She was still, listening. All the doors in the house seemed to open. The house was alive with soft, quick steps and running voices. The green baize door that led to the kitchen regions swung open and shut with a muffled thud. And now there came a long, chuckling absurd sound. It was the heavy piano being moved on its stiff castors. But the air! If you stopped to notice, was the air always like this? Little faint winds were playing chase in at the tops of the windows, out at the doors. And there were two tiny spots of sun, one on the inkpot, one on a silver photograph frame, playing too. Darling little spots. Especially the one on the inkpot lid. It was quite warm. A warm little silver star. She could have kissed it.

The front door bell pealed and there sounded the rustle of Sadie's print skirt on the stairs. A man's voice murmured; Sadie answered, careless, 'I'm sure I don't know. Wait. I'll ask Mrs Sheridan.'

'What is it, Sadie?' Laura came into the hall.

'It's the florist, Miss Laura.'

It was, indeed. There, just inside the door, stood a wide, shallow tray full of pots of pink lilies. No other kind. Nothing but lilies—canna lilies, big pink flowers, wide open, radiant, almost frighteningly alive on bright crimson stems.

'O-oh, Sadie!' said Laura, and the sound was like a little moan. She crouched down as if to warm herself at that blaze of lilies; she felt they were in her fingers, on her lips, growing in her breast.

'It's some mistake,' she said faintly. 'Nobody ever ordered so many. Sadie, go and find mother.'

But at that moment Mrs Sheridan joined them.

'It's quite right,' she said calmly. 'Yes, I ordered them. Aren't they lovely?' She pressed Laura's arm. 'I was passing the shop yesterday, and I saw them in the window. And I suddenly thought for once in my life I shall have enough canna lilies. The garden-party will be a good excuse.'

'But I thought you said you didn't mean to interfere,' said Laura. Sadie had gone. The florist's man was still outside at his van. She put her arm round her mother's neck and gently, very gently, she bit her mother's ear.

'My darling child, you wouldn't like a logical mother, would you? Don't do that. Here's the man.'

He carried more lilies still, another whole tray.

'Bank them up, just inside the door, on both sides of the porch, please,' said Mrs Sheridan. 'Don't you agree, Laura?'

'Oh, I *do*, mother.'

In the drawing-room Meg, Jose, and good little Hans had at last succeeded in moving the piano.

'Now, if we put this chesterfield against the wall and move everything out of the room except the chairs, don't you think?'

'Quite.'

'Hans, move these tables into the smoking-room, and bring a sweeper to take these marks off the carpet and—one moment, Hans—' Jose loved giving orders to the servants and they loved obeying her. She always made them feel they were taking part in some drama. 'Tell mother and Miss Laura to come here at once.'

'Very good, Miss Jose.'

She turned to Meg. 'I want to hear what the piano sounds like, just in case I'm asked to sing this afternoon. Let's try over "This Life is Weary".'

Pom! Ta-ta-ta *Tee*-ta! The piano burst out so passionately that Jose's face changed. She clasped her hands. She looked mournfully and enigmatically at her mother and Laura as they came in.

This Life is *Wee*-ary,
A Tear—a Sigh.
A Love that *Chan*-ges,
This Life is *Wee*-ary,
A Tear—a Sigh.
A Love that *Chan*-ges,
And then . . . Good-bye!

But at the word 'Good-bye', and although the piano sounded more desperate than ever, her face broke into a brilliant, dreadfully unsympathetic smile.

'Aren't I in good voice, mummy?' she beamed.

This Life is *Wee*-ary,
Hope comes to Die,
A Dream—a *Wa*-kening.

But now Sadie interrupted them. 'What is it, Sadie?'

'If you please, m'm, cook says have you got the flags for the sandwiches?'

'The flags for the sandwiches, Sadie?' echoed Mrs Sheridan dreamily. And the children knew by her face that she hadn't got them. 'Let me see.' And she said to Sadie firmly, 'Tell cook I'll let her have them in ten minutes.'

Sadie went.

'Now, Laura,' said her mother quickly, 'come with me into the smoking-room. I've got the names somewhere on the back of an envelope. You'll have to write them out for me. Meg, go upstairs this minute and take that wet thing off your head. Jose, run and finish dressing this instant. Do you hear me, children, or shall I have to tell your father when he comes home to-night? And—and, Jose, pacify cook if you do go into the kitchen, will you? I'm terrified of her this morning.'

The envelope was found at last behind the dining-room clock, though how it had got there Mrs Sheridan could not imagine.

'One of you children must have stolen it out of my bag, because I remember vividly—cream-cheese and lemon-curd. Have you done that?'

'Yes.'

'Egg and—' Mrs Sheridan held the envelope away from her. 'It looks like mice. It can't be mice, can it?'

'Olive, pet,' said Laura, looking over her shoulder.

'Yes, of course, olive. What a horrible combination it sounds. Egg and olive.'

They were finished at last, and Laura took them off to the kitchen. She found Jose there pacifying the cook, who did not look at all terrifying.

'I have never seen such exquisite sandwiches,' said Jose's rapturous voice. 'How many kinds did you say there were, cook? Fifteen?'

'Fifteen, Miss Jose.'

'Well, cook, I congratulate you.'

Cook swept up crusts with the long sandwich knife, and smiled broadly.

'Godber's has come,' announced Sadie, issuing out of the pantry. She had seen the man pass the window.

That meant the cream puffs had come. Godber's were famous for their cream puffs. Nobody ever thought of making them at home.

'Bring them in and put them on the table, my girl,' ordered cook.

Sadie brought them in and went back to the door. Of course Laura and Jose were far too grown-up to really care about such things. All the same, they couldn't help agreeing that the puffs looked very attractive. Very. Cook began arranging them, shaking off the extra icing sugar.

'Don't they carry one back to all one's parties?' said Laura.

'I suppose they do,' said practical Jose, who never liked to be carried back. 'They look beautifully light and feathery, I must say.'

'Have one each, my dears,' said cook in her comfortable voice. 'Yer ma won't know.'

Oh, impossible. Fancy cream puffs so soon after breakfast. The very idea made one shudder. All the same, two minutes later Jose and Laura were licking their fingers with that absorbed inward look that only comes from whipped cream.

'Let's go into the garden, out by the back way,' suggested Laura. 'I want to see how the men are getting on with the marquee. They're such awfully nice men.'

But the back door was blocked by cook, Sadie, Godber's man, and Hans.

Something had happened.

'Tuk-tuk-tuk,' clucked cook like an agitated hen. Sadie had her hand clapped to her cheek as though she had toothache. Han's face was screwed up in the effort to understand. Only Godber's man seemed to be enjoying himself; it was his story.

'What's the matter? What's happened.'

'There's been a horrible accident,' said cook. 'A man killed.'

'A man killed! Where? How? When?'

But Godber's man wasn't going to have his story snatched from under his very nose.

'Know those little cottages just below here, miss?' Know them? Of course she knew them. 'Well, there's a young chap living there, name of *Scott*, a carter. His horse shied at a traction-engine, corner of Hawke Street this morning, and he was thrown out on the back of his head. Killed.'

'Dead!' Laura stared at Godber's man.

'Dead when they picked him up,' said Godber's man with relish. 'They were taking the body home as I come up here.' And he said to the cook, 'He's left a wife and five little ones.'

'Jose, come here.' Laura caught hold of her sister's sleeve and dragged her through the kitchen to the other side of the green baize door. There she paused and leaned against it. 'Jose!' she said, horrified, 'however are we going to stop everything?'

'Stop everything, Laura!' cried Jose in astonishment. 'What do you mean?'

'Stop the garden-party, of course.' Why did Jose pretend?

But Jose was still more amazed. 'Stop the garden-party? My dear Laura, don't be so absurd. Of course we can't do anything of the kind. Nobody expects us to. Don't be so extravagant.'

'But we can't possibly have a garden-party with a man dead just outside the front gate.'

That really was extravagant, for the little cottages were in a lane to themselves at the very bottom of a steep rise that led up to the house. A broad road ran between. True, they were far too near. They were the greatest possible eyesore and they had no right to be in that neighbourhood at all. They were little mean dwellings painted chocolate brown. In the garden patches there was nothing but cabbage stalks, sick hens, and tomato cans. The very smoke coming out of their chimneys was poverty-stricken. Little rags and shreds of smoke, so unlike the great silvery plumes that uncurled from the Sheridans' chimneys. Washerwomen lived in the lane and sweeps and a cobbler and a man whose house-front was studded all over with minute bird-cages. Children swarmed. When the Sheridans were little they were forbidden to set foot there because of the revolting language and of what they might catch. But since they were grown up Laura and Laurie on their prowls sometimes walked through. It was disgusting and sordid. They came out with a shudder. But still one must go everywhere; one must see everything. So through they went.

'And just think of what the band would sound like to that poor woman,' said Laura.

'Oh, Laura!' Jose began to be seriously annoyed. 'If you're going to stop a band playing every time someone has an accident, you'll lead a very strenuous life. I'm every bit as sorry about it as you. I feel just as sympathetic.' Her eyes hardened. She looked at her sister just as she used to when they were little and fighting together. 'You won't bring a drunken workman back to life by being sentimental,' she said softly.

'Drunk! Who said he was drunk?' Laura turned furiously on Jose. She said just as they had used to say on those occasions, 'I'm going straight up to tell mother.'

'Do, dear,' cooed Jose.

'Mother, can I come into your room?' Laura turned the big glass doorknob.

'Of course, child. Why, what's the matter? What's given you such a colour?' And Mrs Sheridan turned round from her dressing-table. She was trying on a new hat.

'Mother, a man's been killed,' began Laura.

'*Not* in the garden?' interrupted her mother.

'No, no!'

'Oh, what a fright you gave me!' Mrs Sheridan sighed with relief and took off the big hat and held it on her knees.

'But listen, mother,' said Laura. Breathless, half choking, she told the dreadful story. 'Of course, we can't have our party, can we?' she pleaded. 'The band and everybody arriving. They'd hear us, mother; they're nearly neighbours!'

To Laura's astonishment her mother behaved just like Jose; it was harder to bear because she seemed amused. She refused to take Laura seriously.

'But, my dear child, use your common sense. It's only by accident we've heard of it. If someone had died there normally—and I can't understand how they keep alive in those poky little holes—we should still be having our party, shouldn't we?'

Laura had to say 'yes' to that, but she felt it was all wrong. She sat down on her mother's sofa and pinched the cushion frill.

'Mother, isn't it really terribly heartless of us?' she asked.

'Darling!' Mrs Sheridan got up and came over to her, carrying the hat. Before Laura could stop her she had popped it on. 'My child!' said her mother, 'the hat is yours. It's made for you. It's much too young for me. I have never seen you look such a picture. Look at yourself!' And she held up her hand-mirror.

'But, mother,' Laura began again. She couldn't look at herself; she turned aside.

This time Mrs Sheridan lost patience just as Jose had done.

'You are being very absurd, Laura,' she said coldly. 'People like that don't expect sacrifices from us. And it's not very sympathetic to spoil everybody's enjoyment as you're doing now.'

'I don't understand,' said Laura, and she walked quickly out of the room into her own bedroom. There, quite by chance, the first thing she saw was this charming girl in the mirror, in her black hat trimmed with gold daisies and a long black velvet ribbon. Never had she imagined she could look like that. Is mother right? she thought. And now she hoped her mother was right. Am I being extravagant? Perhaps it was extravagant. Just for a moment she had another glimpse of that poor woman and those little children and the body being carried into the house. But it all seemed blurred, unreal, like a picture in the newspaper. I'll remember it again after the party's over, she decided. And somehow that seemed quite the best plan. . . .

Lunch was over by half-past one. By half-past two they were all ready for the fray. The green-coated band had arrived and was established in a corner of the tennis-court.

'My dear!' trilled Kitty Maitland, 'aren't they too like frogs for words? You ought to have arranged them round the pond with the conductor in the middle on a leaf.'

Laurie arrived and hailed them on his way to dress. At the sight of him Laura remembered the accident again. She wanted to tell him. If Laurie agreed with the others, then it was bound to be all right. And she followed him into the hall.

'Laurie!'

'Hallo!' He was half-way upstairs, but when he turned round and saw Laura he suddenly puffed out his cheeks and goggled his eyes at her. 'My word, Laura! You do look stunning,' said Laurie. 'What an absolutely topping hat!'

Laura said faintly 'Is it?' and smiled up at Laurie and didn't tell him after all.

Soon after that people began coming in streams. The band struck up; the hired waiters ran from the house to the marquee. Wherever you looked there were couples strolling, bending to the flowers, greeting, moving on over the lawn. They were like bright birds that had alighted in the Sheridans' garden for this one afternoon, on their way to—where? Ah, what happiness it is to be with people who all are happy, to press hands, press cheeks, smile into eyes.

'Darling Laura, how well you look!'

'What a becoming hat, child!'

'Laura, you look quite Spanish. I've never seen you look so striking.'

And Laura, glowing, answered softly, 'Have you had tea? Won't you have an ice? The passion-fruit ices really are rather special.' She ran to her father and begged him: 'Daddy darling, can't the band have something to drink?'

And the perfect afternoon slowly ripened, slowly faded, slowly its petals closed.

'Never a more delightful garden-party . . .' 'The greatest success . . .' 'Quite the most . . .'

Laura helped her mother with the good-byes. They stood side by side in the porch till it was all over.

'All over, all over, thank heaven,' said Mrs Sheridan. 'Round up the others, Laura. Let's go and have some fresh coffee. I'm exhausted. Yes, it's been very successful. But oh, these parties, these parties! Why will you children insist on giving parties!' And they all of them sat down in the deserted marquee.

'Have a sandwich, daddy dear. I wrote the flag.'

'Thanks.' Mr Sheridan took a bite and the sandwich was gone. He took another. 'I suppose you didn't hear of a beastly accident that happened to-day!' he said.

'My dear,' said Mrs Sheridan, holding up her hand, 'we did. It nearly ruined the party. Laura insisted we should put it off.'

'Oh, mother!' Laura didn't want to be teased about it.

'It was a horrible affair all the same,' said Mr Sheridan. 'The chap was married too. Lived just below in the lane, and leaves a wife and half a dozen kiddies, so they say.'

An awkward little silence fell. Mrs Sheridan fidgeted with her cup. Really, it was very tactless of father. . . .

Suddenly she looked up. There on the table were all those sandwiches, cakes, puffs, all uneaten, all going to be wasted. She had one of her brilliant ideas.

'I know,' she said. 'Let's make up a basket. Let's send that poor creature some of this perfectly good food. At any rate, it will be the greatest treat for the children. Don't you agree? And she's sure to have neighbours calling in and so on. What a point to have it all ready prepared. Laura!' She jumped up. 'Get me the big basket out of the stairs cupboard.'

'But, mother, do you really think it's a good idea?' said Laura.

Again, how curious, she seemed to be different from them all. To take scraps from their party. Would the poor woman really like that?

'Of course! What's the matter with you to-day? An hour or two ago you were insisting on us being sympathetic.'

Oh well! Laura ran for the basket. It was filled, it was now heaped by her mother.

'Take it yourself, darling,' said she. 'Run down just as you are. No, wait, take the arum lilies too. People of that class are so impressed by arum lilies.'

'The stems will ruin her lace frock,' said practical Jose.

So they would. Just in time. 'Only the basket, then. And, Laura!'—her mother followed her out of the marquee—'don't on any account—'

'What, mother?'

No, better not put such ideas into the child's head! 'Nothing! Run along.'

It was just growing dusky as Laura shut their garden gates. A big dog ran by like a shadow. The road gleamed white, and down below in the hollow the little cottages were in deep shade. How quiet it seemed after the afternoon. Here she was going down the hill to somewhere where a man lay dead, and she couldn't realize it. Why couldn't she? She stopped a minute. And it seemed to her that kisses, voices, tinkling spoons, laughter, the smell of crushed grass were somehow inside her. She had no room for anything else. How strange! She looked up at the pale sky, and all she thought was, 'Yes, it was the most successful party.'

Now the broad road was crossed. The lane began, smoky and dark. Women in shawls and men's tweed caps hurried by. Men hung over the palings; the children played in the doorways. A low hum came from the mean little cottages. In some of them there was a flicker of light, and a shadow, crab-like, moved across the window. Laura bent her head and hurried on. She wished now she had put on a coat. How her frock shone! And the big hat with the velvet streamer—if only it was another hat! Were the people looking at her? They must be. It was a mistake to have come; she knew all along it was a mistake. Should she go back even now?

No, too late. This was the house. It must be. A dark knot of people stood outside. Beside the gate an old, old woman with a crutch sat in a chair, watching. She had her feet on a newspaper. The voices stopped as Laura drew near. The group parted. It was as though she was expected, as though they had known she was coming here.

Laura was terribly nervous. Tossing the velvet ribbon over her shoulder, she said to a woman standing by, 'Is this Mrs Scott's house?' and the woman, smiling queerly, said, 'It is, my lass.'

Oh, to be away from this! She actually said, 'Help me, God,' as she walked up the tiny path and knocked. To be away from those staring eyes, or to be covered up in anything, one of those women's shawls even. I'll just leave the basket and go, she decided. I shan't even wait for it to be emptied.

Then the door opened. A little woman in black showed in the gloom.

Laura said, 'Are you Mrs Scott?' But to her horror the woman answered, 'Walk in, please, miss,' and she was shut in the passage.

'No,' said Laura, 'I don't want to come in. I only want to leave this basket. Mother sent—'

The little woman in the gloomy passage seemed not to have heard her. 'Step this way, please, miss,' she said in an oily voice, and Laura followed her.

She found herself in a wretched little low kitchen, lighted by a smoky lamp. There was a woman sitting before the fire.

'Em,' said the little creature who had let her in. 'Em! It's a young lady.' She turned to Laura. She said meaningly, 'I'm 'er sister, miss. You'll excuse 'er, won't you?'

'Oh, but of course!' said Laura. 'Please, please don't disturb her. I—I only want to leave—'

But at that moment the woman at the fire turned round. Her face, puffed up, red, with swollen eyes and swollen lips, looked terrible. She seemed as though she couldn't understand why Laura was there. What did it mean? Why was this stranger standing in the kitchen with a basket? What was it all about? And the poor face puckered up again.

'All right, my dear,' said the other. 'I'll thenk the young lady.'

And again she began, 'You'll excuse her, miss, I'm sure,' and her face, swollen too, tried an oily smile.

Laura only wanted to get out, to get away. She was back in the passage. The door opened. She walked straight through into the bedroom, where the dead man was lying.

'You'd like a look at 'im, wouldn't you?' said Em's sister, and she brushed past Laura over to the bed. 'Don't be afraid, my lass'—and now her voice sounded fond and sly, and fondly she drew down the sheet—''e looks a picture. There's nothing to show. Come along, my dear.'

Laura came.

There lay a young man, fast asleep—sleeping so soundly, so deeply, that he was far, far away from them both. Oh, so remote, so peaceful. He was dreaming. Never wake him up again. His head was sunk in the pillow, his eyes were closed; they were blind under the closed eyelids. He was given up to his dream. What did garden-parties and baskets and lace frocks matter to him? He was far from all those things. He was wonderful, beautiful. While they were laughing and while the band was playing, this marvel had come to the lane. Happy . . . happy. . . . All is well, said that sleeping face. This is just as it should be. I am content.

But all the same you had to cry, and she couldn't go out of the room without saying something to him. Laura gave a loud childish sob.

'Forgive my hat,' she said.

And this time she didn't wait for Em's sister. She found her way out of the door, down the path past all those dark people. At the corner of the lane she met Laurie.

He stepped out of the shadow. 'Is that you, Laura?'

'Yes.'

'Mother was getting anxious. Was it all right?'

'Yes, quite, Oh, Laurie!' She took his arm, she pressed up against him.

'I say, you're not crying, are you?' asked her brother.

Laura shook her head. She was.

Laurie put his arm round her shoulder. 'Don't cry,' he said in his warm, loving voice. 'Was it awful?'

'No,' sobbed Laura. 'It was simply marvellous. But, Laurie—' She stopped, she looked at her brother. 'Isn't life,' she stammered, 'isn't life—' But what life was she couldn't explain. No matter. He quite understood.

'*Isn't* it, darling?' said Laurie.

1922

Ethel Wilson

1888-1980

'The short story,' Ethel Wilson said, 'is a curiously interesting art form enormously dependent within its small compass on structure. If structure is faulty a short story may be all at sea, as a well-intentioned ship whose rudder is faulty is all at sea. The ship and the story will probably not arrive at their desired destinations.' The ship is an appropriate simile for a writer who was herself a traveller from her earliest years and whose personal and fictional worlds often focused on her beloved Vancouver with its harbours and inlets and sounds.

Wilson was born in Port Elizabeth, South Africa, where her father was a Methodist missionary. When her mother died, she was taken at the age of two to England. Seven years later her father died, and she came to Vancouver to live with her maternal grandmother. She received her teacher's certificate from the Vancouver Normal School in 1907 and taught in many local elementary schools until her marriage in 1921. In the 1930s Wilson published a few short stories and began a series of family reminiscences which were later transformed into a family chronicle, *The Innocent Traveller* (1949). Her first published novel, *Hetty Dorval*, appeared in 1947, and her writing career ended fourteen years later with the publication of *Mrs Golightly and Other Stories*. Wilson spent her later years in seclusion and ill-health. She died in Vancouver in 1980.

'The short story is slippery—hard to catch and hold in the hand,' Wilson admitted. 'I have written a few short stories, and observe with respect and some pleasure the opportunity for economy of expression, for the recognition of line and contour, and the open opportunity for inference. The short story is a strong, delicate and tricky art, almost done with mirrors.' Inference and nuance are the essence of Wilson's short fiction, which often confronts a major character—and the reader too—with a disturbing situation that raises unanswered questions. Beneath the surface of a Wilson story lurk possible and sometimes realized calamities. According to the epigraph of *Mrs Golightly and Other Stories*, life '. . . is a difficult country, and our home.' Because Wilson viewed the world as 'our home', she considers—sometimes with irony but always with compassion—the hopes and fears, the despair and violence that appear in ordinary situations.

The title character in 'Mr Sleepwalker', a modern ghost story, is a haunting presence who seems to pursue Mrs Manly, a wife often separated from her husband and a victim, like so many Wilson protagonists, of loneliness. The violent act that is the climax of the story fails to break down the aloneness that afflicts Mrs Manly, and Mr Sleepwalker too.

At the beginning of 'Till death us do part', the unnamed narrator is fascinated by, and yet afraid of Kate, her fellow-clerk. In a series of diary entries, these initial feelings give way to pity and perhaps even admiration as the narrator receives a brief glimpse of Kate's tragic home life. Yet the change in feeling does not remove the silence that separates the two clerks.

'Mr Sleepwalker' and 'Till death us do part' were first published in *Mrs Golightly and Other Stories* (1961).

Mr Sleepwalker

During the time that Mary Manly's husband was in Australia, Mrs Manly had an experience that was peculiar. I should like to say that up to the time that her husband went to the war, Mrs Manly had never shown any tendency to undue imagination, nervousness, hysteria, nor any of those weaknesses which are supposed to be the prerogative of her sex, but are not—any of which might have been considered responsible for the mounting episodes which culminated in her nearly killing Mr Sleepwalker. Let us begin with Mary Manly, because we do not know very much about the past of Mr Sleepwalker. It would be provocative, but not fair, to speculate about Mr Sleepwalker's past, but, unless we knew something about his origin and his history, the speculations would be useless, and disturbing.

Mary Davidson married Hugh Manly who was a forester in the government service of British Columbia, and so able a man was Hugh Manly in the matter of conservation of forests, marketing of lumber—especially as these things applied to the Province of British Columbia whose forests are among her noblest treasures—that his government began to send him on long journeys to foreign countries where export trade might be developed, and it became no great surprise—but a source of something like grief—to Mary when Hugh walked in for dinner, and said later on in the evening as he often did, 'Well, it looks as though I'm off again,' and Mary would learn that Hugh was being sent by his government to South Africa, or to the United Kingdom, or to Sweden, and so it was that Mary had to gear herself—as they say—to these absences which became to her a mounting sorrow, because she loved her husband beyond expression, and he loved only her. Each time that Hugh left he said something like this, 'Next time, darling, we'll see if you can't come too,' and Mary would say, 'Yes, next time, Hugh.' But next time Hugh might go to Hyderabad, and how can a young wife whimsically accompany her husband to Hyderabad, when there is a future to look to. I mention all this because it is possible that the unhappiness of repeated separation in a world whose essential limit is bounded by the life and love of two people closely united, may have done something to Mary's otherwise calm and extroverted nature, and may have made her susceptible to outside influence of an esoteric, suprahuman, or even sub-human kind.

Just at the time when it seemed that Hugh had approached the point in his chosen profession at which he could say, "Come with me and be damned to everything and hang the expense,' there came the war. Hugh went to the war, and Mary's sense of separation became exacerbated to the point where it was anguish. Are we who love each other so dearly, she said to herself, always to be deprived of our greatest joy, and have I to accustom myself to the theory that we belong to each other *in absentia* only, for it is an actual fact that the woman in the next apartment and I have lived for seven years with only one wall dividing us, and we do not belong to each other; while Hugh and I, who belong to each other, have lived for seven years with half the world between us most of the time. And now this war!

She busied herself at once, but in spite of being daily involved in responsibility and detail, her other life—that is to say her absent life with Hugh—gradually became more real to her than the life of meetings, administration, billeting, in which her body was engaged, especially after Hugh left for overseas. ('Onlie the body's busy, and pretends.') Again I say that this other-worldness, which developed in Mary, and in many other young women like her during those years, but more in Mary Manly, because absence and frustration had already made some mark on her before the war began, may have been responsible for many queer things, one way and another. Directly the war was over, Hugh came home (fortunately) and was placed at once at the head of his department; and before the two had spent a month together, Hugh was sent to Australia. 'You're coming this time, Mary, and no nonsense about it,' said Hugh, and Mary with rapture prepared to go, broke her left elbow, and Hugh went without her.

To go now to Mr Sleepwalker.

Before Hugh went overseas he was stationed for a while in Winnipeg. Mary camp-followed him to Winnipeg, and it was in Winnipeg that she first saw Mr Sleepwalker. It was in a street car. The street car swinging along Portage Avenue was full, and Mary stood, holding onto a strap. She looked idly about her, and the swaying of the street car so determined that her eyes fell upon this person and that sitting in the row of seats immediately beside the entrance to the street car. She saw a small slim man sitting in this seat, with people on either side of him. Mary's whole attention was taken by this man, although no one else seemed to observe him, and as the body of someone swaying beside her interposed between her and the small man seated, she did not see him, and then she saw him again.

She became violently curious about the small man, and began to speculate about him. He appeared unaware of people around him, and certainly unaware of Mary's occasional scrutiny. If I were accustomed to menservants, thought Mary, or if we lived in a different age, I should think that this little man is, or has been, a 'gentleman's gentleman'. He is drilled in some precision of thought and action, and he hides behind that soft and deferential pose and immobility some definite and different entity. The small man sat erect, looking straight ahead of him, servile yet proud, his hands—in worn black gloves—folded on the head of his walking stick which rested between his knees. His hat was a kind of square obsolete bowler. He wore a wing collar, and a small black tie of the kind known as a string tie. His black suit was old, worn and very neat. Below the anachronistic hat was the face that so attracted and repelled Mary Manly. The features were neat and of a prissy femininity. The eyes were a warm stealthy reddish brown. His hair descended in reddish brown sideburns;

otherwise he was clean-shaven. The hair was soft and unlike the hair of a man; in fact it resembled a soft fur. His mouth was set—so, with gentility. He is a mixture, thought Mary, as she watched the little man, now and again obscured from her, of gentility—a fake product of civilization—and of something feral, I do not know what. I seem to have seen those russet eyes, she continued to herself, in some animal. Is it a fox? No, I know no more about foxes than about gentlemen's gentlemen, and yet it seems like a fox. Or a watching hawk. Or some red-eyed rodent. And why is he in the middle of Canada, in Winnipeg, new city of grain, utility and railroads, looking like this, dressed like this? He is as much a phenomenon in his dreadful respectability, riding on an unlikely street car in the city of Winnipeg as if he wore a crown, or a grey topper, or a sarong. What life does he lead, and why is he here? The small man sat alone, it appeared, in his personal and genteel world, politely apart from those who rubbed shoulders with him or crowded his neatly brushed worn buttoned boots, and he looked straight ahead of him. Mary now avoided looking at the small man, because, so lively had been her interest in his peculiarities, she was afraid that he might become aware of her, and she did not want this to happen; so she turned her back, and faced in the other direction. Then she got off the street car and, for the moment, forgot him.

On the next evening, Hugh came in from barracks, and they had dinner together. Mary tried to tell Hugh about the small man on the street car, but found that she was unable to describe him in such a way as would interest Hugh; and when Hugh told her, as he did, that he was ordered east and that he thought that embarkation would be the next step, this drove other thoughts from Mary's mind and she determined at once to move east also, because, as she said, 'We may as well continue living together, Hugh, in our own peculiar haphazard fashion. I have really loved it in Winnipeg, and who knows but that they may keep you in the east longer than you think. So I shall not go back to Vancouver. I shall go east, too.' Mary then prepared to go east, following Hugh, who left at a day's notice.

She had by this time attained (she thought) a fairly philosophic regard for things as they have to be, realizing of course that she was only one of the millions of persons—friends and enemies—whose lives were dislocated by war; that she could expect no special privilege because she was Mary Manly, wife of Hugh Manly (usually *in absentia);* and that she could and must assume the matter-of-factness which is necessary in the successful conduct of life, which other people achieve so admirably, and which passes very well for courage. So she took life as it came, allowing herself to hope, as was natural, that her husand would be kept in Canada, although a part of each of them wished that he would be sent away and would see action, but safely, with everybody else, and no favours sought or granted. Mary said good-bye to her friends in Winnipeg, many of whom, like herself, were also in motion one way or another, and then, late one night, she boarded the east-bound train.

Because Mary was what is called a good train traveller, she soon bestowed her things neatly away and settled down for the remainder of the night in her lower berth. She slept at once, and only in a half-conscious and comfortable way was she aware of the stopping, starting, moaning, creaking of the great train. Suddenly she was awakened by a quiet. The train was standing still, perhaps in a siding, because there seemed to be no noise, or it may have been in the night-time stillness of the railway station of a town. Mary was half awake, and did not care. She was sleepily aware of stillness, of time and place suspended—and then of persons passing quietly, almost stealthily, in the aisle outside her curtain . . . the porter . . . perhaps . . . passenger . . . porter . . . a murmur . . . a smell . . . earth . . . rotted wood . . . an animal . . . in the sleeping-car . . . impossible . . . a smell . . . earth . . . rotted wood . . . an animal . . . it passed. She fell asleep.

When day broke, the train had left Manitoba and was speeding into the vast western wooded lake-strewn regions of Ontario. The train stopped at Chapleau for twenty minutes. Mary got out, and wandered, as she always did at Chapleau station, to the small stone memorial that bears the name of Louis Hémon. Why, she wondered, did Louis Hémon come to Canada, write his book which, although unknown to most young Canadians, had already dimmed to a reputation faintly classic, and die. And why did Louis Hémon die, still young, at Chapleau, straggling rawly beside its railway station and its forests. A young man stood beside her and studied the carved words. Mary looked up at him and spoke tentatively. 'Do you know why Louis Hémon came here?' she asked.

'Sawry,' said the young man awkwardly, 'I never heard of him. I was kinda wondering myself who he was,' and he strolled away.

Mary turned and walked briskly up and down the platform, with the breeze and against the breeze that blew refreshingly through Chapleau. She heard the cry 'All aboard'. She turned towards her own porter at her own car. As she waited to mount the steps, she saw walking down the platform the small man in black whom she had seen in the Winnipeg street car. She was startled to see the small figure in motion. He walked, one might say, with as much stillness as he sat, regarding no one. He walked with his arms at his sides, guarded, genteel, like a black-suited doll. She climbed on the train, entered her car, and found her seat. She did not see him again.

When she rejoined Hugh in Halifax, there were many urgent things to think about without recalling to mind the small man whose hair was like fur, and so it seemed that he had never been. Hugh's convoy sailed, and Mary Manly went back to Vancouver and put herself at once to work.

It was months later that Mary Manly and Thérèse Leduc went to a movie together. At the end of the first picture, the two people who were sitting beside Mary went out, and, in the dark, another occupant took the seat beside her. Suddenly Mary's attention was taken from the screen by the scent, slight at first, then stronger, of, perhaps, an animal, or, perhaps, rotted wood, thick and dank (but how could it be rotted wood?). This smell was not at first heavy, but pervasive, and was very unpleasant to her. It became at last heavy in the air, and made her uneasy. It recalled to her a journey . . . a what? . . . some smell . . . not train smell . . . something that passed by. She tried to look at the person next to her without appearing to do so. This was difficult. She murmured to Thérèse Leduc, 'Do you smell anything queer?'

'No,' whispered Thérèse. 'What kind of thing?'

'I don't know,' answered Mary.

'I smell nothing,' said Thérèse.

The smell persisted. Suddenly the skin on the back of Mary's neck seemed to prickle. The man (it was a man) who sat beside her, was small, and sat very still. Mary sat still too, and thought, 'I want to get up and leave. I can't. That is unreasonable.' But at last she whispered to Thérèse, 'I'm sorry, Terry, but the man beside me *does* smell. Let's get out . . . perhaps we can move. Let's go your way."

The women got up and shuffled out of the long end of the row.

'How disgusting!' expostulated Thérèse.

'Yes, wasn't it? It really *was,*' said Mary, but she did not explain that the smell was not what Terry though it was. Not dirt. Nothing like dirt. Something animal. Something wild. Thy found other seats, but Mary could not give her attention to the play. After the movie, she discovered also that she could not tell Thérèse about the small man, and about this animal smell which she had begun to associate with him. The thing was fanciful, and Mary did not like to be thought fanciful. Most of all, she did not like to admit to herself that she was fanciful. But there it was. She put her mind to other things, and that was not very difficult.

Some time later, as Mary rose from her knees in church, she did not need to look in order to see who it was that had come into the pew and had now dropped on his knees beside her. The feral scent wafted and then hung heavy. The small man in black drew himself up to his seat, and sat, doll-like, prim, just as (Mary knew) she had seen him sit in the street car on Portage Avenue. She saw him as plainly now as though her physical eyes observed the genteel shape, the russet fur of the sideburns, the prissy set of the mouth. He sat beside her, she knew, correct, genteel, yet vulpine, if it was vulpine. Mary's head began to spin. My imagination plays tricks, or does it? she asked herself . . . Soon, of course, I shall see the two people in front of me move, turn slightly, disturbed by the smell that disturbs me. It cannot be to me, me alone, that it comes. He carried it round with him. Others *must* smell it—always. He is horrible, horrible. But now I can't leave . . . I must stay . . . he can never have observed me (for we never think, do we, that we are the observed ones; always we are the observers), I shall sit here. I shall stay for the service, and out-stay him. But he is horrible. And a revulsion at the proximity of this small being almost overcame her, and she felt faint.

The little man sat still; his worn-gloved hands were on his knees, she could see. He took his Prayer Book and found his place, following the service respectfully, and in an accustomed manner. Mary's mind worked obliquely, directed, in spite of herself, towards the small man.

But the two people in front of her did not turn round, disturbed by the alien smell of rotted wood, of something animal, unknown.

Mary out-sat the service. Then, with elaborate negligence, while the small man was leaving and after he had left, she put on her gloves, leaned back in her pew and awaited the end of the slowly drifting columns of church goers moving with slightly rocking inhibited motion down the aisles. Then she joined the departing stream at its end, went out into the open air, felt refreshed and, by a foolishly roundabout way, returned home.

I shall tell Hugh, she thought, It's very silly. I take this too seriously, and if I tell Hugh, I'll get rid of it. The thing bothers me out of all proportion. What concerns me is the war, and Hugh, and my jobs of work to do, and my life that I have always had; and a small being that smells like—perhaps—a weasel or a musk-rat has no part and does not matter. So she wrote, but when she read the letter that she had written to Hugh, her story seemed idiotic. She tore the letter up, and wrote again and did not mention the small man. Hugh, she thought, would not in any case be amused. She could not make the story amusing. She could just make it sound silly. Hugh might be interested in a man that smelled like an animal (she had seldom smelled an animal), but she would not be able to conceal from him the fact that something was being established that affected her unreasonably and unpleasantly; it seemed to her that the small man, in spite of his apparent immobility and unawareness, was in some peculiar way, aware of her also. This, of course, was possible, yet unlikely and very unpleasant. She neither saw the small man, nor did the strange scent reach her, for a long time.

One night it rained. Mary drove carefully in her little car. She picked up her cousin, Cora Wilmot, and drove through the lashing rain, and through the lights and reflections of lights, cross-hatched in the early dark in splashing pools and pavements, lighted by and left behind by the beams of her own headlights, onto Granville Street Bridge. She drove carefully in the late dinner-time traffic, peering through the rainstorm. She drove rather slowly. Cora, beside her, peered too. Then the thing nearly happened.

Just before Mary reached the narrow span of the bridge, Cora cried out, and stifled her cry. Off the slightly raised platform-like sidewalk of the bridge, into the light of the headlights of Mary's slowly moving car, stepped a small man. He faced the lights of the car, and seemed to look through the windshield of the car and at, or into, the occupants. The lights showed all in one flash the white face (and Mary could see the lighted russet eyes), the intolerable propriety of mouth and chin, dark lines of hair framing the almost rectangular face. The man threw up his arms with the stiff gesture of a marionette. Mary swerved sharply to the left into whatever cars there might be, into the span, if need be, rather than touch, or become involved in any way with the man who had stepped in front of her car. She did not touch him. She touched neither cars nor span. She did not speak. She drove to the end of the bridge, up Granville Street hill, through lights, darkness, and rain, and then she pulled up at the side of the road. She was trembling violently. Cora was voluble.

'That horrible little man!' she said, '*What* was he doing? *Why* did he do it? He did it on purpose! No one crosses the bridge there! There's nothing to cross for! Oh Mary, what a narrow shave! Let's sit here a while. What a face! He looked as if he could see us, as if he was looking at us! I'll never forget him, will you? Do you feel like driving now? Let's get there, and then they'll give us a drink before dinner, and that will help us both.'

'Yes,' said Mary, and she drove on. He saw me, she thought, as I drove so slowly in the lights, and then he stepped out.

Before the end of the year, Hugh came home, the war being incredibly over. And then, as I said, Hugh went to Australia, and Mary, with the complicated fracture of her left arm in a sling, stayed at home.

Many and many a time, towards the end of the war, and now, when alone, when sleeping, and at waking, she seemed to see the doll-like figure of the small man with her motor lights full on his white face. She saw a marionette's gesture—two dark arms flung stiffly upwards, she swerved, she drove on in her dream. And then, the obsession became less frequent. Nevertheless, within herself, she knew that she had begun to be afraid of something.

Hugh wrote from Melbourne, 'I'm going to be here longer than we thought. Just as soon as that elbow is better enough cable me. I'll advise you, and you get a passage by air. And at last . . .' The load of aggravation lifted from Mary, and she began to lie about her elbow in order to get away and to join Hugh in Australia. However, their friend the doctor, Johnny Weston, put her off for a week.

One afternoon she returned from John's surgery with the permission that she might now make arrangements for her flight to Australia, and so she cabled to Hugh. Such a thing as this had never happened to Mary Manly before. She went home, and in her ecstasy, her rapture, she telephoned Thérèse Leduc and Cora, and anybody else that came to mind, to tell them that she was flying to Australia to join Hugh.

There came a ring at the door of the flat. Still careful of her clumsy left arm, Mary went lightly to the door and opened it. A feral smell entered the apartment, followed by the small respectable man who had stood outside Mary's door and had rung her doorbell. The man was dressed as usual in black. As he stepped humbly but without question into the hall, he took off his obsolete square-shaped bowler hat, laid it upon a table, turned and shut the door in a serviceable manner, and then advanced obsequiously on Mary. In his hand he carried a small black valise. Scent hung heavy and it was the smell of fear.

Mary was aghast. Her right hand flew to her mouth. She pressed the back of her hand to her mouth and gazed at the small man over her hand. She did not think, I am alone in this apartment with this unpleasant little creature. She did not think at all. The air was full of the dank wild earthy smell of something old and unknown. She backed, and obsequiously the small man advanced upon her. She saw the russet animal eyes, the reddish animal fur. She saw the prissy gentility of the lips. She smelled the smell.

'Sleepwalker,' said the man softly, looking at her.

Mary snatched up a small bronze vase, and hit the man hard upon the side of the head. He looked at her with infinite surprise and reproach, swayed, and sank to the floor. He lay there like a large black-garbed doll, and blood began to flow from the wound on his head. His eyes were closed and he was very pale.

Mary stood looking down upon him, and tried to measure what she had done. 'Three minutes ago," she thought, 'I was mad with joy because I was going to Hugh, and now perhaps I have killed a man who is a stranger.' She now felt curiously hard and not at all frightened. She went to the telephone and called John Weston at his surgery.

'John,' she said, 'this is Mary Manly. I am at home, I think I have killed a man. Please come.' And she hung up the telephone and went back to the small man who lay as she had left him.

I am very stupid, thought Mary, because I do not know whether he is unconscious or whether he is dead, and I don't know how to find out such things. At least I will bathe his head, and perhaps if he is unconscious he will rally a bit. She got water and a cloth, and although it was repugnant to her, she knelt down and bathed the wound which she had inflicted on the small respectable man. He stirred. He opened his eyes and looked steadily at her. She rose to her feet and looked down at him.

'Dear lady,' whispered the man, still prostrate on the floor, 'whatever made you do that to me?' and his eyes were indeed the eyes of an animal.

Well, thought Mary, I can see that this is going to be a very odd conversation. She could not answer his question, and so she said, 'I am very, very sorry that I have done this to you, but why are you here? And why did you walk into my flat like that? And what was that you said to me when you came in?' It gave her satisfaction that John Weston would soon come, and would act as some kind of a solvent to this situation.

The man sat up slowly, and felt his head. He looked at his red hand with surprise, and again looked up at Mrs Manly.

'Name of Sleepwalker,' he said, 'carrying a line of ladies' underwear samples of special buys in rayon, silk, crêpe, also ladies' hosiery put out by the Silki-Silk company with agents in all major cities of Canada,' and he looked at the black valise which lay where it had fallen.

'Oh,' said Mary, feeling very silly indeed. 'And do you really mean that your name is Sleepwalker?'

'Name of Handel Sleepwalker,' said Mr Sleepwalker, and subsided again into a faint on the floor.

The doorbell rang, and Mary opened the door to Dr Weston. Because Dr Weston was ruffled, and had—unwillingly—left his patients when Mary summoned him so imperatively and strangely, he had, since leaving his consulting-room, built up a genuine and justified annoyance mixed with real uneasiness, and because he could find no other object for his annoyance, he had hung it upon Mary Manly. Therefore by the time Dr Weston arrived at Mary's apartment he was very angry indeed with her for having killed a man at a quarter-past five in the afternoon, for having taken him forcibly from his consultation and for having chosen to do this at a time when Hugh was not at home and therefore was unable to take the matter in hand. Although a very good friend of Hugh and Mary, Dr Weston was not at that moment in the frame of mind to shoulder the results of murder. This is why, when Mary opened the door with a sense of relief, John Weston dismayed her by a complete absence of sympathy; he turned on her an angry face, and roared at her in an injured manner, 'What on earth *have* you been doing?' as if she were guilty. Well, so she was.

Mary, aware of all that had gone before that was so ridiculously unexplainable at that very instant, realized that she had to cope with her own emotions to attend—in the first—to Mr Sleepwalker who lay inert on the living-room floor, and to manage Dr Weston either by returning anger for anger, innocence for anger, or by disregarding anger. This latter she decided to do.

'Come,' she said. She turned and indicated Mr Sleepwalker with an air quite sublime. 'You see!'

When Dr Weston saw the actual body of Mr Sleepwalker lying on the floor of the room in which Dr Weston and his wife had so often enjoyed a cocktail, and saw Mr Sleepwalker's blood upon the carpet, and saw Mary standing there pale, helpless, bandaged and gentle, other feelings began to take possession of him. He kneeled down and examined the prostrate one. Then he looked up and said to Mary in a fretful tone, 'He's not dead at all!'

Well, really, thought Mary, this is too much! Does John expect that she should make sure of *killing* someone before disturbing him! John is going to be aggravating, I can see. But she said simply, 'Oh, John, I am so thankful. This has been very alarming.'

'Did *you* hit him?' asked Dr Weston, scrambling to his feet.

'Oh yes, I hit him.'

'Why . . .?'

'He *terrified* me,' said Mary. 'He stole into the room when I opened the door, and followed me up, and did not explain his business, and then he said something that frightened me very much. And here I was with my bad arm and alone, and before I realized what I was doing, John, I hit him with that little vase.'

'What did he say to you?' asked Dr Weston.

Mr Sleepwalker spoke from the floor. His eyes were closed. He said softly, 'I did not indeed desire to frighten the dear lady; I merely told the dear lady my name.'

Dr Weston shot a very baleful look at Mary; he became suspicious of her again (and there were all those patients in the waiting-room).

'And what *is* your name?' asked Dr Weston.

'Sleepwalker,' said Mr Sleepwalker, opening his eyes.

'And where do you live?' asked Dr Weston.

Mr Sleepwalker closed his eyes again. 'I am afraid,' he said, 'that for the moment I am unable to remember.'

'Well, where would you like us to take you?' asked the doctor.

'Yes, where would you like us to take you?' asked Mary, eagerly.

Mr Sleepwalker paused for a moment. Then, 'I would like to stay ere,' he said.

'That is impossible, quite impossible,' said Dr Weston crossly. 'You can take him to the hospital, Mary. He's all right to move, and a day or two will be all that's needed."

'John,' said Mary, taking the doctor aside, 'do you notice a very queer smell in this room?'

'No, I don't,' said the doctor. 'Do you?'

She did not answer. 'I will get an ambulance if you will arrange with the hospital,' she said.

'I would much prefer,' said a silky voice from the floor, 'if the dear lady would take me to the ospital erself. Far be it indeed to go in an ambulance.'

Mary scowled at the doctor, who said at once, 'No, we'll get an ambulance. See if you can sit up now.'

Mr Sleepwalker obediently sat up, a little black figure with legs outstretched on the floor. The doctor supported him.

'Now into this chair.'

'I am a poor man,' said Mr Sleepwalker, sitting up straight and stiff in the chair, with his disfigured head.

'I will pay for your ambulance, Mr Sleepwalker, and I will pay for your days in the hospital as long as Dr Weston says that you must stay,' said Mary.

'Oh, ow kind, dear lady,' said Mr Sleepwalker humbly, and Mary thought, What a brute I am, I've never abased myself and really apologized for hitting him! 'I shall get you some tea,' she said. Meanwhile, the doctor was busy at the telephone. He looked at his watch. 'Don't leave me!' mumured Mary as she brushed past him in the hall, and Dr Weston gave her an un-affectionate look. She took a tray in to Mr Sleepwalker, who gazed round the room as though he were memorizing it.

'I shall burn this tray, break the cup and saucer, give away the chair, and send the carpet to the cleaners or we can sell it—in fact, we might leave the flat. I can't bear to have had this little horror in the room,' Mary said to herself unfairly, forgetting that she was very lucky.

Mr Sleepwalker coughed. 'One thing may I hask,' he said.

'What,' said Mary.

'I would like to hask,' he said, 'that the dear lady will visit me in the ospital.'

Mary considered. That was the very least she could do.

'Yes, of course I will,' she said, trying to sound hearty.

'Oh, thank you, *thank* you,' said Mr Sleepwalker. The doctor came out of the hall.

'I have arranged for the bed and the ambulance,' he said, looking again at his watch. 'Some time I will hear more about this.' He had one leg out of the door.

'You will stay!' besought Mary with agitation, seizing his arm.

The doctor put down his overcoat again. 'Very well, I will stay,' he said irritably, and thought of his waiting-room. He did not like Mary Manly at all just now, whether because she had or had not killed Mr Sleepwalker (although on the whole he was relieved that she had not); but chiefly he disliked Mary because she had behaved in an irrational manner,—he disapproved of people being irrational—and had called him away from his surgery in the middle of the afternoon. He whirled to the telephone, and Mary heard him say brusquely, 'I'll be back. Keep Mrs Jenkins, and tell Mr Howe I'll see him tomorrow, and explain to the two others that I'll see them tomorrow, and give them a time, and tell Mrs Boniface that I'll drop in on the way home, and don't let the Jackson boy go home till I've seen him, and . . ."

'Oh Lord,' thought Mary, contrite, 'what have I done to all these people! Poor Johnny!' and she tried to look pathetic, but it was no good.

The ambulance arrived, and Dr Weston sped away. Two burly ambulance men helped Mr Sleepwalker; he walked between them in his still fashion. One big man carried his absurdly small valise. The other one took charge of the obsolete hat. Mary stood.

At the door Mr Sleepwalker made as if to turn.

'I do hask, dear lady, that you will recollect your promise?' he said, with a question.

'I will indeed,' said Mary heartily and with the greatest repugnance.

She heard the door close. She turned and opened all the windows, and did what she could to the room. Then she telephoned Cora. 'Cora,' she said, 'a very peculiar thing has happened. I won't tell you over the telephone, but here, but for the grace of God, sits your cousin, the famous murderess . . .' a thought checked her, 'or,' and she laughed, 'the famous huntress.'

'What *do* you mean!' asked Cora.

'Well,' said Mary slowly, 'you remember the night we nearly ran that man down on the bridge?'

'Yes, yes,' said Cora.

'Well,' continued Mary slowly, 'it's the same man. Coincidence of course, of the most extraordinary kind' (was it coincidence?) 'and it's left me rather shaken.'

'Too much happens to you. Come at once and have dinner,' said Cora.

'I will,' said Mary gratefully.

As Mary Manly went to her cousin's house, she asked herself some questions. If I wished to go to the bottom of the queerness of this, if I had any scientific curiosity and not just a detestation of the whole affair, I would take up a notebook and pencil, and question that . . . that . . . person (she avoided even his name). I would say to him, Was your aunt a fox, or your grandmother a weasel, and of course, he would say no, and where should I find myself then? I could ask him if he seeks me in particular, and how, and why. But I am such a coward that I don't want to know. Then I would say, My good sir, do you know that you smell? And if he said yes, I should have to ask him, Do some people (such as I) and not other people, recognize this animal (yes, I should have to say 'animal') scent? I can see how totally impossible such a conversation is, and so I shall leave it alone, and shall admit, to myself, and not to others, only the fact that this man frightens me. . . .

When Mary left Cora the next morning (for Cora easily persuaded her to stay the night), she knew that the talk of her attack upon Mr Sleepwalker would spread among her friends and acquaintances, and that it would be well and properly launched by Cora. She realized that she would be the object of universal pity ('Poor Mrs Manly, wasn't it dreadful for her! The man, my dear, walked straight into the flat, and there was Mary all alone, with a broken arm . . . I think she's very good not to prosecute! And so brave. The most extraordinary coincidence, my dear! Cora Wilmot says . . .') and that this was not quite fair to Mr Sleepwalker who, after all, was the one who had been hit on the temple with a bronze vase and was now in hospital. She knew that she would be decried as soft, foolish, and too kind because she had provided the ambulance and was about to pay the hospital bill. However, she had to choose between all or nothing, and the section of the story which was in Cora's possession and which Cora would launch on all their acquaintances with her well-known energy, approximated to nothing, and that was best.

The following afternoon Mary said to herself as she alighted clumsily with parcels at the hospital, This (calling on this man, I mean) is the most unpleasant thing that I have deliberately done in my whole life. I don't call hitting . . . Mr Sleepwalker . . . deliberate. It was instinctive. If only Hugh were with me it would be easier. However, as she had that afternoon received a cable from Hugh which read: 'Cheers and cheers take first passage and cable me,' she felt more carefree than she would have thought possible. I can tell this . . . individual . . . she thought, that I am going to Australia (that seems far enough away)—which is true—that I'm going tomorrow, which is not true, but it is true enough. And she entered the hospital.

She found Mr Sleepwalker propped up a little on his pillows, looking very pale. His head was bandaged, and when she saw the bandage, she felt much more guilty than when, in the storm of terror, she had struck down Mr Sleepwalker and had seen him lying on the floor, with blood flowing upon the carpet.

Patients in the adjacent beds regarded her apathetically. Mr Sleepwalker looked earnestly, too earnestly, at her. I should, of course, give him my hand, she said to herself, this hand which has struck him down. But she did not wish to do so. She found that her feelings were strangely involved. In order to avoid touching Mr Sleepwalker's hand, and for no more altruistic reason, Mary had filled her good hand with flowers, and carried magazines and a box of chocolates under her arm. As she disposed these articles awkwardly about Mr Sleepwalker's bed, the handshaking moment passed, as she had intended it should. A nurse, seeing her arm in a sling, brought forward a chair. Mary smiled at her, thanked her, and sat down.

'I hope you are not too uncomfortable,' she said.

'Oh, no, thank you, dear lady,' said Mr Sleepwalker. 'This is a very nice ospital, nicer than what I was in in England that time the dogs bit me.'

'Dogs . . .!' said Mary.

'Ounds,' said Mr Sleepwalker.

Mr Sleepwalker's bandages really afflicted Mary. They made her feel more guilty even than her own conscience. However, she could not afford to get soft about Mr Sleepwalker, even though she had hit him with a vase.

'I am sorry that I cannot have a nice long chat,' she said untruthfully, 'but the fact is that I am flying to Australia tomorrow to join my husband.'

'Come a little closer, dear lady,' said Mr Sleepwalker. His reddish eyes were fixed upon her. Mary made hitching noises with her chair, but she was near enough. She began to feel faint, 'I should like to go to Australia,' he said, 'Oh, ow I should like!'

'Australia is, I am sure, a very nice country,' replied Mary with considerable idiocy. I must keep this impersonal, she thought, and proceeded to talk about Australia, of which she knew very little. 'So you see I cannot stay any longer; in fact, I must go. Everthing will be arranged, the bill, you know. I am so very sorry for what I did to you. It was really some terrible misunderstanding.'

The little man in the bed continued to look earnestly at her.

'It has been a pleasure indeed to meet you, dear lady,' he said in his soft voice. (What an extraordinary statement! thought Mary.) 'May I thank you indeed for your kindness, and may I tell you, dear lady, ow grateful I ave always been to you, and ow I ave frequently and in oh ever so many places enjoyed your delicious smell . . . fragrance, I *should* say.'

'My . . .! my . . .!' stammered Mary, and sprang to her feet. She stood for one moment looking down at Mr Sleepwalker. Then she turned and the patients saw her running like a hare out of the ward.

1961

Till death us do part

I have a friend, well I should say an acquaintance, well anyway someone who works with me in the wool shop that is, and she is a very interesting girl not because she says anything, oh no. She is very silent and I don't know whether she is bad tempered or just silent. I think she is proud. Her name is Kate and she is very efficient in the wool shop. If her expression was happier I would say she is beautiful. She is small with a natural golden coiffure or is it coiffeur, well what I mean hair-do and a very clear complexion but I wish she would respond a bit. She silences me. We never laugh and I am used to laughing when I feel like it.

Kate seems to have got a queer defensive thing, I can't imagine why. Perhaps she *has* to defend herself in some way. Me being older than she is although I am junior in the shop, I've had to knock about a bit and I know things happen sometimes so you *have* to defend yourself but she doesn't need to defend herself against me, I'm not going to do her any harm, or is she jealous? oh surely no. I'd like to like her but as it is she won't let me. I think she's scared of intimacy but heavens I don't want to be intimate. Probably she just doesn't like me. Oh well, you can't like everyone.

If I say, Good morning isn't it a lovely day, she says it's going to rain. And if I say, Did you see that warship come into harbour this morning, she says, That wasn't a warship. At first I used to argue a little but that was silly and got nowhere. She'd be better to say just Yes and No. It would save argument and be pleasanter. And better still I'd be wiser not to make a remark of any kind. However.

The result is that neither of us speaks because it is no fun speaking, except to the customers and we are both lovely to the customers. The owner and manager is away sick and I sure hope she comes back soon and sweetens the atmosphere a little. Perhaps Kate has a secret sorrow. Well so have I.

I began to go home at night pretty ruffled. I knew I was being put in my place and supposed to stay there but couldn't see why this should be. I'm a human being too, aren't I.

Today I was very pleased at a good order of wool to a new customer for bed jackets and I thought why not say so.

Yes, said Kate, I saw you. You didn't sell her enough wool for those bed jackets. I could of told you. Then we'll be out of wool when she wants it.

I was really annoyed and said, I always sell that amount for bed jackets and in my experience—and then I thought, This isn't intelligent, and I said no more.

Then I thought What shall I do about this. Shall I

Sit on a stile and continue to smile
That should soften the heart of this cow

but it did not soften the heart. However I had to speak to Kate because the telephone rang and someone asked if Mrs Physick was there. I said I was sorry but Mrs Physick was away ill and could I take a message. And the lady said, Oh dear, well I'll get in touch, but say her aunty called.

I said to Kate, That was Mrs Physick's aunty and I was to say she called.

Kate said, Mrs Physick hasn't got an aunty.

Well really that attitude made me mad if people have to feed their ego that much, so when I got home at night I rang up Mrs Physick's place although I didn't really know her and I said to the person who came to the phone, Oh it's Muriel Brown from the shop, and please would you kindly tell Mrs Physick that her aunty rang up today.

And the person said, Her aunty? Mrs Physick hasn't got an aunty. Oh you must mean Mrs Bonaventure, she always calls her aunty. Was there any message?

I felt very small and said, Oh no, she only rang up and will get in touch, and the lady said, Yes she did.

I sat still on the telephone stool and thought So she's right and there isn't any aunty and I can't win.

I had begun to be very introspective because there were ever so many more silly little things like that and I started not sleeping at night. I've got troubles of my own.

One morning Kate came in late to the shop with her right hand bandaged and began to fumble among the boxes. She didn't seem to want to speak about her hand nor about being so late but turned her face away from me and then she dropped a box because she only had her left hand, and the balls of wool rolled all over the floor.

Oh I said, don't try to pick them up! and I began to pick them up. I looked up at her from where I was on my knees and saw that her face was scarlet and I knew that Kate's pride was hurt to an absurd degree that she should have to be indebted to me, picking up the balls of wool off the floor.

When I had finished I straightened up and looked right at her. I said with authority (a trembling sort of authority I'll tell you, because I had become frightened of Kate and what snub might lie in wait for me), I said, You are not used to letting people do things for you or letting them cooperate with you, but you must let me help you all I can with the boxes and things. It will be a pleasure I assure you except I'm sorry about your hand. Oh what is wrong with your hand?

My hand . . . said Kate turning deathly white, and she had been so scarlet, my hand . . . my hand . . . and a customer came in.

JULY 7.

I began writing this about Kate's hand and her strangeness and then I was much busier for some days and I hadn't time to write down about it. A story has to end and this story hasn't ended yet and I don't know what the end will be.

Kate tried to ignore her hand as much as possible and went back again into her silent way and I went back into my silent way except that I did watch to make things easier if possible, lifting, and boiling the kettle for tea and so on. I do think the shop had the unpleasantest feeling that ever I knew in a place but I decided to go on with it. There's always something.

I got a letter from my sister in Portage la Prairie and she said that when their busy season was over she and Frank would put the boys at his mother's and they might drive to the coast and see how I was getting along, and oh how my heart warmed up under these circumstances. She wrote about Peterborough Edwards too and that was the first time she had mentioned Peterborough Edwards and I found that I didn't mind at all because although it was all on account of Peterborough I had left Portage la Prairie and at first I had felt really badly about it, I found that by this time I was relieved about Peterborough rather than feeling badly. You can go on and on and on with a person till you get past the disappointment point, and then they begin to bore you. I was really just a habit with Peterborough although to my surprise he was awfully shocked when I decided to go off. You never can tell. I like it here in Vancouver except for Kate, it's a change but then I might like to go back to Portage la Prairie some time but no more Peterborough unless he can make up his mind. It seems that he had rung up my sister to see was there any news from me but she was very airy fairy with him she said and she said I was having a wonderful time in Vancouver.

Ha ha.

After a week Kate had the bandage off her hand and it was really very nasty looking. There were still plasters on it as if there were cuts and it was evidently painful, so I helped all I could but not what you'd call ostentatious. There was once that Kate turned to me with such lovely sweetness and gratitude and her pretty customer smile and oh how my heart warmed as it does, foolishly I expect.

That sweetness did not last only long enough for me to think how lovely it would be, because then Mrs Physick rang me up.

All my arrangements with Mrs Physick had been made by mail and so I had not seen her because the doctor said she must have this operation.

But now Mrs Physick asked me to go and see her in the evening if convenient and take the order book and the old order book too, to compare stocks for ordering. She sounded quite young, I was surprised.

After I hung up I said to Kate, is Mrs Physick old or young? She sounds quite young to me.

Kate said coldly, It all depends on what you call young.

Kate was uneasy. At last she said, Why did she ring you not me? Why did she tell *you* to take the order books?

Well really how silly! Mrs Physick probably wanted to give me the once-over but it was no good entering on a silly argument so I said snappishly Better ask her yourself, and we were quits but the atmosphere was nearly unbearable again.

JULY 10.

I took the order books to Mrs Physick's flat where she lived with a woman friend who Mrs Physick told me had a hat shop. Mrs. Physick was lying on a couch and said she was still taking it easy after the operation. She was pleasant looking, youngish but her hair going gray. She had the nice kind of face with some lines on. We went through the order books and she told me to leave them and she'd run through them again and then Kate or I could come and get them. She looked at me and said, How do you get along with Kate?

I said, Oh I get along. And then I said, But I don't think she likes me.

Mrs Physick looked worried and she put out her hand. I know, she said, It's not easy. Don't take it personally.

I was afraid of beginning to discuss Kate which would be a disloyal thing to do and anyway I did not think Mrs Physick would do such a thing, Kate being the senior employee.

Just the same I said, Oh yes it is personal. It would be impossible not to feel that—but I don't take it too seriously. I'll be going now Mrs Physick, is there anything else?

Mrs Physick did not speak for a moment and then she looked down and almost whispered, Kate is a very unhappy young woman.

I was standing up to go. I wondered whether I ought to tell her about Kate's right hand or was even that talking too much. However, I blurted out, She hurt her right hand, I think she had an accident, she didn't say, the bandage is off now and it looks nasty but she can manage more easily.

Mrs Physick stared at me. An accident? she said, an accident to her right hand? It seems to me people always have accidents to their left hand! What kind of accident?

I said, I don't know. She didn't say. It looked to me as if something had hit it.

Mrs Physick was silent and then spoke sort of unhappily, Oh do be good to her, she said, and I said I'll try. I began to think that Mrs Physick might be the whole world to Kate and she couldn't bear to have her friendly to any new person.

JULY 17.

It must have been a few days after I wrote last time and I had been doing what Mrs Physick said, making every allowance and paying no attention and I thought that perhaps Kate seemed happier and I remember feeling happier myself, and easier, when one day I saw a woman in black standing very still outside the door of the shop. Kate was serving a customer at the back of the shop where the new stock of children's small foreign toys are and I was in the front with a customer who wanted to make some baby outfits. There was the wool and there was the pattern book. The customer was taking a long time looking and making little remarks to herself, and in between I happened to look at the glass front door.

The woman began to peer closely this way and that through the glass as though she was looking for someone. She saw me but paid me no attention. I had to attend to my customer and so I could not keep looking at the woman as I wanted to. But I did see that now she was bending down and gazing in and then it seemed to me that she saw what she was looking for. She looked fixedly and with a very unpleasant expression deep into the shop. Between pleasing my customer and advising with her and looking at the woman and looking to see if Kate had seen her, it was all difficult, but the woman (I could see) remained bent down nearly double and peering in.

Next time I could look away from my customer I saw the woman had gone, and I saw that Kate was moving up the shop with her customer who had in her hand one of those little music boxes that seem so funny in a wool shop.

Oh the woman wore a shabby black coat and had her head tied up like an old peasant woman. Her face was sallow, almost yellow, but although I did not know her, there was something familiar about her face and then I knew that if you can have someone ugly look like someone pretty, this woman looked like Kate.

I was very horrified because I thought could this ever be the mother of Kate who is so pretty and so clean and proud and refined and tension-full and—as Mrs Physick said—so unhappy. And I thought Oh how terrible, Kate going home every night to perhaps such a mother in a small place and coming back in the morning full of the feeling of it. How terrible! Next day the woman came again and I found myself watching each day for her and each day she came and bent down to peer through the glass but if Kate was in full view, or on the approach of Kate, she always vanished.

I began to make up stories in my head and I think that Kate had forbidden the mother ever to come near the shop, and so shame her who was so proud, but that in order to annoy her the woman came every day and watched, and that was the kind of woman she was.

Sometimes either Kate or I go into the little back place and get out new stock or paper bags or something, and one of these times when Kate was in the back, the woman came to the door. This time she was bolder. She put her hand on the latch and pushed the door open and stood and I saw more clearly her yellow face which seemed to me terrible and without, well, without humanity. I went up to her (and I felt ready to defend Kate) and said, Can I do anything for you? and the sour smell of cheap whiskey came strong right at me. I did not know what to do. She gave me a look only, and then with a kind of derision she looked slowly round the shop, up and down the shelves, as if to fix in her mind the kind of heaven her daughter came to every day.

I said again, Can I do anything for you? and I wondered Is she foreign or what because she doesn't answer, and all the time the reek of whiskey was on her, when Kate came out from the back and suddenly stopped. The peculiar bright scarlet came up her neck and over her face and then the whiteness and she looked like a frozen woman.

I did not know what was the best thing to do. Everything rushed through my mind in a turmoil about Kate's pride and tension and the hurt right hand and Mrs Physick saying She is unhappy and there was a kind of yawning terribleness of how unhappy she must be to act like she does. There was also this at the same moment, that I must do something at once and that I must not let Kate think in all her pride that I knew that this woman (a hag if every I saw one) could her mother, or the sight of me would always be unbearable to her. So I stepped between them and took the evil-smelling woman gently but firmly by the shoulder and said Let's . . . let's go outside, and I walked her out of the door and shut it.

She was surprised at my action and looked angrily into my face and tried to shake me off.

I got a perfect right, she said, to go into your old shop, and I said, Oh no, you've been drinking, we can't have you in our shop, and she said, I have not so been drinking, and she looked very vicious. Then she spat at me and that made me really mad, a little short and sharp spit.

So I said, You certainly have been drinking and I'll have to get a policeman if you try to come into our shop, there's a policeman at the Bank at the corner, and the woman looked at me like a snake and slipped out of my hand and was gone. There's nothing like the word policeman.

I stood outside in the fresh air for a minute. I felt awful, not just because of this woman but because of Kate. Then I went into the shop but I left the door wide open because it seemed to me the whole place smelled of the stench of that woman. It was lucky there was no customer there, but it would have been just the same if there had been a customer.

Kate was not in the shop. So I wondered What do I do now? It isn't natural for me ever to go to the back and talk to Kate about anything but I'd better do it, casual like, and now. So I went into the back and I think Kate had her head on the desk but she straightened up and looked at me quite wild.

I didn't seem to notice, I hope, and said, Did you see that woman in the store? She'd been drinking so I took her out and told her not to come in. She said she'd come in if she liked but I said No, not when she'd been drinking, in fact I'd have to call a constable if she came in again and she beat it. I kind of hated to speak to an old wom . . . an old lady like that but what could I do. I hope that was all right? I said, anxious like.

Kate nodded her head, still looking at me in that wild way, and I went back into the shop. When the time came to close up I could not bear to think of Kate going home to what she was going home to, but what can you do?

JULY 25.

This has been an uncomfortable week. If it weren't for the fact that business is good and us busy (I think those little foreign dolls and houses and things in the window attract people) I don't think I could stick it. Things seem out of control. Kate is the silentest person I ever did see, but more than that she is so unhappy. It would be no good trying to horn in with a little comfort and what's more she looks ill, in herself, I mean. Her hand was very inflamed this morning and she had it bandaged all over again, but badly. Could I help you fix that, I said, and she said, Well just a bit tighter here, and pin it, and then she actually said Thank you.

I'm not one to tell tales but I just felt that it was too much responsibility and I must go and talk to Mrs Physick after supper. Mrs Physick came to the door herself and she looked better but she moved slowly and we went into the room and sat down.

I said, I'm very worried Mrs Physick about Kate, and I told her about the woman and about Kate's reaction to the woman (all out of proportion, I thought, though it sure was bad enough) and how her hand was infected and red and swollen up her arm and what could we do. I said, I am very willing to go and do things up for her at her home but I don't know where she lives.

No, no, said Mrs Physick. That would never do. Kate is very very proud (I said, I'll say she's proud) and it would spoil your relations together for always if you went into that house and saw it—she'd never forget it. I know it. I'll go. I can drive the car now. You go home. I'll phone later. So I went home.

It was midnight before Mrs Physick phoned and she didn't waste words.

She said, Can you carry on alone tomorrow? Maybe I'll be down for a bit some time. I got Kate into hospital. She's running a fever. When I got there the mother let me in but Kate's bedroom door was closed. Yes it was locked and I had to knock and knock and call but she was suspicious and it was some time before she'd let me in. To think of her barricaded against that woman! I don't blame her. The place was a dirty shambles. Well goodnight Muriel. Do you know my belief: My belief is that bitch hit her on the hand with a bottle.

JULY 29.

I'm carrying on at the shop with Mrs Physick down half days. Kate's been up to the O.R. and they've taken splinters of glass out of her hand. I don't know how I can bear it when Kate comes back, and she will come back, to think of her and that mother going on for ever and ever together and no escape till death comes for one of them, whatever way it comes, but some way death will part them.

There was a letter from Peterborough Edwards tonight when I got home, addressed care of my sister. Peterborough wants to come down to Vancouver on his holiday. He seems upset. I won't answer right away. Do him good to be upset. But my mind turns to Peterborough Edwards as a comfort when I think of Kate and her mother going on until death parts them. I don't say I'd really choose Peterborough Edwards and I never thought I'd turn to Peterborough on account of these circumstances but he might be a comfort and anyway, what can you do.

1961

F. Scott Fitzgerald

1896-1940

In his essays and letters, F. Scott Fitzgerald offers no explicit reflections on the nature of fiction; he does, however, name some of his favourite authors. In 1923 he admitted, 'I'd rather have written Conrad's "Nostromo" than any other novel.' And two years later he wrote that Conrad defined 'the serious business of my profession . . . more clearly, more vividly than any man of our time: "My task is by the power of the written word to make you hear, to make you feel—it is, before all, to make you see".'

In his own fiction Fitzgerald, the social historian of the jazz age and the chronicler—as well as a member—of the American expatriate colony in Europe, captures the hopes and the illusions of his time. Eager for social standing, Fitzgerald pursued the kind of jazz-age high living that he chronicled in his fiction. Yet his novels and short stories, while recording his era, explore and often expose the American dream of material success and happiness.

Born in Saint Paul, Minnesota, the son of a middle-class father whose business failed and a mother from an old upper-class family, Fitzgerald attended private schools and Princeton University, dropping out of college when the United States entered the First World War in 1917. He served in the army for two years, then devoted himself exclusively to the writing of fiction. After his first novel, *This Side of Paradise*, was published in 1920, he divided his time between America and Europe for the next decade. In 1931 he returned permanently to the United States, and later turned to writing for the cinema. He died in Los Angeles.

As he was writing *The Great Gatsby* (1925), Fitzgerald observed that 'the whole burden of this novel' was 'the loss of those illusions that give such colour to the world so that you don't care whether things are true or false as long as they partake of the magical glory.' The beauty of these illusions is equalled by the pathos that follows upon their loss. 'Winter Dreams', a short version, Fitzgerald noted, of *The Great Gatsby*, presents Dexter Green's education in and commitment to the American dream, and then his personal anguish as the enchantment wears off. The centre of Dexter's dream is less financial success, which he easily achieves, than Judy Jones, herself the personification of the American dream, who 'simply made men conscious to the highest degree of her physical loveliness.' Fiction writers such as Henry James and himself, Fitzgerald reflected, 'have to have love as a main concern since our interest lies outside the economic struggle or the life of violence.'

In 'Babylon Revisited', written during Fitzgerald's final long period of residence in Europe, Charlie Watts, widower, reformed alcoholic, and successful businessman, returns to Paris to regain custody of his nine-year-old daughter. Built upon the contrasts between Watts' present life and his former Babylonian lifestyle, between his own generosity and the meanness of spirit of his late wife's sister, the story forces its protagonist to realize that his past never ceases to haunt and to hurt him.

'Winter Dreams' was first published in the December 1922 issue of *Metropolitan Magazine* and then revised and collected in *All the Sad Young Men* (1926). 'Babylon Revisited' was first published in the 21 February 1931 issue of *The Saturday Evening Post* and then revised and collected in *Taps at Reveille* (1935).

Winter Dreams

Some of the caddies were poor as sin and lived in one-room houses with a neurasthenic cow in the front yard, but Dexter Green's father owned the second best grocery-store in Black Bear—the best one was 'The Hub', patronized by the wealthy people from Sherry Island—and Dexter caddied only for pocket-money.

In the fall when the days became crisp and grey, and the long Minnesota winter shut down like the white lid of a box, Dexter's skis moved over the snow that hid the fairways of the golf course. At these times the country gave him a feeling of profound melancholy—it offended him that the links should lie in enforced fallowness, haunted by ragged sparrows for the long season. It was dreary, too, that on the tees where the gay colours fluttered in summer there were now only the desolate sand-boxes knee-deep in crusted ice. When he crossed the hills the wind blew cold as misery, and if the sun was out he tramped with his eyes squinted up against the hard dimensionless glare.

In April the winter ceased abruptly. The snow ran down into Black Bear Lake scarcely tarrying for the early golfers to brave the season with red and black balls. Without elation, without an interval of moist glory, the cold was gone.

Dexter knew that there was something dismal about this Northern spring, just as he knew there was something gorgeous about the fall. Fall made him clinch his hands and tremble and repeat idiotic sentences to himself, and make brisk abrupt gestures of command to imaginary audiences and armies. October filled him with hope which November raised to a sort of ecstatic triumph, and in this mood the fleeting brilliant impressions of the summer at Sherry Island were ready grist to his mill. He became a golf champion and defeated Mr T.A. Hedrick in a marvellous match played a hundred times over the fairways of his imagination, a match each detail of which he changed about untiringly—sometimes he won with almost laughable ease, sometimes he came up magnificently from behind. Again, stepping from a Pierce-Arrow automobile, like Mr Mortimer Jones, he strolled frigidly into the lounge of the Sherry Island Golf Club—or perhaps, surrounded by an admiring crowd, he gave an exhibition of fancy diving from the spring-board of the club raft. . . . Among those who watched him in open-mouthed wonder was Mr Mortimer Jones.

And one day it came to pass that Mr Jones—himself and not his ghost—came up to Dexter with tears in his eyes and said that Dexter was the —— best caddy in the club, and wouldn't he decide not to quit if Mr Jones made it worth his while, because every other —— caddy in the club lost one ball a hole for him—regularly—

'No sir,' said Dexter decisively, 'I don't want to caddy any more.' Then, after a pause: 'I'm too old.'

'You're not more than fourteen. Why the devil did you decide just this morning that you wanted to quit? You promised that next week you'd go over to the state tournament with me.'

'I decided I was too old.'

Dexter handed in his 'A Class' badge, collected what money was due him from the caddy master, and walked home to Black Bear Village.

'The best——caddy I ever saw,' shouted Mr Mortimer Jones over a drink that afternoon. 'Never lost a ball! Willing! Intelligent! Quiet! Honest! Grateful!'

The little girl who had done this was eleven—beautifully ugly as little girls are apt to be who are destined after a few years to be inexpressibly lovely and bring no end of misery to a great number of men. The spark, however, was perceptible. There was a general ungodliness in the way her lips twisted down at the corners when she smiled, and in the—Heaven help us!—in the almost passionate quality of her eyes. Vitality is born in such women. It was utterly in evidence now, shining through her thin frame in a sort of glow.

She had come eagerly out on to the course at nine o'clock with a white linen nurse and five small new golf-clubs in a white canvas bag which the nurse was carrying. When Dexter first saw her she was standing by the caddy house, rather ill at ease and trying to conceal the fact by engaging her nurse in an obviously unnatural conversation graced by startling and irrelevant grimaces from herself.

'Well, it's certainly a nice day, Hilda,' Dexter heard her say. She drew down the corners of her mouth, smiled, and glanced furtively around, her eyes in transit falling for an instant on Dexter.

Then to the nurse:

'Well, I guess there aren't very many people out here this morning, are there?'

The smile again—radiant, blatantly artificial—convincing.

'I don't know what we're supposed to do now,' said the nurse, looking nowhere in particular.

'Oh, that's all right. I'll fix it up.'

Dexter stood perfectly still, his mouth slightly ajar. He knew that if he moved forward a step his stare would be in her line of vision—if he moved backward he would lose his full view of her face. For a moment he had not realized how young she was. Now he remembered having seen her several times the year before—in bloomers.

Suddenly, involuntarily, he laughed, a short abrupt laugh—then, startled by himself, he turned and began to walk quickly away.

'Boy!'

Dexter stopped.

'Boy—'

Beyond question he was addressed. Not only that but he was treated to that absurd smile, that preposterous smile—the memory of which at least a dozen men were to carry into middle age.

'Boy, do you know where the golf teacher is?'

'He's giving a lesson.'

'Well, do you know where the caddy-master is?'

'He isn't here yet this morning.'

'Oh.' For a moment this baffled her. She stood alternately on her right and left foot.

'We'd like to get a caddy,' said the nurse. 'Mrs Mortimer Jones sent us out to play golf, and we don't know how without we get a caddy.'

Here she was stopped by an ominous glance from Miss Jones, followed immediately by the smile.

'There aren't any caddies here except me,' said Dexter to the nurse, 'and I got to stay here in charge until the caddy-master gets here.'

'Oh.'

Miss Jones and her retinue now withdrew, and at a proper distance from Dexter became involved in a heated conversation, which was concluded by Miss Jones taking one of the clubs and hitting it on the ground with violence. For further emphasis she raised it again and was about to bring it down smartly upon the nurse's bosom, when the nurse seized the club and twisted it from her hands.

'You damn little mean old *thing!*' cried Miss Jones wildly.

Another argument ensued. Realizing that the elements of the comedy were implied in the scene, Dexter several times began to laugh, but each time restrained the laugh before it reached audibility. He could not resist the monstrous conviction that the little girl was justified in beating the nurse.

The situation was resolved by the fortuitous appearance of the caddy-master, who was appealed to immediately by the nurse.

'Miss Jones is to have a little caddy, and this one says he can't go.'

'Mr McKenna said I was to wait here till you came,' said Dexter quickly.

'Well, he's here now.' Miss Jones smiled cheerfully at the caddy-master. Then she dropped her bag and set off at a haughty mince toward the first tee.

'Well?' the caddy-master turned to Dexter. 'What you standing there like a dummy for? Go pick up the young lady's clubs.'

'I don't think I'll go out to-day,' said Dexter.

'You don't—'

'I think I'll quit.'

The enormity of his decision frightened him. He was a favourite caddy, and the thirty dollars a month he earned through the summer were not to be made elsewhere around the lake. But he had received a strong emotional shock, and his perturbation required a violent and immediate outlet.

It is not so simple as that, either. As so frequently would be the case in the future, Dexter was unconsciously dictated to by his winter dreams.

II

Now, of course, the quality and the seasonability of these winter dreams varied, but the stuff of them remained. They persuaded Dexter several years later to pass up a business course at the State university—his father, prospering now, would have paid his way—for the precarious advantage of attending an older and more famous university in the East, where he was bothered by his scanty funds. But do not get the impression, because his winter dreams happened to be concerned at first with musings on the rich, that there was anything merely snobbish in the boy. He wanted not association with glittering things and glittering people—he wanted the glittering things themselves. Often he reached out for the best without knowing why he wanted it—and sometimes he ran up against the mysterious denials and prohibitions in which life indulges. It is with one of those denials and not with his career as a whole that this story deals.

He made money. It was rather amazing. After college he went to the city from which Black Bear Lake draws its wealthy patrons. When he was only twenty-three and had been there not quite two years, there were already people who liked to say: 'Now *there's* a boy—' All about him rich men's sons were peddling bonds precariously, or investing patrimonies precariously, or plodding through the two dozen volumes of the 'George Washington Commercial Course', but Dexter borrowed a thousand dollars on his college degree and his confident mouth, and bought a partnership in a laundry.

It was a small laundry when he went into it, but Dexter made a specialty of learning how the English washed fine woollen golf-stockings without shrinking them, and within a year he was catering to the trade that wore knickerbockers. Men were insisting that their Shetland hose and sweaters go to his laundry, just as they had insisted on a caddy who could find golf-balls. A little later he was doing their wives' lingeries as well—and running five branches in different parts of the city. Before he was twenty-seven he owned the largest string of laundries in his section of the country. It was then that he sold out and went to New York. But the part of his story that concerns us goes back to the days when he was making his first big success.

When he was twenty-three Mr Hart—one of the grey-haired men who liked to say 'Now there's a boy'—gave him a guest card to the Sherry Island Golf Club for a week-end. So he signed his name one day on the register, and that afternoon played golf in a foursome with Mr Hart and Mr Sandwood and Mr T.A. Hedrick. He did not consider it necessary to remark that he had once carried Mr Hart's bag over this same links, and that he knew every trap and gully with his eyes shut—but he found himself glancing at the four caddies who trailed them, trying to catch a gleam or gesture that would remind him of himself, that would lessen the gap which lay between his present and his past.

It was a curious day, slashed abruptly with fleeting, familiar impressions. One minute he had the sense of being a trespasser—in the next he was impressed by the tremendous superiority he felt toward Mr T.A. Hedrick, who was a bore and not even a good golfer any more.

Then, because of a ball Mr Hart lost near the fifteenth green, an enormous thing happened. While they were searching the stiff grasses of the rough there was a clear call of 'Fore!' from behind a hill in their rear. And as they all turned abruptly from their search a bright new ball sliced abruptly over the hill and caught Mr T.A. Hedrick in the abdomen.

'By Gad!' cried Mr T.A. Hedrick, 'they ought to put some of these crazy women off the course. It's getting to be outrageous.'

A head and a voice came up together over the hill:

'Do you mind if we go through?'

'You hit me in the stomach!' declared Mr Hedrick wildly.

'Did I?' The girl approached the group of men. 'I'm sorry, I yelled "Fore!"'

Her glance fell casually on each of the men—then scanned the fairway for her ball.

'Did I bounce into the rough?'

It was impossible to determine whether this question was ingenuous or malicious. In a moment, however, she left no doubt, for as her partner came up over the hill she called cheerfully:

'Here I am! I'd have gone on the green except that I hit something.'

As she took her stance for a short mashie shot, Dexter looked at her closely. She wore a blue gingham dress, rimmed at throat and shoulders with a white edging that accentuated her tan. The quality of exaggeration, of thinness, which had made her passionate eyes and down-turning mouth absurd at eleven, was gone now. She was arrestingly beautiful. The colour in her cheeks was centred like the colour in a picture—it was not a 'high' colour, but a sort of fluctuating and feverish warmth, so shaded that it seemed at any moment it would recede and disappear. This colour and the mobility of her mouth gave a continual impression of flux, of intense life, of passionate vitality—balanced only partially by the sad luxury of her eyes.

She swung her mashie impatiently and without interest, pitching the ball into a sand-pit on the other side of the green. With a quick, insincere smile and a careless 'Thank you!' she went on after it.

'That Judy Jones!' remarked Mr Hedrick on the next tee, as they waited—some moments—for her to play on ahead. 'All she needs is to be turned up and spanked for six months and then to be married off to an old-fashioned cavalry captain.'

'My God, she's good-looking!' said Mr Sandwood, who was just over thirty.

'Good-looking!' cried Mr Hedrick contemptuously. 'She always looks as if she wanted to be kissed! Turning those big cow-eyes on every calf in town!'

It was doubtful if Mr Hedrick intended a reference to the maternal instinct.

'She'd play pretty good golf if she'd try,' said Mr Sandwood.

'She has no form,' said Mr Hedrick solemnly.

'She has a nice figure,' said Mr Sandwood.

'Better thank the Lord she doesn't drive a swifter ball,' said Mr Hart, winking at Dexter.

Later in the afternoon the sun went down with a riotous swirl of gold and varying blues and scarlets, and left the dry, rustling night of Western summer. Dexter watched from the veranda of the Golf Club, watched the even overlap of the waters in the little wind, silver molasses under the harvest-moon. Then the moon held a finger to her lips and the lake became a clear pool, pale and quiet. Dexter put on his bathing-suit and swam out to the farthest raft, where he stretched dripping on the wet canvas of the springboard.

There was a fish jumping and a star shining and the lights around the lake were gleaming. Over on a dark peninsula a piano was playing the songs of the last summer and of summers before that—songs from 'Chin-Chin' and 'The Count of Luxemburg' and 'The Chocolate Soldier'—and because the sound of a piano over a stretch of water had always seemed beautiful to Dexter he lay perfectly quiet and listened.

The tune the piano was playing at that moment had been gay and new five years before when Dexter was a sophomore at college. They had played it at a prom once when he could not afford the luxury of proms, and he had stood outside the gymnasium and listened. The sound of the tune precipitated in him a sort of ecstasy and it was with that ecstasy he viewed what happened to him now. It was a mood of intense appreciation, a sense that, for once, he was magnificently attuned to life and that everything about him was radiating a brightness and a glamour he might never know again.

A low, pale oblong detached itself suddenly from the darkness of the Island, spitting forth the reverberate sound of a racing motorboat. Two white streamers of cleft water rolled themselves out behind it and almost immediately the boat was beside him, drowning out the hot tinkle of the piano in the drone of its spray. Dexter raising himself on his arms was aware of a figure standing at the wheel, of two dark eyes regarding him over the lengthening space of water—then the boat had gone by and was sweeping in an immense and purposeless circle of spray round and round in the middle of the lake. With equal eccentricity one of the circles flattened out and headed back toward the raft.

'Who's that!' she called, shutting off her motor. She was so near now that Dexter could see her bathing-suit, which consisted apparently of pink rompers.

The nose of the boat bumped the raft, and as the latter tilted rakishly he was precipitated toward her. With different degrees of interest they recognized each other.

'Aren't you one of those men we played through this afternoon?' she demanded.

He was.

'Well, do you know how to drive a motor-boat? Because if you do I wish you'd drive this one so I can ride on the surf-board behind. My name is Judy Jones'—she favoured him with an absurd smirk—rather, what tried to be a smirk, for, twist her mouth as she might, it was not grotesque, it was merely beautiful—'and I live in a house over there on the Island, and in that house there is a man waiting for me. When he drove up at the door I drove out of the dock because he says I'm his ideal.'

There was a fish jumping and a star shining and the lights around the lake were gleaming. Dexter sat beside Judy Jones and she explained how her boat was driven. Then she was in the water, swimming to the floating surf-board with a sinuous crawl. Watching her was without effort to the eye, watching a branch waving or a sea-gull flying. Her arms, burned to butternut, moved sinuously among the dull platinum ripples, elbow appearing first, casting the forearm back with a cadence of falling water, then reaching out and down, stabbing a path ahead.

They moved out into the lake; turning, Dexter saw that she was kneeling on the low rear of the now uptilted surf-board.

'Go faster,' she called, 'fast as it'll go.'

Obediently he jammed the lever forward and the white spray mounted at the bow. When he looked around again the girl was standing up on the rushing board, her arms spread wide, her eyes lifted toward the moon.

'It's awful cold,' she shouted. 'What's your name?'

He told her.

'Well, why don't you come to dinner to-morrow night?'

His heart turned over like the fly-wheel of the boat, and, for the second time, her casual whim gave a new direction to his life.

III

Next evening while he waited for her to come down-stairs, Dexter peopled the soft deep summer room and the sun-porch that opened from it with the men who had already loved Judy Jones. He knew the sort of men they were—the men who when he first went to college had entered from the great prep schools with graceful clothes and the deep tan of healthy summers. He had seen that, in one sense, he was better than these men. He was newer and stronger. Yet in acknowledging to himself that he wished his children to be like them, he was admitting that he was but the rough, strong stuff from which they eternally sprang.

When the time had come for him to wear good clothes, he had known who were the best tailors in America, and the best tailors in America had made him the suit he wore this evening. He had acquired that particular reserve peculiar to his university, that set it off from other universities. He recognized the value to him of such a mannerism and he had adopted it; he knew that to be careless in dress and manner required more confidence than to be careful. But carelessness was for his children. His mother's name had been Krimplich. She was a Bohemian of the peasant class and she had talked broken English to the end of her days. Her son must keep to the set patterns.

At a little after seven Judy Jones came down-stairs. She wore a blue silk afternoon dress, and he was disappointed at first that she had not put on something more elaborate. This feeling was accentuated when, after a brief greeting she went to the door of a butler's pantry and pushing it open called: 'You can serve dinner, Martha.' He had rather expected that a butler would announce dinner, that there would be a cocktail. Then he put these thoughts behind him as they sat down side by side on a lounge and looked at each other.

'Father and mother won't be here,' she said thoughtfully.

He remembered the last time he had seen her father, and he was glad the parents were not to be here to-night—they might wonder who he was. He had been born in Keeble, a Minnesota village fifty miles farther north, and he always gave Keeble as his home instead of Black Bear Village. Country towns were well enough to come from if they weren't inconveniently in sight and used as footstools by fashionable lakes.

They talked of his university, which she had visited frequently during the past two years, and of the near-by city which supplied Sherry Island with its patrons, and whither Dexter would return next day to his prospering laundries.

During dinner she slipped into a moody depression which gave Dexter a feeling of uneasiness. Whatever petulance she uttered in her throaty voice worried him. Whatever she smiled at—at him, at a chicken liver, at nothing—it disturbed him that her smile could have no root in mirth, or even in amusement. When the scarlet corners of her lips curved down, it was less a smile than an invitation to a kiss.

Then, after dinner, she led him out on the dark sun-porch and deliberately changed the atmosphere.

'Do you mind if I weep a little?' she said.

'I'm afraid I'm boring you,' he responded quickly.

'You're not. I like you. But I've just had a terrible afternoon. There was a man I cared about, and this afternoon he told me out of a clear sky that he was poor as a churchmouse. He'd never even hinted it before. Does this sound horribly mundane?'

'Perhaps he was afraid to tell you.'

'Suppose he was,' she answered. 'He didn't start right. You see, if I'd thought of him as poor—well, I've been mad about loads of poor men, and fully intended to marry them all. But in this case, I hadn't thought of him that way, and my interest in him wasn't strong enough to survive the shock. As if a girl calmly informed her fiancé that she was a widow. He might not object to widows, but—

'Let's start right,' she interrupted herself suddenly. 'Who are you, anyhow?'

For a moment Dexter hesitated. Then:

'I'm nobody,' he announced. 'My career is largely a matter of futures.'

'Are you poor?'

'No,' he said frankly, 'I'm probably making more money than any man my age in the Northwest. I know that's an obnoxious remark, but you advised me to start right.'

There was a pause. Then she smiled and the corners of her mouth drooped and an almost imperceptible sway brought her closer to him, looking up into his eyes. A lump rose in Dexter's throat, and he waited breathless for the experiment, facing the unpredictable compound that would form mysteriously from the elements of their lips. Then he saw—she communicated her excitement to him, lavishly, deeply, with kisses that were not a promise but a fulfilment. They aroused in him not hunger demanding renewal but surfeit that would demand more surfeit . . . kisses that were like charity, creating want by holding back nothing at all.

It did not take him many hours to decide that he had wanted Judy Jones ever since he was a proud, desirous little boy.

IV

It began like that—and continued, with varying shades of intensity, on such a note right up to the dénouement. Dexter surrendered a part of himself to the most direct and unprincipled personality with which he had ever come in contact. Whatever Judy wanted, she went after with the full pressure of her charm. Ther was no divergence of method, no jockeying for position or premeditation of effects—there was a very little mental side to any of her affairs. She simply made men conscious to the highest degree of her physical loveliness. Dexter had no desire to change her. Her deficiencies were knit up with a passionate energy that transcended and justified them.

When, as Judy's head lay against his shoulder that first night, she whispered, 'I don't know what's the matter with me. Last night I thought I was in love with a man and to-night I think I'm in love with you—'—it seemed to him a beautiful and romantic thing to say. It was the exquisite excitability that for the moment he controlled and owned. But a week later he was compelled to view this same quality in a different light. She took him in her roadster to a picnic supper, and after supper she disappeared, likewise in her roadster, with another man. Dexter became enormously upset and was scarcely able to be decently civil to the other people present. When she assured him that she had not kissed the other man, he knew she was lying—yet he was glad that she had taken the trouble to lie to him.

He was, as he found before the summer ended, one of a varying dozen who circulated about her. Each of them had at one time been favoured above all others—about half of them still basked in the solace of occasional sentimental revivals. Whenever one showed signs of dropping out through long neglect, she granted him a brief honeyed hour, which encouraged him to tag along for a year or so longer. Judy made these forays upon the helpless and defeated without malice, indeed half unconscious that there was anything mischievous in what she did.

When a new man came to town every one dropped out—dates were automatically cancelled.

The helpless part of trying to do anything about it was that she did it all herself. She was not a girl who could be 'won' in the kinetic sense—she was proof against cleverness, she was proof against charm; if any of these assailed her too strongly she would immediately resolve the affair to a physical basis, and under the magic of her physical splendour the strong as well as the brilliant played her game and not their own. She was entertained only by the gratification of her desires and by the direct exercise of her own charm. Perhaps from so much youthful love, so many youthful lovers, she had come, in self-defence, to nourish herself wholly from within.

Succeeding Dexter's first exhilaration came restlessness and dissatisfaction. The helpless ecstasy of losing himself in her was opiate rather than tonic. It was fortunate for his work during the winter that those moments of ecstasy came infrequently. Early in their acquaintance it had seemed for a while that there was a deep and spontaneous mutual attraction—that first August, for example—three days of long evenings on her dusky veranda, of strange wan kisses through the late afternoon, in shadowy alcoves or behind the protecting trellises of the garden arbours, of mornings when she was fresh as a dream and almost shy at meeting him in the clarity of the rising day. There was all the ecstasy of an engagement about it, sharpened by his realization that there was no engagement. It was during those three days that, for the first time, he had asked her to marry him. She said 'maybe some day', she said 'kiss me', she said 'I'd like to marry you', she said 'I love you'—she said—nothing.

The three days were interrupted by the arrival of a New York man who visited at her house for half September. To Dexter's agony, rumour engaged them. The man was the son of the president of a great trust company. But at the end of a month it was reported that Judy was yawning. At a dance one night she sat all evening in a motor-boat with a local beau, while the New Yorker searched the club for her frantically. She told the local beau that she was bored with her visitor, and two days later he left. She was seen with him at the station, and it was reported that he looked very mournful indeed.

On this note the summer ended. Dexter was twenty-four, and he found himself increasingly in a position to do as he wished. He joined two clubs in the city and lived at one of them. Though he was by no means an integral part of the stag-lines at these clubs, he managed to be on hand at dances where Judy Jones was likely to appear. He could have gone out socially as much as he liked—he was an eligible young man, now, and popular with down-town fathers. His confessed devotion to Judy Jones had rather solidified his position. But he had no social aspirations and rather despised the dancing men who were always on tap for the Thursday or Saturday parties and who filled in at dinners with the younger married set. Already he was playing with the idea of going East to New York. He wanted to take Judy Jones with him. No disillusion as to the world in which she had grown up could cure his illusion as to her desirability.

Remember that—for only in the light of it can what he did for her be understood.

Eighteen months after he first met Judy Jones he became engaged to another girl. Her name was Irene Scheerer, and her father was one of the men who had always believed in Dexter. Irene was light-haired and sweet and honourable, and a little stout, and she had two suitors whom she pleasantly relinquished when Dexter formally asked her to marry him.

Summer, fall, winter, spring, another summer, another fall—so much he had given of his active life to the incorrigible lips of Judy Jones. She had treated him with interest, with encouragement, with malice, with indifference, with contempt. She had inflicted on him the innumerable little slights and indignities possible in such a case—as if in revenge for having ever cared for him at all. She had beckoned him and yawned at him and beckoned him again and he had responded often with bitterness and narrowed eyes. She had brought him ecstatic happiness and intolerable agony of spirit. She had caused him untold inconvenience and not a little trouble. She had insulted him, and she had ridden over him, and she had played his interest in her against his interest in his work—for fun. She had done everything to him except to criticize him—this she had not done—it seemed to him only because it might have sullied the utter indifference she manifested and sincerely felt toward him.

When autumn had come and gone again it occurred to him that he could not have Judy Jones. He had to beat this into his mind but he convinced himself at last. He lay awake at night for a while and argued it over. He told himself the trouble and the pain she had caused him, he enumerated her glaring deficiencies as a wife. Then he said to himself that he loved her, and after a while he fell asleep. For a week, lest he imagined her husky voice over the telephone or her eyes opposite him at lunch, he worked hard and late, and at night he went to his office and plotted out his years.

At the end of a week he went to a dance and cut in on her once. For almost the first time since they had met he did not ask her to sit out with him or tell her that she was lovely. It hurt him that she did not miss these things—that was all. He was not jealous when he saw that there was a new man to-night. He had been hardened against jealousy long before.

He stayed late at the dance. He sat for an hour with Irene Scheerer and talked about books and about music. He knew very little about either. But he was beginning to be master of his own time now, and he had a rather priggish notion that he—the young and already fabulously successful Dexter Green—should know more about such things.

That was in October, when he was twenty-five. In January, Dexter and Irene became engaged. It was to be announced in June, and they were to be married three months later.

The Minnesota winter prolonged itself interminably, and it was almost May when the winds came soft and the snow ran down into Black Bear Lake at last. For the first time in over a year Dexter was enjoying a certain tranquillity of spirit. Judy Jones had been in Florida, and afterward in Hot Springs, and somewhere she had been engaged, and somewhere she had broken it off. At first, when Dexter had definitely given her up, it had made him sad that people still linked them together and asked for news of her, but when he began to be placed at dinner next to Irene Scheerer people didn't ask him about her any more—they told him about her. He ceased to be an authority on her.

May at last. Dexter walked the streets at night when the darkness was damp as rain, wondering that so soon, with so little done, so much of ecstasy had gone from him. May one year back had been marked by Judy's poignant, unforgivable, yet forgiven turbulence—it had been one of those rare times when he fancied she had grown to care for him. That old penny's worth of happiness he had spent for this bushel of content. He knew that Irene would be no more than a curtain spread behind him, a hand moving among gleaming teacups, a voice calling to children . . . fire and loveliness were gone, the magic of nights and the wonder of the varying hours and seasons . . . slender lips, down-turning, dropping to his lips and bearing him up into a heaven of eyes. . . . The thing was deep in him. He was too strong and alive for it to die lightly.

In the middle of May when the weather balanced for a few days on the thin bridge that led to deep summer he turned in one night at Irene's house. Their engagement was to be announced in a week now—no one would be surprised at it. And to-night they would sit together on the lounge at the University Club and look on for an hour at the dancers. It gave him a sense of solidity to go with her—she was so sturdily popular, so intensely 'great'.

He mounted the steps of the brownstone house and stepped inside.

'Irene,' he called.

Mrs Scheerer came out of the living-room to meet him.

'Dexter,' she said, 'Irene's gone up-stairs with a splitting headache. She wanted to go with you but I made her go to bed.'

'Nothing serious, I—'

'Oh, no. She's going to play golf with you in the morning. You can spare her for just one night, can't you, Dexter?'

Her smile was kind. She and Dexter liked each other. In the living-room he talked for a moment before he said good-night.

Returning to the University Club, where he had rooms, he stood in the doorway for a moment and watched the dancers. He leaned against the door-post, nodded at a man or two—yawned.

'Hello, darling.'

The familiar voice at his elbow startled him. Judy Jones had left a man and crossed the room to him—Judy Jones, a slender enamelled doll in cloth of gold: gold in a band at her head, gold in two slipper points at her dress's hem. The fragile glow of her face seemed to blossom as she smiled at him. A breeze of warmth and light blew through the room. His hands in the pockets of his dinner-jacket tightened spasmodically. He was filled with a sudden excitement.

'When did you get back?' he asked casually.

'Come here and I'll tell you about it.'

She turned and he followed her. She had been away—he could have wept at the wonder of her return. She had passed through enchanted streets, doing things that were like provocative music. All mysterious happenings, all fresh and quickening hopes, had gone away with her, come back with her now.

She turned in the doorway.

'Have you a car here? If you haven't, I have.'

'I have a coupé.'

In then, with a rustle of golden cloth. He slammed the door. Into so many cars she had stepped—like this—like that—her back against the leather, so—her elbow resting on the door—waiting. She would have been soiled long since had there been anything to soil her—except herself—but this was her own self outpouring.

With an effort he forced himself to start the car and back into the street. This was nothing, he must remember. She had done this before, and he had put her behind him, as he would have crossed a bad account from his books.

He drove slowly down-town and, affecting abstraction, traversed the deserted streets of the business section, peopled here and there where a movie was giving out its crowd or where consumptive or pugilistic youth lounged in front of pool halls. The clink of glasses and the slap of hands on the bars issued from saloons, cloisters of glazed glass and dirty yellow light.

She was watching him closely and the silence was embarrassing, yet in this crisis he could find no casual word with which to profane the hour. At a convenient turning he began to zigzag back toward the University Club.

'Have you missed me?' she asked suddenly.

'Everybody missed you.'

He wondered if she knew of Irene Scheerer. She had been back only a day—her absence had been almost contemporaneous with his engagement.

'What a remark!' Judy laughed sadly—without sadness. She looked at him searchingly. He became absorbed in the dashboard.

'You're handsomer than you used to be,' she said thoughtfully. 'Dexter, you have the most rememberable eyes.'

He could have laughed at this, but he did not laugh. It was the sort of thing that was said to sophomores. Yet it stabbed at him.

'I'm awfully tired of everything, darling.' She called every one darling, endowing the endearment with careless, individual camaraderie. 'I wish you'd marry me.'

The directness of this confused him. He should have told her now that he was going to marry another girl, but he could not tell her. He could as easily have sworn that he had never loved her.

'I think we'd get along,' she continued, on the same note, 'unless probably you've forgotten me and fallen in love with another girl.'

Her confidence was obviously enormous. She had said, in effect, that she found such a thing impossible to believe, that if it were true he had merely committed a childish indiscretion—and probably to show off. She would forgive him, because it was not a matter of any moment but rather something to be brushed aside lightly.

"Of course you could never love anybody but me,' she continued, 'I like the way you love me. Oh, Dexter, have you forgotten last year?'

'No, I haven't forgotten.'

'Neither have I!'

Was she sincerely moved—or was she carried along by the wave of her own acting?

'I wish we could be like that again,' she said, and he forced himself to answer:

'I don't think we can.'

'I suppose not. . . . I hear you're giving Irene Scheerer a violent rush.'

There was not the faintest emphasis on the name, yet Dexter was suddenly ashamed.

'Oh, take me home,' cried Judy suddenly; 'I don't want to go back to that idiotic dance—with those children.'

Then, as he turned up the street that led to the residence district, Judy bagan to cry quietly to herself. He had never seen her cry before.

The dark street lightened, the dwellings of the rich loomed up around them, he stopped his coupé in front of the great white bulk of the Mortimer Joneses' house, somnolent, gorgeous, drenched with the splendour of the damp moonlight. Its solidity startled him. The strong walls, the steel of the girders, the breadth and beam and pomp of it were there only to bring out the contrast with the young beauty beside him. It was sturdy to accentuate her slightness—as if to show what a breeze could be generated by a butterfly's wing.

He sat perfectly quiet, his nerves in wild clamour, afraid that if he moved he would find her irresistibly in his arms. Two tears had rolled down her wet face and trembled on her upper lip.

'I'm more beautiful than anybody else,' she said brokenly, 'why can't I be happy?' Her moist eyes tore at his stability—her mouth turned slowly downward with an exquisite sadness: 'I'd like to marry you if you'll have me, Dexter. I suppose you think I'm not worth having, but I'll be so beautiful for you, Dexter.'

A million phrases of anger, pride, passion, hatred, tenderness fought on his lips. Then a perfect wave of emotion washed over him, carrying off with it a sediment of wisdom, of convention, of doubt, of honour. This was his girl who was speaking, his own, his beautiful, his pride.

'Won't you come in?' He heard her draw in her breath sharply.

Waiting.

'All right,' his voice was trembling, 'I'll come in.'

V

It was strange that neither when it was over nor a long time afterward did he regret that night. Looking at it from the perspective of ten years, the fact that Judy's flare for him endured just one month seemed of little importance. Nor did it matter that by his yielding he subjected himself to a deeper agony in the end and gave serious hurt to Irene Scheerer and to Irene's parents, who had befriended him. There was nothing sufficiently pictorial about Irene's grief to stamp itself on his mind.

Dexter was at bottom hard-minded. The attitude of the city on his action was of no importance to him, not because he was going to leave the city, but because any outside attitude on the situation seemed superficial. He was completely indifferent to popular opinion. Nor, when he had seen that it was no use, that he did not possess in himself the power to move fundamentally or to hold Judy Jones, did he bear any malice toward her. He loved her, and he would love her until the day he was too old for loving—but he could not have her. So he tasted the deep pain that is reserved only for the strong, just as he had tasted for a little while the deep happiness.

Even the ultimate falsity of the grounds upon which Judy terminated the engagement that she did not want to 'take him away' from Irene—Judy who had wanted nothing else—did not revolt him. He was beyond any revulsion or any amusement.

He went East in February with the intention of selling out his laundries and settling in New York—but the war came to America in March and changed his plans. He returned to the West, handed over the management of the business to his partner, and went into the first officers' training-camp in late April. He was one of those young thousands who greeted the war with a certain amount of relief, welcoming the liberation from webs of tangled emotion.

VI

This story is not his biography, remember, although things creep into it which have nothing to do with those dreams he had when he was young. We are almost done with them and with him now. There is only one more incident to be related here, and it happens seven years farther on.

It took place in New York, where he had done well—so well that there were no barriers too high for him. He was thirty-two years old, and, except for one flying trip immediately after the war, he had not been West in seven years. A man named Devlin from Detroit came into his office to see him in a business way, and then and there this incident occurred, and closed out, so to speak, this particular side of his life.

'So you're from the Middle West,' said the man Devlin with careless curiosity. 'That's funny—I thought men like you were probably born and raised on Wall Street. You know—wife of one of my best friends in Detroit came from your city. I was an usher at the wedding.'

Dexter waited with apprehension of what was coming.

'Judy Simms,' said Devlin with no particular interest; 'Judy Jones she was once.'

'Yes, I knew her.' A dull impatience spread over him. He had heard, of course, that she was married—perhaps deliberately he had heard no more.

'Awfully nice girl,' brooded Devlin meaninglessly, 'I'm sort of sorry for her.'

'Why?' Something in Dexter was alert, receptive, at once.

'Oh, Lud Simms has gone to pieces in a way. I don't mean he ill-uses her, but he drinks and runs around—'

'Doesn't she run around?'

'No. Stays at home with her kids.'

'Oh.'

'She's a little too old for him,' said Devlin.

'Too old!' cried Dexter. 'Why, man, she's only twenty-seven.'

He was possessed with a wild notion of rushing out into the streets and taking a train to Detroit. He rose to his feet spasmodically.

'I guess you're busy,' Devlin apologized quickly. 'I didn't realize—'

'No, I'm not busy,' said Dexter, steadying his voice. 'I'm not busy at all. Not busy at all. Did you say she was—twenty-seven? No, I said she was twenty-seven.'

'Yes, you did,' agreed Devlin drily.

'Go on, then. Go on.'

'What do you mean?'

'About Judy Jones.'

Devlin looked at him helplessly.

'Well that's—I told you all there is to it. He treats her like the devil. Oh, they're not going to get divorced or anything. When he's particularly outrageous she forgives him. In fact, I'm inclined to think she loves him. She was a pretty girl when she first came to Detroit.'

A pretty girl! The phrase struck Dexter as ludicrous.

'Isn't she—a pretty girl, any more?'

'Oh, she's all right.'

'Look here,' said Dexter, sitting down suddenly. 'I don't understand. You say she was a "pretty girl" and now you say she's "all right". I don't understand what you mean—Judy Jones wasn't a pretty girl, at all. She was a great beauty. Why, I knew her, I knew her. She was—'

Devlin laughed pleasantly.

'I'm not trying to start a row,' he said. 'I think Judy's a nice girl and I like her. I can't understand how a man like Lud Simms could fall madly in love with her, but he did.' Then he added: 'Most of the women like her.'

Dexter looked closely at Devlin, thinking wildly that there must be a reason for this, some insensitivity in the man or some private malice.

'Lots of women fade just like *that,*' Devlin snapped his fingers. 'You must have seen it happen. Perhaps I've forgotten how pretty she was at her wedding. I've seen her so much since then, you see. She has nice eyes.'

A sort of dullness settled down upon Dexter. For the first time in his life he felt like getting very drunk. He knew that he was laughing loudly at something Devlin had said, but he did not know what it was or why it was funny. When, in a few minutes, Devlin went he lay down on his lounge and looked out the window at the New York sky-line into which the sun was sinking in dull lovely shades of pink and gold.

He had thought that having nothing else to lose he was invulnerable at last—but he knew that he had just lost something more, as surely as if he had married Judy Jones and seen her fade away before his eyes.

The dream was gone. Something had been taken from him. In a sort of panic he pushed the palms of his hands into his eyes and tried to bring up a picture of the waters lapping on Sherry Island and the moonlit veranda, and gingham on the golf-links and the dry sun and the gold colour of her neck's soft down. And her mouth damp to his kisses and her eyes plaintive with melancholy and her freshness like new fine linen in the morning. Why, these things were no longer in the world! They had existed and they existed no longer.

For the first time in years the tears were streaming down his face. But they were for himself now. He did not care about mouth and eyes and moving hands. He wanted to care, and he could not care. For he had gone away and he could never go back any more. The gates were closed, the sun was gone down, and there was no beauty but the grey beauty of steel that withstands all time. Even the grief he could have borne was left behind in the country of illusion, of youth, of the richness of life, where his winter dreams had flourished.

'Long ago,' he said, 'long ago, there was something in me, but now that thing is gone. Now that thing is gone, that thing is gone. I cannot cry. I cannot care. That thing will come back no more.'

1922

Babylon Revisited

'And where's Mr Campbell?' Charlie asked.

'Gone to Switzerland. Mr Campbell's a pretty sick man, Mr Wales.'

'I'm sorry to hear that. And George Hardt?' Charlie inquired.

'Back in America, gone to work.'

'And where is the Snow Bird?'

'He was in here last week. Anyway, his friend, Mr Schaeffer, is in Paris.'

Two familiar names from the long list of a year and a half ago. Charlie scribbled an address in his notebook and tore out the page.

'If you see Mr. Schaeffer, give him this,' he said. 'It's my brother-in-law's address. I haven't settled on a hotel yet.'

He was not really disappointed to find Paris was so empty. But the stillness in the Ritz bar was strange and portentous. It was not an American bar any more—he felt polite in it, and not as if he owned it. It had gone back into France. He felt the stillness from the moment he got out of the taxi and saw the doorman, usually in a frenzy of activity at this hour, gossiping with a *chasseur* by the servants' entrance.

Passing through the corridor, he heard only a single, bored voice in the once-clamorous women's room. When he turned into the bar he travelled the twenty feet of green carpet with his eyes fixed straight ahead by old habit; and then, with his foot firmly on the rail, he turned and surveyed the room, encountering only a single pair of eyes that fluttered up from a newspaper in the corner. Charlie asked for the head barman, Paul, who in the latter days of the bull market had come to work in his own custom-built car—disembarking, however, with due nicety at the nearest corner. But Paul was at his country house today and Alix giving him information.

'No, no more,' Charlie said, 'I'm going slow these days.'

Alix congratulated him: 'You were going pretty strong a couple of years ago.'

'I'll stick to it all right,' Charlie assured him. 'I've stuck to it for over a year and a half now.'

'How do you find conditions in America?'

'I haven't been to America for months. I'm in business in Prague, representing a couple of concerns there. They don't know about me down there.'

Alix smiled.

'Remember the night of George Hardt's bachelor dinner here?' said Charlie. 'By the way, what's become of Claude Fessenden?'

Alix lowered his voice confidentially: 'He's in Paris, but he doesn't come here any more. Paul doesn't allow it. He ran up a bill of thirty thousand francs, charging all his drinks and his lunches, and usually his dinner, for more than a year. And when Paul finally told him he had to pay, he gave him a bad cheque.'

Alix shook his head sadly.

'I don't understand it, such a dandy fellow. Now he's all bloated up—' He made a plump apple of his hands.

Charlie watched a group of strident queens installing themselves in a corner.

'Nothing affects them,' he thought. 'Stocks rise and fall, people loaf or work, but they go on forever.' The place oppressed him. He called for the dice and shook with Alix for the drink.

'Here for long, Mr Wales?'

'I'm here for four or five days to see my little girl.'

'Oh-h! You have a little girl?'

Outside, the fire-red, gas-blue, ghost-green signs shone smokily through the tranquil rain. It was late afternoon and the streets were in movement; the *bistros* gleamed. At the corner of the Boulevard des Capucines he took a taxi. The Place de la Concorde moved by in pink majesty; they crossed the logical Seine, and Charlie felt the sudden provincial quality of the left bank.

Charlie directed his taxi to the Avenue de l'Opera, which was out of his way. But he wanted to see the blue hour spread over the magnificent façade, and imagine that the cab horns, playing endlessly the first few bars of *Le Plus que Lent,* were the trumpets of the Second Empire. They were closing the iron grill in front of Brentano's Book-store, and people were already at dinner behind the trim little bourgeois hedge of Duval's. He had never eaten at a really cheap restaurant in Paris. Five-course dinner, four francs fifty, eighteen cents, wine included. For some odd reason he wished that he had.

As they rolled on to the Left Bank and he felt its sudden provincialism, he thought, 'I spoiled this city for myself. I didn't realize it, but the days came along one after another, and then two years were gone, and everything was gone, and I was gone.'

He was thirty-five, and good to look at. The Irish mobility of his face was sobered by a deep wrinkle between his eyes. As he rang his brother-in-law's bell in the Rue Palatine, the wrinkle deepened till it pulled down his brows; he felt a cramping sensation in his belly. From behind the maid who opened the door darted a lovely little girl of nine who shrieked 'Daddy!' and flew up, struggling like a fish, into his arms. She pulled his head around by one ear and set her cheek against his.

'My old pie,' he said.

'Oh, daddy, daddy, daddy, daddy, dads, dads, dads!'

She drew him into the salon, where the family waited, a boy and a girl his daughter's age, his sister-in-law and her husband. He greeted Marion with his voice pitched carefully to avoid either feigned enthusiasm or dislike, but her response was more frankly tepid, though she minimized her expression of unalterable distrust by directing her regard toward his child.

The two men clasped hands in a friendly way and Lincoln Peters rested his for a moment on Charlie's shoulder.

The room was warm and comfortably American. The three children moved intimately about, playing through the yellow oblongs that led to other rooms; the cheer of six o'clock spoke in the eager smacks of the fire and the sounds of French activity in the kitchen. But Charlie did not relax; his heart sat up rigidly in his body and he drew confidence from his daughter, who from time to time came close to him, holding in her arms the doll he had brought.

'Really extremely well,' he declared in answer to Lincoln's question. 'There's a lot of business there that isn't moving at all, but we're doing even better than ever. In fact, damn well. I'm bringing my sister over from America next month to keep house for me. My income last year was bigger than it was when I had money. You see, the Czechs—'

His boasting was for a specific purpose; but after a moment, seeing a faint restiveness in Lincoln's eye, he changed the subject:

'Those are fine children of yours, well brought up, good manners.'

'We think Honoria's a great little girl too.'

Marion Peters came back from the kitchen. She was a tall woman with worried eyes, who had once possessed a fresh American loveliness. Charlie had never been sensitive to it and was always surprised when people spoke of how pretty she had been. From the first there had been an instinctive antipathy between them.

'Well, how do you find Honoria?' she asked.

'Wonderful. I was astonished how much she's grown in ten months. All the children are looking well.'

'We haven't had a doctor for a year. How do you like being back in Paris?'

'It seems very funny to see so few Americans around.'

'I'm delighted,' Marion said vehemently. 'Now at least you can go into a store without their assuming you're a millionaire. We've suffered like everybody, but on the whole it's a good deal pleasanter.'

'But it was nice while it lasted,' Charlie said. 'We were a sort of royalty, almost infallible, with a sort of magic around us. In the bar this afternoon'—he stumbled, seeing his mistake—'there wasn't a man I knew.'

She looked at him keenly. 'I should think you'd have had enough of bars.'

'I only stayed a minute. I take one drink every afternoon, and no more.'

'Don't you want a cocktail before dinner?' Lincoln asked.

'I take only one drink every afternoon, and I've had that.'

'I hope you keep to it,' said Marion.

Her dislike was evident in the coldness with which she spoke, but Charlie only smiled; he had larger plans. Her very aggressiveness gave him an advantage, and he knew enough to wait. He wanted them to initiate the discussion of what they knew had brought him to Paris.

At dinner he couldn't decide whether Honoria was most like them or her mother. Fortunate if she didn't combine the traits of both that had brought them to disaster. A great wave of protectiveness went over him. He thought he knew what to do for her. He believed in character; he wanted to jump back a whole generation and trust in character again as the eternally valuable element. Everything else wore out.

He left soon after dinner, but not to go home. He was curious to see Paris by night with clearer and more judicious eyes than those of other days. He bought a *strapontin* for the Casino and watched Josephine Baker go through her chocolate arabesques.

After an hour he left and strolled toward Montmartre, up the Rue Pigalle into the Place Blanche. The rain had stopped and there were a few people in evening clothes disembarking from taxis in front of cabarets, and *cocottes* prowling singly or in pairs, and many Negroes. He passed a lighted door from which issued music, and stopped with the sense of familiarity; it was Bricktop's, where he had parted with so many hours and so much money. A few doors farther on he found another ancient rendezvous and incautiously put his head inside. Immediately an eager orchestra burst into sound, a pair of professional dancers leaped to their feet and a maître d'hôtel swooped toward him, crying, 'Crowd just arriving, sir!' But he withdrew quickly.

'You have to be damn drunk,' he thought.

Zelli's was closed, the bleak and sinister cheap hotels surrounding it were dark; up in the Rue Blanche there was more light and a local, colloquial French crowd. The Poet's Cave had disappeared, but the two great mouths of the Café of Heaven and the Café of Hell still yawned—even devoured, as he watched, the meagre contents of a tourist bus—a German, a Japanese, and an American couple who glanced at him with frightened eyes.

So much for the effort and ingenuity of Montmartre. All the catering to vice and waste was on an utterly childish scale, and he suddenly realized the meaning of the word 'dissipate'—to dissipate into thin air; to make nothing out of something. In the little hours of the night every move from place to place was an enormous human jump, an increase of paying for the privilege of slower and slower motion.

He remembered thousand-franc notes given to an orchestra for playing a single number, hundred-franc notes tossed to a doorman for calling a cab.

But it hadn't been given for nothing.

It had been given, even the most wildly squandered sum, as an offering to destiny that he might not remember the things most worth remembering, the things that now he would always remember—his child taken from his control, his wife escaped to a grave in Vermont.

In the glare of a *brasserie* a woman spoke to him. He bought her some eggs and coffee, and then, eluding her encouraging stare, gave her a twenty-franc note and took a taxi to his hotel.

II

He woke up on a fine fall day—football weather. The depression of yesterday was gone and he liked the people on the streets. At noon he sat opposite Honoria at Le Grand Vatel, the only restaurant he could think of not reminiscent of champagne dinners and long luncheons that began at two and ended in a blurred and vague twilight.

'Now, how about vegetables? Oughtn't you to have some vegetables?'

'Well, yes.'

'Here's *épinards* and *chou-fleur* and carrot and *haricots.*'

'I'd like *chou-fleur.*'

'Wouldn't you like to have two vegetables?'

'I usually only have one at lunch.'

The waiter was pretending to be inordinately fond of children. *'Qu'elle est mignonne la petite! Elle parle exactement comme une Française.'*

'How about dessert? Shall we wait and see?'

The waiter disappeared. Honoria looked at her father expectantly.

'What are we going to do?'

'First, we're going to that toy store in the Rue Saint-Honoré and buy you anything you like. And then we're going to the vaudeville at the Empire.'

She hesitated. 'I like it about the vaudeville, but not the toy store.'

'Why not?'

'Well, you brought me this doll.' She had it with her. 'And I've got lots of things. And we're not rich any more, are we?'

'We never were. But today you are to have anything you want.'

'All right,' she agreed resignedly.

When there had been her mother and a French nurse he had been inclined to be strict; now he extended himself, reached out for a new tolerance; he must be both parents to her and not shut any of her out of communication.

'I want to get to know you,' he said gravely. 'First let me introduce myself. My name is Charles J. Wales, of Prague.'

'Oh, daddy!' her voice cracked with laughter.

'And who are you, please?' he persisted, and she accepted a rôle immediately: 'Honoria Wales, Rue Palatine, Paris.'

'Married or single?'

'No, not married. Single.'

He indicated the doll. 'But I see you have a child, madame.'

Unwillingly to disinherit it, she took it to her heart and thought quickly: 'Yes, I've been married, but I'm not married now. My husband is dead.'

He went on quickly, 'And the child's name?'

'Simone. That's after my best friend at school.'

'I'm very pleased that you're doing so well at school.'

'I'm third this month,' she boasted. 'Elsie'—that was her cousin—'is only about eighteenth, and Richard is about at the bottom.'

'You like Richard and Elsie, don't you?'

'Oh, yes. I like Richard quite well and I like her all right.'

Cautiously and casually he asked: 'And Aunt Marion and Uncle Lincoln—which do you like best?'

'Oh, Uncle Lincoln, I guess.'

He was increasingly aware of her presence. As they came in, a murmur of '. . . adorable' followed them, and now the people at the next table bent all their silences upon her, staring as if she were something no more conscious than a flower.

'Why don't I live with you?' she asked suddenly. 'Because mamma's dead?'

'You must stay here and learn more French. It would have been hard for daddy to take care of you so well.'

'I don't really need much taking care of any more. I do everything for myself.'

Going out of the restaurant, a man and a woman unexpectedly hailed him.

'Well, the old Wales!'

'Hello there, Lorraine. . . . Dunc.'

Sudden ghosts out of the past: Duncan Schaeffer, a friend from college. Lorraine Quarrles, a lovely pale blonde of thirty; one of a crowd who had helped them make months into days in the lavish times of three years ago.

'My husband couldn't come this year,' she said, in answer to his question. 'We're poor as hell. So he gave me two hundred a month and told me I could do my worst on that. . . . This your little girl?'

'What about coming back and sitting down?' Duncan asked.

'Can't do it.' He was glad for an excuse. As always, he felt Lorraine's passionate, provocative attraction, but his own rhythm was different now.

'Well, how about dinner?' she asked.

'I'm not free. Give me your address and let me call you.'

'Charlie, I believe you're sober,' she said judicially. 'I honestly believe he's sober, Dunc. Pinch him and see if he's sober.'

Charlie indicated Honoria with his head. They both laughed.

'What's your address?' said Duncan sceptically.

He hesitated, unwilling to give the name of his hotel.

'I'm not settled yet. I'd better call you. We're going to see the vaudeville at the Empire.'

There! That's what I want to do,' Lorraine said. 'I want to see some clowns and acrobats and jugglers. That's just what we'll do, Dunc.'

'We've got to do an errand first,' said Charlie. 'Perhaps we'll see you there.'

'All right, you snob. . . . Good-bye, beautiful little girl.'

'Good-bye.'

Honoria bobbed politely.

Somehow, an unwelcome encounter. They liked him because he was functioning, because he was serious; they wanted to see him, because he was stronger than they were now, because they wanted to draw a certain sustenance from his strength.

At the Empire, Honoria proudly refused to sit upon her father's folded coat. She was already an individual with a code of her own, and Charlie was more and more absorbed by the desire of putting a little of himself into her before she crystallized utterly. It was hopeless to try to know her in so short a time.

Between the acts they came upon Duncan and Lorraine in the lobby where the band was playing.

'Have a drink?'

'All right, but not up at the bar. We'll take a table.'

'The perfect father.'

Listening abstractedly to Lorraine, Charlie watched Honoria's eyes leave their table, and he followed them wistfully about the room, wondering what they saw. He met her glance and she smiled.

'I liked that lemonade,' she said.

What had she said? What had he expected? Going home in a taxi afterward, he pulled her over until her head rested against his chest.

'Darling, do you ever think about your mother?'

'Yes, sometimes,' she answered vaguely.

'I don't want you to forget her. Have you got a picture of her?'

'Yes, I think so. Anyhow, Aunt Marion has. Why don't you want me to forget her?'

'She loved you very much.'

'I loved her too.'

They were silent for a moment.

'Daddy, I want to come and live with you,' she said suddenly.

His heart leaped; he had wanted it to come like this.

'Aren't you perfectly happy?'

Yes, but I love you better than anybody. And you love me better than anybody, don't you, now that mummy's dead?'

'Of course I do. But you won't always like me best, honey. You'll grow up and meet somebody your own age and go marry him and forget you ever had a daddy.'

'Yes, that's true,' she agreed tranquilly.

He didn't go in. He was coming back at nine o'clock and he wanted to keep himself fresh and new for the thing he must say then.

'When you're safe inside, just show yourself in that window.'

'All right. Good-bye, dads, dads, dads, dads.'

He waited in the dark street until she appeared, all warm and glowing, in the window above and kissed her fingers out into the night.

III

They were waiting. Marion sat behind the coffee service in a dignified black dinner dress that just faintly suggested mourning. Lincoln was walking up and down with the animation of one who had already been talking. They were as anxious as he was to get into the question. He opened it almost immediately:

'I suppose you know what I want to see you about—why I really came to Paris.'

Marion played with the black stars on her necklace and frowned.

'I'm awfully anxious to have a home,' he continued. 'And I'm awfully anxious to have Honoria in it. I appreciate your taking in Honoria for her mother's sake, but things have changed now'—he hesitated and then continued more forcibly—'changed radically with me, and I want to ask you to reconsider the matter. It would be silly for me to deny that about three years ago I was acting badly—'

Marion looked up at him with hard eyes.

'—but all that's over. As I told you, I haven't had more than a drink a day for over a year, and I take that drink deliberately, so that the idea of alcohol won't get too big in my imagination. You see the idea?'

'No,' said Marion succinctly.

'It's a sort of stunt I set myself. It keeps the matter in proportion.'

'I get you,' said Lincoln. 'You don't want to admit it's got any attraction for you.'

'Something like that. Sometimes I forget and don't take it. But I try to take it. Anyhow, I couldn't afford to drink in my position. The people I represent are more than satisfied with what I've done, and I'm bringing my sister over from Burlington to keep house for me, and I want awfully to have Honoria too. You know that even when her mother and I weren't getting along well we never let anything that happened touch Honoria. I know she's fond of me and I know I'm able to take care of her and—well, there you are. How do you feel about it?'

He knew that now he would have to take a beating. It would last an hour or two hours, and it would be difficult, but if he modulated his inevitable resentment to the chastened attitude of the reformed sinner, he might win his point in the end.

Keep your temper, he told himself. You don't want to be justified. You want Honoria.

Lincoln spoke first: 'We've been talking it over ever since we got your letter last month. We're happy to have Honoria here. She's a dear little thing, and we're glad to be able to help her, but of course that isn't the question—'

Marion interrupted suddenly. 'How long are you going to stay sober, Charlie?' she asked.

'Permanently, I hope.'

'How can anybody count on that?'

'You know I never did drink heavily until I gave up business and came over here with nothing to do. Then Helen and I began to run around with—'

'Please leave Helen out of it. I can't bear to hear you talk about her like that.'

He stared at her grimly; he had never been certain how fond of each other the sisters were in life.

'My drinking only lasted about a year and a half—from the time we came over until I—collapsed.'

'It was time enough.'

'It was time enough,' he agreed.

'My duty is entirely to Helen,' she said. 'I try to think what she would have wanted me to do. Frankly, from the night you did that terrible thing you haven't really existed for me. I can't help that. She was my sister.'

'Yes.'

'When she was dying she asked me to look out for Honoria. If you hadn't been in a sanitarium then, it might have helped matters.'

He had no answer.

'I'll never in my life be able to forget the morning when Helen knocked at my door, soaked to the skin and shivering and said you'd locked her out.'

Charlie gripped the sides of the chair. This was more difficult than he expected; he wanted to launch out into a long expostulation and explanation, but he only said: 'The night I locked her out—' and she interrupted, 'I don't feel up to going over that again.'

After a moment's silence Lincoln said: 'We're getting off the subject. You want Marion to set aside her legal guardianship and give you Honoria. I think the main point for her is whether she has confidence in you or not.'

'I don't blame Marion,' Charlie said slowly, 'but I think she can have entire confidence in me. I had a good record up to three years ago. Of course, it's within human possibilities I might go wrong any time. But if we wait much longer I'll lose Honoria's childhood and my chance for a home.' He shook his head. 'I'll simply lose her, don't you see?'

'Yes, I see,' said Lincoln.

'Why didn't you think of all this before?' Marion asked.

'I suppose I did, from time to time, but Helen and I were getting along badly. When I consented to the guardianship, I was flat on my back in a sanitarium and the market had cleaned me out. I knew I'd acted badly, and I thought if it would bring any peace to Helen, I'd agree to anything. But now it's different. I'm functioning, I'm behaving damn well, so far as—'

'Please don't swear at me,' Marion said.

He looked at her, startled. With each remark the force of her dislike became more and more apparent. She had built up all her fear of life into one wall and faced it toward him. This trivial reproof was possibly the result of some trouble with the cook several hours before. Charlie became increasingly alarmed at leaving Honoria in this atmosphere of hostility against himself; sooner or later it would come out, in a word here, a shake of the head there, and some of that distrust would be irrevocably implanted in Honoria. But he pulled his temper down out of his face and shut it up inside him; he had won a point, for Lincoln realized the absurdity of Marion's remark and asked her lightly since when she had objected to the word 'damn'.

'Another thing,' Charlie said: 'I'm able to give her certain advantages now. I'm going to take a French governess to Prague with me. I've got a lease on a new apartment—'

He stopped, realizing that he was blundering. They couldn't be expected to accept with equanimity the fact that his income was again twice as large as their own.

'I suppose you can give her more luxuries than we can,' said Marion. 'When you were throwing away money we were living along watching every ten francs. . . . I suppose you'll start doing it again.'

'Oh, no,' he said, 'I've learned. I worked hard for ten years, you know—until I got lucky in the market, like so many people. Terribly lucky. It won't happen again.'

There was a long silence. All of them felt their nerves straining, and for the first time in a year Charlie wanted a drink. He was sure now that Lincoln Peters wanted him to have his child.

Marion shuddered suddenly; part of her saw that Charlie's feet were planted on the earth now, and her own maternal feeling recognized the naturalness of his desire; but she had lived for a long time with a prejudice—a prejudice founded on a curious disbelief in her sister's happiness, and which, in the shock of one terrible night, had turned to hatred for him. It had all happened at a point in her life where the discouragement of ill health and adverse circumstances made it necessary for her to believe in tangible villainy and a tangible villain.

'I can't help what I think!' she cried out suddenly. 'How much you were responsible for Helen's death, I don't know. It's something you'll have to square with your own conscience.'

An electric current of agony surged through him; for a moment he was almost on his feet, an unuttered sound echoing in his throat. He hung on to himself for a moment, another moment.

'Hold on there,' said Lincoln uncomfortably. 'I never thought you were responsible for that.'

'Helen died of heart trouble,' Charlie said dully.

'Yes, heart trouble.' Marion spoke as if the phrase had another meaning for her.

Then, in the flatness that followed her outburst, she saw him plainly and she knew he had somehow arrived at control over the situation. Glancing at her husband, she found no help from him, and as abruptly as if it were a matter of no importance, she threw up the sponge.

'Do what you like!' she cried, springing up from her chair. 'She's your child. I'm not the person to stand in your way. I think if it were my child I'd rather see her—' She managed to check herself. 'You two decide it. I can't stand this. I'm sick. I'm going to bed.'

She hurried from the room; after a moment Lincoln said:

'This has been a hard day for her. You know how strongly she feels—' His voice was almost apologetic: 'Where a woman gets an idea in her head.'

'Of course.'

'It's going to be all right. I think she sees now that you—can provide for the child, and so we can't very well stand in your way or Honoria's way.'

'Thank you, Lincoln.'

'I'd better go along and see how she is.'

'I'm going.'

He was still trembling when he reached the street, but a walk down the Rue Bonaparte to the *quais* set him up, and as he crossed the Seine, fresh and new by the *quai* lamps, he felt exultant. But back in his room he couldn't sleep. The image of Helen haunted him. Helen whom he had loved so until they had senselessly begun to abuse each other's love, tear it into shreds. On that terrible February night that Marion remembered so vividly, a slow quarrel had gone on for hours. There was a scene at the Florida, and then he attempted to take her home, and then she kissed young Webb at a table; after that there was what she hysterically said. When he arrived home alone he turned the key in the lock in wild anger. How could he know she would arrive an hour later alone, that there would be a snowstorm in which she wandered about in slippers, too confused to find a taxi? Then the aftermath, her escaping pneumonia by a miracle, and all the attendant horror. They were 'reconciled', but that was the beginning of the end, and Marion, who had seen with her own eyes and who imagined it to be one of many scenes from her sister's martyrdom, never forgot.

Going over it again brought Helen nearer, and in the white, soft light that steals upon half sleep near morning he found himself talking to her again. She said that he was perfectly right about Honoria and that she wanted Honoria to be with him. She said she was glad he was being good and doing better. She said a lot of other things—very friendly things—but she was in a swing in a white dress, and swinging faster and faster all the time, so that at the end he could not hear clearly all that she said.

IV

He woke up feeling happy. The door of the world was open again. He made plans, vistas, futures for Honoria and himself, but suddenly he grew sad, remembering all the plans he and Helen had made. She had not planned to die. The present was the thing—work to do and someone to love. But not to love too much, for he knew the injury that a father can do to a daughter or a mother to a son by attaching them too closely: afterward, out in the world, the child would seek in the marriage partner the same blind tenderness and, failing probably to find it, turn against love and life.

It was another bright, crisp day. He called Lincoln Peters at the bank where he worked and asked if he could count on taking Honoria when he left for Prague. Lincoln agreed that there was no reason for delay. One thing—the legal guardianship. Marion wanted to retain that a while longer. She was upset by the whole matter, and it would oil things if she felt that the situation was still in her control for another year. Charlie agreed, wanting only the tangible, visible child.

Then the question of a governess. Charles sat in a gloomy agency and talked to a cross Béarnaise and to a buxom Breton peasant, neither of whom he could have endured. There were others whom he would see tomorrow.

He lunched with Lincoln Peters at Griffons, trying to keep down his exultation.

'There's nothing quite like your own child,' Lincoln said. 'But you understand how Marion feels too.'

'She's forgotten how hard I worked for seven years there,' Charlie said. 'She just remembers one night.'

'There's another thing.' Lincoln hesitated. 'While you and Helen were tearing around Europe throwing money away, we were just getting along. I didn't touch any of the prosperity because I never got ahead enough to carry anything but my insurance. I think Marion felt there was some kind of injustice in it—you not even working toward the end, and getting richer and richer.'

'It went just as quick as it came,' said Charlie.

'Yes, a lot of it stayed in the hands of *chasseurs* and saxophone players and maîtres d'hôtel—well, the big party's over now. I just said that to explain Marion's feeling about those crazy years. If you drop in about six o'clock tonight before Marion's too tired, we'll settle the details on the spot.'

Back at his hotel, Charlie found a *pneumatique* that had been redirected from the Ritz bar where Charlie had left his address for the purpose of finding a certain man.

> 'Dear Charlie: You were so strange when we saw you the other day that I wondered if I did something to offend you. If so, I'm not conscious of it. In fact, I have thought about you too much for the last year, and it's always been in the back of my mind that I might see you if I came over here. We *did* have such good times that crazy spring, like the night you and I stole the butcher's tricycle, and the time we tried to call on the president and you had the old derby rim and the wire cane. Everybody seems so old lately, but I don't feel old

a bit. Couldn't we get together some time today for old time's sake? I've got a vile hang-over for the moment, but will be feeling better this afternoon and will look for you about five in the sweat-shop at the Ritz.

Always devotedly,
Lorraine.'

His first feeling was one of awe that he had actually, in his mature years, stolen a tricycle and pedalled Lorraine all over the Étoile between the small hours and dawn. In restrospect it was a nightmare. Locking out Helen didn't fit in with any other act of his life, but the tricycle incident did—it was one of many. How many weeks or months of dissipation to arrive at that condition of utter irresponsibility?

He tried to picture how Lorraine had appeared to him then—very attractive; Helen was unhappy about it, though she said nothing. Yesterday, in the restaurant, Lorraine had seemed trite, blurred, worn away. He emphatically did not want to see her, and he was glad Alix had not given away his hotel address. It was a relief to think, instead, of Honoria, to think of Sundays spent with her and of saying good morning to her and of knowing she was there in his house at night, drawing her breath in the darkness.

At five he took a taxi and bought presents for all the Peters—a piquant cloth doll, a box of Roman soldiers, flowers for Marion, big linen handkerchiefs for Lincoln.

He saw, when he arrived in the apartment, that Marion had accepted the inevitable. She greeted him now as though he were a recalcitrant member of the family, rather than a menacing outsider. Honoria had been told she was going; Charlie was glad to see that her tact made her conceal her excessive happiness. Only on his lap did she whisper her delight and the question 'When?' before she slipped away with the other children.

He and Marion were alone for a minute in the room, and on an impulse he spoke boldly:

'Family quarrels are bitter things. They don't go according to any rules. They're not like aches or wounds; they're more like splits in the skin that won't heal because there's not enough material. I wish you and I could be on better terms.'

'Some things are hard to forget,' she answered. 'It's a question of confidence.' There was no answer to this and presently she asked, 'When do you propose to take her?'

'As soon as I can get a governess. I hoped the day after to-morrow.'

'That's impossible. I've got to get her things in shape. Not before Saturday.'

He yielded. Coming back into the room, Lincoln offered him a drink.

'I'll take my daily whisky,' he said.

It was warm here, it was a home, people together by a fire. The children felt very safe and important; the mother and father were serious, watchful. They had things to do for the children more important than his visit here. A spoonful of medicine was, after all, more important than the strained relations between Marion and himself. They were not dull people, but they were very much in the grip of life and circumstances. He wondered if he couldn't do something to get Lincoln out of his rut at the bank.

A long peal at the door-bell; the *bonne à tout faire* passed through and went down the corridor. The door opened upon another long ring, and then voices, and the three in the salon looked up expectantly; Richard moved to bring the corridor within his range of vision, and Marion rose. Then the maid came back along the corridor, closely followed by the voices, which developed under the light into Duncan Schaeffer and Lorraine Quarrles.

They were gay, they were hilarious, they were roaring with laughter. For a moment Charlie was astounded; unable to understand how they ferreted out the Peters' address.

'Ah-h-h!' Duncan wagged his finger roguishly at Charlie. 'Ah-h-h!'

They both slid down another cascade of laughter. Anxious and at a loss, Charlie shook hands with them quickly and presented them to Lincoln and Marion. Marion nodded, scarcely speaking. She had drawn back a step toward the fire; her little girl stood beside her, and Marion put an arm about her shoulder.

With growing annoyance at the intrusion, Charlie waited for them to explain themselves. After some concentration Duncan said:

'We came to invite you out to dinner. Lorraine and I insist that all this shishi, cagy business 'bout your address got to stop.'

Charlie came closer to them, as if to force them backward down the corridor.

'Sorry, but I can't. Tell me where you'll be and I'll phone you in half an hour.'

This made no impression. Lorraine sat down suddenly on the side of a chair, and focusing her eyes on Richard, cried, 'Oh, what a nice little boy! Come here, little boy.' Richard glanced at his mother, but did not move. With a perceptible shrug of her shoulders, Lorraine turned back to Charlie:

'Come and dine. Sure your cousins won' mine. See you so sel'om. Or solemn.'

'I can't,' said Charlie sharply. 'You two have dinner and I'll phone you.'

Her voice became suddenly unpleasant. 'All right, we'll go. But I remember once when you hammered on my door at four A.M. I was enough of a good sport to give you a drink. Come on, Dunc.'

Still in slow motion, with blurred, angry faces, with uncertain feet, they retired along the corridor.

'Good night,' Charlie said.

'Good night!' responded Lorraine emphatically.

When he went back into the salon Marion had not moved, only now her son was standing in the circle of her other arm. Lincoln was still swinging Honoria back and forth like a pendulum from side to side.

'What an outrage!' Charlie broke out. 'What an absolute outrage!'

Neither of them answered. Charlie dropped into an armchair, picked up his drink, set it down again and said:

'People I haven't seen for two years having the colossal nerve—'

He broke off. Marion had made the sound 'Oh!' in one swift, furious breath, turned her body from him with a jerk and left the room.

Lincoln set down Honoria carefully.

'You children go in and start your soup,' he said, and when they obeyed, he said to Charlie:

'Marion's not well and she can't stand shocks. That kind of people make her really physically sick.'

'I didn't tell them to come here. They wormed your name out of somebody. They deliberately—'

'Well, it's too bad. It doesn't help matters. Excuse me a minute.'

Left alone, Charlie sat tense in his chair. In the next room he could hear the children eating, talking in monosyllables, already oblivious to the scene between their elders. He heard a murmur of conversation from a farther room and then the ticking bell of a telephone receiver picked up, and in a panic he moved to the other side of the room and out of earshot.

In a minute Lincoln came back. 'Look here, Charlie, I think we'd better call off dinner for tonight. Marion's in bad shape.'

'Is she angry with me?'

'Sort of,' he said, almost roughly. 'She's not strong and—'

'You mean she's changed her mind about Honoria?'

'She's pretty bitter right now. I don't know. You phone me at the bank tomorrow.'

'I wish you'd explain to her I never dreamed these people would come here. I'm just as sore as you are.'

'I couldn't explain anything to her now.'

Charlie got up. He took his coat and hat and started down the corridor. Then he opened the door of the dining room and said in a strange voice, 'Good night, children.'

Honoria rose and ran around the table to hug him.

'Good night, sweetheart,' he said vaguely, and then trying to make his voice more tender, trying to conciliate something, 'Good night, dear children.'

V

Charlie went directly to the Ritz bar with the furious idea of finding Lorraine and Duncan, but they were not there, and he realized that in any case there was nothing he could do. He had not touched his drink at the

Peters, and now he ordered a whisky-and-soda. Paul came over to say hello.

'It's a great change,' he said sadly. 'We do about half the business we did. So many fellows I hear about back in the States lost eveything, maybe not in the first crash, but then in the second. Your friend George Hardt lost every cent, I hear. Are you back in the States?'

'No, I'm in business in Prague.'

'I heard that you lost a lot in the crash.'

'I did,' he added grimly, 'but I lost everything I wanted in the boom.'

'Selling short.'

'Something like that.'

Again the memory of those days swept over him like a nightmare—the people they had met travelling; then people who couldn't add a row of figures or speak a coherent sentence. The little man Helen had consented to dance with at the ship's party, who had insulted her ten feet from the table; the women and girls carried screaming with drink or drugs out of public places—

—The men who locked their wives out in the snow, because the snow of twenty-nine wasn't real snow. If you didn't want it to be snow, you just paid some money.

He went to the phone and called the Peters' apartment; Lincoln answered.

'I called up because this thing is on my mind. Has Marion said anything definite?'

'Marion's sick,' Lincoln answered shortly. 'I know this thing isn't altogether your fault, but I can't have her go to pieces about it. I'm afraid we'll have to let it slide for six months; I can't take the chance of working her up to this stage again.'

'I see.'

'I'm sorry, Charlie.'

He went back to his table. His whisky glass was empty, but he shook his head when Alix looked at it questioningly. There wasn't much he could do now except send Honoria some things; he would send her a lot of things tomorrow. He thought rather angrily that this was just money—he had given so many people money. . . .

'No, no more,' he said to another waiter. 'What do I owe you?'

He would come back some day; they couldn't make him pay forever. But he wanted his child, and nothing was much good now, beside that fact. He wasn't young any more, with a lot of nice thoughts and dreams to have by himself. He was absolutely sure Helen wouldn't have wanted him to be so alone.

1931

William Faulkner

1897-1962

William Faulkner's fiction is celebrated for its depiction of a regional setting—its history and geography, its characters, climate, and culture. The novels and stories that Faulkner set in Yoknapatawpha County (he called it 'that little postage stamp of native soil') allowed him to explore the change—and the powerful resistance to change—in Southern tradition, particularly in his native Mississippi, that followed the Civil War. But Faulkner always insisted that fiction was an invention, something different from truth: 'I'm a story-teller. I'm telling a story, introducing comic and tragic elements as I like. I'm telling a story—to be repeated and retold. I don't claim to be truthful. Fiction is fiction—not truth; it's make believe. Thus I stack and lie at times, all for the purposes of the story—to entertain.' And even though the specific past of the South haunts Faulkner's fiction with its own particular shadow, his fiction demonstrates how regional settings and themes can resonate universally, rising beyond their time and place, when they are evoked in all their vivid singularity.

The first of four boys, Faulkner was born in New Albany, Mississippi, into a prominent Southern family. He was a lacklustre student, leaving school in 1918 to enlist in the Canadian division of the Royal Air Force. But the First World War ended before Faulkner had completed his training, and he returned to Oxford, Mississippi, having added the 'u' to Falkner, his family name. He attended the University of Mississippi (1919-20), where he published poems and short fiction in the student newspaper. After a brief stint working at a bookstore in New York, he returned to Mississippi and a job at the University post office; increasingly, he was devoting his time to reading and writing, and he left his job in 1924, travelling to New Orleans, where he met Sherwood Anderson. His first book, a collection of poems, was published that year, and his first novel, *Soldier's Pay*, in 1926. By the end of 1929 he had written six novels and published four, but had gained little recognition, although he had completed in 1928 *The Sound and the Fury*, now regarded as one of his masterpieces. He married in 1929 and settled in Oxford, Mississippi. By 1950, having published nineteen works of fiction, he was the most widely respected American writer of his day. He divided the last years of his life between Oxford and Charlottesville, where he became writer-in-residence at the University of Virginia in 1957.

Through its depiction of the isolation of Miss Emily Grierson, 'A Rose for Emily', Faulkner's first published story, dramatizes the passing of an aristocratic way of life in the South. Miss Emily is trapped in the past, bound up in the moribund traditions that are suggested so tellingly by the story's repeated reference to the dust that coats the interior of her house. The revelation that Homer Barron has been lying dead in the house for so many years (and that Miss Emily has probably poisoned him) only confirms this story's poignant exploration of Miss Emily's proud but perverse refusal to acknowledge the force of any change, even that of death itself.

The hot, dry weather at the opening of 'Dry September' accentuates the volatile pitch of the men's emotions. Hawkshaw's attempts to defuse the group's blind bigotry dramatize how powerless reason is in this cultural setting to even consider the possibility of a negro's innocence or of a white woman's lying, and their actions become as inevitable, and as predictable, as the weather.

'A Rose for Emily' was first published in the April 1930 issue of *Forum*, and 'Dry September' in the January 1931 issue of *Scribner's*. Both stories were then collected in *These Thirteen* (1931), with slight revisions to 'A Rose for Emily'.

A Rose for Emily

I

When Miss Emily Grierson died, our whole town went to her funeral: the men through a sort of respectful affection for a fallen monument, the women mostly out of curiosity to see the inside of her house, which no one save an old manservant—a combined gardener and cook—had seen in at least ten years.

It was a big, squarish frame house that had once been white, decorated with cupolas and spires and scrolled balconies in the heavily lightsome style of the seventies, set on what had once been our most select street. But garages and cotton gins had encroached and obliterated even the august names of that neighbourhood; only Miss Emily's house was left, lifting its stubborn and coquettish decay above the cotton wagons and the gasoline pumps—an eyesore among eyesores. And now Miss Emily had gone to join the representatives of those august names where they lay in the cedar-bemused cemetery among the ranked and anonymous graves of Union and Confederate soldiers who fell at the battle of Jefferson.

Alive, Miss Emily had been a tradition, a duty, and a care; a sort of hereditary obligation upon the town, dating from that day in 1894 when Colonel Sartoris, the mayor—he who fathered the edict that no Negro woman should appear on the streets without an apron—remitted her taxes, the dispensation dating from the death of her father on into perpetuity. Not that Miss Emily would have accepted charity. Colonel Sartoris invented an involved tale to the effect that Miss Emily's father had loaned money to the town, which the town, as a matter of business, preferred this way of repaying. Only a man of Colonel Sartoris' generation and thought could have invented it, and only a woman could have believed it.

When the next generation, with its modern ideas, became mayors and aldermen, this arrangement created some little dissatisfaction. On the first of the year they mailed her a tax notice. February came, and there was no reply. They wrote her a formal letter, asking her to call at the sheriff's office at her convenience. A week later the mayor wrote her himself, offering to call or to send his car for her, and received in reply a note on paper of an archaic shape, in a thin, flowing calligraphy in faded ink, to the effect that she no longer went out at all. The tax notice was also enclosed, without comment.

They called a special meeting of the Board of Aldermen. A deputation waited upon her, knocked at her door through which no visitor had passed since she ceased giving china-painting lessons eight or ten years earlier. They were admitted by the old Negro into a dim hall from which a stairway mounted into still more shadow. It smelled of dust and disuse—a close, dank smell. The Negro led them into the parlour. It was furnished in heavy, leather-covered furniture. When the Negro opened the blinds of one window, they could see that the leather was cracked; and when they sat down, a faint dust rose sluggishly about their thighs, spinning with slow motes in the single sun-ray. On a tarnished gilt easel before the fireplace stood a crayon portrait of Miss Emily's father.

They rose when she entered—a small, fat woman in black, with a thin gold chain descending to her waist and vanishing into her belt, leaning on an ebony cane with a tarnished gold head. Her skeleton was small and spare; perhaps that was why what would have been merely plumpness in another was obesity in her. She looked bloated, like a body long submerged in motionless water, and of that pallid hue. Her eyes, lost in the fatty ridges of her face, looked like two small pieces of coal pressed into a lump of dough as they moved from one face to another while the visitors stated their errand.

She did not ask them to sit. She just stood in the door and listened quietly until the spokesman came to a stumbling halt. Then they could hear the invisible watch ticking at the end of the gold chain.

Her voice was dry and cold. 'I have no taxes in Jefferson. Colonel Sartoris explained it to me. Perhaps one of you can gain access to the city records and satisfy yourselves.'

'But we have. We are the city authorities, Miss Emily. Didn't you get a notice from the sheriff, signed by him?'

'I received a paper, yes,' Miss Emily said. 'Perhaps he considers himself the sheriff . . . I have no taxes in Jefferson.'

'But there is nothing on the books to show that, you see. We must go by the—'

'See Colonel Sartoris. I have no taxes in Jefferson.'

'But, Miss Emily—'

'See Colonel Sartoris.' (Colonel Sartoris had been dead almost ten years.) 'I have no taxes in Jefferson. Tobe!' The Negro appeared. 'Show these gentlemen out.'

II

So she vanquished them, horse and foot, just as she had vanquished their fathers thirty years before about the smell. That was two years after her father's death and a short time after her sweetheart—the one we believed would marry her—had deserted her. After her father's death she went out very little; after her sweetheart went away, people hardly saw her at all. A few of the ladies had the temerity to call, but were not received and the only sign of life about the place was the Negro man—a young man then—going in and out with a market basket.

'Just as if a man—any man—could keep a kitchen properly,' the ladies said; so they were not surprised when the smell developed. It was another link between the gross, teeming world and the high and mighty Griersons.

A neighbour, a woman, complained to the mayor, Judge Stevens, eighty years old.

'But what will you have me do about it, madam?' he said.

'Why, send her word to stop it,' the woman said. 'Isn't there a law?'

'I'm sure that won't be necessary,' Judge Stevens said. 'It's probably just a snake or a rat that nigger of hers killed in the yard. I'll speak to him about it.'

The next day he received two more complaints, one from a man who came in diffident deprecation. 'We really must do something about it, Judge. I'd be the last one in the world to bother Miss Emily, but we've got to do something.' That night the Board of Aldermen met—three greybeards and one younger man, a member of the rising generation.

'It's simple enough,' he said. 'Send her word to have her place cleaned up. Give her a certain time to do it in, and if she don't . . .'

'Dammit, sir,' Judge Stevens said, 'will you accuse a lady to her face of smelling bad?'

So the next night, after midnight, four men crossed Miss Emily's lawn and slunk about the house like burglars, sniffing along the base of the brickwork and at the cellar openings while one of them performed a regular sowing motion with his hand out of a sack slung from his shoulder. They broke open the cellar door and sprinkled lime there, and in all the outbuildings. As they recrossed the lawn, a window that had been dark was lighted and Miss Emily sat in it, the light behind her, and her upright torso motionless as that of an idol. They crept quietly across the lawn and into the shadow of the locusts that lined the street. After a week or two the smell went away.

That was when people had begun to feel really sorry for her. People in our town, remembering how old lady Wyatt, her great-aunt, had gone completely crazy at last, believed that the Griersons held themselves a little too high for what they really were. None of the young men were quite good enough for Miss Emily and such. We had long thought of them as a tableau, Miss Emily a slender figure in white in the background, her father a spraddled silhouette in the foreground, his back to her and clutching a horsewhip, the two of them framed by the back-flung front door. So when she got to be thirty and was still single, we were not pleased exactly, but vindicated; even with insanity in the family she wouldn't have turned down all of her chances if they had really materialized.

When her father died, it got about that the house was all that was left to her; and in a way, people were glad. At last they could pity Miss Emily. Being left alone, and a pauper, she had become humanized. Now she too would know the old thrill and the old despair of a penny more or less.

The day after his death all of the ladies prepared to call at the house and offer condolence and aid, as is our custom. Miss Emily met them at the door, dressed as usual and with no trace of grief on her face. She told them that her father was not dead. She did that for three days, with the ministers calling on her, and the doctors, trying to persuade her to let them dispose of the body. Just as they were about to resort to law and force, she broke down, and they buried her father quickly.

We did not say she was crazy then. We believed she had to do that. We remembered all the young men her father had driven away, and we knew that with nothing left, she would have to cling to that which had robbed her, as people will.

III

She was sick for a long time. When we saw her again, her hair was cut short, making her look like a girl, with a vague resemblance to those angels in coloured church windows—sort of tragic and serene.

The town had just let the contracts for paving the sidewalks, and in the summer after her father's death they began the work. The construction company came with niggers and mules and machinery, and a foreman named Homer Barron, a Yankee—a big, dark, ready man, with a big voice and eyes lighter than his face. The little boys would follow in groups to hear him cuss the niggers, and the niggers singing in time to the rise and fall of picks. Pretty soon he knew everybody in town. Whenever you heard a lot of laughing anywhere about the square, Homer Barron would be in the centre of the group. Presently we began to see him and Miss Emily on Sunday afternoons driving in the yellow-wheeled buggy and the matched team of bays from the livery stable.

At first we were glad that Miss Emily would have an interest, because the ladies all said, 'Of course a Grierson would not think seriously of a Northerner, a day labourer.' But there were still others, older people, who said that even grief could not cause a real lady to forget *noblesse oblige*—without calling it *noblesse oblige*. They just said, 'Poor Emily. Her kinsfolk should come to her.' She had some kin in Alabama; but years ago her father had fallen out with them over the estate of old lady Wyatt, the crazy woman, and there was no communication between the two families. They had not even been represented at the funeral.

And as soon as the old people said, 'Poor Emily,' the whispering began. 'Do you suppose it's really so?' they said to one another. 'Of course it is. What else could . . .' This behind their hands; rustling of craned silk and satin behind jalousies closed upon the sun of Sunday afternoon as the thin, swift clop-clop-clop of the matched team passed: 'Poor Emily.'

She carried her head high enough—even when we believed that she was fallen. It was as if she demanded more than ever the recognition of her dignity as the last Grierson; as if it had wanted that touch of earthiness to reaffirm her imperviousness. Like when she bought the rat poison, the arsenic. That was over a year after they had begun to say 'Poor Emily,' and while the two female cousins were visiting her.

'I want some poison,' she said to the druggist. She was over thirty then, still a slight woman, though thinner than usual, with cold, haughty black eyes in a face the flesh of which was strained across the temples and about the eye-sockets as you imagine a lighthouse-keeper's face ought to look. 'I want some poison,' she said.

'Yes, Miss Emily. What kind? For rats and such? I'd recom—'

'I want the best you have. I don't care what kind.'

The druggist named several. 'They'll kill anything up to an elephant. But what you want is—'

'Arsenic,' Miss Emily said. 'Is that a good one?'

'Is . . . arsenic? Yes, ma'am. But what you want—'

'I want arsenic.'

The druggist looked down at her. She looked back at him, erect, her face like a strained flag. 'Why, of course,' the druggist said. 'If that's what you want. But the law requires you to tell what you are going to use it for.'

Miss Emily just stared at him, her head tilted back in order to look him eye for eye, until he looked away and went and got the arsenic and wrapped it up. The Negro delivery boy brought her the package; the druggist didn't come back. When she opened the package at home there was written on the box, under the skull and bones: 'For rats.'

IV

So the next day we all said, 'She will kill herself'; and we said it would be the best thing. When she had first begun to be seen with Homer Barron, we had said, 'She will marry him.' Then we said, 'She will persuade him yet,' because Homer himself had remarked—he liked men, and it was known that he drank with the younger men in the Elks' Club—that he was not a marrying man. Later we said, 'Poor Emily' behind the jalousies as they passed on Sunday afternoon in the glittering buggy, Miss Emily with her head high and Homer Barron with his hat cocked and a cigar in his teeth, reins and whip in a yellow glove.

Then some of the ladies began to say that it was a disgrace to the town and a bad example to the young people. The men did not want to interfere, but at last the ladies forced the Baptist minister—Miss Emily's people were Episcopal—to call upon her. He would never divulge what happened during that interview, but he refused to go back again. The next Sunday they again drove about the streets, and the following day the minister's wife wrote to Miss Emily's relations in Alabama.

So she had blood-kin under her roof again and we sat back to watch developments. At first nothing happened. Then we were sure that they were to be married. We learned that Miss Emily had been to the jeweller's and ordered a man's toilet set in silver, with the letters H. B. on each piece. Two days later we learned that she had bought a complete outfit of men's clothing, including a nightshirt, and we said, 'They are married.' We were really glad. We were glad because the two female cousins were even more Grierson than Miss Emily had ever been.

So we were not surprised when Homer Barron—the streets had been finished some time since—was gone. We were a little disappointed that there was not a public blowing-off, but we believed that he had gone on to prepare for Miss Emily's coming, or to give her a chance to get rid of the cousins. (By that time it was a cabal, and we were all Miss Emily's allies to help circumvent the cousins.) Sure enough, after another week they departed. And, as we had expected all along, within three days Homer Barron was back in town. A neighbour saw the Negro man admit him at the kitchen door at dusk one evening.

And that was the last we saw of Homer Barron. And of Miss Emily for some time. The Negro man went in and out with the market basket, but the front door remained closed. Now and then we would see her at a window for a moment, as the men did that night when they sprinkled the lime, but for almost six months she did not appear on the streets. Then we knew that this was to be expected too; as if that quality of her father which had thwarted her woman's life so many times had been too virulent and too furious to die.

When we next saw Miss Emily, she had grown fat and her hair was turning grey. During the next few years it grew greyer and greyer until it attained an even pepper-and-salt iron-grey, when it ceased turning. Up to the day of her death at seventy-four it was still that vigorous iron-grey, like the hair of an active man.

From that time on her front door remained closed, save for a period of six or seven years, when she was about forty, during which she gave lessons in china-painting. She fitted up a studio in one of the downstairs rooms, where the daughters and granddaughters of Colonel Sartoris' contemporaries were sent to her with the same regularity and in the same spirit that they were sent to church on Sundays with a twenty-five-cent piece for the collection plate. Meanwhile her taxes had been remitted.

Then the newer generation became the backbone and the spirit of the town, and the painting pupils grew up and fell away and did not send their children to her with boxes of colour and tedious brushes and pictures cut from the ladies' magazines. The front door closed upon the last one and remained closed for good. When the town got free postal delivery, Miss Emily alone refused to let them fasten the metal numbers above her door and attach a mailbox to it. She would not listen to them.

Daily, monthly, yearly we watched the Negro grow greyer and more stooped, going in and out with the market basket. Each December we sent her a tax notice, which would be returned by the post office a week later, unclaimed. Now and then we would see her in one of the downstairs windows—she had evidently shut up the top floor of the house—like the carven torso of an idol in a niche, looking or not looking at us, we could never tell which. Thus she passed from generation to generation—dear, inescapable, impervious, tranquil, and perverse.

And so she died. Fell ill in the house filled with dust and shadows, with only a doddering Negro man to wait on her. We did not even know she was sick; we had long since given up trying to get any information from the Negro. He talked to no one, probably not even to her, for his voice had grown harsh and rusty, as if from disuse.

She died in one of the downstairs rooms, in a heavy walnut bed with a curtain, her grey hair propped on a pillow yellow and mouldy with age and lack of sunlight.

V

The Negro met the first of the ladies at the front door and let them in, with their hushed, sibilant voices and their quick, curious glances, and then he disappeared. He walked right through the house and out the back and was not seen again.

The two female cousins came at once. They held the funeral on the second day, with the town coming to look at Miss Emily beneath a mass of bought flowers, with the crayon face of her father musing profoundly above the bier and the ladies sibilant and macabre; and the very old men—some in their brushed Confederate uniforms—on the porch and the lawn, talking of Miss Emily as if she had been a contemporary of theirs, believing that they had danced with her and courted her perhaps, confusing time with its mathematical progression, as the old do, to whom all the past is not a diminishing road but, instead, a huge meadow which no winter ever quite touches, divided from them now by the narrow bottle-neck of the most recent decade of years.

Already we knew that there was one room in that region above stairs which no one had seen in forty years, and which would have to be forced. They waited until Miss Emily was decently in the ground before they opened it.

The violence of breaking down the door seemed to fill this room with pervading dust. A thin, acrid pall as of the tomb seemed to lie everywhere upon this room decked and furnished as for a bridal: upon the valance curtains of faded rose colour, upon the rose-shaded lights, upon the dressing table, upon the delicate array of crystal and the man's toilet things backed with tarnished silver, silver so tarnished that the monogram was obscured. Among them lay a collar and tie, as if they had just been removed, which, lifted, left upon the surface a pale crescent in the dust. Upon a chair hung the suit, carefully folded; beneath it the two mute shoes and the discarded socks.

The man himself lay in the bed.

For a long while we just stood there, looking down at the profound and fleshless grin. The body had apparently once lain in the attitude of an embrace, but now the long sleep that outlasts love, that conquers even the grimace of love, had cuckolded him. What was left of him, rotted beneath what was left of the nightshirt, had become inextricable from the bed in which he lay; and upon him and upon the pillow beside him lay that even coating of the patient and biding dust.

Then we noticed that in the second pillow was the indentation of a head. One of us lifted something from it, and leaning forward, that faint and invisible dust dry and acrid in the nostrils, we saw a long strand of iron-grey hair.

1930

Dry September

I

Through the bloody September twilight, aftermath of sixty-two rainless days, it had gone like a fire in dry grass—the rumour, the story, whatever it was. Something about Miss Minnie Cooper and a Negro. Attacked, insulted, frightened: none of them, gathered in the barber shop on that Saturday evening where the ceiling fan stirred, without freshening it, the vitiated air, sending back upon them, in recurrent surges of stale pomade and lotion, their own stale breath and odours, knew exactly what had happened.

'Except it wasn't Will Mayes,' a barber said. He was a man of middle age; a thin, sand-coloured man with a mild face, who was shaving a client. 'I know Will Mayes. He's a good nigger. And I know Miss Minnie Cooper, too.'

'What do you know about her?' a second barber said.

'Who is she?' the client said. 'A young girl?'

'No,' the barber said. 'She's about forty, I reckon. She aint married. That's why I dont believe—'

'Believe, hell!' a hulking youth in a sweat-stained silk shirt said. 'Wont you take a white woman's word before a nigger's?'

'I dont believe Will Mayes did it,' the barber said. 'I know Will Mayes.'

'Maybe you know who did it, then. Maybe you already got him out of town, you damn niggerlover.'

'I dont believe anybody did anything. I dont believe anything happened. I leave it to you fellows if them ladies that get old without getting married dont have notions that a man cant—'

'Then you are a hell of a white man,' the client said. He moved under the cloth. The youth had sprung to his feet.

'You dont?' he said. 'Do you accuse a white woman of lying?'

The barber held the razor poised above the half-risen client. He did not look around.

'It's this durn weather,' another said. 'It's enough to make a man do anything. Even to her.'

Nobody laughed. The barber said in his mild, stubborn tone: 'I aint accusing nobody of nothing. I just know and you fellows know how a woman that never—'

'You damn niggerlover!' the youth said.

'Shut up, Butch,' another said. 'We'll get the facts in plenty of time to act.'

'Who is? Who's getting them?' the youth said. 'Facts, hell! I—'

'You're a fine white man,' the client said. 'Aint you?' In his frothy beard he looked like a desert rat in the moving pictures. 'You tell them, Jack,' he said to the youth. 'If there aint any white men in this town, you can count on me, even if I aint only a drummer and a stranger.'

'That's right, boys,' the barber said. 'Find out the truth first. I know Will Mayes.'

'Well, by God!' the youth shouted. 'To think that a white man in this town—'

'Shut up, Butch,' the second speaker said. 'We got plenty of time.'

The client sat up. He looked at the speaker. 'Do you claim that anything excuses a nigger attacking a white woman? Do you mean to tell me you are a white man and you'll stand for it? You better go back North where you came from. The South dont want your kind here.'

'North what?' the second said. 'I was born and raised in this town.'

'Well, by God!' the youth said. He looked about with a strained, baffled gaze, as if he was trying to remember what it was he wanted to say or to do. He drew his sleeve across his sweating face. 'Damn if I'm going to let a white woman—'

'You tell them, Jack,' the drummer said. 'By God, if they—'

The screen door crashed open. A man stood in the floor, his feet apart and his heavy-set body poised easily. His white shirt was open at the throat; he wore a felt hat. His hot, bold glance swept the group. His name was McLendon. He had commanded troops at the front in France and had been decorated for valour.

'Well,' he said, 'are you going to sit there and let a black son rape a white woman on the streets of Jefferson?'

Butch sprang up again. The silk of his shirt clung flat to his heavy shoulders. At each armpit was a dark halfmoon. 'That's what I been telling them! That's what I—'

'Did it really happen?' a third said. 'This aint the first man scare she ever had, like Hawkshaw says. Wasn't there something about a man on the kitchen roof, watching her undress, about a year ago?'

'What?' the client said. 'What's that?' The barber had been slowly forcing him back in the chair; he arrested himself reclining, his head lifted, the barber still pressing him down.

McLendon whirled on the third speaker. 'Happen? What the hell difference does it make? Are you going to let the black sons get away with it until one really does it?'

'That's what I'm telling them!' Butch shouted. He cursed, long and steady, pointless.

'Here, here,' a fourth said. 'Not so loud. Dont talk so loud.'

'Sure,' McLendon said; 'no talking necessary at all. I've done my talking. Who's with me?' He poised on the balls of his feet, roving his gaze.

The barber held the drummer's face down, the razor poised. 'Find out the facts first, boys. I know Willy Mayes. It wasn't him. Let's get the sheriff and do this thing right.'

McLendon whirled upon him his furious, rigid face. The barber did not look away. They looked like men of different races. The other barbers had ceased also above their prone clients. 'You mean to tell me,' McLendon said, 'that you'd take a nigger's word before a white woman's? Why, you damn niggerloving—'

The third speaker rose and grasped McLendon's arm; he too had been a soldier. 'Now, now. Let's figure this thing out. Who knows anything about what really happened?'

'Figure out hell!' McLendon jerked his arm free. 'All that're with me get up from there. The ones that aint—' He roved his gaze, dragging his sleeve across his face.

Three men rose. The drummer in the chair sat up. 'Here,' he said, jerking at the cloth about his neck; 'get this rag off me. I'm with him. I dont live here, but by God, if our mothers and wives and sisters—' He smeared the cloth over his face and flung it to the floor. McLendon stood in the floor and cursed the others. Another rose and moved toward him. The remainder sat uncomfortable, not looking at one another, then one by one they rose and joined him.

The barber picked the cloth from the floor. He began to fold it neatly. 'Boys, dont do that. Will Mayes never done it. I know.'

'Come on,' McLendon said. He whirled. From his hip pocket protruded the butt of a heavy automatic pistol. They went out. The screened door crashed behind them reverberant in the dead air.

The barber wiped the razor carefully and swiftly, and put it away, and ran to the rear, and took his hat from the wall. 'I'll be back as soon as I can,' he said to the other barbers. 'I cant let—' He went out, running. The two other barbers followed him to the door and caught it on the rebound, leaning out and looking up the street after him. The air was flat and dead. It had a metallic taste at the base of the tongue.

'What can he do?' the first said. The second one was saying 'Jees Christ, Jees Christ' under his breath. 'I'd just as lief be Will Mayes as Hawk, if he gets McLendon riled.'

'Jees Christ, Jees Christ,' the second whispered.

'You reckon he really done it to her?' the first said.

II

She was thirty-eight or thirty-nine. She lived in a small frame house with her invalid mother and a thin, sallow, unflagging aunt, where each morning between ten and eleven she would appear on the porch in a lace-trimmed boudoir cap, to sit swinging in the porch swing until noon. After dinner she lay down for a while, until the afternoon began to cool. Then, in one of the three or four new voile dresses which she had each summer, she would go downtown to spend the afternoon in the stores with the other ladies, where they would handle the goods and haggle over the prices in cold, immediate voices, without any intention of buying.

She was of comfortable people—not the best in Jefferson, but good people enough—and she was still on the slender side of ordinary looking, with a bright, faintly haggard manner and dress. When she was young she had had a slender, nervous body and a sort of hard vivacity which had enabled her for a time to ride upon the crest of the town's social life as exemplified by the high school party and church social period of her contemporaries while still children enough to be unclassconscious.

She was the last to realize that she was losing ground; that those among whom she had been a little brighter and louder flame than any other were beginning to learn the pleasure of snobbery—male—and retaliation—female. That was when her face began to wear that bright, haggard look. She still carried it to parties on shadowy porticoes and summer lawns, like a mask or a flag, with that bafflement of furious repudiation of truth in her eyes. One evening at a party she heard a boy and two girls, all schoolmates, talking. She never accepted another invitation.

She watched the girls with whom she had grown up as they married and got homes and children, but no man ever called on her steadily until the children of the other girls had been calling her 'aunty' for several years, the while their mothers told them in bright voices about how popular Aunt Minnie had been as a girl. Then the town began to see her driving on Sunday afternoons with the cashier in the bank. He was a widower of about forty—a high-coloured man, smelling always faintly of the barber shop or of whisky. He owned the first automobile in town, a red runabout; Minnie had the first motoring bonnet and veil the town ever saw. Then the town began to say: 'Poor Minnie.' 'But she is old enough to take care of herself,' others said. That was when she began to ask her old schoolmates that their children call her 'cousin' instead of 'aunty.'

It was twelve years now since she had been relegated into adultery by public opinion, and eight years since the cashier had gone to a Memphis bank, returning for one day each Christmas, which he spent at an annual bachelors' part at a hunting club on the river. From behind their curtains the neighbours would see the party pass, and during the over-the-way Christmas day visiting they would tell her about him, about how well he looked, and how they heard that he was prospering in the city, watching with bright, secret eyes her haggard, bright face. Usually by that hour there would be the scent of whisky on her breath. It was supplied by a youth, a clerk at the soda fountain: 'Sure, I buy it for the old gal. I reckon she's entitled to a little fun.'

Her mother kept to her room altogether now; the gaunt aunt ran the house. Against that background Minnie's bright dresses, her idle and empty days, had a quality of furious unreality. She went out in the evenings only with women now, neighbours, to the moving pictures. Each afternoon she dressed in one of the new dresses and went downtown alone, where her young 'cousins' were already strolling in the late afternoons with their delicate, silken heads and thin, awkward arms and conscious hips, clinging to one another or shrieking and giggling with paired boys in the soda fountain when she passed and went on along the serried store fronts, in the doors of which the sitting and lounging men did not even follow her with their eyes any more.

III

The barber went swiftly up the street where the sparse lights, insect-swirled, glared in rigid and violent suspension in the lifeless air. The day had died in a pall of dust; above the darkened square, shrouded by the spent dust, the sky was as clear as the inside of a brass bell. Below the east was a rumor of the twice-waxed moon.

When he overtook them McLendon and three others were getting into a car parked in an alley. McLendon stooped his thick head, peering out beneath the top. 'Changed your mind, did you?' he said. 'Damn good thing; by God, tomorrow when this town hears about how you talked tonight—'

'Now, now,' the other ex-soldier said. 'Hawkshaw's all right. Come on, Hawk; jump in.'

'Will Mayes never done it, boys,' the barber said. 'If anybody done it. Why, you all know well as I do there aint any town where they got better niggers than us. And you know how a lady will kind of think things about men when there aint any reason to, and Miss Minnie anyway—'

'Sure, sure,' the soldier said. 'We're just going to talk to him a little; that's all.'

'Talk hell!' Butch said. 'When we're through with the—'

'Shut up, for God's sake!' the soldier said. 'Do you want everybody in town—'

Tell them, by God!' McLendon said. 'Tell every one of the sons that'll let a white woman—'

'Let's go; let's go: here's the other car.' The second car slid squealing out of a cloud of dust at the alley mouth. McLendon started his car and took the lead. Dust lay like fog in the street. The street lights hung nimbused as in water. They drove on out of town.

A rutted lane turned at right angles. Dust hung above it too, and above all the land. The dark bulk of the ice plant, where the Negro Mayes was night watchman, rose against the sky. 'Better stop here, hadn't we?' the soldier said. McLendon did not reply. He hurled the car up and slammed to a stop, the headlights glaring on the blank wall.

'Listen here, boys,' the barber said; 'if he's here, dont that prove he never done it? Dont it? If it was him, he would run. Dont you see he would?' The second car came up and stopped. McLendon got down;

Butch sprang down beside him. 'Listen, boys,' the barber said.

'Cut the lights off!' McLendon said. The breathless dark rushed down. There was no sound in it save their lungs as they sought air in the parched dust in which for two months they had lived; then the diminishing crunch of McLendon's and Butch's feet, and a moment later McLendon's voice:

'Will! . . . Will!'

Below the east the wan hemorrhage of the moon increased. It heaved above the ridge, silvering the air, the dust, so that they seemed to breathe, live, in a bowl of molten lead. There was no sound of nightbird nor insect, no sound save their breathing and a faint ticking of contracting metal about the cars. Where their bodies touched one another they seemed to sweat dryly, for no more moisture came. 'Christ!' a voice said; 'let's get out of here.'

But they didn't move until vague noises began to grow out of the darkness ahead; then they got out and waited tensely in the breathless dark. There was another sound: a blow, a hissing expulsion of breath and McLendon cursing in undertone. They stood a moment longer, then they ran forward. They ran in a stumbling clump, as though they were fleeing something. 'Kill him, kill the son,' a voice whispered. McLendon flung them back.

'Not here,' he said. 'Get him into the car.' 'Kill him, kill the black son!' the voice murmured. They dragged the Negro to the car. The barber had waited beside the car. He could feel himself sweating and he knew he was going to be sick at the stomach.

'What is it, captains?' the Negro said. 'I aint done nothing. 'Fore God, Mr John.' Someone produced handcuffs. They worked busily about the Negro as though he were a post, quiet, intent, getting in one another's way. He submitted to the handcuffs, looking swiftly and constantly from dim face to dim face. 'Who's here, captains?' he said, leaning to peer into the faces until they could feel his breath and smell his sweaty reek. He spoke a name or two. 'What you all say I done, Mr John?'

McLendon jerked the car door open. 'Get in!' he said.

The Negro did not move. 'What you all going to do with me, Mr John? I aint done nothing. White folks, captains, I aint done nothing: I swear 'fore God.' He called another name.

'Get in!' McLendon said. He struck the Negro. The others expelled their breath in a dry hissing and struck him with random blows and he whirled and cursed them, and swept his manacled hands across their faces and slashed the barber upon the mouth, and the barber struck him also. 'Get him in there,' McLendon said. They pushed at him. He ceased struggling and got in and sat quietly as the others took their places. He sat between the barber and the soldier, drawing his limbs in so as not to touch them, his eyes going swiftly and constantly from face to face. Butch clung to the running board. The car moved on. The barber nursed his mouth with his handkerchief.

'What's the matter, Hawk?' the soldier said.

'Nothing,' the barber said. They regained the highroad and turned away from town. The second car dropped back out of the dust. They went on, gaining speed; the final fringe of houses dropped behind.

'Goddamn, he stinks!' the soldier said.

'We'll fix that,' the drummer in front beside McLendon said. On the running board Butch cursed into the hot rush of air. The barber leaned suddenly forward and touched McLendon's arm.

'Let me out, John,' he said.

'Jump out, niggerlover,' McLendon said without turning his head. He drove swiftly. Behind them the sourceless lights of the second car glared in the dust. Presently McLendon turned into a narrow road. It was rutted with disuse. It led back to an abandoned brick kiln—a series of reddish mounds and weed- and vine-choked vats without bottom. It had been used for pasture once, until one day the owner missed one of his mules. Although he prodded carefully in the vats with a long pole, he could not even find the bottom of them.

'John,' the barber said.

'Jump out, then,' McLendon said, hurling the car along the ruts. Beside the barber the Negro spoke:

'Mr Henry.'

The barber sat forward. The narrow tunnel of the road rushed up and past. Their motion was like an extinct furnace blast: cooler, but utterly dead. The car bounded from rut to rut.

'Mr Henry,' the Negro said.

The barber began to tug furiously at the door. 'Look out, there!' the soldier said, but the barber had already kicked the door open and swung onto the running board. The soldier leaned across the Negro and grasped at him, but he had already jumped. The car went on without checking speed.

The impetus hurled him crashing through dust-sheathed weeds, into the ditch. Dust puffed about him, and in a thin, vicious crackling of sapless stems he lay choking and retching until the second car passed and died away. Then he rose and limped on until he reached the highroad and turned toward town, brushing at his clothes with his hands. The moon was higher, riding high and clear of the dust at last, and after a while the town began to glare beneath the dust. He went on, limping. Presently he heard cars and the glow of them grew in the dust behind him and he left the road and crouched again in the weeds until they passed. McLendon's car came last now. There were four people in it and Butch was not on the running board.

They went on; the dust swallowed them; the glare and the sound died away. The dust of them hung for a while, but soon the eternal dust absorbed it again. The barber climbed back onto the road and limped on toward town.

IV

As she dressed for supper on that Saturday evening, her own flesh felt like fever. Her hands trembled among the hooks and eyes, and her eyes had a feverish look, and her hair swirled crisp and crackling under the comb. While she was still dressing the friends called for her and sat while she donned her sheerest underthings and stockings and a new voile dress. 'Do you feel strong enough to go out?' they said, their eyes bright too, with a dark glitter. 'When you have had time to get over the shock, you must tell us what happened. What he said and did; everything.'

In the leafed darkness, as they walked toward the square, she began to breathe deeply, something like a swimmer preparing to dive, until she ceased trembling, the four of them walking slowly because of the terrible heat and out of solicitude for her. But as they neared the square she began to tremble again, walking with her head up, her hands clenched at her sides, their voices about her murmurous, also with that feverish, glittering quality of their eyes.

They entered the square, she in the centre of the group, fragile in her fresh dress. She was trembling worse. She walked slower and slower, as children eat ice cream, her head up and her eyes bright in the haggard banner of her face, passing the hotel and the coatless drummers in chairs along the curb looking around at her: 'That's the one: see? The one in the pink in the middle.' 'Is that her?' What did they do with the nigger? Did they—?' 'Sure. He's all right.' 'All right, is he?' 'Sure. He went on a little trip.' Then the drug store, where even the young men lounging in the doorway tipped their hats and followed with their eyes the motion of her hips and legs when she passed.

They went on, passing the lifted hats of the gentlemen, the suddenly ceased voices, deferent, protective. 'Do you see?' the friends said. Their voices sounded like long, hovering sighs of hissing exultation. 'There's not a Negro on the square. Not one.'

They reached the picture show. It was like a miniature fairyland with its lighted lobby and colored lithographs of life caught in its terrible and beautiful mutations. Her lips began to tingle. In the dark, when the picture began, it would be all right; she could hold back the laughing so it would not waste away so fast and so soon. So she hurried on before the turning faces, the undertones of low astonishment, and they took their accustomed places where she could see the aisle against the silver glare and the young men and girls coming in two and two against it.

The lights flicked away; the screen glowed silver, and soon life began to unfold, beautiful and passionate and sad, while still the young men and girls entered, scented and sibilant in the half dark, their paired backs in silhouette delicate and sleek, their slim, quick bodies awkward, divinely young, while beyond them the silver dream accumulated, inevitably on and on. She began to laugh. In trying to suppress it, it made more noise than ever; heads began to turn. Still laughing, her friends raised her and led her out, and she stood at the curb, laughing on a high, sustained note, until the taxi came up and they helped her in.

They removed the pink voile and the sheer underthings and the stockings and put her to bed, and cracked ice for her temples, and sent for the doctor. He was hard to locate, so they ministered to her with hushed ejaculations, renewing the ice and fanning her. While the ice was fresh and cold she stopped laughing and lay still for a time, moaning only a little. But soon the laughing welled again and her voice rose screaming.

'Shhhhhhhhhhh! Shhhhhhhhhhhhhh!' they said, freshening the icepack, smoothing her hair, examining it for grey; 'poor girl!' Then to one another: 'Do you suppose anything really happened?' their eyes darkly aglitter, secret and passionate. 'Shhhhhhhhhh! Poor girl! Poor Minnie!'

V

It was midnight when McLendon drove up to his neat new house. It was trim and fresh as a birdcage and almost as small, with its clean, green-and-white paint. He locked the car and mounted the porch and entered. His wife rose from a chair beside the reading lamp. McLendon stopped in the floor and stared at her until she looked down.

'Look at that clock,' he said, lifting his arm, pointing. She stood before him, her face lowered, a magazine in her hands. Her face was pale, strained, and weary-looking. 'Haven't I told you about sitting up like this, waiting to see when I come in?'

'John,' she said. She laid the magazine down. Poised on the balls of his feet, he glared at her with his hot eyes, his sweating face.

'Didn't I tell you?' He went toward her. She looked up then. He caught her shoulder. She stood passive, looking at him.

'Don't, John. I couldn't sleep . . . The heat; something. Please, John. You're hurting me.'

'Didn't I tell you?' He released her and half struck, half flung her across the chair, and she lay there and watched him quietly as he left the room.

He went on through the house, ripping off his shirt, and on the dark, screened porch at the rear he stood and mopped his head and shoulders with the shirt and flung it away. He took the pistol from his hip and laid it on the table beside the bed, and sat on the bed and removed his shoes, and rose and slipped his trousers off. He was sweating again already, and he stooped and hunted furiously for the shirt. At last he found it and wiped his body again, and, with his body pressed against the dusty screen, he stood panting. There was no movement, no sound, not even an insect. The dark world seemed to lie stricken beneath the cold moon and the lidless stars.

1931

Ernest Hemingway

1899-1961

'A writer's job is to tell the truth. His standard of fidelity to the truth should be so high that his invention, out of his experience, should produce a truer account than anything factual can be. For facts can be observed badly; but when a good writer is creating something, he has time and scope to make it of an absolute truth,' said Ernest Hemingway. For him, this heightened truth—the created reality in fiction—is the highest form of truth, partaking finally of timelessness: 'From things that have happened and from things as they exist and from all things that you know and all those that you cannot know, you make something through your invention that is not a representation but a whole new thing truer than anything true and alive, and you make it alive, and if you make it well enough, you give it immortality.'

Born in Oak Park, Illinois, Hemingway worked on his high school newspaper, graduated in 1917, and went to work as a reporter for the Kansas City *Star*. Prevented from enlisting in the army by an earlier eye injury, he became an ambulance driver for the Red Cross in Italy at the end of the First World War. After the war, he worked as a foreign correspondent for the Toronto *Star*, where he met Morley Callaghan, then moved to Paris, where he met Ezra Pound and Gertrude Stein, who christened him and his literary friends a 'lost generation'. In Paris he devoted his attention to fiction writing, beginning with his short-story collection *In Our Time* (1925) and his first major novel, *The Sun Also Rises* (1926). His spare style captured with dramatic understatement the violence and the despair of his generation. He worked as a correspondent on the Loyalist side in the Spanish Civil War and then as a war correspondent in Europe and the Far East during the Second World War. After 1945 he settled in Cuba, and lived there until the Castro government forced him out of the country. In Ketchum, Idaho, in ill health and unable to write, he took his own life.

Journalism did much to shape Hemingway's novels and short stories. If the writer, he commented, 'gets so he can imagine truly, enough people will think that the things he relates all really happened and that he is just reporting.' Fiction, then, becomes a higher form of reporting, where fidelity to truth, complemented by the writer's imagination, creates a new reality for the reader. 'A writer's problem,' Hemingway observed, 'is always how to write truly and having found what is true, to project it in such a way that it becomes a part of the experience of the person who reads it.'

Nada, Spanish for 'nothing', represents the waste land modern man discerns in the universe. The alternative is a clean, well-lighted place, where people can take refuge from the darkness. 'A Clean, Well-Lighted Place' captures, in spare dialogue, humankind's isolation and loneliness in a hostile world.

'A Clean, Well-Lighted Place' was first published in the March 1933 issue of *Scribner's Magazine* and then collected in *Winner Take Nothing* (1933).

A Clean, Well-Lighted Place

It was late and every one had left the café except an old man who sat in the shadow the leaves of the tree made against the electric light. In the day time the street was dusty, but at night the dew settled the dust and the old man liked to sit late because he was deaf and now at night it was quiet and he felt the difference. The two waiters inside the café knew that the old man was a little drunk, and while he was a good client they knew that if he became too drunk he would leave without paying, so they kept watch on him.

'Last week he tried to commit suicide,' one waiter said.

'Why?'

'He was in despair.'

'What about?'

'Nothing.'

'How do you know it was nothing?'

'He has plenty of money.'

They sat together at a table that was close against the wall near the door of the café and looked at the terrace where the tables were all empty except where the old man sat in the shadow of the leaves of the tree that moved slightly in the wind. A girl and a soldier went by in the street. The street light shone on the brass number on his collar. The girl wore no head covering and hurried beside him.

'The guard will pick him up,' one waiter said.

'What does it matter if he gets what he's after?'

'He had better get off the street now. The guard will get him. They went by five minutes ago.'

The old man sitting in the shadow rapped on his saucer with his glass. The younger waiter went over to him.

'What do you want?'

The old man looked at him. 'Another brandy,' he said.

'You'll be drunk,' the waiter said. The old man looked at him. The waiter went away.

'He'll stay all night,' he said to his colleague. 'I'm sleepy now. I never get into bed before three o'clock. He should have killed himself last week.'

The waiter took the brandy bottle and another saucer from the counter inside the café and marched out to the old man's table. He put down the saucer and poured the glass full of brandy.

'You should have killed yourself last week,' he said to the deaf man. The old man motioned with his finger. 'A little more,' he said. The waiter poured on into the glass so that the brandy slopped over and ran down the stem into the top saucer of the pile. 'Thank you,' the old man said. The waiter took the bottle back inside the café. He sat down at the table with his colleague again.

'He's drunk now,' he said.

'He's drunk every night.'

'What did he want to kill himself for?'

'How should I know.'

'How did he do it?'

'He hung himself with a rope.'

'Who cut him down?'

'His niece.'

'Why did they do it?'

'Fear for his soul.'

'How much money has he got?'

'He's got plenty.'

'He must be eighty years old.'

'Anyway I should say he was eighty.'

'I wish he would go home. I never get to bed before three o'clock. What kind of hour is that to go to bed?'

'He stays up because he likes it.'

'He's lonely. I'm not lonely. I have a wife waiting in bed for me.'

'He had a wife once too.'

'A wife would be no good to him now.'

'You can't tell. He might be better with a wife.'

'His niece looks after him. You said she cut him down.'

'I know.'

'I wouldn't want to be that old. An old man is a nasty thing.'

'Not always. This old man is clean. He drinks without spilling. Even now, drunk. Look at him.'

'I don't want to look at him. I wish he would go home. He has no regard for those who must work.'

The old man looked from his glass across the square, then over at the waiters.

'Another brandy,' he said, pointing to his glass. The waiter who was in a hurry came over.

'Finished,' he said, speaking with that omission of syntax stupid people employ when talking to drunken people or foreigners. 'No more tonight. Close now.'

'Another,' said the old man.

'No. Finished.' The waiter wiped the edge of the table with a towel and shook his head.

The old man stood up, slowly counted the saucers, took a leather coin purse from his pocket and paid for the drinks, leaving half a peseta tip.

The waiter watched him go down the street, a very old man walking unsteadily but with dignity.

'Why didn't you let him stay and drink?' the unhurried waiter asked. They were putting up the shutters. 'It is not half-past two.'

'I want to go home to bed.'

'What is an hour?'

'More to me than to him.'

'An hour is the same.'

'You talk like an old man yourself. He can buy a bottle and drink at home.'

'It's not the same.'

'No, it is not,' agreed the waiter with a wife. He did not wish to be unjust. He was only in a hurry.

'And you? You have no fear of going home before your usual hour?'

'Are you trying to insult me?'

'No, *hombre*, only to make a joke.'

'No,' the waiter who was in a hurry said, rising from pulling down the metal shutters. 'I have confidence. I am all confidence.'

'You have youth, confidence, and a job,' the older waiter said. 'You have everything.'

'And what do you lack?'

'Everything but work.'

'You have everything I have.'

'No. I have never had confidence and I am not young.'

'Come on. Stop talking nonsense and lock up.'

'I am of those who like to stay late at the café,' the older waiter said. 'With all those who do not want to go to bed. With all those who need a light for the night.'

'I want to go home and into bed.'

'We are of two different kinds,' the older waiter said. He was now dressed to go home. 'It is not only a question of youth and confidence although those things are very beautiful. Each night I am reluctant to close up because there may be some one who needs the café.'

'*Hombre*, there are *bodegas* open all night long.'

'You do not understand. This is a clean and pleasant café. It is well lighted. The light is very good and also, now, there are shadows of the leaves.'

'Good night,' said the younger waiter.

'Good night,' the other said. Turning off the electric light he continued the conversation with himself. It is the light of course but it is necessary that the place be clean and pleasant. You do not want music. Certainly you do not want music. Nor can you stand before a bar with dignity although that is all that is provided for these hours. What did he fear? It was not fear or dread. It was a nothing that he knew too well. It was all a nothing and a man was nothing too. It was only that and light was all it needed and a certain cleanness and order. Some lived in it and never felt it but he knew it all was *nada y pues nada y nada y pues nada*. Our *nada* who art in *nada, nada* be thy name thy kingdom *nada* thy will be *nada* in *nada* as it is in *nada*. Give us this *nada* our daily *nada* and *nada* us our *nada* as we *nada* our *nadas* and *nada* us not into *nada* but deliver us from *nada; pues nada*.

Hail nothing full of nothing, nothing is with thee. He smiled and stood before a bar with a shining steam pressure coffee machine.

'What's yours?' asked the barman.

'*Nada*.'

'*Otro loco más*,' said the barman and turned away.

'A little cup,' said the waiter.

The barman poured it for him.

'The light is very bright and pleasant but the bar is unpolished,' the waiter said.

The barman looked at him but did not answer. It was too late at night for conversation.

'You want another *copita*?' the barman asked.

'No, thank you,' said the waiter and went out. He disliked bars and *bodegas*. A clean, well-lighted café was a very different thing. Now, without thinking further, he would go home to his room. He would lie in the bed and finally, with daylight, he would go to sleep. After all, he said to himself, it is probably only insomnia. Many must have it.

1933

Morley Callaghan

1903-90

For Morley Callaghan, the author of twenty novels and more than a hundred shorter works of fiction, the essential difference between a novel and a short story is that a novel 'just seems longer, that's all, a story that seems too long to be short. A short story seems to be something that you just see, right there, in a sort of flash. A long story, a novel, is a number of flashes. You see the thing going right on, or you may be dealing with something that you know you just can't do in ten pages.'

Born in Toronto, Callaghan graduated from the University of Toronto and Osgoode Law School. In 1928, the year he was called to the bar, he published his first novel, *Strange Fugitive*; fiction remained his vocation, and he never practised law. In April 1929, he travelled to Paris where his literary circle of friends included Ernest Hemingway, with whom he had worked as a fellow-reporter on the Toronto *Star*, F. Scott Fitzgerald, and James Joyce. He recalled that world in his autobiographical *That Summer in Paris* (1963). In the autumn of 1929 he returned to Toronto, which remained his physical and literary home.

Callaghan's fiction records the drama of ordinary lives, usually of urban people trying to act with dignity in a world of often hostile social forces. 'The writer has for his materials,' Callaghan observed, 'the ways of men and women in their relationship to each other.' And these materials must be presented with accuracy and clarity, and without authorial intrusion. Writing should be, he maintained, 'the right relationship between the words and the thing or person being described: the words should be as transparent as glass, and every time a writer used a brilliant phrase to prove himself witty or clever he merely took the mind of the reader away from the object and directed it to himself; he became simply a performer.'

'When a story came easily,' Callaghan recalled, 'I had suddenly found a structure, or an incident that drew out of me an emotion or a view of things that I had been nursing for a long time . . . there had to be a total poignant impact, and first, of course, this impact had to be in me.' With its contrasts between an illustrious past and a sterile present, 'Ancient Lineage' had such an origin. 'When I was on the *Star*,' Callaghan noted, 'I went down to a town called Campbellford . . . and stumbled on this weird and rather wonderful lady, and I practically wrote the story as I saw it. It's not the story I wrote for the *Star*, naturally, but that was the story as I saw it and I simply wrote it and I told what I saw and I told what I felt.' And the story focuses, to use Callaghan's own words, on 'frustrated people—people who in some mean or desperate way get blocked off from being what they should be.'

'Two Fishermen' focuses on the brief but telling relationship between a young reporter and a hangman. 'The hangman, a necessary figure in society, a man definitely serving the public and the ends of justice, was entitled to a little human dignity. In fact he saw himself as a dignified human being,' Callaghan explained. 'But of course as an instrument of justice he became a despised person, and even his young friend, who understood his wistful humanity, betrayed that humanity when the chips were down.'

'Ancient Lineage' was first published in the Spring 1928 issue of *The Exile* and then collected in *A Native Argosy* (1929) and again in *Morley Callaghan's Stories* (1959). 'Two Fishermen' was first published under the title 'Who Is My Neighbour?' in the February 1934 issue of *Esquire* and then revised and collected under the title 'Two Fishermen' in *Now That April's Here and Other Stories* (1936) and again in *Morley Callaghan's Stories*.

Ancient Lineage

The young man from the Historical Club with a green magazine under his arm got off the train at Clintonville. It was getting dark but the station lights were not lit. He hurried along the platform and jumped down on the sloping cinder path to the sidewalk.

Trees were on the lawns alongside the walk, branches drooping low, leaves scraping occasionally against the young man's straw hat. He saw a cluster of lights, bluish-white in the dusk across a river, many lights for a small town. He crossed the lift-lock bridge and turned on to the main street. A hotel was at the corner.

At the desk a bald-headed man in a blue shirt, the sleeves rolled up, looked critically at the young man while he registered. 'All right, Mr Flaherty,' he said, inspecting the signature carefully.

'Do you know many people around here?' Mr Flaherty asked.

'Just about everybody.'

'The Rowers?'

'The old lady?'

'Yeah, an old lady.'

'Sure, Mrs Anna Rower. Around the corner to the left, then turn to the right on the first street, the house opposite the Presbyterian church on the hill.'

'An old family,' suggested the young man.

'An old-timer all right.' The hotel man made it clear by a twitching of his lips that he was a part of the new town, canal, water power, and factories.

Mr Flaherty sauntered out and turned to the left. It was dark and the street had the silence of small towns in the evening. Turning a corner he heard girls giggling in a doorway. He looked at the church on the hill, the steeple dark against the sky. He had forgotten whether the man had said beside the church or across the road, but could not make up his mind to ask the fellow who was watering the wide church lawn. No lights in the shuttered windows of the rough-cast house beside the church. He came down the hill and had to yell three times at the man because the water swished strongly against the grass.

'All right, thanks. Right across the road,' Mr Flaherty repeated.

Tall trees screened the square brick house. Looking along the hall to a lighted room, Mr Flaherty saw an old lady standing at a sideboard. 'She's in all right,' he thought, rapping on the screen door. A large woman of about forty, dressed in blue skirt and blue waist, came down the stairs. She did not open the screen door.

'Could I speak to Mrs Anna Rower?'

'I'm Miss Hilda Rower.'

'I'm from the University Historical Club.'

'What did you want to see Mother for?'

Mr Flaherty did not like talking through the screen door. 'I wanted to talk to her,' he said firmly.

'Well, maybe you'd better come in.'

He stood in the hall while the large woman lit the gas in the front room. The gas flared up, popped, showing fat hips and heavy lines on her face. Mr Flaherty, disappointed, watched her swaying down the hall to get her mother. He carefully inspected the front room, the framed photographs of dead Conservative politicians, the group of military men hanging over the old-fashioned piano, the faded greenish wallpaper and the settee in the corner.

An old woman with a knot of white hair and good eyes came into the room, walking erectly. 'This is the young man who wanted to see you, Mother,' Miss Hilda Rower said. They all sat down. Mr Flaherty explained he wanted to get some information concerning the Rower genealogical tree for the next meeting of his society. The Rowers, he knew, were a pioneer family in the district, and descended from William the Conqueror, he had heard.

The old lady laughed thinly, swaying from side to side. 'It's true enough, but I don't know who told you. My father was Daniel Rower, who came to Ontario from Cornwall in 1830.'

Miss Hilda Rower interrupted. 'Wait, Mother, you may not want to tell about it.' Brusque and businesslike, she turned to the young man. 'You want to see the family tree, I suppose.'

'Oh, yes.'

'My father was a military settler here,' the old lady said.

'I don't know but what we might be able to give you some notes,' Miss Hilda spoke generously.

'Thanks awfully, if you will.'

'Of course you're prepared to pay something if you're going to print it,' she added, smugly adjusting her big body in the chair.

Mr Flaherty got red in the face; of course he understood, but to tell the truth he had merely wanted to chat with Mrs Rower. Now he knew definitely he did not like the heavy nose and unsentimental assertiveness of the lower lip of this big woman with the wide shoulders. He couldn't stop looking at her thick ankles. Rocking back and forth in the chair she was primly conscious of lineal superiority; a proud unmarried woman, surely she could handle a young man, half-closing her eyes, a young man from the University indeed. 'I don't want to talk to her about the University,' he thought.

Old Mrs Rower went into the next room and returned with a framed genealogical tree of the house of Rower. She handed it graciously to Mr Flaherty, who read, 'The descent of the family of Rower, from William the Conqueror, from Malcolm 1st, and from the Capets, Kings of France.' It bore the *imprimatur* of the College of Arms, 1838.

'It's wonderful to think you have this,' Mr Flaherty said, smiling at Miss Hilda, who watched him suspiciously.

'A brother of mine had it all looked up,' old Mrs Rower said.

'You don't want to write about that,' Miss Hilda said, crossing her ankles. The ankles looked much thicker crossed. 'You just want to have a talk with Mother.'

'That's it,' Mr Flaherty smiled agreeably.

'We may write it up ourselves one day.' Her heavy chin dipped down and rose again.

'Sure, why not?'

'But there's no harm in you talking to Mother if you want to, I guess.'

'You could write a good story about that tree,' Mr Flaherty said, feeling his way.

'We may do it some day but it'll take time,' she smiled complacently at her mother, who mildly agreed.

Mr Flaherty talked pleasantly to this woman, who was so determined he would not learn anything about the family tree without paying for it. He tried talking about the city, then tactfully asked old Mrs Rower what she remembered of the Clintonville of seventy years ago. The old lady talked willingly, excited a little. She went into the next room to get a book of clippings. 'My father, Captain Rower, got a grant of land from the Crown and cleared it,' she said, talking over her shoulder. 'A little way up the Trent River. Clintonville was a small military settlement then . . .'

'Oh, Mother, he doesn't want to know all about that,' Miss Hilda said impatiently.

'It's very interesting indeed.'

The old woman said nervously, 'My dear, what difference does it make? You wrote it all up for the evening at the church.'

'So I did too,' she hesitated, thinking the young man ought to see how well it was written. 'I have an extra copy.' She looked at him thoughtfully. He smiled. She got up and went upstairs.

The young man talked very rapidly to the old lady and took many notes.

Miss Rower returned. 'Would you like to see it?' She handed Mr Flaherty a small grey booklet. Looking quickly through it, he saw it contained valuable information about the district.

'The writing is simply spendid. You must have done a lot of work on it.'

'I worked hard on it,' she said, pleased and more willing to talk.

'Is this an extra copy?'

'Yes, it's an extra copy.'

'I suppose I might keep it,' he said diffidently.

She looked at him steadily. 'Well . . . I'll have to charge you twenty-five cents.'

'Sure, sure, of course, that's fine.' He blushed.

'Just what it costs to get them out,' the old lady explained apologetically.

'Can you change a dollar?' He fumbled in his pocket, pulling the dollar out slowly.

They could not change it but Miss Rower would be pleased to go down to the corner grocery store. Mr Flaherty protested. No trouble, he would go. She insisted on asking the next-door neighbour to change it. She went across the room, the dollar in hand.

Mr Flaherty chatted with the nice old lady and carefully examined the family tree, and wrote quickly in a small book till the screen door banged, the curtains parted, and Miss Hilda Rower came into the room. He wanted to smirk, watching her walking heavily, so conscious of her ancient lineage, a virginal mincing sway to her large hips, seventy-five cents' change held loosely in drooping fingers.

'Thank you,' he said, pocketing the change, pretending his work was over. Sitting back in the chair he praised the way Miss Rower had written the history of the neighbourhood and suggested she might write a spendid story of the family tree, if she had the material, of course.

'I've got the material, all right,' she said, trying to get comfortable again. How would Mr Flaherty arrange it and where should she try to sell it? The old lady was dozing in the rocking-chair. Miss Rower began to talk rather nervously about her material. She talked of the last title in the family and the Sir Richard who had been at the court of Queen Elizabeth.

Mr Flaherty chimed in gaily, 'I suppose you know the O'Flahertys were kings in Ireland, eh?'

She said vaguely, 'I daresay, I daresay,' conscious only of an interruption to the flow of her thoughts. She went on talking with hurried eagerness, all the fine talk about her ancestors bringing her peculiar satisfaction. A soft light came into her eyes and her lips were moist.

Mr Flaherty started to rub his cheek, and looked at her big legs, and felt restive, and then embarrassed, watching her closely, her firm lower lip hanging loosely. She was talking slowly, lazily, relaxing in her chair, a warm fluid oozing through her veins, exhausting but satisfying her.

He was uncomfortable. She was liking it too much. He did not know what to do. There was something immodest about it. She was close to forty, her big body relaxed in the chair. He looked at his watch and suggested he would be going. She stretched her legs graciously, pouting, inviting him to stay a while longer, but he was standing up, tucking his magazine under his arm. The old lady was still dozing. 'I'm so comfortable,' Miss Rower said, 'I hate to move.'

The mother woke up and shook hands with Mr Flaherty. Miss Rower got up to say good-bye charmingly.

Half-way down the path Mr Flaherty turned. She was standing in the doorway, partly shadowed by the tall trees, bright moonlight filtering through leaves touching soft lines on her face and dark hair.

He went down the hill to the hotel unconsciously walking with a careless easy stride, wondering at the change that had come over the heavy, strong woman. He thought of taking a walk along the river in the moonlight, the river on which old Captain Rower had drilled troops on the ice in the winter of 1837 to fight the rebels. Then he thought of having a western sandwich in the café across the road from the hotel. That big woman in her own way had been hot stuff.

In the hotel he asked to be called early so he could get the first train to the city. For a long time he lay awake in the fresh, cool bed, the figure of the woman whose ancient lineage had taken the place of a lover in her life, drifting into his thoughts and becoming important while he watched on the wall the pale moonlight that had softened the lines of her face, and wondered if it was still shining on her bed, and on her throat, and on her contented, lazily relaxed body.

1928

Two Fishermen

The only reporter on the town paper, the *Examiner*, was Michael Foster, a tall, long-legged, eager young fellow, who wanted to go to the city some day and work on an important newspaper.

That morning he went into Bagley's Hotel, he wasn't at all sure of himself. He went over to the desk and whispered to the proprietor, Ted Bagley, 'Did he come here, Mr Bagley?'

Bagley said slowly, 'Two men came here from this morning's train. They're registered.' He put his spatulate forefinger on the open book and said, 'Two men. One of them's a drummer. This one here, T. Woodley. I know because he was through this way last year and just a minute ago he walked across the road to Molson's hardware store. The other one . . . here's his name, K. Smith.'

'Who's K. Smith?' Michael asked.

'I don't know. A mild, harmless-looking little guy.'

'Did he look like the hangman, Mr Bagley?'

'I couldn't say that, seeing as I never saw one. He was awfully polite and asked where he could get a boat so he could go fishing on the lake this evening, so I said likely down at Smollet's place by the power-house.'

'Well, thanks. I guess if he was the hangman, he'd go over to the jail first,' Michael said.

He went along the street, past the Baptist church to the old jail with the high brick fence around it. Two tall maple trees, with branches drooping low over the sidewalk, shaded one of the walls from the morning sunlight. Last night, behind those walls, three carpenters, working by lamplight, had nailed the timbers for the scaffold. In the morning, young Thomas

Delaney, who had grown up in the town, was being hanged: he had killed old Mathew Rhinehart whom he had caught molesting his wife when she had been berry-picking in the hills behind the town. There had been a struggle and Thomas Delaney had taken a bad beating before he had killed Rhinehart. Last night a crowd had gathered on the sidewalk by the lamp-post, and while moths and smaller insects swarmed around the high blue carbon light, the crowd had thrown sticks and bottles and small stones at the out-of-town workmen in the jail yard. Billy Hilton, the town constable, had stood under the light with his head down, pretending not to notice anything. Thomas Delaney was only three years older than Michael Foster.

Michael went straight to the jail office, where Henry Steadman, the sheriff, a squat, heavy man, was sitting on the desk idly wetting his long moustaches with his tongue. 'Hello, Michael, what do you want?' he asked.

'Hello, Mr Steadman, the *Examiner* would like to know if the hangman arrived yet.'

'Why ask me?'

'I thought he'd come here to test the gallows. Won't he?'

'My, you're a smart young fellow, Michael, thinking of that.'

'Is he in there now, Mr Steadman?'

'Don't ask me. I'm saying nothing. Say, Michael, do you think there's going to be trouble? You ought to know. Does anybody seem sore at me? I can't do nothing. You can see that.'

'I don't think anybody blames you, Mr Steadman. Look here, can't I see the hangman? Is his name K. Smith?'

'What does it matter to you, Michael? Be a sport, go on away and don't bother us any more.'

'All right, Mr Steadman,' Michael said very competently, 'just leave it to me.'

Early that evening, when the sun was setting, Michael Foster walked south of the town on the dusty road leading to the power-house and Smollet's fishing pier. He knew that if Mr K. Smith wanted to get a boat he would go down to the pier. Fine powdered road dust whitened Michael's shoes. Ahead of him he saw the power-plant, square and low, and the smooth lake water. Behind him the sun was hanging over the blue hills beyond the town and shining brilliantly on square patches of farm land. The air around the power-house smelt of steam.

Out on the jutting, tumbledown pier of rock and logs, Michael saw a little fellow without a hat, sitting down with his knees hunched up to his chin, a very small man with little grey baby curls on the back of his neck, who stared steadily far out over the water. In his hand he was holding a stick with a heavy fishing-line twined around it and a gleaming copper spoon bait, the hooks brightened with bits of feathers such as they used in the neighbourhood when trolling for lake trout. Apprehensively Michael walked out over the rocks toward the stranger and called, 'Were you thinking of going fishing, mister?' Standing up, the man smiled. He had a large head, tapering down to a small chin, a birdlike neck and a very wistful smile. Puckering his mouth up, he said shyly to Michael, 'Did you intend to go fishing?'

'That's what I came down here for. I was going to get a boat back at the boat-house there. How would you like if we went together?'

'I'd like it first rate,' the shy little man said eagerly. 'We could take turns rowing. Does that appeal to you?'

'Fine. Fine. You wait here and I'll go back to Smollet's place and ask for a row-boat and I'll row around here and get you.'

'Thanks. Thanks very much,' the mild little man said as he began to untie his line. He seemed very enthusiastic.

When Michael brought the boat around to the end of the old pier and invited the stranger to make himself comfortable so he could handle the line, the stranger protested comically that he ought to be allowed to row.

Pulling strongly at the oars, Michael was soon out in the deep water and the little man was letting his line out slowly. In one furtive glance, he had noticed that the man's hair, grey at the temples, was inclined to curl to his ears. The line was out full length. It was twisted around the little man's forefinger, which he let drag in the water. And then Michael looked full at him and smiled because he thought he seemed so meek and quizzical. 'He's a nice little guy,' Michael assured himself and he said, 'I work on the town paper, the *Examiner*.'

'Is it a good paper? Do you like the work?'

'Yes. But it's nothing like a first-class city paper and I don't expect to be working on it long. I want to get a reporter's job on a city paper. My name's Michael Foster.'

'Mine's Smith. Just call me Smitty.'

'I was wondering if you'd been over to the jail yet.'

Up to this time the little man had been smiling with the charming ease of a small boy who finds himself free, but now he became furtive and disappointed. Hesitating, he said, 'Yes, I was over there first thing this morning.'

'Oh, I just knew you'd go there,' Michael said. They were a bit afraid of each other. By this time they were far out on the water which had a millpond smoothness. The town seemed to get smaller, with white houses in rows and streets forming geometric patterns, just as the blue hills behind the town seemed to get larger at sundown.

Finally Michael said, 'Do you know this Thomas Delaney that's dying in the morning?' He knew his voice was slow and resentful.

'No. I don't know anything about him. I never read about them. Aren't there any fish at all in this old lake? I'd like to catch some fish,' he said rapidly. 'I told my wife I'd bring her home some fish.' Glancing at Michael, he was appealing, without speaking, that they should do nothing to spoil an evening's fishing.

The little man began to talk eagerly about fishing as he pulled out a small flask from his hip pocket. 'Scotch,' he said, chuckling with delight. 'Here, take a swig.' Michael drank from the flask and passed it back. Tilting his head back and saying, 'Here's to you, Michael,' the little man took a long pull at the flask. 'The only time I take a drink,' he said still chuckling, 'is when I go on a fishing trip by myself. I usually go by myself,' he added apologetically as if he wanted the young fellow to see how much he appreciated his company.

They had gone far out on the water but they had caught nothing. It began to get dark. 'No fish tonight, I guess, Smitty,' Michael said.

'It's a crying shame,' Smitty said. 'I looked forward to coming up here when I found out the place was on the lake. I wanted to get some fishing in. I promised my wife I'd bring her back some fish. She'd often like to go fishing with me, but of course, she can't because she can't travel around from place to place like I do. Whenever I get a call to go some place, I always look at the map to see if it's by a lake or on a river, then I take my lines and hooks along.'

'If you took another job, you and your wife could probably go fishing together,' Michael suggested.

'I don't know about that. We sometimes go fishing together anyway.' He looked away, waiting for Michael to be repelled and insist that he ought to give up the job. And he wasn't ashamed as he looked down at the water, but he knew that Michael thought he ought to be ashamed. 'Somebody's got to do my job. There's got to be a hangman,' he said.

'I just meant that if it was such disagreeable work, Smitty.'

The little man did not answer for a long time. Michael rowed steadily with sweeping, tireless strokes. Huddled at the end of the boat, Smitty suddenly looked up with a kind of melancholy hopelessness and said mildly, 'The job hasn't been so disagreeable.'

'Good God, man, you don't mean you like it?'

'Oh, no,' he said, to be obliging, as if he knew what Michael expected him to say. 'I mean you get used to it, that's all.' But he looked down again at the water, knowing he ought to be ashamed of himself.

'Have you got any children?'

'I sure have. Five. The oldest boy is fourteen. It's funny, but they're all a lot bigger and taller than I am. Isn't that funny?'

They started a conversation about fishing rivers that ran into the lake farther north. They felt friendly again. The little man, who had an extraordinary gift for story-telling, made many quaint faces, puckered up his lips, screwed up his eyes and moved around restlessly as if he wanted to get up in the boat and stride around for the sake of more expression. Again he brought out the whisky flask and Michael stopped rowing. Grinning, they toasted each other and said together, 'Happy days.' The boat remained motionless on the placid water. Far out, the sun's last rays gleamed on the water-line. And then it got dark and they could only see the town lights. It was time to turn around and pull for the shore. The little man tried to take the oars from Michael, who shook his head resolutely and insisted that he would prefer to have his friend catch a fish on the way back to the shore.

'It's too late now, and we may have scared all the fish away,' Smitty laughed happily. 'But we're having a grand time, aren't we?'

When they reached the old pier by the power-house, it was full night and they hadn't caught a single fish. As the boat bumped against the rocks Michael said, 'You can get out here. I'll take the boat around to Smollet's.'

'Won't you be coming my way?'

'Not just now. I'll probably talk with Smollet a while.'

The little man got out of the boat and stood on the pier looking down at Michael. 'I was thinking dawn would be the best time to catch some fish,' he said. 'At about five o'clock. I'll have an hour and a half to spare anyway. How would you like that?' He was speaking with so much eagerness that Michael found himself saying, 'I could try. But if I'm not here at dawn, you go on without me.'

'All right. I'll walk back to the hotel now.'

'Good night, Smitty.'

'Good night, Michael. We had a fine neighbourly time, didn't we?'

As Michael rowed the boat around to the boat-house, he hoped that Smitty wouldn't realize he didn't want to be seen walking back to town with him. And later, when he was going slowly along the dusty road in the dark and hearing all the crickets chirping in the ditches, he couldn't figure out why he felt so ashamed of himself.

At seven o'clock the next morning Thomas Delaney was hanged in the town jail yard. There was hardly a breeze on that leaden grey morning and there were no small whitecaps out over the lake. It would have been a fine morning for fishing. Michael went down to the jail, for he thought it his duty as a newspaperman to have all the facts, but he was afraid he might get sick. He hardly spoke to all the men and women who were crowded under the maple trees by the jail wall. Everybody he knew was staring at the wall and muttering angrily. Two of Thomas Delaney's brothers, big, strapping fellows with bearded faces, were there on the sidewalk. Three automobiles were at the front of the jail.

Michael, the town newspaperman, was admitted into the courtyard by old Willie Mathews, one of the guards, who said that two newspapermen from the city were at the gallows on the other side of the building. 'I guess you can go around there, too, if you want to,' Mathews said, as he sat down slowly on the step. White-faced, and afraid, Michael sat down on the step with Mathews and they waited and said nothing.

At last the old fellow said, 'Those people outside there are pretty sore, ain't they?'

'They're pretty sullen, all right. I saw two of Delaney's brothers there.'

'I wish they'd go,' Mathews said. 'I don't want to see anything. I didn't even look at Delaney. I don't want to hear anything. I'm sick.' He put his head back against the wall and closed his eyes.

The old fellow and Michael sat close together till a small procession came around the corner from the other side of the yard. First came Mr Steadman, the sheriff, with his head down as though he were crying, then Dr Parker, the physician, then two hard-looking young newspapermen from the city, walking with their hats on the backs of their heads, and behind them came the little hangman, erect, stepping out with military precision and carrying himself with a strange cocky dignity. He was dressed in a long black cut-away coat with grey striped trousers, a gates-ajar collar and a narrow red tie, as if he alone felt the formal importance of the occasion. He walked with brusque precision till he saw Michael, who was standing up, staring at him with his mouth open.

The little hangman grinned and as soon as the procession reached the doorstep, he shook hands with Michael. They were all looking at Michael. As though his work were over now, the hangman said eagerly to Michael, 'I thought I'd see you here. You didn't get down to the pier at dawn?'

'No, I couldn't make it.'

'That was tough, Michael, I looked for you,' he said. 'But never mind. I've got something for you.' As they all went into the jail, Dr Parker glanced angrily at Michael, then turned his back on him. In the office, where the doctor prepared to sign a certificate, Smitty was bending down over his fishing-basket which was in the corner. Then he pulled out two good-sized salmon-bellied trout, folded in a newspaper, and said, 'I was saving these for you, Michael, I got four in an hour's fishing.' Then he said, 'I'll talk about that later, if you'll wait. We'll be busy here, and I've got to change my clothes.'

Michael went out to the street with Dr Parker and the two city newspapermen. Under his arm he was carrying his fish, folded in the newspaper. Outside, at the jail door, Michael thought that the doctor and the two newspapermen were standing a little apart from him. Then the small crowd, with their clothes all dust-soiled from the road, surged forward, and the doctor said to them, 'You might as well go home, boys. It's all over.'

'Where's old Steadman?' somebody demanded.

'We'll wait for the hangman,' somebody else shouted.

The doctor walked away by himself. For a while Michael stood beside the two city newspapermen, and tried to look as nonchalant as they were looking, but he lost confidence in them when he smelled whisky. They only talked to each other. Then they mingled with the crowd, and Michael stood alone. At last he could stand there no longer looking at all the people he knew so well, so he, too, moved out and joined the crowd.

When the sheriff came out with the hangman and two of the guards, they got half-way down to one of the automobiles before someone threw an old boot. Steadman ducked into one of the cars, as the boot hit him on the shoulder, and the two guards followed him. The hangman, dismayed, stood alone on the sidewalk. Those in the car must have thought at first that the hangman was with them for the car suddenly shot forward, leaving him alone on the sidewalk. The crowd threw small rocks and sticks, hooting at him as the automobile backed up slowly towards him. One small stone hit him on the head. Blood trickled from the side of his head as he looked around helplessly at all the angry people. He had the same expression on his face, Michael thought, as he had had last night when he had seemed ashamed and had looked down steadily at the water. Only now, he looked around wildly, looking for someone to help him as the crowd kept pelting him. Farther and farther Michael backed into the crowd and all the time he felt dreadfully ashamed as though he were betraying Smitty, who last night had had such a good neighbourly time with him. 'It's different now, it's different,' he kept thinking, as he held the fish in the newspaper tight under his arm. Smitty started to run toward the automobile, but James Mortimer, a big fisherman, shot out his foot and tripped him and sent him sprawling on his face.

Mortimer, the big fisherman, looking for something to throw, said to Michael, 'Sock him, sock him.'

Michael shook his head and felt sick.

'What's the matter with you, Michael?'

'Nothing. I got nothing against him.'

The big fisherman started pounding his fists up and down in the air. 'He just doesn't mean anything to me at all.' Michael said quickly. The fisherman, bending down, kicked a small rock loose from the road bed and heaved it at the hangman. Then he said, 'What are you holding there, Michael, what's under your arm? Fish. Pitch them at him. Here, give them to me.' Still in a fury, he snatched the fish, and threw them one at a time at the little man just as he was getting up from the road. The fish fell in the thick dust in front of him, sending up a little cloud. Smitty seemed to stare at the fish with his mouth hanging open, then he didn't even look at the crowd. That expression on Smitty's face as he saw the fish on the road made Michael hot with shame and he tried to get out of the crowd.

Smitty had his hands over his head, to shield his face as the crowd pelted him, yelling 'Sock the little rat. Throw the runt in the lake.' The sheriff pulled him into the automobile. The car shot forward in a cloud of dust.

1934

Sinclair Ross

b. 1908

'Despite the sombre tone and the dark themes of Sinclair Ross's short stories,' Margaret Laurence observed, 'man emerges as a creature who can survive—and survive with some remaining dignity—against both outer and inner odds which are almost impossible.' And the outer and inner odds emphasize Ross's unique ability to let his natural settings consistently mirror the minds and moods of his characters. 'Throughout Ross's stories,' Laurence continued, 'the outer situation always mirrors the inner. The emptiness of the landscape, the bleakness of the land, reflect the inability of these people to touch another with assurance and gentleness.'

Born on a homestead in northern Saskatchewan, nineteen kilometres from Shellbrooke and forty kilometres from Prince Rupert, Ross dropped out of school after grade eleven to work in a bank. After working in many small-town banks in Saskatchewan, he transferred to a bank in Winnipeg in 1933. In the thirties he wrote and destroyed two novels, then turned to the short story: 'I am now starting to work on short stories, hoping gradually to build up a better technique without the cramping grind that writing a novel after office hours demands.' In 1941 he published his first novel, *As For Me and My House*. Apart from wartime service in the Canadian army, he continued his banking career in Winnipeg and later in Montreal until his retirement in 1968, when he moved to Europe. He returned to Montreal in 1980, and two years later moved to Vancouver, where he currently resides.

Ross's stories, usually set on the prairies, depict the often tragic struggles of people during the drought, the dust, and the Depression of the 1930s. The centre of the story is the family unit. And the family members lead lives of quiet desperation, trapped in the loneliness of their personal isolation.

'The Lamp at Noon' focuses on the disintegrating marriage of Paul and Ellen, the husband desperate to make a living off the harsh land and terrified of proving inadequate to it, the wife being driven mad by the loneliness of her life on the farm. The land is Paul's enemy, and he seems incapable of letting his wife be his ally; he cannot reach out to her for sympathy or support so that their isolation leads only to tragedy.

In 'The Painted Door', Ann is, like Ellen, a prairie farm wife suffering from loneliness. Frustrated by her husband's complete devotion and equally complete non-understanding of her, she seeks refuge in a brief moment of physical union that also leads only to tragedy.

'The Lamp at Noon' was first published in the Spring 1938 issue of *Queen's Quarterly*. 'The Painted Door' was first published in the Summer 1939 issue of *Queen's Quarterly*. Both stories were collected in *The Lamp at Noon and Other Stories* (1968).

The Lamp at Noon

A little before noon she lit the lamp. Demented wind fled keening past the house: a wail through the eaves that died every minute or two. Three days now without respite it had held. The dust was thickening to an impenetrable fog.

She lit the lamp, then for a long time stood at the window motionless. In dim, fitful outline the stable and oat granary still were visible; beyond, obscuring fields and landmarks, the lower of dust clouds made the farmyard seem an isolated acre, poised aloft above a sombre void. At each blast of wind it shook, as if to topple and spin hurtling with the dust-reel into space.

From the window she went to the door, opening it a little, and peering toward the stable again. He was not coming yet. As she watched there was a sudden rift overhead, and for a moment through the tattered clouds the sun raced like a wizened orange. It shed a soft, diffused light, dim and yellow as if it were the light from the lamp reaching out through the open door.

She closed the door, and going to the stove tried the potatoes with a fork. Her eyes all the while were fixed and wide with a curious immobility. It was the window. Standing at it, she had let her forehead press against the pane until the eyes were strained apart and rigid. Wide like that they had looked out to the deepening ruin of the storm. Now she could not close them.

The baby started to cry. He was lying in a homemade crib over which she had arranged a tent of muslin. Careful not to disturb the folds of it, she knelt and tried to still him, whispering huskily in a singsong voice that he must hush and go to sleep again. She would have liked to rock him, to feel the comfort of his little body in her arms, but a fear had obsessed her that in the dust-filled air he might contract pneumonia. There was dust sifting everywhere. Her own throat was parched with it. The table had been set less than ten minutes, and already a film was gathering on the dishes. The little cry continued, and with wincing, frightened lips she glanced around as if to find a corner where the air was less oppressive. But while the lips winced the eyes maintained their wide, immobile stare. 'Sleep,' she whispered again. 'It's too soon for you to be hungry. Daddy's coming for his dinner.'

He seemed a long time. Even the clock, still a few minutes off noon, could not dispel a foreboding sense that he was longer than he should be. She went to the door again—and then recoiled slowly to stand white and breathless in the middle of the room. She mustn't. He would only despise her if she ran to the stable looking for him. There was too much grim endurance in his nature ever to let him understand the fear and weakness of a woman. She must stay quiet and wait. Nothing was wrong. At noon he would come—and perhaps after dinner stay with her awhile.

Yesterday, and again at breakfast this morning, they had quarrelled bitterly. She wanted him now, the assurance of his strength and nearness, but he would stand aloof, wary, remembering the words she had flung at him in her anger, unable to understand it was only the dust and wind that had driven her.

Tense, she fixed her eyes upon the clock, listening. There were two winds: the wind in flight, and the wind that pursued. The one sought refuge in the eaves, whimpering, in fear; the other assailed it there, and shook the eaves apart to make it flee again. Once as she listened this first wind sprang inside the room, distraught like a bird that has felt the graze of talons on its wing; while furious the other wind shook the walls, and thudded tumbleweeds against the window till its quarry glanced away again in fright. But only to return—to return and quake among the feeble eaves, as if in all this dust-mad wilderness it knew no other sanctuary.

Then Paul came. At his step she hurried to the stove, intent upon the pots and frying-pan. 'The worst wind yet,' he ventured, hanging up his cap and smock. 'I had to light the lantern in the tool shed, too.'

They looked at each other, then away. She wanted to go to him, to feel his arms supporting her, to cry a little just that he might soothe her, but because his presence made the menace of the wind seem less, she gripped herself and thought, 'I'm in the right. I won't give in. For his sake, too, I won't.'

He washed, hurriedly, so that a few dark welts of dust remained to indent upon his face a haggard strength. It was all she could see as she wiped the dishes and set the food before him: the strength, the grimness, the young Paul growing old and hard, buckled against a desert even grimmer than his will. 'Hungry?' she asked, touched to a twinge of pity she had not intended. 'There's dust in everything. It keeps coming faster than I can clean it up.'

He nodded. 'Tonight, though, you'll see it go down. This is the third day.'

She looked at him in silence a moment, and then as if to herself muttered broodingly, 'Until the next time. Until it starts again.'

There was a dark resentment in her voice now that boded another quarrel. He waited, his eyes on her dubiously as she mashed a potato with her fork. The lamp between them threw strong lights and shadows on their faces. Dust and drought, earth that betrayed alike his labour and his faith, to him the struggle had given sternness, an impassive courage. Beneath the whip of sand his youth had been effaced. Youth, zest, exuberance—there remained only a harsh and clenched virility that yet became him, that seemed at the cost of more engaging qualities to be fulfilment of his inmost and essential nature. Whereas to her the same debts and poverty had brought a plaintive indignation, a nervous dread of what was still to come. Her eyes were hollowed, the lips pinched dry and colourless. It was the face of a woman that had aged without maturing, that had loved the little vanities of life, and lost them wistfully.

'I'm afraid, Paul,' she said suddenly. 'I can't stand it any longer. He cries all the time. You will go, Paul—say you will. We aren't living here—not really living—'

The pleading in her voice now, after its shrill bitterness yesterday, made him think that this was only another way to persuade him. He answered evenly, 'I told you this morning, Ellen; we keep on right where we are. At least I do. It's yourself you're thinking about, not the baby.'

This morning such an accusation would have stung her to rage; now, her voice swift and panting, she pressed on, 'Listen, Paul—I'm thinking of all of us—you, too. Look at the sky—what's happening. Are you blind? Thistles and tumbleweeds—it's a desert. You won't have a straw this fall. You won't be able to feed a cow or a chicken. Please, Paul, say we'll go away—'

'Go where?' His voice as he answered was still remote and even, inflexibly in unison with the narrowed eyes and the great hunch of muscle-knotted shoulder. 'Even as a desert it's better than sweeping out your father's store and running his errands. That's all I've got ahead of me if I do what you want.'

'And here—' she faltered. 'What's ahead of you here? At least we'll get enough to eat and wear when you're sweeping out his store. Look at it—look at it, you fool. Desert—the lamp lit at noon—'

'You'll see it come back. There's good wheat in it yet.'

'But in the meantime—year after year—can't you understand, Paul? We'll never get them back—'

He put down his knife and fork and leaned toward her across the table. 'I can't go, Ellen. Living off your people—charity—stop and think of it. This is where I belong. I can't do anything else.'

'Charity!' she repeated him, letting her voice rise in derision. 'And this—you call this independence! Borrowed money you can't even pay the interest on, seed from the government—grocery bills—doctor bills—'

'We'll have crops again,' he persisted. 'Good crops—the land will come back. It's worth waiting for.'

'And while we're waiting, Paul!' It was not anger now, but a kind of sob. 'Think of me—and him. It's not fair. We have our lives, too, to live.'

'And you think that going home to your family—taking your husband with you—'

'I don't care—anything would be better than this. Look at the air he's breathing. He cries all the time. For his sake, Paul. What's ahead of him here, even if you do get crops?'

He clenched his lips a minute, then, with his eyes hard and contemptuous, struck back, 'As much as in town, growing up a pauper. You're the one who wants to go, it's not for his sake. You think that in town you'd have a better time—not so much work—more clothes—'

'Maybe—' She dropped her head defencelessly. 'I'm young still. I like pretty things.'

There was silence now—a deep fastness of it enclosed by rushing wind and creaking walls. It seemed the yellow lamplight cast a hush upon them. Through the haze of dusty air the walls receded, dimmed, and came again. At last she raised her head and said listlessly, 'Go on—your dinner's getting cold. Don't sit and stare at me. I've said it all.'

The spent quietness in her voice was even harder to endure than her anger. It reproached him, against his will insisted that he see and understand her lot. To justify himself he tried, 'I was a poor man when you married me. You said you didn't mind. Farming's never been easy, and never will be.'

'I wouldn't mind the work or the skimping if there was something to look forward to. It's the hopelessness—going on—watching the land blow away.'

'The land's all right,' he repeated. 'The dry years won't last forever.'

'But it's not just dry years, Paul!' The little sob in her voice gave way suddenly to a ring of exasperation. 'Will you never see? It's the land itself—the soil. You've plowed and harrowed it until there's not a root or fibre left to hold it down. That's why the soil drifts—that's why in a year or two there'll be nothing left but the bare clay. If in the first place you farmers had taken care of your land—if you hadn't been so greedy for wheat every year—'

She had taught school before she married him, and of late in her anger there had been a kind of disdain, an attitude almost of condescension, as if she no longer looked upon the farmers as her equals. He sat still, his eyes fixed on the yellow lamp flame, and seeming to know how her words had hurt him, she went on softly, 'I want to help you, Paul. That's why I won't sit quiet while you go on wasting your life. You're only thirty—you owe it to yourself as well as me.'

He sat staring at the lamp without answering, his mouth sullen. It seemed indifference now, as if he were ignoring her, and stung to anger again she cried, 'Do you ever think what my life is? Two rooms to live in—once a month to town, and nothing to spend when I get there. I'm still young—I wasn't brought up this way.'

'You're a farmer's wife now. It doesn't matter what you used to be, or how you were brought up. You get enough to eat and wear. Just now that's all I can do. I'm not to blame that we've been dried out five years.'

'Enough to eat!' she laughed back shrilly. 'Enough salt pork—enough potatoes and eggs. And look—' Springing to the middle of the room she thrust out a foot for him to see the scuffed old slipper. 'When they're completely gone I suppose you'll tell me I can go barefoot—that I'm a farmer's wife—that it's not your fault we're dried out—'

'And what about these?' He pushed his chair away from the table now to let her see what he was wearing. 'Cowhide—hard as boards—but my feet are so calloused I don't feel them any more.'

Then he stood up, ashamed of having tried to match her hardships with his own. But frightened now as he reached for his smock she pressed close to him. 'Don't go yet. I brood and worry when I'm left alone. Please, Paul—you can't work on the land anyway.'

'And keep on like this? You start before I'm through the door. Week in and week out—I've troubles enough of my own.'

'Paul—please stay—' The eyes were glazed now, distended a little as if with the intensity of her dread and pleading. 'We won't quarrel any more. Hear it! I can't work—I just stand still and listen—'

The eyes frightened him, but responding to a kind of instinct that he must withstand her, that it was his self-respect and manhood against the fretful weakness of a woman, he answered unfeelingly, 'In here safe and quiet—you don't know how well off you are. If you were out in it—fighting it—swallowing it—'

'Sometimes, Paul, I wish I was. I'm so caged—if I could only break away and run. See—I stand like this all day. I can't relax. My throat's so tight it aches—'

With a jerk he freed his smock from her clutch. 'If I stay we'll only keep on all afternoon. Wait till tomorrow—we'll talk things over when the wind goes down.'

Then without meeting her eyes again he swung outside and doubled low against the buffets of the wind, fought his way slowly toward the stable. There was a deep hollow calm within, a vast darkness engulfed beneath the tides of moaning wind. He stood breathless a moment, hushed almost to a stupor by the sudden extinction of the storm and the stillness that enfolded him. It was a long, far-reaching stillness. The first dim stalls and rafters led the way into cavern-like obscurity, into vaults and recesses that extended far beyond the stable walls. Nor in these first quiet moments did he forbid the illusion, the sense of release from a harsh, familiar world into one of peace and darkness. The contentious mood that his stand against Ellen had roused him to, his tenacity and clenched despair before the ravages of wind, it was ebbing now, losing itself in the cover of darkness. Ellen and the wheat seemed remote, unimportant. At a whinny from the bay mare, Bess, he went forward and into her stall. She seemed grateful for his presence, and thrust her nose deep between his arm and body. They stood a long time motionless, comforting and assuring each other.

For soon again the first deep sense of quiet and peace was shrunken to the battered shelter of the stable. Instead of release or escape from the assaulting wind, the walls were but a feeble stand against it. They creaked and sawed as if the fingers of a giant hand were tightening to collapse them; the empty loft sustained a pipelike cry that rose and fell but never ended. He saw the dust-black sky again, and his fields blown smooth with drifted soil.

But always, even while listening to the storm outside, he could feel the tense and apprehensive stillness of the stable. There was not a hoof that clumped or shifted, not a rub of halter against manger. And yet, though it had been a strange stable, he would have known, despite the darkness, that every stall was filled. They, too, were all listening.

From Bess he went to the big grey gelding, Prince. Prince was twenty years old, with rib-grooved sides, and high, protruding hipbones. Paul ran his hand over the ribs, and felt a sudden shame, a sting of fear that Ellen might be right in what she said. For wasn't it true—nine years a farmer now on his own land, and still he couldn't even feed his horses? What, then, could he hope to do for his wife and son?

There was much he planned. And so vivid was the future of his planning, so real and constant, that often the actual present was but half felt, but half endured. Its difficulties were lessened by a confidence in what lay beyond them. A new house—land for the boy—land and still more land—or education, whatever he might want.

But all the time was he only a blind and stubborn fool? Was Ellen right? Was he trampling on her life, and throwing away his own? The five years since he married her, were they to go on repeating themselves, five, ten, twenty, until all the brave future he looked forward to was but a stark and futile past?

She looked forward to no future. She had no faith or dream with which to make the dust and poverty less real. He understood suddenly. He saw her face again as only a few minutes ago it had begged him not to leave her. The darkness round him now was as a slate on which her lonely terror limned itself. He went from Prince to the other horses, combing their manes and forelocks with his fingers, but always it was her face before him, its staring eyes and twisted suffering. 'See Paul—I stand like this all day. I just stand still—My throat's so tight it aches—'

And always the wind, the creak of walls, the wild lipless wailing through the loft. Until at last as he stood there, staring into the livid face before him, it seemed that this scream of wind was a cry from her parched and frantic lips. He knew it couldn't be, he knew that she was safe within the house, but still the wind persisted as a woman's cry. The cry of a woman with eyes like those that watched him through the dark. Eyes that were mad now—lips that even as they cried still pleaded, 'See, Paul—I stand like this all day. I just stand still—so caged! If I could only run!'

He saw her running, pulled and driven headlong by the wind, but when at last he returned to the house, compelled by his anxiety, she was walking quietly back and forth with the baby in her arms. Careful, despite his concern, not to reveal a fear or weakness that she might think capitulation to her wishes, he watched a moment through the window, and then went off to the tool shed to mend harness. All afternoon he stitched and riveted. It was easier with the lantern lit and his hands occupied. There was a wind whining high past the tool shed too, but it was only wind. He remembered the arguments with which Ellen had tried to persuade him away from the farm, and one by one he defeated them. There would be rain again—next year or the next. Maybe in his ignorance he had farmed his land the wrong way, seeding wheat every year, working the soil till it was lifeless dust—but he would do better now. He would plant clover and alfalfa, breed cattle, acre by acre and year by year restore to his land its fibre and fertility. That was something to work for, a way to prove himself. It was ruthless wind, blackening the sky with his earth, but it was not his master. Out of his land it had made a wilderness. He now, out of the wilderness, would make a farm and home again.

Tonight he must talk with Ellen. Patiently, when the wind was down, and they were both quiet again. It was she who had told him to grow fibrous crops, who had called him an ignorant fool because he kept on with summer fallow and wheat. Now she might be gratified to find him acknowledging her wisdom. Perhaps she would begin to feel the power and steadfastness of the land, to take a pride in it, to understand that he was not a fool, but working for her future and their son's.

And already the wind was slackening. At four o'clock he could sense a lull. At five, straining his eyes from the tool shed doorway, he could make out a neighbour's buildings half a mile away. It was over—three days of blight and havoc like a scourge—three days so bitter and so long that for a moment he stood still, unseeing, his senses idle with a numbness of relief.

But only for a moment. Suddenly he emerged from the numbness; suddenly the fields before him struck his eyes to comprehension. They lay black, naked. Beaten and mounded smooth with dust as if a sea in gentle swell had turned to stone. And though he had tried to prepare himself for such a scene, though he had known since yesterday that not a blade would last the storm, still now, before the utter waste confronting him, he sickened and stood cold. Suddenly like the fields he was naked. Everything that had sheathed him a little from the realities of existence: vision and purpose, faith in the land, in the future, in himself—it was all rent now, stripped away. 'Desert,' he heard her voice begin to sob. 'Desert, you fool—the lamp lit at noon!'

In the stable again, measuring out their feed to the horses, he wondered what he would say to her tonight. For so deep were his instincts of loyalty to the land that still, even with the images of his betrayal stark upon his mind, his concern was how to withstand her, how to go on again and justify himself. It had not occurred to him yet that he might or should abandon the land. He had lived with it too long. Rather was his impulse still to defend it—as a man defends against the scorn of strangers even his most worthless kin.

He fed his horses, then waited. She too would be waiting ready to cry at him, 'Look now—that crop that was to feed and clothe us! And you'll still keep on! You'll still say "Next year—there'll be rain next year"!'

But she was gone when he reached the house. The door was open, the lamp blown out, the crib empty. The dishes from their meal at noon were still on the table. She had perhaps begun to sweep, for the broom was lying in the middle of the floor. He tried to call, but a terror clamped upon his throat. In the wan, returning light it seemed that even the deserted kitchen was straining to whisper what it had seen. The tatters of the storm still whimpered through the eaves, and in their moaning told the desolation of the miles they had traversed. On tiptoe at last he crossed to the adjoining room; then at the threshold, without even a glance inside to satisfy himself that she was really gone, he wheeled again and plunged outside.

He ran a long time—distraught and headlong as a few hours ago he had seemed to watch her run—around the farmyard, a little distance into the pasture, back again blindly to the house to see whether she had returned—and then at a stumble down the road for help.

They joined him in the search, rode away for others, spread calling across the fields in the direction she might have been carried by the wind—but nearly two hours later it was himself who came upon her. Crouched down against a drift of sand as if for shelter, her hair in matted strands around her neck and face, the child clasped tightly in her arms.

The child was quite cold. It had been her arms, perhaps, too frantic to protect him, or the smother of dust upon his throat and lungs. 'Hold him,' she said as he knelt beside her. 'So—with his face away from the wind. Hold him until I tidy my hair.'

Her eyes were still wide in an immobile stare, but with her lips she smiled at him. For a long time he knelt transfixed, trying to speak to her, touching fearfully with his fingertips the dust-grimed cheeks and eyelids of the child. At last she said, 'I'll take him again. Such clumsy hands—you don't know how to hold a baby yet. See how his head falls forward on your arm.'

Yet it all seemed familiar—a confirmation of what he had known since noon. He gave her the child, then, gathering them up in his arms, struggled to his feet, and turned toward home.

It was evening now. Across the fields a few spent clouds of dust still shook and fled. Beyond, as if through smoke, the sunset smouldered like a distant fire.

He walked with a long dull stride, his eyes before him, heedless of her weight. Once he glanced down and with her eyes she still was smiling. 'Such strong arms, Paul—and I was so tired just carrying him. . . .'

He tried to answer, but it seemed that now the dusk was drawn apart in breathless waiting, a finger on its lips until they passed. 'You were right, Paul. . . .' Her voice came whispering, as if she too could feel the hush. 'You said tonight we'd see the storm go down. So still now, and a red sky—it means tomorrow will be fine.'

1938

each meal they had become more hard-pressed to push each other's buttons and piss the other off

The Painted Door

Straight across the hills it was five miles from John's farm to his father's. But in winter, with the roads impassable, a team had to make a wide detour and skirt the hills, so that from five the distance was more than trebled to seventeen.

'I think I'll walk,' John said at breakfast to his wife. 'The drifts in the hills wouldn't hold a horse, but they'll carry me all right. If I leave early I can spend a few hours helping him with chores, and still be back by suppertime.'

She went to the window, and thawing a clear place in the frost with her breath, stood looking across the snowswept farmyard to the huddle of stables and sheds. 'There was a double wheel around the moon last night,' she countered presently. 'You said yourself we could expect a storm. It isn't right to leave me here alone. Surely I'm as important as your father.'

He glanced up uneasily, then drinking off his coffee tried to reassure her. 'But there's nothing to be afraid of—even supposing it does start to storm. You won't need to go near the stable. Everything's fed and watered now to last till night. I'll be back at the latest by seven or eight.'

She went on blowing against the frosted pane, carefully elongating the clear place until it was oval-shaped and symmetrical. He watched her a moment or two longer, then more insistently repeated, 'I say you won't need to go near the stable. Everything's fed and watered, and I'll see that there's plenty of wood in. That will be all right, won't it?'

'Yes—of course—I heard you—' It was a curiously cold voice now, as if the words were chilled by their contact with the frosted pane. 'Plenty to eat—plenty of wood to keep me warm—what more could a woman ask for?'

'But he's an old man—living there all alone. What is it, Ann? You're not like yourself this morning.'

She shook her head without turning. 'Pay no attention to me. Seven years a farmer's wife—it's time I was used to staying alone.'

Slowly the clear place on the glass enlarged: oval, then round, then oval again. The sun was risen above the frost mists now, so keen and hard a glitter on the snow that instead of warmth its rays seemed shedding cold. One of the two-year-old colts that had cantered away when John turned the horses out for water stood covered with rime at the stable door again, head down and body hunched, each breath a little plume of steam against the frosty air. She shivered, but did not turn. In the clear, bitter light the long white miles of prairie landscape seemed a region alien to life. Even the distant farmsteads she could see served only to intensify a sense of isolation. Scattered across the face of so vast and bleak a wilderness it was difficult to conceive them as a testimony of human hardihood and endurance. Rather they seemed futile, lost, to cower before the implacability of snow-swept earth and clear pale sun-chilled sky.

And when at last she turned from the window there was a brooding stillness in her face as if she had recognized this mastery of snow and cold. It troubled John. 'If you're really afraid,' he yielded, 'I won't go today. Lately it's been so cold, that's all. I just wanted to make sure he's all right in case we do have a storm.'

'I know—I'm not really afraid.' She was putting in a fire now, and he could no longer see her face. 'Pay no attention. It's ten miles there and back, so you'd better get started.'

'You ought to know by now I wouldn't stay away,' he tried to brighten her. 'No matter how it stormed. Before we were married—remember? Twice a week I never missed and we had some bad blizzards that winter too.'

He was a slow, unambitious man, content with his farm and cattle, naïvely proud of Ann. He had been bewildered by it once, her caring for a dull-witted fellow like him; then assured at last of her affection he had relaxed against it gratefully, unsuspecting it might ever be less constant than his own. Even now, listening to the restless brooding in her voice, he felt only a quick, unformulated kind of pride that after seven years his absence for a day should still concern her. While she, his trust and earnestness controlling her again:

'I know. It's just that sometimes when you're away I get lonely. . . . There's a long cold tramp in front of you. You'll let me fix a scarf around your face.'

He nodded. 'And on my way I'll drop in at Steven's place. Maybe he'll come over tonight for a game of cards. You haven't seen anybody but me for the last two weeks.'

She glanced up sharply, then busied herself clearing the table. 'It will mean another two miles if you do. You're going to be cold and tired enough as it is. When you're gone I think I'll paint the kitchen woodwork. White this time—you remember we got the paint last fall. It's going to make the room a lot lighter. I'll be too busy to find the day long.'

'I will though,' he insisted, 'and if a storm gets up you'll feel safer, knowing that he's coming. That's what you need, maybe—someone to talk to besides me.'

She stood at the stove motionless a moment, then turned to him uneasily. 'Will you shave then, John—now—before you go?'

He glanced at her questioningly, and avoiding his eyes she tried to explain, 'I mean—he may be here before you're back—and you won't have a chance then.'

'But it's only Steven—we're not going anywhere.'

'He'll be shaved, though—that's what I mean—and I'd like you too to spend a little time on yourself.'

He stood up, stroking the heavy stubble on his chin. 'Maybe I should—

only it softens up the skin too much. Especially when I've got to face the wind.'

She nodded and began to help him dress, bringing heavy socks and a big woollen sweater from the bedroom, wrapping a scarf around his face and forehead. 'I'll tell Steven to come early,' he said, as he went out. 'In time for supper. Likely there'll be chores for me to do, so if I'm not back by six don't wait.'

From the bedroom window she watched him nearly a mile along the road. The fire had gone down when at last she turned away, and already through the house there was an encroaching chill. A blaze sprang up again when the draughts were opened, but as she went on clearing the table her movements were furtive and constrained. It was the silence weighing upon her—the frozen silence of the bitter fields and sun-chilled sky—lurking outside as if alive, relentlessly in wait, mile-deep between her now and John. She listened to it, suddenly tense, motionless. The fire crackled and the clock ticked. Always it was there. 'I'm a fool,' she whispered, rattling the dishes in defiance, going back to the stove to put in another fire. 'Warm and safe—I'm a fool. It's a good chance when he's away to paint. The day will go quickly. I won't have time to brood.'

Since November now the paint had been waiting warmer weather. The frost in the walls on a day like this would crack and peel it as it dried, but she needed something to keep her hands occupied, something to stave off the gathering cold and loneliness. 'First of all,' she said aloud, opening the paint and mixing it with a little turpentine, 'I must get the house warmer. Fill up the stove and open the oven door so that all the heat comes out. Wad something along the window sills to keep out the draughts. Then I'll feel brighter. It's the cold that depresses.'

She moved briskly, performing each little task with careful and exaggerated absorption, binding her thoughts to it, making it a screen between herself and the surrounding snow and silence. But when the stove was filled and the windows sealed it was more difficult again. Above the quiet, steady swishing of her brush against the bedroom door the clock began to tick. Suddenly her movements became precise, deliberate, her posture self-conscious, as if someone had entered the room and were watching her. It was the silence again, aggressive, hovering. The fire spit and crackled at it. Still it was there. 'I'm a fool,' she repeated. 'All farmers' wives have to stay alone. I mustn't give in this way. I mustn't brood. A few hours now and they'll be here.'

The sound of her voice reassured her. She went on: 'I'll get them a good supper—and for coffee after cards bake some of the little cakes with raisins that he likes. . . . Just three of us, so I'll watch, and let John play. It's better with four, but at least we can talk. That's all I need—someone to talk to. John never talks. He's stronger—doesn't need to. But he likes Steven—no matter what the neighbours say. Maybe he'll have him come again, and some other young people too. It's what we need, both of us, to help keep young ourselves. . . . And then before we know it we'll be into

March. It's cold still in March sometimes, but you never mind the same. At least you're beginning to think about spring.'

She began to think about it now. Thoughts that outstripped her words, that left her alone again with herself and the ever-lurking silence. Eager and hopeful first, then clenched, rebellious, lonely. Windows open, sun and thawing earth again, the urge of growing, living things. Then the days that began in the morning at half-past four and lasted till ten at night; the meals at which John gulped his food and scarcely spoke a word; the brute-tired stupid eyes he turned on her if ever she mentioned town or visiting.

For spring was drudgery again. John never hired a man to help him. He wanted a mortgage-free farm; then a new house and pretty clothes for her. Sometimes, because with the best of crops it was going to take so long to pay off anyway, she wondered whether they mightn't better let the mortgage wait a little. Before they were worn out, before their best years were gone. It was something of life she wanted, not just a house and furniture; something of John, not pretty clothes when she would be too old to wear them. But John of course couldn't understand. To him it seemed only right that she should have the clothes—openly right that he, fit for nothing else, should slave away fifteen hours a day to give them to her. There was in his devotion a baffling, insurmountable humility that made him feel the need of sacrifice. And when his muscles ached, when his feet dragged stolidly with weariness, then it seemed that in some measure at least he was making amends for his big hulking body and simple mind. Year after year their lives went on in the same little groove. He drove his horses in the field; she milked the cows and hoed potatoes. By dint of his drudgery he saved a few months' wages, added a few dollars more each fall to his payments on the mortgage; but the only real difference that it all made was to deprive her of his companionship, to make him a little duller, older, uglier than he might otherwise have been. He never saw their lives objectively. To him it was not what he actually accomplished by means of the sacrifice that mattered, but the sacrifice itself, the gesture—something done for her sake.

And she, understanding, kept her silence. In such a gesture, however futile, there was a graciousness not to be shattered lightly. 'John,' she would begin sometimes, 'you're doing too much. Get a man to help you—just for a month—' but smiling down at her he would answer simply. 'I don't mind. Look at the hands on me. They're made for work.' While in his voice there would be a stalwart ring to tell her that by her thoughtfulness she had made him only the more resolved to serve her, to prove his devotion and fidelity.

They were useless, such thoughts. She knew. It was his very devotion that made them useless, that forbade her to rebel. Yet over and over, sometimes hunched still before their bleakness, sometimes her brush making swift sharp strokes to pace the chafe and rancour that they brought, she persisted in them.

This now, the winter, was their slack season. She could sleep sometimes till eight, and John till seven. They could linger over their meals a little, read, play cards, go visiting the neighbours. It was the time to relax, to indulge and enjoy themselves; but instead, fretful and impatient, they kept on waiting for the spring. They were compelled now, not by labour, but by the spirit of labour. A spirit that pervaded their lives and brought with idleness a sense of guilt. Sometimes they did sleep late, sometimes they did play cards, but always uneasily, always reproached by the thought of more important things that might be done. When John got up at five to attend to the fire he wanted to stay up and go out to the stable. When he sat down to a meal he hurried his food and pushed his chair away again, from habit, from sheer work-instinct, even though it was only to put more wood in the stove, or go down cellar to cut up beets and turnips for the cows.

And anyway, sometimes she asked herself, why sit trying to talk with a man who never talked? Why talk when there was nothing to talk about but crops and cattle, the weather and the neighbours? The neighbours, too—why go visiting them when still it was the same—crops and cattle, the weather and the other neighbours? Why go to the dances in the schoolhouse to sit among the older women, one of them now, married seven years, or to waltz with the work-bent, tired old farmers to a squeaky fiddle tune? Once she had danced with Steven six or seven times in the evening, and they had talked about it for as many months. It was easier to stay at home. John never danced or enjoyed himself. He was always uncomfortable in his good suit and shoes. He didn't like shaving in the cold weather oftener than once or twice a week. It was easier to stay at home, to stand at the window staring out across the bitter fields, to count the days and look forward to another spring.

But now, alone with herself in the winter silence, she saw the spring for what it really was. This spring—next spring—all the springs and summers still to come. While they grew old, while their bodies warped, while their minds kept shrivelling dry and empty like their lives. 'I mustn't,' she said aloud again. 'I married him—and he's a good man. I mustn't keep on this way. It will be noon before long, and then time to think about supper. . . . Maybe he'll come early—and as soon as John is finished at the stable we can all play cards.'

It was getting cold again, and she left her painting to put in more wood. But this time the warmth spread slowly. She pushed a mat up to the outside door, and went back to the window to pat down the woollen shirt that was wadded along the sill. Then she paced a few times round the room, then poked the fire and rattled the stove lids, then paced again. The fire crackled, the clock ticked. The silence now seemed more intense than ever, seemed to have reached a pitch where it faintly moaned. She began to pace on tiptoe, listening, her shoulders drawn together, not realising for a while that it was the wind she heard, thin-strained and whimpering through the eaves.

Then she wheeled to the window, and with quick short breaths thawed the frost to see again. The glitter was gone. Across the drifts sped swift and snakelike little tongues of snow. She could not follow them, where they sprang from, or where they disappeared. It was as if all across the yard the snow were shivering awake—roused by the warnings of the wind to hold itself in readiness for the impending storm. The sky had become a sombre, whitish grey. It, too, as if in readiness, had shifted and lay close to earth. Before her as she watched a mane of powdery snow reared up breast-high against the darker background of the stable, tossed for a moment angrily, and then subsided again as if whipped down to obedience and restraint. But another followed, more reckless and impatient than the first. Another reeled and dashed itself against the window where she watched. Then ominously for a while there were only the angry little snakes of snow. The wind rose, creaking the troughs that were wired beneath the eaves. In the distance, sky and prairie now were merged into one another linelessly. All round her it was gathering; already in its press and whimpering there strummed a boding of eventual fury. Again she saw a mane of snow spring up, so dense and high this time that all the sheds and stables were obscured. Then others followed, whirling fiercely out of hand; and, when at last they cleared, the stables seemed in dimmer outline than before. It was the snow beginning, long lancet shafts of it, straight from the north, borne almost level by the straining wind. 'He'll be there soon,' she whispered, 'and coming home it will be in his back. He'll leave again right away. He saw the double wheel—he knows the kind of storm there'll be.'

She went back to her painting. For a while it was easier, all her thoughts half-anxious ones of John in the blizzard, struggling his way across the hills; but petulantly again she soon began, 'I knew we were going to have a storm—I told him so—but it doesn't matter what I say. Big stubborn fool—he goes his own way anyway. It doesn't matter what becomes of me. In a storm like this he'll never get home. He won't even try. And while he sits keeping his father company I can look after his stable for him, go ploughing through snowdrifts up to my knees—nearly frozen—'

Not that she meant or believed her words. It was just an effort to convince herself that she did have a grievance, to justify her rebellious thoughts, to prove John responsible for her unhappiness. She was young still, eager for excitement and distractions; and John's steadfastness rebuked her vanity, made her complaints seem weak and trivial. She went on, fretfully, 'If he'd listen to me sometimes and not be so stubborn we wouldn't still be living in a house like this. Seven years in two rooms—seven years and never a new stick of furniture. . . . There—as if another coat of paint could make it different anyway.'

She cleaned her brush, filled up the stove again, and went back to the window. There was a void white moment that she thought must be frost formed on the window pane; then, like a fitful shadow through the whirling snow, she recognized the stable roof. It was incredible. The sudden, maniac raging of the storm struck from her face all its pettishness. Her eyes glazed with fear a little; her lips blanched. 'If he starts for home now,' she whispered silently—'But he won't—he knows I'm safe—he knows Steven's coming. Across the hills he would never dare.'

She turned to the stove, holding out her hands to the warmth. Around her now there seemed a constant sway and tremor, as if the air were vibrating with the shudderings of the walls. She stood quite still, listening. Sometimes the wind struck with sharp, savage blows. Sometimes it bore down in a sustained, minute-long blast, silent with effort and intensity; then with a foiled shriek of threat wheeled away to gather and assault again. Always the eave-troughs creaked and sawed. She stared towards the window again, then detecting the morbid trend of her thoughts, prepared fresh coffee and forced herself to drink a few mouthfuls. 'He would never dare,' she whispered again. 'He wouldn't leave the old man anyway in such a storm. Safe in here—there's nothing for me to keep worrying about. It's after one already. I'll do my baking now, and then it will be time to get supper ready for Steven.'

Soon, however, she began to doubt whether Steven would come. In such a storm even a mile was enough to make a man hesitate. Especially Steven, who was hardly the one to face a blizzard for the sake of someone else's chores. He had a stable of his own to look after anyway. It would be only natural for him to think that when the storm blew up John had turned again for home. Another man would have—would have put his wife first.

But she felt little dread or uneasiness at the prospect of spending the night alone. It was the first time she had been left like this on her own resources, and her reaction, now that she could face and appraise her situation calmly, was gradually to feel it a kind of adventure and responsibility. It stimulated her. Before nightfall she must go to the stable and feed everything. Wrap up in some of John's clothes—take a ball of string in her hand, one end tied to the door, so that no matter how blinding the storm she could at least find her way back to the house. She had heard of people having to do that. It appealed to her now because suddenly it made life dramatic. She had not felt the storm yet, only watched it for a minute through the window.

It took nearly an hour to find enough string, to choose the right socks and sweaters. Long before it was time to start out she tried on John's clothes, changing and rechanging, striding around the room to make sure there would be play enough for pitching hay and struggling over snowdrifts; then she took them off again, and for a while busied herself baking the little cakes with raisins that he liked.

Night came early. Just for a moment on the doorstep she shrank back, uncertain. The slow dimming of the light clutched her with an illogical sense of abandonment. It was like the covert withdrawal of an ally, leaving the alien miles unleashed and unrestrained. Watching the hurricane of writhing snow rage past the little house she forced herself, 'They'll never stand the night unless I get them fed. It's nearly dark already, and I've work to last an hour.'

Timidly, unwinding a little of the string, she crept out from the shelter of the doorway. A gust of wind spun her forward a few yards, then plunged her headlong against a drift that in the dense white whirl lay invisible across her path. For nearly a minute she huddled still, breathless and dazed. The snow was in her mouth and nostrils, inside her scarf and up her sleeves. As she tried to straighten a smothering scud flung itself against her face, cutting off her breath a second time. The wind struck from all sides, blustering and furious. It was as if the storm had discovered her, as if all its forces were concentrated upon her extinction. Seized with panic suddenly she threshed out a moment with her arms, then stumbled back and sprawled her length across the drift.

But this time she regained her feet quickly, roused by the whip and batter of the storm to retaliative anger. For a moment her impulse was to face the wind and strike back blow for blow; then, as suddenly as it had come, her frantic strength gave way to limpness and exhaustion. Suddenly, a comprehension so clear and terrifying that it struck all thoughts of the stable from her mind, she realized in such a storm her puniness. And the realization gave her new strength, stilled this time to a desperate persistence. Just for a moment the wind held her, numb and swaying in its vise; then slowly, buckled far forward, she groped her way again towards the house.

Inside, leaning against the door, she stood tense and still a while. It was almost dark now. The top of the stove glowed a deep, dull red. Heedless of the storm, self-absorbed and self-satisfied, the clock ticked on like a glib little idiot. 'He shouldn't have gone,' she whispered silently. 'He saw the double wheel—he knew. He shouldn't have left me here alone.'

For so fierce now, so insane and dominant did the blizzard seem, that she could not credit the safety of the house. The warmth and lull around her was not real yet, not to be relied upon. She was still at the mercy of the storm. Only her body pressing hard like this against the door was staving it off. She didn't dare move. She didn't dare ease the ache and strain. 'He shouldn't have gone,' she repeated, thinking of the stable again, reproached by her helplessness. 'They'll freeze in their stalls—and I can't reach them. He'll say it's all my fault. He won't believe I tried.'

Then Steven came. Quickly, startled to quietness and control, she let him in and lit the lamp. He stared at her a moment, then flinging off his cap crossed to where she stood by the table and seized her arms. 'You're so white—what's wrong? Look at me—' It was like him in such little situations to be masterful. 'You should have known better—for a while I thought I wasn't going to make it here myself—'

'I was afraid you wouldn't come—John left early, and there was the stable—'

But the storm had unnerved her, and suddenly at the assurance of his touch and voice the fear that had been gripping her gave way to an hysteria of relief. Scarcely aware of herself she seized his arm and sobbed against it. He remained still a moment unyielding, then slipped his other arm around her shoulder. It was comforting and she relaxed against it, hushed by a sudden sense of lull and safety. Her shoulders trembled with the easing of the strain, then fell limp and still. 'You're shivering,'—he drew her gently towards the stove. 'It's all right—nothing to be afraid of. I'm going to see to the stable.'

It was a quiet, sympathetic voice, yet with an undertone of insolence, a kind of mockery even, that made her draw away quickly and busy herself putting in a fire. With his lips drawn in a little smile he watched her till she looked at him again. The smile too was insolent, but at the same time companionable; Steven's smile, and therefore difficult to reprove. It lit up his lean, still-boyish face with a peculiar kind of arrogance: features and smile that were different from John's, from other men's—wilful and derisive, yet naïvely so—as if it were less the difference itself he was conscious of, than the long-accustomed privilege that thereby fell his due. He was erect, tall, square-shouldered. His hair was dark and trim, his lips curved soft and full. While John, she made the comparison swiftly, was thickset, heavy-jowled, and stooped. He always stood before her helpless, a kind of humility and wonderment in his attitude. And Steven now smiled on her appraisingly with the worldly-wise assurance of one for whom a woman holds neither mystery nor illusion.

'It was good of you to come, Steven,' she responded, the words running into a sudden, empty laugh. 'Such a storm to face—I suppose I should feel flattered.'

For his presumption, his misunderstanding of what had been only a momentary weakness, instead of angering quickened her, roused from latency and long disuse all the instincts and resources of her femininity. She felt eager, challenged. Something was at hand that hitherto had always eluded her, even in the early days with John, something vital, beckoning, meaningful. She didn't understand, but she knew. The texture of the moment was satisfyingly dreamlike: an incredibility perceived as such, yet acquiesced in. She was John's wife—she knew—but also she knew that Steven standing here was different from John. There was no thought or motive, no understanding of herself as the knowledge persisted. Wary and poised round a sudden little core of blind excitement she evaded him, 'But it's nearly dark—hadn't you better hurry if you're going to do the chores? Don't trouble—I can get them off myself—'

An hour later when he returned from the stable she was in another dress, hair rearranged, a little flush of colour in her face. Pouring warm water for him from the kettle into the basin she said evenly, 'By the time you're washed supper will be ready. John said we weren't to wait for him.'

He looked at her a moment, 'You don't mean you're expecting John tonight? The way it's blowing—'

'Of course.' As she spoke she could feel the colour deepening in her face. 'We're going to play cards. He was the one that suggested it.'

He went on washing, and then as they took their places at the table, resumed, 'So John's coming. When are you expecting him?'

'He said it might be seven o'clock—or a little later.' Conversation with Steven at other times had always been brisk and natural, but now all at once she found it strained. 'He may have work to do for his father. That's what he said when he left. Why do you ask, Steven?'

'I was just wondering—it's a rough night.'

'You don't know John. It would take more than a storm to stop him.'

She glanced up again and he was smiling at her. The same insolence, the same little twist of mockery and appraisal. It made her flinch, and ask herself why she was pretending to expect John—why there should be this instinct of defence to force her. This time, instead of poise and excitement, it brought a reminder that she had changed her dress and rearranged her hair. It crushed in a sudden silence, through which she heard the whistling wind again, and the creaking saw of the eaves. Neither spoke now. There was something strange, almost frightening, about this Steven and his quiet, unrelenting smile; but strangest of all was the familiarity: the Steven she had never seen or encountered, and yet had always known, always expected, always waited for. It was less Steven himself that she felt than his inevitability. Just as she had felt the snow, the silence and the storm. She kept her eyes lowered, on the window past his shoulder, on the stove, but his smile now seemed to exist apart from him, to merge and hover with the silence. She clinked a cup—listened to the whistle of the storm—always it was there. He began to speak, but her mind missed the meaning of his words. Swiftly she was making comparisons again; his face so different to John's, so handsome and young and clean-shaven. Swiftly, helplessly, feeling the imperceptible and relentless ascendancy that thereby he was gaining over her, sensing sudden menace in this new, more vital life, even as she felt drawn towards it.

The lamp between them flickered as an onslaught of the storm sent shudderings through the room. She rose to build up the fire again and he followed her. For a long time they stood close to the stove, their arms almost touching. Once as the blizzard creaked the house she spun around sharply, fancying it was John at the door; but quietly he intercepted her. 'Not tonight—you might as well make up your mind to it. Across the hills in a storm like this—it would be suicide to try.'

Her lips trembled suddenly in an effort to answer, to parry the certainty in his voice, then set thin and bloodless. She was afraid now. Afraid of his face so different from John's—of his smile, of her own helplessness to rebuke it. Afraid of the storm, isolating her here alone with him. They tried to play cards, but she kept starting up at every creak and shiver of the walls. 'It's too rough a night,' he repeated. 'Even for John. Just relax a few minutes—stop worrying and pay a little attention to me.'

But in his tone there was a contradiction in his words. For it implied that she was not worrying—that her only concern was lest it really might be John at the door.

And the implication persisted. He filled up the stove for her, shuffled the cards—won—shuffled—still it was there. She tried to respond to his conversation, to think of the game, but helplessly into her cards instead she began to ask, Was he right? Was that why he smiled? Why he seemed to wait, expectant and assured?

The clock ticked, the fire crackled. Always it was there. Furtively for a moment she watched him as he deliberated over his hand. John, even in the days before they were married, had never looked like that. Only this morning she had asked him to shave. Because Steven was coming—because she had been afraid to see them side by side—because deep within herself she had known even then. The same knowledge, furtive and forbidden, that was flaunted now in Steven's smile. 'You look cold,' he said at last, dropping his cards and rising from the table. 'We're not playing, anyway. Come over to the stove for a few minutes and get warm.

'But first I think we'll hang blankets over the door. When there's a blizzard like this we always do.' It seemed that in sane, commonplace activity there might be release, a moment or two in which to recover herself. 'John has nails to put them on. They keep out a little of the draught.'

He stood on a chair for her, and hung the blankets that she carried from the bedroom. Then for a moment they stood silent, watching the blankets sway and tremble before the blade of wind that spurted around the jamb. 'I forgot,' she said at last, 'that I painted the bedroom door. At the top there, see—I've smeared the blankets.'

He glanced at her curiously, and went back to the stove. She followed him, trying to imagine the hills in such a storm, wondering whether John would come. 'A man couldn't live in it,' suddenly he answered her thoughts, lowering the oven door and drawing up their chairs one on each side of it. 'He knows you're safe. It isn't likely that he'd leave his father, anyway.'

'The wind will be in his back,' she persisted. 'The winter before we were married—all the blizzards that we had that year—and he never missed—'

'Blizzards like this one? Up in the hills he wouldn't be able to keep his direction for a hundred yards. Listen to it a minute and ask yourself.'

His voice seemed softer, kindlier now. She met his smile a moment, its assured little twist of appraisal, then for a long time sat silent, tense, careful again to avoid his eyes.

Everything now seemed to depend on this. It was the same as a few hours ago when she braced the door against the storm. He was watching her, smiling. She dared not move, unclench her hands, or raise her eyes. The flames crackled, the clock ticked. The storm wrenched the walls as if to make them buckle in. So rigid and desperate were all her muscles set, withstanding, that the room around her seemed to swim and reel. So rigid and strained that for relief at last, despite herself, she raised her head and met his eyes again.

Intending that it should be for only an instant, just to breathe again, to ease the tension that had grown unbearable—but in his smile now, instead of the insolent appraisal that she feared, there seemed a kind of warmth and sympathy. An understanding that quickened and encouraged her—that made her wonder why but a moment ago she had been afraid. It was as if the storm had lulled, as if she had suddenly found calm and shelter.

Or perhaps, the thought seized her, perhaps instead of his smile it was she who had changed. She who, in the long, wind-creaked silence, had emerged from the increment of codes and loyalties to her real, unfettered self. She who now felt his air of appraisal as nothing more than an understanding of the unfulfilled woman that until this moment had lain within her brooding and unadmitted, reproved out of consciousness by the insistence of an outgrown, routine fidelity.

For there had always been Steven. She understood now. Seven years—almost as long as John—ever since the night they first danced together.

The lamp was burning dry, and through the dimming light, isolated in the fastness of silence and storm, they watched each other. Her face was white and struggling still. His was handsome, clean-shaven, young. Her eyes were fanatic, believing desperately, fixed upon him as if to exclude all else, as if to find justification. His were cool, bland, drooped a little with expectancy. The light kept dimming, gathering the shadows round them, hushed, conspiratorial. He was smiling still. Her hands again were clenched up white and hard.

'But he always came,' she persisted. 'The wildest, coldest nights—even such a night as this. There was never a storm—'

'Never a storm like this one.' There was a quietness in his smile now, a kind of simplicity almost, as if to reassure her. 'You were out in it yourself for a few minutes. He'd have it for five miles, across the hills. . . . I'd think twice myself, on such a night before risking even one.'

Long after he was asleep she lay listening to the storm. As a check on the draught up the chimney they had left one of the stovelids partly off, and through the open bedroom door she could see the flickerings of flame and shadow on the kitchen wall. They leaped and sank fantastically. The longer she watched the more alive they seemed to be. There was one great shadow that struggled towards her threateningly, massive and black and engulfing all the room. Again and again it advanced, about to spring, but each time a little whip of light subdued it to its place among the others on the wall. Yet though it never reached her still she cowered, feeling that gathered there was all the frozen wilderness, its heart of terror and invincibility.

Then she dozed a while, and the shadow was John. Interminably he advanced. The whips of light still flickered and coiled, but now suddenly they were the swift little snakes that this afternoon she had watched twist and shiver across the snow. And they too were advancing. They writhed and vanished and came again. She lay still, paralysed. He was over her now, so close that she could have touched him. Already it seemed that a deadly tightening hand was on her throat. She tried to scream but her lips were locked. Steven beside her slept on heedlessly.

Until suddenly as she lay staring up at him a gleam of light revealed his face. And in it was not a trace of threat or anger—only calm, and stonelike hopelessness.

That was like John. He began to withdraw, and frantically she tried to call him back. 'It isn't true—not really true—listen, John—' but the words clung frozen to her lips. Already there was only the shriek of the wind again, the sawing eaves, the leap and twist of shadow on the wall.

She sat up, startled now and awake. And so real had he seemed there, standing close to her, so vivid the sudden age and sorrow in his face, that at first she could not make herself understand she had been only dreaming. Against the conviction of his presence in the room it was necessary to insist over and over that he must still be with his father on the other side of the hills. Watching the shadows she had fallen asleep. It was only her mind, her imagination, distorted to a nightmare by the illogical and unadmitted dread of his return. But he wouldn't come. Steven was right. In such a storm he would never try. They were safe, alone. No one would ever know. It was only fear, morbid and irrational; only the sense of guilt that even her new-found and challenged womanhood could not entirely quell.

She knew now. She had not let herself understand or acknowledge it as guilt before, but gradually through the wind-torn silence of the night his face compelled her. The face that had watched her from the darkness with its stonelike sorrow—the face that was really John—John more than his features of mere flesh and bone could ever be.

She wept silently. The fitful gleam of light began to sink. On the ceiling and wall at last there was only a faint dull flickering glow. The little house shuddered and quailed, and a chill crept in again. Without wakening Steven she slipped out to build up the fire. It was burned to a few spent embers now, and the wood she put on seemed a long time catching light. The wind swirled through the blankets they had hung around the door, and then, hollow and moaning, roared up the chimney again, as if against its will drawn back to serve still longer with the onrush of the storm.

For a long time she crouched over the stove, listening. Earlier in the evening, with the lamp lit and the fire crackling, the house had seemed a stand against the wilderness, a refuge of feeble walls wherein persisted the elements of human meaning and survival. Now, in the cold, creaking darkness, it was strangely extinct, looted by the storm and abandoned again. She lifted the stove lid and fanned the embers till at last a swift little tongue of flame began to lick around the wood. Then she replaced the lid, extended her hands, and as if frozen in that attitude stood waiting.

It was not long now. After a few minutes she closed the draughts, and as the flames whirled back upon each other, beating against the top of the stove and sending out flickers of light again, a warmth surged up to relax her stiffened limbs. But shivering and numb it had been easier. The bodily well-being that the warmth induced gave play again to an ever more insistent mental suffering. She remembered the shadow that was John. She saw him bent towards her, then retreating, his features pale and overcast with unaccusing grief. She re-lived their seven years together and, in retrospect, found them to be years of worth and dignity. Until crushed by it all at last, seized by a sudden need to suffer and atone, she crossed to where the draught was bitter, and for a long time stood unflinching on the icy floor.

The storm was close here. Even through the blankets she could feel a sift of snow against her face. The eaves sawed, the walls creaked, and the wind was like a wolf in howling flight.

And yet, suddenly she asked herself, hadn't there been other storms, other blizzards? And through the worst of them hadn't he always reached her?

Clutched by the thought she stood rooted a minute. It was hard now to understand how she could have so deceived herself—how a moment of passion could have quieted within her not only conscience, but reason and discretion too. John always came. There could never be a storm to stop him. He was strong, inured to the cold. He had crossed the hills since his boyhood, knew every creek-bed and gully. It was madness to go on like this—to wait. While there was still time she must waken Steven, and hurry him away.

But in the bedroom again, standing at Steven's side, she hesitated. In his detachment from it all, in his quiet, even breathing, there was such sanity, such realism. For him nothing had happened; nothing would. If she wakened him he would only laugh and tell her to listen to the storm. Already it was long past midnight; either John had lost his way or not set out at all. And she knew that in his devotion there was nothing foolhardy. He would never risk a storm beyond his endurance, never permit himself a sacrifice likely to endanger her lot or future. They were both safe. No one would ever know. She must control herself—be sane like Steven.

For comfort she let her hand rest a while on Steven's shoulder. It would be easier were he awake now, with her, sharing her guilt; but gradually as she watched his handsome face in the glimmering light she came to understand that for him no guilt existed. Just as there had been no passion, no conflict. Nothing but the sane appraisal of their situation, nothing but the expectant little smile, and the arrogance of features that were different from John's. She winced deeply, remembering how she had fixed her eyes on those features, how she had tried to believe that so handsome and young, so different from John's, they must in themselves be her justification.

In the flickering light they were still young, still handsome. No longer her justification—she knew now—John was the man—but wistfully still, wondering sharply at their power and tyranny, she touched them a moment with her fingertips again.

She could not blame him. There had been no passion, no guilt; therefore there could be no responsibility. Looking down at him as he slept, half-smiling still, his lips relaxed in the conscienceless complacency of his achievement, she understood that thus he was revealed in his entirety—all there ever was or ever could be. John was the man. With him lay all the future. For tonight, slowly and contritely through the day and years to come, she would try to make amends.

Then she stole back to the kitchen, and without thought, impelled by overwhelming need again, returned to the door where the draught was bitter still. Gradually towards morning the storm began to spend itself. Its terror blast became a feeble, worn-out moan. Thc lcap of light and shadow sank, and a chill crept in again. Always the eaves creaked, tortured with wordless prophecy. Heedless of it all the clock ticked on in idiot content.

They found him the next day, less than a mile from home. Drifting with the storm he had run against his own pasture fence and overcome had frozen there, erect still, both hands clasping fast the wire.

'He was south of here,' they said wonderingly when she told them how he had come across the hills. 'Straight south—you'd wonder how he could have missed the buildings. It was the wind last night, coming every way at once. He shouldn't have tried. There was a double wheel around the moon.'

She looked past them a moment, then as if to herself said simply, 'If you knew him, though—John would try.'

It was later, when they had left her a while to be alone with him, that she knelt and touched his hand. Her eyes dimmed, it was still such a strong and patient hand; then, transfixed, they suddenly grew wide and clear. On the palm, white even against its frozen whiteness, was a little smear of paint.

1939

Eudora Welty

b. 1909

Eudora Welty's stories, like those of Flannery O'Connor, are often deeply rooted in the South. Welty has observed that southerners are 'born reciters' and 'southern talk is on the narrative side,' explaining that 'if you grew up in the South when things were relatively stable, when there was a lot of talk and so on, you got a great sense of the person's whole life. This is because you know all of the families. You know several generations because they all live together.' The South as a distinctive setting figures strongly in her work: 'I am myself touched off by place,' she explains. 'The place where I am and the place I know, and other places that familiarity with and love for my own make strange and lovely and enlightening to look into, are what set me to writing my stories.'

The importance of the South for Welty is secondary to the necessity for invention and craft: 'stories are *new* things, stories make words new: that is one of their illusions and part of their beauty,' Welty has said. 'The story is a vision; while it's being written, all choices must be its choices, and as these multiply upon one another, their field is growing too. The choices remain inevitable, in fact, through moving in a growing maze of possibilities that the writer, far from being dismayed at his presence on unknown ground . . . has learned to be grateful for, and excited by. The fiction writer has learned . . . that it is the very existence, the very multitude and clamour and threat and lure of *possibility*—all possibilities his work calls up for itself as it goes—that guides his story most delicately.' As these remarks suggest, the story remains Welty's preferred form, although she has written well-received novels and novellas as well.

Welty was born in Jackson, Mississippi, where she went to school, leaving to attend Mississippi State College for Women in Columbus and taking her B.A. (1929) from the University of Wisconsin. In order to find practical employment, she went to the Columbia School of Business the following year, and in 1933 began to work as a publicity agent for the State Office of Works Program Administration, travelling widely across Mississippi and writing feature stories. She drew on this experience when she began writing fiction, publishing her first story, 'Death of a Traveling Salesman', in *Manuscript* in 1936. Her first book of stories, *A Curtain of Green*, appeared in 1941. She continues to make her home in Jackson.

The setting of 'A Worn Path' is the Natchez Trace, a path between Natchez and Nashville originally used by Indians and then by river men and traders returning from the Mississippi. Phoenix Jackson's epic trek along the path, driven by the need to get medicine for her grandson, becomes an exploration of her character in which the old woman's courage, compassion, and selflessness emerge as she deals with the physical, psychological, natural, and man-made challenges to her progress on her errand of mercy.

'Why I Live at the P.O.' exemplifies another of Welty's strengths—the fine use of dialogue, of idiom, and of first-person narration to evoke the small catastrophes of daily life within a family. In this story, as the narrator's own foibles emerge in her minor-key provocations, all of them met with retaliatory escalation from family members with their own grievances to nurse, the collective psyche of the family is laid bare. But the domestic comedy of the story is mitigated by the real anger and sorrow that drive the narrator to take up residence at the post office, so that readers' responses to her situation become more complex.

'A Worn Path' was first published in the February 1941 issue of *Atlantic Monthly*, and 'Why I Live at the P.O.' in the April 1941 issue of the same magazine. Both stories were then collected in *A Curtain of Green*.

A Worn Path

It was December—a bright frozen day in the early morning. Far out in the country there was an old Negro woman with her head tied in a red rag, coming along a path through the pinewoods. Her name was Phoenix Jackson. She was very old and small and she walked slowly in the dark pine shadows, moving a little from side to side in her steps, with the balanced heaviness and lightness of a pendulum in a grandfather clock. She carried a thin, small cane made from an umbrella, and with this she kept tapping the frozen earth in front of her. This made a grave and persistent noise in the still air, that seemed meditative like the chirping of a solitary little bird.

She wore a dark striped dress reaching down to her shoe tops, and an equally long apron of bleached sugar sacks, with a full pocket: all neat and tidy, but every time she took a step she might have fallen over her shoelaces, which dragged from her unlaced shoes. She looked straight ahead. Her eyes were blue with age. Her skin had a pattern all of its own of numberless branching wrinkles and as though a whole little tree stood in the middle of her forehead, but a golden colour ran underneath, and the two knobs of her cheeks were illumined by a yellow burning under the dark. Under the red rag her hair came down on her neck in the frailest of ringlets, still black, and with an odour like copper.

Now and then there was a quivering in the thicket. Old Phoenix said, 'Out of my way, all you foxes, owls, beetles, jack rabbits, coons and wild animals! . . . Keep out from under these feet, little bob-whites. . . . Keep the big wild hogs out of my path. Don't let none of those come running my direction. I got a long way.' Under her small black-freckled hand her cane, limber as a buggy whip, would switch at the brush as if to rouse up any hiding things.

On she went. The woods were deep and still. The sun made the pine needles almost too bright to look at, up where the wind rocked. The cones dropped as light as feathers. Down in the hollow was the mourning dove—it was not too late for him.

The path ran up a hill. 'Seem like there is chains about my feet, time I get this far,' she said, in the voice of argument old people keep to use with themselves. 'Something always takes a hold of me on this hill—pleads I should stay.'

After she got to the top she turned and gave a full, severe look behind her where she had come. 'Up through pines,' she said at length. 'Now down through oaks.'

Her eyes opened their widest, and she started down gently. But before she got to the bottom of the hill a bush caught her dress.

Her fingers were busy and intent, but her skirts were full and long, so that before she could pull them free in one place they were caught in another. It was not possible to allow the dress to tear. 'I in the thorny bush,' she said. 'Thorns, you doing your appointed work. Never want to let folks pass, no sir. Old eyes thought you was a pretty little *green* bush.'

Finally, trembling all over, she stood free, and after a moment dared to stoop for her cane.

'Sun so high!' she cried, leaning back and looking, while the thick tears went over her eyes. 'The time getting all gone here.'

At the foot of this hill was a place where a log was laid across the creek.

'Now comes the trial,' said Phoenix.

Putting her right foot out, she mounted the log and shut her eyes. Lifting her skirt, levelling her cane fiercely before her, like a festival figure in some parade, she began to march across. Then she opened her eyes and she was safe on the other side.

'I wasn't as old as I thought,' she said.

But she sat down to rest. She spread her skirts on the bank around her and folded her hands over her knees. Up above her was a tree in a pearly cloud of mistletoe. She did not dare to close her eyes, and when a little boy brought her a plate with a slice of marble-cake on it she spoke to him. 'That would be acceptable,' she said. But when she went to take it there was just her own hand in the air.

So she left that tree, and had to go through a barbed-wire fence. There she had to creep and crawl, spreading her knees and stretching her fingers like a baby trying to climb the steps. But she talked loudly to herself: she could not let her dress be torn now, so late in the day, and she could not pay for having her arm or her leg sawed off if she got caught fast where she was.

At last she was safe through the fence and risen up out in the clearing. Big dead trees, like black men with one arm, were standing in the purple stalks of the withered cotton field. There sat a buzzard.

'Who you watching?'

In the furrow she made her way along.

'Glad this not the season for bulls,' she said, looking sideways, 'and the good Lord made his snakes to curl up and sleep in the winter. A pleasure I don't see no two-headed snake coming around that tree, where it come once. It took a while to get by him, back in the summer.'

She passed through the old cotton and went into a field of dead corn. It whispered and shook and was taller than her head. 'Through the maze now,' she said, for there was no path.

Then there was something tall, black, and skinny there, moving before her.

At first she took it for a man. It could have been a man dancing in the field. But she stood still and listened, and it did not make a sound. It was as silent as a ghost.

'Ghost,' she said sharply, 'who be you the ghost of? For I have heard of nary death close by.'

But there was no answer—only the ragged dancing in the wind.

She shut her eyes, reached out her hand, and touched a sleeve. She found a coat and inside that an emptiness, cold as ice.

'You scarecrow,' she said. Her face lighted. 'I ought to be shut up for good,' she said with laughter. 'My senses are gone. I too old. I the oldest people I ever know. Dance, old scarecrow,' she said, 'while I dancing with you.'

She kicked her foot over the furrow, and with mouth drawn down, shook her head once or twice in a little strutting way. Some husks blew down and whirled in streamers about her skirts.

Then she went on, patting her way from side to side with the cane, through the whispering field. At last she came to the end, to a wagon track where the silver grass blew between the red ruts. The quail were walking around like pullets, seeming all dainty and unseen.

'Walk pretty,' she said. 'This the easy place. This the easy going.'

She followed the track, swaying through the quiet bare fields, through the little strings of trees silver in their dead leaves, past cabins silver from weather, with the doors and windows boarded shut, all like old women under a spell sitting there. 'I walking in their sleep,' she said, nodding her head vigorously.

In a ravine she went where a spring was silently flowing through a hollow log. Old Phoenix bent and drank. 'Sweet-gum makes the water sweet,' she said, and drank more. 'Nobody know who made this well, for it was here when I was born.'

The track crossed a swampy part where the moss hung as white as lace from every limb. 'Sleep on, alligators, and blow your bubbles.' Then the track went into the road.

Deep, deep the road went down between the high green-coloured banks. Overhead the live-oaks met, and it was as dark as a cave.

A black dog with a lolling tongue came up out of the weeds by the ditch. She was meditating, and not ready, and when he came at her she only hit him a little with her cane. Over she went in the ditch, like a little puff of milkweed.

Down there, her senses drifted away. A dream visited her, and she reached her hand up, but nothing reached down and gave her a pull. So she lay there and presently went to talking. 'Old woman,' she said to herself, 'that black dog come up out of the weeds to stall you off, and now there he sitting on his fine tail, smiling at you.'

A white man finally came along and found her—a hunter, a young man, with his dog on a chain.

'Well, Granny!' he laughed. 'What are you doing there?'

'Lying on my back like a June-bug waiting to be turned over, mister,' she said, reaching up her hand.

He lifted her up, gave her a swing in the air, and set her down. 'Anything broken, Granny?'

'No sir, them old dead weeds is springy enough,' said Phoenix, when she had got her breath. 'I thank you for your trouble.'

'Where do you live, Granny?' he asked while the two dogs were growling at each other.

'Away back yonder, sir, behind the ridge. You can't even see it from here.'

'On your way home?'

'No sir, I going to town.'

'Why, that's too far! That's as far as I walk when I come out myself, and I get something for my trouble.' He patted the stuffed bag he carried, and there hung down a little closed claw. It was one of the bob-whites, with its beak hooked bitterly to show it was dead. 'Now you go on home, Granny!'

'I bound to go to town, mister,' said Phoenix. 'The time come around.'

He gave another laugh, filling the whole landscape. 'I know you old coloured people! Wouldn't miss going to town to see Santa Claus!'

But something held old Phoenix very still. The deep lines in her face went into a fierce and different radiation. Without warning, she had seen with her own eyes a flashing nickel fall out of the man's pocket onto the ground.

'How old are you, Granny?' he was saying.

'There is no telling, mister,' she said, 'no telling.'

Then she gave a little cry and clapped her hands and said, 'Git on away from here, dog! Look! Look at that dog!' She laughed as if in admiration. 'He ain't scared of nobody. He a big black dog.' She whispered, 'Sic him!'

'Watch me get rid of that cur,' said the man. 'Sic him, Pete! Sic him!'

Phoenix heard the dogs fighting, and heard the man running and throwing sticks. She even heard a gunshot. But she was slowly bending forward by that time, further and further forward, the lids stretched down over her eyes, as if she were doing this in her sleep. Her chin was lowered almost to her knees. The yellow palm of her hand came out from the fold of her apron. Her fingers slid down and along the ground under the piece of money with the grace and care they would have in lifting an egg from under a setting hen. Then she slowly straightened up, she stood erect, and the nickel was in her apron pocket. A bird flew by. Her lips moved. 'God watching me the whole time. I come to stealing.'

The man came back, and his own dog panted about them. 'Well, I scared him off that time,' he said, and then he laughed and lifted his gun, and pointed it at Phoenix.

She stood straight and faced him.

'Doesn't that gun scare you?' he said, still pointing it.

'No, sir, I seen plenty go off closer by, in my day, and for less than what I done,' she said, holding utterly still.

He smiled, and shouldered the gun. 'Well, Granny,' he said, 'you must be a hundred years old, and scared of nothing. I'd give you a dime if I had any money with me. But you take my advice and stay home, and nothing will happen to you.'

'I bound to go on my way, mister,' said Phoenix. She inclined her head in the red rag. Then they went in different directions, but she could hear the gun shooting again and again over the hill.

She walked on. The shadows hung from the oak trees to the road like curtains. Then she smelled wood-smoke, and smelled the river, and she saw a steeple and the cabins on their steep steps. Dozens of little black children whirled around her. There ahead was Natchez shining. Bells were ringing. She walked on.

In the paved city it was Christmas time. There were red and green electric lights strung and crisscrossed everywhere, and all turned on in the daytime. Old Phoenix would have been lost if she had not distrusted her eyesight and depended on her feet to know where to take her.

She paused quietly on the sidewalk where people were passing by. A lady came along in a crowd, carrying an armful of red-, green-, and silver-wrapped presents; she gave off perfume like the red roses in hot summer, and Phoenix stopped her.

'Please, missy, will you lace up my shoe?' She held up her foot.

'What do you want, Grandma?'

'See my shoe,' said Phoenix. 'Do all right for out in the country, but wouldn't look right to go in a big building.'

'Stand still then, Grandma,' said the lady. She put her packages down on the sidewalk beside her and laced and tied both shoes tightly.

'Can't lace 'em with a cane,' said Phoenix. 'Thank you, missy. I doesn't mind asking a nice lady to tie up my shoe, when I gets out on the street.'

Moving slowly and from side to side, she went into the big building, and into a tower of steps, where she walked up and around and around until her feet knew to stop.

She entered a door, and there she saw nailed up on the wall the document that had been stamped with the gold seal and framed in the gold frame, which matched the dream that was hung up in her head.

'Here I be,' she said. There was a fixed and ceremonial stiffness over her body.

'A charity case, I suppose,' said an attendant who sat at the desk before her.

But Phoenix only looked above her head. There was sweat on her face, the wrinkles in her skin shone like a bright net.

'Speak up, Grandma,' the woman said. 'What's your name? We must have your history, you know. Have you been here before? What seems to be the trouble with you?'

Old Phoenix only gave a twitch to her face as if a fly were bothering her.

'Are you deaf?' cried the attendant.

But then the nurse came in.

'Oh, that's just old Aunt Phoenix,' she said. 'She doesn't come for herself—she has a little grandson. She makes these trips as regular as clockwork. She lives away back of the Old Natchez Trace.' She bent down. 'Well, Aunt Phoenix, why don't you just take a seat? We won't keep you standing after your long trip.' She pointed.

The old woman sat down, bolt upright in the chair.

'Now, how is the boy?' asked the nurse.

Old Phoenix did not speak.

'I said, how is the boy?'

But Phoenix only waited and stared straight ahead, her face very solemn and withdrawn into rigidity.

'Is his throat any better?' asked the nurse. 'Aunt Phoenix, don't you hear me? Is your grandson's throat any better since the last time you came for the medicine?'

With her hands on her knees, the old woman waited, silent, erect, and motionless, just as if she were in armour.

'You mustn't take up our time this way, Aunt Phoenix,' the nurse said. 'Tell us quickly about your grandson, and get it over. He isn't dead, is he?'

At last there came a flicker and then a flame of comprehension across her face, and she spoke.

'My grandson. It was my memory had left me. There I sat and forgot why I made my long trip.'

'Forgot?' The nurse frowned. 'After you came so far?'

Then Phoenix was like an old woman begging a dignified forgiveness for waking up frightened in the night. 'I never did go to school, I was too old at the Surrender,' she said in a soft voice. 'I'm an old woman without an education. It was my memory fail me. My little grandson, he is just the same, and I forgot it in the coming.'

'Throat never heals, does it?' said the nurse, speaking in a loud, sure voice to old Phoenix. By now she had a card with something written on it, a little list. 'Yes. Swallowed lye. When was it?—January—two, three years ago—'

Phoenix spoke unasked now. 'No, missy, he not dead, he just the same. Every little while his throat begin to close up again, and he not able to swallow. He not get his breath. He not able to help himself. So the time come around, and I go on another trip for the soothing medicine.'

'All right. The doctor said as long as you came to get it, you could have it,' said the nurse. 'But it's an obstinate case.'

'My little grandson, he sit up there in the house all wrapped up, waiting by himself,' Phoenix went on. 'We is the only two left in the world. He suffer and it don't seem to put him back at all. He got a sweet look. He going to last. He wear a little patch quilt and peep out holding his mouth open like a little bird. I remembers so plain now. I not going to forget him again, no, the whole enduring time. I could tell him from all the others in creation.'

'All right.' The nurse was trying to hush her now. She brought her a bottle of medicine. 'Charity,' she said, making a check mark in a book.

Old Phoenix held the bottle close to her eyes, and then carefully put in into her pocket.

'It's Christmas time, Grandma,' said the attendant. 'Could I give you a few pennies out of my purse?'

'Five pennies is a nickel,' said Phoenix stiffly.

'Here's a nickel,' said the attendant.

Phoenix rose carefully and held out her hand. She received the nickel and then fished the other nickel out of her pocket and laid it beside the new one. She stared at her palm closely, with her head on one side.

Then she gave a tap with the cane on the floor.

'This is what come to me to do,' she said. 'I going to the store and buy my child a little windmill they sells, made out of paper. He going to find it hard to believe there such a thing in the world. I'll march myself back where he waiting, holding it straight up in this hand.'

She lifted her free hand, gave a little nod, turned around, and walked out of the doctor's office. Then her slow step began on the stairs, going down.

1941

Why I Live at the P.O.

I was getting along fine with Mama, Papa-Daddy, and Uncle Rondo until my sister Stella-Rondo just separated from her husband and came back home again. Mr Whitaker! Of course I went with Mr Whitaker first, when he first appeared here in China Grove, taking 'Pose Yourself' photos, and Stella-Rondo broke us up. Told him I was one-sided. Bigger on one side than the other, which is a deliberate, calculated falsehood: I'm the same. Stella-Rondo is exactly twelve months to the day younger than I am and for that reason she's spoiled.

She's always had anything in the world she wanted and then she'd throw it away. Papa-Daddy gave her this gorgeous Add-a-Pearl necklace when she was eight years old and she threw it away playing baseball when she was nine, with only two pearls.

So as soon as she got married and moved away from home the first thing she did was separate. From Mr Whitaker! This photographer with the pop-eyes she said she trusted. Came home from one of those towns up in Illinois and to our complete surprise brought this child of two.

Mama said she like to make her drop dead for a second. 'Here you had this marvellous blonde child and never so much as wrote your mother a word about it,' says Mama. 'I'm thoroughly ashamed of you.' But of course she wasn't.

Stella-Rondo just calmly takes off this *hat*, I wish you could see it. She says, 'Why, Mama, Shirley-T.'s adopted, I can prove it.'

'How?' says Mama, but all I says was, 'H'm!' There I was over the hot stove, trying to stretch two chickens over five people and a completely unexpected child into the bargain, without one moment's notice.

'What do you mean—"H'm!"?' says Stella-Rondo, and Mama says, 'I heard that, Sister.'

I said that oh, I didn't mean a thing, only that whoever Shirley-T. was, she was the spit-image of Papa-Daddy if he'd cut off his beard, which of course he'd never do in the world. Papa-Daddy's Mama's papa and sulks.

Stella-Rondo got furious! She said, 'Sister, I don't need to tell you you got a lot of nerve and always did have and I'll thank you to make no future reference to my adopted child whatsoever.'

'Very well,' I said. 'Very well, very well. Of course I noticed once she looks like Mr Whitaker's side too. That frown. She looks like a cross between Mr Whitaker and Papa-Daddy.'

'Well, all I can say is she isn't.'

'She looks exactly like Shirley Temple to me,' says Mama, but Shirley-T. just ran away from her.

So the first thing Stella-Rondo did at the table was turn Papa-Daddy against me.

'Papa-Daddy,' she says. He was trying to cut up his meat. 'Papa-Daddy!' I was taken completely by surprise. Papa-Daddy is about a million years old and's got this long-long beard. 'Papa-Daddy, Sister says she fails to understand why you don't cut off your beard.'

So Papa-Daddy l-a-y-s down his knife and fork! He's real rich. Mama says he is, he says he isn't. So he says, 'Have I heard correctly? You don't understand why I don't cut off my beard?'

'Why,' I says, 'Papa-Daddy, of course I understand, I did not say any such of a thing, the idea!'

He says, 'Hussy!'

I says, 'Papa-Daddy, you know I wouldn't any more want you to cut off your beard than the man in the moon. It was the farthest thing from my mind! Stella-Rondo sat there and made that up while she was eating breast of chicken.'

But he says, 'So the postmistress fails to understand why I don't cut off my beard. Which job I got you through my influence with the government. "Bird's nest"—is that what you call it?'

Not that it isn't the next to smallest P.O. in the entire state of Mississippi.

I says, 'Papa-Daddy,' I says, 'I didn't say any such of a thing, I never dreamed it was a bird's nest, I have always been grateful though this is the next to smallest P.O. in the state of Mississippi, and I do not enjoy being referred to as a hussy by my own grandfather.'

But Stella-Rondo says, 'Yes, you did say it too. Anybody in the world could of heard you, that had ears.'

'Stop right there,' says Mama, looking at *me*.

So I pulled my napkin straight back through the napkin ring and left the table.

As soon as I was out of the room Mama says, 'Call her back; or she'll starve to death,' but Papa-Daddy says, 'This is the beard I started growing on the Coast when I was fifteen years old.' He would of gone on till nightfall if Shirley-T. hadn't lost the Milky Way she ate in Cairo.

So Papa-Daddy says, 'I am going out and lie in the hammock, and you can all sit here and remember my words: I'll never cut off my beard as long as I live, even one inch, and I don't appreciate it in you at all.' Passed right by me in the hall and went straight out and got in the hammock.

It would be a holiday. It wasn't five minutes before Uncle Rondo suddenly appeared in the hall in one of Stella-Rondo's fresh-coloured kimonos, all cut on the bias, like something Mr Whitaker probably thought was gorgeous.

'Uncle Rondo!' I says. 'I didn't know who that was! Where are you going?'

'Sister,' he says, 'get out of my way, I'm poisoned.'

'If you're poisoned stay away from Papa-Daddy,' I says. 'Keep out of the hammock. Papa-Daddy will certainly beat you on the head if you come within forty miles of him. He thinks I deliberately said he ought to cut off his beard after he got me the P.O., and I've told him and told him and told him, and he acts like he just don't hear me. Papa-Daddy must of gone stone deaf.'

'He picked a fine day to do it then,' says Uncle Rondo, and before you could say 'Jack Robinson' flew out in the yard.

What he'd really done, he'd drunk another bottle of that prescription. He does it every single Fourth of July as sure as shooting, and it's horribly expensive. Then he falls over in the hammock and snores. So he insisted on zigzagging right on out to the hammock, looking like a half-wit.

Papa-Daddy woke up with this horrible yell and right there without moving an inch he tried to turn Uncle Rondo against me. I heard every word he said. Oh, he told Uncle Rondo I didn't learn to read till I was eight years old and he didn't see how in the world I ever got the mail put up at the P.O., much less read it all, and he said if Uncle Rondo could only fathom the lengths he had gone to get me that job! And he said on the other hand he thought Stella-Rondo had a brilliant mind and deserved credit for getting out of town. All the time he was just lying there swinging as pretty as you please and looping out his beard, and poor Uncle Rondo was *pleading* with him to slow down the hammock, it was making him as dizzy as a witch to watch it. But that's what Papa-Daddy likes about a hammock. So Uncle Rondo was too dizzy to get turned against me for the time being. He's Mama's only brother and is a good case of a one-track mind. Ask anybody. A certified pharmacist.

Just then I heard Stella-Rondo raising the upstairs window. While she was married she got this peculiar idea that it's cooler with the windows shut and locked. So she has to raise the window before she can make a soul hear her outdoors.

So she raises the window and says, *'Oh!'* You would have thought she was mortally wounded.

Uncle Rondo and Papa-Daddy didn't even look up, but kept right on with what they were doing. I had to laugh.

I flew up the stairs and threw the door open! I says, 'What in the wide world's the matter, Stella-Rondo? You mortally wounded?'

'No,' she says, 'I am not mortally wounded but I wish you would do me the favour of looking out that window there and telling me what you see.'

So I shade my eyes and look out the window.

'I see the front yard,' I says.

'Don't you see any human beings?' she says.

'I see Uncle Rondo trying to run Papa-Daddy out of the hammock,' I says. 'Nothing more. Naturally, it's so suffocating-hot in the house, with all the windows shut and locked, everybody who cares to stay in their right mind will have to go out and get in the hammock before this Fourth of July is over.'

'Don't you notice anything different about Uncle Rondo?' asks Stella-Rondo.

'Why, no, except he's got on some terrible-looking, flesh-coloured contraption I wouldn't be found dead in, is all I can see,' I says.

'Never mind, you won't be found dead in it, because it happens to be part of my trousseau, and Mr Whitaker took several dozen photographs of me in it,' says Stella-Rondo. 'What on earth could Uncle Rondo *mean* by wearing part of my trousseau out in the broad open daylight without saying so much as 'Kiss my foot', *knowing* I only got home this morning after my separation and hung my negligee up on the bathroom door, just as nervous as I could be?'

'I'm sure I don't know, and what do you expect me to do about it?' I says. 'Jump out the window?'

'No, I expect nothing of the kind, I simply declare that Uncle Rondo looks like a fool in it, that's all,' she says, 'It makes me sick to my stomach.'

'Well, he looks as good as he can,' I says. 'As good as anybody in reason could.' I stood up for Uncle Rondo, please remember. And I said to Stella-Rondo, 'I think I would do well not to criticize so freely if I were you and came home with a two-year-old child I had never said a word about, and no explanation whatever about my separation.'

'I asked you the instant I entered this house not to refer one more time to my adopted child, and you gave me your word of honour you would not,' was all Stella-Rondo would say, and started pulling out every one of her eyebrows with some cheap Kress tweezers.

So I merely slammed the door behind me and went down and made some green-tomato pickle. Somebody had to do it. Of course Mama had turned both the Negroes loose; she always said no earthly power could hold one anyway on the Fourth of July, so she wouldn't even try. It turned out that Jaypan fell in the lake and came within a very narrow limit of drowning.

So Mama trots in. Lifts up the lid and says, 'H'm! Not very good for your Uncle Rondo in his precarious condition, I must say. Or poor little adopted Shirley-T. Shame on you!'

That made me tired. I says, 'Well, Stella-Rondo had better thank her lucky stars it was her instead of me came trotting in with that very peculiar-looking child. Now if it had been me that trotted in from Illinois and brought a peculiar-looking child of two, I shudder to think of the reception I'd of got, much less controlled the diet of an entire family.'

'But you must remember, Sister, that you were never married to Mr Whitaker in the first place and didn't go up to Illinois to live,' says Mama, shaking a spoon in my face. 'If you had I would of been just as overjoyed to see you and your littled adopted girl as I was to see Stella-Rondo, when you wound up with your separation and came on back home.'

'You would not,' I says.

'Don't contradict me, I would,' says Mama.

But I said she couldn't convince me though she talked till she was blue in the face. Then I said, 'Besides, you know as well as I do that that child is not adopted.'

'She most certainly is adopted,' says Mama, stiff as a poker.

I says, 'Why, Mama, Stella-Rondo had her just as sure as anything in this world, and just too stuck up to admit it.'

'Why, Sister,' said Mama. 'Here I thought we were going to have a pleasant Fourth of July, and you start right out not believing a word your own baby sister tells you!'

'Just like Cousin Annie Flo. Went to her grave denying the facts of life,' I remind Mama.

'I told you if you ever mentioned Annie Flo's name I'd slap your face,' says Mama, and slaps my face.

'All right, you wait and see,' I says.

'I,' says Mama, '*I* prefer to take my children's word for anything when it's humanly possible.' You ought to see Mama, she weighs two hundred pounds and has real tiny feet.

Just then something perfectly horrible occurred to me.

'Mama,' I says, 'can that child talk?' I simply had to whisper! 'Mama, I wonder if that child can be—you know—in any way? Do you realize,' I says, 'that she hasn't spoken one single, solitary word to a human being up to this minute? This is the way she looks,' I says, and I looked like this.

Well, Mama and I just stood there and stared at each other. It was horrible!

'I remember well that Joe Whitaker frequently drank like a fish,' says Mama. 'I believed to my soul he drank *chemicals*.' And without another word she marches to the foot of the stairs and calls Stella-Rondo.

'Stella-Rondo? O-o-o-o-o! Stella-Rondo!'

'What?' says Stella-Rondo from upstairs. Not even the grace to get up off the bed.

'Can that child of yours talk?' asks Mama.

Stella-Rondo says, 'Can she what?'

'Talk! Talk!' says Mama. 'Burdyburdyburdyburdy!'

So Stella-Rondo yells back, 'Who says she can't talk?'

'Sister says so,' says Mama.

'You didn't have to tell me, I know whose word of honour don't mean a thing in this house,' says Stella-Rondo.

And in a minute the loudest Yankee voice I ever heard in my life yells out, 'OE'm Pop-OE the Sailor-r-r-r Ma-a-an!' and then somebody jumps up and down in the upstairs hall. In another second the house would of fallen down.

'Not only talks, she can tap-dance!' calls Stella-Rondo. 'Which is more than some people I won't name can do.'

'Why, the little precious darling thing!' Mama says, so surprised. 'Just as smart as she can be!' Starts talking baby talk right there. Then she turns on me. 'Sister, you ought to be thoroughly ashamed! Run upstairs this instant and apologize to Stella-Rondo and Shirley-T.'

'Apologize for what?' I says. 'I merely wondered if the child was normal, that's all. Now that she's proved she is, why, I have nothing further to say.'

But Mama just turned on her heel and flew out, furious. She ran right upstairs and hugged the baby. She believed it was adopted. Stella-Rondo hadn't done a thing but turn her against me from upstairs while I stood there helpless over the hot stove. So that made Mama, Papa-Daddy and the baby all on Stella-Rondo's side.

Next, Uncle Rondo.

I must say that Uncle Rondo has been marvellous to me at various times in the past and I was completely unprepared to be made to jump out of my skin, the way it turned out. Once Stella-Rondo did something perfectly horrible to him—broke a chain letter from Flanders Field—and he took the radio back he had given her and gave it to me. Stella-Rondo was furious! For six months we all had to call her Stella instead of Stella-Rondo, or she wouldn't answer. I always thought Uncle Rondo had all the brains of the entire family. Another time he sent me to Mammoth Cave, with all expenses paid.

But this would be the day he was drinking that prescription, the Fourth of July.

So at supper Stella-Rondo speaks up and says she thinks Uncle Rondo ought to try to eat a little something. So finally Uncle Rondo said he would try a little cold biscuits and ketchup, but that was all. So *she* brought it to him.

'Do you think it wise to disport with ketchup in Stella-Rondo's flesh-coloured kimono?' I says. Trying to be considerate! If Stella-Rondo couldn't watch out for her trousseau, somebody had to.

'Any objections?' asks Uncle Rondo, just about to pour out all the ketchup.

'Don't mind what she says, Uncle Rondo,' says Stella-Rondo. 'Sister has been devoting this solid afternoon to sneering out my bedroom window at the way you look.'

'What's that?' says Uncle Rondo. Uncle Rondo has got the most terrible temper in the world. Anything is liable to make him tear the house down if it comes at the wrong time.

So Stella-Rondo says, 'Sister says, "Uncle Rondo certainly does look like a fool in that pink kimono!" '

Do you remember who it was really said that?

Uncle Rondo spills out all the ketchup and jumps out of his chair and tears off the kimono and throws it down on the dirty floor and puts his foot on it. It had to be sent all the way to Jackson to the cleaners and re-pleated.

'So that's your opinion of your Uncle Rondo, is it?' he says. 'I look like a fool, do I? Well, that's the last straw. A whole day in this house with nothing to do, and then to hear you come out with a remark like that behind my back!'

'I didn't say any such of a thing, Uncle Rondo,' I says, 'and I'm not saying who did, either. Why, I think you look all right. Just try to take care of yourself and not talk and eat at the same time,' I says. 'I think you better go lie down.'

'Lie down my foot,' says Uncle Rondo. I ought to of known by that he was fixing to do something perfectly horrible.

So he didn't do anything that night in the precarious state he was in—just played Casino with Mama and Stella-Rondo and Shirley-T. and gave Shirley-T. a nickel with a head on both sides. It tickled her nearly to death, and she called him 'Papa'. But at 6:30 a.m. the next morning, he threw a whole five-cent package of some unsold one-inch firecrackers from the store as hard as he could into my bedroom and they every one went off. Not one bad one in the string. Anybody else, there'd be one that wouldn't go off.

Well, I'm just terribly susceptible to noise of any kind, the doctor has always told me I was the most sensitive person he had ever seen in his whole life, and I was simply prostrated. I couldn't eat! People tell me they heard it as far as the cemetery, and old Aunt Jep Patterson, that had been holding her own so good, thought it was Judgement Day and she was going to meet her whole family. It's usually so quiet here.

And I'll tell you it didn't take me any longer than a minute to make up my mind what to do. There I was with the whole entire house on Stella-Rondo's side and turned against me. If I have anything at all I have pride.

So I just decided I'd go straight down to the P.O. There's plenty of room there in the back, I says to myself.

Well! I made no bones about letting the family catch on to what I was up to. I didn't try to conceal it.

The first thing they knew, I marched in where they were all playing Old Maid and pulled the electric oscillating fan out by the plug, and everything got real hot. Next I snatched the pillow I'd done the needle-point on right off the davenport from behind Papa-Daddy. He went 'Ugh!' I beat Stella-Rondo up the stairs and finally found my charm bracelet in her bureau drawer under a picture of Nelson Eddy.

'So that's the way the land lies,' says Uncle Rondo. There he was, piecing on the ham. 'Well, Sister, I'll be glad to donate my army cot if you got any place to set it up, providing you'll leave right this minute and let me get some peace.' Uncle Rondo was in France.

'Thank you kindly for the cot and "peace" is hardly the word I would select if I had to resort to firecrackers at 6:30 a.m. in a young girl's bedroom,' I says back to him. 'And as to where I intend to go, you seem to forget my position as postmistress of China Grove, Mississippi.' I says. 'I've always got the P.O.'

Well, that made them all sit up and take notice.

I went out front and started digging up some four-o'clocks to plant around the P.O.

'Ah-ah-ah!' says Mama, raising the window. 'Those happen to be my four-o'clocks. Everything planted in that star is mine. I've never known you to make anything grow in your life.'

'Very well,' I says. 'But I take the fern. Even you, Mama, can't stand there and deny that I'm the one watered the fern. And I happen to know where I can send in a box top and get a packet of one thousand mixed seeds, no two the same kind, free.'

'Oh, where?' Mama wants to know.

But I says, 'Too late. You 'tend to your house, and I'll 'tend to mine. You hear things like that all the time if you know how to listen to the radio. Perfectly marvelous offers. Get anything you want free.'

So I hope to tell you I marched in and got that radio, and they could of all bit a nail in two, especially Stella-Rondo, that it used to belong to, and she well knew she couldn't get it back, I'd sue for it like a shot. And I very politely took the sewing-machine motor I helped pay the most on to give Mama for Christmas back in 1929, and a good big calendar, with the first-aid remedies on it. The thermometer and the Hawaiian ukulele certainly were rightfully mine, and I stood on the step-ladder and got all my watermelon-rind preserves and every fruit and vegetable I'd put up, every jar.

Then I began to pull the tacks out of the bluebird wall vases on the archway to the dining room.

'Who told you you could have those, Miss Priss?' says Mama, fanning as hard as she could.

'I bought 'em and I'll keep track of 'em,' I says, 'I'll tack 'em up one on each side of the post-office window, and you can see 'em when you come to ask me for your mail, if you're so dead to see 'em.'

'Not I! I'll never darken the door to that post office again if I live to be a hundred,' Mama says. 'Ungrateful child! After all the money we spent on you at the Normal.'

'Me either,' says Stella-Rondo. 'You can just let my mail lie there and *rot*, for all I care. I'll never come and relieve you of a single, solitary piece.'

'I should worry,' I says. 'And who you think's going to sit down and write you all those big fat letters and postcards, by the way? Mr Whitaker? Just because he was the only man ever dropped down in China Grove and you got him—unfairly—is he going to sit down and write you a lengthy correspondence after you come home giving no rhyme nor reason whatsoever for your separation and no explanation for the presence of that child? I may not have your brilliant mind, but I fail to see it.'

So Mama says, 'Sister, I've told you a thousand times that Stella-Rondo simply got homesick, and this child is far too big to be hers,' and she says, 'Now, why don't you all just sit down and play Casino?'

Then Shirley-T. sticks out her tongue at me in this perfectly horrible way. She has no more manners than the man in the moon. I told her she was going to cross her eyes like that some day and they'd stick.

'It's too late to stop me now,' I says. 'You should have tried that yesterday. I'm going to the P.O. and the only way you can possibly see me is to visit me there.'

So Papa-Daddy says, 'You'll never catch me setting foot in that post office, even if I should take a notion into my head to write a letter some place.' He says, 'I won't have you reachin' out of that little old window with a pair of shears and cuttin' off any beard of mine. I'm too smart for you!'

'We all are,' says Stella-Rondo.

But I said, 'If you're so smart, where's Mr Whitaker?'

So then Unclo Rondo says, 'I'll thank you from now on to stop reading all the orders I get on postcards and telling everybody in China Grove what you think is the matter with them,' but I says, 'I draw my own conclusions and will continue in the future to draw them.' I says, 'If people want to write their inmost secrets on penny postcards, there's nothing in the wide world you can do about it, Uncle Rondo.'

'And if you think we'll ever *write* another postcard you're sadly mistaken,' says Mama.

'Cutting off your nose to spite your face then,' I says. 'But if you're all determined to have no more to do with the U.S. mail, think of this: What will Stella-Rondo do now, if she wants to tell Mr Whitaker to come after her?'

'Wah!' says Stella-Rondo. I knew she'd cry. She had a conniption fit right there in the kitchen.

'It will be interesting to see how long she holds out,' I says. 'And now—I am leaving.'

'Good-bye,' says Uncle Rondo.

'Oh, I declare,' says Mama, 'to think that a family of mine should quarrel on the Fourth of July, or the day after, over Stella-Rondo leaving old Mr Whitaker and having the sweetest little adopted child! It looks like we'd all be glad!'

'Wah!' says Stella-Rondo, and has a fresh conniption fit.

'*He* left *her*—you mark my words,' I says. 'That's Mr Whitaker. I know Mr Whitaker. After all, I knew him first. I said from the beginning he'd up and leave her. I foretold every single thing that's happened.'

'Where did he go?' asks Mama.

'Probably to the North Pole, if he knows whats good for him,' I says.

But Stella-Rondo just bawled and wouldn't say another word. She flew to her room and slammed the door.

'Now look what you've gone and done, Sister,' says Mama. 'You go apologize.'

'I haven't got time, I'm leaving,' I says.

'Well, what are you waiting around for,' asks Uncle Rondo.

So I just picked up the kitchen clock and marched off, without saying 'Kiss my foot' or anything, and never did tell Stella-Rondo good-bye.

There was a girl going along on a little wagon right in front.

'Girl,' I says, 'come help me haul these things down the hill, I'm going to live in the post office.'

Took her nine trips in her express wagon. Uncle Rondo came out on the porch and threw her a nickel.

And that's the last I've laid eyes on any of my family or my family laid eyes on me for five solid days and nights. Stella-Rondo may be telling the most horrible tales in the world about Mr Whitaker, but I haven't heard them. As I tell everybody, I draw my own conclusions.

But oh, I like it here. It's ideal, as I've been saying. You see, I've got everything cater-cornered, the way I like it. Hear the radio? All the war news. Radio, sewing machine, book ends, ironing board and that great big piano lamp—peace, that's what I like. Butter-bean vines planted all along the front where the strings are.

Of course, there's not much mail. My family are naturally the main people in China Grove, and if they prefer to vanish from the face of the earth, for all the mail they get or the mail they write, why, I'm not going to open my mouth. Some of the folks here in town are taking up for me and some turned against me. I know which is which. There are always people who will quit buying stamps just to get on the right side of Papa-Daddy.

But here I am, and here I'll stay. I want the world to know I'm happy.

And if Stella-Rondo should come to me this minute, on bended knees, and *attempt* to explain the incidents of her life with Mr Whitaker, I'd simply put my fingers in both ears and refuse to listen.

1941

Bernard Malamud

1914-86

'I love the pleasures of the short story,' said Bernard Malamud. 'One of them is the fast payoff. Whatever happens happens quickly.' In a 1975 interview, he explained why he liked the short story form: 'I like packing a self or two into a few pages, predicting lifetimes. The drama is terse, happens faster, and is often outlandish. A short story is a way of indicating the complexity of life in a few pages, producing the surprise and effect of a profound knowledge in a short time. There's, among other things, a drama, a resonance, of the reconciliation of opposites: much to say, little time to say it, something like the effect of a poem.' From the beginning of his career, he was attracted to the short story: 'I confess having been longer in love with short fiction. If one begins early in life to make up and tell stories he has a better chance to be heard out if he keeps them short.'

Malamud was born in Brooklyn, New York to immigrant parents who ran a grocery store. After taking his B.A. (1936) from City College in New York and M.A. (1942) from Columbia, Malamud began writing short stories and teaching high school in New York. In 1950 he moved west to teach at Oregon State University. He moved back east in 1961 to Vermont, where he took a teaching position at Bennington College; he remained on the faculty at Bennington until his death.

In novels like *The Natural* (1952), *The Assistant* (1957), and *The Fixer* (1966) as well as in his short stories, Malamud's finest gift is his exploration of characters who live on the margins of society and come through suffering to a measure of insight into their condition and to a renewed sense of relationship with their fellow man. The essential seriousness of his moral vision is often leavened by his sharp comic sense, which emerges in dialogue, description, and deft turns of plot. In 'The Magic Barrel', Leo Finkle, the rabbinical student, must suffer the loss of his idealized and faltering love of God in order to acknowledge his human desire for the marriage broker's fallen daughter; the surprising developments in the relationship between Finkle and Pinye Salzman, which seem at first to accentuate the worldliness of the marriage broker in contrast to Finkle's devoutness, are typical of the reversals Malamud creates to achieve his fictional effects.

'The Jewbird' turns on the several attitudes of the Cohen family toward the needs of the bird for food and shelter, and more vitally, for compassion and community. In their responses to the world-weary (and all too human) reflections of 'Mr Schwartz', Malamud presents his readers with an instructive exploration of intolerance.

'The Magic Barrel' was first published in the November 1954 issue of *Partisan Review* and then collected in 1958 in the book of the same title. 'The Jewbird' was first published in the 11 April 1963 issue of *The Reporter* and then collected in *Idiots First* (1963).

The Magic Barrel

Not long ago there lived in uptown New York, in a small, almost meagre room, though crowded with books, Leo Finkle, a rabbinical student at the Yeshiva University. Finkle, after six years of study, was to be ordained in June and had been advised by an acquaintance that he might find it easier to win himself a congregation if he were married. Since he had no present prospects of marriage, after two tormented days of turning it over in his mind, he called in Pinye Salzman, a marriage broker whose two-line advertisement he had read in the *Forward*.

The matchmaker appeared one night out of the dark fourth-floor hallway of the greystone rooming house where Finkle lived, grasping a black, strapped portfolio that had been worn thin with use. Salzman, who had been long in the business, was of slight but dignified build, wearing an old hat, and an overcoat too short and tight for him. He smelled frankly of fish, which he loved to eat, and although he was missing a few teeth, his presence was not displeasing, because of an amiable manner curiously contrasted with mournful eyes. His voice, his lips, his wisp of beard, his bony fingers were animated, but give him a moment of repose and his mild blue eyes revealed a depth of sadness, a characteristic that put Leo a little at ease although the situation, for him, was inherently tense.

He at once informed Salzman why he had asked him to come, explaining that but for his parents, who had married comparatively late in life, he was alone in the world. He had for six years devoted himself almost entirely to his studies, as a result of which, understandably, he had found himself without time for social life and the company of young women. Therefore he thought it the better part of trial and error—of embarrassing fumbling—to call in an experienced person to advise him on these matters. He remarked in passing that the function of the marriage broker was ancient and honourable, highly approved in the Jewish community, because it made practical the necessary without hindering joy. Moreover, his own parents had been brought together by a matchmaker. They had made, if not a financially profitable marriage—since neither had possessed any worldly goods to speak of—at least a successful one in the sense of their everlasting devotion to each other. Salzman listened in embarrassed surprise, sensing a sort of apology. Later, however, he experienced a glow of pride in his work, an emotion that had left him years ago, and he heartily approved of Finkle.

The two went to their business. Leo had led Salzman to the only clear place in the room, a table near a window that overlooked the lamp-lit city. He seated himself at the matchmaker's side but facing him, attempting by an act of will to suppress the unpleasant tickle in his throat. Salzman eagerly unstrapped his portfolio and removed a loose rubber band from a thin packet of much-handled cards. As he flipped through them, a gesture and sound that physically hurt Leo, the student pretended not to see and gazed steadfastly out the window. Although it was still February, winter was on its last legs, signs of which he had for the first time in years begun to notice. He now observed the round white moon, moving high in the sky through a cloud menagerie, and watched with half-open mouth as it penetrated a huge hen, and dropped out of her like an egg laying itself. Salzman, though pretending through eyeglasses he had just slipped on to be engaged in scanning the writing on the cards, stole occasional glances at the young man's distinguished face, noting with pleasure the long, severe scholar's nose, brown eyes heavy with learning, sensitive yet ascetic lips, and a certain almost hollow quality of the dark cheeks. He gazed around at shelves upon shelves of books and let out a soft, contented sigh.

When Leo's eyes fell upon the cards, he counted six spread out in Salzman's hand.

'So few?' he asked in disappointment.

'You wouldn't believe me how much cards I got in my office,' Salzman replied. 'The drawers are already filled to the top, so I keep them now in a barrel, but is every girl good for a new rabbi?'

Leo blushed at this, regretting all he had revealed of himself in a curriculum vitae he had sent to Salzman. He had thought it best to acquaint him with his strict standards and specifications, but in having done so, felt he had told the marriage broker more than was absolutely necessary.

He hesitantly inquired, 'Do you keep photographs of your clients on file?'

'First comes family, amount of dowry, also what kind promises,' Salzman replied, unbuttoning his tight coat and settling himself in the chair. 'After comes pictures, rabbi.'

'Call me Mr. Finkle. I'm not yet a rabbi.'

Salzman said he would, but instead called him doctor, which he changed to rabbi when Leo was not listening too attentively.

Salzman adjusted his horn-rimmed spectacles, gently cleared his throat, and read in an eager voice the contents of the top card:

'Sophie P. Twenty-four years. Widow one year. No children. Educated high school and two years college. Father promises eight thousand dollars. Has wonderful wholesale business. Also real estate. On the mother's side comes teachers, also one actor. Well known on Second Avenue.'

Leo gazed up in surprise. 'Did you say a widow?'

'A widow doesn't mean spoiled, rabbi. She lived with her husband maybe four months. He was a sick boy she made a mistake to marry him.'

'Marrying a widow has never entered my mind.'

'This is because you have no experience. A widow, especially if she is young and healthy like this girl, is a wonderful person to marry. She will be thankful to you the rest of her life. Believe me, if I was looking now for a bride, I would marry a widow.'

Leo reflected, then shook his head.

Salzman hunched his shoulders in an almost imperceptible gesture of disappointment. He placed the card down on the wooden table and began to read another:

'Lily H. High school teacher. Regular. Not a substitute. Has savings and new Dodge car. Lived in Paris one year. Father is successful dentist thirty-five years. Interested in professional man. Well-Americanized family. Wonderful opportunity.

'I know her personally,' said Salzman. 'I wish you could see this girl. She is a doll. Also very intelligent. All day you could talk to her about books and theyater and what not. She also knows current events.'

'I don't believe you mentioned her age?'

'Her age?' Salzman said, raising his brows. 'Her age is thirty-two years.'

Leo said after a while. 'I'm afraid that seems a little too old.'

Salzman let out a laugh. 'So how old are you, rabbi?'

'Twenty-seven.'

'So what is the difference, tell me, between twenty-seven and thirty-two? My own wife is seven years older than me. So what did I suffer?—Nothing. If Rothschild's a daughter wants to marry you, would you say on account her age, no?'

'Yes,' Leo said dryly.

Salzman shook off the no in the yes. 'Five years don't mean a thing. I give you my word that when you will live with her for one week you will forget her age. What does it mean five years—that she lived more and knows more than somebody who is younger? On this girl, God bless her, years are not wasted. Each one that it comes makes better the bargain.'

'What subject does she teach in high school?'

'Languages. If you heard the way she speaks French, you will think it is music. I am in the business twenty-five years, and I recommend her with my whole heart. Believe me, I know what I'm talking, rabbi.'

'What's on the next card?' Leo said abruptly.

Salzman reluctantly turned up the third card:

'Ruth K. Nineteen years. Honour student. Father offers thirteen thousand cash to the right bridegroom. He is a medical doctor. Stomach specialist with marvelous practice. Brother-in-law owns own garment business. Particular people.'

Salzman looked as if he had read his trump card.

'Did you say nineteen?' Leo asked with interest.

'On the dot.'

'Is she attractive?' He blushed. 'Pretty?'

Salzman kissed his fingertips. 'A little doll. On this I give you my word. Let me call the father tonight and you will see what means pretty.'

But Leo was troubled. 'You're sure she's that young?'

'This I am positive. The father will show you the birth certificate.'

'Are you positive there isn't something wrong with her?' Leo insisted.

'Who says there is wrong?'

'I don't understand why an American girl her age should go to a marriage broker.'

Leo flushed. 'I am pressed for time.'

A smile spread over Salzman's face.

'So for the same reason you went, she comes.'

Salzman, realizing he had been tactless, quickly explained. 'The father came, not her. He wants she should have the best, so he looks around himself. When we will locate the right boy he will introduce him and encourage. This makes a better marriage than if a young girl without experience takes for herself. I don't have to tell you this.'

'But don't you think this young girl believes in love?' Leo spoke uneasily.

Salzman was about to guffaw but caught himself and said soberly, 'Love comes with the right person, not before.'

Leo parted dry lips but did not speak. Noticing that Salzman had snatched a glance at the next card, he cleverly asked, 'How is her health?'

'Perfect,' Salzman said, breathing with difficulty. 'Of course, she is a little lame on her right foot from an auto accident that it happened to her when she was twelve years, but nobody notices on account she is so brilliant and also beautiful.'

Leo got up heavily and went to the window. He felt curiously bitter and upbraided himself for having called in the marriage broker. Finally, he shook his head.

'Why not?' Salzman persisted, the pitch of his voice rising.

'Because I detest stomach specialists.'

'So what do you care what is his business? After you marry her do you need him? Who says he must come every Friday night in your house?'

Ashamed of the way the talk was going, Leo dismissed Salzman, who went home with heavy, melancholy eyes.

Though he had felt only relief at the marriage broker's departure, Leo was in low spirits the next day. He explained it as arising from Salzman's failure to produce a suitable bride for him. He did not care for his type of clientele. But when Leo found himself hesitating whether to seek out another matchmaker, one more polished than Pinye, he wondered if it could be—his protestations to the contrary, and although he honoured his father and mother—that he did not, in essence, care for the matchmaking institution? This thought he quickly put out of mind yet found himself still upset. All day he ran around in the woods—missed an important appointment, forgot to give out his laundry, walked out of a Broadway cafeteria without paying and had to run back with the ticket in his hand; had even not recognized his landlady in the street when she passed with a friend and courteously called out, 'A good evening to you, Doctor Finkle.' By nightfall, however, he had regained sufficient calm to sink his nose into a book and there found peace from his thoughts.

Almost at once there came a knock on the door. Before Leo could say enter, Salzman, commercial cupid, was standing in the room. His face was grey and meagre, his expression hungry, and he looked as if he would expire on his feet. Yet the marriage broker managed, by some trick of the muscles, to display a broad smile.

'So good evening, I am invited?'

Leo nodded, disturbed to see him again, yet unwilling to ask the man to leave.

Beaming still, Salzman laid his portfolio on the table. 'Rabbi, I got for you tonight good news.'

'I've asked you not to call me rabbi. I'm still a student.'

'Your worries are finished. I have for you a first-class bride.'

'Leave me in peace concerning this subject.' Leo pretended lack of interest.

'The world will dance at your wedding.'

'Please, Mr Salzman, no more.'

'But first come back my strength,' Salzman said weakly. He fumbled with the portfolio straps and took out of the leather case an oily paper bag, from which he extracted a hard, seeded roll and a small smoked whitefish. With a quick hand he stripped the fish out of its skin and began ravenously to chew. 'All day in a rush,' he muttered.

Leo watched him eat.

'A sliced tomato you have maybe?' Salzman hesitantly inquired.

'No.'

The marriage broker shut his eyes and ate. When he had finished he carefully cleaned up the crumbs and rolled up the remains of the fish, in the paper bag. His spectacled eyes roamed the room until he discovered, amid some piles of books, a one-burner gas stove. Lifting his hat he humbly asked, 'A glass tea you got, rabbi?'

Conscience-stricken, Leo rose and brewed the tea. He served it with a chunk of lemon and two cubes of lump sugar, delighting Salzman.

After he had drunk his tea, Salzman's strength and good spirits were restored.

'So tell me, rabbi,' he said amiably, 'you considered some more the three clients I mentioned yesterday?'

'There was no need to consider.'

'Why not?'

'None of them suits me.'

'What then suits you?'

Leo let it pass because he could give only a confused answer.

Without waiting for a reply, Salzman asked, 'You remember this girl I talked to you—the high school teacher?'

'Age thirty-two?'

But, surprisingly, Salzman's face lit in a smile. 'Age twenty-nine.'

Leo shot him a look. 'Reduced from thirty-two?'

'A mistake,' Salzman avowed. 'I talked today with the dentist. He took me to his safety deposit box and showed me the birth certificate. She was twenty-nine years last August. They made her a party in the mountains where she went for her vacation. When her father spoke to me the first time I forgot to write the age and I told you thirty-two, but now I remember this was a different client, a widow.'

'The same one you told me about, I thought she was twenty-four?'

'A different. Am I responsible that the world is filled with widows?'

'No, but I'm not interested in them, nor, for that matter, in schoolteachers.'

Salzman pulled his clasped hands to his breast. Looking at the ceiling he devoutly exclaimed, 'Yiddishe kinder, what can I say to somebody that he is not interested in high school teachers? So what then you are interested?'

Leo flushed but controlled himself.

'In what else will you be interested,' Salzman went on, 'if you not interested in this fine girl that she speaks four languages and has personally in the bank ten thousand dollars? Also her father guarantees further twelve thousand. Also she has a new car, wonderful clothes, talks on all subjects and she will give you a first-class home and children. How near do we come in our life to paradise?'

'If she's so wonderful, why wasn't she married ten years ago?'

'Why?' said Salzman with a heavy laugh. '—Why? Because she is *partikiler*. This is why. She wants the *best*.'

Leo was silent, amused at how he had entangled himself. But Salzman had aroused his interest in Lily H., and he began seriously to consider calling on her. When the marriage broker observed how intently Leo's mind was at work on the facts he had supplied, he felt certain they would soon come to an agreement.

Late Saturday afternoon, conscious of Salzman, Leo Finkle walked with Lily Hirschorn along Riverside Drive. He walked briskly and erectly, wearing with distinction the black fedora he had that morning taken with trepidation out of the dusty hat box on his closet shelf, and the heavy black Saturday coat he had thoroughly whisked clean. Leo also owned a walking stick, a present from a distant relative, but quickly put temptation aside and did not use it. Lily, petite and not unpretty, had on something signifying the approach of spring. She was au courant, animatedly, with all sorts of subjects, and he weighed her words and found her surprisingly sound—score another for Salzman, whom he uneasily sensed to be somewhere around, hiding perhaps high in a tree along the street, flashing the lady signals with a pocket mirror; or perhaps a cloven-hoofed Pan, piping nuptial ditties as he danced his invisible way before them, strewing wild buds on the walk and purple grapes in their path, symbolizing fruit of a union, though there was of course still none.

Lily startled Leo by remarking, 'I was thinking of Mr Salzman, a curious figure, wouldn't you say?'

Not certain what to answer, he nodded.

She bravely went on, blushing, 'I for one am grateful for his introducing us. Aren't you?'

He courteously replied, 'I am.'

'I mean,' she said with a little laugh—and it was all in good taste, or at least gave the effect of being not in bad—'do you mind that we came together so?'

He was not displeased with her honesty, recognizing that she meant to set the relationship aright, and understanding that it took a certain amount of experience in life, and courage, to want to do it quite that way. One had to have some sort of past to make that kind of beginning.

He said that he did not mind. Salzman's function was traditional and honourable—valuable for what it might achieve, which, he pointed out, was frequently nothing.

Lily agreed with a sigh. They walked on for a while and she said after a long silence, again with a nervous laugh, 'Woud you mind if I asked you something a little bit personal? Frankly, I find the subject fascinating.' Although Leo shrugged, she went on half embarrassedly, 'How was it that you came to your calling? I mean, was it a sudden passionate inspiration?'

Leo, after a time, slowly replied, 'I was always interested in the Law.'

'You saw revealed in it the presence of the Highest?'

He nodded and changed the subject. 'I understand that you spent a little time in Paris, Miss Hirschorn?'

'Oh, did Mr Salzman tell you, Rabbi Finkle?' Leo winced but she went on, 'It was ages ago and almost forgotten. I remember I had to return for my sister's wedding.'

And Lily would not be put off. 'When,' she asked in a slightly trembly voice, 'did you become enamoured of God?'

He stared at her. Then it came to him that she was talking not about Leo Finkle but a total stranger, some mystical figure, perhaps even passionate prophet that Salzman had dreamed up for her—no relation to the living or dead. Leo trembled with rage and weakness. The trickster had obviously sold her a bill of goods, just as he had him, who'd expected to become acquainted with a young lady of twenty-nine, only to behold, the moment he had laid eyes upon her strained and anxious face, a woman past thirty-five and aging rapidly. Only his self-control had kept him this long in her presence.

'I am not,' he said gravely, 'a talented religious person,' and in seeking words to go on, found himself possessed by shame and fear. 'I think,' he said in a strained manner, 'that I came to God not because I loved Him but because I did not.'

This confession he spoke harshly because its unexpectedness shook him.

Lily wilted. Leo saw a profusion of loaves of bread go flying like ducks high over his head, not unlike the winged loaves by which he had counted himself to sleep last night. Mercifully, then, it snowed, which he would not put past Salzman's machinations.

He was infuriated with the marriage broker and swore he would throw him out of the room the moment he reappeared. But Salzman did not come that night, and when Leo's anger had subsided, an unaccountable despair grew in its place. At first he though this was caused by his disappointment in Lily, but before long it became evident that he had involved himself with Salzman without a true knowledge of his own intent. He gradually realized—with an emptiness that seized him with six hands—that he had called in the broker to find him a bride because he was incapable of doing it himself. This terrifying insight he had derived as a result of his meeting and conversation with Lily Hirschorn. Her probing questions had somehow irritated him into revealing—to himself more than her—the true nature of his relationship to God, and from that it had come upon him, with shocking force, that apart from his parents, he had never loved anyone. Or perhaps it went the other way, that he did not love God so well as he might, because he had not loved man. It seemed to Leo that his whole life stood starkly revealed and he saw himself for the first time as he truly was—unloved and loveless. This bitter but somehow not fully unexpected revelation brought him to a point of panic, controlled only by extraordinary effort. He covered his face with his hands and cried.

The week that followed was the worst of his life. He did not eat and lost weight. His beard darkened and grew ragged. He stopped attending seminars and almost never opened a book. He seriously considered leaving the Yeshiva, although he was deeply troubled at the thought of the loss of all his years of study—saw them like pages torn from a book, strewn over the city—and at the devastating effect of this decision upon his parents. But he had lived without knowledge of himself, and never in the Five Books and all the Commentaries—mea culpa—had the truth been revealed to him. He did not know where to turn, and in all this desolating loneliness there was no *to whom*, although he often thought of Lily but not once could bring himself to go downstairs and make the call. He became touchy and irritable, especially with his landlady, who asked him all manner of personal questions; on the other hand, sensing his own disagreeableness, he waylaid her on the stairs and apologized abjectly, until, mortified, she ran from him. Out of this, however, he drew the consolation that he was a Jew and that a Jew suffered. But gradually, as the long and terrible week drew to a close, he regained his composure and some idea of purpose in life: to go on as planned. Although he was imperfect, the ideal was not. As for his quest of a bride, the thought of continuing afflicted him with anxiety and heartburn, yet perhaps with this new knowledge of himself he would be more successful than in the past. Perhaps love would now come to him and a bride to that love. And for this sanctified seeking who needed a Salzman?

The marriage broker, a skeleton with haunted eyes, returned that very night. He looked, withal, the picture of frustrated expectancy—as if he had steadfastly waited the week at Miss Lily Hirschorn's side for a telephone call that never came.

Casually coughing, Salzman came immediately to the point: 'So how did you like her?'

Leo's anger rose and he could not refrain from chiding the matchmaker: 'Why did you lie to me, Salzman?'

Salzman's pale face went dead white, the world had snowed on him.

'Did you not state that she was twenty-nine?' Leo insisted.

'I give you my word—'

'She was thirty-five, if a day. *At least* thirty-five.'

'Of this don't be sure. Her father told me—'

'Never mind. The worst of it is that you lied to her.'

'How did I lie to her, tell me?'

'You told her things about me that weren't true. You made me out to be more, consequently less than I am. She had in mind a totally different person, a sort of semi-mystical Wonder Rabbi.'

'All I said, you was a religious man.'

'I can imagine.'

Salzman sighed. 'This is my weakness that I have,' he confessed. 'My wife says to me I shouldn't be a salesman, but when I have two fine people that they would be wonderful to be married, I am so happy that I talk too much.' He smiled wanly. 'This is why Salzman is a poor man.'

Leo's anger left him. 'Well, Salzman, I'm afraid that's all.'

The marriage broker fastened hungry eyes on him.

'You don't want any more a bride?'

'I do,' said Leo, 'but I have decided to seek her in another way. I am no longer interested in an arranged marriage. To be frank, I now admit the necessity of premarital love. That is, I want to be in love with the one I marry.'

'Love?' said Salzman, astounded. After a moment he remarked, 'For us, our love is our life, not for the ladies. In the ghetto they—'

'I know, I know,' said Leo. 'I've thought of it often. Love, I have said to myself, should be a product of living and worship rather than its own end. Yet for myself I find it necessary to establish the level of my need and fulfill it.'

Salzman shrugged but answered, 'Listen, rabbi, if you want love, this I can find for you also. I have such beautiful clients that you will love them the minute your eyes will see them.'

Leo smiled unhappily. 'I'm afraid you don't understand.'

But Salzman hastily unstrapped his portfolio and withdrew a manila packet from it.

'Pictures,' he said, quickly laying the envelope on the table.

Leo called after him to take the pictures away, but as if on the wings of the wind, Salzman had disappeared.

March came. Leo had returned to his regular routine. Although he felt not quite himself yet—lacked energy—he was making plans for a more active social life. Of course it would cost something, but he was an expert in cutting corners; and when there were no corners left he would make circles rounder. All the while Salzman's pictures had lain on the table, gathering dust. Occasionally as Leo sat studying, or enjoying a cup of tea, his eyes fell on the manila envelope, but he never opened it.

The days went by and no social life to speak of developed with a member of the opposite sex—it was difficult, given the circumstances of his situation. One morning Leo toiled up the stairs to his room and stared out the window at the city. Although the day was bright his view of it was dark. For some time he watched the people in the street below hurrying along and then turned with a heavy heart to his little room. On the table was the packet. With a sudden relentless gesture he tore it open. For a half hour he stood by the table in a state of excitement, examining the photographs of the ladies Salzman had included. Finally, with a deep sigh he put them down. There were six, of varying degrees of attractiveness, but look at them long enough and they all became Lily Hirschorn: all past their prime, all starved behind bright smiles, not a true personality in the lot. Life, despite their frantic yoohooings, had passed them by; they were pictures in a briefcase that stank of fish. After a while, however, as Leo attempted to return the photographs into the envelope, he found in it another, a snapshot of the type taken by a machine for a quarter. He gazed at it a moment and let out a low cry.

Her face deeply moved him. Why, he could at first not say. It gave him the impression of youth—spring flowers, yet age—a sense of having been used to the bone, wasted; this came from the eyes, which were hauntingly familiar, yet absolutely strange. He had a vivid impression that he had met her before, but try as he might he could not place her although he could almost recall her name, as if he had read it in her own handwriting. No, this couldn't be; he would have remembered her. It was not, he affirmed, that she had an extraordinary beauty—no, though her face was attractive enough; it was that *something* about her moved him. Feature for feature, even some of the ladies of the photographs could do better; but she leaped forth to his heart—had *lived*, or wanted to—more than just wanted, perhaps regretted how she had lived—had somehow deeply suffered: it could be seen in the depths of those reluctant eyes, and from the way the light enclosed and shone from her, and within her, opening realms of possibility: this was her own. Her he desired. His head ached and eyes narrowed with the intensity of his gazing, then as if an obscure fog had blown up in the mind, he experienced fear of her and was aware that he had received an impression, somehow, of evil. He shuddered, saying softly, it is thus with us all. Leo brewed some tea in a small pot and sat sipping it without sugar, to calm himself. But before he had finished drinking, again with excitement he examined the face and found it good: good for Leo Finkle.

Only such a one could understand him and help him seek whatever he was seeking. She might, perhaps, love him. How she had happened to be among the discards in Salzman's barrel he could never guess, but he knew he must urgently find her.

Leo rushed downstairs, grabbed up the Bronx telephone book, and searched for Salzman's home address. He was not listed, nor was his office. Neither was he in the Manhattan book. But Leo remembered having written down the address on a slip of paper after he had read Salzman's advertisement in the 'personals' column of the *Forward*. He ran up to his room and tore through his papers, without luck. It was exasperating. Just when he needed the matchmaker he was nowhere to be found. Fortunately Leo remembered to look in his wallet. There on a card he found his name written and a Bronx address. No phone number was listed, the reason—Leo now recalled—he had originally communicated with Salzman by letter. He got on his coat, put a hat on over his skullcap and hurried to the subway station. All the way to the far end of the Bronx he sat on the edge of his seat. He was more than once tempted to take out the picture and see if the girl's face was as he remembered, but he refrained, allowing the snapshot to remain in his inside coat pocket, content to have her so close. When the train pulled into the station he was waiting at the door and bolted out. He quickly located the street Salzman had advertised.

The building he sought was less than a block from the subway, but it was not an office building, nor even a loft, nor a store in which one could rent office space. It was a very old tenement house. Leo found Salzman's name in pencil on a soiled tag under the bell and climbed three dark flights to his apartment. When he knocked, the door was opened by a thin, asthmatic, grey-haired woman, in felt slippers.

'Yes?' she said, expecting nothing. She listened without listening. He could have sworn he had seen her, too, before but knew it was an illusion.

'Salzman–does he live here? Pinye Salzman,' he said, 'the matchmaker?'

She stared at him a long minute. 'Of course.'

He felt embarrassed. 'Is he in?'

'No.' Her mouth, though left open, offered nothing more.

'The matter is urgent. Can you tell me where his office is?'

'In the air.' She pointed upward.

'You mean he has no office?' Leo asked.

'In his socks.'

He peered into the apartment. It was sunless and dingy, one large room divided by a half-open curtain, beyond which he could see a sagging metal bed. The near side of the room was crowded with rickety chairs, old bureaus, a three-legged table, racks of cooking utensils, and all the apparatus of a kitchen. But there was no sign of Salzman or his magic barrel, probably also a figment of the imagination. An odour of frying fish made Leo weak to the knees.

'Where is he?' he insisted. 'I've got to see your husband.'

At length she answered, 'So who knows where he is? Every time he thinks a new thought he runs to a different place. Go home, he will find you.'

'Tell him Leo Finkle.'

She gave no sign she had heard.

He walked downstairs, depressed.

But Salzman, breathless, stood waiting at his door.

Leo was astounded and overjoyed. 'How did you get here before me?'

'I rushed.'

'Come inside.'

They entered. Leo fixed tea, and a sardine sandwich for Salzman. As they were drinking he reached behind him for the packet of pictures and handed them to the marriage broker.

Salzman put down his glass and said expectantly, 'You found somebody you like?'

'Not among these.'

The marriage broker turned away.

'Here is the one I want.' Leo held forth the snapshot.

Salzman slipped on his glasses and took the picture into his trembling hand. He turned ghastly and let out a groan.

'What's the matter?' cried Leo.

'Excuse me. Was an accident this picture. She isn't for you.' Salzman frantically shoved the manila packet into his portfolio. He thrust the snapshot into his pocket and fled down the stairs.

Leo, after momentary paralysis, gave chase and cornered the marriage broker in the vestibule. The landlady made hysterical outcries but neither of them listened.

'Give me back the picture, Salzman.'

'No.' The pain in his eyes was terrible.

'Tell me who she is then.'

'This I can't tell you. Excuse me.'

He made to depart, but Leo, forgetting himself, seized the matchmaker by his tight coat and shook him frenziedly.

'Please,' sighed Salzman. *'Please.'*

Leo ashamedly let him go. 'Tell me who she is,' he begged. 'It's very important for me to know.'

'She is not for you. She is a wild one—wild, without shame. This is not a bride for a rabbi.'

'What do you mean wild?'

'Like an animal. Like a dog. For her to be poor was a sin. This is why to me she is dead now.'

'In God's name, what do you mean?'

'Her I can't introduce to you,' Salzman cried.

'Why are you so excited?'

'Why, he asks,' Salzman said, bursting into tears. 'This is my baby, my

Stella, she should burn in hell.'

Leo hurried up to bed and hid under the covers. Under the covers he thought his life through. Although he soon fell asleep he could not sleep her out of his mind. He woke, beating his breast. Though he prayed to be rid of her, his prayers went unanswered. Through days of torment he endlessly struggled not to love her; fearing success, he escaped it. He then concluded to convert her to goodness, himself to God. The idea alternately nauseated and exalted him.

He perhaps did not know that he had come to a final decision until he encountered Salzman in a Broadway cafeteria. He was sitting alone at a rear table, sucking the bony remains of a fish. The marriage broker appeared haggard, and transparent to the point of vanishing.

Salzman looked up at first without recognizing him. Leo had grown a pointed beard and his eyes were weighted with wisdom.

'Salzman,' he said, 'love has at last come to my heart.'

'Who can love from a picture?' mocked the marriage broker.

'It is not impossible.'

'If you can love her, then you can love anybody. Let me show you some new clients that they just sent me their photographs. One is a little doll.'

'Just her I want,' Leo murmured.

'Don't be a fool, doctor. Don't bother with her.'

'Put me in touch with her, Salzman,' Leo said humbly. 'Perhaps I can be of service.'

Salzman had stopped eating and Leo understood with emotion that it was now arranged.

Leaving the cafeteria, he was, however, afflicted by a tormenting suspicion that Salzman had planned it all to happen this way.

Leo was informed by letter that she would meet him on a certain corner, and she was there one spring night, waiting under a street lamp. He appeared, carrying a small bouquet of violets and rosebuds. Stella stood by the lamppost, smoking. She wore white with red shoes, which fitted his expectations, although in a troubled moment he had imagined the dress red, and only the shoes white. She waited uneasily and shyly. From afar he saw that her eyes—clearly her father's—were filled with desperate innocence. He pictured, in her, his own redemption. Violins and lit candles revolved in the sky. Leo ran forward with flowers outthrust.

Around the corner, Salzman, leaning against a wall, chanted prayers for the dead.

1954

The Jewbird

The window was open so the skinny bird flew in. Flappity-flap with its frazzled black wings. That's how it goes. It's open, you're in. Closed, you're out and that's your fate. The bird wearily flapped through the open kitchen window of Harry Cohen's top-floor apartment on First Avenue near the lower East River. On a rod on the wall hung an escaped canary cage, its door wide open, but this black-type longbeaked bird—its ruffled head and small dull eyes, crossed a little, making it look like a dissipated crow—landed if not smack on Cohen's thick lamb chop, at least on the table, close by. The frozen-foods salesman was sitting at supper with his wife and young son on a hot August evening a year ago. Cohen, a heavy man with hairy chest and beefy shorts; Edie, in skinny yellow shorts and red halter; and their ten-year-old Morris (after her father)—Maurie, they called him, a nice kid though not overly bright—were all in the city after two weeks out, because Cohen's mother was dying. They had been enjoying Kingston, New York, but drove back when Mama got sick in her flat in the Bronx.

'Right on the table,' said Cohen, putting down his beer glass and swatting at the bird. 'Son of a bitch.'

'Harry, take care with your language,' Edie said, looking at Maurie, who watched every move.

The bird cawed hoarsely and with a flap of its bedraggled wings—feathers tufted this way and that—rose heavily to the top of the open kitchen door, where it perched staring down.

'Gevalt, a pogrom!'

'It's a talking bird,' said Edie in astonishment.

'In Jewish,' said Maurie.

'Wise guy,' muttered Cohen. He gnawed on his chop, then put down the bone. 'So if you can talk, say what's your business. What do you want here?'

'If you can't spare a lamb chop,' said the bird, 'I'll settle for a piece of herring with a crust of bread. You can't live on your nerve forever.'

'This ain't a restaurant,' Cohen replied. 'All I'm asking is what brings you to this address?'

'The window was open,' the bird sighed; adding after a moment, 'I'm running. I'm flying but I'm also running.'

'From whom?' asked Edie with interest.

'Anti-Semeets.'

'Anti-Semites?' they all said.

'That's from who.'

'What kind of anti-Semites bother a bird?' Edie asked.

'Any kind,' said the bird, 'also including eagles, vultures, and hawks. And once in a while some crows will take your eyes out.'

'But aren't you a crow?'

'Me? I'm a Jewbird.'

Cohen laughed heartily. 'What do you mean by that?'

The bird began dovening. He prayed without Book or tallith, but with passion. Edie bowed her head though not Cohen. And Maurie rocked back and forth with the prayers, looking up with one wide-open eye.

When the prayer was done Cohen remarked, 'No hat, no phylacteries?'

'I'm an old radical.'

'You're sure you're not some kind of a ghost or dybbuk?'

'Not a dybbuk,' answered the bird, 'though one of my relatives had such an experience once. It's all over now, thanks God. They freed her from a former lover, a crazy jealous man. She's now the mother of two wonderful children.'

'Birds?' Cohen asked slyly.

'Why not?'

'What kind of birds?'

'Like me. Jewbirds.'

Cohen tipped back in his chair and guffawed. 'That's a big laugh. I heard of a Jewfish but not a Jewbird.'

'We're once removed.' The bird rested on one skinny leg, then on the other. 'Please, could you spare maybe a piece of herring with a small crust of bread?'

Edie got up from the table.

'What are you doing?' Cohen asked her.

'I'll clear the dishes.'

Cohen turned to the bird. 'So what's your name, if you don't mind saying?'

'Call me Schwartz.'

'He might be an old Jew changed into a bird by somebody,' said Edie, removing a plate.

'Are you?' asked Harry, lighting a cigar.

'Who knows?' answered Schwartz. 'Does God tell us everything?'

Maurie got up on his chair. 'What kind of herring?' he asked the bird in excitement.

'Get down, Maurie, or you'll fall,' ordered Cohen.

'If you haven't got matjes, I'll take schmaltz,' said Schwartz.

'All we have is marinated, with slices of onion—in a jar,' said Edie.

'If you'll open for me the jar I'll eat marinated. Do you have also, if you don't mind, a piece of rye bread—the spitz?'

Edie though she had.

'Feed him out on the balcony,' Cohen said. He spoke to the bird. 'After that take off.'

Schwartz closed both bird eyes. 'I'm tired and it's a long way.'

'Which direction are you headed, north or south?'

Schwartz, barely lifting his wings, shrugged.

'You don't know where you're going?'

'Where there's charity I'll go.'

'Let him stay, papa,' said Maurie. 'He's only a bird.'

'So stay the night,' Cohen said, 'but not longer.'

In the morning Cohen ordered the bird out of the house but Maurie cried, so Schwartz stayed for a while. Maurie was still on vacation from school and his friends were away. He was lonely and Edie enjoyed the fun he had playing with the bird.

'He's no trouble at all,' she told Cohen, 'and besides his appetite is very small.'

'What'll you do when he makes dirty?'

'He flies across the street in a tree when he makes dirty, and if nobody passes below, who notices?'

'So all right,' said Cohen, 'but I'm dead set against it. I warn you he ain't gonna stay here long.'

'What have you got against the poor bird?'

'Poor bird, my ass. He's a foxy bastard. He thinks he's a Jew.'

'What difference does it make what he thinks?'

'A Jewbird, what a chutzpah. One false move and he's out on his drumsticks.'

At Cohen's insistence Schwartz lived out on the balcony in a new wooden birdhouse Edie had bought him.

'With many thanks,' said Schwartz, 'though I would rather have a human roof over my head. You know how it is at my age. I like the warm, the windows, the smell of cooking. I would also be glad to see once in a while the *Jewish Morning Journal* and have now and then a schnapps because it helps my breathing, thanks God. But whatever you give me, you won't hear complaints.'

However, when Cohen brought home a bird feeder full of dried corn, Schwartz said, 'Impossible.'

Cohen was annoyed. 'What's the matter, crosseyes, is your life getting too good for you? Are you forgetting what it means to be migratory? I'll bet a helluva lot of crows you happen to be acquainted with, Jews or otherwise, would give their eyeteeth to eat this corn.'

Schwartz did not answer. What can you say to a grubber yung?

'Not for my digestion,' he later explained to Edie. 'Cramps. Herring is better even if it makes you thirsty. At least rainwater don't cost anything.' He laughed sadly in breathy caws.

And herring, thanks to Edie, who knew where to shop, was what Schwartz got, with an occasional piece of potato pancake, and even a bit of soupmeat when Cohen wasn't looking.

When school began in September, before Cohen would once again suggest giving the bird the boot, Edie prevailed on him to wait a little while until Maurie adjusted.

'To deprive him right now might hurt his school work, and you know what trouble we had last year.'

'So okay, but sooner or later the bird goes. That I promise you.'

Schwartz, though nobody had asked him, took on full responsibility for Maurie's performance in school. In return for favours granted, when he was let in for an hour or two at night, he spent most of his time overseeing the boy's lessons. He sat on top of the dresser near Maurie's desk as he laboriously wrote out his homework. Maurie was a restless type and Schwartz gently kept him to his studies. He also listened to him practise his screechy violin, taking a few minutes off now and then to rest his ears in the bathroom. And they afterwards played dominoes. The boy was an indifferent checkers player and it was impossible to teach him chess. When he was sick, Schwartz read him comic books though he personally disliked them. But Maurie's work improved in school and even his violin teacher admitted his playing was better. Edie gave Schwartz credit for these improvements though the bird pooh-poohed them.

Yet he was proud there was nothing lower than C minuses on Maurie's report card, and on Edie's insistence celebrated with a little schnapps.

'If he keeps up like this,' Cohen said, 'I'll get him in an Ivy League college for sure.'

'Oh, I hope so,' sighed Edie.

But Schwartz shook his head. 'He's a good boy—you don't have to worry. He won't be a shicker or a wife beater, God forbid, but a scholar he'll never be, if you know what I mean, although maybe a good mechanic. It's no disgrace in these times.'

'If I was you,' Cohen said, angered, 'I'd keep my big snoot out of other people's private business.'

'Harry, please,' said Edie.

'My goddamn patience is wearing out. That crosseyes butts into everything.'

Though he wasn't exactly a welcome guest in the house, Schwartz gained a few ounces although he did not improve in appearance. He looked bedraggled as ever, his feathers unkempt, as though he had just flown out of a snowstorn. He spent, he admitted, little time taking care of himself. Too much to think about. 'Also outside plumbing,' he told Edie. Still there was more glow to his eyes so that though Cohen went on calling him crosseyes he said it less emphatically.

Liking his situation, Schwartz tried tactfully to stay out of Cohen's way, but one night when Edie was at the movies and Maurie was taking a hot shower, the frozen-foods salesman began a quarrel with the bird.

'For Christ sake, why don't you wash yourself sometimes? Why must you always stink like a dead fish?'

'Mr Cohen, if you'll pardon me, if somebody eats garlic he will smell from garlic. I eat herring three times a day. Feed me flowers and I will smell like flowers.'

'Who's obligated to feed you anything at all? You're lucky to get herring.'

'Excuse me, I'm not complaining,' said the bird. 'You're complaining.'

'What's more,' said Cohen, 'even from out on the balcony I can hear you snoring away like a pig. It keeps me awake nights.'

'Snoring,' said Schwartz, 'isn't a crime, thanks God.'

'All in all you are a goddamn pest and freeloader. Next thing you'll want to sleep in bed next to my wife.'

'Mr Cohen,' said Schwartz, 'on this rest assured. A bird is a bird.'

'So you say, but how do I know you're a bird and not some kind of a goddamn devil?'

'If I was a devil you would know already. And I don't mean because your son's good marks.'

'Shut up, you bastard bird,' shouted Cohen.

'Grubber yung,' cawed Schwartz, rising to the tips of his talons, his long wings outstretched.

Cohen was about to lunge for the bird's scrawny neck but Maurie came out of the bathroom, and for the rest of the evening until Schwartz's bed-time on the balcony, there was pretend peace.

But the quarrel had deeply disturbed Schwartz and he slept badly. His snoring woke him, and awake, he was fearful of what would become of him. Wanting to stay out of Cohen's way, he kept to the birdhouse as much as possible. Cramped by it, he paced back and forth on the balcony ledge, or sat on the birdhouse roof, staring into space. In the evenings, while overseeing Maurie's lessons, he often fell asleep. Awakening, he nervously hopped around exploring the four corners of the room. He spent much time in Maurie's closet, and carefully examined his bureau drawers when they were left open. And once when he found a large paper bag on the floor, Schwartz poked his way into it to investigate what possibilities were. The boy was amused to see the bird in the paper bag.

'He wants to build a nest,' he said to his mother.

Edie, sensing Schwartz's unhappiness, spoke to him quietly.

'Maybe if you did some of the things my husband wants you, you would get along better with him.'

'Give me a for instance,' Schwartz said.

'Like take a bath, for instance.'

'I'm too old for baths,' said the bird. 'My feathers fall out without baths.'

'He says you have a bad smell.'

'Everybody smells. Some people smell because of their thoughts or because who they are. My bad smell comes from the food I eat. What does his come from?'

'I better not ask him or it might make him mad,' said Edie.

In late November Schwartz froze on the balcony in the fog and cold, and especially on rainy days he woke with stiff joints and could barely move his wings. Already he felt twinges of rheumatism. He would have liked to spend more time in the warm house, particularly when Maurie was in school and Cohen at work. But though Edie was goodhearted and might have sneaked him in in the morning, just to thaw out, he was afraid to ask her. In the meantime Cohen, who had been reading articles about the migration of birds, came out on the balcony one night after work when Edie was in the kitchen preparing pot roast, and peeking into the birdhouse, warned Schwartz to be on his way soon if he knew what was good for him. 'Time to hit the flyways.'

'Mr Cohen, why do you hate me so much?' asked the bird. 'What did I do to you?'

'Because you're an A-number-one troublemaker, that's why. What's more, whoever heard of a Jewbird? Now scat or it's open war.'

But Schwartz stubbornly refused to depart so Cohen embarked on a campaign of harassing him, meanwhile hiding it from Edie and Maurie. Maurie hated violence and Cohen didn't want to leave a bad impression. He thought maybe if he played dirty tricks on the bird he would fly off without being physically kicked out. The vacation was over, let him make his easy living off the fat of somebody else's land. Cohen worried about the effect of the bird's departure on Maurie's schooling but decided to take the chance, first, because the boy now seemed to have the knack of studying—give the black bird-bastard credit—and second, because Schwartz was driving him bats by being there always, even in his dreams.

The frozen-foods salesman began his campaign against the bird by mixing watery cat food with the herring slices in Schwartz's dish. He also blew up and popped numerous paper bags outside the birdhouse as the bird slept, and when he had got Schartz good and nervous, though not enough to leave, he brought a full-grown cat into the house, supposedly a gift for little Maurie, who had always wanted a pussy. The cat never stopped springing up at Schwartz whenever he saw him, one day managing to claw out several of his tail feathers. And even at lesson time, when the cat was usually excluded from Maurie's room, though somehow or other he quickly found his way in at the end of the lesson, Schwartz was desperately fearful of his life and flew from pinnacle to pinnacle—light fixture to clothes tree to door top—in order to elude the beast's wet jaws.

Once when the bird complained to Edie how hazardous his existence was, she said, 'Be patient, Mr Schwartz. When the cat gets to know you better he won't try to catch you any more.'

'When he stops trying we will both be in Paradise,' Schwartz answered. 'Do me a favour and get rid of him. He makes my whole life worry. I'm losing feathers like a tree loses leaves.'

'I'm awfully sorry but Maurie likes the pussy and sleeps with it.'

What could Schwartz do? He worried but came to no decision, being afraid to leave. So he ate the herring garnished with cat food, tried hard not to hear the paper bags bursting like firecrackers outside the birdhouse at night, and lived terror-stricken, closer to the ceiling than the floor, as the cat, his tail flicking, endlessly watched him.

Weeks went by. Then on the day after Cohen's mother had died in her flat in the Bronx, when Maurie came home with a zero on an arithmetic test, Cohen, enraged, waited until Edie had taken the boy to his violin lesson, then openly attacked the bird. He chased him with a broom on the balcony and Schwartz frantically flew back and forth, finally escaping into his birdhouse. Cohen triumphantly reached in, and grabbing both skinny legs, dragged the bird out, cawing loudly, his wings wildly beating. He whirled the bird around and around his head. But Schwartz, as he moved in circles, managed to swoop down and catch Cohen's nose in his beak, and hung on for dear life. Cohen cried out in great pain, punched at the bird with his fist, and tugging at its legs with all his might, pulled his nose free. Again he swung the yawking Schwartz around until the bird grew dizzy, then with a furious heave, flung him into the night. Schwartz sunk like a stone into the street. Cohen then tossed the birdhouse and feeder after him, listening at the ledge until they crashed on the sidewalk below. For a full hour, broom in hand, his heart palpitating and nose throbbing with pain, Cohen waited for Schwartz to return, but the brokenhearted bird didn't.

That's the end of the dirty bastard, the salesman thought and went in. Edie and Maurie had come home.

'Look,' said Cohen, pointing to his bloody nose swollen three times its size, 'what that sonofabitchy bird did. It's a permanent scar.'

'Where is he now?' Edie asked, frightened.

'I threw him out and he flew away. Good riddance.'

Nobody said no, though Edie touched a handkerchief to her eyes and Maurie rapidly tried the nine-times table and found he knew approximately half.

In the spring when the winter's snow had melted, the boy, moved by a memory, wandered in the neighbourhood, looking for Schwartz. He found a dead black bird in a small lot by the river, his two wings broken, neck twisted, and both bird-eyes plucked clean.

'Who did it to you, Mr Schwartz?' Maurie wept.

'Anti-Semeets,' Edie said later.

1963

Doris Lessing

b. 1919

'Some writers I know have stopped writing short stories because, as they say, "there is no market for them." Others like myself, the addicts, go on, and I suspect would go on even if there really wasn't any home for them but a private drawer,' Doris Lessing admitted. A self-confessed short-story 'addict', she is frequently associated with the realist tradition in fiction: 'I define realism as an art which springs so vigorously and naturally from a strongly held, though not necessarily intellectually defined, view of life that it absorbs symbolism. I hold the view that the realist novel, the realist story, is the highest form of prose writing.'

Born in Kermanshaw, Persia (now Iran), Lessing moved with her family in 1925 to Southern Rhodesia (now Zimbabwe), where she attended a Dominican convent school and Girls' High School in Salisbury. At the age of fourteen she left school to work as a nursemaid and then as a secretary. In her late twenties she turned her complete attention to the writing of fiction. In 1949, with her first novel and some stories complete, she moved to London, which has remained her home.

Lessing initially worked in the tradition of nineteenth-century realist fiction, focusing on the evils of apartheid in *The Grass Is Singing* (1950). Her interest in Marxism, race relations, psychoanalysis, and the interior life and status of women came together in *The Golden Notebook* (1962), a novel that has had a seminal influence on the women's movement. She then went on to explore subjects such as mysticism and psychic phenomena, which have become an important part of her more recent fiction. Influenced by Sufism, an ascetic and mystic tradition of the Muslim religion, her analysis of extreme psychological states in novels such as *Briefing for a Descent into Hell* (1971) and *Memoirs of a Survivor* (1974), and, later, her experiments with science fiction, have extended the boundaries of realism in her fiction.

'Our Friend Judith' illustrates the way Lessing reveals the inner life of her characters, especially women, by peeling away layers of carefully observed details until a mysterious core is exposed but not reduced to psychological terms. Informed by the literary tradition of continental travels, the story shows how Judith's self-reliance, her insistence on being 'her own person', baffles her friends, who cannot understand how Judith can rely solely on her feelings—which she refuses to explain in conventional terms—to direct her life.

In 'To Room Nineteen', Lessing explores the pains and pitfalls of contemporary marriage. Despite all of the 'intelligence' with which Susan and Matthew plan their marriage, have children, and organize their lives, Susan finds her identity fragmented by the multiple demands of domesticity on one hand and, on the other, by her incomprehensible but ever more powerful desire to be alone, unaccountable to anyone. As the conventions of her marriage—and the larger social world that decrees these conventions—become increasingly empty, inimical to her identity, Susan is forced to rely ever more heavily on her interludes in Room Nineteen.

'Our Friend Judith' was first published in the Summer 1960 issue of *Partisan Review* and then collected in *A Man and Two Women and Other Stories* (1963). 'To Room Nineteen' was published in the same volume.

Our Friend Judith

I stopped inviting Judith to meet people when a Canadian woman remarked, with the satisfied fervour of one who has at last pinned a label on a rare specimen: 'She is, of course, one of your typical English spinsters.'

This was a few weeks after an American sociologist, having elicited from Judith the facts that she was fortyish, unmarried, and living alone, had enquired of me: 'I suppose she has given up?' 'Given up what?' I asked; and the subsequent discussion was unrewarding.

Judith did not easily come to parties. She would come after pressure, not so much—one felt—to do one a favour, but in order to correct what she believed to be a defect in her character. 'I really ought to enjoy meeting new people more than I do,' she said once. We reverted to an earlier pattern of our friendship: odd evenings together, an occasional visit to the cinema, or she would telephone to say: 'I'm on my way past you to the British Museum. Would you care for a cup of coffee with me? I have twenty minutes to spare.'

It is characteristic of Judith that the word spinster, used of her, provoked fascinated speculation about other people. There are my aunts, for instance: aged seventy-odd, both unmarried, one an ex-missionary from China, one a retired matron of a famous London hospital. These two old ladies live together under the shadow of the cathedral in a country town. They devote much time to the Church, to good causes, to letter writing with friends all over the world, to the grandchildren and the great-grandchildren of relatives. It would be a mistake, however, on entering a house in which nothing has been moved for fifty years, to diagnose a condition of fossilized late-Victorian integrity. They read every book reviewed in the *Observer* or the *Times*, so that I recently got a letter from Aunt Rose enquiring whether I did not think that the author of *On the Road* was not—perhaps?—exaggerating his difficulties. They know a good deal about music, and write letters of encouragement to young composers they feel are being neglected—'You must understand that anything new and original takes time to be understood.' Well-informed and critical Tories, they are as likely to dispatch telegrams of protest to the Home Secretary as letters of support. These ladies, my aunts Emily and Rose, are surely what is meant by the phrase *English spinster*. And yet, once the connection has been pointed out, there is no doubt that Judith and they are spiritual cousins, if not sisters. Therefore it follows that one's pitying admiration for women who have supported manless and uncomforted lives needs a certain modification?

One will, of course, never know; and I feel now that it is entirely my fault that I shall never know. I had been Judith's friend for upwards of five years before the incident occurred which I involuntarily thought of—stupidly enough—as 'the first time Judith's mask slipped'.

A mutual friend, Betty, had been given a cast-off Dior dress. She was too short for it. Also she said: 'It's not a dress for a married woman with three children and a talent for cooking. I don't know why not, but it isn't.' Judith was the right build. Therefore one evening the three of us met by appointment in Judith's bedroom, with the dress. Neither Betty nor I were surprised at the renewed discovery that Judith was beautiful. We had both too often caught each other, and ourselves, in moments of envy when Judith's calm and severe face, her undemonstratively perfect body, succeeded in making everyone else in a room or a street look cheap.

Judith is tall, small-breasted, slender. Her light brown hair is parted in the centre and cut straight around her neck. A high straight forehead, straight nose, a full grave mouth are setting for her eyes, which are green, large and prominent. Her lids are very white, fringed with gold, and moulded close over the eyeball, so that in profile she has the look of a staring gilded mask. The dress was of dark green glistening stuff, cut straight, with a sort of loose tunic. It opened simply at the throat. In it Judith could of course evoke nothing but classical images. Diana, perhaps, back from the hunt, in a relaxed moment? A rather intellectual wood nymph who had opted for an afternoon in the British Museum reading room? Something like that. Neither Betty nor I said a word, since Judith was examining herself in a long mirror, and must know she looked magnificent.

Slowly she drew off the dress and laid it aside. Slowly she put on the old cord skirt and woollen blouse she had taken off. She must have surprised a resigned glance between us, for she then remarked, with the smallest of mocking smiles: 'One surely ought to stay in character, wouldn't you say?' She added, reading the words out of some invisible book, written not by her, since it was a very vulgar book, but perhaps by one of us: 'It does everything *for* me, I must admit.'

'After seeing you in it,' Betty cried out, defying her, 'I can't bear for anyone else to have it. I shall simply put it away.' Judith shrugged, rather irritated. In the shapeless skirt and blouse, and without makeup, she stood smiling at us, a woman at whom forty-nine out of fifty people would not look twice.

A second revelatory incident occurred soon after. Betty telephoned me to say that Judith had a kitten. Did I know that Judith adored cats? 'No, but of course she would,' I said.

Betty lived in the same street as Judith and saw more of her than I did. I was kept posted about the growth and habits of the cat and its effect on Judith's life. She remarked for instance that she felt it was good for her to have a tie and some responsibility. But no sooner was the cat out of kittenhood than all the neighbours complained. It was a tomcat, ungelded, and making every night hideous. Finally the landlord said that either the cat or Judith must go, unless she was prepared to have the cat 'fixed'. Judith wore herself out trying to find some person, anywhere in Britain, who would be prepared to take the cat. This person would, however, have to sign a written statement not to have the cat 'fixed'. When Judith took the cat to the vet to be killed, Betty told me she cried for twenty-four hours.

'She didn't think of compromising? After all, perhaps the cat might have preferred to live, if given the choice?'

'Is it likely I'd have the nerve to say anything so sloppy to Judith? It's the nature of a male cat to rampage lustfully about, and therefore it would be morally wrong for Judith to have the cat fixed, simply to suit her own convenience.'

'She said that?'

'She wouldn't have to *say* it, surely?'

A third incident was when she allowed a visiting young American, living in Paris, the friend of a friend and scarcely known to her, to use her flat while she visited her parents over Christmas. The young man and his friends lived it up for ten days of alcohol and sex and marijuana, and when Judith came back it took a week to get the place clean again and the furniture mended. She telephoned twice to Paris, the first time to say that he was a disgusting young thug and if he knew what was good for him he would keep out of her way in the future; the second time to apologize for losing her temper. 'I had a choice either to let someone use my flat, or to leave it empty. But having chosen that you should have it, it was clearly an unwarrantable infringement of your liberty to make any conditions at all. I do most sincerely ask your pardon.' The moral aspects of the matter having been made clear, she was irritated rather than not to receive letters of apology from him—fulsome, embarrassed, but above all, baffled.

It was the note of curiosity in the letters—he even suggested coming over to get to know her better—that irritated her most. 'What do you suppose he means?' she said to me. 'He lived in my flat for ten days. One would have thought that should be enough, wouldn't you?'

The facts about Judith, then, are all in the open, unconcealed, and plain to anyone who cares to study them; or, as it became plain she feels, to anyone with the intelligence to interpret them.

She has lived for the last twenty years in a small two-roomed flat high over a busy West London street. The flat is shabby and badly heated. The furniture is old, was never anything but ugly, is now frankly rickety and fraying. She has an income of £200 a year from a dead uncle. She lives on this and what she earns from her poetry, and from lecturing on poetry to night classes and extramural university classes.

She does not smoke or drink, and eats very little, from preference, not self-discipline.

She studied poetry and biology at Oxford, with distinction.

Shc is a Castlewell. That is, she is a member of one of the academic upper-middle-class families, which have been producing for centuries a steady supply of brilliant but sound men and women who are the backbone of the arts and sciences in Britain. She is on cool good terms with her family who respect her and leave her alone.

She goes on long walking tours, by herself, in such places as Exmoor or West Scotland.

Every three or four years she publishes a volume of poems.

The walls of her flat are completely lined with books. They are scientific, classical and historical; there is a great deal of poetry and some drama. There is not one novel. When Judith says: 'Of course I don't read novels,' this does not mean that novels have no place, or a small place, in literature; or that people should not read novels; but that it must be obvious she can't be expected to read novels.

I had been visiting her flat for years before I noticed two long shelves of books, under a window, each shelf filled with the works of a single writer. The two writers are not, to put it at the mildest, the kind one would associate with Judith. They are mild, reminiscent, vague, and whimsical. Typical English belles-lettres, in fact, and by definition abhorrent to her. Not one of the books in the two shelves has been read; some of the pages are still uncut. Yet each book is inscribed or dedicated to her: gratefully, admiringly, sentimentally and, more than once, amorously. In short, it is open to anyone who cares to examine these two shelves, and to work out dates, to conclude that Judith from the age of fifteen to twenty-five had been the beloved young companion of one elderly literary gentleman, and from twenty-five to thirty-five the inspiration of another.

During all that time she had produced her own poetry, and the sort of poetry, it is quite safe to deduce, not at all likely to be admired by her two admirers. Her poems are always cool and intellectual; that is their form, which is contradicted or supported by a gravely sensuous texture. They are poems to read often; one has to, to understand them.

I did not ask Judith a direct question about these two eminent but rather fusty lovers. Not because she would not have answered, or because she would have found the question impertinent, but because such questions are clearly unnecessary. Having those two shelves of books where they are, and books she could not conceivably care for, for their own sake, is publicly giving credit where credit is due. I can imagine her thinking the thing over, and deciding it was only fair, or perhaps honest, to place the books there; and this despite the fact that she would not care at all for the same attention to be paid to her. There is something almost contemptuous in it. For she certainly despises people who feel they need attention.

For instance, more than once a new emerging wave of 'modern' young poets have discovered her as the only 'modern' poet among their despised and well-credited elders. This is because, since she began writing at fifteen, her poems have been full of scientific, mechanical and chemical imagery. This is how she thinks, or feels.

More than once has a young poet hastened to her flat, to claim her as an ally, only to find her totally and by instinct unmoved by words like modern, new, contemporary. He has been outraged and wounded by her principle, so deeply rooted as to be unconscious, and to need no expression but a contemptuous shrug of the shoulders, that publicity seeking or to want critical attention is despicable. It goes without saying that there is perhaps one critic in the world she has any time for. He has sulked off, leaving her on her shelf, which she takes it for granted is her proper place, to be read by an appreciative minority.

Meanwhile she gives her lectures, walks alone through London, writes her poems, and is seen sometimes at a concert or a play with a middle-aged professor of Greek who has a wife and two children.

Betty and I had speculated about this professor, with such remarks as: Surely she must sometimes be lonely? Hasn't she ever wanted to marry? What about that awful moment when one comes in from somewhere at night to an empty flat?

It happened recently that Betty's husband was on a business trip, her children visiting, and she was unable to stand the empty house. She asked Judith for a refuge until her own home filled again.

Afterwards Betty rang me up to report:

'Four of the five nights Professor Adams came in about ten or so.'

'Was Judith embarrassed?'

'Would you expect her to be?'

'Well, if not embarrassed, at least conscious there was a situation?'

'No, not at all. But I must say I don't think he's good enough for her. He can't possibly understand her. He calls her Judy.'

'Good God.'

'Yes. But I was wondering. Suppose the other two called her Judy—'little Judy'—imagine it! Isn't it awful? But it does rather throw a light on Judith?'

'It's rather touching.'

'I suppose it's touching. But *I* was embarrassed—oh, not because of the situation. Because of how she was, with him. "Judy, is there another cup of tea in that pot?" And she, rather daughterly and demure, pouring him one.'

'Well yes, I can see how you felt.'

'Three of the nights he went to her bedroom with her—very casual about it, because she was being. But he was not there in the mornings. So I asked her. You know how it is when you ask her a question. As if you've been having long conversations on that very subject for years and years, and she is merely continuing where you left off last. So when she says something surprising, one feels such a fool to be surprised?'

'Yes. And then?'

'I asked her if she was sorry not to have children. She said yes, but one couldn't have everything.'

'One can't have everything, she said?'

'Quite clearly feeling she *has* nearly everything. She said she thought it was a pity, because she would have brought up children very well.'

'When you come to think of it, she would, too.'

'I asked about marriage, but she said on the whole the role of a mistress suited her better.'

'She used the word mistress?'

'You must admit it's the accurate word.'

'I suppose so.'

'And then she said that while she liked intimacy and sex and everything, she enjoyed waking up in the morning alone and *her own person*.'

'Yes, *of course*.'

'Of course. But now she's bothered because the professor would like to marry her. Or he feels he ought. At least, he's getting all guilty and obsessive about it. She says she doesn't see the point of divorce, and anyway, surely it would be very hard on his poor old wife after all these years particularly after bringing up two children so satisfactorily. She talks about his wife as if she's a kind of nice old charwoman, and it wouldn't be *fair* to sack her, you know. Anyway. What with one thing and another, Judith's going off to Italy soon in order *to collect herself*.'

'But how's she going to pay for it?'

'Luckily the Third Programme's commissioning her to do some arty programmes. They offered her a choice of The Cid—El Thid, you know—and the Borgias. Well, the Borghese, then. And Judith settled for the Borgias.'

'The Borgias,' I said, '*Judith*?'

'Yes, quite. I said that too, in that tone of voice. She saw my point. She says the epic is right up her street, whereas the Renaissance has never been on her wave length. Obviously it couldn't be, all the magnificence and cruelty and *dirt*. But of course chivalry and a high moral code and all those idiotically noble goings-on are right on her wave length.'

'Is the money the same?'

'Yes. But is it likely Judith would let money decide? No, she said that one should always choose something new, that isn't up one's street. Well, because it's better for her character, and so on, to get herself unsettled by the Renaissance. She didn't say *that*, of course.'

'Of course not.'

Judith went to Florence; and for some months postcards informed us tersely of her doings. Then Betty decided she must go by herself for a holiday. She had been appalled by the discovery that if her husband was away for a night she couldn't sleep; and when he went to Australia for three weeks, she stopped living until he came back. She had discussed this with him, and he had agreed that, if she really felt the situation to be serious, he would despatch her by air, to Italy, in order to recover her self-respect. As she put it.

I got this letter from her: 'It's no use, I'm coming home. I might have known. Better face it, once you're really married you're not fit for man nor beast. And if you remember what I used to be like! *Well!* I moped around Milan. I sunbathed in Venice, then I thought my tan was surely worth something, so I was on the point of starting an affair with another lonely soul, but I lost heart, and went to Florence to see Judith. She wasn't there. She'd gone to the Italian Riviera. I had nothing better to do, so I followed her. When I saw the place I wanted to laugh, it's so much not Judith, you know, all those palms and umbrellas and gaiety at all costs and ever such an ornamental blue sea. Judith is in an enormous stone room up on the hillside above the sea, with grape vines all over the place. You should see her, she's got beautiful. It seems for the last fifteen years she's been going to Soho every Saturday morning to buy food at an Italian shop. I must have looked surprised, because she explained she liked Soho. I suppose because all that dreary vice and nudes and prostitutes and everything prove how right she is to be as she is? She told the people in the shop she was going to Italy, and the *signora* said, what a coincidence, she was going back to Italy too, and she did hope an old friend like Miss Castlewell would visit her there. Judith said to me: 'I felt lacking, when she used the word friend. Our relations have always been formal. Can you understand it?' she said to me. 'For fifteen years,' I said to her. She said: 'I think I must feel it's a kind of imposition, don't you know, expecting people to feel friendship for one.' *Well*. I said: 'You ought to understand it, because you're like that yourself.' 'Am I?' she said. 'Well, think about it,' I said. But I could see she didn't want to think about it. Anyway, she's here, and I've spent a week with her. The widow Maria Rineiri inherited her mother's house, so she came home, from Soho. On the ground floor is a tatty little *rosticcerìa* patronized by the neighbours. They are all working people. This isn't tourist country, up on the hill. The widow lives above the shop with her little boy, a nasty little brat of about ten. Say what you like, the English are the only people who know how to bring up children, I don't care if that's insular. Judith's room is at the back, with a balcony. Underneath her room is the barber's shop, and the barber is Luigi Rineiri, the widow's younger brother. Yes, I was keeping him until the last. He is about forty, tall dark handsome, a great *bull*, but rather a sweet fatherly bull. He has cut Judith's hair and made it lighter. Now it looks like a sort of gold helmet. Judith is all brown. The widow Rineiri has made her a white dress and a green dress. They fit, for a change. When Judith walks down the street to the lower town, all the Italian males take one look at the golden girl and melt in their own oil like ice cream. Judith takes all this in her stride. She sort of acknowledges the homage. Then she strolls into the sea and vanishes into the foam. She swims five miles every day. *Naturally*. I haven't asked Judith whether she has collected herself, because you can see she hasn't. The widow Rineiri is match-making. When I noticed this I wanted to laugh, but luckily I didn't because Judith asked me, really wanting to know: 'Can you see me married to an Italian barber?' (Not being snobbish, but stating the position, so to speak.) 'Well yes,' I said, 'you're the only woman I know who I can see married to an Italian barber.' Because it wouldn't matter who she married, she'd always be her *own person*. 'At any rate, for a time,' I said. At which she said, asperously: 'You can use phrases like for a time in England but not in Italy.' Did you ever see England, at least London, as the home of licence, liberty and free love? No, neither did I, but of course she's right. Married to Luigi it would be the family, the neighbours, the church, and the *bambini*. All the same she's thinking about it, believe it or not. Here she's quite different, all relaxed and free. She's melting in the attention she gets. The widow mothers her and makes her coffee all the time, and listens to a lot of good advice about how to bring up that nasty brat of hers. Unluckily she doesn't take it. Luigi is crazy for her. At mealtimes she goes to the *trattoria* in the upper square and all the workmen treat her like a goddess. Well, a film star then. I said to her, you're mad to come home. For one thing her rent is ten bob a week, and you eat *pasta* and drink red wine till you bust for about one and sixpence. No, she said, it would be nothing but self-indulgence to stay. Why? I said. She said, she's got nothing to stay for. (ho ho.) And besides, she's done her research on the Borghese, though so far she can't see her way to an honest presentation of the facts. What made these people tick? she wants to know. And so she's only staying because of the cat. I forgot to mention the cat. This is a town of cats. The Italians here love their cats. I wanted to feed a stray cat at the table, but the waiter said no; and after lunch, all the waiters came with trays crammed with left-over food and stray cats came from everywhere to eat. And at dark when the tourists go in to feed and the beach is empty—you know how empty and forlorn a beach is at dusk?—well cats appear from everywhere. The beach seems to move, then you see it's cats. They go stalking along the thin inch of grey water at the edge of the sea, shaking their paws crossly at each step, snatching at the dead little fish, and throwing them with their mouths up on to the dry sand. They they scamper after them. You've never seen such a snarling and fighting. At dawn when the fishing boats come in to the empty beach, the cats are there in dozens. The fishermen throw them bits of fish. The cats snarl and fight over it. Judith gets up early and goes down to watch. Sometimes Luigi goes too, being tolerant. Because what he really likes is to join the evening promenade with Judith on his arm around and around the square of the upper town. Showing her off. Can you *see* Judith? But she does it. Being tolerant. But she smiles and enjoys the attention she gets, there's no doubt of it.

'She has a cat in her room. It's a kitten really, but it's pregnant. Judith says she can't leave until the kittens are born. The cat is too young to have kittens. Imagine Judith. She sits on her bed in that great stone room, with her bare feet on the stone floor and watches the cat, and tries to work out why a healthy uninhibited Italian cat always fed on the best from the *rosticcerìa* should be neurotic. Because it is. When it sees Judith watching it gets nervous and starts licking at the roots of its tail. But Judith goes on watching, and says about Italy that the reason why the English love the Italians is because the Italians make the English feel superior. They have no discipline. And that's a despicable reason for one nation to love another. Then she talks about Luigi and says he has no sense of guilt, but a sense of sin; whereas she has no sense of sin but she has guilt. I haven't asked her if this has been an insuperable barrier, because judging from how she looks, it hasn't. She says she would rather have a sense of sin, because sin can be atoned for, and if she understood sin, perhaps she would be more at home with the Renaissance. Luigi is very healthy, she says, and not neurotic. He is a Catholic of course. He doesn't mind that she's an atheist. His mother has explained to him that the English are all pagans, but good people at heart. I suppose he thinks a few smart sessions with the local priest would set Judith on the right path for good and all. Meanwhile the cat walks nervously around the room, stopping to lick, and when it can't stand Judith watching it another second, it rolls over on the floor, with its paws tucked up, and rolls up its eyes, and Judith scratches its lumpy pregnant stomach and tells it to relax. It makes *me* nervous to see her, it's not like her, I don't know why. Then Luigi shouts up from the barber's shop, then he comes up and stands at the door laughing, and Judith laughs, and the widow says: Children, enjoy yourselves. And off they go, walking down to the town eating ice cream. The cat follows them. It won't let Judith out of its sight, like a dog. When she swims miles out to sea, the cat hides under a beach hut until she comes back. Then she carries it back up the hill, because that nasty little boy chases it. *Well.* I'm coming home tomorrow thank God, to my dear old Billy, I was mad ever to leave him. There is something about Judith and Italy that has upset me, I don't know what. The point is, what on earth can Judith and Luigi *talk* about? Nothing. How can they? And of course it doesn't matter. So I turn out to be a prude as well. See you next week.'

It was my turn for a dose of the sun, so I didn't see Betty. On my way back from Rome I stopped off in Judith's resort and walked up through narrow streets to the upper town, where, in the square with the vine-covered *trattoria* at the corner, was a house with *ROSTICCERÌA* written in black paint on a cracked wooden board over a low door. There was a door curtain of red beads, and flies settled on the beads. I opened the beads with my hands and looked in to a small dark room with a stone counter. Loops of salami hung from metal hooks. A glass bell covered some plates of cooked meats. There were flies on the salami and on the glass bell. A few tins on the wooden shelves, a couple of pale loaves, some wine casks, and an open case of sticky pale green grapes covered with fruit flies seemed to be the only stock. A single wooden table with two chairs stood in a corner, and two workmen sat there, eating lumps of sausage and bread. Through another bead curtain at the back came a short, smoothly fat, slender-limbed woman with greying hair. I asked for Miss Castlewell, and her face changed. She said in an offended, off-hand way: 'Miss Castlewell left last week.' She took a white cloth from under the counter, and flicked at the flies on the glass bell. 'I'm a friend of hers,' I said, and she said: '*Si*,' and put her hands palm down on the counter and looked at me, expressionless. The workmen got up, gulped down the last of their wine, nodded, and went. She *ciao'd* them; and looked back at me. Then, since I didn't go, she called: 'Luigi!' A shout came from the back room, there was a rattle of beads, and in came first a wiry sharp-faced boy, and then Luigi. He was tall, heavy-shouldered, and his black rough hair was like a cap, pulled low over his brows. He looked good-natured, but at the moment uneasy. His sister said something, and he stood beside her, an ally, and confirmed: 'Miss Castlewell went away.' I was on the point of giving up, when through the bead curtain that screened off a dazzling light eased a thin tabby cat. It was ugly and it walked uncomfortably, with its back quarters bunched up. The child suddenly let out a 'Ssssss' through his teeth, and the cat froze. Luigi said something sharp to the child, and something encouraging to the cat, which sat down, looked straight in front of it, then began frantically licking at its flanks. 'Miss Castlewell was offended with us,' said Mrs Rineiri suddenly, and with dignity. 'She left early one morning. We did not expect her to go.' I said: 'Perhaps she had to go home and finish some work.'

Mrs Rineiri shrugged, then sighed. Then she exchanged a hard look with her brother. Clearly the subject had been discussed, and closed forever.

'I've known Judith a long time,' I said, trying to find the right note. 'She's a remarkable woman. She's a poet.' But there was no response to this at all. Meanwhile the child, with a fixed bared-teeth grin, was staring at the cat, narrowing his eyes. Suddenly he let out another 'Sssssss' and added a short high yelp. The cat shot backwards, hit the wall, tried desperately to claw its way up the wall, came to its senses and again sat down and began its urgent, undirected licking at its fur. This time Luigi cuffed the child, who yelped in earnest, and then ran out into the street past the cat. Now that the way was clear the cat shot across the floor, up onto the counter, and bounded past Luigi's shoulder and straight through the bead curtain into the barber's shop, where it landed with a thud.

'Judith was sorry when she left us,' said Mrs Rineiri uncertainly. 'She was crying.'

'I'm sure she was.'

'And so,' said Mrs Rineiri, with finality, laying her hands down again, and looking past me at the bead curtain. That was the end. Luigi nodded brusquely at me, and went into the back. I said goodbye to Mrs Rineiri and walked back to the lower town. In the square I saw the child, sitting on the running board of a lorry parked outside the *trattoria*, drawing in the dust with his bare toes, and directing in front of him a blank, unhappy stare.

I had to go through Florence, so I went to the address Judith had been at. No, Miss Castlewell had not been back. Her papers and books were still here. Would I take them back with me to England? I made a great parcel and brought them back to England.

I telephoned Judith and she said she had already written for the papers to be sent, but it was kind of me to bring them. There had seemed to be no point, she said, in returning to Florence.

'Shall I bring them over?'

'I would be very grateful, of course.'

Judith's flat was chilly, and she wore a bunchy sage-green woollen dress. Her hair was still a soft gold helmet, but she looked pale and rather pinched. She stood with her back to a single bar of electric fire—lit because I demanded it—with her legs apart and her arms folded. She contemplated me.

'I went to the Rineiris' house.'

'Oh. Did you?'

'They seemed to miss you.'

She said nothing.

'I saw the cat too.'

'Oh. Oh, I suppose you and Betty discussed it?' This was with a small unfriendly smile.

'Well, Judith, you must see we were likely to?'

She gave this her consideration and said: 'I don't understand why people discuss other people. Oh—I'm not criticizing you. But I don't see why you are so interested. I don't understand human behaviour and I'm not particularly interested.'

'I think you should write to the Rineiris.'

'I wrote and thanked them, of course.'

'I don't mean that.'

'You and Betty have worked it out?'

'Yes, we talked about it. We thought we should talk to you, so you should write to the Rineiris.'

'Why?'

'For one thing, they are both very fond of you.'

'Fond,' she said smiling.

'Judith, I've never in my life felt such an atmosphere of being let down.'

Judith considered this. 'When something happens that shows one there is really a complete gulf in understanding, what is there to say?'

'It could scarcely have been a complete gulf in understanding. I suppose you are going to say we are being interfering?'

Judith showed distaste. 'That is a very stupid word. And it's a stupid idea. No one can interfere with me if I don't let them. No, it's that I don't understand people. I don't understand why you or Betty should care. Or why the Rineiris should, for that matter,' she added with the small tight smile.

'Judith!'

'If you've behaved stupidly, there's no point in going on. You put an end to it.'

'What happened? Was it the cat?'

'Yes, I suppose so. But it's not important.' She looked at me, saw my ironical face, and said: 'The cat was too young to have kittens. That is all there was to it.'

'Have it your way. But that is obviously not all there is to it.'

'What upsets me is that I don't understand at all why I was so upset then.'

'What happened? Or don't you want to talk about it?'

'I don't give a damn whether I talk about it or not. You really do say the most extraordinary things, you and Betty. If you want to know, I'll tell you. What does it matter?'

'I would like to know, of course.'

'*Of course!*' she said. 'In your place I wouldn't care. Well, I think the essence of the thing was that I must have had the wrong attitude to that cat. Cats are supposed to be independent. They are supposed to go off by themselves to have their kittens. This one didn't. It was climbing up onto my bed all one night and crying for attention. I don't like cats on my bed. In the morning I saw she was in pain. I stayed with her all that day. Then Luigi—he's the brother, you know.'

'Yes.'

'Did Betty mention him? Luigi came up to say it was time I went for a swim. He said the cat should look after itself. I blame myself very much. That's what happens when you submerge yourself in somebody else.'

Her look at me was now defiant; and her body showed both defensiveness and aggression. 'Yes. It's true. I've always been afraid of it. And in the last few weeks I've behaved badly. It's because I let it happen.'

'Well, go on.'

'I left the cat and swam. It was late, so it was only for a few minutes. When I came out of the sea the cat had followed me and had had a kitten on the beach. That little beast Michele—the son, you know?—well, he always teased the poor thing, and now he had frightened her off the kitten. It was dead, though. He held it up by the tail and waved it at me as I came out of the sea. I told him to bury it. He scooped two inches of sand away and pushed the kitten in—on the beach, where people are all day. So I buried it properly. He had run off. He was chasing the poor cat. She was terrified and running up the town. I ran too. I caught Michele and I was so angry I hit him. I don't believe in hitting children. I've been feeling beastly about it ever since.'

'You were angry.'

'It's no excuse. I would never have believed myself capable of hitting a child. I hit him very hard. He went off, crying. The poor cat had got under a big lorry parked in the square. Then she screamed. And then a most remarkable thing happened. She screamed just once, and all at once cats just materialized. One minute there was just one cat, lying under a lorry, and the next, dozens of cats. They sat in a big circle around the lorry, all quite still, and watched my poor cat.'

'Rather moving.' I said.

'Why?'

'There was no evidence one way or the other,' I said in inverted commas, 'that the cats were there out of concern for a friend in trouble.'

'No,' she said energetically. 'There isn't. It might have been curiosity. Or anything. How do we know? However, I crawled under the lorry. There were two paws sticking out of the cat's back end. The kitten was the wrong way round. It was stuck. I held the cat down with one hand and I pulled the kitten out with the other.' She held out her long white hands. They were still covered with fading scars and scratches. 'She bit and yelled, but the kitten was alive. She left the kitten and crawled across the square into the house. Then all the cats got up and walked away. It was the most extraordinary thing I've every seen. They vanished again. One minute they were all there, and then they had vanished. I went after the cat, with the kitten. Poor little thing, it was covered with dust—being wet, don't you know. The cat was on my bed. There was another kitten coming, but it got stuck too. So when she screamed and screamed I just pulled it out. The kittens began to suck. One kitten was very big. It was a nice fat black kitten. It must have hurt her. But she suddenly bit out—snapped, don't you know, like a reflex action, at the back of the kitten's head. It died, just like that. Extraordinary, isn't it?' she said, blinking hard, her lips quivering. 'She was its mother, but she killed it. Then she ran off the bed and went downstairs into the shop under the counter. I called to Luigi. You know, he's Mrs Rineiri's brother.'

'Yes, I know.'

'He said she was too young, and she was badly frightened and very hurt. He took the alive kitten to her but she got up and walked away. She didn't want it. Then Luigi told me not to look. But I followed him. He held the kitten by the tail and he banged it against the wall twice. Then he dropped it into the rubbish heap. He moved aside some rubbish with his toe, and put the kitten there and pushed rubbish over it. Then Luigi said the cat should be destroyed. He said she was badly hurt and it would always hurt her to have kittens.'

'He hasn't destroyed her. She's still alive. But it looks to me as if he were right.'

'Yes, I expect he was.'

'What upset you—that he killed the kitten?'

'Oh no, I expect the cat would if he hadn't. But that isn't the point, is it?'

'What is the point?'

'I don't think I really know.' She had been speaking breathlessly, and fast. Now she said slowly: 'It's not a question of right or wrong, is it? Why should it be? It's a question of what one is. That night Luigi wanted to go promenading with me. For him, that was *that*. Something had to be done, and he'd done it. But I felt ill. He was very nice to me. He's a very good person,' she said, defiantly.

'Yes, he looks it.'

'That night I couldn't sleep. I was blaming myself. I should never have left the cat to go swimming. Well, and then I decided to leave the next day. And I did. And that's all. The whole thing was a mistake, from start to finish.'

'Going to Italy at all?'

'Oh, to go for a holiday would have been all right.'

'You've done all that work for nothing? You mean you aren't going to make use of all that research?'

'No. It was a mistake.'

'Why don't you leave it a few weeks and see how things are then?'

'Why?'

'You might feel differently about it.'

'What an extraordinary thing to say. Why should I? Oh, you mean, time passing, healing wounds—that sort of thing? What an extraordinary idea. It's always seemed to me an extraordinary idea. No, right from the beginning I've felt ill at ease with the whole business, not myself at all.'

'Rather irrationally, I should have said.'

Judith considered this, very seriously. She frowned while she thought it over. Then she said: 'But if one cannot rely on what one feels, what can one rely on?'

'On what one thinks, I should have expected you to say.'

'Should you? Why? Really, you people are all very strange. I don't understand you.' She turned off the electric fire, and her face closed up. She smiled, friendly and distant, and said: 'I don't really see any point at all in discussing it.'

1960

To Room Nineteen

This is a story, I suppose, about a failure in intelligence: the Rawlings' marriage was grounded in intelligence.

They were older when they married than most of their married friends: in their well-seasoned late twenties. Both had had a number of affairs, sweet rather than bitter; and when they fell in love—for they did fall in love — had known each other for some time. They joked that they had saved each other 'for the real thing'. That they had waited so long (but not too long) for this real thing was to them a proof of their sensible discrimination. A good many of their friends had married young, and now (they felt) probably regretted lost opportunities; while others, still unmarried, seemed to them arid, self-doubting, and likely to make desperate or romantic marriages.

Not only they, but others, felt they were well matched: their friends' delight was an additional proof of their happiness. They had played the same roles, male and female, in this group or set, if such a wide, loosely connected, constantly changing constellation of people could be called a set. They had both become, by virtue of their modification, their humour, and their abstinence from painful experience people to whom others came for advice. They could be, and were, relied on. It was one of those cases of a man and a woman linking themselves whom no one else had ever thought of linking, probably because of their similarities. But then everyone exclaimed: Of course! How right! How was it we never thought of it before!

And so they married amid general rejoicing, and because of their foresight and their sense for what was probable, nothing was a surprise to them.

Both had well-paid jobs. Matthew was a subeditor on a large London newspaper, and Susan worked in an advertising firm. He was not the stuff of which editors or publicized journalists are made, but he was much more than 'a subeditor', being one of the essential background people who in fact steady, inspire and make possible the people in the limelight. He was content with this position. Susan had a talent for commercial drawing. She was humorous about the advertisements she was responsible for, but she did not feel strongly about them one way or the other.

Both, before they married, had had pleasant flats, but they felt it unwise to base a marriage on either flat, because it might seem like a submission of personality on the part of the one whose flat it was not. They moved into a new flat in South Kensington on the clear understanding that when their marriage had settled down (a process they knew would not take long, and was in fact more a humorous concession to popular wisdom than what was due to themselves) they would buy a house and start a family.

And this is what happened. They lived in their charming flat for two years, giving parties and going to them, being a popular young married couple, and then Susan became pregnant, she gave up her job, and they bought a house in Richmond. It was typical of this couple that they had a son first, then a daughter, then twins, son and daughter. Everything right, appropriate, and what everyone would wish for, if they could choose. But people did feel these two had chosen; this balanced and sensible family was no more than what was due to them because of their infallible sense for *choosing* right.

And so they lived with their four children in their gardened house in Richmond and were happy. They had everything they had wanted and had planned for.

And yet . . .

Well, even this was expected, that there must be a certain flatness. . . .

Yes, yes, of course, it was natural they sometimes felt like this. Like what?

Their life seemed to be like a snake biting its tail. Matthew's job for the sake of Susan, children, house, and garden—which caravanserai needed a well-paid job to maintain it. And Susan's practical intelligence for the sake of Matthew, the children, the house, and the garden—which unit would have collapsed in a week without her.

But there was no point about which either could say: 'For the sake of *this* is all the rest.' Children? But children can't be a centre of life and a reason for being. They can be a thousand things that are delightful, interesting, satisfying, but they can't be a wellspring to live from. Or they shouldn't be. Susan and Matthew knew that well enough.

Matthew's job? Ridiculous. It was an interesting job, but scarcely a reason for living. Matthew took pride in doing it well; but he could hardly be expected to be proud of the newspaper: the newspaper he read, *his* newspaper, was not the one he worked for.

Their love for each other? Well, that was nearest it. If this wasn't a centre, what was? Yes, it was around this point, their love, that the whole extraordinary structure revolved. For extraordinary it certainly was. Both Susan and Matthew had moments of thinking so, of looking in secret disbelief at this thing they had created: marriage, four children, big house, garden, charwomen, friends, cars . . . and this *thing*, this entity, all of it had come into existence, been blown into being out of nowhere, because Susan loved Matthew and Matthew loved Susan. Extraordinary. So that was the central point, the wellspring.

And if one felt that it simply was not strong enough, important enough, to support it all, well whose fault was that? Certainly neither Susan's nor Matthew's. It was in the nature of things. And they sensibly blamed neither themselves nor each other.

On the contrary, they used their intelligence to preserve what they had created from a painful and explosive world: they looked around them, and took lessons. All around them, marriages collapsing, or breaking, or rubbing along (even worse, they felt). They must not make the same mistakes, they must not.

They had avoided the pitfall so many of their friends had fallen into—of buying a house in the country *for the sake of the children*; so that the husband became a weekend husband, a weekend father, and the wife always careful not to ask what went on in the town flat which they called (in joke) a bachelor flat. No, Matthew was a full-time husband, a full-time father, and at nights, in the big married bed in the big married bedroom (which had an attractive view of the river) they lay beside each other talking and he told her about his day, and what he had done, and whom he had met; and she told him about her day (not as interesting, but that was not her fault) for both knew of the hidden resentments and deprivations of the woman who has lived her own life—and above all, has earned her own living—and is now dependent on a husband for outside interests and money.

Nor did Susan make the mistake of taking a job for the sake of her independence, which she might very well have done, since her old firm, missing her qualities of humour, balance, and sense, invited her often to go back. Children needed their mother to a certain age, that both parents knew and agreed on; and when these four healthy wisely brought-up children were of the right age, Susan would work again, because she knew, and so did he, what happened to women of fifty at the height of their energy and ability, with grown-up children who no longer needed their full devotion.

So here was this couple, testing their marriage, looking after it, treating it like a small boat full of helpless people in a very stormy sea. Well, of course, so it was. . . . The storms of the world were bad, but not too close—which is not to say they were selfishly felt: Susan and Matthew were both well-informed and responsible people. And the inner storms and quicksands were understood and charted. So everything was all right. Everything was in order. Yes, things were under control.

So what did it matter if they felt dry, flat? People like themselves, fed on a hundred books (psychological, anthropological, sociological) could scarcely be unprepared for the dry, controlled wistfulness which is the distinguishing mark of the intelligent marriage. Two people, endowed with education, with discrimination, with judgement, linked together voluntarily from their will to be happy together and to be of use to others—one sees them everywhere, one knows them, one even is that thing oneself: sadness because so much is after all so little. These two, unsurprised, turned towards each other with even more courtesy and gentle love: this was life, that two people, no matter how carefully chosen, could not be everything to each other. In fact, even to say so, to think in such a way, was banal, they were ashamed to do it.

It was banal, too, when one night Matthew came home late and confessed he had been to a party, taken a girl home and slept with her. Susan forgave him, of course. Except that forgiveness is hardly the word. Understanding, yes. But if you understand something, you don't forgive it, you are the thing itself: forgiveness is for what you *don't* understand. Nor had he *confessed*—what sort of word is that?

The whole thing was not important. After all, years ago they had joked: Of course I'm not going to be faithful to you, no one can be faithful to one other person for a whole lifetime. (And there was the word *faithful* — stupid, all these words, stupid, belonging to a savage old world.) But the incident left both of them irritable. Strange, but they were both bad-tempered, annoyed. There was something unassimilable about it.

Making love splendidly after he had come home that night, both had felt that the idea that Myra Jenkins, a pretty girl met at a party, could be even relevant was ridiculous. They had loved each other for over a decade, would love each other for years more. Who, then, was Myra Jenkins?

Except, thought Susan, unaccountably bad-tempered, she was (is?) the first. In ten years. So either the ten years' fidelity was not important, or she isn't. (No, no, there is something wrong with this way of thinking, there must be.) But if she isn't important, presumably it wasn't important either when Matthew and I first went to bed with each other that afternoon whose delight even now (like a very long shadow at sundown) lays a long, wand-like finger over us. (Why did I say sundown?) Well, if what we felt that afternoon was not important, nothing is important, because if it hadn't been for what we felt, we wouldn't be Mr and Mrs Rawlings with four children, etc., etc. The whole thing is *absurd*—for him to have come home and told me was absurd. For him not to have told me was absurd. For me to care, or for that matter not to care, is absurd . . . and who is Myra Jenkins? Why, no one at all.

There was only one thing to do, and of course these sensible people did it: they put the thing behind them, and consciously, knowing what they were doing, moved forward into a different phase of their marriage, giving thanks for past good fortune as they did so.

For it was inevitable that the handsome, blond, attractive, manly man, Matthew Rawlings, should be at times tempted (oh, what a word!) by the attractive girls at parties she could not attend because of the four children; and that sometimes he would succumb (a word even more repulsive, if possible) and that she, a good-looking woman in the big well-tended garden at Richmond, would sometimes be pierced as by an arrow from the sky with bitterness. Except that bitterness was not in order, it was out of court. Did the casual girls touch the marriage? They did not. Rather it was they who knew defeat because of the handsome Matthew Rawlings' marriage body and soul to Susan Rawlings.

In that case why did Susan feel (though luckily not for longer than a few seconds at a time) as if life had become a desert, and that nothing mattered, and that her children were not her own?

Meanwhile her intelligence continued to assert that all was well. What if her Matthew did have an occasional sweet afternoon, the odd affair? For she knew quite well, except in her moments of aridity, that they were very happy, that the affairs were not important.

Perhaps that was the trouble? It was in the nature of things that the adventures and delights could no longer be hers, because of the four children and the big house that needed so much attention. But perhaps she was secretly wishing, and even knowing that she did, that the wildness and the beauty could be his. But he was married to her. She was married to him. They were married inextricably. And therefore the gods could not strike him with the real magic, not really. Well, was it Susan's fault that after he came home from an adventure he looked harassed rather than fulfilled? (In fact, that was how she knew he had been *unfaithful*, because of his sullen air, and his glances at her, similar to hers at him: What is it that I share with this person that shields all delight from me?) But none of it by anybody's fault. (But what did they feel ought to be somebody's fault?) Nobody's fault, nothing to be at fault, no one to blame, no one to offer or to take it . . . and nothing wrong, either, except that Matthew never was really struck, as he wanted to be, by joy; and that Susan was more and more often threatened by emptiness. (It was usually in the garden that she was invaded by this feeling: she was coming to avoid the garden, unless the children or Matthew were with her.) There was no need to use the dramatic words, unfaithful, forgive, and the rest: intelligence forbade them. Intelligence barred, too, quarrelling, sulking, anger, silences of withdrawal, accusations, and tears. Above all, intelligence forbids tears.

A high price has to be paid for the happy marriage with the four healthy children in the large white gardened house.

And they were paying it, willingly, knowing what they were doing. When they lay side by side or breast to breast in the big civilized bedroom overlooking the wild sullied river, they laughed, often, for no particular reason; but they knew it was really because of these two small people, Susan and Matthew, supporting such an edifice on their intelligent love. The laugh comforted them; it saved them both, though from what, they did not know.

They were now both fortyish. The older children, boy and girl, were ten and eight, at school. The twins, six, were still at home. Susan did not have nurses or girls to help her: childhood is short; and she did not regret the hard work. Often enough she was bored, since small children can be boring; she was often very tired; but she regretted nothing. In another decade, she would turn herself back into being a woman with a life of her own.

Soon the twins would go to school, and they would be away from home from nine until four. These hours, so Susan saw it, would be the preparation for her own slow emancipation away from the role of hub-of-the-family into woman-with-her-own-life. She was already planning for the hours of freedom when all the children would be 'off her hands'. That was the phrase used by Matthew and by Susan and by their friends, for the moment when the youngest child went off to school. 'They'll be off your hands, darling Susan, and you'll have time to yourself.' So said Matthew, the intelligent husband, who had often enough commended and consoled Susan, standing by her in spirit during the years when her soul was not her own, as she said, but her children's.

What it amounted to was that Susan saw herself as she had been at twenty-eight, unmarried; and then again somewhere about fifty, blossoming from the root of what she had been twenty years before. As if the essential Susan were in abeyance, as if she were in cold storage. Matthew said something like this to Susan one night: and she agreed that it was true—she did feel something like that. What, then, was this essential Susan? She did not know. Put like that it sounded ridiculous, and she did not really feel it. Anyway, they had a long discussion about the whole thing before going off to sleep in each other's arms.

So the twins went off to their school, two bright affectionate children who had no problems about it, since their older brother and sister had trodden this path so successfully before them. And now Susan was going to be alone in the big house, every day of the school term, except for the daily woman who came in to clean.

It was now, for the first time in this marriage, that something happened which neither of them had foreseen.

This is what happened. She returned, at nine-thirty, from taking the twins to the school by car, looking forward to seven blissful hours of freedom. On the first morning she was simply restless, worrying about the twins 'naturally enough' since this was their first day away at school. She was hardly able to contain herself until they came back. Which they did happily, excited by the world of school, looking forward to the next day. And the next day Susan took them, dropped them, came back, and found herself reluctant to enter her big and beautiful home because it was as if something was waiting for her there that she did not wish to confront. Sensibly, however, she parked the car in the garage, entered the house, spoke to Mrs Parkes the daily woman about her duties, and went up to her bedroom. She was possessed by a fever which drove her out again, downstairs, into the kitchen, where Mrs Parkes was making cake and did not need her, and into the garden. There she sat on a bench and tried to calm herself, looking at trees, at a brown glimpse of the river. But she was filled with tension, like a panic: as if an enemy was in the garden with her. She spoke to herself severely, thus: All this is quite natural. First, I spent twelve years of my adult life working, *living my own life*. Then I married, and from the moment I became pregnant for the first time I signed myself over, so to speak, to other people. To the children. Not for one moment in twelve years have I been alone, had time to myself. So now I have to learn to be myself again. That's all.

And she went indoors to help Mrs Parkes cook and clean, and found some sewing to do for the children. She kept herself occupied every day. At the end of the first term she understood she felt two contrary emotions. First: secret astonishment and dismay that during those weeks when the house was empty of children she had in fact been more occupied (had been careful to keep herself occupied) than ever she had been when the children were around her needing her continual attention. Second: that now she knew the house would be full of them, and for five weeks, she resented the fact she would never be alone. She was already looking back at those hours of sewing, cooking (but by herself), as at a lost freedom which would not be hers for five long weeks. And the two months of term which would succeed the five weeks stretched alluringly open to her—freedom. But what freedom—when in fact she had been so careful *not* to be free of small duties during the last weeks? She looked at herself, Susan Rawlings, sitting in a big chair by the window in the bedroom, sewing shirts or dresses, which she might just as well have bought. She saw herself making cakes for hours at a time in the big family kitchen: yet usually she bought cakes. What she saw was a woman alone, that was true, but she had not felt alone. For instance, Mrs Parkes was always somewhere in the house. And she did not like being in the garden at all, because of the closeness there of the enemy—irritation, restlessness, emptiness, whatever it was, which keeping her hands occupied made less dangerous for some reason.

Susan did not tell Matthew of these thoughts. They were not sensible. She did not recognize herself in them. What should she say to her dear friend and husband Matthew? 'When I go into the garden, that is, if the children are not there, I feel as if there is an enemy there waiting to invade me.' 'What enemy, Susan darling?' 'Well I don't know, really. . . .' 'Perhaps you should see a doctor?'

No, clearly this conversation should not take place. The holidays began and Susan welcomed them. Four children, lively, energetic, intelligent, demanding: she was never, not for a moment of her day, alone. If she was in a room, they would be in the next room, or waiting for her to do something for them; or it would soon be time for lunch or tea, or to take one of them to the dentist. Something to do: five weeks of it, thank goodness.

On the fourth day of these so welcome holidays, she found she was storming with anger at the twins, two shrinking beautiful children who (and this is what checked her) stood hand in hand looking at her with sheer dismayed disbelief. This was their calm mother, shouting at them. And for what? They had come to her with some game, some bit of nonsense. They looked at each other, moved closer for support, and went off hand in hand, leaving Susan holding on to the windowsill of the living room, breathing deep, feeling sick. She went to lie down, telling the older children she had a headache. She heard the boy Harry telling the little ones: 'It's all right, Mother's got a headache.' She heard that *It's all right* with pain.

That night she said to her husband: 'Today I shouted at the twins, quite unfairly.' She sounded miserable, and he said gently: 'Well, what of it?'

'It's more of an adjustment than I thought, their going to school.'

'But Susie, Susie darling. . . .' For she was crouched weeping on the bed. He comforted her: 'Susan, what is all this about? You shouted at them? What of it? If you shouted at them fifty times a day it wouldn't be more than the little devils deserve.' But she wouldn't laugh. She wept. Soon he comforted her with his body. She became calm. Calm, she wondered what was wrong with her, and why she should mind so much that she might, just once, have behaved unjustly with the children. What did it matter? They had forgotten it all long ago: Mother had a headache and everything was all right.

It was a long time later that Susan understood that that night, when she had wept and Matthew had driven the misery out of her with his big solid body, was the last time, ever in their married life, that they had been—to use their mutual language—with each other. And even that was a lie, because she had not told him of her real fears at all.

The five weeks passed, and Susan was in control of herself, and good and kind, and she looked forward to the holidays with a mixture of fear and longing. She did not know what to expect. She took the twins off to school (the elder children took themselves to school) and she returned to the house determined to face the enemy wherever he was, in the house, or the garden, or — where?

She was again restless, she was possessed by restlessness. She cooked and sewed and worked as before, day after day, while Mrs Parkes remonstrated: 'Mrs Rawlings, what's the need for it? I can do that, it's what you pay me for.'

And it was so irrational that she checked herself. She would put the car into the garage, go up to her bedroom, and sit, hands in her lap, forcing herself to be quiet. She listened to Mrs Parkes moving around the house. She looked out into the garden and saw the branches shake the trees. She sat defeating the enemy, restlessness. Emptiness. She ought to be thinking about her life, about herself. But she did not. Or perhaps she could not. As soon as she forced her mind to think about Susan (for what else did she want to be alone for?) it skipped off to thoughts of butter or school clothes. Or it thought of Mrs Parkes. She realized that she sat listening for the movements of the cleaning woman, following her every turn, bend, thought. She followed her in her mind from kitchen to bathroom, from table to oven, and it was as if the duster, the cleaning cloth, the saucepan, were in her own hand. She would hear herself saying: No, not like that, don't put that there. . . . Yet she did not give a damn what Mrs Parkes did, or if she did it at all. Yet she could not prevent herself from being conscious of her, every minute. Yes, this was what was wrong with her: she needed, when she was alone, to be really alone, with no one near. She could not endure the knowledge that in ten minutes or in half an hour Mrs Parkes would call up the stairs: 'Mrs Rawlings, there's no silver polish. Madam, we're out of flour.'

So she left the house and went to sit in the garden where she was screened from the house by trees. She waited for the demon to appear and claim her, but he did not.

She was keeping him off, because she had not, after all, come to an end of arranging herself.

She was planning how to be somewhere where Mrs Parkes would not come after her with a cup of tea, or a demand to be allowed to telephone (always irritating since Susan did not care who she telephoned or how often), or just a nice talk about something. Yes, she needed a place, or a state of affairs, where it would not be necessary to keep reminding herself: In ten minutes I must telephone Matthew about . . . and at half past three I must leave early for the children because the car needs cleaning. And at ten o'clock tomorrow I must remember. . . . She was possessed with resentment that the seven hours of freedom in every day (during weekdays in the school term) were not free, that never, not for one second, ever, was she free from the pressure of time, from having to remember this or that. She could never forget herself; never really let herself go into forgetfulness.

Resentment. It was poisoning her. (She looked at this emotion and thought it was absurd. Yet she felt it.) She was a prisoner. (She looked at this thought too, and it was no good telling herself it was a ridiculous one.) She must tell Matthew—but what? She was filled with emotions that were utterly ridiculous, that she despised, yet that nevertheless she was feeling so strongly she could not shake them off.

The school holidays came round, and this time they were for nearly two months, and she behaved with a conscious controlled decency that nearly drove her crazy. She would lock herself in the bathroom, and sit on the edge of the bath, breathing deep, trying to let go into some kind of calm. Or she went up into the spare room, usually empty, where no one would expect her to be. She heard the children calling 'Mother, Mother,' and kept silent, feeling guilty. Or she went to the very end of the garden, by herself, and looked at the slow-moving brown river; she looked at the river and closed her eyes and breathed slow and deep, taking it into her being, into her veins.

Then she returned to the family, wife and mother, smiling and responsible, feeling as if the pressure of these people—four lively children and her husband—were a painful pressure on the surface of her skin, a hand pressing on her brain. She did not once break down into irritation during these holidays, but it was like living out a prison sentence, and when the children went back to school, she sat on a white stone seat near the flowing river, and she thought: It is not even a year since the twins went to school, since *they were off my hands* (What on earth did I think I meant when I used that stupid phrase?) and yet I'm a different person. I'm simply not myself. I don't understand it.

Yet she had to understand it. For she knew that this structure—big white house, on which the mortgage still cost four hundred a year, a husband, so good and kind and insightful, four children, all doing so nicely, and the garden where she sat, and Mrs Parkes the cleaning woman—all this depended on her, and yet she could not understand why, or even what it was she contributed to it.

She said to Matthew in their bedroom: 'I think there must be something wrong with me.'

And he said: 'Surely not, Susan? You look marvellous—you're as lovely as ever.'

She looked at the handsome blond man, with his clear, intelligent, blue-eyed face, and thought: Why is it I can't tell him? Why not? And she said: 'I need to be alone more than I am.'

At which he swung his slow blue gaze at her, and she saw what she had been dreading: Incredulity. Disbelief. And fear. An incredulous blue stare from a stranger who was her husband, as close to her as her own breath.

He said: 'But the children are at school and off your hands.'

She said to herself: I've got to force myself to say: Yes, but do you realize that I never feel free? There's never a moment I can say to myself: There's nothing I have to remind myself about, nothing I have to do in half an hour, or an hour, or two hours. . . .

But she said: 'I don't feel well.'

He said: 'Perhaps you need a holiday.'

She said, appalled: 'But not without you, surely?' For she could not imagine herself going off without him. Yet that was what he meant. Seeing her face, he laughed, and opened his arms, and she went into them, thinking: Yes, yes, but why can't I say it? And what is it I have to say?

She tried to tell him, about never being free. And he listened and said: 'But Susan, what sort of freedom can you possibly want—short of being dead! Am I ever free? I go to the office, and I have to be there at ten— all right, half past ten, sometimes. And I have to do this or that, don't I? Then I've got to come home at a certain time—I don't mean it, you know I don't—but if I'm not going to be back home at six I telephone you. When can I ever say to myself: I have nothing to be responsible for in the next six hours?'

Susan, hearing this, was remorseful. Because it was true. The good marriage, the house, the children, depended just as much on his voluntary bondage as it did on hers. But why did he not feel bound? Why didn't he chafe and become restless? No, there was something really wrong with her and this proved it.

And that word *bondage*—why had she used it? She had never felt marriage, or the children, as bondage. Neither had he, or surely they wouldn't be together lying in each other's arms content after twelve years of marriage.

No, her state (whatever it was) was irrelevant, nothing to do with her real good life with her family. She had to accept the fact that after all, she was an irrational person and to live with it. Some people had to live with crippled arms, or stammers, or being deaf. She would have to live knowing she was subject to a state of mind she could not own.

Nevertheless, as a result of this conversation with her husband, there was a new regime next holidays.

The spare room at the top of the house now had a cardboard sign saying: PRIVATE! DO NOT DISTURB! on it. (This sign had been drawn in coloured chalks by the children, after a discussion between the parents in which it was decided this was psychologically the right thing.) The family and Mrs Parkes knew this was 'Mother's Room' and that she was entitled to her privacy. Many serious conversations took place between Matthew and the children about not taking Mother for granted. Susan overheard the first, between father and Harry, the older boy, and was surprised at her irritation over it. Surely she could have a room somewhere in that big house and retire into it without such a fuss being made? Without it being so solemnly discussed? Why couldn't she simply have announced: 'I'm going to fit out the little top room for myself, and when I'm in it I'm not to be disturbed for anything short of fire'? Just that, and finished; instead of long earnest discussions. When she heard Harry and Matthew explaining it to the twins with Mrs Parkes coming in—'Yes, well, a family sometimes gets on top of a woman'—she had to go right away to the bottom of the garden until the devils of exasperation had finished their dance in her blood.

But now there was a room, and she could go there when she liked, she used it seldom: she felt even more caged there than in her bedroom. One day she had gone up there after a lunch for ten children she had cooked and served because Mrs Parkes was not there, and had sat alone for a while looking into the garden. She saw the children stream out from the kitchen and stand looking up at the window where she sat behind the curtains. They were all—her children and their friends—discussing Mother's Room. A few minutes later, the chase of children in some game came pounding up the stairs, but ended as abruptly as if they had fallen over a ravine, so sudden was the silence. They had remembered she was there, and had gone silent in a great gale of 'Hush! Shhhhhh! Quiet, you'll disturb her. . . .' And they went tiptoeing downstairs like criminal conspirators. When she came down to make tea for them, they all apologized. The twins put their arms around her, from front to back, making a human cage of loving limbs, and promised it would never occur again. 'We forgot, Mummy, we forgot all about it!'

What it amounted to was that Mother's Room, and her need for privacy, had become a valuable lesson in respect for other people's rights. Quite soon Susan was going up to the room only because it was a lesson it was a pity to drop. Then she took sewing up there, and the children and Mrs Parkes came in and out: it had become another family room.

She sighed, and smiled, and resigned herself—she made jokes at her own expense with Matthew over the room. That is, she did from the self she liked, she respected. But at the same time, something inside her howled with impatience, with rage. . . . And she was frightened. One day she found herself kneeling by her bed and praying: 'Dear God, keep it away from me, keep him away from me.' She meant the devil, for she now thought of it, not caring if she were irrational, as some sort of demon. She imagined him, or it, as a youngish man, or perhaps a middle-aged man pretending to be young. Or a man young-looking from immaturity? At any rate, she saw the young-looking face which, when she drew closer, had dry lines about mouth and eyes. He was thinnish, meagre in build. And he had a reddish complexion, and ginger hair. That was he—a gingery, energetic man, and he wore a reddish hairy jacket, unpleasant to the touch.

Well, one day she saw him. She was standing at the bottom of the garden, watching the river ebb past, when she raised her eyes and saw this person, or being, sitting on the white stone bench. He was looking at her, and grinning. In his hand was a long crooked stick, which he had picked off the ground, or broken off the tree above him. He was absent-mindedly, out of an absent-minded or freakish impulse of spite, using the stick to stir around in the coils of a blindworm or a grass snake (or some kind of snakelike creature: it was whitish and unhealthy to look at, unpleasant). The snake was twisting about, flinging its coils from side to side in a kind of dance of protest against the teasing prodding stick.

Susan looked at him thinking: Who is the stranger? What is he doing in our garden? Then she recognized the man around whom her terrors had crystallized. As she did so, he vanished. She made herself walk over to the bench. A shadow from a branch lay across thin emerald grass, moving jerkily over its roughness, and she could see why she had taken it for a snake, lashing and twisting. She went back to the house thinking: Right, then, so I've seen him with my own eyes, so I'm not crazy after all—there *is* a danger because I've seen him. He is lurking in the garden and sometimes even in the house, and he wants *to get into me and to take me over.*

She dreamed of having a room or a place, anywhere, where she could go and sit, by herself, no one knowing where she was.

Once, near Victoria, she found herself outside a news agent that had Rooms to Let advertised. She decided to rent a room, telling no one. Sometimes she could take the train in to Richmond and sit alone in it for an hour or two. Yet how could she? A room would cost three or four pounds a week, and she earned no money, and how could she explain to Matthew that she needed such a sum? What for? It did not occur to her that she was taking it for granted she wasn't going to tell him about the room.

Well, it was out of the question, having a room; yet she knew she must.

One day, when a school term was well established, and none of the children had measles or other ailments, and everything seemed in order, she did the shopping early, explained to Mrs Parkes she was meeting an old school friend, took the train to Victoria, searched until she found a small quiet hotel, and asked for a room for the day. They did not let rooms by the day, the manageress said, looking doubtful, since Susan so obviously was not the kind of woman who needed a room for unrespectable reasons. Susan made a long explanation about not being well, being unable to shop without frequent rests for lying down. At last she was allowed to rent the room provided she paid a full night's price for it. She was taken up by the manageress and a maid, both concerned over the state of her health . . . which must be pretty bad if, living in Richmond (she had signed her name and address in the register), she needed a shelter at Victoria.

The room was ordinary and anonymous, and was just what Susan needed. She put a shilling in the gas fire, and sat, eyes shut, in a dingy armchair with her back to a dingy window. She was alone. She was alone.

She was alone. She could feel pressures lifting off her. First the sounds of traffic came very loud; then they seemed to vanish; she might even have slept a little. A knock on the door: it was Miss Townsend the manageress, bringing her a cup of tea with her own hands, so concerned was she over Susan's long silence and possible illness.

Miss Townsend was a lonely woman of fifty, running this hotel with all the rectitude expected of her, and she sensed in Susan the possibility of understanding companionship. She stayed to talk. Susan found herself in the middle of a fantastic story about her illness, which got more and more improbable as she tried to make it tally with the large house at Richmond, well-off husband, and four children. Suppose she said instead: Miss Townsend, I'm here in your hotel because I need to be alone for a few hours, above all *alone and with no one knowing where I am*. She said it mentally, and saw, mentally, the look that would inevitably come on Miss Townsend's elderly maiden's face. 'Miss Townsend, my four children and my husband are driving me insane, do you understand that? Yes, I can see from the gleam of hysteria in your eyes that comes from loneliness controlled but only just contained that I've got everything in the world you've ever longed for. Well, Miss Townsend, I don't want any of it. You can have it, Miss Townsend. I wish I was absolutely alone in the world, like you. Miss Townsend, I'm besieged by seven devils, Miss Townsend, Miss Townsend, let me stay here in your hotel where the devils can't get me. . . .' Instead of saying all this, she described her anaemia, agreed to try Miss Townsend's remedy for it, which was raw liver, minced, between whole-meal bread, and said yes, perhaps it would be better if she stayed at home and let a friend do shopping for her. She paid her bill and left the hotel, defeated.

At home Mrs Parkes said she didn't really like it, no, not really, when Mrs Rawlings was away from nine in the morning until five. The teacher had telephoned from school to say Joan's teeth were paining her, and she hadn't known what to say; and what was she to make for the children's tea, Mrs Rawlings hadn't said.

All this was nonsense, of course. Mrs Parkes's complaint was that Susan had withdrawn herself spiritually, leaving the burden of the big house on her.

Susan looked back at her day of 'freedom' which had resulted in her becoming a friend to the lonely Miss Townsend, and in Mrs Parkes's remonstrances. Yet she remembered the short blissful hour of being alone, really alone. She was determined to arrange her life, no matter what it cost, so that she could have that solitude more often. An absolute solitude, where no one knew her or cared about her.

But how? She thought of saying to her old employer: I want to back you up in a story with Matthew that I am doing part-time work for you. The truth is that . . . but she would have to tell him a lie too, and which lie? She could not say: I want to sit by myself three or four times a week in a rented room. And besides, he knew Matthew, and she could not really ask him to tell lies on her behalf, apart from his being bound to think it meant a lover.

Suppose she really took a part-time job, which she could get through fast and efficiently, leaving time for herself. What job? Addressing envelopes? Canvassing?

And there was Mrs Parkes, working widow, who knew exactly what she was prepared to give to the house, who knew by instinct when her mistress withdrew in spirit from her responsibilities. Mrs Parkes was one of the servers of this world, but she needed someone to serve. She had to have Mrs Rawlings, her madam, at the top of the house or in the garden, so that she could come and get support from her: 'Yes, the bread's not what it was when I was a girl. . . . Yes, Harry's got a wonderful appetite, I wonder where he puts it all. . . . Yes, it's lucky the twins are so much of a size, they can wear each other's shoes, that's a savings in these hard times. . . . Yes, the cherry jam from Switzerland is not a patch on the jam from Poland, and three times the price. . . .' And so on. That sort of talk Mrs Parkes must have, every day, or she would leave, not knowing herself why she left.

Susan Rawlings, thinking these thoughts, found that she was prowling through the great thicketed garden like a wild cat: she was walking up the stairs, down the stairs, through the rooms, into the garden, along the brown running river, back, up through the house, down again. . . . It was a wonder Mrs Parkes did not think it strange. But on the contrary, Mrs Rawlings could do what she liked, she could stand on her head if she wanted, provided she was *there*. Susan Rawlings prowled and muttered through her house, hating Mrs Parkes, hating poor Miss Townsend, dreaming of her hour of solitude in the dingy respectability of Miss Townsend's hotel bedroom, and she knew quite well she was mad. Yes, she was mad.

She said to Matthew that she must have a holiday. Matthew agreed with her. This was not as things had been once—how they had talked in each other's arms in the marriage bed. He had, she knew, diagnosed her finally as *unreasonable*. She had become someone outside himself that he had to manage. They were living side by side in this house like two tolerably friendly strangers.

Having told Mrs Parkes, or rather, asked for her permission, she went off on a walking holiday in Wales. She chose the remotest place she knew of. Every morning the children telephoned her before they went off to school, to encourage and support her, just as they had over Mother's Room. Every evening she telephoned them, spoke to each child in turn, and then to Matthew. Mrs Parkes, given permission to telephone for instructions or advice, did so every day at lunchtime. When, as happened three times, Mrs Rawlings was out on the mountainside, Mrs Parkes asked that she should ring back at such and such a time, for she would not be happy in what she was doing without Mrs Rawlings' blessing.

Susan prowled over wild country with the telephone wire holding her to her duty like a leash. The next time she must telephone, or wait to be telephoned, nailed her to her cross. The mountains themselves seemed trammelled by her unfreedom. Everywhere on the mountains, where she met no one at all, from breakfast time to dusk, excepting sheep, or a shepherd, she came face to face with her own craziness which might attack her in the broadest valleys, so that they seemed too small; or on a mountain-top from which she could see a hundred other mountains and valleys, so that they seemed too low, too small, with the sky pressing down too close. She would stand gazing at a hillside brilliant with ferns and bracken, jewelled with running water, and see nothing but her devil, who lifted inhuman eyes at her from where he leaned negligently on a rock, switching at his ugly yellow boots with a leafy twig.

She returned to her home and family, with the Welsh emptiness at the back of her mind like a promise of freedom.

She told her husband she wanted to have an *au pair* girl.

They were in their bedroom, it was late at night, the children slept. He sat, shirted and slippered, in a chair by the window, looking out. She sat brushing her hair and watching him in the mirror. A time-hallowed scene in the connubial bedroom. He said nothing, while she heard the arguments coming into his mind, only to be rejected because every one was *reasonable*.

'It seems strange to get one now, after all, the children are in school most of the day. Surely the time for you to have help was when you were stuck with them day and night. Why don't you ask Mrs Parkes to cook for you? She's even offered to—I can understand if you are tired of cooking for six people. But you know that an *au pair* girl means all kinds of problems, it's not like having an ordinary char in during the day. . . .'

Finally he said carefully: 'Are you thinking of going back to work?'

'No,' she said, 'no, not really.' She made herself sound vague, rather stupid. She went on brushing her black hair and peering at herself so as to be oblivious of the short uneasy glances her Matthew kept giving her. 'Do you think we can't afford it?' she went on vaguely, not at all the old efficient Susan who knew exactly what they could afford.

'It's not that,' he said, looking out of the window at dark trees, so as not to look at her. Meanwhile she examined a round, candid, pleasant face with clear dark brows and clear grey eyes. A sensible face. She brushed thick healthy black hair and thought: Yet that's the reflection of a madwoman. How very strange! Much more to the point if what looked back at me was the gingery green-eyed demon with his dry meagre smile. . . . Why wasn't Matthew agreeing? After all, what else could he do? She was breaking her part of the bargain and there was no way of forcing her to keep it: that her spirit, her soul, should live in this house, so that the people in it could grow like plants in water, and Mrs Parkes remain content in their service. In return for this, he would be a good loving husband, and responsible towards the children. Well, nothing like this had been true of either of them for a long time. He did his duty, perfunctorily; she did not even pretend to do hers. And he had become like other husbands, with his real life in his work and the people he met there, and very likely a serious affair. All this was her fault.

At last he drew heavy curtains, blotting out the trees, and turned to force her attention: 'Susan, are you really sure we need a girl?' But she would not meet his appeal at all: She was running the brush over her hair again and again, lifting fine black clouds in a small hiss of electricity. She was peering in and smiling as if she were amused at the clinging hissing hair that followed the brush.

'Yes, I think it would be a good idea on the whole,' she said, with the cunning of a madwoman evading the real point.

In the mirror she could see her Matthew lying on his back, his hands behind his head, staring upwards, his face sad and hard. She felt her heart (the old heart of Susan Rawlings) soften and call out to him. But she set it to be indifferent.

He said: 'Susan, the children?' It was an appeal that *almost* reached her. He opened his arms, lifting them from where they had lain by his sides, palms up, empty. She had only to run across and fling herself into them, onto his hard, warm chest, and melt into herself, into Susan. But she could not. She would not see his lifted arms. She said vaguely: 'Well, surely it'll be even better for them? We'll get a French or a German girl and they'll learn the language.'

In the dark she lay beside him, feeling frozen, a stranger. She felt as if Susan had been spirited away. She disliked very much this woman who lay here, cold and indifferent beside a suffering man, but she could not change her.

Next morning she set about getting a girl, and very soon came Sophie Traub from Hamburg, a girl of twenty, laughing, healthy, blue-eyed, intending to learn English. Indeed, she already spoke a good deal. In return for a room — 'Mother's Room'—and her food, she undertook to do some light cooking, and to be with the children when Mrs Rawlings asked. She was an intelligent girl and understood perfectly what was needed. Susan said: 'I go off sometimes, for the morning or for the day—well, sometimes the children run home from school, or they ring up, or a teacher rings up. I should be here, really. And there's the daily woman. . . .' And Sophie laughed her deep fruity *Fräulein's* laugh, showed her fine white teeth and her dimples, and said: 'You want some person to play mistress of the house sometimes, not so?'

'Yes, that is just so,' said Susan, a bit dry, despite herself, thinking in secret fear how easy it was, how much nearer to the end she was than she thought. Healthy Fräulein Traub's instant understanding of their position proved this to be true.

The *au pair* girl, because of her own common sense, or (as Susan said to herself with her new inward shudder) because she had been *chosen* so well by Susan, was a success with everyone, the children liking her, Mrs Parkes forgetting almost at once that she was German, and Matthew finding her 'nice to have around the house'. For he was now taking things as they came, from the surface of life, withdrawn both as a husband and a father from the household.

One day Susan saw how Sophie and Mrs Parkes were talking and laughing in the kitchen, and she announced that she would be away until teatime. She knew exactly where to go and what she must look for. She took the District Line to South Kensington, changed to the Circle, got off at Paddington, and walked around looking at the smaller hotels until she was satisfied with one which had FRED'S HOTEL painted on windowpanes that needed cleaning. The façade was a faded shiny yellow, like unhealthy skin. A door at the end of a passage said she must knock; she did, and Fred appeared. He was not at all attractive, not in any way, being fattish, and rundown, and wearing a tasteless striped suit. He had small sharp eyes in a white creased face, and was quite prepared to let Mrs Jones (she chose the farcical name deliberately, staring him out) have a room three days a week from ten until six. Provided of course that she paid in advance each time she came? Susan produced fifteen shillings (no price had been set by him) and held it out, still fixing him with a bold unblinking challenge she had not known until then she could use at will. Looking at her still, he took up a ten-shilling note from her palm between thumb and forefinger, fingered it; then shuffled up two half crowns, held out his own palm with these bits of money displayed thereon, and let his gaze lower broodingly at them. They were standing in the passage, a red-shaded light above, bare boards beneath, and a strong smell of floor polish rising about them. He shot his gaze up at her over the still-extended palm, and smiled as if to say: What do you take me for? 'I shan't,' said Susan, 'be using this room for the purposes of making money.' He still waited. She added another five shillings, at which he nodded and said: 'You pay, and I ask no questions.' 'Good,' said Susan. He now went past her to the stairs, and there waited a moment: the light from the street door being in her eyes, she lost sight of him momentarily. Then she saw a sober-suited, white-faced, white-balding little man trotting up the stairs like a waiter, and she went after him. They proceeded in utter silence up the stairs of this house where no questions were asked—Fred's Hotel, which could afford the freedom for its visitors that poor Miss Townsend's hotel could not. The room was hideous. It had a single window, with thin green brocade curtains, a three-quarter bed that had a cheap green satin bedspread on it, a fireplace with a gas fire and a shilling meter by it, a chest of drawers, and a green wicker armchair.

'Thank you,' said Susan, knowing that Fred (if this was Fred, and not George, or Herbert or Charlie) was looking at her, not so much with curiosity, an emotion he would not own to, for professional reasons, but with a philosophical sense of what was appropriate. Having taken her money and shown her up and agreed to everything, he was clearly disapproving of her for coming here. She did not belong here at all, so his look said. (But she knew, already, how very much she did belong: the room had been waiting for her to join it.) 'Would you have me called at five o'clock, please?' and he nodded and went downstairs.

It was twelve in the morning. She was free. She sat in the armchair, she simply sat, she closed her eyes and sat and let herself be alone. She was alone and no one knew where she was. When a knock came on the door she was annoyed, and prepared to show it: but it was Fred himself, it was five o'clock and he was calling her as ordered. He flicked his sharp little eyes over the room—bed, first. It was undisturbed. She might never have been in the room at all. She thanked him, said she would be returning the day after tomorrow, and left. She was back home in time to cook supper, to put the children to bed, to cook a second supper for her husband and herself later. And to welcome Sophie back from the pictures where she had gone with a friend. All these things she did cheerfully, willingly. But she was thinking all the time of the hotel room, she was longing for it with her whole being.

Three times a week. She arrived promptly at ten, looked Fred in the eyes, gave him twenty shillings, followed him up the stairs, went into the room, and shut the door on him with gentle firmness. For Fred, disapproving of her being here at all, was quite ready to let friendship, or at least acquaintanceship, follow his disapproval, if only she would let him. But he was content to go off on her dismissing nod, with the twenty shillings in his hand.

She sat in the armchair and shut her eyes.

What did she *do* in the room? Why, nothing at all. From the chair, when it had rested her, she went to the window, stretching her arms, smiling, treasuring her anonymity, to look out. She was no longer Susan Rawlings, mother of four, wife of Matthew, employer of Mrs Parkes and of Sophie Traub, with these and those relations with friends, schoolteachers, tradesmen. She no longer was mistress of the big white house and garden, owning clothes suitable for this and that activity or occasion. She was Mrs Jones, and she was alone, and she had no past and no future. Here I am, she thought, after all these years of being married and having children and playing those roles of responsibility—and I'm just the same. Yet there have been times I thought that nothing existed of me except the roles that went with being Mrs Matthew Rawlings. Yes, here I am, and if I never saw any of my family again, here I would still be . . . how very strange that is! And she leaned on the sill, and looked into the street, loving the men and women who passed, because she did not know them. She looked at the downtrodden buildings over the street, and at the sky, wet and dingy, or sometimes blue, and she felt she had never seen buildings or sky before. And then she went back to the chair, empty, her mind a blank. Sometimes she talked aloud, saying nothing—an exclamation, meaningless, followed by a comment about the floral pattern on the thin rug, or a stain on the green stain coverlet. For the most part, she wool-gathered — what word is there for it?—brooded, wandered, simply went dark, feeling emptiness run deliciously through her veins like the movement of her blood.

This room had become more her own than the house she lived in. One morning she found Fred taking her a flight higher than usual. She stopped, refusing to go up, and demanded her usual room, Number 19. 'Well, you'll have to wait half an hour then,' he said. Willingly she descended to the dark disinfectant-smelling hall, and sat waiting until the two, man and woman, came down the stairs, giving her swift indifferent glances before they hurried out into the street, separating at the door. She went up to the room, *her* room, which they had just vacated. It was no less hers, though the windows were set wide open, and a maid was straightening the bed as she came in.

After these days of solitude, it was both easy to play her part as mother and wife, and difficult—because it was so easy: she felt an impostor. She felt as if her shell moved here, with her family, answering to Mummy, Mother, Susan, Mrs Rawlings. She was surprised no one saw through her, that she wasn't turned out of doors, as a fake. On the contrary, it seemed the children loved her more; Matthew and she 'got on' pleasantly, and Mrs Parkes was happy in her work under (for the most part, it must be confessed) Sophie Traub. At night she lay beside her husband, and they made love again, apparently just as they used to, when they were really married. But she, Susan, or the being who answered so readily and improbably to the name of Susan, was not there: she was in Fred's Hotel, in Paddington, waiting for the easing hours of solitude to begin.

Soon she made a new arrangement with Fred and with Sophie. It was for five days a week. As for the money, five pounds, she simply asked Matthew for it. She saw that she was not even frightened he might ask what for: he would give it to her, she knew that, and yet it was terrifying it could be so, for this close couple, these partners, had once known the destination of every shilling they must spend. He agreed to give her five pounds a week. She asked for just so much, not a penny more. He sounded indifferent about it. It was as if he were paying her, she thought: *paying her off*—yes, that was it. Terror came back for a moment, when she understood this, but she stilled it: things had gone too far for that. Now, every week, on Sunday nights, he gave her five pounds, turning away from her before their eyes could meet on the transaction. As for Sophie Traub, she was to be somewhere in or near the house until six at night, after which she was free. She was not to cook, or to clean, she was simply to be there. So she gardened or sewed, and asked friends in, being a person who was bound to have a lot of friends. If the children were sick, she nursed them. If teachers telephoned, she answered them sensibly. For the five daytimes in the school week, she was altogether the mistress of the house.

One night in the bedroom, Matthew asked: 'Susan, I don't want to interfere — don't think that, please—but are you sure you are well?'

She was brushing her hair at the mirror. She made two more strokes on either side of her head, before she replied: 'Yes, dear, I am sure I am well.'

He was again lying on his back, his big blond head on his hands, his elbows angled up and part-concealing his face. He said: 'Then Susan, I have to ask you this question, though you must understand, I'm not putting any sort of pressure on you.' (Susan heard the word pressure with dismay, because this was inevitable, of course she could not go on like this.) 'Are things going to go on like this?'

'Well,' she said, going vague and bright and idiotic again, so as to escape: 'Well, I don't see why not.'

He was jerking his elbows up and down, in annoyance or in pain, and, looking at him, she saw he had got thin, even gaunt; and restless angry movements were not what she remembered of him. He said: 'Do you want a divorce, is that it?'

At this, Susan only with the greatest difficulty stopped herself from laughing: she could hear the bright bubbling laughter she *would* have emitted, had she let herself. He could only mean one thing: she had a lover, and that was why she spent her days in London, as lost to him as if she had vanished to another continent.

Then the small panic set in again: she understood that he hoped she did have a lover, he was begging her to say so, because otherwise it would be too terrifying.

She thought this out, as she brushed her hair, watching the fine black stuff fly up to make its little clouds of electricity, hiss, hiss, hiss. Behind her head, across the room, was a blue wall. She realised she was absorbed in watching the black hair making shapes against the blue. She should be answering him. 'Do *you* want a divorce, Matthew?'

He said: 'That surely isn't the point, is it?'

'You brought it up, I didn't,' she said, brightly, suppressing meaningless tinkling laughter.

Next day she asked Fred: 'Have enquiries been made for me?'

He hesitated, and she said: 'I've been coming here a year now. I've made no trouble, and you've been paid every day. I have a right to be told.'

'As a matter of fact, Mrs Jones, a man did come asking.'

'A man from a detective agency?'

'Well, he could have been, couldn't he?'

'I was asking you . . . well, what did you tell him?'

'I told him a Mrs Jones came every weekday from ten until five or six and stayed in Number Nineteen by herself.'

'Describing me?'

'Well Mrs Jones, I had no alternative. Put yourself in my place.'

'By rights I should deduct what that man gave you for the information.'

He raised shocked eyes: she was not the sort of person to make jokes like this! Then he chose to laugh: a pinkish wet slit appeared across his white crinkled face: his eyes positively begged her to laugh, otherwise he might lose some money. She remained grave, looking at him.

He stopped laughing and said: 'You want to go up now?'—returning to the familiarity, and comradeship, of the country where no questions are asked, on which (and he knew it) she depended completely.

She went up to sit in her wicker chair. But it was not the same. Her husband had searched her out. (The world had searched her out.) The pressures were on her. She was here with his connivance. He might walk in at any moment, here, into Room 19. She imagined the report from the detective agency: 'A woman calling herself Mrs Jones, fitting the description of your wife (etc., etc., etc.), stays alone all day in Room No. 19. She insists on this room, waits for it if it is engaged. As far as the proprietor knows, she receives no visitors there, male or female.' A report something on these lines, Matthew must have received.

Well of course he was right: things couldn't go on like this. He had put an end to it all simply by sending the detective after her.

She tried to shrink herself back into the shelter of the room, a snail pecked out of its shell and trying to squirm back. But the peace of the room had gone. She was trying consciously to revive it, trying to let go into the dark creative trance (or whatever it was) that she had found there. It was no use, yet she craved for it, she was as ill as a suddenly deprived addict.

Several times she returned to the room, to look for herself there, but instead she found the unnamed spirit of restlessness, a prickling fevered hunger for movement, an irritable self-consciousness that made her brain feel as if it had coloured lights going on and off inside it. Instead of the soft dark that had been the room's air, were now waiting for her demons that made her dash blindly about, muttering words of hate; she was impelling herself from point to point like a moth dashing itself against a windowpane, sliding to the bottom, fluttering off on broken wings, then crashing into the invisible barrier again. And again and again. Soon she was exhausted, and she told Fred that for a while she would not be needing the room, she was going on holiday. Home she went, to the big white house by the river. The middle of a weekday, and she felt guilty at returning to her own home when not expected. She stood unseen, looking in at the kitchen window. Mrs Parkes, wearing a discarded floral overall of Susan's, was stooping to slide something into the oven. Sophie, arms folded, was leaning her back against a cupboard and laughing at some joke made by a girl not seen before by Susan—a dark foreign girl, Sophie's visitor. In an armchair Molly, one of the twins, lay curled, sucking her thumb and watching the grownups. She must have some sickness, to be kept from school. The child's listless face, the dark circles under her eyes, hurt Susan: Molly was looking at the three grownups working and talking in exactly the same way

Susan looked at the four through the kitchen window: she was remote, shut off from them.

But then, just as Susan imagined herself going in, picking up the little girl, and sitting in an armchair with her, stroking her probably heated forehead, Sophie did just that: she had been standing on one leg, the other knee flexed, its foot set against the wall. Now she let her foot in its ribbon-tied red shoe slide down the wall, stood solid on two feet, clapping her hands before and behind her, and sang a couple of lines in German, so that the child lifted her heavy eyes at her and began to smile. Then she walked, or rather skipped, over to the child, swung her up, and let her fall into her lap at the same moment she sat herself. She said 'Hopla! Hopla! Molly . . .' and began stroking the dark untidy young head that Molly laid on her shoulder for comfort.

Well. . . . Susan blinked the tears of farewell out of her eyes, and went quietly up the house to her bedroom. There she sat looking at the river through the trees. She felt at peace, but in a way that was new to her. She had no desire to move, to talk, to do anything at all. The devils that had haunted the house, the garden, were not there; but she knew it was because her soul was in Room 19 in Fred's Hotel; she was not really here at all. It was a sensation that should have been frightening: to sit at her own bedroom window, listening to Sophie's rich young voice sing German nursery songs to her child, listening to Mrs Parkes clatter and move below, and to know that all this had nothing to do with her: she was already out of it.

Later, she made herself go down and say she was home: it was unfair to be here unannounced. She took lunch with Mrs Parkes, Sophie, Sophie's Italian friend Maria, and her daughter Molly, and felt like a visitor.

A few days later, at bedtime, Matthew said: 'Here's your five pounds,' and pushed them over at her. Yet he must have known she had not been leaving the house at all.

She shook her head, gave it back to him, and said, in explanation, not in accusation: 'As soon as you knew where I was, there was no point.'

He nodded, not looking at her. He was turned away from her: thinking, she knew, how best to handle this wife who terrified him.

He said: 'I wasn't trying to . . . it's just that I was worried.'

'Yes, I know.'

'I must confess that I was beginning to wonder. . .'

'You thought I had a lover?'

'Yes, I am afraid I did.'

She knew that he wished she had. She sat wondering how to say: 'For a year now I've been spending all my days in a very sordid hotel room. It's the place where I'm happy. In fact, without it I don't exist.' She heard herself saying this, and understood how terrified he was that she might. So instead she said: 'Well, perhaps you're not far wrong.'

Probably Matthew would think the hotel proprietor lied: he would want to think so.

'Well,' he said, and she could hear his voice spring up, so to speak, with relief: 'in that case I must confess I've got a bit of an affair on myself.'

She said, detached and interested: 'Really? Who is she?' and saw Matthew's startled look because of this reaction.

'It's Phil. Phil Hunt.'

She had known Phil Hunt well in the old unmarried days. She was thinking: No, she won't do, she's too neurotic and difficult. She's never been happy yet. Sophie's much better: Well Matthew will see that himself, as sensible as he is.

This line of thought went on in silence, while she said aloud: 'It's no point telling you about mine, because you don't know him.'

Quick, quick, invent, she thought. Remember how you invented all that nonsense for Miss Townsend.

She began slowly, careful not to contradict herself: 'His name is Michael' — (*Michael What?*)—'Michael Plant.' (What a silly name!) 'He's rather like you—in looks, I mean.' And indeed, she could imagine herself being touched by no one but Matthew himself. 'He's a publisher.' (Really? Why?) 'He's got a wife already and two children.'

She brought out this fantasy, proud of herself.

Matthew said: 'Are you two thinking of marrying?'

She said, before she could stop herself: 'Good God, *no!*'

She realized, if Matthew wanted to marry Phil Hunt, that this was too emphatic, but apparently it was all right, for his voice sounded relieved as he said: 'It is a bit impossible to imagine oneself married to anyone else, isn't it?' With which he pulled her to him, so that her head lay on his shoulder. She turned her face into the dark of his flesh, and listened to the blood pounding through her ears saying: I am alone, I am alone, I am alone.

In the morning Susan lay in bed while he dressed.

He had been thinking things out in the night, because now he said: 'Susan, why don't we make a foursome?'

Of course, she said to herself, of course he would be bound to say that. If one is sensible, if one is reasonable, if one never allows oneself a base thought or an envious emotion, naturally one says: Let's make a foursome!

'Why not?' she said.

'We could all meet for lunch. I mean, it's ridiculous, you sneaking off to filthy hotels, and me staying late at the office, and all the lies everyone has to tell.'

What on earth did I say his name was?—she panicked, then said: 'I think it's a good idea, but Michael is away at the moment. When he comes back though—and I'm sure you two would like each other.'

'He's away, is he? So that's why you've been . . .' Her husband put his hand to the knot of his tie in a gesture of male coquetry she would not before have associated with him; and he bent to kiss her cheek with the expression that goes with the words: Oh you naughty little puss! And she felt its answering look, naughty and coy, come onto her face.

Inside she was dissolving in horror at them both, at how far they had both sunk from honesty of emotion.

So now she was saddled with a lover, and he had a mistress! How ordinary, how reassuring, how jolly! And now they would make a foursome of it, and go about to theatres and restaurants. After all, the Rawlings could well afford that sort of thing, and presumably the publisher Michael Plant could afford to do himself and his mistress quite well. No, there was nothing to stop the four of them developing the most intricate relationship of civilized tolerance, all enveloped in a charming afterglow of autumnal passion. Perhaps they would all go off on holidays together? She had known people who did. Or perhaps Matthew would draw the line there? Why should he, though, if he was capable of talking about 'foursomes' at all?

She lay in the empty bedroom, listening to the car drive off with Matthew in it, off to work. Then she heard the children clattering off to school to the accompaniment of Sophie's cheerfully ringing voice. She slid down to the hollow of the bed, for shelter against her own irrelevance. And she stretched out her hand to the hollow where her husband's body had lain, but found no comfort there: he was not her husband. She curled herself up in a small tight ball under the clothes: she could stay here all day, all week, indeed, all her life.

But in a few days she must produce Michael Plant, and—but how? She must presumably find some agreeable man prepared to impersonate a publisher called Michael Plant. And in return for which she would—what? Well, for one thing they would make love. The idea made her want to cry with sheer exhaustion. On no, she had finished with all that—the proof of it was that the words 'make love', or even imagining it, trying hard to revive no more than the pleasures of sensuality, let alone affection, or love, made her want to run away and hide from the sheer effort of the thing. . . . Good Lord, why make love at all? Why make love with anyone? Or if you are going to make love, what does it matter who with? Why shouldn't she simply walk into the street, pick up a man and have a roaring sexual affair with him? Why not? Or even with Fred? What difference did it make?

But she had let herself in for it—an interminable stretch of time with a lover, called Michael, as part of a gallant civilized foursome. Well, she could not, and she would not.

She got up, dressed, went down to find Mrs Parkes, and asked her for the loan of a pound, since Matthew, she said, had forgotten to leave her money. She exchanged with Mrs Parkes variations on the theme that husbands are all the same, they don't think, and without saying a word to Sophie, whose voice could be heard upstairs from the telephone, walked to the underground, travelled to South Kensington, changed to the Inner Circle, got out at Paddington, and walked to Fred's Hotel. There she told

Fred that she wasn't going on holiday after all, she needed the room. She would have to wait an hour, Fred said. She went to a busy tearoom-cum-restaurant around the corner, and sat watching the people flow in and out the door that kept swinging open and shut, watched them mingle and merge and separate, felt her being flow into them, into their movement. When the hour was up she left a half crown for her pot of tea, and left the place without looking back at it, just as she had left her house, the big, beautiful white house, without another look, but silently dedicating it to Sophie. She returned to Fred, received the key of No. 19, now free, and ascended the grimy stairs slowly, letting floor after floor fall away below her, keeping her eyes lifted, so that floor after floor descended jerkily to her level of vision, and fell away out of sight.

No. 19 was the same. She saw everything with an acute, narrow, checking glance: the cheap shine of the satin spread, which had been replaced carelessly after the two bodies had finished their convulsions under it; a trace of powder on the glass that topped the chest of drawers; an intense green shade in a fold of the curtain. She stood at the window, looking down, watching people pass and pass and pass until her mind went dark from the constant movement. Then she sat in the wicker chair, letting herself go slack. But she had to be careful, because she did not want, today, to be surprised by Fred's knock at five o'clock.

The demons were not here. They had gone forever, because she was buying her freedom from them. She was slipping already into the dark fructifying dream that seemed to caress her inwardly, like the movement of her blood . . . but she had to think about Matthew first. Should she write a letter for the coroner? But what should she say? She would like to leave him with the look on his face she had seen this morning—banal, admittedly, but at least confidently healthy. Well, that was impossible, one did not look like that with a wife dead from suicide. But how to leave him believing she was dying because of a man—because of the fascinating publisher Michael Plant? Oh, how ridiculous! How absurd! How humiliating! But she decided not to trouble about it, simply not think about the living. If he wanted to believe she had a lover, he would believe it. And he *did* want to believe it. Even when he had found out that there was no publisher in London called Michael Plant, he would think: Oh poor Susan, she was afraid to give me his real name.

And what did it matter whether he married Phil Hunt or Sophie? Though it ought to be Sophie, who was already the mother of those children . . . and what hypocrisy to sit here worrying about the children, when she was going to leave them because she had not got the energy to stay.

She had about four hours. She spent them delightfully, darkly, sweetly, letting herself slide gently, gently, to the edge of the river. Then, with hardly a break in her consciousness, she got up, pushed the thin rug against the door, made sure the windows were tight shut, put two shillings in the meter, and turned on the gas. For the first time since she had been in the room she lay on the hard bed that smelled stale, that smelled of sweat and sex.

She lay on her back on the green satin cover, but her legs were chilly. She got up, found a blanket folded in the bottom of the chest of drawers, and carefully covered her legs with it. She was quite content lying there, listening to the faint soft hiss of the gas that poured into the room, into her lungs, into her brain, as she drifted off into the dark river.

1963

Mavis Gallant

b. 1922

Although Mavis Gallant has written two fine novels, *Green Water, Green Sky* (1959) and *A Fairly Good Time* (1970), she has always preferred the short story. Her stories move through layers of detail to arrive, subtly altered, at their point of departure; as she observes, 'a story usually begins, for me, with people seen in a situation,' explaining that the 'knot' of the situation 'either relaxes or becomes locked in another way.'

Born in Montreal, Gallant spent most of her childhood in boarding schools in Quebec, Ontario, and the United States. At eighteen, she returned to Montreal from New York; four years later, she found a job as a feature writer and reviewer for *The Montreal Standard*, where she worked for six years, leaving the *Standard* in August 1950 and Montreal in September of the same year. Her departure for Europe was closely bound up with her ambition to live an independent life and to make a career as a fiction writer. After living in several European cities—London, Rome, and Madrid among them—Gallant settled in the mid-fifties in Paris, which remains her home.

Gallant was writing fiction while she worked for the *Standard* and published several stories before leaving North America. Her first book of stories, *The Other Paris*, appeared in 1956; of her eight subsequent books of stories, *The Pegnitz Junction* (1973), *From the Fifteenth District* (1979), and *Home Truths* (1981) are generally thought to be her finest.

Gallant's stories are celebrated for their depictions of the disorientation of North American characters in the social, political, and moral landscape of postwar Europe, where the upheavals of two World Wars have left treacherous faultlines in individual and cultural memories. In *The Pegnitz Junction* her fictional territory shifted more particularly to postwar Germany so that she could write about 'where Fascism came from. . . . Not the historical cause of Fascism—just its small possibilities in people.'

Many of Gallant's stories reveal her subtle explorations of the reaches of memory and its deceptions as it reconstructs and reinvents the past. 'In Youth Is Pleasure', the first of six stories about Linnet Muir, is Linnet's first-person recollections of her return to Montreal and her attempt to find out the truth about her father's death. As she resurrects her past, she gains powerful insights into the complexities and ambiguities of her adult recreations of youthful experience. Although there are autobiographical elements in the Linnet Muir stories, Gallant has cautioned against reading them as 'straight autobiography': 'The girl [Linnet Muir] . . . isn't *myself*, but a kind of summary of some of the things I once was. . . . Straight autobiography would be boring. It would bore me. It would bore the reader. The stories are a kind of reality *necessarily* transformed.'

In 'The Moslem Wife', Gallant evokes one of her favourite European settings, Liguria, a region on the Mediterranean coast of northern Italy particularly vulnerable to the hazards of shifting historical forces. Netta Asher leads an impossibly doubled life: first, she is Jack Ross's secluded 'moslem wife'; then, after Jack goes to America during the war, she becomes a woman who experiences historical reality firsthand when the hotel she runs is occupied by soldiers. Haunted by the ghosts of history and by Jack's insistent memories of their prewar happiness, Netta must contend with the several conflicting versions of reality that press in on her.

'In Youth Is Pleasure' was first published in the 24 November 1975 issue of *The New Yorker* and then collected in *Home Truths*. 'The Moslem Wife' was first published in the 24 August 1976 issue of *The New Yorker* and then collected in *From the Fifteenth District*.

In Youth Is Pleasure

My father died, then my grandmother; my mother was left, but we did not get on. I was probably disagreeable with anyone who felt entitled to give me instructions and advice. We seldom lived under the same roof, which was just as well. She had found me civil and amusing until I was ten, at which time I was said to have become pert and obstinate. She was impulsive, generous, in some ways better than most other people, but without any feeling for cause and effect; this made her at the least unpredictable and at the most a serious element of danger. I was fascinated by her, though she worried me; then all at once I lost interest. I was fifteen when this happened. I would forget to answer her letters and even to open them. It was not rejection or anything so violent as dislike but a simple indifference I cannot account for. It was much the way I would be later with men I fell out of love with, but I was too young to know that then. As for my mother, whatever I thought, felt, said, wrote, and wore had always been a positive source of exasperation. From time to time she attempted to alter the form, the outward shape at least, of the creature she thought she was modelling, but at last she came to the conclusion there must be something wrong with the clay. Her final unexpected upsurge of attention coincided with my abrupt unconcern: one may well have been the reason for the other.

It took the form of digging into my diaries and notebooks and it yielded, among other documents, a two-year-old poem, Kiplingesque in its rhythms, entitled 'Why I Am a Socialist'. The first words of the first line were 'You ask . . .', then came a long answer. But it was not an answer to anything she'd wondered. Like all mothers—at least, all I have known—she was obsessed with the entirely private and possibly trivial matter of a daughter's virginity. Why I was a Socialist she rightly conceded to be none of her business. Still, she must have felt she had to say something, and the something was 'You had better be clever, because you will never be pretty.' My response was to take—take, not grab—the poem from her and tear it up. No voices were raised. I never mentioned the incident to anyone. That is how it was. We became, presently, mutually unconcerned. My detachment was put down to the coldness of my nature, hers to the exhaustion of trying to bring me up. It must have been a relief to her when, in the first half of Hitler's war, I slipped quietly and finally out of her life. I was now eighteen, and completely on my own. By 'on my own' I don't mean a show of independence with Papa-Mama footing the bills: I mean that I was solely responsible for my economic survival and that no living person felt any duty toward me.

On a bright morning in June I arrived in Montreal, where I'd been born, from New York, where I had been living and going to school. My luggage was a small suitcase and an Edwardian picnic hamper—a preposterous piece of baggage my father had brought from England some twenty years before; it had been with me since childhood, when his death turned my life into a helpless migration. In my purse was a birth certificate and five American dollars, my total fortune, the parting gift of a Canadian actress in New York, who had taken me to see *Mayerling* before I got on the train. She was kind and good and terribly hard up, and she had no idea that apart from some loose change I had nothing more. The birth certificate, which testified I was Linnet Muir, daughter of Angus and of Charlotte, was my right of passage. I did not own a passport and possibly never had seen one. In those days there was almost no such thing as a 'Canadian'. You were Canadian-born, and a British subject, too, and you had a third label with no consular reality, like the racial tag that on Soviet passports will make a German of someone who has never been to Germany. In Canada you were also whatever your father happened to be, which in my case was English. He was half Scot, but English by birth, by mother, by instinct. I did not feel a scrap British or English, but I was not an American either. In American schools I had refused to salute the flag. My denial of that curiously Fascist-looking celebration, with the right arm stuck straight out, and my silence when the others intoned the trusting '. . . and justice for all' had never been thought offensive, only stubborn. Americans then were accustomed to gratitude from foreigners but did not demand it; they quite innocently could not imagine any country fit to live in except their own. If I could not recognize it, too bad for me. Besides, I was not a refugee—just someone from the backwoods. 'You got schools in Canada?' I had been asked. 'You got radios?' And once, from a teacher, 'What do they major in up there? Basket-weaving?'

My travel costume was a white piqué jacket and skirt that must have been crumpled and soot-flecked, for I had sat up all night. I was reading, I think, a novel by Sylvia Townsend Warner. My hair was thick and long. I wore my grandmother's wedding ring, which was too large, and which I would lose before long. I desperately wanted to look more than my age, which I had already started to give out as twenty-one. I was travelling light; my picnic hamper contained the poems and journals I had judged fit to accompany me into my new, unfettered existence, and some books I feared I might not find again in clerical Quebec—Zinoviev and Lenin's *Against the Stream*, and a few beige pamphlets from the Little Lenin Library, purchased second hand in New York. I had a picture of Mayakovsky torn out of *Cloud in Trousers* and one of Paddy Finucane, the Irish R.A.F. fighter pilot, who was killed the following summer. I had not met either of these men, but I approved of them both very much. I had abandoned my beloved but cumbersome anthologies of American and English verse, confident that I had whatever I needed by heart. I knew every word of Stephen Vincent Benét's 'Litany for Dictatorship' and 'Notes to be Left in a Cornerstone', and the other one that begins:

> They shot the Socialists at half-past five
> In the name of victorious Austria. . . .

I could begin anywhere and rush on in my mind to the end. 'Notes . . .' was the New York I knew I would never have again, for there could be no journeying backward; the words 'but I walked it young' were already a gate shut on a part of my life. The suitcase held only the fewest possible summer clothes. Everything else had been deposited at the various war-relief agencies of New York. In those days I made symbols out of everything, and I must have thought that by leaving a tartan skirt somewhere I was shedding past time. I remember one of those wartime agencies well because it was full of Canadian matrons. They wore pearl earrings like the Duchess of Kent's and seemed to be practising her tiny smile. Brooches pinned to their cashmere cardigans carried some daft message about the Empire. I heard one of them exclaiming, 'You don't expect me, a Britisher, to drink tea made with tea bags!' Good plain girls from the little German towns of Ontario, christened probably Wilma, Jean, and Irma, they had flowing eighteenth-century names like Georgiana and Arabella now. And the Americans, who came in with their arms full of every stitch they could spare, would urge them, the Canadian matrons, to stand fast on the cliffs, to fight the fight, to slug the enemy on the landing fields, to belt him one on the beaches, to keep going with whatever iron rations they could scrape up in Bronxville and Scarsdale; and the Canadians half-shut their eyes and tipped their heads back like Gertrude Lawrence and said in thrilling Benita Hume accents that they would do that—indeed they would. I recorded 'They're all trained nurses, actually. The Canadian ones have a good reputation. They managed to marry these American doctors.'

Canada had been in Hitler's war from the very beginning, but America was still uneasily at peace. Recruiting had already begun; I had seen a departure from New York for Camp Stewart in Georgia, and some of the recruits' mothers crying and even screaming and trying to run alongside the train. The recruits were going off to drill with broomsticks because there weren't enough guns; they still wore old-fashioned headgear and were paid twenty-one dollars a month. There was a song about it: 'For twenty-one dollars a day, once a month.' As my own train crossed the border to Canada I expected to sense at once an air of calm and grit and dedication, but the only changes were from prosperous to shabby, from painted to unpainted, from smiling to dour. I was entering a poorer and a curiously empty country, where the faces of the people gave nothing away. The crossing was my sea change. I silently recited the vow I had been preparing for weeks: that I would never be helpless again and that I would not let anyone make a decision on my behalf.

When I got down from the train at Windsor Station, a man sidled over to me. He had a cap on his head and a bitter Celtic face, with deep indentations along his cheeks, as if his back teeth were pulled. I thought he was asking a direction. He repeated his question, which was obscene. My arms were pinned by the weight of my hamper and suitcase. He brushed the back of his hand over my breasts, called me a name, and edged away. The murderous rage I felt and the revulsion that followed were old friends. They had for years been my reaction to what my diaries called 'their hypocrisy'. 'They' was a world of sly and mumbling people, all of them older than myself. I must have substituted 'hypocrisy' for every sort of aggression, because fright was a luxury I could not afford. What distressed me was my helplessness—I who had sworn only a few hours earlier that I'd not be vulnerable again. The man's gaunt face, his drunken breath, the flat voice which I assigned to the graduate of some Christian Brothers teaching establishment haunted me for a long time after that. 'The man at Windsor Station' would lurk in the windowless corridors of my nightmares; he would be the passenger, the only passenger, on a dark tram. The first sight of a city must be the measure for all second looks.

But it was not my first sight. I'd had ten years of it here—the first ten. After that, and before New York (in one sense, my deliverance), there had been a long spell of grief and shadow in an Ontario city, a place full of mean judgements and grudging minds, of paranoid Protestants and slovenly Catholics. To this day I cannot bear the sight of brick houses, or of a certain kind of empty treeless street on a Sunday afternoon. My memory of Montreal took shape while I was there. It was not a random jumble of rooms and summers and my mother singing 'We've Come to See Miss Jenny Jones', but the faithful record of the true survivor. I retained, I rebuilt a superior civilization. In that drowned world, Sherbrooke Street seemed to be glittering and white; the vision of a house upon that street was so painful that I was obliged to banish it from the memorial. The small hot rooms of a summer cottage became enormous and cool. If I say that Cleopatra floated down the Chateauguay River, that the Winter Palace was stormed on Sherbrooke Street, that Trafalgar was fought on Lake St Louis, I mean it naturally; they were the natural backgrounds of my exile and fidelity. I saw now at the far end of Windsor Station—more foreign, echoing, and mysterious than any American station could be—a statue of Lord Mount Stephen, the founder of the Canadian Pacific, which everyone took to be a memorial to Edward VII. Angus, Charlotte, and the smaller Linnet had truly been: this was my proof; once upon a time my instructions had been to make my way to Windsor Station should I ever be lost and to stand at the foot of Edward VII and wait for someone to find me.

I have forgotten to say that no one in Canada knew I was there. I looked up the number of the woman who had once been my nurse, but she had no telephone. I found her in a city directory, and with complete faith that 'O. Carette' was indeed Olivia and that she would recall and welcome me I took a taxi to the east end of the city—the French end, the poor end. I was so sure of her that I did not ask the driver to wait (to take me where?) but dismissed him and climbed two flights of dark-brown stairs inside a house that must have been built soon after Waterloo. That it was Olivia who came to the door, that the small grey-haired creature I recalled as dark and towering had to look up at me, that she unhesitatingly offered me shelter all seem as simple now as when I broke my fiver to settle the taxi. Believing that I was dead, having paid for years of Masses for the repose of my heretic soul, almost the first thing she said to me was '*Tu vis*?' I understood '*Tu es ici*?' We straightened it out later. She held both my hands and cried and called me *belle et grande*. *Grande* was good, for among American girls I'd seemed a shrimp. I did not see what there was to cry for; I was here. I was as naturally selfish with Olivia as if her sole reason for being was me. I stayed with her for a while and left when her affection for me made her possessive, and I think I neglected her. On her deathbed she told one of her daughters, the reliable one, to keep an eye on me forever. Olivia was the only person in the world who did not believe I could look after myself. Where she and I were concerned I remained under six.

Now, at no moment of this remarkable day did I feel anxious or worried or forlorn. The man at Windsor Station could not really affect my view of the future. I had seen some of the worst of life, but I had no way of judging it or of knowing what the worst could be. I had a sensation of loud, ruthless power, like an enormous waterfall. The past, the part I would rather not have lived, became small and remote, a dark pinpoint. My only weapons until now had been secrecy and insolence. I had stopped running away from schools and situations when I finally understood that by becoming a name in a file, by attracting attention, I would merely prolong my stay in prison—I mean, the prison of childhood itself. My rebellions then consisted only in causing people who were physically larger and legally sovereign to lose their self-control, to become bleached with anger, to shake with such temper that they broke cups and glasses and bumped into chairs. From the malleable, sunny child Olivia said she remembered, I had become, according to later chroniclers, cold, snobbish, and presumptuous. 'You need an iron hand, Linnet.' I can still hear that melancholy voice, which belonged to a friend of my mother's. 'If anybody ever marries you he'd better have an iron hand.' After today I would never need to hear this, or anything approaching it, for the rest of my life.

And so that June morning and the drive through empty, sunlit, wartime streets are even now like a roll of drums in the mind. My life was my own revolution—the tyrants deposed, the constitution wrenched from unwilling hands; I was, all by myself, the liberated crowd setting the palace on fire; I was the flags, the trees, the bannered windows, the flower-decked trains. The singing and the skyrockets of the 1848 I so trustingly believed would emerge out of the war were me, no one but me; and, as in the lyrical first days of any revolution, as in the first days of any love affair, there wasn't the whisper of a voice to tell me, 'You might compromise.'

If making virtue of necessity has ever had a meaning it must be here: for I was independent *inevitably*. There were good-hearted Americans who knew a bit of my story—as much as I wanted anyone to know—and who hoped I would swim and not drown, but from the moment I embarked on my journey I went on the dark side of the moon. 'You seemed so sure of yourself,' they would tell me, still troubled, long after this. In the cool journals I kept I noted that my survival meant nothing in the capitalist system; I was one of those not considered to be worth helping, saving, or even investigating. Thinking with care, I see this was true. What could I have turned into in another place? Why, a librarian at Omsk or a file clerk at Tomsk. Well, it hadn't happened that way; I had my private revolution and I settled in with Olivia in Montreal. Sink or swim? Of course I swam. Jobs were for the having; you could pick them up off the ground. Working for a living meant just what it says—a brisk necessity. It would be the least important fragment of my life until I had what I wanted. The cheek of it, I think now: penniless, sleeping in a shed room behind the kitchen of Olivia's cold-water flat, still I pointed across the wooden balustrade in a long open office where I was being considered for employment and said, 'But I won't sit there.' Girls were *there*, penned in like sheep. I did not think men better than women—only that they did more interesting work and got more money for it. In my journals I called other girls 'coolies'. I did not know if life made them bearers or if they had been born with a natural gift for giving in. 'Coolie' must have been the secret expression of one of my deepest fears. I see now that I had an immense conceit: I thought I occupied a world other people could scarcely envision, let alone attain. It involved giddy risks and changes, stepping off the edge blindfolded, one's hand on nothing more than a birth certificate and a five-dollar bill. At this time of sitting in judgement I was earning nine dollars a week (until I was told by someone that the local minimum wage was twelve, on which I left for greener fields) and washing my white piqué skirt at night and ironing at dawn, and coming home at all hours so I could pretend to Olivia I had dined. Part of this impermeable sureness that I needn't waver or doubt came out of my having lived in New York. The first time I ever heard people laughing in a cinema was there. I can still remember the wonder and excitement and amazement I felt. I was just under fourteen and I had never heard people expressing their feelings in a public place in my life. The easy reactions, the way a poignant moment caught them, held them still—all that was new. I had come there straight from Ontario, where the reaction to a love scene was a kind of unhappy giggling, while the image of a kitten or a baby induced a long flat 'Aaaah', followed by shamed silence. You could image them blushing in the dark for having said that—just that 'Aaaah'. When I heard that open American laughter I thought I could be like these people too, but had been told not to be by everyone, beginning with Olivia: '*Pas si fort*' was something she repeated to me so often when I was small that my father had made a tease out it, called 'passy four'. From a tease it became oppressive too: 'For the love of God, Linnet, passy four.' What were these new people? Were they soft, too easily got at? I wondered that even then. Would a dictator have a field day here? Were they, as Canadian opinion had it, vulgar? Perhaps the notion of vulgarity came out of some incapacity on the part of the refined. Whatever they were, they couldn't all be daft; if they weren't I probably wasn't either. I supposed I stood as good a chance of being miserable here as anywhere, but at least I would not have to pretend to be someone else.

Now, of course there is much to be said on the other side: people who do not display what they feel have practical advantages. They can go away to be killed as if they didn't mind; they can see their sons off to war without a blink. Their upbringing is intended for a crisis. When it comes, they behave themselves. But it is murder in everyday life—truly murder. The dead of heart and spirit litter the landscape. Still, keeping a straight face makes life tolerable under stress. It makes *public* life tolerable—that is all I am saying; because in private people still got drunk, went after each other with bottles and knives, rang the police to complain that neighbours were sending poison gas over the transom, abandoned infant children and aged parents, wrote letters to newspapers in favour of corporal punishment, with inventive suggestions. When I came back to Canada that June, at least one thing had been settled: I knew that it was all right for people to laugh and cry and even to make asses of themselves. I had actually known people like that, had lived with them, and they were fine, mostly—not crazy at all. That was where a lot of my confidence came from when I began my journey into a new life and a dream past.

My father's death had been kept from me. I did not know its exact circumstances or even the date. He died when I was ten. At thirteen I was still expected to believe a fable about his being in England. I kept waiting for him to send for me, for my life was deeply wretched and I took it for granted he knew. Finally I began to suspect that death and silence can be one. How to be sure? Head-on questions got me nowhere. I had to create a situation in which some adult (not my mother, who was far too sharp) would lose all restraint and hurl the truth at me. It was easy: I was an artist at this. What I had not foreseen was the verbal violence of the scene or the effect it might have. The storm that seemed to break in my head, my need to maintain the pose of indifference ('What are you telling me that for? What makes you think I care?') were such a strain that I had physical reactions, like stigmata, which doctors would hopelessly treat on and off for years and which vanished when I became independent. The other change was that if anyone asked about my father I said, 'Oh, he died.' Now, in Montreal, I could confront the free adult world of falsehood and evasion on an equal footing; they would be forced to talk to me as they did to each other. Making appointments to meet my father's friends—Mr Archie McEwen, Mr Stephen Ross-Colby, Mr Quentin Keller—I left my adult name, 'Miss Muir.' These were the men who eight, nine, ten years ago had asked, 'Do you like your school?'—not knowing what else to say to children. I had curtsied to them and said, 'Good night.' I think what I wanted was special information about despair, but I should have known that would be taboo in a place where 'like' and 'don't like' were heavy emotional statements.

Archie McEwen, my father's best friend, or the man I mistook for that, kept me standing in his office on St James Street West, he standing too, with his hands behind his back, and he said the following—not reconstructed or approximate but recalled, like 'The religions of ancient Greece and Rome are extinct' or 'O come, let us sing unto the Lord':

'Of course, Angus was a very sick man. I saw him walking along Sherbrooke Street. He must have just come out of hospital. He couldn't walk upright. He was using a stick. Inching along. His hair had turned grey. Nobody knew where Charlotte had got to, and we'd heard you were dead. He obviously wasn't long for this world either. He had too many troubles for any one man. I crossed the street because I didn't have the heart to shake hands with him. I felt terrible.'

Savage? Reasonable? You can't tell, with those minds. Some recent threat had scared them. The Depression was too close, just at their heels. Archie McEwen did not ask where I was staying or where I had been for the last eight years; in fact, he asked only two questions. In response to the first I said, 'She is married.'

There came a gleam of interest—distant, amused: 'So she decided to marry him, did she?'

My mother was highly visible; she had no secrets except unexpected ones. My father had nothing but. When he asked, 'Would you like to spend a year in England with your Aunt Dorothy?' I had no idea what he meant and I still don't. His only brother, Thomas, who was killed in 1918, had not been married; he'd had no sisters, that anyone knew. Those English mysteries used to be common. People came out to Canada because they did not want to think about the Thomases and Dorothys anymore. Angus was a solemn man, not much of a smiler. My mother, on the other hand—I won't begin to describe her, it would never end—smiled, talked, charmed anyone she didn't happen to be related to, swam in scandal like a partisan among the people. She made herself the central figure in loud, spectacular dramas which she played with the houselights on; you could see the audience too. That was her mistake; they kept their reactions, like their lovemaking, in the dark. You can imagine what she must have been in this world where everything was hushed, muffled, disguised: she must have seemed all they had by way of excitement, give or take a few elections and wars. It sounds like a story about the old and stale, but she and my father had been quite young eight and ten years before. The dying man creeping along Sherbrooke Street was thirty-two. First it was light chatter, then darker gossip, and then it went too far (*he* was ill and he couldn't hide it; *she* had a lover and didn't try); then suddenly it became tragic, and open tragedy was disallowed. And so Mr Archie McEwen could stand in his office and without a trace of feeling on his narrow Lowland face—not unlike my father's in shape—he could say, 'I crossed the street.'

Stephen Ross-Colby, a bachelor, my father's painter chum: the smell of his studio on St Mark Street was the smell of a personal myth. I said timidly, 'Do you happen to have anything of his—a drawing or anything?' I was humble because I was on a private, personal terrain of vocation that made me shy even of the dead.

He said, 'No, nothing. You could ask around. She junked a lot of his stuff and he junked the rest when he thought he wouldn't survive. You might try . . .' He gave me a name or two. 'It was all small stuff,' said Ross-Colby. 'He didn't do anything big.' He hurried me out of the studio for a cup of coffee in a crowded place—the Honey Dew on St Catherine Street, it must have been. Perhaps in the privacy of his studio I might have heard him thinking. Years after that he would try to call me 'Lynn', which I never was, and himself 'Steve'. He'd come into his own as an artist by then, selling wash drawings of Canadian war graves, sun-splashed, wisteria-mauve, lime-green, with drifts of blossom across the name of the regiment; gained a reputation among the heartbroken women who bought these impersonations, had them framed—the only picture in the house. He painted the war memorial at Caen. ('Their name liveth forever.') His stones weren't stones but mauve bubbles—that is all I have against them. They floated off the page. My objection wasn't to 'He didn't do anything big' but to Ross-Colby's way of turning the dead into thistledown. He said, much later, of that meeting, 'I felt like a bastard, but I was broke, and I was afraid you'd put the bite on me.'

Let me distribute demerits equally and tell about my father's literary Jewish friend, Mr Quentin Keller. He was older than the others, perhaps by some twelve years. He had a whispery voice and a long pale face and a daughter older than I. 'Bossy Wendy' I used to call her when, forced by her parents as I was by mine, Bossy Wendy had to take a whole afternoon of me. She had a room full of extraordinary toys, a miniature kitchen in which everything worked, of which all I recall her saying is 'Don't touch.' Wendy Keller had left Smith after her freshman year to marry the elder son of a Danish baron. Her father said to me, 'There is only one thing you need to know and that is that your father was a gentleman.'

Jackass was what I thought. Yes, Mr Quentin Keller was a jackass. But he was a literary one, for he had once written a play called *Forbearance*, in which I'd had a role. I had bounded across the stage like a tennis ball, into the arms of a young woman dressed up like an old one, and cried my one line: 'Here I am, Granny!' Of course, he did not make his living fiddling about with amateur theatricals; thanks to our meeting I had a good look at the inside of a conservative architect's private office—that was about all it brought me.

What were they so afraid of, I wondered. I had not yet seen that I was in a false position where they were concerned; being 'Miss Muir' had not made equals of us but lent distance. I thought they had read my true passport, the invisible one we all carry, but I had neither the wealth nor the influence a provincial society requires to make a passport valid. My credentials were lopsided: the important half of the scales was still in the air. I needed enormous collateral security—fame, an alliance with a powerful family, the power of money itself. I remember how Archie McEwen, trying to place me in some sensible context, to give me a voucher so he could take me home and show me to his wife, perhaps, asked his second question: 'Who inherited the—?'

'The what, Mr McEwen?'

He had not, of course, read 'Why I Am a Socialist'. I did not believe in inherited property. 'Who inherited the—?' could not cross my mind again for another ten years, and then it would be a drawer quickly opened and shut before demons could escape. To all three men the last eight years were like minutes; to me they had been several lives. Some of my confidence left me then. It came down to 'Next time I'll know better,' but would that be enough? I had been buffeted until now by other people's moods, principles, whims, tantrums; I had survived, but perhaps I had failed to grow some outer skin it was now too late to acquire. Olivia thought that; she was the only one. Olivia knew more about the limits of nerve than I did. Her knowledge came out of the clean, swept, orderly poverty that used to be tucked away in the corners of cities. It didn't spill out then, or give anyone a bad conscience. Nobody took its picture. Anyway, Olivia would not have sat for such a portrait. The fringed green rug she put over her treadle sewing machine was part of a personal fortune. On her mantelpiece stood a copper statuette of Voltaire in an armchair. It must have come down to her from some robustly anticlerical ancestor. 'Who is he?' she said to me. 'You've been to school in a foreign country.' 'A governor of New France,' I replied. She knew Voltaire was the name of a bad man and she'd have thrown the figurine out, and it would have made one treasure less in the house. Olivia's maiden name was Ouvrardville, which was good in Quebec, but only really good if you were one of the rich ones. Because of her maiden name she did not want anyone ever to know she had worked for a family; she impressed this on me delicately—it was like trying to understand what a dragonfly wanted to tell. In the old days she had gone home every weekend, taking me with her if my parents felt my company was going to make Sunday a very long day. Now I understood what the weekends were about: her daughters, Berthe and Marguerite, for whose sake she worked, were home from their convent schools Saturday and Sunday and had to be chaperoned. Her relatives pretended not to notice that Olivia was poor or even that she was widowed, for which she seemed grateful. The result of all this elegant sham was that Olivia did not say, 'I was afraid you'd put the bite on me,' or keep me standing. She dried her tears and asked if there was a trunk to follow. No? She made a pot of tea and spread a starched cloth on the kitchen table and we sat down to a breakfast of toast and honey. The honey tin was a ten-pounder decorated with bees the size of hornets. Lifting it for her, I remarked, '*C'est collant*,' a word out of a frozen language that started to thaw when Olivia said, '*Tu vis*?'

On the advice of her confessor, who was to be my rival from now on, Olivia refused to tell me whatever she guessed or knew, and she was far too dignified to hint. Putting together the three men's woolly stories, I arrived at something about tuberculosis of the spine and a butchery of an operation. He started back to England to die there but either changed his mind or was too ill to begin the journey; at Quebec City, where he was to have taken ship, he shot himself in a public park at five o'clock in the morning. That was one version; another was that he died at sea and the gun was found in his luggage. The revolver figured in all three accounts. It was an officer's weapon from the Kaiser's war, that had belonged to his brother. Angus kept it at the back of a small drawer in the tall chest used for men's clothes and known in Canada as a highboy. In front of the revolver was a pigskin stud box and a pile of ironed handkerchiefs. Just describing that drawer dates it. How I happen to know the revolver was loaded and how I learned never to point a gun even in play is another story. I can tell you that I never again in my life looked inside a drawer that did not belong to me.

I know a woman whose father died, she thinks, in a concentration camp. Or was he shot in a schoolyard? Or hanged and thrown in a ditch? Were the ashes that arrived from some eastern plain his or another prisoner's? She invents different deaths. Her inventions have become her conversation at dinner parties. She takes on a child's voice and says 'My father died at Buchenwald.' She chooses and rejects elements of the last act; one avoids mentioning death, shooting, capital punishment, cremation, deportation, even fathers. Her inventions are not thought neurotic or exhibitionist but something sanctioned by history. Peacetime casualties are not like that. They are lightning bolts out of a sunny sky that strike only one house. All around the ashy ruin lilacs blossom, leaves gleam. Speculation in public about the disaster would be indecent. Nothing remains but a silent, recurring puzzlement to the survivors: Why here and not there? Why this and not that? Before July was out I had settled his fate in my mind and I never varied: I thought he had died of homesickness; sickness for England was the consumption, the gun, the everything. 'Everything' had to take it all in, for people in Canada then did not speak of irrational endings to life, and newspapers did not print that kind of news: this was because of the spiritual tragedy for Catholic families, and because the act had long been considered a criminal one in British law. If Catholic feelings were spared it gave the impression no one but Protestants ever went over the edge, which was unfair; and so the possibility was eliminated, and people came to a natural end in a running car in a closed garage, hanging from a rafter in the barn, in an icy lake with a canoe left to drift empty. Once I had made up my mind, the whole story somehow became none of my business: I had looked in a drawer that did not belong to me. More, if I was to live my own life I had to let go. I wrote in my journal that 'they' had got him but would not get me, and after that there was scarcely ever a mention.

My dream past evaporated. Montreal, in memory, was a leafy citadel where I knew every tree. In reality I recognized nearly nothing and had to start from scratch. Sherbrooke Street had been the dream street, pure white. It was the avenue poor Angus descended leaning on a walking stick. It was a moat I was not allowed to cross alone; it was lined with gigantic spreading trees through which light fell like a rain of coins. One day, standing at a corner, waiting for the light to change, I understood that the Sherbrooke Street of my exile—my Mecca, my Jerusalem—was this. It had to be: there could not be two. It was *only* this. The limitless green where in a perpetual spring I had been taken to play was the campus of McGill University. A house, whose beauty had brought tears to my sleep, to which in sleep I'd returned to find it inhabited by ugly strangers, gypsies, was a narrow stone thing with a shop on the ground floor and offices above—if that was it, for there were several like it. Through the bare panes of what might have been the sitting room, with its deep private window seats, I saw neon striplighting along a ceiling. Reality, as always, was narrow and dull. And yet what dramatic things had taken place on this very corner: Once Satan had approached me—furry dark skin, claws, red eyes, the lot. He urged me to cross the street and I did, in front of a car that braked in time. I explained, 'The Devil told me to.' I had no idea until then that my parents did not believe what I was taught in my convent school. (Satan is not bilingual, by the way; he speaks Quebec French.) My parents had no God and therefore no Fallen Angel. I was scolded for lying, which was a thing my father detested, and which my mother regularly did but never forgave in others.

Why these two nonbelievers wanted a strong religious education for me is one of the mysteries. (Even in loss of faith they were unalike, for he was ex-Anglican and she was ex-Lutheran and that is not your same atheist—no, not at all.) 'To make you tolerant' was a lame excuse, as was 'French', for I spoke fluent French with Olivia, and I could read in two languages before I was four. Discipline might have been one reason—God knows, the nuns provided plenty of that—but according to Olivia I did not need any. It cannot have been for the quality of the teaching, which was lamentable. I suspect that it was something like sending a dog to a trainer (they were passionate in their concern for animals, especially dogs), but I am not certain it ever brought me to heel. The first of my schools, the worst, the darkest, was on Sherbrooke Street too. When I heard, years later, it had been demolished, it was like the burial of a witch. I had remembered it penitentiary size, but what I found myself looking at one day was simply a very large stone house. A crocodile of little girls emerged from the front gate and proceeded along the street—white-faced, black-clad, eyes cast down. I knew they were bored, fidgety, anxious, and probably hungry. I should have felt pity, but at eighteen all that came to me was thankfulness that I had been correct about one thing throughout my youth, which I now considered ended: time had been on my side, faithfully, and unless you died you were always bound to escape.

1975

The Moslem Wife

In the South of France, in the business room of a hotel quite near to the house where Katherine Mansfield (whom no one in this hotel had ever heard of) was writing 'The Daughters of the Late Colonel', Netta Asher's father announced that there would never be a man-made catastrophe in Europe again. The dead of that recent war, the doomed nonsense of the Russian Bolsheviks had finally knocked sense into European heads. What people wanted now was to get on with life. When he said 'life', he meant its commercial business.

Who would have contradicted Mr Asher? Certainly not Netta. She did not understand what he meant quite so well as his French solicitor seems to, but she did listen with interest and respect, and then watched him signing papers that, she knew, concerned her for life. He was renewing the long lease her family held on the Hotel Prince Albert and Albion. Netta was then eleven. One hundred years should at least see her through the prime of life, said Mr Asher, only half jokingly, for of course he thought his seed was immortal.

Netta supposed she might easily live to be more than a hundred—at any rate, for years and years. She knew that her father did not want her to marry until she was twenty-six and that she was then supposed to have a pair of children, the elder a boy. Netta and her father and the French lawyer shook hands on the lease, and she was given her first glass of champagne. The date on the bottle was 1909, for the year of her birth. Netta bravely pronounced the wine delicious, but her father said she would know much better vintages before she was through.

Netta remembered the handshake but perhaps not the terms. When the lease had eighty-eight years to run, she married her first cousin, Jack Ross, which was not at all what her father had had in mind. Nor would there be the useful pair of children—Jack couldn't abide them. Like Netta he came from a hotelkeeping family where the young were like blight. Netta had up to now never shown a scrap of maternal feeling over anything, but Mr Asher thought Jack might have made an amiable parent—a kind one, at least. She consoled Mr Asher on one count, by taking the hotel over in his lifetime. The hotel was, to Netta, a natural life; and so when Mr Asher, dying, said, 'She behaves as I wanted her to,' he was right as far as the drift of Netta's behaviour was concerned but wrong about its course.

The Ashers' hotel was not down on the seafront, though boats and sea could be had from the south-facing rooms.

Across the road nearly empty of traffic were handsome villas, and behind and to either side stood healthy olive trees and a large lemon grove. The hotel was painted a deep ochre with white trim. It had white awnings and green shutters and black iron balconies as lacquered and shiny as Chinese boxes. It possessed two tennis courts, a lily pond, a sheltered winter garden, a formal rose garden, and trees full of nightingales. In the summer dark, *belles-de-nuit* glowed pink, lemon, white, and after their evening watering they gave off a perfume that varied from plant to plant and seemed to match the petals' coloration. In May the nights were dense with stars and fireflies. From the rose garden one might have seen the twin pulse of cigarettes on a balcony, where Jack and Netta sat drinking a last brandy-and-soda before turning in. Most of the rooms were shuttered by then, for no traveller would have dreamed of being south except in winter. Jack and Netta and a few servants had the whole place to themselves. Netta would hire workmen and have the rooms that needed it repainted—the blue cardroom, and the red-walled bar, and the white dining room, where Victorian mirrors gave back glossy walls and blown curtains and nineteenth-century views of the Ligurian coast, the work of an Asher great-uncle. Everything upstairs and down was soaked and wiped and polished, and even the pictures were relentlessly washed with soft cloths and ordinary laundry soap. Netta also had the boiler overhauled and the linen mended and new monograms embroidered and the looking glasses resilvered and the shutters taken off their hinges and scraped and made spruce green again for next year's sun to fade, while Jack talked about decorators and expert gardeners and even wrote to some, and banged tennis balls against the large new garage. He also read books and translated poetry for its own sake and practised playing the clarinet. He had studied music once, and still thought that an important life, a musical life, was there in the middle distance. One summer, just to see if he could, he translated pages of St John Perse, which were as blank as the garage wall to Netta, in any tongue.

Netta adored every minute of her life, and she thought Jack had a good life too, with nearly half the year for the pleasures that suited him. As soon as the grounds and rooms and cellar and roof had been put to rights, she and Jack packed and went travelling somewhere. Jack made the plans. He was never so cheerful as when buying Baedekers and dragging out their stickered trunks. But Netta was nothing of a traveller. She would have been glad to see the same sun rising out of the same sea from the window every day until she died. She loved Jack, and what she liked best after him was the hotel. It was a place where, once, people had come to die of tuberculosis, yet it held no trace or feeling of danger. When Netta walked with her workmen through sheeted summer rooms, hearing the cicadas and hearing Jack start, stop, start some deeply alien music (alien even when her memory automatically gave her a composer's name), she was reminded that here the dead had never been allowed to corrupt the living; the dead had been dressed for an outing and removed as soon as their first muscular stiffness relaxed. Some were wheeled out in chairs, sitting, and some reclined on portable cots, as if merely resting.

That is why there is no bad atmosphere here, she would say to herself. Death has been swept away, discarded. When the shutters are closed on a room, it is for sleep or for love. Netta could think this easily because neither she nor Jack was ever sick. They knew nothing about insomnia, and they made love every day of their lives—they had married in order to be able to.

Spring had been the season for dying in the old days. Invalids who had struggled through the dark comfort of winter took fright as the night receded. They felt without protection. Netta knew about this, and about the difference between darkness and brightness, but neither affected her. She was not afraid of death or of the dead—they were nothing but cold, heavy furniture. She could have tied jaws shut and weighted eyelids with native instinctiveness, as other women were born knowing the temperature for an infant's milk.

'There are no ghosts,' she could say, entering the room where her mother, then her father had died. 'If there were, I would know.'

Netta took it for granted, now she was married, that Jack felt as she did about light, dark, death, and love. They were as alike in some ways (none of them physical) as a couple of twins, spoke much the same language in the same accents, had the same jokes—mostly about other people—and had been together as much as their families would let them for most of their lives. Other men seemed dull to Netta—slower, perhaps, lacking the spoken shorthand she had with Jack. She never mentioned this. For one thing, both of them had the idea that, being English, one must not say too much. Born abroad, they worked hard at an Englishness that was innocently inaccurate, rooted mostly in attitudes. Their families had been innkeepers along this coast for a century, even before Dr James Henry Bennet had discovered 'the Genoese Rivieras'. In one of his guides to the region, a 'Mr Ross' is mentioned as a hotel owner who will accept English bank cheques, and there is a 'Mr Asher', reliable purveyor of English groceries. The most trustworthy shipping agents in 1860 are the Montale brothers, converts to the Anglican Church, possessors of a British *laissez-passer* to Malta and Egypt. These families, by now plaited like hair, were connections of Netta's and Jack's and still in business from beyond

Marseilles to Genoa. No wonder that other men bored her, and that each thought the other both familiar and unique. But of course they were unalike too. When once someone asked them, 'Are you related to Montale, the poet?' Netta answered, 'What poet?' and Jack said, 'I wish we were.'

There were no poets in the family. Apart from the great-uncle who had painted landscapes, the only person to try anything peculiar had been Jack, with his music. He had been allowed to study, up to a point; his father had been no good with hotels—had been a failure, in fact, bailed out four times by his cousins, and it had been thought, for a time, that Jack Ross might be a dunderhead too. Music might do him; he might not be fit for anything else.

Information of this kind about the meaning of failure had been gleaned by Netta years before, when she first became aware of her little cousin. Jack's father and mother—the commercial blunderers—had come to the Prince Albert and Albion to ride out a crisis. They were somewhere between undischarged bankruptcy and annihilation, but one was polite: Netta curtsied to her aunt and uncle. Her eyes were on Jack. She could not read yet, though she could sift and classify attitudes. She drew near him, sucking her lower lip, her hands behind her back. For the first time she was conscious of the beauty of another child. He was younger than Netta, imprisoned in a portable-fence arrangement in which he moved tirelessly, crabwise, hanging on a barrier he could easily have climbed. He was as fair as his Irish mother and sunburned a deep brown. His blue gaze was not a baby's—it was too challenging. He was naked except for shorts that were large and seemed about to fall down. The sunburn, the undress were because his mother was reckless and rather odd. Netta—whose mother was perfect—wore boots, stockings, a longsleeved frock, and a white sun hat. She heard the adults laugh and say that Jack looked like a prizefighter. She walked around his prison, staring, and the blue-eyed fighter stared back.

The Rosses stayed for a long time, while the family sent telegrams and tried to raise money for them. No one looked after Jack much. He would lie on a marble step of the staircase watching the hotel guests going into the cardroom or the dining room. One night, for a reason that remorse was to wipe out in a minute, Netta gave him such a savage kick (though he was not really in her way) that one of his legs remained paralyzed for a long time.

'*Why* did you do it?' her father asked her—this in the room where she was shut up on bread and water. Netta didn't know. She loved Jack, but who would believe it now? Jack learned to walk, then to run, and in time to ski and play tennis; but her lifelong gift to him was a loss of balance, a sudden lopsided bend of a knee. Jack's parents had meantime been given a small hotel to run at Bandol. Mr Asher, responsible for a bank loan, kept an eye on the place. He went often, in a hotel car with a chauffeur, Netta perched beside him. When, years later, the families found out that the devoted young cousins had become lovers, they separated them without saying much. Netta was too independent to be dealt with. Besides, her father did not want a rift; his wife had died, and he needed Netta. Jack, whose claim on music had been the subject of teasing until now, was suddenly sent to study in England. Netta saw that he was secretly dismayed. He wanted to be almost anything as long as it was impossible, and then only as an act of grace. Netta's father did think it was his duty to tell her that marriage was, at its best, a parched arrangement, intolerable without a flow of golden guineas and fresh blood. As cousins, Jack and Netta could not bring each other anything except stale money. Nothing stopped them: they were married four months after Jack became twenty-one. Netta heard someone remark at her wedding, 'She doesn't need a husband,' meaning perhaps the practical, matter-of-fact person she now seemed to be. She did have the dry, burned-out look of someone turned inward. Her dark eyes glowed out of a thin face. She had the shape of a girl of fourteen. Jack, who was large, and fair, and who might be stout at forty if he wasn't careful, looked exactly his age, and seemed quite ready to be married.

Netta could not understand why, loving Jack as she did, she did not look more like him. It had troubled her in the past when they did not think exactly the same thing at almost the same time. During the secret meetings of their long engagement she had noticed how even before a parting they were nearly apart—they had begun to 'unmesh', as she called it. Drinking a last drink, usually in the buffet of a railway station, she would see that Jack was somewhere else, thinking about the next-best thing to Netta. The next-best thing might only be a book he wanted to finish reading, but it was enough to make her feel exiled. He often told Netta, 'I'm not holding on to you. You're free,' because he thought it needed saying, and of course he wanted freedom for himself. But to Netta 'freedom' had a cold sound. Is that what I do want, she would wonder. Is that what I think he should offer? Their partings were often on the edge of parting forever, not just because Jack had said or done or thought the wrong thing but because between them they generated the high sexual tension that leads to quarrels. Barely ten minutes after agreeing that no one in the world could possibly know what they knew, one of them, either one, could curse the other out over something trivial. Yet they were, and remained, much in love, and when they were apart Netta sent him letters that were almost despairing with enchantment.

Jack answered, of course, but his letters were cautious. Her exploration of feeling was part of an unlimited capacity she seemed to have for passionate behaviour, so at odds with her appearance, which had been dry and sardonic even in childhood. Save for an erotic sentence or two near the end (which Netta read first) Jack's messages might have been meant for any girl cousin he particularly liked. Love was memory, and he was no good at the memory game; he needed Netta there. The instant he saw her he knew all he had missed. But Netta, by then, felt forgotten, and she came to each new meeting aggressive and hurt, afflicted with the physical signs of her doubts and injuries—cold sores, rashes, erratic periods, mysterious temperatures. If she tried to discuss it he would say, 'We aren't going over all that again, are we?' Where Netta was concerned he had settled for the established faith, but Netta, who had a wilder, more secret God, wanted a prayer a minute, not to speak of unending miracles and revelations.

When they finally married, both were relieved that the strain of partings and of tense disputes in railway stations would come to a stop. Each privately blamed the other for past violence, and both believed that once they could live openly, without interference, they would never have a disagreement again. Netta did not want Jack to regret the cold freedom he had vainly tried to offer her. He must have his liberty, and his music, and other people, and, oh, anything he wanted—whatever would stop him from saying he was ready to let her go free. The first thing Netta did was to make certain they had the best room in the hotel. She had never actually owned a room until now. The private apartments of her family had always been surrendered in a crisis: everyone had packed up and moved as beds were required. She and Jack were hopelessly untidy, because both had spent their early years moving down hotel corridors, trailing belts and raincoats, with tennis shoes hanging from knotted strings over their shoulders, their arms around books and sweaters and gray flannel bundles. Both had done lessons in the corners of lounges, with cups and glasses rattling, and other children running, and English voices louder than anything. Jack, who had been vaguely educated, remembered his boarding schools as places where one had a permanent bed. Netta chose for her marriage a south-facing room with a large balcony and an awning of dazzling white. It was furnished with lemonwood that had been brought to the Riviera by Russians for their own villas long before. To the lemonwood Netta's mother had added English chintzes; the result, in Netta's eyes, was not bizarre but charming. The room was deeply mirrored; when the shutters were closed on hot afternoons a play of light became as green as a forest on the walls, and as blue as seawater in the glass. A quality of suspension, of disbelief in gravity, now belonged to Netta. She became tidy, silent, less introspective, as watchful and as reflective as her bedroom mirrors. Jack stayed as he was, luckily; any alteration would have worried her, just as a change in an often-read story will trouble a small child. She was intensely, almost unnaturally happy.

One day she overheard an English doctor, whose wife played bridge every afternoon at the hotel, refer to her, to Netta, as 'the little Moslem wife'. It was said affectionately, for the doctor liked her. She wondered if he had seen through walls and had watched her picking up the clothing and the wet towels Jack left strewn like clues to his presence. The phrase was collected and passed from mouth to mouth in the idle English colony. Netta, the last person in the world deliberately to eavesdrop (she lacked that sort of interest in other people), was sharp of hearing where her marriage was concerned. She had a special antenna for Jack, for his shades of meaning, secret intentions, for his innocent contradictions. Perhaps 'Moslem wife' meant several things, and possibly it was plain to anyone with eyes that Jack, without meaning a bit of harm by it, had a way with women. Those he attracted were a puzzling lot, to Netta. She had already catalogued them—elegant elderly parties with tongues like carving knives; gentle, clever girls who flourished on the unattainable; untouchable-daughter types, canny about their virginity, wondering if Jack would be father enough to justify the sacrifice. There was still another kind—tough, sunburned, clad in dark colours—who made Netta think in the vocabulary of horoscopes: Her gem—diamonds. Her colour—black. Her language—worse than Netta's. She noticed that even when Jack had no real use for a woman he never made it apparent; he adopted anyone who took a liking to him. He assumed—Netta thought—a tribal, paternal air that was curious in so young a man. The plot of attraction interested him, no matter how it turned out. He was like someone reading several novels at once, or like someone playing simultaneous chess.

Netta did not want her marriage to become a world of stone. She said nothing except, 'Listen, Jack, I've been at this hotel business longer than you have. It's wiser not to be too pally with the guests.' At Christmas the older women gave him boxes of expensive soap. 'They must think someone around here wants a good wash,' Netta remarked. Outside their fenced area of private jokes and private love was a landscape too open, too light-drenched, for serious talk. And then, when? Jack woke up quickly and early in the morning and smiled as naturally as children do. He knew where he was and the day of the week and the hour. The best moment of the day was the first cigarette. When something bloody happened, it was never before six in the evening. At night he had a dark look that went with a dark mood, sometimes. Netta would tell him that she could see a cruise ship floating on the black horizon like a piece of the Milky Way, and she would get that look, for an answer. But it never lasted. His memory was too short to let him sulk, no matter what fragment of night had crossed his mind. She knew, having heard other couples all her life, that at least she and Jack never made the conjugal sounds that passed for conversation and that might as well have been bow-wow and quack quack.

If, by chance, Jack found himself drawn to another woman, if the tide of attraction suddenly ran the other way, then he would discover in himself a great need to talk to his wife. They sat out on their balcony for much of one long night and he told her about his Irish mother. His mother's eccentricity—'Vera's dottiness', where the family was concerned—had kept Jack from taking anything seriously. He had been afraid of pulling her mad attention in his direction. Countless times she had faked tuberculosis and cancer and announced her own imminent death. A telephone call from a hospital had once declared her lost in a car crash. 'It's a new life, a new life,' her husband had babbled, coming away from the phone. Jack saw his father then as beautiful. Women are beautiful when they fall in love, said Jack; sometimes the glow will last a few hours, sometimes even a day or two.

'You know,' said Jack, as if Netta knew, 'the look of amazement on a girl's face . . .'

Well, that same incandescence had suffused Jack's father when he thought his wife had died, and it continued to shine until a taxi deposited dotty Vera with her cheerful announcement that she had certainly brought off a successful April Fool. After Jack's father died she became violent. 'Getting away from her was a form of violence in me,' Jack said. 'But I did it.' That was why he was secretive; that was why he was independent. He had never wanted any woman to get her hands on his life.

Netta heard this out calmly. Where his own feelings were concerned she thought he was making them up as he went along. The garden smelled coolly of jasmine and mimosa. She wondered who his new girl was, and if he was likely to blurt out a name. But all he had been working up to was that his mother—mad, spoiled, devilish, whatever she was—would need to live with Jack and Netta, unless Netta agreed to giving her an income. An income would let her remain where she was—at the moment, in a Rudolf Steiner community in Switzerland, devoted to medieval gardening and to getting the best out of Goethe. Netta's father's training prevented even the thought of spending the money in such a manner.

'You won't regret all you've told me, will you?' she asked. She saw that the new situation would be her burden, her chain, her mean little joke sometimes. Jack scarcely hesitated before saying that where Netta mattered he could never regret anything. But what really interested him now was his mother.

'Lifts give her claustrophobia.' he said. 'She mustn't be higher than the second floor.' He sounded like a man bringing a legal concubine into his household, scrupulously anxious to give all his women equal rights. 'And I hope she will make friends,' he said. 'It won't be easy, at her age. One can't live without them.' He probably meant that he had none. Netta had been raised not to expect to have friends: you could not run a hotel and have scores of personal ties. She expected people to be polite and punctual and to mean what they said, and that was the end of it. Jack gave his friendship easily, but he expected considerable diversion in return.

Netta said dryly, 'If she plays bridge, she can play with Mrs Blackley.' This was the wife of the doctor who had first said 'Moslem wife'. He had come down here to the Riviera for his wife's health; thc two belonged to a subcolony of flat-dwelling expatriates. His medical practice was limited to hypochondriacs and rheumatic patients. He had time on his hands: Netta often saw him in the hotel reading room, standing, leafing—he took pleasure in handling books. Netta, no reader, did not like touching a book unless it was new. The doctor had a trick of speech Jack loved to imitate: he would break up his words with an extra syllable, some words only, and at that not every time. 'It is all a matter of stu-hyle,' he said, for 'style', or, Jack's favourite, 'Oh, well, in the end it all comes down to su-hex.' 'Uh-hebb and flo-ho of hormones' was the way he once described the behaviour of saints—Netta had looked twice at him over that. He was a firm agnostic and the first person from whom Netta heard there existed a magical Dr Freud. When Netta's father had died of pneumonia, the doctor's 'I'm su-horry, Netta' had been so heartfelt she could not have wished it said another way.

His wife, Georgina, could lower her blood pressure or stop her heartbeat nearly at will. Netta sometimes wondered why Dr Blackley had brought her to a soft climate rather than to the man at Vienna he so admired. Georgina was well enough to play fierce bridge, with Jack and anyone good enough. Her husband usually came to fetch her at the end of the afternoon when the players stopped for tea. Once, because he was obliged to return at once to a patient who needed him, she said, 'Can't you be competent about anything?' Netta thought she understood, then, his resigned repetition of 'It's all su-hex.' 'Oh, don't explain. You bore me,' said his wife, turning her back.

Netta followed him out to his car. She wore an India shawl that had been her mother's. The wind blew her hair; she had to hold it back. She said, 'Why don't you kill her?'

'I am not a desperate person,' he said. He looked at Netta, she looking up at him because she had to look up to nearly everyone except children, and he said, 'I've wondered why we haven't been to bed.'

'Who?' said Netta. 'You and your wife? Oh. You mean me.' She was not offended, she just gave the shawl a brusque tug and said, 'Not a hope. Never with a guest,' though of course that was not the reason.

'You might have to, if the guest were a maharaja,' he said, to make it all harmless. 'I am told it is pu-hart of the courtesy they expect.'

'We don't get their trade,' said Netta. This had not stopped her liking the doctor. She pitied him, rather, because of his wife, and because he wasn't Jack and could not have Netta.

'I do love you,' said the doctor, deciding finally to sit down in his car. 'Ee-nee-ormously.' She watched him drive away as if she loved him too, and might never see him again. It never crossed her mind to mention any of this conversation to Jack.

That very spring, perhaps because of the doctor's words, the hotel did get some maharaja trade—three little sisters with ebony curls, men's eyebrows, large heads, and delicate hands and feet. They had four rooms, one for their governess. A chauffeur on permanent call lodged elsewhere. The governess, who was Dutch, had a perfect triangle of a nose and said 'whom' for 'who', pronouncing it 'whum'. The girls were to learn French, tennis, and swimming. The chauffeur arrived with a hairdresser, who cut their long hair; it lay on the governess's carpet, enough to fill a large pillow. Their toe- and fingernails were filed to points and looked like a kitten's teeth. They came smiling down the marble staircase, carrying new tennis racquets, wearing blue linen skirts and navy blazers. Mrs Blackley glanced up from the bridge game as they went by the cardroom. She had been one of those opposed to their having lessons at the English Lawn Tennis Club, for reasons that were, to her, perfectly evident.

She said, loudly, 'They'll have to be in white.'

'End whay, pray?' cried the governess, pointing her triangle nose.

'They can't go on the courts except in white. It is a private club. Entirely white.'

'Whum do they all think they are?' the governess asked, prepared to stalk on. But the girls, with their newly cropped heads, and their vulnerable necks showing, caught the drift and refused to go.

'Whom indeed,' said Georgina Blackley, fiddling with her bridge hand and looking happy.

'My wife's seamstress could run up white frocks for them in a minute,' said Jack. Perhaps he did not dislike children all that much.

'Whom could,' muttered Georgina.

But it turned out that the governess was not allowed to choose their clothes, and so Jack gave the children lessons at the hotel. For six weeks they trotted around the courts looking angelic in blue, or hopelessly foreign, depending upon who saw them. Of course they fell in love with Jack, offering him a passionate loyalty they had nowhere else to place. Netta watched the transfer of this gentle, anxious gift. After they departed, Jack was bad-tempered for several evenings and then never spoke of them again; they, needless to say, had been dragged from him weeping.

When this happened the Rosses had been married nearly five years. Being childless but still very loving, they had trouble deciding which of the two would be the child. Netta overheard 'He's a darling, but she's a sergeant major and no mistake. And so *mean*.' She also heard 'He's a lazy bastard. He bullies her. She's a fool.' She searched her heart again about children. Was it Jack or had it been Netta who had first said no? The only child she had ever admired was Jack, and not as a child but as a fighter, defying her. She and Jack were not the sort to have animal children, and Jack's dotty mother would probably soon be child enough for any couple to handle. Jack still seemed to adopt, in a tribal sense of his, half the women who fell in love with him. The only woman who resisted adoption was Netta—still burned-out, still ardent, in a manner of speaking still fourteen. His mother had turned up meanwhile, getting down from a train wearing a sly air of enjoying her own jokes, just as she must have looked on the day of the April Fool. At first she was no great trouble, though she did complain about an ulcerated leg. After years of pretending, she at last had something real. Netta's policy of silence made Jack's mother confident. She began to make a mockery of his music: 'All that money gone for nothing!' Or else, 'The amount we wasted on schools! The hours he's thrown away with his nose in a book. All that reading—if at least it had got him somewhere.' Netta noticed that he spent more time playing bridge and chatting to cronies in the bar now. She thought hard, and decided not to make it her business. His mother had once been pretty; perhaps he still saw her that way. She came of a ramshackle family with a usable past; she spoke of the Ashers and the Rosses as if she had known them when they were tinkers. English residents who had a low but solid barrier with Jack and Netta were fences-down with his mad mother: they seemed to take her at her own word when it was about herself. She began then to behave like a superior sort of guest, inviting large parties to her table for meals, ordering special wines and dishes at inconvenient hours, standing endless rounds of drinks in the bar.

Netta told herself, Jack wants it this way. It is his home too. She began to live a life apart, leaving Jack to his mother. She sat wearing her own mother's shawl, hunched over a new, modern adding machine, punching out accounts. 'Funny couple,' she heard now. She frowned, smiling in her mind; none of these people knew what bound them, or how tied they were. She had the habit of dodging out of her mother-in-law's parties by saying, 'I've got such an awful lot to do.' It made them laugh, because they thought this was Netta's term for slave-driving the servants. They thought the staff did the work, and that Netta counted the profits and was too busy with bookkeeping to keep an eye on Jack—who now, at twenty-six, was as attractive as he ever would be.

A woman named Iris Cordier was one of Jack's mother's new friends. Tall, loud, in winter dully pale, she reminded Netta of a blond penguin. Her voice moved between a squeak and a moo, and was a mark of the distinguished literary family to which her father belonged. Her mother, a Frenchwoman, had been in and out of nursing homes for years. The Cordiers haunted the Riviera, with Iris looking after her parents and watching their diets. Now she lived in a flat somewhere in Roquebrune with the survivor of the pair—the mother, Netta believed. Iris paused and glanced in the business room where Mr Asher had signed the hundred-year lease. She was on her way to lunch—Jack's mother's guest, of course.

'I say, aren't you Miss Asher?'

'I was.' Iris, like Dr Blackley, was probably younger than she looked. Out of her own childhood Netta recalled a desperate adolescent Iris with middle-aged parents clamped like handcuffs on her life. 'How is your mother?' Netta had been about to say 'How is Mrs Cordier?' but it sounded servile.

'I didn't know you knew her.'

'I remember her well. Your father too. He was a nice person.'

'And still is,' said Iris, sharply. 'He lives with me, and he always will. French daughters don't abandon their parents.' No one had ever sounded more English to Netta. 'And your father and mother?'

'Both dead now. I'm married to Jack Ross.'

'Nobody told me,' said Iris, in a way that made Netta think, Good Lord, Iris too? Jack could not possibly seem like a patriarchal figure where she was concerned; perhaps this time the game was reversed and Iris played at being tribal and maternal. The idea of Jack, or of any man, flinging himself on that iron bosom made Netta smile. As if startled, Iris covered her mouth. She seemed to be frightened of smiling back.

Oh, well, and what of it, Iris too, said Netta to herself, suddenly turning back to her accounts. As it happened, Netta was mistaken (as she never would have been with a bill). That day Jack was meeting Iris for the first time.

The upshot of these errors and encounters was an invitation to Roquebrune to visit Iris's father. Jack's mother was ruthlessly excluded, even though Iris probably owed her a return engagement because of the lunch. Netta supposed that Iris had decided one had to get past Netta to reach Jack—an inexactness if ever there was one. Or perhaps it was Netta Iris wanted. In that case the error became a farce. Netta had almost no knowledge of private houses. She looked around at something that did not much interest her, for she hated to leave her own home, and saw Iris's father, apparently too old and shaky to get out of his armchair. He smiled and he nodded, meanwhile stroking an aged cat. He said to Netta, 'You resemble your mother. A sweet woman. Obliging and quiet. I used to tell her that I longed to live in her hotel and be looked after.'

Not by me, thought Netta.

Iris's amber bracelets rattled as she pushed and pulled everyone through introductions. Jack and Netta had been asked to meet a young American Netta had often seen in her own bar, and a couple named Sandy and Sandra Braunsweg, who turned out to be Anglo-Swiss and twins. Iris's long arms were around them as she cried to Netta, 'Don't you know these babies?' They were, like the Rosses, somewhere in their twenties. Jack looked on, blue-eyed, interested, smiling at everything new. Netta supposed that she was now seeing some of the rather hard-up snobbish—snobbish what? 'Intelligumhen-sia,' she imagined Dr Blackley supplying. Having arrived at a word, Netta was ready to go home; but they had only just arrived. The American turned to Netta. He looked bored, and astonished by it. He needs the word for 'bored', she decided. Then he can go home, too. The Riviera was no place for Americans. They could not sit all day waiting for mail and the daily papers and for the clock to show a respectable drinking time. They made the best of things when they were caught with a house they'd been rash enough to rent unseen. Netta often had them then *en pension* for meals: a hotel dining room was one way of meeting people. They paid a fee to use the tennis courts, and they liked the bar. Netta would notice then how Jack picked up any accent within hearing.

Jack was now being attentive to the old man, Iris's father. Though this was none of Mr Cordier's business, Jack said, 'My wife and I are first cousins, as well as second cousins twice over.'

'You don't look it.'

Everyone began to speak at once, and it was a minute or two before Netta heard Jack again. This time he said, 'We are from a family of great . . .' It was lost. What now? Great innkeepers? Worriers? Skinflints? Whatever it was, old Mr Cordier kept nodding to show he approved.

'We don't see nearly enough of young men like you,' he said.

'True!' said Iris loudly. 'We live in a dreary world of ill women down here.' Netta thought this hard on the American, on Mr Cordier, and on the male Braunsweg twin, but none of them looked offended. 'I've got no time for women,' said Iris. She slapped down a glass of whisky so that it splashed, and rapped on a table with her knuckles. 'Shall I tell you why? Because women don't tick over. They just simply don't tick over.' No one disputed this. Iris went on: Women were underinformed. One could have virile conversations only with men. Women were attached to the past through fear, whereas men had a fearless sense of history. 'Men tick,' she said, glaring at Jack.

'I am not attached to a past,' said Netta, slowly. 'The past holds no attractions.' She was not used to general conversation. She thought that every word called for consideration and for an answer. 'Nothing could be worse than the way we children were dressed. And our mothers—the hard waves of their hair, the white lips. I think of those pale profiles and I wonder if those women were ever young.'

Poor Netta, who saw herself as profoundly English, spread consternation by being suddenly foreign and gassy. She talked the English of expatriate children, as if reading aloud. The twins looked shocked. But she had appealed to the American. He sat beside her on a scuffed velvet sofa. He was so large that she slid an inch or so in his direction when he sat down. He was Sandra Braunsweg's special friend: they had been in London together. He was trying to write.

'What do you mean?' said Netta. 'Write what?'

'Well—a novel, to start,' he said. His father had staked him to one year, then another. He mentioned all that Sandra had borne with, how she had actually kicked and punched him to keep him from being too American. He had embarrassed her to death in London by asking a waitress, 'Miss, where's the toilet?'

Netta said, 'Didn't you mind being corrected?'

'Oh, no. It was just friendly.'

Jack meanwhile was listening to Sandra telling about her English forebears and her English education. 'I had many years of undeniably excellent schooling,' she said. 'Mitten Todd.'

'What's that?' said Jack.

'It's near Bristol. I met excellent girls from Italy, Spain. I took *him* there to visit,' she said, generously including the American. 'I said, "Get a yellow necktie." He went straight out and bought one. I wore a little Schiaparelli. Bought in Geneva but still a real . . . A yellow jacket over a grey . . . Well, we arrived at my excellent old school, and even though the day was drizzly I said, "Put the top of the car back." He did so at once, and then he understood. The interior of the car harmonized perfectly with the yellow and grey.' The twins were orphaned. Iris was like a mother.

'When Mummy died we didn't know where to put all the Chippendale,' said Sandra, 'Iris took a lot of it.'

Netta thought, She is so silly. How can he respond? The girl's dimples and freckles and soft little hands were nothing Netta could have ever described: she had never in her life thought a word like 'pretty'. People were beautiful or they were not. Her happiness had always been great enough to allow for despair. She knew that some people thought Jack was happy and she was not.

'And what made you marry your young cousin?' the old man boomed at Netta. Perhaps his background allowed him to ask impertinent questions; he must have been doing so nearly forever. He stroked his cat; he was confident. He was spokesman for a roomful of wondering people.

'Jack was a moody child and I promised his mother I would look after him,' said Netta. In her hopelessly un-English way she believed she had said something funny.

At eleven o'clock the hotel car expected to fetch the Rosses was nowhere. They trudged home by moonlight. For the last hour of the evening Jack had been skewered on virile conversations, first with Iris, then with Sandra, to whom Netta had already given 'Chippendale' as a private name. It proved that Iris was right about concentrating on men and their ticking—Jack even thought Sandra rather pretty.

'Prettier than me?' said Netta, without the faintest idea what she meant, but aware she said something stupid.

'Not so attractive,' said Jack. His slight limp returned straight out of childhood. *She* had caused his accident.

'But she's not always clear,' said Netta. 'Mitten Todd, for example.'

'Who're you talking about?'

'Who are *you*?'

'Iris, of course.'

As if they had suddenly quarrelled they fell silent. In silence they entered their room and prepared for bed. Jack poured a whisky, walked on the clothes he had dropped, carried his drink to the bathroom. Through the half-shut door he called suddenly, 'Why did you say that asinine thing about promising to look after me?'

'It seemed so unlikely, I thought they'd laugh.' She had a glimpse of herself in the mirrors picking up his shed clothes.

He said, 'Well, is it true?'

She was quiet for such a long time that he came to see if she was still in the room. She said, 'No, your mother never said that or anything like it.'

'We shouldn't have gone to Roquebrune,' said Jack. 'I think those bloody people are going to be a nuisance. Iris wants her father to stay here, with the cat, while she goes to England for a month. How do we get out of that?'

'By saying no.'

'I'm rotten at no.'

'I told you not to be too pally with women,' she said, as a joke again, but jokes were her way of having floods of tears.

Before this had a chance to heal, Iris's father moved in, bringing his cat in a basket. He looked at his room and said, 'Medium large.' He looked at his bed and said, 'Reasonably long.' He was, in short, daft about measurements. When he took books out of the reading room, he was apt to return them with 'This volume contains about 70,000 words' written inside the back cover.

Netta had not wanted Iris's father, but Jack had said yes to it. She had not wanted the sick cat, but Jack had said yes to that too. The old man, who was lost without Iris, lived for his meals. He would appear at the shut doors of the dining room an hour too early, waiting for the menu to be typed and posted. In a voice that matched Iris's for carrying power, he read aloud, alone: 'Consommé. Good Lord, again? Is there a choice between the fish and the cutlet? I can't possibly eat all of that. A bit of salad and a boiled egg. That's all I could possibly want.' That was rubbish, because Mr Cordier ate the menu and more, and if there were two puddings, or a pudding and ice cream, he ate both and asked for pastry, fruit, and cheese to follow. One day, after Dr Blackley had attended him for faintness, Netta passed a message on to Iris, who had been back from England for a fortnight now but seemed in no hurry to take her father away.

'Keith Blackley thinks your father should go on a diet.'

'He can't,' said Iris. 'Our other doctor says dieting causes cancer.'

'You can't have heard that properly,' Netta said.

'It is like those silly people who smoke to keep their figures,' said Iris. 'Dieting.'

'Blackley hasn't said he should smoke, just that he should eat less of everything.'

'My father has never smoked in his life,' Iris cried. 'As for his diet, I weighed his food out for years. He's not here forever. I'll take him back as soon as he's had enough of hotels.'

He stayed for a long time, and the cat did too, and a nuisance they both were to the servants. When the cat was too ailing to walk, the old man carried it to a path behind the tennis courts and put it down on the gravel to die. Netta came out with the old man's tea on a tray (not done for everyone, but having him out of the way was a relief) and she saw the cat lying on its side, eyes wide, as if profoundly thinking. She saw unlicked dirt on its coat and ants exploring its paws. The old man sat in a garden chair, wearing a panama hat, his hands clasped on a stick. He called, 'Oh, Netta, take her away. I am too old to watch anything die. I know what she'll do,' he said, indifferently, his voice falling as she came near. 'Oh, I know that. Turn on her back and give a shriek. I've heard it often.'

Netta disburdened her tray onto a garden table and pulled the tray cloth under the cat. She was angered at the haste and indecency of the ants. 'It would be polite to leave her,' she said. 'She doesn't want to be watched.'

'I always sit here,' said the old man.

Jack, making for the courts with Chippendale, looked as if the sight of the two conversing amused him. Then he understood and scooped up the cat and tray cloth and went away with the cat over his shoulder. He laid it in the shade of a Judas tree, and within an hour it was dead. Iris's father said, 'I've got no one to talk to here. That's my trouble. That shroud was too small for my poor Polly. Ask my daughter to fetch me.'

Jack's mother said that night, 'I'm sure you wish that I had a devoted daughter to take me away too.' Because of the attention given the cat she seemed to feel she had not been nuisance enough. She had taken to saying, 'My leg is dying before I am,' and imploring Jack to preserve her leg, should it be amputated, and make certain it was buried with her. She wanted Jack to be close by at nearly any hour now, so that she could lean on him. After sitting for hours at bridge she had trouble climbing two flights of stairs; nothing would induce her to use the lift.

'Nothing ever came of your music,' she would say, leaning on him. 'Of course, you have a wife to distract you now. I needed a daughter. Every woman does.' Netta managed to trap her alone, and forced her to sit while she stood over her. Netta said, 'Look, Aunt Vera, I forbid you, I absolutely forbid you, do you hear, to make a nurse of Jack, and I shall strangle you with my own hands if you go on saying nothing came of his music. You are not to say it in my hearing or out of it. Is that plain?'

Jack's mother got up to her room without assistance. About an hour later the gardener found her on a soft bed of wallflowers. 'An inch to the left and she'd have landed on a rake,' he said to Netta. She was still alive when Netta knelt down. In her fall she had crushed the plants, the yellow minted *giroflées de Nice*. Netta thought that she was now, at last, for the first time, inhaling one of the smells of death. Her aunt's arms and legs were turned and twisted; her skirt was pulled so that her swollen leg showed. It seemed that she had jumped carrying her walking stick—it lay across the path. She often slept in an armchair, afternoons, with one eye slightly open. She opened that eye now and, seeing she had Netta, said, 'My son.' Netta was thinking, I have never known her. And if I knew her, then it was Jack or myself I could not understand. Netta was afraid of giving orders, and of telling people not to touch her aunt before Dr Blackley could be summoned, because she knew that she had always been mistaken. Now Jack was there, propping his mother up, brushing leaves and earth out of her hair. Her head dropped on his shoulder. Netta thought from the sudden heaviness that her aunt had died, but she sighed and opened that one eye again, saying this time, 'Doctor?' Netta left everyone doing the wrong things to her dying—no, her murdered—aunt. She said quite calmly into a telephone, 'I am afraid that my aunt must have jumped or fallen from the second floor.'

Jack found a letter on his mother's night table that began, 'Why blame Netta? I forgive.' At dawn he and Netta sat at a card table with yesterday's cigarettes still not cleaned out of the ashtray, and he did not ask what Netta had said or done that called for forgiveness. They kept pushing the letter back and forth. He would read it and then Netta would. It seemed natural for them to be silent. Jack had sat beside his mother for much of the night. Each of them then went to sleep for an hour, apart, in one of the empty rooms, just as they had done in the old days when their parents were juggling beds and guests and double and single quarters. By the time the doctor returned for his second visit Jack was neatly dressed and seemed wide awake. He sat in the bar drinking black coffee and reading a travel book of Evelyn Waugh's called *Labels*. Netta, who looked far more untidy and underslept, wondered if Jack wished he might leave now, and sail from Monte Carlo on the Stella Polaris.

Dr Blackley said, 'Well, you are a dim pair. She is not in pu-hain, you know.' Netta supposed this was the roundabout way doctors have of announcing death, very like 'Her sufferings have ended.' But Jack, looking hard at the doctor, had heard another meaning. 'Jumped or fell,' said Dr Blackley. 'She neither fell nor jumped. She is up there enjoying a damned good thu-hing.'

Netta went out and through the lounge and up the marble steps. She sat down in the shaded room on the chair where Jack had spent most of the night. Her aunt did not look like anyone Netta knew, not even like Jack. She stared at the alien face and said, 'Aunt Vera, Keith Blackley says there is nothing really the matter. You must have made a mistake. Perhaps you fainted on the path, overcome by the scent of wallflowers. What would you like me to tell Jack?'

Jack's mother turned on her side and slowly, tenderly, raised herself on an elbow. 'Well, Netta,' she said, 'I daresay the fool is right. But as I've been given quite a lot of sleeping stuff, I'd as soon stay here for now.'

Netta said, 'Are you hungry?'

'I should very much like a ham sandwich on English bread, and about that much gin with a lump of ice.'

She began coming down for meals a few days later. They knew she had crept down the stairs and flung her walking stick over the path and let herself fall hard on a bed of wallflowers—had even plucked her skirt up for a bit of accuracy; but she was also someone returned from beyond the limits, from the other side of the wall. Once she said, 'It was like diving and suddenly realizing there was no water in the sea.' Again, 'It is not true that your life rushes before your eyes. You can see the flowers floating up to you. Even a short fall takes a long time.'

Everyone was deeply changed by this incident. The effect on the victim herself was that she got religion hard.

'We are all hopeless nonbelievers!' shouted Iris, drinking in the bar one afternoon. 'At least, I hope we are. But when I see you, Vera, I feel there might be something in religion. You look positively temperate.'

'I am allowed to love God, I hope,' said Jack's mother.

Jack never saw or heard his mother anymore. He leaned against the bar, reading. It was his favorite place. Even on the sunniest of afternoons he read by the red-shaded light. Netta was present only because she had supplies to check. Knowing she ought to keep out of this, she still said, 'Religion is more than love. It is supposed to tell you why you exist and what you are expected to do about it.'

'You have no religious feelings at all?' This was the only serious and almost the only friendly question Iris was ever to ask Netta.

'None,' said Netta. 'I'm running a business.'

'I love God as Jack used to love music,' said his mother. 'At least he said he did when we were paying for lessons.'

'Adam and Eve had God,' said Netta. 'They had nobody *but* God. A fat lot of good that did them.' This was as far as their dialectic went. Jack had not moved once except to turn pages. He read steadily but cautiously now, as if every author had a design on him. That was one effect of his mother's incident. The other was that he gave up bridge and went back to playing the clarinet. Iris hammered out an accompaniment on the upright piano in the old music room, mostly used for listening to radio broadcasts. She was the only person Netta had ever heard who could make Mozart sound like an Irish jig. Presently Iris began to say that it was time Jack gave a concert. Before this could turn into a crisis Iris changed her mind and said what he wanted was a holiday. Netta thought he needed something: he seemed to be exhausted by love, friendship, by being a husband, someone's son, by trying to make a world out of reading and sense out of life. A visit to England to meet some stimulating people, said Iris. To help Iris with her tiresome father during the journey. To visit art galleries and bookshops and go to concerts. To meet people. To talk.

This was a hot, troubled season, and many persons were planning journeys—not to meet other people but for fear of a war. The hotel had emptied out by the end of March. Netta, whose father had known there would never be another catastrophe, had her workmen come in, as usual. She could hear the radiators being drained and got ready for painting as she packed Jack's clothes. They had never been separated before. They kept telling each other that it was only for a short holiday—for three or four weeks. She was surprised at how neat marriage was, at how many years and feelings could be folded and put under a lid. Once, she went to the window so that he would not see her tears and think she was trying to blackmail him. Looking out, she noticed the American, Chippendale's lover, idly knocking a tennis ball against the garage, as Jack had done in the early summers of their life; he had come round to the hotel looking for a partner, but that season there were none. She suddenly knew to a certainty that if Jack were to die she would search the crowd of mourners for a man she could live with. She would not return from the funeral alone.

Grief and memory, yes, she said to herself, but what about three o'clock in the morning?

By June nearly everyone Netta knew had vanished, or, like the Blackleys, had started to pack. Netta had new tablecloths made, and ordered new white awnings, and two dozen rosebushes from the nursery at Cap Ferrat. The American came over every day and followed her from room to room, talking. He had nothing better to do. The Swiss twins were in England. His father, who had been backing his writing career until now, had suddenly changed his mind about it—now, when he needed money to get out of Europe. He had projects for living on his own, but they required a dose of funds. He wanted to open a restaurant on the Riviera where nothing but chicken pie would be served. Or else a vast and expensive café where people would pay to make their own sandwiches. He said that he was seeing the food of the future, but all that Netta could see was customers asking for their money back. He trapped her behind the bar and said he loved her; Netta made other women look like stuffed dolls. He could still remember the shock of meeting her, the attraction, the brilliant answer she had made to Iris about attachments to the past.

Netta let him rave until he asked for a loan. She laughed and wondered if it was for the chicken-pie restaurant. No—he wanted to get on a boat sailing from Cannes. She said, quite cheerfully, 'I can't be Venus and Barclays Bank. You have to choose.'

He said, 'Can't Venus ever turn up with a letter of credit?'

She shook her head. 'Not a hope.'

But when it was July and Jack hadn't come back, he cornered her again. Money wasn't in it now: his father had not only relented but had virtually ordered him home. He was about twenty-two, she guessed. He could still plead successfully for parental help and for indulgence from women. She said, no more than affectionately, 'I'm going to show you a very pretty room.'

A few days later Dr Blackley came alone to say goodbye.

'Are you really staying?' he asked.

'I am responsible for the last eighty-one years of this lease,' said Netta. 'I'm going to be thirty. It's a long tenure. Besides, I've got Jack's mother and she won't leave. Jack has a chance now to visit America. It doesn't sound sensible to me, but she writes encouraging him. She imagines him suddenly very rich and sending for her. I've discovered the limit of what you can feel about people. I've discovered something else,' she said abruptly. 'It is that sex and love have nothing in common. Only a coincidence, sometimes. You think the coincidence will go on and so you get married. I suppose that is what men are born knowing and women learn by accident.'

'I'm su-horry.'

'For God's sake, don't be. It's a relief.'

She had no feeling of guilt, only of amazement. Jack, as a memory, was in a restricted area—the tennis courts, the cardroom, the bar. She saw him at bridge with Mrs Blackley and pouring drinks for temporary friends. He crossed the lounge jauntily with a cluster of little dark-haired girls wearing blue. In the mirrored bedroom there was only Netta. Her dreams were cleansed of him. The looking glasses still held their blue-and-silver-water shadows, but they lost the habit of giving back the moods and gestures of a Moslem wife.

About five years after this, Netta wrote to Jack. The war had caught him in America, during the voyage his mother had so wanted him to have. His limp had kept him out of the Army. As his mother (now dead) might have put it, all that reading had finally got him somewhere: he had spent the last years putting out a two-pager on aspects of European culture—part of a scrupulous effort Britain was making for the West. That was nearly all Netta knew. A Belgian Red Cross official had arrived, apparently in Jack's name, to see if she was still alive. She sat in her father's business room, wearing a coat and a shawl because there was no way of heating any part of the hotel now, and she tried to get on with the letter she had been writing in her head, on and off, for many years.

'In June, 1940, we were evacuated,' she started, for the tenth or eleventh time. 'I was back by October. Italians had taken over the hotel. They used the mirror behind the bar for target practice. Oddly enough it was not smashed. It is covered with spiderwebs, and the bullet hole is the spider. I had great trouble over Aunt Vera, who disappeared and was found finally in one of the attic rooms.

'The Italians made a pet of her. Took her picture. She enjoyed that. Everyone who became thin had a desire to be photographed, as if knowing they would use this intimidating evidence against those loved ones who had missed being starved. Guilt for life. After an initial period of hardship, during which she often had her picture taken at her request, the Italians brought food and looked after her, more than anyone. She was their mama. We were annexed territory and in time we had the same food as the Italians. The thin pictures of your mother are here on my desk.

'She buried her British passport and would never say where. Perhaps under the Judas tree with Mr Cordier's cat, Polly. She remained just as mad and just as spoiled, and that became dangerous when life stopped being ordinary. She complained about me to the Italians. At that time a complaint was a matter of prison and of death if it was made to the wrong person. Luckily for me, there was also the right person to take the message.

'A couple of years after that, the Germans and certain French took over and the Italians were shut up in another hotel without food or water, and some people risked their well-being to take water to them (for not everyone preferred the new situation, you can believe me). When she was dying I asked her if she had a message for one Italian officer who had made such a pet of her and she said, "No, why?" She died without a word for anybody. She was buried as 'Rossini', because the Italians had changed people's names. She had said she was French, a Frenchwoman named Ross, and so some peculiar civil status was created for us—the two Mrs Rossinis.

'The records were topsy-turvy; it would have meant going to the Germans and explaining my dead aunt was British, and of course I thought I would not. The death certificate and permission to bury are for a Vera Rossini. I have them here on my desk for you with her pictures.

'You are probably wondering where I have found all this writing paper. The Germans left it behind. When we were being shelled I took what few books were left in the reading room down to what used to be the wine cellar and read by candlelight. You are probably wondering where the candles came from. A long story. I even have paint for the radiators, large buckets that have never been opened.

'I live in one room, my mother's old sitting room. The business room can be used but the files are gone. When the Italians were here your mother was their mother, but I was not their Moslem wife, although I still had respect for men. One yelled "*Luce, luce*", because your mother was showing a light. She said, "Bugger you, you little toad." He said, "Granny, I said '*luce*', not '*Duce*'."

'Not long ago we crept out of our shelled homes, looking like cave dwellers. When you see the hotel again, it will be functioning. I shall have painted the radiators. Long shoots of bramble come in through the cardroom windows. There are drifts of leaves in the old music room and I saw scorpions and heard their rustling like the rustle of death. Everything that could have been looted has gone. Sheets, bedding, mattresses. The neighbours did quite a lot of that. At the risk of their lives. When the Italians were here we had rice and oil. Your mother, who was crazy, used to put out grains to feed the mice.

'When the Germans came we had to live under Vichy law, which meant each region lived on what it could produce. As ours produces nothing, we got quite thin again. Aunt Vera died plump. Do you know what it means when I say she used to complain about me?

'Send me some books. As long as they are in English. I am quite sick of the three other languages in which I've heard so many threats, such boasting, such a lot of lying.

'For a time I thought people would like to know how the Italians left and the Germans came in. It was like this: They came in with the first car moving slowly, flying the French flag. The highest-ranking French official in the region. Not a German. No, just a chap getting his job back. The Belgian Red Cross people were completely uninterested and warned me that no one would ever want to hear.

'I suppose that you already have the fiction of all this. The fiction must be different, oh very different, from Italians sobbing with homesickness in the night. The Germans were not real, they were specially got up for the events of the time. Sat in the white dining room, eating with whatever plates and spoons were not broken or looted, ate soups that were mostly water, were forbidden to complain. Only in retreat did they develop faces and I noticed then that some were terrified and many were old. A radio broadcast from some untouched area advised the local population not to attack them as they retreated, it would make wild animals of them. But they were attacked by some young boys shooting out of a window and eight hostages were taken, including the son of the man who cut the maharaja's daughters' black hair, and they were shot and left along the wall of a café on the more or less Italian side of the border. And the man who owned the café was killed too, but later, by civilians—he had given names to the Gestapo once, or perhaps it was something else. He got on the wrong side of the right side at the wrong time, and he was thrown down the deep gorge between the two frontiers.

'Up in one of the hill villages Germans stayed till no one was alive. I was at that time in the former wine cellar, reading books by candlelight.

'The Belgian Red Cross team found the skeleton of a German deserter in a cave and took back the helmet and skull to Knokke-le-Zoute as souvenirs.

'My war has ended. Our family held together almost from the Napoleonic adventures. It is shattered now. Sentiment does not keep families whole—only mutual pride and mutual money.'

This true story sounded so implausible that she decided never to send it. She wrote a sensible letter asking for sugar and rice and for new books; nothing must be older than 1940.

Jack answered at once: there were no new authors (he had been asking people). Sugar was unobtainable, and there were queues for rice. Shoes had been rationed. There were no women's stockings but lisle, and the famous American legs looked terrible. You could not find butter or meat or tinned pineapple. In restaurants, instead of butter you were given miniature golf balls of cream cheese. He supposed that all this must sound like small beer to Netta.

A notice arrived that a CARE package awaited her at the post office. It meant that Jack had added his name and his money to the mailing list. She refused to sign for it; then she changed her mind and discovered it was not from Jack but from the American she had once taken to such a pretty room. Jack did send rice and sugar and delicious coffee but he forgot about books. His letters followed; sometimes three arrived in a morning. She left them sealed for days. When she sat down to answer, all she could remember were implausible things.

Iris came back. She was the first. She had grown puffy in England—the result of drinking whatever alcohol she could get her hands on and grimly eating her sweets allowance: there would be that much less gin and chocolate for the Germans if ever they landed. She put her now wide bottom on a comfortable armchair—one of the few chairs the first wave of Italians had not burned with cigarettes or idly hacked at with daggers—and said Jack had been living with a woman in America and to spare the gossip had let her be known as his wife. Another Mrs Ross? When Netta discovered it was dimpled Chippendale, she laughed aloud.

'I've seen them,' said Iris. 'I mean I saw them together. King Charles and a spaniel. Jack wiped his feet on her.'

Netta's feelings were of lightness, relief. She would not have to tell Jack about the partisans hanging by the neck in the arches of the Place Masséna at Nice. When Iris had finished talking, Netta said, 'What about his music?'

'I don't know.'

'How can you not know something so important?'

'Jack had a good chance at things, but he made a mess of everything,' said Iris. 'My father is still living. Life really is too incredible for some of us.'

A dark girl of about twenty turned up soon after. Her costume, a grey dress buttoned to the neck, gave her the appearance of being in uniform. She unzipped a military-looking bag and cried, in an unplaceable accent, '*Ha*llo, *ha*llo, Mrs Ross? A few small gifts for you,' and unpacked a bottle of Haig, four tins of corned beef, a jar of honey, and six pairs of American nylon stockings, which Netta had never seen before, and were as good to have under a mattress as gold. Netta looked up at the tall girl.

'Remember? I was the middle sister. With,' she said gravely, 'the typical middle-sister problems.' She scarcely recalled Jack, her beloved. The memory of Netta had grown up with her. 'I remember you laughing,' she said, without loving that memory. She was a severe, tragic girl. 'You were the first adult I ever heard laughing. At night in bed I could hear it from your balcony. You sat smoking with, I suppose, your handsome husband. I used to laugh just to hear you.'

She had married an Iranian journalist. He had discovered that political prisoners in the United States were working under lamentable conditions in tin mines. President Truman had sent them there. People from all over the world planned to unite to get them out. The girl said she had been to Germany and to Austria, she had visited camps, they were all alike, and that was already the past, and the future was the prisoners in the tin mines.

Netta said, 'In what part of the country are these mines?'

The middle sister looked at her sadly and said, "Is there more than one part?"

For the first time in years, Netta could seek Jack clearly. They were silently sharing a joke; he had caught it too. She and the girl lunched in a corner of the battered dining room. The tables were scarred with initials. There were no tablecloths. One of the great-uncle's paintings still hung on a wall. It showed the Quai Laurenti, a country road alongside the sea. Netta, who had no use for the past, was discovering a past she could regret. Out of a dark, gentle silence—silence imposed by the impossibility of telling anything real—she counted the cracks in the walls. When silence failed she heard power saws ripping into olive trees and a lemon grove. With a sense of deliverance she understood soon there would be nothing left to spoil. Her great-uncle's picture, which ought to have changed out of sympathetic magic, remained faithful. She regretted everything now, even the three anxious little girls in blue linen. Every calamitous season between then and now seemed to descend directly from Georgina Blackley's having said 'white' just to keep three children in their place. Clad in buttoned-up grey, the middle sister now picked at corned beef and said she had hated her father, her mother, her sisters, and most of all the Dutch governess.

'Where is she now?' said Netta.

'Dead, I hope.' This was from someone who had visited camps. Netta sat listening, her cheek on her hand. Death made death casual: she had always known. Neither the vanquished in their flight nor the victors returning to pick over rubble seemed half so vindictive as a tragic girl who had disliked her governess.

Dr Blackley came back looking positively cheerful. In those days men still liked soldiering. It made them feel young, if they needed to feel it, and it got them away from home. War made the break few men could make on their own. The doctor looked years younger, too, and very fit. His wife was not with him. She had survived everything, and the hardships she had undergone had completely restored her to health—which had made it easy for her husband to leave her. Actually, he had never gone back, except to wind up the matter.

'There are things about Georgina I respect and admire,' he said, as husbands will say from a distance. His war had been in Malta. He had come here, as soon as he could, to the shelled, gnawed, tarnished coast (as if he had not seen enough at Malta) to ask Netta to divorce Jack and to marry him, or live with him—anything she wanted, on any terms.

But she wanted nothing—at least, not from him.

'Well, one can't defeat a memory,' he said. 'I always thought it was mostly su-hex between the two of you.'

'So it was,' said Netta. 'So far as I remember.'

'Everyone noticed. You would vanish at odd hours. Dis-huppear.'

'Yes, we did.'

'You can't live on memories,' he objected. 'Though I respect you for being faithful, of course.'

'What you are talking about is something of which one has no specific memory,' said Netta. 'Only of seasons. Places. Rooms. It is as abstract to remember as to read about. That is why it is boring in talk except as a joke, and boring in books except for poetry.'

'You never read poetry.'

'I do now.'

'I guessed that,' he said.

'That lack of memory is why people are unfaithful, as it is so curiously called. When I see closed shutters I know there are lovers behind them. That is how the memory works. The rest is just convention and small talk.'

'Why lovers? Why not someone sleeping off the wine he had for lunch?'

'No. Lovers.'

'A middle-aged man cutting his toenails in the bathtub,' he said with unexpected feeling. 'Wearing bifocal lenses so that he can see his own feet.'

'No, lovers. Always.'

He said, 'Have you missed him?'

'Missed who?'

'Who the bloody hell are we talking about?'

'The Italian commander billeted here. He was not a guest. He was here by force. I was not breaking a rule. Without him I'd have perished in every way. He may be home with his wife now. Or in that fortress near Turin where he sent other men. Or dead.' She looked at the doctor and said, 'Well, what would you like me to do? Sit here and cry?'

'I can't imagine you with a brute.'

'I never said that.'

'Do you miss him still?'

'The absence of Jack was like a cancer which I am sure has taken root, and of which I am bound to die,' said Netta.

'You'll bu-hury us all,' he said, as doctors tell the condemned.

'I haven't said I won't.' She rose suddenly and straightened her skirt, as she used to do when hotel guests became pally. 'Conversation over,' it meant.

'Don't be too hard on Jack," he said.

'I am hard on myself,' she replied.

After he had gone he sent her a parcel of books, printed on greyish paper, in warped wartime covers. All of the titles were, to Netta, unknown. There was *Fireman Flower* and *The Horse's Mouth* and *Four Quartets* and *The Stuff to Give the Troops* and *Better Than a Kick in the Pants* and *Put Out More Flags*. A note added that the next package would contain Henry Green and Dylan Thomas. She guessed he would not want to be thanked, but she did so anyway. At the end of her letter was 'Please remember, if you mind too much, that I said no to you once before.' Leaning on the bar, exactly as Jack used to, with a glass of the middle sister's drink at hand, she opened *Better Than a Kick in the Pants* and read, '. . . the two Fascists came in, one of them tall and thin and tough looking; the other smaller, with only one arm and an empty sleeve pinned up to his shoulder. Both of them were quite young and wore black shirts.'

Oh, thought Netta, I am the only one who knows all this. No one will ever realize how much I know of the truth, the truth, the truth, and she put her head on her hands, her elbows on the scarred bar, and let the first tears of her after-war run down her wrists.

The last to return was the one who should have been first. Jack wrote that he was coming down from the north as far as Nice by bus. It was a common way of travelling and much cheaper than by train. Netta guessed that he was mildly hard up and that he had saved nothing from his war job. The bus came in at six, at the foot of the Place Masséna. There was a deep-blue late-afternoon sky and pale sunlight. She could hear birds from the public gardens nearby. The Place was as she had always seen it, like an elegant drawing room with a blue ceiling. It was nearly empty. Jack looked out on this sunlighted, handsome space and said, 'Well, I'll just leave my stuff at the bus office, for the moment'—perhaps noticing that Netta had not invited him anywhere. He placed his ticket on the counter, and she saw that he had not come from far away: he must have been moving south by stages. He carried an aura of London pub life; he had been in London for weeks.

A frowning man hurrying to wind things up so he could have his first drink of the evening said, 'The office is closing and we don't keep baggage here.'

'People used to be nice,' Jack said.

'Bus people?'

'Just people.'

She was hit by the sharp change in his accent. As for the way of speaking, which is something else again, he was like the heir to great estates back home after a Grand Tour. Perhaps the estates had run down in his absence. She slipped the frowning man a thousand francs, a new pastel-tinted bill, on which the face of a calm girl glowed like an opal. She said, 'We shan't be long.'

She set off over the Place, walking diagonally—Jack beside her, of course. He did not ask where they were headed, though he did make her smile by saying, 'Did you bring a car?', expecting one of the hotel cars to be parked nearby, perhaps with a driver to open the door; perhaps with cold chicken and wine in a hamper, too. He said, 'I'd forgotten about having to tip for every little thing.' He did not question his destination, which was no farther than a café at the far end of the square. What she felt at that instant was intense revulsion. She thought, I don't want him, and pushed away some invisible flying thing—a bat or a blown paper. He looked at her with surprise. He must have been wondering if hardship had taught Netta to talk in her mind.

This is it, the freedom he was always offering me, she said to herself, smiling up at the beautiful sky.

They moved slowly along the nearly empty square, pausing only when some worn-out Peugeot or an old bicycle, finding no other target, made a swing in their direction. Safely on the pavement, they walked under the arches where partisans had been hanged. It seemed to Netta the bodies had been taken down only a day or so before. Jack, who knew about this way of dying from hearsay, chose a café table nearly under a poor lad's bound, dangling feet.

'I had a woman next to me on the bus who kept a hedgehog all winter in a basketful of shavings,' he said. 'He can drink milk out of a wineglass.' He hesitated. 'I'm sorry about the books you asked for. I was sick of books by then. I was sick of rhetoric and culture and patriotic crap.'

'I suppose it is all very different over there,' said Netta.

'God, yes.'

He seemed to expect her to ask questions, so she said, 'What kind of clothes do they wear?'

'They wear quite a lot of plaids and tartans. They eat at peculiar hours. You'll see them eating strawberries and cream just when you're thinking of having a drink.'

She said, 'Did you visit the tin mines, where Truman sends his political prisoners?'

'*Tin* mines?' said Jack. 'No.'

'Remember the three little girls from the maharaja trade?'

Neither could hear what the other had to say. They were partially deaf to each other.

Netta continued softly, 'Now, as I understand it, she first brought an American to London, and then she took an Englishman to America.'

He had too much the habit of women, he was playing too close a game, to waste points saying, 'Who? What?'

'It was over as fast as it started,' he said. 'But then the war came and we were stuck. She became a friend,' he said. 'I'm quite fond of her'—which Netta translated as, 'It is a subterranean river that may yet come to light.' 'You wouldn't know her,' he said. 'She's very different now. I talked so much about the south, down here, she finally found some land going dirt cheap at Bandol. The major arranged for her to have an orchard next to her property, so she won't have neighbours. It hardly cost her anything. He said to her, "You're very pretty." '

'No one ever had a bargain in property because of a pretty face,' said Netta.

'Wasn't it lucky,' said Jack. He could no longer hear himself, let alone Netta. 'The war was unsettling, being in America. She minded not being active. Actually she was using the Swiss passport, which made it worse. Her brother was killed over Bremen. She needs security now. In a way it was sorcerer and apprentice between us, and she suddenly grew up. She'll be better off with a roof over her head. She writes a little now. Her poetry isn't bad,' he said, as if Netta had challenged its quality.

'Is she at Bandol now, writing poetry?'

'Well, no.' He laughed suddenly. 'There isn't a roof yet. And, you know, people don't sit writing that way. They just think they're going to.'

'Who has replaced you?' said Netta. 'Another sorcerer?'

'Oh, *he* . . . he looks like George II in a strong light. Or like Queen Anne. Queen Anne and Lady Mary, somebody called them.' Iris, that must have been. Queen Anne and Lady Mary wasn't bad—better than King Charles and his spaniel. She was beginning to enjoy his story. He saw it, and said lightly, 'I was too preoccupied with you to manage another life. I couldn't see myself going on and on away from you. I didn't want to grow middle-aged at odds with myself.'

But he had lost her; she was enjoying a reverie about Jack now, wearing one of those purple sunburns people acquire at golf. She saw him driving an open car, with large soft freckles on his purple skull. She saw his mistress's dog on the front seat and the dog's ears flying like pennants. The revulsion she felt did not lend distance but brought a dreamy reality closer still. He must be thirty-four now, she said to herself. A terrible age for a man who has never imagined thirty-four.

'Well, perhaps you have made a mess of it,' she said, quoting Iris.

'What mess? I'm here. *He*—"

'Queen Anne?'

'Yes, well, actually Gerald is his name; he wears nothing but brown. Brown suit, brown tie, brown shoes. I said, "*He* can't go to Mitten Todd. He won't match." '

'Harmonize,' she said.

'That's it. Harmonize with the—'

'What about Gerald's wife? I'm sure he has one.'

'Lucretia.'

'No, really?'

'On my honour. When I last saw them they were all together, talking.'

Netta was remembering what the middle sister had said about laughter on the balcony. She couldn't look at him. The merest crossing of glances made her start laughing rather wildly into her hands. The hysterical quality of her own laughter caught her in midair. What were they talking about? He hitched his chair nearer and dared to take her wrist.

'Tell me, now,' he said, as if they were to be two old confidence men getting their stories straight. 'What about you? Was there ever . . .' The glaze of laughter had not left his face and voice. She saw that he would make her his business, if she let him. Pulling back, she felt another clasp, through a wall of fog. She groped for this other, invisible hand, but it dissolved. It was a lost, indifferent hand; it no longer recognized her warmth. She understood: He is dead . . . Jack, closed to ghosts, deaf to their voices, was spared this. He would be spared everything, she saw. She envied him his imperviousness, his true unhysterical laughter.

Perhaps that's why I kicked him, she said. I was always jealous. Not of women. Of his short memory, his comfortable imagination. And I am going to be thirty-seven and I have a dark, an accurate, a deadly memory.

He still held her wrist and turned it another way, saying, 'Look, there's paint on it.'

'Oh, God, where is the waiter?' she cried, as if that were the one important thing. Jack looked his age, exactly. She looked like a burned-out child who had been told a ghost story. Desperately seeking the waiter, she turned to the café behind them and saw the last light of the long afternoon strike the mirror above the bar—a flash in a tunnel; hands juggling with fire. That unexpected play, at a remove, borne indoors, displayed to anyone who could stare without blinking, was a complete story. It was the brightness on the looking glass, the only part of a life, or a love, or a promise, that could never be concealed, changed, or corrupted.

Not a hope, she was trying to tell him. He could read her face now. She reminded herself, If I say it, I am free. I can finish painting the radiators in peace. I can read every book in the world. If I had relied on my memory for guidance, I would never have crept out of the wine cellar. Memory is what ought to prevent you from buying a dog after the first dog dies, but it never does. It should at least keep you from saying yes twice to the same person.

'I've always loved you,' he chose to announce—it really was an announcement, in a new voice that stated nothing except facts.

The dark, the ghosts, the candlelight, her tears on the scarred bar—*they* were real. And still, whether she wanted to see it or not, the light of imagination danced all over the square. She did not dare to turn again to the mirror, lest she confuse the two and forget which light was real. A pure white awning on a cross street seemed to her to be of indestructible beauty. The window it sheltered was hollowed with sadness and shadow. She said with the same deep sadness, 'I believe you.' The wave of revulsion receded, sucked back under another wave—a powerful adolescent craving for something simple, such as true love.

Her face did not show this. It was set in adolescent stubbornness, and this was one of their old, secret meetings when, sullen and hurt, she had to be coaxed into life as Jack wanted it lived. It was the same voyage, at the same rate of speed. The Place seemed to her to be full of invisible traffic—first a whisper of tires, then a faint, high screeching, then a steady roar. If Jack heard anything, it could be only the blood in the veins and his loud, happy thought. To a practical romantic like Jack, dying to get Netta to bed right away, what she was hearing was only the uh-hebb and flo-ho of hormones, as Dr Blackley said. She caught a look of amazement on his face: *Now* he knew what he had been deprived of. *Now* he remembered. It had been Netta, all along.

Their evening shadows accompanied them over the long square. 'I still have a car,' she remarked. 'But no petrol. There's a train.' She did keep on hearing a noise, as of heavy traffic rushing near and tearing away. Her own quiet voice carried across it, saying, 'Not a hope.' He must have heard that. Why, it was as loud as a shout. He held her arm lightly. He was as buoyant as morning. This *was* his morning—the first light on the mirror, the first cigarette. He pulled her into an archway where no one could see. What could I do, she asked her ghosts, but let my arm be held, my steps be guided?

Later, Jack said that the walk with Netta back across the Place Masséna was the happiest event of his life. Having no reliable counter-event to put in its place, she let the memory stand.

1976

Nadine Gordimer

b. 1923

'A writer is "selected" by his subject—his subject being the consciousness of his own era,' observed Nadine Gordimer. And in her fiction she focuses, as an honest witness of her times, on Africa and the English-speaking whites as well as the black Africans, Asians, and Afrikaners who inhabit it. 'My time and place have been twentieth-century Africa. Emerging from it, immersed in it, the first form in which I wrote was the short story.'

Born in the small gold-mining town of Springs, South Africa, Gordimer studied English literature at the University of the Witwatersrand in Johannesburg. She published her first short stories when she was in her early twenties. Labelled by the South African government a 'very disloyal South African', she has published short fiction and novels that examine her land with care, insight, and affection. Committed to South Africa's problems and choosing to continue residing there, she has asserted, 'I consider myself an intensely loyal South African. I care deeply for my country. If I didn't, I wouldn't still be there.' Although she has served as a visiting lecturer at various universities around the world, including Harvard and Princeton, her home remains Johannesburg.

Gordimer's fiction is a penetrating and painful exploration of the personal and political tragedies in contemporary South Africa. Her often bleak portraits of the society do not permit of facile optimism or easy solutions. And the external tribulations often mirror the internal turmoil of her characters. 'Whites among themselves are shaped by their peculiar position, just as black people are by theirs,' she commented. 'I write about their private selves; often, even in the most private situations, they are what they are because their lives are regulated and their mores formed by the political situation.'

In 'The Train from Rhodesia', Gordimer depicts the white exploitation of blacks. The deceptively simple incident of a young wife's interest in the wooden sculpture of a lion by a black artist becomes a too accurate representation of white domination and its devastating effect on the black population and on some members of the white population.

In a sudden moment of insight, the woman in beige trousers at the centre of 'No Place Like' personally confronts the racial segregation in the land. Nearly a quarter-century separates the publication of this story from the earlier 'The Train from Rhodesia', and the time is reflected in the police-state setting of the latter work.

'The Train from Rhodesia' was first published in the September 1947 issue of *Trek* and then collected in *The Soft Voice of the Serpent, and Other Stories* (1952). 'No Place Like' was first published in the July 1971 issue of *The Southern Review* and then collected in *Livingstone's Companions: Stories* (1971).

The Train from Rhodesia

The train came out of the red horizon and bore down towards them over the single straight track.

The stationmaster came out of his little brick station with its pointed chalet roof, feeling the creases in his serge uniform in his legs as well. A stir of preparedness rippled through the squatting native venders waiting in the dust; the face of a carved wooden animal, eternally surprised, stuck out of a sack. The stationmaster's barefoot children wandered over. From the grey mud huts with the untidy heads that stood within a decorated mud wall, chickens, and dogs with their skin stretched like parchment over their bones, followed the piccanins down to the track. The flushed and perspiring west cast a reflection, faint, without heat, upon the station, upon the tin shed marked 'Goods', upon the walled kraal, upon the grey tin house of the stationmaster, and upon the sand, that lapped all around from sky to sky, cast little rhythmical cups of shadow, so that the sand became the sea, and closed over the children's black feet softly and without imprint.

The stationmaster's wife sat behind the mesh of her veranda. Above her head the hunk of a sheep's carcass moved slightly, dangling in a current of air.

They waited.

The train called out, along the sky; but there was no answer; and the cry hung on: I'm coming . . . I'm coming . . .

The engine flared out now, big, whisking a dwindling body behind it; the track flared out to let it in.

Creaking, jerking, jostling, gasping, the train filled the station.

Here, let me see that one—the young woman curved her body farther out of the corridor window. Missus? smiled the old man, looking at the creatures he held in his hand. From a piece of string on his grey finger hung a tiny woven basket; he lifted it, questioning. No, no, she urged, leaning down towards him, across the height of the train towards the man in the piece of old rug; that one, that one, her hand commanded. It was a lion, carved out of soft dry wood that looked like spongecake; heraldic, black and white, with impressionistic detail burnt in. The old man held it up to her still smiling, not from the heart, but at the customer. Between its vandyke teeth, in the mouth opened in an endless roar too terrible to be heard, it had a black tongue. Look, said the young husband, if you don't mind! And round the neck of the thing, a piece of fur (rat? rabbit? meerkat?); a real mane, majestic, telling you somehow that the artist had delight in the lion.

All up and down the length of the train in the dust the artists sprang, walking bent, like performing animals, the better to exhibit the fantasy held towards the faces on the train. Buck, startled and stiff, staring with round black and white eyes. More lions, standing erect, grappling with strange, thin, elongated warriors who clutched spears and showed no fear in their slits of eyes. How much, they asked from the train, how much?

Give me penny, said the little ones with nothing to sell. The dogs went and sat, quite still, under the dining car, where the train breathed out the smell of meat cooking with onion.

A man passed beneath the arch of reaching arms meeting grey-black and white in the exchange of money for the staring wooden eyes, the stiff wooden legs sticking up in the air; went along under the voices and the bargaining, interrogating the wheels. Past the dogs; glancing up at the dining car where he could stare at the faces, behind glass, drinking beer, two by two, on either side of a uniform railway vase with its pale dead flower. Right to the end, to the guard's van, where the stationmaster's children had just collected their mother's two loaves of bread; to the engine itself, where the stationmaster and the driver stood talking against the steaming complaint of the resting beast.

The man called out to them, something loud and joking. They turned to laugh, in a twirl of steam. The two children careered over the sand, clutching the bread, and burst through the iron gate and up the path through the garden in which nothing grew.

Passengers drew themselves in at the corridor windows and turned into compartments to fetch money, to call someone to look. Those sitting inside looked up: suddenly different, caged faces, boxed in, cut off after the contact of outside. There was an orange a piccanin would like . . . What about that chocolate? It wasn't very nice . . .

A girl had collected a handful of the hard kind, that no one liked, out of the chocolate box, and was throwing them to the dogs, over at the dining car. But the hens darted in and swallowed the chocolates, incredibly quick and accurate, before they had even dropped in the dust, and the dogs, a little bewildered, looked up with their brown eyes, not expecting anything.

— No, leave it, said the young woman, don't take it . . .

Too expensive, too much, she shook her head and raised her voice to the old man, giving up the lion. He held it high where she had handed it to him. No, she said, shaking her head. Three-and-six? insisted her husband, loudly. Yes baas! laughed the old man. *Three-and-six*?—the young man was incredulous. Oh leave it—she said. The young man stopped. Don't you want it? he said, keeping his face closed to the old man. No, never mind, she said, leave it. The old native kept his head on one side, looking at them sideways, holding the lion. Three-and-six, he murmured, as old people repeat things to themselves.

The young woman drew her head in. She went into the coupé and sat down. Out of the window, on the other side, there was nothing; sand and bush; a thorn tree. Back through the open doorway, past the figure of her husband in the corridor, there was the station, the voices, wooden animals waving, running feet. Her eye followed the funny little valance of scrolled wood that outlined the chalet roof of the station; she thought of the lion and smiled. That bit of fur round the neck. But the wooden buck, the hippos, the elephants, the baskets that already bulked out of their brown paper under the seat and on the luggage rack! How will they look at home? Where will you put them? What will they mean away from the places you found them? Away from the unreality of the last few weeks? The young man outside. But he is not part of the unreality; he is for good now. Odd . . . somewhere there was an idea that he, that living with him, was part of the holiday, the strange places.

Outside, a bell rang. The stationmaster was leaning against the end of the train, green flag rolled in readiness. A few men who had got down to stretch their legs sprang onto the train, clinging to the observation platforms, or perhaps merely standing on the iron step, holding the rail; but on the train, safe from the one dusty platform, the one tin house, the empty sand.

There was a grunt. The train jerked. Through the glass the beer drinkers looked out, as if they could not see beyond it. Behind the fly-screen, the stationmaster's wife sat facing back at them beneath the darkening hunk of meat.

There was a shout. The flag drooped out. Joints not yet coordinated, the segmented body of the train heaved and bumped back against itself. It began to move; slowly the scrolled chalet moved past it, the yells of the natives, running alongside, jetted up into the air, fell back at different levels. Staring wooden faces waved drunkenly, there, then gone, questioning for the last time at the windows. Here, one-and-six Baas!—As one automatically opens a hand to catch a thrown ball, a man fumbled wildly down his pocket, brought up the shilling and sixpence and threw them out; the old native, gasping, his skinny toes splaying the sand, flung the lion.

The piccanins were waving, the dogs stood, tails uncertain, watching the train go: past the mud huts, where a woman turned to look up from the smoke of the fire, her hand pausing on her hip.

The stationmaster went slowly in under the chalet.

The old native stood, breath blowing out the skin between his ribs, feet tense, balanced in the sand, smiling and shaking his head. In his opened palm, held in the attitude of receiving, was the retrieved shilling and sixpence.

The blind end of the train was being pulled helplessly out of the station.

The young man swung in from the corridor, breathless. He was shaking his head with laughter and triumph. Here! he said. And waggled the lion at her. One-and-six!

What? she said.

He laughed. I was arguing with him for fun, bargaining—when the train had pulled out already, he came tearing after . . . One-and-six Baas! So there's your lion.

She was holding it away from her, the head with the open jaws, the pointed teeth, the black tongue, the wonderful ruff of fur facing her. She was looking at it with an expression of not seeing, of seeing something different. Her face was drawn up, wryly, like the face of a discomforted child. Her mouth lifted nervously at the corner. Very slowly, cautious, she lifted her finger and touched the mane, where it was joined to the wood.

But how could you, she said. He was shocked by the dismay of her face.

Good Lord, he said, what's the matter?

If you wanted the thing, she said, her voice rising and breaking with the shrill impotence of anger, why didn't you buy it in the first place? If you wanted it, why didn't you pay for it? Why didn't you take it decently, when he offered it? Why did you have to wait for him to run after the train with it, and give him one-and-six? One-and-six!

She was pushing it at him, trying to force him to take the lion. He stood astonished, his hands hanging at his sides.

But you wanted it! You liked it so much?

—It's a beautiful piece of work, she said fiercely, as if to protect it from him.

You liked it so much! You said yourself it was too expensive—

Oh *you*—she said, hopeless and furious. *You* . . . She threw the lion on to the seat.

He stood looking at her.

She sat down again in the corner and, her face slumped in her hands, stared out of the window. Everything was turning round inside her. One-and-six. One-and-six. One-and-six for the wood and the carving and the sinews of the legs and the switch of the tail. The mouth open like that and the teeth. The black tongue, rolling, like a wave. The mane round the neck. To give one-and-six for that. The heat of shame mounted through her legs and body and sounded in her ears like the sound of sand pouring. Pouring, pouring. She sat there, sick. A weariness, a tastelessness, the discovery of a void made her hands slacken their grip, atrophy emptily, as if the hour was not worth their grasp. She was feeling like this again. She had thought it was something to do with singleness, with being alone and belonging too much to oneself.

She sat there not wanting to move or speak, or to look at anything, even; so that the mood should be associated with nothing, no object, word or sight that might recur and so recall the feeling again . . . Smuts blew in grittily, settled on her hands. Her back remained at exactly the same angle, turned against the young man sitting with his hands drooping between his sprawled legs, and the lion, fallen on its side in the corner.

The train had cast the station like a skin. It called out to the sky, I'm coming, I'm coming; and again, there was no answer.

1947

No Place Like

The relief of being down, out, and on the ground after hours in the plane was brought up short for them by the airport building: dirty, full of upended chairs like a closed restaurant. *Transit? Transit?* Some of them started off on a stairway but were shooed back exasperatedly in a language they didn't understand. The African heat in the place had been cooped up for days and nights; somebody tried to open one of the windows but again there were remonstrations from the uniformed man and the girl in her white gloves and leopard-skin pillbox hat. The windows were sealed, anyway, for the air-conditioning that wasn't working; the offender shrugged. The spokesman that every group of travellers produces made himself responsible for a complaint; at the same time some of those sheep who can't resist a hole in a fence had found a glass door unlocked on the far side of the transit lounge—they were leaking to an open passage-way: grass, bougainvillaea trained like standard roses, a road glimpsed there! But the uniformed man raced to round them up and a cleaner trailing his broom was summoned to bolt the door.

The woman in beige trousers had come very slowly across the tarmac, putting her feet down on this particular earth once more, and she was walking even more slowly round the dirty hall. Her coat dragged from the crook of her elbow, her shoulder was weighed by the strap of a bag that wouldn't zip over a package of duty-free European liquor, her bright silk shirt opened dark mouths of wet when she lifted her arms. Fellow-glances of indignance or the seasoned superiority of a sense of humour found no answer in her. As her pace brought her into the path of the black cleaner, the two faces matched perfect indifference: his, for whom the distance from which these people came had no existence because he had been nowhere outside the two miles he walked from his village to the airport; hers, for whom the distance had no existence because she had been everywhere and arrived back.

Another black man, struggling into a white jacket as he unlocked wooden shutters, opened the bar, and the businessmen with their hard-top briefcases moved over to the row of stools. Men who had got talking to unattached women—not much promise in that now; the last leg of the journey was ahead—carried them glasses of gaudy synthetic fruit juice. The Consul who had wanted to buy her a drink with dinner on the plane had found himself a girl in red boots with a small daughter in identical red boots. The child waddled away and flirtation took the form of the two of them hurrying after to scoop it up, laughing. There was a patient queue of ladies in cardigans waiting to get into the lavatories. She passed—once, twice, three times in her slow rounds—a woman who was stitching petit-point. The third time she made out that the subject was a spaniel dog with orange-and-black-streaked ears. Beside the needlewoman was a husband of a species as easily identifiable as the breed of dog—an American, because of the length of bootlace, slotted through some emblem or badge, worn in place of a tie. He sighed and his wife looked up over her glasses as if he had made a threatening move.

The woman in the beige trousers got rid of her chit for Light Refreshment in an ashtray but she had still the plastic card that was her authority to board the plane again. She tried to put it in the pocket of the coat but she couldn't reach, so she had to hold the card in her teeth while she unharnessed herself from the shoulder-bag and the coat. She wedged the card into the bag beside the liquor packages, leaving it to protrude a little so that it would be easy to produce when the time came. But it slipped down inside the bag and she had to unpack the whole thing—the hairbrush full of her own hair, dead, shed; yesterday's newspaper from a foreign town; the book whose jacket tore on the bag's zip as it came out; wads of pink paper handkerchiefs, gloves for a cold climate, the quota of duty-free cigarettes, the Swiss pocket knife that you couldn't buy back home, the wallet of travel documents. There at the bottom was the shiny card. Without it, you couldn't board the plane again. With it, you were committed to go on to the end of the journey, just as the passport bearing your name committed you to a certain identity and place. It was one of the nervous tics of travel to feel for the reassurance of that shiny card. She had wandered to the revolving stand of paperbacks and came back to make sure where she had put the card: yes, it was there. It was not a bit of paper; shiny plastic, you couldn't tear it up—indestructible, it looked, of course they use them over and over again. *Tropic of Capricorn. Kamasutra. Something of Value*. The stand revolved and brought round the same books, yet one turned it again in case there should be a book that had escaped notice, a book you'd been wanting to read all your life. If one were to find such a thing, here and now, on this last stage, this last stop . . . She felt strong hope, the excitation of weariness and tedium perhaps. They came round—*Something of Value, Kamasutra, Tropic of Capricorn*.

She went to the seat where she had left her things and loaded up again, the coat, the shoulder-bag bearing down. Somebody had fallen asleep, mouth open, bottom fly-button undone, an Austrian hat with plaited cord and feather cutting into his damp brow. How long had they been in this place? What time was it where she had left? (Some airports had a whole series of clock-faces showing what time it was everywhere.) Was it still yesterday, there?—Or tomorrow? And where she was going? She thought, I shall find out when I get there.

A pair of curio venders had unpacked their wares in a corner. People stood about in a final agony of indecision: What would he do with a thing like that? Will she appreciate it, I mean? A woman repeated as she must have done in bazaars and shops and market-places all over the world: I've seen them for half the price . . . But this was the last stop of all, the last chance *to take back something*. How else stake a claim? The last place of all the other places of the world.

Bone bracelets lay in a collapsed spiral of overlapping circles. Elephant-hair ones fell into the pattern of the Olympic symbol. There were the ivory paper-knives and the little pictures of palm trees, huts and dancers on black paper. The vender, squatting in the posture that derives from the necessity of the legless beggar to sit that way and has become as much a mark of the street professional—in such towns as the one that must be somewhere behind the airport—as the hard-top briefcase was of the international businessman drinking beer at the bar, importuned her with the obligation to buy. To refuse was to upset the ordination of roles. He was there to sell 'ivory' bracelets and 'African' art; they—these people shut up for him in the building—had been brought there to buy. He had a right to be angry. But she shook her head, she shook her head, while he tried out his few words of German and French (*billig, bon marché*) as if it could only be a matter of finding the right cue to get her to play the part assigned to her. He seemed to threaten, in his own tongue, finally, his head in its white skullcap hunched between jutting knees. But she was looking again at the glass case full of tropical butterflies under the President's picture. The picture was vivid, and new; a general successful in a coup only months ago, in full dress uniform, splendid as the dark one among the Magi. The butterflies, relic of some colonial conservationist society, were beginning to fall away from their pins in grey crumbs and gauzy fragments. But there was one big as a bat and brilliantly emblazoned as the general: something in the soil and air, in whatever existed out there—whatever 'out there' there was—that caused nature and culture to imitate each other . . .?

If it were possible to take a great butterfly. Not take back; just take. But she had the Swiss knife and the bottles, of course. The plastic card. It would see her onto the plane once more. Once the plastic card was handed over, nowhere to go but across the tarmac and up the stairway into the belly of the plane, no turning back past the air-hostess in her leopard-skin pillbox, past the barrier. It wasn't allowed; against regulations. The plastic card would send her to the plane, the plane would arrive at the end of the journey, the Swiss knife would be handed over for a kiss, the bottles would be exchanged for an embrace—she was shaking her head at the curio vender (he had actually got up from his knees and come after her, waving his pictures), *no thanks, no thanks*. But he wouldn't give up and she had to move away, to walk up and down once more in the hot, enclosed course dictated by people's feet, the up-ended chairs and tables, the little shored-up piles of hand-luggage. The Consul was swinging the child in red boots by its hands. It was half-whimpering, half-laughing, yelling to be let down, but the larger version of the same model, the mother, was laughing in a way to make her small breasts shake for the Consul, and to convey to everyone how marvellous such a distinguished man was with children.

There was a gritty crackle and then the announcement in careful, African-accented English, of the departure of the flight. A kind of concerted shuffle went up like a sigh: at last! The red-booted mother was telling her child it was silly to cry, the Consul was gathering their things together, the woman was winding the orange thread for her needlework rapidly round a spool, the sleepers woke and the beer-drinkers threw the last of their foreign small change on the bar counter. No queue outside the Ladies' now and the woman in the beige trousers knew there was plenty of time before the second call. She went in and, once more, unharnessed herself among the crumpled paper towels and spilt powder. She tipped all the liquid-soap containers in turn until she found one that wasn't empty; she washed her hands thoroughly in hot and then cold water and put her wet palms on the back of her neck, under her hair. She went to one of the row of mirrors and looked at what she saw there a moment, and then took out from under the liquor bottles, the Swiss knife and the documents, the hairbrush. It was full of hair; a web of dead hairs that bound the bristles together so that they could not go through a head of live hair. She raked her fingers slowly through the bristles and was aware of a young Indian woman at the next mirror, moving quickly and efficiently about an elaborate toilet. The Indian back-combed the black, smooth hair cut in Western style to hang on her shoulders, painted her eyes, shook her ringed hands dry rather than use the paper towels, sprayed French perfume while she extended her neck, re-pleated the green and silver sari that left bare a small roll of lavender-grey flesh between waist and *choli*.

This is the final call for all passengers.

The hair from the brush was no-colour, matted, and coated with fluff. Twisted round the forefinger (like the orange thread for the spaniel's ears) it became a fibrous funnel, dusty and obscene. She didn't want the Indian girl to be confronted with it and hid it in her palm while she went over to the dustbin. But the Indian girl saw only herself, watching her reflection appraisingly as she turned and swept out.

The brush went easily through the living hair, now. Again and again, until it was quite smooth and fell, as if it had a memory, as if it were cloth that had been folded and ironed a certain way, along the lines in which it had been arranged by professional hands in another hemisphere. A late-comer rushed into one of the lavatories, sounded the flush and hurried out, plastic card in hand.

The woman in the beige trousers had put on lipstick and run a nailfile under her nails. Her bag was neatly packed. She dropped a coin in the saucer set out, like an offering for some humble household god, for the absent attendant. The African voice was urging all passengers to proceed immediately through Gate B. The voice had some difficulty with *l*'s, pronouncing them more like *r*'s; a pleasant, reasoning voice, asking only for everyone to present the boarding pass, avoid delay, come quietly.

She went into one of the lavatories marked 'Western-type toilet' that bolted automatically as the door shut, a patent device ensuring privacy; there was no penny to pay. She had the coat and bag with her and arranged them, the coat folded and balanced on the bag, on the cleanest part of the floor. She thought what she remembered thinking so many times before: not much time, I'll have to hurry. That was what the plastic card was for—surety for not being left behind, never. She had it stuck in the neck of the shirt now, in the absence of a convenient pocket; it felt cool and wafer-stiff as she put it there but had quickly taken on the warmth of her body. Some tidy soul determined to keep up Western-type standards had closed the lid and she sat down as if on a bench—the heat and the weight of the paraphernalia she had been carrying about were suddenly exhausting. She thought she would smoke a cigarette; there was no time for that. But the need for a cigarette hollowed out a deep sigh within her and she got the pack carefully out of the pocket of her coat without disturbing the arrangement on the floor. All passengers delaying the departure of the flight were urged to proceed immediately through Gate B. Some of the words were lost over the echoing intercommunication system and at times the only thing that could be made out was the repetition, Gate B, a vital fact from which all grammatical contexts could fall away without rendering the message unintelligible. Gate B. If you remembered, if you knew Gate B, the key to mastery of the whole procedure remained intact with you. Gate B was the converse of the open sesame; it would keep you, passing safely through it, in the known, familiar, and inescapable, safe from caves of treasure and shadow. *Immediately. Gate B. Gate B.*

She could sense from the different quality of the atmosphere outside the door, and the doors beyond it, that the hall was emptying now. They were trailing, humping along under their burdens—the petit-point, the child in red boots—to the gate where the girl in the leopard-skin pillbox collected their shiny cards.

She took hers out. She looked around the cell as one looks around for a place to set down a vase of flowers or a note that mustn't blow away. It would not flush down the outlet; plastic doesn't disintegrate in water. As she had idly noticed before, it wouldn't easily tear up. She was not at all agitated; she was simply looking for somewhere to dispose of it, now. She heard the voice (was there a shade of hurt embarrassment in the rolling *r*-shaped *l*'s) appealing to the passenger who was holding up flight so-and-so to please . . . She noticed for the first time that there was actually a tiny window, with the sort of pane that tilts outwards from the bottom, just above the cistern. She stood on the seat-lid and tried to see out, just managing to post the shiny card like a letter through the slot.

Gate B, the voice offered, *Gate B*. But to pass through Gate B you had to have a card, without a card Gate B had no place in the procedure. She could not manage to see anything at all, straining precariously from up there, through the tiny window; there was no knowing at all where the card had fallen. But as she half-jumped, half-clambered down again, for a second the changed angle of her vision brought into sight something like a head—the top of a huge untidy palm tree, up in the sky, rearing perhaps between buildings or above shacks and muddy or dusty streets where there were donkeys, bicycles and barefoot people. She saw it only for that second but it was so very clear, she saw even that it was an old palm tree, the fronds rasping and sharpening against each other. And there was a crow—she was sure she had seen the black flap of a resident crow.

She sat down again. The cigarette had made a brown aureole round itself on the cistern. In the corner what she had thought was a date-pit was a dead cockroach. She flicked the dead cigarette butt at it. Heel-taps cluttered into the outer room, an African voice said, Who is there? Please, are you there? She did not hold her breath or try to keep particularly still. There was no one there. All the lavatory doors were rattled in turn. There was a high-strung pause, as if the owner of the heels didn't know what to do next. Then the heels rang away again and the door of the Ladies' swung to with the heavy sound of fanned air.

There were bursts of commotion without, reaching her muffledly where she sat. The calm grew longer. Soon the intermittent commotion would cease; the jets must be breathing fire by now, the belts fastened and the cigarettes extinguished, although the air-conditioning wouldn't be working properly yet, on the ground, and they would be patiently sweating. They couldn't wait for ever, when they were so nearly there. The plane would be beginning to trundle like a huge perambulator, it would be turning, winking, shuddering in summoned power.

Take off. It was perfectly still and quiet in the cell. She thought of the great butterfly; of the general with his beautiful markings of braid and medals. Take off.

So that was the sort of place it was: crows in old dusty palm trees, crows picking the carrion in open gutters, legless beggars threatening in an unknown tongue. Not Gate B, but some other gate. Suppose she were to climb out that window, would they ask her for her papers and put her in some other cell, at the general's pleasure? The general had no reason to trust anybody who did not take Gate B. No sound at all, now. The lavatories were given over to their own internal rumblings; the cistern gulped now and then. She was quite sure, at last, that flight so-and-so had followed its course; was gone. She lit another cigarette. She did not think at all about what to do next, not at all; if she had been inclined to think that, she would not have been sitting wherever it was she was. The butterfly, no doubt, was extinct and the general would dislike strangers, the explanations (everything has an explanation) would formulate themselves, in her absence, when the plane reached its destination. The duty-free liquor could be poured down the lavatory, but there remained the problem of the Swiss pocket knife. And yet—through the forbidden doorway: grass, bougainvillaea trained like standard roses, a road glimpsed there!

1971

Flannery O'Connor

1925-64

Reflecting on what is essential in short fiction, Flannery O'Connor wrote: 'I have decided that it is probably some action, some gesture of a character that is unlike any other in the story, one which indicates where the real heart of the story lies. This would have to be an action or a gesture which was both totally right and totally unexpected; it would have to be one that was both in character and beyond character; it would have to suggest both time and eternity.' This formulation points to several of the strengths of O'Connor's short stories—their reversals of plot, their sudden revelations, and their religious vision at once timebound and hinting at eternal truths. O'Connor's fictional domain is informed both by her Catholicism and her understanding of her Southern heritage. She defined the American South as 'a story-telling section. The Southerner knows he can do more justice to reality by telling a story than he can by discussing problems or proposing abstractions. We live in a complex region and you have to tell stories if you want to be anyway truthful about it.'

O'Connor was born in Savannah, Georgia, moving with her family to Milledgeville in 1938. After taking her B.A. (1945) at the Georgia State College for Women, she received her M.F.A. (1947) from the University of Iowa, where she attended the Writer's Workshop. 'The Geranium', the first story to be published of the thirty-one she wrote in her brief career, appeared in 1946. In 1950 O'Connor became seriously ill with what was later diagnosed as disseminated lupus, the disease that had killed her father in 1941; a year later, she moved with her mother to Andalusia, a dairy farm near Milledgeville, which became her home for the rest of her life. She died at the age of thirty-nine.

'The peculiar problem of the short-story writer,' O'Connor explained, 'is how to make the action he describes reveal as much of the mystery of existence as possible. He has only a short place to do it in and he can't do it by statement. He has to do it by showing, not by saying, and by showing the concrete—so that his problem is really how to make the concrete work for him.' In 'Everything That Rises Must Converge', she shows the reader a number of details and gestures that add up to an indictment of Julian's self-righteous and patronizing attitude towards his mother. But the full 'mystery of existence' that the story evokes in its ending transcends mere condemnation of Julian's shallow behaviour in order to explore his devastating insight into the deeper connections between his mother and himself.

'A Good Man Is Hard to Find' presents the problem of evil in a framework that is both deceptively lurid and deceptively banal. The grandmother's all-too-ordinary foibles and her family's mundane domestic squabbles seem to encounter evil incarnate in the person of the Misfit. But in his spontaneous revulsion at her gesture of charity towards him, the Misfit opens up questions about his grandmother's faith in Jesus, about love, and about his own motivation that invite a reconsideration of the story's apparently gratuitous violence.

'A Good Man Is Hard to Find' was first published in 1953 in *Modern Writing I*, and then became the title story in a 1955 collection. 'Everything That Rises Must Converge' was first published in 1961 in *New World Writing* and then became the title story of O'Connor's last collection (1965).

A Good Man Is Hard to Find

The grandmother didn't want to go to Florida. She wanted to visit some of her connections in east Tennessee and she was seizing at every chance to change Bailey's mind. Bailey was the son she lived with, her only boy. He was sitting on the edge of his chair at the table, bent over the orange sports section of the *Journal*. 'Now look here, Bailey,' she said, 'see here, read this,' and she stood with one hand on her thin hip and the other rattling the newspaper at his bald head. 'Here this fellow that calls himself The Misfit is aloose from the Federal Pen and headed toward Florida and you read here what it says he did to these people. Just you read it. I wouldn't take my children in any direction with a criminal like that aloose in it. I couldn't answer to my conscience if I did.'

Bailey didn't look up from his reading so she wheeled around then and faced the children's mother, a young woman in slacks, whose face was as broad and innocent as a cabbage and was tied around with a green headkerchief that had two points on the top like a rabbit's ears. She was sitting on the sofa, feeding the baby his apricots out of a jar. 'The children have been to Florida before,' the old lady said. 'You all ought to take them somewhere else for a change so they would see different parts of the world and be broad. They never have been to east Tennessee.'

The children's mother didn't seem to hear her but the eight-year-old boy, John Wesley, a stocky child with glasses, said, 'If you don't want to go to Florida, why dontcha stay at home?' He and the little girl, June Star, were reading the funny papers on the floor.

'She wouldn't stay at home to be queen for a day,' June Star said without raising her yellow head.

'Yes and what would you do if this fellow, The Misfit, caught you?' the grandmother asked.

'I'd smack his face,' John Wesley said.

'She wouldn't stay at home for a million bucks,' June Star said. 'Afraid she'd miss something. She has to go everywhere we go.'

'All right, Miss,' the grandmother said. 'Just remember that the next time you want me to curl your hair.'

June Star said her hair was naturally curly.

The next morning the grandmother was the first one in the car, ready to go. She had her big black valise that looked like the head of a hippopotamus in one corner, and underneath it she was hiding a basket with Pitty Sing, the cat, in it. She didn't intend for the cat to be left alone in the house for three days because he would miss her too much and she was afraid he might brush against one of the gas burners and accidentally asphyxiate himself. Her son, Bailey, didn't like to arrive at a motel with a cat.

She sat in the middle of the back seat with John Wesley and June Star on either side of her. Bailey and the children's mother and the baby sat in front and they left Atlanta at eight forty-five with the mileage on the car at 55890. The grandmother wrote this down because she thought it would be interesting to say how many miles they had been when they got back. It took them twenty minutes to reach the outskirts of the city.

The old lady settled herself comfortably, removing her white cotton gloves and putting them up with her purse on the shelf in front of the back window. The children's mother still had on slacks and still had her head tied up in a green kerchief, but the grandmother had on a navy blue straw sailor hat with a bunch of white violets on the brim and a navy blue dress with a small white dot in the print. Her collars and cuffs were white organdy trimmed with lace and at her neckline she had pinned a purple spray of cloth violets containing a sachet. In case of an accident, anyone seeing her dead on the highway would know at once that she was a lady.

She said she thought it was going to be a good day for driving, neither too hot nor too cold, and she cautioned Bailey that the speed limit was fifty-five miles an hour and that the patrolmen hid themselves behind billboards and small clumps of trees and sped out after you before you had a chance to slow down. She pointed out interesting details of the scenery: Stone Mountain; the blue granite that in some places came up to both sides of the highway; the brilliant red clay banks slightly streaked with purple; and the various crops that made rows of green lace-work on the ground. The trees were full of silver-white sunlight and the meanest of them sparkled. The children were reading comic magazines and their mother had gone back to sleep.

'Let's go through Georgia fast so we won't have to look at it much,' John Wesley said.

'If I were a little boy,' said the grandmother, 'I wouldn't talk about my native state that way. Tennessee has the mountains and Georgia has the hills.'

'Tennessee is just a hillbilly dumping ground,' John Wesley said, 'and Georgia is a lousy state too.'

'You said it,' June Star said.

'In my time,' said the grandmother, folding her thin veined fingers, 'children were more respectful of their native states and their parents and everything else. People did right then. Oh look at the cute little pickaninny!' she said and pointed to a Negro child standing in the door of a shack. 'Wouldn't that make a picture now?' she asked and they all turned and looked at the little Negro out of the back window. He waved.

'He didn't have any britches on,' June Star said.

'He probably didn't have any,' the grandmother explained. 'Little niggers in the country don't have things like we do. If I could paint, I'd paint that picture,' she said.

The children exchanged comic books.

The grandmother offered to hold the baby and the children's mother passed him over the front seat to her. She set him on her knee and bounced him and told him about the things they were passing. She rolled her eyes and screwed up her mouth and stuck her leathery thin face into his smooth bland one. Occasionally he gave her a faraway smile. They passed a large cotton field with five or six graves fenced in the middle of it, like a small island. 'Look at the graveyard!' the grandmother said, pointing it out. 'That was the old family burying ground. That belonged to the plantation.'

'Where's the plantation?' John Wesley asked.

'Gone With the Wind,' said the grandmother. 'Ha. Ha.'

When the children finished all the comic books they had brought, they opened the lunch and ate it. The grandmother ate a peanut butter sandwich and an olive and would not let the children throw the box and the paper napkins out the window. When there was nothing else to do they played a game by choosing a cloud and making the other two guess what shape it suggested. John Wesley took one the shape of a cow and June Star guessed a cow and John Wesley said, no, an automobile, and June Star said he didn't play fair, and they began to slap each other over the grandmother.

The grandmother said she would tell them a story if they would keep quiet. When she told a story, she rolled her eyes and waved her head and was very dramatic. She said once when she was a maiden lady she had been courted by a Mr Edgar Atkins Teagarden from Jasper, Georgia. She said he was a very good-looking man and a gentleman and that he brought her a watermelon every Saturday afternoon with his initials cut in it, E. A. T. Well, one Saturday, she said, Mr Teagarden brought the watermelon and there was nobody at home and he left it on the front porch and returned in his buggy to Jasper, but she never got the watermelon, she said, because a nigger boy ate it when he saw the initials, E. A. T.! This story tickled John Wesley's funny bone and he giggled and giggled but June Star didn't think it was any good. She said she wouldn't marry a man that just brought her a watermelon on Saturday. The grandmother said she would have done well to marry Mr Teagarden because he was a gentleman and had bought Coca-Cola stock when it first came out and that he had died only a few years ago, a very wealthy man.

They stopped at The Tower for barbecued sandwiches. The Tower was a part stucco and part wood filling station and dance hall set in a clearing outside of Timothy. A fat man named Red Sammy Butts ran it and there were signs stuck here and there on the building and for miles up and down the highway saying, TRY RED SAMMY'S FAMOUS BARBECUE. NONE LIKE FAMOUS RED SAMMY'S! RED SAM! THE FAT BOY WITH THE HAPPY LAUGH! A VETERAN! RED SAMMY'S YOUR MAN!

Red Sammy was lying on the bare ground outside The Tower with his head under a truck while a grey monkey about a foot high, chained to a small chinaberry tree, chattered nearby. The monkey sprang back into the tree and got on the highest limb as soon as he saw the children jump out of the car and run toward him.

Inside, The Tower was a long dark room with a counter at one end and tables at the other and dancing space in the middle. They all sat down at a board table next to the nickelodeon and Red Sam's wife, a tall burnt-brown woman with hair and eyes lighter than her skin, came and took their order. The children's mother put a dime in the machine and played 'The Tennessee Waltz', and the grandmother said that tune always made her want to dance. She asked Bailey if he would like to dance but he only glared at her. He didn't have a naturally sunny disposition like she did and trips made him nervous. The grandmother's brown eyes were very bright. She swayed her head from side to side and pretended she was dancing in her chair. June Star said play something she could tap to so the children's mother put in another dime and played a fast number and June Star stepped out onto the dance floor and did her tap routine.

'Ain't she cute?' Red Sam's wife said, leaning over the counter. 'Would you like to come be my little girl?'

'No I certainly wouldn't,' June Star said. 'I wouldn't live in a broken-down place like this for a million bucks!' and she ran back to the table.

'Ain't she cute?' the woman repeated, stretching her mouth politely.

'Aren't you ashamed?' hissed the grandmother.

Red Sam came in and told his wife to quit lounging on the counter and hurry up with these people's order. His khaki trousers reached just to his hip bones and his stomach hung over them like a sack of meal swaying under his shirt. He came over and sat down at a table nearby and let out a combination sigh and yodel. 'You can't win,' he said. 'You can't win,' and he wiped his sweating red face off with a grey handkerchief. 'These days you don't know who to trust,' he said. 'Ain't that the truth?'

'People are certainly not nice like they used to be,' said the grandmother.

'Two fellers come in here last week,' Red Sammy said, 'driving a Chrysler. It was a old beat-up car but it was a good one and these boys looked all right to me. Said they worked at the mill and you know I let them fellers charge the gas they bought? Now why did I do that?'

'Because you're a good man!' the grandmother said at once.

'Yes'm, I suppose so,' Red Sam said as if he were struck with this answer.

His wife brought the orders, carrying the five plates all at once without a tray, two in each hand and one balanced on her arm. 'It isn't a soul in this green world of God's that you can trust,' she said. 'And I don't count nobody out of that, not nobody,' she repeated, looking at Red Sammy.

'Did you read about that criminal, The Misfit, that's escaped?' asked the grandmother.

'I wouldn't be a bit surprised if he didn't attact this place right here,' said the woman. 'If he hears about it being here, I wouldn't be none surprised to see him. If he hears it's two cent in the cash register, I wouldn't be a tall surprised if he . . .'

'That'll do,' Red Sam said. 'Go bring these people their Co'-Colas,' and the woman went off to get the rest of the order.

'A good man is hard to find,' Red Sammy said. 'Everything is getting terrible. I remember the day you could go off and leave your screen door unlatched. Not no more.'

He and the grandmother discussed better times. The old lady said that in her opinion Europe was entirely to blame for the way things were now. She said the way Europe acted you would think we were made of money and Red Sam said it was no use talking about it, she was exactly right. The children ran outside into the white sunlight and looked at the monkey in the lacy chinaberry tree. He was busy catching fleas on himself and biting each one carefully between his teeth as if it were a delicacy.

They drove off again into the hot afternoon. The grandmother took cat naps and woke up every few minutes with her own snoring. Outside of Toombsboro she woke up and recalled an old plantation that she had visited in this neighbourhood once when she was a young lady. She said the house had six white columns across the front and that there was an avenue of oaks leading up to it and two little wooden trellis arbours on either side in front where you sat down with your suitor after a stroll in the garden. She recalled exactly which road to turn off to get to it. She knew that Bailey would not be willing to lose any time looking at an old house, but the more she talked about it, the more she wanted to see it once again and find out if the little twin arbours were still standing. 'There was a secret panel in this house,' she said craftily, not telling the truth but wishing that she were, 'and the story went that all the family silver was hidden in it when Sherman came through but it was never found . . .'

'Hey!' John Wesley said. 'Let's go see it! We'll find it! We'll poke all the woodwork and find it! Who lives there? Where do you turn off at? Hey Pop, can't we turn off there?'

'We never have seen a house with a secret panel!' June Star shrieked. 'Let's go to the house with the secret panel! Hey Pop, can't we go see the house with the secret panel!'

'It's not far from here, I know,' the grandmother said. 'It wouldn't take over twenty minutes.'

Bailey was looking straight ahead. His jaw was as rigid as a horseshoe. 'No,' he said.

The children began to yell and scream that they wanted to see the house with the secret panel. John Wesley kicked thc back of the front seat and June Star hung over her mother's shoulder and whined desperately into her ear that they never had any fun even on their vacation, that they could never do what THEY wanted to do. The baby began to scream and John Wesley kicked the back of the seat so hard that his father could feel the blows in his kidney.

'All right!' he shouted and drew the car to a stop at the side of the road. 'Will you all shut up? Will you all just shut up for one second? If you don't shut up, we won't go anywhere.'

'It would be very educational for them,' the grandmother murmured.

'All right,' Bailey said, 'but get this: this is the only time we're going to stop for anything like this. This is the one and only time.'

'The dirt road that you have to turn down is about a mile back,' the grandmother directed. 'I marked it when we passed.'

'A dirt road,' Bailey groaned.

After they had turned around and were headed toward the dirt road, the grandmother recalled other points about the house, the beautiful glass over the front doorway and the candle-lamp in the hall. John Wesley said that the secret panel was probably in the fireplace.

'You can't go inside this house,' Bailey said. 'You don't know who lives there.'

'While you all talk to the people in front, I'll run around behind and get in a window,' John Wesley suggested.

'We'll all stay in the car,' his mother said.

They turned onto the dirt road and the car raced roughly along in a swirl of pink dust. The grandmother recalled the times when there were not paved roads and thirty miles was a day's journey. The dirt road was hilly and there were sudden washes in it and sharp curves on dangerous embankments. All at once they would be on a hill, looking down over the blue tops of trees for miles around, then the next minute, they would be in a red depression with the dust-coated trees looking down on them.

'This place had better turn up in a minute,' Bailey said, 'or I'm going to turn around.'

The road looked as if no one had travelled on it in months.

'It's not much farther,' the grandmother said and just as she said it, a horrible thought came to her. The thought was so embarrassing that she turned red in the face and her eyes dilated and her feet jumped up, upsetting her valise in the corner. The instant the valise moved, the newspaper top she had over the basket under it rose with a snarl and Pitty Sing, the cat, sprang onto Bailey's shoulder.

The children were thrown to the floor and their mother, clutching the baby, was thrown out the door onto the ground; the old lady was thrown into the front seat. The car turned over once and landed right-side-up in a gulch off the side of the road. Bailey remained in the driver's seat with the cat—grey-striped with a broad white face and an orange nose—clinging to his neck like a caterpillar.

As soon as the children saw they could move their arms and legs, they scrambled out of the car, shouting, 'We've had an ACCIDENT!' The grandmother was curled up under the dashboard, hoping she was injured so that Bailey's wrath would not come down on her all at once. The horrible thought she had had before the accident was that the house she had remembered so vividly was not in Georgia but in Tennessee.

Bailey removed the cat from his neck with both hands and flung it out the window against the side of a pine tree. Then he got out of the car and started looking for the children's mother. She was sitting against the side of the red gutted ditch, holding the screaming baby, but she only had a cut down her face and a broken shoulder. 'We've had an ACCIDENT!' the children screamed in a frenzy of delight.

'But nobody's killed,' June Star said with disappointment as the grandmother limped out of the car, her hat still pinned to her head but the broken front brim standing up at a jaunty angle and the violet spray hanging off the side. They all sat down in the ditch, except the children, to recover from the shock. They were all shaking.

'Maybe a car will come along,' said the children's mother hoarsely.

'I believe I have injured an organ,' said the grandmother, pressing her side, but no one answered her. Bailey's teeth were clattering. He had on a yellow sport shirt with bright blue parrots designed in it and his face was as yellow as the shirt. The grandmother decided that she would not mention that the house was in Tennessee.

The road was about ten feet above and they could see only the tops of the trees on the other side of it. Behind the ditch they were sitting in there were more woods, tall and dark and deep. In a few minutes they saw a car some distance away on top of a hill, coming slowly as if the occupants were watching them. The grandmother stood up and waved both arms dramatically to attract their attention. The car continued to come on slowly, disappeared around a bend and appeared again, moving even slower, on top of the hill they had gone over. It was a big black battered hearse-like automobile. There were three men in it.

It came to a stop just over them and for some minutes, the driver looked down with a steady expressionless gaze to where they were sitting, and didn't speak. Then he turned his head and muttered something to the other two and they got out. One was a fat boy in black trousers and a red sweat shirt and a silver stallion embossed on the front of it. He moved around on the right side of them and stood staring, his mouth partly open in a kind of loose grin. The other had on khaki pants and a blue striped coat and a grey hat pulled down very low, hiding most of his face. He came around slowly on the left side. Neither spoke.

The driver got out of the car and stood by the side of it, looking down at them. He was an older man than the other two. His hair was just beginning to grey and he wore silver-rimmed spectacles that gave him a scholarly look. He had a long creased face and didn't have on any shirt or undershirt. He had on blue jeans that were too tight for him and was holding a black hat and a gun. The two boys also had guns.

'We've had an ACCIDENT!' the children screamed.

The grandmother had the peculiar feeling that the bespectacled man was someone she knew. His face was as familiar to her as if she had known him all her life but she could not recall who he was. He moved away from the car and began to come down the embankment, placing his feet carefully so that he wouldn't slip. He had on tan and white shoes and no socks, and his ankles were red and thin. 'Good afternoon,' he said. 'I see you all had you a little spill.'

'We turned over twice!' said the grandmother.

'Oncet,' he corrected. 'We seen it happen. Try their car and see will it run, Hiram,' he said quietly to the boy with the gray hat.

'What you got that gun for?' John Wesley asked. 'Whatcha gonna do with that gun?'

'Lady,' the man said to the children's mother, 'would you mind calling them children to sit down by you? Children make me nervous. I want all you all to sit down right together there where you're at.'

'What are you telling US what to do for?' June Star asked.

Behind them the line of woods gaped like a dark open mouth. 'Come here,' said their mother.

'Look here now,' Bailey began suddenly, 'we're in a predicament! We're in . . .'

The grandmother shrieked. She scrambled to her feet and stood staring. 'You're The Misfit!' she said. 'I recognized you at once!'

'Yes'm,' the man said, smiling slightly as if he were pleased in spite of himself to be known, 'but it would have been better for all of you, lady, if you hadn't of reckernized me.'

Bailey turned his head sharply and said something to his mother that shocked even the children. The old lady began to cry and The Misfit reddened.

'Lady,' he said, 'don't you get upset. Sometimes a man says things he don't mean. I don't reckon he meant to talk to you thataway.'

'You wouldn't shoot a lady, would you?' the grandmother said and removed a clean handkerchief from her cuff and began to slap at her eyes with it.

The Misfit pointed the toe of his shoe into the ground and made a little hole and then covered it up again. 'I would hate to have to,' he said.

'Listen,' the grandmother almost screamed, 'I know you're a good man. You don't look a bit like you have common blood. I know you must come from nice people!'

'Yes mam,' he said, 'finest people in the world.' When he smiled he showed a row of strong white teeth. 'God never made a finer woman than my mother and my daddy's heart was pure gold,' he said. The boy with the red sweat shirt had come around behind them and was standing with his gun at his hip. The Misfit squatted down on the ground. 'Watch them children, Bobby Lee,' he said. 'You know they make me nervous.' He looked at the six of them huddled together in front of him and he seemed to be embarrassed as if he couldn't think of anything to say. 'Ain't a cloud in the sky,' he remarked, looking up at it. 'Don't see no sun but don't see no cloud neither.'

'Yes, it's a beautiful day,' said the grandmother. 'Listen,' she said, 'you shouldn't call yourself The Misfit because I know you're a good man at heart. I can just look at you and tell.'

'Hush!' Bailey yelled. 'Hush! Everybody shut up and let me handle this!' He was squatting in the position of a runner about to sprint forward but he didn't move.

'I pre-chate that, lady,' The Misfit said and drew a little circle in the ground with the butt of his gun.

'It'll take a half a hour to fix this here car,' Hiram called, looking over the raised hood of it.

'Well, first you and Bobby Lee get him and that little boy to step over yonder with you,' The Misfit said, pointing to Bailey and John Wesley. 'The boys want to ask you something,' he said to Bailey. 'Would you mind stepping back in them woods there with them?'

'Listen,' Bailey began, 'we're in a terrible predicament! Nobody realizes what this is,' and his voice cracked. His eyes were as blue and intense as the parrots in his shirt and he remained perfectly still.

The grandmother reached up to adjust her hat brim as if she were going to the woods with him but it came off in her hand. She stood staring at it and after a second she let it fall on the ground. Hiram pulled Bailey up by the arm as if he were assisting an old man. John Wesley caught hold of his father's hand and Bobby Lee followed. They went off toward the woods and just as they reach the dark edge, Bailey turned and supporting himself against a grey naked pine trunk, he shouted, 'I'll be back in a minute, Mamma, wait on me!'

'Come back this instant!' his mother shrilled but they all disappeared into the woods.

'Bailey Boy!' the grandmother called in a tragic voice but she found she was looking at The Misfit squatting on the ground in front of her. 'I just know you're a good man,' she said desperately. 'You're not a bit common!'

'Nome, I ain't a good man,' The Misfit said after a second as if he had considered her statement carefully, 'but I ain't the worst in the world neither. My daddy said I was a different breed of dog from my brothers and sisters. "You know," Daddy said, "it's some that can live their whole life out without asking about it and it's others has to know why it is, and this boy is one of the latters. He's going to be into everything!" ' He put on his black hat and looked up suddenly and then away deep into the woods as if he were embarrassed again. 'I'm sorry I don't have on a shirt before you ladies,' he said, hunching his shoulders slightly. 'We buried our clothes that we had on when we escaped and we're just making do until we can get better. We borrowed these from some folks we met,' he explained.

'That's perfectly all right,' the grandmother said. 'Maybe Bailey has an extra shirt in his suitcase.'

'I'll look and see terrectly,' The Misfit said.

'Where are they taking him?' the children's mother screamed.

'Daddy was a card himself,' The Misfit said. 'You couldn't put anything over on him. He never got in trouble with the Authorities though. Just had the knack of handling them.'

'You could be honest too if you'd only try,' said the grandmother. 'Think how wonderful it would be to settle down and live a comfortable life and not have to think about somebody chasing you all the time.'

The Misfit kept scratching in the ground with the butt of his gun as if he were thinking about it. 'Yes'm, somebody is always after you,' he murmured.

The grandmother noticed how thin his shoulder blades were just behind his hat because she was standing up looking down on him. 'Do you ever pray?' she asked.

He shook his head. All she saw was the black hat wiggle between his shoulder blades. 'Nome,' he said.

There was a pistol shot from the woods, followed closely by another. Then silence. The old lady's head jerked around. She could heard the wind move through the tree tops like a long satisfied insuck of breath. 'Bailey Boy!' she called.

'I was a gospel singer for a while,' The Misfit said. 'I been most everything. Been in the arm service both land and sea, at home and abroad, been twict married, been an undertaker, been with the railroads, plowed Mother Earth, been in a tornado, seen a man burnt alive oncet,' and looked up at the children's mother and the little girl who were sitting close together, their faces white and their eyes glassy; 'I even seen a woman flogged,' he said.

'Pray, pray,' the grandmother began, 'pray, pray . . .'

'I never was a bad boy that I remember of,' The Misfit said in an almost dreamy voice, 'but somewheres along the line I done something wrong and got sent to the penitentiary. I was buried alive,' and he looked up and held her attention to him by a steady stare.

'That's when you should have started to pray,' she said. 'What did you do to get sent to the penitentiary that first time?'

'Turn to the right, it was a wall,' The Misfit said, looking up again at the cloudless sky. 'Turn to the left, it was a wall. Look up it was a ceiling, look down it was a floor. I forget what I done, lady. I set there and set there, trying to remember what it was I done and I ain't recalled it to this day. Oncet in a while, I would think it was coming to me, but it never come.'

'Maybe they put you in by mistake,' the old lady said vaguely.

'Nome,' he said. 'It wasn't no mistake. They had the papers on me.'

'You must have stolen something,' she said.

The Misfit sneered slightly. 'Nobody had nothing I wanted,' he said. 'It was a head-doctor at the penitentiary said what I had done was kill my daddy but I known that for a lie. My daddy died in nineteen ought nineteen of the epidemic flu and I never had a thing to do with it. He was buried in the Mount Hopewell Baptist churchyard and you can go there and see for yourself.'

'If you would pray,' the old lady said, 'Jesus would help you.'

'That's right,' The Misfit said.

'Well then, why don't you pray?' she asked trembling with delight suddenly.

'I don't want no hep,' he said. 'I'm doing all right by myself.'

Bobby Lee and Hiram came ambling back from the woods. Bobby Lee was dragging a yellow shirt with bright blue parrots in it.

'Thow me that shirt, Bobby Lee,' The Misfit said. The shirt came flying at him and landed on his shoulder and he put it on. The grandmother couldn't name what the shirt reminded her of. 'No, lady,' The Misfit said while he was buttoning it up, 'I found out the crime don't matter. You can do one thing or you can do another, kill a man or take a tire off his car, because sooner or later you're going to forget what it was you done and just be punished for it.'

The children's mother had begun to make heaving noises as if she couldn't get her breath. 'Lady,' he asked, 'would you and that little girl like to step off yonder with Bobby Lee and Hiram and join your husband?'

'Yes, thank you,' the mother said faintly. Her left arm dangled helplessly and she was holding the baby, who had gone to sleep, in the other. 'Hep that lady up, Hiram,' The Misfit said as she struggled to climb out of the ditch, 'and Bobby Lee, you hold onto that little girl's hand.'

'I don't want to hold hands with him,' June Star said. 'He reminds me of a pig.'

The fat boy blushed and laughed and caught her by the arm and pulled her off into the woods after Hiram and her mother.

Alone with The Misfit, the grandmother found that she had lost her voice. There was not a cloud in the sky nor any sun. There was nothing around her but woods. She wanted to tell him that he must pray. She opened and closed her mouth several times before anything came out. Finally she found herself saying, 'Jesus, Jesus,' meaning, Jesus will help you, but the way she was saying it, it sounded as if she might be cursing.

'Yes'm,' The Misfit said as if he agreed. 'Jesus thown everything off balance. It was the same case with Him as with me except He hadn't committed any crime and they could prove I had committed one because they had the papers on me. Of course,' he said, 'they never shown me my papers. That's why I sign myself now. I said long ago, you get you a signature and sign everything you do and keep a copy of it. Then you'll know what you done and you can hold up the crime to the punishment and see do they match and in the end you'll have something to prove you ain't been treated right. I call myself The Misfit,' he said, 'because I can't make what all I done wrong fit what all I gone through in punishment.'

There was a piercing scream from the woods, followed closely by a pistol report. 'Does it seem right to you, lady, that one is punished a heap and another ain't punished at all?'

'Jesus!' the old lady cried. 'You've got good blood! I know you wouldn't shoot a lady! I know you come from nice people! Pray! Jesus, you ought not to shoot a lady. I'll give you all the money I've got!'

'Lady,' The Misfit said, looking beyond her far into the woods, 'there never was a body that give the undertaker a tip.'

There were two more pistol reports and the grandmother raised her head like a parched old turkey hen crying for water and called, 'Bailey Boy, Bailey Boy!' as if her heart would break.

'Jesus was the only One that ever raised the dead.' The Misfit continued, 'and He shouldn't have done it. He thrown everything off balance. If He did what He said, then it's nothing for you to do but throw away everything and follow Him, and if He didn't then it's nothing for you to do but enjoy the few minutes you got left the best way you can—by killing somebody or burning down his house or doing some other meanness to him. No pleasure but meanness,' he said and his voice had become almost a snarl.

'Maybe He didn't raise the dead,' the old lady mumbled, not knowing what she was saying and feeling so dizzy that she sank down in the ditch with her legs twisted under her.

'I wasn't there so I can't say He didn't,' The Misfit said. 'I wisht I had of been there,' he said, hitting the ground with his fist. 'It ain't right I wasn't there because if I had of been there I would of known. Listen lady,' he said in a high voice, 'if I had of been there I would of known and I wouldn't be like I am now.' His voice seemed about to crack and grandmother's head cleared for an instant. She saw the man's face twisted close to her own as if he were going to cry and she murmured, 'Why you're one of my babies. You're one of my own children!' She reached out and touched him on the shoulder. The Misfit sprang back as if a snake had bitten him and shot her three times through the chest. Then he put his gun down on the ground and took off his glasses and began to clean them.

Hiram and Bobby Lee returned from the woods and stood over the ditch, looking down at the grandmother who half sat and half lay in a puddle of blood with her legs crossed under her like a child's and her face smiling up at the cloudless sky.

Without his glasses, The Misfit's eyes were red-rimmed and pale and defenceless-looking. 'Take her off and throw her where you thrown the others,' he said, picking up the cat that was rubbing itself against his leg.

'She was a talker, wasn't she?' Bobby Lee said, sliding down the ditch with a yodel.

'She would of been a good woman,' The Misfit said, 'if it had been somebody there to shoot her every minute of her life.'

'Some fun!' Bobby Lee said.
'Shut up, Bobby Lee,' The Misfit said. 'It's no real pleasure in life.'

1953

Everything That Rises Must Converge

Her doctor had told Julian's mother that she must lose twenty pounds on account of her blood pressure, so on Wednesday nights Julian had to take her downtown on the bus for a reducing class at the Y. The reducing class was designed for working girls over fifty, who weighed from 165 to 200 pounds. His mother was one of the slimmer ones, but she said ladies did not tell their age or weight. She would not ride the buses by herself at night since they had been integrated, and because the reducing class was one of her few pleasures, necessary for her health, and *free*, she said Julian could at least put himself out to take her, considering all she did for him. Julian did not like to consider all she did for him, but every Wednesday night he braced himself and took her.

She was almost ready to go, standing before the hall mirror, putting on her hat, while he, his hands behind him, appeared pinned to the door frame, waiting like Saint Sebastian for the arrows to begin piercing him. The hat was new and had cost her seven dollars and a half. She kept saying, 'Maybe I shouldn't have paid that for it. No, I shouldn't have. I'll take it off and return it tomorrow. I shouldn't have bought it.'

Julian raised his eyes to heaven. 'Yes, you should have bought it,' he said. 'Put it on and let's go.' It was a hideous hat. A purple velvet flap came down on one side of it and stood up on the other; the rest of it was green and looked like a cushion with the stuffing out. He decided it was less comical than jaunty and pathetic. Everything that gave her pleasure was small and depressed him.

She lifted the hat one more time and set it down slowly on top of her head. Two wings of grey hair protruded on either side of her florid face, but her eyes, sky-blue, were as innocent and untouched by experience as they must have been when she was ten. Were it not that she was a widow who had struggled fiercely to feed and clothe and put him through school and who was supporting him still, 'until he got on his feet', she might have been a little girl that he had to take to town.

'It's all right, it's all right,' he said. 'Let's go.' He opened the door himself and started down the walk to get her going. The sky was a dying violet and the houses stood out darkly against it, bulbous liver-coloured monstrosities of a uniform ugliness though no two were alike. Since this had been a fashionable neighbourhood forty years ago, his mother persisted in thinking they did well to have an apartment in it. Each house had a narrow collar of dirt around it in which sat, usually, a grubby child. Julian walked with his hands in his pockets, his head down and thrust forward and his eyes glazed with the determination to make himself completely numb during the time he would be sacrificed to her pleasure.

The door closed and he turned to find the dumpy figure, surmounted by the atrocious hat, coming toward him. 'Well,' she said, 'you only live once and paying a little more for it, I at least won't meet myself coming and going.'

'Some day I'll start making some money,' Julian said gloomily—he knew he never would—'and you can have one of those jokes whenever you take the fit.' But first they would move. He visualized a place where the nearest neighbours would be three miles away on either side.

'I think you're doing fine,' she said, drawing on her gloves. 'You've only been out of school a year. Rome wasn't built in a day.'

She was one of the few members of the Y reducing class who arrived in hat and gloves and who had a son who had been to college. 'It takes time,' she said, 'and the world is in such a mess. This hat looked better on me than any of the others, though when she brought it out I said, "Take that thing back. I wouldn't have it on my head," and she said, "Now wait till you see it on," and when she put it on me, I said, "We-ull," and she said, "If you ask me, that hat does something for you and you do something for the hat, and besides,' she said, 'with that hat, you won't meet yourself coming and going." '

Julian thought he could have stood his lot better if she had been selfish, if she had been an old hag who drank and screamed at him. He walked along, saturated in depression, as if in the midst of his martyrdom he had lost his faith. Catching sight of his long, hopeless, irritated face, she stopped suddenly with a grief-stricken look, and pulled back on his arm. 'Wait on me,' she said. 'I'm going back to the house and take this thing off and tomorrow I'm going to return it. I was out of my head. I can pay the gas bill with the seven-fifty.'

He caught her arm in a vicious grip. 'You are not going to take it back,' he said. 'I like it.'

'Well,' she said, 'I don't think I ought . . .'

'Shut up and enjoy it,' he muttered, more depressed than ever.

'With the world in the mess it's in,' she said, 'it's a wonder we can enjoy anything. I tell you, the bottom rail is on the top.'

Julian sighed.

'Of course,' she said, 'if you know who you are, you can go anywhere.' She said this every time he took her to the reducing class. 'Most of them in it are not our kind of people,' she said, 'but I can be gracious to anybody. I know who I am.'

'They don't give a damn for your graciousness,' Julian said savagely. 'Knowing who you are is good for one generation only. You haven't the foggiest idea where you stand now or who you are.'

She stopped and allowed her eyes to flash at him. 'I most certainly do know who I am,' she said, 'and if you don't know who you are, I'm ashamed of you.'

'Oh hell,' Julian said.

'Your great-grandfather was a former governor of this state,' she said. 'Your grandfather was a prosperous landowner. Your grandmother was a Godhigh.'

'Will you look around you,' he said tensely, 'and see where you are now?' and he swept his arm jerkily out to indicate the neighbourhood, which the growing darkness at least made less dingy.

'You remain what you are,' she said. 'Your great-grandfather had a plantation and two hundred slaves.'

'There are no more slaves,' he said irritably.

'They were better off when they were,' she said. He groaned to see that she was off on that topic. She rolled onto it every few days like a train on an open track. He knew every stop, every junction, every swamp along the way, and knew the exact point at which her conclusion would roll majestically into the station: 'It's ridiculous. It's simply not realistic. They should rise, yes, but on their own side of the fence.'

'Let's skip it,' Julian said.

'The ones I feel sorry for,' she said, 'are the ones that are half white. They're tragic.'

'Will you skip it?'

'Suppose we were half white. We would certainly have mixed feelings.'

'I have mixed feelings now,' he groaned.

'Well let's talk about something pleasant,' she said. 'I remember going to Grandpa's when I was a little girl. Then the house had double stairways that went up to what was really the second floor—all the cooking was done on the first. I used to like to stay down in the kitchen on account of the way the walls smelled. I would sit with my nose pressed against the plaster and take deep breaths. Actually the place belonged to the Godhighs but your grandfather Chestny paid the mortgage and saved it for them. They were in reduced circumstances,' she said, 'but reduced or not, they never forgot who they were.'

'Doubtless that decayed mansion reminded them,' Julian muttered. He never spoke of it without longing. He had seen it once when he was a child before it had been sold. The double stairways had rotted and been torn down. Negroes were living in it. But it remained in his mind as his mother had known it. It appeared in his dreams regularly. He would stand on the wide porch, listening to the rustle of oak leaves, then wander through the high-ceilinged hall into the parlour that opened onto it and gaze at the worn rugs and faded draperies. It occurred to him that it was he, not she, who could have appreciated it. He preferred its threadbare elegance to anything he could name and it was because of it that all the neighbourhoods they had lived in had been a torment to him—whereas she had hardly known the difference. She called her insensitivity 'being adjustable'.

'And I remember the old darky who was my nurse, Caroline. There was no better person in the world. I've always had a great respect for my coloured friends,' she said. 'I'd do anything in the world for them and they'd . . .'

'Will you for God's sake get off that subject?' Julian said. When he got on a bus by himself, he made it a point to sit down beside a Negro, reparation as it were for his mother's sins.

'You're mighty touchy tonight,' she said. 'Do you feel all right?'

'Yes I feel all right,' he said. 'Now lay off.'

She pursed her lips. 'Well, you certainly are in a vile humour,' she observed. 'I just won't speak to you at all.'

They had reached the bus stop. There was no bus in sight and Julian, his hands still jammed in his pockets and his head thrust forward, scowled down the empty street. The frustration of having to wait on the bus as well as ride on it began to creep up his neck like a hot hand. The presence of his mother was borne in upon him as she gave a pained sigh. He looked at her bleakly. She was holding herself very erect under the preposterous hat, wearing it like a banner of her imaginary dignity. There was in him an evil urge to break her spirit. He suddenly unloosened his tie and pulled it off and put it in his pocket.

She stiffened. 'Why must you look like *that* when you take me to town?' she said. 'Why must you deliberately embarrass me?'

'If you'll never learn where you are,' he said, 'you can at least learn where I am.'

'You look like a—thug,' she said.

'Then I must be one,' he murmured.

'I'll just go home,' she said. 'I will not bother you. If you can't do a little thing like that for me . . .'

Rolling his eyes upward, he put his tie back on. 'Restored to my class,' he muttered. He thrust his face toward her and hissed, 'True culture is in the mind, the *mind*,' he said, and tapped his head, 'the mind.'

'It's in the heart,' she said, 'and in how you do things and how you do things is because of who you *are*.'

'Nobody in the damn bus cares who you are.'

'I care who I am,' she said icily.

The lighted bus appeared on top of the next hill and as it approached, they moved out into the street to meet it. He put his hand under her elbow and hoisted her up on the creaking step. She entered with a little smile, as if she were going into a drawing room where everyone had been waiting for her. While he put in the tokens, she sat down on one of the broad front seats for three which faced the aisle. A thin woman with protruding teeth and long yellow hair was sitting on the end of it. His mother moved up beside her and left room for Julian beside herself. He sat down and looked at the floor across the aisle where a pair of thin feet in red and white canvas sandals were planted.

His mother immediately began a general conversation meant to attract anyone who felt like talking. 'Can it get any hotter?' she said and removed from her purse a folding fan, black with a Japanese scene on it, which she began to flutter before her.

'I reckon it might could,' the woman with the protruding teeth said, 'but I know for a fact my apartment couldn't get no hotter.'

'It must get the afternoon sun,' his mother said. She sat forward and looked up and down the bus. It was half filled. Everybody was white. 'I see we have the bus to ourselves,' she said. Julian cringed.

'For a change,' said the woman across the aisle, the owner of the red and white canvas sandals. 'I come on one the other day and they were thick as fleas—up front and all through.'

'The world is in a mess everywhere,' his mother said. 'I don't know how we've let it get in this fix.'

'What gets my goat is all those boys from good families stealing automobile tires,' the woman with the protruding teeth said. 'I told my boy, I said you may not be rich but you been raised right and if I ever catch you in any such mess, they can send you on to the reformatory. Be exactly where you belong.'

'Training tells,' his mother said. 'Is your boy in high school?'

'Ninth grade,' the woman said.

'My son just finished college last year. He wants to write but he's selling typewriters until he gets started,' his mother said.

The woman leaned forward and peered at Julian. He threw her such a malevolent look that she subsided against the seat. On the floor across the aisle there was an abandoned newspaper. He got up and got it and opened it out in front of him. His mother discreetly continued the conversation in a lower tone but the woman across the aisle said in a loud voice, 'Well that's nice. Selling typewriters is close to writing. He can go right from one to the other.'

'I tell him,' his mother said, 'that Rome wasn't built in a day.'

Behind the newspaper Julian was withdrawing into the inner compartment of his mind where he spent most of his time. This was a kind of mental bubble in which he established himself when he could not bear to be a part of what was going on around him. From it he could see out and judge but in it he was safe from any kind of penetration from without. It was the only place where he felt free of the general idiocy of his fellows. His mother had never entered it but from it he could see her with absolute clarity.

The old lady was clever enough and he thought that if she had started from any of the right premises, more might have been expected of her. She lived according to the laws of her own fantasy world, outside of which he had never seen her set foot. The law of it was to sacrifice herself for him after she had first created the necessity to do so by making a mess of things. If he had permitted her sacrifices, it was only because her lack of foresight had made them necessary. All of her life had been a struggle to act like a Chestny with the Chestny goods, and to give him everything she thought a Chestny ought to have; but since, said she, it was fun to struggle, why complain? And when you had won, as she had won, what fun to look back on the hard times! He could not forgive her that she had enjoyed the struggle and that she thought *she* had won.

What she meant when she said she had won was that she had brought him up successfully and had sent him to college and that he had turned out so well—good looking (her teeth had gone unfilled so that his could be straightened), intelligent (he realized he was too intelligent to be a success), and with a future ahead of him (there was of course no future ahead of him). She excused his gloominess on the grounds that he was still growing up and his radical ideas on his lack of practical experience. She said he didn't yet know a thing about 'life', that he hadn't even entered the real world—when already he was as disenchanted with it as a man of fifty.

The further irony of all this was that in spite of her, he had turned out so well. In spite of going to only a third-rate college, he had, on his own initiative, come out with a first-rate education; in spite of growing up dominated by a small mind, he had ended up with a large one; in spite of all her foolish views, he was free of prejudice and unafraid to face facts. Most miraculous of all, instead of being blinded by love for her as she was for him, he had cut himself emotionally free of her and could see her with complete objectivity. He was not dominated by his mother.

The bus stopped with a sudden jerk and shook him from his meditation. A woman from the back lurched forward with little steps and barely escaped falling in his newspaper as she righted herself. She got off and a large Negro got on. Julian kept his paper lowered to watch. It gave him a certain satisfaction to see injustice in daily operation. It confirmed his view that with a few exceptions there was no one worth knowing within a radius of three hundred miles. The Negro was well dressed and carried a briefcase. He looked around and then sat down on the other end of the seat where the woman with the red and white canvas sandals was sitting. He immediately unfolded a newspaper and obscured himself behind it. Julian's mother's elbow at once prodded insistently into his ribs. 'Now you see why I won't ride on these buses by myself,' she whispered.

The woman with the red and white canvas sandals had risen at the same time the Negro sat down and had gone further back in the bus and taken the seat of the woman who had got off. His mother leaned forward and cast her an approving look.

Julian rose, crossed the aisle, and sat down in the place of the woman with the canvas sandals. From his position, he looked serenely across at his mother. Her face had turned an angry red. He stared at her, making his eyes the eyes of a stranger. He felt his tension suddenly lift as if he had openly declared war on her.

He would have liked to get in conversation with the Negro and to talk with him about art or politics or any subject that would be above the comprehension of those around them, but the man remained entrenched behind his paper. He was either ignoring the change of seating or had never noticed it. There was no way for Julian to convey his sympathy.

His mother kept her eyes fixed reproachfully on his face. The woman with the protruding teeth was looking at him avidly as if he were a type of monster new to her.

'Do you have a light?' he asked the Negro.

Without looking away from his paper, the man reached in his pocket and handed him a packet of matches.

'Thanks,' Julian said. For a moment he held the matches foolishly. A NO SMOKING sign looked down upon him from over the door. This alone would not have deterred him; he had no cigarettes. He had quit smoking some months before because he could not afford it. 'Sorry,' he muttered and handed back the matches. The Negro lowered the paper and gave him an annoyed look. He took the matches and raised the paper again.

His mother continued to gaze at him but she did not take advantage of his momentary discomfort. Her eyes retained their battered look. Her face seemed to be unnaturally red, as if her blood pressure had risen. Julian allowed no glimmer of sympathy to show on his face. Having got the advantage, he wanted desperately to keep it and carry it through. He would have liked to teach her a lesson that would last her a while, but there seemed no way to continue the point. The Negro refused to come out from behind his paper.

Julian folded his arms and looked stolidly before him, facing her but as if he did not see her, as if he had ceased to recognize her existence. He visualized a scene in which, the bus having reached their stop, he would remain in his seat and when she said, 'Aren't you going to get off?' he would look at her as at a stranger who had rashly addressed him. The corner they got off on was usually deserted, but it was well lighted and it would not hurt her to walk by herself the four blocks to the Y. He decided to wait until the time came and then decide whether or not he would let her get off by herself. He would have to be at the Y at ten to bring her back, but he could leave her wondering if he was going to show up. There was no reason for her to think she could always depend on him.

He retired again into the high-ceilinged room sparsely settled with large pieces of antique furniture. His soul expanded momentarily but then he became aware of his mother across from him and the vision shrivelled. He studied her coldly. Her feet in little pumps dangled like a child's and did not quite reach the floor. She was training on him an exaggerated look of reproach. He felt completely detached from her. At that moment he could with pleasure have slapped her as he would have slapped a particularly obnoxious child in his charge.

He began to imagine various unlikely ways by which he could teach her a lesson. He might make friends with some distinguished Negro professor or lawyer and bring him home to spend the evening. He would be entirely justified but her blood pressure would rise to 300. He could not push her to the extent of making her have a stroke, and moreover, he had never been successful at making any Negro friends. He had tried to strike up an acquaintance on the bus with some of the better types, with ones that looked like professors or ministers or lawyers. One morning he had sat down next to a distinguished-looking dark brown man who had answered his questions with a sonorous solemnity but who had turned out to be an undertaker. Another day he had sat down beside a cigar-smoking Negro with a diamond ring on his finger, but after a few stilted pleasantries, the Negro had rung the buzzer and risen, slipping two lottery tickets into Julian's hand as he climbed over him to leave.

He imagined his mother lying desperately ill and his being able to secure only a Negro doctor for her. He toyed with that idea for a few minutes and then dropped it for a momentary vision of himself participating as a sympathizer in a sit-in demonstration. This was possible but he did not linger with it. Instead, he approached the ultimate horror. He brought home a beautiful suspiciously Negroid woman. Prepare yourself, he said. There is nothing you can do about it. This is the woman I've chosen. She's intelligent, dignified, even good, and she's suffered and she hasn't thought it *fun*. Now persecute us, go ahead and persecute us. Drive her out of here, but remember, you're driving me too. His eyes were narrowed and through the indignation he had generated, he saw his mother across the aisle, purple-faced, shrunken to the dwarf-life proportions of her moral nature, sitting like a mummy beneath the ridiculous banner of her hat.

He was tilted out of his fantasy again as the bus stopped. The door opened with a sucking hiss and out of the dark a large, gaily dressed, sullen-looking coloured woman got on with a little boy. The child, who might have been four, had on a short plaid suit and a Tyrolean hat with a blue feather in it. Julian hoped that he would sit down beside him and that the woman would push in beside his mother. He could think of no better arrangement.

As she waited for her tokens, the woman was surveying the seating possibilities—he hoped with the idea of sitting where she was least wanted. There was something familiar-looking about her but Julian could not place what it was. She was a giant of a woman. Her face was set not only to meet opposition but to seek it out. The downward tilt of her large lower lip was like a warning sign: DON'T TAMPER WITH ME. Her bulging figure was encased in a green crêpe dress and her feet overflowed in red shoes. She had on a hideous hat. A purple velvet flap came down on one side of it and stood up on the other; the rest of it was green and looked like a cushion with the stuffing out. She carried a mammoth red pocketbook that bulged throughout as if it were stuffed with rocks.

To Julian's disappointment, the little boy climbed up on the empty seat beside his mother. His mother lumped all children, black and white, into the common category, 'cute', and she thought little Negroes were on the whole cuter than little white children. She smiled at the little boy as he climbed on the seat.

Meanwhile the woman was bearing down upon the empty seat beside Julian. To his annoyance, she squeezed herself into it. He saw his mother's face change as the woman settled herself next to him and he realized with satisfaction that this was more objectionable to her that it was to him. Her face seemed almost grey and there was a look of dull recognition in her eyes, as if suddenly she had sickened at some awful confrontation. Julian saw that it was because she and the woman had, in a sense, swapped sons. Though his mother would not realize the symbolic significance of this, she would feel it. His amusement showed plainly on his face.

The woman next to him muttered something unintelligible to herself. He was conscious of a kind of bristling next to him, muted growling like that of an angry cat. He could not see anything but the red pocketbook upright on the bulging green thighs. He visualized the woman as she had stood waiting for her tokens—the ponderous figure, rising from the red shoes upward over the solid hips, the mammoth bosom, the haughty face, to the green and purple hat.

His eyes widened.

The vision of the two hats, identical, broke upon him with the radiance of a brilliant sunrise. His face was suddenly lit with joy. He could not believe that Fate had thrust upon his mother such a lesson. He gave a loud chuckle so that she would look at him and see that he saw. She turned her eyes on him slowly. The blue in them seemed to have turned a bruised purple. For a moment he had an uncomfortable sense of her innocence, but it lasted only a second before principle rescued him. Justice entitled him to laugh. His grin hardened until it said to her as plainly as if he were saying aloud: Your punishment exactly fits your pettiness. This should teach you a permanent lesson.

Her eyes shifted to the woman. She seemed unable to bear looking at him and to find the woman preferable. He became conscious again of the bristling presence at his side. The woman was rumbling like a volcano about to become active. His mother's mouth began to twitch slightly at one corner. With a sinking heart, he saw incipient signs of recovery on her face and realized that this was going to strike her suddenly as funny and was going to be no lesson at all. She kept her eyes on the woman and an amused smile came over her face as if the woman were a monkey that had stolen her hat. The little Negro was looking up at her with large fascinated eyes. He had been trying to attract her attention for some time.

'Carver!' the woman said suddenly. 'Come heah!'

When he saw that the spotlight was on him at last, Carver drew his feet up and turned himself toward Julian's mother and giggled.

'Carver!' the woman said. 'You heah me? Come heah!'

Carver slid down from the seat but remained squatting with his back against the base of it, his head turned slyly around toward Julian's mother, who was smiling at him. The woman reached a hand across the aisle and snatched him to her. He righted himself and hung backwards on her knees, grinning at Julian's mother. 'Isn't he cute?' Julian's mother said to the woman with the protruding teeth.

'I reckon he is,' the woman said without conviction.

The Negress yanked him upright but he eased out of her grip and shot across the aisle and scrambled, giggling wildly, onto the seat beside his love.

'I think he likes me,' Julian's mother said, and smiled at the woman. It was the smile she used when she was being particularly gracious to an inferior. Julian saw everything lost. The lesson had rolled off her like rain on a roof.

The woman stood up and yanked the little boy off the seat as if she were snatching him from contagion. Julian could feel the rage in her at having no weapon like his mother's smile. She gave the child a sharp slap across the leg. He howled once and then thrust his head into her stomach and kicked his feet against her shins. 'Behave,' she said vehemently.

The bus stopped and the Negro who had been reading the newspaper got off. The woman moved over and set the little boy down with a thump between herself and Julian. She held him firmly by the knee. In a moment he put his hands in front of his face and peeped at Julian's mother through his fingers.

'I see yoooooooo!' she said and put her hand in front of her face and peeped at him.

The woman slapped his hand down. 'Quit yo' foolishness,' she said, 'before I knock the living Jesus out of you!'

Julian was thankful that the next stop was theirs. He reached up and pulled the cord. The woman reached up and pulled it at the same time. Oh my God, he thought. He had the terrible intuition that when they got off the bus together, his mother would open her purse and give the little boy a nickel. The gesture would be as natural to her as breathing. The bus stopped and the woman got up and lunged to the front, dragging the child, who wished to stay on, after her. Julian and his mother got up and followed. As they neared the door, Julian tried to relieve her of her pocketbook.

'No,' she murmured, 'I want to give the little boy a nickel.'

'No!' Julian hissed. 'No!'

She smiled down at the child and opened her bag. The bus door opened and the woman picked him up by the arm and descended with him, hanging at her hip. Once in the street she set him down and shook him.

Julian's mother had to close her purse while she got down the bus step but as soon as her feet were on the ground, she opened it again and began to rummage inside. 'I can't find but a penny,' she whispered, 'but it looks like a new one.'

'Don't do it!' Julian said fiercely between his teeth. There was a streetlight on the corner and she hurried to get under it so that she could better see into her pocketbook. The woman was heading off rapidly down the street with the child still hanging backward on her hand.

'Oh little boy!' Julian's mother called and took a few quick steps and caught up with them just beyond the lamppost. 'Here's a bright new penny for you,' and she held out the coin, which shone bronze in the dim light.

The huge woman turned and for a moment stood, her shoulders lifted and her face frozen with frustrated rage, and stared at Julian's mother. Then all at once she seemed to explode like a piece of machinery that had been given one ounce of pressure too much. Julian saw the black fist swing out with the red pocketbook. He shut his eyes and cringed as he heard the woman shout, 'He don't take nobody's pennies!' When he opened his eyes, the woman was disappearing down the street with the little boy staring wide-eyed over her shoulder. Julian's mother was sitting on the sidewalk.

'I told you not to do that,' Julian said angrily. 'I told you not to do that!'

He stood over her for a minute, gritting his teeth. Her legs were stretched out in front of her and her hat was on her lap. He squatted down and looked her in the face. It was totally expressionless. 'You got exactly what you deserved,' he said. 'Now get up.'

He picked up her pocketbook and put what had fallen out back in it. He picked the hat up off her lap. The penny caught his eye on the sidewalk and he picked that up and let it drop before her eyes into the purse. Then he stood up and leaned over and held his hands out to pull her up. She remained immobile. He sighed. Rising above them on either side were black apartment buildings, marked with irregular rectangles of light. At the end of the block a man came out of a door and walked off in the opposite direction. 'All right,' he said, 'suppose somebody happens by and wants to know why you're sitting on the sidewalk?'

She took the hand and, breathing hard, pulled heavily up on it and then stood for a moment, swaying slightly as if the spots of light in the darkness were circling around her. Her eyes, shadowed and confused, finally settled on his face. He did not try to conceal his irritation. 'I hope this teaches you a lesson,' he said. She leaned forward and her eyes raked his face. She seemed trying to determine his identity. Then, as if she found nothing familiar about him, she started off with a headlong movement in the wrong direction.

'Aren't you going on to the Y?' he asked.

'Home,' she muttered.

'Well, are we walking?'

For answer she kept going. Julian followed along, his hands behind him. He saw no reason to let the lesson she had had go without backing it up with an explanation of its meaning. She might as well be made to understand what had happened to her. 'Don't think that was just an uppity Negro woman,' he said. 'That was the whole coloured race which will no longer take your condescending pennies. That was your black double. She can wear the same hat as you, and to be sure,' he added gratuitously (because he thought it was funny), 'it looked better on her than it did on you. What all this means,' he said, 'is that the old world is gone. The old manners are obsolete and your graciousness is not worth a damn.' He thought bitterly of the house that had been lost for him. 'You aren't who you think you are,' he said.

She continued to plow ahead, paying no attention to him. Her hair had come undone on one side. She dropped her pocketbook and took no notice. He stooped and picked it up and handed it to her but she did not take it.

'You needn't act as if the world had come to an end,' he said, 'because it hasn't. From now on you've got to live in a new world and face a few realities for a change. Buck up,' he said, 'it won't kill you.'

She was breathing fast.

'Let's wait on the bus,' he said.

'Home,' she said thickly.

'I hate to see you behave like this,' he said. 'Just like a child. I should be able to expect more of you.' He decided to stop where he was and make her stop and wait for a bus. 'I'm not going any farther,' he said, stopping. 'We're going on the bus.'

She continued to go on as if she had not heard him. He took a few steps and caught her arm and stopped her. He looked into her face and caught his breath. He was looking into a face he had never seen before. 'Tell Grandpa to come get me,' she said.

He stared, stricken.

'Tell Caroline to come get me,' she said.

Stunned, he let her go and she lurched forward again, walking as if one leg were shorter than the other. A tide of darkness seemed to be sweeping her from him. 'Mother!' he cried. 'Darling, sweetheart, wait!' Crumpling, she fell to the pavement. He dashed forward and fell at her side, crying, 'Mamma, Mamma!' He turned her over. Her face was fiercely distorted. One eye, large and staring, moved slightly to the left as if it had become unmoored. The other remained fixed on him, raked his face again, found nothing and closed.

'Wait here, wait here!' he cried and jumped up and began to run for help toward a cluster of lights he saw in the distance ahead of him. 'Help, help!' he shouted, but his voice was thin, scarcely a thread of sound. The lights drifted farther away the faster he ran and his feet moved numbly as if they carried him nowhere. The tide of darkness seemed to sweep him back to her, postponing from moment to moment his entry into the world of guilt and sorrow.

1961

Margaret Laurence

1926-87

Margaret Laurence found the short story form as challenging as the novel: 'I don't feel that the short story is any less difficult a form; in fact in some ways it's more difficult. I think generally speaking, with my short stories anyway, I've had one sort of main theme into which I go fairly deeply, whereas with the novel I have a whole lot of interrelated themes and dilemmas. I don't think you necessarily do more in the novel—it doesn't attract me any more than the short story—it's just that the material itself chooses the form.'

Jean Margaret Wemyss was born in Neepawa, Manitoba—a small town that she was to transform into Manawaka, the setting of much of her finest fiction. Her parents died when she was a very young girl, and she was brought up by an aunt who had become her stepmother. She left Neepawa to attend the University of Winnipeg, graduating in 1947; that same year she began to write for the *Winnipeg Citizen* and she married Jack Laurence. The couple moved to England in 1949 and then to Africa for seven years, returning to Vancouver in 1957. In 1962, Laurence moved back to England, where she lived and wrote for ten years, returning in the early seventies to make her home in Ontario, where she spent summers in a cottage on the Otonabee river near Peterborough and eventually settled in the town of Lakefield.

Laurence's most enduring gifts are as a creator of place—for many readers, Manawaka has the power of Faulkner's Yoknapatawpha—and of character. Her fiction resonates with the deeply felt conflicts of characters whom Laurence often felt inhabiting her as she wrote: 'The main concern of a writer remains that of somehow creating the individual on the printed page, of catching the tones and accents of human speech, of setting down the conflicts of people who are as real to him as himself.'

In 'The Tomorrow-Tamer' Laurence drew on her experience in Africa to dramatize the conflicts between a traditional way of life and the colonizing forces that she saw transforming it. Outlined in the tragic path of Kofi's life is the fate of a whole culture as it struggles to align its ancestral beliefs with modern ideals of progress.

'To Set Our House in Order' is part of a collection of stories that Laurence describes as her only venture into 'semi-autobiographical' fiction: 'I have never written anything that is directly autobiographical, except for one book of short stories, *A Bird in the House*, which was based on my own childhood, myself as a child, and my family.' Vanessa MacLeod's changing perceptions of her parents, her grandmother, and finally of the alleged 'order' of the universe within and beyond the MacLeod household culminates in her realization that life is capricious, and therefore at once more dangerous and beautiful.

'The Tomorrow-Tamer' was first published in the Fall 1961 issue of *Prism International* and then collected in 1963 in the book of the same title. 'To Set Our House in Order' was first published in abridged form in the March 1964 issue of *Ladies' Home Journal* and then collected in *A Bird in the House* (1970).

The Tomorrow–Tamer

The dust rose like clouds of red locusts around the small stampeding hooves of taggle-furred goats and the frantic wings of chickens with all their feathers awry. Behind them the children darted, their bodies velvety with dust, like a flash and tumble of brown butterflies in the sun.

The young man laughed aloud to see them, and began to lope after them. Past the palms where the tapsters got wine, and the sacred grove that belonged to Owura, god of the river. Past the shrine where Nana Ayensu poured libation to the dead and guardian grandsires. Past the thicket of ghosts, where the graves were, where every leaf and flower had fed on someone's kin, and the wind was the thin whisper-speech of ancestral spirits. Past the deserted huts, clay walls runnelled by rain, where rats and demons dwelt in unholy brotherhood. Past the old men drowsing in doorways, dreaming of women, perhaps, or death. Past the good huts with their brown baked walls strong against any threatening night-thing, the slithering snake carrying in its secret sac the end of life, or red-eyed Sasabonsam, huge and hairy, older than time and always hungry.

The young man stopped where the children stopped, outside Danquah's. The shop was mud and wattle, like the huts, but it bore a painted sign, green and orange. Only Danquah could read it, but he was always telling people what it said. *Hail Mary Chop-Bar & General Merchant.* Danquah had gone to a mission school once, long ago. He was not really of the village, but he had lived here for many years.

Danquah was unloading a case of beer, delivered yesterday by a lorry named *God Helps Those*, which journeyed fortnightly over the bush trail into Owurasu. He placed each bottle in precisely the right place on the shelf, and stood off to admire the effect. He was the only one who could afford to drink bottled beer, except for funerals, maybe, when people made a show, but he liked to see the bright labels in a row and the bottle-tops winking a gilt promise of forgetfulness. Danquah regarded Owurasu as a mudhole. But he had inherited the shop, and as no one in the village had the money to buy it and no one outside had the inclination, he was fixed here for ever.

He turned when the children flocked in. He was annoyed at them, because he happened to have taken his shirt off and was also without the old newspaper which he habitually carried.

The children chuckled surreptitiously, hands over mouths, for the fat on Danquah's chest made him look as though the breasts of a young girl had been stuck incongruously on his scarred and ageing body.

'A man cannot even go about his work,' Danquah grumbled, 'without a whole pack of forest monkeys gibbering in his doorway. Well, what is it?'

The children bubbled their news, like a pot of soup boiling over, fragments cast here and there, a froth of confusion.

Attah the ferryman—away, away downriver (half a mile)—had told them, and he got the word from a clerk who got it from the mouth of a government man. A bridge was going to be built, and it was not to be at Atware, where the ferry was, but—where do you think? At Owurasu! This very place. And it was to be the biggest bridge any man had ever seen—big, really big, and high—look, like this (as high as a five-year-old's arms).

'A bridge, eh?' Danquah looked reflectively at his shelves, stacked with jars of mauve and yellow sweets, bottles of jaundice bitters, a perfume called *Bint el Sudan*, the newly-arranged beer, two small battery torches which the village boys eyed with envy but could not afford. What would the strangers' needs be? From the past, isolated images floated slowly to the surface of his mind, like weed shreds in the sluggish river. Highland Queen whisky. De Reszke cigarettes. Chivers marmalade. He turned to the young man.

'Remember, a year ago, when those men from the coast came here, and walked all around with sticks, and dug holes near the river? Everyone said they were lunatics, but I said something would come of it, didn't I? No one listened to me, of course. Do you think it's true, this news?'

The boy grinned and shrugged. Danquah felt irritated at himself, that he had asked. An elder would not have asked a boy's opinion. In any event, the young man clearly had no opinion.

'How do I know?' the boy said. 'I will ask my father, who will ask Nana Ayensu.'

'I will ask Nana Ayensu myself,' Danquah snapped, resenting the implication that the boy's father had greater access to the chief than he did, although in fact this was the case.

The young man's broad blank face suddenly frowned, as though the news had at last found a response in him, an excitement over an unknown thing.

'Strangers would come here to live?'

'Of course, idiot,' Danquah muttered. 'Do you think a bridge builds itself?'

Danquah put on his pink rayon shirt and his metal-rimmed spectacles so he could think better. But his face remained impassive. The boy chewed thoughtfully on a twig, hoisted his sagging loincloth, gazed at a shelf piled with patterned tradecloth and long yellow slabs of soap. He watched the sugar ants trailing in amber procession across the termite-riddled counter and down again to the packed-earth floor.

Only the children did not hesitate to show their agitation. Shrilling like cicadas, they swarmed and swirled off and away, bearing their tidings to all the world.

Danquah maintained a surly silence. The young man was not surprised, for the villagers regarded Danquah as a harmless madman. The storekeeper had no kin here, and if he had relatives elsewhere, he never mentioned them. He was not son or father, nephew or uncle. He lived by himself in the back of his shop. He cooked his own meals and sat alone on his stoep in the evenings, wearing food-smirched trousers and yellow shoes. He drank the costly beer and held aloft his ragged newspaper, bellowing the printed words to the toads that slept always in clusters in the corners, or crying sadly and drunkenly, while the village boys peered and tittered without pity.

The young man walked home, his bare feet making light crescent prints in the dust. He was about seventeen, and his name was Kofi. He was no one in particular, no one you would notice.

Outside the hut, one of his sisters was pounding dried cassava into *kokonte* meal, raising the big wooden pestle and bringing it down with an unvaried rhythm into the mortar. She glanced up.

'I saw Akua today, and she asked me something.' Her voice was a teasing singsong.

Kofi pretended to frown. 'What is that to me?'

'Don't you want to know?'

He knew she would soon tell him. He yawned and stretched, languidly, then squatted on his heels and closed his eyes, miming sleep. He thought of Akua as she had looked this morning, early, coming back from the river with the water jar on her head, and walking carefully, because the vessel was heavy, but managing also to sway her plump buttocks a little more than was absolutely necessary.

'She wants to know if you are a boy or a man,' his sister said.

His thighs itched and he could feel the slow full sweetness of his amiable lust. He jumped to his feet and leapt over the mortar, clumsy-graceful as a young goat. He sang softly, so his mother inside the hut would not hear.

'*Do you ask a question,*
Akua, Akua?
In a grove dwells an oracle,
Oh Akua—
Come to the grove when the village sleeps—'

The pestle thudded with his sister's laughter. He leaned close to her.

'Don't speak of it, will you?'

She promised, and he sat cross-legged on the ground, and drummed on the earth with his outspread hands, and sang in the cool heat of the late afternoon. Then he remembered the important news, and put on a solemn face, and went in the hut to see his father.

His father was drinking palm wine sorrowfully. The younger children were crawling about like little lizards, and Kofi's mother was pulling out yams and red peppers and groundnuts and pieces of fish from bowls and pots stacked in a corner. She said 'Ha—ei—' or 'True, true—' to everything the old man said, but she was not really listening—her mind was on the evening meal.

Kofi dutifully went to greet his grandmother. She was brittle and small and fleshless as the empty shell of a tortoise. She rarely spoke, and then only to recite in her tenuous bird voice her genealogy, or to complain of chill. Being blind, she liked to run her fingers over the faces of her grandchildren. Kofi smiled so that she could touch his smile. She murmured to him, but it was the name of one of his dead brothers.

'And when I think of the distance we walked,' Kofi's father was saying, 'to clear the new patch for the cocoyam, and now it turns out to be no good, and the yams are half the size they should be, and I ask myself why I should be afflicted in this way, because I have no enemies, unless you want to count Donkor, and he went away ten years ago, so it couldn't be him, and if it is a question of libation, who has been more generous than I, always making sure the gods drank before the planting—'

He went on in this vein for some time, and Kofi waited. Finally his father looked up.

'The government men will build a bridge at Owurasu,' Kofi said. 'So I heard.'

His father snorted.

'Nana Ayensu told me this morning. He heard it from Attah, but he did not believe it. Everyone knows the ferry-man's tongue has diarrhoea. Garrulity is an affliction of the soul.'

'It is not true, then?'

'How could it be true? We have always used the Atware ferry. There will be no bridge.'

Kofi got out his adze and machete and went outside to sharpen them. Tomorrow he and his father would begin clearing the fallow patch beside the big baobab tree, for the second planting of cassava. Kofi could clear quickly with his machete, slicing through underbrush and greenfeather ferns. But he took no pride in the fact, for every young man did the same.

He was sorry that there would be no bridge. Who knows what excitement might have come to Owurasu? But he knew nothing of such things. Perhaps it was better this way.

A week later, three white men and a clerk arrived, followed by a lorry full of tents and supplies, several cooks, a mechanic and four carpenters.

'Oh, my lord,' groaned Gerald Wain, the Contractor's Superintendent, climbing out of the Land-Rover and stretching his travel-stiffened limbs, 'is this the place? Eighteen months—it doesn't bear thinking about.'

The silence in the village broke into turbulence. The women who had been filling the water vessels at the river began to squeal and shriek. They giggled and wailed, not knowing which was called for. They milled together, clambered up the clay bank, hitched up their long cloths and surged down the path that led back to the village, leaving the unfilled vessels behind.

The young men were returning from the farms, running all together, shouting hoarsely. The men of Owurasu, the fathers and elders, had gathered outside the chief's dwelling and were waiting for Nana Ayensu to appear.

At the *Hail Mary* Danquah found two fly-specked pink paper roses and set them in an empty jam jar on his counter. He whipped out an assortment of bottles—gin, a powerful red liquid known as Steel wine, the beer with their gleaming tops, and several sweet purple Doko-Doko which the villagers could afford only when the cocoa crop was sold. Then he opened wide his door. In the centre of the village, under the sacred fire tree, Nana Ayensu and the elders met the new arrivals. The leader of the white men was not young, and he had a skin red as fresh-bled meat. Red was the favoured colour of witches and priests of witchcraft, as everyone knew, so many remarks were passed, especially when some of the children, creeping close, claimed to have seen through the sweat-drenched shirt a chest and belly hairy as the Sasabonsam's. The other two white men were young and pale. They smoked many cigarettes and threw them away still burning, and the children scrambled for them.

Badu, the clerk-interpreter, was an African, but to the people of Owurasu he was just as strange as the white men, and even less to be trusted, for he was a coast man. He wore white clothes and pointed shoes and a hat like an infant umbrella. The fact that he could speak their language did not make the villagers any less suspicious.

'The stranger is like a child,' Nana Ayensu said, 'but the voice of an enemy is like the tail of a scorpion—it carries the sting.'

The clerk, a small man, slight and nervous as a duiker, sidled up to weighty Opoku, the chief's spokesman, and attempted to look him in the eye. But when the clerk began to speak his eyes flickered away to the gnarled branches of the old tree.

'The wise men from the coast,' Badu bawled in a voice larger than himself, 'the government men who are greater than any chief—they have said that a bridge is to be built here, an honour for your small village. Workmen will be brought in for the skilled jobs, but we will need local men as well. The bungalows and labourers' quarters will be started at once, so we can use your young men in that work. Our tents will be over there on the hill. Those who want to work can apply to me. They will be paid for what they do. See to it that they are there tomorrow morning early. In this job we waste no time.'

The men of Owurasu stood mutely with expressionless faces. As for the women, they felt only shame for the clerk's mother, whoever she might be, that she had taught her son so few manners.

Badu, brushing the dust from his white sleeves, caught their soft deploring voices and looked defiant. These people were bush—they knew nothing of the world of streets and shops. But because they had once thrown their spears all along the coast, they still scorned his people, calling them cowards and eaters of fish-heads. He felt, as well, a dismal sense of embarrassment at the backwardness of rural communities, now painfully exposed to the engineers' eyes. He turned abruptly away and spoke in rapid stuttering English to the Superintendent.

With a swoosh and a rattle, the strangers drove off towards the river, scattering goats and chickens and children from the path, and filling the staring villagers' nostrils with dust. Then—pandemonium. What was happening? What was expected of them? No one knew. Everyone shouted at once. The women and girls fluttered and chattered like parrots startled into flame-winged flight. But the faces of the men were sombre.

Kofi came as close as he dared to the place where Nana Ayensu and the elders stood. Kofi's father was speaking. He was a small and wiry man. He plucked at his yellow and black cloth, twirling one end of it across his shoulder, pulling it down, flinging it back again. His body twitched in anger.

'Can they order us about like slaves? We have men who have not forgotten their grandfathers were warriors—'

Nana Ayensu merely flapped a desolate hand. 'Compose yourself, Kobla. Remember that those of our spirit are meant to model their behaviour on that of the river. We are supposed to be calm.'

Nana Ayensu was a portly man, well-fleshed. His bearing was dignified, especially when he wore his best *kente* cloth, as he did now, having hastily donned it upon being informed of the strangers' approach. He was, however, sweating a great deal—the little rivers formed under the gold and leather amulets of his headband, and trickled down his forehead and nose.

'Calm,' he repeated, like an incantation. 'But what do they intend to do with our young men? Will there be the big machines? I saw them once, when I visited my sister in the city. They are very large, and they feed on earth, opening their jaws—thus. Jaws that consume earth could consume a man. If harm comes to our young men, it is upon my head. But he said they would be paid, and Owurasu is not rich—'

Okomfo Ofori was leaning on his thornwood stick, waiting his turn to speak. He was older than the others. The wrinkled skin of his face was hard and cracked, as though he had been sun-dried like an animal hide. He had lived a long time in the forest and on the river. He was the priest of the river, and there was nothing he did not know. Watching him covertly, Kofi felt afraid.

'We do not know whether Owura will suffer his river to be disturbed,' Okomfo Ofori said. 'If he will not, then I think the fish will die from the river, and the oil palms will wither, and the yams will shrink and dwindle in the planting places, and plague will come, and river-blindness will come, and the snake will inhabit our huts because the people are dead, and the strangler vine will cover our dwelling places. For our life comes from the river, and if the god's hand is turned against us, what will avail the hands of men?'

Kofi, remembering that he had casually, without thought, wished the bridge to come, felt weak with fear. He wanted to hide himself, but who can hide from his own fear and from the eyes of a god?

That night, Kofi's father told him they were to go to the sacred grove beside the river. Without a word or question, the boy shook off sleep and followed his father.

The grove was quiet. The only sounds were the clicking of palm boughs and the deep low voice of Owura the river. Others were there—Kofi never knew who—young men and old, his friends and his uncles, all now changed, distorted, grown ghostly and unknown in the grey moonlight.

'Here is wine from our hands,' Okomfo Ofori said. 'God of the river, come and accept this wine and drink.'

The palm wine was poured into the river. It made a faint far-off splash, then the river's voice continued unchanged, like muted drums. The priest lifted up a black earthen vessel, an ordinary pot fashioned from river clay, such as the women use for cooking, but not the same, for this one was consecrated. Into the pot he put fresh river water, and leaves he had gathered from the thicket of ghosts, and eggs, and the blood and intestines of a fowl whose neck he wrung, and white seeds, and a red bead, and a cowrie shell. He stirred the contents, and he stared for a long time, for this was the vessel wherein the god could make himself known to his priest. And no one moved.

Then—and the night was all clarity and all madness—the priest was possessed of his god, Owura the river. Kofi could never afterwards remember exactly what had happened. He remembered a priest writhing like a snake with its back broken, and the clothing trance-torn, and the god's voice low and deep. Finally, dizzied with sleeplessness and fear, he seemed to see the faces and trees blurred into a single tree face, and his mind became as light and empty as an overturned water vessel, everything spilled out, drained, gone.

Back at the hut, Kofi's father told him the outcome. Libation would be poured to the ancestors and to the god of the river, as propitiation for the disturbance of the waters. Also, one young man had been selected to go to the bridge work. In order that the village could discover what the bridgemen would do to the sons of Owurasu, one young man had been chosen to go, as a man will be sent to test the footing around a swamp.

Kofi was to be that young man.

He was put to work clearing a space for the bridgemen's dwellings. He knew his machete and so he worked well despite his apprehension, swinging the blade slowly, bending low from the waist and keeping his legs straight. The heat of the sun poured and filtered down the leaves and bushes, through the fronds and hairy trunks of the oil palms. The knotted grasses and the heavy clots of moss were warm and moist to the feet, and even the ferns, snapping easily under the blade, smelled of heat and damp.

Kofi wore only his loincloth, but the sweat ran down his sides and thighs, making his skin glossy. He worked with his eyes half closed. The blade lifted and fell. Towards mid-day, when the river had not risen to drown him, he ventured to sing.

'We are listening, we are listening.
Vine, do not harm us, for we ask your pardon.
We are listening, River, for the drums.
Thorn, do not tear us, for we ask your pardon.
River, give the word to Crocodile.
The crocodile, he drums in the river.
Send us good word, for we ask your pardon.'

Before he left at nightfall, he took the gourd bottle he had brought with him and sprinkled the palm oil on the ground where his machete had cleared.

'Take this oil,' he said to the earth, 'and apply it to your sores.'

Kofi returned home whole, day after day, and finally Nana Ayensu gave permission for other young men to go, as many as could be spared from the farming and fishing.

Six bungalows, servants' quarters, latrines and a long line of labourers' huts began to take shape. The young men of Owurasu were paid for their work. The village had never seen so much cash money before. The white men rarely showed their faces in the village, and the villagers rarely ventured into the strangers' camp, half a mile upriver. The two settlements were as separate as the river fish from the forest birds. They existed beside one another, but there was no communication between them. Even the village young men, working on the bungalows, had nothing to do with the Europeans, whose orders filtered down to them through Badu or the head carpenter. The bridgemen's cooks came to the village market to buy fruit and eggs, but they paid good prices and although they were haughty they did not bother anyone. The carpenters and drivers came to Danquah's in the evening, but there were not many of them and the villagers soon took them for granted. The village grew calm once more in the prevailing atmosphere of prosperity.

In the *Hail Mary Chop-Bar* the young men of Owurasu began to swagger. Some of them now kept for themselves a portion of the money they earned. Danquah, bustling around his shop, pulled out a box of new shirts and showed them off. They were splendid; they shimmered and shone. Entranced, the young men stared. A bottle of beer, Danquah urged. Would the young men have another bottle of beer while they considered the new shirts? They drank, and pondered, and touched the glittering cloth.

Kofi was looked up to now by the other young men. Some of them called him the chief of the young men. He did not admit it, but he did not deny, either. He stretched to his full height, yawned luxuriously, drank his beer in mighty gulps, laughed a little, felt strength flooding through his muscles, walked a trifle crookedly across the room to Danquah, who, smiling, was holding up a blue shirt imprinted with great golden trees. Kofi reached out and grabbed the shirt.

When he left the *Hail Mary* that night, Kofi found Akua waiting for him in the shadows. He remembered another purchase he had made. He drew it out and handed it to her, a green bottle with a picture of flowers. Akua seized it.

'For me? Scent?'

He nodded. She unstopped it, sniffed, laughed, grasped his arm.

'Oh, it is fine, a wonder. Kofi—when will you build the new hut?'

'Soon,' he promised. 'Soon.'

It was all settled between their two families. He did not know why he hesitated. When the hut was built, and the gifts given and received, his life would move in the known way. He would plant his crops and his children. Some of his crops would be spoiled by worm or weather; some of his children would die. He would grow old, and the young men would respect him. That was the way close to him as his own veins. But now his head was spinning from the beer, and his mouth was bitter as lime rind. He took Akua by the hand and they walked down the empty path together, slowly, in the dark, not speaking.

The next week the big machines came rolling and roaring into Owurasu. Lorries brought gangs of skilled labourers, more Europeans and more cooks. The tractor drivers laughed curses at the gaping villagers and pretended to run them down until they shrieked and fled in humiliation like girls or mice.

Gong-gong beat in Owurasu that night, and the drums did not stop their rumble until dawn. The village was in an uproar. What would the machines do? Who were these men? So many and so alien. Low-born coast men, northern desert men with their tribal marks burned in long gashes onto their cheeks and foreheads, crazy shouting city men with no shame. What would become of the village? No one knew.

Nana Ayensu visited the shrine where the carved and blackened state stools of dead chiefs were kept and where the ancestral spirits resided.

'Grandsires, we greet you. Stand behind us with a good standing. Protect us from the evils we know and from the evils we do not know. We are addressing you, and you will understand.'

Danquah sat at the counter of the *Hail Mary* with a hurricane lamp at his elbow. He was laboriously scrawling a letter to his cousin in the city, asking him to arrange for four cases of gin and ten of beer, together with fifty cartons of cigarettes, to be sent on the next mammy-lorry to Owurasu.

Okomfo Ofori scattered sacred *summe* leaves to drive away spirits of evil, and looked again into his consecrated vessel. But this time he could see only the weeping faces of his father and his mother, half a century dead.

When morning came, the big machines began to uproot the coconut palms in the holy grove beside the river. The village boys, who had been clearing the coarse grass from the river bank, one by one laid down their machetes and watched in horrified fascination as the bulldozers assaulted the slender trees. Everyone had thought of the river's being invaded by strangers. But it had never occurred to anyone that Owura's grove would be destroyed.

Kofi watched and listened. Under the noise of the engines he could hear the moaning of Owura's brown waters. Now would come the time of tribulation; the plague and the river-blindness would strike now. The bulldozer rammed another tree, and it toppled, its trunk snapping like a broken spine. Kofi felt as though his own bones were being broken, his own body assaulted, his heart invaded by the massive blade. Then he saw someone approaching from the village.

Okomfo Ofori was the river's priest, and there was nothing he did not know. Except this day, this death. Kofi stared, shocked. The old priest was running like a child, and his face was wet with his tears.

At the work site, the Superintendent listened wearily while the old man struggled to put his anguish into words.

'What's he saying, Badu? If it isn't one damn thing, it's another—what's the trouble now?'

'He says the grove belongs to the gods,' Badu explained.

'All right,' Wain sighed. 'Ask him how much he wants. It's a racket, if you ask me. Will ten pounds do it? It can be entered under Local Labour.'

The village boys looked towards Kofi, who stood unmoving, his machete dangling uselessly from his hand.

'What does it mean? What will happen?'

He heard their questioning voices and saw the question in their eyes. Then he turned upon them in a kind of fury.

'Why do you ask me? I know nothing, nothing, nothing!'

He dropped his machete and ran, not knowing where he was going, not seeing the paths he took.

His mother was a woman vast as mountains. Her blue cloth, faded and tinged with a sediment of brown from many washings in river water, tugged and pulled around her heavy breasts and hips. She reached out a hand to the head of her crouched son.

So the grove was lost, and although the pleas were made to gods and grandsires, the village felt lost, too, depleted and vulnerable. But the retribution did not come. Owura did not rise. Nothing happened. Nothing at all.

In the days following, Kofi did not go to the bridge work. He built the new hut, and when the gifts were given and taken, Akua made a groundnut stew and half the villagers were invited to share this first meal. Kofi, drinking palm wine and eating the food as though he could never get enough, was drawn into his new wife's smile and lapped around with laughter.

After a week, the young men of Owurasu went back to work for the bridgemen.

The approaches were cleared and the steamy river air was filled with the chunking of the pile-driver and the whirr of the concrete-mixer, as the piers and anchor blocks went in.

To the villagers, the river bank no longer seemed bald without the grove. Kofi could scarcely remember how the palms had looked when they lived there. Gradually he forgot that he had been afraid of the machines. Even the Europeans no longer looked strange. At first he had found it difficult to tell them apart, but now he recognized each.

Akua bought a new cloth and an iron cooking-pot. On one memorable day, Kofi came home from the *Hail Mary* with a pocket torch. It was green and handsome, with silver on its end and silver on the place one touched to make the light come on. Kofi flicked the switch and in the tiny bulb a faint glow appeared. Akua clapped her hands in pleasure.

'Such a thing. It is yours, Kofi?'

'Mine. I paid for it.'

The glow trembled, for the battery was almost worn out from the village boys' handling. Kofi turned it off hastily. Danquah had forgotten to tell him and so he did not know that the power could be replaced.

At the bridge, Kofi's work had changed. Now he helped in the pouring of the concrete as the blocks were made. He unloaded steel. He carried tools. He was everywhere. Sweat poured from him. His muscles grew tough as liana vines. He talked with the ironworkers, some of whom spoke his tongue. They were brash, easy-laughing, rough-spoken men, men of the city. Their leader was a man by the name of Emmanuel, a man with a mighty chest, hugely strong. Emmanuel wore a green felt hat enlivened with the white and lightly dancing feathers of the egrets that rode the cattle on the grasslands of the coast. He spoke often to Kofi, telling of the places he had been, the things he had seen.

'The money goes, but who cares? That's an ironworker's life—to make money and spend it. Someday I will have a car—you'll see. Ahh—it'll be blue, like the sea, with silver all over it. Buick—Jaguar—you don't know those names. Learn them, hear me? I'm telling them to you. Wait until you see me on the high steel. Then you'll know what an ironworker does. Listen—I'll tell you something—only men like me can be ironworkers, did you know that? Why? Because I know I won't fall. If you think you might fall, then you do. But not me. I'll never fall, I tell you that.'

Kofi listened, his mouth open, not understanding what Emmanuel was talking about, but understanding the power of the man, the fearlessness. More and more Kofi was drawn to the company of the bridgeman in the evenings at the *Hail Mary*. Akua would click her tongue disapprovingly.

'Kofi—why do you go there so much?'

'I am going,' he would reply, not looking into her eyes. 'It is not for you to say.'

He still went each evening to see his father and his mother. His father was morose, despite the money, and had taken to quoting proverbs extensively.

'Man is not a palm-nut that he should be self-centred. At the word of the elder, the young bends the knee. If you live in an evil town, the shame is yours.'

He would continue interminably, and Kofi would feel uneasy, not certain why his father was offended, not knowing where his own offence lay. But after he had returned to his own hut and had filled himself with bean soup and *kokonte*, he would feel better and would be off again to the *Hail Mary*.

One evening Kofi's father sent the women and younger children away and began to speak to his son. The old man frowned, trying to weave into some pattern the vast and spreading spider-web of his anxieties.

'The things which are growing from the river—we did not know the bridge would be like this, a defiance. And these madmen who go about our village—how many girls are pregnant by them already? And what will the children be like? Children of no known spirit—'

Kofi said nothing at all. He listened silently, and then he turned and walked out of the hut. It was only when he was halfway to the *Hail Mary* that he realized he had forgotten to greet or say farewell to the grandmother who sat, blind and small, in the darkened hut, repeating in her far-off voice the names of the dead.

At the *Hail Mary*, Kofi went over to Emmanuel, who was drinking beer and talking with Danquah. Danquah no longer complained about the village. These days he said that he had always known something wonderful would happen here; he had prayed and now his prayers had been answered. Emmanuel nodded and laughed, shrugging his shoulders rhythmically to the highlife music bellowed by the gramophone, a recent investment of Danquah's. Kofi put one hand on Emmanuel's arm, touching the crimson sheen of the ironworker's shirt.

'I am one of the bridgemen,' he said. 'Say it is true.'

Emmanuel clapped him on the shoulder.

'Sure,' he said. 'You are a bridgeman, bush boy. Why not?'

He winked at Danquah, who stifled a guffaw. But Kofi did not notice.

The dry *harmattan* wind came down from the northern deserts and across the forest country, parching the lips and throats of fishermen who cast their moon-shaped nets into the Owura river, and villagers bent double as they worked with their hoes in the patches of yam and cassava, and labourers on the sun-hot metal of the bridge.

More than a year had passed, and the bridge had assumed its shape. The towers were completed, the main cables sang in the scorching wind.

Kofi, now a mechanic's helper, scurried up and down the catwalks. He wore only a loincloth and he had a rag tied around his forehead as slight insulation against the fiery sun. He had picked up from the mechanics and ironworkers some of the highlife songs, and now as he worked he sang of the silk-clad women of the city.

Badu, immaculate in white shirt and white drill trousers, called to him.

'Hey, you, Kofi!'

Kofi trotted over to him.

'The bridge will be completed soon,' Badu said. 'Do you want to stay on as painter? We will not need so many men. But you have worked well. Shall I put your name down?'

'Of course,' Kofi said promptly. 'Am I not a bridgeman?'

Badu gave him a quizzical glance.

'What will you do when the bridge is finished? What will you do when we leave?'

Kofi looked at him blankly.

'You will be leaving? Emmanuel, he will be leaving?'

'Naturally,' Badu said. 'Did you think we would stay for ever?'

Kofi did not reply. He merely walked away. But Badu, watching him go, felt uneasily that something somewhere was disjointed, but he could not exactly put his finger on it.

To the people of Owurasu, the bridge was now different. It had grown and emerged and was an entity. And so another anxiety arose. Where the elders had once been concerned only over the unseemly disturbance of Owura's waters and grove, now they wondered how the forest and river would feel about the presence of this new being.

The forest was alive, and everywhere spirit acted upon spirit, not axe upon wood, nor herb upon wound, nor man upon steel. But what sort of spirit dwelt in the bridge? They did not know. Was it of beneficent or malicious intent? If a being existed, and you did not know whether it meant you good or ill, nor what it required of you, how could you possibly have peace of mind?

A series of calamities enforced the villagers' apprehension. Two of the pirogues drifted away and were found, rock-battered and waterlogged, some distance downriver. A young child fell prey to the crocodile that dwelt under the river bank. Worst of all, three of the best fishermen, who worked downstream near the rapids where the waterflies flourished, developed river-blindness.

When the council of elders met, Kofi was told to attend. He was not surprised, for he had now been the spokesman of the village youth for some time. Nana Ayensu spoke.

'The bridge is beside us, and we live beside this bridge, but we do not know it. How are we to discover its nature?'

Danquah, who was there by reason of his wealth, flatly stated that the bridge had brought good fortune to the village. Business was brisk; money flowed. He could not see why anyone should be worried.

Kofi's father leapt to his feet, quavering with rage. The bridge might have brought good fortune to Danquah, but it had brought ill fortune to everyone else.

'What of my son, spending all his time in the company of strangers? What of Inkumsah's child, buried in the river mud until his limbs rot soft enough for the crocodile to consume? What of—'

'Kobla, Kobla, be calm,' Nana Ayensu soothed. 'Remember the river.'

'The river itself will not be calm,' Kofi's father cried. 'You will see—Owura will not suffer this thing to remain.'

Okomfo Ofori and Opoku the linguist were nodding their heads. They agreed with Kobla. Kofi looked from face to face, the wise and wizened faces of his father, his uncles, his chief and his priest.

'Something is dwelling in it—something strong as Owura himself.'

Silence. All of them were staring at him. Only then did Kofi realize the enormity of his utterance. He was terrified at what he had done. He could not look up. The strength was drained from his body. And yet—the belief swelled and grew and put forth the leaf. The being within the bridge was powerful, perhaps as powerful as Owura, and he, Kofi, was a man of the bridge. He knew then what was meant to happen. The other bridgemen might go, might desert, might falter, but he would not falter. He would tend the bridge as long as he lived. He would be its priest.

When the paint began to appear on the bridge, the people of Owurasu gathered in little groups on the river bank and watched. The men shook their heads and lifted their shoulders questioningly. The women chirped like starlings.

'What's the matter with them?' Gerald Wain asked. 'Don't they like the aluminium paint?'

'They like it,' Badu replied. 'They think it is real silver.'

'What next?' the Superintendent said. 'I hope they don't start chipping it off.'

But the villagers were not primarily concerned with monetary value. The bridge was being covered with silver, like the thin-beaten silver leaf on a great queen's chair. Silver was the colour of queen mothers, the moon's daughters, the king-makers. The villagers wondered, and pondered meanings, and watched the bridge grow moon-bright in the kingly sun.

Kofi, who had been shunned at home ever since his insolence, himself brightened and shone with every brushful of paint he splashed and slapped on the metal. He painted like one possessed, as though the task of garbing the bridge lay in him alone.

In the *Hail Mary* he questioned Emmanuel.

'Where will you go, when you go from here?'

'Back to the city. First I'll have a good time. Everything a man does in the city, I'll do it—hear me? Then I'll look around for another job.'

Kofi was amazed. 'You do not know where you will go?'

'I'll find out,' Emmanuel said easily. 'What about you, bush boy?'

'I will tend the bridge,' Kofi said in a low voice.

Emmanuel's laughter boomed. 'Do you think it needs looking after? Do you think it would fall down tomorrow if no one was here?'

That was not what Kofi had meant. But he did not perceive the difference in their outlooks. He heard only one thing—the bridge did not need a priest. Emmanuel must be wrong. But if he were not? Kofi thought once again of the bridgemen, coming together for a while and then separating once more, going away to look for other places, somewhere. The thought could not be borne. He clicked it off like the little light of the green and silver torch.

He could return to his father's farm. That would please Akua and his mother. His father would welcome another pair of hands at the planting. He thought of his machete and adze. They would need a lot of sharpening. He stood up indecisively, looking from the counter to the door and back again. In his pocket the silver shillings clashed softly as he moved. He pulled them out and held them in his hand, staring at the last of the tin bright discs. Then he grasped Emmanuel's arm, clutching it tightly.

'What will I do? What will I do now?'

Emmanuel looked at him in astonishment.

'Why ask me?'

The towers were painted from small platforms run up on pulleys, and the cables were painted from the catwalks. Then the day came for painting the cross-members at the top of the towers. It was not a job which many men would have wanted, for one had to leave the safety of the catwalk and crawl gingerly out onto the steel beam.

Kofi at once volunteered. He swung himself lightly over the catwalk and onto the exposed steel. He straddled the beam two hundred feet above the river, and began to paint.

On either side of the brown waters lay the forest, green and dense, heavy-hanging, sultry and still at mid-day. The palms rose above the tangle of underbrush and fern, and the great buttressed hardwoods towered above the palms. Through and around it all, the lianas twisted and twined. Poinsettia and jungle lily blood-flecked the greens with their scarlet.

Kofi listened to the steely twanging of the cables. The sound, high and sweet as bees or bells, clear as rain, seemed to grow louder and louder, obscuring the bird-voiced forest, surpassing even the deep-throated roar of Owura the river.

Squinting, Kofi could make out other villages, huts like small calabashes in the sun. Then he saw something else. At a distance a straight red-gold streak pierced like a needle through the forest. It was the new road. He had heard about it but he had not seen it before and had not believed it was really there. Now he saw that it would emerge soon here and would string both village and bridge as a single bead on its giant thread.

Emmanuel would ride along there in a mammy-lorry, shouting his songs. At some other village, some other bridge, Emmanuel would find his brothers waiting for him, and he would greet them and be with them again.

Then Kofi knew what to do. He was no longer the bridge's priest, but now the thought could be borne. He was fearless, fearless as Emmanuel. He knew the work of the bridge. In the far places, men would recognize him as a bridgeman. The power of it went with him and in him. Exultant, he wanted to shout aloud his own name and his praises. There was nothing he could not do. Slowly, deliberately, he pulled himself up until he was standing there on the steel, high above the forest and the river. He was above even the bridge itself. And above him, there was only the sky.

Then he did something that Emmanuel would never have done on the high steel—he looked up. The brightness of the bridge seemed strangely to pale in the sunfire that filled his eyes. For an instant he looked straight into the sun. Then, blinded, he swayed and his foot slipped on the silver paint. He pitched forward, missing the bridge entirely, and arched into the river like a thrown spear.

The bridgeworkers' shouted alarm, as they saw him, was each man's cry of terror for himself, who might have been the one to fall. The pirogues went out, and the men of the village dragged the river. But Kofi's body was not found.

'What could have possessed the idiot?' the Superintendent cried, in anger and anguish, for it was the only fatal accident on the job.

'He did not believe the bridge would hurt him, perhaps,' Badu said.

'Did he think it was alive?' Wain said despairingly. 'Won't they ever learn?'

But looking up now, and hearing the metallic humming of the cables, it seemed to him that the damn thing almost was alive. He was beginning to have delusions; it was time he went on leave.

As for the people of Owurasu, they were not surprised. They understood perfectly well what had happened. The bridge, clearly, had sacrificed its priest in order to appease the river. The people felt they knew the bridge now. Kofi had been the first to recognize the shrine, but he had been wrong about one thing. The bridge was not as powerful as Owura. The river had been acknowledged as elder. The queenly bridge had paid its homage and was a part of Owurasu at last.

The boy's father quoted, stoically and yet with pride, and proverb—'A priest cannot look upon his god and live.' Kofi's mother and his widow mourned him, and were not much consoled by the praises they heard of him. But even they, as they listened, felt a certain awe and wondered if this was indeed the Kofi they had known.

Many tales were woven around his name, but they ended always in the same way, always the same.

'The fish is netted and eaten; the antelope is hunted and fed upon; the python is slain and cast into the cooking-pot. But—oh, my children, my sons—a man consumed by the gods lives forever.'

1961

To Set Our House in Order

When the baby was almost ready to be born, something went wrong and my mother had to go into hospital two weeks before the expected time. I was wakened by her crying in the night, and then I heard my father's footsteps as he went downstairs to phone. I stood in the doorway of my room, shivering and listening, wanting to go to my mother but afraid to go lest there be some sight there more terrifying than I could bear.

'Hello—Paul?' my father said, and I knew he was talking to Dr Cates. 'It's Beth. The waters have broken, and the fetal position doesn't seem quite—well, I'm only thinking of what happened the last time, and another like that would be—I wish she were a little huskier, damn it—she's so—no, don't worry. I'm quite all right. Yes, I think that would be the best thing. Okay, make it as soon as you can, will you?'

He came back upstairs, looking bony and dishevelled in his pyjamas, and running his fingers through his sand-coloured hair. At the top of the stairs, he came face to face with Grandmother MacLeod, who was standing there in her quilted black satin dressing gown, her slight figure held straight and poised, as though she were unaware that her hair was bound grotesquely like white-feathered wings in the snare of her coarse nighttime hairnet.

'What is it, Ewen?'

'It's all right, Mother. Beth's having—a little trouble. I'm going to take her into the hospital. You go back to bed.'

'I told you,' Grandmother MacLeod said in her clear voice, never loud, but distinct and ringing like the tap of a sterling teaspoon on a crystal goblet, 'I did tell you, Ewen, did I not, that you should have got a girl in to help her with the housework? She would have rested more.'

'I couldn't afford to get anyone in,' my father said. 'If you thought she should've rested more, why didn't you ever—oh God, I'm out of my mind tonight—just go back to bed, Mother, please. I must get back to Beth.'

When my father went down to the front door to let Dr Cates in, my need overcame my fear and I slipped into my parents' room. My mother's black hair, so neatly pinned up during the day, was startlingly spread across the white pillowcase. I stared at her, not speaking, and then she smiled and I rushed from the doorway and buried my head upon her.

'It's all right, honey,' she said. 'Listen, Vanessa, the baby's just going to come a little early, that's all. You'll be all right. Grandmother MacLeod will be here.'

'How can she get the meals?' I wailed, fixing on the first thing that came to mind. 'She never cooks. She doesn't know how.'

'Yes, she does,' my mother said. 'She can cook as well as anyone when she has to. She's just never had to very much, that's all. Don't worry—she'll keep everything in order, and then some.'

My father and Dr Cates came in, and I had to go, without ever saying anything I had wanted to say. I went back to my own room and lay with the shadows all around me. I listened to the night murmurings that always went on in that house, sounds which never had a source, rafters and beams, contracting in the dry air, perhaps, or mice in the walls, or a sparrow that had flown into the attic through the broken skylight there. After a while, although I would not have believed it possible, I slept.

The next morning I questioned my father. I believed him to be not only the best doctor in Manawaka, but also the best doctor in the whole of Manitoba, if not in the entire world, and the fact that he was not the one who was looking after my mother seemed to have something sinister about it.

'But it's always done that way, Vanessa,' he explained. 'Doctors never attend members of their own family. It's because they care so much about them, you see, and—'

'And what?' I insisted, alarmed at the way he had broken off. But my father did not reply. He stood there, and then he put on that difficult smile with which adults seek to conceal pain from children. I felt terrified, and ran to him, and he held me tightly.

'She's going to be fine,' he said. 'Honestly she is. Nessa, don't cry—'

Grandmother MacLeod appeared beside us, steel-spined despite her apparent fragility. She was wearing a purple silk dress and her ivory pendant. She looked as though she were all ready to go out for afternoon tea.

'Ewen, you're only encouraging the child to give way,' she said. 'Vanessa, big girls of ten don't make such a fuss about things. Come and get your breakfast. Now, Ewen, you're not to worry. I'll see to everything.'

Summer holidays were not quite over, but I did not feel like going out to play with any of the kids. I was very superstitious, and I had the feeling that if I left the house, even for a few hours, some disaster would overtake my mother. I did not, of course, mention this feeling to Grandmother MacLeod, for she did not believe in the existence of fear, or if she did, she never let on. I spent the morning morbidly, in seeking hidden places in the house. There were many of these—odd-shaped nooks under the stairs, small and loosely nailed-up doors at the back of clothes closets, leading to dusty tunnels and forgotten recesses in the heart of the house where the only things actually to be seen were drab oil paintings stacked upon the rafters, and trunks full of outmoded clothing and old photograph albums. But the unseen presences in these secret places I knew to be those of every person, young or old, who had ever belonged to the house and had died, including Uncle Roderick who got killed on the Somme, and the baby who would have been my sister if only she had managed to come to life. Grandfather MacLeod, who had died a year after I was born, was present in the house in more tangible form. At the top of the main stairs hung the mammoth picture of a darkly uniformed man riding upon a horse whose prancing stance and dilated nostrils suggested that the battle was not yet over, that it might indeed continue until Judgement Day. The stern man was actually the Duke of Wellington, but at the time I believed him to be my grandfather MacLeod, still keeping an eye on things.

We had moved in with Grandmother MacLeod when the Depression got bad and she could no longer afford a housekeeper, but the MacLeod house never seemed like home to me. Its dark red brick was grown over at the front with Virginia creeper that turned crimson in the fall, until you could hardly tell brick from leaves. It boasted a small tower in which Grandmother MacLeod kept a weedy collection of anaemic ferns. The veranda was embellished with a profusion of wrought-iron scrolls, and the circular rose-window upstairs contained glass of many colours which permitted an outlooking eye to see the world as a place of absolute sapphire or emerald, or if one wished to look with a jaundiced eye, a hateful yellow. In Grandmother MacLeod's opinion, their features gave the house style.

Inside, a multitude of doors led to rooms where my presence, if not actually forbidden, was not encouraged. One was Grandmother MacLeod's bedroom, with its stale and old-smelling air, the dim reek of medicines and lavender sachets. Here resided her monogrammed dresser silver, brush and mirror, nail-buffer and button hook and scissors, none of which must even be fingered by me now, for she meant to leave them to me in her will and intended to hand them over in the same flawless and unused condition in which they had always been kept. Here, too, were the silver-framed photographs of Uncle Roderick—as a child, as a boy, as a man in his Army uniform. The massive walnut spool bed had obviously been designed for queens or giants, and my tiny grandmother used to lie within it all day when she had migraine, contriving somehow to look like a giant queen.

The living room was another alien territory where I had to tread warily, for many valuable objects sat just-so on tables and mantelpiece, and dirt must not be tracked in upon the blue Chinese carpet with its birds in eternal motionless flight and its water-lily buds caught forever just before the point of opening. My mother was always nervous when I was in this room.

'Vanessa, honey,' she would say, half apologetically, 'why don't you go and play in the den, or upstairs?'

'Can't you leave her, Beth?' my father would say. 'She's not doing any harm.'

'I'm only thinking of the rug,' my mother would say, glancing at Grandmother MacLeod, 'and yesterday she nearly knocked the Dresden shepherdess off the mantel. I mean, she can't help it, Ewen, she has to run around—'

'Goddamn it, I know she can't help it,' my father would growl, glaring at the smirking face of the Dresden shepherdess.

'I see no need to blaspheme, Ewen,' Grandmother MacLeod would say quietly, and then my father would say he was sorry, and I would leave.

The day my mother went to the hospital, Grandmother MacLeod called me at lunch-time, and when I appeared, smudged with dust from the attic, she looked at me distastefully as though I had been a cockroach that had just crawled impertinently out of the woodwork.

'For mercy's sake, Vanessa, what have you been doing with yourself? Run and get washed this minute. Here, not that way—you use the back stairs, young lady. Get along now. Oh—your father phoned.'

I swung around. 'What did he say? How is she? Is the baby born?'

'Curiosity killed a cat,' Grandmother MacLeod said, frowning. 'I cannot understand Beth and Ewen telling you all these things, at your age. What sort of vulgar person you'll grow up to be, I dare not think. No, it's not born yet. Your mother's just the same. No change.'

I looked at my grandmother, not wanting to appeal to her, but unable to stop myself. 'Will she—will she be all right?'

Grandmother MacLeod straightened her already-straight back. 'If I said definitely yes, Vanessa, that would be a lie, and the MacLeods do not tell lies, as I have tried to impress upon you before. What happens is God's will. The Lord giveth, and the Lord taketh away.'

Appalled, I turned away so she would not see my face and my eyes. Surprisingly, I heard her sigh and felt her papery white and perfectly manicured hand upon my shoulder.

'When your Uncle Roderick got killed,' she said, 'I thought I would die. But I didn't die, Vanessa.'

At lunch, she chatted animatedly, and I realized she was trying to cheer me in the only way she knew.

'When I married your Grandfather MacLeod,' she related, 'he said to me, "Eleanor, don't think because we're going to the prairies that I expect you to live roughly. You're used to a proper house, and you shall have one." He was as good as his word. Before we'd been in Manawaka three years, he'd had this place built. He earned a good deal of money in his time, your grandfather. He soon had more patients than either of the other doctors. We ordered our dinner service and all our silver from Birks' in Toronto. We had resident help in those days, of course, and never had less than twelve guests for dinner parties. When I had a tea, it would always be twenty or thirty. Never any less than half a dozen different kinds of cake were ever served in this house. Well, no one seems to bother much these days. Too lazy, I suppose.'

'Too broke,' I suggested. 'That's what Dad says.'

'I can't bear slang,' Grandmother MacLeod said. 'If you mean hard up, why don't you say so? It's mainly a question of management, anyway. My accounts were always in good order, and so was my house. No unexpected expenses that couldn't be met, no fruit cellar running out of preserves before the winter was over. Do you know what my father used to say to me when I was a girl?'

'No,' I said. 'What?'

'God loves Order,' Grandmother MacLeod replied with emphasis. 'You remember that, Vanessa. God loves Order—he wants each one of us to set our house in order. I've never forgotten those words of my father's. I was a MacInnes before I got married. The MacInnes is a very ancient clan, the lairds of Morven and the constables of the Castle of Kinlochaline. Did you finish that book I gave you?'

'Yes,' I said. Then, feeling some additional comment to be called for, 'It was a swell book, Grandmother.'

This was somewhat short of the truth. I had been hoping for her cairngorm brooch on my tenth birthday, and had received instead the plaid-bound volume entitled *The Clans and Tartans of Scotland*. Most of it was too boring to read, but I had looked up the motto of my own family and those of some of my friends' families. *Be then a wall of brass. Learn to suffer. Consider the end. Go carefully*. I had not found any of these slogans reassuring. What with Mavis Duncan learning to suffer, and Laura Kennedy considering the end, and Patsy Drummond going carefully, and I spending my time in being a wall of brass, it did not seem to me that any of us were going to lead very interesting lives. I did not say this to Grandmother MacLeod.

'The MacInnes motto is *Pleasure Arises from Work*,' I said.

'Yes,' she agreed proudly. 'And an excellent motto it is, too. One to bear in mind.'

She rose from the table, rearranging on her bosom the looped ivory beads that held the pendant on which a fullblown ivory rose was stiffly carved.

'I hope Ewen will be pleased,' she said.

'What at?'

'Didn't I tell you?' Grandmother MacLeod said. 'I hired a girl this morning, for the housework. She's to start tomorrow.'

When my father got home that evening, Grandmother MacLeod told him her good news. He ran one hand distractedly across his forehead.

'I'm sorry, Mother, but you'll just have to unhire her. I can't possibly pay anyone.'

'It seems distinctly odd,' Grandmother MacLeod snapped, 'that you can afford to eat chicken four times a week.'

'Those chickens,' my father said in an exasperated voice, 'are how people are paying their bills. The same with the eggs and the milk. That scrawny turkey that arrived yesterday was for Logan MacCardney's appendix, if you must know. We probably eat better than any family in Manawaka, except Niall Cameron's. People can't entirely dispense with doctors or undertakers. That doesn't mean to say I've got any cash. Look, Mother, I don't know what's happening with Beth. Paul thinks he may have to do a Caesarean. Can't we leave all this? Just leave the house alone. Don't touch it. What does it matter?'

'I have never lived in a messy house, Ewen,' Grandmother MacLeod said, 'and I don't intend to begin now.'

'Oh Lord,' my father said. 'Well, I'll phone Edna, I guess, and see if she can give us a hand, although God knows she's got enough, with the Connor house and her parents to look after.'

'I don't fancy having Edna Connor in to help,' Grandmother MacLeod objected.

'Why not?' my father shouted. 'She's Beth's sister, isn't she?'

'She speaks in such a slangy way,' Grandmother MacLeod said. 'I have never believed she was a good influence on Vanessa. And there is no need for you to raise your voice to me, Ewen, if you please.'

I could barely control my rage. I thought my father would surely rise to Aunt Edna's defence. But he did not.

'It'll be all right,' he soothed her. 'She'd only be here for part of the day, Mother. You could stay in your room.'

Aunt Edna strode in the next morning. The sight of her bobbed black hair and her grin made me feel better at once. She hauled out the carpet sweeper and the weighted polisher and got to work. I dusted while she polished and swept, and we got through the living room and front hall in next to no time.

'Where's her royal highness, kiddo?' she enquired.

'In her room,' I said. 'She's reading the catalogue from Robinson & Cleaver.'

'Good Glory, not again?' Aunt Edna cried. 'The last time she ordered three linen tea-clothes and two dozen serviettes. It came to fourteen dollars. Your mother was absolutely frantic. I guess I shouldn't be saying this.'

'I knew anyway,' I assured her. 'She was at the lace handkerchiefs section when I took up her coffee.'

'Let's hope she stays there. Heaven forbid she should get onto the banqueting cloths. Well, at least she believes the Irish are good for two things—manual labour and linen-making. She's never forgotten Father used to be a blacksmith, before he got the hardware store. Can you beat it? I wish it didn't bother Beth.'

'Does it?' I asked, and immediately realized this was a wrong move, for

Aunt Edna was suddenly scrutinizing me.

'We're making you grow up before your time,' she said. 'Don't pay any attention to me, Nessa. I must've got up on the wrong side of the bed this morning.'

But I was unwilling to leave the subject.

'All the same,' I said thoughtfully, 'Grandmother MacLeod's family were the lairds of Morven and the constables of the Castle of Kinlochaline. I bet you didn't know that.'

Aunt Edna snorted. 'Castle, my foot. She was born in Ontario, just like your Grandfather Connor, and her father was a horse doctor. Come on, kiddo, we'd better shut up and get down to business here.'

We worked in silence for a while.

'Aunt Edna—' I said at last, 'what about Mother? Why won't they let me go and see her?'

'Kids aren't allowed to visit maternity patients. It's tough for you, I know that. Look, Nessa, don't worry. If it doesn't start tonight, they're going to do the operation. She's getting the best of care.'

I stood there, holding the feather duster like a dead bird in my hands. I was not aware that I was going to speak until the words came out.

'I'm scared,' I said.

Aunt Edna put her arms around me, and her face looked all at once stricken and empty of defences.

'Oh, honey, I'm scared, too,' she said.

It was this way that Grandmother MacLeod found us when she came stepping lightly down into the front hall with the order in her hand for two dozen lace-bordered handkerchiefs of pure Irish linen.

I could not sleep that night, and when I went downstairs, I found my father in the den. I sat down on the hassock beside his chair, and he told me about the operation my mother was to have the next morning. He kept on saying it was not serious nowadays.

'But you're worried,' I put in, as though seeking to explain why I was.

'I should at least have been able to keep from burdening you with it,' he said in a distant voice, as though to himself. 'If only the baby hadn't got itself twisted around—'

'Will it be born dead, like the little girl?'

'I don't know,' my father said. 'I hope not.'

'She'd be disappointed, wouldn't she, if it was?' I said bleakly, wondering why I was not enough for her.

'Yes, she would,' my father replied. 'She won't be able to have any more, after this. It's partly on your account that she wants this one, Nessa. She doesn't want you to grow up without a brother or sister.'

'As far as I'm concerned, she didn't need to bother,' I retorted angrily.

My father laughed. 'Well, let's talk about something else, and then maybe you'll be able to sleep. How did you and Grandmother make out today?'

'Oh, fine, I guess. What was Grandfather MacLeod like, Dad?'

'What did she tell you about him?'

'She said he made a lot of money in his time.'

'Well, he wasn't any millionaire,' my father said, 'but I suppose he did quite well. That's not what I associate with him, though.'

He reached across to the bookshelf, took out a small leather-bound volume and opened it. On the pages were mysterious marks, like doodling, only much neater and more patterned.

'What is it?' I asked.

'Greek,' my father explained. 'This is a play called *Antigone*. See, here's the title in English. There's a whole stack of them on the shelves there. *Oedipus Rex*. *Electra*. *Medea*. They belonged to your Grandfather MacLeod. He used to read them often.'

'Why?' I enquired, unable to understand why anyone would pore over those undecipherable signs.

'He was interested in them,' my father said. 'He must have been a lonely man, although it never struck me that way at the time. Sometimes a thing only hits you a long time afterwards.'

'Why would he be lonely?' I wanted to know.

'He was the only person in Manawaka who could read these plays in the original Greek,' my father said. 'I don't suppose many people, if anyone, had even read them in English translations. Maybe he would have liked to be a classical scholar—I don't know. But his father was a doctor, so that's what he was. Maybe he would have liked to talk to somebody about these plays. They must have meant a lot to him.'

It seemed to me that my father was talking oddly. There was a sadness in his voice that I had never heard before, and I longed to say something that would make him feel better, but I could not, because I did not know what was the matter.

'Can you read this kind of writing?' I asked hesitantly.

My father shook his head. 'Nope. I was never very intellectual, I guess. Rod was always brighter than I, in school, but even he wasn't interested in learning Greek. Perhaps he would've been later, if he'd lived. As a kid, all I ever wanted to do was go into the merchant marine.'

'Why didn't you, then?'

'Oh well,' my father said offhandedly, 'a kid who'd never seen the sea wouldn't have made much of a sailor. I might have turned out to be the seasick type.'

I had lost interest now that he was speaking once more like himself.

'Grandmother MacLeod was pretty cross today about the girl,' I remarked.

'I know,' my father nodded. 'Well, we must be as nice as we can to her. Nessa, and after a while she'll be all right.'

Suddenly I did not care what I said.

'Why can't she be nice to us for a change?' I burst out. 'We're always the ones who have to be nice to her.'

My father put his hand down and slowly tilted my head until I was forced to look at him.

'Vanessa, he said, 'she's had troubles in her life which you really don't know much about. That's why she gets migraine sometimes and has to go to bed. It's not easy for her these days, either—the house is still the same, so she thinks other things should be, too. It hurts her when she finds they aren't.'

'I don't see—' I began.

'Listen,' my father said, 'you know we were talking about what people are interested in, like Grandfather MacLeod being interested in Greek plays? Well, your grandmother was interested in being a lady, Nessa, and for a long time it seemed to her that she was one.'

I thought of the Castle of Kinlochaline, and of horse doctors in Ontario.

'I didn't know—' I stammered.

'That's usually the trouble with most of us,' my father said. 'You go on up to bed now. I'll phone tomorrow from the hospital as soon as the operation's over.'

I did sleep at last, and in my dreams I could hear the caught sparrow fluttering in the attic, and the sound of my mother crying, and the voices of the dead children.

My father did not phone until afternoon. Grandmother MacLeod said I was being silly, for you could hear the phone ringing all over the house, but nevertheless I refused to move out of the den. I had never before examined my father's books, but now, at a loss for something to do, I took them out one by one and read snatches here and there. After I had been doing this for several hours, it dawned on me that most of the books were of the same kind. I looked again at the titles.

Seven-League Boots. Arabia Deserta. The Seven Pillars of Wisdom. Travels in Tibet. Count Lucknor the Sea Devil. And a hundred more. On a shelf by themselves were copies of the *National Geographic* magazine, which I looked at often enough, but never before with the puzzling compulsion which I felt now, as though I were on the verge of some discovery, something which I had to find out and yet did not want to know. I riffled through the picture-filled pages. Hibiscus and wild orchids grew in a soft-petalled confusion. The Himalayas stood lofty as gods, with the morning sun on their peaks of snow. Leopards snarled from the vined depths of a thousand jungles. Schooners buffetted their white sails like the wings of giant angcls against the great sea winds.

'What on earth are you doing?' Grandmother MacLeod enquired waspishly, from the doorway. You've got everything scattered all over the place. Pick it all up this minute, Vanessa, do you hear?'

So I picked up the books and magazines, and put them all neatly away, as I had been told to do.

When the telephone finally rang, I was afraid to answer it. At last I picked it up. My father sounded faraway, and the relief in his voice made it unsteady.

'It's okay, honey. Everything's fine. The boy was born alive and kicking after all. Your mother's pretty weak, but she's going to be all right.'

I could hardly believe it. I did not want to talk to anyone. I wanted to be by myself, to assimilate the presence of my brother, towards whom, without ever having seen him yet, I felt such tenderness and such resentment.

That evening, Grandmother MacLeod approached my father, who, still dazed with the unexpected gift of neither life now being threatened, at first did not take her seriously when she asked what they planned to call the child.

'Oh, I don't know. Hank, maybe, or Joe. Fauntleroy, perhaps.'

She ignored his levity.

'Ewen,' she said, 'I wish you would call him Roderick.'

My father's face changed. 'I'd rather not.'

'I think you should,' Grandmother MacLeod insisted, very quietly, but in a voice as pointed and precise as her silver nail-scissors.

'Don't you think Beth ought to decide?' my father asked.

'Beth will agree if you do.'

My father did not bother to deny something that even I knew to be true. He did not say anything. Then Grandmother MacLeod's voice, astonishingly, faltered a little.

'It would mean a great deal to me,' she said.

I remembered what she had told me—*When your Uncle Roderick got killed, I thought I would die. But I didn't die.* All at once, her feeling for that unknown dead man became a reality for me. And yet I held it against her, as well, for I could see that it had enabled her to win now.

'All right,' my father said tiredly. 'We'll call him Roderick.'

Then, alarmingly, he threw back his head and laughed.

'Roderick Dhu!' he cried. 'That's what you'll call him, isn't it? Black Roderick. Like before. Don't you remember? As though he were a character out of Sir Walter Scott, instead of an ordinary kid who—'

He broke off, and looked at her with a kind of desolation in his face.

'God, I'm sorry, Mother,' he said. 'I had no right to say that.'

Grandmother MacLeod did not flinch, or tremble, or indicate that she felt anything at all.

'I accept your apology, Ewen,' she said.

My mother had to stay in bed for several weeks after she arrived home. The baby's cot was kept in my parents' room, and I could go in and look at the small creature who lay there with his tightly closed fists and his feathery black hair. Aunt Edna came in to help each morning, and when she had finished the housework, she would have coffee with my mother. They kept the door closed, but this did not prevent me from eavesdropping, for there was an air register in the floor of the spare room, which was linked somehow with the register in my parents' room. If you put your ear to the iron grille, it was almost like a radio.

'Did you mind very much, Beth?' Aunt Edna was saying.

'Oh, it's not the name I mind,' my mother replied. 'It's just the fact that Ewen felt he had to. You know that Rod had only had the sight of one eye, didn't you?'

'Sure, I knew. So what?'

'There was only a year and half between Ewen and Rod,' my mother said, 'so they often went around together when they were youngsters. It was Ewen's air-rifle that did it.'

'Oh Lord,' Aunt Edna said heavily. 'I suppose she always blamed him?'

'No, I don't think it was so much that, really. It was how he felt himself. I think he even used to wonder sometimes if—but people shouldn't let themselves think like that, or they'd go crazy. Accidents do happen, after all. When the war came, Ewen joined up first. Rod should never have been in the Army at all, but he couldn't wait to get in. He must have lied about his eyesight. It wasn't so very noticeable unless you looked at him closely, and I don't suppose the medicals were very thorough in those days. He got in as a gunner, and Ewen applied to have him in the same company. He thought he might be able to watch out for him, I guess, Rod being—at a disadvantage. They were both only kids. Ewen was nineteen and Rod was eighteen when they went to France. And then the Somme. I don't know, Edna, I think Ewen felt that if Rod had had proper sight, or if he hadn't been in the same outfit and had been sent somewhere else—you know how people always think these things afterwards, not that it's ever a bit of use. Ewen wasn't there when Rod got hit. They'd lost each other somehow, and Ewen was looking for him, not bothering about anything else, you know, just frantically looking. Then he stumbled across him quite by chance. Rod was still alive, but—'

'Stop it, Beth,' Aunt Edna said. 'You're only upsetting yourself.'

'Ewen never spoke of it to me,' my mother went on, 'until once his mother showed me the letter he'd written to her at the time. It was a peculiar letter, almost formal, saying how gallantly Rod had died, and all that. I guess I shouldn't have, but I told him she'd shown it to me. He was very angry that she had. And then, as though for some reason he were terribly ashamed, he said—*I had to write something to her, but men don't really die like that, Beth. It wasn't that way at all.* It was only after the war that he decided to come back and study medicine and go into practice with his father.'

'Had Rod meant to?' Aunt Edna asked.

'I don't know,' my mother said slowly. 'I never felt I should ask Ewen that.'

Aunt Edna was gathering up the coffee things, for I could hear the clash of cups and saucers being stacked on the tray.

'You know what I heard her say to Vanessa once, Beth? *The MacLeods never tell lies*. Those were her exact words. Even then, I didn't know whether to laugh or cry.'

'Please, Edna—' my mother sounded worn out now. 'Don't.'

'Oh Glory,' Aunt Edna said remorsefully, 'I've got all the delicacy of a two-ton truck. I didn't mean Ewen, for heaven's sake. That wasn't what I meant at all. Here, let me plump up your pillows for you.'

Then the baby began to cry, so I could not hear anything more of interest. I took my bike and went out beyond Manawaka, riding aimlessly along the gravel highway. It was later summer, and the wheat had changed colour, but instead of being high and bronzed in the fields, it was stunted and desiccated, for there had been no rain again this year. But in the bluff where I stopped and crawled under the barbed wire fence and lay stretched out on the grass, the plentiful poplar leaves were turning to a luminous yellow and shone like church windows in the sun. I put my head down very close to the earth and looked at what was going on there. Grasshoppers with enormous eyes ticked and twitched around me, as though the dry air were perfect for their purposes. A ladybird laboured mightily to climb a blade of grass, fell off, and started all over again, seeming to be unaware that she possessed wings and could have flown up.

I thought of the accidents that might easily happen to a person—or, of course, might not happen, might happen to somebody else. I thought of the dead baby, my sister, who might as easily have been I. Would she, then, have been lying here in my place, the sharp grass making its small toothmarks on her brown arms, the sun warming her to the heart? I thought of the leather-bound volumes of Greek, and the six different kinds of iced cakes that used to be offered always in the MacLeod house, and the pictures of leopards and green seas. I thought of my brother, who had been born alive after all, and now had been given his life's name.

I could not really comprehend these things, but I sensed their strangeness, their disarray. I felt that whatever God might love in this world, it was certainly not order.

1970

Alice Munro

b. 1931

'I think the most attractive kind of writing at all is the single short story,' Alice Munro maintains. 'It satisfies me the way nothing else does.' Although Munro has written what she calls an 'episodic novel', *Lives of Girls and Women* (1971), and a book of 'linked stories', *Who Do You Think You Are?* (1978), she sees herself as 'essentially a short story writer'; she cannot explain precisely how this came to be: 'I've never known why I've chosen the short story form. I guess in a short story you impose discipline rather soon.'

Born in Wingham, Ontario, Munro grew up in small-town southwestern Ontario—the setting that has come to be her most favoured fictional terrain—and at the age of eighteen went to the University of Western Ontario. After two years at university, she married and moved to Vancouver. For more than two decades she lived in British Columbia, then returned to southwestern Ontario, and now lives in Clinton, a small town near Wingham.

Although Munro recognizes that writing fiction always involves what she calls 'trickery', she tries to write in a way that is 'as unobtrusive as possible, where there has been an attempt, as honest an attempt as one can make to get at what is really there.' In all her fiction, she achieves her finest effects by focusing on 'the surface of life', as she calls it: 'to me, just things in themselves are very important. I'm not a writer who is very concerned with ideas. I'm not an intellectual writer. I'm very, very excited by what you might call the surface of life, and it must be that this seems to me meaningful in a way I can't analyze or describe.'

As Munro's art develops, the plots of her stories become less linear, relying more on seemingly random memories to weave in and out of episodes that reveal the outlines of a character's past, the climate of a household or a relationship, or the ambience of a small town. Often characters will seem to present at least two faces to the world: one as mundane as kitchen linoleum, the other idiosyncratic, eccentric, or unpredictably violent. Her characters, and the lives they lead, come to appear both mundane and mysterious, banal and quirky at the same time. This is how 'Royal Beatings' unfolds, inviting readers to wonder at the relationships among Flo, Rose, and her father; looping backwards in time as Flo narrates the seemingly disconnected episode involving Hat Nettleton; and then moving into the future, beyond the moment of Rose's father beating her, to depict Flo in old age.

'Friend of My Youth' shows how seemingly effortlessly a Munro story can move from one layer of memory—here, the narrator's recurring dream of meeting her mother—into a deeper layer that takes us into another past, another story that at first seems unrelated to the opening episode. As the narrator recounts her mother's memories of boarding with Flora, Ellie, and Robert, the focus shifts away from the mother to the improbabilities of the relationships among this trio. At the same time, as the narrator and her mother imagine alternate stories to explain Flora's character, the story begins to return to its larger frame, depicting the relationship between mother and daughter; finally, the daughter begins to articulate an insight into her changed perception of her mother. Telling or remembering stories, then, becomes an imaginative pathway for narrators, characters, and readers, leading all of them to reconsider the shape and meaning of their lives.

'Royal Beatings' was first published in the 14 March 1977 issue of *The New Yorker* and then revised and collected in *Who Do You Think You Are?* 'Friend of My Youth' was first published in the 22 January 1990 issue of *The New Yorker* and then collected that year in the book of stories of the same title.

Royal Beatings

Royal Beating. That was Flo's promise. You are going to get one Royal Beating.

The word Royal lolled on Flo's tongue, took on trappings. Rose had a need to picture things, to pursue absurdities, that was stronger than the need to stay out of trouble, and instead of taking this threat to heart she pondered: how is a beating royal? She came up with a tree-lined avenue, a crowd of formal spectators, some white horses and black slaves. Someone knelt, and the blood came leaping out like banners. An occasion both savage and splendid. In real life they didn't approach such dignity, and it was only Flo who tried to supply the event with some high air of necessity and regret. Rose and her father soon got beyond anything presentable.

Her father was king of the royal beatings. Those Flo gave never amounted to much; they were quick cuffs and slaps dashed off while her attention remained elsewhere. You get out of my road, she would say. You mind your own business. You take that look off your face.

They lived behind a store in Hanratty, Ontario. There were four of them: Rose, her father, Flo, Rose's young half brother Brian. The store was really a house, bought by Rose's father and mother when they married and set up here in the furniture and upholstery repair business. Her mother could do upholstery. From both parents Rose should have inherited clever hands, a quick sympathy with materials, an eye for the nicest turns of mending, but she hadn't. She was clumsy, and when something broke she couldn't wait to sweep it up and throw it away.

Her mother had died. She said to Rose's father during the afternoon, 'I have a feeling that is so hard to describe. It's like a boiled egg in my chest, with the shell left on.' She died before night, she had a blood clot on her lung. Rose was a baby in a basket at the time, so of course could not remember any of this. She heard it from Flo, who must have heard it from her father. Flo came along soon afterwards, to take over Rose in the basket, marry her father, open up the front room to make a grocery store. Rose, who had known the house only as a store, who had known only Flo for a mother, looked back on the sixteen or so months her parents spent here as an orderly, far gentler, and more ceremonious time, with little touches of affluence. She had nothing to go on but some egg cups her mother had bought, with a pattern of vines and birds on them, delicately drawn as if with red ink; the pattern was beginning to wear away. No books or clothes or pictures of her mother remained. Her father must have got rid of them, or else Flo would. Flo's only story about her mother, the one about her death, was oddly grudging. Flo like the details of a death: the things people said, the way they protested or tried to get out of bed or swore or laughed (some did those things), but when she said that Rose's mother mentioned a hard-boiled egg in her chest she made the comparison sound slightly foolish, as if her mother really was the kind of person who might think you could swallow an egg whole.

Her father had a shed out behind the store, where he worked at his furniture repairing and restoring. He caned chair seats and backs, mended wickerwork, filled cracks, put legs back on, all most admirably and skillfully and cheaply. That was his pride: to startle people with such fine work, such moderate, even ridiculous charges. During the Depression people could not afford to pay more, perhaps, but he continued the practice through the war, through the years of prosperity after the war, until he died. He never discussed with Flo what he charged or what was owing. After he died she had to go out and unlock the shed and take all sorts of scraps of paper and torn envelopes from the big wicked-looking hooks that were his files. Many of these she found were not accounts or receipts at all but records of the weather, bits of information about the garden, things he had been moved to write down.

Ate new potatoes 25th June. Record.
Dark Day, 1880's, nothing supernatural. Clouds of ash from forest fire.
Aug 16, 1938. Giant thunderstorm in evng. Lightning str. Pres. Church, Turberry Twp. Will of God?
Scald strawberries to remove acid.
All things are alive. Spinoza.

Flo thought Spinoza must be some new vegetable he planned to grow, like broccoli or eggplant. He would often try some new thing. She showed the scrap of paper to Rose and asked, did she know what Spinoza was? Rose did know, or had an idea—she was in her teens by that time—but she replied that she did not. She had reached an age where she thought she could not stand to know any more, about her father, or about Flo; she pushed any discovery aside with embarrassment and dread.

There was a stove in the shed, and many rough shelves covered with cans of paint and varnish, shellac and turpentine, jars of soaking brushes and also some dark sticky bottles of cough medicine. Why should a man who coughed constantly, whose lungs took in a whiff of gas in the War (called, in Rose's earliest childhood, not the First, but the Last, War) spend all his days breathing fumes of paint and turpentine? At the time, such questions were not asked as often as they are now. On the bench outside Flo's store several old men from the neighbourhood sat gossiping, drowsing, in the warm weather, and some of these old men coughed all the time too. The fact is they were dying, slowly and discreetly, of what was called, without any particular sense of grievance, 'the foundry disease'. They had worked all their lives at the foundry in town, and now they sat still, with their wasted yellow faces, coughing, chuckling, drifting into aimless obscenity on the subject of women walking by, or any young girl on a bicycle.

From the shed came not only coughing, but speech, a continual muttering, reproachful or encouraging, usually just below the level at which separate words could be made out. Slowing down when her father was at a tricky piece of work, taking on a cheerful speed when he was doing something less demanding, sandpapering or painting. Now and then some words would break through and hang clear and nonsensical on the air. When he realized they were out, there would be a quick bit of cover-up coughing, a swallowing, an alert, unusual silence.

'Macaroni, pepperoni, Botticelli, beans—'

What could that mean? Rose used to repeat such things to herself. She could never ask him. The person who spoke these words and the person who spoke to her as her father were not the same, though they seemed to occupy the same space. It would be the worst sort of taste to acknowledge the person who was not supposed to be there; it would not be forgiven. Just the same, she loitered and listened.

The cloud-capped towers, she heard him say once.

'The cloud-capped towers, the gorgeous palaces.'

That was like a hand clapped against Rose's chest, not to hurt, but astonish her, to take her breath away. She had to run then, she had to get away. She knew that was enough to hear, and besides, what if he caught her? It would be terrible.

This was something the same as bathroom noises. Flo had saved up, and had a bathroom put in, but there was no place to put it except in a corner of the kitchen. The door did not fit, the walls were only beaverboard. The result was that even the tearing of a piece of toilet paper, the shifting of a haunch, was audible to those working or talking or eating in the kitchen. They were all familiar with each other's nether voices, not only in their more explosive moments but in their intimate sighs and growls and pleas and statements. And they were all most prudish people. So no one ever seemed to hear, or be listening, and no reference was made. The person creating the noises in the bathroom was not connected with the person who walked out.

They lived in a poor part of town. There was Hanratty and West Hanratty, with the river flowing between them. This was West Hanratty. In Hanratty the social structure ran from doctors and dentists and lawyers down to foundry workers and factory workers and draymen; in West Hanratty it ran from factory workers and foundry workers down to large improvident families of casual bootleggers and prostitutes and unsuccessful thieves. Rose thought of her own family as straddling the river, belonging nowhere, but that was not true. West Hanratty was where the store was and they were, on the straggling tail end of the main street. Across the road from them was a blacksmith shop, boarded up about the time the war started, and a house that had been another store at one time. The Salada Tea sign had never been taken out of the front window; it remained as a proud and interesting decoration though there was no Salada Tea for sale inside. There was just a bit of sidewalk, too cracked and tilted for roller-skating, though Rose longed for roller skates and often pictured herself whizzing along in a plaid skirt, agile and fashionable. There was one street light, a tin flower; then the amenities gave up and there were dirt roads and boggy places, front-yard dumps and strange-looking houses. What made the houses strange-looking were the attempts to keep them from going completely to ruin. With some the attempt had never been made. These were grey and rotted and leaning over, falling into a landscape of scrub hollows, frog ponds, cattails and nettles. Most houses, however, had been patched up with tarpaper, a few fresh shingles, sheets of tin, hammered-out stovepipes, even cardboard. This was, of course, in the days before the war, days of what would later be legendary poverty, from which Rose would remember mostly low-down things—serious-looking anthills and wooden steps, and a cloudy, interesting, problematical light on the world.

There was a long truce between Flo and Rose in the beginning. Rose's nature was growing like a prickly pineapple, but slowly, and secretly, hard pride and scepticism overlapping, to make something surprising even to herself. Before she was old enough to go to school, and while Brian was still in the baby carriage, Rose stayed in the store with both of them—Flo sitting on the high stool behind the counter, Brian asleep by the window; Rose knelt or lay on the wide creaky floorboards working with crayons on pieces of brown paper too torn or irregular to be used for wrapping.

People who came to the store were mostly from the houses around. Some country people came too, on their way home from town, and a few people from Hanratty, who walked across the bridge. Some people were always on the main street, in and out of stores, as if it was their duty to be always on display and their right to be welcomed. For instance, Becky Tyde.

Becky Tyde climbed upon Flo's counter, made room for herself beside an open tin of crumbly jam-filled cookies.

'Are these any good?' she said to Flo, and boldly began to eat one. 'When are you going to give us a job, Flo?'

'You could go and work in the butcher shop,' said Flo innocently. 'You could go and work for your brother.'

'Roberta?' said Becky with a stagey sort of contempt. 'You think I'd work for him?' Her brother who ran the butcher shop was named Robert but often called Roberta, because of his meek and nervous ways. Becky Tyde laughed. Her laugh was loud and noisy like an engine bearing down on you.

She was a big-headed loud-voiced dwarf, with a mascot's sexless swagger, a red velvet tam, a twisted neck that forced her to hold her head on one side, always looking up and sideways. She wore little polished high-heeled shoes, real lady's shoes. Rose watched her shoes, being scared of the rest of her, of her laugh and her neck. She knew from Flo that Becky Tyde had been sick with polio as a child, that was why her neck was twisted and why she had not grown any taller. It was hard to believe that she had started out differently, that she had ever been normal. Flo said she was not cracked, she had as much brains as anybody, but she knew she could get away with anything.

'You know I used to live out here?' Becky said, noticing Rose. 'Hey! What's-your-name! Didn't I used to live out here, Flo?'

'If you did it was before my time,' said Flo, as if she didn't know anything.

'That was before the neighbourhood got so downhill. Excuse me saying so. My father built his house out here and he built his slaughterhouse and we had half an acre of orchard.'

'Is that so?' said Flo, using her humouring voice, full of false geniality, humility even. 'Then why did you ever move away?'

'I told you, it got to be such a downhill neighbourhood,' said Becky. She would put a whole cookie in her mouth if she felt like it, let her cheeks puff out like a frog's. She never told any more.

Flo knew anyway, as who didn't. Everyone knew the house, red brick with the veranda pulled off and the orchard, what was left of it, full of the usual outflow—car seats and washing machines and bedsprings and junk. The house would never look sinister, in spite of what had happened in it, because there was so much wreckage and confusion all around.

Becky's old father was a different kind of butcher from her brother according to Flo. A bad-tempered Englishman. And different from Becky in the matter of mouthiness. His was never open. A skinflint, a family tyrant. After Becky had polio he wouldn't let her go back to school. She was seldom seen outside the house, never outside the yard. He didn't want people gloating. That was what Becky said, at the trial. Her mother was dead by that time and her sisters married. Just Becky and Robert at home. People would stop Robert on the road and ask him, 'How about your sister, Robert? Is she altogether better now?'

'Yes.'

'Does she do the housework? Does she get your supper?'

'Yes.'

'And is your father good to her, Robert?'

The story being that the father beat them, had beaten all his children and beaten his wife as well, beat Becky more now because of her deformity, which some people believed he had caused (they did not understand about polio). The stories persisted and got added to. The reason that Becky was kept out of sight was now supposed to be her pregnancy, and the father of the child was supposed to be her own father. Then people said it had been born, and disposed of.

'What?'

'Disposed of,' Flo said. 'They used to say go and get your lamp chops at Tyde's, get them nice and tender! It was all lies in all probability,' she said regretfully.

Rose could be drawn back—from watching the wind shiver along the old torn awning, catch in the tear—by this tone of regret, caution, in Flo's voice. Flo telling a story—and this was not the only one, or even the most lurid one, she knew—would incline her head and let her face go soft and thoughtful, tantalizing, warning.

'I shouldn't even be telling you this stuff.'

More was to follow.

Three useless young men, who hung around the livery stable, got together—or were got together, by more influential and respectful men in town—and prepared to give old man Tyde a horsewhipping, in the interests of the public morality. They blacked their faces. They were provided with whips and a quart of whisky apiece, for courage. They were: Jelly Smith, a horse-racer and a drinker; Bob Temple, a ball-player and strongman; and Hat Nettleton, who worked on the town dray, and had his nickname from a bowler hat he wore, out of vanity as much as for the comic effect. (He still worked on the dray, in fact; he had kept the name if not the hat, and could often be seen in public—almost as often as Becky Tyde—delivering sacks of coal, which blackened his face and arms. That should have brought to mind his story, but didn't. Present time and past, the shady melodramatic past of Flo's stories, were quite separate, at least for Rose. Present people could not be fitted into the past. Becky herself, town oddity and public pet, harmless and malicious, could never match the butcher's prisoner, the cripple daughter, a white streak at the window: mute, beaten, impregnated. As with the house, only a formal connection could be made.)

The young men primed to do the horsewhipping showed up late, outside Tyde's house, after everybody had gone to bed. They had a gun, but they used up their ammunition firing it off in the yard. They yelled for the butcher and beat on the door; finally they broke it down. Tyde concluded they were after his money, so he put some bills in a handkerchief and sent Becky down with them, maybe thinking those men would be touched or scared by the sight of a little wry-necked girl, a dwarf. But that didn't content them. They came upstairs and dragged the butcher out from under his bed, in his nightgown. They dragged him outside and stood him in the snow. The temperature was four below zero, a fact noted later in court. They meant to hold a mock trial but they could not remember how it was done. So they began to beat him and kept beating him until he fell. They yelled at him, *Butcher's meat*! and continued beating him while his nightgown and the snow he was lying in turned red. His son Robert said in court that he had not watched the beating. Becky said that Robert had watched at first but had run away and hid. She herself had watched all the way through. She watched the men leave at last and her father make his delayed bloody progress through the snow and up the steps of the veranda. She did not go out to help him, or open the door until he got to it. Why not? she was asked in court, and she said she did not go out because she just had her nightgown on, and she did not open the door because she did not want to let the cold into the house.

Old man Tyde then appeared to have recovered his strength. He sent Robert to harness the horse, and made Becky heat water so that he could wash. He dressed and took all the money and with no explanation to his children got into the cutter and drove to Belgrave where he left the horse tied in the cold and took the early morning train to Toronto. On the train he behaved oddly, groaning and cursing as if he was drunk. He was picked up on the streets of Toronto a day later, out of his mind with fever, and was taken to hospital, where he died. He still had all the money. The cause of death was given as pneumonia.

But the authorities got wind, Flo said. The case came to trial. The three men who did it all received long prison sentences. A farce, said Flo. Within a year they were all free, had all been pardoned, had jobs waiting for them. And why was that? It was because too many higher-ups were in on it. And it seemed as if Becky and Robert had no interest in seeing justice done. They were left well-off. They bought a house in Hanratty. Robert went into the store. Becky after her long seclusion started on a career of public sociability and display.

That was all. Flo put the lid down on the story as if she was sick of it. It reflected no good on anybody.

'Imagine,' Flo said.

Flo at this time must have been in her early thirties. A young woman. She wore exactly the same clothes that a woman of fifty, or sixty, or seventy, might wear: print housedresses loose at the neck and sleeves as well as the waist; bib aprons, also of print, which she took off when she came from the kitchen into the store. This was a common costume at the time, for a poor though not absolutely poverty-stricken woman; it was also, in a way, a scornful deliberate choice. Flo scorned slacks, she scorned the outfits of people trying to be in style, she scorned lipstick and permanents. She wore her own black hair cut straight across, just long enough to push behind her ears. She was tall but fine-boned, with narrow wrists and shoulders, a small head, a pale, freckled, mobile, monkeyish face. If she had thought it worthwhile, and had the resources, she might have had a black-and-pale, fragile, nurtured sort of prettiness; Rose realized that later. But she would have to have been a different person altogether; she would have to have learned to resist making faces, at herself and others.

Rose's earliest memories of Flo were of extraordinary softness and hardness. The soft hair, the long, soft, pale cheeks, soft almost invisible fuzz in front of her ears and above her mouth. The sharpness of her knees, hardness of her lap, flatness of her front.

When Flo sang:

Oh the buzzin' of the bees in the cigarette trees
And the soda-water fountain . . .

Rose thought of Flo's old life before she married her father, when she worked as a waitress in the coffee shop in Union Station, and went with her girl friends Mavis and Irene to Centre Island, and was followed by men on dark streets and knew how pay-phones and elevators worked. Rose heard in her voice the reckless dangerous life of cities, the gum-chewing sharp answers.

And when she sang:

Then slowly, slowly, she got up
And slowly she came nigh him
And all she said, that she ever did say,
Was young man I think, you're dyin'!

Rose thought of a life Flo seemed to have had beyond that, earlier than that, crowded and legendary, with Barbara Allen and Becky Tyde's father and all kinds of old outrages and sorrows jumbled up together in it.

The royal beatings. What got them started?

Suppose a Saturday, in spring. Leaves not out yet but the doors open to the sunlight. Crows. Ditches full of running water. Hopeful weather. Often on Saturdays Flo left Rose in charge of the store—it's a few years now, these are the years when Rose was nine, ten, eleven, twelve—while she herself went across the bridge to Hanratty (going uptown they called it) to shop and see people, and listen to them. Among the people she listened to were Mrs Lawyer Davies, Mrs Anglican Rector Henley-Smith, and Mrs Horse-Doctor McKay. She came home and imitated them at supper: their high-flown remarks, their flibberty voices. Monsters, she made them seem; of foolishness, and showiness, and self-approbation.

When she finished shopping she went into the coffee shop of the Queen's Hotel and had a sundae. What kind? Rose and Brian wanted to know when she got home, and they would be disappointed if it was only pineapple or butterscotch, pleased if it was a Tin Roof, or Black and White. Then she smoked a cigarette. She had some ready-rolled, that she carried with her, so that she wouldn't have to roll one in public. Smoking was the one thing she did that she would have called showing off in anybody else. It was a habit left over from her working days, from Toronto. She knew it was asking for trouble. Once the Catholic priest came over to her right in the Queen's Hotel, and flashed his lighter at her before she could get her matches out. She thanked him but did not enter into conversation, lest he should try to convert her.

Another time, on the way home, she saw at the town end of the bridge a boy in a blue jacket, apparently looking at the water. Eighteen, nineteen years old. Nobody she knew. Skinny, weakly looking, something the matter with him, she saw at once. Was he thinking of jumping? Just as she came up even with him, what does he do but turn and display, holding his jacket open, also his pants. What he must have suffered from the cold, on a day that had Flo holding her coat collar tight around her throat.

When she first saw what he had in his hand, Flo said, all she could think of was, what is he doing out here with a baloney sausage?

She could say that. It was offered as truth; no joke. She maintained that she despised dirty talk. She would go out and yell at the old men sitting in front of her store.

'If you want to stay where you are you better clean your mouths out!'

Saturday, then. For some reason Flo is not going uptown, has decided to stay home and scrub the kitchen floor. Perhaps this has put her in a bad mood. Perhaps she was in a bad mood anyway, due to people not paying their bills, or the stirring-up of feelings in spring. The wrangle with Rose has already commenced, has been going on forever, like a dream that goes back and back into other dreams, over hills and through doorways, maddeningly dim and populous and familiar and elusive. They are carting all the chairs out of the kitchen preparatory to the scrubbing, and they have also got to move some extra provisions for the store, some cartons of canned goods, tins of maple syrup, coal-oil cans, jars of vinegar. They take these things out to the woodshed. Brian who is five or six by this time is helping drag the tins.

'Yes,' says Flo, carrying on from our lost starting-point. 'Yes, and that filth you taught to Brian.'

'What filth?'

'And he doesn't know any better.'

There is one step down from the kitchen to the woodshed, a bit of carpet on it so worn Rose can't ever remember seeing the pattern. Brian loosens it, dragging a tin.

'Two Vancouvers,' she says softly.

Flo is back in the kitchen. Brian looks from Flo to Rose and Rose says again in a slightly louder voice, an encouraging sing-song, 'Two Vancouvers—'

'Fried in snot!' finishes Brian, not able to control himself any longer.

'Two pickled arseholes—'

'—tied in a knot!'

There it is. The filth.

Two Vancouvers fried in snot!
Two pickled arseholes tied in a knot!

Rose has known that for years, learned it when she first went to school. She came home and asked Flo, what is a Vancouver?

'It's a city. It's a long ways away.'

'What else besides a city?'

Flo said, what did she mean, what else? How could it be fried, Rose said, approaching the dangerous moment, the delightful moment, when she would have to come out with the whole thing.

'Two Vancouvers fried in snot!/Two pickled arseholes tied in a knot!'

'You're going to get it!' cried Flo in a predictable rage. 'Say that again and you'll get a good clout!'

Rose couldn't stop herself. She hummed it tenderly, tried saying the innocent words aloud, humming through the others. It was not just the words snot and arsehole that gave her pleasure, though of course they did. It was the pickling and tying and the unimaginable Vancouvers. She saw them in her mind shaped rather like octopuses, twitching in the pan. The tumble of reason; the spark and spit of craziness.

Lately she has remembered it again and taught it to Brian, to see if it has the same effect on him, and of course it has.

'Oh, I heard you!' says Flo. 'I heard that! And I'm warning you!'

So she is. Brian takes the warning. He runs away, out the woodshed door, to do as he likes. Being a boy, free to help or not, involve himself or not. Not committed to the household struggle. They don't need him anyway, except to use against each other, they hardly notice his going. They continue, can't help continuing, can't leave each other alone. When they seem to have given up they were really just waiting and building up steam.

Flo gets out the scrub pail and the brush and the rag and the pad for her knees, a dirty red rubber pad. She starts to work on the floor. Rose sits on the kitchen table, the only place left to sit, swinging her legs. She can feel the cool oilcloth, because she is wearing shorts, last summer's tight faded shorts dug out of the summer-clothes bag. They smell a bit mouldy from winter storage.

Flo crawls around underneath, scrubbing with the brush, wiping with the rag. Her legs are long, white and muscular, marked all over with blue veins as if somebody had been drawing rivers on them with an indelible pencil. An abnormal energy, a violent disgust, is expressed in the chewing of the brush at the linoleum, the swish of the rag.

What do they have to say to each other? It doesn't really matter. Flo speaks of Rose's smart-aleck behaviour, rudeness and sloppiness and conceit. Her willingness to make work for others, her lack of gratitude. She mentions Brian's innocence, Rose's corruption. Oh, don't you think you're somebody, says Flo, and a moment later, Who do you think you are? Rose contradicts and objects with such poisonous reasonableness and mildness, displays theatrical unconcern. Flo goes beyond her ordinary scorn and self-possession and becomes amazingly theatrical herself, saying it was for Rose that she sacrificed her life. She saw her father saddled with a baby daughter and she thought, what is that man going to do? So she married him, and here she is, on her knees.

At that moment the bell rings, to announce a customer in the store. Because the fight is on, Rose is not permitted to go into the store and wait on whoever it is. Flo gets up and throws off her apron, groaning—but not communicatively, it is not a groan whose exasperation Rose is allowed to share—and goes in and serves. Rose hears her using her normal voice.

'About time! Sure is!'

She comes back and ties on her apron and is ready to resume.

'You never have a thought for anybody but your ownself! You never have a thought for what I'm doing.'

'I never asked you to do anything. I wished you never had. I would have been a lot better off.'

Rose says this smiling directly at Flo, who has not yet gone down on her knees. Flo sees the smile, grabs the scrub rag that is hanging on the side of the pail, and throws it at her. It may be meant to hit her in the face but instead it falls against Rose's leg and she raises her foot and catches it, swinging it negligently against her ankle.

'All right,' says Flo. 'You've done it this time. All right.'

Rose watches her go to the woodshed door, hears her tramp through the woodshed, pause in the doorway, where the screen door hasn't yet been hung, and the storm door is standing open, propped with a brick. She calls Rose's father. She calls him in a warning, summoning voice, as if against her will preparing him for bad news. He will know what this is about.

The kitchen floor has five or six different patterns of linoleum on it. Ends, which Flo got for nothing and ingeniously trimmed and fitted together, bordering them with tin strips and tacks. While Rose sits on the table waiting, she looks at the floor, at this satisfying arrangement of rectangles, triangles, some other shape whose name she is trying to remember. She hears Flo coming back through the woodshed, on the creaky plank walk laid over the dirt floor. She is loitering, waiting, too. She and Rose can carry this no further, by themselves.

Rose hears her father come in. She stiffens, a tremor runs through her legs, she feels them shiver on the oilcloth. Called away from some peaceful, absorbing task, away from the words running in his head, called out of himself, her father has to say something. He says, 'Well? What's wrong?'

Now comes another voice of Flo's. Enriched, hurt, apologetic, it seems to have been manufactured on the spot. She is sorry to have called him from his work. Would never have done it, if Rose was not driving her to distraction. How to distraction? With her back-talk and impudence and her terrible tongue. The things Rose has said to Flo are such that, if Flo had said them to her mother, she knows her father would have thrashed her into the ground.

Rose tries to butt in, to say this isn't true.

What isn't true?

Her father raises a hand, doesn't look at her, says, 'Be quiet.'

When she says it isn't true, Rose means that she herself didn't start this, only responded, that she was goaded by Flo, who is now, she believes, telling the grossest sort of lies, twisting everything to suit herself. Rose puts aside her other knowledge that whatever Flo has said or done, whatever she herself has said or done, does not really matter at all. It is the struggle itself that counts, and that can't be stopped, can never be stopped, short of where it has got to, now.

Flo's knees are dirty, in spite of the pad. The scrub rag is still hanging over Rose's foot.

Her father wipes his hands, listening to Flo. He takes his time. He is slow at getting into the spirit of things, tired in advance, maybe, on the verge of rejecting the role he has to play. He won't look at Rose, but at any sound or stirring from Rose, he holds up his hand.

'Well we don't need the public in on this, that's for sure,' Flo says, and she goes to lock the door of the store, putting in the store window the sign that says 'Back Soon', a sign Rose made for her with a great deal of fancy curving and shading of letters in black and red crayon. When she comes back she shuts the door to the store, then the door to the stairs, then the door to the woodshed.

Her shoes have left marks on the clean wet part of the floor.

'Oh, I don't know,' she says now, in a voice worn down from its emotional peak. 'I don't know what to do about her.' She looks down and sees her dirty knees (following Rose's eyes) and rubs at them viciously with her bare hands, smearing the dirt around.

'She humiliates me,' she says, straightening up. There it is, the explanation. 'She humiliates me,' she repeats with satisfaction. 'She has no respect.'

'I do not!'

'Quiet, you!' says her father.

'If I hadn't called your father you'd still be sitting there with that grin on your face! What other way is there to manage you?'

Rose detects in her father some objections to Flo's rhetoric, some embarrassment and reluctance. She is wrong, and ought to know she is wrong, in thinking that she can count on this. The fact that she knows about it, and he knows she knows, will not make things any better. He is beginning to warm up. He gives her a look. This look is at first cold and challenging. It informs her of his judgement, of the hopelessness of her position. Then it clears, it begins to fill up with something else, the way a spring fills up when you clear the leaves away. It fills with hatred and pleasure. Rose sees that and knows it. Is that just a description of anger, should she see his eyes filling up with anger? No. Hatred is right. Pleasure is right. His face loosens and changes and grows younger, and he holds up his hand this time to silence Flo.

'All right,' he says, meaning that's enough, more than enough, this part is over, things can proceed. He starts to loosen his belt.

Flo has stopped anyway. She has the same difficulty Rose does, a difficulty in believing that what you know must happen really will happen, that there comes a time when you can't draw back.

'Oh, I don't know, don't be too hard on her.' She is moving around nervously as if she has thoughts of opening some escape route. 'Oh, you don't have to use the belt on her. Do you have to use the belt?'

He doesn't answer. The belt is coming off, not hastily. It is being grasped at the necessary point. *All right you.* He is coming over to Rose. He pushes her off the table. His face, like his voice, is quite out of character. He is like a bad actor, who turns a part grotesque. As if he must savour and insist on just what is shameful and terrible about this. That is not to say he is pretending, that he is acting, and does not mean it. He is acting, and he means it. Rose knows that, she knows everything about him.

She has since wondered about murders, and murderers. Does the thing have to be carried through, in the end, partly for the effect, to prove to the audience of one—who won't be able to report, only register, the lesson—that such a thing can happen, that there is nothing that can't happen, that the most dreadful antic is justified, feelings can be found to match it?

She tries again looking at the kitchen floor, that clever and comforting geometrical arrangement, instead of looking at him or his belt. How can this go on in front of such daily witnesses—the linoleum, the calendar with the mill and creek and autumn trees, the old accommodating pots and pans?

Hold out your hand!

Those things aren't going to help her, none of them can rescue her. They turn bland and useless, even unfriendly. Pots can show malice, the patterns of linoleum can leer up at you, treachery is the other side of dailiness.

At the first, or maybe the second, crack of pain, she draws back. She will not accept it. She runs around the room, she tries to get to the doors. Her father blocks her off. Not an ounce of courage or of stoicism in her, it would seem. She runs, she screams, she implores. Her father is after her, cracking the belt at her when he can, then abandoning it and using his hands. Bang over the ear, then bang over the other ear. Back and forth, her head ringing. Bang in the face. Up against the wall and bang in her face again. He shakes her and hits her against the wall, he kicks her legs. She is incoherent, insane, shrieking. *Forgive me! Oh please, forgive me*!

Flo is shrieking too. *Stop, stop*!

Not yet. He throws Rose down. Or perhaps she throws herself down. He kicks her legs again. She has given up on words but is letting out a noise, the sort of noise that makes Flo cry, *Oh, what if people can hear her*? The very last-ditch willing sound of humiliation and defeat it is, for it seems Rose must play her part in this with the same grossness, the same exaggeration, that her father displays, playing his. She plays his victim with a self-indulgence that arouses, and maybe hopes to arouse, his final, sickened contempt.

They will give this anything that is necessary, it seems, they will go to any lengths.

Not quite. He has never managed to really injure her, though there are times, of course, when she prays that he will. He hits her with an open hand, there is some restraint in his kicks.

Now he stops, he is out of breath. He allows Flo to move in, he grabs Rose up and gives her a push in Flo's direction, making a sound of disgust. Flo retrieves her, opens the stair door, shoves her up the stairs.

'Go on up to your room now! Hurry!'

Rose goes up the stairs, stumbling, letting herself stumble, letting herself fall against the steps. She doesn't bang her door because a gesture like that could still bring him after her, and anyway, she is weak. She lies on the bed. She can hear through the stovepipe hole Flo snuffling and remonstrating, her father saying angrily that Flo should have kept quiet then, if she did not want Rose punished she should not have recommended it. Flo says she never recommended a hiding like that.

They argue back and forth on this. Flo's frightened voice is growing stronger, getting its confidence back. By stages, by arguing, they are being drawn back into themselves. Soon it's only Flo talking; he will not talk any more. Rose has had to fight down her noisy sobbing, so as to listen to them, and when she loses interest in listening, and wants to sob some more, she finds she can't work herself up to it. She has passed into a state of calm, in which outrage is perceived as complete and final. In this state events and possibilities take on a lovely simplicity. Choices are mercifully clear. The words that come to mind are not the quibbling, seldom the conditional. Never is a word to which the right is suddenly established. She will never speak to them, she will never look at them with anything but loathing, she will never forgive them. She will punish them; she will finish them. Encased in these finalities, and in her bodily pain, she floats in curious comfort, beyond herself, beyond responsibility.

Suppose she dies now? Suppose she commits suicide? Suppose she runs away? Any of these things would be appropriate. It is only a matter of choosing, of figuring out the way. She floats in her pure superior state as if kindly drugged.

And just as there is a moment, when you are drugged, in which you feel perfectly safe, sure, unreachable, and then without warning and right next to it a moment in which you know the whole protection has fatally cracked, though it is still pretending to hold soundly together, so there is a moment now—the moment, in fact, when Rose hears Flo step on the stairs—that contains for her both present peace and freedom and a sure knowledge of the whole down-spiralling course of events from now on.

Flo comes into the room without knocking, but with a hesitation that shows it might have occurred to her. She brings a jar of cold cream. Rose is hanging on to advantage as long as she can, lying face down on the bed, refusing to acknowledge or answer.

'Oh come on,' Flo says uneasily. 'You aren't so bad off, are you? You put some of this on and you'll feel better.'

She is bluffing. She doesn't know for sure what damage has been done.

She has the lid off the cold cream. Rose can smell it. The intimate, babyish, humiliating smell. She won't allow it near her. But in order to avoid it, the big ready clot of it in Flo's hand, she has to move. She scuffles, resists, loses dignity, and lets Flo see there is not really much the matter.

'All right,' Flo says. 'You win. I'll leave it here and you can put it on when you like.'

Later still a tray will appear. Flo will put it down without a word and go away. A large glass of chocolate milk on it, made with Vita-Malt from the store. Some rich streaks of Vita-Malt around the bottom of the glass. Little sandwiches, neat and appetizing. Canned salmon of the first quality and reddest color, plenty of mayonnaise. A couple of butter tarts from a bakery package, chocolate biscuits with a peppermint filling. Rose's favourites, in the sandwich, tart and cookie line. She will turn away, refuse to look, but left alone with these eatables will be miserably tempted, roused and troubled and drawn back from thoughts of suicide or flight by the smell of salmon, the anticipation of crisp chocolate, she will reach out a finger, just to run it around the edge of one of the sandwiches (crusts cut off!) to get the overflow, get a taste. Then she will decide to eat one, for strength to refuse the rest. One will not be noticed. Soon, in helpless corruption, she will eat them all. She will drink the chocolate milk, eat the tarts, eat the cookies. She will get the malty syrup out of the bottom of the glass with her finger, though she sniffles with shame. Too late.

Flo will come up and get the tray. She may say, 'I see you got your appetite still,' or, 'Did you like the chocolate milk, was it enough syrup in it?' depending on how chastened she is feeling, herself. At any rate, all advantage will be lost. Rose will understand that life has started up again, that they will all sit around the table eating again, listening to the radio news. Tomorrow morning, maybe even tonight. Unseemly and unlikely as that may be. They will be embarrassed, but rather less than you might expect considering how they have behaved. They will feel a queer lassitude, a convalescent indolence, not far off satisfaction.

One night after a scene like this they were all in the kitchen. It must have been summer, or at least warm weather, because her father spoke of the old men who sat on the bench in front of the store.

'Do you know what they're talking about now?' he said, and nodded his head towards the store to show who he meant, though of course they were not there now, they went home at dark.

'Those old coots,' said Flo. 'What?'

There was about them both a geniality not exactly false but a bit more emphatic than was normal, without company.

Rose's father told them then that the old men had picked up the idea somewhere that what looked like a star in the western sky, the first star that came out after sunset, the evening star, was in reality an airship hovering over Bay City, Michigan, on the other side of Lake Huron. An American invention, sent up to rival the heavenly bodies. They were all in agreement about this, the idea was congenial to them. They believed it to be lit by ten thousand electric light bulbs. Her father had ruthlessly disagreed with them, pointing out that it was the planet Venus they saw, which had appeared in the sky long before the invention of an electric light bulb. They had never heard of the planet Venus.

'Ignoramuses,' said Flo. At which Rose knew, and knew her father knew, that Flo had never heard of the planet Venus either. To distract them from this, or even apologize for it, Flo put down her teacup, stretched out with her head resting on the chair she had been sitting on and her feet on another chair (somehow she managed to tuck her dress modestly between her legs at the same time), and lay stiff as a board, so that Brian cried out in delight, 'Do that! Do that!'

Flo was double-jointed and very strong. In moments of celebration or emergency she would do tricks.

They were silent while she turned herself around, not using her arms at all but just her strong legs and feet. Then they all cried out in triumph, though they had seen it before.

Just as Flo turned herself Rose got a picture in her mind of that airship, an elongated transparent bubble, with its strings of diamond lights, floating in the miraculous American sky.

'The planet Venus!' her father said, applauding Flo. 'Ten thousand electric lights!'

There was a feeling of permission, relaxation, even a current of happiness, in the room.

Years later, many years later, on a Sunday morning, Rose turned on the radio. This was when she was living by herself in Toronto.

Well sir.

It was a different kind of a place in our day. Yes it was.

It was all horses then. Horses and buggies. Buggy races up and down the main street on the Saturday nights.

'Just like the chariot races,' says the announcer's, or interviewer's, smooth encouraging voice.

I never seen a one of them.

'No sir, that was the old Roman chariot races I was referring to. That was before your time.'

Musta been before my time. I'm a hunerd and two years old.

'That's a wonderful age, sir.'

It is so.

She left it on, as she went around the apartment kitchen, making coffee for herself. It seemed to her that this must be a staged interview, a scene from some play, and she wanted to find out what it was. The old man's voice was so vain and belligerent, the interviewer's quite hopeless and alarmed, under its practised gentleness and ease. You were surely meant to see him holding the microphone up to some toothless, reckless, preening centenarian, wondering what in God's name he was doing here, and what would he say next?

'They must have fairly dangerous.'

What was dangerous?

'Those buggy races.'

They was. Dangerous. Used to be the runaway horses. Used to be a-plenty of accidents. Fellows was dragged along on the gravel and cut their face open. Wouldna matter so much if they was dead. Heh.

Some of them horses was the high-steppers. Some, they had to have the mustard under their tail. Some wouldn step out for nothin. That's the thing it is with the horses. Some'll work and pull till they drop down dead and some wouldn pull your cock out of a pail of lard. Hehe.

It must be a real interview after all. Otherwise they wouldn't have put that in, wouldn't have risked it. It's all right if the old man says it. Local colour. Anything rendered harmless and delightful by his hundred years.

Accidents all the time then. In the mill. Foundry. Wasn't the precautions.

'You didn't have so many strikes then, I don't suppose? You didn't have so many unions?'

Everybody taking it easy nowadays. We worked and we was glad to get it. Worked and was glad to get it.

'You didn't have television.'

Didn't have no T.V. Didn't have no radio. No picture show.

'You made your own entertainment.'

That's the way we did.

'You had a lot of experiences young men growing up today will never have.'

Experiences.

'Can you recall any of them for us?'

I eaten groundhog meat one time. One winter. You wouldna cared for it. Heh.

There was a pause, of appreciation, it would seem, then the announcer's voice saying that the foregoing had been an interview with Mr Wilfred Nettleton of Hanratty, Ontario, made on his hundred and second birthday, two weeks before his death, last spring. A living link with our past. Mr Nettleton had been interviewed in the Wawanash County Home for the Aged.

Hat Nettleton.

Horsewhipper into centenarian. Photographed on his birthday, fussed over by nurses, kissed no doubt by a girl reporter. Flash bulbs popping at him. Tape recorder drinking in the sound of his voice. Oldest resident. Oldest horsewhipper. Living link with our past.

Looking out from her kitchen window at the cold lake, Rose was longing to tell somebody. It was Flo who would enjoy hearing. She thought of her saying *Imagine*! in a way that meant she was having her worst suspicions gorgeously confirmed. But Flo was in the same place Hat

Nettleton had died in, and there wasn't any way Rose could reach her. She had been there even when that interview was recorded, though she would not have heard it, would not have known about it. After Rose put her in the Home, a couple of years earlier, she had stopped talking. She had removed herself, and spent most of her time sitting in a corner of her crib, looking crafty and disagreeable, not answering anybody, though she occasionally showed her feelings by biting a nurse.

1977

Friend of My Youth

I used to dream about my mother, and though the details in the dream varied, the surprise in it was always the same. The dream stopped, I suppose because it was too transparent in its hopefulness, too easy in its forgiveness.

In the dream I would be the age I really was, living the life I was really living, and I would discover that my mother was still alive. (The fact is, she died when I was in my early twenties and she in her early fifties.) Sometimes I would find myself in our old kitchen, where my mother would be rolling out piecrust on the table, or washing the dishes in the battered cream-coloured dishpan with the red rim. But other times I would run into her on the street, in places where I would never have expected to see her. She might be walking through a handsome hotel lobby, or lining up in an airport. She would be looking quite well—not exactly youthful, not entirely untouched by the paralysing disease that held her in its grip for a decade or more before her death, but so much better than I remembered that I would be astonished. Oh, I just have this little tremor in my arm, she would say, and a little stiffness up this side of my face. It is a nuisance but I get around.

I recovered then what in waking life I had lost—my mother's liveliness of face and voice before her throat muscles stiffened and a woeful, impersonal mask fastened itself over her features. How could I have forgotten this, I would think in the dream—the casual humour she had, not ironic but merry, the lightness and impatience and confidence? I would say that I was sorry I hadn't been to see her in such a long time—meaning not that I felt guilty but that I was sorry I had kept a bugbear in my mind, instead of this reality—and the strangest, kindest thing of all to me was her matter-of-fact reply.

Oh, well, she said, better late than never. I was sure I'd see you someday.

When my mother was a young woman with a soft, mischievous face and shiny, opaque silk stockings on her plump legs (I have seen a photograph of her, with her pupils), she went to teach at a one-room school, called Grieves School, in the Ottawa Valley. The school was on a corner of the farm that belonged to the Grieves family—a very good farm for that country. Well-drained fields with none of the Precambrian rock shouldering through the soil, a little willow-edged river running alongside, a sugar bush, log barns, and a large, unornamented house whose wooden walls had never been painted but had been left to weather. And when wood weathers in the Ottawa Valley, my mother said, I do not know why this is, but it never turns grey, it turns black. There must be something in the air, she said. She often spoke of the Ottawa Valley, which was her home—she had grown up about twenty miles away from Grieves School—in a dogmatic, mystified way, emphasizing things about it that distinguished it from any other place on earth. Houses turn black, maple syrup has a taste no maple syrup produced elsewhere can equal, bears amble within sight of farmhouses. Of course I was disappointed when I finally got to see this place. It was not a valley at all, if by that you mean a cleft between hills; it was a mixture of flat fields and low rocks and heavy bush and little lakes—a scrambled, disarranged sort of country with no easy harmony about it, not yielding readily to any description.

The log beams and unpainted house, common enough on poor farms, were not in the Grieveses' case a sign of poverty but of policy. They had the money but they did not spend it. That was what people told my mother. The Grieveses worked hard and they were far from ignorant, but they were very backward. They didn't have a car or electricity or a telephone or a tractor. Some people thought this was because they were Cameronians—they were the only people in the school district who were of that religion—but in fact their church (which they themselves always called the Reformed Presbyterian) did not forbid engines or electricity or any inventions of that sort, just card playing, dancing, movies, and, on Sundays, any activity at all that was not religious or unavoidable.

My mother could not say who the Cameronians were or why they were called that. Some freak religion from Scotland, she said from the perch of her obedient and lighthearted Anglicanism. The teacher always boarded with the Grieveses, and my mother was a little daunted at the thought of going to live in that black board house with its paralytic Sundays and coal-oil lamps and primitive notions. But she was engaged by that time, she wanted to work on her trousseau instead of running around the country having a good time, and she figured she could get home one Sunday out of three. (On Sundays at the Grieveses' house, you could light a fire for heat but not for cooking, you could not even boil the kettle to make tea, and you were not supposed to write a letter or swat a fly. But it turned out that my mother was exempt from these rules. 'No, no,' said Flora Grieves, laughing at her. 'That doesn't mean you. You must just go on as you're used to doing.' And after a while my mother had made friends with Flora to such an extent that she wasn't even going home on the Sundays when she'd planned to.)

Flora and Ellie Grieves were the two sisters left to the family. Ellie was married, to a man called Robert Deal, who lived there and worked the farm but had not changed its name to Deal's in anyone's mind. By the way people spoke, my mother expected the Grieves sisters and Robert Deal to be middle-aged at least, but Ellie, the younger sister, was only about thirty, and Flora seven or eight years older. Robert Deal might be in between.

The house was divided in an unexpected way. The married couple didn't live with Flora. At the time of their marriage, she had given them the parlour and the dining room, the front bedrooms and staircase, the winter kitchen. There was no need to decide about the bathroom, because there wasn't one. Flora had the summer kitchen, with its open rafters and uncovered brick walls, the old pantry made into a narrow dining room and sitting room, and the two back bedrooms, one of which was my mother's. The teacher was housed with Flora, in the poorer part of the house. But my mother didn't mind. She immediately preferred Flora, and Flora's cheerfulness, to the silence and sickroom atmosphere of the front rooms. In Flora's domain it was not even true that all amusements were forbidden. She had a crokinole board—she taught my mother how to play.

The division had been made, of course, in the expectation that Robert and Ellie would have a family, and that they would need the room. This hadn't happened. They had been married for more than a dozen years and there had not been a live child. Time and again Ellie had been pregnant, but two babies had been stillborn, and the rest she had miscarried. During my mother's first year, Ellie seemed to be staying in bed more and more of the time, and my mother thought that she must be pregnant again, but there was no mention of it. Such people would not mention it. You could not tell from the look of Ellie, when she got up and walked around, because she showed a stretched and ruined though slack-chested shape. She carried a sickbed odour, and she fretted in a childish way about everything. Flora took care of her and did all the work. She washed the clothes and tidied up the rooms and cooked the meals served in both sides of the house, as well as helping Robert with the milking and separating. She was up before daylight and never seemed to tire. During the first spring my mother was there, a great housecleaning was embarked upon, during which Flora climbed the ladders herself and carried down the storm windows, washed and stacked them away, carried all the furniture out of one room after another so that she could scrub the woodwork and varnish the floors. She washed every dish and glass that was sitting in the cupboards supposedly clean already. She scalded every pot and spoon. Such need and energy possessed her that she could hardly sleep—my mother would wake up to the sound of stovepipes being taken down, or the broom, draped in a dish towel, whacking at the smoky cobwebs. Through the washed uncurtained windows came a torrent of unmerciful light. The cleanliness was devastating. My mother slept now on sheets that had been bleached and starched and that gave her a rash. Sick Ellie complained daily of the smell of varnish and cleansing powders. Flora's hands were raw. But her disposition remained topnotch. Her kerchief and apron and Robert's baggy overalls that she donned for the climbing jobs gave her the air of a comedian—sportive, unpredictable.

My mother called her a whirling dervish.

'You're a regular whirling dervish, Flora,' she said, and Flora halted. She wanted to know what was meant. My mother went ahead and explained, though she was a little afraid lest piety should be offended. (Not piety exactly—you could not call it that. Religious strictness.) Of course it wasn't. There was not a trace of nastiness or smug vigilance in Flora's observance of her religion. She had no fear of heathens—she had always lived in the midst of them. She like the idea of being a dervish, and went to tell her sister.

'Do you know what the teacher says I am!'

Flora and Ellie were both dark-haired, dark-eyed women, tall and narrow-shouldered and long-legged. Ellie was a wreck, of course, but Flora was still superbly straight and graceful. She could look like a queen, my mother said—even riding into town in that cart they had. For church they used a buggy or a cutter, but when they went to town they often had to transport sacks of wool—they kept a few sheep—or of produce, to sell, and they had to bring provisions home. The trip of a few miles was not made often. Robert rode in front, to drive the horse—Flora could drive a horse perfectly well, but it must always be the man who drove. Flora would be standing behind holding on to the sacks. She rode to town and back standing up, keeping an easy balance, wearing her black hat. Almost ridiculous but not quite. A gypsy queen, my mother thought she looked like, with her black hair and her skin that always looked slightly tanned, and her lithe and bold serenity. Of course she lacked the gold bangles and the bright clothes. My mother envied her her slenderness, and her cheekbones.

Returning in the fall for her second year, my mother learned what was the matter with Ellie.

'My sister has a growth,' Flora said. Nobody then spoke of cancer.

My mother had heard that before. People suspected it. My mother knew many people in the district by that time. She had made particular friends with a young woman who worked in the post office; this woman was going to be one of my mother's bridesmaids. The story of Flora and Ellie and Robert had been told—or all that people knew of it—in various versions. My mother did not feel that she was listening to gossip, because she was always on the alert for any disparaging remarks about Flora—she would not put up with that. But indeed nobody offered any. Everybody said that Flora had behaved like a saint. Even when she went to extremes, as in dividing up the house—that was like a saint.

Robert came to work at Grieveses' some months before the girls' father died. They knew him already, from church. (Oh, that church, my mother said, having attended it once, out of curiosity—that drear building miles on the other side of town, no organ or piano and plain glass in the windows and a doddery old minister with his hours-long sermon, a man hitting a tuning fork for the singing.) Robert had come out from Scotland and was on his way west. He had stopped with relatives or people he knew, members of the scanty congregation. To earn some money, probably, he came to Grieveses'. Soon he and Flora were engaged. They could not go to dances or to card parties like other couples, but they went for long walks. The chaperone—unofficially—was Ellie. Ellie was then a wild tease, a long-haired, impudent, childish girl full of lolloping energy. She would run up hills and smite the mullein stalks with a stick, shouting and prancing and pretending to be a warrior on horseback. That, or the horse itself. This when she was fifteen, sixteen years old. Nobody but Flora could control her, and generally Flora just laughed at her, being too used to her to wonder if she was quite right in the head. They were wonderfully fond of each other. Ellie, with her long skinny body, her long pale face, was like a copy of Flora—the kind of copy you often see in families, in which because of some carelessness or exaggeration of features or colouring, the handsomeness of one person passes into the plainness—or almost plainness—of the other. But Ellie had no jealousy about this. She loved to comb out Flora's hair and pin it up. They had great times, washing each other's hair. Ellie would press her face into Flora's throat, like a colt nuzzling its mother. So when Robert laid claim to Flora, or Flora to him—nobody knew how it was—Ellie had to be included. She didn't show any spite toward Robert, but she pursued and waylaid them on their walks; she sprung on them out of the bushes or sneaked up behind them so softly that she could blow on their necks. People saw her do it. And they heard of her jokes. She had always been terrible for jokes and sometimes it had got her into trouble with her father, but Flora had protected her. Now she put thistles in Robert's bed. She set his place at the table with the knife and fork the wrong way around. She switched the milk pails to give him the old one with the hole in it. For Flora's sake, maybe, Robert humoured her.

The father had made Flora and Robert set the wedding day a year ahead, and after he died they did not move it any closer. Robert went on living in the house. Nobody knew how to speak to Flora about this being scandalous, or looking scandalous. Flora would just ask why. Instead of putting the wedding ahead, she put it back—from next spring to early fall, so that there should be a full year between it and her father's death. A year from wedding to funeral—that seemed proper to her. She trusted fully in Robert's patience and in her own purity.

So she might. But in the winter a commotion started. There was Ellie, vomiting, weeping, running off and hiding in the haymow, howling when they found her and pulled her out, jumping to the barn floor, running around in circles, rolling in the snow. Ellie was deranged. Flora had to call the doctor. She told him that her sister's period had stopped—could the backup of blood be driving her wild? Robert had had to catch her and tie her up, and together he and Flora had put her to bed. She would not take food, just whipped her head from side to side, howling. It looked as if she would die speechless. But somehow the truth came out. Not from the doctor, who could not get close enough to examine her, with all her thrashing about. Probably, Robert confessed. Flora finally got wind of the truth, through all her high-mindedness. Now there had to be a wedding, though not the one that had been planned.

No cake, no new clothes, no wedding trip, no congratulations. Just a shameful hurry-up visit to the manse. Some people, seeing the names in the paper, thought the editor must have got the sisters mixed up. They thought it must be Flora. A hurry-up wedding for Flora! But no—it was Flora who pressed Robert's suit—it must have been—and got Ellie out of bed and washed her and made her presentable. It would have been Flora who picked one geranium from the window plant and pinned it to her sister's dress. And Ellie hadn't torn it out. Ellie was meek now, no longer flailing and crying. She let Flora fix her up, she let herself be married, she was never wild from that day on.

Flora had the house divided. She herself helped Robert build the necessary partitions. The baby was carried full term—nobody even pretended that it was early—but it was born dead after a long, tearing labour. Perhaps Ellie had damaged it when she jumped from the barn beam and rolled in the snow and beat on herself. Even if she hadn't done that, people would have expected something to go wrong, with that child or maybe one that came later. God dealt out punishment for hurry-up marriages—not just Presbyterians but almost everybody else believed that. God rewarded lust with dead babies, idiots, harelips and withered limbs and clubfeet.

In this case the punishment continued. Ellie had one miscarriage after another, then another stillbirth and more miscarriages. She was constantly pregnant, and the pregnancies were full of vomiting fits that lasted for days, headaches, cramps, dizzy spells. The miscarriages were as agonizing as full-term births. Ellie could not do her own work. She walked around holding on to chairs. Her numb silence passed off, and she became a complainer. If anybody came to visit, she would talk about the peculiarities of her headaches or describe her latest fainting fit, or even—in front of men, in front of unmarried girls or children—go into bloody detail about what Flora called 'disappointments'. When people changed the subject or dragged the children away, she turned sullen. She demanded new medicine, reviled the doctor, nagged Flora. She accused Flora of washing the dishes with a great clang and clatter, out of spite, of pulling her—Ellie's—hair when she combed it out, of stingily substituting water-and-molasses for her real medicine. No matter what she said, Flora soothed her. Everybody who came into the house had some story of that kind to tell. Flora said, 'Where's my little girl, then? Where's my Ellie? This isn't my Ellie, this is some crosspatch got in here in place of her!'

In the winter evenings after she came in from helping Robert with the barn chores, Flora would wash and change her clothes and go next door to read Ellie to sleep. My mother might invite herself along, taking whatever sewing she was doing, on some item of her trousseau. Ellie's bed was set up in the big dining room, where there was a gas lamp over the table. My mother sat on one side of the table, sewing, and Flora sat on the other side, reading aloud. Sometimes Ellie said, 'I can't hear you.' Or if Flora paused for a little rest Ellie said, 'I'm not asleep yet.'

What did Flora read? Stories about Scottish life—not classics. Stories about urchins and comic grandmothers. The only title my mother could remember was *Wee Macgregor*. She could not follow the stories very well, or laugh when Flora laughed and Ellie gave a whimper, because so much was in Scots dialect or read with that thick accent. She was surprised that Flora could do it—it wasn't the way Flora ordinarily talked, at all.

(But wouldn't it be the way Robert talked? Perhaps that is why my mother never reports anything that Robert said, never has him contributing to the scene. He must have been there, he must have been sitting there in the room. They would only heat the main room of the house. I see him black-haired, heavy-shouldered, with the strength of a plow horse, and the same kind of sombre, shackled beauty.)

Then Flora would say, 'That's all of that for tonight.' She would pick up another book, an old book written by some preacher of their faith. There was in it such stuff as my mother had never heard. What stuff? She couldn't say. All the stuff that was in their monstrous old religion. That put Ellie to sleep, or made her pretend she was asleep, after a couple of pages.

All that configuration of the elect and the damned, my mother must have meant—all the arguments about the illusion and necessity of free will. Doom and slippery redemption. The torturing, defeating, but for some minds irresistible pileup of interlocking and contradictory notions. My mother could resist it. Her faith was easy, her spirits at that time robust. Ideas were not what she was curious about, ever.

But what sort of thing was that, she asked (silently), to read to a dying woman? This was the nearest she got to criticizing Flora.

The answer—that it was the only thing, if you believed it—never seemed to have occurred to her.

By spring a nurse had arrived. That was the way things were done then. People died at home, and a nurse came in to manage it.

The nurse's name was Audrey Atkinson. She was a stout woman with corsets as stiff as barrel hoops, marcelled hair the colour of brass candlesticks, a mouth shaped by lipstick beyond its own stingy outlines. She drove a car into the yard—her own car, a dark-green coupé, shiny and smart. News of Audrey Atkinson and her car spread quickly. Questions were asked. Where did she get the money? Had some rich fool altered his will on her behalf? Had she exercised influence? Or simply helped herself to a stash of bills under the mattress? How was she to be trusted?

Hers was the first car ever to sit in the Grieveses' yard overnight.

Audrey Atkinson said that she had never been called out to tend a case in so primitive a house. It was beyond her, she said, how people could live in such a way.

'It's not that they're poor, even,' she said to my mother. 'It isn't, is it? That I could understand. Or it's not even their religion. So what is it? They do not care!'

She tried at first to cozy up to my mother, as if they would be natural allies in this benighted place. She spoke as if they were around the same age—both stylish, intelligent women who liked a good time and had modern ideas. She offered to teach my mother to drive the car. She offered her cigarettes. My mother was more tempted by the idea of learning to drive than she was by the cigarettes. But she said no, she would wait for her husband to teach her. Audrey Atkinson raised her pinkish-orange eyebrows at my mother behind Flora's back, and my mother was furious. She disliked the nurse far more than Flora did.

'I knew what she was like and Flora didn't,' my mother said. She meant that she caught a whiff of a cheap life, maybe even of drinking establishments and unsavoury men, of hard bargains, which Flora was too unworldly to notice.

Flora started into the great housecleaning again. She had the curtains spread out on stretchers, she beat the rugs on the line, she leapt up on the stepladder to attack the dust on the moulding. But she was impeded all the time by Nurse Atkinson's complaining.

'I wondered if we could have a little less of the running and clattering?' said Nurse Atkinson with offensive politeness. 'I only ask for my patient's sake.' She always spoke of Ellie as 'my patient' and pretended that she was the only one to protect her and compel respect. But she was not so respectful of Ellie herself. 'Allee-oop,' she would say, dragging the poor creature up on her pillows. And she told Ellie she was not going to stand for fretting and whimpering. 'You don't do yourself any good that way,' she said. 'And you certainly don't make me come any quicker. What you just as well might do is learn to control yourself.' She exclaimed at Ellie's bedsores in a scolding way, as if they were a further disgrace of the house. She demanded lotions, ointments, expensive soap—most of them, no doubt, to protect her own skin, which she claimed suffered from the hard water. (How could it be hard, my mother asked her—sticking up for the household when nobody else would—how could it be hard when it came straight from the rain barrel?)

Nurse Atkinson wanted cream, too—she said that they should hold some back, not sell it all to the creamery. She wanted to make nourishing soups and puddings for her patient. She did make puddings, and jellies, from packaged mixes such as had never before entered this house. My mother was convinced that she ate them all herself.

Flora still read to Ellie, but now it was only short bits from the Bible. When she finished and stood up, Ellie tried to cling to her. Ellie wept, sometimes she made ridiculous complaints. She said there was a horned cow outside, trying to get into the room and kill her.

'They often get some kind of idea like that,' Nurse Atkinson said. 'You mustn't give in to her or she won't let you go day or night. That's what they're like, they only think about themselves. Now, when I'm here alone with her, she behaves herself quite nice. I don't have any trouble at all. But after you been in here I have trouble all over again because she sees you and she gets upset. You don't want to make my job harder for me, do you? I mean, you brought me here to take charge, didn't you?'

'Ellie, now, Ellie dear, I must go,' said Flora, and to the nurse she said, 'I understand. I do understand that you have to be in charge and I admire you, I admire you for your work. In your work you have to have so much patience and kindness.'

My mother wondered at this—was Flora really so blinded, or did she hope by this underserved praise to exhort Nurse Atkinson to the patience and kindness that she didn't have? Nurse Atkinson was too thick-skinned and self-approving for any trick like that to work.

'It is a hard job, all right, and not many can do it,' she said. 'It's not like those nurses in the hospital, where they got everything laid out for them.' She had no time for more conversation—she was trying to bring in 'Make-Believe Ballroom' on her battery radio.

My mother was busy with the final exams and the June exercises at the school. She was getting ready for her wedding in July. Friends came in cars and whisked her off to the dressmaker's, to parties, to choose the invitations and order the cake. The lilacs came out, the evenings lengthened, the birds were back and nesting, my mother bloomed in everybody's attention, about to set out on the deliciously solemn adventure of marriage. Her dress was to be appliquéd with silk roses, her veil held by a cap of seed pearls. She belonged to the first generation of young women who saved their money and paid for their own weddings—far fancier than their parents could have afforded.

On her last evening, the friend from the post office came to drive her away, with her clothes and her books and the things she had made for her trousseau and the gifts her pupils and others had given her. There was great fuss and laughter about getting everything loaded into the car. Flora came out and helped. This getting married is even more of a nuisance than

I thought, said Flora, laughing. She gave my mother a dresser scarf, which she had crocheted in secret. Nurse Atkinson could not be shut out of an important occasion—she presented a spray bottle of cologne. Flora stood on the slope at the side of the house to wave good-bye. She had been invited to the wedding, but of course she had said she could not come, she could not 'go out' at such a time. The last my mother ever saw of her was this solitary, energetically waving figure in her housecleaning apron and bandanna, on the green slope by the black-walled house, in the evening light.

'Well, maybe now she'll get what she should've got the first time round,' the friend from the post office said. 'Maybe now they'll be able to get married. Is she too old to start a family? How old is she, anyway?'

My mother thought that this was a crude way of talking about Flora and replied that she didn't know. But she had to admit to herself that she had been thinking the very same thing.

When she was married and settled in her own home, three hundred miles away, my mother got a letter from Flora. Ellie was dead. She had died firm in her faith, Flora said, and grateful for her release. Nurse Atkinson was staying on for a little while, until it was time for her to go off to her next case. This was late in the summer.

News of what happened next did not come from Flora. When she wrote at Christmas, she seemed to take for granted that information would have gone ahead of her.

'You have in all probability heard,' wrote Flora, 'that Robert and Nurse Atkinson have been married. They are living on here, in Robert's part of the house. They are fixing it up to suit themselves. It is very impolite of me to call her Nurse Atkinson, as I see I have done. I ought to have called her Audrey.'

Of course the post-office friend had written, and so had others. It was a great shock and scandal and a matter that excited the district—the wedding as secret and surprising as Robert's first one had been (though surely not for the same reason), Nurse Atkinson permanently installed in the community, Flora losing out for the second time. Nobody had been aware of any courtship, and they asked how the woman could have enticed him. Did she promise children, lying about her age?

The surprises were not to stop with the wedding. The bride got down to business immediately with the 'fixing up' that Flora mentioned. In came the electricity and then the telephone. Now Nurse Atkinson—she would always be called Nurse Atkinson—was heard on the party line lambasting painters and paperhangers and delivery services. She was having everything done over. She was buying an electric stove and putting in a bathroom, and who knew where the money was coming from? Was it all hers, got in her deathbed dealings, in shady bequests? Was it Robert's, was he claiming his share? Ellie's share, left to him and Nurse Atkinson to enjoy themselves with, the shameless pair?

All these improvements took place on one side of the house only. Flora's side remained just as it was. No electric lights there, no fresh wallpaper or new venetian blinds. When the house was painted on the outside—cream with dark-green trim—Flora's side was left bare. This strange open statement was greeted at first with pity and disapproval, then with less sympathy, as a sign of Flora's stubbornness and eccentricity (she could have bought her own paint and made it look decent), and finally as a joke. People drove out of their way to see it.

There was always a dance given in the schoolhouse for a newly married couple. A cash collection—called 'a purse of money'—was presented to them. Nurse Atkinson sent out word that she would not mind seeing this custom followed, even though it happened that the family she had married into was opposed to dancing. Some people thought it would be a disgrace to gratify her, a slap in the face to Flora. Others were too curious to hold back. They wanted to see how the newlyweds would behave. Would Robert dance? What sort of outfit would the bride show up in? They delayed a while, but finally the dance was held, and my mother got her report.

The bride wore the dress she had worn at her wedding, or so she said. But who would wear such a dress for a wedding at the manse? More than likely it was bought specially for her appearance at the dance. Pure-white satin with a sweetheart neckline, idiotically youthful. The groom was got up in a new dark-blue suit, and she had stuck a flower in his buttonhole. They were a sight. Her hair was freshly done to blind the eye with brassy reflections, and her face looked as if it would come off on a man's jacket, should she lay it against his shoulder in the dancing. Of course she did dance. She danced with every man present except the groom, who sat scrunched into one of the school desks along the wall. She danced with every man present—they all claimed they had to do it, it was the custom—and then she dragged Robert out to receive the money and to thank everybody for their best wishes. To the ladies in the cloakroom she even hinted that she was feeling unwell, for the usual newlywed reason. Nobody believed her, and indeed nothing ever came of this hope, if she really had it. Some of the women thought that she was lying to them out of malice, insulting them, making them out to be so credulous. But nobody challenged her, nobody was rude to her—maybe because it was plain that she could summon a rudeness of her own to knock anybody flat.

Flora was not present at the dance.

'My sister-in-law is not a dancer,' said Nurse Atkinson. 'She is stuck in the olden time.' She invited them to laugh at Flora, whom she always called her sister-in-law, though she had no right to do so.

My mother wrote a letter to Flora after hearing about all these things. Being removed from the scene, and perhaps in a flurry of importance due to her own newly married state, she may have lost sight of the kind of person she was writing to. She offered sympathy and showed outrage, and said blunt disparaging things about the woman who had—as my mother say it—dealt Flora such a blow. Back came a letter from Flora saying that she did not know where my mother had been getting her information, but it seemed she had misunderstood, or listened to malicious people, or jumped to unjustified conclusions. What happened in Flora's family was nobody else's business, and certainly nobody needed to feel sorry for her or angry on her behalf. Flora said that she was happy and satisfied in her life, as she always had been, and she did not interfere with what others did or wanted, because such things did not concern her. She wished my mother all happiness in her marriage and hoped that she would soon be too busy with her own responsibilities to worry about the lives of people that she used to know.

This well-written letter cut my mother, as she said, to the quick. She and Flora stopped corresponding. My mother did become busy with her own life and finally a prisoner in it.

But she thought about Flora. In later years, when she sometimes talked about the things she might have been, or done, she would say, 'If I could have been a writer—then I would have written the story of Flora's life. And do you know what I would have called it? "The Maiden Lady". '

The Maiden Lady. She said these words in a solemn and sentimental tone of voice that I had no use for. I knew, or thought I knew, exactly the value she found in them. The stateliness and mystery. The hint of derision turning to reverence. I was fifteen or sixteen years old by that time, and I believed that I could see into my mother's mind. I could see what she would do with Flora, what she had already done. She would make her into a noble figure, one who accepts defection, treachery, who forgives and stands aside, not once but twice. Never a moment of complaint. Flora goes about her cheerful labours, she cleans the house and shovels out the cow byre, she removes some bloody mess from her sister's bed, and when at last the future seems to open up for her—Ellie will die and Robert will beg forgiveness and Flora will silence him with the proud gift of herself—it is time for Audrey Atkinson to drive into the yard and shut Flora out again, more inexplicably and thoroughly the second time than the first. She must endure the painting of the house, the electric lights, all the prosperous activity next door. 'Make-Believe Ballroom', 'Amos 'n' Andy'. No more Scottish comedies or ancient sermons. She must see them drive off to the dance—her old lover and that coldhearted, stupid, by no means beautiful woman in the white satin wedding dress. She is mocked. (And of course she has made over the farm to Ellie and Robert, of course he has inherited it, and now everything belongs to Audrey Atkinson.) The wicked flourish. But it is all right. It is all right—the elect are veiled in patience and humility and lighted by a certainty that events cannot disturb.

That was what I believed my mother would make of things. In her own plight her notions had turned mystical, and there was sometimes a hush, a solemn thrill in her voice that grated on me, alerted me to what seemed a personal danger. I felt a great fog of platitudes and pieties lurking, an incontestable crippled-mother power, which could capture and choke me. There would be no end to it. I had to keep myself sharp-tongued and cynical, arguing and deflating. Eventually I gave up even that recognition and opposed her in silence.

This is a fancy way of saying that I was no comfort and poor company to her when she had almost nowhere else to turn.

I had my own ideas about Flora's story. I didn't think that I could have written a novel but that I would write one. I would take a different tack. I saw through my mother's story and put in what she left out. My Flora would be as black as hers was white. Rejoicing in the bad turns done to her and in her own forgiveness, spying on the shambles of her sister's life. A Presbyterian witch, reading out of her poisonous book. It takes a rival ruthlessness, the comparatively innocent brutality of the thick-skinned nurse, to drive her back, to flourish in her shade. But she is driven back; the power of sex and ordinary greed drive her back and shut her up in her own part of the house with the coal-oil lamps. She shrinks, she caves in, her bones harden and her joints thicken, and—oh, this is it, this is it, I see the bare beauty of the ending I will contrive!—she becomes crippled herself, with arthritis, hardly able to move. Now Audrey Atkinson comes into her full power—she demands the whole house. She wants those partitions knocked out that Robert put up with Flora's help when he married Ellie. She will provide Flora with a room, she will take care of her. (Audrey Atkinson does not wish to be seen as a monster, and perhaps she really isn't one.) So one day Robert carries Flora—for the first and last time he carries her in his arms—to the room that his wife Audrey has prepared for her. And once Flora is settled in her well-lit, well-heated corner Audrey Atkinson undertakes to clean out the newly vacated rooms, Flora's rooms. She carries a heap of old books out into the yard. It's spring again, housecleaning time, the season when Flora herself performed such feats, and now the pale face of Flora appears behind the new net curtains. She has dragged herself from her corner, she sees the light-blue sky with its high skidding clouds over the watery fields, the contending crows, the flooded creeks, the reddening tree branches. She sees the smoke rise out of the incinerator in the yard, where her books are burning. Those smelly old books, as Audrey has called them. Words and pages, the ominous dark spines. The elect, the damned, the slim hopes, the mighty torments—up in smoke. There was the ending.

To me the really mysterious person in the story, as my mother told it, was Robert. He never has a word to say. He gets engaged to Flora. He is walking beside her along the river when Ellie leaps out at them. He finds Ellie's thistles in his bed. He does the carpentry made necessary by his and Ellie's marriage. He listens or does not listen while Flora reads. Finally he sits scrunched up in the school desk while his flashy bride dances by with all the men.

So much for his public acts and appearances. But he was the one who started everything, in secret. He *did it to* Ellie. He did it to that skinny wild girl at a time when he was engaged to her sister, and he did it to her again and again when she was nothing but a poor botched body, a failed child-bearer, lying in bed.

He must have done it to Audrey Atkinson, too, but with less disastrous results.

Those words, *did it to*—the words my mother, no more than Flora, would never bring herself to speak—were simply exciting to me. I didn't feel any decent revulsion or reasonable indignation. I refused the warning. Not even the fate of Ellie could put me off. Not when I thought of that first encounter—the desperation of it, the ripping and striving. I used to sneak longing looks at men in those days. I admired their wrists and their necks and any bit of their chests a loose button let show, and even their ears and their feet in shoes. I expected nothing reasonable of them, only to be engulfed by their passion. I had similar thoughts about Robert.

What made Flora evil in my story was just what made her admirable in my mother's—her turning away from sex. I fought against everything my mother wanted to tell me on this subject; I despised even the drop in her voice, the gloomy caution, with which she approached it. My mother had grown up in a time and in a place where sex was a dark undertaking for women. She knew that you could die of it. So she honoured the decency, the prudery, the frigidity, that might protect you. And I grew up in horror of that very protection, the dainty tyranny that seemed to me to extend to all areas of life, to enforce tea parties and white gloves and all other sorts of tinkling inanities. I favoured bad words and a breakthough, I teased myself with the thought of a man's recklessness and domination. The odd thing is that my mother's ideas were in line with some progressive notions of her times, and mine echoed the notions that were favoured in my time. This in spite of the fact that we both believed ourselves independent, and lived in backwaters that did not register such changes. It's as if tendencies that seem most deeply rooted in our minds, most private and singular, have come in as spores on the prevailing wind, looking for any likely place to land, any welcome.

Not long before she died, but when I was still at home, my mother got a letter from the real Flora. It came from that town near the farm, the town that Flora used to ride to, with Robert, in the cart, holding on to the sacks of wool or potatoes.

Flora wrote that she was no longer living on the farm.

'Robert and Audrey are still there,' she wrote. 'Robert has some trouble with his back but otherwise he is very well. Audrey has poor circulation and is often short of breath. The doctor says she must lose weight but none of the diets seem to work. The farm has been doing very well. They are out of sheep entirely and into dairy cattle. As you may have heard, the chief thing nowadays is to get your milk quota from the government and then you are set. The old stable is all fixed up with milking machines and the latest modern equipment, it is quite a marvel. When I go out there to visit I hardly know where I am.'

She went on to say that she had been living in town for some years now, and that she had a job clerking in a store. She must have said what kind of a store this was, but I cannot now remember. She said nothing, of course, about what had led her to this decision—whether she had in fact been put off her own farm, or hd sold out her share, apparently not to much advantage. She stressed the fact of her friendliness with Robert and Audrey. She said her health was good.

'I hear that you have not been so lucky in that way,' she wrote. 'I ran into Cleta Barnes who used to be Cleta Stapleton at the post office out at home, and she told me that there is some problem with your muscles and she said your speech is affected too. This is sad to hear but they can do such wonderful things nowadays so I am hoping that the doctors may be able to help you.'

An unsettling letter, leaving so many things out. Nothing in it about God's will or His role in our afflictions. No mention of whether Flora still went to that church. I don't think my mother ever answered. Her fine legible handwriting, her schoolteacher's writing, had deteriorated, and she had difficulty holding a pen. She was always beginning letters and not finishing them. I would find them lying around the house. *My dearest Mary*, they began. *My darling Ruth, My dear little Joanne (though I realize you are not little anymore), My dear old friend Cleta, My lovely Margaret.* These women were friends from her teaching days, her Normal School days, and from high school. A few were former pupils. I have friends all over the country, she would say defiantly. I have dear, dear friends.

I remember seeing one letter that started out: *Friend of my Youth*. I don't know whom it was to. They were all friends of her youth. I don't recall one that began with *My dear and most admired Flora*. I would always look at them, try to read the salutation and the few sentences she had written, and because I could not bear to feel sadness I would feel an impatience with the flowery language, the direct appeal for love and pity. She would get more of that, I thought (more from myself, I meant), if she could manage to withdraw with dignity, instead of reaching out all the time to cast her stricken shadow.

I had lost interest in Flora by then. I was always thinking of stories, and by this time I probably had a new one on my mind.

But I have thought of her since. I have wondered what kind of a store. A hardware store or a five-and-ten, where she has to wear a coverall, or a drugstore, where she is uniformed like a nurse, or a Ladies' Wear, where she is expected to be genteelly fashionable? She might have had to learn about food blenders or chain saws, negligees, cosmetics, even condoms. She would have to work all day under electric lights, and operate a cash register. Would she get a permanent, paint her nails, put on lipstick? She must have found a place to live—a little apartment with a kitchenette, overlooking the main street, or a room in a boarding house. How could she go on being a Cameronian? How could she get to that out-of-the-way church unless she managed to buy a car and learned to drive it? And if she did that she might drive not only to church but to other places. She might go on holidays. She might rent a cottage on a lake for a week, learn to swim, visit a city. She might eat meals in a restaurant, possibly in a restaurant where drinks were served. She might make friends with women who were divorced.

She might meet a man. A friend's widowed brother, perhaps. A man who did not know that she was a Cameronian or what Cameronians were. Who knew nothing of her story. A man who had never heard about the partial painting of the house or the two betrayals, or that it took all her dignity and innocence to keep her from being a joke. He might want to take her dancing, and she would have to explain that she could not go. He would be surprised but not put off—all that Cameronian business might seem quaint to him, almost charming. So it would to everybody. She was brought up in some weird religion, people would say. She lived a long time out on some godforsaken farm. She is a little bit strange but really quite nice. Nice-looking, too. Especially since she went and got her hair done.

I might go into a store and find her.

No, no. She would be dead a long time now.

But suppose I had gone into a store—perhaps a department store. I see a place with the brisk atmosphere, the straightforward displays, the old-fashioned modern look of the fifties. Suppose a tall, handsome woman, nicely turned out, had come to wait on me, and I had known, somehow, in spite of the sprayed and puffed hair and the pink or coral lips and fingernails—I had known that this was Flora. I would have wanted to tell her that I knew, I knew her story, though we had never met. I imagine myself trying to tell her. (This is a dream now, I understand it as a dream.) I imagine her listening, with a pleasant composure. But she shakes her head. She smiles at me, and in her smile there is a degree of mockery, a faint, self-assured malice. Weariness, as well. She is not surprised that I am telling her this, but she is weary of it, of me and my idea of her, my information, my notion that I can know anything about her.

Of course it's my mother I'm thinking of, my mother as she was in those dreams, saying, It's nothing, just this little tremor; saying with such astonishing lighthearted forgiveness, Oh, I knew you'd come someday. My mother surprising me, and doing it almost indifferently. Her mask, her fate, and most of her affliction taken away. How relieved I was, and happy. But I now recall that I was disconcerted as well. I would have to say that I felt slightly cheated. Yes. Offended, tricked, cheated, by this welcome turnaround, this reprieve. My mother moving rather carelessly out of her old prison, showing options and powers I never dreamed she had, changes more than herself. She changes the bitter lump of love I have carried all this time into a phantom—something useless and uncalled for, like a phantom pregnancy.

The Cameronians, I have discovered, are or were an uncompromising remnant of the Covenanters—those Scots who in the seventeenth century bound themselves, with God, to resist prayer books, bishops, any taint of popery or interference by the King. Their name comes from Richard Cameron, an outlawed, or 'field', preacher, soon cut down. The Cameronians—for a long time they have preferred to be called the Reformed Presbyterians—went into battle singing the seventy-fourth and the seventy-eighth Psalms. They hacked the haughty Bishop of St Andrews to death on the highway and rode their horses over his body. One of their ministers, in a mood of firm rejoicing at his own hanging, excommunicated all the other preachers in the world.

1990

Edna O'Brien

b. 1932

Novelist and short story writer, playwright and screenwriter, Edna O'Brien examines in her writings the lives of women, their search for love and their seemingly inevitable disappointment. With frank and sympathetic understanding, she allows her characters to examine the loneliness and pain at the centre of human relationships. 'When I look back on the graph of my own life and the things I've done, and the things I've sought out, it seems to me that I have always pursued pain and humiliation, and always emerged as a kind of auditor or surgeon in order to write about it,' she admitted. 'So I suppose it not only fulfils me, I suppose it's as necessary to me and maybe more necessary than relationships. This sounds terribly callous and maybe it is terribly callous, but I have gone into relationships, I mean intense relationships with men, obviously knowing that I was eventually going to write about them.'

Born in Tuamgraney, County Clare, Ireland, O'Brien was educated at the Convent of Mercy at Loughrea and then obliged to attend the Pharmaceutical College of Ireland, from which she graduated in 1950. But writing, a vocation she had chosen at the age of nine, commanded her attention. In 1959 she moved to London, which remains her home. She left Ireland 'in order to write about it. Because one needs the formality and perspective that distance gives in order to write calmly about a place,' she later observed. Her first novel, *The Country Girls* (1960), along with *The Lonely Girl* (1962) and *Girls in Their Married Bliss* (1964), form a trilogy of an Irish country girl's maturation and disappointment in love.

Ireland is the primary setting of O'Brien's fiction. 'A state of mind as well as an actual country', Ireland is, for her, 'moments of its history, and its geography, a few people who embody its strange quality, the features of a face, a holler, a line from a Synge play, the whiff of night air, but Ireland insubstantial like the goddesses poets dream of, who lead them down into strange circles. I live out of Ireland because something in me warns me that I might stop if I lived there, that I might cease to feel what it has meant to have such a heritage, might grow placid when in fact I want yet again and for indefinable reasons to trace that same route, that trenchant childhood route, in the hope of finding some clue that will, or would, or could, make possible the leap that would restore one to one's original place and state of consciousness, to the radical innocence of the moment just before birth.'

In a long analytic soliloquy, the narrator of 'Over' relives her love affair with a younger man. Her stream-of-consciousness meanderings reflect her shifting moods and desires, the agony of her aloneness, and even the predictability of the affair itself.

On her belated honeymoon in the Irish countryside, the young wife of 'Honeymoon' experiences a Joycean epiphany as she confronts the true nature of her marriage and her feelings for her husband.

'Over' was first published in the 2 December 1972 issue of *The New Yorker* and then revised and collected in *A Scandalous Woman and Other Stories*. 'Honeymoon' was first published in the December 1973 issue of *Cosmopolitan* and then collected in *A Scandalous Woman and Other Stories* (1974).

Over

Oh my dear I would like to be something else, anything else, an albatross. In short I wish I never knew you. Or could forget. Or be a bone—you could suck it. Or a stone in the bottom of your pocket, slipped down if you like, through one of the holes in the lining and wedged into the hem more or less forever, until you threw the coat away or gave it to one of your relations. I never saw you in a coat only in a sort of jacket, what they call an anorak. A funny word.

The first time you came to see me you were on the point of leaving as I opened the door. Leaving already. Yes you were that intrepid. So was I. You asked me where you might put your coat, or rather that anorak thing and I couldn't think, there being no hall stand. Do you remember the room was too big for us. I remember. Seeing you sitting an ocean away, on a print-covered chair, ill at ease, young, younger than your thirty years and I thought how I would walk across somehow or even stride across and cradle you. It was too grand the room, the upright piano, the cut glass chandelier. I have had notions of grandeur in the past but they are vanishing. Oh my God, everything is vanishing, except you.

A younger man. I go over our years ahead; jump ahead if you will. I will be grey before you. What a humbling thing. I will dye my tresses, all my tresses. Perhaps I should experiment now with a bottle of brown dye and a little soft brush, experiment even with my hidden hairs. I must forestall you always, always. Leave no loopholes, nothing that will disappoint, or disenchant you. What nonsense, when you have already gone. I don't expect to see you again unless we bump into one another. I think I am getting disappointed in you and that is good. Excellent. You told me yourself how you lied to me. You are back from your lecturing and probably thinking of getting in touch with me, probably at this very moment. Your hand on the telephone, debating, all of you debating. Now you've taken your hand away. You've put it off. You know you can, you can put it aside like a treat a childhood treat.

I did that as a child with a watch. Not a real watch but still a watch. It was the colour of jam, raspberry colour and I left it somewhere in fact in a vestibule in order that I could go and look at it, in order to see it there, mine, mine.

I did it. I crossed the room and what you did was to feel my hair over and over again and in different ways, touch it, with the palm of your hand, your drink was in your other hand (at first you refused a drink), felt it, strands of hair with your fingers, touched it as if it were cloth, the way a child touches its favourite surfaces such as a doll or a toy.

I keep saying child. It was like that, and you staring, staring, right through me, into me.

No knowing what I surrendered that night, what I gave up. I gave up most people, and I gave up the taste for clothes and dinners and anything that could be called frivolous. I even gave up my desire to talk to intrude or make my presence felt. I went right back; that is true, right back to the fields, so to speak, where I grew up. All of the features of that place, the simplest things, the sensations repossessed me. Crystal clear. A gate, a hasp, a water trough, the meadows and the way one can flow down into the corner of a field, a hay field. Dew again. And the image I had was of the wetness that babies and calves and foals have when they are just born and are about to be licked, and yet I was the mother.

Undoubtedly I was the mother when I gave you that soup and peeled a potato for you and cut it in half and mashed it as if you couldn't do it yourself and you said 'I have a poor appetite.' You thought I should have been more imposing. Even my kitchen you liked, the untidiness and the laurel leaves in a jug. They last a long time and I am told that they are lucky.

I should have enjoyed that night, that first unplanned meeting. As a matter of fact I did but it has been overlayed with so much else that it is like something crushed, something smothered, something at the bottom of a cupboard that has been forgotten, its very shape destroyed, its denomination ignored, and yet it is something that will always be there, except that no one will know or care about it, and no one will want to retrieve it and in the years to come if the cupboard should be cleaned out, if for instance, the occupants are leaving, it will indeed be found but it will be so crumpled as to be useless.

I dreamt of you before I met you. That was rash. I dream of you still, quite unedifying dreams where you are embracing me and whispering and we are interrupted the way we are constantly interrupted in life. You once told me that there was only ten minutes left for us because you had to buy a piece of perspex for a painting, make sure of getting it before the shops closed. The painting was a present to you both. It must have been in lieu of a wedding present.

Yes, I believe you are afraid of her. You say it's pity that holds you. But I believe that you are afraid of her and don't know it, and I believe that you love her and don't know it. You don't know very much about yourself, you shirk that. I asked you once, I went down on my knees I asked you to go away for three days, without her or me or anyone and you looked at me as if I were sending you to Van Diemen's Land.

And another thing, you told me the same stories the same escapades. You seem to forget that you have already told me that story when you broke bottles of champagne, stole them and then broke them. In your youth. And how you pity chambermaids, make the bed with them, that is to say help them with the tuckings. Another virtue of yours is that you never flirt. You don't trade on your good looks and really you deserve a beautiful young girl. I don't think you are in your right mind. Neither am I. We should never have met. I do believe it's a tribal thing. When I saw your daughter I thought it was me. No, not quite. I thought, or rather I knew I was once her. She looked at me like a familiar. That gaze. She didn't make strange. I touched her all over. I had to touch her. I had to tickle her, her toes, her soft knees, (like blancmange she was) her little crevices, and she smiled up at me and you said 'Smile for your auntie' and I was glad you called me Auntie, it was so ordinary and so plain and put me in the same circle as you.

Couldn't we all live together, couldn't we try. I used to be so jealous, green with it as they say, eaten up. I still am but couldn't we ride that way, the way the waves, the white horses, ride the sea. When I said it to you the mere suggestion made you panic, which makes me realize of course that you are not able for it, you are not up to it, you are only able for lies, you are only able for deceit.

So one day you will disappear for ever. Maybe you have. Isn't there some way of letting me know. I had so many wishes concerning us, but I had one in particular the smallest most harmless one and it was this: that one day I would come in from the outside and you would be here, already waiting for me, quite at home, maybe the kettle on or a drink poured. Not an outlandish wish. I suppose you wouldn't have wanted to make the journey without the certainty of seeing me. You said that going up the street you always wondered what I would look like and what I would be wearing. I wear brown now. I suppose it's to be sombre.

After your baby smiled you put her on the swivel chair and I watched her and you watched me, and your friend whom you'd brought as a safety measure, was watching you watching me and the baby watched over us all. It was a perfect moment. I know that. None of us wanted it to end. Your friend knew. He knew how much I loved you and maybe he knew how much you loved me but neither you nor I knew it because we didn't dare to and possibly never will.

Possibly and perhaps—your two favourite words. Damn it. You see, I had just got used to the possibility of nobody, a barren life, when you came along. Of course you don't believe that, you think with all my frocks and my bracelets and my platform shoes that I am always gallivanting. The truth is I used to. I have collected those garments over the years and that parasol you saw was given to me once on my way to a bullfight. About a year ago—I stopped gallivanting. It is not that I want to be good, no. If anything I want to be bad because I would like it to end without its being too sickly. Endings are hideous. Take flowers for instance, some go putrid, the very sweetest smelling of all go putrid—so does parsley. I would like it just to shrivel away. It mustn't though.

The strangest thing is he lost his parents too at a young age. My father that is. You see, I am mixing you up with everyone, my father, my mother, my former husband, myself. Could you not come, could you not contact me now, so I could tell you about them, their customs and their ways. The whole parish I know. The lady called Josie walking out for three evenings with a man and saying 'I have no story to tell,' meaning was he going to propose to her, and next day he sent for a tray of engagement rings. He must have done it out of fright. Later she went mad. People depend on each other so much. Too much. You listen to me all right, in fact you repeat things that I say. My thoughts are like sprouts, like sprouts on the branch of your brain. Why are you so cold so silent. Your element is mercury.

All sorts of things remind me of you. On a dump today I saw a remains of a gas cooker and a Christmas tree though we're bang in the middle of the year. Christmas. That will rankle. You will celebrate it with your family as you did last year. Well anyhow it looked pathetic, out in the rain—a small gas oven and a Christmas tree and a stump of clay around it. I stood and looked at it. I had a feeling that you might come around the corner, swiftly the way you do. We would not have needed to say anything, you would have understood. That is the worse thing that at times you understand.

We were seen twice in public. I hated you buying me drinks but you refused to allow me to. I wanted to slip you a note but couldn't. As a matter of fact I lost all my confidence and quite a few of my movements. I was ashamed to remove my coat even though I was sweating. I thought it would make me seem too much at home and after all I had asked you there and you hadn't wanted to come, you had resisted even to the extent that you couldn't think of the name of a pub despite the fact that it was your district and what I had to do was go there and prowl around and find a quiet one and ring you. You allowed me to ring because she was away, staying with her sister. Her sister is an invalid. You seemed to imply that she had harmed herself. Are they a hysterical family, are they musical. Shall we call her Bimba. I can't use her name, that would be too friendly. I dream of her death, in her sleep, in an aeroplane crash. Anyhow in the pub you made me promise, take an oath, that I would never ring again. I took an oath. Is that commendable. I was thinking of you even as I sat there and promised, I was thinking of you, in another state altogether, a former state, a state of grace, a you saying 'I'll always come back to you, always, there's nothing else,' and I was thinking of the expression attached to that time, the sad eyes and so forth. Your eyes pierce people. You may say it again with your sad true eyes. Anything may happen, anything.

Anyhow, to get back to my father and yours. There are resemblances and there are differences. Yours loved his wife and died soon after her, to rejoin her in the next world. You felt left out maybe, excluded as a child. In the middle of a family, neither the youngest nor the eldest. My father's parents also died within a short space of one another. Pneumonia. Winter time and snow at the funeral and snow falling in on the coffin and then the four children divided up among cousins and the method of division was that each child was told to choose which pony and trap it wanted to be in, and in so doing choose its future home. Not a scrap of love had he. Once when he was sick he hid in the harness room and when he was found the woman of the house gave him a good thrashing and then a laxative. Not a scrap of love had he.

Maybe you're like him somewhere in the centre of you, maybe you're alike. No you're not. You're as unalike as chalk and cheese. You have nature. He lacks it. Not many people have nature. And not many people have gentleness. Take my next-door neighbours, they shout and go around in dressing gowns, and as their friends arrive they shout even louder, and the hostess puts on a horrible red raincoat when she wants to go out and get something from her car and it happens to be raining. I have a dreadful feeling that she's trying to impress me with her shouting and her car and her rain wear.

It's teeming today. Wouldn't you know. I have a feeling a very definite feeling that it might not cease, might turn into a second flood. We will all be incarcerated wherever we happen to be. Are you indoors, are you addressing a meeting, are you, or rather were you on your way to a bus stop and been obliged to take shelter under a tree. You said you had no knowledge of ever in your life missing anybody. Yes I think it might rain forever or at least for forty days and forty nights. That is a form of ever. I will smash these chandeliers bit by bit. It won't be difficult. They break easily, once when we were washing them a few of the pieces crumbled. The woman who was helping me couldn't understand why I laughed, neither could I.

She gave me a bit of advice, said by loving you I was closing the door to all other suitors.

Maybe you are in bed making love to her, or just caressing, the curtains drawn. Anyhow your rooms are so small that if you are indoors you are bound to be very close. I can see it, the little room, the sofa, the cushions, and, I never told you this but there are three ornaments in that room identical to three ornaments of mine. I shall not tell you now either as I am leaving you to guess.

If only we had been more exuberant. I went there three times in all, two of them against your will. The last time I was hungry as it happened. You offered me nothing. Are you by any chance a miserly man. I dearly wanted a keepsake of you and true enough on one of these unfortunate visits you gave me a handkerchief to dry my eyes, but it was a new one and had nothing of your person on it. I cried a lot. I wonder who washed it. You wash your own trousers because when I enquired about the white round stains on them you said it was where you had spattered on the undiluted bleach. I could have told you. I wish I had them. If I could hold them now—I would hold them and hug them and press them to me.

It is not right to love so. I suppose there is a sickness of heart as well as a sickness of mind and body. Yes when you first came I really had reached a point where I had stopped looking and you appeared at my door with a pamphlet and you were leaving again and I liked the look of you and I invited you in. They call it fate. I still see your face in window pane, appearing, disappearing, re-appearing. Oh my god, a face.

Don't get married, or if you do, tell me, give me warning so that I can get used to it. I won't give you a wedding present. What an ugly thing to say. Yes it's ugly. This house is upside down, that drawing room that you saw, well, it's a shambles and there are glasses lying around and the plants haven't been watered, or if they have it has been reckless, too much water one day so that they brimmed over, then none for days. There are little pools of water on the floor and those that have dried up have left white marks upon the parquet not unlike the bleach on your trousers. How long is it now. My God it is all a matter of how long it is. The days are jumbled. Just now, lying on my bed—another fatal habit—I saw the tree that I always see, the plane tree, its leaves, and would you believe it it seemed to me that the bits of sky that I saw through the leaves were leaves also, different-coloured leaves, serrated at the edges, so I saw tree leaves and cloud leaves. I am losing my reason. The garden is soggy, a wreck. And although it is summer I definitely smell autumn. I keep thinking that by autumn it will have improved a bit. Then again I think that you will have come back as you threatened to, and that we will be together in the darkest light, under covers, talking, touching the most terrible reconciliations uttered, uttering. Do you know that in your sleep I stroke and stroke you and when you waken, no matter how late the hour you always say 'A lovely way to waken' and you always stayed a few minutes longer, defied time, and yes, come to think of it those were our most valuable moments. You were at your best then and without fear. I stood at the door to see you off and only once did you look back. I expect you hate farewells.

The last fling I had was not like this at all, except that he was actually hitched, married. An odd fellow. A Harry. We spent five days away from his country and mine, though in a country much similar, dark and craggy and with a heavy rainfall. Some interesting excavations there, skeletons intact in peat. We drove a lot. He told me how he loved his wife, always did, always would. Wives do not come out too badly in the human maul. We had the same thing each day for lunch—salt bread, and herrings and a small glass of spirit. When we got to our destination we had a suite and one set of windows faced the sea and another set faced the dormitory town. We picked stones the first morning. I found a beautiful white stone, nearly pearl. I wanted to give it to you. I gave it to a friend of yours, a man you brought here. I didn't do it to make you jealous but rather to let you know that if all this weight didn't exist between us I would be able to be nice to you and maybe you in your turn would be nice to me and even funny and even frivolous. Yes we once made the noise of turkeys, beeping.

As I got to know this man Harry, he decreased in my estimation. He made a point of telling me about other loves of his and there was always a lot of blood in question. One story of his concerned a very beautiful Spanish virgin, all about her beauty and her moisture, etc. On the very last evening just as he was consulting the menu fór dinner he said he hoped I had money because he hadn't brought very much. You see I was ashamed of him and that is why I paid. Whereas when we went to an hotel, you, who could scarcely afford it, paid. And you set the clock twenty minutes before we were due to waken up so that we could be together for one of those lovely moments those lovely series of moments. Even you who profess to miss nothing, can you tell me you don't miss those. That morning in the hotel was when you first talked of love and made a plan for the future, our future. That morning you lost your head. You must have imagined yourself as someone else or that you could have explained it all to her, ironed it all out. You were quite practical. You said it would take five weeks, but instead of that you were back in a week and I might have known something was amiss because you came early and you drank heavily and you said could we talk could we talk. We talked. You said you had two rows with her, two dirty rows and then at the very end you said you collapsed into one another.

Sweet Jesus never have I known such a stab. That collapse, I could actually see it and feel it. I saw the hour, it was dawn and your tiredness and hers and both of you washed out and one or other of you saying—it matters not which of you—saying 'What am I saying, what am I doing' and then the collapse, lying down, in your clothes, fitting in a bit of sleep until your baby stirred, and one of you went to tend to it while the other prepared two cups of tea. Maybe while you were shaving you called in and said 'hey, I hope I didn't give you a black eye.' Of course it was not all erased, nor indeed forgotten, but it was over, it was behind you and you had accomplished something, shown your ugly colours and got nearer to one another.

I brought you nearer, God help us. Most probably you went out for the day maybe you went to the library. But no doubt you said roughly what time you would be back and that is the thing. You made it known that you would be back whatever the hour. That was the second bitterest thing for there is another.

The evening—one of the three occasions when I telephoned and dropped the phone out of shock and then re-dialled and later saw you in the pub—I asked if I could have a child of yours. You told me point blank that it was impossible, also you inferred that I was too old, what, with my divorce and my children reared and all that. Then after a few whiskies you decided to invite me back to your house and on the way back you allowed me to link you until we got near your street and then you ran on ahead so as not to be spied upon and I followed slightly ashamed, and as I said, like a dog.

Still inside the house you were different. The moment you discovered that your baby hadn't smothered itself or wasn't kidnapped or wasn't choking you kissed me fondly, fond kisses, many of them, and you removed my coat, and later as we fell talking you said that in the morning you had got someone to mind your child and you had gone to market and bought razor blades and white cotton handkerchiefs, one of which you offered me—and then came the second and bitterest blow, because as you were telling me I realized that you had had free time, that you could have seen me that you could have contacted me that for once you were not tied to her but you didn't and I realized that it wasn't she who always came between us. Sometimes it was you.

Guessing my thoughts you said you loved no one and were only interested in your educational work. When you remember that night, that is if ever you let loose the hogs of memory, if they stalk, do you remember the subsequent time, the goat skin, you, me, us, perfect, then. You can't have forgotten it all. Couldn't you have written. Ah yes you did. A circumspect little letter about how you mustn't get out of your depth how it mustn't be allowed to blossom. Well it didn't. Yes it did. It blossomed and what's more it caught fire, a whole forest of fire.

And another thing you have softened me towards others. I am prepared to nurse my aged father and my aged mother when the time comes and they call on me. Shall I tell you why. I think by your expression and by one or two things that you say that you did want to be by my side, and constantly, but that a sense of duty restrained you and a compassion. I needed you less than her. It seems to you that I have advantages over her. Which reminds me I haven't told you about the boy who died. I feel responsible, no not responsible but somehow involved.

The day I met you I also met another good-looking young man, a doctor in fact. He was a new doctor that I had gone to and he took a bit of a shine to me. I'd gone about my depression. A thing I didn't want you to know. He saw how it was and he prescribed accordingly. Later that day I met you having taken the first set of tablets and already believing that magic was at work.

The young doctor visited me in a private capacity that is after I had met you. He kissed me, yes. By then I was so enraptured with you that I was nice to everybody. I let him kiss me. I remember our exact conversation, his describing a caesarean birth, putting his two hands in and lifting the imaginary baby out. He said caesarean babies had less gumption because they didn't have to push. He was telling me all this and I was remarking to myself how deftly his nostrils flared in and out and then he went a bit far demonstrating this caesarean to me and I jumped up off the cushions. That was another thing. He arranged the cushions for us to loll on. You never did that. You sat at a distance. We talked stiffly. After a long time and nearly always as you were about to leave you asked if you might come and kiss me and quite often we met half way across the room like two animals, little animals charging into one another. Only once did you rebuff me altogether, you said did I have to be so demonstrative. I rushed towards you and embraced you and you threw me off. You even said that if we did make love it would preclude its ever happening again.

Why did you say that? To punish me for going to your house for pleading with you. And on the way out I said 'Are you angry' and you said no but that maybe I was, a little. Of course I was. Not a little, a lot. Another time you said did I have to talk so much. The trouble is I talked to no one else in between. That is the worst of putting all one's eggs in one basket. I loved your smell. You may have heard it from others but you smell of gardens, not flower gardens but herb gardens and grasses and plants and dock and all those rampant things.

Do you use the same words exactly, and exactly the same caresses, the same touch, the same hesitation, the same fingering. Are you as shy with her as with me. If only you had had courage and a braver heart.

I do believe we would have been happy. It is perhaps foolish to say so but there was nothing in you that I did not like and admire. Even your faults even your forgetfulness. There was nothing in you that clashed with me. You were startled once by the flowers very white flowers they were with very thick blossom. You admired them. It was as if you had never seen flowers before, or certainly never seen those. You made me feel as if I had cultivated them as if they were an extension of me.

I heard from that friend you brought that she is more demanding, makes her needs felt. You found a lack in me. You told me I am kind. I did a favour for your friend but that was only to woo you.

I am not kind, I cut people off as with the shears and I drop them, like nettles. At this moment there are several people who could do with my company and I withhold it and that poor cat sits day after day on the window ledge or outside the door and when I open it to take in the milk that poor black cat tries to slink in but I kick it with my shoe, in fact with the heel of my shoe. The same black cat as I held on my breast one night when you came and I was lounging. That was a false moment but I had to vary things because the previous time you said it was unnatural to spend so many hours over a dinner table and I felt that already it was all getting a bit stale, and I wished in my heart that you would invent something, that you would think up some new plan, some diversion, arrange for us to meet elsewhere. Of course you couldn't. There was a matter of secrecy and shortage of money. When I am short of money I borrow and to tell you the truth my debts are catching up with me, but when you are short you go without. I wanted to give a big cushion to your child. You refused. At the same time as you swore me to secrecy I broke that pledge. I told a few of my women friends and then you introduced me to a few of your men friends. I think you were showing me off. Come to think of it we were like children. It is just as well it got nowhere.

Yes there are times when I think the whole thing seems ridiculous. For instance the night you were to come to dinner or rather one of the nights you were to come to dinner and after waiting for about two hours I got restless and began to walk back and forth, paced, and did little things hoping that would speed you up—changed my shoes, brushed my hair, thumped the piano, kept opening and shutting the door. It was winter then and I could tell the seconds passing by a lot of ways but most of all by the candle burning down. It was a blue candle. At length I couldn't bear it any longer so I turned down the stove—I always had food that could be kept hot—and went out without a coat to wait at the bus stop. And do you know something, there was a moment standing there, an absolute moment when I mistook someone else for you. Yes I was convinced. I saw him at the top of the bus, wild hair, the anorak and then I saw him rise and I saw his back as he went down the stairs of the bus and I got myself ready to smile, to kiss, to reach out my hand, and yes I was shaking and excited as if it were you.

I wish it had been. That was the second occasion I went to your house. A very cold reception. You kept on the television. I was prepared to end it and the next day you appeared out of breath and you sat and you talked and you said how it would all improve and everything would be better between us.

Did you believe that then? I must confess I did. That particular evening, the objects—the room getting dark, the end of the blue candle, the two of us thinking that the worst of our troubles were behind us.

You had to go away next day. Away. Of course there are ruses for passing the time. I didn't see my friends, alas I have abandoned my friends but what I did do was go to cafés where it was very full and very noisy. I searched them out but no matter how full a café is, there is always room for one, usually at someone else's table. The way they argued or looked into one another's eyes. I was having a rest from you. I could tell the lesbians even though they couldn't tell and those who would be together forever and those who wouldn't. I had such a way of seeing into them, such clarity. That is another thing. I often see you as an old man and you are in a trenchcoat, white with the belt hanging down, one of those stiff trenchcoats, with perforations under the arm, and you are recuperating from some illness and you are, yes, a disillusioned man. It will all be behind you then, she and I, and your daughter and your life's work, and how will you remember it, how?

In those restaurants they play waltzes. I loved the first bars of the waltz. I often stood up to dance, with my mind meandering. Yes that has been my life of late, restaurants, people saying to each other, 'Happy?', and people saying what François said and how much of that hair they should cut.

I did something awful. Friends of mine were going away on a boat forever, and I didn't see them off. It was my godson going away forever and I didn't see him off. I thought you might have been ringing and I didn't want to be out.

My lovely godson. I sent him a cup and saucer to the cabin but it is not the same thing. You see I had a moment with him, unique, I think it was tantamount to a sexual moment. It was this.

I had been in his house once, or rather in their garden and there was a party in full swing. A lot of people, a lot of drinking and jabber, and he and I sat far apart from the others, under a tree, asking riddles. There were flies bothering us and we used to blow them away and he told me about his dreams when he was always winning and then he said would I like to walk around, to go out of the garden. And we did that, we went out and walked all around the clapboard fence, and met a lady, a sort of serving lady going in with a platter of strawberries, and he held my hand and squeezed it on and off, and when we got back to our starting point and were just about to go in by the lych gate he pointed to the nearby woods and told me there was a dirty man in there who pulled down his trousers and showed his butt and then we hurried in. I didn't see him off.

And another thing, I bought fire irons—don't ask me why, because it's summer—and I tried to beat the lady down about the price. I went to her private house having got the address from the assistant and when she opened the door I saw that I was confronted by a hunchback and still I tried to beat her down about the price. It was nothing. A matter of shillings. I stood there waiting for her to concede and she did. We are to be pitied.

Another haunt of mine is cinemas, before they open. Oh my God, they have to be seen to be believed. Shabby. Quite a long way from Strauss and the waltzes. Usherettes, mostly elderly ladies and people like myself, killing time in the afternoon. I want all my teeth drawn out of me and other teeth, molars, if you will, stuck back into my gums. I want to grind these new teeth, these molars to a pulp. Perhaps I want to eat you alive. Ah yes the seat of this love must indeed be a hate. So the smart alecs would tell me. The hate extends to others. Good friends. How boring they have become. They tell me the shape of their new rooms, or the colours of their walls and what they eat in restaurants. Most terrible bilge. I get listless. Then I get angry. I have to leave right in the middle of their conversations. Mostly I don't see them.

I don't work now. Waiting. It gets on one's nerves. I can keep going a little longer but only a little. One good thing about being out is that I imagine you telephoning. I exist on that little ploy for hours. I even live your disappointment with you. Your phoning once, then again immediately then asking the operator to get the number, then phoning again in about an hour and another hour, and concluding that I have gone somewhere, abroad maybe as far as Morocco, when all the time I am in one of those cafés listening to one of those waltzes, thinking of you or in one of those cinemas waiting for the performance to start, reading a sign that says

'Fruits and ices', unable to stop thinking of you. It can't be hate. Do you ever imagine me with another man. You offered me one of your friends once, the night we were all together, here, dancing, cavorting and laughing. Laughing we were. 'Why don't you have Mike' you said. But your arms were all around me and anyhow we were on the landing, on our way to bed. Believe me, I even wanted you to feed and drink off me. I wanted to waste away in your service. To be a bone.

Am I saying wanted when I actually mean want? It is still my purpose, still my intention. You forbade me the gift of having your child and I was too honest or else too cowardly to betray you, to dupe you. Maybe you have taken the plunge, maybe you have got married and that is why you are not showing yourself. You told me once that you muttered something about it. You mutterer. That doctor I mentioned got killed in a plane crash along with a hundred others. You may get killed. Do you know what I hate about myself, I have never done a brave thing, I have never risked death. If only I had done something you could have admired me by. If only I'd renounced you. She is by your side. Your guardian angel, perhaps your little help mate? Not from what I know of her. You told me little but you inferred a lot. We are so hard on ourselves. Ah yes, those waltzes in those restaurants make me cry, and so do mushrooms. If only I could hear your voice for a minute, half a minute, less. You go from place to place. She is by your side, whether you like it or not. I often imagine you in trains sitting opposite each other saying the odd word, then getting off, the two of you sharing the carrier cot. What bliss.

Tell me, is she pretty, is she soft, your lady, or does she have what is called a whim of iron? I did ask you once if she had blue eyes and you professed not to know. You must know. It is not that I am a lover of blue eyes, the question simply cropped up. You must have seen them in all lights, and at all moments, maybe even in childbirth. On these numerous train journeys, do you ever think of me? I know you do. I am certain of it. I can feel you thinking of me even now. You may carry the thought through. You may contact me. Yes he died, that young doctor. I am glad that I didn't make love to him. I would not care to have made love to a dead man. Yes it got killed between us, you and I. Contravened. That is a fact, a bitter fact. It wasn't that it didn't happen, oh it did. Oh how it happened. Your face and mine, your voice and mine. Evening. Just like milking time, and the cows lowing as if we were in the byre. Then the moon came up. Our faces shone. I could have touched the stars. One should be thankful for a moment, even grateful, and not be plaintive like this. Yes, it is nothing short of a miracle, the way you met me, more than half way. The way you came out of your innerness and complexity and came to me, and I told you things, nonsense things. I told you for instance about the one wooden sweet, which was mixed up with all the other sweets in a carnival assortment. This wooden sweet had bright wrapping like all the others, and more than once I got it and I didn't know whether to be glad or sorry, and neither of us could tell why it was in the box in the first place, whether it was some sort of joke or the like. And you told me about having to undress at the doctors and having a dirty vest on, and being scolded by your mother. She was ashamed.

It is when I think about you suffering that I cannot bear it. I think of you crying. You cried lest you could never see me again and I said you always could and that I would always understand and be womanly and be patient. King Lear says women must be kind, or something to that effect. Yes that is what I must be, kind and womanly. I know what I will do. I will talk to your friend, Mike, the friend you brought here. I will tell him some little pleasantry and he will pass it on to you, and you will be touched, regaled. I will do that now.

Oh God, I have done it. I rang. He told me. You have gone away to a new country, a young country at that. Gone with your family. I knew it. It seems she did something silly like her sister, something extreme. Oh how mad I was to think that she would give you up, that we would all share. Oh how cracked one's thoughts get. You did the right thing, the only thing. Yes, I will see you when you are old, just as I visualized it, in the off-white mackintosh with the perforations under the armpit and you will be convalescing. I suppose you're married. And yes, you have no nature. Oh God, send me some word, some sign, some token. Tell me if you are married, or if you've forgotten, tell me how you are. It has all been for nothing, tell me something, I have to know . . . I will never know, I do not want to know now.

1972

Honeymoon

Elizabeth knew that honeymoons were likely to be fraught, and were not pleasant occasions that the send-off of rice, or confetti suggested. She remembered a cousin who had to be taken to hospital for an operation for haemorrhoids after hers, and another girl whose husband had conked her with a beach ball, whereby she had to have six stitches, and still another man—middle aged—who ordered plates and plates of oysters the better to consummate his marriage and at the end of two weeks declared he was still a bachelor.

Her honeymoon was different in that she had lived with the man in question for six months before actually becoming married to him. The reason was that he had difficulties in securing his divorce. Then, when it did take place, the marriage itself was so like none other, since it passed without a Mass or relatives or a wedding breakfast, or anything that could be called celebration. It was in the sacristy of a chapel on a weekday with two strangers—builders—as witnesses, and the ceremony presided over by an elderly and somewhat disgruntled priest. Theirs was a mixed marriage, which was why it took place in a sacristy and the parish priest as much as told her that it would not last.

The honeymoon came months later, after he had fixed up the old sports car and secured a workman to keep an eye to the sheep scattered over the mountainy farm. The little sports car was in perfect working order and they set off with the hood down. Soon they passed the poor hungry fields and descended the narrow rough road towards the valley, towards houses and pasture land and green hedges; saying goodbye for a while to their own single-storied white-cemmed lodge, to the grim mountain and to the lake where he had set a trap to catch pike. Down in the valley it was warm and sunny, and she remembered her own home and her own childhood as she saw the clothes on the line, and the women painting piers, and the little children waving endlessly at whatever passed. Although it was only six months since she had eloped with him, that part of her life seemed far away, and almost forbidden to her, to recall. And still it resided in her, somewhere, her parents' cut-stone house, the big empty rooms with the blond blinds drawn through the summer days, the hosts of daffodils, and the one narcissus in a dead child's hand, and once the soft tar on the road ruining a pair of white canvas shoes that had been given her.

From time to time he would ask her to look at the map, or pronounce the name of a town they were about to approach; and when they had driven for about three hours he decided that they should stop for tea. They stopped in a town where there had once been a dreadful battle and she told him what she remembered of it, from her schooldays. He was not a native and sometimes she got the feeling that he had no pity for those people, her people, who had for so long lived in subjugation and who like her were ashamed to confront themselves. He was twice her age, and she obeyed him in everything, even in the type of shoes she was to wear—completely flat shoes which as it happened gave her a pain in her instep.

The tea turned out to be delicious, what with home-made bread, tart, barely-ripened tomatoes, and salmon that had been cooked in muslin. Setting out again they were almost gay, as if no great divide of age or temperament lay between them. He had had two other wives of different nationalities and she often wondered if they were as biddable and obedient as herself. In this she despised herself because at heart she was quite wilful and rebellious and her earliest memory was of herself refusing to remember the names of grown-up people whom she resented. She had developed these traits of niceness and agreeableness simply to get away from people—to keep them from pestering her.

The first night they slept in the car, in a hay field, alongside a river. The smell of newly-mown hay possessed the air, and what with that, and the gurgle of the river, and the birds roosting in the trees, and now and then a car or a lorry on the main road, they found it hard to get a wink of sleep at all. They were wakened by crows in the very early morning, and were up and on their way to secure a can of milk long before the farm woman had rounded up her two cows.

They set out soon after breakfast and passed a little town where he bought fishing flies and a pound of eating apples. Before long they entered that part of the country where there were hedges of fuchsia, and consequently they were greeted by the dangling earrings of vivid red no matter where they looked. She felt like adorning herself with them. They parked the car and crossed some fields down to an ancient fort, where they encountered an old woman, a caretaker, from whom they had to get the big key.

On the spur of the moment, and for no reason, this woman asked them if they would like to rent a cottage, and just as rashly he agreed. The cottage belonged to her daughter and she gave them exact instructions where to find it. To enter the fort they had to stoop and once inside it was damp and grimy, with grey powdery stone peeling out of the walls, and a strange intimation of some other life, a relentless life that had gone on there.

The woman watched them, wrapt in curiosity, as if something weird might happen, or as if once, some other visitor had been compelled to do something untoward there. Obviously she hated her job and was doing it only out of necessity. She had no historical information whatsoever and said the place couldn't be worse for her sciatica.

When they arrived at the daughter's cottage they were delighted that it overlooked the sea and that there were great sweeps of sand, fine black sand; an uncanny smooth black vista like none that she had ever seen. The loose grains crept along the surface of it, playing an endless game. As they knocked on the open door, the shy daughter crawled out from under a table, a hunchbacked figure, in silver shoes, wearing a richly embroidered shawl. Her delight in seeing them was matched only by her agitation and she kept saying 'yes sir' before being asked anything at all. They crossed a little kitchen garden disturbing a hen who was on the point of laying, entered a little paddock where a goat was tethered, to reach the cottage that was smothered in roses and shrubs. All the time Rose clapped her hands and kept saying 'ha-ha'. The cottage comprised two rooms, a huge bare swept hearth, a low bamboo table and a churn resting on its side, which was as she said an antique. There was a single iron bed and the floor exhaled steam and damp. The hunchback saw them look at each other, shake their heads and as they declined she threw some evil word at them. Her vexation was as vivid as moments before her excitement had been. Then she pelted stones after them, and told them to get out of her sight.

That night, their sleep was less restless because of becoming more accustomed to the outdoors, the sounds, the smells, and the cramped environment of the car, with its little sponge mattress. In the morning he decided to do some fishing and they were able to follow the source of the river from the very spot where they were parked. Though sad at being left alone Elizabeth was pleased to see him set off, in his thigh-high wellington boots, with his new rod, and his lid of newly-dug wriggling worms. She folded the mattress, washed the breakfast things, ate some chocolate, and then sat down with the intention of talking to herself, and telling herself little stories to pass the time. She could hear the river, and tried to make out what sort of words it was saying to itself, and once she ran across to take a look at the brown water and the stones that were richly covered in a green luxurious moss. The time just crawled by, and she thought of snails and wished that she were one, and wondered about the little child she felt certain was in her; and what its sex was likely to be. She plaited her hair, then sat facing the sun, staring directly ahead at the two houses, the only two, about a mile distant, on a hill. They were identical houses of grey stone, with very blue slates, and red hall doors. She took to thinking of the occupants and wondered if they were friends, and if they had children, and if so, how they got to and from school. Just then a man appeared from the road-side with a sack of flour on his back, and she said hello almost at the exact same moment as he did. He commented on the fine weather and seeing that she smiled, he put down the sack and started to look at the little car and to touch the headlights. Then he stooped down and looked inside it. He was intrigued by it. She leant in and turned on the wireless and within seconds he was clapping his hands to the music, and letting out a yodel as if he were a guest at a house dance. She conveyed him across the field, and he told her how he lived with his wife Nora and how she pined for company, and how the previous summer hikers had called on them and taken tea with them. She was on the point of turning back when he asked if she would like to come up and meet Nora. He badly wanted her to go, so she went both to please him and to inspect one of the two houses that a short while before had been like a house in a mystery story, never to be entered.

She had to take off her shoes, as they crossed the various little brooks. Some stones carried the time-worn footprints of people and animals. One stone had the shape of a heel in it and he told her it was there since he was a small child. As they approached the house he called Nora, in a high excited voice, and a youngish woman came running down the steps, wiping her hands on her apron. The moment she saw he was not alone, she quit smiling, and began to pant, and drew her long tongue out and raised it to the tip of her nose, touching her nose over and over again, making some important signal with it, and demanding of him to do the exact same thing. They looked identical, like brother and sister, having the same lugubrious features, the same gravel eyes, and these elongated tongues, with which they could touch the tips of their noses. Once inside the house Nora began to jump up and down, throw cutlery, splash water, and whimper so that the man was obliged to take her to the next room where they spent several minutes.

When they emerged the woman was calm, but reserved, shook hands with her guest, put a newspaper on the chair, made tea in a china pot, and left it to draw in the middle of the kitchen floor, well away from coals or sparks from the fire. She gabbled on about what a nice day it was, and how it was Tuesday, St Anthony's day, and how hikers had called the summer before and would call again. He told her about the little blonde sports car, the mudguard, the headlights, and the dashboard with the various knobs of light; and then he told her about the radio and the tunes that came pouring out of it, like milk out of the separator, he said. She jumped up and down, took off her skull cap, threw it in the air and started to dance with joy. They proposed that after milking time, they would come down and visit the little car, and listen to the wireless. They shook both her hands when she left, repeated the arrangements, and said they would bring a bottle of milk and a jug of cream.

Elizabeth headed down the lane, over the field, across the various brooks, and down the last soggy field to where she knew her husband would be waiting. As she approached she saw a herd of cattle centred round the car, some lowing, some making louder, more ominous noises and she picked up a few rocks in case she be accosted.

Her husband called to her, to please hurry and asked where on earth she had got herself to. A small black bull was butting its way through the radiator, while some other members of the herd were sampling the canvas hood, licking it with their thick, pink tongues. She shouted out to her husband that she was afraid. He repeated that she had better hurry, since the car was in danger of being slashed and gored, and throwing two rocks somewhat rashly and randomly she managed to make three of the animals rear up towards the mudguard, and make her passage to the door all the more treacherous. Just then he began to blow the hooter, mercilessly; and shocked by the implosion and obviously unaccustomed to it, the cattle shied away, and scattered in all directions, enabling her to get in.

He asked what she meant, disappearing like that, with some strange yokel. The bull was still adhering to the radiator, and starting up the car he had to battle his way, forcing the animal back on its hind legs, and finally capsizing it altogether. The last she saw were the animals, like a raging swarm, threatening to chase them as they drove out of the field, and then she remembered how they could not leave because of the promise she had made. She told him about the visitors, and their identical faces, and he said how very interesting as he drove on. She thought of sundown, and their excitement, she even pictured them coming hand in hand, down the lane and across the stepping stones, probably dressed up, and she imagined their disappointment and then she thought how she had thought that her own husband was a man she had loved, but that she had been mistaken, and she remembered the phrase 'marry in haste, repent in leisure' and she began to cry quietly and unobtrusively, and yet she cried from the very depth of her young, and about to be chastised, being.

1973

Alistair MacLeod

b. 1936

'From time to time there are writers who come riding out of the hinterlands of this country called Canada. And they are writing about a life that they really know down to its smallest detail. And it is a life that is fierce and hard and beautiful and close to the bone.' Although Alistair MacLeod used these words to describe other fiction writers, his phrases apply equally well to his own short stories.

Born in North Battleford, Saskatchewan, MacLeod grew up in a coal-mining area of Alberta until the age of ten when his parents moved back to the family farm in Inverness County, Cape Breton. After obtaining his teacher's certificate from the Nova Scotia Teachers College, he took his B.A. and B.Ed. (1960) from St Francis Xavier University, his M.A. (1961) from the University of New Brunswick, and his Ph.D. (1968) from the University of Notre Dame. He taught at Indiana University from 1966 until 1969, then moved to the University of Windsor, where he is currently Professor of English and Creative Writing.

The settings of MacLeod's two collections of short fiction, *The Lost Salt Gift of Blood* (1976) and *As Birds Bring Forth the Sun and Other Stories* (1986), are usually the rugged and turbulent terrain of Cape Breton, where life is indeed 'fierce and hard and beautiful and close to the bone.' His characters tend to be stern individualists who make their living from the sea and find solace in their deep-rooted traditions. MacLeod captures the conflicts and traditions of the sturdy Scottish families from Cape Breton, and his stories root themselves in carefully defined details only to transcend their settings in humane explorations of the personal struggles that often defeat men and women of all time.

In 'The Boat', the narrator looks back on the winter when he was fifteen, recalling the harbour, the wharf, and the boat that evoke memories of his family. Unlike his mother, whose horizons were 'the very literal ones she scanned with her dark and fearless eyes,' he had sought more distant and more challenging horizons. As he recaptures his Cape Breton childhood, he comes to know and appreciate his feelings for his parents and to understand the emotional price he has paid for his advanced education.

In his aged father's final moments of mortality, the narrator of 'As Birds Bring Forth the Sun' recaptures not only childhood memories but family lore that dates back five generations. These tales from the past transcend time and prove the power and timelessness of family traditions at the very moment when the narrator witnesses his father's death.

'The Boat' was first published in the Spring 1968 issue of *The Massachusetts Review* and then collected in *The Lost Salt Gift of Blood*. 'As Birds Bring Forth the Sun' was first published in *event* (Volume 14, Number 2, 1985) and then collected in *As Birds Bring Forth the Sun and Other Stories*.

The Boat

There are times even now, when I awake at four o'clock in the morning with the terrible fear that I have overslept; when I imagine that my father is waiting for me in the room below the darkened stairs or that the shore-bound men are tossing pebbles against my window while blowing their hands and stomping their feet impatiently on the frozen steadfast earth. There are times when I am half out of bed and fumbling for socks and mumbling for words before I realize that I am foolishly alone, that no one waits at the base of the stairs and no boat rides restlessly in the waters by the pier.

At such times only the grey corpses on the overflowing ashtray beside my bed bear a witness to the extinction of the latest spark and silently await the crushing out of the most recent of their fellows. And then because I am afraid to be alone with death, I dress rapidly, make a great to-do about clearing my throat, turn on both faucets in the sink and proceed to make loud splashing ineffectual noises. Later I go out and walk the mile to the all-night restaurant.

In the winter it is a very cold walk and there are often tears in my eyes when I arrive. The waitress usually gives a sympathetic little shiver and says, 'Boy, it must be really cold out there; you got tears in your eyes.'

'Yes,' I say, 'it sure is; it really is.'

And then the three or four of us who are always in such places at such times make uninteresting little protective chit-chat until the dawn reluctantly arrives. Then I swallow the coffee which is always bitter and leave with a great busy rush because by that time I have to worry about being late and whether I have a clean shirt and whether my car will start and about all the other countless things one must worry about when he teaches at a great Midwestern university. And I know then that that day will go by as have all the days of the past ten years, for the call and the voices and the shapes and the boat were not really there in the early morning's darkness and I have all kinds of comforting reality to prove it. They are only shadows and echoes, the animals a child's hands make on the wall by lamplight, and the voices from the rain barrel; the cuttings from an old movie made in the black and white of long ago.

I first became conscious of the boat in the same way and at almost the same time that I became aware of the people it supported. My earliest recollection of my father is a view from the floor of gigantic rubber boots and then of being suddenly elevated and having my face pressed against the stubble of his cheek, and of how it tasted of salt and of how he smelled of salt from his red-soled rubber boots to the shaggy whiteness of his hair.

When I was very small, he took me for my first ride in the boat. I rode the half-mile from our house to the wharf on his shoulders and I remember the sound of his rubber boots galumphing along the gravel beach, the tune of the indecent little song he used to sing, and the odour of the salt.

The floor of the boat was permeated with the same odour and in its constancy I was not aware of change. In the harbour we made our little circle and returned. He tied the boat by its painter, fastened the stern to its permanent anchor and lifted me high over his head to the solidity of the wharf. Then he climbed up the little iron ladder that led to the wharf's cap, placed me once more upon his shoulders and galumphed off again.

When we returned to the house everyone made a great fuss over my precocious excursion and asked, 'How did you like the boat?' 'Were you afraid in the boat?' 'Did you cry in the boat?' They repeated 'the boat' at the end of all their questions and I knew it must be very important to everyone.

My earliest recollection of my mother is of being alone with her in the mornings while my father was away in the boat. She seemed to be always repairing clothes that were 'torn in the boat', preparing food 'to be eaten in the boat' or looking for 'the boat' through our kitchen window which faced upon the sea. When my father returned about noon, she would ask, 'Well, how did things go in the boat today?' It was the first question I remember asking: 'Well, how did things go in the boat today?' 'Well, how did things go in the boat today?'

The boat in our lives was registered at Port Hawkesbury. She was what Nova Scotians called a Cape Island boat and was designed for the small inshore fishermen who sought the lobsters of the spring and the mackerel of summer and later the cod and haddock and hake. She was thirty-two feet long and nine wide, and was powered by an engine from a Chevrolet truck. She had a marine clutch and a high speed reverse gear and was painted light green with the name *Jenny Lynn* stencilled in black letters on her bow and painted on an oblong plate across her stern. Jenny Lynn had been my mother's maiden name and the boat was called after her as another link in the chain of tradition. Most of the boats that berthed at the wharf bore the names of some female member of their owner's household.

I say this now as if I knew it all then. All at once, all about boat dimensions and engines, and as if on the day of my first childish voyage I noticed the difference between a stencilled name and a painted name. But of course it was not that way at all, for I learned it all very slowly and there was not time enough.

I learned first about our house which was one of about fifty which marched around the horseshoe of our harbour and the wharf which was its heart. Some of them were so close to the water that during a storm the sea spray splashed against their windows while others were built farther along the beach as was the case with ours. The houses and their people, like those of the neighbouring towns and villages, were the result of Ireland's discontent and Scotland's Highland Clearances and America's War of Independence. Impulsive emotional Catholic Celts who could not bear to live with England and shrewd determined Protestant Puritans who, in the years after 1776, could not bear to live without.

The most important room in our house was one of those oblong old-fashioned kitchens heated by a wood- and coal-burning stove. Behind the stove was a box of kindlings and beside it a coal scuttle. A heavy wooden table with leaves that expanded or reduced its dimensions stood in the middle of the floor. There were five wooden homemade chairs which had been chipped and hacked by a variety of knives. Against the east wall, opposite the stove, there was a couch which sagged in the middle and had a cushion for a pillow, and above it a shelf which contained matches, tobacco, pencils, odd fish-hooks, bits of twine, and a tin can filled with bills and receipts. The south wall was dominated by a window which faced the sea and on the north there was a five-foot board which bore a variety of clothes hooks and the burdens of each. Beneath the board there was a jumble of odd footwear, mostly of rubber. There was also, on this wall, a barometer, a map of the marine area and a shelf which held a tiny radio. The kitchen was shared by all of us and was a buffer zone between the immaculate order of ten other rooms and the disruptive chaos of the single room that was my father's.

My mother ran her house as her brothers ran their boats. Everything was clean and spotless and in order. She was tall and dark and powerfully energetic. In later years she reminded me of the women of Thomas Hardy, particularly Eustacia Vye, in a physical way. She fed and clothed a family of seven children, making all of the meals and most of the clothes. She grew miraculous gardens and magnificent flowers and raised broods of hens and ducks. She would walk miles on berry-picking expeditions and hoist her skirts to dig for clams when the tide was low. She was fourteen years younger than my father, whom she had married when she was twenty-six and had been a local beauty for a period of ten years. My mother was of the sea as were all of her people, and her horizons were the very literal ones she scanned with her dark and fearless eyes.

Between the kitchen clothes rack and barometer, a door opened into my father's bedroom. It was a room of disorder and disarray. It was as if the wind which so often clamoured about the house succeeded in entering this single room and after whipping it into turmoil stole quietly away to renew its knowing laughter from without.

My father's bed was against the south wall. It always looked rumpled and unmade because he lay on top of it more than he slept within any folds it might have had. Beside it, there was a little brown table. An archaic goose-necked reading light, a battered table radio, a mound of wooden matches, one or two packages of tobacco, a deck of cigarette papers and an overflowing ashtray cluttered its surface. The brown larvae of tobacco shreds and the grey flecks of ash covered both the table and the floor beneath it. The once-varnished surface of the table was disfigured by numerous black scars and gashes inflicted by the neglected burning cigarettes of many years. They had tumbled from the ashtray unnoticed and branded their statements permanently and quietly into the wood until the odour of their burning caused the snuffing out of their lives. At the bed's foot there was a single window which looked upon the sea.

Against the adjacent wall there was a battered bureau and beside it there was a closet which held his single ill-fitting serge suit, the two or three white shirts that strangled him and the square black shoes that pinched. When he took off his more friendly clothes, the heavy woollen sweaters, mitts and socks which my mother knitted for him and the woollen and doeskin shirts, he dumped them unceremoniously on a single chair. If a visitor entered the room while he was lying on the bed, he would be told to throw the clothes on the floor and take their place upon the chair.

Magazines and books covered the bureau and competed with the clothes for domination of the chair. They further overburdened the heroic little table and lay on top of the radio. They filled a baffling and unknowable cave beneath the bed, and in the corner by the bureau they spilled from the walls and grew up from the floor.

The magazines were the most conventional: *Time, Newsweek, Life, Maclean's, Family Herald, Reader's Digest*. They were the result of various cut-rate subscriptions or of the gift subscriptions associated with Christmas, 'the two whole years for only $3.50'.

The books were more varied. There were a few hard-cover magnificents and bygone Book-of-the-Month wonders and some were Christmas or birthday gifts. The majority of them, however, were used paperbacks which came from those second-hand bookstores which advertise in the backs of magazines: 'Miscellaneous Used Paperbacks 10¢ Each.' At first he sent for them himself, although my mother resented the expense, but in later years they came more and more often from my sisters who had moved to the cities. Especially at first they were very weird and varied. Mickey Spillane and Ernest Haycox vied with Dostoyevsky and Faulkner, and the Penguin Poets edition of Gerard Manley Hopkins arrived in the same box as a little book on sex technique called *Getting the Most Out of Love*. The former had been assiduously annotated by a very fine hand using a very blue-inked fountain pen while the latter had been studied by someone with very large thumbs, the prints of which were still visible in the margins. At the slightest provocation it would open almost automatically to particularly graphic and well-smudged pages.

When he was not in the boat, my father spent most of his time lying on the bed in his socks, the top two buttons of his trousers undone, his discarded shirt on the ever-ready chair and the sleeves of the woollen Stanfield underwear, which he wore both summer and winter, drawn half way up to his elbows. The pillows propped up the whiteness of his head and the goose-necked lamp illuminated the pages in his hands. The cigarettes smoked and smouldered on the ashtray and on the table and the radio played constantly, sometimes low and sometimes loud. At midnight and at one, two, three and four, one could sometimes hear the radio, his occasional cough, the rustling thud of a completed book being tossed to the corner heap, or the movement necessitated by his sitting on the edge of the bed to roll the thousandth cigarette. He seemed never to sleep, only to doze, and the light shone constantly from his window to the sea.

My mother despised the room and all it stood for and she had stopped sleeping in it after I was born. She despised disorder in rooms and in houses and in hours and in lives, and she had not read a book since high school. There she had read *Ivanhoe* and considered it a colossal waste of time. Still the room remained, like a solid rock of opposition in the sparkling waters of a clear deep harbour, opening off the kitchen where we really lived our lives, with its door always open and its contents visible to all.

The daughters of the room and of the house were very beautiful. They were tall and willowy like my mother and had her fine facial features set off by the reddish copper-coloured hair that had apparently once been my father's before it turned to white. All of them were very clever in school and helped my mother a great deal about the house. When they were young they sang and were very happy and very nice to me because I was the youngest and the family's only boy.

My father never approved of their playing about the wharf like the other children, and they went there only when my mother sent them on an errand. At such times they almost always overstayed, playing screaming games of tag or hide-and-seek in and about the fishing shanties, the piled traps and tubs of trawl, shouting down to the perch that swam languidly about the wharf's algae-covered piles, or jumping in and out of the boats that tugged gently at their lines. My mother was never uneasy about them at such times, and when her husband criticized her she would say, 'Nothing will happen to them there,' or 'They could be doing worse things in worse places.'

By about the ninth or tenth grade my sisters one by one discovered my father's bedroom and then the change would begin. Each would go into the room one morning when he was out. She would go with the ideal hope of imposing order or with the more practical objective of emptying the ashtray, and later she would be found spell-bound by the volume in her hand. My mother's reaction was always abrupt, bordering on the angry. 'Take your nose out of that trash and come and do your work,' she would say, and once I saw her slap my youngest sister so hard that the print of her hand was scarletly emblazoned upon her daughter's cheek while the broken-spined paperback fluttered uselessly to the floor.

Thereafter my mother would launch a campaign against what she had discovered but could not understand. At times although she was not overly religious she would bring in God to bolster her arguments, saying, 'In the next world God will see to those who waste their lives reading useless books when they should be about their work.' Or without theological aid, 'I would like to know how books help anyone to live a life.' If my father were in, she would repeat the remarks louder than necessary, and her voice would carry into his room where he lay upon his bed. His usual reaction was to turn up the volume of the radio, although that action in itself betrayed the success of the initial thrust.

Shortly after my sisters began to read the books, they grew restless and lost interest in darning socks and baking bread, and all of them eventually went to work as summer waitresses in the Sea Food Restaurant. The restaurant was run by a big American concern from Boston and catered to the tourists that flooded the area during July and August. My mother despised the whole operation. She said the restaurant was not run by 'our people', and 'our people' did not eat there, and that it was run by outsiders for outsiders.

'Who are these people anyway?' she would ask, tossing back her dark hair, 'and what do they, though they go about with their cameras for a hundred years, know about the way it is here, and what do they care about me and mine, and why should I care about them?'

She was angry that my sisters should even conceive of working in such a place and more angry when my father made no move to prevent it, and she was worried about herself and about her family and about her life. Sometimes she would say softly to her sisters, 'I don't know what's the matter with my girls. It seems none of them are interested in any of the right things.' And sometimes there would be bitter savage arguments. One afternoon I was coming in with three mackerel I'd been given at the wharf when I heard her say, 'Well I hope you'll be satisfied when they come home knocked up and you'll have had your way.'

It was the most savage thing I'd ever heard my mother say. Not just the words but the way she said them, and I stood there in the porch afraid to breathe for what seemed like the years from ten to fifteen, feeling the damp moist mackerel with their silver glassy eyes growing clammy against my leg.

Through the angle in the screen door I saw my father who had been walking into his room wheel around on one of his rubber-booted heels and look at her with his blue eyes flashing like clearest ice beneath the snow that was his hair. His usually ruddy face was drawn and grey, reflecting the exhaustion of a man of sixty-five who had been working in those rubber boots for eleven hours on an August day, and for a fleeting moment I wondered what I would do if he killed my mother while I stood there in the porch with those three foolish mackerel in my hand. Then he turned and went into his room and the radio blared forth the next day's weather forecast and I retreated under the noise and returned again, stamping my feet and slamming the door too loudly to signal my approach. My mother was busy at the stove when I came in, and did not raise her head when I threw the mackerel in a pan. As I looked into my father's room, I said, 'Well how did things go in the boat today?' and he replied, 'Oh not too badly, all things considered.' He was lying on his back and lighting the first cigarette and the radio was talking about the Virginia coast.

All of my sisters made good money on tips. They bought my father an electric razor which he tried to use for a while and they took out even more magazine subscriptions. They bought my mother a great many clothes of the type she was very fond of, the wide-brimmed hats and the brocaded dresses, but she locked them all in trunks and refused to wear any of them.

On one August day my sisters prevailed upon my father to take some of their restaurant customers for an afternoon ride in the boat. The tourists with their expensive clothes and cameras and sun glasses awkwardly backed down the iron ladder at the wharf's side to where my father waited below, holding the rocking *Jenny Lynn* in snug against the wharf with one hand on the iron ladder and steadying his descending passengers with the other. They tried to look both prim and wind-blown like the girls in the Pepsi-Cola ads and did the best they could, sitting on the thwarts where the newspapers were spread to cover the splattered blood and fish entrails, crowding to one side so that they were in danger of capsizing the boat, taking the inevitable pictures or merely trailing their fingers through the water of their dreams.

All of them liked my father very much and, after he'd brought them back from their circles in the harbour, they invited him to their rented cabins which were located high on a hill overlooking the village to which they were so alien. He proceeded to get very drunk up there with the beautiful view and the strange company and the abundant liquor, and late in the afternoon he began to sing.

I was just approaching the wharf to deliver my mother's summons when he began, and the familiar yet unfamiliar voice that rolled down from the cabins made me feel as I had never felt before in my young life or perhaps as I had always felt without really knowing it, and I was ashamed yet proud, young yet old and saved yet forever lost, and there was nothing I could do to control my legs which trembled nor my eyes which wept for what they could not tell.

The tourists were equipped with tape recorders and my father sang for more than three hours. His voice boomed down the hill and bounced off the surface of the harbour, which was an unearthly blue on that hot August day, and was then reflected to the wharf and the fishing shanties where it was absorbed amidst the men who were baiting their lines for the next day's haul.

He sang all the old sea chanties which had come across from the old world and by which men like him had pulled ropes for generations, and he sang the East Coast sea songs which celebrated the sealing vessels of Northumberland Strait and the long liners of the Grand Banks, and of Anticosti, Sable Island, Grand Manan, Boston Harbor, Nantucket and Block Island. Gradually he shifted to the seemingly unending Gaelic drinking songs with their twenty or more verses and inevitable refrains, and the men in the shanties smiled at the coarseness of some of the verses and at the thought that the singer's immediate audience did not know what they were applauding nor recording to take back to staid old Boston. Later as the sun was setting he switched to the laments and the wild and haunting Gaelic war songs of those spattered Highland ancestors he had never seen, and when his voice ceased, the savage melancholy of three hundred years seemed to hang over the peaceful harbour and the quiet boats and the men leaning in the doorways of their shanties with their cigarettes glowing in the dusk and the women looking to the sea from their open windows and their children in their arms.

When he came home he threw the money he had earned on the kitchen table as he did with all his earnings but my mother refused to touch it and the next day he went with the rest of the men to bait his trawl in the shanties. The tourists came to the door that evening and my mother met them there and told them that her husband was not in although he was lying on the bed only a few feet away with the radio playing and the cigarette upon his lips. She stood in the doorway until they reluctantly went away.

In the winter they sent him a picture which had been taken on the day of the singing. On the back it said, 'To Our Ernest Hemingway' and the 'Our' was underlined. There was also an accompanying letter telling how much they had enjoyed themselves, how popular the tape was proving and explaining who Ernest Hemingway was. In a way it almost did look like one of those unshaven, taken-in-Cuba pictures of Hemingway. He looked both massive and incongruous in the setting. His bulky fisherman's clothes were too big for the green and white lawn chair in which he sat, and his rubber boots seemed to take up all of the well-clipped grass square. The beach umbrella jarred with his sunburned face and because he had already been singing for some time, his lips which chapped in the winds of spring and burned in the water glare of summer had already cracked in several places, producing tiny flecks of blood at their corners and on the whiteness of his teeth. The bracelets of brass chain which he wore to protect his wrists from chafing seemed abnormally large and his broad leather belt had been slackened and his heavy shirt and underwear were open at the throat revealing an uncultivated wilderness of white chest hair bordering on the semi-controlled stubble of his neck and chin. His blue eyes had looked directly into the camera and his hair was whiter than the two tiny clouds which hung over his left shoulder. The sea was behind him and its immense blue flatness stretched out to touch the arching blueness of the sky. It seemed very far away from him or else he was so much in the foreground that he seemed too big for it.

Each year another of my sisters would read the books and work in the restaurant. Sometimes they would stay out quite late on the hot summer nights and when they came up the stairs my mother would ask them many long and involved questions which they resented and tried to avoid. Before ascending the stairs they would go into my father's room and those of us who waited above could hear them throwing his clothes off the chair before sitting on it or the squeak of the bed as they sat on its edge. Sometimes they would talk to him a long time, the murmur of their voices blending with the music of the radio into a mysterious vapour-like sound which floated softly up the stairs.

I say this again as if it all happened at once and as if all of my sisters were of identical ages and like so many lemmings going into another sea and, again, it was of course not that way at all. Yet go they did, to Boston, to Montreal, to New York with the young men they met during the summers and later married in those far-away cities. The young men were very articulate and handsome and wore fine clothes and drove expensive cars and my sisters, as I said, were very tall and beautiful with their copper-coloured hair and were tired of darning socks and baking bread.

One by one they went. My mother had each of her daughters for fifteen years, then lost them for two and finally forever. None married a fisherman. My mother never accepted any of the young men, for in her eyes they seemed always a combination of the lazy, the effeminate, the dishonest and the unknown. They never seemed to do any physical work and she could not comprehend their luxurious vacations and she did not know whence they came nor who they were. And in the end she did not really care, for they were not of her people and they were not of her sea.

I say this now with a sense of wonder at my own stupidity in thinking I was somehow free and would go on doing well in school and playing and helping in the boat and passing into my early teens while streaks of grey began to appear in my mother's dark hair and my father's rubber boots dragged sometimes on the pebbles of the beach as he trudged home from the wharf. And there were but three of us in the house that had at one time been so loud.

Then during the winter that I was fifteen he seemed to grow old and ill at once. Most of January he lay upon the bed, smoking and reading and listening to the radio while the wind howled about the house and the needle-like snow blistered off the ice-covered harbour and the doors flew out of people's hands if they did not cling to them like death.

In February when the men began overhauling their lobster traps he still did not move, and my mother and I began to knit lobster trap headings in the evenings. The twine was as always very sharp and harsh, and blisters formed upon our thumbs and little paths of blood snaked quietly down between our fingers while the seals that had drifted down from distant Labrador wept and moaned like human children on the ice-floes of the Gulf.

In the daytime my mother's brother who had been my father's partner as long as I could remember also came to work upon the gear. He was a year older than my mother and was tall and dark and the father of twelve children.

By March we were very far behind and although I began to work very hard in the evenings I knew it was not hard enough and that there were but eight weeks left before the opening of the season on May first. And I knew that my mother worried and my uncle was uneasy and that all of our very lives depended on the boat being ready with her gear and two men, by the date of May the first. And I knew then that *David Copperfield* and *The Tempest* and all of those friends I had dearly come to love must really go forever. So I bade them all good-bye.

The night after my first full day at home and after my mother had gone upstairs he called me into his room where I sat upon the chair beside his bed. 'You will go back tomorrow,' he said simply.

I refused then, saying I had made my decision and was satisfied.

'That is no way to make a decision,' he said, 'and if you are satisfied I am not. It is best that you go back.' I was almost angry then and told him as all children do that I wished he would leave me alone and stop telling me what to do.

He looked at me a long time then, lying there on the same bed on which he had fathered me those sixteen years before, fathered me his only son, out of who knew what emotions when he was already fifty-six and his hair had turned to snow. Then he swung his legs over the edge of the squeaking bed and sat facing me and looked into my own dark eyes with his of crystal blue and placed his hand upon my knee. 'I am not telling you to do anything,' he said softly, 'only asking you.'

The next morning I returned to school. As I left, my mother followed me to the porch and said, 'I never thought a son of mine would choose useless books over the parents that gave him life.'

In the weeks that followed he got up rather miraculously and the gear was ready and the *Jenny Lynn* was freshly painted by the last two weeks of April when the ice began to break up and the lonely screaming gulls returned to haunt the silver herring as they flashed within the sea.

On the first day of May the boats raced out as they had always done, laden down almost to the gunwales with their heavy cargoes of traps. They were almost like living things as they plunged through the waters of the spring and manoeuvred between the still floating icebergs of crystal-white and emerald green on their way to the traditional grounds that they sought out every May. And those of us who sat that day in the high school on the hill, discussing the water imagery of Tennyson, watched them as they passed back and forth beneath us until by afternoon the piles of traps which had been stacked upon the wharf were no longer visible but were spread about the bottoms of the sea. And the *Jenny Lynn* went too, all day, with my uncle tall and dark, like a latter-day Tashtego standing at the tiller with his legs wide apart and guiding her deftly between the floating pans of ice and my father in the stern standing in the same way with his hands upon the ropes that lashed the cargo to the deck. And at night my mother asked, 'Well, how did things go in the boat today?'

And the spring wore on and the summer came and school ended in the third week of June and the lobster season on July first and I wished that the two things I loved so dearly did not exclude each other in a manner that was so blunt and too clear.

At the conclusion of the lobster season my uncle said he had been offered a berth on a deep sea dragger and had decided to accept. We all knew that he was leaving the *Jenny Lynn* forever and that before the next lobster season he would buy a boat of his own. He was expecting another child and would be supporting fifteen people by the next spring and could not chance my father against the family that he loved.

I joined my father then for the trawling season, and he made no protest and my mother was quite happy. Through the summer we baited the tubs of trawl in the afternoon and set them at sunset and revisited them in the darkness of the early morning. The men would come tramping by our house at four a.m. and we would join them and walk with them to the wharf and be on our way before the sun rose out of the ocean where it seemed to spend the night. If I was not up they would toss pebbles to my window and I would be very embarrassed and tumble downstairs to where my father lay fully clothed atop his bed, reading his book and listening to his radio and smoking his cigarette. When I appeared he would swing off his bed and put on his boots and be instantly ready and then we would take the lunches my mother had prepared the night before and walk off toward the sea. He would make no attempt to wake me himself.

It was in many ways a good summer. There were few storms and we were out almost every day and we lost a minimum of gear and seemed to land a maximum of fish and I tanned dark and brown after the manner of my uncles.

My father did not tan—he never tanned—because of his reddish complexion, and the salt water irritated his skin as it had for sixty years. He burned and reburned over and over again and his lips still cracked so that they bled when he smiled, and his arms, especially the left, still broke out into the oozing salt-water boils as they had ever since as a child I had first watched him soaking and bathing them in a variety of ineffectual solutions. The chafe-preventing bracelets of brass linked chain that all the men wore about their wrists in early spring were his the full season and he shaved but painfully and only once a week.

And I saw then, that summer, many things that I had seen all my life as if for the first time and I thought that perhaps my father had never been intended for a fisherman either physically or mentally. At least not in the manner of my uncles; he had never really loved it. And I remembered that, one evening in his room when we were talking about *David Copperfield*, he had said that he had always wanted to go to the university and I had dismissed it then in the way one dismisses his father's saying he would like to be a tight-rope walker, and we had gone on to talk about the Peggottys and how they loved the sea.

And I thought then to myself that there were many things wrong with all of us and all our lives and I wondered why my father, who was himself an only son, had not married before he was forty and then I wondered why he had. I even thought that perhaps he had had to marry my mother and checked the dates on the flyleaf of the Bible where I learned that my oldest sister had been born a prosaic eleven months after the marriage, and I felt myself then very dirty and debased for my lack of faith and for what I had thought and done.

And then there came into my heart a very great love for my father and I thought it was very much braver to spend a life doing what you really do not want rather than selfishly following forever your own dreams and inclinations. And I knew then that I could never leave him alone to suffer the iron-tipped harpoons which my mother would forever hurl into his soul because he was a failure as a husband and a father who had retained none of his own. And I felt that I had been very small in a little secret place within me and that even the completion of high school was for me a silly shallow selfish dream.

So I told him one night very resolutely and very powerfully that I would remain with him as long as he lived and we would fish the sea together. And he made no protest but only smiled through the cigarette smoke that wreathed his bed and replied, 'I hope you will remember what you've said.'

The room was now so filled with books as to be almost Dickensian, but he would not allow my mother to move or change them and he continued to read them, sometimes two or three a night. They came with great regularity now, and there were more hard covers, sent by my sisters who had gone so long ago and now seemed so distant and so prosperous, and sent also pictures of small red-haired grandchildren with baseball bats and dolls which he placed upon his bureau and which my mother gazed at wistfully when she thought no one would see. Red-haired grandchildren with baseball bats and dolls who would never know the sea in hatred or in love.

And so we fished through the heat of August and into the cooler days of September when the water was so clear we could almost see the bottom and the white mists rose like delicate ghosts in the early morning dawn. And one day my mother said to me, 'You have given added years to his life.'

And we fished on into October when it began to roughen and we could no longer risk night sets but took our gear out each morning and returned at the first sign of the squalls; and on into November when we lost three tubs of trawl and the clear blue water turned to a sullen grey and the trochoidal waves rolled rough and high and washed across our bows and decks as we ran within their troughs. We wore heavy sweaters now and the awkward rubber slickers and the heavy woollen mitts which soaked and froze into masses of ice that hung from our wrists like the limbs of gigantic monsters until we thawed them against the exhaust pipe's heat. And almost every day we would leave for home by noon, driven by the blasts of the northwest wind, coating our eyebrows with ice and freezing our eyelids closed as we leaned into a visibility that was hardly there, charting our course from the compass and the sea, running with the waves and between them but never confronting their towering might.

And I stood at the tiller now, on these homeward lunges, stood in the place and in the manner of my uncle, turning to look at my father and to shout over the roar of the engine and the slop of the sea to where he stood in the stern, drenched and dripping with the snow and the salt and the spray and his bushy eyebrows caked in ice. But on November twenty-first, when it seemed we might be making the final run of the season, I turned and he was not there and I knew even in that instant that he would never be again.

On November twenty-first the waves of the grey Atlantic are very very high and the waters are very cold and there are no signposts on the surface of the sea. You cannot tell where you have been five minutes before and in the squalls of snow you cannot see. And it takes longer than you would believe to check a boat that has been running before a gale and turn her ever so carefully in a wide and stupid circle, with timbers creaking and straining, back into the face of storm. And you know that it is useless and that your voice does not carry the length of the boat and that even if you knew the original spot, the relentless waves would carry such a burden perhaps a mile or so by the time you could return. And you know also, the final irony, that your father like your uncles and all the men that form your past, cannot swim a stroke.

The lobster beds off the Cape Breton coast are still very rich and now, from May to July, their offerings are packed in crates of ice, and thundered by the gigantic transport trucks, day and night, through New Glasgow, Amherst, Saint John and Bangor and Portland and into Boston where they are tossed still living into boiling pots of water, their final home.

And though the prices are higher and the competition tighter, the grounds to which the *Jenny Lynn* once went remain untouched and unfished as they have for the last ten years. For if there are no signposts on the sea in storm there are certain ones in calm and the lobster bottoms were distributed in calm before any of us can remember and the grounds my father fished were those his father fished before him and there were others before and before and before. Twice the big boats have come from forty and fifty miles, lured by the promise of the grounds, and strewn the bottom with their traps and twice they have returned to find their buoys cut adrift and their gear lost and destroyed. Twice the Fisheries Officer and the Mounted Police have come and asked many long and involved questions and twice they have received no answers from the men leaning in the doors of their shanties and the women standing at their windows with their children in their arms. Twice they have gone away saying: 'There are no legal boundaries in the Marine area'; 'No one can own the sea'; 'Those grounds don't wait for anyone.'

But the men and women, with my mother dark among them, do not care for what they say, for to them the grounds are sacred and they think they wait for me.

It is not an easy thing to know that your mother lives alone on an inadequate insurance policy and that she is too proud to accept any other aid. And that she looks through her lonely window onto the ice of winter and the hot flat calm of summer and the rolling waves of fall. And that she lies awake in the early morning's darkness when the rubber boots of the men scrunch upon the gravel as they pass beside her house on their way down to the wharf. And she knows that the footsteps never stop, because no man goes from her house, and she alone of all the Lynns has neither son nor son-in-law that walks toward the boat that will take him to the sea. And it is not an easy thing to know that your mother looks upon the sea with love and on you with bitterness because the one has been so constant and the other so untrue.

But neither is it easy to know that your father was found on November twenty-eighth, ten miles to the north and wedged between two boulders at the base of the rock-strewn cliffs where he had been hurled and slammed so many many times. His hands were shredded ribbons as were his feet which had lost their boots to the suction of the sea, and his shoulders came apart in our hands when we tried to move him from the rocks. And the fish had eaten his testicles and the gulls had pecked out his eyes and the white-green stubble of his whiskers had continued to grow in death, like the grass on graves, upon the purple, bloated mass that was his face. There was not much left of my father, physically, as he lay there with the brass chains on his wrists and the seaweed in his hair.

1968

As Birds Bring Forth the Sun

Once there was a family with a Highland name who lived beside the sea. And the man had a dog of which he was very fond. She was large and grey, a sort of staghound from another time. And if she jumped up to lick his face, which she loved to do, her paws would jolt against his shoulders with such force that she would come close to knocking him down and he would be forced to take two or three backward steps before he could regain his balance. And he himself was not a small man, being slightly over six feet and perhaps one hundred and eighty pounds.

She had been left, when a pup, at the family's gate in a small handmade box and no one knew where she had come from or that she would eventually grow to such a size. Once, while still a small pup, she had been run over by the steel wheel of a horse-drawn cart which was hauling kelp from the shore to be used as fertilizer. It was in October and the rain had been falling for some weeks and the ground was soft. When the wheel of the cart passed over her, it sunk her body into the wet earth as well as crushing some of her ribs; and apparently the silhouette of her small crushed body was visible in the earth after the man lifted her to his chest while she yelped and screamed. He ran his fingers along her broken bones, ignoring the blood and urine which fell upon his shirt, trying to soothe her bulging eyes and her scrabbling front paws and her desperately licking tongue.

The more practical members of his family, who had seen run-over dogs before, suggested that her neck be broken by his strong hands or that he grasp her by the hind legs and swing her head against a rock, thus putting an end to her misery. But he would not do it.

Instead, he fashioned a small box and lined it with woollen remnants from a sheep's fleece and one of his old and frayed shirts. He placed her within the box and placed the box behind the stove and then he warmed some milk in a small saucepan and sweetened it with sugar. And he held open her small and trembling jaws with his left hand while spooning in the sweetened milk with his right, ignoring the needle-like sharpness of her small teeth. She lay in the box most of the remaining fall and into the early winter, watching everything with her large brown eyes.

Although some members of the family complained about her presence and the odour from the box and waste of time she involved, they gradually adjusted to her; and as the weeks passed by, it became evident that her ribs were knitting together in some form or other and that she was recovering with the resilience of the young. It also became evident that she would grow to a tremendous size, as she outgrew one box and then another and the grey hair began to feather from her huge front paws. In the spring she was outside almost all of the time and followed the man everywhere; and when she came inside during the following months, she had grown so large that she would no longer fit into her accustomed place behind the stove and was forced to lie beside it. She was never given a name but was referred to in Gaelic as *cù mòr glas*, the big grey dog.

By the time she came into her first heat, she had grown to a tremendous height, and although her signs and her odour attracted many panting and highly aroused suitors, none was big enough to mount her and the frenzy of their disappointment and the longing of her unfulfilment were more than the man could stand. He went, so the story goes, to a place where he knew there was a big dog. A dog not as big as she was, but still a big dog, and he brought him home with him. And at the proper time he took the *cù mòr glas* and the big dog down to the sea where he knew there was a hollow in the rock which appeared only at low tide. He took some sacking to provide footing for the male dog and he placed the *cù mòr glas* in the hollow of the rock and knelt beside her and steadied her with his left arm under her throat and helped position the male dog above her and guided his blood-engorged penis. He was a man used to working with the breeding of animals, with the guiding of rams and bulls and stallions and often with the funky smell of animal semen heavy on his large and gentle hands.

The winter that followed was a cold one and ice formed on the sea and frequent squalls and blizzards obliterated the offshore islands and caused the people to stay near their fires much of the time, mending clothes and nets and harness and waiting for the change in season. The *cù mòr glas* grew heavier and even more large until there was hardly room for her around the stove or even under the table. And then one morning, when it seemed that spring was about to break, she was gone.

The man and even his family, who had become more involved than they cared to admit, waited for her but she did not come. And as the frenzy of spring wore on, they busied themselves with readying their land and their fishing gear and all of the things that so desperately required their attention. And then they were into summer and fall and winter and another spring which saw the birth of the man and his wife's twelfth child. And then it was summer again.

That summer the man and two of his teenaged sons were pulling their herring nets about two miles offshore when the wind began to blow off the land and the water began to roughen. They became afraid that they could not make it safely back to shore, so they pulled in behind one of the offshore islands, knowing that they would be sheltered there and planning to outwait the storm. As the prow of their boat approached the gravelly shore, they heard a sound above them, and looking up they saw the *cù mòr glas* silhouetted on the brow of the hill which was the small island's highest point.

'*M'eudal cù mòr glas*' shouted the man in his happiness—*m'eudal* meaning something like dear or darling; and as he shouted, he jumped over the side of his boat into the waist-deep water, struggling for footing on the rolling gravel as he waded eagerly and awkwardly towards her and the shore. At the same time, the *cù mòr glas* came hurtling down towards him in a shower of small rocks dislodged by her feet; and just as he was emerging from the water, she met him as she used to, rearing up on her hind legs and placing her huge front paws on his shoulders while extending her eager tongue.

The weight and speed of her momentum met him as he tried to hold his balance on the sloping angle and the water rolling gravel beneath his feet, and he staggered backwards and lost his footing and fell beneath her force. And in that instant again, as the story goes, there appeared over the brow of the hill six more huge grey dogs hurtling down towards the gravelled strand. They had never seen him before; and seeing him stretched prone beneath their mother, they misunderstood, like so many armies, the intention of their leader.

They fell upon him in a fury, slashing his face and tearing aside his lower jaw and ripping out his throat, crazed with blood-lust or duty or perhaps starvation. The *cù mòr glas* turned on them in her own savagery, slashing and snarling and, it seemed, crazed by their mistake; driving them bloodied and yelping before her, back over the brow of the hill where they vanished from sight but could still be heard screaming in the distance. It all took perhaps little more than a minute.

The man's two sons, who were still in the boat and had witnessed it all, ran sobbing through the salt water to where their mauled and mangled father lay; but there was little they could do other than hold his warm and bloodied hands for a few brief moments. Although his eyes 'lived' for a small fraction of time, he could not speak to them because his face and throat had been torn away, and of course there was nothing they could do except to hold and be held tightly until that too slipped away and his eyes glazed over and they could no longer feel his hands holding theirs. The storm increased and they could not get home and so they were forced to spend the night huddled beside their father's body. They were afraid to try to carry the body to the rocking boat because he was so heavy and they were afraid that they might lose even what little of him remained and they were afraid also, huddled on the rocks, that the dogs might return. But they did not return at all and there was no sound from them, no sound at all, only the moaning of the wind and the washing of the water on the rocks.

In the morning they debated whether they should try to take his body with them or whether they should leave it and return in the company of older and wiser men. But they were afraid to leave it unattended and felt that the time needed to cover it with protective rocks would be better spent in trying to get across to their home shore. For a while they debated as to whether one should go in the boat and the other remain on the island, but each was afraid to be alone and so in the end they managed to drag and carry and almost float him towards the bobbing boat. They laid him facedown and covered him with what clothes there were and set off across the still-rolling sea. Those who waited on the shore missed the large presence of the man within the boat and some of them waded into the water and others rowed out in skiffs, attempting to hear the tearful message called out across the rolling waves.

The *cù mòr glas* and her six young dogs were never seen again, or perhaps I should say they were never seen again in the same way. After some weeks, a group of men circled the island tentatively in their boats but they saw no sign. They went again and again but found nothing. A year later, and grown much braver, they beached their boats and walked the island carefully, looking into the small sea caves and the hollows at the base of the wind-ripped trees, thinking perhaps that if they did not find the dogs, they might at least find their whitened bones; but again they discovered nothing.

The *cù mòr glas*, though, was supposed to be sighted here and there for a number of years. Seen on a hill in one region or silhouetted on a ridge in another or loping across the valleys or glens in the early morning or the shadowy evening. Always in the area of the half perceived. For a while she became rather like the Loch Ness Monster or the Sasquatch on a smaller scale. Seen but not recorded. Seen when there were no cameras. Seen but never taken.

The mystery of where she went became entangled with the mystery of whence she came. There was increased speculation about the handmade box in which she had been found and much theorizing as to the individual or individuals who might have left it. People went to look for the box but could not find it. It was felt she might have been part of a *buidseachd* or evil spell cast on the man by some mysterious enemy. But no one could go much farther than that. All of his caring for her was recounted over and over again and nobody missed any of the ironies.

What seemed literally known was that she had crossed the winter ice to have her pups and had been unable to get back. No one could remember ever seeing her swim; and in the early months at least, she could not have taken her young pups with her.

The large and gentle man with the smell of animal semen often heavy on his hands was my great-great-great-grandfather, and it may be argued that he died because he was too good at breeding animals or that he cared too much about their fulfilment and well-being. He was no longer there for his own child of the spring who, in turn, became my great-great-grandfather, and he was perhaps too much there in the memory of his older sons who saw him fall beneath the ambiguous force of the *cù mòr glas*. The youngest boy in the boat was haunted and tormented by the awfulness of what he had seen. He would wake at night screaming that he had seen the *cù mòr glas a'bhàis*, the big grey dog of death, and his screams filled the house and the ears and minds of the listeners, bringing home again and again the consequences of their loss. One morning, after a night in which he saw the *cù mòr glas a'bhàis* so vividly that his sheets were drenched with sweat, he walked to the high cliff which faced the island and there he cut his throat with a fish knife and fell into the sea.

The other brother lived to be forty, but, again so the story goes, he found himself in a Glasgow pub one night, perhaps looking for answers, deep and sodden with the whisky which had become his anaesthetic. In the half darkness he saw a large, grey-haired man sitting by himself against the wall and mumbled something to him. Some say he saw the *cù mòr glas a'bhàis* or uttered the name. And perhaps the man heard the phrase through ears equally affected by drink and felt he was being called a dog or a son of a bitch or something of that nature. They rose to meet one another and struggled outside into the cobblestoned passageway behind the pub where, most improbably, there were supposed to be six other large, grey-haired men who beat him to death on the cobblestones, smashing his bloodied head into the stone again and again before vanishing and leaving him to die with his face turned to the sky. The *cù mòr glas a'bhàis* had come again, said his family, as they tried to piece the tale together.

This is how the *cù mòr glas a'bhàis* came into our lives, and it is obvious that all of this happened a long, long time ago. Yet with succeeding generations it seemed the spectre had somehow come to stay and that it had become *ours*—not in the manner of an unwanted skeleton in the closet from the family's ancient past but more in the manner of something close to a genetic possibility. In the deaths of each generation, the grey dog was seen by some—by women who were to die in childbirth; by soldiers who went forth to the many wars but did not return; by those who went forth to feuds or dangerous love affairs; by those who answered mysterious midnight messages; by those who swerved on the highway to avoid the real or imagined grey dog and ended in masses of crumpled steel. And by one professional athlete who, in addition to his ritualized athletic superstitions, carried another fear or belief as well. Many of the man's descendants moved like careful hemophiliacs, fearing that they carried unwanted possibilities deep within them. And others, while they laughed, were like members of families in which there is a recurrence over the generations of repeated cancer or the diabetes which comes to those beyond middle age. The feeling of those who may say little to others but who may say often and quietly to themselves, 'It has not happened to me,' while adding always the cautionary '*yet*'.

I am thinking all of this now as the October rain falls on the city of Toronto and the pleasant, white-clad nurses pad confidently in and out of my father's room. He lies quietly amidst the whiteness, his head and shoulders elevated so that he is in that hospital position of being neither quite prone nor yet sitting. His hair is white upon his pillow and he breathes softly and sometimes unevenly, although it is difficult ever to be sure.

My five grey-haired brothers and I take turns beside his bedside, holding his heavy hands in ours and feeling their response, hoping ambiguously that he will speak to us, although we know that it may tire him. And trying to read his life and ours into his eyes when they are open. He has been with us for a long time, well into our middle age. Unlike those boys in that boat of so long ago, we did not see him taken from us in our youth. And unlike their youngest brother who, in turn, became our great-great-grandfather, we did not grow into a world in which there was no father's touch. We have been lucky to have this large and gentle man so deep into our lives.

No one in this hospital has mentioned the *cù mòr glas a'bhàis*. Yet as my mother said ten years ago, before slipping into her own death as quietly as a grownup child who leaves or enters her parents' house in the early hours, 'It is hard to *not* know what you do know.'

Even those who are most skeptical, like my oldest brother who has driven here from Montreal, betray themselves by their nervous actions. 'I avoided the Greyhound bus stations in both Montreal and Toronto,' he smiled upon his arrival, and then added, 'Just in case.'

He did not realize how ill our father was and has smiled little since then. I watch him turning the diamond ring upon his finger, knowing that he hopes he will not hear the Gaelic phrase he knows too well. Not having the luxury, as he once said, of some who live in Montreal and are able to pretend they do not understand the 'other' language. You cannot *not* know what you do know.

Sitting here, taking turns holding the hands of the man who gave us life, we are afraid for him and for ourselves. We are afraid of what he may see and we are afraid to hear the phrase born of the vision. We are aware that it may become confused with what the doctors call 'the will to live' and we are aware that some beliefs are what others would dismiss as 'garbage'. We are aware that there are men who believe the earth is flat and that the birds bring forth the sun.

Bound here in our own peculiar mortality, we do not wish to see or see others see that which signifies life's demise. We do not want to hear the voice of our father, as did those other sons, calling down his own particular death upon him.

We would shut our eyes and plug our ears, even as we know such actions to be of no avail. Open still and fearful to the grey hair rising on our necks if and when we hear the scrabble of the paws and the scratching at the door.

1985

Raymond Carver

1938-88

Raymond Carver's short fiction presents his working-class American characters in a style and idiom that seem naturally suited to the hard circumstances of their lives. But in its spare simplicity, his narration is beautifully crafted to summon up his characters' values and their transforming moments of insight, despair, and love. Carver believed that good fiction conveys moral truths: 'In fiction that matters, the significance of the action inside the story translates to the lives of people outside the story. Do we need to remind ourselves of this? In the best novels and short stories, goodness is recognized as such. Loyalty, love, fortitude, courage, integrity may not always be rewarded, but they are recognized as good or noble actions or qualities; and evil or base or simply stupid behaviour is seen and held up for what it is: evil, base, or stupid behaviour.'

Carver was born to working-class parents in Clatskanie, a logging town in Oregon, and grew up in Yakima, Washington, where he worked at a series of odd jobs in his teens. He married at nineteen, then moved to Paradise, California, where he enrolled at Chico State College. He published his first story, 'The Furious Seasons', in 1961, and took his B.A. (1963) from Humboldt State. After another series of odd jobs, he began to write full-time in 1970; the publication of the collection *Will You Please Be Quiet, Please?* (1976) was followed by *Furious Seasons* (1977) and *What We Talk About When We Talk About Love* (1981). Carver lived in Port Angeles, Washington for the last five years of his life.

'What creates tension in a piece of fiction,' Carver explained in 1984, 'is partly the way the concrete words are linked up to make the visible action of the story. But it's also the things that are left out, that are implied, the landscape just under the smooth (but sometimes broken and unsettled) surface of things.' In 'Why Don't You Dance?' the surface is at once banal and quirky: a man has moved all his belongings out of his house into the driveway. But rather than exploring his motivations, the story shifts its focus to the young couple who buy the man's belongings. It is the 'things that are left out, that are implied' in the couple's responses to the man that shape the story into a disquieting reflection on their lives.

In 'Cathedral', Carver explores a crucial transformation in the values of his first-person narrator. Annoyed and suspicious at the visit of the blind man who has been his wife's friend and confidant for ten years, the narrator plainly reveals his distrust and unease; but as the story traces his evolution over the course of an evening, his own voice modulates to reveal his awakening into wonder at the strangeness of experience. Finally, the cathedral that he draws with the blind man becomes a rich symbol of the changed quality in his perceptions.

'Why Don't You Dance?' was first published in the Autumn 1978 issue of *Quarterly West* and then collected in *What We Talk About When We Talk About Love*. 'Cathedral' was first published in the September 1981 issue of *Atlantic Monthly* and then collected in *The Best American Short Stories 1982* before becoming the title story of Carver's 1983 collection.

Why Don't You Dance?

In the kitchen, he poured another drink and looked at the bedroom suite in his front yard. The mattress was stripped and the candy-striped sheets lay beside two pillows on the chiffonier. Except for that, things looked much the way they had in the bedroom—nightstand and reading lamp on his side of the bed, nightstand and reading lamp on her side.

His side, her side.

He considered this as he sipped the whisky.

The chiffonier stood a few feet from the foot of the bed. He had emptied the drawers into cartons that morning, and the cartons were in the living room. A portable heater was next to the chiffonier. A rattan chair with a decorator pillow stood at the foot of the bed. The buffed aluminum kitchen set took up a part of the driveway. A yellow muslin cloth, much too large, a gift, covered the table and hung down over the sides. A potted fern was on the table, along with a box of silverware and a record player, also gifts. A big console-model television set rested on a coffee table, and a few feet away from this stood a sofa and chair and a floor lamp. The desk was pushed against the garage door. A few utensils were on the desk, along with a wall clock and two framed prints. There was also in the driveway a carton with cups, glasses, and plates, each object wrapped in newspaper. That morning he had cleared out the closets, and except for the three cartons in the living room, all the stuff was out of the house. He had run an extension cord on out there and everything was connected. Things worked, no different from how it was when they were inside.

Now and then a car slowed and people stared. But no one stopped.

It occurred to him that he wouldn't, either.

'It must be a yard sale,' the girl said to the boy.

This girl and this boy were furnishing a little apartment.

'Let's see what they want for the bed,' the girl said.

'And for the TV,' the boy said.

The boy pulled into the driveway and stopped in front of the kitchen table.

They got out of the car and began to examine things, the girl touching the muslin cloth, the boy plugging in the blender and turning the dial to MINCE, the girl picking up a chafing dish, the boy turning on the television set and making little adjustments.

He sat down on the sofa to watch. He lit a cigarette, looked around, flipped the match into the grass.

The girl sat on the bed. She pushed off her shoes and lay back. She thought she could see a star.

'Come here, Jack. Try this bed. Bring one of those pillows,' she said.

'How is it?' he said.

'Try it,' she said.

He looked around. The house was dark.

'I feel funny,' he said. 'Better see if anybody's home.'

She bounced on the bed.

'Try it first,' she said.

He lay down on the bed and put the pillow under his head.

'How does it feel?' she said.

'It feels firm,' he said.

She turned on her side and put her hand to his face.

'Kiss me,' she said.

'Let's get up,' he said.

'Kiss me,' she said.

She closed her eyes. She held him.

He said, 'I'll see if anybody's home.'

But he just sat up and stayed where he was, making believe he was watching the television.

Lights came on in houses up and down the street.

'Wouldn't it be funny if,' the girl said and grinned and didn't finish.

The boy laughed, but for no good reason. For no good reason, he switched the reading lamp on.

The girl brushed away a mosquito, whereupon the boy stood up and tucked in his shirt.

'I'll see if anybody's home,' he said. 'I don't think anybody's home. But if anybody is, I'll see what things are going for.'

'Whatever they ask, offer ten dollars less. It's always a good idea,' she said. 'And, besides, they must be desperate or something.'

'It's a pretty good TV,' the boy said.

'Ask them how much,' the girl said.

The man came down the sidewalk with a sack from the market. He had sandwiches, beer, whisky. He saw the car in the driveway and the girl on the bed. He saw the television set going and the boy on the porch.

'Hello,' the man said to the girl. 'You found the bed. That's good.'

'Hello,' the girl said, and got up. 'I was just trying it out.' She patted the bed. 'It's a pretty good bed.'

'It's a good bed,' the man said, and put down the sack and took out the beer and whisky.

'We thought nobody was here,' the boy said. 'We're interested in the bed and maybe in the TV. Also maybe the desk. How much do you want for the bed?'

'I was thinking fifty dollars for the bed,' the man said.

'Would you take forty?' the girl asked.

'I'll take forty,' the man said.

He took a glass out of the carton. He took the newspaper off the glass. He broke the seal on the whisky.

'How about the TV?' the boy said.
'Twenty-five.'
'Would you take fifteen?' the girl said.
'Fifteen's okay. I could take fifteen,' the man said.
The girl looked at the boy.
'You kids, you'll want a drink,' the man said. 'Glasses in that box. I'm going to sit down. I'm going to sit down on the sofa.'
The man sat on the sofa, leaned back, and stared at the boy and the girl.

The boy found two glasses and poured whisky.
'That's enough,' the girl said. 'I think I want water in mine.'
She pulled out a chair and sat at the kitchen table.
'There's water in that spigot over there,' the man said. 'Turn on the spigot.'
The boy came back with the watered whisky. He cleared his throat and sat down at the kitchen table. He grinned. But he didn't drink anything from his glass.
The man gazed at the television. He finished his drink and started another. He reached to turn on the floor lamp. It was then that his cigarette dropped from his fingers and fell between the cushions.
The girl got up to help him find it.
'So what do you want?' the boy said to the girl.
The boy took out the chequebook and held it to his lips as if thinking.
'I want the desk,' the girl said. 'How much money is the desk?'
The man waved his hand at this preposterous question.
'Name a figure,' he said.
He looked at them as they sat at the table. In the lamplight, there was something about their faces. It was nice or it was nasty. There was no telling.

'I'm going to turn off this TV and put on a record,' the man said. 'This record-player is going, too. Cheap. Make me an offer.'
He poured more whisky and opened a beer.
'Everything goes,' said the man.
The girl held out her glass and the man poured.
'Thank you,' she said. 'You're very nice,' she said.
'It goes to your head,' the boy said. I'm getting it in the head.' He held up his glass and jiggled it.
The man finished his drink and poured another, and then he found the box with the records.
'Pick something,' the man said to the girl, and he held the records out to her.
The boy was writing a cheque.
'Here,' the girl said, picking something, picking anything, for she did not know the names on these labels. She got up from the table and sat

down again. She did not want to sit still.

'I'm making it out to cash,' the boy said.

'Sure,' the man said.

They drank. They listened to the record. And then the man put on another.

Why don't you kids dance? he decided to say, and then he said it, 'Why don't you dance?'

'I don't think so,' the boy said.

'Go ahead,' the man said. 'It's my yard. You can dance if you want to.'

Arms about each other, their bodies pressed together, the boy and the girl moved up and down the driveway. They were dancing. And when the record was over, they did it again, and when that one ended, the boy said, 'I'm drunk.'

The girl said, 'You're not drunk.'

'Well, I'm drunk,' the boy said.

The man turned the record over and the boy said, 'I am.'

'Dance with me,' the girl said to the boy and then to the man, and when the man stood up, she came to him with her arms wide open.

'Those people over there, they're watching,' she said.

'It's okay,' the man said. 'It's my place,' he said.

'Let them watch,' the girl said.

'That's right,' the man said. 'They thought they'd seen everything over here. But they haven't seen this, have they?' he said.

He felt her breath on his neck.

'I hope you like your bed,' he said.

The girl closed and then opened her eyes. She pushed her face into the man's shoulder. She pulled the man closer.

'You must be desperate or something,' she said.

Weeks later, she said: 'The guy was about middle-aged. All his things right there in his yard. No lie. We got real pissed and danced. In the driveway. Oh, my God. Don't laugh. He played us these records. Look at this record-player. The old guy gave it to us. And all these crappy records. Will you look at this shit?'

She kept talking. She told everyone. There was more to it, and she was trying to get it talked out. After a time, she quit trying.

1978

Cathedral

This blind man, an old friend of my wife's, he was on his way to spend the night. His wife had died. So he was visiting the dead wife's relatives in Connecticut. He called my wife from his in-laws'. Arrangements were made. He would come by train, a five-hour trip, and my wife would meet him at the station. She hadn't seen him since she worked for him one summer in Seattle ten years ago. But she and the blind man had kept in touch. They made tapes and mailed them back and forth. I wasn't enthusiastic about his visit. He was no one I knew. And his being blind bothered me. My idea of blindness came from the movies. In the movies, the blind moved slowly and never laughed. Sometimes they were led by seeing-eye dogs. A blind man in my house was not something I looked forward to.

That summer in Seattle she had needed a job. She didn't have any money. The man she was going to marry at the end of the summer was in officers' training school. He didn't have any money, either. But she was in love with the guy, and he was in love with her, etc. She'd seen something in the paper: HELP WANTED—*Reading to Blind Man*, and a telephone number. She phoned and went over, was hired on the spot. She'd worked with this blind man all summer. She read stuff to him, case studies, reports, that sort of thing. She helped him organize his little office in the county social-service department. They'd become good friends, my wife and the blind man. How do I know these things? She told me. And she told me something else. On her last day in the office, the blind man asked if he could touch her face. She agreed to this. She told me he touched his fingers to every part of her face, her nose—even her neck! She never forgot it. She even tried to write a poem about it. She was always trying to write a poem. She wrote a poem or two every year, usually after something really important had happened to her.

When we first started going out together, she showed me the poem. In the poem, she recalled his fingers and the way they had moved around her face. In the poem, she talked about what she had felt at the time, about what went through her mind when the blind man touched her nose and lips. I can remember I didn't think much of the poem. Of course, I didn't tell her that. Maybe I just don't understand poetry. I admit it's not the first thing I reach for when I pick up something to read.

Anyway, this man who'd first enjoyed her favours, the officer-to-be, he'd been her childhood sweetheart. So okay. I'm saying that at the end of the summer she let the blind man run his hands over her face, said goodbye to him, married her childhood etc., who was now a commissioned officer, and she moved away from Seattle. But they'd kept in touch, she and the blind man. She made the first contact after a year or so. She called him up one night from an Air Force base in Alabama. She wanted to talk. They talked. He asked her to send him a tape and tell him about her life.

She did this. She sent the tape. On the tape, she told the blind man about her husband and about their life together in the military. She told the blind man she loved her husband but she didn't like it where they lived and she didn't like it that he was a part of the military-industrial thing. She told the blind man that she'd written a poem and he was in it. She told him that she was writing a poem about what it was like to be an Air Force officer's wife. The poem wasn't finished yet. She was still writing it. The blind man made a tape. He sent her the tape. She made a tape. This went on for years. My wife's officer was posted to one base and then another. She sent tapes from Moody AFB, McGuire, McConnell, and finally Travis, near Sacramento, where one night she got to feeling lonely and cut off from people she kept losing in that moving-around life. She got to feeling she couldn't go it another step. She went in and swallowed all the pills and capsules in the medicine chest and washed them down with a bottle of gin. Then she got into a hot bath and passed out.

But instead of dying, she got sick. She threw up. Her officer—why should he have a name? he was the childhood sweetheart, and what more does he want?—came home from somewhere, found her, and called the ambulance. In time, she put it all on a tape and sent the tape to the blind man. Over the years, she put all kinds of stuff on tapes and sent the tapes off lickety-split. Next to writing a poem every year, I think it was her chief means of recreation. On one tape, she told the blind man she'd decided to live away from her officer for a time. On another tape, she told him about her divorce. She and I began going out, and of course she told her blind man about it. She told him everything, or so it seemed to me. Once she asked if I'd like to hear the latest tape from the blind man. This was a year ago. I was on the tape, she said. So I said okay, I'd listen to it. I got us drinks and we settled down in the living room. We made ready to listen. First she inserted the tape into the player and adjusted a couple of dials. Then she pushed a lever. The tape squeaked and someone began to talk in this loud voice. She lowered the volume. After a few minutes of harmless chitchat, I heard my own name in the mouth of this stranger, this blind man I didn't even know! And then this: 'From all you've said about him, I can only conclude—' But we were interrupted, a knock at the door or something, and we didn't ever get back to the tape. Maybe it was just as well. I'd heard all I wanted to.

Now this same blind man was coming to sleep in my house.

'Maybe I could take him bowling,' I said to my wife. She was at the draining board doing scalloped potatoes. She put down the knife she was using and turned around.

'If you love me,' she said, 'you can do this for me. If you don't love me, okay. But if you had a friend, any friend, and the friend came to visit, I'd make him feel comfortable.' She wiped her hands with the dish towel.

'I don't have any blind friends,' I said.

'You don't have *any* friends,' she said. 'Period. Besides,' she said, 'goddamn it, his wife's just died! Don't you understand that! The man's lost his wife!'

I didn't answer. She'd told me a little about the blind man's wife. Her name was Beulah. Beulah! That's a name for a coloured woman.

'Was his wife a Negro?' I asked.

'Are you crazy?' my wife said. 'Have you just flipped or something?' She picked up a potato. I saw it hit the floor, then roll under the stove. 'What's wrong with you?' she said. 'Are you drunk?'

'I'm just asking,' I said.

Right then my wife filled me in with more detail than I cared to know. I made a drink and sat at the kitchen table to listen. Pieces of the story began to fall into place.

Beulah had gone to work for the blind man the summer after my wife had stopped working for him. Pretty soon Beulah and the blind man had themselves a church wedding. It was a little wedding—who'd want to go to such a wedding in the first place?—just the two of them, plus the minister and the minister's wife. But it was a church wedding just the same. It was what Beulah had wanted, he'd said. But even then Beulah must have been carrying cancer in her glands. After they had been inseparable for eight years—my wife's word, *inseparable*—Beulah's health went into a rapid decline. She died in a Seattle hospital room, the blind man sitting beside the bed and holding on to her hand. They'd married, lived and worked together, slept together—had sex, sure—and then the blind man had to bury her. All this without his having ever seen what the goddamned woman looked like. It was beyond my understanding. Hearing this, I felt sorry for the blind man for a little bit. And then I found myself thinking what a pitiful life this woman must have led. Imagine a woman who could never see herself as she was seen in the eyes of her loved one. A woman who could go on day after day and never receive the smallest compliment from her beloved. A woman whose husband could never read the expression on her face, be it misery or something better. Someone who could wear makeup or not—what difference to him? She could, if she wanted, wear green eyeshadow around one eye, a straight pin in her nostril, yellow slacks and purple shoes, no matter. And then to slip off into death, the blind man's hand on her hand, his blind eyes streaming tears—I'm imagining now—her last thought maybe this: that he never even knew what she looked like, and she on an express to the grave. Robert was left with a small insurance policy and half of a twenty-peso Mexican coin. The other half of the coin went into the box with her. Pathetic.

So when the time rolled around, my wife went to the depot to pick him up. With nothing to do but wait—sure, I blamed him for that—I was having a drink and watching the TV when I heard the car pull into the drive. I got up from the sofa with my drink and went to the window to have a look.

I saw my wife laughing in the parked car. I saw her get out of the car and shut the door. She was still wearing a smile. Just amazing. She went around to the other side of the car to where the blind man was already starting to get out. This blind man, feature this, he was wearing a full beard! A beard on a blind man! Too much, I say. The blind man reached into the back seat and dragged out a suitcase. My wife took his arm, shut the car door, and, talking all the way, moved him down the drive and then up the steps to the front porch. I turned off the TV. I finished my drink, rinsed the glass, dried my hands. Then I went to the door.

My wife said, 'I want you to meet Robert. Robert, this is my husband. I've told you all about him.' She was beaming. She had this blind man by his coat sleeve.

The blind man let go of his suitcase and up came his hand.

I took it. He squeezed hard, held my hand, and then he let it go.

'I feel like we've already met,' he boomed.

'Likewise,' I said. I didn't know what else to say. Then I said, 'Welcome. I've heard a lot about you.' We began to move then, a little group, from the porch into the living room, my wife guiding him by the arm. The blind man was carrying his suitcase in his other hand. My wife said things like, 'To your left here, Robert. That's right. Now watch it, there's a chair. That's it. Sit down right here. This is the sofa. We just bought this sofa two weeks ago.'

I started to say something about the old sofa. I'd liked that old sofa. But I didn't say anything. Then I wanted to say something else, small-talk, about the scenic ride along the Hudson. How going *to* New York, you should sit on the right-hand side of the train, and coming *from* New York, the left-hand side.

'Did you have a good train ride?' I said. 'Which side of the train did you sit on, by the way?'

'What a question, which side!' my wife said. 'What's it matter which side?' she said.

'I just asked,' I said.

'Right side,' the blind man said. 'I hadn't been on a train in nearly forty years. Not since I was a kid. With my folks. That's been a long time. I'd nearly forgotten the sensation. I have winter in my beard now,' he said. 'So I've been told, anyway. Do I look distinguished, my dear?' the blind man said to my wife.

'You look distinguished, Robert,' she said. 'Robert,' she said. 'Robert, it's just so good to see you.'

My wife finally took her eyes off the blind man and looked at me. I had the feeling she didn't like what she saw. I shrugged.

I've never met, or personally known, anyone who was blind. This blind man was late forties, a heavy-set, balding man with stooped shoulders, as if he carried a great weight there. He wore brown slacks, brown shoes, a light-brown shirt, a tie, a sports coat. Spiffy. He also had this full beard. But he didn't use a cane and he didn't wear dark glasses. I'd always thought dark glasses were a must for the blind. Fact was, I wished he had a pair. At first glance, his eyes looked like anyone else's eyes. But if you looked close, there was something different about them. Too much white in the iris, for one thing, and the pupils seemed to move around in the sockets without his knowing it or being able to stop it. Creepy. As I stared at his face, I saw the left pupil turn toward his nose while the other made an effort to keep in one place. But it was only an effort, for that eye was on the roam without his knowing it or wanting it to be.

I said, 'Let me get you a drink. What's your pleasure? We have a little of everything. It's one of our pastimes.'

'Bub, I'm a Scotch man myself,' he said fast enough in this big voice.

'Right,' I said. Bub! 'Sure you are. I knew it.'

He let his fingers touch his suitcase, which was sitting alongside the sofa. He was taking his bearings. I didn't blame him for that.

'I'll move that up to your room,' my wife said.

'No, that's fine,' the blind man said loudly. 'It can go up when I go up.'

'A little water with the Scotch?' I said.

'Very little,' he said.

'I knew it,' I said.

He said, 'Just a tad. The Irish actor, Barry Fitzgerald? I'm like that fellow. When I drink water, Fitzgerald said, I drink water. When I drink whisky, I drink whisky.' My wife laughed. The blind man brought his hand up under his beard. He lifted his beard slowly and let it drop.

I did the drinks, three big glasses of Scotch with a splash of water in each. Then we made ourselves comfortable and talked about Robert's travels. First the long flight from the West Coast to Connecticut, we covered that. Then from Connecticut up here by train. We had another drink concerning that leg of the trip.

I remembered having read somewhere that the blind didn't smoke because, as speculation had it, they couldn't see the smoke they exhaled. I thought I knew that much and that much only about blind people. But this blind man smoked his cigarette down to the nubbin and then lit another one. This blind man filled his ashtray and my wife emptied it.

When we sat down at the table for dinner, we had another drink. My wife heaped Robert's plate with cube steak, scalloped potatoes, green beans. I buttered him up two slices of bread. I said, 'Here's bread and butter for you.' I swallowed some of my drink. 'Now let us pray,' I said, and the blind man lowered his head. My wife looked at me, her mouth agape. 'Pray the phone won't ring and the food doesn't get cold,' I said.

We dug in. We ate everything there was to eat on the table. We ate like there was no tomorrow. We didn't talk. We ate. We scarfed. We grazed that table. We were into serious eating. The blind man had right away located his foods, he knew just where everything was on his plate. I watched with admiration as he used his knife and fork on the meat. He'd cut two pieces of meat, fork the meat into his mouth, and then go all out for the scalloped potatoes, the beans next, and then he'd tear off a hunk of buttered bread and eat that. He'd follow this up with a big drink of milk. It didn't seem to bother him to use his fingers once in a while, either.

We finished everything, including half a strawberry pie. For a few moments, we sat as if stunned. Sweat beaded on our faces. Finally, we got up from the table and left the dirty plates. We didn't look back. We took ourselves into the living room and sank into our places again. Robert and my wife sat on the sofa. I took the big chair. We had us two or three more drinks while they talked about the major things that had come to pass for them in the past ten years. For the most part, I just listened. Now and then I joined it. I didn't want him to think I'd left the room, and I didn't want her to think I was feeling left out. They talked of things that had happened to them—to them!—these past ten years. I waited in vain to hear my name on my wife's sweet lips: 'And then my dear husband came into my life'—something like that. But I heard nothing of the sort. More talk of Robert. Robert had done a little of everything, it seemed, a regular blind jack-of-all-trades. But most recently he and his wife had had an Amway distributorship, from which, I gathered, they'd earned their living, such as it was. The blind man was also a ham radio operator. He talked in his loud voice about conversations he'd had with fellow operators in Guam, in the Philippines, in Alaska, and even in Tahiti. He said he'd have a lot of friends there if he ever wanted to go visit those places. From time to time, he'd turn his blind face toward me, put his hand under his beard, ask me something. How long had I been in my present position? (Three years.) Did I like my work? (I didn't.) Was I going to stay with it? (What were the options?) Finally, when I thought he was beginning to run down, I got up and turned on the TV.

My wife looked at me with irritation. She was heading toward a boil. Then she looked at the blind man and said, 'Robert, do you have a TV?'

The blind man said, 'My dear, I have two TVs. I have a colour set and a black-and-white thing, an old relic. It's funny, but if I turn the TV on, and I'm always turning it on, I turn on the colour set. It's funny, don't you think?'

I didn't know what to say to that. I had absolutely nothing to say to that. No opinion. So I watched the news program and tried to listen to what the announcer was saying.

'This is a colour TV,' the blind man said. 'Don't ask me how, but I can tell.'

'We traded up a while ago,' I said.

The blind man had another taste of his drink. He lifted his beard, sniffed it, and let it fall. He leaned forward on the sofa. He positioned his ashtray on the coffee table, then put the lighter to his cigarette. He leaned back on the sofa and crossed his legs at the ankles.

My wife covered her mouth, and then she yawned. She stretched. She said, 'I think I'll go upstairs and put on my robe. I think I'll change into something else. Robert, you make yourself comfortable,' she said.

'I'm comfortable,' the blind man said.

'I want you to feel comfortable in this house,' she said.

'I am comfortable,' the blind man said.

After she'd left the room, he and I listened to the weather report and then to the sports roundup. By that time, she'd been gone so long I didn't know if she was going to come back. I thought she might have gone to bed. I wished she'd come back downstairs. I didn't want to be left alone with a blind man. I asked him if he wanted another drink, and he said sure. Then I asked if he wanted to smoke some dope with me. I said I'd just rolled a number. I hadn't, but I planned to do so in about two shakes.

'I'll try some with you,' he said.

'Damn right,' I said. 'That's the stuff.'

I got our drinks and sat down on the sofa with him. Then I rolled us two fat numbers. I lit one and passed it. I brought it to his fingers. He took it and inhaled.

'Hold it as long as you can,' I said. I could tell he didn't know the first thing.

My wife came back downstairs wearing her pink robe and her pink slippers.

'What do I smell?' she said.

'We thought we'd have us some cannabis,' I said.

My wife gave me a savage look. Then she looked at the blind man and said, 'Robert, I didn't know you smoked.'

He said, 'I do now, my dear. There's a first time for everything. But I don't feel anything yet.'

'This stuff is pretty mellow,' I said. 'This stuff is mild. It's dope you can reason with,' I said. 'It doesn't mess you up.'

'Not much it doesn't, bub,' he said, and laughed.

My wife sat on the sofa between the blind man and me. I passed her the number. She took it and toked and then passed it back to me. 'Which way is this going?' she said. Then she said, 'I shouldn't be smoking this. I can hardly keep my eyes open as it is. That dinner did me in. I shouldn't have eaten so much.'

'It was the strawberry pie,' the blind man said. 'That's what did it,' he said, and he laughed his big laugh. Then he shook his head.

'There's more strawberry pie,' I said.

'Do you want some more, Robert?' my wife said.

'Maybe in a little while,' he said.

We gave our attention to the TV. My wife yawned again. She said, 'Your bed is made up when you feel like going to bed, Robert. I know you must have had a long day. When you're ready to go to bed, say so.' She pulled his arm, 'Robert?'

He came to and said, 'I've had a real nice time. This beats tapes, doesn't it?'

I said, 'Coming at you,' and I put the number between his fingers. He inhaled, held the smoke, and then let it go. It was like he'd been doing it since he was nine years old.

'Thanks, bub,' he said. 'But I think this is all for me. I think I'm beginning to feel it,' he said. He held the burning roach out for my wife.

'Same here,' she said. 'Ditto. Me, too.' She took the roach and passed it to me. 'I may just sit here for a while between you two guys with my eyes closed. But don't let me bother you, okay? Either one of you. If it bothers you, say so. Otherwise, I may just sit here with my eyes closed until you're ready to go to bed,' she said. 'Your bed's made up, Robert, when you're ready. It's right next to our room at the top of the stairs. We'll show you up when you're ready. You wake me up now, you guys, if I fall asleep.' She said that and then she closed her eyes and went to sleep.

The news program ended. I got up and changed the channel. I sat back down on the sofa. I wished my wife hadn't pooped out. Her head lay across the back of the sofa, her mouth open. She'd turned so that her robe had slipped away from her legs, exposing a juicy thigh. I reached to draw the robe back over her, and it was then that I glanced at the blind man. What the hell! I flipped the robe open again.

'You say when you want some strawberry pie,' I said.

'I will,' he said.

I said, 'Are you tired? Do you want me to take you up to your bed? Are you ready to hit the hay?'

'Not yet,' he said. 'No, I'll stay up with you, bub. If that's all right. I'll stay up until you're ready to turn in. We haven't had a chance to talk. Know what I mean? I feel like me and her monopolized this evening.' He lifted his beard and he let it fall. He picked up his cigarettes and his lighter.

'That's all right,' I said. Then I said, 'I'm glad for the company.'

And I guess I was. Every night I smoked dope and stayed up as long as I could before I fell asleep. My wife and I hardly ever went to bed at the same time. When I did go to sleep, I had these dreams. Sometimes I'd wake up from one of them, my heart going crazy.

Something about the church and the Middle Ages was on the TV. Not your run-of-the-mill TV fare. I wanted to watch something else. I turned to the other channels. But there was nothing on them, either. So I turned back to the first channel and apologized.

'Bub, it's all right,' the blind man said. 'It's fine with me. Whatever you want to watch is okay. I'm always learning something. Learning never ends. It won't hurt me to learn something to-night. I got ears,' he said.

We didn't say anything for a time. He was leaning forward with his head turned at me, his right ear aimed in the direction of the set. Very disconcerting. Now and then his eyelids drooped and then they snapped open again. Now and then he put his fingers into his beard and tugged, like he was thinking about something he was hearing on the television.

On the screen, a group of men wearing cowls was being set upon and tormented by men dressed in skeleton costumes and men dressed as devils. The men dressed as devils wore devil masks, horns, and long tails. This pageant was part of a procession. The Englishman who was narrating the thing said it took place in Spain once a year. I tried to explain to the blind man what was happening.

'Skeletons,' he said. 'I know about skeletons,' he said, and he nodded.

The TV showed this one cathedral. Then there was a long, slow look at another one. Finally, the picture switched to the famous one in Paris, with its flying buttresses and its spires reaching up to the clouds. The camera pulled away to show the whole of the cathedral rising above the skyline.

There were times when the Englishman who was telling the thing would shut up, would simply let the camera move around over the cathedrals. Or else the camera would tour the countryside, men in fields walking behind oxen. I waited as long as I could. Then I felt I had to say something. I said, 'They're showing the outside of this cathedral now. Gargoyles. Little statues carved to look like monsters. Now I guess they're in Italy. Yeah, they're in Italy. There's paintings on the walls of this one church.'

'Are those fresco paintings, bub?' he asked, and he sipped from his drink.

I reached for my glass. But it was empty. I tried to remember what I could remember. 'You're asking me are those frescoes?' I said. 'That's a good question. I don't know.'

The camera moved to a cathedral outside Lisbon. The differences in the Portuguese cathedral compared with the French and Italian were not that great. But they were there. Mostly the interior stuff. Then something occurred to me, and I said, 'Something has occurred to me. Do you have any idea what a cathedral is? What they look like, that is? Do you follow me? If somebody says cathedral to you, do you have any notion what they're talking about? Do you know the difference between that and a Baptist church, say?'

He let the smoke dribble from his mouth. 'I know they took hundreds of workers fifty or a hundred years to build,' he said. 'I just heard the man say that, of course. I know generations of the same families worked on a cathedral. I heard him say that, too. The men who began their life's work on them, they never lived to see the completion of their work. In that wise, bub, they're no different from the rest of us, right?' He laughed. Then his eyelids drooped again. His head nodded. He seemed to be snoozing. Maybe he was imagining himself in Portugal. The TV was showing another cathedral now. This one was in Germany. The Englishman's voice droned on. 'Cathedrals,' the blind man said. He sat up and rolled his head back and forth. 'If you want the truth, bub, that's about all I know. What I just said. What I heard him say. But maybe you could describe one to me?

I wish you'd do it. I'd like that. If you want to know, I really don't have a good idea.'

I stared hard at the shot of the cathedral on the TV. How could I even begin to describe it? But say my life depended on it. Say my life was being threatened by an insane guy who said I had to do it or else.

I stared some more at the cathedral before the picture flipped off into the countryside. There was no use. I turned to the blind man and said, 'To begin with, they're very tall.' I was looking around the room for clues. 'They reach way up. Up and up. Toward the sky. They're so big, some of them, they have to have these supports. To help hold them up, so to speak. These supports are called buttresses. They remind me of viaducts, for some reason. But maybe you don't know viaducts, either? Sometimes the cathedrals have devils and such carved into the front. Sometimes lords and ladies. Don't ask me why this is,' I said.

He was nodding. The whole upper part of his body seemed to be moving back and forth.

'I'm not doing so good, am I?' I asked.

He stopped nodding and leaned forward on the edge of the sofa. As he listened to me, he was running his fingers through his beard. I wasn't getting through to him, I could see that. But he waited for me to go on just the same. He nodded, like he was trying to encourage me. I tried to think what else to say. 'They're really big,' I said. 'They're massive. They're built of stone. Marble, too, sometimes. In those olden days, when they built cathedrals, men wanted to be close to God. In those olden days, God was an important part of everyone's life. You could tell this from their cathedral-building. I'm sorry,' I said, 'but it looks like that's the best I can do for you. I'm just no good at it.'

'That's all right, bub,' the blind man said. 'Hey, listen. I hope you don't mind my asking you. Can I ask you something? Let me ask you a simple question, yes or no. I'm just curious and there's no offence. You're my host. But let me ask if you are in any way religious? You don't mind my asking?'

I shook my head. He couldn't see that, though. A wink is the same as a nod to a blind man. 'I guess I don't believe in it. In anything. Sometimes it's hard. You know what I'm saying?'

'Sure, I do,' he said.

'Right,' I said.

The Englishman was still holding forth. My wife sighed in her sleep. She drew a long breath and went on with her sleeping.

'You'll have to forgive me,' I said. 'But I can't tell you what a cathedral looks like. It just isn't in me to do it. I can't do any more than I've done.'

The blind man sat very still, his head down, as he listened to me.

I said, 'The truth is, cathedrals don't mean anything special to me. Nothing. Cathedrals. They're something to look at on late-night TV. That's all they are.'

It was then that the blind man cleared his throat. He brought something up. He took a handkerchief from his back pocket. Then he said, 'I get it, bub. It's okay. It happens. Don't worry about it,' he said. 'Hey, listen to me. Will you do me a favour? I got an idea. Why don't you find us some heavy paper? And a pen. We'll do something. We'll draw one together. Get us a pen and some heavy paper. Go on, bub, get the stuff,' he said.

So I went upstairs. My legs felt like they didn't have any strength in them. They felt like they did after I'd done some running. In my wife's room, I looked around. I found some ballpoints in a little basket on her table. And then I tried to think where to look for the kind of paper he was talking about.

Downstairs, in the kitchen, I found a shopping bag with onion skins in the bottom of the bag. I emptied the bag and shook it. I brought it into the living room and sat down with it near his legs. I moved some things, smoothed the wrinkles from the bag, spread it out on the coffee table.

The blind man got down from the sofa and sat next to me on the carpet.

He ran his fingers over the paper. He went up and down the sides of the paper. The edges, even the edges. He fingered the corners.

'All right,' he said. 'All right, let's do her.'

He found my hand, the hand with the pen. He closed his hand over my hand. 'Go ahead, bub, draw,' he said. 'Draw. You'll see. I'll follow along with you. It'll be okay. Just begin now like I'm telling you. You'll see. Draw,' the blind man said.

So I began. First I drew a box that looked like a house. It could have been the house I lived in. Then I put a roof on it. At either end of the roof, I drew spires. Crazy.

'Swell,' he said. 'Terrific. You're doing fine,' he said. 'Never thought anything like this could happen in your lifetime, did you, bub? Well, it's a strange life, we all know that. Go on now. Keep it up.'

I put in windows with arches. I drew flying buttresses. I hung great doors. I couldn't stop. The TV station went off the air. I put down the pen and closed and opened my fingers. The blind man felt around over the paper. He moved the tips of his fingers over the paper, all over what I had drawn, and he nodded.

'Doing fine,' the blind man said.

I took up the pen again, and he found my hand. I kept at it. I'm no artist. But I kept drawing just the same.

My wife opened up her eyes and gazed at us. She sat up on the sofa, her robe hanging open. She said, 'What are you doing? Tell me, I want to know.'

I didn't answer her.

The blind man said, 'We're drawing a cathedral. Me and him are working on it. Press hard,' he said to me. 'That's right. That's good,' he said. 'Sure. You got it, bub. I can tell. You didn't think you could. But you can, can't you? You're cooking with gas now. You know what I'm saying?

We're going to really have us something here in a minute. How's the old arm?' he said. 'Put some people in there now. What's a cathedral without people?'

My wife said, 'What's going on? Robert, what are you doing? What's going on?'

'It's all right,' he said to her. 'Close your eyes now,' the blind man said to me.

I did it. I closed them just like he said.

'Are they closed?' he said. 'Don't fudge.'

'They're closed,' I said.

'Keep them that way,' he said. He said, 'Don't stop now. Draw.'

So we kept on with it. His fingers rode my fingers as my hand went over the paper. It was like nothing else in my life up to now.

Then he said, 'I think that's it. I think you got it,' he said. 'Take a look. What do you think?'

But I had my eyes closed. I thought I'd keep them that way for a little longer. I thought it was something I ought to do.

'Well?' he said. 'Are you looking?'

My eyes were still closed. I was in my house. I knew that. But I didn't feel like I was inside anything.

'It's really something,' I said.

1981

Joyce Carol Oates

b. 1938

'I am concerned with only one thing: the moral and social conditions of my generation,' Joyce Carol Oates has observed, and in her novels and short stories this concern has remained constant among many different fictional forms and structures. For Oates, the demands of moral and social realism merge with the invitation that she wants her fiction to extend to the 'sympathetic' reader: 'I would like to create the psychological and emotional equivalent of an experience so completely and in such exhausting detail, that anyone who reads it sympathetically will have *experienced* that event in his mind (which is where we live anyway).' Faithfulness to experience also demands that fiction not be falsely optimistic, Oates explains: 'A melancholy vision, a tragic vision, [is] inevitable. Uplifting endings and resolutely cheerful world views are appropriate to television commercials but insulting elsewhere. It is not only wicked to pretend otherwise, it is futile.'

Born in Lockport, New York, Oates grew up on her grandparents' farm in Erie County. She took her B.A. (1960) from Syracuse University and her M.A. (1961) from the University of Wisconsin. Her first collection of stories, *By the North Gate*, appeared in 1963. She moved to Detroit—a setting that figures powerfully in much of her fiction—in 1962, living there for six years and teaching at the University of Detroit until 1967. She then moved across the river to the University of Windsor, where she taught until 1978, when she joined the faculty of Princeton University.

'Where Are You Going, Where Have You Been?' takes place in familiar Oates territory—the troubled interior life of a teenage girl growing into her own sexuality and struggling within the confines of her family and of her own misconceptions about life. But it is not the girl's individual problems that the story dramatizes; rather, the story reveals the perverseness of the larger social world that surrounds her—particularly the world of violent male sexuality, personified in the boy/man, Arnold 'Friend' who terrifies her, transforming the initiation she has been dreaming of into an imminent nightmare.

As implied in its title, 'How I Contemplated the World from the Detroit House of Correction and Began My Life Over Again' is a story in which the style and form reveal not only the narrator's intentions, but also the fragmented nature of the consciousness she is trying to reassemble. The notes for a high-school English essay prove to be an apt model for the girl's scattered recollections as she sketches a contrast between the harsh street-life of downtown Detroit—the world of Simon and ultimately of the House of Correction, where she is beaten up—and the rich but sterile upper-class family environment she has been brought up in. Her return to the apparent comforts of home are complicated by the story's suggestion that perhaps the only real act of kindness has been the brutal beating, and that her search for love at home remains futile.

'Where Are You Going, Where Have You Been?' was first published in the Fall 1966 issue of *Epoch* and then collected in *The Best American Short Stories 1967*. 'How I Contemplated the World from the Detroit House of Correction and Began My Life Over Again' was first published in the Spring 1969 issue of *Triquarterly* and then collected in *The Wheel of Love and Other Stories* (1970).

Where Are You Going, Where Have You Been?

FOR BOB DYLAN

Her name was Connie. She was fifteen and she had a quick, nervous giggling habit of craning her neck to glance into mirrors or checking other people's faces to make sure her own was all right. Her mother, who noticed everything and knew everything and who hadn't much reason any longer to look at her own face, always scolded Connie about it. 'Stop gawking at yourself. Who are you? You think you're so pretty?' she would say. Connie would raise her eyebrows at these familiar old complaints and look right through her mother, into a shadowy vision of herself as she was right at that moment: she knew she was pretty and that was everything. Her mother had been pretty once too, if you could believe these old snapshots in the album, but now her looks were gone and that was why she was always after Connie.

'Why don't you keep your room clean like your sister? How've you got your hair fixed—what the hell stinks? Hair spray? You don't see your sister using that junk.'

Her sister June was twenty-four and still lived at home. She was a secretary in the high school Connie attended, and if that wasn't bad enough—with her in the same building—she was so plain and chunky and steady that Connie had to hear her praised all the time by her mother and her mother's sisters. June did this, June did that, she saved money and helped clean the house and cooked and Connie couldn't do a thing, her mind was all filled with trashy daydreams. Their father was away at work most of the time and when he came home he wanted supper and he read the newspaper at supper and after supper he went to bed. He didn't bother talking much to them, but around his bent head Connie's mother kept picking at her until Connie wished her mother was dead and she herself was dead and it was all over. 'She makes me want to throw up sometimes,' she complained to her friends. She had a high, breathless, amused voice that made everything she said sound a little forced, whether it was sincere or not.

There was one good thing: June went places with girl friends of hers, girls who were just as plain and steady as she, and so when Connie wanted to do that her mother had no objections. The father of Connie's best girl friend drove the girls the three miles to town and left them at a shopping plaza so they could walk through the stores or go to a movie, and when he came to pick them up again at eleven he never bothered to ask what they had done.

They must have been familiar sights, walking around the shopping plaza in their shorts and flat ballerina slippers that always scuffed the sidewalk, with charm bracelets jingling on their thin wrists; they would lean together to whisper and laugh secretly if someone passed who amused or interested them. Connie had long dark blond hair that drew anyone's eye to it, and she wore part of it pulled up on her head and puffed out and the rest of it she let fall down her back. She wore a pull-over jersey blouse that looked one way when she was at home and another way when she was away from home. Everything about her had two sides to it, one for home and one for anywhere that was not home: her walk, which could be childlike and bobbing, or languid enough to make anyone think she was hearing music in her head; her mouth, which was pale and smirking most of the time, but bright and pink on these evenings out; her laugh, which was cynical and drawling at home—'Ha, ha, very funny,'—but high-pitched and nervous anywhere else, like the jingling of the charms on her bracelet.

Sometimes they did go shopping or to a movie, but sometimes they went across the highway, ducking fast across the busy road, to a drive-in restaurant where older kids hung out. The restaurant was shaped like a big bottle, though squatter than a real bottle, and on its cap was a revolving figure of a grinning boy holding a hamburger aloft. One night in midsummer they ran across, breathless with daring, and right away someone leaned out a car window and invited them over, but it was just a boy from high school they didn't like. It made them feel good to be able to ignore him. They went up through the maze of parked and cruising cars to the bright-lit, fly-infested restaurant, their faces pleased and expectant as if they were entering a sacred building that loomed up out of the night to give them what haven and blessing they yearned for. They sat at the counter and crossed their legs at the ankles, their thin shoulders rigid with excitement, and listened to the music that made everything so good: the music was always in the background, like music at a church service; it was something to depend upon.

A boy named Eddie came in to talk with them. He sat backwards on his stool, turning himself jerkily around in semicircles, and then stopping and turning back again, and after a while he asked Connie if she would like something to eat. She said she would and so she tapped her friend's arm on her way out—her friend pulled her face up into a brave, droll look—and Connie said she would meet her at eleven, across the way. 'I just hate to leave her like that,' Connie said earnestly, but the boy said that she wouldn't be alone for long. So they went out to his car, and on the way Connie couldn't help but let her eyes wander over the windshields and faces all around her, her face gleaming with a joy that had nothing to do with Eddie or even this place; it might have been the music. She drew her shoulders up and sucked in her breath with the pure pleasure of being alive, and just at that moment she happened to glance at a face just a few feet from hers. It was a boy with shaggy black hair, in a convertible jalopy painted gold. He stared at her and then his lips widened into a grin. Connie slit her eyes at him and turned away, but she couldn't help glancing back and there he was, still watching her. He wagged a finger and laughed and said, 'Gonna get you, baby,' and Connie turned away again without

Eddie noticing anything.

She spent three hours with him, at the restaurant where they ate hamburgers and drank Cokes in wax cups that were always sweating, and then down an alley a mile or so away, and when he left her off at five to eleven only the movie house was still open at the plaza. Her girl friend was there, talking with a boy. When Connie came up, the two girls smiled at each other and Connie said, 'How was the movie?' and the girl said, '*You* should know.' They rode off with the girl's father, sleepy and pleased, and Connie couldn't help but look at the darkened shopping plaza with its big empty parking lot and its signs that were faded and ghostly now, and over at the drive-in restaurant where cars were still circling tirelessly. She couldn't hear the music at this distance.

Next morning June asked her how the movie was and Connie said, 'So-so.'

She and that girl and occasionally another girl went out several times a week, and the rest of the time Connie spent around the house—it was summer vacation—getting in her mother's way and thinking, dreaming about the boys she met. But all the boys fell back and dissolved into a single face that was not even a face but an idea, a feeling, mixed up with the urgent insistent pounding of the music and the humid night air of July. Connie's mother kept dragging her back to the daylight by finding things for her to do or saying suddenly, 'What's this about the Pettinger girl?'

And Connie would say nervously, 'Oh, her. That dope.' She always drew thick clear lines between herself and such girls, and her mother was simple and kind enough to believe it. Her mother was so simple, Connie thought, that it was maybe cruel to fool her so much. Her mother went scuffling around the house in old bedroom slippers and complained over the telephone to one sister about the other, then the other called up and the two of them complained about the third one. If June's name was mentioned her mother's tone was approving, and if Connie's name was mentioned it was disapproving. This did not really mean she disliked Connie, and actually Connie thought that her mother preferred her to June just because she was prettier, but the two of them kept up a pretence of exasperation, a sense that they were tugging and struggling over something of little value to either of them. Sometimes, over coffee, they were almost friends, but something would come up—some vexation that was like a fly buzzing suddenly around their heads—and their faces went hard with contempt.

One Sunday Connie got up at eleven—none of them bothered with church—and washed her hair so that it could dry all day long in the sun. Her parents and sister were going to a barbecue at an aunt's house and Connie said no, she wasn't interested, rolling her eyes to let her mother know just what she thought of it. 'Stay home alone then,' her mother said sharply. Connie sat out back in a lawn chair and watched them drive away, her father quiet and bald, hunched around so that he could back the car out, her mother with a look that was still angry and not at all softened through the windshield, and in the back seat poor old June, all dressed up as if she didn't know what a barbecue was, with all the running yelling kids and the flies. Connie sat with her eyes closed in the sun, dreaming and dazed with the warmth about her as if this were a kind of love, the caresses of love, and her mind slipped over onto thoughts of the boy she had been with the night before and how nice he had been, how sweet it always was, not the way someone like June would suppose but sweet, gentle, the way it was in movies and promised in songs; and when she opened her eyes she hardly knew where she was, the back yard ran off into weeds and a fence-like line of trees and behind it the sky was perfectly blue and still. The asbestos 'ranch house' that was now three years old startled her—it looked small. She shook her head as if to get awake.

It was too hot. She went inside the house and turned on the radio to drown out the quiet. She sat on the edge of her bed, barefoot, and listened for an hour and a half to a program called XYZ Sunday Jamboree, record after record of hard, fast, shrieking songs she sang along with, interspersed by exclamations from 'Bobby King': 'An' look here, you girls at Napoleon's—Son and Charley want you to pay real close attention to this song coming up!'

And Connie paid close attention herself, bathed in a glow of slow-pulsed joy that seemed to rise mysteriously out of the music itself and lay languidly about the airless little room, breathed in and breathed out with each gentle rise and fall of her chest.

After a while she heard a car coming up the drive. She sat up at once, startled, because it couldn't be her father so soon. The gravel kept crunching all the way in from the road—the driveway was long—and Connie ran to the window. It was a car she didn't know. It was an open jalopy, painted a bright gold that caught the sunlight opaquely. Her heart began to pound and her fingers snatched at her hair, checking it, and she whispered, 'Christ, Christ,' wondering how bad she looked. The car came to a stop at the side door and the horn sounded four short taps, as if this were a signal Connie knew.

She went into the kitchen and approached the door slowly, then hung out the screen door, her bare toes curling down off the step. There were two boys in the car and now she recognized the driver: he had shaggy, shabby black hair that looked crazy as a wig and he was grinning at her.

'I ain't late, am I?' he said.

'Who the hell do you think you are?' Connie said.

'Toldja I'd be out, didn't I?'

'I don't even know who you are.'

She spoke sullenly, careful to show no interest or pleasure, and he spoke in a fast, bright monotone. Connie looked past him to the other boy, taking her time. He had fair brown hair, with a lock that fell onto his forehead. His sideburns gave him a fierce, embarrassed look, but so far he hadn't even bothered to glance at her. Both boys wore sunglasses. The driver's glasses were metallic and mirrored everything in miniature.

'You wanta come for a ride?' he said.

Connie smirked and let her hair fall loose over one shoulder.

'Don'tcha like my car? New paint job,' he said. 'Hey.'

'What?'

'You're cute.'

She pretended to fidget, chasing flies away from the door.

'Don'tcha believe me, or what?' he said.

'Look, I don't even know who you are,' Connie said in disgust.

'Hey, Ellie's got a radio, see. Mine broke down. He lifted his friend's arm and showed her the little transistor radio the boy was holding, and now Connie began to hear the music. It was the same program that was playing inside the house.

'Bobby King?' she said.

'I listen to him all the time. I think he's great.'

'He's kind of great,' Connie said reluctantly.

'Listen, that guy's *great*. He knows where the action is.'

Connie blushed a little, because the glasses made it impossible for her to see just what this boy was looking at. She couldn't decide if she liked him or if he was just a jerk, and so she dawdled in the doorway and wouldn't come down or go back inside. She said, 'What's all that stuff painted on your car?'

'Can'tcha read it?' He opened the door very carefully, as if he were afraid it might fall off. He slid out just as carefully, planting his feet firmly on the ground, the tiny metallic world in his glasses slowing down like gelatine hardening, and in the midst of it Connie's bright green blouse. 'This here is my name, to begin with,' he said. ARNOLD FRIEND was written in tarlike black letters on the side, with a drawing of a round, grinning face that reminded Connie of a pumpkin, except it wore sunglasses. 'I wanta introduce myself, I'm Arnold Friend and that's my real name and I'm gonna be your friend, honey, and inside the car's Ellie Oscar, he's kinda shy.' Ellie brought his transistor radio up to his shoulder and balanced it there. 'Now, these numbers are a secret code, honey,' Arnold Friend explained. He read off the numbers 33, 19, 17 and raised his eyebrows at her to see what she thought of that, but she didn't think much of it. The left rear fender had been smashed and around it was written, on the gleaming gold background: DONE BY CRAZY WOMAN DRIVER. Connie had to laugh at that. Arnold Friend was pleased at her laughter and looked up at her. 'Around the other side's a lot more—you wanta come and see them?'

'No.'

'Why not?'

'Why should I?'

'Don'tcha wanta see what's on the car? Don'tcha wanta go for a ride?'

'I don't know.'

'Why not?'

'I got things to do.'

'Like what?'

'Things.'

He laughed as if she had said something funny. He slapped his thighs. He was standing in a strange way, leaning back against the car as if he were balancing himself. He wasn't tall, only an inch or so taller than she would be if she came down to him. Connie liked the way he dressed, which was the way all of them dressed: tight faded jeans stuffed into black, scuffed boots, a belt that pulled his waist in and showed how lean he was, and a white pull-over shirt that was a little soiled and showed the hard small muscles of his arms and shoulders. He looked as if he probably did hard work, lifting and carrying things. Even his neck looked muscular. And his face was a familiar face, somehow: the jaw and chin and cheeks slightly darkened because he hadn't shaved for a day or two, and the nose long and hawklike, sniffing as if she were a treat he was going to gobble up and it was all a joke.

'Connie, you ain't telling the truth. This is your day set aside for a ride with me and you know it,' he said, still laughing. The way he straightened and recovered from his fit of laughing showed that it had been all fake.

'How do you know what my name is?' she said suspiciously.

'It's Connie.'

'Maybe and maybe not.'

'I know my Connie,' he said, wagging his finger. Now she remembered him even better, back at the restaurant, and her cheeks warmed at the thought of how she had sucked in her breath just at the moment she passed him—how she must have looked to him. And he had remembered her. 'Ellie and I come out here especially for you,' he said. 'Ellie can sit in back. How about it?'

'Where?'

'Where what?'

'Where're we going?'

He looked at her. He took off the sunglasses and she saw how pale the skin around his eyes was, like holes that were not in shadow but instead in light. His eyes were like chips of broken glass that catch the light in an amiable way. He smiled. It was as if the idea of going for a ride somewhere, to someplace, was a new idea to him.

'Just for a ride, Connie sweetheart.'

'I never said my name was Connie,' she said.

'But I know what it is. I know your name and all about you, lots of things,' Arnold Friend said. He had not moved yet but stood still leaning back against the side of his jalopy. 'I took a special interest in you, such a pretty girl, and found out all about you—like I know your parents and sister are gone somewheres and I know where and how long they're going to be gone, and I know who you were with last night, and your best friend's name is Betty. Right?'

He spoke in a simple lilting voice, exactly as if he were reciting the words to a song. His smile assured her that everything was fine. In the car Ellie turned up the volume on his radio and did not bother to look around at them.

'Ellie can sit in the back seat,' Arnold Friend said. He indicated his friend with a casual jerk of his chin, as if Ellie did not count and she should not bother with him.

'How'd you find out all that stuff?' Connie said.

'Listen: Betty Schultz and Tony Fitch and Jimmy Pettinger and Nancy Pettinger,' he said in a chant. 'Raymond Stanley and Bob Hutter—'

'Do you know all those kids?'

'I know everybody.'

'Look, you're kidding. You're not from around here.'

'Sure.'

'But—how come we never saw you before?'

'Sure you saw me before,' he said. He looked down at his boots, as if he were a little offended. 'You just don't remember.'

'I guess I'd remember you,' Connie said.

'Yeah?' He looked up at this, beaming. He was pleased. He began to mark time with the music from Ellie's radio, tapping his fists lightly together. Connie looked away from his smile to the car, which was painted so bright it almost hurt her eyes to look at it. She looked at that name, ARNOLD FRIEND. And up at the front fender was an expression that was familiar—MAN THE FLYING SAUCERS. It was an expression kids had used the year before but didn't use this year. She looked at it for a while as if the words meant something to her that she did not yet know.

'What're you thinking about? Huh?' Arnold Friend demanded. 'Not worried about your hair blowing around in the car, are you?'

'No.'

'Think I maybe can't drive good?'

'How do I know?'

'You're a hard girl to handle. How come?' he said. 'Don't you know I'm your friend? Didn't you see me put my sign in the air when you walked by?'

'What sign?'

'My sign.' And he drew an X in the air, leaning out toward her. They were maybe ten feet apart. After his hand fell back to his side the X was still in the air, almost visible. Connie let the screen door close and stood perfectly still inside it, listening to the music from her radio and the boy's blend together. She stared at Arnold Friend. He stood there so stiffly relaxed, pretending to be relaxed, with one hand idly on the door handle as if he were keeping himself up that way and had no intention of ever moving again. She recognized most things about him, the tight jeans that showed his thighs and buttocks and the greasy leather boots and the tight shirt, and even that slippery friendly smile of his, that sleepy dreamy smile that all the boys used to get across ideas they didn't want to put into words. She recognized all this and also the singsong way he talked, slightly mocking, kidding, but serious and a little melancholy, and she recognized the way he tapped one fist against the other in homage to the perpetual music behind him. But all these things did not come together.

She said suddenly, 'Hey, how old are you?'

His smile faded. She could see then that he wasn't a kid, he was much older—thirty, maybe more. At this knowledge her heart began to pound faster.

'That's a crazy thing to ask. Can'tcha see I'm your own age?'

'Like hell you are.'

'Or maybe a coupla years older. I'm eighteen.'

'Eighteen?' she said doubtfully.

He grinned to reassure her and lines appeared at the corners of his mouth. His teeth were big and white. He grinned so broadly his eyes became slits and she saw how thick the lashes were, thick and black as if painted with a black tarlike material. Then, abruptly, he seemed to become embarrassed and looked over his shoulder at Ellie. '*Him*, he's crazy,' he said. 'Ain't he a riot? He's a nut, a real character.' Ellie was still listening to the music. His sunglasses told nothing about what he was thinking. He wore a bright orange shirt unbuttoned halfway to show his chest, which was a pale, bluish chest and not muscular like Arnold Friend's. His shirt collar was turned up all around and the very tips of the collar pointed out past his chin as if they were protecting him. He was pressing the transistor radio up against his ear and sat there in a kind of daze, right in the sun.

'He's kinda strange,' Connie said.

'Hey, she says you're kinda strange! Kinda strange!' Arnold Friend cried. He pounded on the car to get Ellie's attention. Ellie turned for the first time and Connie saw with shock that he wasn't a kid either—he had a fair, hairless face, cheeks reddened slightly as if the veins grew too close to the surface of his skin, the face of a forty-year-old baby. Connie felt a wave of dizziness rise in her at this sight and she stared at him as if waiting for something to change the shock of the moment, make it all right again. Ellie's lips kept shaping words, mumbling along with the words blasting in his ear.

'Maybe you two better go away,' Connie said faintly.

'What? How come?' Arnold Friend cried. 'We come out here to take you for a ride. It's Sunday.' He had the voice of the man on the radio now. It was the same voice, Connie thought. 'Don'tcha know it's Sunday all day? And honey, no matter who you were with last night, today you're with Arnold Friend and don't you forget it! Maybe you better step out here,' he said, and this last was in a different voice. It was a little flatter, as if the heat was finally getting to him.

'No. I got things to do.'

'Hey.'

'You two better leave.'

'We ain't leaving until you come with us.'

'Like hell I am—'

'Connie, don't fool around with me. I mean—I mean, don't fool *around*,' he said, shaking his head. He laughed incredulously. He placed his sunglasses on top of his head, carefully, as if he were indeed wearing a wig, and brought the stems down behind his ears. Connie stared at him, another wave of dizziness and fear rising in her so that for a moment he wasn't even in focus but was just a blur standing there against his gold car, and she had the idea that he had driven up the driveway all right but had come from nowhere before that and belonged nowhere and that everything about him and even about the music that was so familiar to her was only half real.

'If my father comes and sees you—'

'He ain't coming. He's at a barbecue.'

'How do you know that?'

'Aunt Tillie's. Right now they're—uh—they're drinking. Sitting around,' he said vaguely, squinting as if he were staring all the way to town and over to Aunt Tillie's back yard. Then the vision seemed to get clear and he nodded energetically. 'Yeah. Sitting around. There's your sister in a blue dress, huh? And high heels, the poor sad bitch—nothing like you, sweetheart! And your mother's helping some fat woman with the corn, they're cleaning the corn—husking the corn—'

'What fat woman?' Connie cried.

'How do I know what fat woman, I don't know every goddamn fat woman in the world!' Arnold Friend laughed.

'Oh, that's Mrs Hornsby . . . Who invited her?' Connie said. She felt a little lightheaded. Her breath was coming quickly.

'She's too fat. I don't like them fat. I like them the way you are, honey,' he said, smiling sleepily at her. They stared at each other for a while through the screen door. He said softly, 'Now, what you're going to do is this: you're going to come out that door. You're going to sit up front with me and Ellie's going to sit in the back, the hell with Ellie, right? This isn't Ellie's date. You're my date. I'm your lover, honey.'

'What? You're crazy—'

'Yes, I'm your lover. You don't know what that is but you will,' he said. 'I know that too. I know all about you. But look: it's real nice and you couldn't ask for nobody better than me, or more polite. I always keep my word. I'll tell you how it is, I'm always nice at first, the first time. I'll hold you so tight you won't think you have to try to get away or pretend anything because you'll know you can't. And I'll come inside you where it's all secret and you'll give in to me and you'll love me—'

'Shut up! You're crazy!' Connie said. She backed away from the door. She put her hands up against her ears as if she'd heard something terrible, something not meant for her. 'People don't talk like that, you're crazy,' she muttered. Her heart was almost too big now for her chest and its pumping made sweat break out all over her. She looked out to see Arnold Friend pause and then take a step toward the porch, lurching. He almost fell. But, like a clever drunken man, he managed to catch his balance. He wobbled in his high boots and grabbed hold of one of the porch posts.

'Honey?' he said. 'You still listening?'

'Get the hell out of here!'

'Be nice, honey. Listen.'

'I'm going to call the police—'

He wobbled again and out of the side of his mouth came a fast spat curse, an aside not meant for her to hear. But even this 'Christ!' sounded forced. Then he began to smile again. She watched this smile come, awkward as if he were smiling from inside a mask. His whole face was a mask, she thought wildly, tanned down to his throat but then running out as if he had plastered make-up on his face but had forgotten about his throat.

'Honey—? Listen, here's how it is. I always tell the truth and I promise you this: I ain't coming in that house after you.'

'You better not! I'm going to call the police if you—if you don't—'

'Honey,' he said, talking right through her voice, 'honey, I'm not coming in there but you are coming out here. You know why?'

She was panting. The kitchen looked like a place she had never seen before, some room she had run inside but that wasn't good enough, wasn't going to help her. The kitchen window had never had a curtain, after three years, and there were dishes in the sink for her to do—probably—and if you ran your hand across the table you'd probably feel something sticky there.

'You listening, honey? Hey?'

'—going to call the police—'

'Soon as you touch the phone I don't need to keep my promise and can come inside. You won't want that.'

She rushed forward and tried to lock the door. Her fingers were shaking. 'But why lock it,' Arnold Friend said gently, talking right into her face. 'It's just a screen door. It's just nothing.' One of his boots was at a strange angle, as if his foot wasn't in it. It pointed out to the left, bent at the ankle. 'I mean, anybody can break through a screen door and glass and wood and iron or anything else if he needs to, anybody at all, and specially Arnold Friend. If the place got lit up with a fire, honey, you'd come runnin' out into my arms, right into my arms an' safe at home—like you knew I was your lover and'd stopped fooling around. I don't mind a nice shy girl but I don't like no fooling around.' Part of those words were spoken with a slight rhythmic lilt, and Connie somehow recognized them—the echo of a song from last year, about a girl rushing into her boy friend's arms and coming home again—

Connie stood barefoot on the linoleum floor, staring at him. 'What do you want?' she whispered.

'I want you,' he said.

'What?'

'Seen you that night and thought, that's the one, yes sir. I never needed to look anymore.'

'But my father's coming back. He's coming to get me. I had to wash my hair first—' She spoke in a dry, rapid voice, hardly raising it for him to hear.

'No, your daddy is not coming and yes, you had to wash your hair and you washed it for me. It's nice and shining and all for me. I thank you sweetheart,' he said with a mock bow, but again he almost lost his balance. He had to bend and adjust his boots. Evidently his feet did not go all the way down; the boots must have been stuffed with something so that he would seem taller. Connie stared out at him and behind him at Ellie in the car, who seemed to be looking off toward Connie's right, into nothing. This Ellie said, pulling the words out of the air one after another as if he were just discovering them, 'You want me to pull out the phone?'

'Shut your mouth and keep it shut,' Arnold Friend said, his face red from bending over or maybe from embarrassment because Connie had seen his boots. 'This ain't none of your business.'

'What—what are you doing? What do you want?' Connie said. 'If I call the police they'll get you, they'll arrest you—'

'Promise was not to come in unless you touch that phone, and I'll keep that promise,' he said. He resumed his erect position and tried to force his shoulders back. He sounded like a hero in a movie, declaring something important. But he spoke too loudly and it was as if he were speaking to someone behind Connie. 'I ain't made plans for coming in that house where I don't belong but just for you to come out to me, the way you should. Don't you know who I am?'

'You're crazy,' she whispered. She backed away from the door but did not want to go into another part of the house, as if this would give him permission to come through the door. 'What do you . . . you're crazy, you. . . .'

'Huh? What're you saying, honey?'

Her eyes darted everywhere in the kitchen. She could not remember what it was, this room.

'This is how it is, honey: you come out and we'll drive away, have a nice ride. But if you don't come out we're gonna wait till your people come home and then they're all going to get it.'

'You want that telephone pulled out?' Ellie said. He held the radio away from his ear and grimaced, as if without the radio the air was too much for him.

'I toldja shut up, Ellie,' Arnold Friend said, 'you're deaf, get a hearing aid, right? Fix yourself up. This little girl's no trouble and's gonna be nice to me, so Ellie keep to yourself, this ain't your date—right? Don't hem in on me, don't hog, don't crush, don't bird dog, don't trail me,' he said in a rapid, meaningless voice, as if he were running through all the expressions he'd learned but was no longer sure which of them was in style, then rushing on to new ones, making them up with his eyes closed. 'Don't crawl under my fence, don't squeeze in my chipmunk hole, don't sniff my glue, suck my popsicle, keep your own greasy fingers on yourself!' He shaded his eyes and peered in at Connie, who was backed against the kitchen table. 'Don't mind him, honey, he's just a creep. He's a dope. Right? I'm the boy for you and like I said, you come out here nice like a lady and give me your hand, and nobody gets hurt, I mean, your nice old bald-headed daddy and your mummy and your sister in her high heels. Because listen: why bring them in this?'

'Leave me alone,' Connie whispered.

'Hey, you know that old woman down the road, the one with the chickens and stuff—you know her?'

'She's dead!'

'Dead? What? You know her?' Arnold Friend said.

'She's dead—'

'Don't you like her?'

'She's dead—she's—she isn't here any more—'

'But don't you like her, I mean, you got something against her? Some grudge or something?' Then his voice dipped as if he were conscious of a rudeness. He touched the sunglasses perched up on top of his head as if to make sure they were still there. 'Now, you be a good girl.'

'What are you going to do?'

'Just two things, or maybe three,' Arnold Friend said. 'But I promise it won't last long and you'll like me the way you get to like people you're close to. You will. It's all over for you here, so come on out. You don't want your people in any trouble, do you?'

She turned and bumped against a chair or something, hurting her leg, but she ran into the back room and picked up the telephone. Something roared in her ear, a tiny roaring, and she was so sick with fear that she could do nothing but listen to it—the telephone was clammy and very heavy and her fingers groped down to the dial but were too weak to touch it. She began to scream into the phone, into the roaring. She cried out, she cried for her mother, she felt her breath start jerking back and forth in her lungs as if it were something Arnold Friend was stabbing her with again and again with no tenderness. A noisy sorrowful wailing rose all about her and she was locked inside it the way she was locked inside this house.

After a while she could hear again. She was sitting on the floor with her wet back against the wall.

Arnold Friend was saying from the door, 'That's a good girl. Put the phone back.'

She kicked the phone away from her.

'No, honey. Pick it up. Put it back right.'

She picked it up and put it back. The dial tone stopped.

'That's a good girl. Now, you come outside.'

She was hollow with what had been fear but what was now just an emptiness. All that screaming had blasted it out of her. She sat, one leg cramped under her, and deep inside her brain was something like a pinpoint of light that kept going and would not let her relax. She thought, I'm not going to see my mother again. She thought, I'm not going to sleep in my bed again. Her bright green blouse was all wet.

Arnold Friend said, in a gentle-loud voice that was like a stage voice, 'The place where you came from ain't there any more, and where you had in mind to go is cancelled out. This place you are now—inside your daddy's house—is nothing but a cardboard box I can knock down any time. You know that and always did know it. You hear me?'

She thought, I have got to think. I have got to know what to do.

'We'll go out to a nice field, out in the country here where it smells so nice and it's sunny,' Arnold Friend said. 'I'll have my arms tight around you so you won't need to try to get away and I'll show you what love is like, what it does. The hell with this house! It looks solid all right,' he said. He ran a fingernail down the screen and the noise did not make Connie shiver, as it would have the day before. 'Now, put your hand on your heart, honey. Feel that? That feels solid too but we know better. Be nice to me, be sweet like you can because what else is there for a girl like you but to be sweet and pretty and give in?—and get away before her people come back?'

She felt her pounding heart. Her hand seemed to enclose it. She thought for the first time in her life that it was nothing that was hers, that belonged to her, but just a pounding, living thing inside this body that wasn't really hers either.

'You don't want them to get hurt,' Arnold Friend went on. 'Now, get up, honey. Get up all by yourself.'

She stood.

'Now, turn this way. That's right. Come over here to me.—Ellie, put that away, didn't I tell you? You dope. You miserable creepy dope,' Arnold Friend said. His words were not angry but only part of an incantation. The incantation was kindly. 'Now, come out through the kitchen to me, honey, and let's see a smile, try it, you're a brave, sweet little girl and now they're eating corn and hot dogs cooked to bursting over an outdoor fire, and they don't know one thing about you and never did and honey, you're better than them because not a one of them would have done this for you.'

Connie felt the linoleum under her feet; it was cool. She brushed her hair back out of her eyes. Arnold Friend let go of the post tentatively and opened his arms for her, his elbows pointing in toward each other and his wrists limp, to show that this was an embarrassed embrace and a little mocking, he didn't want to make her self-conscious.

She put out her hand against the screen. She watched herself push the door slowly open as if she were back safe somewhere in the other doorway, watching this body and this head of long hair moving out into the sunlight where Arnold Friend waited.

'My sweet little blue-eyed girl,' he said in a half-sung sigh that had nothing to do with her brown eyes but was taken up just the same by the vast sunlit reaches of the land behind him and on all sides of him—so much land that Connie had never seen before and did not recognize except to know that she was going to it.

1966

How I Contemplated the World from the Detroit House of Correction and Began My Life Over Again

NOTES FOR AN ESSAY FOR AN ENGLISH CLASS AT BALDWIN COUNTRY DAY SCHOOL; POKING AROUND IN DEBRIS; DISGUST AND CURIOSITY; A REVELATION OF THE MEANING OF LIFE; A HAPPY ENDING. . .

I EVENTS

I. The girl (myself) is walking through Branden's, that excellent store. Suburb of a large famous city that is a symbol for large famous American cities. The event sneaks up on the girl, who believes she is herding it along with a small fixed smile, a girl of fifteen, innocently experienced. She dawdles in a certain style by a counter of costume jewelry. Rings, earrings, necklaces. Prices from $5 to $50, all within reach. All ugly. She eases over to the glove counter, where everything is ugly too. In her close-fitted coat with its black fur collar she contemplates the luxury of Branden's, which she has known for many years: its many mild pale lights, easy on the eye and the soul, its elaborate tinkly decorations, its women shoppers with their excellent shoes and coats and hairdos, all dawdling gracefully, in no hurry.

Who was ever in a hurry here?

2. The girl seated at home. A small library, panelled walls of oak. Someone is talking to me. An earnest, husky, female voice drives itself against my ears, nervous, frightened, groping around my heart, saying, 'If you wanted gloves, why didn't you say so? Why didn't you ask for them?' That store, Branden's, is owned by Raymond Forrest who lives on Du Maurier Drive. We live on Sioux Drive. Raymond Forrest. A handsome man? An

ugly man? A man of fifty or sixty, with grey hair, or a man of forty with earnest, courteous eyes, a good golf game; who is Raymond Forrest, this man who is my salvation? Father has been talking to him. Father is not his physician; Dr Berg is his physician. Father and Dr Berg refer patients to each other. There is a connection. Mother plays bridge with . . . On Mondays and Wednesdays our maid Billie works at . . . The strings draw together in a cat's cradle, making a net to save you when you fall. . . .

3. *Harriet Arnold's*. A small shop, better than Branden's. Mother in her black coat, I in my close-fitted blue coat. Shopping. Now look at this, isn't this cute, do you want this, why don't you want this, try this on, take this with you to the fitting room, take this also, what's wrong with you, what can I do for you, why are you so strange . . .? 'I wanted to steal but not to buy,' I don't tell her. The girl droops along in her coat and gloves and leather boots, her eyes scan the horizon, which is pastel pink and decorated like Branden's, tasteful walls and modern ceilings with graceful glimmering lights.

4. Weeks later, the girl at a bus stop. Two o'clock in the afternoon, a Tuesday; obviously she has walked out of school.

5. The girl stepping down from a bus. Afternoon, weather changing to colder. Detroit. Pavement and closed-up stores; grill-work over the windows of a pawnshop. What is a pawnshop, exactly?

II CHARACTERS

I. The girl stands five feet five inches tall. An ordinary height. Baldwin Country Day School draws them up to that height. She dreams along the corridors and presses her face against the Thermoplex glass. No frost or steam can ever form on that glass. A smudge of grease from her forehead . . . could she be boiled down to grease? She wears her hair loose and long and straight in suburban teen-age style, 1968. Eyes smudged with pencil, dark brown. Brown hair. Vague green eyes. A pretty girl? An ugly girl? She sings to herself under her breath, idling in the corridor, thinking of her many secrets (the thirty dollars she once took from the purse of a friend's mother, just for fun, the basement window she smashed in her own house just for fun) and thinking of her brother who is at Susquehanna Boys' Academy, an excellent preparatory school in Maine, remembering him unclearly . . . he has long manic hair and a squeaking voice and he looks like one of the popular teen-age singers of 1968, one of those in a group, *The Certain Forces, The Way Out, The Maniacs Responsible*. The girl in her turn looks like one of those fieldsful of girls who listen to the boys' singing, dreaming and mooning restlessly, breaking into high sullen laughter, innocently experienced.

2. The mother. A Midwestern woman of Detroit and suburbs. Belongs to the Detroit Athletic Club. Also the Detroit Golf Club. Also the Bloomfield Hills Country Club. The Village Women's Club at which lectures are given each winter on Genet and Sartre and James Baldwin, by the Director of the Adult Education Program at Wayne State University. . . . The Bloomfield Art Association. Also the Founders Society of the Detroit Institute of Arts. Also . . . Oh, she is in perpetual motion, this lady, hair like blown-up gold and finer than gold, hair and fingers and body of inestimable grace. Heavy weighs the gold on the back of her hairbrush and hand mirror. Heavy heavy the candlesticks in the dining room. Very heavy is the big car, a Lincoln, long and black, that on one cool autumn day split a squirrel's body in two unequal parts.

3. The father. Dr. He belongs to the same clubs as #2. A player of squash and golf; he has a golfer's umbrella of stripes. Candy stripes. In his mouth nothing turns to sugar, however; saliva works no miracles here. His doctoring is of the slightly sick. The sick are sent elsewhere (to Dr Berg?), the deathly sick are sent back for more tests and their bills are sent to their homes, the unsick are sent to Dr Coronet (Isabel, a lady), an excellent psychiatrist for unsick people who angrily believe they are sick and want to do something about it. If they demand a male psychiatrist, the unsick are sent by Dr (my father) to Dr Lowenstein, a male psychiatrist, excellent and expensive, with a limited practice.

4. Clarita. She is twenty, twenty-five, she is thirty or more? Pretty, ugly, what? She is a woman lounging by the side of a road, in jeans and a sweater, hitchhiking, or she is slouched on a stool at a counter in some roadside diner. A hard line of jaw. Curious eyes. Amused eyes. Behind her eyes processions move, funeral pageants, cartoons. She says, 'I never can figure out why girls like you bum around down here. What are you looking for anyway?' An odour of tobacco about her. Unwashed underclothes, or no underclothes, unwashed skin, gritty toes, hair long and falling into strands, not recently washed.

5. Simon. In this city the weather changes abruptly, so Simon's weather changes abruptly. He sleeps through the afternoon. He sleeps through the morning. Rising, he gropes around for something to get him going, for a cigarette or a pill to drive him out to the street, where the temperature is hovering around 35°. Why doesn't it drop? Why, why doesn't the cold clean air come down from Canada; will he have to go up into Canada to get it? will he have to leave the Country of his Birth and sink into Canada's frosty fields . . .? Will the FBI (which he dreams about constantly) chase him over the Canadian border on foot, hounded out in a blizzard of broken glass and horns . . .?

'Once I was Huckleberry Finn,' Simon says, 'but now I am Roderick

Usher.' Beset by frenzies and fears, this man who makes my spine go cold, he takes green pills, yellow pills, pills of white and capsules of dark blue and green . . . he takes other things I may not mention, for what if Simon seeks me out and climbs into my girl's bedroom here in Bloomfield Hills and strangles me, what then . . .? (As I write this I begin to shiver. Why do I shiver? I am now sixteen and sixteen is not an age for shivering.) It comes from Simon, who is always cold.

III WORLD EVENTS

Nothing.

IV PEOPLE & CIRCUMSTANCES CONTRIBUTING TO THIS DELINQUENCY

Nothing.

V SIOUX DRIVE

George, Clyde G. 240 Sioux. A manufacturer's representative; children, a dog, a wife. Georgian with the usual columns. You think of the White House, then of Thomas Jefferson, then your mind goes blank on the white pillars and you think of nothing. Norris, Ralph W. 246 Sioux. Public relations. Colonial. Bay window, brick, stone, concrete, wood, green shutters, sidewalk, lantern, grass, trees, blacktop drive, two children, one of them my classmate Esther (Esther Norris) at Baldwin. Wife, cars. Ramsey, Michael D. 250 Sioux. Colonial. Big living room, thirty by twenty-five, fireplaces in living room, library, recreation room, panelled walls wet bar five bathrooms five bedrooms two lavatories central air conditioning automatic sprinkler automatic garage door three children one wife two cars a breakfast room a patio a large fenced lot fourteen trees a front door with a brass knocker never knocked. Next is our house. Classic contemporary. Traditional modern. Attached garage, attached Florida room, attached patio, attached pool and cabana, attached roof. A front door mail slot through which pour *Time Magazine, Fortune, Life, Business Week*, the *Wall Street Journal*, the *New York Times*, the *New Yorker*, the *Saturday Review, M.D., Modern Medicine, Disease of the Month* . . . and also. . . . And in addition to all this, a quiet sealed letter from Baldwin saying: *Your daughter is not doing work compatible with her performance on the Stanford-Binet*. . . . And your son is not doing well, not well at all, very sad. Where is your son anyway? Once he stole trick-and-treat candy from some six-year-old kids, he himself being a robust ten. The beginning. Now your daughter steals. In the Village Pharmacy she made off with, yes she did, don't deny it, she made off with a copy of *Pageant Magazine* for no reason, she swiped a roll of Life Savers in a green wrapper and was in no need of saving her life or even in need of sucking candy; when she was no more than eight years old she stole, don't blush, she stole a package of Tums only because it was out on the counter and available, and the nice lady behind the counter (now dead) said nothing. . . . Sioux Drive. Maples, oaks, elms. Diseased elms cut down. Sioux Drive runs into Roosevelt Drive. Slow, turning lanes not streets, all drives and lanes and ways and passes. A private police force. Quiet private police, in unmarked cars. Cruising on Saturday evenings with paternal smiles for the residents who are streaming in and out of houses, going to and from parties, a thousand parties, slightly staggering, the women in their furs alighting from automobiles bought of Ford and General Motors and Chrysler, very heavy automobiles. No foreign cars. Detroit. In 275 Sioux, down the block in that magnificent French-Normandy mansion, lives himself, who has the C account itself, imagine that! Look at where he lives and look at the enormous trees and chimneys, imagine his many fireplaces, imagine his wife and children, imagine his wife's hair, imagine her fingernails, imagine her bathtub of smooth clean glowing pink, imagine their embraces, his trouser pockets filled with odd coins and keys and dust and peanuts, imagine their ecstasy on Sioux Drive, imagine their income tax returns, imagine their little boy's pride in his experimental car, a scaled-down C, as he roars around the neighbourhood on the sidewalks and frightening dogs and Negro maids, oh imagine all these things, imagine everything, let your mind roar out all over Sioux Drive and Du Maurier Drive and Roosevelt Drive and Ticonderoga Pass and Burning Bush Way and Lincolnshire Pass and Lois Lane.

When spring comes, its winds blow nothing to Sioux Drive, no odours of hollyhocks or forsythia, nothing Sioux Drive doesn't already possess, everything is planted and performing. The weather vanes, had they weather vanes, don't have to turn with the wind, don't have to contend with the weather. There is no weather.

VI DETROIT

There is always weather in Detroit. Detroit's temperature is always 32°. Fast-falling temperatures. Slow-rising temperatures. Wind from the north-northeast four to forty miles an hour, small-craft warnings, partly cloudy today and Wednesday changing to partly sunny through Thursday . . . small warnings of frost, soot warnings, traffic warnings, hazardous lake conditions for small craft and swimmers, restless Negro gangs, restless cloud formations, restless temperatures aching to fall out the very bottom of the thermometer or shoot up over the top and boil everything over in red mercury.

Detroit's temperature is 32°. Fast-falling temperatures. Slow-rising temperatures. Wind from the north-northeast four to forty miles an hour. . . .

VII EVENTS

I. The girl's heart is pounding. In her pocket is a pair of gloves! In a plastic bag! Airproof breathproof plastic bag, gloves selling for twenty-five dollars on Branden's counter! In her pocket! Shoplifted! . . . In her purse is a blue comb, not very clean. In her purse is a leather billfold (a birthday present from her grandmother in Philadelphia) with snapshots of the family in clean plastic windows, in the billfold are bills, she doesn't know how many bills. . . . In her purse is an ominous note from her friend Tykie *What's this about Joe H. and the kids hanging around at Louise's Sat. night? You heard anything?* . . . passed in French class. In her purse is a lot of dirty yellow Kleenex, her mother's heart would break to see such very dirty Kleenex, and at the bottom of her purse are brown hairpins and safety pins and a broken pencil and a ballpoint pen (blue) stolen from somewhere forgotten and a purse-size compact of Cover Girl Make-Up, Ivory Rose. . . . Her lipstick is Broken Heart, a corrupt pink; her fingers are trembling like crazy; her teeth are beginning to chatter; her insides are alive; her eyes glow in her head; she is saying to her mother's astonished face *I want to steal but not to buy.*

2. At Clarita's. Day or night? What room is this? A bed, a regular bed, and a mattress on the floor nearby. Wallpaper hanging in strips. Clarita says she tore it like that with her teeth. She was fighting a barbaric tribe that night, high from some pills; she was battling for her life with men wearing helmets of heavy iron and their faces no more than Christian crosses to breathe through, every one of those bastards looking like her lover Simon, who seems to breathe with great difficulty through the slits of mouth and nostrils in his face. Clarita has never heard of Sioux Drive. Raymond Forrest cuts no ice with her, nor does the C account and its millions; Harvard Business School could be at the corner of Vernor and 12th Street for all she cares, and Vietnam might have sunk by now into the Dead Sea under its tons of debris, for all the amazement she could show . . . her face is overworked, overwrought, at the age of twenty (thirty?) it is already exhausted but fanciful and ready for a laugh. Clarita says mournfully to me *Honey somebody is going to turn you out let me give you warning*. In a movie shown on late television Clarita is not a mess like this but a nurse, with short neat hair and a dedicated look, in love with her doctor and her doctor's patients and their diseases, enamoured of needles and sponges and rubbing alcohol. . . . Or no: she is a private secretary. Robert Cummings is her boss. She helps him with fantastic plots, the canned audience laughs, no, the audience doesn't laugh because nothing is funny, instead her boss is Robert Taylor and they are not boss and secretary but husband and wife, she is threatened by a young starlet, she is grim, handsome, wifely, a good companion for a good man. . . . She is Claudette Colbert. Her sister too is Claudette Colbert. They are twins, identical! Her husband Charles Boyer is a very rich handsome man and her sister, Claudette Colbert, is plotting her death in order to take her place as the rich man's wife, no one will know because they are *twins*. . . . All these marvellous lives Clarita might have lived, but she fell out the

bottom at the age of thirteen. At the age when I was packing my overnight case for a slumber party at Toni Deshield's she was tearing filthy sheets off a bed and scratching up a rash on her arms. . . . Thirteen is uncommonly young for a white girl in Detroit, Miss Brock of the Detroit House of Correction said in a sad newspaper interview for the *Detroit News*; fifteen and sixteen are more likely. Eleven, twelve, thirteen are not surprising in coloured . . . they are more precocious. What can we do? Taxes are rising and the tax base is falling. The temperature rises slowly but falls rapidly. Everything is falling out of the bottom, Woodward Avenue is filthy, Livernois Avenue is filthy! Scraps of paper flutter in the air like pigeons, dirt flies up and hits you right in the eye, oh Detroit is breaking up into dangerous bits of newspaper and dirt, watch out. . . .

Clarita's apartment is over a restaurant. Simon her lover emerges from the cracks at dusk. Mrs Olesko, a neighbour of Clarita's, an aged white wisp of a woman, doesn't complain but sniffs with contentment at Clarita's noisy life and doesn't tell the cops, hating cops, when the cops arrive. I should give more fake names, more blanks, instead of telling all these secrets. I myself am a secret; I am a minor.

3. My father reads a paper at a medical convention in Los Angeles. There he is, on the edge of the North American continent, when the unmarked detective put his hand so gently on my arm in the aisle of Branden's and said, 'Miss, would you like to step over here for a minute?'

And where was he when Clarita put her hand on my arm, that wintry dark sulphurous aching day in Detroit, in the company of closed-down barber shops, closed-down diners, closed-down movie houses, homes, windows, basements, faces . . . she put her hand on my arm and said, 'Honey, are you looking for somebody down here?'

And was he home worrying about me, gone for two weeks solid, when they carried me off . . . .? It took three of them to get me in the police cruiser, so they said, and they put more than their hands on my arm.

4. I work on this lesson. My English teacher is Mr Forest, who is from Michigan State. Not handsome, Mr Forest, and his name is plain, unlike Raymond Forrest's, but he is sweet and rodentlike, he has conferred with the principal and my parents, and everything is fixed . . . treat her as if nothing has happened, a new start, begin again, only sixteen years old, what a shame, how did it happen?—nothing happened, nothing could have happened, a slight physiological modification known only to a gynecologist or to Dr Coronet. I work on my lesson. I sit in my pink room. I look around the room with my sad pink eyes. I sigh, I dawdle, I pause, I eat up time, I am limp and happy to be home, I am sixteen years old suddenly, my head hangs heavy as a pumpkin on my shoulders, and my hair

has just been cut by Mr Faye at the Crystal Salon and is said to be very becoming.

(Simon too put his hand on my arm and said, 'Honey, you have got to come with me,' and in his six-by-six room we got to know each other. Would I go back to Simon again? Would I lie down with him in all that filth and craziness? Over and over again.

a Clarita is being betrayed as in front of a Cunningham Drug Store she is nervously eying a coloured man who may or may not have money, or a nervous white boy of twenty with sideburns and an Appalachian look, who may or may not have a knife hidden in his jacket pocket, or a husky red-faced man of friendly countenance who may or may not be a member of the Vice Squad out for an early twilight walk.)

I work on my lesson for Mr Forest. I have filled up eleven pages. Words pour out of me and won't stop. I want to tell everything . . . what was the song Simon was always humming, and who was Simon's friend in a very new trench coat with an old high school graduation ring on his finger . . .? Simon's bearded friend? When I was down too low for him, Simon kicked me out and gave me to him for three days, I think, on Fourteenth Street in Detroit, an airy room of cold cruel drafts with newspapers on the floor. . . . Do I really remember that or am I piecing it together from what they told me? Did they tell the truth? Did they know much of the truth?

VIII CHARACTERS

1. Wednesdays after school, at four; Saturday mornings at ten. Mother drives me to Dr Coronet. Ferns in the office, plastic or real, they look the same. Dr Coronet is queenly, an elegant nicotine-stained lady who would have studied with Freud had circumstances not prevented it, a bit of a Catholic, ready to offer you some mystery if your teeth will ache too much without it. Highly recommended by Father! Forty dollars an hour, Father's forty dollars! Progress! Looking up! Looking better! That new haircut is so becoming, says Dr Coronet herself, showing how normal she is for a woman with an IQ of 180 and many advanced degrees.

2. Mother. A lady in a brown suede coat. Boots of shiny black material, black gloves, a black fur hat. She would be humiliated could she know that of all the people in the world it is my ex-lover Simon who walks most like her . . . self-conscious and unreal, listening to distant music, a little bow-legged with craftiness. . . .

3. Father. Tying a necktie. In a hurry. On my first evening home he put his hand on my arm and said, 'Honey, we're going to forget all about this.'

4. Simon. Outside, a plane is crossing the sky, in here we're in a hurry. Morning. It must be morning. The girl is half out of her mind, whimpering and vague; Simon her dear friend is wretched this morning . . . he is wretched with morning itself . . . he forces her to give him an injection with that needle she knows is filthy, she has a dread of needles and surgical instruments and the odour of things that are to be sent into the blood, thinking somehow of her father. . . . This is a bad morning, Simon says that his mind is being twisted out of shape, and so he submits to the needle that he usually scorns and bites his lip with his yellowish teeth, his face going very pale. *Ah baby!* he says in his soft mocking voice, which with all women is a mockery of love, *do it like this—Slowly*—And the girl, terrified, almost drops the precious needle but manages to turn it up to the light from the window . . . is it an extension of herself then? She can give him this gift then? *I wish you wouldn't do this to me*, she says, wise in her terror, because it seems to her that Simon's danger—in a few minutes he may be dead—is a way of pressing her against him that is more powerful than any other embrace. She has to work over his arm, the knotted corded veins of his arm, her forehead wet with perspiration as she pushes and releases the needle, staring at the mixture of liquid now stained with Simon's bright blood. . . . When the drug hits him she can feel it herself, she feels that magic that is more than any woman can give him, striking the back of his head and making his face stretch as if with the impact of a terrible sun. . . . She tries to embrace him but he pushes her aside and stumbles to his feet. *Jesus Christ*, he says. . . .

5. Princess, a Negro girl of eighteen. What is her charge? She is closed-mouth about it, shrewd and silent, you know that no one had to wrestle her to the sidewalk to get her in here; she came with dignity. In the recreation room she sits reading *Nancy Drew and the Jewel Box Mystery*, which inspires in her face tiny wrinkles of alarm and interest: what a face! Light brown skin, heavy shaded eyes, heavy eyelashes, a serious sinister dark brow, graceful fingers, graceful wristbones, graceful legs, lips, tongue, a sugar-sweet voice, a leggy stride more masculine than Simon's and my mother's, decked out in a dirty blouse and dirty white slacks; vaguely nautical is Princess' style. . . . At breakfast she is in charge of clearing the table and leans over me, saying, *Honey you sure you ate enough?*

6. The girl lies sleepless, wondering. Why here, why not there? Why Bloomfield Hills and not jail? Why jail and not her pink room? Why downtown Detroit and not Sioux Drive? What is the difference? Is Simon all the difference? The girl's head is a parade of wonders. She is nearly sixteen, her breath is marvellous with wonders, not long ago she was colouring with crayons and now she is smearing the landscape with paints that won't come off and won't come off her fingers either. She says to the matron *I am not talking about anything*, not because everyone has warned her

not to talk but because, because she will not talk; because she won't say anything about Simon, who is her secret. And she says to the matron, *I won't go home*, up until that night in the lavatory when everything was changed. . . . 'No, I won't go home I want to stay here,' she says, listening to her own words with amazement, thinking that weeds might climb everywhere over that marvellous $180,000 house and dinosaurs might return to muddy the beige carpeting, but never never will she reconcile four o'clock in the morning in Detroit with eight o'clock breakfasts in Bloomfield Hills. . . . oh, she aches still for Simon's hands and his caressing breath, though he gave her little pleasure, he took everything from her (five-dollar bills, ten-dollar bills, passed into her numb hands by men and taken out of her hands by Simon) until she herself was passed into the hands of other men, police, when Simon evidently got tired of her and her hysteria. . . . *No, I won't go home, I don't want to be bailed out.* The girl thinks as a *Stubborn and Wayward Child* (one of several charges lodged against her), and the matron understands her crazy white-rimmed eyes that are seeking out some new violence that will keep her in jail, should someone threaten to let her out. Such children try to strangle the matrons, the attendants, or one another . . . they want the locks locked forever, the doors nailed shut . . . and this girl is no different up until that night her mind is changed for her. . . .

IX THAT NIGHT

Princess and Dolly, a little white girl of maybe fifteen, hardy however as a sergeant and in the House of Correction for armed robbery, corner her in the lavatory at the farthest sink and the other girls look away and file out to bed, leaving her. God, how she is beaten up! Why is she beaten up? Why do they pound her, why such hatred? Princess vents all the hatred of a thousand silent Detroit winters on her body, this girl whose body belongs to me, fiercely she rides across the Midwestern plains on this girl's tender bruised body . . . . revenge on the oppressed minorities of America! revenge on the slaughtered Indians! revenge on the female sex, on the male sex, revenge on Bloomfield Hills, revenge revenge. . . .

X DETROIT

In Detroit, weather weighs heavily upon everyone. The sky looms large. The horizon shimmers in smoke. Downtown the buildings are imprecise in the haze. Perpetual haze. Perpetual motion inside the haze. Across the choppy river is the city of Windsor, in Canada. Part of the continent has bunched up here and is bulging outward, at the tip of Detroit; a cold hard rain is forever falling on the expressways. . . . Shoppers shop grimly, their cars are not parked in safe places, their windshields may be smashed and graceful ebony hands may drag them out through their shatterproof smashed windshields, crying, *Revenge for the Indians!* Ah, they all fear leaving Hudson's and being dragged to the very tip of the city and thrown off the parking roof of Cobo Hall, that expensive tomb, into the river. . . .

XI CHARACTERS WE ARE FOREVER ENTWINED WITH

I. Simon drew me into his tender rotting arms and breathed gravity into me. Then I came to earth, weighed down. He said, *You are such a little girl*, and he weighed me down with his delight. In the palms of his hands were teeth marks from his previous life experiences. He was thirty-five, they said. Imagine Simon in this room, in my pink room: he is about six feet tall and stoops slightly, in a feline cautious way, always thinking, always on guard, with his scuffed light suede shoes and his clothes that are anyone's clothes, slightly rumpled ordinary clothes that ordinary men might wear to not-bad jobs. Simon has fair long hair, curly hair, spent languid curls that are like . . . exactly like the curls of wood shavings to the touch, I am trying to be exact . . . and he smells of unheated mornings and coffee and too many pills coating his tongue with a faint green-white scum. . . . Dear Simon, who would be panicked in this room and in this house (right now Billie is vacuuming next door in my parents' room; a vacuum cleaner's roar is a sign of all good things), Simon who is said to have come from a home not much different from this, years ago, fleeing all the carpeting and the polished banisters . . . Simon has a deathly face, only desperate people fall in love with it. His face is bony and cautious, the bones of his cheeks prominent as if with the rigidity of his ceaseless thinking, plotting, for he has to make money out of girls to whom money means nothing, they're so far gone they can hardly count it, and in a sense money means nothing to him either except as a way of keeping on with his life. *Each Day's Proud Struggle*, the title of a novel we could read at jail. . . . Each day he needs a certain amount of money. He devours it. It wasn't love he uncoiled in me with his hollowed-out eyes and his courteous smile, that remnant of a prosperous past, but a dark terror that needed to press itself flat against him, or against another man . . . but he was the first, he came over to me and took my arm, a claim. We struggled on the stairs and I said, *Let me loose, you're hurting my neck, my face*, it was such a surprise that my skin hurt where he rubbed it, and afterward we lay face to face and he breathed everything into me. In the end I think he turned me in.

2. Raymond Forrest. I just read this morning that Raymond Forrest's father, the chairman of the board at   , died of a heart attack on a plane bound for London. I would like to write Raymond Forrest a note of sympathy. I would like to thank him for not pressing charges against me one hundred years ago, saving me, being so generous . . . well, men like Raymond Forrest are generous men, not like Simon. I would like to write him a letter telling of my love, or of some other emotion that is positive and

healthy. Not like Simon and his poetry, which he scrawled down when he was high and never changed a word . . . but when I try to think of something to say, it is Simon's language that comes back to me, caught in my head like a bad song, it is always Simon's language:

There is no reality only dreams
Your neck may get snapped when you wake
My love is drawn to some violent end
She keeps wanting to get away
My love is heading downward
And I am heading upward
She is going to crash on the sidewalk
And I am going to dissolve into the clouds

XII EVENTS

I. Out of the hospital, bruised and saddened and converted, with Princess' grunts still tangled in my hair . . . and Father in his overcoat looking like a prince himself, come to carry me off. Up the expressway and out north to home. Jesus Christ, but the air is thinner and cleaner here. Monumental houses. Heartbreaking sidewalks, so clean.

2. Weeping in the living room. The ceiling is two stories high and two chandeliers hang from it. Weeping, weeping, though Billie the maid is *probably listening*. I will never leave home again. Never. Never leave home. Never leave this home again, never.

3. Sugar doughnuts for breakfast. The toaster is very shiny and my face is distorted in it. Is that my face?

4. The car is turning in the driveway. Father brings me home. Mother embraces me. Sunlight breaks in movieland patches on the roof of our traditional-contemporary home, which was designed for the famous automotive stylist whose identity, if I told you the name of the famous car he designed, you would all know, so I can't tell you because my teeth chatter at the thought of being sued . . . or having someone climb into my bedroom window with a rope to strangle me. . . . The car turns up the blacktop drive. The house opens to me like a doll's house, so lovely in the sunlight, the big living room beckons to me with its walls falling away in a delirium of joy at my return, Billie the maid is *no doubt* listening from the kitchen as I burst into tears and the hysteria Simon got so sick of. Convulsed in Father's arms, I say I will never leave again, never, why did I leave, where did I go, what happened, my mind is gone wrong, my body is one big bruise, my backbone was sucked dry, it wasn't the men who hurt me and Simon never hurt me but only those girls . . . my God, how they

hurt me . . . I will never leave home again. . . . The car is perpetually turning up the drive and I am perpetually breaking down in the living room and we are perpetually taking the right exit from the expressway (Lahser Road) and the wall of the rest room is perpetually banging against my head and perpetually are Simon's hands moving across my body and adding everything up and so too are Father's hands on my shaking bruised back, far from the surface of my skin on the surface of my good blue cashmere coat (dry-cleaned for my release). . . . I weep for all the money here, for God in gold and beige carpeting, for the beauty of chandeliers and the miracle of a clean polished gleaming toaster and faucets that run both hot and cold water, and I tell them, *I will never leave home, this is my home, I love everything here, I am in love with everything here*. . . .

I am home.

1969

Margaret Atwood

b. 1939

In Atwood's diverse career as essayist, poet, novelist, short-story writer, editor, cartoonist, and critic, it has been her fiction that has won her the widest audience. Distinguishing between her poetry and her fiction, Atwood observes that poetry is 'the heart of the language, the activity through which language is renewed and kept alive. I believe fiction is the guardian of the moral and ethical sense of the community.' She wants her fiction 'to do something that surprises me, the writer, and therefore, I hope, will surprise you, the reader.'

Born in Ottawa, Atwood moved to Sault Ste Marie when she was six and the following year to Toronto, spending her early summers in northern Ontario and Quebec. She took her B.A. (1961) from the University of Toronto and her M.A. (1962) from Radcliffe College and pursued doctoral studies at Harvard University. She has lectured and taught at several universities in Canada, the United States, and Europe. She makes her permanent home in Toronto.

Although widely regarded as a Canadian nationalist and a feminist, Atwood believes that her writing, which explores the social, sexual, and political conflicts in the lives of contemporary women, transcends issues of nationality and gender. She sees 'Canadian nationalism and the concern for women's rights as part of a larger, non-exclusive picture.'

Atwood's female characters, she cautions, should not be read as paragons: 'you know, women are equal human beings. That also means they're equally fallible.' In seven novels and four collections of stories, she presents her readers with a wide range of female characters—mothers and daughters, wives, women in various careers—and an equally wide range of fictional forms, including the comic and parodic romance, *Lady Oracle* (1976) and the dystopian *The Handmaid's Tale* (1985). Her narration is often marked by experiments with point of view and, above all, by irony, which enhances both her comic and cutting social commentary and her more sombre dramatizations of conflicts within individual psyches.

Atwood sees the difference between the novel and the short story in the kind of changes that characters can undergo in each form: 'In a novel you hope there's more than one of those moments. In a short story there may only be one such moment. And it may not be their whole life changing. It may be one thing they've thought which they can no longer think. It may not be their entire life, it may just be an area. I don't have any thoughts about what *has* to happen in a story beyond the fact that *something* has to happen.' 'Significant Moments in the Life of My Mother' gathers its quiet momentum from Atwood's assembly of the narrator's recollections; what 'happens' is less a matter of event than of the narrator's gathering of her memories.

The plot of 'Bluebeard's Egg' seems on one level to be more direct: Sally discovers that her perception of her husband's character and conduct has been dramatically wrong. But because of the ways in which the narrative also unfolds at other levels—such as Sally's reflections on the story she has to write for her night course in fiction—'Bluebeard's Egg' becomes a richly complex and metaphorical presentation of a marriage and its partners' apprehensions of each other.

'Significant Moments in the Life of My Mother' was first published in the Autumn 1983 issue of *Queen's Quarterly*, and 'Bluebeard's Egg' in the November 1983 issue of *Chatelaine*. Both stories were then collected in *Bluebeard's Egg* (1983).

Significant Moments in the Life of My Mother

When my mother was very small, someone gave her a basket of baby chicks for Easter. They all died.

'I didn't know you weren't supposed to pick them up,' says my mother. 'Poor little things. I laid them out in a row on a board, with their little legs sticking out straight as pokers, and wept over them. I'd loved them to death.'

Possibly this story is meant by my mother to illustrate her own stupidity, and also her sentimentality. We are to understand she wouldn't do such a thing now.

Possibly it's a commentary on the nature of love; though, knowing my mother, this is unlikely.

My mother's father was a country doctor. In the days before cars he drove a team of horses and a buggy around his territory, and in the days before snow ploughs he drove a team and a sleigh, through blizzards and rainstorms and in the middle of the night, to arrive at houses lit with oil lamps where water would be boiling on the wood range and flannel sheets warming on the plate rack, to deliver babies who would subsequently be named after him. His office was in the house, and as a child my mother would witness people arriving at the office door, which was reached through the front porch, clutching parts of themselves—thumbs, fingers, toes, ears, noses—which had accidentally been cut off, pressing these severed parts to the raw stumps of their bodies as if they could be stuck there like dough, in the mostly vain hope that my grandfather would be able to sew them back on, heal the gashes made in them by axes, saws, knives, and fate.

My mother and her younger sister would loiter near the closed office door until shooed away. From behind it would come groans, muffled screams, cries for help. For my mother, hospitals have never been glamorous places, and illness offers no respite or holiday. 'Never get sick,' she says, and means it. She hardly ever does.

Once, though, she almost died. It was when her appendix burst. My grandfather had to do the operation. He said later that he shouldn't have been the person to do it: his hands were shaking too much. This is one of the few admissions of weakness on his part that my mother has ever reported. Mostly he is portrayed as severe and in charge of things. 'We all respected him, though,' she says. 'He was widely respected.' (This is a word which has slipped a little in the scale since my mother's youth. It used to outrank *love*.)

It was someone else who told me the story of my grandfather's muskrat farm: how he and one of my mother's uncles fenced in the swamp at the back of their property and invested my mother's maiden aunt's savings in muskrats. The idea was that these muskrats would multiply and eventually be made into muskrat coats, but an adjoining apple farmer washed his spraying equipment upstream, and the muskrats were all killed by the poison, as dead as doornails. This was during the Depression, and it was no joke.

When they were young—this can cover almost anything these days, but I put it at seven or eight—my mother and her sister had a tree house, where they spent some of their time playing dolls' tea parties and so forth. One day they found a box of sweet little bottles outside my grandfather's dispensary. The bottles were being thrown out, and my mother (who has always hated waste) appropriated them for use in their dolls' house. The bottles were full of yellow liquid, which they left in because it looked so pretty. It turned out that these were urine samples.

'We got Hail Columbia for that,' says my mother. 'But what did we know?'

My mother's family lived in a large white house near an apple orchard, in Nova Scotia. There was a barn and a carriage-house; in the kitchen there was a pantry. My mother can remember the days before commercial bakeries, when flour came in barrels and all the bread was made at home. She can remember the first radio broadcast she ever heard, which was a singing commercial about socks.

In this house there were many rooms. Although I have been there, although I have seen the house with my own eyes, I still don't know how many. Parts of it were closed off, or so it seemed; there were back staircases. Passages led elsewhere. Five children lived in it, two parents, a hired man and a hired girl, whose names and faces kept changing. The structure of the house was hierarchical, with my grandfather at the top, but its secret life—the life of pie crusts, clean sheets, the box of rags in the linen closet, the loaves in the oven—was female. The house, and all the objects in it, crackled with static electricity; undertows washed through it, the air was heavy with things that were known but not spoken. Like a hollow log, a drum, a church, it amplified, so that conversations whispered in it sixty years ago can be half-heard even today.

In this house you had to stay at the table until you had eaten everything on your plate. ' "Think of the starving Armenians," mother used to say,' says my mother. 'I didn't see how eating my bread crusts was going to help them out one jot.'

It was in this house that I first saw a stalk of oats in a vase, each oat wrapped in the precious silver paper which had been carefully saved from a chocolate box. I thought it was the most wonderful thing I had ever seen, and began saving silver paper myself. But I never got around to wrapping the oats, and in any case I didn't know how. Like many other art forms of vanished civilizations, the techniques for this one have been lost and cannot quite be duplicated.

'We had oranges at Christmas,' says my mother. 'They came all the way from Florida; they were very expensive. That was the big treat: to find an orange in the toe of your stocking. It's funny to remember how good they tasted, now.'

When she was sixteen, my mother had hair so long she could sit on it. Women were bobbing their hair by then; it was getting to be the twenties. My mother's hair was giving her headaches, she says, but my grandfather, who was very strict, forbade her to cut it. She waited until one Saturday when she knew he had an appointment with the dentist.

'In those days there was no freezing,' says my mother. 'The drill was worked with a foot pedal, and it went *grind, grind, grind*. The dentist himself had brown teeth: he chewed tobacco, and he would spit the tobacco juice into a spittoon while he was working on your teeth.'

Here my mother, who is a good mimic, imitates the sounds of the drill and the tobacco juice: '*Rrrrr! Rrrrr! Rrrrr! Phtt! Rrrrr! Rrrrr! Rrrrr! Phtt!* It was always sheer agony. It was a heaven-sent salvation when gas came in.'

My mother went into the dentist's office, where my grandfather was sitting in the chair, white with pain. She asked him if she could have her hair cut. He said she could do anything in tarnation as long as she would get out of there and stop pestering him.

'So I went out straight away and had it all chopped off,' says my mother jauntily. 'He was furious afterwards, but what could he do? He'd given his word.'

My own hair reposes in a cardboard box in a steamer trunk in my mother's cellar, where I picture it becoming duller and more brittle with each passing year, and possibly moth-eaten; by now it will look like the faded wreaths of hair in Victorian funeral jewellery. Or it may have developed a dry mildew; inside its tissue-paper wrappings it glows faintly, in the darkness of the trunk. I suspect my mother has forgotten it's in there. It was cut off, much to my relief, when I was twelve and my sister was born. Before that it was in long curls: 'Otherwise,' says my mother, 'it would have been just one big snarl.' My mother combed it by winding it around her index finger every morning, but when she was in the hospital my father couldn't cope. 'He couldn't get it around his stubby fingers,' says my mother. My father looks down at his fingers. They are indeed broad compared with my mother's long elegant ones, which she calls boney. He smiles a pussy-cat smile.

So it was that my hair was sheared off. I sat in the chair in my first beauty parlour and watched it falling, like handfuls of cobwebs, down over my shoulders. From within it my head began to emerge, smaller, denser, my face more angular. I aged five years in fifteen minutes. I knew I could go home now and try out lipstick.

'Your father was upset about it,' says my mother, with an air of collusion. She doesn't say this when my father is present. We smile, over the odd reactions of men to hair.

I used to think that my mother, in her earlier days, led a life of sustained hilarity and hair-raising adventure. (That was before I realized that she never put in the long stretches of uneventful time that must have made up much of her life: the stories were just the punctuation.) Horses ran away with her, men offered to, she was continually falling out of trees or off the ridgepoles of barns, or nearly being swept out to sea in rip-tides; or, in a more minor vein, suffering acute embarrassment in trying circumstances.

Churches were especially dangerous. 'There was a guest preacher one Sunday,' she says. 'Of course we had to go to church every Sunday. There he was, in full career, preaching hellfire and damnation'—she pounds an invisible pulpit—'and his full set of false teeth shot out of his mouth—*phoop*!—just like that. Well, he didn't miss a stride. He struck his hand up and caught them and popped them back into his mouth, and he kept right on, condemning us all to eternal torment. The pew was shaking! The tears were rolling down our faces, and the worst of it was, we were in the front pew, he was looking right at us. But of course we couldn't laugh out loud: father would have given us Hail Columbia.'

Other people's parlours were booby-trapped for her; so were any and all formal social occasions. Zippers sprang apart on her clothes in strategic places, hats were unreliable. The shortage of real elastic during the war demanded constant alertness: underpants then had buttons, and were more taboo and therefore more significant than they are now. 'There you would be,' she says, 'right on the street, and before you knew it they'd be down around your galoshes. The way to do was to step out of them with one foot, then kick them up with your other foot and whip them into your purse. I got quite good at it.'

This particular story is told only to a few, but other stories are for general consumption. When she tells them, my mother's face turns to rubber. She takes all the parts, adds the sound effects, waves her hands around in the air. Her eyes gleam, sometimes a little wickedly, for although my mother is sweet and old and a lady, she avoids being a sweet old lady. When people are in danger of mistaking her for one, she flings in something from left field; she refuses to be taken for granted.

But my mother cannot be duped into telling stories when she doesn't want to. If you prompt her, she becomes self-conscious and clams up. Or she will laugh and go out into the kitchen, and shortly after that you will hear the whir of the Mixmaster. Long ago I gave up attempting to make her do tricks at parties. In gatherings of unknown people, she merely listens intently, her head tilted a little, smiling a smile of glazed politeness. The secret is to wait and see what she will say afterwards.

At the age of seventeen my mother went to the Normal School in Truro. This name—'Normal School'—once held a certain magic for me. I thought it had something to do with learning to be normal, which possibly it did, because really it was where you used to go to learn how to be a school-teacher. Subsequently my mother taught in a one-room school house not far from her home. She rode her horse to and from the school house every day, and saved up the money she earned and sent herself to university with it. My grandfather wouldn't send her: he said she was too frivolous-minded. She liked ice-skating and dancing too much for his taste.

At Normal School my mother boarded with a family that contained several sons in more or less the same age group as the girl boarders. They all ate around a huge dining-room table (which I pictured as being of dark wood, with heavy carved legs, but covered always with a white linen tablecloth), with the mother and father presiding, one at each end. I saw them both as large and pink and beaming.

'The boys were great jokers,' says my mother. 'They were always up to something.' This was desirable in boys: to be great jokers, to be always up to something. My mother adds a key sentence: 'We had a lot of fun.'

Having fun has always been high on my mother's agenda. She has as much fun as possible, but what she means by this phrase cannot be understood without making an adjustment, an allowance for the great gulf across which this phrase must travel before it reaches us. It comes from another world, which, like the stars that originally sent out the light we see hesitating in the sky above us these nights, may be or is already gone. It is possible to reconstruct the facts of this world—the furniture, the clothing, the ornaments on the mantelpiece, the jugs and basins and even the chamber pots in the bedrooms, but not the emotions, not with the same exactness. So much that is now known and felt must be excluded.

This was a world in which guileless flirtation was possible, because there were many things that were simply not done by nice girls, and more girls were nice then. To fall from niceness was to fall not only from grace: sexual acts, by girls at any rate, had financial consequences. Life was more joyful and innocent then, and at the same time permeated with guilt and terror, or at least the occasions for them, on the most daily level. It was like the Japanese haiku: a limited form, rigid in its perimeters, within which an astonishing freedom was possible.

There are photographs of my mother at this time, taken with three or four other girls, linked arm in arm or with their arms thrown jestingly around each other's necks. Behind them, beyond the sea or the hills or whatever is in the background, is a world already hurtling towards ruin, unknown to them: the theory of relativity has been discovered, acid is accumulating at the roots of trees, the bull-frogs are doomed. But they smile with something that from this distance you could almost call gallantry, their right legs thrust forward in parody of a chorus line.

One of the great amusements for the girl boarders and the sons of the family was amateur theatre. Young people—they were called 'young people'—frequently performed in plays, which were put on in the church basement. My mother was a regular actor. (I have a stack of the scripts somewhere around the house, yellowing little booklets with my mother's parts checked in pencil. They are all comedies, and all impenetrable.) 'There was no television then,' says my mother. 'You made your own fun.'

For one of these plays a cat was required, and my mother and one of the sons borrowed the family cat. They put it into a canvas bag and drove to the rehearsal (there were cars by then), with my mother holding the cat on her lap. The cat, which must have been frightened, wet itself copiously, through the canvas bag and all over my mother's skirt. At the same time it made the most astonishingly bad smell.

'I was ready to sink through the floorboards,' says my mother. 'But what could I do? All I could do was sit there. In those days things like that'—she means cat pee, or pee of any sort—'were not mentioned.' She means in mixed company.

I think of my mother driven through the night, skirts dripping, overcome with shame, the young man beside her staring straight ahead, pretending not to notice anything. They both feel that this act of unmentionable urination has been done, not by the cat, but by my mother. And so they continue, in a straight line that takes them over the Atlantic and past the curvature of the earth, out through the moon's orbit and into the dark reaches beyond.

Meanwhile, back on earth, my mother says: 'I had to throw the skirt out. It was a good skirt, too, but nothing could get rid of the smell.'

'I only heard your father swear once,' says my mother. My mother herself never swears. When she comes to a place in a story in which swearing is called for, she says 'dad-ratted' or 'blankety-blank'.

'It was when he mashed his thumb, when he was sinking the well, for the pump.' This story, I know, takes place before I was born, up north, where there is nothing underneath the trees and their sheddings but sand and bedrock. The well was for a hand pump, which in turn was for the first of the many cabins and houses my parents built together. But since I witnessed later wells being sunk and later hand pumps being installed, I know how it's done. There's a pipe with a point at one end. You pound it into the ground with a sledge hammer, and as it goes down you screw other lengths of pipe onto it, until you hit drinkable water. To keep from ruining the thread on the top end, you hold a block of wood between the sledge hammer and the pipe. Better, you get someone else to hold it for you. This is how my father mashed his thumb: he was doing both the holding and the hammering himself.

'It swelled up like a radish,' says my mother. 'He had to make a hole in the nail, with his toad-sticker, to ease the pressure. The blood spurted out like pips from a lemon. Later on the whole nail turned purple and black and dropped off. Luckily he grew another one. They say you only get two chances. When he did it though, he turned the air blue for yards around. I didn't even know he knew those words. I don't know where he picked them up.' She speaks as if these words are a minor contagious disease, like chicken pox.

Here my father looks modestly down at his plate. For him, there are two worlds: one containing ladies, in which you do not use certain expressions, and another one—consisting of logging camps and other haunts of his youth, and of gatherings of acceptable sorts of men—in which you do. To let the men's world slip over verbally into the ladies' would reveal you as a mannerless boor, but to carry the ladies' world over into the men's brands you a prig and maybe even a pansy. This is the word for it. All of this is well understood between them.

This story illustrates several things: that my father is no pansy, for one; and that my mother behaved properly by being suitably shocked. But my mother's eyes shine with delight while she tells this story. Secretly, she thinks it funny that my father got caught out, even if only once. The thumbnail that fell off is, in any significant way, long forgotten.

There are some stories which my mother does not tell when there are men present: never at dinner, never at parties. She tells them to women only, usually in the kitchen, when they or we are helping with the dishes or shelling peas, or taking the tops and tails off the string beans, or husking corn. She tells them in a lowered voice, without moving her hands around in the air, and they contain no sound effects. These are stories of romantic betrayals, unwanted pregnancies, illnesses of various horrible kinds, marital infidelities, mental breakdowns, tragic suicides, unpleasant lingering deaths. They are not rich in detail or embroidered with incident: they are stark and factual. The women, their own hands moving among the dirty dishes or the husks of vegetables, nod solemnly.

Some of these stories, it is understood, are not to be passed on to my father, because they would upset him. It is well known that women can deal with this sort of thing better than men can. Men are not to be told anything they might find too painful; the secret depths of human nature, the sordid physicalities, might overwhelm or damage them. For instance, men often faint at the sight of their own blood, to which they are not accustomed. For this reason you should never stand behind one in the line at the Red Cross donor clinic. Men, for some mysterious reason, find life more difficult than women do. (My mother believes this, despite the female bodies, trapped, diseased, disappearing, or abandoned, that litter her stories.) Men must be allowed to play in the sandbox of their choice, as happily as they can, without disturbance; otherwise they get cranky and won't eat their dinners. There are all kinds of things that men are simply not equipped to understand, so why expect it of them? Not everyone shares this belief about men; nevertheless, it has its uses.

'She dug up the shrubs from around the house,' says my mother. This story is about a shattered marriage: serious business. My mother's eyes widen. The other women lean forward. 'All she left him were the shower curtains.' There is a collective sigh, an expelling of breath. My father enters the kitchen, wondering when the tea will be ready, and the women close ranks, turning to him their deceptive blankly smiling faces. Soon afterwards, my mother emerges from the kitchen, carrying the tea pot, and sets it down on the table in its ritual place.

'I remember the time we almost died,' says my mother. Many of her stories begin this way. When she is in a certain mood, we are to understand that our lives have been preserved only by a series of amazing coincidences and strokes of luck; otherwise the entire family, individually or collectively, would be dead as doornails. These stories, in addition to producing adrenalin, serve to reinforce our sense of gratitude. There is the time we almost went over a waterfall, in a canoe, in a fog; the time we almost got caught in a forest fire; the time my father almost got squashed, before my mother's very eyes, by a ridgepole he was lifting into place; the time my brother almost got struck by a bolt of lightning, which went by him so close it knocked him down. 'You could hear it sizzle,' says my mother.

This is the story of the hay wagon. 'Your father was driving,' says my mother, 'at the speed he usually goes.' We read between the lines: *too fast*. 'You kids were in the back.' I can remember this day, so I can remember how old I was, how old my brother was. We were old enough to think it was funny to annoy my father by singing popular songs of a type he disliked, such as 'Mockingbird Hill'; or perhaps we were imitating bagpipe music by holding our noses and humming, while hitting our Adam's apples with the edges of our hands. When we became too irritating my father would say, 'Pipe down.' We weren't old enough to know that his irritation could be real: we thought it was part of the game.

'We were going down a steep hill,' my mother continues, 'when a hay wagon pulled out right across the road, at the bottom. Your father put on the brakes, but nothing happened. The brakes were gone! I thought our last moment had come.' Luckily the hay wagon continued across the road, and we shot past it, missing it by at least a foot. 'My heart was in my mouth,' says my mother.

I didn't know until afterwards what had really happened. I was in the back seat, making bagpipe music, oblivious. The scenery was the same as it always was on car trips: my parents' heads, seen from behind, sticking up above the front seat. My father had his hat on, the one he wore to keep things from falling off the trees into his hair. My mother's hand was placed lightly on the back of his neck.

'You had such an acute sense of smell when you were younger,' says my mother.

Now we are on more dangerous ground: my mother's childhood is one thing, my own quite another. This is the moment at which I start rattling the silverware, or ask for another cup of tea. 'You used to march into houses that were strange to you, and you would say in a loud voice, "What's that funny smell?" ' If there are guests present, they shift a little away from me, conscious of their own emanations, trying not to look at my nose.

'I used to be so embarrassed,' says my mother absentmindedly. Then she shifts gears. 'You were such an easy child. You used to get up at six in the morning and play by yourself in the play room, singing away. . . .' There is a pause. A distant voice, mine, high and silvery, drifts over the space between us. 'You used to talk a blue streak. Chatter, chatter, chatter, from morning to night.' My mother sighs imperceptibly, as if wondering why I have become so silent, and gets up to poke the fire.

Hoping to change the subject, I ask whether or not the crocuses have come up yet, but she is not to be diverted. 'I never had to spank you,' she says. 'A harsh word, and you would be completely reduced.' She looks at me sideways; she isn't sure what I have turned into, or how. 'There were just one or two times. Once, when I had to go out and I left your father in charge.' (This may be the real point of the story: the inability of men to second-guess small children.) 'I came back along the street, and there were you and your brother, throwing mud balls at an old man out of the upstairs window.'

We both know whose idea this was. For my mother, the proper construction to be put on this event is that my brother was a hell-raiser and I was his shadow, 'easily influenced', as my mother puts it. 'You were just putty in his hands.'

'Of course, I had to punish both of you equally,' she says. Of course. I smile a forgiving smile. The real truth is that I was sneakier than my brother, and got caught less often. No front-line charges into enemy machine-gun nests for me, if they could be at all avoided. My own solitary acts of wickedness were devious and well concealed; it was only in partnership with my brother that I would throw caution to the winds.

'He could wind you around his little finger,' says my mother. 'Your father made each of you a toy box, and the rule was—' (my mother is good at the devising of rules) '—the rule was that neither of you could take the toys out of the other one's toy box without permission. Otherwise he would have got all your toys away from you. But he got them anyway, mind you. He used to talk you into playing house, and he would pretend to be the baby. Then he would pretend to cry, and when you asked what he wanted, he'd demand whatever it was out of your toy box that he wanted to play with at the moment. You always gave it to him.'

I don't remember this, though I do remember staging World War Two on the living-room floor, with armies of stuffed bears and rabbits; but surely some primal patterns were laid down. Have these early toy-box experiences—and 'toy box' itself, as a concept, reeks with implications—have they made me suspicious of men who wish to be mothered, yet susceptible to them at the same time? Have I been conditioned to believe that if I am not solicitous, if I am not forthcoming, if I am not a never-ending cornucopia of entertaining delights, they will take their collections of milk-bottle tops and their mangy one-eared teddy bears and go away into the woods by themselves to play snipers? Probably. What my mother thinks was merely cute may have been lethal.

But this is not her only story about my suckiness and gullibility. She follows up with the *coup de grâce*, the tale of the bunny-rabbit cookies.

'It was in Ottawa. I was invited to a government tea,' says my mother, and this fact alone should signal an element of horror: my mother hated official functions, to which however she was obliged to go because she was the wife of a civil servant. 'I had to drag you kids along; we couldn't afford a lot of babysitters in those days.' The hostess had made a whole plateful of decorated cookies for whatever children might be present, and my mother proceeds to describe these: wonderful cookies shaped like bunny rabbits, with faces and clothes of coloured icing, little skirts for the little girl bunny rabbits, little pants for the little boy bunny rabbits.

'You chose one,' says my mother. 'You went off to a corner with it, by yourself. Mrs X noticed you and went over. 'Aren't you going to eat your cookie?' she said. 'Oh, no,' you said. 'I'll just sit here and talk to it.' And there you sat, as happy as a clam. But someone had made the mistake of leaving the plate near your brother. When they looked again, there wasn't a single cookie left. He'd eaten every one. He was very sick that night, I can tell you.'

Some of my mother's stories defy analysis. What is the moral of this one? That I was a simp is clear enough, but on the other hand it was my brother who got the stomach ache. Is it better to eat your food, in a straightforward materialistic way, and as much of it as possible, or go off into the corner and talk to it? This used to be a favourite of my mother's before I was married, when I would bring what my father referred to as 'swains' home for dinner. Along with the dessert, out would come the bunny-rabbit cookie story, and I would cringe and twiddle my spoon while my mother forged blithely on with it. What were the swains supposed to make of it? Were my kindliness and essential feminity being trotted out for their inspection? Were they being told in a roundabout way that I was harmless, that they could expect to be talked to by me, but not devoured? Or was she, in some way, warning them off? Because there is something faintly crazed about my behaviour, some tinge of the kind of person who might be expected to leap up suddenly from the dinner table and shout, 'Don't eat that! It's alive!'

There is, however, a difference between symbolism and anecdote. Listening to my mother, I sometimes remember this.

'In my next incarnation,' my mother said once, 'I'm going to be an archaeologist and go around digging things up.' We were sitting on the bed that had once been my brother's, then mine, then my sister's; we were sorting out things from one of the trunks, deciding what could now be given away or thrown out. My mother believes that what you save from the past is mostly a matter of choice.

At that time something wasn't right in the family; someone wasn't happy. My mother was angry: her good cheer was not paying off.

This statement of hers startled me. It was the first time I'd ever heard my mother say that she might have wanted to be something other than what she was. I must have been thirty-five at the time, but it was still shocking and slightly offensive to me to learn that my mother might not have been totally contented fulfilling the role in which fate had cast her: that of being my mother. What thumbsuckers we all are, I thought, when it comes to mothers.

Shortly after this I became a mother myself, and this moment altered for me.

While she was combing my next-to-impossible hair, winding it around her long index finger, yanking out the snarls, my mother used to read me stories. Most of them are still in the house somewhere, but one has vanished. It may have been a library book. It was about a little girl who was so poor she had only one potato left for her supper, and while roasting it the potato got up and ran away. There was the usual chase, but I can't remember the ending: a significant lapse.

'That story was one of your favourites,' says my mother. She is probably still under the impression that I identified with the little girl, with her hunger and her sense of loss; whereas in reality I identified with the potato.

Early influences are important. It took that one a while to come out; probably until after I went to university and started wearing black stockings and pulling my hair back into a bun, and having pretentions. Gloom set in. Our next-door neighbour, who was interested in wardrobes, tackled my mother: ' "If she would only *do* something about herself," ' my mother quotes, ' "she could be *quite attractive*." '

'You always kept yourself busy,' my mother says charitably, referring to this time. 'You always had something cooking. Some project or other.'

It is part of my mother's mythology that I am as cheerful and productive as she is, though she admits that these qualities may be occasionally and temporarily concealed. I wasn't allowed much angst around the house. I had to indulge it in the cellar, where my mother wouldn't come upon me brooding and suggest I should go out for a walk, to improve my circulation. This was her answer to any sign, however slight, of creeping despondency. There wasn't a lot that a brisk sprint through dead leaves, howling winds, or sleet couldn't cure.

It was, I knew, the *zeitgeist* that was afflicting me, and against it such simple remedies were powerless. Like smog I wafted through her days, dankness spreading out from around me. I read modern poetry and histories of Nazi atrocities, and took to drinking coffee. Off in the distance, my mother vacuumed around my feet while I sat in chairs, studying, with car rugs tucked around me, for suddenly I was always cold.

My mother has few stories to tell about these times. What I remember from them is the odd look I would sometimes catch in her eyes. It struck me, for the first time in my life, that my mother might be afraid of me. I could not even reassure her, because I was only dimly aware of the nature of her distress, but there must have been something going on in me that was beyond her: at any time I might open my mouth and out would come a language she had never heard before. I had become a visitant from outer space, a time-traveller come back from the future, bearing news of a great disaster.

1983

Bluebeard's Egg

Sally stands at the kitchen window, waiting for the sauce she's reducing to come to a simmer, looking out. Past the garage the lot sweeps downwards, into the ravine; it's a wilderness there, of bushes and branches and what Sally thinks of as vines. It was her idea to have a kind of terrace, built of old railroad ties, with wild flowers growing between them, but Edward says he likes it the way it is. There's a playhouse down at the bottom, near the fence; from here she can just see the roof. It has nothing to do with Edward's kids, in their earlier incarnations, before Sally's time; it's more ancient than that, and falling apart. Sally would like it cleared away. She thinks drunks sleep in it, the men who live under the bridges down there, who occasionally wander over the fence (which is broken down, from where they step on it) and up the hill, to emerge squinting like moles into the light of Sally's well-kept back lawn.

Off to the left is Ed, in his windbreaker; it's officially spring, Sally's blue scylla is in flower, but it's chilly for this time of year. Ed's windbreaker is an old one he won't throw out; it still says WILDCATS, relic of some team he was on in high school, an era so prehistoric Sally can barely imagine it; though picturing Ed at high school is not all that difficult. Girls would have had crushes on him, he would have been unconscious of it; things like that don't change. He's puttering around the rock garden now; some of the rocks stick out too far and are in danger of grazing the side of Sally's Peugeot, on its way to the garage, and he's moving them around. He likes doing things like that, puttering, humming to himself. He won't wear work gloves, though she keeps telling him he could squash his fingers.

Watching his bent back with its frayed, poignant lettering, Sally dissolves; which is not infrequent with her. *My darling Edward*, she thinks. *Edward Bear, of little brain. How I love you.* At times like this she feels very protective of him.

Sally knows for a fact that dumb blondes were loved, not because they were blonde, but because they were dumb. It was their helplessness and confusion that were so sexually attractive, once; not their hair. It wasn't false, the rush of tenderness men must have felt for such women. Sally understands it.

For it must be admitted: Sally is in love with Ed because of his stupidity, his monumental and almost energetic stupidity: energetic, because Ed's stupidity is not passive. He's no mere blockhead; you'd have to be working at it to be that stupid. Does it make Sally feel smug, or smarter than he is, or even smarter than she really is herself? No; on the contrary, it makes her humble. It fills her with wonder that the world can contain such marvels as Ed's colossal and endearing thickness. He is just so *stupid*. Every time he gives her another piece of evidence, another tile that she can glue into place in the vast mosaic of his stupidity she's continually piecing together, she wants to hug him, and often does; and he is so stupid he can never figure out what for.

Because Ed is so stupid he doesn't even know he's stupid. He's a child of luck, a third son who, armed with nothing but a certain feeble-minded amiability, manages to make it through the forest with all its witches and traps and pitfalls and end up with the princess, who is Sally, of course. It helps that he's handsome.

On good days she sees his stupidity as innocence, lamblike, shining with the light of (for instance) green daisied meadows in the sun. (When Sally starts thinking this way about Ed, in terms of the calendar art from the service-station washrooms of her childhood, dredging up images of a boy with curly golden hair, his arm thrown around the neck of an Irish setter—a notorious brainless beast, she reminds herself—she knows she is sliding over the edge, into a ghastly kind of sentimentality, and that she must stop at once, or Ed will vanish, to be replaced by a stuffed facsimile, useful for little else but an umbrella stand. Ed is a real person, with a lot more to him than these simplistic renditions allow for; which sometimes worries her.) On bad days though, she sees his stupidity as wilfulness, a stubborn determination to shut things out. His obtuseness is a wall, within which he can go about his business, humming to himself, while Sally, locked outside, must hack her way through the brambles with hardly so much as a transparent raincoat between them and her skin.

Why did she choose him (or, to be precise, as she tries to be with herself and sometimes is even out loud, *hunt him down*), when it's clear to everyone she had other options? To Marylynn, who is her best though most recent friend, she's explained it by saying she was spoiled when young by reading too many Agatha Christie murder mysteries, of the kind in which the clever and witty heroine passes over the equally clever and witty first-lead male, who's helped solve the crime, in order to marry the second-lead male, the stupid one, the one who would have been arrested and condemned and executed if it hadn't been for her cleverness. Maybe this is how she sees Ed: if it weren't for her, his blundering too-many-thumbs kindness would get him into all sorts of quagmires, all sorts of sink-holes he'd never be able to get himself out of, and then he'd be done for.

'Sink-hole' and 'quagmire' are not flattering ways of speaking about other women, but this is what is at the back of Sally's mind; specifically, Ed's two previous wives. Sally didn't exactly extricate him from their clutches. She's never even met the first one, who moved to the west coast fourteen years ago and sends Christmas cards, and the second one was middle-aged and already in the act of severing herself from Ed before Sally came along. (For Sally, 'middle-aged' means anyone five years older than she is. It has always meant this. She applies it only to women, however. She doesn't think of Ed as middle-aged, although the gap between them is considerably more than five years).

Ed doesn't know what happened with these marriages, what went wrong. His protestations of ignorance, his refusal to discuss the finer points, is frustrating to Sally, because she would like to hear the whole story. But it's also cause for anxiety: if he doesn't know what happened with the other two, maybe the same thing could be happening with her and he doesn't know about that, either. Stupidity like Ed's can be a health hazard, for other people. What if he wakes up one day and decides that she isn't the true bride after all, but the false one? Then she will be put into a barrel stuck full of nails and rolled downhill, endlessly, while he is sitting in yet another bridal bed, drinking champagne. She remembers the brand name, because she bought it herself. Champagne isn't the sort of finishing touch that would occur to Ed, though he enjoyed it enough at the time.

But outwardly Sally makes a joke of all this. 'He doesn't *know*,' she says to Marylynn, laughing a little, and they shake their heads. If it were them, they'd know, all right. Marylynn is in fact divorced, and she can list every single thing that went wrong, item by item. After doing this, she adds that her divorce was one of the best things that ever happened to her. 'I was just a nothing before,' she says. 'It made me pull myself together.'

Sally, looking across the kitchen table at Marylynn, has to agree that she is far from being a nothing now. She started out re-doing people's closets, and has worked that up into her own interior-design firm. She does the houses of the newly rich, those who lack ancestral furniture and the confidence to be shabby, and who wish their interiors to reflect a personal taste they do not in reality possess.

'What they want are mausoleums,' Marylynn says, 'or hotels,' and she cheerfully supplies them. 'Right down to the ash-trays. Imagine having someone else pick out your ash-trays for you.'

By saying this, Marylynn lets Sally know that she's not including her in that category, though Sally did in fact hire her, at the very first, to help with a few details around the house. It was Marylynn who redesigned the wall of closets in the master bedroom and who found Sally's massive Chinese mahogany table, which cost her another seven hundred dollars to have stripped. But it turned out to be perfect, as Marylynn said it would. Now she's dug up a nineteenth-century keyhole desk, which both she and Sally know will be exactly right for the bay-windowed alcove off the living room. 'Why do you need it?' Ed said in his puzzled way. 'I thought you worked in your study.' Sally admitted this, but said they could keep the telephone bills in it, which appeared to satisfy him. She knows exactly what she needs it for: she needs it to sit at, in something flowing, backlit by the morning sunlight, gracefully dashing off notes. She saw a 1940's advertisement for coffee like this once; and the husband was standing behind the chair, leaning over, with a worshipful expression on his face.

Marylynn is the kind of friend Sally does not have to explain any of this to, because it's assumed between them. Her intelligence is the kind Sally respects.

Marylynn is tall and elegant, and makes anything she is wearing seem fashionable. Her hair is prematurely grey and she leaves it that way. She goes in for loose blouses in cream-coloured silk, and eccentric scarves gathered from interesting shops and odd corners of the world, thrown carelessly around her neck and over one shoulder. (Sally has tried this toss in the mirror, but it doesn't work.) Marylynn has a large collection of unusual shoes; she says they're unusual because her feet are so big, but Sally knows better. Sally, who used to think of herself as pretty enough and now thinks of herself as doing quite well for her age, envies Marylynn her bone structure, which will serve her well when the inevitable happens.

Whenever Marylynn is coming to dinner, as she is today—she's bringing the desk too—Sally takes especial care with her clothes and make-up. Marylynn, she knows, is her real audience for such things, since no changes she effects in herself seem to affect Ed one way or the other, or even to register with him. 'You look fine to me,' is all he says, no matter how she really looks. (But does she want him to see her more clearly, or not? Most likely not. If he did he would notice the incipient wrinkles, the small pouches of flesh that are not quite there yet, the network forming beneath her eyes. It's better as it is.)

Sally has repeated this remark of Ed's to Marylynn, adding that he said it the day the Jacuzzi overflowed because the smoke alarm went off, because an English muffin she was heating to eat in the bathtub got stuck in the toaster, and she had to spend an hour putting down newspaper and mopping up, and only had half an hour to dress for a dinner they were going to. 'Really I looked like the wrath of God,' said Sally. These days she finds herself repeating to Marylynn many of the things Ed says: the stupid things. Marylynn is the only one of Sally's friends she has confided in to this extent.

'Ed is cute as a button,' Marylynn said. 'In fact, he's just like a button:

he's so bright and shiny. If he were mine, I'd get him bronzed and keep him on the mantel-piece.'

Marylynn is even better than Sally at concocting formulations for Ed's particular brand of stupidity, which can irritate Sally: coming from herself, this sort of comment appears to her indulgent and loving, but from Marylynn it borders on the patronizing. So then she sticks up for Ed, who is by no means stupid about everything. When you narrow it down, there's only one area of life he's hopeless about. The rest of the time he's intelligent enough, some even say brilliant: otherwise, how could he be so successful?

Ed is a heart man, one of the best, and the irony of this is not lost on Sally: who could possibly know less about the workings of hearts, real hearts, the kind symbolized by red satin surrounded by lace and topped by pink bows, than Ed? Hearts with arrows in them. At the same time, the fact that he's a heart man is a large part of his allure. Women corner him on sofas, trap him in bay-windows at cocktail parties, mutter to him in confidential voices at dinner parties. They behave this way right in front of Sally, under her very nose, as if she's invisible, and Ed lets them do it. This would never happen if he were in banking or construction.

As it is, everywhere he goes he is beset by sirens. They want him to fix their hearts. Each of them seems to have a little something wrong—a murmur, a whisper. Or they faint a lot and want him to tell them why. This is always what the conversations are about, according to Ed, and Sally believes it. Once she'd wanted it herself, that mirage. What had she invented for him, in the beginning? A heavy heart, that beat too hard after meals. And he'd been so sweet, looking at her with those stunned brown eyes of his, as if her heart were the genuine topic, listening to her gravely as if he'd never heard any of this twaddle before, advising her to drink less coffee. And she'd felt such triumph, to have carried off her imposture, pried out of him that minuscule token of concern.

Thinking back on this incident makes her uneasy, now that she's seen her own performance repeated so many times, including the hand placed lightly on her heart, to call attention of course to the breasts. Some of these women have been within inches of getting Ed to put his head down on their chest, right there in Sally's living room. Watching all this out of the corners of her eyes while serving the liqueurs, Sally feels the Aztec rise within her. *Trouble with your heart? Get it removed*, she thinks. *Then you'll have no more problems.*

Sometimes Sally worries that she's a nothing, the way Marylynn was before she got a divorce and a job. But Sally isn't a nothing; therefore, she doesn't need a divorce to stop being one. And she's always had a job of some sort; in fact she has one now. Luckily Ed has no objection; he doesn't have much of an objection to anything she does.

Her job is supposed to be full-time, but in effect it's part-time, because Sally can take a lot of the work away and do it at home, and, as she says, with one arm tied behind her back. When Sally is being ornery, when she's playing the dull wife of a fascinating heart man—she does this with people she can't be bothered with—she says she works in a bank, nothing important. Then she watches their eyes dismiss her. When, on the other hand, she's trying to impress, she says she's in P.R. In reality she runs the in-house organ for a trust company, a medium-sized one. This is a thin magazine, nicely printed, which is supposed to make the employees feel that some of the boys are doing worthwhile things out there and are human beings as well. It's still the boys, though the few women in anything resembling key positions are wheeled out regularly, bloused and suited and smiling brightly, with what they hope will come across as confidence rather than aggression.

This is the latest in a string of such jobs Sally has held over the years: comfortable enough jobs that engage only half of her cogs and wheels, and that end up leading nowhere. Technically she's second-in-command: over her is a man who wasn't working out in management, but who couldn't be fired because his wife was related to the chairman of the board. He goes out for long alcoholic lunches and plays a lot of golf, and Sally runs the show. This man gets the official credit for everything Sally does right, but the senior executives in the company take Sally aside when no one is looking and tell her what a great gal she is and what a whiz she is at holding up her end.

The real pay-off for Sally, though, is that her boss provides her with an endless supply of anecdotes. She dines out on stories about his dim-wittedness and pomposity, his lobotomized suggestions about what the two of them should cook up for the magazine; *the organ*, as she says he always calls it. 'He says we need some fresh blood to perk up the organ,' Sally says, and the heart men grin at her. 'He actually said that?' Talking like this about her boss would be reckless—you never know what might get back to him, with the world as small as it is—if Sally were afraid of losing her job, but she isn't. There's an unspoken agreement between her and this man: they both know that if she goes, he goes, because who else would put up with him? Sally might angle for his job, if she were stupid enough to disregard his family connections, if she coveted the trappings of power. But she's just fine where she is. Jokingly, she says she's reached her level of incompetence. She says she suffers from fear of success.

Her boss is white-haired, slender, and tanned, and looks like an English gin ad. Despite his vapidity he's outwardly distinguished, she allows him that. In truth she pampers him outrageously, indulges him, covers up for him at every turn, though she stops short of behaving like a secretary: she doesn't bring him coffee. They both have a secretary who does that anyway. The one time he made a pass at her, when he came in from lunch visibly reeling, Sally was kind about it.

Occasionally, though not often, Sally has to travel in connection with her job. She's sent off to places like Edmonton, where they have a branch.

She interviews the boys at the middle and senior levels; they have lunch, and the boys talk about ups and downs in oil or the slump in the real-estate market. Then she gets taken on tours of shopping plazas under construction. It's always windy, and grit blows into her face. She comes back to home base and writes a piece on the youthfulness and vitality of the West.

She teases Ed, while she packs, saying she's going off for a rendezvous with a dashing financier or two. Ed isn't threatened; he tells her to enjoy herself, and she hugs him and tells him how much she will miss him. He's so dumb it doesn't occur to him she might not be joking. In point of fact, it would have been quite possible for Sally to have had an affair, or at least a one- or two-night stand, on several of these occasions: she knows when those chalk lines are being drawn, when she's being dared to step over them. But she isn't interested in having an affair with anyone but Ed.

She doesn't eat much on the planes; she doesn't like the food. But on the return trip, she invariably saves the pre-packaged parts of the meal, the cheese in its plastic wrap, the miniature chocolate bar, the bag of pretzels. She ferrets them away in her purse. She thinks of them as supplies, that she may need if she gets stuck in a strange airport, if they have to change course because of snow or fog, for instance. All kinds of things could happen, although they never have. When she gets home she takes the things from her purse and throws them out.

Outside the window Ed straightens up and wipes his earth-smeared hands down the sides of his pants. He begins to turn, and Sally moves back from the window so he won't see that she's watching. She doesn't like it to be too obvious. She shifts her attention to the sauce: it's in the second stage of a *sauce suprême*, which will make all the difference to the chicken. When Sally was learning this sauce, her cooking instructor quoted one of the great chefs, to the effect that the chicken was merely a canvas. He meant as in painting, but Sally, in an undertone to the woman next to her, turned it around. 'Mine's canvas anyway, sauce or no sauce,' or words to that effect.

Gourmet cooking was the third night course Sally has taken. At the moment she's on her fifth, which is called *Forms of Narrative Fiction*. It's half reading and half writing assignments—the instructor doesn't believe you can understand an art form without at least trying it yourself—and Sally purports to be enjoying it. She tells her friends she takes night courses to keep her brain from atrophying, and her friends find this amusing: whatever else may become of Sally's brain, they say, they don't see atrophying as an option. Sally knows better, but in any case there's always room for improvement. She may have begun taking the courses in the belief that this would make her more interesting to Ed, but she soon gave up on that idea: she appears to be neither more nor less interesting to Ed now than she was before.

Most of the food for tonight is already made. Sally tries to be well organized: the overflowing Jacuzzi was an aberration. The cold watercress soup with walnuts is chilling in the refrigerator, the chocolate mousse ditto. Ed, being Ed, prefers meatloaf to sweetbreads with pine nuts, butterscotch pudding made from a package to chestnut purée topped with whipped cream. (Sally burnt her fingers peeling the chestnuts. She couldn't do it the easy way and buy it tinned.) Sally says Ed's preference for this type of food comes from being pre-programmed by hospital cafeterias when he was younger: show him a burned sausage and a scoop of instant mashed potatoes and he salivates. So it's only for company that she can unfurl her *boeuf en daube* and her salmon *en papillote*, spread them forth to be savoured and praised.

What she likes best about these dinners though is setting the table, deciding who will sit where and, when she's feeling mischievous, even what they are likely to say. Then she can sit and listen to them say it. Occasionally she prompts a little.

Tonight will not be very challenging, since it's only the heart men and their wives, and Marylynn, whom Sally hopes will dilute them. The heart men are forbidden to talk shop at Sally's dinner table, but they do it anyway. 'Not what you really want to listen to while you're eating,' says Sally. 'All those tubes and valves.' Privately she thinks they're a conceited lot, all except Ed. She can't resist needling them from time to time.

'I mean,' she said to one of the leading surgeons, 'basically it's just an exalted form of dress-making, don't you think?'

'Come again?' said the surgeon, smiling. The heart men think Sally is one hell of a tease.

'It's really just cutting and sewing, isn't it?' Sally murmured. The surgeon laughed.

'There's more to it than that,' Ed said, unexpectedly, solemnly.

'What more, Ed?' said the surgeon. 'You could say there's a lot of embroidery, but that's in the billing.' He chuckled at himself.

Sally held her breath. She could hear Ed's verbal thought processes lurching into gear. He was delectable.

'Good judgement,' Ed said. His earnestness hit the table like a wet fish. The surgeon hastily downed his wine.

Sally smiled. This was supposed to be a reprimand to her, she knew, for not taking things seriously enough. *Oh, come on, Ed*, she could say. But she knows also, most of the time, when to keep her trap shut. She should have a light-up JOKE sign on her forehead, so Ed would be able to tell the difference.

The heart men do well. Most of them appear to be doing better than Ed, but that's only because they have, on the whole, more expensive tastes and fewer wives. Sally can calculate these things and she figures Ed is about par.

These days there's much talk about advanced technologies, which Sally tries to keep up on, since they interest Ed. A few years ago the heart men got themselves a new facility. Ed was so revved up that he told Sally about it, which was unusual for him. A week later Sally said she would drop by the hospital at the end of the day and pick Ed up and take him out for dinner; she didn't feel like cooking, she said. Really she wanted to check out the facility; she likes to check out anything that causes the line on Ed's excitement chart to move above level.

At first Ed said he was tired, that when the day came to an end he didn't want to prolong it. But Sally wheedled and was respectful, and finally Ed took her to see his new gizmo. It was in a cramped, darkened room with an examining table in it. The thing itself looked like a television screen hooked up to some complicated hardware. Ed said that they could wire a patient up and bounce sound waves off the heart and pick up the echoes, and they would get a picture on the screen, an actual picture, of the heart in motion. It was a thousand times better than an electrocardiogram, he said: they could see the faults, the thickenings and cloggings, much more clearly.

'Colour?' said Sally.

'Black and white,' said Ed.

Then Sally was possessed by a desire to see her own heart, in motion, in black and white, on the screen. At the dentist's she always wants to see the X-rays of her teeth, too, solid and glittering in her cloudy head. 'Do it,' she said, 'I want to see how it works,' and though this was the kind of thing Ed would ordinarily evade or tell her she was being silly about, he didn't need much persuading. He was fascinated by the thing himself, and he wanted to show it off.

He checked to make sure there was nobody real booked for the room. The he told Sally to slip out of her clothes, the top half, brassière and all. He gave her a paper gown and turned his back modestly while she slipped it on, as if he didn't see her body every night of the week. He attached electrodes to her, the ankles and one wrist, and turned a switch and fiddled with the dials. Really a technician was supposed to do this, he told her, but he knew how to run the machine himself. He was good with small appliances.

Sally lay prone on the table, feeling strangely naked. 'What do I do?' she said.

'Just lie there,' said Ed. He came over to her and tore a hole in the paper gown, above her left breast. The he started running a probe over her skin. It was wet and slippery and cold, and felt like the roller on a roll-on deodorant.

'There,' he said, and Sally turned her head. On the screen was a large grey object, like a giant fig, paler in the middle, a dark line running down the centre. The sides moved in and out; two wings fluttered in it, like an uncertain moth's.

'That's it?' said Sally dubiously. Her heart looked so insubstantial, like a bag of gelatin, something that would melt, fade, disintegrate, if you squeezed it even a little.

Ed moved the probe and they looked at the heart from the bottom, then the top. Then he stopped the frame, then changed it from a positive to a negative image. Sally began to shiver.

'That's wonderful,' she said. He seemed so distant, absorbed in his machine, taking the measure of her heart, which was beating over there all by itself, detached from her, exposed and under his control.

Ed unwired her and she put on her clothes again, neutrally, as if he were actually a doctor. Nevertheless this transaction, this whole room, was sexual in a way she didn't quite understand; it was clearly a dangerous place. It was like a massage parlour, only for women. Put a batch of women in there with Ed and they would never want to come out. They'd want to stay in there while he ran his probe over their wet skins and pointed out to them the defects of their beating hearts.

'Thank you,' said Sally.

Sally hears the back door open and close. She feels Ed approaching, coming through the passages of the house towards her, like a small wind or a ball of static electricity. The hair stands up on her arms. Sometimes he makes her so happy she thinks she's about to burst; other times she thinks she's about to burst anyway.

He comes into the kitchen, and she pretends not to notice. He puts his arms around her from behind, kisses her on the neck. She leans back, pressing herself into him. What they should do now is go into the bedroom (or even the living room, even the den) and make love, but it wouldn't occur to Ed to make love in the middle of the day. Sally often comes across articles in magazines about how to improve your sex life, which leave her feeling disappointed, or reminiscent: Ed is not Sally's first and only man. But she knows she shouldn't expect too much of Ed. If Ed were more experimental, more interested in variety, he would be a different kind of man altogether: slyer, more devious, more observant, harder to deal with.

As it is, Ed makes love in the same way, time after time, each movement following the others in an exact order. But it seems to satisfy him. Of course it satisfies him: you can always tell when men are satisfied. It's Sally who lies awake, afterwards, watching the pictures unroll across her closed eyes.

Sally steps away from Ed, smiles at him, 'How did you make out with the women today?' she says.

'What women?' says Ed absently, going towards the sink. He knows what women.

'The ones out there, hiding in the forsythia,' says Sally. 'I counted at least ten. They were just waiting for a chance.'

She teases him frequently about these troops of women, which follow him around everywhere, which are invisible to Ed but which she can see as plain as day.

'I bet they hang around outside the front door of the hospital,' she will say, 'just waiting till you come out. I bet they hide in the linen closets and jump out at you from behind, and then pretend to be lost so you'll take them by the short cut. It's the white coat that does it. None of those women can resist the white coats. They've been conditioned by Young Doctor Kildare.'

'Don't be silly,' says Ed today, with equanimity. Is he blushing, is he embarrassed? Sally examines his face closely, like a geologist with an aerial photograph, looking for telltale signs of mineral treasure: markings, bumps, hollows. Everything about Ed means something, though it's difficult at times to say what.

Now he's washing his hands at the sink, to get the earth off. In a minute he'll wipe them on the dish towel instead of using the hand towel the way he's supposed to. Is that complacency, in the back turned to her? Maybe there really are these hordes of women, even though she's made them up. Maybe they really do behave that way. His shoulders are slightly drawn up: is he shutting her out?

'I know what they want,' she goes on. 'They want to get into that little dark room of yours and climb up onto your table. They think you're delicious. They'll gobble you up. They'll chew you into tiny pieces. There won't be anything left of you at all, only a stethoscope and a couple of shoelaces.'

Once Ed would have laughed at this, but today he doesn't. Maybe she's said it, or something like it, a few times too often. He smiles though, wipes his hands on the dish towel, peers into the fridge. He likes to snack.

'There's some cold roast beef,' Sally says, baffled.

Sally takes the sauce off the stove and sets it aside for later: she'll do the last steps just before serving. It's only two-thirty. Ed has disappeared into the cellar, where Sally knows he will be safe for a while. She goes into her study, which used to be one of the kids' bedrooms, and sits down at her desk. The room has never been completely redecorated: there's still a bed in it, and a dressing table with a blue flowered flounce Sally helped pick out, long before the kids went off to university: 'flew the coop', as Ed puts it.

Sally doesn't comment on the expression, though she would like to say that it wasn't the first coop they flew. Her house isn't even the real coop, since neither of the kids is hers. She'd hoped for a baby of her own when she married Ed, but she didn't want to force the issue. Ed didn't object to the idea, exactly, but he was neutral about it, and Sally got the feeling he'd had enough babies already. Anyway, the other two wives had babies, and look what happened to them. Since their actual fates have always been vague to Sally, she's free to imagine all kinds of things, from drug addiction to madness. Whatever it was resulted in Sally having to bring up their kids, at least from puberty onwards. The way it was presented by the first wife was that it was Ed's turn now. The second wife was more oblique: she said that the child wanted to spend some time with her father. Sally was left out of both these equations, as if the house wasn't a place she lived in, not really, so she couldn't be expected to have any opinion.

Considering everything, she hasn't done badly. She likes the kids and tries to be a friend to them, since she can hardly pretend to be a mother. She describes the three of them as having an easy relationship. Ed wasn't around much for the kids, but it's him they want approval from, not Sally; it's him they respect. Sally is more like a confederate, helping them get what they want from Ed.

When the kids were younger, Sally used to play Monopoly with them, up at the summer place in Muskoka Ed owned then but has since sold. Ed would play too, on his vacations and on the weekends when he could make it up. These games would all proceed along the same lines. Sally would have an initial run of luck and would buy up everything she had a chance at. She didn't care whether it was classy real estate, like Boardwalk or Park Place, or those dingy little houses on the other side of the tracks; she would even buy train stations, which the kids would pass over, preferring to save their cash reserves for better investments. Ed, on the other hand, would plod along, getting a little here, a little there. Then, when Sally was feeling flush, she would blow her money on next-to-useless luxuries such as the electric light company; and when the kids started to lose, as they invariably did, Sally would lend them money at cheap rates or trade them things of her own, at a loss. Why not? She could afford it.

Ed meanwhile would be hedging his bets, building up blocks of property, sticking houses and hotels on them. He preferred the middle range, respectable streets but not flashy. Sally would land on his spaces and have to shell out hard cash. Ed never offered deals, and never accepted them. He played a lone game, and won more often than not. Then Sally would feel thwarted. She would say she guessed she lacked the killer instinct; or she would say that for herself she didn't care, because after all it was only a game, but he ought to allow the kids to win, once in a while. Ed couldn't grasp the concept of allowing other people to win. He said it would be condescending towards the children, and anyway you couldn't arrange to have a dice game turn out the way you wanted it to, since it was partly a matter of chance. If it was chance, Sally would think, why were the games so similar to one another? At the end, there would be Ed, counting up his paper cash, sorting it out into piles of bills of varying denominations, and Sally, her vast holdings dwindled to a few shoddy blocks on Baltic Avenue, doomed to foreclosure: extravagant, generous, bankrupt.

On these nights, after the kids were asleep, Sally would have two or three more rye-and-gingers than were good for her. Ed would go to bed early—winning made him satisfied and drowsy—and Sally would ramble about the house or read the endings of murder mysteries she had already read once before, and finally she would slip into bed and wake Ed up and stroke him into arousal, seeking comfort.

Sally has almost forgotten these games. Right now the kids are receding, fading like old ink; Ed on the contrary looms larger and larger, the outlines around him darkening. He's constantly developing, like a Polaroid print, new colours emerging, but the result remains the same: Ed is a surface, one she has trouble getting beneath.

'Explore your inner world,' said Sally's instructor in *Forms of Narrative Fiction*, a middle-aged woman of scant fame who goes in for astrology and the Tarot pack and writes short stories, which are not published in any of the magazines Sally reads. 'Then there's your outer one,' Sally said afterwards, to her friends. 'For instance, she should really get something done about her hair.' She made this trivial and mean remark because she's fed up with her inner world; she doesn't need to explore it. In her inner world is Ed, like a doll within a Russian wooden doll, and in Ed is Ed's inner world, which she can't get at.

She takes a crack at it anyway: Ed's inner world is a forest, which looks something like the bottom part of their ravine lot, but without the fence. He wanders around in there, among the trees, not heading in any special direction. Every once in a while he comes upon a strange-looking plant, a sickly plant choked with weeds and briars. Ed kneels, clears a space around it, does some pruning, a little skilful snipping and cutting, props it up. The plant revives, flushes with health, sends out a grateful red blossom. Ed continues on his way. Or it may be a conked-out squirrel, which he restores with a drop from his flask of magic elixir. At set intervals an angel appears, bringing him food. It's always meatloaf. That's fine with Ed, who hardly notices what he eats, but the angel is getting tired of being an angel. Now Sally begins thinking about the angel: why are its wings frayed and dingy grey around the edges, why is it looking so withered and frantic? This is where all Sally's attempts to explore Ed's inner world end up.

She knows she thinks about Ed too much. She knows she should stop. She knows she shouldn't ask, 'Do you still love me?' in the plaintive tone that sets even her own teeth on edge. All it achieves is that Ed shakes his head, as if not understanding why she would ask this, and pats her hand. 'Sally, Sally,' he says, and everything proceeds as usual; except for the dread that seeps into things, the most ordinary things, such as rearranging the chairs and changing the burnt-out lightbulbs. But what is it she's afraid of? She has what they call everything: Ed, their wonderful house on a ravine lot, something she's always wanted. (But the hill is jungly, and the house is made of ice. It's held together only by Sally, who sits in the middle of it, working on a puzzle. The puzzle is Ed. If she should ever solve it, if she should ever fit the last cold splinter into place, the house will melt and flow away down the hill, and then. . . .) It's a bad habit, fooling around with her head this way. It does no good. She knows that if she could quit she'd be happier. She ought to be able to: she's given up smoking.

She needs to concentrate her attention on other things. This is the real reason for the night courses, which she picks almost at random; to coincide with the evenings Ed isn't in. He has meetings, he's on the boards of charities, he has trouble saying no. She runs the courses past herself, mediaeval history, cooking, anthropology, hoping her mind will snag on something; she's even taken a course in geology, which was fascinating, she told her friends, all that magma. That's just it: everything is fascinating, but nothing enters her. She's always a star pupil, she does well on the exams and impresses the teachers, for which she despises them. She is familiar with her brightness, her techniques; she's surprised other people are still taken in by them.

Forms of Narrative Fiction started out the same way. Sally was full of good ideas, brimming with helpful suggestions. The workshop part of it was anyway just like a committee meeting, and Sally knew how to run those, from behind, without seeming to run them: she'd done it lots of times at work. Bertha, the instructor, told Sally she had a vivid imagination and a lot of untapped creative energy. 'No wonder she never gets anywhere, with a name like Bertha,' Sally said, while having coffee afterwards with two of the other night-coursers. 'It goes with her outfits, though.' (Bertha sports the macramé look, with health-food sandals and bulky-knit sweaters and hand-weave skirts that don't do a thing for her square figure and too many Mexican rings on her hands, which she doesn't wash often enough.) Bertha goes in for assignments, which she calls learning by doing. Sally likes assignments: she likes things that can be completed and then discarded, and for which she gets marks.

The first thing Bertha assigned was The Epic. They read *The Odyssey* (selected passages, in translation, with a plot summary of the rest); then they poked around in James Joyce's *Ulysses*, to see how Joyce had adapted the epic form to the modern-day novel. Bertha had them keep a Toronto notebook, in which they had to pick out various spots around town as the ports of call in *The Odyssey*, and say why they had chosen them. The notebooks were read out loud in class, and it was a scream to see who had chosen what for Hades. (The Mount Pleasant Cemetery, McDonald's, where, if you eat the forbidden food, you never get back to the land of the living, the University Club with its dead ancestral souls, and so forth.) Sally's was the hospital, of course; she had no difficulty with the trench filled with blood, and she put ghosts in wheelchairs.

After that they did The Ballad, and read gruesome accounts of murders and betrayed love. Bertha played them tapes of wheezy old men singing traditionally, in the Doric mode, and assigned a newspaper scrapbook, in which you had to clip and paste up-to-the-minute equivalents. The *Sun* was the best newspaper for these. The fiction that turned out to go with this kind of plot was the kind Sally liked anyway, and she had no difficulty concocting a five-page murder mystery, complete with revenge.

But now they are on Folk Tales and the Oral Tradition, and Sally is having trouble. This time, Bertha wouldn't let them read anything. Instead she read to them, in a voice, Sally said, that was like a gravel truck and was not conducive to reverie. Since it was the Oral Tradition, they weren't even allowed to take notes; Bertha said the original hearers of these stories couldn't read, so the stories were memorized. 'To recreate the atmosphere,' said Bertha, 'I should turn out the lights. These stories were always told at night.' 'To make them creepier?' someone offered. 'No,' said Bertha. 'In the days, they worked.' She didn't do that, though she did make them sit in a circle.

'You should have seen us,' Sally said afterwards to Ed, 'sitting in a circle, listening to fairy stories. It was just like kindergarten. Some of them even had their mouths open. I kept expecting her to say, "If you need to go, put up your hand." ' She was meaning to be funny, to amuse Ed with this account of Bertha's eccentricity and the foolish appearance of the students, most of them middle-aged, sitting in a circle as if they had never grown up at all. She was also intending to belittle the course, just slightly. She always did this with her night courses, so Ed wouldn't get the idea there was anything in her life that was even remotely as important as he was. But Ed didn't seem to need this amusement or this belittlement. He took her information earnestly, gravely, as if Bertha's behaviour was, after all, only the procedure of a specialist. No one knew better than he did that the procedures of specialists often looked bizarre or incomprehensible to onlookers. 'She probably has her reasons,' was all he would say.

The first stories Bertha read them, for warm-ups ('No memorizing for *her*,' said Sally), were about princes who got amnesia and forgot about their true loves and married girls their mothers had picked out for them. Then they had to be rescued, with the aid of magic. The stories didn't say what happened to the women the princes had already married, though Sally wondered about it. Then Bertha read them another story, and this time they were supposed to remember the features that stood out for them and write a five-page transposition, set in the present and cast in the realistic mode. ('In other words,' said Bertha, 'no real magic.') They couldn't use the Universal Narrator, however: they had done that in their Ballad assignment. This time they had to choose a point of view. It could be the point of view of anyone or anything in the story, but they were limited to one only. The story she was about to read, she said, was a variant of the Bluebeard motif, much earlier than Perrault's sentimental rewriting of it. In Perrault, said Bertha, the girl has to be rescued by her brothers; but in the earlier version things were quite otherwise.

This is what Bertha read, as far as Sally can remember:

There were once three young sisters. One day a beggar with a large basket on his back came to the door and asked for some bread. The eldest sister brought him some, but no sooner had she touched him than she was compelled to jump into his basket, for the beggar was really a wizard in disguise. ('So much for United Appeal,' Sally murmured. 'She should have said, "I gave at the office." ') The wizard carried her away to his house in the forest, which was large and richly furnished. 'Here you will be happy with me, darling,' said the wizard, 'for you will have everything your heart could desire.'

This lasted for a few days. Then the wizard gave the girl an egg and a bunch of keys. 'I must go away on a journey,' he said, 'and I am leaving the house in your charge. Preserve this egg for me, and carry it about with you everywhere; for a great misfortune will follow from its loss. The keys open every room in the house. You may go into each of them and enjoy what you find there, but do not go into the small room at the top of the house, on pain of death.' The girl promised, and the wizard disappeared.

At first the girl contented herself with exploring the rooms, which contained many treasures. But finally her curiosity would not let her alone. She sought out the smallest key, and, with beating heart, opened the little door at the top of the house. Inside it was a large basin full of blood, within which were the bodies of many women, which had been cut to pieces; nearby were a chopping block and an axe. In her horror, she let go of the egg, which fell into the basin of blood. In vain did she try to wipe away the stain: every time she succeeded in removing it, back it would come.

The wizard returned, and in a stern voice asked for the egg and the keys. When he saw the egg, he knew at once she had disobeyed him and gone into the forbidden room. 'Since you have gone into the room against my will,' he said, 'you shall go back into it against your own.' Despite her pleas he threw her down, dragged her by the hair into the little room, hacked her into pieces and threw her body into the basin with the others.

Then he went for the second girl, who fared no better than her sister. But the third was clever and wily. As soon as the wizard had gone, she set the egg on a shelf, out of harm's way, and then went immediately and opened the forbidden door. Imagine her distress when she saw the cut-up bodies of her two beloved sisters; but she set the parts in order, and they joined together and her sisters stood up and moved, and were living and well. They embraced each other, and the third sister hid the other two in a cupboard.

When the wizard returned he at once asked for the egg. This time it was spotless. 'You have passed the test,' he said to the third sister. 'You shall be my bride.' ('And second prize,' said Sally, to herself this time, 'is *two* weeks in Niagara Falls.') The wizard no longer had any power over her, and had to do whatever she asked. There was more, about how the wizard met his come-uppance and was burned to death, but Sally already knew which features stood out for her.

At first she thought the most important thing in the story was the forbidden room. What would she put in the forbidden room, in her present-day realistic version? Certainly not chopped-up women. It wasn't that they were too unrealistic, but they were certainly too sick, as well as being too obvious. She wanted to do something more clever. She thought it might be a good idea to have the curious woman open the door and find nothing there at all, but after mulling it over she set this notion aside. It would leave her with the problem of why the wizard would have a forbidden room in which he kept nothing.

That was the way she was thinking right after she got the assignment, which was a full two weeks ago. So far she's written nothing. The great temptation is to cast herself in the role of the cunning heroine, but again it's too predictable. And Ed certainly isn't the wizard; he's nowhere near sinister enough. If Ed were the wizard, the room would contain a forest, some ailing plants and feeble squirrels, and Ed himself, fixing them up; but then, if it were Ed the room wouldn't even be locked, and there would be no story.

Now, as she sits at the desk, fiddling with her felt-tip pen, it comes to Sally that the intriguing thing about the story, the thing she should fasten on, is the egg. Why an egg? From the night course in Comparative Folklore she took four years ago, she remembers that the egg can be a fertility symbol, or a necessary object in African spells, or something the world hatched out of. Maybe in this story it's a symbol of virginity, and that is why the wizard requires it unbloodied. Women with dirty eggs get murdered, those with clean ones get married.

But this isn't useful either. The concept is so outmoded. Sally doesn't see how she can transpose it into real life without making it ridiculous, unless she sets the story in, for instance, an immigrant Portuguese family, and what would she know about that?

Sally opens the drawer of her desk and hunts around in it for her nail file. As she's doing this, she gets the brilliant idea of writing the story from the point of view of the egg. Other people will do the other things: the clever girl, the wizard, the two blundering sisters, who weren't smart enough to lie, and who will have problems afterwards, because of the thin red lines running all over their bodies, from where their parts are joined together. But no one will think of the egg. How does it feel, to be the innocent and passive cause of so much misfortune?

(Ed isn't the Bluebeard: Ed is the egg. Ed Egg, blank and pristine and lovely. Stupid, too. Boiled, probably. Sally smiles fondly.)

But how can there be a story from the egg's point of view, if the egg is so closed and unaware? Sally ponders this, doodling on her pad of lined paper. Then she resumes the search for her nail file. Already it's time to begin getting ready for her dinner party. She can sleep on the problem of the egg and finish the assignment tomorrow, which is Sunday. It's due on Monday, but Sally's mother used to say she was a whiz at getting things done at the last minute.

After painting her nails with *Nuit Magique*, Sally takes a bath, eating her habitual toasted English muffin while she lies in the tub. She begins to dress, dawdling; she has plenty of time. She hears Ed coming up out of the cellar; then she hears him in the bathroom, which he has entered from the hall door. Sally goes in through the other door, still in her slip. Ed is standing at the sink with his shirt off, shaving. On the weekends he leaves it until necessary, or until Sally tells him he's too scratchy.

Sally slides her hands around his waist, nuzzling against his naked back. He has very smooth skin, for a man. Sally smiles to herself: she can't stop thinking of him as an egg.

'Mmm,' says Ed. It could be appreciation, or the answer to a question Sally hasn't asked and he hasn't heard, or just an acknowledgement that she's there.

'Don't you ever wonder what I think about?' Sally says. She's said this more than once, in bed or at the dinner table, after dessert. She stands behind him, watching the swaths the razor cuts in the white of his face, looking at her own face reflected in the mirror, just the eyes visible above his naked shoulder. Ed, lathered, is Assyrian, sterner than usual; or a frost-covered Arctic explorer; or demi-human, a white-bearded forest mutant. He scrapes away at himself, methodically destroying the illusion.

'But I already know what you think about,' says Ed.

'How?' Sally says, taken aback.

'You're always telling me,' Ed says, with what might be resignation or sadness; or maybe this is only a simple statement of fact.

Sally is relieved. If that's all he's going on, she's safe.

Marylynn arrives half an hour early, her pearl-coloured Porsche leading two men in a delivery truck up the driveway. The men install the keyhole desk, while Marylynn supervises: it looks, in the alcove, exactly as Marylynn has said it would, and Sally is delighted. She sits at it to write the cheque. Then she and Marylynn go into the kitchen, where Sally is finishing up her sauce, and Sally pours them each a Kir. She's glad Marylynn is here: it will keep her from dithering, as she tends to do just before people arrive. Though it's only the heart men, she's still a bit nervous. Ed is more likely to notice when things are wrong than when they're exactly right.

Marylynn sits at the kitchen table, one arm draped over the chairback, her chin on the other hand; she's in soft grey, which makes her hair look silver, and Sally feels once again how banal it is to have ordinary dark hair like her own, however well-cut, however shiny. It's the confidence she envies, the negligence. Marylynn doesn't seem to be trying at all, ever.

'Guess what Ed said today?' Sally says.

Marylynn leans further forward. 'What?' she says, with the eagerness of one joining in a familiar game.

'He said, "Some of these femininists go too far."' Sally reports.

' "*Femininists*". Isn't that sweet?'

Marylynn holds the pause too long, and Sally has a sudden awful thought: maybe Marylynn thinks she's showing off, about Ed. Marylynn has always said she's not ready for another marriage yet; still, Sally should watch herself, not rub her nose it it. But then Marylynn laughs indulgently, and Sally, relieved, joins in.

'Ed is unbelievable,' says Marylynn. 'You should pin his mittens to his sleeves when he goes out in the morning.'

'He shouldn't be let out alone,' says Sally.

'You should get him a seeing-eye dog,' says Marylynn, 'to bark at women.'

'Why?' says Sally, still laughing but alert now, the cold beginning at the ends of her fingers. Maybe Marylynn knows something she doesn't; maybe the house is beginning to crumble, after all.

'Because he can't see them coming,' says Marylynn. 'That's what you're always telling me.'

She sips her Kir; Sally stirs the sauce. 'I bet he thinks I'm a femininist,' says Marylynn.

'You?' says Sally. 'Never.' She would like to add that Ed has given no indication of thinking anything at all about Marylynn, but she doesn't. She doesn't want to take the risk of hurting her feelings.

The wives of the heart men admire Sally's sauce; the heart men talk shop, all except Walter Morly, who is good at by-passes. He's sitting beside Marylynn, and paying far too much attention to her for Sally's comfort. Mrs Morly is at the other end of the table, not saying much of anything, which Marylynn appears not to notice. She keeps on talking to Walter about St Lucia, where they've both been.

So after dinner, when Sally has herded them all into the living room for coffee and liqueurs, she takes Marylynn by the elbow. 'Ed hasn't seen our desk yet,' she says, 'not up close. Take him away and give him your lecture on nineteenth-century antiques. Show him all the pigeon-holes. Ed loves pigeon-holes.' Ed appears not to get this.

Marylynn knows exactly what Sally is up to. 'Don't worry,' she says, 'I won't rape Dr Morly; the poor creature would never survive the shock,' but she allows herself to be shunted off to the side with Ed.

Sally moves from guest to guest, smiling, making sure everything is in order. Although she never looks directly, she's always conscious of Ed's presence in the room, any room; she perceives him as a shadow, a shape seen dimly at the edge of her field of vision, recognizable by the outline. She likes to know where he is, that's all. Some people are on their second cup of coffee. She walks towards the alcove: they must have finished with the desk by now.

But they haven't, they're still in there. Marylynn is bending forward, one hand on the veneer. Ed is standing too close to her, and as Sally comes up behind them she sees his left arm, held close to his side, the back of it pressed against Marylynn, her shimmering upper thigh, her ass to be exact. Marylynn does not move away.

It's a split second, and then Ed sees Sally and the hand is gone; there it is, on top of the desk, reaching for a liqueur glass.

'Marylynn needs more Tia Maria,' he says. 'I just told her that people who drink a little now and again live longer.' His voice is even, his face is as level as ever, a flat plain with no signposts.

Marylynn laughs. 'I once had a dentist who I swear drilled tiny holes in my teeth, so he could fix them later,' she says.

Sally sees Ed's hand outstretched towards her, holding the empty glass. She takes it, smiling, and turns away. There's a roaring sound at the back of her head; blackness appears around the edges of the picture she is seeing, like a television screen going dead. She walks into the kitchen and puts her cheek against the refrigerator and her arms around it, as far as they will go. She remains that way, hugging it; it hums steadily, with a sound like comfort. After a while she lets go of it and touches her hair, and walks back into the living room with the filled glass.

Marylynn is over by the french doors, talking with Walter Morly. Ed is standing by himself, in front of the fireplace, one arm on the mantelpiece, his left hand out of sight in his pocket.

Sally goes to Marylynn, hands her the glass. 'Is that enough?' she says.

Marylynn is unchanged. 'Thanks, Sally,' she says, and goes on listening to Walter, who has dragged out his usual piece of mischief: some day, when they've perfected it, he says, all hearts will be plastic, and this will be a vast improvement on the current model. It's an obscure form of flirtation. Marylynn winks at Sally, to show that she knows he's tedious. Sally, after a pause, winks back.

She looks over at Ed, who is staring off into space, like a robot which has been parked and switched off. Now she isn't sure whether she really saw what she thought she saw. Even if she did, what does it mean? Maybe it's just that Ed, in a wayward intoxicated moment, put his hand on the nearest buttock, and Marylynn refrained from a shriek or a flinch out of good breeding or the desire not to offend him. Things like this have happened to Sally.

Or it could mean something more sinister: a familiarity between them, an understanding. If this is it, Sally has been wrong about Ed, for years, forever. Her version of Ed is not something she's perceived but something that's been perpetrated on her, by Ed himself, for reasons of his own. Possibly Ed is not stupid. Possibly he's enormously clever. She thinks of moment after moment when this cleverness, this cunning, would have shown itself if it were there, but didn't. She has watched him so carefully. She remembers playing Pick Up Sticks, with the kids, Ed's kids, years ago: how if you moved one stick in the tangle, even slightly, everything else moved also.

She won't say anything to him. She can't say anything: she can't afford to be wrong, or to be right either. She goes back into the kitchen and begins to scrape the plates. This is unlike her—usually she sticks right with the party until it's over—and after a while Ed wanders out. He stands silently, watching her. Sally concentrates on the scraping: dollops of *sauce suprême* slide into the plastic bag, shreds of lettuce, rice, congealed and lumpy. What is left of her afternoon.

'What are you doing out here?' Ed says at last.

'Scraping the plates,' Sally says, cheerful, neutral. 'I just thought I'd get a head start on tidying up.'

'Leave it,' says Ed. 'The woman can do that in the morning.' That's how he refers to Mrs Rudge, although she's been with them for three years now: *the woman*. And Mrs Bird before her, as though they are interchangeable. This has never bothered Sally before. 'Go on out there and have a good time.'

Sally puts down the spatula, wipes her hands on the hand towel, puts her arms around him, holds on tighter than she should. Ed pats her shoulder. 'What's up?' he says; then, 'Sally, Sally.' If she looks up, she will see him shaking his head a little, as if he doesn't know what to do about her. She doesn't look up.

Ed has gone to bed. Sally roams the house, fidgeting with the debris left by the party. She collects empty glasses, picks up peanuts from the rug. After a while she realizes that she's down on her knees, looking under a chair, and she's forgotten what for. She goes upstairs, creams off her make-up, does her teeth, undresses in the darkened bedroom and slides into bed beside Ed, who is breathing deeply as if asleep. *As if.*

Sally lies in bed with her eyes closed. What she sees is her own heart, in black and white, beating with that insubstantial moth-like flutter, a ghostly heart, torn out of her and floating in space, an animated valentine with no colour. It will go on and on forever; she has no control over it. But now she's seeing the egg, which is not small and cold and white and inert but larger than a real egg and golden pink, resting in a nest of brambles, glowing softly as though there's something red and hot inside it. It's almost pulsing; Sally is afraid of it. As she looks it darkens: rose-red, crimson. This is something the story left out, Sally thinks: the egg is alive, and one day it will hatch. But what will come out of it?

1983

Bharati Mukherjee

b. 1940

'The oldest paradox of prejudice is that it renders its victims simultaneously invisible and over-exposed,' Bharati Mukherjee commented on one of the main themes of her writing. Using her own experience of prejudice as the basis of fiction, she has written a body of work in which the personal and the political often converge.

Born in Calcutta, India, the daughter of a Brahmin pharmaceutical chemist, Mukherjee and her family moved to London, England, where she learned English. Educated at a convent school in Switzerland, she received her B.A. (1959) from the University of Calcutta, M.A. (1961) from the University of Baroda, and M.F.A. (1963) and Ph.D. (1969) from the University of Iowa. While studying at the University of Iowa, she met Canadian novelist Clark Blaise, whom she married. She emigrated from the United States to Canada in 1966, and, after living in Montreal and Toronto, returned in 1980 to the United States. She has taught at many colleges and universities, including McGill University and the University of Iowa. She currently resides in New York City.

'A Third World writer isn't limited as a First World writer is in choosing her contemporaries,' Mukherjee observed. 'Having been born in a city that prided itself as the second city of the British Empire, and having been brought up on British literature, especially on Victorian and Edwardian literature, I felt as close to Jane Austen, Galsworthy, Wilde, and Conrad as to Bernard Malamud, Alice Munro, Mavis Gallant, Ann Beattie, and Raymond Carver.'

Mukherjee's fiction, like her life, is an exploration of cultural displacement as her East Indian protagonists confront personal and social struggles both in India and in North America. She writes about India from the vantage point of being Indian, and about the plight of immigrants and expatriates with the urgency of first-hand experience. And her novels and short stories frequently focus on women who are trying to invent themselves in an often hostile place.

'Short stories don't always occur to me as being about a character. Sometimes a line or a possible title will set me going,' Mukherjee reflected. ' "The Lady from Lucknow", for instance, began with the title. In stories the hard thing is to find the right "voice", by which I mean locating a centre.' The voice in 'The Lady from Lucknow,' ironic with the detachment that she has learned as an outsider, narrates her experience as an East Indian woman living with her husband, an IBM executive, in Atlanta. When her affair with a successful older American is discovered by his wife, the confrontation brings home to her how invisible she remains in the eyes of the dominant culture.

'Jasmine', which was later expanded into the novel by the same title (1989), traces the progress of another of Mukherjee's immigrants seeking to invent herself in a foreign culture. Jasmine's path from the Caribbean to Ann Arbor is marked by the transformations she undergoes to become another person, culminating in her abandonment to Bill, which will take her a step further from the past and towards a different identity.

'The Lady from Lucknow' was first published in the Fall 1985 issue of *Missouri Review* and then collected in *Darkness* (1985). 'Jasmine' was first published in *The Middleman and Other Stories* (1988).

The Lady from Lucknow

When I was four, one of the girls next door fell in love with a Hindu. Her father intercepted a love note from the boy, and beat her with his leather sandals. She died soon after. I was in the room when my mother said to our neighbour, 'The Nawab-*sahib* had no choice, but Husseina's heart just broke, poor dear.' I was an army doctor's daughter, and I pictured the dead girl's heart—a rubbery squeezable organ with auricles and ventricles—first swelling, then bursting and coating the floor with thick, slippery blood.

We lived in Lucknow at the time, where the Muslim community was large. This was just before the British took the fat, diamond-shaped subcontinent and created two nations, a big one for the Hindus and a littler one for us. My father moved us to Rawalpindi in Pakistan two months after Husseina died. We were a family of soft, voluptuous children, and my father wanted to protect us from the Hindus' shameful lust.

I have fancied myself in love many times since, but never enough for the emotions to break through tissue and muscle. Husseina's torn heart remains the standard of perfect love.

At seventeen I married a good man, the fourth son of a famous poet-cum-lawyer in Islamabad. We have a daughter, seven, and a son, four. In the Muslim communities we have lived in, we are admired. Iqbal works for IBM, and because of his work we have made homes in Lebanon, Brazil, Zambia, and France. Now we live in Atlanta, Georgia, in a wide, new house with a deck and a backyard that runs into a golf course. IBM has been generous to us. We expect to pass on this good, decent life to our children. Our children are ashamed of the dingy cities where we got our start.

Some Sunday afternoons when Iqbal isn't at a conference halfway across the world, we sit together on the deck and drink gin and tonics as we have done on Sunday afternoons in a dozen exotic cities. But here, the light is different somehow. A gold haze comes off the golf course and settles on our bodies, our new house. When the light shines right in my eyes, I pull myself out of the canvas deck chair and lean against the railing that still smells of forests. Everything in Atlanta is so new!

'Sit,' Iqbal tells me. 'You'll distract the golfers. Americans are crazy for sex, you know that.'

He half rises out of his deck chair. He lunges for my breasts in mock passion. I slip out of his reach.

At the bottom of the backyard, the golfers, caddies, and carts are too minute to be bloated with lust.

But, who knows? One false thwock! of their golfing irons, and my little heart, like a golf ball, could slice through the warm air and vanish into the jonquil-yellow beyond.

It isn't trouble that I want, though I do have a lover. He's an older man, an immunologist with the Center of Disease Control right here in town. He comes to see me when Iqbal is away at high-tech conferences in sunny, remote resorts. Just think, Beirut was once such a resort! Lately my lover comes to me on Wednesdays even if Iqbal's in town.

'I don't expect to live till ninety-five,' James teases on the phone. His father died at ninety-three in Savannah. 'But I don't want a bullet in the brain from a jealous husband right now.'

Iqbal owns no firearms. Jealousy would inflame him.

Besides, Iqbal would never come home in the middle of the day. Not even for his blood pressure pills. The two times he forgot them last month, I had to take the bottle downtown. One does not rise through the multinational hierarchy coming home in midday, arriving late, or leaving early. Especially, he says, if you're a 'not-quite' as we are. It is up to us to set the standards.

Wives who want to be found out will be found out. Indiscretions are deliberate. The woman caught in mid-shame is a woman who wants to get out. The rest of us carry on.

James flatters me indefatigably; he makes me feel beautiful, exotic, responsive. I am a creature he has immunized of contamination. When he is with me, the world seems a happy enough place.

Then he leaves. He slips back into his tweed suit and backs out of my driveway.

I met James Beamish at a reception for foreign students on the Emory University campus. Iqbal avoids these international receptions because he thinks of them as excuses for looking back when we should be looking forward. These evenings are almost always tedious, but I like to go; just in case there's someone new and fascinating. The last two years, I've volunteered as host in the 'hospitality program'. At Thanksgiving and Christmas, two lonely foreign students are sent to our table.

That first evening at Emory we stood with name tags on lapels, white ones for students and blue ones for hosts. James was by a long table, pouring Chablis into a plastic glass. I noticed him right off. He was dressed much like the other resolute, decent men in the room. But whereas the other men wore white or blue shirts under their dark wool suits, James's shirt was bright red.

His wife was with him that evening, a stoutish woman with slender ankles and expensive shoes.

'Darling,' she said to James. 'See if you can locate our Palestinian.' Then she turned to me, and smiling, peered into my name tag.

'I'm Nafeesa Hafeez,' I helped out.

'Na-fee-sa,' she read out. 'Did I get that right?'

'Yes, perfect,' I said.

'What a musical name,' she said. 'I hope you'll be very happy here. Is this your first time abroad?'

James came over with a glass of Chablis in each hand. 'Did we draw this lovely lady? Oops, I'm sorry, you're a *host*, of course.' A mocking blue light was in his eyes. 'Just when I thought we were getting lucky, dear.'

'Darling, ours is a Palestinian. I told you that in the car. This one is obviously not Palestinian, are you, dear?' She took a bright orange notebook out of her purse and showed me a name.

I had to read it upside-down. Something Waheed. School of Dentistry.

'What are you drinking?' James asked. He kept a glass for himself and gave me the other one.

Maybe James Beamish said nothing fascinating that night, but he was attentive, even after the Beamishes' Palestinian joined us. Mrs Beamish was brave, she asked the dentist about his family and hometown. The dentist described West Beirut in detail. The shortage of bread and vegetables, the mortar poundings, the babies bleeding. I wonder when aphasia sets in. When does a dentist, even a Palestinian dentist, decide it's time to cut losses.

Then my own foreign student arrived. She was an Indian Muslim from Lucknow, a large, bold woman who this far from our common hometown claimed me as a country-woman. India, Pakistan, she said, not letting go of my hand, what does it matter?

I'd rather have listened to James Beamish but I couldn't shut out the woman's voice. She gave us her opinions on Thanksgiving rituals. She said, 'It is very odd that the pumpkin vegetable should be used for dessert, no? We are using it as vegetable only. Chhi! Pumpkin as a sweet. The very idea is horrid.'

I promised that when she came to our house for Thanksgiving, I'd make sweetmeats out of ricotta cheese and syrup. When you live in as many countries as Iqbal has made me, you can't tell if you pity, or if you envy, the women who stayed back.

I didn't hear from James Beamish for two weeks. I thought about him. In fact I couldn't get him out of my mind. I went over the phrases and gestures, the mocking light in the eyes, but they didn't add up to much. After the first week, I called Amina and asked her to lunch. I didn't know her well but her husband worked at the Center for Disease Control. Just talking to someone connected with the Center made me feel good. I slipped his name into the small talk with Amina and her eyes popped open, 'Oh, he's famous!' she exclaimed, and I shrugged modestly. I stayed home in case he should call. I sat on the deck and in spite of the cold, pretended to read Barbara Pym novels. Lines from Donne and Urdu verses about love floated in my skull.

I wasn't sure Dr Beamish would call me. Not directly, that is. Perhaps he would play a subtler game, get his wife to invite Iqbal and me for drinks. Maybe she'd even include their Palestinian and my Indian and make an international evening out of it. It sounded plausible.

Finally James Beamish called me on a Tuesday afternoon, around four. The children were in the kitchen, and a batch of my special chocolate sludge cookies was in the oven.

'Hi,' he said, then nothing for a bit. Then he said, 'This is James Beamish from the CDC. I've been thinking of you.'

He was between meetings, he explained. Wednesday was the only flexible day in his week, his day for paperwork. Could we have lunch on Wednesday?

The cookies smelled gooey hot, not burned. My daughter had taken the cookie sheet out and put in a new one. She'd turned the cold water faucet on so she could let the water drip on a tiny rosebud burn on her arm.

I felt all the warm, familiar signs of lust and remorse. I dabbed the burn with an ice cube wrapped in paper towel and wondered if I'd have time to buy a new front-closing bra after Iqbal got home.

James and I had lunch in a Dekalb County motel lounge.

He would be sixty-five in July, but not retire till sixty-eight. Then he would live in Tonga, in Fiji, see the world, travel across Europe and North America in a Winnebago. He wouldn't be tied down. He had five daughters and two grandsons, the younger one aged four, a month older than my son. He had been in the navy during the war (*his* war), and he had liked that.

I said, "Goodbye, Mama, I'm off to Yokohama." It was silly, but it was the only war footage I could come up with, and it made him laugh.

'You're special,' he said. He touched my knee under the table. 'You've already been everywhere.'

'Not because I've wanted to.'

He squeezed my knee again, then paid with his Master-Card card.

As we were walking through the parking lot to his car (it was a Cougar or a Buick, and not German or British as I'd expected), James put his arm around my shoulders. I may have seen the world but I haven't gone through the American teenage rites of making out in parked cars and picnic grounds, so I walked briskly out of his embrace. He let his hand slide off my shoulder. The hand slid down my back. I counted three deft little pats to my bottom before he let his hand fall away.

Iqbal and I are sensual people, but secretive. The openness of James Beamish's advance surprised me.

I got in his car, wary, expectant.

'Do up the seatbelt,' he said.

He leaned into his seatbelt and kissed me lightly on the lips. I kissed him back, hard. 'You don't panic easily, do you?' he said. The mocking blue light was in his eyes again. His tongue made darting little thrusts and probes past my lips.

Yes, I do, I would have said if he'd let me.

We held hands on the drive to my house. In the driveway he parked behind my Honda. 'Shall I come in?'

I said nothing. Love and freedom drop into our lives. When we have to beg or even agree, it's already too late.

'Let's go in.' He said it very softly.

I didn't worry about the neighbours. In his grey wool slacks and tweed jacket, he looked too old, too respectable, for any sordid dalliance with a not-quite's wife.

Our house is not that different in size and shape from the ones on either side. Only the inside smells of heavy incense, and the walls are hung with rows of miniature paintings from the reign of Emperor Akbar. I took James's big wrinkled hand in mine. Adultery in my house is probably no different, no quieter, than in other houses in this neighbourhood.

Afterwards it wasn't guilt I felt (guilt comes with desire not acted), but wonder that while I'd dashed out Tuesday night and bought myself silky new underwear, James Beamish had worn an old T-shirt and lemon-pale boxer shorts. Perhaps he hadn't planned on seducing a Lucknow lady that afternoon. Adventure and freedom had come to him out of the blue, too. Or perhaps only younger men like Iqbal make a fetish of doing sit-ups and dieting and renewing their membership at the racquet club when they're on the prowl.

October through February our passion held. When we were together, I felt cherished. I only played at being helpless, hysterical, cruel. When James left, I'd spend the rest of the afternoon with a Barbara Pym novel. I kept the novels open at pages in which excellent British women recite lines from Marvell to themselves. I didn't read. I watched the golfers trudging over brown fairways instead. I let the tiny golfers—clumsy mummers—tell me stories of ambitions unfulfilled. Golf carts lurched into the golden vista. I felt safe.

In the first week of March we met in James's house for a change. His wife was in Madison to babysit a grandson while his parents flew to China for a three-week tour. It was a thrill to be in his house. I fingered the book spines, checked the colour of sheets and towels, the brand names of cereals and detergents. Jane Fonda's Workout record was on the VCR. He was a man who took exceptional care of himself, this immunologist. Real intimacy, at last. The lust of the winter months had been merely foreplay. I felt at home in his house, in spite of the albums of family photographs on the coffee table and the brutish metal vulvas sculpted by a daughter in art school and stashed in the den. James was more talkative in his own house. He showed me the photos he wanted me to see, named real lakes and mountains. His family was real, and not quite real. The daughters were hardy, outdoor types. I saw them hiking in Zermatt and bicycling through Europe. They had red cheeks and backpacks. Their faces were honest and marvellously ordinary. What would they say if they knew their father, at sixty-five, was in bed with a married woman from Lucknow? I feared and envied their jealousy more than any violence in my husband's heart.

Love on the decline is hard to tell from love on the rise. I have lived a life perched on the edge of ripeness and decay. The traveller feels at home everywhere, because she is never at home anywhere. I felt the hot red glow of blood rushing through capillaries.

His wife came back early, didn't call, caught a ride from Hartsfield International with a friend. She had been raised in Saskatchewan, and she'd remained thrifty.

We heard the car pull into the driveway, the loud 'thank yous' and 'no, I couldn'ts' and then her surprised shout, 'James? Are you ill? What're you doing home?' as she shut the front door.

We were in bed, sluggish cozy and still moist under the goosedown quilt that the daughter in Madison had sent them as a fortieth anniversary gift some years before. His clothes were on top of a long dresser; mine were on the floor, the stockings wrinkled and looking legless.

James didn't go to pieces. I had to admire that. He said, 'Get in the bathroom. Get dressed. I'll take care of this.'

I am submissive by training. To survive, the Asian wife will usually do as she is told. But this time I stayed in bed.

'How are you going to explain me away, James? Tell her I'm the new cleaning woman?' I laughed, and my laugh tinkled flirtatiously, at least to me.

'Get in the bathroom.' This was the fiercest I'd ever heard him.

'I don't think so,' I said. I jerked the quilt off my body but didn't move my legs.

So I was in bed with the quilt at my feet, and James was by the dresser buttoning his shirt when Kate Beamish stood at the door.

She didn't scream. She didn't leap for James's throat—or mine. I'd wanted passion, but Kate didn't come through. I pulled the quilt over me.

I tried insolence. 'Is your wife not the jealous kind?' I asked.

'Let's just get over this as quietly and quickly as we can, shall we?' she said. She walked to the window in her brown Wallabies. 'I don't see any unfamiliar cars, so I suppose you'll expect James to drive you home.'

'She's the jealous type,' James said. He moved toward his wife and tried to guide her out of the bedroom.

'I'm definitely the jealous kind,' Kate Beamish said. 'I might have stabbed you if I could take you seriously. But you are quite ludicrous lounging like a Goya nude on my bed.' She gave a funny little snort. I noticed straggly hairs in her nostrils and looked away.

James was running water in the bathroom sink. Only the panicky ones fall apart and call their lawyers from the bedroom.

She sat on my side of the bed. She stared at me. If that stare had made me feel secretive and loathsome, I might not have wept, later. She plucked the quilt from my breasts as an internist might, and snorted again. 'Yes,' she said, 'I don't deny a certain interest he might have had,' but she looked through my face to the pillow behind, and dropped the quilt as she stood. I was a shadow without depth or colour, a shadow-temptress who would float back to a city of teeming millions when the affair with James had ended.

I had thought myself provocative and fascinating. What had begun as an adventure had become shabby and complex. I was just another involvement of a white man in a pokey little outpost, something that 'men do' and then come to their senses while the *memsahibs* drink gin and tonic and fan their faces. I didn't merit a stab wound through the heart.

It wasn't the end of the world. It was humorous, really. Still. I let James call me a cab. That half hour wait for the cab, as Kate related tales of the grandson to her distracted husband was the most painful. It came closest to what Husseina must have felt. At least her father, the Nawab-*sahib*, had beaten her.

I have known all along that perfect love has to be fatal. I have survived on four of the five continents. I get by because I am at least moderately charming and open-minded. From time to time, James Beamish calls me. 'She's promised to file for divorce.' Or 'Let's go away for a weekend. Let's go to Bermuda. Have lunch with me this Wednesday.' Why do I hear a second voice? She has laughed at me. She has mocked my passion.

I want to say yes. I want to beg him to take me away to Hilton Head in his new, retirement Winnebago. The golden light from the vista is too yellow. Yes, *please*, let's run away, keep this new and simple.

I can hear the golf balls being thwocked home by clumsy mummers far away where my land dips. My arms are numb, my breathing loud and ugly from pressing hard against the cedar railing. The pain in my chest will not go away. I should be tasting blood in my throat by now.

1985

Jasmine

Jasmine came to Detroit from Port-of-Spain, Trinidad, by way of Canada. She crossed the border at Windsor in the back of a grey van loaded with mattresses and box springs. The plan was for her to hide in an empty mattress box if she heard the driver say, 'All bad weather seems to come down from Canada, doesn't it?' to the customs man. But she didn't have to crawl into a box and hold her breath. The customs man didn't ask to look in.

The driver let her off at a scary intersection on Woodward Avenue and gave her instructions on how to get to the Plantations Motel in Southfield. The trick was to keep changing vehicles, he said. That threw off the immigration guys real quick.

Jasmine took money for cab fare out of the pocket of the great big raincoat that the van driver had given her. The raincoat looked like something that nuns in Port-of-Spain sold in church bazaars. Jasmine was glad to have a coat with wool lining, though; and anyway, who would know in Detroit that she was Dr Vassanji's daughter?

All the bills in her hand looked the same. She would have to be careful when she paid the cabdriver. Money in Detroit wasn't pretty the way it was back home, or even in Canada, but she liked this money better. Why should money be pretty, like a picture? Pretty money is only good for putting on your walls maybe. The dollar bills felt businesslike, serious. Back home at work, she used to count out thousands of Trinidad dollars every day and not even think of them as real. Real money was worn and green, American dollars. Holding the bills in her fist on a street corner meant she had made it in okay. She'd outsmarted the guys at the border. Now it was up to her to use her wits to do something with her life. As her Daddy kept saying, 'Girl, is opportunity come only once.' The girls she'd worked with at the bank in Port-of-Spain had gone green as bananas when she'd walked in with her ticket on Air Canada. Trinidad was too tiny. That was the trouble. Trinidad was an island stuck in the middle of nowhere. What kind of place was that for a girl with ambition?

The Plantations Motel was run by a family of Trinidad Indians who had come from the tuppenny-ha'penny country town, Chaguanas. The Daboos were nobodies back home. They were lucky, that's all. They'd gotten here before the rush and bought up a motel and an ice cream parlour. Jasmine felt very superior when she saw Mr Daboo in the motel's reception area. He was a pumpkin-shaped man with very black skin and Elvis Presley sideburns turning white. They looked like earmuffs. Mrs Daboo was a bumpkin, too; short, fat, flapping around in house slippers. The Daboo daughters seemed very American, though. They didn't seem to know that they were nobodies, and kept looking at her and giggling.

She knew she would be short of cash for a great long while. Besides, she wasn't sure she wanted to wear bright leather boots and leotards like Viola and Loretta. The smartest move she could make would be to put a down payment on a husband. Her Daddy had told her to talk to the Daboos first chance. The Daboos ran a service fixing up illegals with islanders who had made it in legally. Daddy had paid three thousand back in Trinidad, with the Daboos and the mattress man getting part of it. They should throw in a good-earning husband for that kind of money.

The Daboos asked her to keep books for them and to clean the rooms in the new wing, and she could stay in 16B as long as she liked. They showed her 16B. They said she could cook her own roti; Mr Daboo would bring in a stove, two gas rings that you could fold up in a metal box. The room was quite grand, Jasmine thought. It had a double bed, a TV, a pink sink and matching bathtub. Mrs Daboo said Jasmine wasn't the big-city Port-of-Spain type she'd expected. Mr Daboo said that he wanted her to stay because it was nice to have a neat, cheerful person around. It wasn't a bad deal, better than stories she'd heard about Trinidad girls in the States.

All day every day except Sundays Jasmine worked. There wasn't just the bookkeeping and the cleaning up. Mr Daboo had her working on the match-up marriage service. Jasmine's job was to check up on social security cards, call clients' bosses for references, and make sure credit information wasn't false. Dermatologists and engineers living in Bloomfield Hills, store owners on Canfield and Woodward: she treated them all as potential liars. One of the first things she learned was that Ann Arbor was a magic word. A boy goes to Ann Arbor and gets an education, and all the barriers come crashing down. So Ann Arbor was the place to be.

She didn't mind the work. She was learning about Detroit, every side of it. Sunday mornings she helped unload packing crates of Caribbean spices in a shop on the next block. For the first time in her life, she was working for a black man, an African. So what if the boss was black? This was a new life, and she wanted to learn everything. Her Sunday boss, Mr Anthony, was a courtly, Christian, church-going man, and paid her the only wages she had in her pocket. Viola and Loretta, for all their fancy American ways, wouldn't go out with blacks.

One Friday afternoon she was writing up the credit info on a Guyanese Muslim who worked in an assembly plant when Loretta said that enough was enough and that there was no need for Jasmine to be her father's drudge.

'Is time to have fun,' Viola said. 'We're going to Ann Arbor.'

Jasmine filed the sheet on the Guyanese man who probably now would never get a wife and got her raincoat. Loretta's boyfriend had a Cadillac parked out front. It was the longest car Jasmine had ever been in and louder than a country bus. Viola's boyfriend got out of the front seat. 'Oh, oh, sweet things,' he said to Jasmine. 'Get in front.' He was a talker. She'd learned that much from working on the matrimonial match-ups. She didn't believe him for a second when he said that there were dudes out there dying to ask her out.

Loretta's boyfriend said, 'You have eyes I could leap into, girl.'

Jasmine knew he was just talking. They sounded like Port-of-Spain boys of three years ago. It didn't surprise her that these Trinidad country boys in Detroit were still behind the times, even of Port-of-Spain. She sat very stiff between the two men, hands on her purse. The Daboo girls laughed in the back seat.

On the highway the girls told her about the reggae night in Ann Arbor. Kevin and the Krazee Islanders. Malcolm's Lovers. All the big reggae groups in the Midwest were converging for the West Indian Students Association fall bash. The ticket didn't come cheap but Jasmine wouldn't let the fellows pay. She wasn't that kind of girl.

The reggae and steel drums brought out the old Jasmine. The rum punch, the dancing, the dreadlocks, the whole combination. She hadn't heard real music since she got to Detroit, where music was supposed to be so famous. The Daboo girls kept turning on rock stuff in the motel lobby whenever their father left the area. She hadn't danced, really *danced*, since she'd left home. It felt so good to dance. She felt hot and sweaty and sexy. The boys at the dance were more than sweet talkers; they moved with assurance and spoke of their futures in America. The bartender gave her two free drinks and said, 'Is ready when you are, girl.' She ignored him but she felt all hot and good deep inside. She knew Ann Arbor was a special place.

When it was time to pile back into Loretta's boyfriend's Cadillac, she just couldn't face going back to the Plantations Motel and to the Daboos with their accounting books and messy files.

'I don't know what happen, girl,' she said to Loretta. 'I feel all crazy inside. Maybe is time for me to pursue higher studies in this town.'

'This Ann Arbor, girl, they don't just take you off the street. It *cost* like hell.'

She spent the night on a bashed-up sofa in the Student Union. She was a well-dressed, respectable girl, and she didn't expect anyone to question her right to sleep on the furniture. Many others were doing the same thing. In the morning, a boy in an army parka showed her the way to the Placement Office. He was a big, blond, clumsy boy, not bad-looking except for the blond eyelashes. He didn't scare her, as did most Americans. She let him buy her a Coke and a hotdog. That evening she had a job with the Moffitts.

Bill Moffitt taught molecular biology and Lara Hatch-Moffitt, his wife, was a performance artist. A performance artist, said Lara, was very different from being an actress, though Jasmine still didn't understand what the difference might be. The Moffitts had a little girl, Muffin, whom Jasmine was to look after, though for the first few months she might have to help out with the housework and the cooking because Lara said she was deep into performance rehearsals. That was all right with her, Jasmine said, maybe a little too quickly. She explained she came from a big family and was used to heavy-duty cooking and cleaning. This wasn't the time to say anything about Ram, the family servant. Americans like the Moffitts wouldn't understand about keeping servants. Ram and she weren't in similar situations. Here mother's helpers, which is what Lara had called her—Americans were good with words to cover their shame—seemed to be as good as anyone.

Lara showed her the room she would have all to herself in the finished basement. There was a big, old TV, not in colour like the motel's and a portable typewriter on a desk which Lara said she would find handy when it came time to turn in her term papers. Jasmine didn't say anything about not being a student. She was a student of life, wasn't she? There was a scary moment after they'd discussed what she could expect as salary, which was three times more than anything Mr Daboo was supposed to pay her but hadn't. She thought Bill Moffitt was going to ask her about her visa or her green card number and social security. But all Bill did was smile and smile at her—he had a wide, pink, baby face—and play with a button on his corduroy jacket. The button would need sewing back on, firmly.

Lara said, 'I think I'm going to like you, Jasmine. You have a something about you. A something real special. I'll just bet you've acted, haven't you?' The idea amused her, but she merely smiled and accepted Lara's hug. The interview was over.

Then Bill opened a bottle of Soave and told stories about camping in northern Michigan. He'd been raised there. Jasmine didn't see the point in sleeping in tents; the woods sounded cold and wild and creepy. But she said, 'Is exactly what I want to try out come summer, man. Campin and huntin.'

Lara asked about Port-of-Spain. There was nothing to tell about her hometown that wouldn't shame her in front of nice white American folk like the Moffitts. The place was shabby, the people were grasping and cheating and lying and life was full of despair and drink and wanting. But by the time she finished, the island sounded romantic. Lara said, 'It wouldn't surprise me one bit if you were a writer, Jasmine.'

Ann Arbor was a huge small town. She couldn't imagine any kind of school the size of the University of Michigan. She meant to sign up for courses in the spring. Bill brought home a catalogue bigger than the phonebook for all of Trinidad. The university had courses in everything. It would be hard to choose; she'd have to get help from Bill. He wasn't like a professor, not the ones back home where even high school teachers called themselves professors and acted like little potentates. He wore blue jeans and thick sweaters with holes in the elbows and used phrases like 'in vitro' as he watched her curry up fish. Dr Parveen back home—he called himself 'doctor' when everybody knew he didn't have even a Master's degree—was never seen without his cotton jacket which had gotten really ratty at the cuffs and lapel edges. She hadn't learned anything in the two years she'd put into college. She'd learned more from working in the bank for two months than she had at college. It was the assistant manager, Personal Loans Department, Mr Singh, who had turned her on to the Daboos and to smooth, bargain-priced emigration.

Jasmine like Lara. Lara was easygoing. She didn't spend the time she had between rehearsals telling Jasmine how to cook and clean American-style. Mrs Daboo did that in 16B. Mrs Daboo would barge in with a plate of stale samosas and snoop around giving free advice on how mainstream Americans did things. As if she were dumb or something! As if she couldn't keep her own eyes open and make her mind up for herself.

Sunday mornings she had to share the butcher-block workspace in the kitchen with Bill. He made the Sunday brunch from new recipes in *Gourmet* and *Cuisine*. Jasmine hadn't seen a man cook who didn't have to or wasn't getting paid to do it. Things were topsy-turvy in the Moffitt house. Lara went on two- and three-day road trips and Bill stayed home. But even her Daddy, who'd never poured himself a cup of tea, wouldn't put Bill down as a woman. The mornings Bill tried out something complicated, a Cajun shrimp, sausage, and beans dish, for instance, Jasmine skipped church services. The Moffitts didn't go to church, though they seemed to be good Christians. They just didn't talk church talk, which suited her fine.

Two months passed. Jasmine knew she was lucky to have found a small, clean, friendly family like the Moffitts to build her new life around. 'Man!' she'd exclaim as she vacuumed the wide-plank wood floors or ironed (Lara wore pure silk or pure cotton). 'In this country Jesus givin out good luck only!' By this time they knew she wasn't a student, but they didn't care and said they wouldn't report her. They never asked if she was illegal on top of it.

To savour her new sense of being a happy, lucky person, she would put herself through a series of 'what ifs': what if Mr Singh in Port-of-Spain hadn't turned her on to the Daboos and loaned her two thousand! What if she'd been ugly like the Mintoo girl and the manager hadn't even offered! What if the customs man had unlocked the door of the van! Her Daddy liked to say, 'You is a helluva girl, Jasmine.'

'Thank you, Jesus,' Jasmine said, as she carried on.

Christmas Day the Moffitts treated her just like family. They gave her a red cashmere sweater with a V neck so deep it made her blush. If Lara had worn it, her bosom wouldn't hang out like melons. For the holiday weekend Bill drove her to the Daboos in Detroit. 'You work too hard,' Bill said to her. 'Learn to be more selfish. Come on, throw your weight around.' She'd rather not have spent time with the Daboos, but that first afternoon of the interview she'd told Bill and Lara that Mr Daboo was her mother's first cousin. She had thought it shameful in those days to have no papers, no family, no roots. Now Loretta and Viola in tight, bright pants seemed trashy like girls at Two-Johnny Bissoondath's Bar back home. She was stuck with the story of the Daboos being family. Village bumpkins, ha! She would break out. Soon.

Jasmine had Bill drop her off at the RenCen. The Plantations Motel, in fact, the whole Riverfront area, was too seamy. She'd managed to cut herself off mentally from anything too islandy. She loved her Daddy and Mummy, but she didn't think of them that often anymore. Mummy had expected her to be homesick and come flying right back home. 'Is blowin sweat-of-brow money is what you doin, Pa,' Mummy had scolded. She loved them, but she'd become her own person. That was something that Lara said: 'I am my own person.'

The Daboos acted thrilled to see her back. 'What you drinkin, Jasmine girl?' Mr Daboo kept asking. 'You drinkin sherry or what?' Pouring her little glasses of sherry instead of rum was a sure sign he thought she had become whitefolk-fancy. The Daboo sisters were very friendly, but Jasmine considered them too wild. Both Loretta and Viola had changed boyfriends. Both were seeing black men they'd danced with in Ann Arbor. Each night at bedtime, Mr Daboo cried. 'In Trinidad we stayin we side, they stayin they side. Here, everything mixed up. Is helluva confusion, no?'

On New Year's Eve the Daboo girls and their black friends went to a dance. Mr and Mrs Daboo and Jasmine watched TV for a while. Then Mr Daboo got out a brooch from his pocket and pinned it on Jasmine's red sweater. It was a Christmasy brooch, a miniature sleigh loaded down with snowed-on mistletoe. Before she could pull away, he kissed her on the lips. 'Good luck for the New Year!' he said. She lifted her head and saw tears. 'Is year for dreams coming true.'

Jasmine started to cry, too. There was nothing wrong, but Mr Daboo, Mrs Daboo, she, everybody was crying.

What for? This is where she wanted to be. She'd spent some damned uncomfortable times with the assistant manager to get approval for her loan. She thought of Daddy. He would be playing poker and fanning himself with a magazine. Her married sisters would be rolling out the dough for stacks and stacks of roti, and Mummy would be steamed purple from stirring the big pot of goat curry on the stove. She missed them. But. It felt strange to think of anyone celebrating New Year's Eve in summery clothes.

In March Lara and her performing group went on the road. Jasmine knew that the group didn't work from scripts. The group didn't use a stage, either; instead, it took over supermarkets, senior citizens' centres, and school halls, without notice. Jasmine didn't understand the performance world. But she was glad that Lara said, 'I'm not going to lay a guilt trip on myself. Muffie's in super hands,' before she left.

Muffie didn't need much looking after. She played Trivial Pursuit all day, usually pretending to be two persons, sometimes Jasmine, whose accent she could imitate. Since Jasmine didn't know any of the answers she couldn't help. Muffie was a quiet, precocious child with see-through blue eyes like her dad's, and red braids. In the early evenings Jasmine cooked supper, something special she hadn't forgotten from her island days. After supper she and Muffie watched some TV, and Bill read. When Muffie went to bed, Bill and she sat together for a bit with their glasses of Soave. Bill, Muffie, and she were a family, almost.

Down in her basement room that late, dark winter, she had trouble sleeping. She wanted to stay awake and think of Bill. Even when she fell asleep it didn't feel like sleep because Bill came barging into her dreams in his funny, loose-jointed, clumsy way. It was mad to think of him all the time, and stupid and sinful; but she couldn't help it. Whenever she put back a book he'd taken off the shelf to read or whenever she put his clothes through the washer and dryer, she felt sick in a giddy, wonderful way. When Lara came back things would get back to normal. Meantime she wanted the performance group miles away.

Lara called in at least twice a week. She said things like, 'We've finally obliterated the margin between realspace and performancespace.' Jasmine filled her in on Muffie's doings and the mail. Bill always closed with, 'I love you. We miss you, hon.'

One night after Lara had called—she was in Lincoln, Nebraska—Bill said to Jasmine, 'Let's dance.'

She hadn't danced since the reggae night she'd had too many rum punches. Her toes began to throb and clench. She untied her apron and the fraying, knotted-up laces of her running shoes.

Bill went around the downstairs rooms turning down lights. 'We need atmosphere,' he said. He got a small, tidy fire going in the living room grate and pulled the Turkish scatter rug closer to it. Lara didn't like anybody walking on the Turkish rug, but Bill meant to have his way. The hissing logs, the plants in the dimmed light, the thick patterned rug: everything was changed. This wasn't the room she cleaned every day.

He stood close to her. She smoothed her skirt down with both hands.

'I want you to choose the record,' he said.

'I don't want your music.'

She brought her hand high to his face. His skin was baby smooth.

'I want *you* to pick,' he said. 'You are your own person now.'

'You got island music?'

He laughed, 'What do you think?' The stereo was in a cabinet with albums packed tight alphabetically into the bottom three shelves. 'Calypso has not been a force in my life.'

She couldn't help laughing. 'Calypso? Oh, man.' She pulled dust jackets out at random. Lara's records. The Flying Lizards. The Violent Ferns. There was so much still to pick up on!

'This one,' she said, finally.

He took the record out of her hand. 'God! he laughed. 'Lara must have found this in a garage sale!' He laid the old record on the turntable. It was 'Music for Lovers', something the nuns had taught her to foxtrot to way back in Port-of-Spain.

They danced so close that she could feel his heart heaving and crashing against her head. She liked it, she liked it very much. She didn't care what happened.

'Come on,' Bill whispered. 'If it feels right, do it.' He began to take her clothes off.

'Don't, Bill,' she pleaded.

'Come on, baby,' he whispered again. 'You're a blossom, a flower.'

He took off his fisherman's knit pullover, the corduroy pants, the blue shorts. She kept pace. She'd never had such an effect on a man. He nearly flung his socks and Adidas into the fire. 'You feel so good,' he said. 'You smell so good. You're really something, flower of Trinidad.'

'Flower of Ann Arbor,' she said, 'not Trinidad.'

She felt so good she was dizzy. She'd never felt this good on the island where men did this all the time, the girls went along with it always for favours. You couldn't feel really good in a nothing place. She was thinking this as they made love on the Turkish carpet in front of the fire: she was a bright, pretty girl with no visa, no papers, and no birth certificate. No nothing other than what she wanted to invent and tell. She was a girl rushing wildly into the future.

His hand moved up her throat and forced her lips apart and it felt so good, so right, that she forgot all the dreariness of her new life and gave herself up to it.

1988

Index of Authors and Titles